Song *of the* Silent Harp

This popular novel of the Famine period glows with love and faith amid the hardships, and even cruelty, of life under absentee landlords in nineteenth-century Ireland.

The author has created a cast of complex characters in a panorama that stretches from County Mayo to Dublin, London, and eventually New York, where the Kavanaghs are to work out their destiny.

All the color and imagery of a film enliven this story as it unfolds against a background of aborted revolution, disappointed love, the elemental struggle for life fulfillment in a harsh society.

Rarely has a novel captured so authentically the enduring faith of the Irish peasant that sustains Nora Kavanagh through the tribulation and struggle of that harrowing period.

A compelling and uplifting read that adds to an understanding of Ireland in the last century.

DR. EOIN MCKIERNAN,
FOUNDER, IRISH AMERICAN CULTURAL INSTITUTE

The Emerald Ballad Series

BY BJ HOFF

Song *of the* Silent Harp

THE EMERALD BALLAD

BJ HOFF

HARVEST HOUSE PUBLISHERS

EUGENE, OREGON

Cover by Koechel Peterson & Associates, Inc., Minneapolis, Minnesota

Cover photos © iStockphoto; Thinkstockphotos; Shutterstock; Dreamstime; Stock.xchng

BJ Hoff: Published in association with the Books & Such Literary Agency, 52 Mission Circle, Suite 122, PMB 170, Santa Rosa, CA 95409-5370, www.booksandsuch.biz.

Previously published as *Song of the Silent Harp*, book one of An Emerald Ballad series, Bethany House Publishers.

SONG OF THE SILENT HARP
Copyright © 1991 by BJ Hoff
Published 2010 by Harvest House Publishers
Eugene, Oregon 97402
www.harvesthousepublishers.com

Library of Congress Cataloging-in-Publication Data
   Hoff, B. J., 1940-
   Song of the silent harp / BJ Hoff.
      p. cm. — (The emerald ballad ; bk. 1)
   ISBN 978-0-7369-2788-8 (pbk.)
   1. Families—Ireland—Fiction. 2. Irish Americans—Fiction. 3. Ireland—History—Famine,
1845-1852—Fiction. I. Title.
   PS3558.O34395S6 2010
   813'.54—dc22

                                                                        2010004618

Printed in the United States of America

          10 11 12 13 14 15 16 17 18 / RDM-SK / 10 9 8 7 6 5 4 3 2 1

For Jim—My Hero...
My Husband...My Best Friend.

Acknowledgments

My warmest thanks and appreciation to Harvest House Publishers for publishing this new edition of *Song of the Silent Harp*, the first book of The Emerald Ballad series, and for their ongoing support and encouragement of my work.

Much gratitude is due the late Dr. Eoin McKiernan for the information and assistance he so kindly and patiently provided throughout the development of this series.

Thanks also to the following: Ivor Hamrock of the Mayo County Council, Castlebar, County Mayo, Ireland; John R. Podracky of the New York City Police Museum; and the late Thomas Gallagher of New York City.

A special note of appreciation to the librarians at the Fairfield County District Library, Lancaster, Ohio, for their continuing and always cheerful assistance.

About BJ Hoff

BJ Hoff's bestselling historical novels continue to cross the boundaries of religion, language, and culture to capture a worldwide reading audience. In addition to The Emerald Ballad series, her books include such popular titles as *Song of Erin* and *American Anthem* and bestselling series such as The Riverhaven Years and The Mountain Song Legacy. Her stories, although set in the past, are always relevant to the present. Whether her characters move about in Ireland or America, in small country towns or metropolitan areas, reside in Amish settlements  or in coal company houses, she creates *communities* where people can form relationships, raise families, pursue their faith, and experience the mountains and valleys of life. BJ and her husband make their home in Ohio.

For a complete listing of BJ's books published by
Harvest House Publishers, turn to page 429.

Contents

PART THREE
SONG OF FAREWELL • THE PASSAGE

A Pronunciation Guide for Proper Names

Aidan . . . . Ā'den

Aine . . . . Än'ya
(Anne)

Caomhanach . . . . Kavanagh

Conal . . . . Kôn'al

Connacht . . . . Kôn'ot

Drogheda . . . . Draw'he guh

Eoin . . . . Ôwen
(older form of John)

Killala . . . . Kil lä'lä

Padraic . . . . Paw'rig
(Patrick)

Sean . . . . Shôn
(form of John)

Tahg . . . . Tīge

Tierney . . . . Teer'ney

On the willow trees in the midst of Babylon we hung our harps.
For there they who led us captive required of us a song.... Our
tormentors and they who wasted us required of us mirth.

PSALM 137:2-3 (AMP)

Eoín

These are the clouds about the fallen sun,
The majesty that shuts his burning eye:
The weak lay hand on what the strong has done,
Till that be tumbled that was lifted high.

W. B. YEATS (1865–1939)

Drogheda, Ireland
1649

Eoin Caomhanach, your harp will sing no more until the evil of Black Cromwell has been forgotten in the land and the survivors of his butchery return from exile."

Eoin's harp rode his shoulder in silent obedience as his grandfather's command echoed throughout the dim upstairs room. For a moment the old man looked as if he would say more; instead, he turned and went to stand at the narrow window, where a pale blade of late evening light struggled to pierce the gloom. Like a shadowed statue, Conal stood gazing down upon the ruins below.

Drogheda had finally fallen. After a seemingly endless siege and a three-day orgy of savagery and slaughter, the town's destruction was complete. The massacre of its defenders had been swift and thorough, the slaying of its innocent people brutal and merciless. The streets, now virtually deserted, were haunted by the eerie hush that follows disaster. The only sounds to break the silence were the cries of the wounded, an occasional angry shout between soldiers, and the screaming of the gulls over the River Boyne.

13

Yesterday, Eoin had crouched on one of the breastworks with his bow, watching as the wall around the town was breached by the hordes of Cromwell's New Model Army. He had stared in stunned disbelief as the first wave of shouting, blood-crazed troopers came pouring through the break. Today his heart raced and pounded in his ears as he remembered the surging tide of round black helmets and rust-red doublets exploding on the town in demented fury, chanting psalms and screaming curses in the same breath. On foot and on horseback, with muskets cracking and swords clanging, they hacked and shot and stabbed until the breach was soaked with blood and littered with fallen soldiers.

Losing his bow, Eoin was quickly swept up in the wave of retreating men, then stalled in the chaos and press of the massacre. From there he gazed in sick horror as Sir Arthur Aston, the defending commander of the city, was upended by a mob of jeering troopers, then bludgeoned to death on the bridge with his own wooden leg. As if in a daze, the lad watched the brightly colored feather from Aston's hat wave bravely in the warm harvest breeze before sailing to the ground in final defeat.

Eoin could no longer remember his route of escape. He vaguely recalled hearing the voices of the people at St. Peter's singing the *Gloria* just before the wooden steeple roared to a blaze; within seconds the church's shelter became a funeral pyre. He dimly remembered trying to avoid stepping on the dead bodies as he raced toward home. His ears still rang with the ominous drum of marching boots on cobblestones, and his nostrils still burned with the stench of smoke and gunpowder and death.

Somehow he made his way through the alleys and back streets to his house, only to find his mild-natured father slain just outside the open door, his young mother and two sisters savaged and mutilated within.

Blood...his home had been a river of blood.

Half-crazed with shock and grief, he had stumbled blindly down St. John's Street, deep into the Irish quarter to the home of his grandfather. Now the two of them waited, as did the other survivors of Drogheda, to learn their fate. Already lands had been seized, the garrison destroyed, their clergy and scholars humiliated, then slain alongside the town's defenders.

They would be driven from their home, his grandfather said, then either killed or taken prisoner. Rumors ran wild, but most believed that survivors would be sent to Barbados as slaves or relocated to barren Connacht in western Ireland. Eoin thought he would prefer death to being a slave or a prisoner—not that he would have a choice.

"Did you hear me, lad?"

Eoin blinked, forced back to his surroundings by his grandfather's voice. Conal had left the window and stood watching him. "I did, Grandfather. But—"

"I am charging you with the custody of the Harp of Caomhanach. You have been taught the covenant."

"Aye, sir," Eoin said softly. The harp was the symbol of a generations-old covenant between the Caomhanach family and their God. A clan chief in the time of the kings had decreed that the harp was to remain silent in time of exile, that it should sing only for a free people.

"So it has ever been with our ancestors," Conal now intoned, "and so it is to be with you, Eoin, the eldest and only surviving son of Dermot."

A fierce conflict of emotions flooded Eoin. He was still raw with pain at the loss of his parents and sisters, still bewildered by the enormity of what had happened to him and his neighbors, and while he loved Conal deeply, he resented the old man's stern directive, especially at this moment.

Lifting his eyes to the ruins of his grandfather's craggy face, Eoin realized that the old man would be woefully unprepared for the rebellion of his only surviving grandson. No less than the fullest measure of respect would be anticipated, for no less had ever been given.

In his prime, the old warrior, like past generations of male Caomhanachs, had been a giant of a man. Year after year of battle and bloodshed, however, had finally defeated him, leaving him shrunken and wasted, a scarecrow whose flesh draped his once mighty frame like the useless folds of a tattered cloak. Now his hair and beard were purest white, his eyes faded, his hand unsteady. His tunic and breeches hung loosely on his bones.

Eoin answered Conal carefully, denying the pity that rose deep within him. Such an emotion in the face of a chieftain would be an unforgivable insult. "I'm sorry, Grandfather, but I cannot abide by the old ways. The Harp of Caomhanach will no longer be a silent harp of exile. I intend to let her have her voice."

"No!" Conal pounded a fist on the wooden table in front of him, causing Eoin to jump back into a large Venetian vase. It tipped, crashing to the floor. Mindless of the broken vase, the old man went on shouting. "It is forbidden! The harp is to sing only in its own land, to its own people! You would not *dare* break the covenant."

Anticipating his grandfather's opposition to what he was about to say, Eoin nevertheless longed for the old man's understanding. "Grandfather, please, hear me. I can no longer be faithful to the old order, don't you see? To remain silent is to ignore all that has gone before. If we allow our past to be forgotten, we lose not only our land, but our hope as well. Surely you would not have it so. *God* would not have it so."

Ashen-faced, Conal stared at Eoin in breathless silence. "And so, do you now speak for God, Eoin?" he questioned softly. "Would you truly break a vow with our Lord?"

"But don't you see, Grandfather, I wouldn't be breaking the covenant! The vow between our family and God was that the harp would sing for our people as long as the Lord is among us and freedom is ours. If—"

Shaking his head like an angry lion and pointing a thin, accusing finger, Conal leaned toward Eoin. "You forget the rest of the vow! We are about to be an exiled people—perhaps even a people *enslaved!* Whether we flee to the west or go to the islands in chains, we will be slaves. The devil Cromwell and his demons will have our freedom and our faith at their feet."

"No, Grandfather, they will not," Eoin said quietly. "Wherever they send us, we will take our memories. And our faith. And as long as we have our past and our faith, do we not also possess at least a remnant of dignity and freedom—and a future? The Lord promised us 'a future and a hope,' did He not?"

Conal's disdainful glare made Eoin rush to defend his own words. "We will not be leaving God behind, after all, will we? Nor will God desert us. Has He not promised that He would never forsake us?" Forcing a strength into his voice he did not feel, Eoin pressed on. "As long as our God is with us, Grandfather, I say we are free. Free, and at liberty to allow the harp to declare our freedom, to call to mind our heritage and our hope of what God in His mercy will do for us in a new day."

"You rave like a roaming minstrel! An unseasoned child of fourteen years, and you dare to break the pledge of centuries between a people and their God?"

With a stab first of uneasiness, then anger at his grandfather's words, Eoin hesitated, struggling to control his feelings. "I am no child," he answered harshly. "I have seen my family butchered, my townsmen massacred, my land stolen. I have seen evil of a kind that men three times my years have not witnessed."

He moved a step closer to Conal, intent now on making his grandfather understand. "I saw him. Cromwell. I saw that pious hypocrite on his knees. He was praying, Grandfather. Only moments before he himself stood in the blood-soaked breach of the wall and urged his soldiers to break through and slaughter our people—*he...was...praying.* I saw his rage—he was wild with it, in a white-hot passion for our blood! 'No quarter,' he said. 'Kill them all!' Our soldiers said he intends to bring all Ireland to its knees. They said he believes himself to be the divine instrument of God's judgment upon the Irish!"

Even now the memory of the Puritan general's gaunt, sour face, the sound of his vile name, made Eoin's head roar. "Would you have the ugly truth about that monster go untold? Would you have his name remain free of the guilt it ought to bear?"

At last Eoin stopped. His heartbeat slowed, and the ringing in his ears subsided. He was drained, his anger cooled, his passion depleted.

After a long, tense silence, Conal nodded sadly. "What you say is true. The Puritan and his army purport to carry out the will of our merciful Lord, while in truth they have no mercy at all—none at all. But, then, Drogheda is not the first, nor will it likely be the last field of battle where the Hatchet of Hell proclaims itself the Sword of Heaven."

Their eyes met, and Eoin drew a deep breath. "Grandfather, two nights past, before the massacre, I had a dream. In the dream, God"—he faltered—"God spoke to me."

Conal's chin lifted, his eyes flashing first with incredulity, then something akin to dread as he listened.

"Our Lord has given me a clear vision of—of His will for my life." Eoin spoke haltingly, yet he felt his conviction grow as he went on. "That's how I know I am to take the harp into exile, wherever we go. And not as a silent harp, but as a voice. A voice for our people. The Harp of Caomhanach will be our emblem of freedom, an unchanging reminder of God's presence with us and His promise for us: a promise that one day we will be truly free. A free *Ireland*, Grandfather."

Silence hung between them. When Conal finally spoke, his voice trembled as violently as his hands, causing Eoin's heart to wrench at the pain he knew he had inflicted. Gone was the challenge in the old man's eyes; instead, there was only sorrow.

"Do what you must do, then, Eoin. I will only caution you this one last time, for soon I will no longer be with you to dampen that fiery spirit you possess."

Eoin stared at him. "What do you mean, Grandfather? Of course, you will be with me."

Conal shook his head. "No, lad. I'm old, and I'm ill, and I'll lay my head down for the last time on my own sod. As Drogheda has been my home, so will it be my tomb."

Stunned, Eoin moved toward him, but Conal stopped him with an upraised hand. "I do not fear those stone-faced zealots, lad. With what can they threaten me? Death?" He made a small sound of laughter. "They cannot threaten a sick old man with heaven, now can they?

No," he said, again shaking his head slowly, "I do not fear death, so long as I can die in Drogheda."

When Eoin opened his mouth to protest, Conal ignored him. "But as for you, if indeed God has spoken to you, then of course you must obey."

Tears scalded Eoin's eyes, and he quickly lowered his head to hide them.

"Come here, lad," Conal beckoned him kindly. "Come here to me now."

Eoin went to him. Standing with one hand behind his back, the other steadying the harp on his shoulder, he suddenly felt very much the child Conal had accused him of being.

"If indeed you are leaving, Eoin, you must leave now. Go by the river. Use the opening in the cellar, behind the stone. Go up the river, not down, where the ships are. Swim until you find a boat. Go tonight," he said, his voice urgent, "before the moon rises."

"But I can't—"

"You must!" The old man clutched at Eoin's arm. "There's a sack of coins beneath the cellar floor—take it with you. Hide it somehow; you may need the gold later, to buy your safety."

Conal paused, then tugged at Eoin's arm to draw him still closer. "If you believe with all your heart the words you have spoken to me, Eoin, that the harp is free to sing, then let it sing for me this one last time. Sing a lament for Conal Caomhanach, whose spirit has already departed the land and waits for his flesh to follow."

Eoin stared at his grandfather for a moment. At last he eased away from Conal and turned, knowing the old man would not wish to see the tears that now spilled from his eyes. Steadying the harp, which some long-dead ancestor had hollowed from a single block of willow, he slowly began to pluck the strings.

He sang in a voice still boyishly high. He sang for his grandfather, and he sang for himself.

"My harp will sing across the land across the past and years to be...."

Eoin's voice caught, and he had to stop and swallow hard before going on.

"No loss or grief nor death itself
will still its faithful melody...
To sing the presence of a God
who conquers even exile's pain—
Who heals the wandering pilgrim's wound
and leads him home, in joy again..."

PART ONE

SONG OF SORROW

The Hunger

*They who are slain with the sword are more fortunate
than they who are the victims of hunger.*

LAMENTATIONS 4:9 (AMP)

IRELAND
1847

Atlantic
Ocean

DONEGAL

LONDONDERRY

ANTRIM

ULSTER

Belfast

TYRONE

DOWN

Killala
Bay

Killala

Ballina

FERMANAGH

ARMAGH

MONAGHAN

SLIGO

LEITRIM

CAVAN

LOUTH

MAYO

Castlebar

ROSCOMMON

LONG-
FORD

MEATH

CONNACHT

WEST MEATH

Dublin

GALWAY

OFFALY

DUBLIN

KILDARE

LEINSTER

QUEENS

WICKLOW

CLARE

CARLOW

Limerick

KILKENNY

LIMERICK

TIPPERARY

WEXFORD

MUNSTER

WATERFORD

KERRY

CORK

Cork

St. George's
Channel

1

Daniel

Write his merits on your mind;
Morals pure and manners kind;
In his head, as on a hill,
Virtue placed her citadel.

WILLIAM DRENNAN (1754–1820)

Killala, County Mayo (Western Ireland)
January, 1847

Ellie Kavanagh died at the lonesome hour of two o'clock in the morning—a time, according to the Old Ones, when many souls left their bodies with the turning of the tide. A small, gaunt specter with sunken eyes and a vacant stare, she died a silent death. The Hunger had claimed even her voice at the end. She was six years old, and the third child in the village of Killala to die that Friday.

Daniel kept the death watch with his mother throughout the evening. Tahg, his older brother, was too ill to sit upright, and with their da gone— killed in a faction fight late last October—it was for Daniel to watch over his little sister's corpse and see to his mother.

The small body in the corner of the cold, dimly lit kitchen seemed less than human to Daniel; certainly it bore little resemblance to wee Ellie. Candles flickering about its head mottled the ghastly pallor of the skull- like face, and the small, parchment-thin hands clasping the Testament on top of the white sheet made Daniel think uneasily of claws. Even the col- ored ribbons adorning the sheet mocked his sister's gray and lifeless body.

23

The room was thick with shadows and filled with weeping women. Ordinarily it would have been heavy with smoke as well, but the men in the village could no longer afford tobacco. The only food smells were faint: a bit of sour cheese, some onion, stale bread, a precious small basket of shellfish. There was none of the illegal poteen—even if potatoes had been available from which to distill the stuff, Grandfar Dan allowed no spirits inside the cottage; he and Daniel's da had both taken the pledge some years before.

All the villagers who came and went said Ellie was laid out nicely. Daniel knew their words were meant to be a comfort, but he found them an offense. Catherine Fitzgerald had done her best in tidying the body—Catherine had no equal in the village when it came to attending at births or deaths—but still Daniel could see nothing at all *nice* about Ellie's appearance.

He hated having to sit and stare at her throughout the evening, struggling to keep the sight of her small, wasted corpse from permanently imbedding itself in his mind. He was determined to remember his black-haired little sister as she had been before the Hunger, traipsing along behind him and chattering at his back to the point of exasperation.

Old Mary Larkin had come to keen, and her terrible shrieking wail now pierced the cottage. Squatting on the floor beside the low fire, Mary was by far the loudest of the women clustered around her. Her tattered skirt was drawn up almost over her head, revealing a torn and grimy red petticoat that swayed as her body twisted and writhed in the ancient death mime.

The woman's screeching made Daniel's skin crawl. He felt a sudden fierce desire to gag her and send her home. He didn't think his feelings were disrespectful of his sister—Ellie had liked things quiet; besides, she had been half-afraid of Old Mary's odd ways.

Ordinarily when Mary Larkin keened the dead, the entire cottage would end up in a frenzy. Everyone knew she was the greatest keener from Killala to Castlebar. At this moment, however, as Daniel watched the hysterical, withered crone clutch the linen sheet and howl with a force that would turn the thunder away, he realized how weak were the combined cries of the mourners. The gathering was pitifully small for a wake—six months ago it would have been twice the size, but death had become too commonplace to attract much attention. And it was evident from the subdued behavior in the room that the Hunger had sapped the strength of even the stoutest of them.

Daniel's head snapped up with surprise when he saw Grandfar Dan haul himself off the stool and go trudging over to the howling women grouped around Ellie's body. He stood there a few moments until at last Mary Larkin glanced up and saw him glaring at her. Behind the stringy wisps of white hair falling over her face, her black eyes looked wild and fierce with challenge. Daniel held his breath, half-expecting her to lash out physically at his grandfather when he put a hand to her shoulder and began speaking to her in the Irish. But after a moment she struggled up from the floor and, with a display of dignity that Daniel would have found laughable under different circumstances, smoothed her skirts and made a gesture to her followers. The lot of them got up and huddled quietly around the dying fire, leaving the cottage quiet again, except for the soft refrain of muffled weeping.

Daniel's mother had sat silent and unmoving throughout the entire scene; now she stirred. "Old Dan should not have done that," Nora said softly. "He should not have stopped them from the keening."

Daniel turned to look at her, biting his lip at her appearance. His mother was held in high esteem for her good looks. "Nora Kavanagh's a grand-looking woman," he'd heard people in the village say, and she was that. Daniel thought his small, raven-haired mother was, in fact, the prettiest woman in Killala. But in the days after his da was killed and the fever had come on Ellie, his mother had seemed to fade, not only in her appearance but in her spirit as well. She seemed to have retreated to a place somewhere deep inside herself, a distant place where Daniel could not follow. Her hair had lost its luster and her large gray eyes their quiet smile; she spoke only when necessary, and then with apparent effort. Hollow-eyed and deathly quiet, she continued to maintain her waxen, lifeless composure even in the face of her grief, but Daniel sometimes caught a glimpse of something shattering within her.

At times he found himself almost wishing his mother would give way to a fit of weeping or womanly hysteria. Then at least he could put an arm about her narrow shoulders and try to console her. This silent stranger beside him seemed beyond comfort; in truth, he suspected she was often entirely unaware of his presence.

In the face of his mother's wooden stillness, Daniel himself turned inward, to the worrisome question that these days seldom gave him any peace.

What was to become of them?

The potato crop had failed for two years straight, and they were now more than half the year's rent in arrears. Grandfar was beginning to fail. And Tahg—his heart squeezed with fear at the thought of his older brother—Tahg was no longer able to leave his bed. His mother continued to insist that Tahg would recover, that the lung ailment which had plagued him since childhood was responsible for his present weakness. Perhaps she was right, but Daniel was unable to convince himself. Tahg had a different kind of misery on him now—something dark and ugly and evil.

A tight, hard lump rose to his throat. It was going to be the same as with Ellie. First she'd grown weak from the hunger; later the fever had come on her until she grew increasingly ill. And then she died.

As for his mother, Daniel thought she still seemed healthy enough, but too much hard work and too little food were fast wearing her down. She was always tired lately, tired and distracted and somber. Even so, she continued to mend and sew for two of the local magistrates. Her earnings were less than enough to keep them, now that they lacked his da's wages from Reilly the weaver, yet she had tried in vain to find more work.

The entire village was in drastic straits. The Hunger was on them all; fever was spreading with a vengeance. Almost every household was without work, and the extreme winter showed no sign of abating. Most were hungry; many were starving; all lived in fear of eviction.

Still, poor as they were as tenant farmers, Daniel knew they were better off than many of their friends and neighbors. Thomas Fitzgerald, for example, had lost his tenancy a few years back when he got behind in his rent. Unable thereafter to get hold of a patch of land to lease, he barely managed to eke out an existence for his family by means of conacre, wherein he rented a small piece of land season by season, with no legal rights to it whatever. The land they occupied was a mere scrap. Their cabin, far too small for such a large family, was scarcely more than a buffer against the winter winds, which this year had been fierce indeed.

Daniel worried as much about the Fitzgeralds as he did about his own family. His best friend, Katie, was cramped into that crude, drafty hut with several others. She was slight, Katie was, so thin and frail that Daniel's blood chilled at the thought of what the fever might do to her. His sister had been far sturdier than Katie, and it had destroyed Ellie in such a short time.

Katie was more than his friend—she was his sweetheart as well. She was only eleven, and he thirteen, but they would one day marry—of that he was certain. Together they had already charted their future.

When he was old enough, Daniel would make his way to Dublin for his physician's training, then come back to set up his own practice in Castlebar. Eventually he'd be able to build a fine house for himself and Katie—and for his entire family.

There was the difference of their religions to be considered, of course. Katie was a Roman and he a Protestant. But they would face that hurdle later, when they were older. In the meantime, Katie was his lass, and that was that. At times he grew almost desperate for the years to pass so they could get on with their plans.

A stirring in the room yanked Daniel out of his thoughts. He glanced up and caught a sharp breath. Without thinking, he popped off his stool, about to cry out a welcome until he remembered his surroundings.

The man ducking his head to pass through the cottage door was a great tower of a fellow, with shoulders so broad he had to ease himself sideways through the opening. Yet he was as lean and as wiry as a whip. He had a mane of curly copper hair and a lustrous, thick beard the color of a fox's pelt. He carried himself with the grace of a cat-a-mountain, yet he seemed to fill the room with the restrained power of a lion.

As Daniel stood watching impatiently, the big man straightened, allowing his restless green eyes to sweep the room. His gaze gentled for an instant when it came to rest on Ellie's corpse, softening even more at the sight of Daniel's mother, to whom he offered a short, awkward nod of greeting. Only when he locked eyes with Daniel did his sun-weathered face at last break into a wide, pleased smile.

He started toward them, and it seemed to Daniel that even clad humbly as he was in dark frieze and worn boots, Morgan Fitzgerald might just as well have been decked with the steel and colors of a warrior chief, so imposing and awe-inspiring was his presence. He stopped directly in front of them, and both he and Daniel stood unmoving for a moment, studying each other's faces. Then, putting hands the size of dinner plates to Daniel's shoulders, Morgan pulled him into a hard, manly embrace. Daniel breathed a quiet sigh of satisfaction as he buried his cheek against

Morgan's granite chest, knowing the bond between him and the bronze giant to be renewed.

After another moment, Morgan tousled Daniel's hair affectionately, released him, and turned to Nora. The deep, rumbling voice that could shake the walls of a cabin was infinitely soft when he spoke. "I heard about Owen and the lass, Nora. 'Tis a powerful loss."

As Daniel watched, his mother lifted her shadowed eyes to Morgan. She seemed to grow paler still, and her small hands began to wring her handkerchief into a twisted rope. Her voice sounded odd when she acknowledged his greeting, as if she might choke on her words. "'Tis good of you to come, Morgan."

"Nora, how are you keeping?" he asked, leaning toward her still more as he scrutinized her face.

Her only reply was a small, stiff nod of her head before she looked away.

Daniel wondered at the wounded look in Morgan's eyes, even more at his mother's strained expression. The room was still, and he noticed that the lank-haired Judy Hennessey was perched forward on her chair as far as she could get in an obvious attempt to hear their conversation. He shot a fierce glare in her direction, but she ignored him, craning her neck even farther.

Just then Grandfar Dan moved from his place by the fire and began to lumber toward them, his craggy, gray-bearded face set in a sullen scowl. Daniel braced himself. For as long as he could remember, there had been bad blood between his grandfather and Morgan Fitzgerald. Grandfar had carried some sort of a grudge against Morgan for years, most often referring to him as "that worthless rebel poet."

"Sure, and that long-legged rover thinks himself a treasure," Grandfar would say. "Well, a *scoundrel* is what he is! A fresh-mouthed scoundrel with a sweet-as-honey tongue and a string of wanton ways as long as the road from here to Sligo, that's your Fitzgerald! What he's learned from all his books and his roaming is that it's far easier to sing for your supper than to work for it."

Now, watching the two of them square off, Daniel held his breath in anticipation of a fracas. A warning glint flared in Morgan's eye, and the old man's face was red. They stared at each other for a tense moment. Then, to Daniel's great surprise, Morgan greeted Grandfar with a bow of respect and, instead of goading him as he might have done in the past, he said quietly, "'Tis a bitter thing, Dan. I'm sorry for your troubles."

Even shrunken as he was by old age and hard labor, Grandfar was a taller man than most. Still, he had to look up at Morgan. His mouth thinned as they eyed each other, but the expected sour retort did not come. Instead, the old man inclined his head in a curt motion of acknowledgment, then walked away without a word, his vest flapping loosely against his wasted frame.

Morgan stared after him, his heavy brows drawn together in a frown. "'Tis the first time I have known Dan Kavanagh to show his years," he murmured, as if to himself. "It took the Hunger to age him, it would seem."

He turned back to Daniel's mother. "So, then, where is Tahg? I was hoping to see him."

Nora glanced across the kitchen. Tahg lay abed in a small, dark alcove at the back of the room, where a tattered blanket had been hung for his privacy. "He's sleeping. Tahg is poorly again."

Morgan looked from her to Daniel. "How bad? Not the fever?"

"No, it is *not* the fever!" she snapped, her eyes as hard as her voice. "'Tis his lungs."

Daniel stared down at the floor, unable to meet Morgan's eyes for fear his denial would be apparent. "Nora—"

Daniel raised his head to see Morgan searching his mother's face, a soft expression of compassion in his eyes. "Nora, is there anything I can do?"

Daniel could not account for his mother's sudden frown. Couldn't she tell that Morgan only wanted to help? "Thank you, but there's no need."

Morgan looked doubtful. "Are you sure, Nora? There must be something—"

She interrupted him, her tone making it clear that he wasn't to press. "It's kind of you to offer, Morgan, but as I said, there is no need."

Morgan continued to look at her for another moment. Finally he gave a reluctant nod. "I should be on my way, then. The burial—will it be tomorrow?"

Her mouth went slack. "The burial...aye, the burial will be tomorrow."

Hearing her voice falter, Daniel started to take her hand, but stopped at the sight of the emptiness in her eyes. She was staring past Morgan to Ellie's corpse, seemingly unaware of anyone else in the room.

Morgan shot Daniel a meaningful glance. "I'll just be on my way, then. Will you walk outside with me, lad?" Without waiting for Daniel's reply, he lifted a hand as if to place it on Nora's shoulder but drew it away before he touched her. Then, turning sharply, he started for the door.

Eager to leave the gloom of the cottage, and even more eager to be with Morgan after months of separation, Daniel nevertheless waited for his mother's approval. When he realized she hadn't even heard Morgan's question, he went to lift his coat from the wall peg by the door. With a nagging sense of guilt for the relief he felt upon leaving, he hurried to follow Morgan outside.

2

Morgan

Oh, blame not the bard if he flies to the bowers
Where pleasure lies carelessly smiling at fame;
He was born for much more, and in happier hours
His soul might have burned with a holier flame.

THOMAS MOORE (1779–1852)

Despite the frigid evening air, they walked all the way to the edge of town, heading toward the pier. The lines of Killala's low, grim buildings were smudged by the gathering darkness, their stains from the wet Atlantic winds scarcely visible. It was a heavy, menacing dusk, thick with the inhospitable silence of a village in mourning.

Although he held a near-sentimental fondness for the village, Morgan had long ago observed that Killala was much like Ireland throughout: at a distance it presented an alluring appearance, with its gently sloping grounds, its fertile meadows and groves, and its picturesque setting by the bay; seen closer up, however, the beauty was spoiled by disorder and squalor, by a dismal aimlessness among its winding streets and its poverty-stricken inhabitants.

Despite its location in Mayo, the wildest and poorest county in all Ireland, Killala had once been a cheerful, bustling town, the center of episcopal authority. Years ago, however, most of the trade had moved south to

Ballina, destroying Killala's economy. Eventually the church consolidated its jurisdiction in Tuam, adding to the village's declining prosperity.

The cathedral still stood at the center of the town, as did an ancient round tower, from which Killala's three main streets diverged—one turning west toward the miserable hamlet of Palmerstown, one going south toward a site known as the "Acres," and the other leading east. The tower was the only building of any real interest; even the cathedral was spare and plain. In addition, Killala boasted the handsome residence of the Protestant clergyman—still referred to as "the palace"—a small Wesleyan meetinghouse, a Roman chapel, and a schoolhouse that was often without a master.

As they walked through the town, Morgan's distress for its ruinous conditions grew. Still, he should not have been surprised; the same oppressive death pall that now hung over Killala had draped all the other villages he had passed through during the last few months. Like the dreaded potato blight that had settled over the country's fields for two consecutive growing seasons, an uneasy hush seemed to permeate the whole of Ireland. It was, Morgan knew, the silence of a people whose hope was dying, a people who had lost sight of tomorrow. The sound of the fiddle and pipes had been exchanged for the mourners' keen; the rhythm of dancing feet had slowed to the dirge of the death cart, the cadence of the burial march, and the desperate, shuffling steps of a homeless people in search of refuge.

They must have passed twenty or more poor, uprooted wretches before they came to the outskirts of the village. Most of them stood huddled and shivering around their tumbled cottages, waiting for night to fall so they could creep back beneath the remains of their roof and walls to shelter themselves until daybreak.

Morgan knew their ways, for he had encountered hundreds like them. For days they would hover close to what was left of their houses—houses often destroyed for payment by some of their own neighbors. Unwilling to break the final tie to the land on which their homes and those of their ancestors had long stood, they would spend the night in the tumbled shelter, then crawl outside before dawn to avoid discovery by one of the agent's henchmen. Making themselves scarce until evening, they would then repeat the ritual all over again. Eventually they would have to leave and take to the road.

Evictions were routine now, the sufferings of the homeless a pandemic tragedy in Ireland. The nation was fast becoming an open graveyard, burying its memories, its traditions, its spirit—and its people.

People were dying by the thousands: dying from hunger, from the vicious fevers that never failed to accompany a famine, and from the total despair of utter hopelessness. From their ancient beginnings the Irish had been a valiant, generous people of open doors and open hearts, who in the very worst of times were never without their poems and songs, so gregarious by nature they made a festival out of a wake. Now they lurked behind locked doors, quaking in fear and dread and defeat.

And it was killing them. Morgan had seen the dying wherever he went—not all of it physical, not by far. The people were losing their sense of themselves—their homes, their dreams, their pride, their very *identity*—to a faceless, seemingly invincible enemy.

And who would bear the guilt for the changes that ravaged Ireland? People blamed the British, who continued to claim Ireland as her own personal breadbasket, ruling her with an incredible lack of Christian conscience. They accused the greedy absentee landlords, who owned enormous chunks of the small island, yet cared nothing about their properties except for the collection of exorbitant rents. They condemned the land agents, who managed estates for the absentee landlords, often with a total disregard for the lives and health of their tenants. And they vilified the disease itself, which was, with a vengeance, claiming the children of Eire by the thousands.

But despite so many areas to which communal guilt could be apportioned, Morgan reflected, Ireland's great destroyer was the *ukrosh*. The Hunger. The life-destroying, heart-freezing, soul-stealing Hunger—

"Morgan? Morgan, look!"

The lad's voice at his side brought him up short from his brooding. He looked at Daniel John, then followed the boy's gaze to see what had caught his attention.

Across from them, in a ditch off the right side of the road, huddled a woman and two wee girls, all clothed in rags. Both the mother and the children were without coats or shawls, and their dresses were so tattered they might as well have been wearing paper ribbons. Even in his cloak, Morgan was chilled; he could not imagine how these poor souls could bear the cold with no protective outer clothing. They were clearly half-frozen and in the throes of starvation. The woman appeared to be watching their approach through glazed, dull eyes; but as they drew nearer, Morgan saw that her gaze was the empty, fixed stare of one whose strength is so depleted she could see nothing beyond the mists of gathering death.

He glanced down the road and saw others on their way out of the village: an old man and woman, both coatless, plus a number of other walking skeletons covered only by rags or torn sacks. Some hovered lifelessly in the ditches on both sides, while others marched in the wooden, moribund gait of impending death. Some were grown; some were children; many were carrying infants.

Where had they all come from? Not from the village, Morgan suspected. Killala was a wee place, fourteen or fifteen hundred at most. Besides, from the looks of these stricken souls, many had been traveling for days. Most likely they were refugees from other towns in search of work or relief or shelter—none of which they were likely to find.

As they came abreast of the woman and her little girls, Morgan put a hand to Daniel's shoulder, indicating the lad should wait for him. He turned toward the ditch where the small family huddled. The woman watched his approach with no real show of interest or emotion. One of the girls, the smaller of the two, fastened dazed, unseeing eyes upon Morgan; he sensed she was but hours away from death. The older lass seemed to be holding the smaller one up, as if to keep her from falling into the ditch. Both were gaunt like their mother, with skin hanging in folds and cavernous eyes that burned a tunnel to Morgan's heart.

"Sure, and you'd not be on the road, you and your lasses?" he ventured by way of greeting.

The woman stared at him. When she opened her mouth to speak, it seemed to require great effort. "We are that."

"Where is your man, then?"

Again the woman gave him a blank look, as if she didn't understand. She was shaking so hard and her voice was so weak and phlegmy that Morgan could scarcely make out her words. "Dead two weeks now, from the fever."

"Here, in Killala?"

She shook her head. "We come from Rathroeen. The agent turned us out yesterday."

What kind of man, Morgan wondered, *could throw a starving woman and two wee girls into the snow?* But he already knew—a man such as their own local agent, George Cotter. More beast than some, less man than others. And the island had more than her share of them.

"Do you have someone here in the village?" he asked. "Family, perhaps?"

Shivering, the woman drew her children close against her, as if to gather some warmth from them. Neither showed any sign of awareness, but simply continued to stare at Morgan with hollow eyes. "Not here," she answered dully, her voice shaking as hard as her body. "We are going to Kilcummin; my man's family is there."

"Kilcummin?" Morgan stared at them with dismay. "Your little girls are not up to the road. Haven't you anyone nearby?"

The woman turned her head without replying, as if she had not heard. Morgan looked from her to the tiny girls, clutching their mother's ragged dress. With a mutter of frustration, he pried open the pouch tied about his waist. "Here," he said, fishing out a coin and handing it to her. "There's a woman on the Rathlackan road who lets rooms. It's not a tavern, mind, but a decent place. Give her this and tell her Morgan Fitzgerald says she should give you a room and some food until you're able to go on to Kilcummin."

The woman stared at Morgan's outstretched hand as if it held a rainbow. Her eyes went from his hand to his face, then back to the money he was thrusting on her. At last her stiff fingers reached for the money with a jerk. "God bless you, man," she mumbled, stuffing the coin down the front of her dress. "May God in His mercy bless you. You have saved us."

Morgan started back to the road, but before he could reach Daniel John, he was stopped. As if a call had been sounded to a host of phantoms, raggedy marchers swept in upon him like a flock of buzzards, grasping, crying, whimpering—all reaching for him at once. They clawed at his clothes, wailing and pleading that he must help them, too.

"I can't—I'm sorry, but I can't—" In vain he tried to make himself heard, but his protests were lost amid the clamor.

Throwing up his arms as a shield, he tried to draw back without striking out. He stood more than a head above them all, yet so desperate and determined was the press of their bodies that he knew a moment of alarm for fear they'd bring him down and trample him.

He was shouting now, but in vain. Afraid they might turn and swarm the woman and her little girls, Morgan twisted around and shot her a warning look, jerking his head toward the road. It took her a moment to react, but at last she moved, dragging the children with her. Stumbling and weaving, they finally managed to leave the ditch for the road.

Over the heads of the crowd, Morgan saw Daniel John; the lad had left the road and was running toward him. *"No!"* Morgan shouted above the din. "Stay there!"

Still unwilling to turn the power of his own large, healthy body against the starving, pathetic scarecrows encircling him, Morgan flung his arms up, snapping himself sideways like a whip through the first opening he spotted. The force of his movement caused a tear in the frenzied crowd, and they began to fall back.

Finally free of them, Morgan felt himself seared by their accusing eyes as they followed his retreat. A hot, irrational flash of guilt struck him in rebuke of his own well-being.

Daniel John had managed to skirt the mob and rushed to his side, his face milk-white. "Are you all right, Morgan? Did they hurt you?"

"No, no, lad, I'm fine," Morgan assured him, straightening his clothing. "How could the poor creatures hurt me, and them so near death?"

Not wanting the boy to know just how badly the incident had shaken him, Morgan forced a note of gruffness into his voice. "We must be getting back. Your mother will be furious with the both of us—especially with me, keeping you out in this cold so long."

"Let's just go the rest of the way to the pier first, Morgan. Please, can't we? Like we used to?"

Morgan hesitated, then slung his arm around the lad's shoulders, catching his breath at the sharpness of bone he could feel beneath the thin coat. "All right, laddie, but only for a moment, and then we must be off."

They reached the edge of the rude pier and stood in silence, staring across the dark, sullen waters of the bay, now thick with ice. Wind laced with mist stung their faces, and Morgan pulled the scarf from his neck and wrapped it about the boy's throat. "So, now, is it true what I've heard— there have been numerous deaths in the village from the Hunger?"

Daniel John nodded, touching the scarf at his throat with a grateful smile. "Aye. From the Hunger or the fever—or both."

Morgan stooped to clasp the boy's shoulders. "I want the truth now, Daniel John. Have you food, you and your family?"

The lad hesitated, and Morgan could almost see Nora's pride at work in her son. He knew a sudden stab of anger with her for shifting her own stubborn self-sufficiency onto those young shoulders, and yet he understood. In her fierce need to better herself, Nora had learned to suppress any hint of weakness. He supposed he might have expected Daniel to be struck with the same branch.

"You're to tell me the truth, lad," he insisted softly.

The boy looked away. "Mother is proud, you know."

Morgan nodded. *Proud and stone-stubborn,* he thought. "Aye, she is that, and pride has its place. But it's not among friends such as us." He paused for a moment before asking, "Owen had nothing put by, then?"

Again Daniel John avoided meeting his eyes. "He did, but it's long gone."

Morgan tightened his hold on the boy's shoulders. "Well, see here, now, you're not to worry. I'll work something out for you and your family."

"But *how?*" the boy blurted out. "Grandfar says your pockets are as empty as your promises." Too late, he threw a hand over his mouth, his eyes wide with dismay at his words.

Morgan grinned, dropped his hands away from the boy's shoulders, and straightened. "True enough. But I believe I can still help a friend when the need is there."

Stretching up on the balls of his feet, he looked up for a moment at the night sky, so heavy with clouds they looked to be dropping into the bay. "What about evictions, lad? Have there been many so far?"

"Aye, and more every week. The Conlons were turned out just last Saturday, in the worst of the ice storm. They're living in one of the squatters' abandoned huts near the shore."

Morgan looked at him. "Brian Conlon, is it?"

Daniel John nodded. "Cotter had their place tumbled practically around their heads."

Morgan frowned angrily and spit out the agent's name like an oath. *"Cotter!"* The memory of the swine-featured agent was still all too clear in his mind. He was the devil's own spawn, that one.

A question nagged at the fringe of his thoughts, but he wasn't sure he should ask it. Still the boy seemed to feel easy about confiding in him. "And what about *your* rent, Daniel John? Do you know if you're behind at all?"

"We owe for the last half year," the boy said quietly, without hesitation.

He bit his lower lip for a moment, and added, "Grandfar says it will be the road for us before spring if we can't pay what we owe to date and the next half as well."

The old anger and resentment flared up in Morgan as he searched the lad's worried eyes. Impulsively, he pulled him into the circle of his arms and held him. "Didn't I say I would help, and that you're not to worry?"

"Aye, Morgan."

He heard the uncertainty in the boy's muffled reply. Taking him by the shoulders, he set him away from him just enough that he could see his face. "Let's have a smile now," he said, forcing one of his own.

"You must not forget that your granddaddy is a great one for making big out of little." He tousled Daniel John's unruly black curls. "Well, am I wrong?"

Shaking his head, the boy managed a small smile. Morgan opened his cloak, pulling Daniel John into its shelter, close beside him. "Come along, now," he ordered, putting his arm around the boy's shoulders and turning him back toward town. "Suppose while we walk you advise me of your progress with the harp. Yours and Tahg's."

Daniel John grinned up at him. "Do you know, you always say that, in the exact same way, each time you come back home?"

"And haven't I the right, being the one who taught you all your music?"

"Tahg says I'm sounding more and more like you all the time when I play."

Morgan grinned down at him as they walked. "Oh, does he, now? Well, we shall have to be seeing about that, I expect." He felt a tug at his heart at the boy's pleasure, and he found himself wishing, not for the first time, that this tenderhearted lad with the wise blue eyes were his own.

As well he might have been, man, had you not been so intent on playing the fool. The thought stabbed Morgan before he could shield his heart against it. *But best not to turn down that road,* "And Tahg, then? How does he fare with the harp?"

The boy's face clouded. "Tahg isn't strong enough to play these days. He can scarcely sit up in bed now."

The image of Nora's oldest son fastened itself upon Morgan's mind— all pale skin and slashes of bone; good, guileless eyes, and a heart equally pure. Tahg was the sober one, the down-to-earth, sensible planner and doer. A lovely lad, destined to be a fine, strong man. But now?

They walked the rest of the way in silence, both ducking their heads against the sting of the snow and the wind whipping at their skin. Neither spoke again until they reached the walk to Daniel John's cottage.

"I'll leave you here," Morgan said. "Your mother will be anxious and want you with her."

The boy clung to his hand, and Morgan could see Daniel John's reluctance to go inside. "Morgan…"

"Aye, lad?" The boy's eyes were fastened on Morgan in a look of mingled trust and confusion.

"Do you believe—" He stopped, then went on. "You know how we're always saying 'God is good'?"

Morgan frowned down at him and nodded.

The boy hesitated. "Well…do you believe it?"

Morgan stared at him. "Why would you ask such a question, lad?"

Daniel John didn't answer, but simply stood staring up at him, waiting.

Morgan sucked in a deep breath, glancing over his shoulder toward the road for a moment as he attempted to form his reply. When he turned back, the lad was still watching him expectantly. "Aye, Daniel John, of course I believe that God is good. But that doesn't mean," he went on, running a hand through his hair as he measured his words, "that all His *creatures* are good. Though He made us in His image, there are those who have badly distorted His original notion, it seems to me."

He paused, sensing that the struggle going on inside the boy was the same kind of conflict between faith and doubt that took place all too often in his own spirit.

"You see, lad, what seems to happen is that God's goodness is often overshadowed by His creation's meanness. Do you understand what I'm saying?"

After a moment the boy nodded. "I think so. But ever since Da was killed and Ellie died and Tahg was taken so ill—" He stopped, as if unable to capture the words he needed to explain himself.

Morgan waited, comprehending the boy's struggle all too well. "It's a hard thing, I know. If God is truly good, you're wondering why He gives evil so much quarter, isn't that it?"

Daniel John nodded, his gaze clearing somewhat. "Some of the villagers are even saying that God has abandoned Ireland altogether."

"Well, lad, I confess to having had that thought myself upon occasion," Morgan admitted. At the boy's expression of surprise, he tried to explain. "Being a man doesn't necessarily mean you cease to doubt and to question, Daniel John. But I have come to believe that God's ways were never meant to be entirely understood. Perhaps the fact that I cannot perceive the reasons for His doing what He does or does not do only serves to point out that I am human, and He divine."

The boy seemed to consider Morgan's words for a moment, but his eyes were still troubled. "It seems so unfair, the bad things that are happening. Like Ellie's dying. She suffered so before she went, and Ellie never hurt a living soul."

"Ah, lad, don't make the mistake of expecting life to have the qualities of God. Learn now, while you're young, not to compare the two, or it may well drive you mad one day. Life is life, and God is God, and it's nothing but folly to confuse the two. Life will never be fair, Daniel John, but we must *believe* that God is never *less* than fair. That is the truth, even though it's often a hard truth to cling to, especially in times like these."

Morgan was grateful to see a faint light of understanding dawn in the boy's eyes. "I will have to think on that, Morgan."

"Aye, lad," he said, putting a hand to the boy's shoulder. "I am sure you will. But it's inside with you for now."

"Morgan?" The boy still made no move toward the door. "Will you be staying for a while this time?"

Seeing Daniel John's hopeful gaze, Morgan felt a pang of sorrow for all the losses the lad's young heart had suffered, the loneliness he now must be bearing. His delay in answering caused the boy to press. "Will you, Morgan?"

"I have something I must do first," he began. Seeing Daniel John's eyes cloud with disappointment, Morgan hurried to reassure him. "It will not take but two or three days, I'm sure. Then I'll come back, and when I do—yes, lad, I plan to stay for a time. These long legs of mine are growing stiff and sore from roaming about in the cold. Perhaps a nice long rest would be just the thing for me."

The boy beamed. "I should think so, Morgan. A *very* long rest at home, that's what you need."

Home. The word struck a note of regret in Morgan. For more years than he could remember, home had been the road—or, at best, a bed in a friend's house or a pallet of straw in a kind farmer's barn. Home had never been much more than a word, never meant more than a dream or two of what might have been if he had been a different man, a good enough man, for Nora.

Ah, well. Home tonight was a corner near the fire in his brother's kitchen. After seeing the lad safe inside, Morgan turned and, pushing his hands into his pockets to keep them warm, went on down the road.

3

Nora

But I, being poor, have only my dreams;
I have spread my dreams under your feet;
Tread softly because you tread on my dreams.

W. B. YEATS (1865–1939)

Squeezing her eyes shut against the pain grinding at her temples, Nora stopped her spinning wheel and waited for the dizziness to pass. There was still enough late afternoon light in the kitchen that she could work, but she was so weary she thought she could not possibly go on.

She was weak to the point of collapse. There seemed to be no end to the days, and the nights dragged on forever. The daylight hours brought enough work for two women, but it was the darkness she minded most. No matter how exhausted she might be when she threw herself onto her bed, sleep refused to come. Night after night, her mind continued its torture, forcing her to relive Owen's death, then Ellie's, before assaulting her with a fresh seizure of fear for Tahg and the threat of imminent disaster for them all.

Only a week had passed since Ellie's burial, but things had gone from bad to worse throughout the village. The Hunger was upon them with a fury now, and its companion, disease, continued to seek out more and more victims, afflicting entire families at once. Mary Conlon had died just last night, and before dawn death claimed her youngest son. Last week alone, half a dozen families or more had been evicted and turned out on the road; before week's end the bitter January gales had felled three of the homeless children.

Though the Kavanaghs fared better than some, in their own cottage Old Dan was visibly failing. Night before last, while trying to plug a hole in the thatch on the roof, he had grown faint and come close to falling. He would not admit his weakness, of course, but it had been painfully obvious that he was spent. Nora had found Daniel in tears beside the fire shortly afterward; he was a brave lad, never crying for the pain in his own empty belly, yet unable to disguise his worry for those he loved.

Nora's hope was stretched thin, hard put to find even a slender thread to cling to. She had heard talk of soup kitchens and new relief centers to be added. Some said help would come any day now; others believed it would be spring before aid would arrive here, in one of the most remote sections of Mayo.

Spring would be too late. Their pig was gone, and the hens; the cow alone was left, and she was starving. Only her milk and a few old turnips stood between the family and starvation. There was grain in the barn, but it was marked with the landlord's cross for rent and could not be touched. Old Dan said they must begin to sneak a bit of it for food, but if they were caught it could bring eviction.

Nora shuddered at the thought of being homeless. With the old man so weak, and Tahg growing worse every day, they would die in the ditch in no time.

Tahg. He was suffering his life away. Every night he coughed and groaned until Nora thought she would surely go mad from the sounds of his misery. Old Dan suspected that Tahg had the fever, but she would not even consider the possibility. The boy's lungs had been poorly ever since he'd had pneumonia as a wee wane; he'd always been frail, Tahg had. This fierce winter had simply weakened him even more, but when spring came, he would be stronger. *Please, God.*

Dropping her hands to her lap, she began to rub them together. The cottage was cold; she kept the fire low, for the turf was nearly gone. Soon the only thing left to burn would be the few sticks of furniture they hadn't already sold, not nearly enough to see them through the rest of the winter.

A wave of despair rolled over her. It was impossible not to speculate on what might lie ahead. She had tried, at least until recently, to fix her mind on God's promises of provision for the future; but lately she lived with such fear, such dread, that it was becoming nearly impossible not to surrender to utter despair. The very act of living, of *surviving*, required such a fierce effort that there was little strength left over for its added burdens.

Who would ever have dreamed that the appearance just two summers past of some small brown spots on the potato plants would herald the nationwide disaster they now faced? Even when the dreaded blight had come again in '46, stealing its way across the land in a great white, silent cloud, those who had felt the eerie, unnatural quiet could not have envisioned the doom about to fall on Ireland's fields. The vile, sulphurous stench on the wind might well have been that of hell itself, so disastrous was its onslaught.

Some said the blight was God's judgment on the land, that Ireland's own sin had condemned her. Old Dan had remarked testily that only the British would believe that kind of foolishness, but Nora no longer knew *what* to believe. It was difficult to fathom how a merciful God could allow infants and children to starve to death or die in the agony of the fever, yet the horrors now sweeping Ireland seemed to defy any hint of mercy. The all-powerful God who could have stayed the destruction at any moment had not moved to do so; indeed, the storm of pestilence and devastation raged more fiercely than ever.

More and more often, questions came to nag Nora's conscience and attack her faith. If, as some insisted, the Hunger *was* an act of God's judgment, then how high a payment would He exact from her—from them all—before His divine justice was satisfied?

In the curtained alcove behind her, Tahg coughed and gasped, and Nora got up to go to him. When she stepped inside the small, windowless room, she saw that he was still sleeping. As she stood, unmoving, watching him, an ugly phantom of fear rounded the corner of her mind to assail her. *First Owen, then Ellie. Would Tahg be next?*

Owen had once accused her of being partial to their eldest, though of course she had vigorously denied it. Now she seemed to hear a guilty whisper in her mind, repeating her husband's accusation.

It's true…you know it's true; you've always favored Tahg…

It was *not* true, she silently insisted—at least not entirely. It was more that she had always been able to *know* Tahg, to understand him. He was so much like her, so close in spirit that she seemed to know his heart as well as her own. The two of them seemed to share a special communion, an unspoken sameness.

Daniel John, on the other hand, had been a mystery to her almost since his first word. At thirteen the boy already had the look of a long-armed, long-legged plowboy, but his head held the mind of a dreamer, a scholar, a poet. The lad was as starved for books and knowledge as most boys his age were for food and fun. Forever running to the schoolhouse when there was a master, he would soak up what he could of history and the old language and the heroes' tales, then run home to share all he had learned. His deepest pleasure was found in reading from a tattered book of poems or strumming achingly lovely tunes on the ancient Kavanagh Harp, tunes that somehow made Nora want to weep.

She had long ago accepted the fact that her youngest son would forever be a question, perhaps an exasperation, to her own cautious, practical nature. No matter how deeply she cared for Daniel John, she knew she would never really understand him.

Indeed, she wondered if *anyone* would, except perhaps for Morgan Fitzgerald, who had once called Daniel John a "boy-bard with a soul of old sorrows and a heart born to break." But, then, Morgan Fitzgerald was cut from the same cloth, she thought with a bitterness she refused to examine too closely. Hadn't the man been a dreamer his life long, with his precious books and his songs and his poems—his *words*?

Words. Morgan was never without them. They were living things to him, riches such as jewels would be to a king. Well, much good had they done him. He lived the life of a penniless vagabond, traipsing about the country, teaching in one schoolhouse after another, then wandering off to barter an occasional poem for food and lodging. He seemed to care not at all for hearth fire and comfort, but was more at home with the wind at his back and an untraveled road just ahead.

Ah, but once, Nora…once you would have died for the lad…

With a start, Nora gave the curtain a yank and returned to the kitchen, where Old Dan had come in from outside and was punching at the fire. "Work as if there is a fire under your skin," he muttered, straightening, "and there will ever be a fire in your hearth. Ha! No truth at all in that old saying, not in these times."

Nora smiled at him. "You've got it burning well enough, though. It will ease the chill, at least."

The old man's concern with the fire was a recent concession to Nora's worsening fatigue. As the woman of the house, maintaining the hearth fire was entirely her responsibility. In the old days no housewife would have thought of letting the fire go out, day or night; it was the heart of the home, the perpetual symbol of family unity. That an old one like her father-in-law would deign to share this traditional woman's chore was a distinct act of love, an act that endeared him to her that much more.

"Where's the lad?" he asked now, clasping his hands behind his back to warm them.

Nora sighed, knowing the truth would bring a sour retort. "I believe he went to the Fitzgeralds."

As she'd anticipated, the old man uttered a grunt of disgust. "With his harp, I suppose."

Nora felt a quick stirring of defense for her son and an even sharper stab of anger at Morgan Fitzgerald. No sooner had he left Ellie's burial site than he'd taken to the road again, leaving behind a disappointed, but still loyal, Daniel John. Every day since, the lad had watched the road or gone to the Fitzgerald cabin to inquire, never saying a word about Morgan's defection.

"Well?" the old man pressed.

"His harp? No, he left his harp at home today."

"Ach, so he's given up on the rogue for now, eh?"

Not answering, Nora went back to the spinning wheel and, after smoothing the lumps from a roll of thin wool, set the wheel singing with a hard spin. Old Dan crossed to the small, narrow window at the front of the kitchen and peered out.

"It's going to snow again," he said with a heavy sigh. "What a winter this has been. 'Tis the worst I remember since Peg died."

Nora watched him as she worked, frowning with concern at his wasted appearance. Old Dan was seventy-three, but he still had a full head of curly gray hair, and his beard was as thick as cotton batting. He was toothless, but this was seldom noticed since he was a solemn man, not given to many smiles. Until a few months ago, he had been a strong man, healthy and vigorous for his age. Now he appeared to be little more than bone, with his tall, stooped frame and his long, rope-thin arms. Lately, Nora thought, his skin had turned as gray as his beard.

"I'm thinking of sending Daniel John for the doctor tomorrow," she said. "Tahg is getting no rest at night."

The old man turned around from the window. His face was glum. "And how is it we will be paying him?"

"He's been kind enough to take fresh milk before. I'm sure he'll do so again." Nora paused, then ventured her next words with care. "I thought we might have him take a look at you as well."

"Well, keep your thoughts to yourself, woman. There's not a thing wrong with me that a good meal wouldn't cure! And as for the fresh milk— the cow is going dry, and well you know it! She can't live on roots and rocks any more than the lot of us."

Groping for patience with the irritable old man, Nora stopped the wheel and gave him a level look. "Sure, and weren't you the one recently reminding me that this winter will not last forever? 'Spring will come,' I heard you say only days ago."

He uttered something unintelligible and crossed the room with a stiff, unsteady gait. "I'll sit with our boyo a bit," he said, disappearing behind the curtain.

Once he was out of sight, Nora wiped a hand over her eyes to blot the tears of weakness and frustration she'd fought to hide. The raking dryness of her palm caused her to frown at her hand with distaste. She had always been vain about her hands, had done her best to keep them smooth and soft while Owen lived, for he had liked to hold them between his when they sat by the fire in the evening. Now her skin was as rough as tree bark, her nails peeled and broken.

Again she lifted a hand, this time to her hair. Another vanity, God forgive her. It was still long and thick, but had grown dull and felt nearly as dry as her skin. *What more?* she wondered wearily. *What more?*

Merciful God, don't let me lose my teeth, too!

She shuddered against the sudden thought, then just as quickly breathed a prayer to ask forgiveness for her wicked vanity. Of course, she would eventually be toothless. These days more women were than not, at least those she had seen in the village. The Hunger spared no one from its ravages, not even foolish women with forbidden pride.

"Nora! You'd best come!"

Her father-in-law's cry from Tahg's room shocked her out of her thoughts, and she knocked the stool over in her haste to get up. Old Dan was holding the boy awkwardly by the shoulders as Tahg writhed and choked in the throes of a coughing spasm.

Nora went to him, forcing a note of calm into her voice as she took Old Dan's place by the bed. "Here, now, *asthore*," she crooned, bending over to take him in her arms. Holding him gently, she grieved at his appearance. At fifteen Tahg looked more like a man in his middle years, so great had been the toll of his illness. The angry flush on his hollow cheeks, the wildness in his fevered blue eyes, the limp strands of dark hair falling raggedly over his forehead gave him a peculiar, deranged look. Gripped as he was with a furious fit of coughing, he seemed even weaker than usual. The look of him tore Nora's heart and stabbed her with fear, but she forced a smile and continued to make small sounds of comfort until the spasm passed.

Finally he drew an easier breath, then another. A thin ribbon of blood trickled from the side of his mouth, and he lifted a frail hand to wipe it away. When he finally looked up at her, his eyes were still glazed with pain, and for an instant Nora thought he didn't recognize her. But after a moment his lips moved with the effort to smile, and he whispered, "I'm fine now, Mum."

At her side, she was aware of the old man shaking his head and mumbling a prayer.

"God have mercy on him," Old Dan murmured. "Ah, dear God, have mercy on him…"

And on us all, Nora added silently. *And on us all.*

4

Michael

I am come of the seed of the people,
The people that sorrow,
That have no treasure but hope,
No riches laid up but a memory
Of an ancient glory.

P. H. PEARSE (1879–1916)

New York City

Michael Burke loved New York—except, that is, in the winter. In the spring the city was a capricious, blood-stirring flirt of a lass, but in the winter she turned to a bad-tempered woman, spitting her nastiness and flaunting her ill breeding as if to put a man off. Her sky became a grim, pewter shield, her avenues teemed with dirty snow and frozen refuse, and her sullen harbor waters churned with ice and floating debris.

January in New York meant driving snow and bitter wind, and today had brought a relentless attack of both. It was still snowing hard as Michael turned down Pearl Street and headed toward home. He pulled the collar of his greatcoat higher about his throat, feeling uncommonly relieved that his watch was over.

He was tired, bone-tired. Fridays were always the worst of his week, but this one had been even more trying than most, with two murders, a series of knifings, and a vicious attack on Sal Folio, the grocer—all within the last three hours. One of the murder victims had been a newsboy, a small, scrawny lad who routinely turned over his wages to one of the countless gangs that ran the streets day and night. More than likely a member of that same gang had done the killing, but since the incident had gone unobserved, the chances of ever catching the murderer were slim indeed.

It was becoming increasingly difficult these days for the police force to make any real mark on the wave of violent crime sweeping the city. The force had grown appreciably, but was still far too small for a city of New York's size. Until '44, there hadn't even been a professional police force—merely two constables, a small group of appointed marshals, and a "watch" made up of men who patrolled the streets at night. Even with the significantly larger new force of day and night policemen, the city's lawlessness remained out of control. Jails were badly overcrowded, laws remained inadequate, and widespread corruption existed throughout the entire legal system.

More and more these days, Michael found himself angry and frustrated with his job, discouraged one minute and furious the next at the way the entire force seemed to be losing ground to the criminals. Even worse, a rising number of Irish immigrants were to be found among the thugs roving the streets. Hundreds of his own were fast becoming the very kind of predators from which they'd thought themselves to be escaping when they'd fled the auld sod. Once they found the golden streets of their dreams to be paved with garbage instead of gold, and once they learned that the good jobs were seldom if ever available to anyone whose name began with *Mac* or *O* in front, they often turned on the city with a vengeance and seized whatever they could from her.

A bitter root was taking hold in the leprous tenements these days, a root Michael knew would yield even more hatred and a vast new crop of crime and corruption. It had been bad before, but never more so than in the months since Ireland and other parts of Europe had been devastated by famine. They were coming by the thousands now, arriving hungry and ill and desperate, and neither New York nor any other American city was prepared to handle the problems the people brought with them. The streets were filled with a variety of races and nationalities, and there seemed to be no end to the continuing flood of immigrants deluging the shores of the East.

Michael's eyes took in his surroundings. A crush of people crowded along the gaslight-lined streets. Nobody seemed aware of the lateness of the evening or even the bitter wind and stinging snow. There was such a busy, noisy stream of bodies, he felt certain every nation in Europe must be represented somewhere amid the throng. Over there was the fez of a Mohammedan; just ahead the brimless hat of a Persian; farther up a cluster of Italian women with brightly colored shawls and heavy skirts. Mixed in among them were Irish newsboys, Negro laborers, Germans and Spaniards and Orientals—they were all here in the streets, making their fortunes, chasing their dreams, loving and marrying, robbing their countrymen, even killing their neighbors. What was to become of them all, he couldn't imagine.

He was nearing Krueger's bakery now, and he managed a pallid smile for Margaret O'Handley, who worked for the German. As was often the case lately, the woman appeared to be waiting for him, giving him one of her long-toothed grins and a coquettish wave as she watched his approach. Michael instinctively quickened his step as he passed by the storefront, anxious to avoid an encounter.

He was hungry and could smell the bakery's delights, but his step didn't falter as he hurried on. The widow O'Handley had taken to pushing small packages on him once a week or more, insisting they were the leavings from the day and that he "might just as well take them home to the boyo." The leftover pastries were always grand, but Michael was determined to avoid any further kindnesses from the woman.

Some had hinted that he could do worse than consider Margaret O'Handley as a wife. But it was impossible for him to think of the stout, eager-eyed woman as a replacement for his Eileen. Not only did he suspect the widow O'Handley to be considerably older than himself, but he saw a certain meanness in her nature that made him wary of her outward geniality. In short, he simply did not trust the woman.

Aside from his mother, Michael had loved only two women in his thirty-six years, and he wasn't at all convinced he had it in him to attempt a relationship with another. Perhaps his Eileen had been no beauty, but she'd been fair enough in her way, small and sweet-natured, with a quiet voice that gentled his world and an adoring smile that never failed to make his heart leap. He had loved his wife, truly loved her. Her death from the stillbirth of their second child would have crushed him had it not been for the need to go on and look after their son, Tierney. Gone ten years this winter, Eileen still warmed his memories like the tender touch of sunlight on a bitter day.

Before Eileen there had been only Nora Doyle—Nora *Kavanagh*—but they had been little more than children when he'd fancied her.

Besides, she had never been able to see him; Morgan Fitzgerald stood ever in the way. Except for those times when a brief letter from Morgan would send his thoughts straying back to Killala, he had given Nora little thought over the years.

From time to time he considered marrying, but mostly out of concern for Tierney. His son wasn't a bad boy, just motherless since he was four. Growing up as he had, in a city that viewed all things Irish with contempt and in a neighborhood that keened with the endless sorrows of its people, it was small wonder that the lad inclined toward rebellion. A woman's touch might just be the thing to bring some gentling to Tierney's fiery spirit and volatile temper, but only the *right* woman could ever hope to—

A cry from the midst of the dense crowd just ahead brought Michael to a dead stop. It took him only an instant to spot the trouble and take off running, shouting as he went.

A sandwich-board man—one of the numerous fellows who walked about with two advertising signs slung over his shoulders—was down in the street, shrieking at the top of his lungs. A row of young toughs had formed a menacing circle around the poor man, who lay on his back, a virtual prisoner of his signboards. The thugs—four of them, Michael noted as he ran—were kicking the man and brandishing knives as they taunted him and jeered at his terror.

"Here, you!" Michael shouted. Twirling his stick from under his arm, he blew his whistle and took off running, pushing pedestrians out of his way as he went. Some scowled or cursed at him, and one dark-skinned Arab spit in his direction.

A crowd had gathered to watch the assault on the sandwich-board man, and the press of their bodies kept the thugs from seeing Michael until he was nearly on top of them.

"Leave off, scum!" he roared at the largest of the four. This one was whipping a knife dangerously close to the sandwich-board man's horror-stricken face.

"*Copper!*" The warning shout was from one of the punks, a small, ferret-faced boy with freckles.

Michael lunged for the big brute first, clubbing him with a fist as he waved off the other thugs with his stick. Out of the corner of his eye he saw the other three take off and go darting down the street. There was nothing to do but to let them go and concentrate on this one.

The crowd was cheering vigorously, and Michael wasn't surprised to realize that the cheers weren't for him: they were rooting for the tough with the knife. A piercing flash of hot rage surged through him as he hurled himself at the wild-eyed thug and knocked the knife from his hand.

Pressing his stick across the throat of the pimply-faced youth, glaring into his defiant eyes, Michael was tempted to inflict a well-deserved blow. Instead, he fought for control. "It will require no effort at all on my part to snap your scrawny neck if you've a mind to resist arrest," he grated out in a tightly controlled voice. "It's your decision entirely, punk."

At that moment Denny Price, another policeman, parted the crowd, approaching Michael and his captive. "Thought you might need some help, Sergeant, but I can see you don't. I'll tend to the sandwich-board man."

The sandwich-board man seemed shaken, but otherwise unharmed. Price helped the man to his feet, straightened his signs, and turned back to Michael.

"Sure, and your watch is over, Sergeant. Why don't you go along home and let me take this worthless pup in for you? I can manage him without a bit of help at all."

Too tired to argue, Michael gladly took Price's suggestion. As he resumed his trek homeward, he wondered, not for the first time, whatever had possessed him to take on this thankless job.

The answer, of course, was the same as always: It was one of the few decent jobs available to an Irishman in New York City.

5

Do You See Your Children Weeping, Lord?

Pale mothers, wherefore weeping?
Would to God that we were dead—
Our children swoon before us,
And we cannot give them bread!

LADY WILDE [SPERANZA] (1820–1896)

Killala

The road to the Fitzgerald cabin was a highway of the dead and dying. Frozen corpses lay heaped in ditches on either side. Some, Daniel knew, had died of starvation and the cold; others of fever. Meanwhile, the living continued their death march, limping silently down the snow-pitted road. Few expected to escape their inevitable doom, but simply wandered in a bewildered haze of aimlessness and dejection.

They fell when least expected, one by one or at times as an entire family. Many died on their way into the village in search of food or shelter. Others died as they left Killala to seek survival elsewhere.

Encountering former friends and neighbors dead along the road was almost past the bearing, and yet there was no escaping the evidence of the famine's unyielding hand. Daniel's heart was laden with feelings so heavy he thought the weight of them would stop him in his tracks. He always seemed to carry with him a bitter mixture of fear, confusion, and anger.

He *did* stop now, standing off to the side of the road, his gaze falling for a moment on the round tower on Steeple Hill. Its dark silhouette thrust into the late afternoon sky filled him as always with a mixture of wonder and yearning. Again he found himself questioning how long it had stood there, this monument to a past no man could date. What battles had it seen throughout the centuries? How many generations had it watched from birthing to burial?

The past beckoned and tugged at Daniel's imagination. He longed to look across the years and see what had gone before, study it, and perhaps preserve its memory as a part of his own.

In truth, he believed there was no real separation between past and present and future. He felt that somehow, in a way known only to God, the three were one and the same. Mere humans were incapable of seeing things from beginning to end, and so they had to isolate the times, one from the other. But God, he was certain, had no need for such distinctions; He could undoubtedly view at once everything that had ever been and everything that would ever be.

He had once attempted to explain his thoughts to Morgan, who'd had a word for his theory. Morgan had a word for everything, of course, but this was a particularly grand one, which Daniel had never forgotten: *panorama*. "God's panorama," Morgan called it, saying, "I believe, lad, you may have excavated a great truth for yourself, one well worth a measure of careful study."

Now, as Daniel stood staring at the tower, he was convinced that if God were sharing this moment with him, He would more than likely be seeing not only a black-haired boy gazing at a round tower but the mysterious builders of that curious structure as well. Morgan said the towers scattered throughout Ireland had long been a source of controversy among the scholars and the poets. For his part, Morgan held that the ancient buildings had been watchtowers from which the approach of the enemy could be seen in advance. Probably, he said, they had once served as places of refuge, into which the monks could retreat when the barbarous Norsemen invaded the island.

But, wise as he was about most things, even Morgan could not be certain of the towers' origins. God *did* know, however, and Daniel thought that was a wondrous thing indeed. God could see the giants and the heroes who had walked the land before the coming of St. Patrick, the ancient warriors and mythical creatures from which the great legends and epic poems had arisen. God could see the inhabitants of the *raths*—the stone ring-forts, where hundreds of jagged stone stakes enclosed the dwellings of pre-Christian inhabitants. God knew all about the clan chiefs and the druids, the high kings and the bards, and He could see the French fleet landing in the bay during the ill-fated rising of 1798.

Knowing that, believing it, Daniel also had to assume that God saw the corpses of the children and the elderly lying along the road, the starving infants in the dim, unheated cabins, and all the dreadful atrocities taking place beneath the watchful eye of the old round tower. What puzzled him was how God could see it all and do nothing about it. The very One who could end the suffering and the dying in a whisper of an instant made no move to do so.

Knotting his hands into tight fists, Daniel thrust them deep inside his pockets. *Life is life and God is God, and it's nothing but folly to confuse the two.*

The words Morgan had spoken the night of Ellie's wake returned again, as they often had in the days since. They didn't actually help to ease the worrying, and certainly they answered none of his questions. Yet Daniel found an inexplicable measure of comfort when he considered them. Somehow the words relieved his need to *blame* God, thereby allowing him to maintain faith in the Lord's compassion. He sensed there was much, much more to Morgan's words than he'd so far been able to glean, some important truth that continued to elude him.

Perhaps, he thought with a sigh, he simply needed to pray harder about it. Grandfar said too much thinking was a waste, that time and effort were far better spent on one's knees. But Daniel found it virtually impossible to separate the two. It seemed his thoughts were forever interfering with his prayers.

A frigid blast of wind-driven snow shook him out of his reverie for the time being, and he hurried on. He passed half a dozen *scalpeens* on the way to Thomas Fitzgerald's cabin. Their numbers were increasing every day. The hastily built lean-tos were thrown together from whatever thatch and beams and rafters could be salvaged, then anchored against a roadside bank or stone ledge to secure them. Inadequate as they were for one alone, most were crowded with whole families and sometimes even a "lodger" or two. In these hard times, the people inside the rude shelters counted themselves fortunate to have even this much respite from the weather.

Hunched stiffly against the shrieking wind and snow, Daniel was eager for some shelter of his own. His boots, entirely too small for his feet, were worn so thin they provided little protection. His cramped toes felt like chunks of ice, and his stomach was empty, making him lightheaded and a bit queasy. He felt a growing need to see Morgan, and he prayed his friend might have returned by now.

Veering across the road, he started through the field leading to the Fitzgerald cabin. In truth, the "cabin" was little more than a hut in the hollow of a hill. Its walls were shaped by the hillside itself, its front made of mud, its roof sparsely thatched with fern and straw.

Deep ice-glazed ruts in the field sucked at Daniel's feet, slowing him down and freezing his toes. He lifted his face to catch some snow in his mouth, hoping to appease the gnawing in his belly; instead, he caught a sharp breath at the sight of the doctor's trap in front of the Fitzgerald place.

His heart pounding, he began to run. Catherine Fitzgerald had been poorly most of the winter; Daniel had heard his mother voice her concern more than once about her friend's failing health. If the doctor were there, it could only mean Catherine had taken a turn for the worse.

He gave a perfunctory knock, then opened the door and stepped inside. The Kavanaghs and Fitzgeralds went in and out of each other's dwellings freely, like family. His automatic greeting of "God bless all here" met no response, for the only Fitzgerald in sight was ten-year-old Johanna, who was both deaf and mute. She stood staring at Daniel, a fist stuffed against her mouth. Thinner yet than her older sister, Katie, the girl looked pale and not entirely well. Her torn frieze dress, mended more times than the cloth could bear, hung on her like a sack, and her dark red hair was tangled and wild. Her face was so pinched and pale that the freckles banding the bridge of her nose appeared almost black.

Daniel gave her a smile, but she didn't respond. He was struck by a keen sense of something wrong. The cabin was silent. Silent and cold. No family was gathered about the table, and the peat fire had gone out. There was no sign of life, except for Johanna, who stood still as a stone, watching Daniel with frightened eyes.

The Fitzgeralds were a family given to noisy laughter and much teasing— all except for Thomas, who tended to be solemn. Their cabin was normally a loud and lively place, even in these bitter times. The present hush was entirely unnatural, and Daniel's apprehension sharpened still more.

At that moment the curtain at the back of the room parted, and Katie Fitzgerald appeared. As soon as Daniel saw her red-rimmed eyes, he knew she had been crying.

As if anticipating the reason for Daniel's visit, she shook her head. "Morgan isn't back yet, Daniel John."

"But the doctor is here, I see."

Katie nodded. "Mum is awful sick again, she is."

She came the rest of the way into the room then, and Daniel frowned at her appearance. A terrible pallor had settled over her skin, fading it to an almost unhealthy gray. Her face and neck were thin, almost transparent; she looked sad and troubled and somewhat ill.

"Where is your da?" Daniel asked, looking around the room.

Johanna came to stand beside her older sister, and Katie clasped her hand. "He took Little Tom to stay with the grandmother, so he wouldn't be pestering Mum." She paused and her voice faltered. "And...and then he was to go for Father Joseph."

Daniel looked at her with dismay.

"Dr. Browne said he should." Katie's voice had dropped to little more than a whisper.

Daniel stood staring at the two sisters, not knowing what to say. Katie's reddish-blonde hair was damp around her thin face, her eyes desperate. At her side, Johanna continued to stare down at the floor, clinging to Katie's hand.

If the Hunger could fell the once strong and steady Catherine Fitzgerald, how much more easily could it devastate his small, frail mother?

Unbidden, the question struck Daniel with a force that made him sway. For one dreadful moment he wanted to run, to flee the Fitzgeralds and their tragedy. But the look of utter helplessness and pleading in Katie's face held him captive.

Johanna was tugging demandingly at her sister, whining in an odd, voiceless manner, but Katie seemed scarcely aware of her presence. "Daniel John...do you think you could go for your mother? Perhaps it would help Mum if Aunt Nora were here...They're such friends..."

"Aye, I'll go straightaway. Katie, I—" At a loss, Daniel fumbled for some word of comfort. Finding none, he simply repeated, "I'll go now."

Ashamed of his eagerness to get away, he turned and started for the door, willing himself not to run.

As soon as he closed the door behind him, however, he *did* run. Paying no heed to his half-frozen feet or the sharp wind knifing his face, he ran as fast as he could over the field to the road. He ran until he thought his chest would explode, furious with himself for his lack of courage.

I don't understand You, God. Why are You letting this happen to Catherine...to Katie and—and to all of us? You're allowing the good to die with the bad, and even if You're not the one doing the killing, You're letting it happen, and that's the same now, isn't it? It's not fair! You know it isn't the least bit fair to take mothers from their children and let little babes die. What have we done to make You turn on us so, to make You so angry with all Ireland? Don't You see what is happening to us? Don't You care?

It was almost dusk as Morgan tramped the last half mile toward his brother's cabin. He was relieved to be back in the village, though disgruntled that his expedition had not been as successful as he'd hoped. His men had given generously of their meager supply, but they, too, had families to feed—some, entire villages.

There were few ships to plunder on these stormy winter waters, and those that did brave the sea usually did so with naval escorts. Ever since the looting in Blacksod Bay a few months past, the government had been more cautious with their sea trafficking. Still, the lads had provided him with a measure of barley, flour, and dried beef. Morgan had carefully limited his portion, taking only what he could carry on his back; he dared not chance discovery of his mount, leaving it, as always, with his men in the hills.

He neither knew nor cared which particular land agent might be short a few head of cattle or a barrel of flour. He had closed the door on any personal guilt when he'd come to grips with the truth about England's handling of the famine: While Ireland starved, British ships sailed out of her harbors with enough Irish-grown oats and wheat and cattle in a year's time to feed twice the population of the entire island.

Other countries—France, Germany, Holland—had also suffered from the potato blight during the last year, but these, not being ruled by the British, stopped all exports of other food at once in order that their own people would not go hungry. Not so in Ireland. Under the pitiless hand of British rule, tons of home-grown food left the country's harbors every day on British ships, leaving the already starving Irish to survive on nothing but their failed potato crop. Even the grain stored in the farmers' barns was not available to the people; it was marked for rent, to be collected by the agents, while the very ones who had grown it died lingering deaths from the Hunger.

No, Morgan no longer allowed his conscience to keep him awake nights with recriminations. He had no illusions about the road he had taken: He was a wordsmith turned outlaw, a patriot turned rebel, and if he were caught he would die at the end of a rope.

If he were caught...

Should that be the case, he suspected that even the Young Ireland movement—which presently viewed him as an influential, if not entirely irreproachable, member—might be less than eager to claim him as well. All the essays and verses he had written for their journal, *The Nation*—not to mention the funds he and his lads had poured into their coffers—would not inspire them to come to the rescue of a common brigand. While he had done his part to convince Ireland's masses that "peaceful negotiation" with Britain would never bring about a free Ireland, his writings stopped a bit short of the militant, inflammatory tirades some members of the movement would have preferred. He was no favorite of Mitchel or Thomas Meagher, and the fanatical Lalor despised him.

In truth, the entire movement had progressed to an extremism Morgan found both ineffective and foolhardy, and *The Nation* was fueling its fire. He had held both its chief contributor, the now deceased Thomas Davis, and its founder, Charles Gavan Duffy, in high regard. But besides himself, only a few supporters, like Smith O'Brien, still shared the original concepts on which the Young Ireland movement had been founded—that of an Ireland with its own identity, a right to its independence, and a nationalism of the spirit that would embrace both Protestant and Catholic, peasantry and gentry.

No, there would be little help for him from the movement. No matter; he wrote what he wrote, not for the movement, but for himself and the few in the country who still wanted to hear the truth. As for the rest of his "labors," he liked to think they were for those who were too weak or oppressed to save themselves. And, of course, for those few he loved: Thomas and Catherine, their little ones...and Nora and her lads.

He had reached the top of the hill behind his brother's cabin now and, stopping, he shifted the bag of provisions from one shoulder to the other. He frowned when he saw no sign of life below—no smoke from the fire, nobody moving about. But in the remaining gray mist of evening he could just make out blurred hoofprints and tracks from a carriage.

His uneasiness grew as he stared down at the desolate-looking cabin. Finally he moved, taking the hill at a leap, sliding most of the way down in his urgency to reach the bottom.

He knew it was bad as soon as he was through the door. Thomas sat at the table with Johanna in his arms, both of them weeping. His brother's face was stricken, his eyes stunned and vacant.

Then he saw Nora Kavanagh, and knew it all. Joseph Mahon was leading her and Katie from the curtained room at the back. Nora's thin shoulders were stooped beneath the priest's supportive arm, and she was sobbing quietly. The silver-haired Mahon met Morgan's gaze with a sorrowful shake of his head.

Swallowing down his own sense of loss—for he had set a great store by Catherine, fine Christian woman that she was—Morgan dropped his bag onto a chair by the door, then crossed the room to Thomas. His brother wiped his eyes and grabbed for Morgan's hand; Morgan could feel the wet from Thomas's tears on his own skin. "She just…slipped away, Morgan. So quietly…so quickly…"

Katie now came to stand beside Johanna, and Morgan released his brother to gather both little girls into his arms, giving them a hug and some feeble words of comfort before handing them back to their da. He turned and walked uncertainly toward Nora. When she lifted her face to look up at him, her grief was a raw, painful thing.

Gently he eased her away from the priest, and she came to him with a choked sound of despair. As he held her, Morgan felt her trembling, sensed her frailty. The knife of sorrow dug even deeper into his heart, sharpened by a sudden thrust of fear for the small woman in his arms. Instinctively he tightened his embrace.

"She is gone, Morgan. Catherine is gone." Muffled against his chest, Nora's voice was little more than a whisper.

"Shhh, Nora." He rested his chin gently on top of her head. "Catherine rests now. Her struggle is done."

While the priest prayed with Thomas and the girls, Nora went on crying softly in Morgan's arms. He longed to console her, but at this moment he, who had spent most of his life fashioning just the right words for his feelings, could summon none at all to assuage her grief. He could only hold her steady and let her weep.

After a time, her trembling subsided and she backed away, avoiding his eyes. "The old man is ailing now," she said abruptly. "He took to his bed late this afternoon and has not got up since."

"Old Dan?" Morgan frowned. He shouldn't be surprised; the elderly and small children were among those hardest hit by the Hunger and its companion diseases. But Big Dan Kavanagh had always seemed as invincible as the mountains of Mayo themselves, as enduring as the round tower on Steeple Hill.

"I must get home," Nora said, taking another step backward to free herself from his arms. "There's no more I can do here for now, and I left Daniel John to see to Tahg and the grandfather."

Morgan nodded, noting the sooty smudges of exhaustion beneath her eyes, the ashen pallor of her thin, drawn face. "I'll see you home, then."

"That's not necessary," she said stiffly.

"It will soon be dark. Besides, you may need me to go for the doctor for Old Dan."

She shook her head. "I wanted to go myself this afternoon, but he wouldn't hear of it."

"Even so, I'll see you home."

She looked at him, saying nothing, then turned and went to have a word with Thomas.

Outside, the last light of day had almost faded. The gloom-draped dusk was heavy with snow, and the sorrow from the cabin seemed to be carried on the wind.

They walked along without speaking until Morgan broke the silence between them. "So then, how is Tahg? Any change at all?"

Nora stumbled on a jutting ridge of ice, and he took her arm to steady her, tucking it firmly inside his own. "He's so terribly weak," she answered worriedly. "It's as though he's coughed away all his strength and has no more left inside himself. He coughs all the time now, night and day. The medicine Dr. Browne left with us doesn't seem to help at all."

Morgan pressed her hand. "This cold weather is hard on a cough. Sure, and he'll do better once spring comes."

When she said nothing, he added, "You must get some rest yourself, Nora. You'll be no help to your family if you're ill."

She gave a small, apathetic shrug but didn't answer. Morgan felt her shiver and attempted to pull her closer to his side, but she firmly resisted.

"It was all so much easier when we were young," he said with a sigh, primarily to himself. He was remembering other walks they had taken through the snow, in happier days. "Life was kinder then."

"For you, perhaps," she said tersely. "I hated being a child."

He looked at her. "Because of your mother." It was no question, merely a statement of what they both knew.

"There was that," she said quietly. He winced at the hurt in her voice, remembering all too clearly Nora's shame.

"Nobody thought the less of you for her, Nora," he said awkwardly, meaning it.

"Nor the better of me either, I'm sure." A harsh, choked sound of derision escaped her.

"Many thought you were a grand girl," Morgan said evenly after a moment. "I, for one. And Michael, another."

He could scarcely hear her reply, so soft were her words. "Aye, I remember."

He looked down at her, but her eyes were fixed straight ahead. "Have you heard from him of late?" she asked.

"Michael? Not since last fall."

A ghost of a smile touched the corners of her mouth as if she, too, were remembering. "You were the lads, the two of you. You, always in trouble, with Michael guarding your back."

"And both of us playing the fools over you." He said it quietly, not thinking. She didn't seem to hear. If Nora was remembering, she was keeping her thoughts to herself.

Where had it gone, that time in the sun? The years of being young and brimming with life, when every wish was a promise and every dream still within reach...when Nora had been but a slip of a lass, with him and Michael standing as tall as heroes in her eyes?

Ah, where had it gone...and so quickly?

❧

Where have the years gone? Nora wondered, a terrible sense of loss pervading her spirit. Had it really been so long ago that the three of them roamed the village as childhood friends and adventurers?

They had been great companions, those three, young and more than a little foolish at times, but faithful one to the other for all their youthful follies...so different in so many ways, and yet somehow so close in spirit that each could finish the other's thoughts.

Nora had been in Killala first, before either Michael or Morgan. Born in the village, the only other town she had ever stepped foot in was Ballina. She was a child of shame, the oldest of four children, all born on the wrong side of the blanket to a woman who was the scandal of the village. Their father had been a womanizing British sailor who promised Nora's mother the stars and delivered only stones. It was thought he had left a wife in England, for when Nora was eight years old he went back to the sea and never returned.

After that, her mother had taken in one man after another until she became such a slattern she could find no companion but the bottle. Nora and the younger children were left to fend for themselves as best they knew how, and over the years Nora provided what she could in the way of motherly care to the little ones.

She grew up in abject shame: the shame of her mother, their mean, dilapidated hut, her own raggedy clothing and the cast-off garments she and her siblings were forced to wear—but, most of all, the shame of rejection: that of her mother for her own offspring and that of the village for the lot of them. So heavy had been the burden of that shame throughout the years that when her mother died only weeks before Nora gave birth to Tahg, her first thought—may God forgive her—was one of relief: relief that her own children would never need to know their maternal grandmother.

Michael came to the village the year Nora turned nine, the same year a diphtheria epidemic took the lives of her two younger sisters, leaving only her and her wee brother, Rory, to defend themselves against their abusive mother. Three years her senior and already possessing the instincts of a born leader, Michael Burke had immediately taken Nora under his protection. He took his self-appointed guardianship seriously; no longer did the children of the village dare to wag about Nora and her brother, much less taunt them face-to-face. Michael was brawny and rock-solid even then, and he had a look about him that clearly said he was not to be trifled with.

To the lonely, timid Nora, the Burkes were a great wonder of a family, and she often made believe they were her own. Michael's Roman Catholic mother had been an actress in Dublin; his Protestant father the son of a clergyman. Both had defied their families and their churches to wed, eventually settling with their two sons in Killala on a small square of land that had once belonged to Michael's grandparents.

Unloved and neglected, Nora was charmed and entirely in awe of the gregarious, unconventional Burkes. Their generosity of affection, their intelligence and wit, their flair for the dramatic, and, more than anything else, their enthusiastic love for one another attracted her to them like the warm sun draws a dying blossom from the snow. The statuesque, vibrant Madeline Burke appeared to Nora as grand as the legendary warrior-queen Maeve of Connacht. She was beautiful, clever, and endowed with a heart as big as the Irish Sea. The men in Madeline's family adored her, as did the Doyle waifs, who over the years put their feet under the Burkes' kitchen table far more than under their own.

Then came Morgan. In Nora's twelfth year, a long, lean man named Aidan Fitzgerald appeared out of nowhere one autumn day with his two sons in tow and a poke on his back that appeared to hold the sum of their worldly possessions.

Aidan Fitzgerald claimed to be from the southern County Kerry—a long way, indeed, from Killala. He said he was on the road in search of a schoolmaster's position, and when he learned there was an empty schoolhouse in the village he simply moved himself and his lads into an abandoned hillside cabin and stayed. Over the years he kept a school of surprising excellence, managing at the same time to keep the nearby taverns busy accommodating his thirst, which was considerable.

A great deal of mystery surrounded the new schoolmaster and his sons. Aidan was obviously a highly educated, even cultured man, despite the fact that he routinely drank himself witless. He never seemed to be without funds, yet they lived a crude, Spartan life in their womanless cabin. Not a mean-spirited man, he nevertheless appeared to be indifferent to his sons. Indeed, the only time he appeared to show them any interest at all was when he was instructing them in some long-dead poet like Virgil or, more appropriately to Nora's thinking, in the legends and history of ancient

Ireland. Of course, Aidan might just as well have been whistling jigs to a milestone with poor Thomas, who cared for nothing but the land; but Morgan soaked it up like the bog in a downpour, always eager for more.

Never a word was spoken of Morgan's mother, and for a reason Nora did not entirely understand, she knew she was not to ask. Once, when they were older, Michael did make a cautious attempt to inquire, but Morgan's curt "I never knew her" was the only reply.

Rumors circulated the village, as was always the case where a mystery was involved. One particularly popular story had it that Aidan was a fugitive from the law, on the run from some terrible deed in his past. Nora found it difficult to imagine Morgan's distant, hollow-eyed father possessing either the passion or the energy to commit a dastardly crime. Other tales hinted of scandal or tragedy somewhere in the Fitzgeralds' background, and Nora found these far more likely. Another account, one that was never entirely put down, had to do with Aidan's family being gentry of means, who, for reasons never quite fully defined, had disowned him and set him and his boys on the road.

Whatever his past, Morgan was nearly as much on his own as was Nora. They were the same age, though to Nora it seemed that Morgan was years older than she—older, even, than Michael. Considering the friendship that quickly developed among the three of them, it seemed entirely natural that Morgan and his brother, Thomas, would soon pull up their chairs at the Burkes' supper table and be assimilated into the family. Thus Nora found herself with two protectors rather than one.

She soon recognized, however, that while Morgan might enjoy the companionship of Michael and his family, his solitary, restless nature had no real need of a permanent family unit. In contrast to the serious-minded, land-loving Thomas, Morgan had a yen for the road and could often be seen wandering in or out of town, his harp riding his shoulder, his poke slung over his back.

Differences among the three of them might have been expected. In matters of faith, for example, Nora and Michael were closest, both being a part of the small remnant of Protestants in the village. Nora had sought out the small Wesleyan meetinghouse on her own when still a wee girl; her mother was held in such disgrace by most of the Catholics in Killala that Nora could not bear to attend the Roman chapel. As for Michael, although his younger brother Tim had opted for the Catholic faith, Michael himself was impatient with what he termed the "fuss and bother" of it all. He liked the orderly but simple style of worship he found at the meetinghouse.

Morgan was of a different cut entirely. His da never went to church at all, although Aidan was widely known as a "lapsed Catholic." But while Thomas faithfully attended mass whenever it was offered, Morgan went only occasionally. Nora knew that Morgan was a believer, but he claimed no particular denomination or doctrine. Sometimes he showed up at the meetinghouse; sometimes he attended mass with his brother. His odd churchgoing habits made him suspect in the village, of course. Even Nora was bothered by his lack of interest in any formal religious practice. Still, she had to admit that the freedom of Morgan's faith somehow seemed to suit him.

She had a fierce love for both her defenders, though a far different kind for each. She adored Michael Burke as a grand older brother, but Morgan she loved with all her heart. Morgan loved her, too, at least he claimed to as they grew older, and for a time she clung to her hopes that they would one day wed. However, near the time when she reached an age to marry, Morgan left Killala. Apparently there were enough nuggets left in Aidan's mysterious pot of gold to pay for the furthering of his son's education, so Morgan set off for France.

To Nora's dismay, the Burkes took it upon themselves shortly thereafter to announce their intention to leave Ireland as well. They were of a mind to travel to Van Diemen's Land—Australia. Michael, however, having no interest in his parents' plans, declared that *he* would be sailing for America and stunned Nora by asking her to accompany him as his wife.

Once she recovered from her shock, Nora was sorely tempted to accept Michael's proposal. The prospect of losing both Morgan and the entire Burke family terrified her; she could scarcely bear to face life in the village without them. But in spite of her despair, she knew she could not marry Michael Burke. She simply did not love him in the way a woman *should* love the man she weds. Nor could she find it in her heart to leave Ireland and start her life anew in a foreign land among strangers.

So she reluctantly let Michael go, and when Owen Kavanagh began paying her great attention at the meetinghouse and eventually came calling, she put aside her memories of both Michael Burke and Morgan Fitzgerald. Older than Nora by several years, Owen was still a handsome man. More importantly to Nora, he was a *good* man: sober, industrious, and sensible, with goals she could share and the respect of the entire village. Owen's dreams were simple but worthy ones, and closely related to Nora's own. He had it in mind to make a proper marriage, farm a piece of land, supplement his income by working for Reilly the weaver, and raise a family.

Nora was happy as Owen's wife. If she sometimes allowed a longing thought of Morgan Fitzgerald to cross her mind, she immediately dismissed it and asked forgiveness. Although he drifted in and out of her life now and then, making an appearance in the village whenever he'd a mind to, their paths crossed only casually. She could not help the way he looked at her with those searching, sorrowful eyes of his; but she was a woman grown, a wife and mother, and so she quickly turned away and pretended not to see.

Seventeen years had passed since Nora had kissed Michael Burke goodbye and wished him the blessing of God as he left for America. Now she was a widow who had buried her little girl as well as her husband, lost her dearest friend to death, and given up her only brother to a life on the sea as a sailor. She had gray in her hair and winter in her bones and a brimming cup of sorrow in her heart. It was nearly impossible to believe there had once been a time when she had run through a mountain field of wild flowers on the arm of a tall copper-haired lad who played her love songs on his harp and wrote verses about her smoke-gray eyes.

Nora Kavanagh looked up at the bronze-bearded man leading her over the snow, and unwillingly found her heart aching, not only for Owen and wee Ellie and Catherine, but for the young Nora Doyle and Morgan Fitzgerald, for their now silent laughter and long-forgotten dreams.

The time for dreams, Nora knew, had come and gone.

6

And the Fool Has Condemned the Wise

From Boyne to the Linn
Has the mandate been given,
That the children of Finn
From their country be driven.

FEARFLATHA O'GNIVE (SIXTEENTH CENTURY)

Killala
Early February

George Cotter, land agent for Sir Roger Gilpin's holdings in County Mayo, considered himself a victim. He was given to brooding about the various acts of unfairness he had been forced to suffer since childhood. This continual litany of woes had long since become much more than a means of reconciling himself to his miserable existence; indeed, it had become the very *essence* of that existence.

Among his afflictions he numbered poor health, a short, round physique with a flat-featured face, and a history of unfortunate financial circumstances. The bane of his entire life, however, was his father. George could not remember a time when he had not hated his father, hated him with an almost debilitating passion.

Richard Cotter had been a Dublin barrister with a terrible thirst for the spirits and an even greater lust for gambling. He would bet on anything, no matter how foolish the risk, and he proved to be incredibly unlucky in all his endeavors. While still a young man, he had gambled away not only his own small inheritance from his physician father, but most of his British-born wife's humble dowry as well. It was widely held in the village and surrounding countryside that Richard Cotter was a weak, dissipated, totally immoral man whose lifelong conduct would have shamed a field of tinkers.

Fortunately for the family, George's maternal grandparents owned a modest estate and two small but successful farms in Connacht, which, taken together, provided the Cotters with a home and an adequate livelihood. Even so, George grew up a bitter, rebellious young man: bitter because of what he considered their humble station in life, and rebellious in response to his father's frequently expressed contempt for his only son.

George's mother died before he reached his eighteenth year, and his father's excesses finally took their toll a few months later. Richard Cotter's only legacy to his son was more than a decade of verbal and sometimes physical abuse, and George felt nothing but relief and even a sense of satisfaction when he buried the man.

Cotter was left with virtually nothing. His grandparents' lands had so many liens on them by then that they immediately fell to Hamilton Gilpin, an "absentee landlord" who owned vast tracts of property throughout County Mayo—but who was never seen to step foot on any one of them. When Gilpin's agent, a kind enough man, offered the penniless young George Cotter a job on the Gilpin estates, he saw nothing else to do but take him up on it, albeit grudgingly.

Cotter had worked for the Gilpin family ever since, rising to his present position as land agent not through any real ambition or even competence, but because he was one of the few men in the area who could read, write, and do sums. The "big lord" was now Sir Roger Gilpin, who like his father before him, avoided any involvement with his Irish holdings, except what was required to collect the rents.

It was a Friday night, and Cotter sat morosely in his shabby fireside chair, his gouty leg propped up on a stool, his belt unbuckled to free his protruding stomach. He scowled at the letter in his hand. His mood was as ugly as the wild, shrieking snowstorm he'd only recently escaped. Chilled and in agony with the gout that plagued him more and more bitterly these days, he lifted his tumbler of whiskey and drained it dry.

It was easy enough for these absentee landlords like Gilpin to wave their pens over their fancy stationery and sign eviction orders, he thought.

It would not be *their* hides if a mob of village riffraff took it upon themselves to have their revenge on those responsible for turning them out. Agents like himself suffered the consequences of the landlords' greed. And all because they had no choice but to do as they were told.

Retaliation by some of the locals was a distinct possibility. Cotter had heard enough, all right, to know it was happening all across Ireland, even right here in backward Mayo. Displaced tenants were striking out, venting their rage like a bunch of mindless savages on the land agents. Just last month an agent near Ballina had been knifed and clubbed to death by a group of peasants he'd evicted.

Mass eviction. That was the cause of it. Not just tumbling a few squatters' cabins or the huts of those worthless whiners who were continually in arrears, but the large-scale eviction of dozens of families who had lived in Killala and similar communities all their lives.

His throat tightened. It would be easy to imagine men like O'Malley, a known faction fighter, and Rafferty, the worst kind of drunken troublemaker, rising up and taking arms against their betters.

Head pounding, Cotter tipped the tumbler to his lips. Finding it empty, he hauled his ponderous, aching frame from the chair, grunting with the effort. He went to the window and looked out, down the hill toward the village, but there was nothing to be seen except sheets of wind-driven snow piercing the night. His anger swelled along with the pain in his head, and he limped across the room to pour another whiskey.

The thing to do, he thought as he swilled his drink, *the expedient thing, would be to torch the entire dismal village.* Not only would it remove an unsightly blot from the landscape, but it would settle those miserable wretches in their hovels once and for all, before they took it upon themselves to make trouble up here on the hill.

With a stab of apprehension, Cotter recalled the rumors blowing about the county: tales of a band of rebels and malcontents, sweeping down from the mountains just long enough to fire the houses and barns of agents throughout the county, stealing their livestock and pantry contents, then depositing their spoils in the yards of the starving peasants.

One band in particular raised the hair on his neck—the rabble who followed the brigand called the *Red Wolf.* Outlaws, every last one of them, and not beyond stirring up an enraged peasantry to rebellion. Thugs was what they were: low-browed, hulking primitives, for certain, and their leader—the one they fancifully called the Red Wolf—was undoubtedly the worst of them all. Tales mounted weekly about that one, most of them undoubtedly blown all out of proportion. They tended to make him a creature far bigger than life and more a menace than the predator from which he took his name. George had his suspicions about their Red Wolf's identity, and while the great brute might be entirely human, he was still a formidable enough enemy.

A hot pain stabbed upward from his foot to his knee, and he cried out, fumbling for the desk to steady himself. At last he staggered across the room, sinking weakly down into his chair and leaning back with a moan. As the pain subsided, he tried to think what to do. One thing was certain: he would need every man of the constabulary he could get. First thing in the morning he'd call in the bailiff and have him alert the police. It was best to begin at once, before some of the riffraff in the village got wind of what was coming, as they seemed to have a way of doing.

Cotter started to crumple his employer's letter, then stopped, realizing it might not be smart to destroy Gilpin's written orders. It also occurred to him that he might be wise to arrange for protection for himself when he talked with the bailiff. No point in taking chances. Considering the fate to which he would be subjecting these poor devils, it wouldn't do to relax his guard.

There was an unmistakable smell of trouble in the air, and he didn't intend to be caught unawares. Those starving barbarians in the village were capable of anything, of that he had no doubt. Once the evictions began, who could tell what mischief they might wreak?

Two weeks after Catherine's burial, Morgan was still trying to soften Nora's reserve toward him, with no success. He thought he understood the way she had retreated into herself after Catherine died. On the heels of the death of both her little girl and husband, losing her dearest friend had to be near devastating, both physically and emotionally.

But he wanted to see her, to help if he could, to comfort if she'd let him. He wasn't dim-witted enough to try to start things up with her again. Not only was she in mourning, but the two of them had long ago faced the truth that no matter how deep their feelings for each other, they simply had no future together. He was one way, and she another; involving himself in her life in any manner other than as a friend could only lead to problems, even pain, for them both.

That being resolved, why, then, did she still flicker like a flame in the shadows of his mind? Why did his heart ache so when she deliberately ignored his overtures to see her? If he called at the cottage, she merely exchanged a few words with him at the door, never once inviting him inside. If he passed by her place—which he made it a point to do at least once a day—and happened to spot her in the yard tending to the cow, she offered a distant greeting, then hurried inside before he could stop her. She was deliberately avoiding him, he had no doubt; as to why, he wasn't sure.

Although getting past that iron-hard stubbornness of hers had been a bit like boring through a mountain, he had finally convinced her to accept the provisions he'd brought back with him from the hills. At first she had argued, her mulish pride resisting the suggestion that she needed his help. God forbid that she should accept charity from one such as Morgan Fitzgerald! Finally, though, she had acquiesced and accepted his offering. It had been the last real conversation they had shared.

Thus, he reluctantly decided to attend tonight's farewell to-do for Tim O'Malley. Ordinarily he would have avoided the event. He had never been the man for these provincial traditions, nor did he particularly enjoy being a part of a group. Added to his solitary nature, however, was his physical discomfort this night; he had a monster of a toothache that had been paining him since sunup, and the O'Malley's cabin was cold as a grave, which only served to aggravate the pain.

He was here for one reason only—to see Nora, who so far had been maddeningly successful at ignoring him entirely. He had expected that, of course, but it scalded him nevertheless, the way she would look in a different direction each time he managed to catch her eye.

The "American wake," as it was called throughout most counties— or more commonly here in Mayo, the "feast of departure"—had been observed only on rare occasions before the famine. Lately, however, it had become commonplace, although the nature of the event had changed drastically, given the destitute conditions across the country. For many of them, indeed, the act of leaving Ireland seemed the closest thing to death itself. Dying was epitomized by the departure from home. The ship came

to represent a coffin, separating the voyager from his loved ones and setting him on his way to "Paradise"—America.

During the best of times the custom made for a bittersweet occasion.
The evening ordinarily began with dancing and singing, drinking and eating, then declined to a maudlin wallow in nostalgia and painful farewells.
Until recently it was not uncommon for a family to go the entire affair on
tick—on credit—depending on the one going across to repay the debt
once he attained his fortune. With the extreme poverty in the village these
days, however, tonight's gathering for Sean O'Malley's Tim held little hint
of merriment and even less of a feast. Without the luxuries of tobacco or the
illegally distilled poteen, the occasion was a solemn, almost dismal affair.

By late in the evening the talk had drifted round to the heart of the
wake: America, and her limitless opportunities for success, wealth, and
happiness. The men, most of them gaunt and somewhat desperate-looking,
stood with their arms folded across their sunken chests, listening with avid
expressions to young Tim and another hopeful emigrant repeat their collected tales about the promised land. Most of the stories were based upon
letters received by other village residents who had family already settled in
America, family "growing richer by the day."

The women, hunched for the most part in a dimly lighted corner across
the room, were noisily reviewing the contents of the letters to which they
had been privy. This group, while loud enough in its own right, was far
more somber and inclined to expound in great detail about the horrors
inflicted upon unsuspecting voyagers who, alas, had not lived long enough
to see the sweet shores of America.

Morgan noted that Nora didn't seem to be a part of either group, nor
of the smaller cluster of young girls who sat off to themselves, giggling and
casting an occasional flirtatious glance toward the lads across the room.
Instead, she stood off to herself, her eyes dull and fixed.

An unexpected rush of desire to comfort her seized him, only to ebb
as he accepted the fact there was nothing he could do. The kind of loss
Nora had suffered over the past months was a grief only God Himself
could relieve. Still, he could not quite dismiss the frustration of wanting
to encourage her, all the while knowing that Nora would no more turn to
him for consolation than she might to an Englishman for mercy.

When Daniel John walked up at that moment, Morgan spoke before
he could conceal his annoyance with the situation.

"Ah, I was beginning to think I was invisible to the Kavanaghs this evening."

The boy gave him a blank look.

"Your mother has as yet been unable to see me."

Daniel John was quick to reassure him, but Morgan didn't miss the lad's troubled expression. "Mother is sad, is all, Morgan. She...she has very little to say these days, even at home."

Disgusted with his own churlishness, Morgan forced a smile. "I know, lad. I suppose I've always been a bit touchy where your mother is concerned."

"But why, Morgan?"

The question on the boy's face was entirely innocent, and Morgan hesitated, uncertain as to how to reply. "Well, now, I expect it's because I've always valued her good opinion, you see. Your mother is a grand woman, and why wouldn't I want her to think well of me?"

"Oh, but she *does*, Morgan! I know she does! You were great friends once, after all. It's just that..."

The boy faltered, and Morgan hastily changed the subject. "Pay me no mind, Daniel John. I've a toothache that's been driving a dagger up my skull for most of the day; it's made me as cross as a bag of cats. Come along now," he said cheerfully, slinging an arm about the boy's thin shoulders, "let us go and say hello to your mother."

At their approach, Nora's eyes took on the startled expression of a skittish foal. Morgan sensed with impatience that she was vastly uncomfortable in his presence. He supposed he deserved that from her, but it grieved him to see her look at him so.

More than her awkwardness around him, though, he was concerned about her appearance. Her always willow-slim frame was thin to the point of gauntness; she looked wan and frail and not entirely well. He wondered if she were eating, wondered as quickly if she and the family still had food left from what he'd given her. He would make it a point to get Daniel John alone before the evening ended and see what he could learn about their situation.

She finally managed a smile—for her son's sake, Morgan suspected—and a murmured "Hello." They exchanged stiff, uncomfortable bits of conversation for a time, with the boy doing his best to alleviate the tension. Morgan did manage to learn that Tahg was no better—he was, in fact, worse—and that Old Dan's condition had also deteriorated.

When Daniel John eventually drifted off to talk with another lad from the village, Morgan stepped closer to Nora to prevent her from escaping him. "And you, then, Nora, how is it with you?"

She tensed, avoiding his gaze as he stared down at her. "We're getting on. As well as the next, I'm sure."

"That's not entirely reassuring, given conditions in the village."

She shrugged, still not meeting his eyes. "They say we're to have more relief soon. New soup kitchens and distribution centers." Clearly she was unconvinced. "Have you heard so?"

She looked at him, her eyes so large and anxious that he hadn't the heart to tell her what he knew. Even if more relief *were* to come to their all-but-forgotten village, it would likely be too late for most of Killala, just as it had been too late for so many other towns throughout the country. True, numerous centers had been established all across Ireland, but they were far too few, and the soup served by most of them was little more than worthless greasy water, a pitiful excuse for even the most meager nourishment.

"Aye, I have heard," he mumbled. Now he was the one to look away.

"What requirements will there be, do you know?"

He looked back at her. "Requirements?"

She nodded. "Sean O'Malley is saying you must meet certain requirements to be eligible for the relief. He says the rules are strict."

"I would expect so." *Strict and entirely unrealistic,* he thought bitterly.

When he said no more, Nora went on. "I must be certain we will qualify. For Tahg and the Old Man, especially."

For a moment, Morgan felt a hot stab of resentment and anger at the helpless fear in her eyes: resentment that one so innocent and good should be degraded to such dependency, and anger at himself for being virtually powerless to help her.

"As I understand it," he said, carefully choking back the bitterness he felt, "recipients must be certified to have no means of support. They must have no animals, and their potato patch must be a total waste." Pausing, he then added, "And you must give up all land more than a quarter acre."

Her eyes widened with alarm. "But the land is all we have!"

Wanting more and more to avoid this conversation, he gave a small nod of agreement. "They know that only too well, I should imagine."

A reluctant understanding dawned in her eyes. "You're saying they don't *want* us to survive, aren't you? That even when the famine ends, they mean for us to die."

"That possibility has occurred to some," he answered sourly. "The land, you see, will be far more profitable to the landlords as grazing land, rather than parceled out as it presently is, in tenant farms. Some believe that Mother England intends to clear the land of people so she can populate it with cattle. Perhaps," he finished, "the lads like young Tim there are doing the Queen a great turn by sailing for America."

Nora searched his eyes for a moment. "And is that what you believe?"

He answered her question with a shrug, feeling a tinge of relief when Sean O'Malley walked up just then, sparing him the need to say more.

"Did I see you bringing your harp inside this evening, Morgan?"

"You did, Sean."

The older man's expression was sober and somewhat strained. "Would you give us a tune, then? A song for Tim and his mother, perhaps?"

Morgan put a hand to O'Malley's once burly shoulder, keenly aware of the sharp protrusion of bone beneath his fingers. "I will do that, Sean, and gladly. Have you a special one you fancy?"

"One of your own, I should think, Morgan, if it's no trouble. Something just for the lad, if you would."

Ashamed of his eagerness to escape the pain in the grieving father's eyes, Morgan gave a short nod and started for the corner by the fireplace to retrieve his harp. Even as he crossed the room, a song began to form on his tongue. Words and melodies had ever been within easy reach for him. From the time he was a lad it seemed that the Lord had placed a storage box of songs within his heart, from which he never had to do more than simply lift the lid and reach inside to select the one he wanted. He knew that he was known more for his words—his verses, and lately his essays in *The Nation*—but in truth he found his greatest pleasure in choosing words to fit melodies equally his own.

And so he sang his song for Tim O'Malley, and although it was a sad song that poured forth from him, he was able to give it a touch of hope as well. For while the lad undoubtedly had a terrible, bitter time ahead of him, he was at least doing something to save himself and perhaps eventually some of his family, too.

Morgan cradled the harp against his shoulder and plucked the brass strings with his fingers. The sound vibrated into his chest as he caressed the ancient instrument with the familiar touch of a lover returning to his beloved. For a moment—for just a moment—his heart vibrated, too, with the hope of something better to come. But the fleeting echo died as quickly as it had begun, and when the last strains of Morgan Fitzgerald's song for Tim O'Malley had ceased, darkness closed in around the poet's soul once more.

By the time he had finished, the "wake" had reached the hardest moment of all, the time of the final parting. The guests would commiserate with the family, then make their tearful goodbyes before departing to allow the O'Malleys a private farewell. Afterward, young Timothy would exchange embraces with his family, then turn and leave, for the last time, the cabin in which he had grown to manhood. Off he would go with his paltry worldly goods and a brave wave of his hand as he put behind him forever his loved ones, his past, and his heritage.

The closing of the coffin, as it were. How many from the village, Morgan wondered, would repeat this same scene in the weeks and months to come? Indeed, how many would *survive* long enough to repeat it?

His eyes went to Nora. Her face was stricken, drawn with grief for her friends and, he sensed, dread for her own family. At her side, Daniel John's face was ashen and taut with his own bewilderment and unanswered questions.

At that instant Morgan felt a suffocating hand of apprehension slip down and close around his throat. He was struck so hard he almost reeled at the power of his unspoken but ever-present love for these two. The small woman in the coarse black dress was as lovely and as noble to his eyes as if she were a princess in satin, and the long-legged boy at her side might have been his own son, so dear to his heart had he long been.

Sudden fear for them both loomed up as strong as a physical presence, and he knew at last why he had returned to Killala long before he had planned. His intention had been to stay with the lads in the hills, dropping down at night only when he had a need to. There he could think and write and even find a bit of temporary peace. But something had called him back, some urge he could neither name nor resist.

He recognized it now and was infinitely thankful to have heeded its call. Without knowing how he would accomplish it, he knew he was here to save Nora and her sons from the darkness gathering on Killala's horizon.

How much he could do and how soon he should act depended in part on Michael's response to the letter he had written him—the letter he should have received by now.

If Michael were willing to help, and if Nora were willing to go, there was still hope for her and the boys. But one thing was certain: Every day that went by eroded their hope and compounded the danger. To wait too long might well mean disaster.

And yet wait he must. In the meantime, he would do what he could to help them survive.

If Nora would let him, that is.

~

Nora asked young Moira Sullivan from up the road to pay a call at the cottage while she and Daniel John attended the O'Malley farewell supper. Old Dan had grown far too weak to be of any real help to Tahg; more and more Nora feared the old man might fall, with nobody nearby to help *him*.

Moira had already gone when they returned home, so Nora went immediately to check on the old man, then Tagh. Both were asleep, though Tagh was tossing and moaning. Ashamed that she had left him for so long, Nora hurried from the room to get a cloth and some cool water.

She stopped just inside the kitchen at the sight of Daniel John, framed in the open doorway, standing as still as a statue.

"Ach, Daniel John, close the door! 'Tis cold enough in here as it is, without—" His white, stricken face stopped her in mid-sentence. "What is it? What's wrong?"

"The cow is gone!" he blurted out, his eyes wide and frightened. "Someone has taken Sadie!"

Fear clutched at Nora's heart as she stood staring at him. Then she bolted across the kitchen and out the door. Coatless, she scarcely noticed the damp, stinging cold of the night as she ran around the side of the cottage with Daniel John right behind her.

As he'd said, the cow was gone, rope and all. Panic rose like a flood tide as the dreadful reality of their situation washed over her. Their one remaining source of food was gone.

"Perhaps she wasn't taken, though…perhaps she simply broke her rope and is roaming about…somewhere." She heard the trembling in her voice, felt her knees threaten to buckle beneath her.

"Aye, that could be," Daniel John agreed quickly. Too quickly. "I'll have a look. She's probably nearby."

"But you can't be wandering about in the dead of night, not in this cold."

He looked at her. "And we can't afford to lose Sadie, Mother. I don't think I should wait."

If the cow had been stolen, a few hours wouldn't matter, Nora realized with dismay. Still, she knew he was right; they had to try.

"If she's only wandered off, I won't be long. Sadie will come to the sound of my voice," he said uncertainly.

A nagging whisper somewhere deep inside Nora told her the cow had not wandered off. The theft of livestock, even in broad daylight, had been on the increase for weeks now, not only in Killala, but throughout all Ireland. People were doing whatever they must to survive. They had taken to eating horses, even dogs. A cow would seem a treasure.

She could see in Daniel John's eyes that he, too, held little hope of finding Sadie. But neither of them dared to give voice to their thoughts.

"Go, then," she said, averting her eyes. "But not too far. It will do us no good to find the cow if you catch your death in the searching."

He put a hand to her arm. "I'll find her, Mother. You go back inside now."

She nodded, still unable to meet his eyes.

Hugging her arms to her body against the cold, Nora stood, watching him start for the road. She turned once to look at the empty barn, then glanced around the yard.

She was suddenly struck by the memory of Morgan's words when he had named off the requirements for relief distributions. No animals, he had said; no animals, no potatoes, and less than a quarter acre of land.

Well, then, it would seem we are now eligible for relief, she thought, nearly choking on her own bitterness.

The question was, would they live long enough to apply for it?

7

A Gaunt Crowd
on the Highway

When tyranny's pampered and purple-clad minions
Drive forth the lone widow and orphan to die,
Shall no angel of vengeance unfurl his red pinions,
And grasping sharp thunderbolts, rush from on high?

RICHARD DALTON WILLIAMS (1822–1862)

Morgan spent the weekend at Frank Grehan's place near Ballina, working on a piece they were writing for *The Nation,* the journal of the Young Ireland movement. He had hoped a day or two away from the village might be just the tonic for his troubled thoughts about Nora and his own family. Instead, he spent an altogether dismal two days, wishing he had never come at all.

Why had he ever agreed to collaborate with the blustering, irascible Grehan anyhow? The man was more trying than ever, to the point that Morgan could scarcely wait to get away from him.

Grehan was an embittered man in his forties who lived alone in a gloomy, drafty old farmhouse. A loyal Young Irelander who fancied himself a radical and a revolutionary, he unfailingly turned a visit from an acquaintance into a political forum. Unfortunately, his acquaintance with the bottle went deeper than his knowledge of politics.

He had spent most of the weekend attempting to badger Morgan into assuming a more active leadership role in the movement, accompanying each argument with the statement that Morgan could "make a real difference."

Even as he ushered Morgan out the heavy front door, instead of sending him off with a friendly farewell, Grehan blasted him with still more rhetoric. "You think on it, Fitzgerald; you're ripe to lead. The movement is made up of mostly Protestants as yet, but your golden tongue and gift of reason can make the Catholic voice heard within the ranks at last."

Morgan ground his teeth as he reminded Frank that he was merely an out-of-work schoolmaster and a dilettante writer, not a politician. "And I have no 'Catholic voice,' as I have pointed out to you before. Why, neither Catholic nor Protestant would want to claim the likes of me, man. I'm a heathen in the eyes of both."

His attempt at levity went unnoticed. Grehan accompanied him out the door and into the yard, waist high with weeds. "The people are going to rise, Fitzgerald. It's in the wind, even now. Aye, there will be a rising, that's sure, and you should be one of its leaders."

With a great deal of firmness mixed with laughter, Morgan finally managed to free himself from his host's cloying grasp and take his leave. Hoisting his harp a bit higher, he whipped his cloak around his shoulders and started down the road.

The weather seemed grimly appropriate to his mood. Within moments he found himself in the midst of a savage storm of wind-driven, freezing rain and snow. Drawing his cloak a bit tighter around his throat, he ducked his head and turned his face toward Killala.

Despite the weather, he was glad to have escaped when he did. Had Grehan continued to press him, he might have lost his temper and revealed more of his personal displeasure with the "movement" than Firebrand Frank would care to hear.

An entire host of objections to the antics of Grehan and his bunch swarmed in his head like angry bees. He was particularly disgruntled about the new militant organization being formed out of the Young Ireland movement—the "Irish Confederation," they were calling themselves. He knew the plan. They intended to spread their influence by forming clubs in every city and town, whereby more and more pressure might be brought to bear on the British government. Repeal of the union between England and Ireland was one of their primary objectives, arguing as always that only absolute freedom could save their country from total destruction.

It sounded fine in theory, but in reality it had as many holes as a sieve. Oh, he knew well enough who Frank and his wild-eyed rebels had been listening to, all right: Fintan Lalor, a dark-natured, brooding recluse who had isolated himself on a farm in Queens County to agonize over Ireland's tragedy.

Lalor argued for a "moral insurrection," his premise being that only the rising up of tenants against their landlords would eventually free the Irish from England's chains. He used his considerable facility with words to incite farmers to withhold their rent payments until they were granted coequal ownership of the land.

But Lalor's ideals would never be realized except by revolution: armed insurrection, not moral. And while he shared, with reservations, Lalor's contention that Ireland's only future lay in reclaiming her own lands from the British, Morgan knew beyond a doubt that these angry, "courageous" peasants were more figments of Lalor's imagination than fact. In reality, Ireland's farmers were dying in the ditches—frozen, starved, and decimated by disease. He found it incomprehensible that these raving visionaries could entertain the notion of an armed uprising by a starving, defeated people. Even a fool could see that the Irish peasantry were too enfeebled, too demoralized, and too broken to think of anything at all beyond survival. Moreover, it was commonly agreed that the famine had not yet reached its full horror. Morgan knew in his soul that a cataclysm of unimaginable proportions was yet to come.

With a failed potato crop for the second year in a row, the half-naked, poverty-stricken men and women who had managed to survive on the outdoor public works now had no employment at all. The public works were at an end; the workhouses were full and running over; thousands upon thousands of peasants were severely in arrears on their rents. To fall behind meant certain eviction, and to be homeless during this, the most severe winter in Ireland's memory, meant certain death.

Revolution, indeed! When a man had no food and no work, no health and no strength, no home and no hope—was such a man equipped for rebellion?

Morgan was convinced that before insurrection could even be considered, the people must be fed—fed and healed. Education, too, was vital. The Lord knew the Irish loved all manner of learning, but with years of their own Gaelic language forbidden and their schoolmasters and clergy in hiding, any traditional form of real education had gone by the wayside. In addition, there was the desperate need to end the hatred between

Protestant and Catholic, which played a very real part in dividing the country.

We are forever fighting one another, Morgan mused bitterly, *the Irish against the Irish.* He could not help but wonder who, themselves or the British, had harmed the island most.

It was midafternoon before Morgan reached the edge of Killala. In spite of his heavy cloak, he was drenched and thoroughly chilled. So absorbed had he been in some lines for a new poem that he was jolted harshly back to reality by a sound like approaching thunder.

He whirled around. Cotter, the land agent, came bearing down on him from the west fork in the road, astride a foaming, wild-eyed stallion. Throwing a wall of mud and ice in Morgan's path, the agent wielded his riding crop like a lunatic. His heavy-jowled, bloated face was raw and windwhipped. Below his hat, sparse, wet strands of red hair capped his ears.

The agent's small round eyes betrayed a meanness, an expression of bestial excitement that chilled Fitzgerald's blood. The man looked for all the world like a demon turned loose from hell's pit. Following him, also mounted, were the bailiff and two ruffians known to be Cotter's personal bodyguards. Running behind and struggling to keep up came a raggedy bunch of housewreckers, all brandishing crowbars.

Morgan leaped out of the way, twisting his ankle as he hurled himself into the slush-filled ditch to avoid being run down. Watching them charge by, fury slammed at his ribcage, and he raised a fist to their backs, wanting nothing so much as to hurl the lot of them into the bay. Instead, he could only stand unmoving in the ditch, stunned and impotent in his rage, watching as the mob came to a halt in front of Aine Quigley's cottage.

Anger gave way to sick horror as Morgan realized what was happening. Mass eviction. He had seen it before in Galway and Sligo, still carried the nightmare scenes in his mind. His stomach knotted and his breathing grew labored as he stood watching.

The Quigley place, sorely rundown and neglected, had not always been in such a sad state. Once the dwelling of Michael Burke's family, the large two-story house with its slate roof and tall, narrow windows had been one of the finest homes in the village. But according to Thomas, poor Aine had been at her wits' end for months now, trying to keep food in the bellies of her three small children after her husband died of pneumonia. The house had steadily gone to ruin.

There were three homes there at the turn in the road: Aine Quigley's, Sean O'Malley's, and, directly across from these two, the Gaffneys', all looking forlorn and uncared-for in the icy winter rain hammering down on them. Within the hour, Morgan knew with a terrible certainty, three families—two of them with children—would face death in a ditch.

For a long time he stood watching the scene unfold in front of the Quigley's, anger and outrage hitting him like waves. Finally he stirred. His feet were half frozen in his boots, his hands stiff from cold in spite of wool gloves. He lurched out of the ditch, starting in the direction of the wrecking crew.

With every step, the fire of his rage increased. A moan of physical pain escaped his lips as he stumbled, then lunged ahead. Nearly mindless now with fury, he charged through the icy slush on the road, as intent on his prey as a mad bull.

Nora stood in the middle of the road outside her cottage, tented beneath Old Dan's *bawneen* and wearing his boots as she searched the surroundings for a glimpse of Daniel. This was the third day straight the boy had gone looking for the missing Sadie. In spite of Nora's insistence that the cow was surely lost to them, he simply refused to give up; he had been out almost all morning in this terrible, freezing rain.

A noise made her turn back to look toward the opposite end of town. The sound came rolling up the road, an advancing roar of angry voices.

With the gloom of the day and the pouring rain, it was difficult to see much of anything, but she could look down the road and make out the Quigley house and one side of the O'Malley place. A crowd seemed to be gathered in front of Aine Quigley's—some on horseback, but most on foot. Nora stared for another moment. Then, dropping the old man's work coat down to her shoulders, she quickly slipped it on and began walking.

She was over halfway down the road when Cotter, the land agent, came into view. He was sitting astride his big, dirty gray stallion, shouting orders to a group of men nearby. A sickening wave of foreboding engulfed her as she recalled a conversation she'd had with Aine Quigley only days before. Apparently Cotter had been threatening them with eviction for weeks. They had fallen behind with the rent some months before, and, according to Aine, only the fact that the agent had his unholy eye on Padraic's younger brother had kept him from turning them out before now.

The sick-minded land agent's attraction to young boys had been rumored in the village for years. Speculation had turned to outrage just last summer, however, when Dr. Browne's son let it slip to some of the lads that his father had treated young Fursey Lynch for "wounds" inflicted by Cotter.

An orphan boy from Kilcummin, Fursey Lynch had been given a place in the agent's barn, as well as his meals, in exchange for doing odd jobs around the property. Although the doctor's son had been vague about Fursey's "wounds," he let it be known that the lad's injuries were severe enough to keep him at Browne's house for nearly two weeks before his return to Kilcummin.

Aine Quigley, convinced that Cotter's leniency with their back rent hinged on his fascination for Padraic's brother, told Nora in hushed tones it was "the end for them," since the lad had left the village to live with an aunt in Ballina. "Cotter will turn us out without mercy now," she whispered to Nora, her eyes wide with fear. "And what will become of my babes, then? They won't last a day on the road!" Nora had done her best to reassure the distraught widow, but at the same time she feared that Aine was justified in expecting the worst.

A terrible dread welled up in her as she approached the Quigley house. She nodded a greeting to Mary Larkin, whose grim shake of the head indicated that the worst was about to happen. A silence had fallen over the group as she drew near, a strange, oppressive stillness, as if the entire assembly was waiting for someone to die. The faces of the people, both men and women, were lined with a mixture of fear and sympathy, disbelief and hostility.

Her gaze went from the bailiff, mounted on a scrawny brown horse, to Cotter, who sat scowling down at the crowd from his snorting gray stallion. It took her a moment to comprehend the significance of several raggedy-looking men standing near the horses, but when she did she nearly gasped aloud.

"Destructives," murmured a man nearby, as if voicing her dismay. Nora shuddered. These were the despised housewreckers, those who, after being evicted from their own homes, managed to survive by tearing down the houses of their neighbors for food or pay.

God have mercy, are they going to tumble Aine's house as well as turn her out? Nora wondered.

One of the local constables was reading off a list in a loud, imperious voice. Nora heard the names of the O'Malleys and the Quigleys called, then the Gaffneys. When no one appeared from any of the three cottages, Cotter spurred his horse forward, prodding the constable with his riding crop. Startled, the short, rotund man jumped, then took off running to the front door of the Quigley house, giving it three hard raps with his fist.

Nora's breath quickened with dismay when Aine appeared at the door. In her arms she held her youngest babe, a thin, fine-boned boy with hair the color of old ivory; two wee girls stood on either side of their mother. Every face, with the exception of the babe in his mother's arms, was pale with fright.

The constable started to speak, but Cotter went charging up the yard on his mount, his gruff voice drowning out the policeman. "Where's the man of this house?"

Nora could just barely hear Aine's reply.

"Why, my husband is dead, sir. More than four months past now." The woman's voice trembled almost as violently as the thin hand clinging to the door frame.

Cotter turned to the bailiff, who was dismounting. "What have they got? Any animals?"

"A goat and a horse," the other man replied carelessly, handing over the reins of his horse to one of the housewreckers standing nearby. "They had a cow, but it seems it died on them in December—"

"The horse and the goat are dead, too, sir," Aine quickly interrupted. "We have no animals now, none at all."

"Well, your rent is in arrears, and since you've no way of paying it, you'll have to leave," Cotter ordered. "Get what you want from inside and get out. Now!"

Aine flinched as if the agent had struck her in the face with his riding crop. Wincing from the plight of her friend's pain, Nora instinctively took a step forward. She stopped when Cotter whirled around to eye the crowd that had gradually begun to close in.

"Stay back, the lot of you!" he bellowed. "You'd be wise to take heed of what is happening here. Any one of you behind in his rent—you'll be next if it's not paid in full when you're told!"

From somewhere in the crowd a woman cried out, and soon others began to weep with her. Aine Quigley, however, seemed resolved to fight. "Sure, and you can't mean what you say, sir! I've three small babes and not a coat among us. We've no food and no health! You'll be sending us to our deaths if you turn us out."

"Then apply for admission to the workhouse!" snapped Cotter, turning to glare down at the bailiff. "Get those men started at once!

And you"—he wagged a finger at the bald-headed constable still in the yard—"see to the other tenant across the road."

A red-faced Sean O'Malley had come out of his cottage and now stood, his wife pressed behind him, halfway between his own place and Aine Quigley's. "There's no room in the workhouse, and well you know it!" O'Malley shouted at Cotter. "Would you have the woman and her babes die in the ditch before sundown?"

By now the crowd had again started to close their ranks and were gathering in around Cotter. Some of the women were still weeping, but the men's voices rose in an angry buzz that burst into a roar of fury when the destructives swung out and, dividing, began to swarm on all three houses.

"God have mercy on us!" wailed a silver-haired woman to Nora's left. "They mean to see us all dead."

Nora watched in horror as one of the housewreckers yanked Aine and the children away from the door and shoved them roughly out into the yard. Aine Quigley sent up the keening cry of the mourner as she watched her meager possessions being tossed out of the house into the mud and sleet. Pushing the babe in her arms at a woman nearby, she ran back inside, screaming.

The distressed murmurs of the watching crowd had swelled to a rumble of mounting fury when a roar rose up from somewhere behind them. Nora spun around with the others at the sound. Stunned, she watched Morgan Fitzgerald charging his way through their midst, his face livid, his eyes blazing.

Two of the housewreckers had just come out the front door, their arms filled with kettles and dishes. They froze at the sight of the fiery-haired giant tearing his way through the crowd, which was now parting to give him room.

One of the destructives shot a glance of alarm at Cotter, then scurried back inside the house. The other dropped the contents in his arms where he stood and took off running around the side of the yard.

They needn't have feared, for Morgan's objective was plainly Cotter. Stunned, Nora watched him charge the agent, who still sat astride his horse, his bloated red face a mask of incredulity. The wild-eyed stallion snorted, then reared with a force that sent Cotter flying. His riding crop sailed out of his hand and landed in the mud as he fell.

Morgan went for the agent, now lying on his back, feet up, in a pool of icy slush. Cotter was paunchy and awkward, no match at all for the frenzied giant towering over him. Grasping him roughly beneath his arms, Morgan jerked him upright and spun him around. The terrified agent squawked and let fly a string of oaths. Undaunted, Morgan lifted him into the air as if he were no more than a lumpy sack of potatoes. He held him there, feet dangling above the ground, arms flailing wildly as he faced the crowd.

Horrified, Nora could hear Morgan's words to the bug-eyed Cotter as he demanded, *"Call them off!* Get your riffraff out of that house, or I'll snap your cowardly spine, I swear I will!"

The agent's red face looked like a melon about to burst. He continued to rage and squeal as Morgan dangled him in front of the people.

At that moment the constable who had started for Michael Gaffney's place came racing across the road, his pistol drawn. He fired once into the air, then again. *"Put him down, Fitzgerald!* Release him at once or you're a dead man!"

Morgan swiveled to look, dragging Cotter around with him. As he pivoted, he set the agent rudely on his feet, but continued to grasp him firmly under the arms. Pushing Cotter in front of him as he went, he edged his way toward the policeman. "A grand idea, Constable! Go ahead, shoot! Shoot this devil and bless us all!"

A roar went up from the crowd, and several of the men now began to converge on the policeman. The man stood gaping for another instant, then lowered his gun and backed away.

Nora saw the other constable and Cotter's two bodyguards edge up behind Morgan's back. *"Morgan!* Look out—behind you!"

Morgan whipped around, dragging the agent as if the man were weightless. "Get back!" he warned, his face hard and determined. "His death will be on your heads, lads."

They halted, but didn't retreat, and Morgan shouted again, "I mean it! Just give me an excuse, why don't you? Wouldn't I just love to snap his fat neck!"

Nora shivered in the hush that had fallen over the crowd as Morgan dared his attackers with a grim smile. Didn't the lunatic realize he was endangering not only himself, but all of them? Cotter would turn out the entire village for his madness!

"Well? Get on with it, then—him or me?"

The constables lowered their weapons, and the bodyguards took a few reluctant steps backward.

"I'll have the pistols on the ground, lads," Morgan demanded.

The policemen exchanged uncomfortable glances, but dropped their guns as he instructed.

A growl of rage exploded from Cotter. Morgan yanked him back against his chest, hard enough that Nora heard the man's bones snap as he cried out in pain. She cringed again, anger at Morgan and his mindless temper surging through her. The man he was threatening held the life of every person here in his very hands.

"Now, then, *Mister* Cotter—your honor, *sir*," Morgan sneered, his mouth close to the agent's temple as he slurred his words in an exaggerated brogue, "you'll be after ending this little incident right away. Just send your boys along like good lads, and I'll turn you loose as well. We'll be having no more of this eviction talk today, if you please." His eyes went to the destructives. "But first, boyos, let's be putting the Missus Quigley's furniture back inside her house where it belongs."

"*No!*" Cotter twisted and squirmed, struggling in vain to free himself from Morgan's iron grip. "Stay where you are! Do you hear? *Stay where you are!*"

Nora's hand flew to her mouth as Morgan's grasp on the man tightened. Cotter shrieked, but Morgan merely pressed his mouth even closer to Cotter's ear and grated, "I think you'd best heed what I say, man, and heed it well. I have some lads of my own, you see, who are far more fierce than these miserable *spalpeens* of yours." One brawny arm locked under Cotter's chin. "Now here's the way it will be, unless you do as you're told: Some night very soon my men and I will come calling. We'll come while you sleep, and you'll not even know we're about." His voice hardened. "Until we've spread-eagled you in the yard and set you ablaze, that is."

The agent had stopped his squirming—indeed, he seemed to have stopped breathing. "Aye," Morgan finished smoothly, "you'll be ashes among the cow dung before anyone even suspects what has happened."

Cotter's eyes looked about to pop as Morgan tightened his hold on his throat. The agent frantically began to nod his agreement.

"Ah, so we understand each other then, your honor?"

Again Cotter wagged his head vigorously, tears tracking down his fat cheeks.

"Well, that's grand, then," Morgan said cheerfully, inclining his head toward O'Malley. "Bring me one of those pistols, Sean, why don't you? And perhaps you might want to hold on to the other one yourself."

The lithe, square-shouldered O'Malley didn't hesitate. He passed one pistol to Morgan, then leveled the other gun on the agent.

"All right, now," Morgan said evenly, releasing Cotter's throat to palm the gun. "We'll just be waiting until your lads put Missus Quigley's house back in order."

Morgan continued to hold Cotter firmly until all Aine's belongings had been returned to her cottage. Finally, he gave the agent a rough shove, pushing him toward his horse and training the pistol on him.

All eyes followed Cotter and the officials as they jumped on their mounts and started to ride away, their henchmen running behind them. Unexpectedly Cotter jerked his stallion around to face Morgan. "Know this, Fitzgerald," he grated out, his face flushed with hatred and humiliation, "this day you have signed your death ticket!"

An impudent grin spread over Morgan's face as he lifted his chin and cocked his head, but his eyes glittered as hard as ice chips. "That being the case, your honor, *sir*, you might do well to remember that *your* ticket is attached to my own."

The agent swore, then yanked his horse around and took off at a frenzied gallop. Behind him, the crowd of watchers broke into a militant cheer.

Nora stiffened, feeling her face grow hot as Morgan caught her eye and began walking toward her. She could sense the interested stares of her neighbors and wanted desperately to run.

"You saved my back, lass," he said quietly in the Irish. "I thank you for the warning."

Nora stared resolutely down at the frozen mire, not answering.

Acutely aware of his eyes on her, she finally dragged her gaze up to meet his, encountering a faint glint of amusement that made her blood boil. His eyes went over her, traveling past Old Dan's worn, shapeless coat and her sodden brown skirt, down to her feet, lost in the old man's heavy boots.

His eyes met hers again and held. He said nothing; his smile said it all. It suddenly occurred to Nora how desperately woebegone she must appear to him, standing there like a drowned ragamuffin in the old man's clothes. Well, and what did she care *how* she looked to Morgan Fitzgerald?

Irked by his insolence, Nora snapped at him. "You do know he's right, don't you? Not only has your madness signed your ticket to the gallows, but you've most likely sealed the fate of the entire village!"

His arrogant smile fled as he stood studying her face. When he finally spoke, his tone was guarded. "The fate of the village and all Ireland was sealed long before this day. If you did not know that before, then at least face the truth now."

"Just what is the truth?" she whispered savagely. "What, Morgan Fitzgerald, did you mean when you warned the agent about 'your lads,' as you called them? What is it you're hiding, with your wandering about and your gifting us with provisions from the Lord knows where and—"

Suddenly Nora stopped, shaking her head wearily. She dared not finish the question or play out her accusations to the end. There were some things, she realized with self-disgust, that were better left unknown.

When she looked up at Morgan again his eyes were hard, and for a moment Nora thought he was simply going to turn and walk away. Instead, he shoved the pistol into his belt, took her firmly by the arm, and started walking, pulling her along beside him. "Come along, Nora Ellen, I will see you home before you catch your death."

Mortified by his insufferable air of proprietorship, Nora tried to twist her arm free. Ignoring her, he merely tightened his hold and stepped up his pace.

Nora deliberately lowered her voice to avoid calling further attention to herself. "You haven't changed at all, Morgan Fitzgerald," she spit out bitterly, stumbling along beside him. "You still have more gall than sense."

He glanced down at her, not breaking his stride in the least as he gave her a measuring look. "And you, Nora lass, have not changed all that much yourself," he countered with just the faintest hint of a smile. "Yours is still a terrible beauty when you're vexed with me. Now, tell me, what were you doing out in this miserable weather to begin with?"

Nora flushed at his words. "I was looking for Daniel John."

She explained then about the stolen cow, being careful to conceal her feelings of desperation. "I told him to give it up, but he insisted on going out again this morning. The cow is gone for good. I know it, and I think he knows it as well."

"He feels as if he has to do *something*," Morgan replied softly. "With both Tahg and his granddaddy ill now, I imagine the lad is doing his best to take his place as the man of the house."

Startled at his perception—for she had already recognized her son's efforts to do just that—Nora glanced up at him. "Aye, I'm sure that's how it is with him." It made her heart ache to see her youngest trying so hard to become a man overnight. Fortunately for them all, the boy had always seemed far older than his years. True, he was a dreamer, but despite his fanciful imagination, he was a lad who could be counted on when he was needed.

"How is the old man?"

"Growing weaker by the day. He was still abed when I left the house." Nora's voice betrayed her worry. "I can't remember him ever lying in so late before." She paused, struck by a thought which she expressed, mostly to herself. "It seems that nothing is the same these days. Everything is changing. Even people."

Morgan looked at her, nodding slowly. "There are even more changes coming, you know. You'd do well to be prepared for them."

They had reached the front yard of the cottage. Morgan stopped and turned to face her, catching her hand in his. "Nora—I'm going to be gone for a few days, but before I leave I want to know that you've food enough to last until I get back. Especially now, with the cow gone, can you manage?"

Trying to ignore the sharp stab of disappointment she felt upon learning that he was leaving again, Nora nodded, avoiding his eyes.

With his free hand he caught her chin and tilted it up, forcing her to meet his gaze. "I must know the truth, Nora," he said urgently. "I'll bring some more provisions with me when I come back, but I need to be sure you'll be all right until then. Don't lie to me, lass—your pride will not keep your family alive."

Stung by his words, Nora stiffened. She would *not* become dependent on him. She had no idea what he was up to, with this sudden concern for their well-being, but she must not allow herself to grow used to
his presence in her life again. Morgan was quicksilver—unstable, unreliable, unpredictable. As for her pride, he was being entirely unfair. What he
took to be pride was simply self-respect, and she thought he should have
understood her need to retain what she could of it.

"Nora?" His eyes narrowed, challenging her.

"I—yes. We'll be fine."

Still he searched her eyes, as if he were trying to read her heart.

"Your concern is misplaced, Morgan," she said evenly. "Thomas and his
children are your family. If you're determined to look after anyone, then
see to them."

He let his hand fall away from her chin. "Thomas is a man grown," he
said, drawing back slightly. "He takes responsibility for his own family."

"Well, it's not for you to take responsibility for *mine*." Her words
sounded sharper than she'd intended. Still, she meant them. "We—will
be all right," she said, gentling her tone a bit. "Truly, we will."

Morgan's eyes softened, a look Nora did not want to remember. "And
that is all I'm wanting, Nora—for you and yours to be safe and well. Can
you not accept that much from me, at least—that I still care for you?"

She could not look at him. She *wouldn't*. She would not look at him or
listen to him or believe in him or feel anything at all for him. Not ever.

Mustering as impersonal a tone as she could manage, Nora fixed her
gaze on a spot just past his shoulder. "Thank you...for what you did for
Aine today, Morgan. It was very brave. I really must go inside now and see
to Tahg and the old man."

She sensed that he was about to say more—something nasty, by the
looks of his frown—but he held his tongue. His expression cleared as he
gave a short nod and said agreeably, "Aye, and even more do you need to
be getting out of those wet things."

She started to turn, but he reached out and put a hand to her arm.
"Nora—"

She turned back to him.

"Tell Daniel John that I'll be back in a few days. Tell him I said goodbye."

She nodded, and started for the cottage. Already she dreaded the look she would see in her son's eyes when he learned that Morgan was leaving again. But then he might just as well get used to doing without the man. Perhaps Morgan meant what he said, this time, about coming back in a few days, but that was only for now. The day would come—and soon, more than likely—when he would go wandering off again, not to be seen for months or even years. Morgan would never be—*could* never be— anything else but what he was. She must not allow Daniel John to believe, even for a moment, that the man would ever change.

And she must not allow herself to believe it either.

8

Winter Memories

All through the night did I hear the banshee keening:
Somewhere you are dying, and nothing can I do:
My hair with the wind, and my two hands clasped in anguish;
Bitter is your trouble—and I am far from you.

DORA SIGERSON SHORTER (1866–1917)

New York City

The snow that had begun at dawn increased with a vengeance throughout the day. Several inches already blanketed the city, and still it slashed relentlessly against the kitchen window facing the street.

Home from his watch and relaxing with his tea, Michael Burke propped his elbows on the table and stared down onto the street below. In the quickly gathering dusk, the snow wove a blowing veil about the gas-lights, allowing the mean, cluttered streets to masquerade as a quaint, even charming winter scene. A flow of pedestrians hurrying home from work pushed urgently along, holding their caps as their coattails and scarves whipped sharply in the wind. Much of the garbage that bordered them on either side was disguised, distorted by flickering shadows from the snow swirling about the lamplight.

Michael checked his pocket watch; Tierney should be along soon from his after-school job at the hotel. Wiping a hand over the back of his neck, he yawned and glanced again at the newspaper on the table in front of him. He suspected much of his gloomy mood could be attributed to the *Tribune's* front-page report of the troubles in Ireland. These days the

papers were filled with accounts of the Great Famine, as they were calling it; indeed, it was a rare edition that carried no news of the mounting
disaster across the sea.

Compassion for Ireland's plight seemed nationwide. Young as she was,
America was a land with an enormous heart, a generous heart. Oh, there
was no denying Tierney's frequent complaints about New York's resistance to the Irish. The hostilities were real enough, even among the Irish
themselves. The Protestants continued to view their Catholic countrymen with contempt, just as they had back in Ireland, thinking them ignorant, superstitious peasants who were incapable of bettering their lot in
life even if they had a mind to do so. Such disaffection for the "papists,"
some years past, had led to a number of Protestant Irish-Americans identifying themselves as "Scotch-Irish" to dissociate themselves from their
Roman countrymen.

On the other side, the Catholic immigrants had transferred their
native resentment of the normally wealthier and better-educated Protestants to the same class here in the States. Distrust and bitterness fed the old
antagonism, creating new rifts between the two groups. In addition, new
barriers rose between the Irish and other emigrants, especially the Germans. The German Catholics, for example, found the Irish too grim and
defeatist for their own energetic, practical religious beliefs, while the Irish
thought the Germans somewhat naive and pompous.

Despite their differences, however, Americans simply were not a people
who could ignore the large-scale suffering of an entire country, especially
a country that had apparently been abandoned by her own "Mother England." Already meetings were being held—not only here in New York, but
throughout the country—to respond to Ireland's needs.

Railways offered to carry free all shipments marked *Ireland*, and public carriers delivered at no cost all boxes going toward Irish aid. Relief committees throughout the nation hastened to put thousands of dollars and
shiploads of food at the disposal of the Society of Friends—the Quakers—
who were energetically organizing the United States' aid to Ireland.

Here in New York, Tammany Hall collected thousands of dollars, as
did both Catholic and Protestant churches nationwide. "Donation parties"
were held by all denominations, along with concerts and teas. Young ladies
in private schools volunteered to make useful articles that could be sold
for the benefit of Ireland. Jewish synagogues sent their weekly collections.

A group of Choctaw Indians worked to collect an offering of $170, and in villages and towns all over America, women and children pooled their pennies and sent them to Ireland.

Such a flood of enthusiasm had swept the land that not enough ships could be found to transport the bounty. Aye, it was a grand thing that was happening, but it rankled Michael that it should require a disaster of such tragic proportions to unite his countrymen. Especially those who claimed to be Christians.

Michael sighed and tapped his fingers impatiently on the newspapers, then rose and went to stand at the window, looking up and down the street for some sign of Tierney. He, too, longed to do more in the way of donations, but he had already dipped deep into their small savings. Tierney, however, exhibiting his characteristic cleverness and knack for money raising, had organized a host of lads from school into teams, and among them they'd pestered a number of shopkeepers and tradesmen into donating generous amounts for the school's "Friends in Ireland" fund.

These days Michael found himself thinking more and more of his own "friends in Ireland." Morgan and Nora were frequently on his mind. Back in November, when news reports of the famine had begun to pour across the sea, he had written an anxious letter to Morgan in care of his brother, Thomas. Each day that passed he watched with growing impatience for a reply.

Strange—after so many years and an ocean between them, his mind could still see the two of them clearly. Nora was now a woman grown, a wife and mother; yet it was difficult to imagine her as anything but a small, sober-faced lass with enormous sad eyes and the tiniest waist in Killala. He hoped she'd been happy with the husband she'd chosen; Nora deserved happiness, she did, for she'd had little enough of it as a girl.

As for Morgan Fitzgerald, he supposed *that* rogue could take care of himself well enough. Michael smiled at the thought of his old friend, with his harp and his poems and his roaming ways—and, always, his fatalistic but fervent love for Ireland. He was a vagabond, Morgan was. Ever the dreamer, he had been smitten with the wanderlust as a lad and seemingly never recovered.

The man was a puzzle of many pieces, one or two of which might never be found. Michael thought he had as much love for his homeland as any respectable Irishman, but with Morgan it was more than love of country.

It was an obsession. He could still remember the great oaf's words to him when Michael had first told Morgan of his dream to see America, trying to convince him they should go together.

Backed up against a gnarled old tree, Morgan had stretched his long arms, locked his hands behind his head, and smiled that thoroughly impudent grin of his. "Ach, Michael, I could never do that, and you know it. You intend to go and never come back. I could never leave our Lady Ireland for good."

To Michael's way of thinking, Ireland was more the fallen woman than the lady, and he said as much.

Morgan had laughed, shaking his head. "Aye, she's a miserable island at that, but she's claimed me entirely, don't you see? There never was a woman quite so bent on owning a man as our *Eire*. She's a fierce and terrible mistress, I admit, and most likely she'll be my destruction. But beloved as she is to me, I could no more give her up than rip out my own heart."

Did Morgan still cling to his beloved, even now? Michael wondered. He prayed not, for surely she would drag him to his death along beside her—

"Well, Da—I am here, but where are you?"

Startled, Michael jumped and whirled around to see Tierney standing just inside the door, grinning at him.

"Wool-gathering, it seems. I didn't even hear you come up the stairs."

Tierney tossed his gloves on a nearby chair, then hung his coat and cap on a peg by the door. A shock of dark auburn hair, wet from the snow, hung insolently over one eye. The boy's other eye was still dark from a mouse he'd incurred in last week's scrap with the Dolan boy.

The thought of Tierney's frequent fights brought a sour frown to Michael's face. "That eye is a grand sight."

The boy came to the table, his grin still in place. "Now, don't go starting on me, Da. What's for supper?"

"There's a pot of brown beans, and Mrs. Gallagher sent up a pan of corn bread. And I'm telling you again to quit calling me 'Da.' We're not living in Ireland—talk like the American you are."

"Irish-American," Tierney corrected, going to the stove to check the beans. "And you still say, 'aye,' you know. Can we eat now, Da? I'm starved."

"As you always are," Michael retorted, getting up from his chair. "Set the table and I'll fix our plates."

Tierney whisked around the kitchen getting the dishes out, flipping them carelessly onto the table as if they were unbreakable—which, Michael reminded him again, they weren't.

"Have you heard, Da? Eleven ships are sailing from here to Ireland tomorrow with food!" Tierney's voice was boyishly high with excitement, though more often than not these days it tended to crack with the gruffness of approaching manhood.

Michael nodded as he dished up a plate of beans and handed it to the boy. "Aye, and four more leaving from Philadelphia the day after. It's in the paper."

"Can we go to the harbor and watch them sail out? You're off duty tomorrow, aren't you?"

"I am, but need I remind you that you will be in school?" Michael shot him a stern look as he sat down across from him.

The boy shrugged and reached for the corn bread. "I won't miss that much. Not for just one day. Come on, Da—say we'll go."

"I will say a prayer if you'll hush long enough to listen." Michael glared at him, but the boy's tilted grin made him give over.

"Besides, I hate that school, and you know it," Tierney continued after Michael gave their thanks. "I wish I could go to the Catholic school."

"Catholics go to Catholic school."

"I know, and that's my point," Tierney muttered.

Michael put down his fork. "We are not going to have this conversation again, are we, Tierney?"

The boy shrugged, a gesture Michael increasingly disliked. "I will never understand why a lad born as a Protestant and raised as a Protestant has this cracked notion about becoming a Catholic."

"It's the Irish way," Tierney said, reaching for the butter.

"I said we weren't going to have this conversation again, and I meant it, boyo. But let me remind you of one thing: Ireland has bred a few Protestants as well as Catholics—myself, for one, and your mother as well, God bless her."

"I know that. But it's different here in New York. The other Irish kids are all Catholic; they think I'm some kind of freak. And I'm just about the only Irish kid in the whole school. All my friends on the block go to Catholic school."

"What *difference* does it make, Tierney?" Exasperated with the boy,

Michael was far too tired and cross to be patient. "Christ is the same Savior to Protestant or Catholic—if they accept Him as such."

"Sure," Tierney muttered, pulling his mouth down in contempt. "And is that why the Catholics say theirs is the only church, and the Protestants say a Catholic church is no church at all—and anyone who disagrees with either one of them is a heathen?"

Michael drew a deep sigh and picked up his fork. "That's not the way with all Catholics or Protestants, lad," he said between bites. "The thing that matters is your heart, don't you see? I've told you about my friend back in Ireland, Morgan Fitzgerald?"

Tierney's face lighted up, and he nodded eagerly. Again Michael sighed. Morgan had become a bit of a hero to the lad, and he supposed he could blame himself for that. Tierney was charmed by all the tales of Morgan's exploits repeated over the years. Ah, well, perhaps he'd pay more attention to Morgan's words than those of his stodgy old dad.

"Well, Morgan was never entirely convinced that the Lord is all that interested in our church buildings and doctrines and religious symbols. He seemed to think the Almighty would be more concerned about *relationships*: our relationship with Him, and with one another as well. And do you know, Tierney, the longer I live, the more truth I find in my old friend's words."

The boy merely grunted, then shoveled another heaping spoon of beans into his mouth. His eyes danced as he chewed. "Well," he said, swallowing, "when I'm grown and go to Ireland, I may not take to either church. Perhaps I'll look up old Morgan Fitzgerald and become a heathen, like him."

"Morgan is *not* a heathen—and will you stop with that foolish talk about going to Ireland!" Michael exploded, banging his fork down on his plate. "Why would you even think of it?"

He was unsettled by the way Tierney met his gaze without wavering. The boy's blue eyes, so much like his mother's, turned hard and cold. "You've always known that's what I want."

"Aye," Michael growled, "and never have I understood why! Ireland is a corpse. Can you not get that into your skull? She is dead and rotting above ground. There is nothing there for us, nothing for anyone except death. Why do you think I left it in the first place?"

If only he could help the boy to see what *he* had seen—the poverty, the defeat, the squalor...the *misery*.

"Morgan didn't leave," the boy said with a calm that fired Michael's anger even more. "He chose to stay and work to make things better."

"Morgan is Morgan—and perhaps a bit of a fool! Thousands upon thousands are fighting to get out of Ireland, to come here to America! They want what you already have—what you seem to hold so cheaply. Doesn't it strike you as a bit odd that all those hordes of people are so anxious to leave behind what you seem to think is so grand?"

"I still want to go. I want to go because I'm Irish." The maturity and strength in the boy's voice chilled Michael.

"You're an *American*. And you should thank God every day for it!"

Tierney stared at him and, not for the first time, Michael felt a stirring of apprehension at the hooded, unreadable expression in his son's eyes.

Furious with the boy—and even more with himself for once again losing his temper with his son—Michael shoved his chair back from the table. "Eat your supper. Your foolishness has cost me my appetite. I'll be doing some reading."

He half-expected the boy to defy him; he did so often lately. But Tierney simply lowered his eyes and went on eating.

In the bedroom, Michael sank down onto the rocking chair that had been Eileen's. For a long time he sat there, unmoving, staring at the bed he had slept in alone for so many years. A longing for his wife welled up in him, bringing him close to tears. He had not missed her this much in a long, long time, and he suddenly felt a dreadful, cold loneliness. His wife was lost to him, and he was beginning to wonder if his son wouldn't one day be lost to him as well. He did not understand the boy—in truth, he never had—but that did not diminish his love for the lad. He only wanted...what? For Tierney to be like him?

Sure, and that was a joke. Tierney was like no one else—not himself, nor Eileen, nor anyone else that Michael could think of. Tierney was different. And it was a difference Michael did not understand, a difference that almost frightened him at times. What would the boy come to down the years?

He had such dreams for his son—for both of them. He wasn't going to stay a police sergeant forever. He had set his sights on Tammany Hall, had already made some contacts he believed would take him there. By the time Tierney was fully grown, he hoped to be in a position to help him become whatever he wanted to be. But the boy seemed to have no dream, no dream at all, except to be as…as *Irish* as possible. And what kind of a dream was that?

Michael closed his eyes, letting his head fall back against the cushion of the chair. Suddenly he wished he didn't feel so old. So old and so tired and so fiercely alone.

Da would never understand. He expected his son to share his dreams, not to have dreams of his own.

Tierney pushed his plate away and propped one elbow on the table, resting his chin in his hand. Well, he *did* have his dreams, and they had nothing at all to do with his father's.

It wasn't that he didn't love his da. Of course, he loved him, and he didn't relish making him sad. But he couldn't help the way he was nor would he change. Sometimes he wished that a man like Morgan Fitzgerald had been his father. He would have understood, would have encouraged his love for Ireland. Da never would. He loved New York and simply could not understand anyone who did not.

Well, *he* did not love New York—he *hated* it. He hated its filth and noise, its churning masses of people. He hated it most of all for the way the entire city hated the Irish.

Tierney got up, walked to the window, and looked out upon the snow falling into the city night.

They'd keep us beggars if they could. In their eyes we're nothing but dumb animals, fit only for hauling the manure from their streets, killing their rats, ironing their clothes, putting out their fires—or policing their precious city.

Well, he wanted no part of this ugly place—he would *be* no part of it, not ever. He belonged to Ireland. In a way he couldn't begin to understand, in a way he could never have put into words, the country owned him.

One day he would go. He would travel the length and breadth of it, absorb it, merge with it, become one with it. Ireland was his home as New York could never be. Ireland was the mother he longed for, the bosom friend he craved, the missing part of his heart.

Somewhere in Ireland, Tierney Burke would find his destiny.

9

Evan's Adventure

Ill fares the land, to hastening ills a prey,
Where wealth accumulates, and men decay.

OLIVER GOLDSMITH (1728–1774)

London

R oger Gilpin was no gentleman.

Evan Whittaker had been in the man's employ only days before making that judgment, and now, eleven years of service later, his opinion had changed not a whit. Sir Roger could be incredibly crude in his manners and attitudes; he had a problem with spirits, and his behavior when he had been drinking ranged from disagreeable to intolerable. He seemed to delight in ignoring the authorities, insulting his contemporaries, and destroying his enemies—who numbered many. Even in the eyes of his few friends, he was often a bore. To his servants, he was thoughtless, bullying, and downright intimidating. Evan seemed to be the only soul in his employ to whom Sir Roger gave even a measure of grudging respect. More surprising yet, he seemed to have actually become somewhat dependent on his reserved, mild-mannered secretary.

Evan supposed he was nearly indispensable to his difficult employer. He didn't arrive at this conclusion by way of conceit; it was just the way things appeared to be, however inexplicable the reasons. It was a fact that he wasn't in the least intimidated by Sir Roger. He stood steady in the face of Gilpin's frequent storms of rage. Indeed, Evan's mother had always called him "unflappable," though his father had thought him hardheaded.

At any rate, his phlegmatic disposition seemed immune to whatever cruelty Roger Gilpin had a mind to inflict.

Evan Whittaker was, in fact, the only employee who had ever remained at Gilpin Manor for longer than a year. The vulgar, self-important Sir Roger certainly did not inspire loyalty on the part of those who worked for him. Evan was an oddity, and perhaps that was a part of his appeal.

He had often been asked by his peers, and on occasion by one or more of Gilpin's acquaintances, why he *had* stayed with the difficult Sir Roger all this time. He had been offered a number of other positions over the years, and admittedly, he had considered leaving more than once. After careful thought, however, he always managed to talk himself out of the idea. His wages were outstanding, his living quarters more than comfortable, and he had grown used to the irascible widower.

Another possibility loomed in his mind, but he preferred not to dwell on it—it made him appear so *dull,* even to himself. Could he have become so complacent about his life and indifferent to the monotony of his days that he was unwilling to muster either the energy or the courage to make a change?

Of course, there *had* been a time when he would have welcomed an adventure. A shy, quiet youngster, he'd grown up as the only son—and a somewhat frail one, at that—of an aging clergyman in a small, depressed village near Portsmouth.

As a boy, Evan had been plagued by a dreadful stammer, mocked, and ostracized by his peers in the schoolyard. His father had encouraged him to be brave and to trust God, and the lad had managed to obey at least half of his father's injunction. He learned to trust God, but the bravery never seemed to follow.

And so Evan retreated into his books. Only there did the young outcast find what he was looking for—adventure, romance, the opportunity, through his imagination, to become the swashbuckling hero of his dreams. There he did not stutter; there he was not ridiculed by pig-faced schoolboys; there, at last, he liked himself.

Evan Whittaker found his courage, and he found his faith. But he never seemed to find both in the same place.

Even now, in his mid-thirties, Evan had difficulty reconciling the two. He still read avidly, and his literary tastes remained very much the same. He *did* enjoy a good adventure novel about explorers or pirates, and he had no trouble at all imagining himself as the danger-defying hero, complete with a cape slung casually over his shoulder and a sword on his hip.

And Evan still trusted God. His faith, marked by a simple life of devotion, sustained him in his encounters with his ill-tempered employer and supported him in the mundane execution of his duties.

Have faith and be brave, his father had said. Well, Evan's life incorporated both—his heart rooted in the reality of Christ, his imagination caught up in the vast possibilities of fantasy.

Yet something was missing. When Evan allowed himself the luxury of thinking about it, he realized with a pang of regret that the two significant parts of his life had never merged. There was no bravery in his faith, no courageous acting out of his love for God. And there was no faith in the bravery of his imaginative heroism—no spiritual life beyond the sheer joy of adventuring with the fictional characters that populated his books.

Something, indeed, was missing. Somehow, somewhere, the two should have come together.

These days, however, he had little time for considering such philosophical imponderables; he had all he could do to keep up with his regular duties. This exasperating business in Ireland kept Sir Roger in a continual fit of temper, which in turn kept the household in a constant state of chaos. Evan invariably found himself with more letters to pen, more dinners to plan, and more frequent tantrums and bouts of rage to placate.

At the moment, Sir Roger was using Whittaker's presence in the library as an audience for his rage. And, as always seemed to be the case these days, the object of his wrath was Ireland.

"Killala!" Sir Roger spit out, pacing the length of the library. "I have never laid eyes on the squalid little pit—only *God* knows and cares where it is!"

His employer's reference to God made Evan blink and draw a tired sigh, for the man certainly had no acquaintance whatever with the Creator. "I believe it's located near a bay in western Ireland, sir," Evan offered, going on with his careful copying of the letter Gilpin had just dictated to George Cotter. "Very remote."

"I know *that!"* Gilpin snarled. Sir Roger had been pacing the room for the better part of an hour as he dictated. At last he stopped and turned to Evan, who lifted his eyes from the letter he was transcribing.

A tall, gaunt man with long legs, white hair, and large, slightly bulging eyes, Roger Gilpin never failed to remind Evan of an aging, frost-coated grasshopper. Indeed, "Grasshopper" was Evan's private name for his employer.

"I *asked* you your opinion of that fool Cotter's letter!" Sir Roger crossed his long, thin arms over his chest and fixed Evan with a baleful glare. "Well?"

Clearing his throat, Evan stared at the pen in his hand. "Ah, w-well, of course, the agent had no right...n-no right at all...to defy your instructions, Sir Roger." Knowing how annoying the Grasshopper found his habitual stammer, Evan now gave it free rein. "Ah...although I must s-say I can appreciate that an undertaking of this n-n-nature might well contain difficulties we haven't c-c-considered. P-perhaps, if m-mass eviction is the only feasible solution, we need to give the agent m-more time." Evan beamed a slightly vacuous smile at his employer from his chair at the desk.

"Oh, for pity's sake, man, can't you just say whatever you mean and stop that hemming and hawing?" Sir Roger's mouth thinned even more. "Can't you get that fixed somehow, that tic of yours?"

So now it was a tic. Only last week it had been a plague. Over the years the dreaded stammer had evoked such misnomers as "croak," "twitch," and "splutter." Perhaps the Grasshopper was mellowing.

"I'm sorry, s-sir, but I don't b-believe there's any...f-fixing for it." Evan did his best to look humiliated.

Sir Roger grunted and again began to pace. "Well, as to Cotter— he's supposed to be in charge out there! He's the land agent, and the land agent's job is to take charge of the tenants, isn't that so?"

Matching his words to his quickening pace, he spilled them out in a frenzy. "I don't pay him to let those shiftless freeloaders make a monkey out of him! Not that it wouldn't be easy enough to do—the man is a fool!"

After one more pass across the room, he stopped in front of the fireplace, where only a thin, feeble flame continued to fight its way between the logs. Reaching for the poker, Sir Roger began punching the fire back to life. When he straightened, he resorted to a mannerism Evan had always found oddly intriguing: after opening his mouth to a wide, gaping cavern, he snapped it shut with a smacking sound. *The Grasshopper.*

He now came back to the desk and picked up the letter from Cotter which lay near Evan's hand. "What were you able to find out about this—Fitzgerald creature?"

Evan shifted slightly on his chair, fastening his eyes on the book-lined wall across the room. Intense concentration seemed to relieve the stammer somewhat, and at the moment he thought it best to be precise. "Apparently, Morgan Fitzgerald is something of a...an enigma. Part p-poet, part vagabond, and p-part folk hero. He sounds f-formidable: big—very big—with an unruly m-mane of copper hair and, according to Quincy Moore, our c-correspondent, the 'strength of a Druid oak tree.'" Evan felt a delicious shiver wind its way down his spine; Moore's description could have been right from the pages of one of his favorite adventure novels.

Aware of Gilpin's impatient squirming but entirely unperturbed by it, Evan smoothed the sheet of vellum in front of him, aligning its four corners with those of the desk, just so. Then, fastening his eyes once more on the bookshelves—this time on the brass candlesticks—he continued. "Apparently F-Fitzgerald is a writer held in great esteem—a 'poet p-patriot,' Moore says." Evan glanced from the candlesticks to Sir Roger. "Ah...then there's the...association with the Y-Young Irelanders, as you know."

Sir Roger swore and again waved the letter in his hand. "The man is a common thug! He almost killed George Cotter!" He paused, then added sourly, "Not that it would be any great loss."

Evan bristled. Fitzgerald might be a great many things, but he was certainly no common thug. No, indeed. The man sounded anything but common.

Perversely enjoying his employer's agitation, Evan warmed to his subject, paraphrasing parts of Moore's letter as he went on. "Fitzgerald s-seems to be quite well known f-for his writings in the...*The Nation.*" Oh, dear, now he'd done it. Even the mention of the radical Young Ireland news journal was enough to set Sir Roger's teeth to rattling.

Hurrying on before his employer could let fly one of his florid streams of profanity, Evan explained, "Fitzgerald seems to be a highly...educated m-man. Until recently, he was best known for his p-poems and satirical essays, but it seems these days he's d-dipping his pen more and more into the ink of rebellion."

Sir Roger's eyes bugged out, and his mandible dropped down, presumably preparing for an expression of disgust, but Evan hurried on; he had saved the juiciest morsel for last and was not about to be denied his thunder. "As for this next observation: Moore stresses that it's p-purely rumor, although George Cotter is apparently convinced it's so."

The letter in Sir Roger's hand now crumpled as he clenched both fists and waited, his long, homely face set in a terrible scowl.

Evan drew a long, steadying breath and set his gaze on the list of instructions he'd been copying. "It seems that for months now there have been…s-stories of a mysterious rebel leader and his men who are up to all manner of mischief in C-Connacht, especially in County Mayo."

Gilpin's eyes narrowed, and he looked to be in the throes of some sort of fit. "A *rebel leader?*"

"Yes. Well…Mr. Moore says these p-primitive folk in the west have a tendency to imbue their outlaws, as well as their heroes, with l-larger-than-life attributes, even supernatural traits. This rebel leader would seem to be a case in point. They c-call him the, ah, the Red Wolf." A chill of delight gripped Evan as he uttered the name. What a *splendid* tale this was!

"Those who claim to have seen him, this…Red Wolf…say he and his marauders ride only at night. They say he has a head of c-curly copper hair and rides an enormous wild red stallion. Supposedly he and his men come charging down out of the hills when least expected, d-do their dirty work, and then simply…d-disappear back into the mountains and the mist."

Really, this would make the most wonderful novel…

Realizing Sir Roger had asked him a question, Evan blinked, then looked up at him. "I'm s-sorry, sir?"

"I *said*, what *sort* of dirty work?"

"Oh—well, nothing too violent, actually. They've k-killed some c-cattle from time to time—a few head of yours, I'm afraid, Sir Roger. They steal grain, drive horses out of their p-paddocks, provide p-protection to men on the run—that kind of thing. The peasants adore them, it seems, because they drop…b-baskets of food at cottages throughout the villages and do other miscellaneous…good deeds for the poor unfortunates."

Evan sighed. *An Irish Robin Hood, no less.*

"Is that all?"

Evan looked at him. "Well…yes…except that there are some, Cotter included, who suspect Morgan Fitzgerald of being this, ah, Red Wolf."

Sir Roger actually growled—a choked, phlegmy rumble. For a moment Evan feared it might be the beginning of a seizure, but the Grasshopper was simply grinding his jaws in rage.

Leaning forward, Gilpin hurled the crumpled letter to the desk. "I want you to leave for County Mayo at once! At *once*, do you hear?" He made a jabbing motion with his head to the letter in front of Evan. "You'll deliver those instructions to Cotter personally, as my emissary!"

Wagging a long talon of a finger in Evan's face, he went on shouting. "And you'll stay in Killala until you see my orders carried out, do you understand? I want those...*creatures*...off my land and those...*bandits*... hanged!"

Good heavens, the man was *serious!* Evan squirmed. *He*—go to Ireland? Worse yet, to *Mayo*? Why, according to Quincy Moore the place was nothing more than a bleak, desolate rock pile, its inhabitants unwashed savages and wild men, most of whom still spoke some ancient, unintelligible tongue! *Furious fools,* Tennyson called them. Oh my, no—it was impossible!

"I'm afraid that's...quite impossible, Sir Roger," he said as firmly as he could manage. "I have a slight lung condition, you remember"—he cleared his throat—"and I understand the c-climate in western Ireland is abysmal. Besides," he hastened to add for good measure, "who would assume my responsibilities in my absence? My workload is heavier than it's ever b-been before." There.

That should take care of *that.*

"You'll do as I say or your *workload,*" Sir Roger snarled, "will be considerably lightened. Considerably."

Evan lifted his chin in what he hoped was a gesture of defiance. "S-see here, Sir Roger—"

The Grasshopper was already hopping to his next thought. "Naturally," he said in a more conciliatory tone, turning his back on Evan, "you'll be generously recompensed for your travel expenses and your inconvenience. And of course, once you return you'll be due a sizable increase in wages." He paused, then turned back with a somewhat malicious smile to add, "And perhaps a vacation, as well, eh?"

Evan swallowed. He hadn't had a vacation in years. Perhaps the climate wasn't all *that* wretched. "A vacation, did you say?"

The Grasshopper showed his teeth.

"Think of it as—an adventure, Whittaker! Yes, that's it, an adventure! I should think a young, handsome fellow like yourself would be eager for a bit of travel and excitement."

Dear heaven, the man was actually patting him on the shoulder! Evan cringed. An adventure might be well and good, but he hardly thought a forced visit to Ireland qualified as such. Still, it would be a change of scenery. And there was the promise of a vacation...

"Well, if you're certain it's absolutely necessary—"

"Absolutely!" Gilpin boomed, thumping him solidly on the back. "This is excellent. You'll be able to give me a firsthand account of the famine conditions, as well."

Evan rose from his chair to avoid another bone jarring back pounding. "I thought Mr. C-Cotter and some of our other c-correspondents had already done that, sir. I'm sure they d-didn't exaggerate—the newspaper accounts c-confirm—"

"I should hope they didn't exaggerate!" Gilpin gave a short laugh, crossing the room to the gleaming mahogany sideboard. He poured himself a drink from a crystal decanter and tossed it down in one enormous gulp. "For my part," he said, wiping his lips on the back of his hand, "I consider these potato blights heaven-sent. Yes, indeed," he went on, pouring himself another tumbler of whiskey, "a distinct act of Providence, I should think. So do Elwood and Combs and some of the other landlords at the Club. Why, it's the very solution to the Irish problem!"

He downed his drink, rolling the tumbler around in the palm of one large hand as he continued. "God knows we need to rid the land of those scavengers, and this famine has got them dropping like flies!"

Setting the tumbler down, he crossed to the fireplace, backing up close to it and clasping his hands behind him. "Cattle and horses, that's what we'll replace them with. It's Divine Providence, all right, Whittaker," he said, shooting Evan a pleased smile. "The Irish were starving anyway, dying of their own indolence. Why, the only thing those savages have ever known is poverty! They're too lazy, the lot of them, to turn an honest day's work. We landlords have to save ourselves before they bleed us dry! Once we get those *papists* off the land, we can turn it over to grazing and protect our investment in that wretched island."

From what Evan had read, not all the starving Irish were of the Roman Catholic faith, but he doubted that this fact would matter one way or the other to his employer.

"It's just as Trevelyan says," Sir Roger went on in a somewhat sanctimonious voice, "the Irish overpopulation and immoral character are altogether beyond our power to correct. Only God Himself can deal with those idolaters. And it would seem that He is doing just that at last."

Trevelyan, assistant secretary of the treasury, had indeed seconded the Prime Minister's belief that the famine was the work of a benign Providence. And numerous members of Parliament seemed eager to echo that sentiment.

Evan wasn't entirely sure just what he thought about the Irish. But he was fairly certain that the God he knew would not share Roger Gilpin's attitude. He recalled his father—a clergyman for forty-odd years now—making a remark in one of his recent letters about the "suddenly pious Trevelyan is convinced that God has cheerfully set about starving to death thousands of infants and children, simply because their parents placed some statues in their churches."

Not being personally affected by the conditions in Ireland, Evan had given the matter little thought. Now, it seemed, he would have the chance—albeit unwelcome—to see for himself whether or not the devastation was, indeed, the judgment of God upon an idolatrous people.

Sir Roger roused Evan from his thoughts. "Well, then, it's settled! You'll leave for Killala right away. By the end of the week at the latest."

Evan forced an unhappy smile. "Yes, I suppose I shall."

"Good man." Sir Roger stretched up, poised on the balls of his feet, then dropped down. The Grasshopper preened. "Write up whatever papers you may need, and I'll sign them in the morning. Just be sure that Cotter understands there's to be no more delay—they're *all* to be turned out, with no exceptions! And if he doesn't do the job this time, I'll hire a man who *will*!"

A thought struck Evan, and he moistened his lips. "About this Fitzgerald person—"

"*Fitzgerald be hanged!* And I'll see that he is! Cotter says he has family there, in the village, and they're as destitute as the rest of the peasantry. Perhaps you can use them to bring Fitzgerald into line, eh?"

Evan nodded vaguely, chafing to get away from his employer. Sir Roger was quite a disgusting man, actually.

"Come, now, Whittaker, you needn't look so despondent! Perhaps you'll find yourself one of those saucy little Irish tarts to brighten up your trip. Make a man of you!" Gilpin gave his loud, abrasive laugh, obviously delighted with himself. "Just see that you don't bring her home with you. London has quite enough of them scurrying through the sewers as it is."

For a moment Evan feared the man was about to cross the room and slap him soundly on the back again. He edged his way to the door and, calling up an immense amount of self-control, managed not to bolt and run.

When at last he escaped the library, he went directly to the front door, dragged it open, and stepped outside. Pulling in a long, cleansing breath of cold air, he willed the frigid wind to wash away the stench that seemed to have settled over him.

10

The Letter

And my heart flies back to Erin's isle,
To the girl I left behind me.

THOMAS OSBORNE DAVIS (1814–1845)

New York City

Not for the first time, Michael Burke found himself wishing for a uniformed police force. The idea of uniforms had been discussed and dismissed any number of times, mostly due to the men's fierce complaints. Many of the Irish lads, who comprised the majority of the total police force, were virulently opposed to the idea. Equating uniforms with the livery worn by English footmen, they remained adamant in their resistance to being decked out like "British lackeys."

From the beginning, Michael had disagreed, seeing the uniform as a means of gaining a bit more authority on the street. He was convinced that the instant recognition afforded by a uniform would automatically give a man greater influence, and thereby more control, among the rabble—at least a good deal more than their present copper badges could provide. From what he had seen in the streets of New York, Michael would have welcomed the edge of intimidation a mass of blue uniforms could effect.

He sighed and donned the blue woolen shirt lying on the bed, rubbing a calloused thumb over the copper badge affixed to his chest. For now, this makeshift uniform would have to do.

Michael headed for the kitchen, tucking in his shirttail as he went. Tierney, standing at the door, was just stepping aside to admit a stranger.

"Someone to see you, Da," Tierney said, studying the stranger with obvious curiosity.

"Sergeant Burke?"

Michael gave a short nod, taking in the stranger's appearance. Although he was dressed decently enough in the clothes of a working man, a furtive look filled the hooded dark eyes, and a hard set to his mouth immediately put Michael on guard.

"I've a letter for you," the man said without preamble.

Irish. There was no mistaking the accent.

Michael frowned. "Have we met, then?"

The man shook his head, volunteering nothing further as he pulled an envelope from his pocket and handed it to Michael.

"I was to see this safely into your hands," said the stranger. He paused, then added, "And I was asked to collect your reply as quickly as possible."

Michael recognized the large, untidy scrawl across the front of the envelope immediately. "Morgan," he said, surprised. "Morgan Fitzgerald."

The stranger gave a brief nod.

"But how—why the personal delivery?"

"I was told only that it's urgent, sir, and would you please send an answer back with me as soon as possible."

Michael studied the man's impassive face. "I didn't get your name."

The stranger met his gaze. "Barry will do. Do you think I could collect your answer by tomorrow, sir?"

Again Michael looked at the envelope in his hand. "You're going back to Ireland that soon?"

"Aye. I have some business to attend to in the city; then I'll be leaving."

"How is it that you know Morgan?" Michael pressed.

"I'm sorry, sir, did I lead you to think that? I don't actually know him at all. We have some mutual friends, you see, and when they learned I was coming over they asked me to deliver this for Mr. Fitzgerald."

Tierney had come to peer over his shoulder. "Aren't you going to open it, Da?" he asked eagerly.

Michael lifted his hand to silence the lad. "You say you need my reply by tomorrow?"

"If at all possible, sir. I need to get back straightaway."

"All right, then, I'll have it ready." Anxious now for the man to leave, Michael followed him to the door.

Tierney was at him again as soon as he turned around. "Is it really from your friend Morgan, Da? Why do you suppose he had it carried by messenger?"

"It's from Morgan right enough," Michael said, ripping open the envelope.

Tierney hovered at his shoulder. "What does he say? Is something wrong?"

"Hush, now, and let me read it so we'll know."

As soon as he began reading, Michael realized the letter had not been written in answer to his own, mailed back in November. If Morgan had received it at all, he made no mention. Neither was it typical of the hastily scratched notes Morgan usually wrote; it was several pages long and written in a careful hand.

"Aren't you going to read it aloud, Da?"

Hearing the impatience in Tierney's voice, Michael shook his head distractedly. "It's too long. You can read it a page at a time as I do."

The further he read, the more disturbed he became. The news accounts he'd been following for weeks leaped to life through Morgan's vivid descriptions and uncompromising accounts of Ireland's tragedy. Michael felt as if Morgan were here, in this very room, telling him face-to-face of the devastation, the horrors that had fallen upon their country. All the ugliness he had heretofore only imagined became dreadfully real. And behind every line, he could sense Morgan's pain and his rage at his utter helplessness.

Handing the pages to Tierney as he finished each one, Michael's heart began to pound. The more he read, the worse it got. Morgan reeled off news about his own family and others Michael knew and remembered. *Nora...*

She had lost her husband—and her little girl! Dear heaven, her oldest son was failing, too? Michael realized he had moaned aloud for her pain when Tierney put a hand to his arm.

The only hope for her at all is to leave Killala...to leave Ireland. While I know I'll have the time of it, convincing her to go, somehow I must find a way. Although Nora has not faced it yet, I doubt that Tahg, her oldest lad, will last until spring, and her father-in-law—do you remember Old Dan Kavanagh?—will most certainly be gone before then. If she does not leave, and soon, Michael, she will perish with all the others.

I have told her nothing of this yet, but with the help of some of my lads, I'm sure I can raise passage money for her and those of her family left alive, as well as for Thomas and his young ones, to come across. But I'll be needing some help, and that's where you come in, old friend, though what I'm about to ask is not an easy thing.

Curious, Michael frowned and scanned ahead, reading beyond the words of apology until he reached the next page.

And so, keeping in mind that you've been without your Eileen some years now, and remembering there was a time when you had a true fondness for Nora, I'm anxiously wondering if you could find it in your heart, Michael—you and Tierney—to take Nora and what remains of her family by then, into your home.

Stunned, Michael's eyes fastened on the last line for a long moment before Tierney's voice broke through his incredulity. Looking at his son, Michael hesitated, then handed him the page he had just read. His pulse skipped, then lunged and raced ahead as he went on with Morgan's letter.

The only chance I stand of making her listen to reason is to give her the security of knowing someone will be there, waiting for her, when she arrives. In truth, what I am asking, Michael, is that you consider marrying our Nora...

Marry her? Marry Nora?

Michael's eyes went back over the words again, the blood roaring to his head.

I know there was a time when you had a great fondness for

her, and with that in mind, I'm hoping an arrangement such as I suggest might not be entirely to your disliking.

By now I'm sure you're newly astounded at my always considerable nerve, but I must stretch your patience even further. Knowing Nora's infernal pride and insistence on propriety, I believe the only way she would ever entertain such an extreme idea would be if you were to write her yourself—just as if all this were your doing, rather than mine. Perhaps—and only perhaps—if she thought the need were more yours than her own, she might be willing to start a new life in America.

The room swayed around Michael. His mouth went dry, and his heart pumped wildly. But there was more.

You have a right to ask, and are wondering, I'm sure, why I do not wed Nora and bring her over myself. I cannot deny that I love the lass and have for most of my life long. But we both know it would be worse than folly for a woman like Nora to wed a man like me—even if she would have me, which I doubt. I can offer her nothing but a heart forever chained to a dying country. I cannot leave; besides, Nora deserves far more than the fool I am. And so I'm praying you will find it in your heart to make room for her and her youngest, Daniel John—and, should Tahg survive, him as well. I'm sure the old man would never leave, even if he should recover enough to travel.

I hope to secure passage for both families and perhaps raise some extra funds as well. I know the increased financial burden in this is no small matter.

In closing, I would ask that you send me a private answer by the lad who delivered this letter to you, and if, please God, your answer is yes, then send Nora a letter by him as well. I will see to it she never knows but what the idea was entirely your own.

If you must forgive me for anything, my friend, then

forgive me for remembering your utter selflessness and your eager willingness to help others.

I thank you, and as always, I remain...your loyal friend,

Morgan Fitzgerald.

Michael stared at the last lines of the letter for a long time. He felt oddly detached from his surroundings—lightheaded, isolated, weak. The only reality seemed to be the letter in his hand and the sound of his heart pounding violently in his ears.

When Tierney reached for the last page of the letter, prying it carefully from his father's fingers, Michael was only vaguely aware of releasing it. Finally he blinked and turned to look at his son.

The boy was gaping at him with a dazed look of disbelief that Michael was sure mirrored his own dumbfounded expression.

"What in the world are you going to do, Da?"

Numb, Michael stared at the boy. Then a thought struck him, jerking him back to reality.

"The question is, what are *we* going to do?"

Tierney stood watching him, the letter clutched in his hand. "What do you mean?"

Michael willed himself to think. "This affects you every bit as much as me, lad. We're talking about taking in an entire family—I can't make a decision like that alone." He stopped, swallowing down the panic swelling up in him. "Dear God, how can I make a decision like this at *all?*"

Silence stretched between them until Tierney finally broke it. "I still remember Mother. Does that surprise you?"

The boy's soft words caught Michael completely off guard. "Of course, you do, son. Tierney, no one is suggesting that Nora could ever take your mother's place, nor would she—"

Tierney shook his head. "I didn't mean that, Da."

Michael waited. "What, then?"

The boy looked away, embarrassed. "It's just that...sometimes I wonder if it wouldn't be nice, having someone—a woman—" He looked up, his face tight and pinched. "It might make it seem more like a home." His shoulders relaxed a little, and he released a long breath.

Michael's face must have mirrored the dismay he felt at the boy's words, for Tierney quickly tried to retract them. "I don't mean we don't already have a home, Da, nothing like that—I—"

With a small wave of his hand, Michael nodded. "I know. I know exactly what you mean, and it's all right. I've had the same thoughts myself, lad."

"You have? Honestly, Da?"

Again Michael nodded. Going to the stove, he set the kettle on for tea. Then he turned back to Tierney, who stood watching him, clenching and unclenching his hands.

"Da? What did Morgan mean—about your once having a—a fondness for Nora?"

Michael moistened his lips. He had not noticed before now the spurt of growth the boy seemed to have taken—he was nearly as tall as Michael himself—or the faint dusting of fuzz on his upper lip and cheeks, the newly angled lines and planes of his face. His son would soon be a man.

And so he would talk with him as a man. "Sit down, son. We'll have some breakfast, and I'll tell you about Nora…and how she was special to both Morgan and me. And then—then we must be deciding what to do."

Only then did Michael manage to admit to himself that he did not necessarily find Morgan's astounding request all that unthinkable.

Dublin

Two young men, both in knit caps and dock workers' jackets waited in the darkness between the side of a warehouse and a pub on the wharf. It was late, past midnight, and the only light was a thin ribbon from the moon that barely managed to squeeze between the buildings.

The taller of the two was a year older than his companion and had dark hair and a hard mouth; he stood so still he scarcely seemed to be breathing. Hair the color of corn silk straggled below the cap of the smaller man, who was pulling nervously at his gloved fingers.

Neither had ever met Morgan Fitzgerald before tonight, but he was said to be a great steeple of a bearded man with dark red hair. They heard the sound of boots scraping the dock, and in another moment a dark, towering shadow loomed before them in the opening between the buildings.

"*I nanabhruid fen ama ge—*" the tall, cloaked stranger intoned by way of identifying himself. *My harp will sound a joyful chord.*

"*Gach saorbhile samh—*" Both men completed the greeting in unison. *For the Gaels will be free!*

Fitzgerald slipped into the space where they stood. "Any word yet?"

The fair-haired youth gaped at him openly, trying to get a better look in the dark, while the taller of the two shook his head. "None. But we've got your tickets. And some money."

The giant's copper hair could barely be seen in the shadows. His voice was oddly gentle for such a large man. "That's grand, lads. And what about the ship?"

The dark-haired man opened his coat and withdrew a small packet, handing it to him. "It's yours, sir. But we'll need a date."

The big man in the cape took the packet, and there was a hint of a smile in his voice. "You're efficient as well as generous. I do thank you. But as to a date, I'm waiting for a response to my letter. Your lad was to wait on it and return it himself?"

"Aye, sir. Those were his orders, and he's dependable."

Fitzgerald nodded. "Well, then, we'll simply go ahead with the plan. I'll have to trust my friend in New York to come through for me as I believe he will." He paused, running one hand down his beard. "Whether he does or he doesn't, I *must* get them onto that ship. Let's plan for the last weekend of March."

"Time enough," answered the dark-haired man without delay. "The ship is ready, as is the crew. The other passengers will be boarded before she sails into Killala Bay. One good thing, the weather should improve some by then." He paused, adding, "It's a small ship, sir, but American-built. Safer than any of those British coffins."

"I appreciate it, lads. It's my family—and others dear to me—who will be sailing on it."

The younger man spoke for the first time. "It's treacherous, sailing out of such a small harbor, sir."

He felt the big man's eyes on him and worried that he'd spoken out of turn.

But the voice in the darkness was kind when it came. "I know. But it's the only way, you see. There will be some going who are ill, if they last long enough to go at all. They will do well to make it to the bay, much less survive the trek to a distant port."

The youth was quick to reassure him. "Sure, and they'll be fine sailing out of Killala, sir."

Fitzgerald's heavy sigh filled the darkness. "If I can convince them to sail at all." After a brief lull, he said, "Well, lads, you can reach me through Duffy or Smith O'Brien for another day or so. Then I'll be starting for Killala—I dare not stay away any longer. You'll see that any message from New York reaches me there right away?"

"You'll be contacted just as soon as our man returns, sir. You can count on that," the dark-haired one assured him.

"Sir—"

The big man had turned to go, but stopped at the youth's voice, waiting.

"You've heard about O'Connell? They're saying he's a broken man."

Fitzgerald nodded and again sighed. "He has exhausted himself entirely."

"For Ireland," the youth said stoutly.

"Aye" came Fitzgerald's soft answer. "For Ireland."

The two men watched him disappear into the mist-veiled night. "He's not at all as I had pictured him," said the younger.

"How is that?"

"I expected him to be a somewhat—harder man. A bit loud and fiery, perhaps even gruff."

His dark-haired companion murmured agreement.

"Still, he calls himself a simple schoolmaster and a poet," said the youth.

"That he does," replied the older man. "But in County Mayo, they call him the Red Wolf."

11

The Sorrowful Spring

For the vision of hope is decayed,
Though the shadows still linger behind.
THOMAS DERMODY (1775–1802)

March came to Killala with no song of spring, no hint of hope.
Ordinarily it was a month greeted with relief and lighter
hearts. March meant the approaching end of winter and the drawing
near of spring, the promise of warm breezes and planting time, the welcome escape from long months of indoor confinement and idleness. Soon
the days would turn gentle, the evenings soft with the scent of sea and
heather.

That had been March before the Hunger. Now the month arrived
with the sobs of starving children and the endless clacking of death carts
in the streets. Heralded by the lonely keening of those who mourned their
dead and the shuffling footsteps of homeless peasants on the road, the
winds of March moaned across the land with no respite from the winter's cruelty.

In every county, in every province, evictions were commonplace, starvation was rampant, and disease raged through village after village with
the fury of a host of demons. By March the reality of an epidemic was
undeniable. Fever hospitals dotted the countryside, but they were so few
and so poorly equipped as to be almost negligible; the workhouses, too,
were impossibly overcrowded and had long since closed their doors. The
afflicted had little choice other than to suffer at home—if indeed they

still had a roof over their heads—or to surrender their lives in a ditch by the road.

The Kavanagh household was no exception. They had depleted their paltry supply of food days ago, and with no cow or other stock to slaughter, they were facing imminent starvation. Nora had even found herself praying for Morgan Fitzgerald's return, in the far-reaching hope that he might bring another precious store of provisions with him.

Daniel John had gone outside just before midday to look for food—a futile effort, Nora knew only too well, and she had tried to dissuade him. The poor lad was trying so desperately these days to be a man, to be strong for them all, but there was nothing he could do. There was nothing *anyone* could do.

Her spirit had always been set against the wind, opposed to giving in to hardship or despair. But she had very nearly reached the point where she no longer had the strength or the desire to drag herself through another hopeless day. Were it not for her sons and the old man needing her so desperately, she could easily lie down and welcome death.

But they *did* need her, and as long as they did she could not give up. She sat watching them now, her ailing son and father-in-law. Daniel John had helped her move his grandfather's bed into the alcove next to Tahg's so she could more easily attend to the two of them at once. They were both sleeping, Tahg fitfully, his forehead furrowed with pain as he shivered beneath the threadbare blanket. Old Dan lay somewhere in the shadowed place where he'd been for days, waiting for the angels to come for him. Except for the heaving of his sunken chest, he moved not at all.

Nora leaned her head back, closing her eyes against the painful sight of their misery. Not for the first time, she was stirred by anger and resentment at the thought of all that had been taken from the old man and his descendants. This was *his* land, after all, his and that of his ancestors before him. Ever since the youthful Eoin Caomhanach—the first John Kavanagh—had fled to the west after Cromwell's invasion, this land had been worked and farmed by the Kavanagh family. Driven across the country like cattle fleeing from a storm, those early refugees from Cromwell's cruelty had learned to make the best of the land as they found it.

But over the years, history repeated itself, and the people of Killala, like those throughout all Ireland, found themselves plundered and stripped of all they owned, reduced to the station of destitute serfs upon their own land.

At a moan from Tahg, Nora's eyes snapped open. Dragging herself up from the chair, she gave her head a moment to clear, then went to wipe a trail of blood-tinged spittle from Tahg's chin. His face was white, with that awful transparency that seemed to reflect the dim light of the room. In spite of the cold—for there had been no turf to burn for days now—his skin was hot and damp with unhealthy perspiration.

The pain in her head throbbed fiercely as she tended to Tahg. Turning to Old Dan, she tucked his blanket more closely about his shoulders, then braced her hands on either side of his wasted body to steady herself. Straightening, she gasped as a hot wave of nausea washed over her. Her ears were ringing, the room spinning. She grabbed for the bedstead, but missed.

She fell, tumbling slowly at first, then faster and faster toward a deep, dark pit. Again she reached out, clutching at something, anything, to break her fall. But it was too late. The pit yawned and widened, sucking her into a dizzying whirlpool of darkness, then hurled her into oblivion.

Daniel hadn't intended to go so far; certainly he had not thought of ending up here, on the hill where the land agent lived.

But he had promised himself not to return to the cottage until he'd found some sort of provisions for his family. Tahg was so terribly ill, as was Grandfar—and lately Mother looked nearly as weak and sick as they did. He had to get help for them all—he simply *had* to!

Now, after searching for more than two hours and finding not even a rotten old turnip, he stood staring up at the bleak gray house of the agent, attempting to muster his courage. Perched almost at the very top of the hill, it was a grim, ill-kept block of a place, square and ugly and battered by the Atlantic winds. It stood there in all its drab coldness, glowering down on the village as if to mirror its occupant's contempt.

In spite of his earlier promise to himself, Daniel shivered, longing to turn back. But he knew in his heart that this might be the one place he would find food—food that could very well mean his family's survival. And so he began to walk, hesitatingly at first, then with more purpose.

About a quarter of the way up, he stopped to read a notice tacked up on a fencepost. It was the same warning he'd seen in numerous places throughout the village. Thomas Fitzgerald had said the stranger in town had nailed up the notices, the one sent from London by the Big Lord. Gilpin's lackey.

The tenantry on Sir Roger Gilpin's estate, residing in the village of Killala and surrounding manor, are requested to pay into my office on the 30th of March, all rent and rent in arrears due up to that date. Otherwise summary steps will be taken to recover same.

It was signed by the agent, *George Cotter.*

Daniel wanted to rip the notice from the post and burn it. No one in the village—including his own family—was in a position to pay the rent.

Anger and fear churned together inside him, making his empty, bloated stomach cramp even more. Clenching his hands into tight fists, he resumed his trek up the hill with more determination. He passed a stone fence that followed a wild thicket up to the stables, and, farther up, a rough-hewn storage barn. It was a forlorn, wild-looking property that appeared to have had no attention for years. The buildings were in need of paint, the weeds overgrown; and paper and other debris littered the yard.

Out of breath, his chest heaving from the effort of the climb, Daniel stopped. Partially concealed by a tumble of overgrown brush, he stood unmoving, taking a long, careful look around his surroundings. Satisfied that nobody was about, he broke into a run, heading toward the back of the house. As soon as he came around the side, he spotted a large bin and some barrels, but they were dangerously close to the door. He crouched, again scanning his surroundings.

The backyard led straight into the woods with a path leading off to the right, toward the stables. There was no one in sight, no sound from the house. With the wind whipping his face, he broke toward the barrels near the door.

He made it as far as the nearest barrel when he froze, paralyzed by the sound of approaching hoofbeats.

A horse snorted, and somebody shouted, *"Halt! You—stay where you are!"*

Daniel whipped around to see the agent bearing down on him on his enormous gray stallion. Behind him, on a black mare, sat a small, slender man with fair hair and round spectacles. He was dressed like a gentleman, and Daniel knew at once this must be Lord Gilpin's man from London.

Instinctively, he stiffened, bracing himself for the blow he was sure would come.

Cotter drew his horse to a sharp halt, and the other man stopped beside him. The agent's eyes were blazing, his face flushed and slick with perspiration. In his upraised hand he held a riding crop.

"What the devil are you up to, you little nit?" he shouted, waving the crop in Daniel's direction. "Thinking to rob me, is that it?"

Daniel tried not to shrink beneath the agent's fierce gaze. His tongue seemed glued to the roof of his mouth, and his heart threatened to explode, but he stood his ground, waiting.

Cotter looked as slovenly as he was rumored to be. Stains spotted his coat and a tear showed in one sleeve; he was unshaven and appeared to need a wash.

Daniel's only thought was to run, and he did lunge forward. As if the agent had anticipated his move, Cotter turned the big stallion's lathered body sideways to block him.

"Stay where you are, you thieving little wretch! I want your name!"

Daniel opened his mouth, but the words wouldn't come. He swallowed, trying again. "Daniel...Daniel Kavanagh."

"From the village?"

"Aye, sir."

"How many more of you are hiding in the bushes?" Cotter glanced toward the woods.

"None...none, sir. I'm alone." Daniel's heart was hammering crazily, and he feared that, in an instant of terror, he was going to humiliate himself by breaking into tears. But he fought for a deep breath, seeing something in the agent's eyes that said it would go even worse for him if the man sensed his fear.

"Well, then—what are you doing here? Have you come to steal or to beg?"

"I—neither, sir." Shame crept over Daniel as he tried to explain. "I was hoping you wouldn't mind if I helped myself...to some of your leavings."

Cotter's lips turned up in disgust. "You thought to steal from the garbage? What are you, then, a rat?"

Angered, Daniel refused to shrink from this bleary-eyed man. "No, sir," he muttered harshly. "I am simply hungry. As is everyone else in the village."

The agent leaned forward on his horse, his small, glazed eyes boring into Daniel. "Well, then, perhaps you'd like to beg," he sneered. "Any lad hungry enough to eat a man's garbage should certainly be humble enough to beg, I would think."

Daniel stiffened, blinking furiously against the tears threatening to spill from his eyes. He looked at the younger man on the horse beside Cotter, surprised to see him studying the agent with a look of open contempt.

"Who are your people, boy?"

Daniel's gaze returned to Cotter. A faint shift in the agent's tone made him wary. Cotter's anger seemed to have faded; in its place was another expression that sent a ripple of uneasiness coursing through him.

"My people? My da was Owen Kavanagh, sir, but he's dead now. My mother's name is Nora, and I'm called after my granddaddy, Dan Kavanagh."

"And how many more nits at home?"

"Just my brother and me, sir," Daniel replied grudgingly. "My little sister died of the fever."

Cotter rubbed the side of one hand across his stubbled chin. "And you're hungry, is that it? You and your family?"

Daniel gave a curt nod, bitter that the agent would feign ignorance of the widespread starvation in the village.

"Lazy, too, I'll wager," Cotter sniped, leaning forward still more.

Daniel was struck by a roaring wave of rage, and with it a sudden desperate wish to be a man grown. A big man, as big as Morgan, so he need not stand here and be disgraced by this disgusting, loathsome creature. For the first time in his life he knew the intense, almost debilitating desire to harm another human being.

"But perhaps you're not as lazy as some, after all, eh?" the agent was saying. "At least you had the industry to go in search of food."

Daniel frowned, puzzled as to what Cotter was getting at. "I'm not lazy, sir. I'd work if there were work to be had."

The agent straightened a bit, giving Daniel a long look of appraisal. "You'd welcome a job, would you?"

"Aye, sir," Daniel said uncertainly. "It's not that I haven't tried to find work."

Cotter smiled, but the smile only increased Daniel's apprehension. Something lay behind the look that he did not understand. "What's your age, boy?"

"My—I'm thirteen, sir."

"Mmm." Cotter went on studying him carefully. "You're old enough, I suppose. None too strapping, though you're tall for your age. Are you strong enough for hard work, do you think?"

Daniel now began to feel a surge of hope. "Oh, I'm that fit, sir! I could do any work I set my hand to."

Again the agent stroked his chin, and Daniel squirmed inwardly under his keen inspection. He felt as if every inch of his frame was being measured. Even as his hope increased, his stomach knotted. There were stories about the agent, murmured stories and accusations about some terrible, unspeakable aberration in his nature that was only spoken of in whispers.

"I suppose there's always work to be found around this place for a boy who is fit," Cotter proclaimed loudly, jarring Daniel out of his uncomfortable thoughts. "How soon could you start?"

He was offering a job! The ground tilted beneath Daniel's feet, and his legs went weak with relief.

Forgetting the rumors, dismissing his feelings of uncertainty, Daniel answered him quickly before the man had time to change his mind. "As soon as you'd want, sir! Today, if you wish."

Cotter slapped the open palm of his hand with the riding crop. "Good enough. I'll give you bed and board and a fair wage."

Bed and board? "I—I wouldn't have to stay here, would I, sir? I can come up in the mornings just as early as you like, and stay late in the evenings, but—"

The agent's eyes narrowed, and his mouth thinned to a tight line. "If you work here, you stay here. I need somebody I can count on, day or night."

Daniel's mind reeled. His mother couldn't do without him, couldn't manage Tahg and Grandfar on her own. But the money—he *must* take the job!

His eyes went to the fair-haired man, who was studying him with an expression that startled Daniel. *Pity.* The man was staring at him with open pity.

Daniel looked away, pretending he hadn't seen. He lifted his chin; he wanted no pity, least of all from an *Englishman.*

"All right, sir. I'll have to go home and tell my mother, but I'll come back whenever you say."

Cotter twisted his mouth to one side, raking Daniel's face with his eyes. "See that you're back before sunset this evening." He raised a hand, pointing a finger warningly. "If you're *not* back when I say, you need not come at all, do you mind? I'll find a boy I can *depend* on."

Daniel nodded, eager now to get away and tell his mother the good news. As soon as Cotter waved him off, he bolted around the side of the house.

He ran all the way down the hill, ignoring the cramps in his stomach and the burning pain in his chest.

Sure, and I do thank You, Lord...I can't tell how much it means to know You're looking after us after all...

He couldn't wait to see his mother's face, to see relief in her large sad eyes instead of the ever-present fear that lately seemed to grow darker and darker. Perhaps she would be able to smile again. It had been so long since he had seen her do more than force a thin smile for Tahg's sake.

Reaching the bottom of the hill now, he slowed and started down the road toward home. Despite his exhaustion and dizziness, he knew a sense of hope and expectation he had not felt for a long, long time.

Suddenly, in the midst of his relief and excitement, he recalled something he'd overheard Sean O'Malley say to Morgan the night of Timothy's wake: *"Sure, and I'd go to work for the devil himself, Morgan, would it put food in my family's bellies again."*

At the time, Daniel had caught his breath at the man's blasphemy. Now, he could only try to ignore the possibility that he might be about to do what Sean O'Malley had only threatened.

❧

She was coming to. Morgan quickly rose from the chair, bending over her as she attempted to focus her eyes in the dim light from the lantern.

"Nora?" He had covered her with his cloak and now tucked it more snugly under her chin.

A large bruise discolored her left cheekbone, just below the small cut near her eye. Her hair had come loose from its pins, and he moved to smooth it away from her face. She watched him through heavy, dull eyes.

"How do you feel?" he asked her, taking her hand. She blinked, her eyes still uncomprehending. "You must have blacked out. I found you on the floor."

She squeezed her eyes shut, then opened them again. "My head…"

"Aye, I expect it hurts." Again he stroked her hair back from her forehead, and turned to tug the chair closer to the bed.

Suddenly her eyes widened, and she tried to lift her head from the pillow. "Tahg—"

"Tahg and the old man are both all right," Morgan quickly assured her, putting a hand to her shoulder until she dropped her head weakly back onto the pillow. "You must rest, now. Just lie still."

He sat down, taking her hand between the two of his. "I got worried when nobody came to the door, so I came inside to check on you. You gave me quite a fright, lass." *Frightened him out of his wits was what she did.* "Nora…how long since you've eaten?"

She turned her head away.

"Nora?"

Keeping her face turned from him, she gave a small, weak shrug beneath his cloak.

"I've brought food, Nora," he told her. "Enough for several days." When she still made no reply, he went on. "Did you hear me, lass? As soon as Daniel John comes in, we'll have something to eat. Where is he, by the way?"

At last she turned back to him and spoke. "He went looking for food. He's not back yet?"

Morgan shook his head. Guilt lay heavy on his heart. He should never have stayed away so long. The small, forlorn figure beneath his cloak was little more than a ghost of herself. He shuddered involuntarily as a memory of the young Nora flashed across his mind. Gone were the laughing eyes of her youth, the vibrant energy of her nature. The raven tresses that had shone in the summer sun hung lank and graying around her ashen face. Cheekbones jutted above sunken hollows, and her deep gray eyes were darkly shadowed. He had known a moment of total, blood-chilling panic when he found her slumped on the floor beside the old man's bed, looking for all the world as if the life had left her body.

Well, he would not leave her again. From this time on, for as long as she remained in the village, he would be here, too, to take care of her.

Without thinking, he lifted her hand and brushed his lips across her knuckles. "It will be all right, *ma girsha*," he murmured. "Everything will be all right, you'll see. But you must continue to fight for a little while longer."

As if she had not heard him, she turned her face to the wall. "I just want it finished," she said woodenly.

He lifted his head, frowning at the defeat he heard in her voice. "No," he said firmly. "You must not allow yourself to think so. You have to fight, Nora."

Slowly, she dragged her gaze back to his face. "Fight?" A low moan of bitterness escaped her. "For *what?*"

He rose from the chair, and, bending over her, pressed his hands into the mattress on either side of her shoulders. "For your sons. For yourself. For *life*, Nora. You must fight for life."

She closed her eyes as if to block out the sight of him, and he was struck anew by the frailty of her fine, delicate features. Dear God, she was so small, so thin and weak!

"Nora—look at me."

Her eyes opened, and he saw the unshed tears. Stabbed by the fear and misery in her eyes, he dropped down beside her and scooped her up in his arms. "Cry, lass…it's all right to cry…cry it out…"

She made a small, choked sound and allowed him to press her face against his chest. "I'm so *afraid*, Morgan," she whispered against him. He felt her shoulders sag, then begin to shake. "I know it's wrong…I should have more faith. But I'm so frightened all the time. I try not to show it to the others, but I'm…terrified, Morgan…*I'm terrified*…"

The dam of her grief and fear burst then, and Morgan felt a spasm of shudders wrack her fragile body. As he held her, he tried to will some of his own strength into her.

After a long time, she turned in his arms, her face damp, her eyes haunted and glistening. When he saw a look of uncertainty, then embarrassment, steal over her features, he tightened his embrace before she could free herself.

She stared up at him. "I—I'm sorry…I can't think what—"

"Shhh, none of that," he said firmly, resisting her effort to slip out of his arms. "Nora, listen to me, now. As soon as the boy comes in, we'll have some supper, and then we'll talk. There's something I need to tell you, and I want Daniel John here when I do."

"What?"

"It will keep," he said, drinking in her face and her hair tumbling free over his arm, cherishing this rare, precious moment of holding her again, if only to comfort her. "We must get some food into you before—"

"*Mother?*"

They broke apart at the sound of Daniel John's voice, calling out from the kitchen.

Morgan got to his feet. "In here, lad."

The boy's eyes were large with excitement as he came charging into Nora's bedroom. "Mother, wait till you hear my news! I—"

He stopped, his eyes going from Nora to Morgan. "Morgan? What is it? What's wrong?"

"Your mother has had a fall, lad."

Nora extended her hand to the boy, and he hurried to her side to grasp it.

"Are you all right?"

"It's nothing," Nora assured him. "I—I fell, that's all, and Morgan found me. I'm perfectly fine. Now, what's this about your having news?"

Daniel John straightened, still holding her hand. Morgan thought the boy's enthusiasm seemed a bit strained, but there was little doubt as to his eagerness to tell Nora.

"I have a job!" he announced. "A real job."

Nora's hand went to her mouth. "A *job*, Daniel John? But how—"

Smiling at her surprise, the boy nodded eagerly. "Didn't I tell you things would be getting better for us soon?"

"That's grand news indeed, lad," Morgan said carefully, sensing the boy's forced cheerfulness. "And what is this job you have found for yourself?"

Daniel John blinked, hesitating for only an instant. "I'm going to be working for the land agent," he said, not looking at either Morgan or his mother. "I start tonight."

12

Night Voices

Borne on the wheel of night, I lay
And dreamd as it softly sped—
Toward the shadowy hour that spans the way
Whence spirits come, 'tis said:
And my dreams were three—
The first and worst
Was of a land alive, yet cursed,
That burn'd in bonds it couldn't burst—
And thou wert the land, Erie!

THOMAS D'ARCY MCGEE (1825–1868)

Sprawled indolently in a tattered armchair, Cotter smirked at Evan over his tumbler. "You look a mite green, Whittaker. Was our tour of Sir Roger's holdings a bit much for your delicate sensibilities?"

Evan simply shook his head, unwilling to expose what he privately thought of as his "sentimentality" to anyone as coarse and unfeeling as Cotter. His normal reserve was so shaken he did not have the energy to dissemble, so he could only keep silent.

For hours, his head had been hammering with a fury that threatened to prostrate him—indeed it had made him violently nauseous for a time. The hour's rest he'd taken late in the afternoon had done little to ease his misery. At the moment, he was only vaguely aware of the agent's drunken rambling, which had been going on for the better part of the evening. His mind still reeled from the ghastly scenes he had witnessed earlier in the day, and he felt a desperate need to flee the room, knowing he needed both time and solitude to absorb the day's events. No matter how much he might wish to avoid doing so, he had to confront his rioting emotions.

Never in his wildest imaginings could he have conceived the succession of horrors he had encountered in this suffering village. Dante's nine levels of hell seemed little more than a glimpse of the misery of Killala. Within hours, the nightmarish experience had engulfed him, reaching deep into his spirit to pierce some dark, undiscovered depth, touching and altering something vital to his very being. Instinctively, he knew he would never be quite the same man he had been before today.

Across from him, Cotter downed another long pull of whiskey, then nodded to himself. "They're a disgusting bunch, eh? Live like pigs and die like dogs. The esteemed Sir Roger will be well rid of the lot of them, wouldn't you say?"

Evan didn't miss the way the agent slurred his employer's name as if it were an obscenity. He was appalled by this dull, slovenly creature, and could scarcely believe that Roger Gilpin continued to allow him to manage his properties. For his own part, he had all he could do to remain in the same room with the man.

A sudden thought of the comely boy with the soulful blue eyes struck Evan, and he found himself greatly relieved that the youngster had not returned to the agent's house that evening. Watching Cotter when they'd first encountered the boy, Evan had sensed something in the agent's rapacious stare that had both sickened and alarmed him. Only now did he identify the man's glazed, oddly feverish expression as one of undeniable lust.

Most likely the boy's failure to show up accounted for the agent's foul mood. As the evening wore on, Cotter had grown increasingly surly, until now, intoxicated and hostile, he no longer made the slightest attempt to be anything less than offensive.

"To my way of thinking, we can't turn them out fast enough," the agent muttered, seemingly as much to himself as to Evan. "Worthless bunch of savages."

His patience about to snap, Evan fought to keep his voice even. "I-I'm sure," he said, "that when I r-report to Sir Roger the extreme circumstances of his tenants, he will d-do the Christian thing and d-delay all scheduled evictions." Even as he voiced the words, Evan knew he was attempting to convince himself as much as the agent.

"At any rate," he added more firmly, "I shall send a letter to London immediately t-to apprise him of the conditions here."

Cotter uttered a short, ugly laugh and straightened a bit in his chair. "Oh, he knows the conditions here well enough! Why do you think he chose to turn the lot of them out when he did?"

Evan looked at him. "Wh-what, exactly, do you mean?"

Cotter stared at his near-empty glass for a moment, then lifted his eyes to Evan. His smirk plainly said he thought the younger man a fool. "You saw it for yourself, did you not? Those poor devils are in no shape to defend themselves! Why, they're starved to the point of death. They'll not be lifting so much as a hand for their own protection. Sure, and we won't have to *force* them out of their squalid huts—we'll simply let the death cart driver *drag* them out! Oh, yes," he said, grunting out a sound that might have been amusement, "old Gilpin knows what he's doing well enough."

Evan could feel the sour taste of revulsion bubbling up in his throat, and he had all he could do not to choke on his own words. "Nevertheless, Sir Roger has not seen the circumstances of his tenants for himself. I shall spare no details of their plight."

Cotter fastened a bleary-eyed, contemptuous stare on him, all the while rooting inside his ear with his little finger. "How long have you worked for Gilpin, Whittaker? Ten years or more by now, I shouldn't wonder."

"Eleven," Evan replied coldly.

The wide gap between the agent's upper front teeth seemed to divide his mouth in half each time he flashed his insolent grin. "Well, then, you can't possibly believe for a shake that the old goat has so much as a hair of charity in his soul. You needn't defend him to *me*, man. Haven't I been working for either him or his blackhearted father for nigh on twenty years by now? I know full well what a devil he is."

Evan rose from his chair, disturbed as much by his uneasy awareness of the truth in Cotter's remarks as by the agent's crude disrespect. "Mr. Cotter," he said stiffly, placing his empty teacup on the scarred table beside the chair, "I hardly think it p-proper to discuss our employer in this fashion. Besides, I find m self quite exhausted, and I still have to write to Sir Roger. If you don't mind, I'll retire to my room now."

The agent's only response was a distracted smirk and a drunken wave of the empty tumbler in his hand.

Steeling himself not to run, Evan held his breath as he crossed the dimly lighted room. So unsteady did he feel, so furiously was his stomach pitching, he feared taking a deep breath lest he disgrace himself by losing his dinner in full view of the leering agent.

The initial shock of Daniel John's announcement about Cotter's job offer had finally waned, although the boy's frustration was still evident. It had taken an hour or more of argument among the three of them, no lack of pleading on Nora's part, and, finally, a few stern words from Morgan, but eventually they'd managed to talk without shouting at one another.

The bedroom was swathed in deep shadows, lighted by only one squat candle. Nora sat ashen-faced on the edge of the sagging bed, watching her son, wringing her hands worriedly. Daniel John stood as fixed as a rock in the middle of the room, his fists tightly clenched, his eyes sullen.

Morgan's own emotions were scarcely less turbulent. Upon learning of Cotter's attempt to lure the lad into his employ, a fresh surge of hatred for the degenerate land agent had roared through him. Even now, his temper was still stretched tight as an archer's bow.

"*Whatever* possessed you to go to the hill in the first place?" He hurled the question at the boy more sharply than he'd intended, immediately aware that his anxiety was making him unreasonable.

From his rigid stance in the middle of the room, Daniel John met Morgan's eyes without flinching. "Hunger," he said evenly. "I only went as a last resort. I had looked everywhere else I knew for food, and found none. The big house seemed the only possibility left."

"And Cotter came upon you by surprise."

The boy nodded.

"And offered you a job."

"He did."

"Which you accepted without conferring with your mother first," Morgan said, making no attempt to soften the rebuke in his tone.

Daniel John lifted his chin. "I thought my having a job would please her." He paused, then added defensively, "At the least, I thought it might save us."

"Oh, Daniel John, I still can't believe you did such a foolish thing!"

Nora exclaimed, pushing herself up off the bed and making an effort to stand. "To resort to stealing? You know that's wrong; it is *sin*! And to think that you might have been shot!"

"And is it less sin to watch my family starve while that pig on the hill wallows in his greed?"

The boy's quiet retort made Nora pale. Seeing her sway, Morgan grabbed her. "Nora! Here, sit down; you're entirely too weak to be up yet." Carefully, he helped her onto the chair beside the bed before turning back to Daniel John.

"Your mother has told you that you must not take Cotter's job, lad, and she is right. You have heard the stories about the agent, have you not?" When the boy made no reply, Morgan pressed. "Well?"

"I—rumors, is all," Daniel John muttered, looking away.

"No, and they are not *rumors*!" Morgan closed the distance between them to snatch the boy roughly by the shoulders. "There is all too much truth to the tales, and you'd do well to mind what you have heard. Cotter is a sick, depraved man—don't be thinking you're a match for the likes of him!"

Daniel John surprised him by twisting free. "I can take care of myself!" he burst out. "And I still say it's foolish to turn down such a job when we're starving to death!"

For an instant Morgan's own temper flared, but just as quickly he banked it. "Now, you listen to me, lad. The subject is no longer up for discussion—your mother has said you're not to go back on the hill, and that is that. If you need any further explanation as to why Cotter was so eager to get you under his roof, the two of us will go outside and I'll explain it to you more clearly. But for now I want your word that you will obey your mother."

He winced at the desperation in the boy's eyes. No longer a child, yet not quite a man, the lad looked like a young animal caught in a trap. Morgan could almost feel the conflict raging within Daniel John.

The boy stared at him another moment, then turned to Nora. "And what are we to do, then, Mother? What choice do we have?" His voice sounded thin and childlike, and Morgan yearned to pull the boy into his arms and somehow shelter him from all the ugliness hovering just outside the cottage walls.

His mind went to the letter he had written Michael. With every day that passed, his impatience grew. He had been so sure that this time when he returned to Killala, he would come with a letter in hand. The ship was to be in the bay in a matter of days; he must broach the subject of emigration to Nora before much longer, or it would be too late entirely.

He cast a look at Daniel John. Even as lean and coltish as he was, with his long arms and legs, and his shoulders crowding the seams of his shirt, there was no denying that he was growing into a winsome, grand-looking lad. God only knew what that demented animal Cotter might yet try to get the boy into his clutches. He would not be stopped by one failed attempt. Not Cotter. He had tried once, and he would try again, perhaps something more devious or even dangerous next time.

His eyes went to Nora. Dear Lord, she was so terribly weak, so frail! Just to look at her and see the way she had failed made him heartsore. No wonder the boy had been driven by desperation.

Daniel John's question, asked for the second time, roused Morgan from his grim musings. "Mother? What choice do we have? What can we do?"

When Nora did not answer, Morgan made his decision. Clenching his fists, he looked first at the boy, then to Nora. "You can leave Ireland," he said at last, making no attempt to gentle his words. "There is that choice, and it would seem the time has come for the both of you to give it serious consideration."

Daniel John's eyes grew large with surprise, and Nora gasped aloud. Deliberately avoiding their gaze for the moment, Morgan turned and walked toward the blanket-draped opening of the room. Keeping his back to them both, he stopped just short of the threshold. "Daniel John, I want you to come help me with the meal while your mother rests. We will have something to eat, and then we will talk."

Saying no more, he turned, feeling their astonished eyes on his back.

The night's rest for which Evan so desperately longed refused to come. He lay on his back, as rigid as a paralyzed man, his eyes frozen on the ceiling in the darkness. Only in the vaguest sense was he aware of the musty dampness of the room, the faint clinking of glass downstairs where Cotter, he assumed, still sat drinking.

After a time he felt himself falling into a gray, trancelike state between wakefulness and sleep; he seemed to dream, yet remained dimly aware of his surroundings. Against his will, he again found himself walking the streets of Killala, streets lined on either side by the frozen dead. Once more he saw himself surrounded by entire families of corpses. Parents and grandparents, young children and infants lay heaped like worthless rubbish in ditches along the road—skeletons clad only in thin rags, many entirely naked.

A silent scream froze in his throat as some unseen, determined force urged him back inside the same dark, cold cabin he had visited earlier that day. Once more he was made to breathe the fetid stench of fever and death. There, in the same corner, lay the emaciated corpse of a small child; beside it, the wild-eyed, filthy mother, totally devoid of her senses, crouched on the floor, weeping and shrieking some unintelligible plea. The gaunt, mute man who might have been either young or old was still hunched close to his wife, watching her with blank, unfeeling eyes.

Outside, sprawled on the road, were the leavings of a dog's carcass, its near-frozen remains being consumed by a woman and three small children. Off to one side a voiceless procession of half-dead townsmen trudged by, seemingly blind, or at least indifferent, to the gruesome scene.

Against his dream-drugged will Evan continued to travel through the hideous labyrinth of the day. Staring in numb helplessness, he watched a young mother, obviously half-starved and ill with fever herself, drag the lifeless body of her little girl outside their cottage and leave it, partially covered with rocks and straw, in the open yard. Starting back to the door, she stumbled and fell, then lay unmoving only feet away from the improvised grave of her dead child.

Cotter appeared at his side—only this Cotter seemed more demon than man. With a gaping black hole where his mouth should have been and the yellow, soulless eyes of some otherworld fiend, he grinned and gestured that Evan should come along with him.

Evan's stomach heaved, and he tried to pull free of Cotter's clawlike hand on his arm, but the creature urged him across the road to a hovel, familiar in its wretchedness. A neglected one-room cabin with a dunghill at the door and a sloppy mud floor inside, it looked to be abandoned. Its only furnishings consisted of a dilapidated bedstead with some straw and a tattered blanket tossed across it, an empty iron cooking pot, and two rickety wooden boxes. Five cadaverous children clad only in paper huddled near the crumbling hearth, while the father, ragged and barefooted, lay in a stupor on the bed. The dead mother had been left to herself on a soiled pallet near the cold fireplace.

Cotter pushed him outside, cackling. *"What did I tell you, eh? They live like pigs and die like dogs!"*

Back on the wet, ice-glazed road their horses were forced to halt and wait while a death cart passed by. It was filled with corpses tied in sacks, heaped on top of one another in random piles.

"Nowadays they mostly tie them up in sacks or sheets and dump them into the pits as is," Cotter explained in a voice that echoed with indifference. *"Else they use a false bottom casket, so's they can dump one corpse out before going for another. We've long since run out of coffins, you know."*

The children terrified Evan the most. Not the weak, helpless children he had encountered throughout the day; but the nightmare children, vengeful, malicious sprites who clawed at his face and dug at his eyes until he thought he would surely die from the horror. As if performing some dark, macabre dance, they spiraled through the chambers of his mind, fleshless wraiths not quite alive and yet not dead.

He recognized them for what they were: obscene, horribly mutated effigies of those innocents he had observed earlier in the day. But those children had neither cried nor spoken; indeed, they had made no sound at all, but simply stared in vacant despair and utter helplessness, as if biding their time until the death carts would stop for them. With their partially bald scalps, cavernous eyes, and deep facial lines, they had appeared to be wearing death masks. Even more terrible was the peculiar growth of soft, downy hair sprouting from their chins and cheeks, giving them the chilling look of ancient little monkeys.

Caught in the midst of the nightmare children twisting and writhing all around him, Evan felt himself hurled from one to the other as he was swept faster and faster into the depths of their tormented frenzy. He tried to cry out, but his throat seemed paralyzed by terror. Panicked, he turned to Cotter for help. But Cotter was gone, absorbed by the churning darkness just outside the ring of children.

Small hands grabbed for Evan, stuck to his skin, covered his mouth, and stole his breath. They were chanting something in voiceless whispers... taunting him, threatening him, warning him...

"God, help me!"

Evan shot bolt upright in bed, terror-stricken by the sound of his own strangled cry. For a long time he couldn't move, could scarcely breathe. Huddled beneath the blankets, chilled by his own clammy skin, he trembled so violently that he shook the entire bed. He was wide awake, but unable to see anything in the thick, damp darkness of the bedroom.

Yet even now he could not escape the children. In the black silence of the night, their sunken, horror-filled eyes continued to accuse him as they took up the chant of Cotter's complaint:

"We've long since run out of coffins, you know... We've long since run out of coffins."

13

A Starless Night

Was sorrow ever like to our sorrow?
Oh, God above!
Will our night never change into a morrow
Of joy and love?

LADY WILDE [SPERANZA] (1820–1896)

Nora's cottage was hushed, the silence in the kitchen thick and strained.

It had been over two hours since they shared the meal. The candle on the table had burned nearly to the bottom, but there was still a dim light from the fire Morgan had built out of a half-rotted log and some old copies of *The Nation*. The only sound to be heard was an occasional lapping of flames against wood and the low, mournful wailing of the wind outside.

Morgan sat across the table from Nora, watching her stare into the fire. She was still wrapped in his cloak and appeared almost childlike beneath its weight. He was again struck by the alarming pallor of her skin, even dappled as it was by the soft glow of firelight. She had not met his eyes for what seemed an interminable time, but merely sat, wooden and silent, almost as if she had forgotten his presence.

Moments before, Daniel John had retreated to his room—most likely, Morgan suspected, because he was unwilling to face the possibility of another argument. The heated exchange that had broken out between Morgan and Nora earlier had obviously upset the boy—and it had lasted the better part of an hour before finally being halted by a strangled fit of coughing from Tahg.

Tahg. Morgan could not help but wonder what was keeping the lad alive. He had reached the point in his illness where he would often become extremely agitated, sometimes even incoherent, often a seizure. Morgan had seen it before with lung fever; the afflicted would panic and begin to thrash about with a kind of savage energy before collapsing once again into a stupor. This time it had taken both him and Daniel John to hold the boy down while Nora worked to cool his skin with wet cloths.

Mercifully, he slept now; Morgan hoped that Daniel John might, too, although he thought it unlikely. What with the events of the day and the commotion of the evening, he feared the boy would find little peace this night.

This was not the way he had wanted it, not at all the way he had planned for it to be. He had hoped that his first mention of emigration would come only after a comfortable length of time spent in preparing Nora and her family to face the truth: that leaving Ireland was their only choice if they were to live.

Had there only been more time, perhaps he might have talked them around to the idea with some degree of calm and common sense. As it was, however, he had more or less been forced to hurl the suggestion at them with no warning at all. Their reactions had been predictably stormy.

At first Daniel John had responded with little more than bewildered amazement, saying nothing. Later, though, Morgan realized the lad's aloofness had only been the precursor to a kind of dazed confusion. Even when the boy left the room and ascended the ladder to his bed in the loft, his stiff movements and glazed stare were unmistakably the mannerisms of one who has been badly stunned.

Nora, however, had been far more vocal, exhibiting a feverish kind of anger, protesting every point Morgan attempted to raise with a vigor he would not have expected, given her frailty. Finally, unwilling to risk her collapsing again, he deliberately broke off the conversation, urging her to at least consider the possibility he had raised.

He had left the cottage then, on the pretense of foraging for more wood. When he returned, he found her as she was now, silent and unyielding. At first he assumed her withdrawal to be the result of anger with him and his "daft ideas." He had taken his time poking up the fire, then looking in on Tahg and the old man—both were sleeping—before finally coming to draw up a chair opposite her. Only after several moments had passed, moments during which neither of them spoke, did he see her lips moving faintly and realize that she was praying.

He took this to be a good sign. If she was praying, then she must also be thinking. Could he dare to hope that the Lord might be his ally in all this? Certainly he had thought to do his own praying about things, but given the sin-stained condition of his soul, why should he think any prayer of his would reach heaven?

Now, as he watched the firelight play over her face, memories of the young girl she had been unexpectedly filled his thoughts. Without warning, a crest of longing rose deep inside him, a wave of remembrance of lost joy so powerful and poignant he nearly moaned aloud. He *did* turn his face away so that he could no longer see the gentle curve of her cheek, the graceful line of her throat, and the softly pursed lips moving ever so faintly in petition.

Oh, Lord, I must not let her see…even suspect…the burden of love I still carry for her. There are times I ache to tell her the truth, to gather her into my arms and plead with her to love me again as she once did, to be mine for whatever time we might be able to steal together. Oh, God, for once help me turn a deaf ear to my own selfish desires and make me mindful instead of Nora's good…

≈

Aware that she had been praying—or at least making a numb attempt at it—Nora felt a sudden rush of guilt when she realized that she could scarcely recall her words. How long, she wondered, had she been sitting here, mouthing vain repetitions and meaningless pleas?

Forgive me, Lord. I cannot think…I simply cannot think…

She glanced over at Morgan, who sat staring into the dying fire as if oblivious to his surroundings. Something about his profile caused Nora to scrutinize him. Was it the uncharacteristic sag to his heavy shoulders, a slackness to his face she had not noticed there before? Surprised, she saw that there was an unkempt look about his appearance, and that in itself was enough to make her inspect him all the more closely. Careless as he might be about the company he kept or the manner in which he spent his days, Morgan had never been untidy or neglectful of his person. Tonight, however, an air of resignation seemed to hang about him. His always unruly curly hair was messed—was that why she had not noticed until now the thick brushing of silver at his temples? Even his clothing looked rumpled and worn—and so did Morgan. Faint webs fanned out from the corners of his eyes, deep grooves bracketed his mouth, and his usually bronzed complexion had grayed with the distinct shading of fatigue.

An unexpected, irrational stirring of sadness rose in Nora at the realization that, like herself, Morgan was growing older. Just as quickly she chided herself for her foolishness. She and Morgan were the same age, after all—neither of them chicks any longer after thirty-three years. Besides, considering the dissipated life some said the man had led, he actually looked quite fit.

As if sensing her appraisal, Morgan turned, smiling at her. Inexplicably, Nora felt a sharp stab of pain at the tenderness reflected in that smile.

"Tell me, *ma girsha*," he said, "how is it that I've become an old dog while you've remained but a pup?"

Nora caught her breath at the way he seemed to have read her thoughts. "'Tis not a dog you've turned into, or so I've heard," she stammered, "but a wolf. A *red* wolf," she added pointedly.

When he did not reply, she continued to challenge him. "Did you think you would not be found out? Who else could it be? 'Tis said that the leader of this mountain gang of bandits is a 'huge tower of a man with wild red hair and an even wilder red stallion.' Connacht's own *Robin Hood*, they call him."

Morgan lifted a questioning eyebrow, saying nothing.

"Oh, I know about England's outlaw-hero well enough!" Nora snapped, irritated that he seemed bent on ignoring her accusation. "Was it not your father himself who taught me, at the school?" Her mouth thinned with indictment. "Daniel John knows, too. And aren't you setting a fine example for him and the other children in the village, leading them to believe that it's righteous to steal so long as it's for a good purpose? Sure, and haven't we seen the results this very day of such thinking?"

"Who else knows?"

"And is that all you will say for yourself, then—*who else knows?*"

"In the village. Who else in the village knows?" he repeated impatiently.

"There is talk. Did you think there would not be?"

He made a scornful, dismissing gesture with his hand. "There is always talk. I can't recall you being one for village gossip, Nora."

"And is that all it is, then? Village gossip?"

A shrug was his only reply.

A chill went over Nora, and she drew a shuddering breath. Until now she had only suspected the truth. In spite of believing him to be capable of the thievery and rebellion attributed to the notorious outlaw, a part of her had managed to resist the idea. Perhaps a foolish, lingering fidelity to their childhood friendship and young love had made her want to keep his memory unsullied. But the steady green gaze he leveled on her forced Nora to acknowledge what she had tried to deny for so long: Morgan Fitzgerald was indeed *an mhac tire run*. The Red Wolf.

A sudden torrent of anger surged through her, and she leaned toward him. "*Why*, Morgan? How did you come to such a thing? You with your fine education, your brilliant mind, your poetry and songs—how could you throw it all away as if it had no meaning and turn into a—a common *outlaw*? Is it the political business, then…this Young Ireland movement? Is it that?"

Morgan drew in a long breath, expelling it slowly. Shaking his head, he answered, "No. Oh, most of the lads are of the movement, I suppose, but the movement has no part in this business. That is one thing, this is another. No," he went on in a weary voice, rubbing the back of his neck with one hand, "this is about hunger. And survival. The survival of our families—our villages."

Nora stared at him with dismay, awareness gradually dawning. "That is where the food comes from," she said, watching him. "The supplies you bring into the village—to *us*—the medicine for Tahg, the money you said would pay our passage to America—" Appalled, she stopped. "Oh, you foolish, foolish man!" she cried. "Don't you realize the destruction you are bringing down upon your head? They will *hang* you! Don't you care at all?"

Morgan's gaze never wavered as he reached for her. Feeling the warm, unyielding strength of his large, calloused hands closing over her own, Nora stiffened and tried to draw back. But Morgan held her firmly, leaning across the table, thrusting his face close to hers, so close she felt herself trapped by his eyes. "Do *you* care, *asthore*?"

My treasure. The old endearment from their youth brought scalding tears to Nora's eyes.

"Do you care, Nora?" he repeated softly, bringing her hand to his face and laying her palm against his bearded cheek.

Panic seized Nora at his touch, the unexpected softness of his beard against her hand.

"Well, of course, I care," she said, averting her gaze from his. "I would hardly want to see any man on the gallows."

"Even a fool like me?" he prompted, a tender touch of amusement in his voice.

"Indeed." She could not look at him.

"Nora?"

Unable to stop herself, she met his eyes, and the enveloping warmth she encountered there—an entire tide of feeling—was achingly familiar. Familiar, and somehow frightening.

Nora's mouth went dry, her heart rocked, and for one mad moment no years of pain stood between them. She was a girl again, and Morgan her hero-lad. Startled, she squeezed her eyes shut to close him out. But when she opened them again she found him staring at her with a searching look that seemed to hold a myriad of questions. And in that brief, suspended breath in time, a knowing passed between them, an awareness that long-ago hopes had languished, but not died, that young love had paled, but not entirely fled.

And then it was gone.

He released her hands and rose from the chair. "I should go now," he said roughly. "But will you promise me to think, Nora—really think—about what I have suggested to you this night? You must be the one to make the decision; you are still the mother, and responsible for the safety of your family."

When Nora would have interrupted his admonition, he lifted a hand to stop her. "Remember, now, you need not worry about funds to pay your passage. As I told you, a number of passages are already paid, and a ship is on the way." He hesitated, and for just an instant Nora caught a sense that he wanted to say more—indeed, was withholding something from her.

But his gaze quickly cleared, and he said firmly, "I will help you get Tahg and the old man...if he's still living...to the pier. And I'll see to your food supplies as well, getting them boxed and loaded onto the ship. The only thing that will be left for you to do is to pack the few personal things you may have need of."

He looked away, then started for the door. Without warning, Nora was struck by the suspicion that Morgan was not so much concerned for their welfare as he was desperately eager to be rid of them. He had clearly gone to a great deal of trouble to make sure they would have no excuse for *not* leaving.

Why hadn't she realized before now that they had become a burden to him? Of *course*, he would be anxious to see them out of Killala! For some unfathomable reason—a stroke of uncharacteristic Christian conscience, she supposed—he had assumed a kind of guardianship for her and her family. Clearly, he now had second thoughts, could scarcely wait to pack the lot of them off to America.

A sharp thrust of disillusionment tore at her heart. "How very neatly you have arranged my life for me, Morgan. I don't suppose it even once occurred to you that you might be assuming too much!"

Her voice trembled with humiliation and anger as she continued to rail at him. "I can't think what possessed you to feel responsible for me and my sons, but I can assure you it's entirely unnecessary. Whether we do or we don't choose to leave Ireland is none of your concern, you see. We will manage, and you're not to fret yourself about us another moment."

Morgan had nearly reached the door, but now he whipped around to face her, his eyes flashing a warning. Closing the distance between them in two broad steps, he hauled her up from the chair, his large hands completely engulfing her shoulders. "You can be the most *infuriating* woman!"

When Nora made no reply but simply stared up at him, he scowled and uttered a groan of frustration. "Can you not get it through that stubborn head that I'm only trying to help you?"

In truth, Nora seemed unable to do anything more than gape at him, wide-eyed. His immense frame filled the room, his burning eyes seared her skin, and for one wild instant she thought he might shake her soundly. But after another long moment his hands went limp and the fire in his eyes died away. Releasing her, he turned and, without another word, stalked out of the cottage.

Staring after him, Nora drew in a ragged breath. She glanced down, vaguely aware that she was still wrapped in his cloak. She started to call out to him but stopped, knowing he wouldn't hear. Numbly, she lifted the corner of the rough, heavy frieze of his cloak and brought it to her face. The scent of winter, woodsmoke, and the vast outdoors flooded her senses; hunched over in weakness and regret, she moaned aloud.

Mother? Mother, are you all right?" Daniel John's alarmed voice behind her made Nora straighten and turn.

He came to her at once. He was in his nightclothes, and Nora knew from the pinched look of concern and anguish on his face that he had heard at least a part of the argument between her and Morgan.

"I'm fine, son," she said in an unsteady voice. "But why are you not sleeping?"

He shook his head. "There's too much to think about."

Nora studied his young face, lined too soon with the cares and burdens life had thrust upon him. Putting a hand to his arm, she said gently, "Still, you must rest, Daniel John."

"Mother..."

Nora waited, taken aback, as she often was lately, by the change in her youngest son: his soaring height, his spreading shoulders, the sharpening angles and planes of his long, handsome face, so like his father's. He was only thirteen—almost fourteen, she reminded herself—but soon the last trace of boyhood would be gone, exchanged for the mantle of a man.

So quickly gone, that wondrous time of childhood, when worries were the responsibility of grown-ups, when dreams seemed more real than life itself, and almost as precious. Would Daniel John ever find time for his own dreams? Or was he simply to make the leap from child to man with nothing to bridge the distance? Indeed, she sometimes wondered if her son had *ever* been a child. Always, he had seemed older—stronger, wiser, maturer than many of the other children. Had she made him this way with her ever-increasing dependence on him?

"Mother, can we talk?" His tone held an urgency that pulled Nora back to their surroundings.

"I thought...now that Morgan is gone...we could discuss what he— what he suggested."

She looked at him. "About leaving Ireland?"

He nodded.

"'Tis late, Daniel John," Nora reminded him feebly, knowing herself to be too weak, too exhausted and...wounded to handle anything further this night.

He peered into her face. "Yes," he said finally. "All right, then. I don't want to tire you. But will you just answer me one thing, Mother?"

"Of course, son. If I can."

"Do you—do you think perhaps Morgan might be right? He seems so determined that we leave Ireland. Do you agree with him, that emigration is our only hope of survival? Are things truly that desperate, Mother?"

Unable for the moment to meet his searching eyes, Nora looked down at the floor. She wasn't at all certain exactly *what* she believed. At least for now, she seemed incapable of getting beyond the degrading suspicion that Morgan merely wanted to unburden himself of them in the easiest way possible. Why couldn't he simply have realized from the beginning how vastly unsuited he was for the role of benefactor? It would have been so much better for them all.

She could not stop her anger from spilling over. "Of course not!" she snapped out. "He's only making things sound worse to frighten us into doing what *he* has decided we *should* do!"

Daniel John stood staring at her with an expression that was both puzzled and hurt. "I...I don't think Morgan would do that, Mother. He's not like that, not a bit."

Suddenly irritated with the boy's adoration for the man—which Morgan clearly did not deserve—Nora proceeded to tell her son exactly what she thought to be the truth behind his hero's professed concern for their welfare.

14

Choices and Wishes

Day and night we are wrapped in a desperate strife,
Not for national glory, but personal life.

JOHN DE JEAN FRAZER (1809–1852)

Early the next morning, Morgan stopped at Nora's cottage with an axe and a cart, explaining that he was on his way to fell a tree and asking if Daniel John wished to come along.

The two walked and climbed for nearly an hour before stopping halfway up a steep, dense hillside. They stood appraising a medium-sized elm tree and a smaller beech for firewood.

Although it was a cold, damp morning with mist bleeding down the hill, the sky was clear; indeed, it looked as if the sun might actually be about to shine upon Killala for the first time in weeks. Looking down on the village from this far up, its streets veiled by the shimmering mist, Daniel could hardly believe it was teeming with death and disease. The bodies heaped along the road weren't visible from up here, nor were the beggars, those few still able to stumble through the town. But here and there a ragged tunnel of smoke from a torched cottage rose to meet the mist in a grim reminder that the Reaper of Death was still on the prowl in Killala.

And, as always, silence reigned—the terrible, ominous silence, somehow more agonizing than actual cries of human misery. Even here, far above the town, the unnatural silence of the famine seemed to hover. Other than the occasional snap of a twig underfoot or the brushing of branches in the light morning wind, the same awful stillness that permeated the entire village shrouded the hill.

Morgan finally broke the silence. "The beech will do best," he said decisively, slipping out of the cloak he had retrieved only that morning. "We can be done with it faster, and it will burn just as long."

Daniel nodded shortly, not looking at him. Feeling ill at ease in Morgan's company was a new experience for him, and a distressing one. The harsh words spoken in haste the evening before seemed to have raised a wall between them. He had spent a long, restless night trying to sort out an entire parade of troubled feelings, not the least of which was humiliation.

Their argument over Cotter's job offer had provoked the first sharp words Morgan had ever uttered to him, and the scene had left Daniel feeling ignorant. He resented being scolded like a wee wane. Even if he *had* been foolish in going to the agent's house, he would have expected Morgan to understand the desperation that drove him there, rather than reprimanding him for it.

As for Cotter—certainly Daniel had heard the tales about the land agent. But what Morgan—and his mother as well—seemed bent on ignoring was the fact that Daniel was no longer a child. If he had not thought himself up to handling a weak, dull-witted man like Cotter, he wouldn't have agreed to accept the job in the first place.

Morgan's unexpected rebuke had been bad enough, but even more disturbing had been the abrupt, uncompromising manner in which he had forced upon them the subject of emigration. Obviously, he had upset Mother a great deal; the bitter, scathing things she said after Morgan left the cottage had been painful and impossible to believe.

Her accusation that Morgan wanted only to be rid of them had gone straight to Daniel's heart, piercing like a bandit's knife. When he attempted to protest on Morgan's behalf, she had ignored him. "Morgan is a man after living for himself—and himself alone!" she'd snapped. "And for his precious Ireland, of course! He cares for nothing else and never will. Why, he's even managed to coax Thomas and the children to go along with this daft scheme! Sure, and won't he be as free as a sea bird, once he gets the lot of us onto a ship?"

Despite his own conflicting emotions, Daniel still thought his mother's allegations unfair. Both she and Grandfar had always accused Morgan of being selfish and irresponsible, indifferent to the feelings of others. But Daniel had never seen him in that light. Admittedly, Morgan was a solitary man—perhaps even a bit peculiar, as some in the village insinuated. He was lonely, often melancholy, at times even aloof. But never uncaring—especially with Mother. He had seen the way Morgan sometimes looked at her when he thought nobody was watching, as if she were a rare and precious jewel, a treasure to cherish. Daniel could not put a name to the expression that came over Morgan's face, but there was no mistaking the endless depth of caring there.

And yet, if Morgan *truly* cared, would he be so determined to send them away? To emigrate might mean they would never see one another again, after all. Mother said Morgan had no intention whatsoever of leaving Ireland, not now, not ever. If he had any real affection for them, would he be quite so eager to set them on their way to America?

America. The word had once been magic to Daniel. Often he had dreamed of visiting the liberty-loving young country. Like Morgan, he doubted that any true Irish heart could help but be stirred by the tale of America's struggle for independence from the British.

But how could Morgan think Daniel would want to *stay* there? Didn't he understand that he wasn't the only one who loved Ireland? Wasn't this *his* country as well as Morgan's? Killala, the mountains—the entire island—this was *home.* Everything he'd ever known and loved was here. Did Morgan think he could simply turn his back on it, leave and forget it altogether?

"Daniel John? Are you going to help me?"

Morgan's voice yanked him out of his troubled thoughts. He whipped around and, without thinking, blurted out, "Morgan—I don't want to go! I don't *want* to leave Ireland!"

Clearly taken aback, Morgan stared at him a moment before answering. "Of course you don't want to leave, lad," he finally said, his voice quiet. "You think I do not know that?"

"Then why did you even bring it up? You saw how weak Mother is! All you did was upset her!" Daniel's earlier hurt and confusion parted to make way for a growing wave of doubt. "Is it true, then, what Mother thinks—that you simply want to be rid of us?"

Morgan stood leaning on the axe, his eyes hooded. "Your mother said that, did she?"

Miserable, already wishing he had held his silence, Daniel turned away without answering.

Behind him, Morgan's voice was soft and oddly uncertain. "And you, Daniel John? Is that what *you* think?"

Daniel John swallowed, feeling torn and bewildered and even a little frightened. "I don't know," he muttered, still keeping his back to Morgan. "I don't suppose I know *what* I think anymore."

                                              ?

And how could he? Morgan thought with despair. *He is but thirteen years old. A boy, not a man. A boy who has lost his father, his little sister—and is now losing his grandfather and older brother as well. And as if that were not enough to crush the spirit out of him, here am I, suggesting that he forsake his home and his country in the bargain. Of course he does not know what to think, except perhaps that his life has become a tale of madness, a cruel and heartless jest.*

"Mother was right, you know." Daniel John finally turned to face him when he spoke. "Even if we were of a mind to leave, it would be impossible. Tahg cannot walk—he scarcely even speaks anymore. And Grandfar—"

Morgan nodded. "Yes, lad, I know," he said, trying to be gentle. "Your granddaddy is dying. And I am sorry, Daniel John, deeply sorry." He paused. "But can you not understand, lad, that it is only because I don't want to see you and your mother die as well that I'm trying to make you face reality—face it and do something about it?"

"You know Mother will never be able to bring herself to leave!" the boy argued, his voice breaking for an instant in his frustration. "Not only because of Grandfar and Tahg." He paused, as if debating as to whether he had the right to say what came next. "Mother...Mother would be afraid, Morgan. Why, she'd be terrified, don't you see? She's never been farther than Ballina in her life! Her entire world is here, in Killala."

Again Morgan nodded, unable to dispute the lad's insight about his mother. Yes, of course, Nora would be frightened. Hadn't he known all along that fear might prove to be the one obstacle he could not overcome? Everything else was within the realm of possibility: money for passage, a ship, even the hope of a livelihood once they arrived. But what to do about Nora's fear?

Wasn't that the reason he had counted on Michael's willingness to help?

His hope was that having somebody to depend on, somebody *familiar*, once they reached the States would make all the difference for Nora.

Ah, Michael, Michael, why haven't you answered me, man? Have I hoped for too much, after all?

"Morgan?"

The boy seemed to be looking everywhere else but at him. "If…if *you* were to go, Mother might not be so frightened. It would make all the difference if you were with us. I don't believe she considers me any protection at all—she still thinks of me as a child, you know."

Stricken, Morgan groped for an answer; it was a question he had not anticipated. Not that he hadn't already thought of the possibility. In the event that Michael did not answer his letter, or if he answered but was unwilling to help, he had considered accompanying Nora and the others across, then returning once they were settled.

But the timing could not be worse. The new Confederation was planning a rising—a plan doomed to failure before it began. How else could it end but in defeat? Their army would be made up mostly of hungry men and starving boys, with any number of wild-eyed fanatics thrown in who had no real conception at all as to what they were fighting for. An army of starving peasants and visionaries was hardly a match for the mighty British Empire.

Despite his conviction that defeat was the only possible outcome for such an undertaking, however, Morgan could not bring himself to turn his back on Smith O'Brien. His friendship with the leader of the Young Ireland movement—and hence the leader, albeit a reluctant one, of the planned rising—made it impossible for Morgan to walk away. Besides— as Smith O'Brien had pointed out to those members like Morgan who tended to be less radical—a few cool heads might help to temper the heat of the rebellion's real fire, the impassioned militant, John Mitchel. This strong-willed son of a Unitarian minister could not be a more dramatic contrast to O'Brien, a reserved, Protestant country gentleman; yet the two had somehow managed to engulf themselves and the entire movement in a gathering storm that could explode into open rebellion at any time.

Because of his friendship with O'Brien, Morgan had promised his pen—and his men—to the Young Ireland movement, and hence the rising. He would not renege. He was committed.

But was he not also committed to the boy who stood across from him, staring at him with entreating eyes? And to the lad's mother?

Nora. Dear God, don't make me choose between her and Ireland again. I made my choice once, and I have lived with it. But, please, God, not again... not again...

Raking a hand through his hair, he looked away, turning his gaze toward the mountains. "Daniel John, please try to understand. I am deeply involved in some things right now that I must see through to the end. I have committed myself to a plan, and to some people, and to leave Ireland at this time would be akin to betrayal."

Unexpectedly, the boy nodded and said, "You're talking about a rising."

Morgan shot him a surprised look. "What do you know of a rising?"

"I've heard Grandfar talking," Daniel John said with a shrug. "Him and the other men in the village. And at meeting some weeks ago we were warned about such a possibility. The speaker said we should have no part in it." He stopped, managing a small, bitter smile. "As if anyone in the village has the strength left to take up arms."

He lifted his eyes to Morgan's, his expression sad but knowing. "I'm sorry, Morgan," he said quietly. "I shouldn't have said what I did. I understand why you can't go."

Morgan took a step toward him with the intention of explaining himself still further, but Daniel John shook his head. "No, really, it's all right," he said in a choked voice. "I do understand, at least I think I do, how it is with you...how it has always been. It's as if Ireland has absorbed your very spirit, made you a part of her."

Morgan had never loved the lad quite so much as he did at that moment. He thought his heart would surely explode as he laid his hands lightly on the boy's shoulders, saying, "Aye, it is as you say. But do you also understand, lad, that though it is a different kind of love, it is no greater than my feelings for you and your mother?"

Daniel John gave a short, stiff nod, averting his eyes. "Aye, I do know that, Morgan. I have always known."

The ache in Morgan's heart swelled. "Then know this as well, lad: I would never, ever, wish you or your mother separated from me. It crushes me to even think of it. But what I *do* wish is for you to live, Daniel John— to live and have a chance for a good life, a better life than this suffering island can ever offer you."

Daniel John looked up at him, and Morgan saw with dismay that the boy's eyes were filled with tears. Impulsively, he caught him in a brief embrace, then held him away. "You are growing up quickly, lad," he said, still holding him loosely by the shoulders. "And you will grow to be a fine man—a *great* man, I am thinking."

The boy flushed, but Morgan went on. "You have a noble, heroic heart, Daniel John. You will do your mother proud." He stopped, searching for the words to express what he so desperately wanted to say. "There is something I want to tell you, lad, and no matter what may happen in the days and years to come, I pray you will always remember it." He tightened his grip on the boy's shoulders, regarding him with pride and approval. "If I had ever had a son, Daniel John, I would have been pleased had he been a lad like you, exactly like you. Many is the time I have wished you mine."

For a silent moment they stood so, each searching the gaze of the other. Suddenly, Daniel John threw his arms about Morgan's neck and clung to him. "Go with us, Morgan!" he choked out, the words muffled against Morgan's shoulder. *"Please! Go with us!"*

Morgan held him tightly, squeezing his eyes shut against the pain. Obviously, none of this was going to be as simple as he had hoped.

Part Two

SONG OF SILENCE

The Waiting

The Lord himself has scattered them; he no longer watches over them. The priests are shown no honor, the elders no favor. Our eyes failed, looking in vain for help; from our towers we watched for a nation that could not save us.

Lamentations 4:16–17 (niv)

15

Night Watches

For where is Faith, or Purity, or Heaven in us now?
In power alone the times believe—to gold alone they bow.

RICHARD D'ALTON WILLIAMS (1822–1862)

Cotter sat alone in the large, drafty front room, nursing his whiskey along with his rage.

He had spent most of the day fuming about the Kavanagh boy, plotting his revenge on the thieving little rat. He was vaguely aware that night had fallen. The darkness around him was relieved only by the low fire across the room, which had almost burned itself out. A candle had been flickering earlier, but when the draft from the ill-fitting windows snuffed it out, he hadn't bothered to light it again.

He was completely alone in the house, except for Whittaker, who had secreted himself in his room upstairs immediately after supper. Cook had returned to her cottage in the village after the evening meal; and since the latest in a succession of housekeepers had quit only last week, there were no other domestics presently on the grounds.

From time to time Cotter shot a furious glare at the ceiling, angrily willing the milksop Englishman in the room above to feel the heat of his wrath. For the most part, however, he merely sat, sprawled drunkenly in his chair, drinking and cursing. Sometimes aloud, more often to himself, he cursed Daniel Kavanagh, his family, and the useless inhabitants of the village.

As for the boy, that impudent *gorsoon* would pay, he would. He could not imagine what had possessed the young pup, pretending to be so eager for a job, then deliberately defying him. Well, he would rue his insolence, and soon. Tomorrow the foolhardy young buck would find out the hard way that he could not afford to flout Georges Cotter's authority.

The agent tossed down the rest of his whiskey. Aye, tomorrow young Kavanagh would learn to his misfortune the consequences of rebuffing those in authority. Indeed, many of the disrespectful savages in this squalid village would have themselves a taste of their agent's authority tomorrow.

Mastery was the thing, he concluded with a self-satisfied smirk. Mastery, not mercy. The English dandy upstairs liked to run on about mercy. Well, Whittaker would also be learning soon enough that mercy had no place in this hellhole. Power was the thing that got the job done—*British* power. The power of the British landlord.

He laughed aloud. To these ignorant Irish peasants, what other power was there?

Upstairs, on his knees, his head resting on clasped hands atop the bed, his brow beaded with perspiration, Evan Whittaker pleaded with his Lord.

He pleaded for control over the hot anger coursing through him, an anger fueled by disgust and targeted at Cotter, yet somehow directed at his own homeland at the same time. He found it incomprehensible that one people could devastate another in such a way, with such blatant inhumanity and indifference. The question that had confronted him, nagged at him all day, was how a nation like England, perceived as a nation of greatness and nobility by other lands throughout the world, could simply turn its back on a starving country—a country from which they had drawn huge quantities of grain, produce, cattle, and manufactured goods for years. The accusation that they were allowing the Irish to starve to death was no longer a point of debate; a number of Protestant churchmen throughout both countries had begun to add their outraged protests to those of the Catholic clergy, confirming what had been, up until a few months past, merely rumor and insinuation. Facts were facts, and Evan no longer attempted to deny the truth. But what dumbfounded him most was the arrogant detachment, the glib ease with which they had condemned this suffering island.

Why?

The question had been on his lips for hours, and he still had no answer. But it seemed to him that at the heart of England's unmerciful treatment of the Irish, there had to be something larger than neglect, more significant than bigotry. Or did he only cling to that assumption because he could not bring himself to accept the fact that his own country had condemned an entire people out of greed? Greed and apathy.

And so as he prayed for an ebbing of his anger, as he pleaded for mercy and divine intervention in the lives of the suffering Irish, he prayed for God's mercy upon his own land as well, for England and her hardened heart.

So intent was Evan upon his supplications that the noise below scarcely penetrated his awareness. When it came again, he raised his head to listen.

He heard the sound of breaking glass, then a low, guttural roar, followed by an instant of silence. Evan held his breath, waiting. After another moment came a high-pitched shriek, then an explosion of laughter.

The sound of madness.

Evan shuddered, swallowed against his fear, then squeezed his eyes shut. Clasping his hands even more tightly, he bowed his head and returned to the Quiet, to the secure shelter of his Hiding Place.

༈

The letter from Michael came that night.

Morgan was sitting at the kitchen table, fiddling with a piece of writing by a young medical student in Dublin, a member of the Young Ireland movement named Richard D'Alton Williams. Williams wrote for *The Nation* under the *nom-de-plume,* "Shamrock." He was a talented lad who on more than one occasion had asked Morgan to critique his poems. Tonight, however, he was finding it difficult to concentrate on Williams' work, in spite of its usual excellence.

It was late, past midnight. The children had been in bed for hours. Thomas, his shaggy hair falling over his forehead, sat nodding and dozing by the fire. Earlier he had been reading from the Scriptures. His large hands still held his Bible securely in his lap.

Pushing his pen and paper aside, Morgan rose to go and wake his brother lest he topple from the chair. He was halfway across the room when someone pounded on the door. Morgan jumped, and Thomas awakened with a startled grunt.

As soon as Morgan opened the door and saw the young, sober-faced Colin Ward, he knew that at long last he had his reply from Michael.

A diminutive, wiry lad, Ward wore an eye patch to cover his missing left eye, lost in a brawl on the Dublin docks. At the moment he appeared half-frozen and nearly exhausted. Morgan urged him inside, but the youth refused to sit down and rest.

"No, thank you, sir. I'll take but a moment to warm myself, and then I must be off to Castlebar. I have one more delivery yet tonight."

Reaching into a pouch on a rope tied about his waist, he pulled out a large, thick envelope and handed it to Morgan. "Here you are, sir. All the way from New York City—and safe and dry at that, though it has passed through many hands, I should imagine."

His heart pounding, Morgan reached for the envelope with one hand while squeezing Ward's shoulder with the other. "I cannot thank you enough, lad. I had almost given this up."

Morgan glanced at the hefty envelope, pulling in a sharp breath of anticipation when he saw that it was addressed in Michael's hand. So impatient was he to open the letter he had to make an effort not to be rude to Ward. But he need not have worried, for the lad seemed as eager to be gone as Morgan was to read his letter. After a brief introduction to Thomas and a few observations about O'Connell's failing health and Smith O'Brien's troubles, Ward started to leave. Morgan saw him out, then turned to Thomas.

"So it has come," his brother said, watching Morgan with the first spark of interest he had exhibited since Catherine's death.

Morgan nodded. He had told Thomas of the letter to Michael, omitting his proposal regarding Nora. So far as his brother was aware, Morgan had simply contacted his old friend to ask assistance for his family in matters of lodging and employment.

"Go on, then," Thomas said, returning to his chair. "I am as anxious as you to hear his reply."

Standing in the middle of the kitchen, Morgan opened the outside envelope, his hands trembling when he realized it contained two separate letters, each in its own sealed envelope. One was addressed to him, the other to Nora.

Putting aside for now the torrent of emotions surging up inside his chest, he ripped open the letter addressed to him. He read in silence for a moment, his eyes scanning the words quickly but thoroughly.

As he had hoped—hoped and half-feared, he admitted to himself— Michael declared himself willing to do what he could to help Nora and her family, as well as Thomas and his children. Though it was not an overly long letter, it was warm and plainly sincere. The decision, Michael said, had not been his alone, but had been made only after much prayer and lengthy discussion with his son, Tierney.

> We are agreed that Nora should come to us, along with those family members who manage to survive the terrible events you have described. And so I have written a separate letter to Nora, as you so insightfully suggested, to make an honorable proposal of marriage, explaining that I greatly need the companionship of a wife, and that Tierney even more needs the mothering influence and nurture she could provide.
>
> I have tried my best, Morgan, to be entirely sincere and convincing. In truth, I do fervently pray that Nora will come. I am not exaggerating when I say that Tierney and I need her, but in all honesty I might never have come to this realization if you had not written when you did. While I have attempted to build a good life for the both of us, I fear it is often a somewhat lonely life; I know the boy, to say nothing of myself, would benefit greatly from Nora's presence.

Not only was he in full agreement with Morgan's suggestions, Michael went on to say, but he was enclosing some money inside Nora's letter, "just in case additional funds might be needed once her passage is paid."

Bless the man, he had even gone so far as to inquire into employment opportunities for Thomas before writing, saying he thought he might have "something lined up for him by the time they arrive."

As Morgan neared the end of the letter, he was feeling a bit better about things—at least until he came to Michael's closing remarks, which seemed to leap up off the page as if to challenge him.

It's entirely true, of course, that when we were young, I was that mad for Nora. Yet, although I did ask her to accompany me to America as my wife, I was never fool enough to hope she could care for me in any way other than as a friend. We both know that she never saw me apart from your shadow, and I was never so blind as to be unaware of your love for her as well. That being the case, I must ask you, man: Are you absolutely certain this is how you want things to be?

Ah, no, Michael, this is not the way I want things to be! Were I a different man and this a different time, I would make Nora mine in a shake, if she would have me.

Dragging his gaze back to the letter, Morgan continued to read.

Please know, Morgan, that by raising this question I am in no way attempting to renege on anything, but am only trying to be absolutely certain you realize what you are doing. If you are indeed convinced, then know this: If we do this thing, if Nora agrees to come to me and be my wife, then it will be for the duration.

What I mean to say is that, if you bid her goodbye once, you will be saying goodbye forever. For I will commit my heart to her—and what is left of my life—in an attempt to give her whatever happiness is within my power to give. Do not think that if you should have a change of heart at some time in the future I will simply step aside to make way for you, for indeed I will not.

Morgan gave a small, grim smile, for he could not help but remember Michael's tenacity, once he made a decision.

So consider your feelings well, old friend, for there will be no going back. That done, if your decision still stands, then do your utmost to convince Nora to come to me, and to come quickly. Do not let her delay and die in Ireland. Convince her to come now, before it is too late. And I thank you, Morgan, for your trust, for I know in my heart that by doing this you are giving up the only thing you have ever truly loved besides that wretched, dying island….

For a long moment, Morgan continued to stare at the pages in his hand, though he knew Thomas was growing impatient. He felt a cold, desolate hole begin to open somewhere deep inside him, and for a moment the image of Nora's wounded, fearful eyes froze in his mind with a pain he thought could not be borne.

At last he lifted his eyes from the letter to meet Thomas's questioning gaze. "You are going," he said quietly. "It is all arranged. Your fares are more than paid for, and Michael has even explored some job possibilities for you. And it would seem—" He faltered, then managed to go on with forced cheerfulness. "It would seem that he intends to ask Nora to marry him when she arrives. Perhaps that is the very thing that will finally convince her to go."

Thomas's eyes on Morgan were grave and searching as he slowly got to his feet. "I'm thinking it should not be Michael Burke asking Nora to be his wife. You have loved that lass since you were a boy."

Shaking his head, Morgan made no attempt to answer. Instead, he deliberately changed the subject. "You can be ready soon, you said."

After another long look, Thomas nodded. "Aye, there's little enough to pack." He paused, again searching Morgan's face. "It's grateful I am to you, brother, for making this possible. You have kept us alive for weeks now, and it would seem that once more you are saving me and my children. I owe you much. But won't you at least give thought to going with us? I know—"

Morgan interrupted as if he had not heard. "I will count on you, Thomas, to be a help to Nora—assuming I can convince her to go."

"She is still resisting, then?"

Morgan uttered a short, dry laugh. "Adamantly. I am hoping Michael's letter will help to bring her around."

"You said the other night when we first talked that things were set, with the ship."

"Aye. It should be in the bay anytime now. Possibly as soon as the end of this week."

Thomas said nothing more for a moment, but Morgan could see that he was troubled. "What is it, then? You're not having a change of heart?"

Thomas shook his head. "No, none of that. But I cannot help thinking of that coffin ship that sailed from the bay last year," he said, raking a hand down one side of his beard-stubbled face. "I'm not worried for myself, you understand. It's the children."

The *Elizabeth and Sarah* to which Thomas referred had sailed from the bay the past summer only to lose forty-two of her passengers to death during the voyage. Morgan had learned from one of the Young Ireland men in Quebec that the ship had actually broken down and had to be towed the rest of the way into the St. Lawrence.

"That ship was greatly overloaded with passengers and understocked with provisions," Morgan reminded Thomas. "You will be going on a much finer ship—an American vessel. They're far better constructed and more ably commanded, in addition to being much faster than the British vessels. My men arranged this especially for my family, Thomas; they promised to do their best to secure a safe, fast ship. I understand your concern, but—"

Thomas put up a hand to stop him. "I'd not be much of a father if I did not fear for my children's safety. But risking their lives on a voyage across the Atlantic still appears to be a far safer venture than keeping them here to die in Killala."

Morgan was relieved at his brother's good sense. If only he could convince Nora to see things the same way. "I will go to Nora first thing tomorrow morning," he said, carefully folding the pages of Michael's letter and tucking it back inside the envelope. "You will get the children ready as quickly as possible?"

"Aye, they will think it's a great adventure, no doubt." Thomas's expression darkened. "Perhaps it will even help to ease their grieving for their mother."

With a distracted nod, Morgan lay the envelope on the table. He was weary, almost aching with fatigue and a somber sense of impending loss. Yet he knew he would manage little sleep this night.

"You should get some rest, brother," Thomas said, his own eyes red-rimmed and heavy. "It is late."

"You go on. I want to work a bit longer on Williams' poem."

After Thomas left the room, Morgan continued to stare at the envelope on the table for a long time. Finally, he sighed, and cupping the candle's flame with the palm of his hand, snuffed it out.

Still he could not bring himself to move, but merely stood like a cold marble statue in the darkness of his brother's cabin.

The breaking of his heart was now complete.

16

So Many Partings

Famine and plague, what havoc have ye made?
And was it thus that stalwart men should die?

JEREMIAH O'RYAN (1770–1855)

Old Dan drew his last breath early the next morning.

An icy rain had returned during the night, and even now, long past dawn, its gray chill seemed to drape the entire cottage in gloom. Sensing that the old man's death was imminent, Nora had sat by his bed most of the night. When at last she heard the death rattles in his throat, she rose and went to call Daniel John in from the kitchen.

"You will want to say your goodbyes to your grandfather now, son," she told him gently. "He will soon be gone."

With anguish in his eyes, the boy parted the curtain and entered the alcove. Nora followed, waiting at the foot of the bed as Daniel John slipped in between Tahg and the old man. Tahg was awake—one of his increasingly rare lucid times—and lay watching as his brother took their grandfather by the hand.

"Can he hear me, do you think?" Daniel John asked, not taking his gaze from the unconscious old man.

"Only God knows," Nora answered. Tortured by her son's grief, she put a hand to her throat, swollen painfully with unshed tears.

In the silent shadows of the alcove, Tahg suddenly reached out a thin, white hand to his brother, who turned to look at him. "I'm sure he hears," Tahg said in a strained whisper. "Tell him for me, too, Danny. I can't—" He broke off when a fit of coughing stole his breath.

Daniel John's eyes filled as he stared at his older brother for a long moment. Finally, he nodded and turned back to Old Dan, then began speaking in the Irish.

The ache in Nora's heart grew fierce as she listened to her son's last farewell to his grandfather. He thanked him for the countless sacrifices he had made for the family, acknowledging the noble menory, the legacy of love and goodness and integrity Old Dan would be leaving behind.

"I will do my best...to be true to your name, Grandfar...to bring honor to you. I will remember for all my life that the name of Daniel Kavanagh is one to wear with pride."

Nora sobbed aloud as the boy bent to kiss the old man's sunken cheek. She had said her own goodbyes earlier that morning, but God help her, it was still hard to let him go. Dan Kavanagh had been the only father she had ever known, and in truth he had treated her as his own flesh and blood. She could not imagine this cottage, which he had built with his own two hands—or, for that matter, life itself—without him.

For the next hour, the three of them kept their vigil, praying together, then mourning together when it was finally over. Both boys cried, and Nora felt it was a tribute to their da that they were able to do so. Owen had raised both his sons to be strong in heart and tender in spirit. He had been a fine father, Owen had, as fine a father as a husband, and she missed him deeply, especially at times like these.

Before she realized what she was doing, she found herself wishing that Morgan would come. Just as quickly, she despised herself for her own weakness, for she knew it was his *strength* for which she longed, not merely his presence.

She was so tired, so utterly exhausted. The very thought of having to deal with yet another death overwhelmed her to the point of desperation. But deal with it she must, and right away, especially with Tahg so ill; he must not have to lie there, in a bed alongside his dead grandfather, for any length of time. Obviously, she could not send for Morgan. After their words two nights past, she was certain he was as bent on avoiding her as she him. He had been noticeably ill at ease the day before, when he'd stopped by the cottage for Daniel John. No, Morgan would not be coming round again soon—if ever.

On the heels of this thought came a fierce longing for Catherine Fitzgerald. Nora herself had never laid out a body. Catherine had tended to the pitiful wee babe who had been stillborn, between Tahg and Daniel John. When Owen died, Catherine laid him out, and she had been there again for Ellie. But now Catherine was gone, and this time Nora was on her own. She would not ask Daniel John to help; she simply couldn't. The boy was still only thirteen, not yet a man grown. And this was his grandfather, after all—he should not have to do what it was her place to do.

What she *would* do, however, was to send him for Thomas Fitzgerald. Thomas had promised that when the time came he would make a coffin for Old Dan. It would be a simple one, of course, for they had only some scrap wood and part of an old table she had saved with this day in mind. But at least the old man would not be dropped into the ground from one of those awful hinged "trap coffins" used by the death-cart drivers. Dan Kavanagh had been a man of great pride and dignity before the Hunger had stripped most of it away, and Nora was immensely grateful to Thomas for offering to spare her father-in-law the final humiliation of a pauper's grave.

There would be no wake, of course, and this distressed her. The old dear should have had a proper mourning. For years Dan Kavanagh had been treated to the respect and confidence of the entire village. Why, he was one of the very oldest residents, he was. In the old days, he would have been a tribal chieftain. His ancestors dated back to the time of Cromwell's invasion, when the young Eoin Caomhanach—John Kavanagh— had fled across the island to Connacht rather than risk exile to Barbados.

Still, there would be no wake. The few villagers who might yet possess the strength to make their way to the cottage had all they could do to see to their own families. Besides, with the fever now on the rage throughout the district, few were willing to risk public gatherings, even to show respect for the dead.

There was nothing to do but lay out the old man in private and see to it that he at least had a proper burial. *Thank God for friends like Thomas,* she thought with a deep sigh. She would send Daniel John for him right away.

Morgan dumped an armload of wood next to the fireplace, then went to the table to drain the last of his tea. Replacing his empty cup, he picked up the envelope containing the letters and, after giving it a long look, tucked it securely inside the pouch tied at his waist.

This morning he would deliver Michael's letter to Nora. It must be done now, before his foolish feelings allowed him to delay any longer. He had spent most of the night at odds with himself, sleeping hardly at all as he mulled over and over again what lay ahead. By dawn he had almost managed to convince himself to simply keep quiet about the letter. He would take Nora and the others across, to the States, and once they arrived he would—

He would do *what?* The lack of an answer to that question ultimately forced him to face the utter absurdity of his plan. Unless he were willing to stay in America and build a life together with Nora—and why would he even imagine she would have him?—then there was no conceivable reason to go with her.

He squatted down to punch up the fire, putting aside his foolish thoughts. Thomas was going, and Michael was waiting; Nora would be perfectly fine. The best thing for her—indeed the *only* thing, if she was to find the happiness she so deserved—was for her to marry Michael Burke. He was a grand lad, a veritable rock of a man: sober, hardworking, ambitious, a man of unimpeachable integrity. And hadn't he already committed himself to Nora's happiness? He would give her a new life, a good life in America. In addition, he could provide Daniel John opportunities the likes of which the boy would never see here in Ireland.

He would take the letter to Nora this morning. Then the only thing remaining would be to convince her to go.

He would never see her again, never again feel his heart melt from the warmth of her huge gray eyes or hear her soft, uncertain laugh or touch the silk of her raven hair…Daniel John would be lost to him as well…He would not see him grow to manhood, would not be allowed to feed his hunger for learning, share his dreams, encourage his music. So much would be lost to him, so much…

But so much would be *gained* by *Nora,* he reminded himself, straightening. And that would somehow have to make his own loss bearable. Besides, who could say he would not see her again? He could always pay a visit to the States.

But by then she would be another man's wife.

He uttered a sharp sound of disgust at himself. Had she not been another man's wife for years? It was time for him to stop playing the fool for the woman and get a grip on himself.

Squaring his shoulders, he crossed to the table and sliced off a crust of bread, chewing it without really tasting it. Little Tom came trudging out from his bed just then, and, as always, ran to Morgan, climbing him as he would a tree.

Morgan scooped the little fellow the rest of the way up, hoisting him onto his shoulder. He was scarcely out of didies, this one, but already the stunned, morose look of the Hunger was on him. His enormous green eyes—as green as Morgan's own—held, instead of a childish glint of fun, the faintly suspicious, watchful stare of a stray pup trying to gauge an unpredictable master's intentions.

Yet this wee wane was healthier by far than most of the other children in the village. *Pity those little ones,* Morgan thought grimly, *who had no outlaw uncle to fill their bellies.*

"Your sisters are still asleep?" Morgan asked the tyke in the Irish. As he most often did with his own family, he spoke the ancient language, determined that the children should grow up entirely at ease with the original tongue of their people. Morgan loved the language, and because he knew himself to be one of the last remaining Gaelic poets and writers, he was determined to do his part in keeping this much of their heritage alive. As long as their language survived, perhaps there was hope that all things Irish would not perish under Britain's colonization.

The little boy nodded and put his arms around Morgan's neck in a tight hug.

"Say the words, Tom," Morgan demanded.

"They are sleeping, Uncle Morgan," the little boy replied in the Irish.

"Ah, then to you is appointed the privilege of waking them," Morgan said, grinning at his nephew as he swung him down to his feet. "You have my permission to tug their ears, if that's what it takes. Just a tiny tug, though; you must not hurt them. Girls are very tender, don't forget." Swatting the little boy lightly on his bottom, he stood and watched him go trundling off to the back of the cottage, where his sisters slept.

"And what is he about so early?" Thomas asked, rubbing the sleep from his eyes as he entered the room.

"I thought it might be well to wake the lasses. There will be much to do over these next days, and they could be of help to Nora as well."

"Johanna, perhaps," Thomas agreed solemnly, tucking his shirttail inside his breeches. "Katie is that weak, though. She seems to tire with the least effort."

Fear lurked in his brother's eyes, and Morgan didn't wonder at it. He, too, had seen the frailty of his eldest niece. Katie had a blotched, feverish look about her. The girl had never been a sturdy child, and lately she appeared even more wan, almost wraithlike. Morgan suspected the lass had long been plagued with a heart malady; she seemed to gasp for her breath with the slightest exertion and never appeared to feel entirely well.

"Little Tom can help," Morgan said reassuringly. "He's growing fast, that one."

Thomas's expression cleared somewhat. "Aye, he'll be a brawny lad. He's the stoutest of the three. Catherine used to say the boy was—"

He stopped at the sound of a rap on the door, immediately followed by Daniel John's voice. "Thomas?" Pushing the door open a bit, the boy stuck his head inside.

Thomas motioned him in. "What are you doing out so early in the day, lad?"

Entering, Daniel John looked from Morgan to Thomas. "Grandfar," he said quietly. "He...he is gone. Mother said I should ask if you would come."

"Of course, lad," Thomas answered without hesitation. "Of course, I will come. Let me just finish dressing and wake the girls so they can see to Little Tom."

Morgan went to the boy and clasped his shoulder. "When, lad?"

"An hour ago, no more."

"I will come with Thomas," Morgan said, "if you want me to, that is."

Daniel John nodded soberly. "Please."

"When does your mother want the burial, do you know?"

"This afternoon. Since there can't be a wake, she thought it best for Tahg if we had the burial right away. That is," the boy added, "if Thomas can get the...the coffin ready soon enough."

Morgan nodded, squeezing Daniel John's shoulder. "We will help him. Your mother is right—it will be best this way." He paused, aware of something more than grief reflected in the lad's eyes. "You're troubled about the lack of a wake, is that it?"

The boy nodded. "I know it can't be helped. But I wish there could be...*something* for him. Something special, you know." For an instant his eyes brightened. "Morgan, do you think—" He stopped, looking uncomfortable.

"What, lad?" Morgan prompted, turning the boy toward him.

Daniel John looked up at him uncertainly. "I know that you and Grandfar were not friends," he said, his voice faltering for an instant, "but...I thought if you could write something...a poem that would be just for him...it might somehow make the burial more special."

It pained Morgan that the boy would be so reluctant to ask. "I had great respect for your granddaddy, Daniel John," he said quietly.

"As it happens, I would consider it an honor to write a lament for Dan Kavanagh."

Daniel John smiled, his gratitude boyishly transparent. "I do thank you, Morgan. I know Mother will be pleased as well."

The thought of Nora reminded Morgan of the letter he had yet to deliver. Old Dan's death had created still another delay. For just an instant he was relieved, then felt ashamed of his selfishness. At this point, every delay only served to tighten the net of peril around Nora and his own family.

This evening, then. This evening, after the burial, he must give her the letter. He simply did not dare to wait any longer.

17

A Most Unlikely Hero

And to him, who as hero and martyr hath striven,
Will the Crown, and the Throne,
and the Palm-branch be given.

LADY WILDE (1820–1896)

At three-thirty that same afternoon, Evan Whittaker arose from another intense hour on his knees before the Lord, and began to pace. Cracking his knuckles, chewing his lip, he walked the floor from one end of the room to the other, trying desperately to decide what he should do—what he *could* do.

Evan had always considered himself a tolerant person. He had adopted his father's philosophy that even the best of men had their flaws and the worst of men could be expected to have at least one redeeming feature, if not more. Consequently, he thought he was reasonably objective and forbearing with his fellowman. That had been his father's way, and over the years he had conscientiously striven to make it his own.

Of course, Father had never met George Cotter, and by now Evan heartily wished he could say the same. After spending the better part of a week in the scurrilous agent's company, Evan was forced to admit that thus far he had been unable to find a single redeeming feature in the man. Bearing with the agent's "flaws" was turning out to be a monumental challenge.

Cotter seemed determined to force this eviction business, despite every attempt Evan made to delay things. Until less than an hour ago, he thought he had managed to stall the agent from carrying out Sir Roger's original demand to implement mass eviction. Insisting they wait until their employer had an opportunity to reconsider his instructions, Evan had almost managed to convince himself that once Sir Roger learned the dire nature of his tenants' plight, he would indeed grant them at least a measure of mercy.

This afternoon, however, Cotter belligerently announced that, one, he had his orders; and, two, Evan was "only a secret'ry and not the one to be telling him his job." Thus, he would proceed to carry out Sir Roger's original instructions that very afternoon—and he would start with the family of that "heathen Fitzgerald." If the outlaw was lodging with his brother, as was rumored in the village, he would soon find himself without a hiding place.

Evan was aware that Thomas Fitzgerald had only recently buried his wife, and that he and his three children were just barely surviving in some godforsaken hillside cabin. Moved by feelings of pity he chose not to analyze, he met the agent's brash announcement with as much cunning as he could muster, attempting to gain a temporary grace period for the ill-fortuned family. Only by convincing Cotter that Thomas Fitzgerald offered the best chance of apprehending his outlaw brother was Evan finally able to delay the Fitzgeralds' eviction another day.

Cotter seemed to take a great deal of delight in Evan's discomfiture, fixing him with a glare of contempt and a threat: "This being your idea and all, Whittaker, you can handle the Fitzgeralds yourself; I have a number of others to attend to today and tomorrow. Why, you may turn out to be the very man who brings down our infamous Red Wolf," he added with an ugly laugh. "Oh, and speaking of that good-for-nothing marauder," he went on, "I've asked the magistrate to see to a warrant for Morgan Fitzgerald's arrest as soon as possible. I'm having some *Wanted* posters prepared, offering a three-month rent extension to anybody who gives information leading to his capture."

Angered by the man's insolence, Evan had ventured to remind Cotter of the limits of his power. "Th-that is presumptuous and n-not at all within your authority!"

"Ah, but I am entirely within my authority!" Cotter shot back. "Didn't you bring me Gilpin's instructions yourself? 'Get this Fitzgerald outlaw locked up,'" he said, quoting Sir Roger's letter, "'and use whatever means necessary to do so.'" He paused, shooting Evan a look of smug triumph.

Evan attempted one last argument, but Cotter merely scowled and wagged a meaty finger in front of his face. "You just handle the brother! I'm way behind schedule now in carrying out my duties, thanks to you and your simpering, and I'll not delay any longer!"

Thus Evan prepared to leave for Thomas Fitzgerald's cabin, ostensibly to question the man about his brother before serving an eviction notice on him. What Cotter did not know was that Evan also intended to warn Fitzgerald that his notorious brother was about to become a hunted criminal.

Pacing the floor, Evan admitted to himself that, while his sympathy for Thomas Fitzgerald might be understandable—the poor man was newly widowed and making every effort to save his small family—his concern for the man's fugitive brother was something else. Morgan Fitzgerald was, by all accounts, an outlaw. He flagrantly defied the authorities, flaunting his lawlessness by wandering in and out of the village whenever he chose. Still, Evan felt some sort of incomprehensible bond to the man, a strong enough affinity that he was intent on warning him of Cotter's vengeful plan to do him in.

Outlaw or not, the Red Wolf had undeniably managed to save a number of lives, and had done so without wreaking any known physical harm on those in authority. A few discreet conversations with some of the villagers had revealed not only an overwhelming sense of gratitude, but no small amount of admiration for the Irish raider. Apparently he had become a kind of folk hero to much of Mayo's populace—understandable, Evan thought, considering the way the outlaw and his men continued to risk their own skins in an effort to save the people from annihilation.

Evan could not deny that he found the tales surrounding this local legend intriguing. The Red Wolf was no ordinary, brutish scoundrel. The mixture of adulation and intimidation he seemed to inspire argued that he was anything but ordinary and certainly far from brutish.

In addition, Evan grew increasingly convinced that it was not Roger Gilpin's orders that had brought him here, to Killala, but rather the leading of the Lord. He was here for an entirely different purpose than the unpleasant tasks Sir Roger had assigned to him. As he prayed he sensed a whisper in his spirit: he was to be, in some inexplicable manner, *responsible* for Morgan Fitzgerald, perhaps for others in the village also.

He stopped pacing to adjust his flawless cravat and smooth his waistcoat. Suddenly, he felt somewhat foolish, wondering if he could possibly be allowing his penchant for melodrama, a suppressed longing for adventure, to cloud his normally sound judgment. After all, Morgan Fitzgerald *was* an outlaw, an *Irish* outlaw who was likely to be a vulgar, swaggering sort and not at all kindly disposed toward anyone reckless enough to present him with a warning about his freedom.

Especially if the bearer of such bad tidings happened to be an Englishman.

Still, there *was* that inner sense of responsibility for the man—indeed, for this entire village—which continued to pervade his being every time he prayed. It had to mean *something*.

Fogging his eyeglasses with his breath, Evan cleaned the lenses with an immaculate handkerchief, then carefully settled them over the bridge of his nose. His headache was returning with a vengeance, and he longed to simply collapse on the bed and forget about the Red Wolf, George Cotter, and Killala. Instead, he sighed and collected his legal case and gloves from the scarred, wobbly desk, then opened the bedroom door and left the room.

Evan was halfway down the long, dim hallway when his attention was caught by raised voices coming from downstairs, at the front of the house. He recognized Cotter's surly tone, but there were others—two, he thought, both gruff and coarse—which he assumed belonged to the agent's roughnecks. Evan was not one to eavesdrop, but he could not help but overhear Cotter's words.

What he heard made his heart thud to a stop, then begin to race. Drawing back, he stood, unmoving, listening.

"That's what I said!" Cotter snarled. "*Kavanagh. Daniel Kavanagh.* You're to nab the young scoundrel and bring him here, just as soon as you can lay your hands on him! He bargained with me," the agent went on in an outraged whine, "and agreed to take a job days ago. Why, I paid the deceitful *gorsoon* a day's wage already! He will work it off or go to gaol! He'll find he can't steal from this landlord without paying a dear price for it!"

Evan nearly choked at the blatant lie. He had witnessed the entire encounter between Cotter and young Kavanagh, and there had been no exchange of money. Of that much he was certain.

Holding his breath, he took a step backward, concealing himself in the shadows. The replies of the other men were muffled, but Cotter's loud voice boomed all the way up the stairs.

"You just be sure and have him here by this evening! Tell the mother that her son is a thief, and if she doesn't want him in gaol by dusk, she'll send him along with you. If they refuse to cooperate, turn them out on the spot." He let go a high-pitched laugh. "They'll be out by nightfall anyway, but that's for our ears only, until later. You just bring me the boy!"

Rage hit Evan like a massive blow. He had all he could do not to go flying down the steps and attack the besotted land agent. But Cotter was still giving orders, so Evan steeled himself to stand and listen, intent on learning all he could. He could almost see the odious man's slick, fat face and self-satisfied smile as he went on with his instructions.

"You collect the bailiff and the police right away—take care of the evictions in the Acres first, before you go to the Kavanagh shanty. And mind your orders, now: no extensions, and no exceptions!"

There were some brief, muffled words from the other men, then, "I don't want to hear about widows and orphans, you fool! My orders are to turn out anyone more than three months in arrears, and to turn them out at once! *Burn* them out if you must, what do I care? At any rate, their filthy huts are to be torched before evening! The fever is rampant out there!"

Evan stood, scarcely breathing, his mind scrambling to take in what he had just overheard. Dear heaven, the man was a lying blackguard! He was going to have that boy picked up like a common criminal and then throw his family out in this ghastly weather, not to mention all the other poor souls who would suffer the same fate.

Stunned and weak, Evan swallowed hard, then began to back up toward the bedroom. Once inside, he quietly closed the door and leaned against it, trying to think.

He must *do* something, of course. But *what?* Cotter had his ruffians and a number of armed police at his command. And, to make matters worse, he had legal authorization from Sir Roger for what he was about to do.

Evan turned his fury inward for a moment. Like a fool, he had handed over Sir Roger's signed instructions to the agent when he first arrived. All Cotter had to do was wave the orders under the nose of the bailiff and the police, and they would comply with whatever the agent demanded. As for those thugs who had been ordered to lure that poor unsuspecting boy up here, they were probably paid well enough that they would go to any lengths to satisfy Cotter's whims. It would be the Kavanagh boy's word against the land agent's, a foregone judgment against the youth.

Tossing his gloves and legal case onto the desk, Evan crossed the room and sank down onto the bed. For a long moment he could do nothing but stare at the floor in frustration. Finally, he turned to the bedside table, picked up his Bible, and opened it. *What can I do, Lord?*

He was only a frail, stammering Englishman who knew nothing about bravery except for what he read in adventure novels. He did not understand these people, none of them—Cotter, his toughs, the suffering villagers. Nor did he understand or even care about this wretched island. He had never in his life felt so isolated, so alone. What was one man against an entire army of wickedness?

His eyes fell on the open page, and the words leaped out at him: *A king is not saved by his great army; a warrior is not delivered by his great strength... the eye of the Lord is on those who fear him, on those who hope in his steadfast love, that he may deliver their soul from death, and keep them alive in famine.*

Evan squirmed, clutching the open Bible more tightly. "I'm hardly cut out for the...business of deliverance, Lord, and even if I were, I wouldn't know where to begin. B-besides, I'm really not a bit stout—my lungs, You remember—and while I'm not altogether fearful, I suppose it's fair to say that I am somewhat t-timid about certain things. Oh—and of course You know that I st-stammer in the most disconcerting way, especially when I'm...tense or nervous..."

He fidgeted, flipping through the pages aimlessly. At last his fingers stopped, and he looked down again.

Then the Lord said to Moses: "Who has made man's mouth? Who makes him dumb, or deaf, or seeing, or blind? Is it not I, the Lord? Now therefore go, and I will be with your mouth and teach you what you shall speak."

"Lord, p-perhaps this isn't important...but wasn't it Aaron who actually ended up d-doing most of the talking for M-Moses? Besides, I'm afraid I don't quite understand what it is, exactly, You want me to do. I wouldn't even kn-know where to start."

Evan drew a deep breath and shut the Bible. The words rang in his mind—not audibly spoken, but very clear: *Your ears shall hear a word behind you, saying, "This is the way, walk in it," when you turn to the right or when you turn to the left.*

"Lord...the th-thing is," Evan objected, "ah, well...this is Ireland, You see, and I'm...an Englishman, and, well...You know how they feel about us. I'm not at all sure I have any credibility whatsoever with these people."

Have we not all one father? Has not one God created us? Why then are we faithless to one another?

"But, Lord, wouldn't I be betraying my employer? As much as I d-dislike the man, I've worked for Roger Gilpin for years, and he does...trust me to carry out his instructions."

Should you serve the wicked and love those who hate the Lord? Choose this day whom you will serve, Evan...choose now.

"Lord! Lord, I...I chose *You* years ago! Nothing can change that, not ever." Evan moistened his lips. "But I still don't see *how*, Lord."

Not by might, not by power, but by my Spirit.

Evan squeezed his eyes shut and waited in self-imposed darkness. He didn't want to do this—he wasn't even certain he *could* do it, and yet something pushed him on. Something had always been missing in his life; he loved God, but his faith had never been tried in action. Now, as he sat in silence, a calmness began to wash over him. He felt as if he were in the center of a dark tunnel: from both sides light advanced toward him, at last converging where he waited.

The light flooded into him, illuminating not his surroundings, but some hidden inner reservoir of his own soul. From the deep recesses of his memory, Evan's mind recalled the words, *"Who knows if you have come to the king's court for such a time as this?"*

He drew a deep breath, and in his own exhaled sigh, he heard his father's familiar voice: *"Trust God, and be brave."*

At last Evan opened his eyes. Replacing the Bible on the table, he got up from the bed and went to the desk, once more collecting his legal case and gloves. He was amazed at the peace that filled him, relieved that he seemed to know what he must do. Not *how* he was going to do it, at least not yet. But for now, it was enough to know that he must act, and that God would be with him when he did.

The nasty business at the Fitzgerald cabin would have to wait, he decided, opening the bedroom door. First, he must find a way to thwart the capture of Daniel Kavanagh.

18

Dan Kavanagh's Lament

In all my wanderings round this world of care,
In all my griefs—and God has given me my share—
I still had hopes, my latest hours to crown,
Amidst these humble bowers to lay me down.

OLIVER GOLDSMITH (1728-1774)

Death had become so much a part of every day in the village of Killala that the passing of yet another soul went more or less unnoticed. Still, there were those who claimed that a number of dark portents had warned of Dan Kavanagh's approaching demise.

Old Mary Larkin, for example, claimed to have seen a *badhb*—the crow symbolizing death—hovering near the Kavanagh cottage late in the afternoon. And Judy Hennessey, who grew more and more demented by the day, insisted that she had heard the *banshee*—the female angel of death—wail her eerie song just past midnight. When her mother-in-law pointed out that only family members or others in close relationship to the dying could hear the white-robed phantom of the night, Judy snapped back that as one of the Kavanaghs' nearest neighbors she guessed she knew what she'd heard well enough.

In truth, however, the only event that might have drawn attention to yet another death was the fact that the deceased was being buried in a proper coffin after a traditional procession; someone had even thought to toll the church bell in advance of the mourners.

When the word finally circulated the village that it was Old Dan Kavanagh on the way to the graveyard, a few heads nodded wisely, as if to imply that you could expect it of the Kavanaghs to observe convention, even during a time of widespread disaster. Didn't they always do things according to the old ways? To some, the family's strict adherence to tradition might hint of excess pride, but most of the townspeople would have disagreed. The Kavanaghs were an old established Christian family, early settlers in Connacht and a well-respected name in the village for generations. If it was their way to observe the proprieties, who, then, should be denouncing them for it?

The cold rain that had begun that morning and continued steadily throughout the day was considered by all to be a good omen for a burial. A few villagers still strong enough to walk the distance to the graveyard joined the funeral procession—some in remembrance of kindnesses done by Dan Kavanagh, others out of affection for Nora and her family. It was a grim, blood-chilling sight, this mourners' march. Gaunt and hollow-eyed, some scarcely clothed or at best wrapped only in thin rags against the rain and driving wind, they tramped in silence along the traditional route to Killala's graveyard. Ill and doomed and defeated, they looked like a macabre parade of the walking dead on their way to a mass burial service of their own.

In this poor, sad village, as in hundreds of others all across Ireland, the graveyard was filled to overflowing. Only those farsighted persons who had in better days secured their plots were still laid to rest in the traditional burial site. Improvised graves marred the entire town—indeed the whole countryside. Roadside ditches, backyards, hillside slopes, even the shore by the bay hosted makeshift coffins, or corpses wrapped in sacks or papers. Open pits into which corpse after corpse had been tossed and heaped, one upon the other, were simply covered over with a thin layer of dirt. Cabins where fever and disease raged were most often knocked down, then torched, turning them into funeral pyres.

Priests could no longer keep up in their efforts to administer last rites; indeed, many were dying in large numbers themselves, a consequence of exhaustion and giving up their own food to feed their parishioners. The Protestant clergy, though the numbers of their fold were fewer, also felt the sting of frustration in their attempts to comfort the sick and perform a seemingly endless number of funeral services. Roman and Protestant clerics served side by side in the beleaguered fever hospitals, where suffering and death provided a natural focus for unity.

There were never enough gravediggers. Frail, emaciated survivors excavated the graves for their loved ones; in their weakness, they dug scarcely deeper than they might have for potato plants. Tombstones were no longer given a thought. A pile of stones or a piece of cloth on a stick were the only monuments erected to mark the countless unknown graves.

Once recognized as a land of vigilant, painstaking respect for the dead, Ireland's growing apathy seemed a terrible and piercing commentary on the country's present wretchedness. But on this day of further loss in Killala, there was grief. Even the mist-shrouded, ancient round tower appeared to mourn and weep over the suffering village, much as Christ must have sorrowed over Jerusalem.

Daniel stood at the graveside in the rain, watching them bury his grandfather. The rough-hewn, simple coffin Morgan and Thomas had hastily constructed was lowered into the grave the same two men had dug. A few shawled women drew nearer to commence the ancient keen.

The traditionally silent funeral procession had followed the coffin to Killala's graveyard, laying Grandfar to rest with simple prayers, some reading of Scripture and, finally, a wonderful Irish lament that Morgan had written. But Daniel offered the final tribute to his grandfather's memory. Strumming the Kavanagh harp in the way of the ancient harpers, which Morgan had taught him, he began to play and sing the lament that had been passed down through generations of Kavanagh men. Originally written for *his* grandfather by Eoin Caomhanach, the piece had been preserved from the seventeenth century; for almost two hundred years it had concluded the burial services of male members of the Kavanagh clan.

Daniel had always felt a strong sense of kinship with the ancestor who had composed the lament. After losing his entire family to Cromwell's bloodthirsty soldiers when he was only fourteen years old, Eoin Caomhanach had been forced to flee his lifelong home in Drogheda for the unknown, untamed western coast of Ireland. Today, that special affinity seemed even stronger. Both had lost precious family members; both had been placed in the position of lamenting a beloved grandfather. And, like Eoin, Daniel knew that soon he, too, might be forced to leave his home for the uncertainty of an unknown land.

Pain stabbed his heart, and it took all the will he could muster to keep his voice from breaking as he fixed his eyes upon his grandfather's grave and began to sing.

> "My harp will sing across the land,
>   across the past and years to be.
>   No loss or grief nor death itself
>   will still its faithful melody."

Daniel faltered only once, but at the touch of Morgan's hand upon his shoulder, he caught a long breath and went on:

> "To sing the presence of a God
>   who conquers even exile's pain—
>   Who heals the wandering pilgrim's wound
>   and leads him home in joy again."

At the end of the ceremony, Thomas shoveled an ample amount of thick, wet clay over the coffin, finally placing the spade and shovel on top of the grave in the form of a cross. Daniel led his mother away, with Thomas at her other side and Morgan following closely behind. Along with the rest of the mourners, they turned and set their faces against the cold, rain-swept wind and started for home.

Daniel wondered as they walked if Grandfar could see them from heaven. Was he aware of how much they already missed him? Somehow he hoped that the old man had heard Morgan's moving lament at the graveside and had been pleased with it. In heaven, of course, Grandfar's bad feelings toward Morgan would have been wiped away by now, but Daniel still wanted him to know the respect Morgan had paid him.

On the wordless march toward home, Daniel prayed—for his grandfather's peace, for the "blessed rest of heaven" for which the old man had so often yearned.

I pray that Grandfar is with You already, Lord...that he's resting his head on a giant pillow of a cloud, as he used to speak of doing, and that he's feasting on the beauty and grandeur of heaven.

He could almost hear his grandfather's deep, gruff voice as he spoke of the place prepared for him:

"Sure, and don't I hope that the mansion the Lord has built for me is a snug, warm place where these old bones can be thawing out at last? It won't matter at all whether it's grand in any way, just so long as it's warm. Not that I'd mind a table heaped with some meat and potatoes as well…"

Daniel was struck by a fresh wave of loneliness for the old man who had been as much friend and companion as grandfather to him throughout his years of childhood. With Grandfar gone and Tahg naught but a shadow of himself, it was officially up to him to assume the role of head of the house.

In truth, at this moment he felt shamefully young and filled with fear. It struck him again that everything he had ever trusted in or counted on was being ripped away from him, one piece at a time. His da, now Grandfar—even Tahg, ill as he was—all were lost to him.

And his home: Was that to be his next loss? His home, his village, his country?

The questions that frequently assailed him these days once again came hurtling through his thoughts, questions he could not seem to avoid, no matter how much they distressed him. When this nightmare of death and destruction finally ended—if indeed it ever *did*—would there be anyone…or anything…left that he cared about? Or was this, as some in the village seemed to believe, the end of all that they loved, perhaps even the end of the world?

Again rose the awful possibility that God had abandoned the island entirely. That being the case, there was indeed no hope, no hope at all, left to any of them.

And if there were no hope, even the few who might manage to survive would be just as well off dead. Grandfar himself had said that life without hope was no life at all.

Daniel was only now beginning to understand what his grandfather had meant.

On his way into the village, Evan was so engrossed in his anxious thoughts that he was almost upon the odd, straggling procession before he actually became aware of them.

He reined in his horse and sat watching their dispirited approach. Huddled and shivering in their wet, ragged clothing, they appeared to be coming away from the graveyard, even though Cotter had made it sound as if formal burial services were a thing of the past.

Leaning forward on his mount, Evan's attention was quickly caught by a tall, thin youth at the front of the procession. The boy had an ancient-looking wire-strung harp slung over one shoulder, and appeared to be supporting the small, black-clad woman at his side, as if she were too frail to stand alone. Both were thoroughly drenched from the soaking rain.

Apparently sensing Evan's eyes on him, the boy slowed his pace, then stopped and lifted his head.

Daniel Kavanagh.

Evan caught his breath. He had not expected to encounter the boy like this, in the open, surrounded by people. He darted a glance at the woman, whom he took to be the lad's mother. But who was the gaunt, graying fellow at her side? Hadn't the boy told Cotter that his father was dead?

Young Kavanagh now tipped his chin even higher. A wary glint just short of defiance, hardened the boy's expression, and Evan caught a glimpse of the same quiet, unbending courage he had sensed in the youth that day on the hill behind Cotter's house.

Evan's gaze left the boy to scan the crowd, locking almost at once, on a man standing just behind young Kavanagh and his mother, towering over them like some sort of threatening guardian angel. Again his breath caught in his throat, and his entire body began to vibrate with a blend of fascination and dread. Unable to tear his gaze away from the copper-haired giant, Evan fought to regain his wits.

The man was a mountain in frieze, a colossus decked in a homespun cloak and worn leather boots. Swallowing hard, Evan found himself staring into the most intense, dangerous green eyes he had ever encountered, and he knew at once he was looking into the face of the notorious outlaw-patriot, Morgan Fitzgerald.

The Red Wolf.

19

An Encounter on the Road

A fighting-man he was...
A copper-skinned six-footer,
Hewn out of the rock,
Who would stand up against
His hammer-knock?
A goodly man, A Gael....
JOSEPH CAMPBELL (1879–1944)

The Irish giant's intimidating size, the thick, wild russet hair tossed wetly about his head, and the full bronze beard perfectly mirrored what Quincy Moore had written of him. Fitzgerald's features were neither coarse nor heavy, as Evan had anticipated. Indeed, had it not been for the terrible scowl fixed upon his face, the man might have been considered almost handsome in appearance, if a bit rustic.

Evan now became aware that the entire procession had stopped where they were on the side of the road, and that all eyes were fixed on him in a combined force of open hostility. Still he found it impossible to drag his gaze away from the giant, who seemed determined to annihilate him with his blazing stare. The man stepped out in front of the boy and his mother as if to shield the two of them with his body, and his size was such that he almost totally concealed them both.

Up until this moment, Evan had viewed the stories about the Irish brigand with a mixture of intrigue, skepticism, and a certain sense of excitement. Confronted with the legend face-to-face, however, he was struck by a reaction he could not have anticipated. To his surprise, his mind now registered a distinct quake of panic.

Not only was the rogue even larger in life than the tales told about him, but a carefully controlled energy seemed to emanate from him, a power that, while temporarily under restraint, threatened to break loose at any instant. The big man's obvious calm and ease of posture suggested, if not actual arrogance, at least absolute confidence; yet Evan sensed an inferno blazing inside the man, constrained only by sheer force of will.

For a moment the granite-faced Irishman simply stared at Evan as if he were no more than an irritating toad. When he finally did move, he took only two broad steps, then stopped, his eyes traveling slowly up the height of the horse until they came to rest on Evan's face.

Evan steeled himself to meet the man's patently contemptuous stare, praying he wouldn't stammer. He cleared his throat and took a deep breath before speaking. "Good…day to you, sir. My name is—" He stopped, determinedly pushing the words from his mouth. "Whittaker. Evan Whittaker."

The man's cloak had fallen open, revealing a harp similar to the boy's riding high on one shoulder, and what appeared to be the handle of a pistol tucked into the waist of his breeches. The Irishman again stepped forward, this time coming close enough that he could easily have reached up and yanked Evan from his mount if so inclined. It did not escape Evan that one hard tug from that hammer of a hand would most likely break his arm, and for a moment he had all he could do not to lash his horse and go tearing off down the road.

Despite his apprehension, however, he had to admit that coming upon both Fitzgerald and the Kavanagh boy together seemed too propitious an occurrence to be written off as mere chance. If this were God's way of providing him a means of carrying out His will, he could hardly afford to retreat out of cowardice.

The giant stood in menacing silence, his eyes shooting out a blast of disgust strong enough to make Evan flinch. Driven by an increasing urgency, he reminded himself that the chap was a poet, a back-country schoolmaster—not an armor-decked warlord. Best not to dwell on the unsettling fact that he was also reputed to be a revolutionary and an outlaw—an *armed* outlaw.

"A-a—am I correct in assuming that you are M-M-Morgan F-F-Fitzgerald?" Evan felt his skin heat as the humiliating stammer now exploded full-force.

A murmur behind Fitzgerald was silenced with a slight lift of the giant's hand. Again his contemptuous expression pinned Evan in place. The green eyes narrowed, the wide, generous mouth thinned to a slash, and finally the big Irishman spoke. "I am Fitzgerald. And what is that to you?" he countered in a voice deadly in its quiet.

Feeling increasingly threatened, Evan groped to maintain a calm of his own. "As I said, my n-name is Whittaker." He paused, waiting.

"Aye. The *Englishman*."

An entire history of contempt echoed from those quiet words, and Evan thought he would never again feel quite the same about himself. His hands went clammy inside his gloves, and the knot in his throat swelled to a fist. "I...really must t-talk with you right away, Fitzgerald." Hesitating, he then added, "And...the boy as well."

The fire in Fitzgerald's eyes now died, to be replaced by a glacial stare. "And what boy would that be?"

Evan managed a stiff nod in Daniel Kavanagh's direction. The Irishman's bearded chin seemed to slide forward and lock in place as his voice turned even softer and more menacing. "Now what possible business could the Big Lord's lackey have with an ignorant Paddy like myself and a poor village lad?"

Evan swallowed with great difficulty, but refused to let the man goad him. "I assure you, it's im...p-portant. For you *and* the boy."

"Ah, indeed."

"Is there s-somewhere we could talk alone?" Evan pressed. "You m-must believe me, it's for your own good."

"Oh, of *course* it is," Fitzgerald answered. His tone was openly mocking, but a warning still lurked in his eyes.

Evan's exasperation with the man overcame his caution. "N-now see here, F-Fitzgerald, you're in t-terrible jeopardy, as is young Kavanagh! It would b-be to your advantage to hear me out."

Fitzgerald's expression darkened, and when he spoke the mask of the cynic had disappeared. "Have a care, man. This is not the day to be dallying with me."

Evan could no longer contain his frustration. "For the love of heaven, m-man, I'm not *dallying* with you! I'm t-trying to save your neck! And the boy's as well!"

He cringed as Fitzgerald's ruddy complexion paled with fury, but he also thought that at last he might have penetrated the stubborn Irishman's guard. The man turned away for a moment, saying something in the barbaric tongue Evan recognized as Gaelic. Immediately, the mourners began to move, a few at a time, continuing their doleful march down the road. Only the boy, his mother, and the craggy-faced man at her side remained.

Young Kavanagh suddenly moved, starting toward Fitzgerald, who motioned him off with an upraised hand and a firm shake of his head. Again, he muttered something in their unpronounceable language, and the boy stopped, leveling a dark, furious frown on Evan.

Turning back, Fitzgerald searched Evan's face with narrowed eyes for a long moment. "You'll understand if I seem to question your interest," he said in a voice as deep as a drum roll. "It's a new thing for me entirely, you see, having an Englishman concerned for my well-being." Searching frantically for just the right words to break through Fitzgerald's antagonism, Evan pulled in a deep, steadying breath.

Oh, Lord, please take this abominable stammer away, at least for the moment, so Fitzgerald won't think me such a joke. I can't possibly be of any help to him or the boy if he won't even take me seriously!

Vaguely recollecting that the heroes in his favorite adventure novels always tightened their jaws when faced with a challenge, Evan now clenched his own. Facing his adversary with rigid resolve, he decided to go right to the heart of things. "I thought you should know that Cotter's bully-boys will be at the Kavanagh cottage before evening," he said, trying to keep his voice low enough that only Fitzgerald could hear "They, ah…they have orders to collect the boy and take him to Cotter on…on the pretext that he was paid a day's wages he never earned."

"That's a *lie*!" His face contorted with rage, Fitzgerald reached to lay a hand on the mare's neck. "The boy owes that blackheart nothing! Nothing!"

"I understand that," Evan quickly assured him, flinching at Fitzgerald's abrupt movement. "I'm telling you what I heard, nothing else."

Evan shuddered in spite of himself at the fury that seemed to shake the big man's powerful frame. The quiet voice cracked like a whiplash, and fire leaped in Fitzgerald's eyes. "And how is it that you know what Cotter and his rabble are up to?"

"I overheard them. His two thugs are supposed to assist with some evictions in the—the *Acres*—then come back to town and pick up the boy.

They're to take him directly to Cotter," Evan explained. He was vaguely aware that his stammer had fled as his words came tumbling out in a rush—confirmation, perhaps, that God was indeed enabling him.

Fitzgerald started to speak, but Evan stopped him. "That's not all," he said, pressing his lips together nervously. "I'm…supposed to be serving an eviction notice on your brother even now. He and his family are to be out of their dwelling by tomorrow morning."

Evan felt almost driven now, engulfed by a need to deliver all the sordid facts into Fitzgerald's hands as quickly as possible. "As for you," he went on, "you'll be arrested the minute they catch sight of you. Cotter's putting out *Wanted* posters all over the village, and there will be a warrant for your arrest issued yet today, if there isn't one already. You *must* get away!" He paused, then added urgently, "And the boy—he dare not return to his home!"

Fitzgerald took a step back, measuring Evan with suspicious eyes. "What are you about, man? What, exactly, is your game?"

The blunt question stopped Evan for only an instant. "We can't afford to waste time sparring about my motives! In truth, I…I'm not at all sure I understand them myself. You'll simply have to trust me."

A sharp, ugly laugh exploded from Fitzgerald. "You are an Englishman," he said, as if that explained it all.

Evan bristled. "I am also a *Christian*."

"Aye," Fitzgerald bit out, his tone thick with scorn. "As was Oliver Cromwell."

Grinding his teeth to keep from screaming at the man, Evan challenged him. "I thought perhaps *you* might be a believer."

Fitzgerald lifted an eyebrow in feigned surprise. "Ach, and could a Paddy be a Christian like yourself?" he drawled. "Ah, no, we're but cowherds and bogmen, don't you know? Heathens, every last mother's son of us."

Evan was taken aback by the faint light in Fitzgerald's eyes, which seemed to alter his entire appearance. The militant chieftain had suddenly taken on a lively, if sardonic wit.

Flustered by the quicksilver change in the man, Evan snapped defensively, "You are wasting precious time, Fitzgerald! It was my understanding that you have…some concern for the Kavanagh boy; certainly you must have a care for yourself. Will you do nothing to save your life and his?"

"You have not answered my question," Fitzgerald said, his expression turning hard as he dropped the exaggerated brogue. "Why are you doing this? You *are* Gilpin's man, are you not?"

By now Evan was feeling decidedly peevish. His chest ached from the miserable wet weather, his nose was dripping, and his backside was sore from spending a great deal more time on horseback than he was used to. Moreover, he was out of patience with Fitzgerald's mulishness. "I am Roger Gilpin's secretary!" he snapped, gripped for a moment by a coughing seizure. When he could again speak, he added, "I'm employed by the man. That doesn't necessarily mean that I...agree with all his methods."

Fitzgerald said nothing, but merely crossed his arms over his spacious chest and gave Evan another long, studying look.

Forcing himself not to shrink beneath the Irishman's fierce glare, Evan chose his words carefully. "Quite frankly," he said, "I'm not at all certain my employer would approve of Cotter's conduct. That man is utterly despicable! And I know he's lying about the boy, because I was there that day when he offered young Kavanagh a job. There was no money exchanged—none at all." He paused. "As for what he intends to do with *you*—"

Something glinted in Fitzgerald's eyes, and Evan faltered. The man *was* an outlaw, after all; who was to say he wouldn't shoot him on the spot if he didn't like what he heard?

"Cotter believes you to be...ah, I believe the name he used was...the *Red Wolf*. In addition," Evan continued cautiously, "you seem to have... threatened him at some time, I take it? He makes no secret of his hatred for you."

Fitzgerald seemed thoroughly unruffled about his own peril. "You say Cotter's men will be back in the village by evening?"

Relieved that the man finally seemed to be listening, Evan nodded eagerly. "You *must* get yourself and the boy out of sight! Do you have a place where you can go?"

Ignoring his question, Fitzgerald raked a hand down one side of his face in a gesture of frustration. "You're sure Thomas—my brother—has until morning before he's turned out?"

Evan nodded. "Supposedly because the bailiff and the bully-boys have their hands full with other evictions this afternoon. Frankly, I believe Cotter is giving your brother some notice on purpose, hoping to flush you out of your hiding place. He thinks you're staying there, at least part of the time. I imagine he's expecting you either to try to stop the eviction or, at the very least, to delay it." He paused, then added pointedly, "He's determined to see you hang."

"And I'm just as determined that he won't," Fitzgerald said absently, casting a sweeping gaze around their surroundings. "So, then, it would seem we have only tonight to get ready to leave."

"You must find a safe place for yourself and the others," Evan urged. "They'll tear the village apart looking for you."

"My family will be leaving for the States soon—there is a ship coming any day. Until then, I know of a place where we can stay."

"You're going with them to America, I hope?"

Fitzgerald shrugged. "Who knows what I will do?" he said cryptically "In the meantime, there is a place where we can go." He paused, fixing Evan with a studying look. "And you will come with us."

Startled, Evan hurried to protest. "Now, see here, I can't—"

"You will come with us," Fitzgerald repeated in a tone that left no room for argument. "I may need you. First, however, we must hide Daniel John, then get Tahg and Nora away from the cottage. That will take some doing, I fear."

"Tahg? Who is Tahg?"

"Daniel John's elder brother. He is ill. Mortally ill." Fitzgerald turned a bitter look on Evan. "There are many in the village just like him—one night on the road will kill them all."

Evan gripped the horse's reins more tightly. "I'll do whatever I can to help move him."

Fitzgerald waved him off. "It's not that at all. I could carry the lad with one arm, he's that frail. But to take him out in this cold rain…" His words died away, unfinished. For a long moment he stood in silence, tugging mindlessly at the wet hair at the back of his neck as he stared off into the distance.

"Fitzgerald?" Evan waited until the Irishman turned to meet his eyes. "Once Cotter realizes he's been thwarted, you can expect that he'll be wild. He'll stop at nothing to get the boy. I think he's obsessed."

"He's a devil," Fitzgerald said.

"But a dull-witted one," Evan pointed out.

Fitzgerald looked at him, then began to nod, slowly. "Aye, there was a great deal of sense left outside his head," he answered dryly. "What is your point?"

"That your wits and mine should be more than enough to foil him."

Fitzgerald studied him for a moment more. "How far are you willing to go with what you've started, man?"

"What do you mean?"

"I mean that you may be able to save some lives here," Fitzgerald replied, his gaze steady. "But only if you're willing to risk your soft position with Gilpin and perhaps your English honor as well."

Uncertain as to what the man was getting at, Evan nevertheless nodded, waiting.

"There's no more time for talk," Fitzgerald muttered, still peering into Evan's face. "Just answer me this, for once you commit yourself, there can be no turning back. You say you are a Christian; but which is dearer to you, Evan Whittaker—your Savior or your Saxon neck?"

For a long, silent moment Evan felt himself turned inside out, as if his very soul were being laid open to the burning eyes of his inquisitor. And in the same moment he somehow knew that the answer to Morgan Fitzgerald's piercing question was even more important to Evan himself than it was to the Gael.

He shut his eyes, allowing his spirit a moment of quiet before he answered. Then he faced Fitzgerald with a level look of his own. "I should imagine that I value my...*Saxon neck* quite as much as you do your stubborn Irish hide. But not so much that I would ever betray my Savior." He swallowed with some difficulty, adding, "I shall do whatever I can to help rescue you...and those who are dear to you, Fitzgerald. You have my word on that."

As Evan watched, a slow, wondering light seemed to soften and gentle the big man's face, a light so faint Evan almost thought he might be imagining it. But, no, the warmth rose in Fitzgerald's eyes, a glow that somehow hinted of approval. And without ever questioning why this brash Irishman's affirmation should matter in the slightest, Evan found himself basking in its warmth.

"By all that is holy," Fitzgerald said quietly, his great leonine head thrown back as the rain slashed his face, "it would seem that I have found myself an Englishman with a noble heart. Now, *there* is a wonder for us all."

Evan flushed. He knew himself to have been saluted by this great tower of a man, and he savored it.

"All right, then, Whittaker," Fitzgerald said, still examining Evan as if he were some sort of a rare oddity, "let us get on with it. We have much to do, and from the looks of you we'll need to do it quickly before you catch your death. First, though, we need a plan as to how we can hold off Cotter's thugs until I can get some of my lads and an extra horse or two down from the hills."

"I'm still the official emissary of their landlord," Evan pointed out. "I should think I'm more than capable of managing those roughnecks." Even as he spoke, he was hoping he sounded more confident than he felt.

Fitzgerald permitted himself a ghost of a smile. "Aye, somehow I think you can."

"Before anything else, though," Evan said urgently, "we *must* get young Daniel hidden away."

Fitzgerald nodded. "He can go with Thomas for now."

"Good. But I'm afraid Mrs. Kavanagh needs to come with us. Things may get unpleasant if Cotter's toughs show up, but with her help I believe I can get rid of them."

"Give me a moment," Fitzgerald said with a short nod. Turning, he walked off, tossing out a stream of Gaelic to the others as he approached.

Not long after he reached them, the Kavanagh lad shot a look of disbelief in Evan's direction, while the woman's face went white with visible alarm. Only the tall, haggard-looking man next to her appeared unshaken as Fitzgerald went to him and, gripping his shoulders, began to speak. Seeing the two men together, Evan immediately noted the resemblance. Evidently, this gaunt, sad-eyed man was the brother he had been ordered to evict. Feeling suddenly ill, he was struck by a fresh blow of guilt for his years of association with Roger Gilpin, and renewed shame for himself and his country.

The woman and the boy continued to stare, first at Fitzgerald, then at Evan, with incredulous, frightened eyes. He attempted a lame smile of reassurance, but his face quickly froze in the effort. Seized by a sudden wave of uncertainty, he fought down a surge of panic. These people despised him, as well as everything he stood for; in their eyes, he was the enemy, a man to be feared and shunned. What had ever possessed him to think he could gain their trust, especially within such a short period of time? There was no earthly reason, even if they were to accept his *willingness* to help, that they should trust his *ability* to help. For that matter, there was no earthly reason why *he* should trust *himself*.

Still, it wasn't *himself* he was trusting, any more than it had been an *earthly* reason that had brought him this far. *"Trust God,"* his father had said. *"Trust God, and be brave."*

Less than an hour later, Nora sat rigidly on a chair in her kitchen, struggling to accept the fact that her entire life was about to change.

The whirlwind in which she found herself seemed to be gathering strength. What had started when they encountered the Englishman on the way back from the graveyard had continued to build until she thought she would go mad from fear and confusion.

First, Morgan had sent Daniel John rushing off with Thomas, offering no more than a hurried explanation about getting the boy "out of Cotter's reach," and a reminder to "use the space beneath the cabin if it's needed"— whatever *that* meant.

Scarcely a heartbeat later, he scooped Nora up and set her squarely on the horse with the Englishman, ordering them to take the back road around the village to her cottage, that he would meet them there "in a shake."

All the way down the road the Englishman mumbled what sounded like words of apology and reassurance, but Nora had been far too distraught and bewildered to catch more than a few bits and pieces of his British blather. The only thing she *had* understood was that Cotter meant to abduct Daniel John, and this was enough to take her to the very edge of hysteria.

By the time they reached the cottage, she was trembling so violently she thought she would fly to pieces before Whittaker could get her off the horse. She went through the motions of tending to Tahg, doing her best not to let him see her terror, but she was aware of the lad watching her with uneasy eyes, as if he sensed something was wrong. When she mumbled a hurried, awkward explanation about Whittaker being a "friend of Morgan's," the boy stared at her incredulously but offered no argument.

During the entire time she busied herself with Tahg, Whittaker hovered nearby, peering at her through those odd little spectacles of his as if he feared that any moment she might run screaming from the cottage. As soon as Morgan arrived, the two of them closeted themselves in a corner of the kitchen, doing a great deal of muttering and nodding, virtually ignoring her.

Now, leaving Whittaker in the back of the cottage, Morgan crossed the room to pull up a chair and sit down, facing her. Nora had all she could do not to shout at him. For a moment he simply searched her eyes, saying nothing. Then, drawing a deep sigh, he reached for her hand, seemingly mindless of the way she immediately knotted it into a tight, unrelenting fist.

"Nora, I am sorry," he said, studying her. "I would not have yanked you about as I did had there been more time."

Nora stiffened, glaring at him. "Why are you listening to that *Englishman*, Morgan? What is he doing here, in *my* cottage, telling us what to do?" She was aware that her voice was shaking as hard as the rest of her. "Does he not work for the landlord himself?"

Morgan was still in his cloak, and with his free hand he reached now to shrug it off, letting it fall over the back of the chair. "Believe it or not," he said, sliding his harp off his shoulder and placing it carefully on the table, "he is trying to help us. In truth, he means to save our lives."

"You are cracked!" Nora exploded. She heard the shrillness of her voice, tasted the fear that caused it, but she could not stop. "And since when do you heed the words of an Englishman, Morgan Fitzgerald?"

Morgan smiled grimly and nodded. "Aye, it is an incredible thing, I admit. Still, I believe the man, Nora. He is risking a great deal to help us. But listen to me, now," he said, his expression sobering, "there is more that you must know, much more than I had time to explain before. Did Whittaker tell you anything at all," he asked quietly, "about the evictions?"

"Evictions?" His expression was inscrutable, but something in the way he watched her made Nora sit stock-still, unable to breathe. "What evictions?"

Dragging in a long breath, Morgan enfolded both her hands between his. "Nora," he said gently, "you will have to be very strong. What I have to say is not easy."

Squeezing her hands, he seemed to choose his words with great care. He spoke in a quiet, level voice of the horrors to come—of their imminent homelessness and what Nora could only view as their approaching doom.

When he was done, she began to rock back and forth, trying mindlessly to still the shaking of her body. "God help us," she whispered, and then again, "God help us, what are we to do?"

"We are going to get you and Tahg out of here as quickly as possible," Morgan said grimly. "You and the boys will stay at Thomas's cabin for a few hours. Later tonight, I will take you to a place in the hills where you will be safe until the ship for America comes."

Nora felt her face crumble with fear and disbelief. "Are you *daft*? Tahg cannot leave the cottage!"

He gripped her hands even more tightly. "He *must* leave, lass. There is no other way."

Nora twisted, trying to tug her hands free, but he held her. *"No!* No, you are mad!" she burst out. "It would *kill* him to be taken out in this weather, after all this time and him so ill. Sure, and you must see that, Morgan— Tahg would die!"

In spite of his hands gripping hers, she managed to pull herself up off the chair, still wrenching in vain to twist free. Morgan, too, shot to his feet, catching her by the shoulders. *"Nora, listen to me!"* he shouted, his eyes burning into hers as he held her. "There is nothing else we can do! They will tumble the place down around your head if you resist. *Then* what will become of Tahg? You can't think he would survive *that!"*

Nora stopped struggling, her mind finally beginning to register the awful truth in his words.

His grip on her shoulders relaxed only slightly. "Hush, now, and hear me out, *ma girsha*," he said, his voice dropping to a low, soothing tone. "There is a way out of this, after all. But you must mind what I say."

She shook her head in hopeless protest. "Do not try to deceive me, Morgan," she choked out brokenly, no longer even trying to stop the tears. "You know as well as I that nothing can save us now! 'Tis the road for us… oh, God help us, how will we manage? What am I to do with Tahg?"

"Stop that!" His voice cracked like a whip, and he shook her soundly. "You must not give way, do you hear me? I will do all I can, but you must keep your wits while I am gone."

"Gone?" The word struck her like a blow.

He nodded, watching her closely. "Only for a short time—an hour, perhaps two. I'm going to bring some of my men down from the hills, with extra horses. They will help us to get away."

"But Tahg—"

He slid his hands down her shoulders to grip her forearms. "There's a cabin where we're going. Tahg will be warm and safe until the ship arrives."

Nora gaped at him. "But what of Cotter's men while you're gone? What if they turn us out before you get back?"

His hands tightened on her arms. "You'll be all right until I return with the lads. Whittaker is going to make certain of that. In the meantime, you must get some things together for you and the boys. Pack only what you need—no more. When I come back, you must have Tahg ready to leave, and yourself as well. Can you do that, Nora? Whittaker will help you."

When she hesitated, trembling, he pulled her to him. Dipping his head to make her meet his relentless gaze, he cupped her face between his hands. "You will be all right, lass, I promise you. I will let no harm come to you or your sons, but you must do your part. And you must not give in to your fear."

Nora closed her eyes. Her head was pounding, her mind reeling. "Nora? Look at me."

She opened her eyes, slowly dragging her gaze to lock with his. Still framing her face with his hands, he again spoke her name. "Nora . . you used to trust me, do you remember, lass?"

Nora could not answer, but merely nodded, all the while allowing his eyes to hold her captive.

"Can't you trust me again, *ma girsha*? At least once more? For the sake of your life, and that of your sons, Nora? Please?"

She searched his eyes, still unable to allow herself to hope. Yet he seemed so determined…so sure.

"Nora?"

Slowly, she nodded, unable to wrest her eyes from his.

"There's my good lass," he said, his voice softening to a hoarse whisper, his gaze brimming with an old, familiar fondness. "It will be all right. You will see."

At the unexpected touch of his lips on her forehead, Nora caught her breath sharply. She stood unmoving as he tipped her face up to look at him. "I will go now," he said, his eyes searching hers, "and fetch our English hero. First, though, you must promise me that you will do whatever he might ask of you while I am gone."

When she would have protested, he touched a finger to her lips. "Nora, impossible as it may be to comprehend, I know in my heart that Evan Whittaker is a good man, an honorable man. And a clever one as well, if I'm any judge. For now, we will simply have to trust him."

He held her gaze until she finally gave him a small, uncertain nod of assent. Then, with seeming reluctance, he released her, picked up his cloak and harp, and hurried out of the room.

Moments later, behind the cottage, Evan watched the small mare Cotter had given him to ride sag as Fitzgerald swung himself up on her back.

"How long will it t-take you?" he asked, convinced the little black mare could not carry so heavy a burden for very long.

"Two hours at the most—one is more likely," Fitzgerald replied, raking Evan with a measuring stare. "It's not far, but I'll be stopping at my brother's on the way out of town. To make sure Daniel John is safely hidden, and to have a word with Thomas about what to do should Cotter's thugs decide to come calling."

Evan was uncomfortably aware that he was being appraised. He sensed that Fitzgerald, if not actually having second thoughts about his trustworthiness, was at least making one last attempt to reassure himself.

"You saw how frail she is?" he asked Evan abruptly.

"Mrs. Kavanagh? Yes, I did. I told you, I shall help her however I c-can. If she w-will allow me to help her, that is," he amended.

Still delaying, Fitzgerald glanced up at the rain-heavy clouds. "We will need bedding for Tahg—several layers, if she has it. I'll try to borrow one or two cloaks from my lads as well." He paused. "You are absolutely certain you can turn away Cotter's men?"

Hooding his coat over his head, Evan fidgeted impatiently. He was going to have the most ghastly chest cold after all this came to an end—if indeed it ever *did* come to an end. "Yes, yes, of c-course, I'm certain," he reassured Fitzgerald, ignoring the immediate twist of doubt that followed his words. "You really *m-must* go now! You dare not be caught here!"

"Aye, I am going," the other man answered, starting to turn the horse.

Both of them jumped at the distant sound of hoofbeats. Fitzgerald whipped around, shooting a startled look first toward the road, then back to Evan. "It's too soon! What are they doing back in town—"

Panicked, the blood pounding in his ears, Evan stared at him. "Get *out* of here!"

Fitzgerald slanted him one last warning look as he yanked the mare around. "If anything happens to her or her sons," he bit out in a murderous voice, "you are a dead man!" Hauling up sharply on the reins, he tore off in a frenzy across the field, throwing rocks and splattering mud as he went.

At that moment, Evan knew with absolute certainty what he had only suspected before: *Fitzgerald was in love with the Kavanagh woman!*

His mouth went dry. Pressing the knuckles of one hand to his forehead, he groaned aloud. Fitzgerald was not the kind of man to make idle threats; of that, Evan had no doubt. And now that he was aware of the real motivation behind the big Irishman's actions, he knew with chilling conviction that his own life depended on his being able to save Nora Kavanagh and her sons.

The drumming sound of approaching horses was growing louder by the second. Evan watched Fitzgerald's back for an instant more before hurrying around the side of the cottage, cringing as the deep, sludge-filled ruts sucked his feet down and filled his boots with cold, muddy water.

He shuddered, more from desperation than cold, and went back inside. As yet he had no idea what he was going to do to turn Cotter's bully-boys away.

But he must do *something*. There was too much at stake for him to fail. *Lives* were at stake.

Lord, I don't know where to start...Please show me the next step to take. Help me not to fail these people. Lord...help me not to fail You.

20

The Wind Is Risen

Many times man lives and dies
Between his two eternities,
That of race and that of soul.

W. B. YEATS (1865–1939)

The Fitzgerald cabin was cold and dank. There was plenty of wood left from Morgan's recent trip to the hills, but Thomas had ordered them not to light a fire. "We'll not be wanting to call attention to ourselves in any way," he explained. "We will keep warm by packing for the journey. There is much to do this night."

Daniel admired Thomas for the way he had risen to this most recent crisis. Many of the villagers considered Morgan's brother a dull, plodding man, albeit a kindhearted, honorable one. Through the years-long friendship between their families, however, Daniel had come to know Thomas Fitzgerald as a quiet, orderly individual, unswervingly devoted to his God, his family, and his friends, in that order.

The two brothers were more alike than was usually perceived, especially in their mutual love for the land. While Morgan's passion was more inclined toward Ireland's culture, her history, and her always questionable destiny, Thomas found his fulfillment in working the land itself, coaxing it to yield its maximum bounty. Despite their differences, both men shared a basic bond with all that was Irish and a common instinct to preserve it.

At the moment, Thomas was showing keener instincts than most of the townspeople would have credited him with. As soon as he shoved

Daniel safely inside the cabin, he set him and the children, including Little Tom, to preparing for their forthcoming "adventure." Deliberately fueling their excitement about the voyage to America, he assigned each of them specific jobs, encouraging their efforts with occasional words of approval. In the midst of a dilemma that might well spell ruin for them all, he still managed to convey a sense of expectation to his children for what lay ahead, reminding them that God was very much a part of this, as He was in all things.

While the silent Johanna and wee Tom helped their father to pack the most essential of their meager belongings, Daniel and Katie worked hurriedly to collect the few remaining bottles of Catherine's homemade medications and herb ointments. Opening the wooden box that held her midwifery instruments, they emptied its contents onto the kitchen table, replacing them with precious containers of medicine, as well as vinegar, soap, needles, and dressings.

While they worked, they talked sparingly, speaking in low, strained voices. Mostly they watched one another with anxious eyes. Daniel was more than a little worried by Katie's appearance. In spite of the food Morgan had managed to provide, she appeared to be failing at an alarming pace. She was wretchedly thin, so slight her bones seemed to protrude through her skin, all sharp angles and knobs. She wheezed with every breath, as if the slightest movement required great effort.

He tried his utmost to be cheerful as they worked, making frequent efforts to reassure her. But his own mounting anxiety about his family, combined with a nagging whisper of guilt, made it nearly impossible to keep his mind on what he was doing. While Morgan had not pointed a finger of blame, Daniel knew he had set something in motion during his ill-fated encounter with George Cotter. Apparently, his actions were going to exact a dear price from them all—and for that he was deeply grieved and ashamed.

"Daniel John?" Katie's soft voice tugged him back from his troubled thoughts, and he looked over at her.

"What did you mean when you said Cotter had made your mother's decision for her?"

Forcing a note of brightness into his voice, Daniel replied, "Just that she can't very well refuse to go to America now, since after today we'll have nowhere *else* to go."

Katie tucked a small vial of ointment in between some dressings. "But you don't really want to go, do you?" she asked.

Daniel shrugged, avoiding her gaze. "This is not the time to think of what I want or don't want," he replied. "From what Morgan told your da, we'll either go to America or go on the road."

"I never thought it would happen to us," Katie said in a choked voice. "I suppose I've always thought that somehow Uncle Morgan would *keep* it from happening to us."

Her eyes seemed enormous as she stared into the distance, biting her lip. Daniel fumbled for words that might ease the haunted look about her, but his own throat was treacherously swollen. "Your uncle Morgan has done all he could, and more," he said lamely. "At least our passage is paid, and our families will be crossing together."

"But Uncle Morgan *isn't* going," said Katie dejectedly, dragging her gaze back to his. "And nobody seems to understand why."

"I don't suppose anyone but Morgan could understand that," Daniel said. "He is tied to Ireland in a special way, a way that only he can fathom. It's almost as if his heart is somehow…chained to the land itself."

"I—I really don't want to go either, you know," Katie said in little more than a whisper. Clutching at the knuckles on both hands, she added, "I suppose I'm afraid."

The woeful expression in her large green eyes told Daniel this was no time to play the brave man. "To be sure, I might be a bit afraid, too."

Her quick, grateful look made him glad he'd been honest. "Are you, Daniel John? Truly?"

He nodded. "I am. But I'd rather be afraid in America and have some hope for a future than to stay here in Killala, and have to be afraid every day of dying on the road. That would be a harder thing, I am thinking."

As he spoke, he absently touched the harp on the end of the table. The sight of the ancient instrument that had been passed down through so many generations made him wonder if his youthful ancestor, Eoin Caomhanach, had also suffered this same unmanly fear at the idea of leaving his home for an unknown land.

Katie seemed to consider his words. "It helps me to know that you will be going with us," she said with her usual directness. "I'm sure I won't be quite as frightened with you there."

Daniel wished he shared some of her confidence in him. He didn't think he'd ever been quite this frightened, except perhaps the day Cotter had caught him trying to loot the agent's garbage barrels.

"Daniel John…why is this happening?"

"What do you mean, Katie?"

"The Hunger. So many people starving and dying, losing their homes—I don't understand. Doesn't God care about us at all anymore?"

Staring down at the open box in front of him, Daniel shifted from one foot to the other. He had no answers for Katie, none for himself.

When he made no reply, she continued. "I once heard your mum tell mine that maybe God had placed a curse on Ireland," Katie remarked gravely. "She said the Hunger might be His way of punishing us for our sins."

Daniel looked at her. Her eyes were glazed, her skin a waxen white. Even as they stood there, scarcely moving, he could hear her laboring wheeze. He wished for a cheerful answer to give her, but could think of none. His mother often spoke of punishment and sin, and he was aware that she believed Ireland to be suffering the hand of God's wrath. He wasn't at all sure he agreed with her—at least not altogether. He still had a problem with the thought that a God who loved enough to send His own Son to die for depraved sinners would just as easily punish innocent babes.

At times even Grandfar had seemed to chafe at his mother's grim comments, actually scolding her upon occasion for such "talk of doom." His da had known best how to deal with what he called her "dark moods," had always seemed to know instinctively when to tease, when to cajole, or when to simply leave her alone until the despondency passed.

"Is that what you believe, Daniel John?" Katie asked, snapping him out of his thoughts. "That we are cursed by God?"

Slowly, Daniel shook his head. "No, in truth I don't," he said, feeling a faint nudge of guilt, as if he were somehow betraying his mother. "Da used to say it was England who had cursed us, not God."

"I never knew a country could curse another country," said Katie skeptically.

"It's more that they condemn us, I should think. By keeping us slaves on our own land and taking the very food out of our mouths—food we have grown ourselves—they've condemned us to poverty and hopelessness."

Closing the lid of the medicine box, Katie looked at him thoughtfully. "You sound just like Uncle Morgan."

Daniel gave her a faint, sheepish smile. "Well, in truth, they are his words, not mine."

"Why do the English hate us so, Daniel John?" she asked abruptly. "They don't even know us, not really. How can they hate us so fiercely when they don't *know* us?"

Daniel looked into the dead fireplace. "Morgan says it isn't so much hate as indifference."

When he turned back to her, Katie was staring at him with a blank, uncomprehending look.

"It's as if they don't consider us—*worthy*," he tried to explain. "We're not so much human beings in their estimation as we are beasts. Animals. They believe us to be wild and ignorant savages that must be kept in our place. They've always held that Ireland belongs to them, you see, not to the Irish. They colonized a part of it, and so as far as they're concerned, they have every right to do whatever they please with their own land."

"But it's *not* their land, it's ours!"

"Aye, Katie, but what we look at from one side, they look at from the other—and neither they nor we are seeing the entire picture."

"That sounds like Uncle Morgan, too," she said testily, running her hand over the top of the wooden box.

Daniel shrugged. "What do *you* think?"

She gave him a long, burning look. "I think," she replied fiercely "that I *hate* England! It's an evil country entirely."

Tying a rope around the box to secure it, Daniel glanced over at her. "I don't know that an entire country can be evil," he said carefully. The last thing he wanted, with her feeling so poorly, was an argument, but she was obviously cross with him.

"Well, people *can* be evil," she countered, "and I think the English people must be very evil indeed!"

"Sure, and the English have no sole claim on wickedness, lass." Thomas had crossed the room and now stood at the end of the table, watching the two of them. Bracing both hands on the back of a chair, he added quietly, "Evil abounds wherever the old, sinful nature rules the heart, and many are the places throughout this world where that is the case, Ireland being no exception. You both must know by now that only our Lord can change hearts, and change them He does, Katie Frances. Even English hearts, at that."

Katie shot him a skeptical look. "That may be so, Da," she muttered grudgingly, "but soon there will be neither good nor evil folks in Ireland. They will all either be dead or gone to America."

Daniel felt a chill skate down his spine. There was no denying the bitter truth of her words. He was grateful when Thomas ended the exchange, calling everyone to gather around the table for a time of prayer.

Hearing Thomas Fitzgerald pray was much like listening in on an intimate conversation between good friends, Daniel thought. Thomas never so much seemed to talk *to* the Lord as to talk *with* Him. So forthright, so earnest were his words—and so frequent his silences—that at times Daniel found himself trying to imagine what the Lord might be saying in response.

At the moment, however, he was finding it nearly impossible to keep his thoughts focused on Thomas's prayer. The day had simply been too much. He felt as if he had been swept up in a rolling ball of thunder, a storm hurtling faster and faster toward destruction. He was almost ill with fear: fear for his mother, for Tahg, for Katie and her family—and for Morgan. It was a new kind of fear, an overwhelming, cloying sort of terror that seized both his mind and his body and held them prisoner. He had never felt quite so young and utterly helpless in his life.

"*…Aye, preserve our young, Lord God, that they might have many tomorrows to live for You…*"

As Thomas's quiet words finally penetrated the turmoil in Daniel's mind, he willed himself to listen, to focus his attention on the simple but fervent prayer being lifted up. Gradually, his pulse stuttered and slowed to a normal beat. Catching a deep, steadying breath, he now added his own silent assent as Thomas went on praying.

"*Guard us all and see us safely through this night and the days to come, Lord. Protect Nora and young Tahg and the courageous Englishman who is risking himself to help us. Shelter Daniel John and all the rest of us as well in the shadow of Your love, and see us safely to Your appointed destination. And, as always, Lord God, I pray for the soul of my brother, Morgan, who has not yet recognized the fact of his love for You or the depth of his need for You, but who is, without even knowing it, a man much like Your chosen prophet, the sorrowful Jeremiah, whose great heart was broken by his own country…*"

Surprised, Daniel's eyes shot open. Moved at the look of intense pleading on Thomas's good, plain face, he found himself wondering if Morgan had any idea at all how very much his brother loved him.

Then he thought of Tahg, and quickly added a fervent prayer for his *own* brother. He was convinced that Tahg, more than any of the rest of them this night, would need the merciful intervention and protection of a loving God.

The silence inside the Kavanagh cottage was broken only by the sound of anxious breathing. Nora had heard the horses ride up, followed by the muffled sound of men's voices. Evan had no time for anything more than a whispered warning to the widow to stay close to her ailing son, advising that it might be good to "hover over him and allow her maternal concern to show, as instinct might indicate."

Instinct had indicated nothing at all to *him* as yet, and he was uncomfortably close to panic. Glancing across the bed of the barely conscious boy, he met the gaze of Nora Kavanagh. Her morose gray eyes were wide with fear, and her hands had caught the bedding in a death grip. Given the terrors this woman had endured, Evan wouldn't have been at all surprised if she had shattered into a fit of hysteria.

From the first, Nora Kavanagh had struck him as a timid, weary woman whom life had beaten down one time too many. Lovely as she was—for she possessed a winsome beauty that even the ravages of the famine had not been able to destroy completely—she nevertheless bore the appearance of one wholly exhausted, physically and emotionally depleted. Moreover, she gave off a sense of unmitigated despair, much like a cornered animal whose only choices ran to a hunter's gun or a trap.

Evan had not missed the fact that her eyes darkened with suspicion each time she so much as glanced in his direction. There was no telling what she might do. That uncertainty, added to his own impending panic, made Evan wish, at least for an instant, that he had never heard of this wretched village or its inhabitants.

He looked at young Tahg Kavanagh and was immediately ashamed of his own cowardly selfishness. Pity coursed through him as he took in the boy's smudged, sunken eyes, glassy with fever and heavy with weakness. The youth's skin was waxen and pale, except for an angry flush blotting his cheeks.

"What will we do?"

Nora Kavanagh's slightly shrill question made Evan straighten and pull in a deep breath. "I will answer the d-door," he said, clearing his throat. "You...stay with your son and just...say n-nothing." He stopped, then added, "I believe I, ah, would perhaps feel somewhat b-better about things if I knew you were p-praying while I'm...talking with these fellows."

"Mr. Whittaker?"

Evan darted a startled glance at the boy. It was the first time he had heard him speak, and the lad's voice was little more than a hoarse whisper.

"I...will pray, too," young Tahg managed to say, moistening his parched lips. "I can still...pray."

Unexpectedly, Evan's eyes filled, and he blinked. Nora Kavanagh bent over her son, bringing her lips close to his ear to whisper an endearment and give his shoulder a gentle squeeze. When she straightened, Evan thought the fear in her eyes might have abated, just a little. "Yes, we can do that much, at least, Mr. Whittaker. Both Tahg and I will be praying."

Evan was surprised and reassured to see her struggling for—and seemingly gaining—her composure. "Th-thank you, Mrs. Kavanagh. It helps me to know that."

Just then a furious pounding began at the door. Evan and Nora locked eyes for another instant before she sank down onto the chair beside her son's bed. Gently tugging the boy's hand out from under the bedclothes, she clung to it, saying softly, "We are praying, Mr. Whittaker...we are praying."

Feeling oddly bolstered, Evan nodded and started for the door, then stopped. Turning, he checked the curtain to be sure both the woman and her son could be seen from the kitchen.

After a hurried stop at Thomas's cabin, Morgan had left the village by the back road. Now he sat his horse, looking down on the village from the crest of the hill one last time.

A deadly quiet covered the hillside, the only sounds being the horse's snorting and the rain dancing off the tree limbs. He could still make out Nora's cottage, though at this distance the horses in front scarcely looked real, more like tiny brush strokes on a painting.

But they were real enough, all right, as were the thugs to whom they belonged.

Morgan was aware of his own labored breathing—not from exertion, but from his burden of dread for Nora and others. Now that he was out of Whittaker's presence, he wondered what had possessed him to set such store by the man. What had he done, leaving Nora and her ailing son to the questionable protection of a frail-looking Englishman who was a stranger to them all? How had the thin, bespectacled Saxon managed to inspire his confidence and capture his trust so quickly? He had left everyone he loved at the mercy of this slight, stammering Britisher who had no reason at all to care one way or the other whether they lived or died.

And yet Morgan had sensed that Whittaker *did* care, and cared a great deal. He shook his head as if to rid himself of the sudden doubts that threatened to stop him in his tracks. He had done all he knew to do, and in truth the Englishman was the only hope they had.

Something stirred within him, and he recognized it reluctantly as fear. He did not frighten easily, for the very fact of his size and its effect on others had made it easy to assume a certain invulnerability over the years. Without ever meaning to, he had long ago relegated fear to the distant fields of childhood.

But this was different. This present dryness of his mouth and racing of his heart had nothing at all to do with little-boy terrors or childish nightmares. This was the very reality of fear—close-up, tangible fear for the only people in his life he really cared about, the only people in his life who cared, at least a little, about *him*. It was a fear borne of his own helplessness, for when all was said and done he was only a man, even if a bit larger and stronger than most. A man vulnerable, with limitations and weaknesses and all too little hope.

How long has it been since I have prayed? he wondered abruptly. *Really prayed, with a desperate heart and a longing soul…and enough faith to send my pleas heavenward?*

Years. Years of wandering and doubting, years of bitterness, denial, and an unrepentant spirit. Years of ignoring God because he was sure that God had chosen to ignore him.

And yet something inside him was rising up and fighting for a voice, fighting to cry out, to be heard, to make its pain known.

Fighting to pray.

He yanked on the reins so savagely the little mare squealed and reared up, then surged forward as if to free herself of the wild giant on her back.

"Oh, God!" Morgan roared, his face locked in a fierce grimace of agony as he galloped furiously into the slashing rain. *"God! Do You remember me? After all this time and all my sin, do You even know my name? Does Morgan Fitzgerald still exist for You?*

"Do You see me, do You see my people? We are Ireland, God! Do You remember Ireland? Do You?"

21

A Gathering of Heroes

O brave young men, my love, my pride, my promise,
'Tis on you my hopes are set.

SAMUEL FERGUSON (1810–1886)

Evan turned for one last look at the mother and her son before opening the door. It was a touching scene, he thought, reassured. The woman leaned across the bed, clinging desperately to the boy's hand as if she feared he would be taken from her any moment; the boy lay still and quiet, his eyes closed, his sunken cheeks stained with angry red.

Despite the fact that he knew the boy's eyes were closed because he was praying, Evan felt a chill of eerie premonition trace his spine. There was a macabre reality about the vignette, the boy's apparent lifelessness, that sent a huge lump surging to his throat.

The mother was weeping. For some reason, the sight of her tears caught him up short, although why that should be, he had no notion; if ever a woman had reason to weep, surely Nora Kavanagh did.

Turning toward the door, he attempted to swallow down his panic and effect a visage of calm.

Lord, use me...free me of my fear and make me...adequate.

Dragging in one enormous steadying breath, he threw the bolt and swung the door open. An armed policeman and Cotter's two brutish bodyguards stood scowling at him. Behind them stood half a dozen or more men, all with crowbars.

Evan stiffened, but granted them not so much as the blink of an eye as he nodded formally. "Gentlemen?"

The bigger of Cotter's toughs stepped up and put a hand on the door frame. "What are *you* doing here?" He was a decidedly unpleasant creature, Evan considered, with his skin deeply pitted from pox scars and a nose so far off center it appeared almost deformed.

Returning the man's contemptuous appraisal, Evan replied, "I was hoping to find Thomas Fitzgerald here." Evan replied coldly. "I have e-eviction orders to serve on him."

"Well, sure and you won't find him *here!*" the thug growled with disgust. "The Fitzgerald hut is down the road."

"I…am quite aware of that," Evan said coldly. Praying they would not take note of his horse's absence, he hurried to add, "Fitzgerald was not at home. Cotter m-mentioned the families were close, so I thought perhaps I m-might find him here." He shot a meaningful glance toward the invalid boy and his mother, then shook his head with a sympathy he did not have to pretend. "Helping out with the b-boy, you know."

The hateful stutter was out of control again. Most likely that accounted for the blistering stares of disdain both ruffians now fastened on him. Still, if the despised affliction worked to divert their attention, perhaps he could bear it with more grace. Obviously, he was nothing more than a lame joke to these burly barbarians, and that just might work to his advantage.

"I say," he ventured now with affected anxiety, "this Fitzgerald chap… he's not the outlaw his b-brother is, is he?"

The two thugs exchanged looks, then grins. "Ah, no," said the bigger of the two, "not a bit. Thomas Fitzgerald is just a slow-witted farmer is all. But," he added with a sneer, "you'll not want to be close by if his renegade brother turns up, Whittaker! He'd have you for dinner, he would!"

All the men laughed, even the constable. It was just as Evan thought: In their eyes, he was a milksop—somewhat comical, highly contemptible, but utterly harmless. So much the better. He would play his part to the hilt.

Thinking fast, Evan leveled his eyeglasses over his nose. "Ah, good, at least I d-don't have to worry about *him!*" he burst out with feigned relief. "More than likely, he won't b-be b-back in the village before tomorrow."

The big bully with the pockmarked face abruptly sobered. "What's that you say?" he snapped, his eyes narrowing to mean slits. "What do you know about the outlaw?"

"Well, I d-don't know *anything,*" Evan said guilelessly, "other than

what's rumored in the village. Somebody saw this...M-Morgan Fitzgerald ride out of town earlier." Again Evan dropped his voice to a whisper
and leaned toward the men. "Supposedly, he's g-gone to a nearby town for
supplies," he said slyly, "but if he's as sweet on the wo-woman as they say,
I'd be inclined to b-believe he's gone to fetch a surgeon for her son. The
boy's dying, you know," he said, pursing his lips and clucking his tongue.
"So sad, isn't it?"

"What town? Did they say what town?"

"Town? Oh yes, I b-believe it was, ah, B-Ballina. Yes, that was it. B-Ballina."

The two men again locked gazes. With an air of conspiracy, Evan
motioned them outside the door, then followed. "Do you think that's
where the other b-boy is?" he questioned in a hushed tone. "The one you're
supposed to, ah, fetch for Cotter? He's certainly n-nowhere around *here*."

The shorter of the two men, who had hair the color of old rust and an
incredible number of ginger freckles on his face, jumped on Evan's remark.
"The younger brat? He's not here, then?"

"Oh no," Evan answered, widening his eyes. "I inquired after him,
knowing of Cotter's...interest. No, he's not here."

"Where did the woman say he is?"

Evan made a small dismissing motion with one hand. "Her? Poor
soul, she can't t-talk at all, she's simply d-devastated. Her son is dying, you
know." For emphasis, he leveled an icy look of rebuke on the man.

The big man studied him. "You're sure the outlaw is headed for Ballina? That's what you heard?"

"Well, I can't be *certain*," Evan said haughtily. "All these Irish names
sound alike to me. But, yes, I b-believe that was the place. B-Ballina." *Oh,
Lord, forgive me...I know most of this isn't true, not at all, but I simply don't
know what else I can do.*

The rusty-haired man turned toward his companion. "He's probably
right about the younger boy. The brat's forever tagging after Fitzgerald
when he's in the village. If they're together, we could take the both of them
at once. That should be worth a dear bonus, wouldn't you say?"

The taller, meaner looking of the two shook his head. "Our orders is
to empty this place tonight."

"Aye, and our orders were first and foremost to deliver the Kavanagh
gorsoon to Cotter! You know him well enough to know which job will

please him most, presenting him with both the boy and that devil Fitzgerald, or tumbling some worthless widow from her cottage."

Evan saw his chance and pressed it. "Oh, I say, you're n-not thinking of evicting the woman *tonight*, are you?" He reached to straighten his eyeglasses. "Oh, that won't do at all! Why, Sir Roger would have a stroke if he knew we had tossed a widow and her dying son out into the cold! Oh, dear, n-no! I simply won't hear of it."

The big man glowered at him. "It's not for you to say. It's for Cotter."

Squaring his shoulders, Evan fixed the man with a freezing glare. "B-Begging your pardon, but George Cotter is only an *employee* of Sir Roger Gilpin. And I," he bit out precisely, "am Sir Roger's *assistant*, and I'm telling you that you will not evict this woman to-tonight. N-not if you want to continue in the employ of Gilpin estates."

The two men exchanged long looks. "I think we ought to go directly on to Ballina," said the freckle-faced man. "We're wasting time here."

"We may do that," agreed the other, "but if his honor doesn't mind, we will first have us a look inside." The man's eyes were hard with an unreadable glint.

Evan could almost feel the perspiration fighting to break out along his forehead. Did he see malice lurking behind those small gray eyes? Had he, in his haste and his nervousness, given himself away somehow?

Please, Lord, get them out of here quickly...please...

"Why, of c-course," he stammered, stepping aside to allow them entrance. "You'll want to dry out a bit before going on, I'm sure."

The big man motioned to the others in the yard that they should wait, then followed his rusty-haired cohort inside the cottage. They stopped in the middle of the kitchen, their gazes sweeping their surroundings until they spied the woman and the boy within the alcove.

Evan shot her a look, but it went unheeded. It was also unnecessary, he saw at once. Nora Kavanagh was clearly up to what was expected of her. Her eyes were fastened on her son as she wept copious tears, shaking her head over and over in gesture of desolation. She dragged her eyes away from Tahg only once to glance at the men standing in her kitchen, immediately breaking into loud sobs as if the very sight of them had triggered a fresh outburst of grief.

"As I said," Evan murmured discreetly, "the b-boy is in a terrible way. He'll be gone before n-nightfall, I should imagine." With a flash of inspiration, he added, "I say, you Irish *do* t-take on in this sort of thing, don't you? She's b-been wailing like that ever since I got here."

With obvious resentment, the freckle-faced man shot him an angry glare. "You think it be unnatural to grieve over a dying lad? Your own, at that?"

Feigning indignation, Evan bristled. "Certainly n-not! But you *do* have so many, after all. I suppose I didn't expect…well, you know…"

The other man twisted his lip in disgust. "Aye, I do know." Turning to his tall, broad-shouldered partner, he snapped, "Come on, then. It's Ballina for us."

The big man with the bad skin studied the mother and her son for what seemed to Evan an interminable time before giving a short nod. "Aye, we're off, then. But mind," he said, scowling at Evan, "if Thomas Fitzgerald shows up here, you question him good. If he has word of his brother and the boy being anywhere else but Ballina, send a message by the bailiff. We'll leave him in the village, just in case. Or would you rather he stay here, should there be trouble with Fitzgerald?"

Evan's mind raced. "Why should there be t-trouble? I'm simply going to serve his papers and be off. He has until tomorrow to leave; I'm certainly not g-going to wait around here until morning. No," he said firmly, "there's no need for anyone to stay. If Fitzgerald d-doesn't show up before long, I'm going back to Cotter's house, where it's warm."

Both men gave him one more long look, then stalked impatiently out of the cottage. Evan waited until the entire dastardly crew was safely out of the yard and back on the road before shoving the door closed and bolting it. He leaned against it for a moment, his eyes squeezed shut.

Forgive me, Lord, for lying as I did. I just couldn't think of another way.

After a moment, he opened his eyes to find Nora Kavanagh still weeping. Taking a deep breath, he crossed the room, going to stand at the curtained alcove. "You were splendid, Mrs. K-Kavanagh," he said with total sincerity. "You are a very b-brave woman."

She glanced up, staring at him almost as if she had only then become aware of his presence. Tears continued to spill over her cheeks, but she said nothing.

The boy finally broke the silence. "And you…are a very brave man, Mr. Whittaker. My mother and I…we both thank you."

Feeling too awkward to reply, Evan glanced away. "Well, now," he said briskly, "if you'll just tell me what to do, I shall help you with your packing,

Mrs. K-Kavanagh. I suppose we should get b-busy with it, since Fitzgerald said he would be returning soon."

The woeful look she turned on him made Evan long to comfort her. Clearly, the poor woman was only a step this side of utter collapse. But once more she rallied and, pulling herself up off the chair, brushed her lips across the boy's cheek. "Aye," she said wearily, leaving her bedside vigil, "let us have done with it, then."

Evan had never seen such raw, exposed pain in another human being's eyes as he encountered when Nora Kavanagh passed by him to enter the kitchen.

Pat Gleeson had been Cotter's bodyguard for nearly six years, long enough to know that the agent turned vicious when foiled. The memory of Cotter's rages helped him make his decision.

Turning to the man on the horse beside him, he said bluntly, "We'll stop at the Fitzgerald hut before heading for Ballina."

Sharkey, a short, muscular man with a nasty streak, shot Gleeson an impatient glance. "For what? You heard what the Britisher said."

Ignoring Sharkey's irritation, Gleeson said, as much to himself as to his companion, "Something about that stuttering little fop puts me off. He may be Gilpin's man, but I don't trust him." Turning his horse, he gave a sharp jerk of his head to indicate Sharkey should do likewise. "We'll just have ourselves a look," he said. "I'll not be easy unless we do."

Sharkey glowered, but turned his horse, signaling the men behind them to follow. "That one has never trusted a soul in his entire wretched life, I'd wager," he muttered under his breath. "Pity he cannot see that not all men are as deceitful as himself." His scowl deepened, as did his impatience, when a sudden blast of rain let loose from the clouds, a downpour that drenched them all within seconds.

"Men, Da!" Katie cried, peering out the small front window. "Men on horses are coming!"

Thomas was hoisting a trunk to his shoulders and had it halfway up in the air when Katie called her warning. Setting it to the floor, he hurriedly pushed it beneath the bed where the Kavanagh harp had already been safely stored.

Morgan had feared that Cotter's toughs would come to check out the cabin. Thomas's mind raced, trying desperately to remember his brother's exact instructions.

"Katie Frances, did you mind what I told you? About what you are to say to the men if they ask questions about me or your uncle Morgan—or Daniel John?" Without waiting for her answer, he jerked his arm toward the small deal table in the middle of the floor. "Hurry, boy!" he whispered harshly to Daniel. "There is no time!"

The lad scooted the table off its platform bottom, and Thomas quickly eased the wooden plank away so they could lower themselves into the hole it concealed. As soon as Daniel dropped down, out of sight, Thomas looked at his wide-eyed daughter and warned, "You'll not forget to replace the plank and the table, lass?"

She shook her head, but Thomas still hesitated, worried for the stark look of fear on her face. "It will be all right, *asthore*. Try not to be afraid— God is with us."

Katie nodded, biting at her lower lip. "I know, Da."

With a short nod, Thomas turned to the other two children. Using a hand language Morgan had helped him to develop, he once more reminded Johanna to take Little Tom to the back bedroom, and to stay there until the men were gone.

As soon as the children left the kitchen, he followed Daniel into the hole. Total darkness enveloped him the instant Katie slid the table back to its place. The black pit was actually a tunnel that led a distance away from the cabin; he and Morgan had started it over a year ago. When Morgan was in the village, he helped with it, but Thomas had done most of the digging himself, he and the two girls. In the beginning, he had used it as storage for their precious extra food supplies. Later, when the food was gone, he'd continued to tunnel, always with the thought at the back of his mind that Morgan might someday need a hidey-hole nearby; he had never expected to be hiding in it himself.

In the thick, unrelieved darkness, he could not see the boy at his side, but he was aware of Daniel John's trembling. Lifting a hand, he fumbled until he found the lad's shoulder.

"God help us, Thomas," the boy murmured.

"God *will* help us, Daniel John," Thomas replied, silently praying a psalm of refuge even as he voiced his reassurance.

When Morgan found the mountain cabin empty, he almost panicked. Only the leavings of some stirabout and bread crumbs gave him hope that the lads could be found close by.

He was soaked all the way through his cloak to his skin, his hair dripping down over his shoulders, but he took no time to dry off or warm himself. Gathering some blankets from the back room, he crashed out the door, hurriedly tugging the small mare around to the back of the cabin to a rude lean-to deep in the woods.

As soon as he entered the shed, the immense red stallion tethered at the back began to snort excitedly. Morgan crossed to the horse and soothed him, speaking the Irish. He saddled him quickly, tossing the blankets across his broad back, then tied the mare to a lead rope.

"Aye, I have missed you, too, Pilgrim," he murmured, making a soft clicking noise with his tongue between his teeth, which immediately quieted the big stallion. "But tonight we will ride together again."

Leading both horses from the shed, Morgan silenced Pilgrim with a sharp warning as the stallion began to fight the mare's presence. After checking the lead rope, he swung himself up into the saddle. "So, then, where are the lads, Pilgrim? Where have they gone, eh?"

He thought he knew. Two priests and a country clergyman had thrown up a tent near Kilcummin, where they aided those on the road with what food and remnants of clothing they could collect. The lads made a practice of helping them out in any way they could, going down in the evening once or twice a week to drop off a bit of this or that, as well as to lend a strong back where needed.

The smudged tracings of hoofprints in the mud proved him right; at least they had headed in that direction. He had counted on finding the men at the cabin, and he resented the need to spend precious time running them down. He knew his anger was unreasonable, his impatience unjustified, but he was bone tired, anxious, and growing more apprehensive by the moment.

His mind went to those he had left behind in the village. Try as he would, he could not imagine the frail, mild Whittaker facing down Cotter's bully-boys. Even less would he allow himself to entertain the consequences of Daniel being discovered at Thomas's cabin before he could get back.

Suddenly the sound of hoofbeats and tree limbs brushing together made him look up, startled. Colin Ward and the other five lads galloped out of the woods toward him, hailing him as if he'd been gone for a month. Morgan actually gasped aloud with relief.

He yanked Pilgrim up short, waiting. "I need the lot of you in the village," he bit out when they reached him, wasting no time on a greeting. "Bring in any extra horses we have from the woods and ride as hard as you can." His eyes went over the six men, resting on the biggest of them all. "Cassidy, you meet me at Nora Kavanagh's cottage, with at least one extra horse. The rest of you go to my brother's cabin—go down the back road, and make sure you're not seen. Cassidy and I will meet you there." He paused, then added, "We will be bringing my family and the Kavanaghs up here this night."

"*All* of them?" questioned Cassidy, his heavy black brows drawn together. "The children as well?"

Morgan looked at him. "All of them," he said. "The children especially."

He saw the men exchange glances. As briefly as possible, he explained, giving them only a hurried sketch of the events that had taken place that day. When he had finished, Cassidy spoke without hesitation. "We will get them out, Morgan."

The others nodded their assent, and Morgan drew a long breath. "Remember, we must not be seen. If we are taken, it will mean disaster for them all."

"We will not be taken," Colin Ward announced in a hard voice. Morgan knew from past experience that the young man with the black eye patch had the courage legends were made of and wits enough for two men. Just hearing Ward's reassurance made him feel easier.

"The other horses are nearby," said Ward, nodding toward the small mare on the lead rope. "Why don't you send that one with us, sir? She'll only slow you down."

Morgan quickly released the mare, handing her off to Ward. Cassidy parted his way through the other riders, pulling his horse up sharply beside Morgan.

With a short nod, Morgan turned his horse, and together he and the burly Cassidy started down the mountain for Killala.

22

Undertones

We are fainting in our misery,
But God will hear our groan.
LADY WILDE (1820-1896)

The two rough-looking men burst into the cabin as soon as Katie cracked open the door. Flinging it aside, they shoved her backward into the kitchen with such force she cried out.

The bigger of the two, the one with the scarred skin and mean-looking eyes, glared at her. "Where is your da, girl?"

"He's not at home right now, sir," Katie finally managed, nearly choking on her own voice. She was trembling, not from the cold cabin, but from fear.

"Well, and where *is* he, then?" grated the same man.

Katie's mind groped for just the right words, knowing that what she said and how she acted might be terribly important to her da and Daniel—indeed, to them all. "I'm...not exactly sure *where* he might be, sir. Just that he's away for now. I'm sure he won't be gone long, though."

Both men continued to pin her in place with their cold, threatening stares, but it was the big man with the heavy shoulders and cruel eyes who questioned her. "And what of your uncle, then? Morgan Fitzgerald?"

Katie swallowed hard but forced herself to meet the man's gaze, "My uncle Morgan, sir? Sure, and I don't know where he is. He doesn't live here with us, you know."

"We hear otherwise," pressed the second man.

His face was peppered generously with freckles, his mouth seemingly trapped in a permanent frown. Still, he acted a bit less gruff than his companion, so Katie fixed her eyes on him as she spoke. "Oh no, sir! Uncle Morgan stops for a visit now and then, he does, but he never stays for any length of time at all."

The freckle-faced man raked a hand through his straight red hair. "Are you satisfied at last, Gleeson? Can we get on with it now?"

Ignoring him, the big man swept the cabin with his eyes. "Who else is here with you, girl?"

Katie's heart lurched, then raced. She could not shake the image of her da and Daniel huddled in the dark pit below the cabin. "Who else, sir?"

His eyes on her were hard and impatient. "Aye," he snarled, *who else?*"

Katie was certain the trembling of her chin must be apparent to both men. "Only my younger sister and wee brother, sir. Johanna is putting Little Tom to bed. My mum is dead, you see."

Katie held her breath. The man finally gave a short nod. "Check in the back!" he snapped. The freckle-faced man let go with a violent oath, but made his way across the room toward the rear of the cabin.

Seconds later he returned with Little Tom, clinging tightly to the hand of Johanna, who was white with fear. The big, burly man shot the same questions at Johanna as he had Katie, but the girl simply stared at him with huge, frightened eyes.

"My sister cannot hear or speak, sir," Katie quickly explained. "She has no way of knowing what you want."

He looked at her, then again at Johanna before turning to his partner with a scowl. "We will go now," he said shortly, starting for the door, then stopping. "Let us hope that you are telling the truth, girl," he said roughly. "It will go hard for your da and your entire family if you are lying."

He watched her closely, as if he half expected her to deny everything she'd said. Her heart pounding, Katie met his eyes with as level a look as she could manage.

As soon as the two men were out the door, she rushed to throw the bolt. Turning, she sank back against the door, staring at Johanna, waiting until the fierce trembling of her legs subsided enough that she could finally cross the room and move the table away from the hidey-hole.

Evan would never have believed he could feel such monumental relief at the sight of two outlaws. When Fitzgerald and the great brawny creature called Cassidy first edged themselves through the back door of the cottage, he could have fallen at their feet in welcome.

Fitzgerald's first move, of course, was to see to Mrs. Kavanagh. Evan found himself surprised and quite touched to see the gentleness which the Irish giant afforded the small, pale widow. It occurred to him, watching Fitzgerald's courtly tenderness with the woman, that this big, heavy-chested Gael was at heart, if not in breeding, a consummate gentleman.

When Fitzgerald quizzed him briefly but thoroughly on his handling of Cotter's thugs, Evan once again encountered a glint of approval in the Irishman's gaze.

"You have my thanks, Evan Whittaker," Fitzgerald said quietly across the boy's bed. "You are a brave man."

He turned his attention to Tahg. "We will make you as warm and as comfortable as humanly possible, lad," Fitzgerald said in a gentle voice, taking the boy's frail hand and bending over him. "This will not be an easy thing for you, Tahg. But it is necessary."

His eyes shut, Tahg nodded. "'Tis all right, Morgan. I understand. I'm only sorry to be such a burden…making everything so difficult—"

The boy's mother choked out a protest, but it was Fitzgerald who, bracing a huge hand on either side of the boy's thin shoulders, silenced him. "I'll not be listening to such foolishness from a man grown," he said with a stern frown. "There is no burden about it. Once we get you into some warm wrappings, you will ride out of here on Pilgrim's back, and that will be that."

Evan would have thought Tahg Kavanagh to be beyond enthusiasm of any sort, but the boy's eyes shot open and actually appeared to brighten. "Pilgrim? Is that your horse, Morgan? Is he a stallion?"

"He is," replied Morgan, straightening, "and as hardheaded and cantankerous a great brute as you are likely to find trampling Irish sod. Now, then," he said briskly, "let us get you ready for your journey."

The boy gave a weak nod. "You are going, too, Morgan?"

Carefully freeing Tahg's arms from the bedding, Fitzgerald looked at him. "Well, of course, I am going. Would I set you on old Pilgrim by yourself?"

Tahg shook his head. "No...I mean, you are going to America with us, are you not?"

Fitzgerald stopped his movements for only an instant, his wide mouth straining at a smile. "Not this time," he said, quickly adding, "perhaps later."

Tahg tried to push himself up. "But, Morgan, you must go! You dare not stay here, in Killala, after—"

Fitzgerald brought a finger to his own lips. "We will save our talking for later, lad. For now, we must hurry; there is little time."

With obvious reluctance, the boy sank back onto his pillow, remaining silent as both Fitzgerald and Cassidy worked to wrap him, first in Morgan's heavy frieze cloak, then in several layers of bedding. Throughout the entire process, the boy followed Fitzgerald's movements with a mournful expression and pain-filled eyes.

Watching him, Evan felt certain that a part of the pain in young Tahg's gaze was, for a change, not entirely physical.

23

As the Shadows Advance

Through the woods let us roam,
Through the wastes wild and barren;
We are strangers at home!
We are exiles in Erin!

FEARFLATHA O'GNIVE (C. 1560)
[TR. SAMUEL FERGUSON]

The road from Nora's cottage to Thomas's cabin at the edge of town spanned only a short distance, but tonight it seemed an endless trek. Indeed, Morgan felt as if he had been riding for hours.

His heart was stretched tight enough to crack. How long had it been since he'd last drawn an easy breath? Not since hoisting Tahg onto Pilgrim's back, that was certain. Instinctively, he tightened his embrace around the boy, snugly wrapped in several layers of bedding. Even so, Morgan felt the lad's trembling, heard him utter a soft moan with Pilgrim's every step.

The rain had stopped. Other than an occasional errant cloud moving across the face of the moon, the night sky was beginning to clear. He looked ahead. Nora was riding with Cassidy, with Whittaker just behind them on the extra roan. The horses took the wet, rocky hillside at a slow walk. Even Pilgrim, ordinarily a daredevil, had tempered his impatience, as if aware of the need for caution.

Morgan had fallen a ways behind the others, but in the faint spray of moonlight he could see them clearly. Too clearly. Although relieved for Tahg's sake that the rain had ended, he would have preferred the safety of

227

cloud cover. Still, they should soon be well concealed by the fog drifting down from the mountains.

Despite the fact that the wind was cold and he wore no cloak, perspiration ribbed the back of his head, trickling down his back beneath his shirt. Anxiety. The thought of the ordeal ahead, and all that could go wrong gripped him with dread. And yet there was nothing he could do but go on.

And so they rode into the night, like prisoners already condemned to the gallows. Their only hope of survival lay in the hands of a God who seemed to have forgotten their very existence. A God who was absent.

Morgan's gaze traveled down over the hill, to the ancient round tower, then back to the night sky with its faintly shadowed moon. Lately he had found himself brooding over this...*absence* of God. Was it a fact? And, if so, did that *absence* somehow signify the *presence* of something else? Something evil?

All through history, it seemed that a common seed of evil sprouted its corrupt fruit, the spoiled and worthless crowding out the healthy and good. Civilization was much like the potato blight, he thought: As long as the plants blossomed prettily, grew healthy and strong in the sun, they were taken for granted but not really prized for their value. It was only after the pestilence struck, blighting the leaves and seizing the roots, finally wiping out an entire country's livelihood, that the worth of the now destroyed crop was finally realized.

With a shudder, Morgan pulled Tahg closer, as if to shelter him and will him to survive. To endure.

If only the good can ever hope to supplant the evil...if only what is innocent can ever hope to uproot the defiled, then what hope was there for this wasted island? The best of Ireland was dying or fleeing... What would be left behind to bloom in Ireland for a future day?

Oh, God...what would be left?

꙳

Daniel watched through the jagged tear in the paper-covered window. Any instant now he hoped to catch a glimpse of Morgan and the others.

Behind him, the dim room was crowded. Boxes bound with rope, one large trunk and a smaller one, three sacks of miscellaneous items—all were heaped randomly in the middle of the floor. Morgan's men were there, three of them; the other two had slipped out of the cabin earlier to scout the village and watch for Morgan as he brought his charges across the hill.

"You'll not see them coming until they're at the door." Katie had edged up beside him. "They will come down on the other side of hill, not around the front way."

Daniel nodded, but continued to peer out into the moon-dusted darkness. "I know. It's just that I thought they would be here by now."

She touched his arm. "They will come soon, Daniel John. Uncle Morgan will see them safely here."

He looked at her then, managing a smile.

"Aye, he will that. Sure, there is nowhere safer to be than under your uncle Morgan's protection." Still studying her flushed, thin face, he added, "You did well tonight, Katie, turning Cotter's men away from the cabin as you did. You were brave."

She shook her head. "I did not feel brave, I can tell you! I was frightened out of my wits! I still can scarcely believe I didn't ruin things for us all by breaking down like a crybaby."

"Well, you didn't," he said. "And besides, *feeling* brave isn't the same as *being* brave, you know. It's how you behave that counts the most, not how you feel—"

They both heard the sounds at the side of the cabin at the same time— the low murmur of voices, the wet slap of hoofs in the mud. Daniel caught a glimpse of his mother as she rounded the corner of the cabin, then Morgan.

"*It's them!*" he cried, motioning to Katie to throw the bolt.

Morgan came in first, carrying Tahg in his arms like a baby in its wrappings. Daniel's mother and a big, gruff-looking man with a barrel chest came next, followed by the Englishman.

Without stopping, Morgan inclined his head to Daniel, motioning him to follow as he carried Tahg directly to the back of the cabin and eased him onto the bed. Daniel started to loosen the bedding from around Tahg's face, stopping for a quick embrace from his mother. When she began to fuss over Tahg, he moved aside to give her room.

As the blankets dropped away from Tahg's face, Daniel choked back a gasp of dismay. His brother's eyes were pinched shut, his lips cracked and tinged a milky shade of blue against the stark white of his skin. For a moment his heart stopped at the terrible thought that his brother was dead.

Finally Tahg began to cough. His eyes fluttered open, and Daniel caught his breath in relief. Glancing across the bed at Morgan, however, his relief immediately died. Morgan's eyes were fixed on Tahg with a grim, watchful expression. As if sensing Daniel's gaze, he looked up. Their eyes met, and in that instant Daniel knew with a stab of anguish that Morgan held no hope at all for Tahg's survival.

Instinctively he took a protective stance closer to his brother. Tahg looked up, moistening his parched lips in a weak attempt to smile. "Danny…"

"Aye, Tahg, I am here," Daniel said quickly, putting a hand to Tahg's thin shoulder.

"Are we ready, then, Danny?"

"Ready, Tahg?"

His brother gave a small jerk of a nod. "Aye…are we ready to go to America?"

Daniel stared at his brother, his throat tightening even more. "Aye, Tahg, we are almost ready at last."

Again the older boy nodded. "We must…we must convince Morgan to go with us, Danny…tell him…tell him he must go, too…"

It was the fever talking, Daniel knew. And yet he could not help but look across the bed to Morgan, who avoided his gaze by staring resolutely at Tahg.

"Do not wear yourself out, lad," Morgan said, his voice gruff. "We will soon be leaving for the mountain. You must save your strength for yet another ride."

Tahg's eyes rolled out of focus, then closed, and Daniel knew that he had once again drifted off to the place the fever took him.

⁂

Two miles outside of town, Pat Gleeson reined in his mount so sharply the stallion reared on his haunches and pawed the sky. Snorting, the horse hit the ground hard as he came down. Beside him, Sharkey pulled up his own horse with an oath. "What do you think you're doing, you—"

Gleeson sat his horse with his brawny arms braced straight out, his hands knotted tightly on the reins. "Where was the Englishman's mount, do you suppose?"

Sharkey stared at him as if he'd taken leave of his senses.

"Whittaker's *horse!*" Gleeson demanded impatiently. "Where was it? And why was he so intent on hanging about the widow's cottage—and not evicting her, eh?"

His partner twisted his face into a grimace of disbelief. "What do I know—or care—where the Englishman's *horse* is? What kind of madness is on you now?"

Gleeson didn't answer. Thinking hard, he sat staring into the night with fixed eyes and a growing certainty.

"Come on," he said, turning his horse, "we're going back."

Again Sharkey swore. "What's wrong with you, man? It's the boy and the outlaw we want, not some slow-witted farmer or widow woman! I should think—"

"Well, don't—you haven't the mind for it! Now, ride! We are going back!"

Without another word, Gleeson squeezed his legs against the stallion's sides and took off at a mad gallop.

Sharkey hurled a stream of evil epithets at him as he tore off, but after an instant spurred his mount and followed.

They had the cart nearly loaded and hitched to one of the extra horses when the sound of approaching hoofbeats came tearing out of the night. Crouched down on one knee to tighten a wheel, Morgan raised his head to listen, then lunged to his feet.

O'Dwyer and Quigley had returned from their scouting mission around the village. Waiting, Morgan wiped the oil from his hands onto his trousers.

"Is all quiet, then?" he asked the fair-haired Quigley as the men reined up in front of him.

The words were hardly out of his mouth when young Quigley blurted out, "The ship is in, sir! It's coming into the harbor now!"

For a moment Morgan could only stare at them, his brain refusing to take in what they had said.

"An American packet, it is," spluttered the red-faced O'Dwyer with a huge grin. "A small one, but it looks fit."

"The ship is in." Morgan tested their news on his own lips. "You are certain?"

Daniel John walked up just then, staring wide-eyed, first at Morgan, then at the men on horseback. He started to speak, but Morgan stopped him with an upraised hand.

"Oh, there's no mistaking it," O'Dwyer assured him. "There's a green silk hanging from the steerage deck, just as we were told! Aye, it is your ship, right enough. There will be no need to head for the mountain this night," the man went on. "We can take your people directly to the pier."

Disoriented by this unexpected turn of events, Morgan's mind groped to change directions. "Tonight? But will they let them board tonight, do you suppose?"

O'Dwyer's grin turned sly. "Sure, and we will convince them to do so."

"Mind, we can't afford to take any more risks than are absolutely necessary," Morgan cautioned. "Especially with an ailing boy on our hands. We dare not have him jostled about or lying in the cold."

"The lass did say that most of the agent's thugs had started on for Ballina," Quigley reminded him. "That should leave only the bailiff and Cotter himself. It's not likely the two of *them* would give us any grief."

Morgan nodded vaguely. It was beginning to make sense. Indeed, it occurred to him that their chances were now better than they might have hoped, with Cotter's bodyguards and the constables out of the picture. Still, he could not feel altogether easy with their circumstances—not yet. It seemed too smooth, and it had been his experience that when things appeared too smooth, trouble was often lurking nearby.

"All right, then," he said, still apprehensive as he scanned their thickly shadowed surroundings. "We will get them ready to go at once. You men will need to give us all the guard you can, in front and in the rear." He paused, glancing at Daniel John, who stood listening to the exchange with a mixture of excitement and uneasiness in his eyes.

Returning his gaze to O'Dwyer and Quigley, Morgan continued. "We cannot be stopped," he said quietly. "No matter what happens, we cannot be stopped. We *must* get them aboard that ship."

"Morgan, *you* dare not be seen!" O'Dwyer exclaimed. "They'll have you on the gallows by dawn if you're caught! Let us take the ailing boy with us, and you go on to the mountain!"

Shaking his head emphatically, Morgan dismissed the suggestion with a wave of his hand. "I will see them aboard that ship first."

"But if you are spotted, man—"

Again he cut O'Dwyer's protest short. "I must go back inside. Stay here and keep watch while I tell the others."

Beside him, Daniel John put a hand to his arm. "Morgan—"

Morgan looked at him, then shook his head. "We have said what is to be said, lad. Come with me now. Your mother will need your help."

The boy studied him for another moment, then dropped his hand away.

Thomas was just coming out the door with another box as they approached. "This is the last of it, except—"

He stopped in mid-sentence, his eyes going from Morgan's face to Daniel John's.

"The ship is in," Morgan said without preamble. "There is no longer a need to go to the mountain. We will ride directly to the harbor instead."

His brother stared at him. A combination of surprise, regret, and long years of unspoken feelings hung between them.

"Put that in the cart, Thomas," Morgan said quietly, gesturing to the box. "We are leaving at once."

Still Thomas hesitated, his eyes going over Morgan's face. At last he gave a small nod and took off down the mud-slicked path, loping awkwardly toward the cart that held his meager belongings.

Morgan watched him for a moment, then turned to the boy. "Let us go and tell the others," he said quietly. "The waiting is over."

The waiting was over...and still he had not given Nora the letter, Michael's letter...

Now she would have no privacy for reading it—yet read it she must. As yet she did not know that on the other side of the ocean help was waiting.

Ah, well, there was no more opportunity to choose the proper moment. He would have to give her the letter before they left the cabin, let her read it wherever and whenever she could—after they boarded the ship, if need be. At least she would leave Ireland with the assurance that she would not be without security, without protection, once she reached the States.

Michael, Michael, she is coming. Be there for her. Be good to her, old friend...be everything to her that I could never be...

It was a rare night that George Cotter was still sober by eleven o'clock; tonight was such an occasion. So great was his anxiety that the two drinks he had downed earlier might just as well have been water. So when Harry Macken, the bailiff, appeared at his door in an obvious state of agitation, Cotter was alert enough to make sense of the man's ranting.

"There is a ship in the bay! I saw it myself!" Macken exclaimed, brushing past Cotter.

"What are you raving about?" Cotter snapped as he stepped aside to let him enter. Closing the door, he turned to face the excited bailiff. "And what are you doing *here*? I thought you were with Gleeson and Sharkey."

Worrying his hat between both hands, the hatchet-faced Macken scowled. "I *did* go with them—at least, that is, until they left for Ballina. They felt I should stay behind in case Fitzgerald turns up back in the village."

"Ballina?" Cotter's head began to throb. "What do you mean, they left for Ballina? Make sense, man! Are you saying they have not found the boy yet?"

Macken shook his head. "Your Mr. Whittaker seems to think that Fitzgerald and the Kavanagh boy are on their way to Ballina, that they won't be back until tomorrow at the earliest."

"Fitzgerald *and* the Kavanagh boy?" Deep inside Cotter's belly a fire flared to life, adding even more agony to the already hammering pain in his head. "Gone to Ballina?" he choked out.

"Aye, so the Englishman claims to have heard. Anyway, Gleeson and Sharkey took the others and started out. I was headed home and saw the ship making anchor. I thought it best to make you aware of it right away."

"I know about a ship!" Cotter snapped, leaning toward the bailiff. "Gilpin himself paid for a number of passages, just to get the rabble off his land." He stopped, rubbing the stubble on his chin with an unsteady hand. "What kind of ship does it look to be?"

Macken shrugged. "It flies the Stars and Stripes. It's not such a big vessel, though. Mid-sized, from what I could tell in the fog."

"Stars and Stripes?" The tremor in Cotter's hand grew worse. "An American ship?"

Macken nodded. "Aye, it was that, I'm sure."

Enraged, Cotter let out an oath. The passages Gilpin had paid for were booked on a British vessel!

Cotter's mind raced. Hatred boiled up inside of him, hatred for the outlaw Fitzgerald and for the sniveling young scoundrel who was obviously depending on the bandit for protection.

"You said the Englishman told you about Fitzgerald and the boy—" he burst out suddenly. "Where did you see him? Where was Whittaker?"

Macken lifted a quizzical brow. "Why, at the widow's cottage. He was waiting for Fitzgerald's brother."

"Why there?"

As Macken explained. Cotter's fury rose. He stared at the bailiff for a moment. Abruptly, he turned, going to the closet under the stairway. "Wait—I'll need my coat."

Macken stared at him. "Your *coat?* Where would you be going at this time of night?"

"To the harbor, that's where!" Cotter shot over his shoulder. "And you are going with me!"

They thought him a fool, that was clear enough. Fitzgerald, Whittaker, even the boy—they thought him too dull-witted to see past their traitorous scheming.

Well, they would find out their mistake soon enough. He would show them that George Cotter was not nearly the fool they liked to think.

Killala slept as the American packet drifted into the harbor. Here and there a dim flicker of candlelight could be seen behind a cabin window, but most of the village was shrouded in fog and darkness. Even the sluggish, tarnished waters of the bay were black now, except for the reflected wash of moonlight around the ship.

Nobody in the village would have suspected that escape lay just beyond the weathered, drab buildings near the bay. Nobody would have dreamed that deliverance waited at the end of the pier. It would have made little difference if they had, for the few remaining residents of the village with health enough to travel would have had no money for passage to America.

The packet had already dropped anchor and now rocked gently in the waters, her silhouette forlorn in the fog-wrapped moonlight. Waiting in the deserted harbor, shifting silently in the dead of night, the lonely ship might have been one of the ghost vessels from the old tales repeated by the fireside in better days. Draped in mist and distorted by shadows, she was eerily quiet, except for an occasional creak or groan from the hull. Even the ocean beneath her seemed to whisper, as if reluctant to disturb whatever presence might wait above.

She was small but fully rigged, with three masts and a graceful, apple-cheeked bow. Sturdily constructed and buoyant in appearance, she was not a new vessel by any means. A seasoned cargo ship, she had originally been built to carry cotton and corn eastward, iron and machinery westward. These days she carried emigrants—mostly Irish—to North America.

She was the *Green Flag*, and only her crew knew that she was not all she might appear to be.

24

Flight of Terror

The last may be first! Shall our country's glory
Ever flash light on the path we have trod?
Who knows? Who knows? for our future story
Lies hid in the great sealed Book of God.

LADY WILDE (1824–1896)

Leaving Thomas's home was almost as painful for Nora as leaving her own. Spartan and plain as it was, the small cabin echoed with memories: the sound of Catherine's soft humming in the kitchen as they worked together, the children's laughter and the men arguing politics beside the fire, the long waiting throughout the night of wee Tom's birth...

God in heaven, how many goodbyes can a heart survive before it is broken beyond repair?

She sat on the edge of the bed beside Tahg, studying the dimly lit cabin as if to memorize it. They were ready to leave. The ship was in, most of their belongings loaded in the cart, the candles extinguished, all but one. Whittaker was holding the door to let the children file outside with some small bags and boxes. After a moment he followed them out, leaving Nora alone with Tahg and Morgan.

Still wrapped in his bedding like a babe, Tahg lay drifting in and out of his feverish dreams. Watching him, Nora stroked his arm beneath the rough wool blanket. His face was pinched and bloodless, white as a winding sheet except for his spotted red cheeks. His eyes were closed, his long, dark lashes edging lids that looked swollen and bruised. One thin hand clutched the bedding, and she reached to enfold it gently with her own.

He had never been strong, her eldest son. Even as a little boy he had appeared frail and delicate, tiring easily for no apparent reason. Could he possibly survive this night…and the nights to come?

Oh, merciful Lord, help my son. Wrap love and strength around him like these blankets, and protect him from the dangers of this night. Protect us all from the dangers of this night…

"I will bring the boy and his mother," she heard Morgan say to the burly man who had just stepped up to the door. "Keep a close eye on the children."

The man nodded, leaving the door ajar as he left.

"Nora?"

She looked up. Morgan had come to stand in front of her, a wool blanket tossed carelessly about his shoulders like a makeshift cloak. His face was lined with worry and fatigue, his eyes somber. He was holding something in his hand—an envelope.

"I should have given this to you before now," he said, "and did intend to. But one thing or another kept happening. Now"—his voice faltered, and he glanced away for an instant before going on—"now there is no time left. You will have to read it after you're aboard."

He seemed awkward, uncertain; a rare thing for Morgan. Nora's eyes went to the envelope in his hand.

"This is for you," he said quietly, pressing the envelope into the palm of her hand and closing her fingers around it. "It's from Michael."

Nora stared at him, then glanced down at the envelope in her hand. "Michael?" she repeated, frowning in confusion as she read her name on the front of the envelope.

He nodded. "Aye, our Michael. Michael Burke. I have written him much of the Hunger and the sad state of things across Ireland."

"But why is he writing to *me*?" Nora gaped up at him. "And how…why did he send it to you?"

Raking a hand through his hair, Morgan looked everywhere in the cabin but at her. "I received a letter as well," he said, turning away to stand at the window. "When I last wrote to Michael, I told him I hoped to convince you to make the voyage with Thomas and the children. He is simply offering to help you get settled, once you arrive. I…I imagine your letter is much the same as mine."

When he turned to face her, his expression had brightened, though it seemed to Nora that his tight smile was forced. "He has done well for himself, Michael has, being a policeman in New York City. He knows people—he'll be a great help to all of you."

Nora stared blankly at the envelope. "He still remembers us?"

"Did you think he wouldn't?" Morgan interrupted, crossing the room. "Michael was a good friend, still is. But tuck the letter away for now, Nora. We dare not delay our leaving any longer. After you're safely aboard the ship, you can—"

"Morgan!"

The harsh cry came from the large, powerfully built Cassidy. He stood framed in the open doorway, his face taut and white. "Riders coming! From the east!"

Morgan seemed to freeze, but only for an instant. Uttering a choked groan, he spun around, swinging Nora into his arms. "Take the lad with you!" he shouted to Cassidy, jerking his head toward Tahg's motionless form on the bed.

The brawny Cassidy scooped Tahg into his arms, hastily pulling the bedding about the boy's face.

By the time they reached the road, the others were already mounted, waiting. As Morgan swung Nora onto his own stallion's back, she saw Daniel John with Whittaker, astride the small mare.

"Get those children out of the cart!" Morgan shouted to his men. "Ward—bring the little boy here! Daniel John—get off the mare! I want you on a horse to yourself, up here with me and your mother! One of the lasses can ride with Whittaker. *Hurry!*" He swiveled then to Cassidy, and together they anchored Tahg securely on the big man's albino mount.

A youthful-looking man with an eye patch ran up and plopped Little Tom into Nora's arms, immediately trotting off. Even as she attempted to soothe the whimpering child, Nora quaked with fear. As if sensing his rider's panic, the big stallion threatened to shy. Snorting, he lashed out with his forefeet, quieting at once at an angry command from Morgan, who was frantically tossing some of the heavier tools over the side of the cart as an anguished Thomas looked on in despair.

Nora realized she was still clutching the letter from Michael in her hand; with trembling fingers she now tucked it down inside the front of her dress. Waiting for Morgan to return, she sat shivering at the feel of restrained power in the enormous creature beneath her. So long of leg and broad in girth was the red stallion that she could almost imagine she sat upon one of the giant steeds of ancient legend.

When Morgan finally swung up into the saddle behind her, she choked out a deep sigh of relief. Again the horse snorted, tossing his mane, but Morgan quickly settled him with a sharp litany in the Irish, hauling on the reins to turn him around. "Ride hard and keep your heads," he bit out, meeting the eyes of his men one by one for an instant. "We must not be stopped!"

He paused, turning his mount even more in order to appraise the caravan he would lead. "Ward," he said, jerking his head toward the youth with the eye patch, "you and Quigley stay behind. Do what you can to delay them. Stop them altogether if you can! We need time!"

He yanked the horse around, and the stallion reared as if to expel some of his excess energy. Coming down, he pawed the ground, then tore off down the road in a fury.

The wind smacked at Nora's face, sucking the breath out of her. Terrified, she felt her heart slam hard against her chest and begin to race wildly, mimicking the frantic rhythm of the thundering hoofbeats beneath her. She caught Little Tom against her in a smothering embrace, praying for divine protection as they flew over the mud-slicked, deeply rutted road.

From behind, Morgan's big arms locked her in a vise. She could feel his labored breathing at the back of her head. Just the thought that Morgan was rattled was enough to parlay her own fear into panic, but she fought it down. She must not pass her terror on to the child in her arms.

It was a ride straight out of a ghastly dream, a nightmare flight of horror through the fog-fingered darkness. The treacherous highway seemed to leap up like a snake as they pounded over it, while on either side trees strained their naked, gnarled branches toward them. The fog thickened as they neared the bay, wrapping its dank, cloying tendrils around both horse and rider until they were all but lost from one another's sight.

As they rode, Nora's blood chilled with a sense of evil all about them. She imagined the arms of the rag-clad corpses along the road reaching out, groping upward in a macabre attempt to pluck them from their horses, forcing them to join the roadside legion of the dead. It seemed for all the world as if the very pit of hell had opened, spewing its horde of demons into the fog to run them down. She could almost smell the stench of sulphur at her back.

The night seemed filled with the sounds of their desperation. Lathered horses pounded and snorted, anxious men lashed them to an even greater frenzy. Amid the smothered sobs of the children, Nora was certain she heard Tahg moan from somewhere behind her.

Suddenly wee Tom made a sharp cry, and Nora realized she must have clutched the boy too tightly in her terror. Quickly she dipped her head to murmur a comforting word in his ear, squeezing her eyes shut for an instant.

"There, ahead!"

At Morgan's cry, Nora's eyes snapped open. Directly ahead of them, at the far west end of the harbor, lay a three-masted ship bobbing gently in the bay waters. Draped in fog and silhouetted against the pale, moon-lit sky, the aging vessel looked like an eerie apparition.

A mixture of relief and alarm welled up in Nora at the sight of the ship. This was their goal, then, the end of the road. It might just as well have marked the end of her world. The very ground was being torn from under her feet. Any moment now she would be hurled into a vast unknown as dark and unfathomable as the great Atlantic itself.

Tears scalded her eyes as she glanced at Daniel John. His face set straight ahead, he leaned far forward on his brown-and-white horse, his eyes locked on the ship ahead.

"Morgan! They come!"

It was the youth with the eye patch, the one called Ward. He came roaring up through their ranks, his horse lathered and wild-eyed. *"Cotter's men!* They are coming through the village! Riding hard!"

As soon as they reached the pier, Morgan hurled himself down off the stallion, swinging Nora and Little Tom onto the ground.

Immediately he turned to yank Daniel John from the mare's back, giving him a firm shove toward Nora.

"Stay with your mother!" he ordered, meeting Ward as he dismounted.

The youth was clearly shaken. "They were too many!" he exclaimed, his face ashen. "They got past us! Quigley was shot—he is dead!" He stopped, wiped the back of his arm over his mouth, as he gasped for breath. "They are right behind us, Morgan! You must get away before you're taken!"

Except for Thomas and Johanna, who were still coming with the cart, the others had arrived and were dismounting. Now they gathered in close to listen.

Cassidy grabbed Morgan's arm. "Ward is right! For the love of heaven, man, get yourself out of here! We will see to your people!"

Morgan shook him off without a reply, then sent both him and Ward off to join the others.

For a moment, Nora could not think beyond the horror of the young Quigley lad, murdered on their behalf. Her gaze abruptly flew to Morgan, who had pulled his pistol free from his waistband and stood, waiting anxiously for Thomas.

Only now did the full extent of his sacrifice for his family—for them all—strike her. It could just as easily be *Morgan* lying back there in the mud, his life forfeited for their sake.

Hiking Little Tom against her shoulder, she clutched at Morgan's arm with her free hand. "He is right, Morgan! You *must* come with us! It's the only way! Sure, and you will hang if you stay here!"

He looked down at her, briefly covering her hand with his, his eyes searching hers as if to read her heart. "Believe me, *ma girsha,* you will never know just how much I want to come with you." He lifted his hand to her cheek.

They stood in silence for another moment. *Weariness. So much weariness filled those eyes that had once laughed and danced with the reflection of her love for him.*

Gradually a ribbon of fog wound its way between them, momentarily clouding their faces before drifting off over the water. Finally, with obvious reluctance, Morgan dropped his hand away. Taking Little Tom from her arms, he started off to help Thomas, who had just arrived with the cart.

Nora watched him go, his great, broad back bent as if straining beneath a formidable weight. For the first time in a long time she sensed the conflict in his soul, the fires that drove him. A terrible sorrow gripped her, a rush of loneliness to which she could give no name.

God in heaven, I do not want to leave him...how can I leave him so? He will be alone entirely...without Thomas...the children...Daniel John. Without me...

She forced the thought from her mind with the bitter reminder that

Morgan did not need her or anyone else. Hadn't he lived his entire life as if to prove that very fact?

Once the cart was unhitched, Morgan returned with Daniel John and Cassidy, who was again carrying Tahg in his strong arms. Grasping Daniel John's hand, Morgan pressed it to Nora's, joining them. "You must go now! Cotter's men will be on us any moment. It will not do for them to see you, especially, Daniel John. Thomas has all the passages," he said, glancing toward the ship. "You've only to go aboard. Cassidy will carry Tahg on for you."

Nora followed his gaze. A few shadowed figures had begun to appear on the lower deck, ghostly in the swirling mist. Some now started down the gangplank while others remained on the deck.

"The crew," Morgan said. "They will help you board." He paused, then urged her again, "Please, Nora—you dare not wait any longer!"

Their eyes met and held one last time. His gaze was hooded, distant. Nora felt as if a great chasm had opened between them.

"I will try to come aboard before you sail, to say goodbye," he said gruffly. "If not—" He stopped, looked at her, then at Daniel John, abruptly pulling them both into his arms. "If not, know that I will keep you both forever in my heart. There will never be a time when you are not with me."

Daniel John's eyes brimmed with tears, and Nora thought she would strangle on the knot of grief in her throat. Just as she would have made a last attempt to change Morgan's mind, the moment was shattered by a panicky shout from Thomas.

"Morgan! They are here!" His son in his arms, his little girls on either side of him, Thomas came lumbering toward them. In the distance behind him came a band of shouting men on horseback.

Morgan shoved Nora and Daniel John toward two of his men, yanking his pistol free as he spun around. "Sullivan, O'Dwyer—get everyone aboard! *Now!*"

Cotter's men came charging up, reining in their mounts just short of the pier.

"Go!" Morgan roared, shooting a look over his shoulder as he feverishly herded Thomas and the children onto the pier.

Somebody fired a shot. Horses shied, screaming and rearing. Morgan's two men lunged into the midst of the emigrants, frantically driving them toward the ship, shouting at the crew to help.

Gripping Daniel John's hand, Nora began to run. She looked back to find Cassidy, saw him coming right behind them, Tahg locked securely in his arms. Suddenly Nora stumbled, wrenching her ankle. She cried out, and Daniel John caught her around the waist, then pulled her onto the gangplank.

Halfway up, she looked back. Her last sight of Morgan saw him striding resolutely toward Cotter's men, his head high, his pistol aimed.

25

To Stand with the Gael

Shall mine eyes behold thy glory, O my country?
Shall mine eyes behold thy glory?
Or shall the darkness close around them, ere the sunblaze
Break at last upon thy story?

FANNY PARNELL (1854–1882)

Frozen by indecision, Evan teetered on the end of the pier, just outside the ragged line of emigrants hurrying toward the ship. He watched them in their race to get aboard for only a moment before turning and going back the way he came.

With three of his men diverted at the ship and Quigley dead, Fitzgerald was left with only the youth called Ward and Blake, a thin man with graying hair and a sharp edge of flint in his eyes. These three now stood together a short distance away from the entrance to the pier, guns leveled at Cotter's men.

The two rough-looking bodyguards, Gleeson and Sharkey, along with the constable, had already dismounted and stood glaring angrily at Fitzgerald and his men across the slight rise of muddy ground that sloped between them. At their backs waited half a dozen others, still mounted in an undisciplined row, like ill-trained troops reluctant to attack.

Evan was unarmed, but he felt a need to at least stand with Fitzgerald. Moving cautiously, he went to stand almost directly behind the three Irishmen. Just as he did, Fitzgerald stepped out, his pistol aimed directly at the head of the biggest and most brutish of the two bodyguards.

His voice was deceptively soft, laced with an unmistakable threat when he spoke. "You are outnumbered, Pat. You'd do well to be off with your lads right now while you still can."

Gleeson glanced over his shoulder at the line of men mounted behind him, then turned back to Fitzgerald and said pointedly, "I think not."

"Then think again," Fitzgerald said quietly. "One of my lads is worth three or more of those poor *goms*. That is no secret to either of us."

"Don't be a fool, Fitzgerald! Whatever daft scheme you and that traitorous Englishman have cooked up, it is over and done with now! You and the boy are coming with us, so flush him out and be quick about it!"

Gleeson was waving his gun in every direction, his eyes as unfocused as those of a drunken sailor. Swallowing nervously, Evan moved up a step, then another, edging over to the side of young Ward.

Fitzgerald was smiling—a terrible rictus of a smile that brought a chill to Evan's blood. "Ah, Pat, just drop your pistol, why don't you? Else I will have to drop *you* and leave my men to finish off the rest of your lads while your dust is still settling. Be the good fellow, now, and lay down the gun. We both know you never could shoot straight enough to hit the side of a barn. You're next to blind, and that's the truth."

It did seem to Evan that Fitzgerald and his men had the others at a distinct disadvantage, despite the fact they were outnumbered. The men still on horseback looked to be the very dregs of the village—paid housewreckers, most likely—and, as best as he could tell, unarmed. The constable, a pawnchy, seemingly timid soul, was brandishing his pistol in a palsied hand, but if he managed to wound anyone at all, Evan felt sure it would be entirely by accident. As for Fitzgerald and his men, they all had weapons, and Evan felt certain they were more than adept at using them.

Yet something in the eyes of the two named Gleeson and Sharkey made the back of his neck prickle. *Hatred.* The kind of mindless, depraved hatred that seemed to have no purpose beyond destroying the object of its malice. They would kill Fitzgerald simply because they were paid to kill him, never mind that he was one of their own countrymen, and a patriot at that.

Unexpectedly, the constable made a stab at asserting his authority. "Now, see here, Fitzgerald," he said lamely, "you're deep enough into the stew as it is! You are a wanted man! Throw down your weapon and deliver up the Kavanagh boy before this goes any further. To persist will only bring more grief upon your family and you!"

It was the wrong thing to say; Evan knew it at once. He had already seen Fitzgerald's fierce protectiveness for his brother and family, his unshakable resolve to ensure the safety of his loved ones. Watching him now, Evan sensed the rage shuddering behind every taut line of that powerful frame.

The burning green eyes seemed to bore a path right through the constable's weak bravado. "Well, then, if my hanging is already assured," Fitzgerald said, his voice hard, "I see no reason for further caution, do you? Ah, perhaps you'd step just a bit closer to Gleeson and his comrade, constable—in case I'm forced to deal with the three of you at once."

The policeman blanched, hesitating. Fitzgerald's deadly smile remained locked in place, and after another moment the constable stumbled backward, lowering his gun and finally dropping it to the ground. Immediately the man shot a furious glare at the backs of Gleeson and Sharkey, as if this entire debacle were their doing.

"Thank you, constable," Fitzgerald said with that same icy calm. "Now, Pat, if you and Mr. Sharkey there will oblige me by doing likewise, all you lads can still manage a night's sleep in your own beds."

When Gleeson and Sharkey made no move but simply stood, glaring at him, Fitzgerald glanced at Ward, who gave him a brief, answering nod. With faultless timing and before anyone knew what was happening, they shot the pistols from the hands of the other two men.

Murder in his eyes, Gleeson started to lunge, curbing his charge when Fitzgerald raised the gun and aimed it steadily at the man's head. "I will not miss, Pat," he said quietly. "We both know that I will not miss." He stood waiting, as still and as implacable as a mountain. At the same time, Ward sprang across the rise and collected both weapons.

Gleeson cursed Fitzgerald with an obscene oath but dropped back. Beside him, Sharkey now raised his hands in the air, shaking his head as if to indicate he was finished with it all.

Watching them with the keen eye of a hawk, Fitzgerald nodded slowly. "Aye, that's better. Now, then, you may get back onto your horses and take yourselves off to your homes and hearth fires. But carefully, lads," he warned, his voice tightening, "very carefully."

Seconds passed, during which the two men cast surly looks at each other. Behind them, the rank of mounted men sat deadly silent, as if holding a collective breath. Finally, their faces set in grudging defeat, both Gleeson and Sharkey began to back away, then turned and stalked off to mount their horses. Gleeson gave the reins a vicious snap, shouting to the others to follow as he spurred his horse hard and galloped off like a man possessed.

Moments later—though it seemed hours—Evan was still struggling to catch a steadying breath. Shaking his head a little to clear it, he leveled his eyeglasses on the bridge of his nose with an index finger. "Well," he said pointlessly, then again. "Well, that would seem to b-be that."

Fitzgerald turned to him with a faint, grim smile. "And what did you have in mind by sticking around here, Mr. Whittaker? Were you planning to plead for my life if it became necessary?"

Evan twisted his mouth with distaste. "I thought to d-do just that, if you really want to know, though the idea of groveling to those…heathens made me almost ill."

"Don't you realize at all the fix you are in, man?" Fitzgerald asked with a wondering frown. "By now you are as much a priority on Cotter's hanging list as I am."

"Oh, I kn-know that well enough, of course," Evan replied. He was only too well aware of what he had done to himself, had been aware of it since the moment he made his decision to go against Cotter. "I suppose I was hoping *they* didn't know it yet."

His eyes glinting with tired amusement, Fitzgerald put a hand to Evan's shoulder and started toward the pier. "Walk with me, my friend. We will go on board to say a proper goodbye."

With the moon hidden behind a thick bank of clouds, it was difficult to make out anything other than shadows on the ship. As they started down the old, sagging pier, Evan was keenly aware of being dwarfed by Fitzgerald's towering shadow. He realized, though, that he was no longer intimidated by the Gael's impressive size. The big Irishman now treated him with respect—indeed, had called him "my friend," and the warmth behind his manner somehow served as a vast equalizer.

Fitzgerald stopped for a moment, drawing in a long sigh of exhaustion. "So, then, Whittaker, what do you do now? Go back to England and seek different employment? Or will you try to mend things with Gilpin?"

Evan felt something warm begin to swell inside him, and he knew before the words ever left his mouth that they were not altogether his own. "No, I really d-don't think I'm meant to go back to England. At least n-not yet."

Glancing down at him, Fitzgerald lifted a questioning brow. "What, then?"

"I suppose," Evan replied uncertainly, "I suppose I m-might just as well stay here for now. Perhaps I could be of some assistance to you and your men?" he posed hopefully.

Fitzgerald shot Evan a look that plainly questioned his sanity. "You can't do that, man! Why, Cotter would have a noose around your neck before sundown tomorrow! You're mad to even think it! Go and get on that ship, why don't you? There are extra passages paid in full—use one of them for yourself! You've more than earned it."

Boarding the ship had already occurred to Evan. He had some money with him, more saved, and indeed he had always wanted to see the States. But something in him was loathe to leave Fitzgerald just yet.

What, Lord? What more can I possibly do for this man? He's obviously dead set on braving it out here in Ireland.

"What about *you*?" he blurted out, turning to face the big man at his side. "You've a p-price on your head, your family and…and friends…will be gone—what would keep *you* here now?"

Fitzgerald looked off into the bay, delaying his answer. When he finally spoke, his tone was vague and infinitely weary. "Madness, some would say, and I'm not so sure but what they would be right." He stood, facing the ship, his magnificent head lifted slightly to the sky as if he had in mind any moment to fling heavenward a myriad of unanswered questions. One long-fingered hand absently chafed the ragged neckline of his improvised cloak, the other clenched and unclenched at his side in a kind of mindless rhythm.

Watching him, Evan caught a fleeting glimpse of one of the medieval clan chieftains: a provincial Irish prince, perhaps, with a torn woolen blanket for his royal robe and an elusive veil of fog for his crown. A prince who ruled a ruined kingdom in which his own dying populace was breaking his heart.

"I wed myself to an island," Fitzgerald was saying, tugging Evan back from his thoughts as they resumed walking. "For better or for worse, she is mine. There are changes on the wind, things coming, to which I am committed, both for country and out of loyalty to friends. I will stay," Fitzgerald said quietly, "because I must. More than that, I cannot explain."

They were almost at the ship. A raw, wet wind was whipping up again, and Evan shivered, both from the sting in the air and from the aura of fatalism he sensed in Fitzgerald's manner. He smelled the brackish waters of the bay, felt the heavy gloom and dread of this night closing in, threatening to engulf him.

A few scattered crew members were milling about on the decks and along the wharf. Looking toward the steerage deck, Evan could just make out Fitzgerald's brother and the others standing in a line, as if waiting to be shown where to go. Ship lanterns, combined with thin wisps of moonlight, haloed the dull waters of the bay, washing both him and Fitzgerald in a dim, wavering glow.

Fitzgerald lifted a hand to those on deck, then stepped onto the broad wooden gangplank. Impulsively, Evan caught his arm, stopping him. "I *wish* I could help you!" he choked out, meaning it with all his being.

Fitzgerald turned, raking Evan's face with a searching look. "Do you mean that, *mo chara*...my friend?" he asked quietly. "Because you *can* help me."

"Of course, I m-mean it! You've only to tell me how."

"If you really want to help me, man, then get on board that ship with my family! It breaks my heart every time I think of the fear they must be feeling, will be feeling throughout the days and weeks ahead. Thomas and Nora—they know nothing of cities, of strangers...of the world. They are innocents." He paused, then added grimly, "And both of us know, do we not, what evil the world is capable of wreaking upon the innocent?"

Evan stared at the man, seized by the burning, desperate appeal in his eyes.

Is this it, then, Lord? Is this what You want me to do?

Almost at once, filling his heart, illuminating his thoughts, the answer came. "All right," he said quietly, turning to stare at the ship. "I will go."

"Do you mean it?" Fitzgerald pressed Evan's hand with a dangerously tight grip. "You will go with them? Look after them?"

"As if they were m-my own," Evan replied softly, knowing in his heart that, in a way he would never understand, they had indeed become his own.

Stepping up onto the deck, Fitzgerald continued to grip Evan's arm. "You are a rare man, Evan Whittaker, a truly good and noble man." He paused, giving a small nod. "And a brave one as well."

Evan uttered a short, dry laugh. "I am anything but b-brave, Fitzgerald.

Most of my life, at least, I have been the m-milksop Cotter believes me to be." Evan pulled in a long sigh. "No," he said, shaking his head, feeling inexplicably sad, "I am not b-brave."

"No coward would do what you have done this night, Whittaker, certainly not for a family of strangers. Only a man with a heroic heart."

"You are wrong about that, my friend," Evan said softly. "Only a m-man with a changed heart, a captured heart."

Fitzgerald stared at him quizzically. "I do not believe your heart has ever required changing, Evan Whittaker. I believe it has always been good and brave."

"My heart is the heart of a *c-coward!*" Evan bit out, making no attempt to mask his self-contempt. "Until this past week, the only courage or daring I've ever known, I managed to experience from reading adventure novels! No," he protested, unwilling that Fitzgerald should see him for anything other than what he was, "only the yoke of Christ gives my heart any goodness or worth whatsoever."

Fitzgerald's eyes narrowed skeptically, and Evan hurried to explain. "Christ said to shoulder His yoke, to take His b-burden and learn from Him. But when I first accepted that burden and said yes to His yoke, I did not dream I was agreeing to help bear the burden of the entire world—a burden that includes the suffering of all mankind, throughout the ages."

He paused, gratified by Fitzgerald's intent expression. Growing more and more aware of the Lord's loving desire to communicate with this hurting, complex man, Evan stopped to wait on his Savior's leading.

When it came, even *he* was surprised. "I think, Morgan Fitzgerald, that you have tried in your own way to d-do exactly that...to take on the burden of your entire country, your people, and help them bear their suffering. But in doing so, you have neglected—even rejected—the very p-power that would enable you to withstand such an infinite, insufferable burden."

He was listening. He was hearing. At least for this brief moment, the Lord finally had Morgan Fitzgerald's attention.

Evan put a hand to the Irishman's brawny arm, felt the muscles tense beneath his touch. "When I was just a boy, my father told me, 'Trust God, and be brave.' I always thought I trusted God, but I never had it in me to be brave." He paused. "Now, I think I understand. When I finally trusted God fully, to lead me as He wished, the bravery followed."

Evan looked intently into Fitzgerald's eyes. "The two are connected, don't you see? In trusting God, I ultimately found the courage to do His will. And you, Morgan Fitzgerald—" He took a deep breath, then rushed to his conclusion. "Perhaps in being *courageous*, you will ultimately find your way to *trusting* God."

Evan paused, amazed at his ability to speak to this Irish giant so directly. "My friend, you are a very b-big man, a strong, powerful man. But even *you* are not man enough to bear the pain of a nation, to carry the burden of an entire people, unless you in turn allow Jesus Christ to hold *your* heart and carry *you*."

The silence that hung between them was crowned with Fitzgerald's unvoiced questions and Evan's unanswered prayers. To Evan's surprise, the other man did not appear offended; on the contrary, the big Irishman was watching him with a look of keen interest and something else—something Evan thought might have been regret.

"Fitzgerald…if I go with your family as you have asked…if I d-do that, will you promise to do something for *me*?"

The Irishman's eyes grew even narrower, and Evan hurried to assure him. "Actually, it's not for me. It's for you. But it will give me a certain peace if you agree."

Fitzgerald's nod was grudging, his blanket-cloak falling back from his shoulders as he crossed his massive arms on his chest.

"All I ask," Evan said quietly, "is that you take the time to think about what I've said…about your burdened heart, and what Christ can do with it."

"He owned my heart once, when I was a lad," Fitzgerald said tightly. "These days He has no use for it. It is far too worn and tarnished."

"God is not put off by tarnished hearts, my friend. The only kind of heart He cannot use is one of stone that can no longer be broken." Evan swallowed down his compassion for the look of utter pain that now passed over the Irishman's face. "Fitzgerald, I do not know very much about you—not very much at all. But this much I *do* know—your heart has most assuredly not turned to stone."

He paused. He could see the other man struggling to conceal whatever tide of emotion was assailing him, but he made the decision to plunge ahead and finish what he had begun. "A man like you, empowered by a God like ours, would be a formidable instrument of change. For your people, for your nation—perhaps even for other nations. I believe with all my heart that God intends to shake you. I don't pretend for a moment to know how, but I believe He means to have your attention...and your heart...and that one way or another, He will. Be warned, Morgan Fitzgerald, for the Ancient of Days and the Shepherd of your soul is in pursuit of you...*and there is no hiding from Him.*"

26

One Last Goodbye

But alas for his country!—her pride is gone by,
And that spirit is broken which never would bend.
O'er the ruin her children in secret must sigh,
For 'tis treason to love her, and death to defend.

THOMAS MOORE (1779–1852)

Morgan sent his men off the ship as soon as he went on board. "I want you to split up," he said. "Tell Ward and Blake to ride to Cotter's place and wait for me there. I'll be along shortly." When Cassidy would have interrupted, he waved him off. "You knew we would settle with Cotter. That is for later. For now, the rest of you go back up the road and stand guard while you wait for me. Gleeson and the others could always change their minds and turn back, you know."

The emigrants were still waiting on the steerage deck when Morgan went aboard. He found Nora crouched in a dim corner, huddled over Tahg, who lay quietly where Cassidy had placed him; both little girls and wee Tom sat one on either side of her. Daniel John, his knees pulled up to his chin, was perched close by, leaning against a stack of boxes as he watched two rough-looking sailors arguing in front of a rusted porthole. A few feet away, at the railing, stood Thomas and Whittaker, gazing out at the pier.

Morgan intended to have a look at their quarters below, before leaving, but for now it was more important that he see Nora alone. Watching her, crouched there in the shadows with her ailing son, he hesitated, then touched her lightly on the shoulder. "Nora?"

254

She looked up, and he caught her hands, raising her to her feet. "I want to talk with your mother," he told Daniel John. "Stay here with Tahg until we return."

Guiding her amidships, he sought an isolated corner and led her to it. "We've only a moment," he said. "I should be getting off soon, and I still want to see your quarters before you sail."

There was just enough reflection from the ship's lanterns that he could see her face. Her eyes were enormous, glistening in the shadows as she stared up at him.

Morgan was all too aware of her fear. Taking her hand, he lifted it to his mouth and pressed his lips to it. "It will be all right, *ma girsha*," he said, lowering her hand but holding on to it. "Truly it will. I know this is a hard thing, but it is the *right* thing, for all of you. I do believe that with all my heart."

Looking down at their clasped hands, Nora said in a voice that was little more than a whisper, "Sure, it might not be quite so hard a thing if you were going with us, Morgan."

He winced. Releasing her hand, he tilted her chin upward, forcing her to meet his gaze. The anguish in her eyes made him want to weep.

"Morgan, please. It's not too late."

Gently, he pressed a finger to her lips to silence her, sadly shaking his head. "Hush, *macushla*. We will not spend these last few moments arguing with each other. There has already been enough of that."

He had not expected her to cry. When he saw the tears spilling over from her eyes, he caught her to him and held her. "Nora...ah, lass, don't, please don't. You will unman me...you are tearing me to pieces."

She stunned him entirely by flinging her arms about his neck, crying, "Morgan, go with us! *Please*—go with us!"

His heart aching, he eased her away from him just enough to frame her face between his hands, to lose himself in her eyes one last time. "A part of me *does* go with you, will always be with you. Ah, lass, I could never forget you. Don't you know that by now? But won't you at least try to understand, for my sake? If ever you loved me, even a little, please try to understand why I must stay."

Weeping openly now, Nora clung to him. "I have *always* loved you, Morgan! Always! Even with Owen, there was a part of me that still belonged to you!"

As soon as she uttered the words, she put a fist to her mouth as if to stop them, too late. Seeing her dismay, Morgan tried to soothe her, but instead only seemed to make things worse. Now she sobbed even more furiously. "God *forgive* me! I should never have said such a thing to you."

She was destroying him. With a soft moan, Morgan buried his face in her hair, fighting back his own scalding tears. "I am a great fool, Nora, but loving you as you deserved to be loved would have taken so much more than I had to give. Loving you, I would have lived for you, rather than for what I have always known my destiny to be. Forgive me, sweetheart," he whispered into the damp warmth of her hair. "Forgive this fool."

Blinded by his own unshed tears, he gave in to his heart, surrendering the last remaining part of the love he had tried all these years to withhold from her. He kissed her, despising himself for all the joy he had lost, all the years he had wasted, yet all the while knowing she had been better off without him.

She amazed him by kissing him back, fiercely, desperately. He felt his heart fall away, completely shattered. Dragging his mouth from hers, he gripped her shoulders, pleading with his eyes. He dared not hold her a moment more or he would never leave the ship. "We must get back," he murmured with regret, setting her gently away from him.

Unable to face the desolation in her eyes, he looked away for an instant. "Your passages are paid and your belongings have been loaded, so you are ready." Groping for something to ease the pain of the moment, he faced her again. "Did I tell you, our friend Whittaker has decided to go with you?"

"Whittaker?" she said, wiping at her eyes with both hands. "Whittaker is going to America?"

Morgan forced a smile. "Aye, that he is. So you will have the benefit of his considerable wits at your disposal for whatever you may need. He is already half in love with you, you see, so whatever you want, sure, and you've only to ask."

When his teasing failed to bring the hoped-for smile, Morgan lifted his hand to brush away a strand of hair clinging to her temple, then bent to kiss her lightly on the cheek. "Go with God, Nora *a gra*," he said, strangling on the words. "And know that the best part of my heart goes with you."

"Touching, Fitzgerald. Touching, indeed. In truth, your heart will be the only part of you going anywhere at all—now or ever."

Nora screamed and Morgan, stunned, pulled her with him as he whipped around in the direction of the voice.

Smiling an ugly, vengeful smile, George Cotter hauled himself through the open doorway of a nearby hatch, the bailiff on his heels. Each was holding a gun.

✥

Daniel heard his mother scream and scrambled to his feet, his heart pounding like a wild thing as he tore around the corner.

He saw them at once, standing toward the middle of the ship—his mother and Morgan, held at gunpoint by two men. The gunmen's backs were toward him, but it took only an instant to recognize Cotter and Harry Macken, the bailiff.

Whittaker and Thomas ran up alongside him, but Daniel could not take his eyes from the scene amidships.

"Get *back*, boy!" Whittaker ordered in a harsh whisper. "You must not let them see you!"

Daniel stared at the Englishman with incredulity, his pulse thundering in his ears. "How did *they* get aboard? Where are Morgan's men?"

Whittaker shook his head in frustration. "The men are already gone— I saw them leave." He paused. "As for how those two got aboard, I doubt a bailiff would have much difficulty talking his way onto a ship docked in a harbor under his jurisdiction."

"We must *do* something! They will kill them both! *What can we do?*"

The three of them looked on in horror as Morgan, facing them, pushed Daniel's mother behind his own large body and then stood, one hand lifted as if in warning, the other at his waist, close to his pistol.

Thomas put a restraining hand on Daniel's arm. "They won't hurt Nora, lad—it's Morgan they—"

He jumped, as did Daniel and Whittaker when Cotter shot his gun into the air. Morgan threw up both hands, as if in surrender.

Daniel could just make out the taut mask of rage contorting Morgan's face as he stood, hands raised, legs spread, facing Cotter and Macken.

Alarmed, he saw his mother step forward, moving up to Morgan's side.

Thomas tugged at his arm, whispering urgently, "Come, lad! Go back to your brother and stay there! If they see you, it will only make things worse!"

Daniel, only vaguely aware of Thomas's plea, was intent on figuring a way to help Morgan and his mother. At that moment, two sailors rounded the corner near the hatch where Cotter and the bailiff were standing. Daniel's hopes rose, but only for a moment. The crewmen stopped short as Macken turned his gun on them and motioned them toward the hatch, where they quickly disappeared.

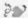

As soon as the sailors backed down the hatch, Cotter again demanded they produce Daniel John. Lowering his gun, he leveled it directly at Morgan's heart. "You will turn over the boy, Fitzgerald, or I will kill you—right after I shoot the mother, that is." He glanced at Nora with a malevolent smile that made Morgan ache to smash his face in.

"No!" Nora cried, clutching Morgan's arm, staring at him in terror. "Morgan—" She broke off and turned back to Cotter. "My son isn't here!" she cried. "He's still back in the village—"

Morgan cringed. She was rambling, and he feared she would try something foolish. His mind raced furiously as he gripped her arm.

"You will watch her die, Fitzgerald," snarled Cotter. "Is that what you want?"

Morgan's brain boiled in rage and uncertainty. Never had he felt such hatred. Were it not for Nora, he would take his chances and go for both of them, never mind the guns.

Suddenly Nora twisted free of his grasp. *"No!"* she screamed wildly, flying at Cotter. *"You'll not have my son!"*

Morgan gaped in horror, then snaked out his arm to stop her. Too late. He lunged, charging forward. Now he had her, yanked her back, shoved her hard behind him.

Suddenly a wave of shouts came rolling toward them. His head shot up to see Daniel John and Thomas barreling up the deck, followed by Whittaker, all three charging madly into their midst.

Cotter whipped around, his gun flailing. Seeing him, Thomas flung one long arm out, knocking Daniel John to the right, toward the railing and out of the way.

At the same time, Whittaker rushed toward Macken. The bailiff aimed his gun at the Englishman, fired, and missed.

Seeing his chance, Morgan shoved Nora toward the railing and Daniel John. Pulling his pistol as he spun, he hurled himself at Cotter.

Too late, he saw the agent raise the gun and aim it toward Thomas.

"*No*, Thomas, stop!" Morgan shouted, throwing himself at Cotter. Cotter fired once, then again as Morgan tackled him.

꙳

Thomas had began to run the instant Daniel John broke loose. He had ever been slow, but now he prayed wings for his heels as he went roaring up the deck, shouting like a madman in hopes of diverting the armed men from Nora and Morgan, slowing only enough to fling Daniel John out of the way.

His mind registered the sight of Morgan grabbing Nora, pushing her away, toward the railing. For an instant Thomas thought he did fly as he flung himself toward Cotter.

Then a hot, jagged pain pierced his chest, stopping him in mid-flight. Amazed, saddened, he felt himself drop from the sky.

As he fell, he cried—first, his brother's name, and then his Savior's.

꙳

Mad with rage and horror, Morgan saw Thomas fall, then Whittaker. With a thunderous roar, he yanked Cotter away from his brother's body, downing him with one vicious blow to the head, then another before finally putting a bullet through his chest. The agent's gun went spinning crazily across the deck and into the bay.

Morgan turned. Whittaker lay huddled on the deck, his face a grimace of pain, blood gushing from between his fingers as he clutched his upper left arm.

For a fleeting instant Morgan glanced from Whittaker to his brother's still form, sprawled on the deck, blood pouring from the gaping hole in his chest. An ancient blood-beast reared up inside him. His lungs exploded with a murderous scream, and he hurled the full force of his powerful frame at Harry Macken.

The bailiff was already backing away, stumbling and waving his gun in midair as he went. Morgan closed the distance between them in two great leaps. He sprang, throwing himself on the bailiff's back, knocking Macken's pistol from his hand with a fierce blow.

The bailiff was down, spread-eagled on his back and jabbering wildly. Morgan pinned him in place with one huge hand splayed in the middle of his chest, raised the gun in his other hand and leveled it at the bailiff's head.

He stared at the wailing man beneath him, saw the spittle running out of the side of his mouth, the tears of terror pouring down his cheeks. Cursing him, he tossed his own gun onto the deck and began to batter Macken with his bare hands.

It wasn't enough. Yanking him up from the deck, he started to slam the nearly unconscious man up and down on the deck, hard enough to shatter his spine.

All the while the monster inside him raged, urging him on, whipping him into madness.

It took three sailors to pull Fitzgerald off the bailiff, barely in time to save Macken's life.

Evan looked on in sick horror as Fitzgerald, torn free of the man he would have killed, stretched to his full height, raving. More awful still was the slow look of devastation that settled over his face when he turned his wild-eyed gaze upon his slain brother, still sprawled grotesquely at his feet.

Weak as he was from the gunshot wound in his upper arm, Evan could only make a feeble attempt to comfort the grieving Irishman before dropping to the deck in a near-faint. Nora Kavanagh and the boy, Daniel, did their best to get through to Fitzgerald, but there was no reaching him. Throwing them off, he flung himself across his brother's body, then lifted the dead man into his arms and clutched him against his chest. There he remained, rocking his slain brother, his stunned, vacant stare fixed on nothing.

Those close by could just make out the soft muttering that fell from his lips like tears that had found a voice.

"Why, Thomas...*why*? *Yours* was the life worth saving, not *mine*...not mine...why did you do it, brother? Why?"

Almost an hour later, some of the crew returned with a magistrate and two constables. It took every man of them, plus a number of sailors, to pry the stricken, dazed Fitzgerald from his brother's body and clamp his legs in irons.

෨෨

When it was over, both Thomas Fitzgerald and Cotter lay dead, Macken injured almost past reviving.

The authorities arrested Morgan Fitzgerald, as well as Ward and Blake, who were captured while waiting for their leader outside Cotter's house. The other three Young Irelanders got away.

Evan wept with Nora Kavanagh and young Daniel as the police led Fitzgerald off in irons. The Gael spoke not a word as he stumbled into the night, his shoulders sagging, his great head bowed. Evan had all he could do to keep the devastated young widow and her son from bolting from the ship and running after him. He eventually managed to restrain them only with the reminder that the three orphaned children would desperately need their help.

Long past midnight, Tahg Kavanagh died, before the ship ever set sail for America.

PART THREE

SONG OF FAREWELL

The Passage

My harp is tuned to mourning,
and my flute to the sound of wailing.
JOB 30:31 (NIV)

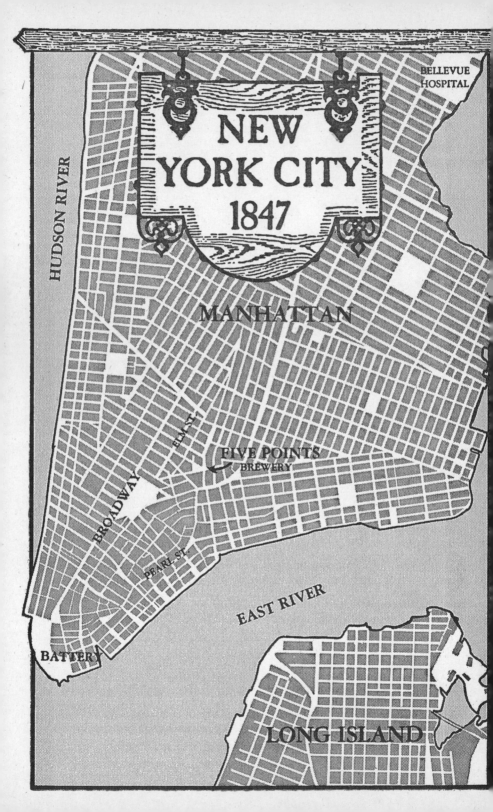

27

27

Erin, Farewell

The minstrel fell—but the foeman's chain
Could not bring his proud soul under;
The harp he loved ne'er spoke again,
For he tore its chords asunder;
And said, "No chains shall sully thee,
Thou soul of love and bravery!
Thy songs were made for the pure and free,
They shall never sound in slavery!"

Thomas Moore (1779–1852)

A day had come and gone, and soon it would be dawn again. They were now twenty-four hours away from Killala. A full day separated from home. A lifetime removed from all that was safely familiar.

They had set sail just before daybreak, stealing as silently and smoothly out of the bay as the mind drifts from the edge of wakefulness to a dream. Indeed, to Daniel the *Green Flag* did seem more dream than fact. As soon as he realized they were weighing anchor, he felt himself suspended in a web between reality and illusion. He knew where he was and where he was going, and yet he felt as if at any moment he might awaken in his own bed at home.

He had done his utmost to commit to memory one last view of Mayo's wild, forlorn coast—the sheltering mountains, the immense, heavy sky, the dark waters of the bay, the round tower. But at the last moment there had been such confusion, so much panic and commotion, he could only turn his back on the harbor and stumble to his quarters with the others.

Afterward, he had felt the most terrible dread that he was leaving behind something infinitely precious, something essential to his very being. It was more than the anxiety of being uprooted, more than grief for all he was losing. Throughout the sleepless night, the dark shadows of foreboding deepened, engulfing him, overwhelming him. He felt as if a piece of his heart had been torn from his body and hurled overboard into the sea.

Now he sat on the hard edge of his bunk, staring into the darkness of the steerage quarters, absorbing the sounds and smells of the ship—all unpleasant. It was still dark outside the four small portholes, and almost as dark inside, amid the rancid, filthy bunks. Only two lanterns swayed from the wooden ceiling to shed a dim light on their crowded quarters.

Above the constant creaks and groans of the aging hull droned a steady wailing from passengers who had boarded at other ports before Killala. Much louder were the breathless, agonized moans of those suffering from seasickness. From at least half a dozen bunks came the unmistakable sound of retching. The very walls seemed to ooze dank, foul odors, saturating the air itself with despair.

Daniel's stomach pitched suddenly, then settled. He glanced in his mother's direction, two aisles across, but the coarse jute curtain separating the women's quarters from the men's had been pulled almost all the way closed. He could catch only a glimpse of her berth. He hoped she was sleeping, hoped even more she would not dream.

His gaze now came to rest on Whittaker, in the bunk beside him. The Englishman lay unmoving, eyes closed, his breathing shallow. His arm had been tended by the ship's surgeon, a Dr. Leary, a tall, gruff man who seemed kind enough, though he fairly reeked of the pungent odor of whiskey and tobacco.

The berths were unbelievably small and crowded—pine shelves with iron bedsteads connected to the beams. They were less than the width of the back of a man's coat, yet each bunk housed at least four people. Daniel, Whittaker, and Little Tom had been assigned a berth already occupied by a widowed farmer from Galway, while Daniel's mother shared hers with the two Fitzgerald girls and a surly young woman named Alice.

Daniel gripped his knees with his hands, staring down at the floor. He still felt somewhat dazed, oddly detached from his present surroundings. Like a sleepwalker wandering through a house crammed with unfamiliar occupants, he was aware of his fellow passengers only as they hindered his freedom of movement, not with any real awareness of their individual needs or misery.

There had been no true goodbyes for them—no final farewells, no pipes to play them off, no women to keen for their going. Tragedy had set the wind at their backs. Death had been their valedictory, grief their song of farewell.

Even now, hearing the groaning of the ship's timbers, the mournful bleat of a fog horn, the echoing cries of misery from other voyagers who lay suffering in the depths of steerage, Daniel felt a strangely painful need, an aching urgency to say goodbye, to *separate* himself from all that had gone before this moment. He was seized by an inexplicable longing to make a final farewell to the small whitewashed cottage in which he had been born and spent his childhood, to the ancient round tower upon which he had focused so many of his questions and dreams—and, of course, to Morgan, who had sacrificed the one thing he prized most—his freedom—in order to guarantee theirs.

His eyes traveled down to the foot of his bunk, where he had placed the Kavanagh harp. Despite the fact that his brother had seldom played the ancient instrument, by rights it had belonged to Tahg, as the eldest son. Now it fell to Daniel to preserve it and the long history of tradition that went with it. The sight of the well-loved instrument should have been comforting, he supposed, if for nothing else but its familiarity and ties to the past. But at this moment he could find no comfort in the harp, or in anything else.

Instead, he found himself wondering what had become of *Morgan's* harp, and the thought made the fist of grief in his throat swell even more. Morgan's harp, his hefty box of writings, his few worn books—all had been tucked inside the saddlebags across Pilgrim's back.

A new thought struck him now, bringing a flood of hot tears to his eyes: What would become of *Pilgrim*? Nobody else could ride that great beast, nobody other than Morgan, who, though he ranted and raved at the animal, was fiercely attached to him.

He did not know which pain pierced most deeply—the loss of Tahg and Thomas to death, or the loss of Morgan to Ireland. Each stab of sorrow seemed to rip at a different part of his heart.

God, help me…help me to get past my own pain so I can help my mother,

be a source of strength to her, and to Katie and Johanna and wee Tom. God,
help me to be a man...

⁊⊛⋗

Nora had known loneliness as a child—the pain of rejection, the shame
of being the daughter of the village strumpet, hungry and ragged and
unloved. But never had she known the loneliness, the emptiness of spirit
that seized her now.

Over the past months she had forced herself to move through one tide
of grief after another, staggering, stumbling through her own agony without ever completely surrendering to it. Tahg's illness, his dependence on
her, had been enough to keep her going.

Now Tahg was gone, and she suddenly found herself not only paralyzed by the enormity of all she had lost but, for the first time in years,
unneeded. There was no longer a loving husband depending on her, no
wide-eyed little girl, no ailing father-in-law, no bedridden son. She still
had Daniel John, of course, but he didn't need her, not really. He was
healthy, would soon be a man grown, and already was showing the first
stirrings of independence.

So much change, so much loss. Family, home, even country—gone.
Friends, too. Catherine...Thomas...Morgan—

She would not think about Morgan...

But she could not stop the thought of Thomas—dear, good, kindhearted Thomas, who had ever put his family and friends before himself,
even to the point of sacrificing his own life for his brother. They had buried
him at sea, along with Tahg, only hours after the ship left the bay. Somehow Whittaker, weak as he was, had convinced the ship's captain to allow
it, thereby sparing them all the agony of leaving their loved ones behind
to lie in unmarked graves.

That alone was a great deal more concession, Nora was certain, than
would ultimately be afforded Morgan Fitzgerald.

Again she tried to shake off the thought of him. Odd, how the sound
of his name still pierced her heart, even now. Should it not have made
a difference, she wondered dully, finally hearing from his own lips that
his love for her had been as real, as impossible to deny as hers for him?
Shouldn't it have helped somehow, made things easier?

No, no, of course it made no difference. He was lost to her, as good as dead. They would hang him, that much was sure. They would lock him inside an airless cell, and that in itself would all but kill him. Then they would hang him and toss him into a common pit on the bog.

And hadn't the man done everything but lead himself there by his own rope?

Oh, Morgan, Morgan, you fool! Was it really worth it all, now that it is over? Was it worth the death of your brother, the death of your honor…and our love? Was it worth your life, Morgan?

Gone—everything was gone, torn away from her one piece at a time, like old fabric heedlessly rent and discarded. Daniel John was all she had left, and even for him she could not stir herself to feel, to care again.

She heard him come up beside her bunk, sensed his troubled gaze on her back. But she lay still, eyes closed, unwilling—unable—to encounter the sorrow she knew she would see in that haunted blue gaze. Her own pain would not allow her to face his, and so she pretended to be asleep. She was his mother, and undoubtedly he needed her comfort; but she had no comfort to give him, not now.

Nora felt his light, uncertain touch on her shoulder, but she didn't move. After a moment, he released her, his boots kicking the sawdust on the floor as he walked away.

She opened her eyes and watched the two sleeping girls across from her. Katie's face was flushed and pinched in sleep. She lay huddled close to Johanna, whose dark red hair fell in wild tangles about her face. Only now did it strike her that the girls were orphans. God in heaven, what would become of them and Little Tom? What would become of them all?

She should be weeping. How could she not weep, mourning her son, her friends? How could she feel—*nothing*? Her heart seemed a dark, frozen pit, empty of all human feelings, even pain.

At the very least she should feel guilt. God had withdrawn His blessing from them, that was clear. Aye, He had removed everything—His blessing, His Spirit, His love—everything but His wrath. It was just as she had long suspected: He was punishing them for their sin. Punishing *her*.

Oh, she *had* sinned, and in such vile ways! She had been conceived in sin, raised in sin, then gone on to compound it all by withholding a part of her heart from her husband, wantonly allowing her thoughts at times to drift from that good man to Morgan and their foolish, childish love for each other.

And Tahg. Perhaps Owen had been right all along, accusing her of favoring their eldest son over and above the other children. She had not seen it, but Owen had. God had seen. God could not be fooled; He knew her heart.

Now only Daniel John was left to her, and yet her heart was too empty, too dead to take him in.

Her hand went absently to cover her heart as if to see if it were still beating. Through her dress she touched the envelope Morgan had given her, surprised for an instant to discover it there. She had forgotten the letter entirely.

Michael's letter. Morgan had insisted she read it as soon as possible. She thought about it for a moment, then let her hand fall away. What did a letter matter now? What did *anything* matter now?

Later. She would read it later.

Evan was doing his best to reassure the worried boy, but obviously his efforts were having little effect. Still, he persisted. "I'm sure she'll b-be all right, son. You must give her time, however. She's had a t-terrible loss, she's utterly exhausted and still st-stunned from it all. It may take some time before she's herself again, so you must be patient with her."

Sitting on his side of the berth, young Daniel gave him a morose look. "You do think she's all right, then? Physically, I mean? You don't think she's ill?"

"Ill?" Evan tried to consider his reply with care, but his shoulder was burning with such a vengeance he found it almost impossible to concentrate on anything but his pain. He was beginning to question what, exactly, that bleary-eyed surgeon had done to him.

Shifting from his back to his right side, he grimaced with the effort. "No, of course not, though she will undoubtedly require your close attention. Your m-mother seemed somewhat…frail to me, lad, even before tonight's tragedy. The combination of grief and fatigue, added to her already weakened physical condition—well, it was simply t-too much."

Pushing himself up onto one elbow, Evan watched the boy. "To be p-perfectly frank, Daniel, I believe your mother has endured enough to devastate even a p-person in splendid health. She was weak to begin with, and so it's only natural that she would be…d-dis-traught…perhaps somewhat disoriented for a time."

His head bowed, the boy nodded miserably. "I wish I knew what to do for her." He looked up, and Evan winced at the frustration and pain in those magnificent eyes. "She—she doesn't seem to want me near her, you see."

Evan stared at him with dismay. "Oh, n-no, son, you mustn't think that! Why, your mother is utterly *devoted* to you—that's as evident as can be. No, I think she has simply…withdrawn. Just for now. She's had more than enough to crush her spirit: losing her home, your brother, seeing Thomas Fitzgerald slain so brutally…" Evan shook his head, his words dying away.

"And Morgan," the boy choked out. "The way they took him off—it grieved her something fierce, did you see?"

Evan felt a lump swell in his own throat at the thought of his last sight of Morgan Fitzgerald, clamped in irons like a common felon, his back bent in defeat. "Yes, yes, I saw," he said. With a deep sigh, he rolled over onto his back, keeping his face turned toward the boy.

"I never knew…before last night," Daniel murmured, staring down at the floor, "that Mother cared so about Morgan. More often she acted as if he were naught but a nuisance when he came round. They always seemed to argue, they did." He paused, and Evan sensed his confusion. "But she must have counted him as a real friend, after all. I thought—I thought she would fly apart when they took him away, she was that shattered. She did care, much more than I knew."

Evan looked away. "Yes, yes, I'm sure you're right," he said softly. "And Fitzgerald cared greatly for your mother and you, as well."

He had cared enough to risk his life, indeed to give up the freedom he prized, even *more* than life.

Dear Lord, have mercy on that valiant man…he may have done some wrong things, Lord, but his heart struggles to do right, it truly does…have mercy on him, Lord…have mercy on his tortured soul…

Seemingly lost in his own thoughts, Daniel lay down. Soon his eyes closed, and his breathing grew deep and rhythmic with sleep. Evan, however, remained wide awake. The muddled Dr. Leary had indicated he might be "somewhat uncomfortable" for a day or so; obviously, the man had been right.

He did hope the rheumy-eyed surgeon wasn't representative of the rest of the ship's crew or its facilities. Fortunately, the captain seemed efficient enough, if uncompromisingly cold. Evan wondered about the stiff-spined Captain Schell. He was a disturbing sort of man, defying every preconceived notion Evan had ever held about brawny, adventuresome sea captains. The novels he read most often portrayed ship commanders as large and loud—brash, beefy characters who barked out their orders in a decided brogue and were rarely if ever clean-shaven.

The enigmatic Captain Schell, however, was neither brawny nor brash, and his beardless face appeared to have been waxed, so smooth and tight was the skin. There *was* just the slightest hint of an accent in the man's precise speech—Germanic, Evan thought—but it only served to strengthen the overall impression of quality education and unquestionable authority. The only flaw in Schell's otherwise marble-smooth skin was an ugly red slash of a scar carved almost the entire length of the left side of his face, from temple to jawbone.

The scar drew immediate attention, but not so much as the strange pale blue eyes that bored through round-rimmed spectacles. Those eyes seemed to mock the object of their attention one moment, only to freeze into a glacial stare the next.

Still, the man had surprised him twice before they ever set sail—first by remaining adamant in his refusal to delay weighing anchor when the authorities would have detained the ship, and again in his ready willingness to provide a burial at sea for the Kavanagh lad and Thomas Fitzgerald.

Neatly uniformed and precise in behavior, the captain seemed a stark contrast to the ship he commanded. Evan had read about the superiority of American vessels over British ships. That information, plus the knowledge that Fitzgerald himself had arranged for these passages, had led him to believe that conditions would be, if not luxurious, at least clean and comfortable.

Accommodations on the *Green Flag* were neither. Had Fitzgerald observed firsthand the immature crew—most appeared to be mere youngsters, a fact that Evan found unnerving—and the crowded, squalid conditions in steerage, he would undoubtedly have removed his family from the ship with all haste.

He supposed he might be judging the ship too quickly. He really hadn't seen much of it, after all, having spent the last twenty-four hours in this abominable, rancid bunk. And things always looked bleak when lying flat on one's back. At any rate, he couldn't afford to allow conditions around him to affect him too greatly. He sighed. With this miserable gunshot wound in his arm, it was going to be difficult enough to keep his word to Fitzgerald about looking after his loved ones; fretting over the ship's accommodations would only make things more difficult.

Besides, no matter how unappealing their circumstances aboard the *Green Flag,* they could not help but be vastly superior to what Fitzgerald must be facing just now.

The unsettling image of the great Gael caged in a remote Mayo prison cell was enough to drive Evan off his bunk. Staggering from the hot pain in his shoulder, he sank to unsteady knees and began to pray.

For the first time in his life, Morgan was confined to a place where he could not see the sky, could not open the door and walk out a free man. God knew he had earned himself a cell—more than once, if truth be told. The real wonder was that his lawless and careless ways had only now caught up to him.

The gaol in Castlebar was a miserable hole, a dark, dank room reeking of vermin and unwashed bodies and years of mold. A filthy blanket tossed over a lumpy mattress of straw served as a bed, a bucket as a privy. There was no window, no chair, no water pitcher. The only sound was an occasional scurrying of a rat making its way from one corner to the other.

Morgan could not stand upright, nor could he take more than four broad steps from wall to wall. Had there been any furnishings he would have tripped over them, for the darkness was almost totally unrelieved, save for the palest wash of light from a candle outside in the corridor.

At the moment he sat on the edge of the mattress, his elbows propped on his knees, his head supported by his hands. He was neither fully awake nor quite asleep; his bad tooth throbbed just enough to keep him from getting any rest. It occurred to him for an instant that there was a dubious irony in a man plagued by a toothache when about to be hanged, and he smiled grimly to himself in the darkness.

He heard the jingle of keys and looked up with no real interest as the gaoler opened the door to allow Joseph Mahon entrance.

"I'll be just outside, Father," said Cummins, the gaoler, waiting for the priest to enter the cell. "You've only to call if you need me. Have a care with that one—he's big and mean clear through."

Mahon came the rest of the way in, his arms filled with some packages and Morgan's harp.

"Morgan," he said with a nod, coming to stand near the bed. "How are you, lad? Here, I've brought you clean clothes. And some of your things from your saddlebags. They said you could have them."

In the shadows, Morgan noted that the priest was as lean as sorrow, his long, narrow face drawn and hollowed out, his silver hair thinned to a web across his skull. The Hunger exempted no man, not even a man of God.

Morgan thanked him for his things, laying them at the head of the bed.

"So, Morgan, what is this they are saying you have done? 'Tis a real fix you've gotten yourself into this time."

Morgan patted the mattress beside him, and the other man sat down. "Aye, I'm in trouble for sure, if they've sent the priest," he said. "With things that bad, it's not likely I'll have time enough for the books, Joseph."

"You needn't play the *googeen* with me, Morgan," the priest said quietly. "We have known each other too long for that."

Morgan turned his gaze to the floor, disconcerted by the man's undisguised sympathy.

"I came to see if there is anything you need," said Mahon. "And to tell you how sorry I am about Thomas. Your brother was a good man, a truly good man."

"What have they done with him, do you know?" Morgan asked, cracking the knuckles of both hands.

"They allowed me to go aboard and administer the last rites. He was then to be buried at sea." Mahon paused. "Along with the Kavanagh lad—young Tahg."

Morgan lifted his head to face the priest. "Tahg?"

Mahon nodded. "He died before they sailed."

Morgan stared at him for a moment, then again cupped his head between his hands, digging at his beard with his fingers. "Oh, God," he whispered. "Oh, God, how much more?"

"You at least have the peace of knowing Thomas died in a state of grace," said the priest.

"Thomas *lived* in a state of grace," Morgan bit out.

"Aye, more than most," agreed Mahon.

"And just see his profit from it."

"We do not live a godly life for profit, lad, but to the glory of our Lord. Your brother would have been one of the first to testify to that."

Morgan said nothing, involuntarily drawing away when the priest reached to touch his arm.

"Morgan, you are a tormented man. Let me help you."

"*Help me?*" Morgan jerked to his feet. "What, then? Shall I confess to you? Is that what you'd have me do?"

"Ach, if only you would."

"You know I have never believed in that way."

"Then confess to your *Savior*, Morgan. Sure, and you still believe in Him, I would hope."

"Are you saying I don't have to go through *you*, then, Joseph? Strange words for a priest."

"Do not mock me, Morgan. I only came to help, and to tell you of your brother."

Morgan unclenched his hands, splayed them on his knees. "Aye, I do know that," he said with a sigh. "And it was kindness itself for you to come, Joseph. You are a good man. You have done much for my family and for the village."

"Morgan, 'tis no secret to you and to my people that I myself have questioned certain tenets of the church from time to time. I've never been the one to say that every word handed down from Rome is divinely given."

"That's so. I think you must be as much a renegade of the cloth as I am of the law, Joseph," Morgan said, managing a thin smile.

In truth, he greatly admired the slight, aging priest. The man had poured himself out for the villagers year after year, spent himself completely, never complaining, with not a thing to show for it other than the stoop of age and an occasional kiss on the hand.

"Well, then, reject the Church if you must, but for the sake of your soul, lad, do not reject our Lord. He does know what He is about, even if we cannot see it."

Unwilling to subject himself to a theological discussion, Morgan ignored the priest's caution. "Did you see the others when you went aboard, Joseph? Thomas's children…Nora?"

Mahon shook his head. "They wouldn't let me below decks. I was allowed only a moment with Thomas, they were that eager to set sail." He stopped and clasped his hands together in his lap. "Morgan—for what it may be worth, I understand what you did last night. Cotter would have killed you if you had not got to him first. You and perhaps several others as well."

Morgan shook his head. "Have no illusions about what I did, Joseph. I went mad, and that's the truth. I would have murdered George Cotter even if he hadn't shot my brother; more than likely I would have killed him even if he had no gun. And no doubt I would have finished off poor old Macken as well, had they not pulled me off him when they did." Rubbing his jaw against the pain of the aching tooth, he went on. "No, the truth is that something inside me tore loose, changed me into more beast than man. But don't ask me to repent of killing the agent. God Himself could not convince me that George Cotter deserved to live."

Wringing his hands, Mahon studied him. "That is not for us to decide, Morgan. We cannot know why God chooses to give life to some or withdraw it from others. But one thing I do know: There is an entire well of hatred and bitterness in you, lad, that must be emptied if you are ever to find your way back to the Lord." He drew a shaky breath. "Morgan…you know they will hang you."

Morgan looked at him. "Aye, they will."

Mahon seemed flustered by his directness. "You must not die with all this hatred on your soul, Morgan, and with such…lawlessness, such sin. Please, at least let me pray with you."

Morgan saw in the priest's face what he had seen in few others: a pure, selfless compassion and concern for another human being. It should have moved him, but in truth it only made him sad. "Don't waste your efforts on me, Joseph," he said, turning his back to the other man. "There are too many others in the village who need you. Save what strength you have for them. I deserve the hanging they are going to do, and we both know there is no stopping it."

Behind him, Mahon's quiet words sounded unexpectedly stern. "Do not let your brother's death be in vain, Morgan! Even worse, do not let our *Savior's* death be in vain."

Morgan felt a muscle near his right eye twitch. When he turned, the priest had risen to his feet and stood watching him.

"Say what you mean, Joseph."

"Thomas loved you to the point of despair, Morgan," the other man said firmly. "He agonized over you—over your soul. The man literally stormed the gates of heaven for your return to God's arms, time after time, year after year, never once conceding that his efforts might be in vain. And at the end—" Mahon stopped, but his gaze never wavered. "At the end he died in order that you might live. Sure, I do believe that you owe Thomas's noble memory at least a prayer in your own behalf."

Angry at the man's intrusion into his grief, Morgan scowled, opening his mouth to shoot back a caustic reply.

But the priest ignored him. "God in heaven, lad, do you not see it, even now? Your brother's unselfish death, our Savior's sacrifice on the cross—both were for *you*. Thomas died to spare your flesh, but our Lord died to spare your soul. Morgan, Morgan," the priest said, shaking his head sadly, "you belonged to Him once. Why have you turned from Him all these years? Let Thomas's final gift to you be your way back to the Savior!"

Steeling himself against the storm of emotion battering at his heart, more mindful than ever of the ache throbbing against his jaw, Morgan again turned his back on the other man. "I am not up for this, Joseph," he said unsteadily. "I know what you are trying to do, and I know you mean well. But I ask you to leave me. Please."

There was silence for a moment, then the sound of Mahon's weary footsteps scraping the stone floor as he came to stand beside him. "I will go, then, Morgan. But I want you to know that I will do whatever I can to change some minds. I will go this very day to speak with the authorities."

In reply, Morgan gave only the ghost of a knowing smile. Finally, the priest gave his arm a light squeeze, hesitating another moment before calling the gaoler.

"I will come if you need me, Morgan. Night or day, I will come. You've only to call."

Morgan nodded shortly, waiting until the priest was gone before crossing the room and sinking down onto the mattress. Idly, he began to finger through the things Mahon had brought: some worn books, a stack of poems and articles for *The Nation*, a clean shirt and pants. At last his hand went to the harp. He lifted it, placed it on his lap, and sat staring at it for a long time.

Finally, his face twisted with pain and rage, he began to yank at the strings, pulling them free one at a time until all dangled brokenly.

Then he stood, and with an agonized cry ripping up from the very center of his soul, gave the useless instrument a fierce toss, hurling it against the stone wall of the cell.

It fell to the floor with a voiceless thud.

28

Changes and Challenges

New York City

Michael Burke stood staring at his reflection in the bedroom mirror, a practice to which he was not ordinarily given. Lately, however, he had become increasingly concerned about his appearance.

At the oddest times and in the most unlikely places he would catch himself trying to measure just how much he had changed in seventeen years. It embarrassed him, caused him no end of impatience with himself, to realize that this recent preoccupation with his looks had been brought on entirely by the unsettling question of how he might appear to Nora after so long a time.

This morning he felt neither pleased nor displeased by the image staring back at him, only anxious. Walking a beat, chasing the pigs from city streets, and running at least one gang member to the ground every day kept him fit and lean enough. And there was more than one advantage in not being a drinker; his middle was as trim as it had been the day he sailed out of Killala Bay.

A few lines in the face could not be denied, mostly about the mouth, which, according to Eileen, had always been a bit grim at best. Ah, well, at least his hair was still thick and dark, though lately some silver had begun to peep through here and there.

He leaned a bit closer to the mirror in order to inspect his face more thoroughly. After Eileen's death, he had considered growing a beard, or at least a mustache. Now he decided it would be best to remain clean-shaven—at least until Nora had had a chance to get used to him again.

If she came.

Unwilling for the moment to dwell on whether she would or would not make the journey to America, he began to comb his hair. The room reflected in the mirror caught his attention—a small room, too small, and too drab entirely. Somehow Eileen had managed to fill it with color and freshness, but her cheerful influence had long since faded. He had changed nothing since her death, yet the room did not appear the same at all. The ruffled curtains and pillows she had made, the coverlet she had quilted, the rough pine she had faithfully waxed—it was all the same, yet altogether different. The iron bedstead needed polishing, the vanity was scratched and dull, and the curtains hung as limp as a cow's tail on a hot summer's day.

He frowned at himself and the bedroom in the mirror. It was a faded, dull room, in sore need of a woman.

And that's what I've become, he thought. *A faded, dull man in sore need of a woman.*

He pulled back from the mirror and went to stand by the window. If Nora were coming, she might well be on her way, even now. According to the messenger who had come for his return letter to Morgan, the ship was to sail from Killala some time near the end of March. That being the case, they could arrive in New York as early as the end of April or the first part of May. It would take at least five weeks, perhaps longer, depending on the type of ship and the weather. Some of the packets were said to be crossing in as little as thirty days. His own voyage had lasted for nearly six weeks; his seasickness, however, had made it seem far longer. It had been a miserable time, despite his youthful excitement at the adventure that lay before him.

Unless Nora had changed greatly, he doubted she would be excited. Frightened, perhaps, and even resentful at having to leave her own Ireland for a strange land, but not excited. Nora had never been one for adventure or change, had ever held back when it came to daring the unknown.

Why, then, was he so foolish as to think she would marry him?

Perhaps because he wanted it so—wanted it selfishly, to fill his emptiness, ease his loneliness. But he *could* help her and her boys, after all. The flat might not be much, but it *had* to be better than what she was used to in Killala. He knew the cottages in the village well enough: even the best of them boasted only dirt floors, patched windows, and turf fires. Besides, now that he had the promise of a promotion, he might soon afford a better place in a nicer neighborhood. Just because he worked Sixth Ward didn't mean he had to live here forever, especially with a wife and a family.

Until this moment he had not admitted to himself how very much he *wanted* her to come, how greatly he was anticipating it. And it was not an anticipation he would have felt for just *any* woman. No, it was *Nora* he could not get out of his mind, shy Nora from Killala whom he longed to see.

Oh, Lord, if she is on that ship, bring her safely to me. It's a terrible journey at best, and to a shy lass like Nora it will be a torment. Give her the courage to leave, Lord, and then give her the stamina to survive the crossing. I'll be good to her, I promise I will…I'll do all that I can to make her glad she came—

"Da?"

The bedroom door came flying open as Tierney charged into the room. Michael sighed. The boy never walked, it seemed, could only run or leap or trot; indeed, sometimes he seemed to fly.

"I thought we recently had us a talk about knocking before bursting into someone's room," Michael said. He had to force a frown, for this morning his spirits were too high for more than a token sternness.

His son grinned at him, as if sensing his good humor. "Don't fret yourself, Da. Once your Nora arrives, I promise I'll knock before I come crashing into the bedroom."

Now Michael *did* frown. "That'll do, Tierney! Don't be fresh. And she is not 'my Nora'!"

"Not yet," Tierney shot back, still grinning as he plopped down onto the bed. "So, then, d'you think they are coming?"

"There's no way to know that."

"But if they do come, you think Nora will marry you, right?"

Uncomfortable with the boy's scrutiny, Michael turned back to the mirror and pretended to straighten his collar. "And how would I know the answer to such a foolish question? No man can say what a woman will do."

"Mmm. Well, I hope they come. And I hope she marries you. But then, I'm sure she will, since she already knows what a fine fellow you are."

Pleased, Michael exchanged grins with him in the mirror, then turned. "You really mean that, don't you, Tierney? You *do* want them to come?"

"Sure I do, Da, I've already told you so. It'll be grand! You'll have a wife, and I'll have myself a brother. Well, perhaps not a brother," he said, folding his arms over his chest, "but at least a friend from Ireland. I can't wait to ask him all sorts of questions!"

"Nora has two sons, Tierney," Michael reminded him.

"Oh, I know," the boy put in quickly. "It's too bad about the older one. He must be very ill."

Michael shook his head. "Aye, it sounds so. But we can continue to pray for the lad, you know."

"Sure, Da. Listen, I've got news!" He stood, and Michael saw now that his face was flushed with excitement. "I'm to have a raise in pay, starting next week. That'll be a help if we're to take on a new family, won't it?"

"Why, that's fine, son, just fine," Michael said, crossing the room to make up the bed. "Help me with this, won't you? And before you tell me more about that raise, I'll hear your reason for coming home so late last night."

Tierney talked as he worked. "Mr. Walsh stopped by and asked me to stay over a bit—that's when I found out about the raise."

"Walsh himself talked to you? Isn't that a bit unusual?"

Tierney flung the coverlet up on his side, then smoothed the pillows. Walking over to the bureau, he picked up the previous day's newspaper and, rolling it into a tube, began to tap it against the palm of his hand. "He told me he's pleased with my work—*greatly* pleased, he said. So, starting next week, I'm to handle the desk until eleven."

Michael straightened, frowning. "That's too late for you to be out, Tierney. Too late entirely. You have your schoolwork to do, and you must get your sleep as well. Besides, what's the man thinking of, giving a boy your age such a responsible job?"

"He knows I can do it," Tierney said, color rising to his cheeks as he slapped the paper harder against his hand. "He trusts me, you know."

Michael could not argue with that, not in good conscience. Tierney *was* responsible, at least when it came to his job.

The lad had always seemed older than his years; at times his maturity worried Michael, for he wanted a normal childhood for his son. More than likely Walsh had seen that same maturity, and he could hardly fault the man for that. It would not do to have the boy think he was criticizing him for being dependable.

"Tierney, understand, son, I am glad Mr. Walsh thinks so highly of you, but—"

"Come on, Da," the boy interrupted, tossing the newspaper back onto the bureau. "You know I don't have to put in all that many hours to get my grades. Even if I did, that's just another advantage to the job: I can mind the desk and study at the same time. Mr. Walsh said so, said I can do whatever I please just so long as I don't neglect the desk."

"Tierney—" Michael stopped, uncertain as to how to phrase his reservations. "Mind, now, I think it's grand that you've done so well, and I'm proud to hear that you're appreciated. It's only that I don't want you getting too tight with Patrick Walsh. There is plenty of talk about the man, and not all of it good; I've told you that already. I've heard questions raised all too often about the nature of his businesses—and the legitimacy of them."

Tierney scowled. "You've also told me I should never mind gossip," he bit out. "And I *won't* listen to it about Mr. Walsh! It's jealousy talking, that's all. He's smart and ambitious, and he's good to those who work for him, which is more than you can say about most of the other swells in this city."

"That may be true," Michael countered, "but you must admit, it's a rare thing entirely for an Irishman to make his mark in New York at all, much less in only a few years, as Walsh has. I'm only saying that you should have a care, Tierney, that's all."

The boy's casual nod told Michael he would remember his caution no longer than it took to repeat it. "Sure, Da, I'll be careful. But I'm telling you, you've nothing to worry about with Mr. Walsh. Anyway, guess what else? I told him about Thomas Fitzgerald, how he'd be needing a job and a place to stay, and he said if he's any good at all at gardening, he just might have a place for him. His present man is going west next month, so he'll be needing somebody to replace him. There's even a gardener's cottage on the grounds—he has a grand estate on Staten Island, you know. And that's not all," the boy went on, his words spilling out in a breathless rush. "He also told me he has some extra work for me some Saturdays if I want it, up at his house. Odd jobs, he said, but he'll pay me well."

Michael regarded his son with troubled eyes. Something about Patrick Walsh's easy generosity bothered him. Irishmen in New York City nearly always fell into one of two categories: Either they remained unemployed, or they worked at low-paying, undesirable jobs that "respectable" citizens refused to touch. Yet Patrick Walsh had managed to become a wealthy, successful businessman in only a few years. He owned at least half a dozen boardinghouses near the docks and in other low-rent districts, plus a couple of nicer hotels farther uptown. There was no telling how many saloons belonged to the man, no figuring how he had wangled his way into the political establishment at Tammany Hall. The fact that Walsh seemed to enjoy wealth, influence, and respectability—all uncommon to the Irish in New York City—made him immediately suspect in Michael's mind.

Still, he hated to spoil the lad's news. "Just remember what I've told you, Tierney—have a care. Things—and people—are not always as they seem. Now, then," he said, shoving his hands down deep into his pockets, "I've some news for *you*. It seems that I am up for assistant captain."

Tierney crossed the room in three broad strides to grab Michael by the shoulder. "But that's *grand*, Da! Is it definite, d'you know?"

"Well, nothing is certain until it's announced, but I was told by Captain Hart I should expect it."

"And you deserve it! You're one of the best they have, and it's time they were knowing it!"

Surprised at this rare affirmation from his son, Michael beamed at him. "So, then, it would seem that we will both be getting a raise in pay. Perhaps this is a sign from the Lord that we are indeed about to expand our family."

"Could be, Da, could be," Tierney said negligently, reverting now to his usual noncommittal manner as he moved to check his own appearance in the mirror. "You'd know more about that sort of thing than I would." He started for the door. "I must be off, or I'll be late. Are you leaving now?"

"Not yet, but soon. I have to go in a bit early today. Price and I are to escort some ladies from one of those benevolent societies into Five Points later this morning."

Tierney made a face, and Michael nodded in agreement. The thought was enough to dampen his cheerful spirits. Like every other policeman on the force, he dreaded the notorious Five Points slum with a vengeance.

"Why in the world would a bunch of rich old ladies want to venture into that place?" Tierney asked, starting for the door.

"Well, with some, of course, it's little more than curiosity," Michael answered, following him out of the bedroom. "Others, I suppose, truly want to help, but mean to see where their money will be spent before making any sort of commitment."

Tierney gave a small grunt of disgust. "I doubt they'll much like what they see."

"Their intentions are more than likely the best," Michael replied with a sigh, going to the stove to put some water on for tea. "But they've no idea—none at all—what they're letting themselves in for."

"I'll wager they won't be staying very long once they get a close look at the place. I'm going now, Da."

Michael turned around, watching him shrug into his jacket. "Mind, don't be late again tonight. I'll pick up some pork on the way home and we'll have us a meal together for a change."

"Right." Halfway through the open door, Tierney stopped and turned back. "Say, Da, I've been wondering, have you given any thought to where you're going to put all those people once they get here? There's quite a bunch of them, after all."

Michael stared at him, then gave a brief shrug and a lame smile. "Aye, I have given a great *deal* of thought to it, but so far I've not come up with any answer."

"Ah, well, we'll work it out. The lads can bunk with me, and of course you and Nora will share a room—" He stopped, shot Michael a rakish grin. "Once you're married, that is." Before Michael could add a word, he went on, his expression all innocence. "We'd better hope that Thomas Fitzgerald and his family get a situation soon—otherwise it could get a bit crowded around here."

He waved, then bolted out the door, leaving Michael staring after him.

Michael carried his tea to the kitchen table and sank down onto a chair, looking around the room. The boy had a point, one that had already given him a sleepless night or two.

Where *was* he going to put all those people if they came? Especially Thomas and his little boy and lassies?

Tierney seemed willing enough to have Nora's lads share his room, though they'd be severely crowded in that wee hidey-hole. And Nora...

He found himself reluctant to think about Nora at the moment. More than likely she would not even consider marriage for some time. She had been widowed for only a few months, after all. And, even if they should happen to wed right away, for the sake of propriety if nothing else, he mustn't think she'd be ready for marital intimacy right off. Why, they didn't even know each other anymore. Anything more than a marriage in name only was highly unlikely for a long, long time. He did not know quite how he felt about that, nor was he willing to examine his feelings.

Meanwhile, he was still faced with the problem of providing housing for as many as seven additional lodgers in a three-room flat. The Irish in New York were used to bundling up together—Michael had seen as many as six or seven families in one room many a time. But he'd like to be able to give them all a bit more than just a roof over their heads and a place to eat and sleep.

His heart began to race again, a common occurence these days. Worry, he supposed. Worry and nervousness and perhaps even a bit of fear. His life might well be about to change in a most significant way.

He raked both hands down his face, then propped his elbows on the table and rested his head atop his folded hands.

All I can do is trust You, Lord—trust and make the little I have available to the rest of them. I know You'll work it out for us, Lord, and work it out for the best, so help me to stop worrying and show a bit more faith in Your providence.

A Visit to Five Points

They shall carry to the distant land
A teardrop in the eye,
And some shall go uncomforted—
Their days an endless sigh.

ETHNA CARBERY (1866–1902)

The ladies under the protection of Michael Burke and Denny Price had made a good show up till now of containing their horror and controlling their shock. Michael knew from past experience, however, that their hard-won composure would not survive the next stop on their tour. He could only hope that one of them had brought along some smelling salts.

This was at least the fifth group of society women he had escorted through the gutters and garrets of Five Points. He supposed it had never occurred to a one of them that New York's finest might have a few other things to do besides conducting private tours through the most infamous slum in the city. Apparently, the thought had eluded Chief Matsell and Mayor Brady as well. Otherwise, this foolishness would have been stopped long ago.

The results of these silly excursions were always the same, never amounting to anything more than a few offended sensibilities. At least two would faint, and a fresh sense of hopelessness would convince the well-intentioned ladies that, indeed, they could do little for the poor wretches trapped in Five Points—unless, of course, they happened to be willing to invest the rest of their lives and a considerable chunk of their wealth into providing a whole new way of life for the entire populace. Those who knew the district best—its inhabitants, the police, and a few priests—would be quick to agree that only a dedicated team of strong hearts and even stronger backs could ever hope to make the slightest difference in this place.

Today's half dozen ladies had thus far seen only the fringes of the notorious slums, but already they had to stop and collect their nerves before going on. Watching them, Michael had to admit that this group seemed a bit different than most—more observant, less frivolous, and, he thought, genuinely devastated by the misery they encountered.

At the moment they stood clustered about Denny Price, who was doing his best to brace them a bit with some Irish charm and futile reassurances. Denny *was* a charmer, all right, handsome enough that the women could not resist him, and as clever as he was good-looking. This was one of those times, however, when Michael found his partner's charm somewhat thin and the women's smiling response to it a bit grating. Five Points never failed to have a negative effect on his disposition.

Leaning against a wooden fence, his grim gaze left the women long enough to scan the area where so many of his countrymen lived in unrelieved misery. Although the district was inhabited by refugees from other countries, the Irish comprised the bulk of its population. Indeed, it seemed the only place in New York City—other than the police force—where the Irish were entirely welcome.

The brightness of the morning did nothing to disguise the gloom of the slum. In fact, it seemed strange to Michael that the sun did actually shine on Five Points. Its deceptive, cheerful warmth could almost tempt the unaware into believing this was just another neighborhood, housing its share of good and bad residents going about the normal business of living.

Michael knew better. Five Points was an abomination, possibly the habitat of more vice and wretchedness than any other one place on earth. Even the sun's cleansing, nourishing rays must surely die the very moment they touched its contaminated soul.

It had not always been so. Standing on the site of a low, swampy pond, the area had been a fairly decent residential community until about 1820. But the landfill hadn't been properly packed, and gradually the buildings began to sink into the swamp, their doors tearing free of their hinges, their facades crumbling. The more respectable families moved on to better parts of the city, and the destitute Irish moved in. The entire district had long ago degenerated to a breeding ground of drunkenness, crime, and depravity.

Five Points was so named because of the five streets that emptied themselves into the center. The slum lay only a short walk from Broadway's center of wealth and elegance, another moment from City Hall. From where Michael now stood, he could look directly onto the small, triangular courtyard at the center of the point where the streets converged, a parklike place dubiously named "Paradise Square." This was where the ladies in his party had congregated, casting uncertain glances at their surroundings.

There was not a redeeming feature to Five Points, not one. A maze of dilapidated, rotting buildings with patched and broken windows, its commerce consisted of grog shops and brothels in abundance. The neighborhood was populated by brutal men with vicious eyes, squalid, dispirited women, and filthy, neglected children in rags whose mothers were often drunk right along with the fathers—though in many cases, of course, there *were* no fathers.

With no proper sewage or garbage disposal, the alleys teemed with offal and trash. Both the streets and the buildings constantly reeked from the stench of animal and human waste, kerosene stoves, and whiskey. Beneath the dank cellars and fetid garrets ran dozens of underground passages connecting blocks of houses on different streets, affording ideal getaway routes for the hardened criminals who drifted in and out of the district and certain death for anyone else foolish enough to enter.

The place was the terror of the police force and every decent citizen who was aware of its existence. Home for entire gangs of gun-fighting Irish, thieves, and murderers, it also housed rampant disease and utter hopelessness. Buried in ignorance, filth, pestilence, and poverty, Five Points was a pool of concentrated, unchecked evil. And at the heart of it all stood the predominant landmark of Five Points, the ugly, infamous building to which Michael and his partner were about to escort the unsuspecting ladies. The Old Brewery.

Lurking in the square, ringed on one side by "Murderer's Alley," the old Coulter's Brewery building had long ago been converted into a multiple dwelling. It was a veritable monstrosity of a place—mustard-colored, sagging, hideous as a misshapen toad. It squatted in defiance of all decency and authority, the acknowledged headquarters of corruption and perversion for all to see.

Michael hated the very sight of the place. Every trek through its diseased passages brought on nightmares, and he knew tonight would be no exception. His stomach heaved at the thought of what waited inside, but the ladies would not consent to forego their exploration of this most disreputable of the slum's many dens of corruption.

Wanting only to have it over and done with, Michael sighed and detached himself from the fence, heading toward Price and the women. "Ladies, if you insist," he said with a somewhat rude jerk of his head in the direction of the building.

Ignoring at least three sets of raised eyebrows, Michael parted their numbers and started across the square. With himself in front and Price bringing up the rear, he resolutely marched them straight toward the Old Brewery.

᠈᠉

If human misery and degradation could be measured, Michael thought, then certainly the weight of it within these walls would be enough to sink the city into the ocean. Over the years, any number of journalists and social chroniclers had attempted to depict the stark horror of conditions inside the Old Brewery. All had failed, for indeed there was a point at which raw evil could not be described, only—to the observer's peril— seen and felt.

Such was the iniquity running rampant throughout the Brewery's dark, winding passageways. Michael led the way with a lantern in hand, cautioning the ladies to have a care where they stepped. "The whole of the building is rickety and unsafe," he warned, parting two drunks sprawled at the bottom of the steps.

A spur of annoyance nipped at him as they made their way up the tottering stairs and started down the hall. He found something almost obscene in these well-dressed, impeccably coiffed uptown ladies injecting their presence into the squalor and hopelessness of this place. What, exactly, did they think to see or hope to accomplish?

The boards creaked and groaned in protest as they moved along the hallway. Almost in unison the women lifted their skirts to keep their hemlines from touching the begrimed floor, all the while casting apprehensive glances into the darkness around them.

Great mounds of what appeared to be filthy rags lay in heaps against the wall, but as they passed by the rags would stir, then attempt to rise, revealing the pathetic forms of human beings, both Negro and white. In the dim glow of the lantern, dozens of half-naked children could be seen cowering or playing in the shadows.

Too cross by now to make any concession toward the ladies' delicate breeding, Michael could not resist pointing out a patched section of floor just ahead. "That place was dug up a while back," he informed them, "after finding some of the boards sawed free. There were human bones underneath—the remains of two bodies." He stood aside, waiting for the women to tiptoe around the area, their faces pale and taut as they minced away from the shabby repair job.

His sense of decency overcame his petulance, however, when he realized the sounds coming from a dark alcove just to their left were those of a couple taking their pleasure right there in the hallway—a common enough occurrence in this pit of immorality. With a deft pivot to the side, he managed to divert the group's attention to himself by swinging the lantern and pretending to stumble as he hurried them past the alcove.

A few of the rooms were open to view, the doors either ajar or ripped from their hinges. They passed by one, slowing almost to a stop at the sight of three elderly women inside, all lying on a bed of filthy rags pushed into a corner. Each appeared to be feeble and emaciated. Across the room two other women, these younger, sat at a dilapidated table crowded with whiskey bottles and what looked to be the remains of several meals. Beneath the table three children, one but an infant, played with a dog.

Michael had been down these halls of horror far too many times to react to the cloying hands of the beggars that groped at them as they moved on. The ladies, however, made the mistake of digging into their handbags so often he was sure they would go home without a coin.

From every shadowed corner came the sounds of weeping or groaning, whether from sickness or desolation no one could say. By now most of the women had gone pale and begun to look somewhat ill, making Michael feel a bit ashamed of his earlier crankiness. They had, more than likely, never experienced anything near the squalor of Five Points before today.

He did not doubt their sincerity. The simple act of submitting to a tour through such a vile place indicated they at least had the sensitivity to think of others less fortunate than themselves. There was little enough human decency and Christian charity in this city; certainly he had no right to be faulting the few who displayed a measure of it.

Michael stepped out of the way, allowing the ladies to sidestep a drunk sprawled face down in the hall. Waiting for the women to pass, his attention was caught by one in particular, who appeared to be lagging a bit behind the others. A slender, straight-backed young woman, her rich chestnut hair was caught in a thick chignon that seemed to defy the frivolous bonnet perched on top of her head. She walked with a slight limp, scarcely noticeable, and her expression was not so much one of revulsion as compassion. Her attention seemed to have been caught by something just ahead, and he turned to look in the direction of her gaze.

Her eyes were fastened on a little girl who was huddled just outside a closed door. The young woman stopped when she reached the child, separating herself from the rest of the group who walked on, accompanied by Officer Price. Michael was about to urge the straggler on, but he hesitated when she stooped down to gaze into the child's face.

When she spoke, her voice was low, and, as he would have expected, unmistakably refined. But it was also a voice touched with genuine warmth and concern.

The woman had soft hazel eyes and a small oval face with a nearly pointed chin. So fine-boned was her frame that she seemed to bend beneath the heavy weight of her hair. But a note of firmness in her voice and the strong line of her jaw belied any hint of frailty.

Smiling, she reached out a hand to the child, who regarded her with a mixture of distrust and awe. "Hello," said the young woman, withdrawing her hand when the little girl ignored it. "Is this where you live?"

Suspicious eyes burned out of a dirty, bruised face. The little girl, about five years old, was clad only in a filthy sack of a dress. Her body was covered with grime and sores, and Michael knew a moment of rage at the thought of parents who would allow a child to go around in such a state.

"My name is Sara," said the soft-voiced young woman. "Won't you tell me yours?"

The child studied her for another moment, then answered in a whisper, "Maggie."

"Maggie," the woman repeated. "Why, that's a *lovely* name! And is this where you live, Maggie?"

The little girl nodded, staring at the woman across from her. The distrust in her eyes had given way to puzzlement, and as she gaped, she sucked the thumb of a grimy hand.

To Michael's amazement, the young woman dropped down to her knees in front of the child, seemingly mindless of the fact that her fine wool suit would be instantly ruined by the grime covering the floor. "Do you have any sisters or brothers, Maggie?" she asked, touching the child lightly on the forearm.

The little girl jumped back, as if unaccustomed to being touched, at least in so gentle a manner. The young woman immediately dropped her hand away.

"Brothers," the child finally answered in the same hushed tone. "Me has two brothers."

Michael noted the thick brogue as southern Ireland, most likely County Kerry. Appraising the child more carefully, he decided she'd be a fair little thing were that wee pinched face scrubbed clean and her long black curls combed free of their tangles.

"Aren't you frightened out here in the dark, Maggie?" the woman asked. "Shouldn't you go inside, with your mother?"

The child hunched her shoulders. "Uh-uh," she murmured, shaking her head. "Not allowed."

The young woman—Sara—looked confused for a moment. "You're not allowed to go inside your rooms, Maggie? Why is that?"

"Mum is visiting."

"I see. Well, couldn't you visit, too?"

Again the child shook her head. "Not allowed. Mr. Tully wouldn't like it."

Sara's eyes narrowed. "Mr. Tully? That's your mother's guest?"

The little girl stared as if she didn't understand.

"Mr. Tully only visits with your mother?" Sara asked tersely.

When the child bobbed her head stiffly up and down, Michael expected the refined young woman to either blanch or blush. She did neither. Remaining as she was, on her knees, she put a hand to the riot of black hair falling over the little girl's face, smoothing it back from her temple. "Well, Maggie, I can see that you're a very good girl, obeying your mother as you do. I wonder if she would allow you to have a sweet?"

The child's face brightened, though her eyes still held a glint of uncertainty. "A sweet?"

"A peppermint," Sara said, fumbling inside the pocket of her skirt. "Would you like one?"

The little girl's eyes went from the young woman's face to the piece of candy she held out to her. Finally, she nodded, extending a dirty hand. Sara smiled, pressed the candy into the outstretched hand, then got to her feet.

"I must go now, Maggie," she said, "but if I may, I'd like to come back soon and visit with you."

The child stuffed the peppermint into her mouth like a greedy baby bird, then looked up. "Will you bring more sweets, then?"

"I certainly will. Now, you must stay right here, Maggie, close to your own door, until your mother is...is finished with her visit. It's not a good idea for you to go wandering about the building. Will you do that, Maggie?"

The little girl nodded distractedly, her attention wholly absorbed in the peppermint. Michael moved to escort the young woman on down the hall.

"I suppose there are hundreds of others just like her trapped in this dreadful place," the woman said after a bit.

"Aye, and she's in better shape than most," Michael bit out. "See here, Mrs.—"

"It's *Miss*, Sergeant Burke. Miss Sara Farmington."

"Yes, well, Miss Farmington, you told the child you'd be back—"

"And so I shall."

"I don't mean to offend you, Miss Farmington," Michael said with an edge in his voice, "but a lady would not dare to enter Five Points without a police escort. And, begging your pardon, these little...junkets into the district take a great deal more of our time than we can actually spare on such—"

"Foolishness?" she finished for him, then stopped, and turned to look into his face.

Michael was somewhat taken aback by her direct scrutiny. Behind that gentle, unassuming gaze he caught a glimpse of a formidable, iron-clad will. He was also struck by the fact that Miss Sara Farmington reminded him a little of Nora—at least Nora as he remembered her.

"Do you know, Sergeant Burke," she said thoughtfully, "you're quite right. I don't believe any of us ever stopped to consider the ramifications of taking you away from your duties."

Her frown of concern left no doubt as to her sincerity, and Michael suddenly felt awkward. She seemed a true lady, after all; he hadn't meant to insult her. "Don't take offense, Miss Far—"

"Oh, I'm not," she hastened to reassure him. "Not at all. It's just that you're absolutely right. We simply didn't think. Crime is running rampant in our city, and here we are, expecting the police to play bodyguard so we can go exploring. It's really quite unforgivable. And totally unnecessary."

"Well, now, you can't be coming into this terrible place by yourself, Miss Farmington. You can see that it's no place for a woman at all, much less a woman alone."

"Oh, you needn't worry about that!" she said, laughing. "None of us is brave enough to come down here *alone*! But in the future we shall enlist the help of some of the gentlemen from our congregation. They should be more than capable of providing us an escort."

"Miss Farmington, even the *police* dread coming in here! And we *never* come in unarmed!" Michael was horrified at the thought of some silk-vested deacon attempting to see to the safety of this fine young woman and her friends. "If you *must* come, then it should be only with a police escort. But I cannot help wondering—why are you so determined to come at *all*?"

She seemed to enjoy his discomfiture, her eyes twinkling with amusement. But as he watched, her expression abruptly sobered. "Sergeant Burke, we want to help these people—and we believe we can. I know this probably sounds like nothing more than womanly idealism to you, working as you must amid truly deplorable conditions. But we happen to think that, with enough planning and financial backing, we can make a real difference in Five Points. We're prepared to plan for years, if necessary, and to spend a considerable sum of money in order to turn this into a decent place to live."

Michael shook his head. "It's been talked about before, Miss Farmington, many a time, with no results, none at all. You've seen the poor souls for yourself—their wretchedness. What could you possibly hope to accomplish that would make any difference for them?"

She straightened her shoulders and looked him square in the eye. "What we will do, Sergeant Burke, is to pray, praise, and proceed."

Michael stared at her. "Begging your pardon, I—?"

She smiled. "That is the scriptural order of things for God's people when they prepare to conquer a heathen nation. Read your Bible, Officer Burke—oh, I'm sorry, your faith doesn't really encourage that, does it?"

Michael could not contain a slight smile at her flustered expression. "Well, as a matter of fact, Miss Farmington, I am that rare creature, an Irish Protestant who can actually read—and *does* read, especially the Scriptures. I might point out that some of my Catholic friends can also read. And do."

One eyebrow went up in challenge. "But not the Bible."

He shrugged. "Some do, some don't. That would not seem to be any of my business." He gave her a look to remind her it was also none of hers.

"Your rebuke is noted, Sergeant," she retorted with a dryness that made a grin break across his face.

They walked the rest of the way in silence, Michael pacing his stride to her slight limp. When they reached the downstairs landing, the others were waiting to continue the tour, giving Michael no opportunity to apologize to the young woman for his rudeness.

By early afternoon they concluded their tour and led the ladies out of Five Points to their waiting carriages. Turning onto Broadway, Michael pulled in a deep, cleansing breath of fresh air, his first since entering the slum that morning.

He felt a faint edge of disappointment that he'd been unable to talk more with the plucky Sara Farmington. Just as quickly, he was struck by a feeling akin to shame. How could he be seeking the company of another woman when he had only recently committed himself to marriage with Nora? But he immediately justified his attraction to Sara Farmington by deciding it was her vague resemblance to Nora that had piqued his interest in her in the first place.

He spent the rest of the way back to headquarters in prayerful thanks that Morgan had written when he did, asking for help for his family and Nora's. If the lot of them had taken it upon themselves to make the crossing with nobody waiting on this side, they might well have ended up in Five Points, with all the rest of its hopeless victims.

Through Morgan's intervention, Nora and her family would be spared that particular hell. With that thought—and the thought that in only a few weeks he might be a husband again—Michael quickened his step and lifted his face to catch the sun. Giving his nightstick a bit of a twist, he then continued up Broadway with the jaunty, purposeful step of a man whose life has taken on new purpose and challenge.

30

NORA'S TURNING

I know where I'm going,
I know who's going with me,
I know who I love,
But the dear knows who I'll marry....

OLD IRISH BALLAD (ANONYMOUS)

The Green Flag

They had been at sea almost three full days before Nora finally read Michael's letter.

The first day out she had been too devastated, too dazed to think, much less read. The second, she had suffered the assault of a peculiar sort of illness—not seasickness, exactly, at least not like that of the other passengers close by. She had not endured the same painful retching, had not even lost the contents of her stomach. All the same, she'd been ill enough that she could do nothing more than lie weakly on her berth, staring up at the ribs of the moldy ceiling as the bile from her stomach rose and ebbed, filling her mouth with a bitter, nauseating acid.

Today her stomach had stopped its pitching, but she still felt lifeless, enervated and lay in the same benumbed stupor. Only in the vaguest sense was she aware of her surroundings. Her bunk mate, the young woman who had glared at her so fiercely their first day at sea, now lay flat on her back, moaning and weeping in despair between bouts of retching. Katie Frances was curled in a tight ball at the bottom of the bunk, wheezing with every breath she took, while the silent Johanna looked nearly as dazed as Nora felt.

All around them rose the mingled sounds of suffering. Those with the strength to cry out filled the air with a mixed chorus of prayers and curses, pleas for mercy and screams of agony. Babes wailed, grown men raged, and women keened.

Throughout the day, Daniel John had appeared often, at times coaxing her to eat or take water. When she refused, he would go away, only to return later—mostly, she supposed, to satisfy himself that she still lived. Evan Whittaker had come around once or twice, staying only long enough to ask if there was anything he could do for her, shuffling back to his bunk when she quietly assured him she needed nothing.

By evening of the third day, she still had not made the slightest effort to move further from the bunk than the privy, had not bathed or combed her hair or taken food. Part of her nagged that she had no right to continue in this fashion, that it was thoughtless and selfish to ignore her own family and the orphaned Fitzgerald children; another part dully responded that it no longer mattered.

A terrible, vile stench surrounded her, and she made the effort to pull herself up on the bunk to look around, throwing a hand to her head when it began to spin. Knowing she was weak to the point of collapse, she caught two or three deep breaths, then waited until the danger of fainting had passed.

Finally she was able to haul herself the rest of the way up. Dragging her legs over the side of the berth, she glanced around at her surroundings, appalled at what she saw and smelled.

Alice, her bunk mate, and the two little girls at the foot of the berth were asleep, all three lying in their own messes from being ill. Nora's stomach pitched, and she fought against being sick. She put a hand to her sticky, brittle hair, then to her face, grimacing when she saw the dirt and oil that smudged her palm.

Her throat was sore and painfully dry. Mostly, she felt disheveled and disoriented—and disgusted with herself and the putrid conditions around them. Instinctively, she attempted to smooth her bodice, staying her hand when she touched the envelope close to her heart.

Retrieving Michael's letter from inside her dress, she glanced around, hesitating. She supposed she should make an effort to clean up their berth, but she wasn't at all sure she had the strength. Besides, she had put off reading the letter long enough; the berth could wait.

Her head ached with a dull, nagging throb, and her hands trembled as she opened the envelope, pulled the letter free, and began to read:

Dear Nora Ellen...I hope you will remember your long-ago friend, who still remembers you with much affection....

Evan Whittaker had been brooding for most of the evening. He knew what he wanted to say to Nora Kavanagh, had prayed over it as much as he was able, given his light-headed state. As yet, he had been unable to muster the courage to approach her with his suggestion.

There was always the chance she would take him the wrong way, become offended or even angry. His intention—his *only* intention—was to help, if he could. He could not deny his growing admiration and somewhat unsettling concern for the grieving young widow. She *was* lovely, after all—even in her frailty and her unhappiness, she was like a rare, delicate wildflower, exquisite and fragile and elusive.

Obviously, she should not be alone. She needed someone to look after her. He had promised Morgan Fitzgerald to care for her and the others as if they were his own. And he would keep that promise if at all possible. Admittedly, it would be no sacrifice on his part to look after Nora Kavanagh; she was the kind of woman who somehow called forth one's manly, protective instincts. In her own unique way, she was really quite wonderful.

In thirty-six years, Evan had never loved a woman, had never had a romance. Always too shy to initiate a relationship—and too set in his ways to respond in the unlikely event that a woman should take the initiative with *him*—he had resigned himself to living his life alone. It was not such a bad life, really: he had his work, his church, his books. He managed. Now that he would be starting a new life in a new country, however, he thought it might be wise to give some consideration to starting over in other ways as well. Where was it written, after all, that he need remain a bachelor for the rest of his years?

Suddenly realizing the direction his thoughts had taken, he blinked, then pressed a hand to his mouth in dismay. It might not be *written*, but he had always assumed as much, and now was certainly no time to be thinking about changing his spots. What he must do, above all else, was to make every effort to fulfill his vow to Fitzgerald. He would do his best to look after Nora Kavanagh, ease the journey, help with the children. To anticipate anything more was absurd.

Still, if she came to depend on him, trust him…who could say? Perhaps later…

꒰꒱

Nora still sat on the side of the berth, her feet planted heavily on the floor. Stunned, frozen in place by what she had just read, she stared into the shadows.

Her mind could not take it in. Added to everything else, this was simply too much. An offer of marriage from a man she had not seen for more than seventeen years? How else could she respond but with shock and bitterness—a bitterness directed not at Michael Burke, but at Morgan Fitzgerald.

Morgan. She had seen his clever, conniving hand in it at once. It was all too clear what he had done. Hadn't he admitted, just before leaving Thomas's cabin, that he, too, had received a letter from Michael? He had played the innocent, like the consummate rogue he was, telling her as little as possible, all the while knowing exactly what he'd been up to. Obviously, he had taken it upon himself, in his proprietary, arrogant way, to try to order her life for her. Why would he do such a thing? Sure, and he must have realized it would humiliate her.

Anger and the pain of betrayal nearly doubled Nora over. She hugged her arms to her breast as if to hold herself together. Choking on unshed tears of fury and humiliation, she drew deep, shuddering breaths to control her trembling.

She had believed he truly cared for her. At the last, she had cherished his outburst of emotion, had clung to it. Had it all been a lie, then, just another attempt to pacify poor little Nora, to keep her from going to pieces on him and making things more difficult?

No. No, she did not, *could* not, believe that. His heart had been in his eyes, his true heart revealed at last. What she had seen in his face had been real, at least at that moment.

It was obvious what had driven him to do such a daft thing. As always, he simply believed her to be too weak, too helpless to manage on her own.

The man had ever believed she needed a keeper; since childhood, he had treated her like a wee, frail thing to be pampered and patronized.

For an instant—only an instant—the thought skirted her mind that perhaps, out of the depths of his caring, he had simply taken it upon himself to ensure her safety and well-being, that he had not meant to be so heavy-handed. But just as quickly came a fresh wave of shame at the position in which he had placed her, *whatever* his motives might have been.

Merciful Lord, what had he told Michael? That they were destitute, starving, in dire need of charity?

Just as we are…

She squeezed her eyes shut against the painful truth, willing herself not to weep. She *hated* being dependent on others, had always despised the shame of it, yet had been forced to endure all too much of it in her life, from her childhood on.

Nora opened her eyes. What if she were wrong? What if Michael meant all he said, that his son was in sore need of mothering, that he himself was in need of a partner to share his life? What if he *did* remember her with affection, after all, and did truly want her as his wife?

Don't be a fool! Nora's mind argued. *Morgan's stamp is all over this thing! Why would any decent man with a brain in his head go offering to wed a used-up woman he hasn't seen or heard from in years?*

Besides, whatever was behind it, did they really think she would consent to marry a man she no longer knew, a man she didn't love? She had rejected Michael once; had he and Morgan forgotten that? If she had not loved him enough to marry him then, when they were close and knew each other well, what in heaven's name led them to believe she would marry him *now*, and the two of them strangers?

She sat up a little straighter, trying to ignore the throbbing at the base of her skull. Glancing down at the pages of the letter strewn across her side of the berth, she grabbed them up in one angry sweep, intending to shred them to pieces.

Startled, Nora jumped as Evan Whittaker moved out of the shadows. Still clutching the letter in one hand, she nodded to him.

"I hope I didn't startle you, Mrs. K-Kavanagh," he said uncertainly, stopping a few feet away from the berth. "It's…good to see you sitting up at last. I hope you're feeling b-better?"

"Aye, a bit, thank you. But how are *you*, Mr. Whittaker? Is your arm giving you much pain?"

"Some. But nothing I c-can't tolerate." With his good hand, Whittaker moved a small stool closer to the bunk. "May I?" he said, waiting for her nod of assent before he sat down.

To Nora, the Englishman looked ghastly pale, ill, and more than a little shaky. Pain had lined his smooth forehead and carved deep brackets on either side of his mouth, adding years to his once almost boyish countenance.

"Am I disturbing you?" he asked abruptly, half rising from the stool as his gaze went to the letter in her hand.

"No—no, not a bit," she assured him.

"Yes, well…" He relaxed only a little. Then, clearing his throat, he leaned forward. "I, ah, was wondering if we might…talk? There's something…I'd like to, ah, d-discuss with you. If it's no b-bother, that is."

Nora shook her head, sensing the man's difficulty. Obviously, he was struggling to find words for whatever he intended to say. "It's no bother at all, Mr. Whittaker."

"Yes, well…you see, k-keeping in mind that you've been through a great deal…you've had a terrible time of things, after all…and it does seem to me that it must be rather frightening for a woman, crossing the ocean more or less alone. Oh, you have your son, of course, I don't m-mean to denigrate Daniel. He's such a fine boy, so c-collected and mature for his age. Still, it has to be most difficult…"

He stopped, his expression frozen in dismay. "Oh, dear, I'm saying this b-badly…I knew I would…"

Having no idea how to help him, Nora offered a weak smile.

Whittaker rose suddenly, reaching out to a nearby beam to steady himself. "I would like," he said, his voice gaining a bit of strength, "to offer my p-protection to you, Mrs. K-Kavanagh. For the duration of our journey… and for as long as you might desire, afterward."

Nora's mouth went slack as she stared at the man. "I'm sorry?"

"Please, Mrs. K-Kavanagh understand that in no way do I mean to be forward!" he blurted out. "I wouldn't want you to think—"

Whittaker stopped and swallowed with difficulty. Even in the dull glow from the lantern, Nora could see him flush and was torn between conflicting emotions of sympathy and annoyance. *Even to a mild-mannered man such as this, she appeared helpless and weak, in need of an overseer!*

As he stood there, looking none too steady on his feet, he clenched and unclenched the fingers of one hand. "I only meant to say, Mrs. K-Kavanagh, that it would be my pleasure to act as your...ah...protector...for the duration of our voyage...and for as long as necessary after we reach New York. After that...well, ah, I'd b-be most flattered if you would consider me as a...a friend, at least."

The poor man looked about to faint. Nora was at a loss. Half fearful that he might topple over at any moment, half angry that yet another man perceived her as helpless, she forced a note of steady calm into her voice. "I—truly, I don't know what to say, Mr. Whittaker. I'm very grateful to you, of course...but you've already done so much for me and my family—"

"Oh, please," Whittaker interrupted, pulling a handkerchief from his vest pocket and wiping it over his brow with a trembling hand, "you need say n-nothing! Nothing at all. I only wanted to m-make you aware of the fact that...that I respect you greatly, and care deeply about your welfare. And that of your son, of course," he added quickly. "D-Daniel and I have been getting to know each other quite well, and he's a wonderful b-boy. Wonderful..."

His words trailed off, unfinished. Nora felt an unjustified stirring of anger. She was being entirely unfair. This good, shy man was willingly making himself miserable on her account, pledging his protection to a virtual stranger, to a woman who must look no better than a deranged harridan at the moment. And, clearly, the very act of making himself understood was a torment, timid soul that he seemed to be.

Indeed, she *liked* Evan Whittaker and owed him much; that his intentions were the best, she had no doubt. But he, too, had seen something in her, some flaw in her character, that marked her as inadequate. God in heaven, what was there in her demeanor that made her appear simpleminded and incompetent to these men?

She sat up a bit straighter, having to grope at the limp mattress when she was hit by a new surge of dizziness. Seeing her sway, Whittaker put a hand to her shoulder. "I've upset you! I'm so sorry—"

"No, no, it's not that!" Nora protested, forcing herself to sit upright, unassisted. "I'm still...a bit weak, is all. No, I'm—my goodness, Mr. Whittaker, I'm not perturbed with you at all, simply overwhelmed—by your kindness."

He stooped slightly to peer into her face. "Please d-don't feel you need to say anything more, Mrs. K-Kavanagh. You're really quite weak, and I didn't intend to cause you additional d-distress. I—just b-bear in mind that I will count it a privilege to d-do whatever I can to make this journey easier for you. Now then," he said with more firmness, "I'm going to leave you alone so you can rest."

He turned to go, then stopped. "You will let me know if there's anything I can d-do?"

Nora nodded and managed another faint smile. "Of course. And—I do thank you, Mr. Whittaker."

Still somewhat dazed, she watched him stumble off to the men's quarters. Truly, she did not know what to make of the man.

At the moment, she wasn't sure she cared. She had had her fill, and then some, of coming across as incompetent to the men with whom she came in contact. From now on, she would do whatever she must to avoid even a hint of weakness, any sign of dependency. She was a woman grown, after all, with a son and three orphaned children who had nobody else in the world.

Deliberately, and with a strange new sense of purpose, she took the pages of Michael Burke's letter and, one by one, tore them into pieces. As she watched them flutter to the floor, she knew an instant of panic.

Perhaps she should have at least saved his address…what if— Shaking off the thought, she closed her eyes.

Dear Lord, I am sick to death of being a weak, clinging woman. I ask You now to do whatever You must to make me strong…strong in Your power, strong enough, Lord, so that others will no longer feel such a need to take care of me, indeed strong enough that I might begin to look after others for a change. Oh, I'm that frightened, Lord. Sure, and You know I am terrified of what may lie ahead for all of us. But in the future, Blessed Savior, couldn't we just let my terrors be our secret—Yours and mine? Please, Lord?

Nora opened her eyes and, for the first time in her life, stretched her hands up, toward heaven. Crying out in a harsh, desperate whisper of a plea, she begged, *"God, change me! Oh, my Lord—change me!*

31

The Most Fearful Dread of All

The fell Spectre advanc'd—who the horrors shall tell
Of his galloping stride, as he sounded the knell.

AUTHOR UNKNOWN (1858)

They had been at sea nearly a week when Evan took a turn for the worse. His fever soared, and his wound began to fester and burn as if somebody held a fiery brand to his skin. Still, there were others in sadder condition, and it was their need, not his own, that sent him stumbling to the surgeon's quarters late at night.

He found Dr. Leary sprawled in his bunk, his eyes glazed. He looked about to pass out.

"I'm sorry," Evan said stiffly, not meaning it. "I know it's late, but you're d-desperately needed in steerage. We have people down there in their extremities."

The surgeon lolled where he was, peering at Evan with eyes that would not quite focus.

Dr. Leary's quarters were cramped and reeked of whiskey and mold. Evan was struck by a bout of weakness and, head pounding, his wound on fire, he groped for the open door to keep from falling.

"There's something terribly wrong b-below," he said thickly. "Not seasickness. M-much worse. Please—you *must* come! People are dying!" The surgeon had not been seen in steerage since the day after they sailed, and Evan found it almost impossible to keep from screaming at the drunken man to do his job.

"The Irish are always dying," muttered Leary drunkenly. "Why should I be the one to circumvent their destiny?"

A terrible fury rose in Evan as he stood studying the dissipated wreck of a man across the room. Was this all the help they could expect, this drunken failure who could scarcely speak? God help them all, they *would* perish!

"You are Irish yourself, man!"

The surgeon grunted. "Don't be reminding me."

"Dr. Leary," Evan tried again, the words sticking to his palate, "we have two c-corpses in steerage, and from the looks of things this night, we will have m-many more before sunrise. If you do not c-come with me and come now, I promise you I will return with a number of the largest, b-brawniest men on board and we will *drag* you below! Good heavens, man, you're a *physician!*"

Leary glared at Evan for another full minute. At last, he hauled himself up from the berth, teetering wildly as he stood. He grabbed at the corner of the desk to break his fall. After another moment, he yanked his bag off the desk and pitched toward Evan. "Let's go, then."

Fighting back his revulsion, Evan put a hand to the man's arm to help steady him, but the surgeon shook him off with a grunt of protest.

"C'mon, Englishman, show me your corpses. And don't be getting so rattled about it." He stopped long enough to wag a finger in Evan's face. "You'll be seeing plenty more of them before this crossing is done."

The surgeon laughed, then lurched through the open doorway. "That's the truth, you know. There'll be plenty of corpses for the greedy old Atlantic on this voyage. She'll claim those she wants—she always does!"

The doctor looked back over his shoulder, squinting at Evan with a peculiar grimace of a smile. "And who can say but what they all would not be better off in the bosom of the sea than where they're going, eh?"

⟩⬤⟩

Less than an hour later, Leary, white-faced and suddenly sober, faced the captain in his quarters.

"I tell you it's the *Black Fever!*" the surgeon exploded, ducking his head beneath the low rough-beamed ceiling. A big man, he felt more confined in Schell's cabin than in his own, though the captain's room was far more spacious. Schell's Spartan quarters were oddly inhibiting, like a foreign laboratory. Sterile, cold, and restricted.

"Typhus?" Schell sat calmly, his smooth hands folded on his desk.

As always, the desk top was uncluttered and bare, except for the ship's log and a sextant.

"Call it what you will," Leary spat out, "it's certain doom! This is disaster aboard a ship, and well you know it!"

Frigid blue eyes fixed the physician in place like a bug on a pin. Even in the somber lantern glow, the red scar on Schell's face blazed its anger. "How many?"

"Dead, do you mean? Two so far; at least half a dozen down with it, though. It can take the lot of them before it's done—but, then, I don't have to tell you that, now do I? You've seen it all before."

The captain's thin mouth pulled down only enough to cause a faint break in the marble mask of his face. "Tell no one but the bosun and First Mate Clewes. They will confine steerage below decks."

"*All* of them?"

Schell lifted his eyes to regard Leary with a cold, exaggerated patience. "Of course, *all* of them," he said, still not raising his voice. "It would hardly make sense to isolate only a few, now would it?"

"They'll have no chance, none at all, locked in there together like rats in a barrel!"

Schell remained silent, watchful. Leary could hear the man's shallow breathing, saw the cold eyes freeze over, but just enough of the whiskey remained to dull his normal sense of caution. "I should think you'd want to deliver most of your cargo alive, Captain, if you're to earn your fee."

"*Our* cargo," Schell said smoothly, his accent thickening somewhat, "has already been paid for, the fee collected—from *your* countrymen. The only thing left for us to do is to put them ashore in New York. After that, it's entirely the problem of the...what do you call them? The *runners*."

Leary glared at the man across from him. Schell was an unfeeling, cold-blooded monster. The man had no soul. No soul at all.

"Send Clewes and the bosun to me," said the captain, turning his back. "And stay sober."

Leary stared at the back of Schell's head, debating whether his surgeon's knife would penetrate that granite-hewn skull. At last he turned and lunged out of the room, in a mad race for his bottle.

Fiabhras dubh…

The Black Fever. Typhus. The fearful malediction began to circulate steerage within hours, bouncing from berth to berth, striking raw terror into the hearts of all who heard it whispered or moaned.

No disease was more dreaded, none more horrifying than the prolonged, agonizing terrors of typhus. No swift, merciful death, this, but days of suffering and slow destruction, a lingering agony that transcended every other known form of human misery. Even to speak its name aloud was to unleash a blast of hell's wrath.

Black Fever aboard ship meant unavoidable epidemic and unimaginable suffering. Tonight, aboard the *Green Flag,* it meant sorrow upon sorrow.

In the Castlebar gaol, Morgan Fitzgerald thought about Nora aboard the ship to America and Daniel John at her side. He thought about his fine horse, Pilgrim, wondering what had become of him. He even thought about Whittaker, the Englishman. Then, despite his intentions to avoid the subject, he turned his thoughts to his approaching death.

There had been no trial—not that he had expected one. He knew well enough how things would be. One night soon, his cell would open. Hooded men would lead him out and put him onto a horse. He would be taken outside the town, to a deserted stand of trees—convenient for a hanging—and that, as they say, would be that. The end of him.

It had happened before, and it would happen again, was going to happen, to *him* this time. He had no hopes of a surprise or a last-minute miracle. He doubted that God was of a mind to perform miracles for an outlaw. And that was what he was, all right—an outlaw.

To the magistrates, he was the worst kind of outlaw—an Irish rebel who happened to have a passing good education, who could write a fair essay that might stir Gaelic blood and heat nationalist passions. He had robbed and raided. He had insulted the authorities and embarrassed their superiors. Of course, he might have survived all that if he had been ignorant—ignorant and entirely lacking in political interests.

Oh, he was a dead man, and that was the truth.

He should pray for his soul, Joseph Mahon had said, and Morgan knew the priest had it right. The thing was, he didn't know how—where to begin, what to say. He had gone too far. Over the years the stains of his sins had run together, eventually draining into the sea of a past from which he could no longer draw the slightest hope of a future.

Besides, only a penitent should pray for his own soul, one who sorrowed for his sin and wished it gone. Morgan supposed he was sorry for whatever wrongs he had committed in his lifetime, was *deeply* sorry for any that might have brought hurt or harm to his fellowman. But, in truth, the greatest sorrows in his soul were mostly self-centered: He grieved the loss of his loved ones, and he grieved the desolation of his country.

Had he known a way to create remorse within himself, he would have done so. But there was a terrible deadness in his spirit that seemed beyond reach. And so he waited, strangely impassive, knowing he would swing. Other than wondering when it would come, he was not as overwhelmed by the thought as he probably should have been.

Joseph Mahon, the priest, felt swept under by a great wave of defeat as he prepared to pray for the neck—and the soul—of Morgan Fitzgerald.

Joseph Mahon, the man, felt despair and anger as he knelt beside the bed in his room behind the chapel and considered the kind of death the brash young poet would endure.

Joseph had seen men hang, had rubbed his own neck at the snap of the noose, beheld the final agony of their last moments. He could not bear the thought of Morgan Fitzgerald facing such an end. The man was an outlaw, a renegade, a rogue. But, oh, what God could do with such a man, with such a valiant heart and mighty spirit!

Yet only a fool could not anticipate Fitzgerald's end. There would be no trial; the rumor was all over the village and the county, and Joseph had not been at all surprised to hear of it.

He had tried to stop this mad rush to the gallows, had spent days pounding on the door of every magistrate in the area who might have helped to stay the hangman's rope. But everywhere he went, he heard the same sound: the toll of doom for Morgan Fitzgerald.

And yet he knew that somehow it must be stopped. The man waiting in the Castlebar gaol, waiting to die, must be saved, spared from the noose at all costs. The country was in dire need of this man, would be in even greater need of him in the days to come.

The priest had a single hope—only one—to save Morgan from the gallows. Aidan Fitzgerald, Morgan's father, had given him that hope with his final confession, before he died of the drink.

But how could he salvage that hope, how could he use it in Morgan's behalf, without violating both Aidan's confession and his wishes for his son? *How, Lord?*

There was a man. One man, in Dublin, who could turn the tide. If he would.

Joseph prayed. Prayed for light, for a word of wisdom, for a work of power that would save a man's life—and his soul as well.

32

Secrets Aboard the Green Flag

Abandoned, forsaken,
To grief and to care,
Will the sea ever waken
Relief from Despair?

(ANONYMOUS—NINETEENTH CENTURY)

Daniel and his mother fought their way up the ladder to the hatch, gripping the splintery rungs with fierce determination. Behind them, hands grasped and shoved in an effort to push upward and free themselves from the stench of illness and death that now permeated steerage.

At the first clang of the morning bell just after daybreak, the ladder became a prize sought by every able-bodied person in steerage. Reaching the foredeck first didn't necessarily guarantee an early place at the stove; that boon was reserved for those holding bargaining power with the deck cook, such as bribe money or flattery from a pretty lass. Still, there was a mad rush every morning to reach the caboose, the fireplace that served as a cooking stove for steerage passengers.

The race for the hatch was even more frantic than usual this morning. All were in a fever to flee the misery of their quarters—not so much to gain the advantage at the caboose, but to escape the common dread of being confined with dead bodies.

Two had died late in the night, an elderly grandmother and a wee lass. Not long after, wild rumors had begun to sweep the entire deck.

There was even talk of the Black Fever, though nobody seemed willing to say for certain as yet.

The victims had been left to lie in their bunks after the surgeon's cursory examinations. Dr. Leary had been in a fierce hurry to leave, ignoring the questions and pleas of the frightened passengers trying to crowd him.

With the surgeon himself in such a bother, Daniel thought bitterly, *is there any wonder the passengers are eager to flee?*

Despite the pall of death and the ominous rumors, his own heart felt lighter this morning than it had in days. For the first time since boarding the *Green Flag,* his mother seemed to be her old self again. Oh, her sadness was still painfully apparent, but at least she had eaten her meals two days in a row.

Today she had come for him before the morning bell, not long after he awakened. He'd seen at once that she had combed her hair and scrubbed her face.

Smiling at him, she handed him one of the two cooking pots she was carrying. "You must have a warm breakfast this day, Daniel John," she said, much as she might have had they still been at home in the village. "It's important to eat and build our strength, so we can ward off the fever."

"Then you believe that's what it is, the Black Fever?"

Averting her eyes, she nodded, then answered in a strained voice. "I have seen it before, several years ago in the village. From what they're saying about the bodies, I've no doubt it's the typhus."

Instead of the fear Daniel would have expected, she seemed surprisingly steady and matter-of-fact.

Now, as they clung to the ladder, waiting for the hatch to open, she still appeared resolute and in control. Glancing back over her shoulder, she said, "We'll bring breakfast back for Katie and Johanna. They're minding Little Tom so I can go above decks. And we'll fix enough for Mr. Whittaker as well, though if he's as ill as you say, I doubt he'll be able to eat."

The Englishman had grown worse all through the night, flush-faced and hollow-eyed with the fever, going on like a crazy man in his sleep. "I'll have a look at him as soon as we come back," his mother went on. "Oh— and Daniel John, I'll need the medicine box. Katie is some fevered, too."

"It's under my bunk," Daniel John said, his spirits plummeting with her comment about Katie. Uneasily, he remembered how pale his friend had looked the day before, how listless and weak she appeared every time they were together. "Mother, you don't think Katie—"

He broke off when the hatch suddenly opened, letting in a thin veil of light from early dawn. Behind him, the big-bellied, peevish man from a neighboring bunk prodded his back, and Daniel instinctively kicked out a leg to keep from being knocked off the ladder.

Only five or six people were in front of him and his mother, so he had no trouble hearing the sailor who now stood in the hatchway, staring down at them with hard black eyes. "Go back to your quarters, all of you! No one is allowed above decks this day! You're under quarantine until further notice from the captain!"

"*Quarantine*? For *what*?" A redheaded man at the very top of the ladder blasted out the question.

"There's two of you dead of the Black Fever, that's for what!" the sailor retorted, his mouth screwing up with contempt.

"By whose say-so are we quarantined?" called out another man, this one halfway down the ladder.

"The surgeon's! Now get below, the lot of you!"

"But how long will you be keeping us down here?" cried out the man at the top.

"I wasn't told." The crewman started to close the hatch, then stopped when a thin, gray-faced woman standing near the bottom of the ladder cried out. "You can't just be keeping us locked up down here, in this—pit! Why, we won't be able to cook our food! We can't even get to the privies!"

Her outrage caught fire and set off a round of furious protests. People began to fight their way higher up the ladder, toward the hatch. Those still on the floor now started to move, until soon a swarm of hands was clawing at the ladder, threatening to topple everybody on it.

"You'll stay below deck until you're told otherwise!" shouted the sailor, shaking his fist through the opening of the hatch. "Now get down to your hole where you belong!"

With two meaty hands, he gave the redheaded man at the top of the ladder a hard shove, enough to cause him to reel backward. The man shouted as he swayed, then toppled helplessly from the ladder, causing the woman and little girl at his back to lose their balance. The ladder itself creaked and shook.

Daniel grabbed his mother around the waist with one hand, bracing the two of them against the hull with his other arm as their cooking pots went clanging to the floor. The burly man at his back let go an oath. Daniel shot him a look over his shoulder, shouting, "Get down! Get off the ladder!"

The man cursed him again, but turned and yelled the same warning to those behind him. Finally, one by one, they lowered themselves to the floor. After a moment, Daniel and his mother followed.

While some went to help those who had fallen, others clustered at the foot of the ladder, murmuring and looking about in fear and anger.

An elderly hawk-nosed man on a cane yelled up at the sailor, who still stood in the hatchway, scowling down at them. "God have mercy, man, you must at least help us to get the corpses out of here! We can't be leaving dead bodies lying about!"

The sailor glared at him, cursed, then heaved the door shut with a bang.

Within seconds, the angry murmurs of the crowd swelled to enraged threats and invective. Daniel could smell the fear in the air. Questions flew among the bunks, met by dread predictions and cries of alarm. Soon a general wailing went up. Women wept, children whined, and the men cursed and raged among themselves.

Suddenly, from across the room came a high-pitched shout of terror. "*Fiabhras dubh! Fiabhras dubh!* It is the Black Fever!"

Careful not to crack his head against the low ceiling—which was actually the underside of the main deck—Daniel stretched, craning his neck forward to see where the cry was coming from. At the opposite end of the men's quarters, a fair-haired boy who looked to be about his own age was hunched over a lower bunk, wide-eyed with fear. *"Their faces! Oh, God, have mercy, their faces—they're almost black!"*

Daniel lunged forward, but his mother grabbed his arm, holding him back. *"No!* Stay away!" He froze, staring at her.

"Let only those who have had the fever and survived it go near the bodies," she said, clutching his arm. "It's not as dangerous for them. The rest of us must do whatever we can to slow its spread!" Her eyes bored into his. "We have too many people depending on us to come down with the fever, Daniel John. We must stay well!"

Daniel looked from his mother to the bunk across the room. A number of men had gathered near the frightened boy and now stood staring at the occupants of the berth. "But what can we do? How can we possibly *not* come down with it, locked up in this…*dungeon!*"

He broke off, dismayed at how easily he had surrendered to his fear. Even in his own ears, he sounded like a panicky child.

"We will do what we must," said his mother, her voice unexpectedly gentle. Still clasping his arm, she added, "And you can be sure there will be much to do. But, first, we must see to Mr. Whittaker. Now, hurry and get the medicine box for me."

Daniel looked at her, confused as much by this new, unsettling show of strength as by the chaos surrounding them.

"Daniel John, *please*. I'm frightened, too. But we must do what we can while we're still strong!"

He saw the look in her eyes, a plea for him to be a man, at least for the moment.

The panic rising in his throat threatened to reduce him to blubbering, but, catching a deep breath, he nodded and followed her down the aisle.

ॐ

Evan strained to focus his eyes on the face lowered to his. The bunk, the stinking lantern hanging from the ceiling—even the woman's face—swayed drunkenly in front of him.

Now he stared into twin faces, two Nora Kavanaghs. He saw himself reflected in both pairs of eyes. The eyes were worried…or was it fear that stared back at him?

He tried to speak, but someone had sewn his mouth shut. There was a weight on his tongue, a hot coal…

In lieu of speech, he attempted to lift his hand, to make a signal of sorts. But his arm had been tied to the bunk. Pain held it fast; his other hand was free, but stiff and numb, lifeless.

He struggled to sit up, but hands held him down, pressing him into the bunk.

"It's all right, Mr. Whittaker. We'll take care of you. Be easy now, just rest yourself and be easy…it's all right." Both faces spoke as one, smiling with kindness.

Hot…he was so hot…and a host of knives stabbed, slicing into his shoulder.

The twin Nora Kavanaghs were saying something, their voices echoing, drifting away.... Young Daniel hovered closer, frowning, his eyes burning, heating Evan's skin even more. Why did the boy look so frightened?

Again he tried to speak. Nothing came. Humiliated, he felt tears track his cheeks...hot tears...scalding hot, like his skin and the pain in his shoulder.

"Please don't struggle, Mr. Whittaker. We'll take care of you...try to rest." The boy's voice was thin, distant, fading...

Something cool touched his forehead...so good. He mustn't weep... what would she think? He didn't want her to think him weak. He was supposed to be taking care of *her*...

33

Where Is God?

If it be stormy,
Fear not the sea;
Jesus upon it
Is walking by thee.

JOSEPH SHERIDAN LEFANU (1814–1873)

Daniel straightened, his gaze going from Evan Whittaker, who lay writhing on his berth in obvious agony, to his mother, her eyes frantic, her face pale with alarm in the swaying light from the overhead lantern.

With trembling hands she gingerly parted the torn sleeve of the Englishman's shirt to examine his bandaged shoulder. The vile odor issuing from the blood-soaked wrappings forced Daniel to turn away momentarily, but his mother continued to hover over Whittaker, shaking her head worriedly while tending to him as best she could.

"Daniel John, we *must* have the surgeon, and soon!" she whispered hoarsely. "His wound is infected, I'm sure of it. He's failing badly!"

"I *tried*, Mother!" Both he and Hugh MacCabe, the farmer in the next bunk, had made three futile attempts that day to get a crewman's attention by banging on the closed door to the hatch. "They wouldn't answer us!"

His mother glanced toward the ladder, unused for over two days now, except for those times when someone would ascend it out of sheer desperation, to hammer on the door in appeal. They *were* desperate; a number among them were bordering on hysteria. They might just as well be in prison, so hopeless did their plight seem.

The stench in steerage, intolerable before, was now unbearable. The very act of breathing had become another kind of misery. Beneath most bunks lurked wet, soiled rags, rotting food scraps, even feces. Without ventilation, the overpowering odors of stale air, human waste, and rank filth filled the entire dungeonlike hold with fumes deadly enough to fell a sailor—had one taken it upon himself to venture down into this pit of horrors.

Barred from the latrines, without access to fresh air or cooked food, the doomed passengers were falling ill by the dozens from seasickness, diarrhea, and fevers. Three new cases of suspected Black Fever had developed. Even now, a new corpse lay in the men's section, an old man who had screamed the entire night before dying.

Nothing in Daniel's worst nightmares could have prepared him for the horror of this pit in which they were trapped. He felt himself to be existing in a dark abyss, as if the sea itself had swallowed the *Green Flag* and was now bearing it upon some dread course of doom.

Darkness engulfed them, a shroud of evil drawing them in, closer and closer each day. Last night he had fallen asleep to the cries of the suffering and dying, his last thought a silent cry of his own: *Where is God in the midst of all this madness, this misery? When evil is so powerful a presence... where is God?*

Just as quickly, another question seized his thoughts to torment him. *How could Morgan have done this to us?*

Hadn't he bothered to investigate the ship and its crew? Daniel couldn't believe he would have set them aboard had he held even the slightest suspicion about the ship. Yet how could he *not* have known? He had made the arrangements, after all.

But what did it matter now? There was no turning back, no escape.

And no Morgan to settle their grievances. It was up to *him* now to do whatever he could to protect his mother and the children. And to help Evan Whittaker.

Daniel looked down at the Englishman. Drenched with perspiration from the fever, the man was out of his head with pain. His once-neat white shirt was ripped and bloodstained, his thin face smudged with grime. Daniel was struck by the thought that without the odd little spectacles Whittaker always wore, he looked surprisingly young and vulnerable. Strange, up until now he had not thought of Whittaker as young, and certainly not as a vulnerable human being like himself.

A fresh surge of emotion coursed through him as he realized anew the debt of gratitude they owed this man who had involved himself in their misery and now lay suffering in their midst—all because he had tried to help them.

Greater love hath no man than this, that he lay down his life for his friends...

But they weren't *his friends,* Daniel thought, a lump rising to his throat. *They were virtual strangers, even enemies, when Evan Whittaker risked his life for them. They were nothing to him, nothing more than unfamiliar names and foreign faces.*

From somewhere deep inside his spirit, something stirred. A slow, gentle kind of warmth began to rise from the very depths of his being.

And suddenly Daniel had the answer to his question. He knew where God was.

He was *here*, in the throes of their wretchedness. In the midst of their suffering. In the sacrificial love of the pain-racked Evan Whittaker. In this humble heart from which the love of Christ had so freely flowed. God was *here*.

Still stronger and brighter than the evil that lurked all around them, seeking an opportunity to conquer, *God was here—*

"Daniel John?"

He blinked at the sound of his mother's voice, looked from her to Whittaker.

"You must try again. Perhaps someone will come this time."

"Yes, all right. I'll go right now, Mother. I'll go and pound on the door of the hatch until *somebody* comes. I'll *make* them open it, or drive them mad trying!"

Nora's eyes swept over her son with a questioning look. Then she nodded and turned back to Whittaker. Crooning to the delirious man as she might have a child who needed soothing, she continued to swab his flushed face with gentle strokes. "Aye, you try again, Daniel John. Mr. Whittaker cannot go on so. We must get help for him at once!"

Daniel scurried up the ladder, ignoring the splinters that pierced his hands. Reaching the top, he pounded as hard as he could on the door. When his efforts were met by silence, he shinnied back down to grab an iron pot lying discarded amid some rubbish in a corner.

This time when he reached the top of the ladder, he began to crash the pot against the door, over and over again, shouting like a wild thing as he pummeled the rotting wood. *"We've a dead body in here! Open the hatch and help us take him out!"*

At last, the door flew open, and the sailor in charge of passing down their daily ration of water appeared in the opening. His face was ugly with rage as he glared at Daniel. "Stop with that racket, you little Mick!"

Daniel reared. Flinging the cooking pot to the floor, he squeezed his left arm and leg through the opening, past the sailor's brawny frame. Then, grabbing hold of the coaming, he managed to push by the crewman, throwing him off as he hit the deck at a run.

He had no idea which direction to go, where he would find Dr. Leary, but he headed aft, toward the stern, hurtling down the deck like a fired arrow in search of a target.

It came as no surprise to William Leary, the surgeon, that Abidas Schell had a stone for a heart. He had known the man too long to believe otherwise. Thus far this voyage had only served to confirm what he already knew.

Schell stood now, stiff and straight on the quarterdeck, entirely indifferent to Leary's protests on behalf of the poor wretches in steerage.

Leary was sober for a change, a condition in which his temper flared far more quickly than when numbed with whiskey. Schell's arrogant coldness had already torched the surgeon's anger, and with every minute's passing the flame blazed that much higher.

To make matters worse, Leary was as edgy as a wounded polecat about the storm blowing up. Already the Atlantic breezes had increased to strong winds. The tightly tuned rigging hummed and keened as the waves lifted the ship's stern, sweeping the deck with spray.

Leary wiped the salt foam from his face and raked a hand over the muscles at the back of his neck, strung tight with tension. The thought of a storm at sea never failed to make his blood run cold, but battling a storm with a daredevil captain like Schell at the helm made it freeze in his veins.

The grim-visaged captain was using the pretext of preparing for the approaching storm to ignore Leary's presence, but the surgeon wasn't fooled. This man was entirely capable of barking out a set of clipped, precise orders while absorbing half a dozen other conversations at the same time.

Schell simply had no interest in, no compassion for the poor devils below.

Leary almost wished he were as heartless.

He felt a sudden, vicious stab of spite at the expression on the captain's face as he watched the crew work feverishly to bring in some of the standing sails and double-reef the topsails.

He knew it set Schell's teeth on edge, having to haul in canvas. The man would fly every possible square foot of sail he dared, running the ship to the limit of her potential. The few knowledgeable seamen on board—and they *were* few—grumbled nervously from time to time that they would all eventually suffer for their captain's irresponsibility. One or two had even dared to challenge Schell's orders, but he had ordered them flogged senseless, thereby putting an end to any further questioning of his judgment.

Making another attempt to get Schell's attention, Leary now moved to stand directly in front of the man. "At least let them take turns coming up, just long enough to suck in some fresh air," he said. "A few at a time will do no harm, and the healthier we can keep them, the better off we will all be."

"The entire steerage is under quarantine and will be until I'm assured of no further outbreak of typhus." Schell's reply was distracted, his gaze set above, to where a nimble-footed youngster was climbing a towering mast.

Finally, he lowered his eyes to look at Leary. "As the surgeon, I should think your concern would be for the welfare of the entire ship, not just the few Irish paupers in steerage."

"Few?" Leary shot an incredulous look at Schell. "There are over two hundred of them down there!"

The captain shrugged.

"And what about those poor Chinese girls you've got locked up in the cabins with the opium? They're children, God help us! Just children! Is there *nothing* that means as much to you as gold?"

He paused, enraged at the other man's lack of response. "Well, answer me this, man, what happens if you deliver your Irish unfortunates and your little-girl whores dead instead of alive? Where will that leave your *business* then, eh?"

Schell's icy blue gaze never wavered, but the threat in his voice was unmistakable. "I believe our arrangement had your blessing, *Doctor*. It was you, after all, who handled the negotiations."

Leary swallowed. "You gave me no choice, and you know it," he muttered, forcing himself not to shrink beneath Schell's frigid stare of contempt.

"Doctor! Dr. Leary—please, sir, you must come!"

Leary whirled around, and Schell blinked in surprise as a wild-eyed boy came upon them at a run.

It was the young colt of a lad who was traveling with the injured Englishman. Gasping for breath, he looked faint, perhaps even ill.

"What are you doing here?" Schell's voice cracked like a gunshot. "How did you get abovedecks?"

Panting, the boy looked from Leary to the captain. "Please, sir, I'm sorry, but we need the surgeon badly! My friend, Mr. Whittaker, may be dying!"

Schell glared at the boy as if he were a worm. "Denker, here!" he called out to a nearby crewman. "Put this beggar back down in steerage where he belongs."

"No. Not unless the surgeon comes with me!"

Schell made no move for an instant. Then, without warning, his hand shot out to slap the boy across the cheek with enough force to make him reel.

Instinctively Leary put up a hand, as much to ward off the enraged captain as to steady the boy. But Schell had already dropped his arm, the implacable mask once more in place.

The sailor he had summoned now moved behind the boy, yanking both his arms hard behind him. The lad struggled, crying out. His eyes flashed with fury as he stood, legs outspread, facing Schell.

"Our fares are paid," he said, his voice trembling with resentment. "We're entitled to a doctor, and that's all I'm asking!"

"You're entitled to be strung up on the ratlines," retorted Schell, pointing to the tarred ropes used as a ladder, "if you so much as open your mouth once more. As it is, you've earned yourself a night in the wheelhouse."

"Oh, give over!" Leary blurted out. "I was going below tonight anyway, to check the lot of them. I'll go with him now instead of waiting."

For an instant he thought Schell would refuse, would stick to his intention of locking the boy up. A muscle tightened at the corner of one eye, and the nasty scar seemed to pulse and blaze. But at last he gave a short nod of dismissal, telling the sailor, "Let him go. There's more important work to be done than wasting time with an Irish beggar boy."

"Come on, you little fool!" Leary snapped, now angry with himself for stepping in. His impulsive defense of the boy would serve neither of them well.

Taking the lad by the arm, he half dragged him back up the deck, grumbling all the way. "Why would you be fretting yourself so over a stinking Englishman is what I'd like to know? What is he to you? Not worth incurring the wrath of a man like Schell, I can tell you."

"Mr. Whittaker saved our lives!" The boy twisted in an attempt to tug himself free from Leary's grasp. "We can do no less for him."

Leary looked at him. "What you'd best be doing is staying out of the captain's way from now on unless you've a mind to end up at the end of a lash! He makes no distinction for age."

"He has no right to flog a passenger! I know that much!"

"You know nothing at all!" Leary shouted, again grabbing him by the arm and bringing him to a stop. *"Nothing!* Schell is the law on this ship, and you are no more than a flyspeck to him. If you value your skin, you'll stay out of his sight!"

The boy was quiet for a moment, his piercing blue eyes making Leary increasingly uncomfortable.

"What kind of a ship *is* this?" he asked in a low voice. "Not what we were told, that much is certain."

Leary flared, tightening his grasp on the lad's arm. "I don't know what you were told, boy, but you'd best listen to what *I'm* telling you. You'll do neither yourself nor your family any good by making trouble. Stay quiet and stay out of the way if you hope to see America."

Leary studied the boy for a moment more, relaxing his grip slightly but still holding on to him with care.

"All right, come on now," he ordered, somewhat mollified as he again started to tug the lad along beside him. "If you want me to have a look at your Englishman, give me no more grief. And if you've more than a pea for a brain between your ears, you'll not show your face outside steerage again until you're told. This ship is a dangerous place for meddlesome children."

The boy's gaze stabbed at Leary's conscience. For an instant he felt as if his defenses were being cut away, layer by layer, and his soul laid bare. Something in those eyes belied the youthful countenance, something old and wise beyond the lad's years.

Chilled by the thought that he had been seen for what he was, Leary gave the boy's arm a vicious yank and quickened his pace still more.

Nora pressed her clasped hands against her lips, her gaze going back and forth between the scowling physician and the semiconscious Evan Whittaker.

In his delirium, the Englishman had struggled so fiercely against the surgeon that Daniel had to help hold him down.

"Please, Doctor, can you give him something for the pain?" Nora ventured uncertainly, somewhat intimidated by the doctor's rough impatience.

Ignoring her, he straightened, his shoulders bent slightly to keep his head from grazing the ceiling. For a moment he continued to stare down at Whittaker's shoulder, his lined face twisted into a taut, resentful grimace.

"There's nothing for it but to take the arm."

The words were spoken with such a resentment it almost sounded as if he were indicting Whittaker for his failure to heal.

The room swayed. Nora stared at the surgeon, then Whittaker. *"No... oh, no!* Please, there must be another way...some medicine—"

"I said I'll have to amputate!" snapped the surgeon, still not looking at anyone but Whittaker. "It's his arm or his life."

"But he's not aware enough to even have a say in it—"

The physician turned to look at her. "He *has* no say in it, woman, if he wants to live!"

Dear Lord, all this is happening to him because of us! It's so unfair; he saved our lives, and now...this?

"If you...if you amputate, will he live?" Daniel John's voice sounded thin, tremulous. Nora saw the dismay in her heart mirrored in her son's eyes.

The surgeon's lower lip rolled down even farther. "I can't promise that. He might live if I take the arm. But he'll die for certain if I *don't!"*

Doesn't he care? Whittaker might be a stranger to him, but he is a doctor, after all.

Nora stepped closer to Whittaker, looking down on him. His face was tracked with perspiration and grime, etched with pain. She felt ill. Ill and sad. And guilty.

He did it for us. It's because of us this is happening to him.

"I'll have to go and get my instruments," Dr. Leary said. "We'd best get to it right away. He's in bad shape."

"Just be sure that's *all* you get. You'll be sober when you operate on him."

Nora's head shot up at Daniel John's sharp words. The surgeon whipped around to face him, eyes flashing.

"I saw the shape you were in when you treated his wound." The lad's voice was as hard as any man's. "You were *drunk!* I wouldn't be surprised if it wasn't your fault the wound went bad."

"Why, you!"

"You know I'm right!" Daniel John stood, stepping out from Whittaker's bunk to face the surgeon. "I'm only asking for your word that you'll come back sober. He's important to us."

"He's English," the surgeon sneered.

"He's our *friend,*" countered the boy. "He saved our lives. Now you will save his."

Nora stared in wonder as the surgeon's angry glare slowly wilted, then dropped away entirely.

His shoulders sagged, his face went slack, and then he gave a short nod. "See to him until I get back," he muttered gruffly. "I won't be long."

As soon as the doctor walked away, Nora let go the tears she'd been choking back. Daniel John came to her, pulling her gently into his arms.

She could feel her son's trembling as she wept against his shoulder, but his arms were strong and his voice still steady. "At least this way, he has a better chance to live, Mother. That's the important thing—that he live."

Wetting his shoulder with her tears, Nora desperately hoped that Evan Whittaker would feel the same when he awakened.

34

The Keen Comes Wailing on the Wind

I hear all night as through a storm
Hoarse voices calling, calling
My name upon the wind.

JAMES CLARENCE MANGAN (1803–1849)

Morgan Fitzgerald stood in the middle of his cell, wondering why the gaol was so uncommonly quiet tonight.

For more than an hour he had heard none of Cummins the gaoler's vigorous cursing, no prisoner complaints, no rattling of chains or slamming of doors.

It was as dark as it was quiet. Even the candle that usually lighted the corridor seemed to have been forgotten.

Outside, the wind set up a mournful wail, and Morgan shivered. A breath of dread whispered at the back of his neck—from the keening of the wind or the cold of the cell, he couldn't say.

Not for the first time since being locked up, he thought of the flask he had once carried. He'd given up the drink years before, while still a young man, once he saw himself headed down the same road as his father. Tonight, though, he thought he would not mind a taste or two.

He smiled grimly in the darkness. Had he known back then that his choices ran to dying with a noose around his neck or a tumbler in his hand, he might not have been so quick to smash the flask.

He was exceedingly bored. The candle he'd managed to badger from

Cummins had burned itself up last evening, so he couldn't see to read or write. This would have been bad enough in itself, but it was more vexing than it might have been, thanks to that sly priest, Joseph Mahon.

The man had slipped a worn copy of the Scriptures inside his belongings. On the cover was fastened a note.

Now Joseph knew him well enough to know he could never resist a good tale. His vague message had been meant to pique Morgan's curiosity, and so it had.

Morgan, the note had read, *there's a tale inside about a foolish fellow who thought he could escape God by running in the opposite direction. More than a little like you, I should imagine. I thought perhaps you might want to see for yourself the lengths to which our Lord will go to get our attention and change our course. His name was Jonah, by the way, if you care to look him up...*

Morgan knew the story of Jonah, of course, but, partly to appease Joseph and partly out of idle interest, he had read it again.

And again.

Even now he found himself wanting to read it once more, at length. Something about Jonah and his great fish captured Morgan's attention in an odd sort of way.

At times, like now, he even found himself musing that this cell was not unlike the fish's belly—cold and wet and dark.

At any rate, he was eager for Cummins to bring his evening meal so he could nag him for another candle.

In the meantime, he wondered where the irascible rat who had become his nighttime companion was hiding himself.

Oliver, Morgan had named him, in memory of Cromwell, of course. And wasn't the dull-witted rodent nearly as predictable as old Oliver himself had reportedly been?

Each evening just after Cummins left Morgan's plate, the rat would slink out of its hole and actually try to beat him to his supper.

For the first two or three days, Morgan had let the creature have the offensive mess in its entirety, for he could not stomach it. At that rate, however, he would have ended up too weak to attend his own hanging, and so he determined to teach the greedy Oliver some manners, making him wait until he himself arrived at the last few bites and set the plate to the floor.

Either the rat had tired of his paltry leavings, or else the gruel had finally killed him off. Morgan suspected the gruel.

The cursed tooth had begun to ache again this afternoon. Morgan wished he had the stomach to yank it out, but the thing was a piece of himself, and these days he was not eager to part with even a rotting tooth. If nothing else, the pain was a reminder that he was still alive.

He heard the jingle of keys and turned. The door opened to frame both Cummins, the gaoler, and Joseph Mahon, the priest, in the flickering glow from the candle Cummins held.

In the dim, weaving light the men's faces took on an eerie pall, giving them an almost spectral appearance. The gaoler's heavy-jowled face was set in a fierce, relentless expression, while the priest stared at Morgan with a peculiar, speculative look in his eye.

Morgan met his stare with a questioning look of his own, then turned to Cummins.

His shoulders tightened instinctively as the cold finger of doom began a slow descent down his backbone.

The question no longer seemed to be whether Whittaker would survive the amputation of his arm, but whether he would live long enough for the amputation to take place.

Daniel watched the Englishman with anxious eyes, his own face flushed with dread of what was to come. Whittaker had not spoken for over an hour, other than to moan or mumble something entirely incoherent.

Much to Daniel's relief, the doctor had returned in a short time, sober. With him he brought a number of ominous-looking medical instruments, the sight of which had made Daniel's mother quickly turn her head away.

Whittaker lay on a rough wooden table at the end of the steerage compartment. The surgeon, an apron bound around him, had just returned from scrubbing his hands in a bowl of hot water, water he had taken time to heat before returning. He snapped at a number of inquisitive onlookers, chasing them off to their own quarters with a string of curses and threats.

Now he stood, studying Whittaker. After a moment he raised his eyes to look first at Daniel, then at his mother.

"One of you will have to stay and help," he said shortly.

Daniel's heart slammed hard against his ribcage. He looked at his mother's ashen face, swallowed, and said, "I'll stay."

He didn't miss the pool of relief that instantly welled up in his mother's eyes. But, pressing her lips into a tight line, she shook her head. "No, Daniel John, I will stay. You—"

"Mother," he interrupted, "I'm going to be a surgeon, remember? This is something I will have to do myself one day. I will stay with Whittaker."

Their eyes held briefly; then she gave a slight nod and backed away, retreating to a nearby place against the hull.

"If he starts to wake up, give him as many drops of this as he can manage."

Dr. Leary's graveled voice jerked Daniel's attention back to the table and Whittaker. Taking the small bottle the surgeon handed him, he asked, "What is it?"

"Laudanum. Opium. It'll ease the pain some."

"Some? Don't you have anything stronger?"

The surgeon glanced up from assembling his instruments on a tray beside the table. "Even if I did, I wouldn't chance giving it to him, the shape he's in. His heart is battling for every beat. Pain never killed a man," he finished curtly. "Too much opiate has killed more than one."

Daniel swallowed down his growing panic. "I'd like to pray, please."

The surgeon turned. "As you like."

"I'd...I'd feel better about things if you would pray as well."

"I'm not a praying man," replied the doctor, turning away.

"And what kind of man are you, then, Doctor?"

Daniel's quiet question seemed to fluster the surgeon. Pretending to search the inside of his medical case, he delayed his answer. "A man who has seen far too much to believe in a God who hears prayer," he finally muttered, turning back to Whittaker.

Daniel scrutinized the stooped, weathered-looking surgeon. Something in this man belied the gruffness he seemed so determined to project, and he found himself wondering if the doctor's hard exterior was as impenetrable as he had first believed.

Daniel hesitated another instant, then bowed his head and closed his eyes. In a soft, not altogether steady voice, he prayed for the skill of Dr. Leary, for the success of the operation, and for angels to stand guard and minister to the unsuspecting Evan Whittaker.

"And I pray that when he awakens, Lord, he will forgive us for the tragedy we have brought upon him."

Daniel opened his eyes, blinking at the sight of the knife the surgeon now held in his hand.

"Come around to this side," the doctor ordered. "You scrubbed your hands as I said?"

Daniel nodded and crossed to the other side of the table, where the doctor had laid out the instruments.

He tried to swallow, but found his throat swollen shut.

"This is the saw I will need when I'm finished with the knife," the surgeon said, pointing out each instrument as he reeled off their names.

"This other is the Hey's saw," he went on. "Silk for sutures, here. Now, then, you stay close, hand me each as I ask for it." He glanced at Daniel. "You all right, boy?"

Daniel moistened his lips, nodded.

The surgeon studied him. "You must not get sick on me, mind. You're sure you are up to this?"

Daniel dragged his eyes away from the instruments, looked at the doctor, and nodded stiffly.

The physician bent over Whittaker and set to work. "So you've a mind to be a surgeon yourself, then?"

"Aye," Daniel replied in a shaky voice, his eyes widening as the doctor ripped off what remained of Whittaker's torn shirt, then flushed away the blood from the wound with a bucket of cold water.

"Tonight may just change your mind."

Daniel's eyes went to the knife in the surgeon's hand, followed the movement of the blade as it targeted Whittaker's upper arm.

The room swayed. The table rocked back and forth.

Daniel panicked, sure he was about to be ill—or, even worse, that he might faint.

Then he saw the knife suspended in the air and the surgeon lift his head, frowning as he let go an oath. "It's the storm," he growled, holding the scalpel poised until the rocking ebbed. "This ship is damned, that's certain! I told Schell, I told him he would pay…"

Daniel could make no sense of the man's wild muttering. But he knew well enough the importance of a steady hand on the knife.

Grinding his teeth, he hugged both arms to his body, holding his breath as the surgeon began to cut.

Whittaker's eyes were still shut, but he screamed—a terrible, piercing scream.

Tightening his own arms around himself, Daniel screamed, too, a silent, suffocating scream that tore at the walls of his heart and made his chest swell until he thought it would explode.

Dimly he became aware of the doctor's rough demand. "The saw, boy! *Hand me the saw!*"

Whittaker screamed once more when the saw met bone. Then his head lolled to the side as if he were dead.

The ship rocked, creaking and groaning, swaying like a drunken whale. The table danced on the floor.

The surgeon stopped, waited, then returned to his task. His face was flushed, slick with sweat, his eyes boring through the bone along with the saw.

The ship rolled, and Daniel pitched forward. He reached to steady himself and the table, to hold fast.

His stomach recoiled at the motion of the ship, the sight of the surgeon's blood-soaked apron, the sound of the saw severing Whittaker's arm.

Oh, dear Lord, I am sick…so sick…I mustn't retch…I mustn't faint…

Seawater streamed through the overhead vents, spraying the table, Whittaker, the surgeon.

Passengers shrieked. Prayers and curses were lifted, fighting to be heard against the squeal and crack of the ship's timbers, the crash of the waves.

The wind itself seemed to be screaming with pain as the surgeon finally separated Whittaker's arm from his body.

Daniel squeezed his eyes shut against Evan Whittaker's tragedy and cupped both hands to his ears to shut out the hellish sound of torment shaking the very hull of the ship.

The demented face of a woman rode the storm aboard the *Green Flag.* Sheathed in a gossamer gown, hair flowing, her twisted features were set straight ahead. One arm was raised, the hand balled to a fist. The fist gripped a piece of green silk, flapping madly in the wind.

The wild eyes of the *Green Flag's* masthead seemed to follow the frenzied movement of the crewmen as they fought the gale-driven waves splashing over the deck.

The force of the waves knocked sailors off their feet, hurtling them forward, sweeping some the entire length of the deck. Timbers cracked, blocks fell, spars broke loose and went down in a tangle of rigging.

On into the howling night the woman leaped across the waves, pointing the way with the flag in her upraised arm, daring the gale to slow her speed.

Engulfed by the blackness of the sea and the night, the woman appeared to be fleeing a different Darkness.

35

To Set the Captive Free

And thus we rust
Life's iron chain
Degraded and alone:
And some men curse, and some men weep,
And some men make no moan:
But God's eternal Laws are kind
And break the heart of stone.

OSCAR WILDE (1854–1900)

It was taking Cummins and the priest a powerful long time to get around to telling him he was about to swing.

After fifteen minutes or more of idle blather, Morgan had enough. They might just as well get to it, since all three knew exactly why they had come.

Joseph Mahon obviously still hoped to shrive him, and Cummins no doubt wanted to be the lad to lead him to the noose.

Joseph had already sat down twice, only to haul himself up again and go pacing around the cell as if *he* were the one confined. Morgan thought it a bit peculiar that a priest like Mahon, who by now had to be an old hand at hearing the confessions of the condemned, should have such a difficult time of things with yet another sinner.

Cummins, too, seemed in an odd mood. Rather than the glee Morgan would have expected from him, the man's face was so sour it could have curdled a pail of new milk.

"So, then, Joseph, where have you been hiding yourself these days? You haven't been ill, I hope?"

Even as Morgan said the words, it struck him that indeed the priest *did* look ill, so lean you could blow him off your hand. Joseph Mahon was killing himself over his parish. Morgan would have wagered that both he and Oliver the rat had been eating better than the priest.

Mahon stopped his pacing and came to stand directly in front of Morgan, in the middle of the cell. In his right hand he held an envelope and a paper rolled into a tube—the legal go-ahead for his hanging, Morgan assumed. The hand holding the papers trembled so fiercely Morgan's instinct was to reach out and steady it with his own.

Instead, he shot the priest a grim smile in an attempt to make things easier for him. Splaying his hands on his hips, he stood, legs wide, studying Mahon with a rueful expression.

"It's all right, Joseph. Haven't we both known it was coming, and soon at that?"

The priest contemplated Morgan for what seemed a very long time, looking away only once to glance at Cummins.

"Morgan," Joseph Mahon finally said, his quivering hand tightening on the papers, "it is not what you think, lad."

Morgan frowned, waiting.

"Morgan," Joseph Mahon said again, lifting the paper in his hand and holding it up like a signpost, "you have been granted a pardon. A *conditional* pardon, mind you. But you are saved, Morgan. You are saved from the rope."

Morgan stared at him. He dropped his hands down to his sides, looked about him. The room seemed to swim. Even the ceiling tilted a bit, and the floor on which he was standing rose as if to hurl him backward.

"What are you saying to me, Joseph?" he grated out.

The priest reached out to put a hand to Morgan's forearm. "It's true, lad. You will not hang."

His heart pounding, Morgan looked to Cummins. The gaoler sat, hunched over like a lump on the sagging mattress. He wore the dark, angry face of one who has had the rug yanked out from under him.

"A pardon, is it?" Morgan parroted, turning back to Joseph Mahon.

"Aye, lad," said the priest, quickly adding, "a *conditional* pardon."

"I don't believe it," said Morgan, then repeated the words softly.

"I don't believe it. How could this be, Joseph?"

"It is true, Morgan," the priest assured him. "You are saved. By God's grace, you will live."

For one appalling instant, Morgan felt he would disgrace himself by bursting into tears of stunned relief. Recovering, he looked at the papers in Joseph's hand.

"Is that—"

The priest nodded. "This is your pardon, Morgan. And a letter."

"A letter? A letter from whom?"

Morgan reached for the papers, but Joseph put up a restraining hand. "Wait, lad. Sit down, now, for we must talk."

Morgan managed a jerky nod. "How, Joseph? How could such a thing happen?"

The priest gave him a long look, then took his arm and motioned him toward the bed. Cummins immediately jumped to his feet and went to stand on the opposite side of the cell, as if Morgan's nearness might contaminate him.

"It came about," said the priest, waiting for Morgan to sit down, "through your grandfather."

While Morgan sat staring at him with burning eyes, struggling to shake off the buzzing in his head, Joseph Mahon turned to Cummins. "I will talk with him alone now."

The sullen line of the gaoler's mouth pulled down even more. "I'm to see the pardon delivered," he said, crossing his arms over his chest, "and its terms accepted before the prisoner is released."

Mahon narrowed his eyes. "The pardon will be *delivered*, and will tell you when the prisoner can be released! Will you insult your own priest by doubting his honor, Francis Cummins?"

The gaoler grumbled but finally turned and let himself out the door.

The priest sat down beside Morgan. "I know you are surprised, Morgan. I will explain what I can."

Morgan's own hand was shaking as he rubbed one side of his beard. He looked at the priest.

"Surprised?" Morgan repeated blankly. "Oh, I am not surprised, Joseph. I am dumbfounded!"

Avoiding Morgan's eyes, Joseph sat staring down at the floor.

Morgan noted that the priest's hands were still trembling. *Weakness,* he realized. *It isn't dread over approaching doom after all, but illness and exhaustion that has made him quake so.*

"Much of what you will want to know, Morgan, is in this letter," said Joseph, handing both the envelope and the scrolled sheet of paper to Morgan without looking at him. "There are some things I cannot tell you, not without violating your father's last confession."

Morgan looked down at the papers in Joseph's hand, then took them. "My father's—" Morgan stopped, groping to make some sense of the priest's words. "What is all this you are telling me, Joseph? About my father—and a grandfather? I have no grandfather, at least none I ever knew."

He paused, and Joseph Mahon turned and met his eyes, nodding. "Aye, lad, I know that. You thought you had no real family, other than your father and Thomas."

"That's the truth. But how is it that *you* know?"

"I have just returned from Dublin, Morgan. That's why I have not come to the gaol for some days now."

"Dublin? What is in Dublin?"

"Your grandfather. Your mother's father."

"My—Joseph, what is this about?" Morgan put a heavy hand to Joseph's arm, but, feeling the thin, fragile bones beneath the sleeve of the priest's cassock, he immediately gentled his touch.

Mahon looked away. "Do you remember your mother at all, Morgan?"

"No. I never knew her."

Still staring at the floor, Joseph asked quietly, "Did you know that she was half English?"

"Aye, I knew that, well enough," Morgan muttered.

The priest turned to look at him, his eyes widening with surprise. "Aidan told you, then—about your mother?"

Morgan shook his head. "Thomas. Thomas told me. Our da spilled it to him one night when he was on the bottle," he said tightly, remembering how his young heart had sickened at the thought of British blood in his veins.

"How much did Thomas know?"

"How much?" Morgan looked at him, then shrugged. "That was most of it. Our mother was the daughter of an English politician and a Dublin woman who left the church to marry."

"That was all? Did you never wonder what happened to your mother?"

"She died," Morgan said quietly, avoiding the priest's probing gaze. "When I was still a babe. I never knew her at all. She died, and his grief for her set our father on the road. He never got over her death, you know. Her dying killed him as well."

"It was hard for you lads, you and Thomas," said Joseph softly, as if remembering. "Aidan was a…a difficult man. A broken man. You must have wondered about your mother, what she was like?"

"Aye, we did," Morgan admitted. "Da would not speak of her, told us nothing of their life together, and so I made up a picture of her in my mind when I was small. The picture became so real that she almost seemed to live, at least at night, in my dreams. Even now," he said with a faint smile, "I can see the face I gave to her. It was a lovely face—"

Catching the maudlin note in his voice, he broke off and got to his feet. "Ah, well, what boy does not want a lovely mother? Joseph, I will ask you again: How is it that you know these things, and what is all this leading up to?"

"Aidan told both you and Thomas that your mother's people were dead as well as herself, did he not?"

Morgan nodded. "He did."

The priest sighed, his eyes roaming over the dark, barren cell. "I suppose he felt it best, safer for you boys." He regarded Morgan with a thoughtful gaze for a moment. "But it was a lie. Your grandfather still lives, Morgan. And it is to him you owe your freedom."

For a fleeting instant, Joseph caught a rare glimpse of vulnerability in Morgan, and it pierced his heart all through.

He had known this immense, strapping young man since he was a lad—long enough to know he was not the callous outlaw his reputation suggested. The Morgan Fitzgerald Joseph knew might very well possess the ferocity of a lion and the cunning of the wolf after which he was called. But he was also a man with an infinitely tender heart that belied his strength, a heart easily pierced and supremely capable of deep, intense pain.

Joseph remembered the boy Morgan had been, with his wild copper curls and his too-long legs and his habit of hurling endless unanswerable questions during the catechism classes. Brilliant and eclectic, he had been

a rebel even then, a rebel with a hunger for knowledge and a fierce intolerance of easy answers. The lad had often reminded Joseph of a young animal, stalking the most elusive prey known to man—Truth.

"Sit down, Morgan," he said. "Sit down here beside me."

Morgan did as he was told, but the look he gave Joseph was guarded
and not altogether friendly.

"The letter you hold is from your maternal grandfather. He has written
to you with an explanation of the terms of your pardon, which he secured
on your behalf. I will tell you the little I can without violating the confessional, but the rest you must learn for yourself, inside that letter."

Morgan studied the envelope in his hand for an instant. "How did you
know where to find him?"

"Oh, *finding* him was no problem," Joseph said. "He is a well-known,
powerful man—a member of the aristocracy. He sat in Parliament for
years, owns vast estates both in England and in Ireland, and has great
influence. No, it wasn't difficult at all to find him," he repeated. "He's an
old man now, of course, retired because of age and poor health. But your
friend, Smith O'Brien, helped me gain an audience with him. He knew a
man who knew another man, don't you see, and the next thing that happened, I found myself in your grandfather's library."

Joseph leaned toward Morgan. "And what a library it *is*, Morgan! You
would lie down and die of ecstasy just to see it, and that's the truth!"

"Joseph, I care nothing about my—about this man's library! Just tell me
whatever it is you think I should know and be done with it. If it's true that
I am about to be freed from this place, the sooner the better for me!"

Joseph nodded. He thought he understood Morgan's confusion. To
spend years with no family at all and then one day to learn of a grandfather who is no more than a stranger—an English stranger—would be a
hard thing. A hard thing, indeed.

"Your father's family was ancient Gaelic—among the very oldest of
Irish stock. Not wealthy at all, but learned people, most of them teachers and priests. Aidan was educated, first in France and later in Dublin at
great financial sacrifice. To his family, knowledge was all, nearly as important as life itself."

"Aye, the old man often rambled on about the sanctity of education
when he was drunk," Morgan commented brusquely.

Nodding, Joseph went on. "Your mother's family—at least on her father's side—was English, only a step or two removed from nobility. Wealthy, influential—"

"—and thoroughly Protestant," Morgan finished dryly.

"That's the truth. Your grandmother left the church in a great rush to marry her English lover, and it was immediately hushed up that their spotless Saxon bloodline had been some tainted with a touch of the Roman Irish.

"Your father was a poor student when he met and fell in love with your mother. By that time her family was so entrenched in their wealthy English Protestantism that the news of their only daughter's love for a starving Roman Catholic brought as much horror as if she had asked their leave to wed a leper.

"Your father's family was no more pleased. They cherished their Irishness and their Catholicism every bit as much as the girl's family did their Anglican ways. Both families threatened the young lovers with expulsion if they did not part.

"Well, the long and short of it," Joseph continued, feeling a renewed wave of sadness for the young couple who wanted only to be left alone with their love for each other, "was that your mother and father *would* be married, and so they defied their families—and their religions—and ran off to some godforsaken village in County Kerry to be married by a civil official.

"Over the years their poverty forced them to move from town to town. Aidan kept a school wherever he was needed, or else worked at odd jobs to keep food in their mouths.

"When Thomas was born, Aidan's father—his mother had died— relented and asked them to come home with their babe. Things were better for them for a time, but when the old man died, nothing was left to them except a house on which they could not pay the rent.

"Your mother was carrying you by then, and after you were born, she sickened for some weeks, then died. Aidan tried to keep you boys with him, but he had no money and was drinking something fierce all the time. So he went to your mother's family and offered the two of you—you and Thomas—to them."

As Joseph watched, a stricken look came over Morgan's face. "He gave us *away*? Is that the truth?"

"It wasn't like that! He was wild with grief, desperate to save you and your brother from starving. The family agreed to take you both, and gave Aidan some money to go away. He had to sign papers giving up all claim to you, had to promise he would never attempt to see you again. At the last minute, he couldn't do it. The papers were signed, the money in his pocket, but he reneged on the agreement and ran away, taking both you and Thomas with him.

"Apparently they tried for months to locate the three of you—even offered a reward. But Aidan went on the road like a common outlaw, hiding in the woods, stopping off in remote villages, until the family finally lost his scent. After that…well, as you know, he did the best he could. But by then he was a beaten man.

"The rest of it…no longer matters. There are private, personal things a father would not want his sons to know, only his priest."

Morgan was silent for a long time. He sat slumped over on the bed, his broad shoulders sagging, his rugged face pensive. Joseph reached once to touch him, thought better of it, and dropped his hand away.

"So that is where the money for my education came from," Morgan said softly. "He stole it from *them*." He was silent for a moment, thinking. "How did my grandfather manage a pardon for me? And *why*?" He turned to look at Joseph. "And these *conditions* you mentioned—what are they?"

"Your grandfather has the power to obtain most anything he pleases," Joseph replied. "As to *why*, you are his blood—his only grandson, Morgan—and he is sorry for what he did to your parents. Truly sorry."

"Of course, he is," Morgan sneered. "You still haven't told me what the conditions are."

"Morgan, he is an old, sick man. Probably he has little time left on this earth. It is altogether likely his remorse is genuine. I believe it is," Joseph said firmly. "As for the conditions, they are more than fair. He asks only that you refrain from further 'illegal activities.' And he wants to see you. He wants you to come to Dublin once you're released."

"He wants to *see* me?" Morgan uttered a short, ugly laugh. *"When hell is an iceberg!"*

Again Joseph reached to clasp Fitzgerald's shoulder. "Morgan—"

Morgan shook him off with a violent shrug. He shot to his feet and went to stand in the center of the shadowed cell. "If seeing him is a part of the pardon, tell him I'll whistle as I swing!"

He tossed the envelope and the pardon to the floor.

"Don't be a *fool!*" Ignoring the pain in his back, Joseph got to his feet and hurried to rescue the papers.

Facing Morgan, he pressed the envelope and the pardon into his hand. "I understand your bitterness, lad, and I don't blame you. But it will gain you nothing to go on nursing your poison. That paper is your freedom! Do not let your anger get in the way of your good sense!"

His face livid, Morgan waved the papers in the air. "Why, after all these years, Joseph? Answer me that! Why should I go toadying to a man who as good as murdered my parents? His own *daughter*, for the love of heaven! Why should I do anything for a man like that?"

Joseph looked at him, choosing his words carefully. "Because he is soon to die and wants to see his only grandson while there is still time."

At Morgan's grunt of disgust, Joseph shook his head and put up a hand to quiet him. "And because *you* will die if you do not go, if you refuse to let him help you. You should do this thing out of mercy for him, and for the sake of your own life most of all. I cannot think you would need more reason than that."

The younger man's back stiffened. He squared his shoulders, lifted his chin. Standing there, so straight and towering, he looked for all the world like one of the ancient warlords.

Oh, God, soften his pride, the priest prayed silently. *Quench his anger! Do not let him be such a fool as to deny the freedom he holds within his hand even now...*

When Morgan turned back to him, Joseph was amazed to see the lad's eyes glazed with unshed tears. So, then, a struggle *was* going on.

Indeed, Joseph wondered, had there ever been a time when a battle was *not* going on inside that searching, tormented spirit?

Savior...tender Shepherd of our souls, reach out to Your prodigal son and draw him back into your loving arms. Give him, at last, the peace that has eluded him all his life...

Moments passed, and the silence in the room hung heavy and thick with dread.

Finally Morgan turned, his face set in an unreadable mask. "I suppose," he said in a strangled voice, "I do not want to hang, after all. I will accept the pardon. I will go to Dublin."

Their eyes locked and held. "God be praised," murmured Joseph. "God be praised."

An hour later, Morgan walked out the back door of the Castlebar gaol into a clear, star-studded night.

He stopped just outside the door. There, a few feet away, stood Pilgrim, tethered to a fence rail.

As soon as Pilgrim saw Morgan, he went berserk, pawing the ground and squealing with excitement.

Stunned, Morgan bolted toward the horse. He crooned to the big stallion in the Irish, stroking his sides, patting his noble head.

At last he swung around to Joseph, just coming out the door. "How did you manage this?" he asked, a smile breaking across his face. "Where was he?"

With one arm tucked behind his back, the priest started toward him. "Cassidy hid him in the woods, took care of him. I found out where he was only last night."

Then, fixing a stern frown on Morgan, he withdrew what he had been holding behind his back.

Morgan's harp. His *broken* harp.

"What is the meaning of *this*?" The priest's voice was sharp.

Morgan shrugged.

"Can it be fixed?" Joseph asked, handing it to Morgan.

Hesitating, Morgan glanced at the strings hanging limply from the broken block of willow. Finally, he reached for it, nodding. "Aye, it just needs to be glued and restrung."

The priest studied him for a long moment. "The same is true of yourself, I'm thinking."

Morgan looked at him.

"God is calling you back, Morgan Fitzgerald," Joseph said, his tone softening. "How long will you turn deaf ears to His voice?"

Morgan stared at the diminutive, frail priest with real affection. "I have much to thank you for, Joseph Mahon. My freedom, my life—even my horse, it seems. How do I tell you what is in my heart?"

"You have *God* to thank," the priest replied. "I was only His hands and feet. It's Him you should be telling what is in your heart."

Morgan inclined his head, smiling ruefully at the priest. "As you say, Joseph. Still, I owe you much."

"Then repay me by grieving for your sins and turning back to your Savior. I could hope for no greater payment."

Morgan studied him, wondering at the kind of great soul it took to make such a man. "You mean that."

"Of course, I *mean* it! I have stormed the doors of heaven for you, Morgan Fitzgerald! Can you not at least go knocking on your own behalf?"

Morgan managed a lame smile. "I suppose I can try, Joseph. But do not be surprised if the doors are permanently locked against me."

"Even if they are, lad, you hold the one key that will open them."

"The key, Joseph? What key would that be?"

"Christ in your heart, Morgan."

"Ah, I doubt He would live in a heart like mine, Joseph. Not now, not after all I've done."

From a great distance away, as if floating down from the ancient mountains of Mayo, came the memory of the Englishman Evan Whittaker's voice: *"He means to have your attention...and your heart...and one way or another, He will. Be warned, Morgan Fitzgerald, for the Ancient of Days and the Shepherd of your soul is in pursuit of you...and there is no hiding from Him."*

Morgan suddenly thought of Jonah...the cold, dark belly of the fish... his gaol cell. Had the Castlebar gaol been his fish?

God, what was happening? He was sniveling, sniveling like a boy...

"Will you pray with me, Morgan?"

"Now, Joseph?"

"Now, Morgan."

And so they knelt there, on the cold, wet earth in back of the Castlebar gaol.

With the weary priest at his side, the warm, familiar breath of his horse at his back, the prodigal prayed. And listened.

Above them in the night sky, the stars of heaven blinked in wonder.

"Do you still believe in the Man named *Jesus,* Morgan...the Man who was nailed to a cross on Calvary?"

"I do, yes," Morgan said softly, silently voicing the precious name in his heart for the first time in what seemed an age.

Jesus...

"And do you still believe," the priest went on, "it was the very Son of God whose hands and feet were nailed to that tree, Morgan?"

"Aye, I do." His voice grew softer still, choking on a wave of long-suppressed tears.

"And do you know that He died for you...indeed, would have died upon His cross even if there had been no sinner in the world that day *apart* from you?"

God, oh, God, that's the truth, isn't it? You died for me, would have died for me alone...

Morgan Fitzgerald was weeping, his heart breaking.

"Lord, oh, Lord Jesus, forgive this sinner..."

Morgan, My son, I love you. You are Mine.

"Even now, Lord? Even now?"

I have always loved you, Morgan. Even now...now and forever.

The priest and the prodigal wept, and heaven sang.

36

Whisper of Darkness

Be Thou my wisdom, Thou my true word;
I ever with Thee, Thou with me, Lord.
Be Thou my battle-shield, sword for the fight,
Be Thou my dignity, Thou my delight.
Thou my soul's shelter, Thou my high tower;
Raise Thou me heavenward, power of my power.

ANONYMOUS (EIGHTH CENTURY)

For three days Evan Whittaker lay suspended between life and death. Unconscious, seemingly unaware of everything but pain, he seldom moved except to thrash back and forth in the throes of his suffering. He made no sound except to add his intermittent groans and cries to the cacophony of despair that rang throughout the steerage quarters day and night.

Throughout the entire time, Nora felt that Whittaker had somehow escaped the *Green Flag*, had managed to slip away to a secret place, where he now awaited the Lord's decision as to his fate.

When, on the evening of the third day, he began to rouse, she nearly panicked. From the hour of the surgery, she had prayed for his recovery, yet dreaded his awakening. What would she say to him when and if he finally came to and found himself missing an arm?

Even as his eyes fluttered open to fix a glazed, uncomprehending stare on her, Nora looked frantically around the men's quarters for Daniel John. He was nowhere in sight. Only moments before, he had taken Little Tom to the back of the compartment to relieve himself, and they had not yet returned. MacCabe, the Galway farmer who was Whittaker's bunk mate, was gone as well.

A garbled word from Whittaker made Nora turn back to him.

"Hurts..."

Leaning close, Nora put a cloth to his head. "Shhh, now, Mr. Whittaker, I know it must hurt something fierce, but you are going to be all right, truly you are. You will be just fine."

His eyes closed for an instant, then opened again. Nora thought she saw a faint glimmer of recognition.

"Mrs.... Kavanagh..."

He was coming around! He would need the surgeon...somebody. "Daniel John! Oh, thank the Lord!"

The sight of her son coming up the aisle, tugging wee Tom by the hand, made relief spill over Nora.

"Take Little Tom to the girls, and come back. *Hurry!*"

Glancing from her to Whittaker with surprise, Daniel turned before the words were out of her mouth. Pulling the little boy up into his arms, he hurried him off to Katie and Johanna.

He was back in a moment, his eyes anxious as he came to stand next to his mother.

As if sensing the movement, Whittaker's eyes flickered open. His lips were cracked and bleeding, his face still bruised and scraped from the fall he'd taken at the time of his shooting.

"What...happened?" he finally managed.

Nora's throat ached with despair as she reached out to smooth a strand of limp blond hair away from his forehead, gently, as she might have touched an ailing child.

Merciful Lord, what do I say? There are no words that can make this any easier for him.

"You...you have had surgery, Mr. Whittaker," she choked out. "Three days past now."

"Surgery?" His head lolled to one side, and his eyes closed again, only for an instant. "What sort of...surgery?" When he opened his eyes again, his gaze was more focused.

Oh, God, how do I tell him the terrible truth? I want to comfort him, but there is no comfort for such a thing as this.

"Your arm, Mr. Whittaker…the wound was badly infected, you see. The surgeon…Dr. Leary…he—" She glanced at Daniel John for support, but the boy's attention was fixed on Whittaker, his eyes glistening with pain and sympathy.

Nora's mouth went dry as she turned back to Whittaker. "The doctor said there was…no other way if you were to live. He said…it was the only thing to do." The words stuck in her throat.

Whittaker's eyes met hers, and Nora suddenly felt the man absorb her horror. Slowly, he reached his right hand across his chest to touch the empty space at his left side.

Nora could feel his shock—the sudden, awful emptiness—as if it were her own. She swallowed, held her breath, nodding at the anguished question in his eyes.

"He *had* to do it, Mr. Whittaker," she managed to say, strangling on the words. "You would have died if he had not…operated."

Whittaker's hand continued to move, fumbling, passing over the blanket once, then again. All the while he continued to stare at Nora, as if expecting her at any instant to tell him he was dreaming, that his arm was right there, just as it had always been.

"I'm so sorry, Mr. Whittaker," Nora choked out. "It was the only way."

His eyes froze on her face, bleak and mute. Nora swallowed down the knot of despair in her throat, unable to speak. At last Whittaker squeezed his eyes tightly shut and turned his head away.

Nora cast a pleading glance at Daniel John, and he put an arm around her waist to steady her. "We'll take care of you, Mr. Whittaker," he said, his voice trembling as he repeated the assurance. "We'll take care of you. You'll be fine in no time at all."

Nora wasn't sure exactly what she had expected from the Englishman. She would not have been surprised if he had screamed or lashed out in a fit of hysterics.

What she had not anticipated was the stillness of the man, the lack of even the slightest display of horror or anger or outrage. He lay there on the bunk, eyes closed, quiet as a shadow. Once he opened his mouth in a soft, sobbing sound. Other than that, the only indication of his grief was a silent tear that crept from the corner of his eye, then made a slow descent down his scraped, lightly bearded cheek.

Instinctively, Nora reached to blot it gently with her fingers. Its dampness mingled with her own tears as she lifted a hand to brush them away.

꿈

To Daniel's surprise, Dr. Leary came again that night to check on Whittaker.

He had appeared each day since the surgery, briefly, but showing what appeared to be genuine interest in his patient. During each visit, Daniel had thought him to be reasonably sober.

Until tonight. As had been the case when he'd first tended Whittaker's wound, the surgeon showed up reeking of whiskey, obviously unsteady on his feet.

Angry, Daniel was relieved that his mother had gone to lie down. He would not want her exposed to the surgeon's foul mood—or his foul mouth—when he was drunk.

Glaring at the man, he kept him under close scrutiny as Leary checked Whittaker's bandages with clumsy hands. Once, Whittaker gasped with pain at the doctor's careless touch, spurring Daniel to lunge forward and throw a restraining hand on Leary's arm.

The surgeon shot him a glazed look, then glanced angrily down at the hand clutching his arm.

Daniel didn't move. "Why did you come here like this?" he challenged.

"Like *what*?" the surgeon snarled. "Keep your hands to yourself!"

"You're *drunk!*"

"You're impertinent!" Leary shot back, shaking him off.

"What is it with you?" Daniel pressed in a low voice. "You seem a *good* surgeon when you're sober enough to mind what you're doing. Why do you do this to yourself, and to those who depend on you?"

The surgeon straightened, brushing the back of his hand across his brow as he fixed Daniel with a sullen glare. Beneath the swaying glow from the overhead lantern, Daniel saw a subtle change in Leary's expression. Resentment gave way to a look of weariness. The doctor's features, indeed his entire body, seemed to slump in defeat.

"That's the truth," he mumbled, averting his eyes. "I *was* a good surgeon once. More than good, some said."

"You still are," Daniel countered awkwardly. "Or you *could* be if you'd only leave the whiskey alone."

Replacing a roll of bandages in his case, the doctor slanted a disdainful glance at Daniel. "You know nothing, boy. Nothing at all. Let it be."

"I know your hands were deft and steady the other night when you performed Mr. Whittaker's surgery. Just watching you…it made me want to be the best physician I can be."

It was true, Daniel realized. In spite of the agony of watching Whittaker lose his arm, the terror of the entire procedure, he had been fascinated, even inspired, by the surgeon's obvious skill. He could not comprehend how a man of Leary's ability could descend to such an abysmal level.

Daniel stared at him for a moment. Then, sensing the futility of trying to reason with the man in his drunken state, he asked, "Did you bring more laudanum as you said you would? He's in fierce pain most of the time."

The surgeon gave him a blank look.

"You forgot!" Daniel accused him. "He needs *something* for the pain!"

Leary nodded distractedly, waving him off. "I'll bring it down later. Later tonight."

"No, you won't," Daniel grated, knowing full well the surgeon would be passed out on his bunk within the hour. "I'll go with you and get it myself. He needs it *now*."

The doctor twisted his mouth into an obstinate pout. "You're not allowed above decks. You're in quarantine."

"You're the surgeon!" Daniel challenged. "Sure, and you have the authority to make an exception. Besides, it will save you a trip," he added spitefully. "You must have more important things to do."

Leary leveled an exasperated look on Daniel. "Oh, all right, then!" he said, snapping his medical case closed. "Come along!"

Daniel took time to ask that Hugh MacCabe keep a close watch on Whittaker until he returned, then leaned over to reassure Whittaker himself. "I'm going with the surgeon to get something for your pain. You'll be all right until I get back?"

Whittaker's attempt at a smile failed, but he managed a light squeeze on Daniel's hand to indicate he had heard.

Looking at him, Daniel felt a great rush of affection course through him. Who would have thought this quiet, retiring man would own such an infinitely heroic heart, such a brave, steadfast spirit?

A renewed determination to help his English friend rose up in Daniel.

Indeed, thanks to Evan Whittaker, his faith in the Spirit of God working in mankind had been restored.

In spite of men like Dr. Leary.

꒢꒳

A fierce, overwhelming wave of homesickness slammed into Daniel as soon as he crawled out onto the open deck. He stood, breathing in the smell of the salt sea, letting the cold, clean air wash over him like a gift.

Unbidden came the thought of home, the dark waters of the bay, the sagging pier, the sea-stained cottages, Killala...

Home! So strong were the memories, so powerful the longing, he nearly went to his knees. Shaking off the yearning thoughts, he gave the surgeon a hand up. Leary swayed a bit, grabbing for the rail to steady himself.

In an attempt to throw off his melancholy, Daniel started up a running conversation with the physician—mostly one-sided—as they headed aft.

"How long have you been a ship's surgeon?" he asked, lifting his face to catch the spray off the water.

"Years" was the only reply from the doctor.

"Why did you do it?"

The surgeon darted a startled look at him, making Daniel wonder at the man's jumpiness. "Why did I do *what?*"

"Take on a shipboard practice instead of one in the city? Do you love the sea so much?"

An indecipherable look crossed the doctor's face. "No," he bit out, "I've no love for the sea."

"Then why?"

"Why are you so blasted curious?" Leary grumbled, making it clear further questions would not be tolerated.

Daniel shrugged, turning his attention to the night sky, the dark, vast Atlantic surrounding them. A dizzying sense of space and freedom...*precious freedom*...swirled around him as they walked. He could almost ignore the stiffness in his legs from inactivity, the weakness of his body from lack of proper nourishment.

All that mattered was being out in the open, the stench of dying and misery replaced, at least for the moment, by the clean, sharp scent of salt air, weathered canvas, and sea-aged wood. His heart swelled to hear, instead of the requiem of hopelessness that rose from steerage, the chorus of gusty ocean winds and flapping sails.

So keen was his temporary sense of well-being he forgot the surgeon's impatience and blurted out another question, one that had nagged at him almost from the time they had come aboard. "Why is it I never see any of the cabin passengers?"

The doctor's shuffling gait faltered for an instant. "And how would you be seeing anything at all when you are confined to the kennel?"

Ignoring the man's jibe, Daniel tried another tack. "Are they afraid to come out because of the typhus?"

"You need not concern yourself with the cabins! We are carrying only a scant few passengers, as it happens. This is not an ordinary passenger ship, at least not this voyage."

"True enough," Daniel said softly. "I had already figured out this is no ordinary ship."

The surgeon was not so drunk as to miss Daniel's pointed remark. "And what is that supposed to mean?"

Daniel shrugged, deliberately not answering.

Without warning, the doctor seized his arm, stopping them both where they stood. Three sailors standing nearby, playing out a line, glanced over at Daniel and the surgeon with no real interest.

"Boy, you are entirely too fresh! You'd do well to forget what you may *think* you know and concentrate on minding your own business—which has nothing at all to do with this ship!"

In reply to the doctor's outburst, Daniel appraised him with a growing sense that the man harbored an entire horde of guilty secrets—secrets that somehow involved every passenger on board.

The nagging at the back of his mind had been there almost from the beginning. There was something very wrong about the *Green Flag,* and he was convinced Dr. Leary was a part of it.

❧

On his way back from the surgeon's quarters, laudanum in hand, Daniel gave in to his curiosity. He would have a closer look at the cabin area.

The mention of the cabin passengers had seemed to set off an alarm in the furtive surgeon. Whatever secrets the *Green Flag* was hiding could be found, he was convinced, in the cabin area.

If he were discovered, he could truthfully claim permission from the surgeon to be out of steerage. If it came down to it, he would pretend he had lost his way going back to his quarters.

Nervously glancing behind him every few steps, he started up the deck, staying inboard and stopping to hide in the shadows when he spotted a member of the crew.

He was only a few feet from the cabins when the sound of angry voices stopped him. Ducking down behind a stack of wooden chests, Daniel peered around the corner, watching.

He saw a big hulk of a sailor framed in the doorway of one of the cabins. He appeared to be adjusting his clothing. Almost nose to nose with him stood Captain Schell.

They were having a terrible row about something. A few feet away another seaman stood and watched.

Shivering in the damp shadows, Daniel crouched down a little lower. He could still see what was taking place, could hear every word of their angry exchange. *"You were warned!"*

The captain's steel-edged voice grated with fury. He held a lantern high, trapping the sailor in its light. "You were told not to go near the cabins! What do you think you are doing?"

The crewman attempted a wide-gapped smile. "I thought I heard something, is all, Captain. Thought I'd best have a look. The door was unlocked."

Schell froze the man in place with a threatening glare. "You thought you'd have a look, all right!" The captain's voice cracked like a pistol shot. "Thought you'd take your pleasure like the rutting pig you are, that's what you were doing!"

"Aw, Captain, what's the harm? I was just breaking one of them in, you know. What difference does it make? That's what they're for."

Schell's face went livid, engorged with contempt. "Yes, that's what they're for! But not for the likes of *you!*" He broke off, backhanding the sailor across the face.

The man's head reeled. Daniel caught his breath, and put a hand to his cheek at the memory of his own encounter with the captain's vicious temper.

"Garbage!" Schell hurled at the sailor. *"You are garbage!* That is *cargo* in there, do you understand? This entire ship is *cargo!* And you are to have nothing to do with the *cargo* beyond loading it and unloading it!"

The blood pounded in Daniel's head, making his ears ring. His stomach knotted even tighter as he went on watching.

The captain reached past the man to yank the cabin door closed, then turned to bark an order over his shoulder.

The crewman behind him stepped up. "I want to know who left that door unlocked!" Schell grated, pointing to the cabin. "And you pass the word that if I hear tell of another man interfering with the cargo of this ship, he will be flogged until the deck runs red with blood!"

Turning back to the offending sailor, he moved the lantern closer to his face. "Well, you stupid fool, let us hope she was worth a keelhauling." His voice was low but thick with menace. A brief slash of a smile appeared, then faded as he stood watching the crewman drag the protesting sailor down the deck.

Holding his breath, Daniel watched Schell turn the handle on the cabin door and push it open. He stood just inside the doorway, lifting the lantern to inspect whatever lay within. *Somebody inside the cabin was crying!*

Daniel pulled in a ragged breath, biting down on his bottom lip hard enough to bring blood.

After a moment, the captain turned and closed the door, this time locking it with a key before walking away.

Daniel stayed where he was for a long time after Schell disappeared. His heart banged wildly against his ribcage as he huddled in the shadows, trying to understand what he had just witnessed.

At last he got up his nerve to creep over to the cabin door and put his ear to it. Hearing nothing, he lifted his hand and touched the door, hesitating a moment before rapping lightly. When there was no answering reply, he again tapped softly on the door.

After another long silence, he glanced around uncertainly. With the lantern gone, the darkness on the deck was thick and relentless. But it wasn't the darkness of the night that gripped Daniel, trapping him in a surging wave of panic. It was another kind of darkness, one so cold and reeking of corruption it could almost be touched.

It was the darkness that rode the waves with the *Green Flag,* a presence that permeated the entire ship. He could hear its whisper above the tormented cries in steerage, over the roar of the waves above decks, in the secret shadows of the passenger cabins, even in the wind that flew the sails.

He had sensed the darkness before, had heard its whisper, felt its touch, smelled its decay. Tonight he thought he at last understood what it was.

The darkness had taken on a soul of its own. The soul of the *Green Flag*.

Back in steerage, Daniel gave Whittaker a dose of the laudanum, then propped himself up in the bunk next to the Englishman, watching him.

What he would give to tell Whittaker about this night: what he had seen and heard, what he suspected. But Whittaker was in pain most of the time, and when he wasn't, he was sleeping. It wouldn't do to bother him with anything that might cause him upset.

He would have to wait until the Englishman was stronger, had at least begun to mend. Then he would tell him. Perhaps Whittaker would understand, would know what to do.

With a rush of dread, Daniel felt the presence of an Enemy aboard the ship. Unseen, unknown…but real. Terribly real.

He was suddenly frightened, as frightened as he had ever been. How could he hope to defend himself or his loved ones against what he could not see?

We are not contending against flesh and blood, but against the powers of an unseen world.

How did one fight against a whisper, an elusive presence, a shadow of evil?

Put on the entire armor of God…the belt of truth, the breastplate of righteousness, the shoes of peace, the shield of faith, the helmet of salvation, the sword of the Spirit—God's Word.

Pray…plead…watch.

Slipping down off the bunk, Daniel dropped to his knees and began to pray.

Afternoon Encounters

A little love, a little trust,
A soft impulse, a sudden dream,
And life as dry as desert dust
Is fresher than a mountain stream.
So simple is the heart of man,
So ready for new hope and joy;
Ten thousand years since it began
Have left it younger than a boy.

STOPFORD A. BROOKE (1822–1916)

New York City
Late April

It was an almost springlike afternoon in New York. The air was gentle, the sky was clear, and on this part of the street in front of the Tombs—the Hall of Justice—there was no ripe smell of manure droppings or piled up garbage.

The entrance door had been propped open, but Michael Burke had come all the way outside and stood leaning up against one of the huge Greek columns that guarded the front of the building. At his feet, a baby boy lay sleeping in a basket.

He had found the infant abandoned in the dark hallway of a Mulberry Street tenement, wrapped only in thin rags, hidden in the same basket in which he now slept. When a thorough questioning of the building's tenants and surrounding neighbors yielded no clue as to the baby's parents,

Michael had brought him back to the station and filed a report. Now he waited for an agency volunteer to pick up the foundling and take it to one of the designated hospitals or protectories.

While he waited, he read over the ship arrival notices in *The New York Packet*. These days he faithfully checked every issue of the *Packet*. If the ship had left Killala near the end of March, it had been at sea for nigh on four weeks by now. That being the case, it could arrive in the harbor as early as next week.

Of course, he had no way of knowing exactly when it set sail. Nor had he any certainty that Nora and her family were aboard.

The past few weeks of waiting and wondering, hoping—and occasionally dreading—had been the most exasperating, nerve-wracking experience in Michael's memory. Not to know if Nora was coming, and if she were, how she would react to him after so long a time; whether she would be willing to marry him; how her boys and Tierney would get along if they *should* wed; where he was going to put so many people…

He could not remember a time when his mind had felt so cluttered, so heavy, so fragmented.

Added to this was his concern over the increasing amount of time Tierney was spending in the employ of Patrick Walsh.

The boy was working almost every Saturday, from daylight to dark, out at Walsh's posh palace on Staten Island—and that was in addition to his regular after-school job at the hotel.

Lately Michael sensed a gap widening between him and his son. It grated on him, but he had to concede a certain amount of jealousy about Tierney's adulation for his employer. Walsh had achieved an impressive record of successes for an Irish immigrant. But Michael wanted Tierney to value some things more than money and influence and achievement—things like integrity and Christian principles, for example.

Yet, every time he raised the subject with the boy, Tierney would fire back that *he* was the one always encouraging him to "better himself." Since Michael could not deny the truth in the challenge, their debates always ended in a deadlock.

It was no wonder he was sleeping poorly, when he slept at all, and even less wonder he could not seem to concentrate on anything more complicated than the ship arrival notices.

His attention was suddenly diverted by a hackney cab slowing in front

of the building. As soon as the two gray horses clopped to a halt, the driver
leaped down to assist his passenger.

Surprised, Michael watched as Sara Farmington stepped from the carriage, gave instructions to the driver, then started toward the front steps.

Again he noted a faint limp in her stride, though her posture was
straight and confident. She was wearing a fine spring suit, soft blue with
white piping, and a somewhat more sensible wee hat than he observed on
most women.

She smiled as soon as she saw him. Michael straightened, stepped out
from the column and greeted her.

"Miss Farmington? Don't tell me you're here for another jaunt into
Five Points so soon."

Still smiling, she glanced from him to the sleeping infant in the basket
behind him. "Not today, Sergeant Burke, although I *did* intend to request
an escort for next week. This afternoon, however, I'm here to relieve you
of your little burden."

She went to the foundling and, stooping down, lifted him carefully
from the basket. The infant slept on as she cradled him gently against her
shoulder.

"You've come for the child, then?"

"That's right," she said distractedly, studying the face of the sleeping
infant. "I volunteer for the Infants Hospital on Wednesdays and Thursdays."

"You are a busy young woman, Miss Farmington," said Michael, gazing at her with interest.

She shrugged. "There's no need to be idle in New York City. Especially
these days, with the population exploding as it is."

Her eyes went to *The New York Packet* Michael held. "Do you have
family scheduled to arrive soon, Sergeant Burke?" she asked, rubbing the
baby's back as she inclined her head toward the paper.

Michael glanced at the *Packet* in his hand. "No. That is, not family.
But friends."

"I see. When do you expect them?"

"As early as next week, possibly. But I don't even know for certain they
are coming," he added. "I've been watching the notices, just in case."

The infant stirred a bit, cooed, and Sara Farmington smiled down at
him. "Well, I hope they arrive safely. What ship are they booked on?"

"The *Green Flag*. It's a small packet, I believe."

"I'm not familiar with the name. I'll have to ask my father. Perhaps he'd have some information for you."

"Your father?"

"Yes, he's very informed about the vessels coming into New York," she replied, shifting the infant to her other shoulder. "I'll see if he knows anything about your friends' ship."

"Is your father employed at the harbor?"

She looked at him, her eyes glinting with a faint light that appeared to be amusement. "Well, actually," she said, "Father's in the business of building ships. But he haunts the harbor all the same, so he might have some information for you."

A bell went off in Michael's mind.

Sara *Farmington*.

Lewis Farmington, the millionaire shipbuilder! Farmington was a contemporary and close friend of John Jacob Astor. Astor, himself an immigrant from Germany, had made his fortune by investing the profits from his fur trade in farmland on Manhattan Island. Farmington, like McKay of Boston, had amassed a sizable fortune of his own by building some of the finest—and fastest—sailing ships in the world.

"You're not Lewis Farmington's daughter?" Michael blurted out, immediately dismayed by his lack of tact.

To her credit, Sara Farmington grinned at him. Her response was genuinely unaffected. "I'm afraid I am."

"Oh, I'm sorry!" Michael stammered, suddenly feeling awkward and crude and—very *Irish*. "I didn't mean to be rude; I simply hadn't connected the names."

"It's all right," she quickly assured him. "You weren't rude at all."

Michael still felt the fool, but wasn't she being grand about it?

Sara Farmington changed the subject with ease. "I think I'd like to walk for a bit, with the baby, before taking him back to the hospital—it's so beautiful today. Would you like to keep me company, Sergeant Burke? Do you have time?"

"Yes, of course," Michael said, pleased that she asked. "But let me carry the little fellow. He's underfed, but still a bit of a chunk."

"Why do you suppose he was abandoned?"

Michael frowned, reaching for the baby. "We find dozens just like him every month, many already dead. I suppose it's often a case where the mother is unmarried or unable to care for them. At any rate, the number is increasing as the city grows."

"It's difficult for me to understand how a mother could actually abandon her own baby," she said quietly, her gaze lingering on the fair-haired infant's face.

"No offense, Miss Farmington," Michael said grimly, "but if you've never been hungry and frightened—perhaps even desperate—it's not a thing you *would* understand."

His remark brought her up short, and he felt impatient with his own gruffness. But it was the truth, after all. How could those who had never known want even hope to understand those who had never known anything else?

Miss Farmington seemed a fine lady—a compassionate one, that much was certain—but to his way of thinking she could spend the rest of her life doing her bit of work in the slums and still never fathom the hopelessness of the poor wretches she was so determined to help.

There was, after all, no changing the fact that she was a Farmington, not a Flanagan.

His blunt statement made Sara stop and think.

"Yes," she said quietly, "I'm sure you're right." Watching the brawny sergeant heft the infant against his chest with one large hand, she couldn't help but wonder if the man spoke from experience. Had *he* ever been hungry or desperate? He *was* an Irish immigrant, so it was more than possible he knew whereof he spoke.

Holding the infant with one hand, the sergeant offered a supporting arm to Sara until they reached the bottom of the steps. Watching him as he instructed the hackney driver to wait, she noted how very small the baby looked in his arms.

He seemed a man of many facets, this Sergeant Burke. One might think him a hard man were it not for his eyes. His handsome face—and indeed it *was* handsome—at first glance appeared somewhat stern, perhaps because of the deep lines that bracketed his mouth and webbed out from his eyes.

But the eyes spoke a different tale. They reflected the varying colors of the man. They were wounded eyes. Sara sensed that the strapping Irish·man had endured deep, personal pain. Not to mention the fact that he must daily encounter things no decent man could ever hope to forget. But they were also eyes that loved life, good-natured eyes that looked out upon the world with humor and tolerance and great kindness, as if they liked most of what they saw.

While he wore the marks of an old pain, the scars appeared to be fading. Sergeant Burke was a strong, determined man, unless Sara was very much mistaken. A survivor.

And most likely married.

The unbidden thought made Sara blink.

Well, what if he were? It was certainly of no concern to her, she reminded herself as they walked. "How long have you been in New York, Sergeant?" she asked, feeling a need to lighten her own tension.

"Almost seventeen years now."

Sara would have guessed a shorter time. The Irish lilt in his speech was still evident.

"I see. And do you have…family?" she asked as they started up Franklin Street.

He nodded, glancing over at her with a faint smile. "A son. Tierney. He'll soon be fifteen, though I'm finding it hard to believe."

"Tierney? That's an Irish name, I imagine."

"Aye, my wife chose it."

So there was a wife. "I see. Then your wife is also Irish?"

"She was, yes." He hesitated only an instant, then volunteered, "My wife died when the lad was small."

"Oh, I'm sorry," Sara said softly. *An old pain…*

"I'll be marrying again, perhaps," he said abruptly, darting a glance at her that made Sara wonder if he had spoken without thinking. "If my friends do come over, that is," he added quickly. "And if my proposal is accepted."

"That's…wonderful for you," Sara said lamely, unsettled and somewhat confused by the faint edge of disappointment she felt at his blunt announcement.

"It's nothing definite, mind," he put in. "I've written to ask, that's all. Nora may have a different notion entirely."

"Nora," Sara repeated softly. "Such a lovely name."

"We were children together," he offered in his brusque way. "Grew up in the same village. Her husband died last year, as did her little girl. Things have been hard for her, with the famine and all…" He let his words die away, unfinished.

"I see," Sara said awkwardly, "Well, I hope things work out for both of you."

He gave a small nod, but said nothing more. They walked on in silence for a time before Sara stopped. "I should get back with the baby, I suppose."

"Aye, he seems to be waking up," said the sergeant, glancing down at the squirming infant against his chest.

For a moment he stood regarding Sara with a questioning gaze. A smile flickered in his eyes, then reached his mouth. "I'm curious, Miss Sara Farmington," he said. "Why is it you do what you do?"

She frowned. "I beg your pardon?"

He continued to study her. The intensity of his gaze would have seemed bold from any other man, but Sara felt not the least bit offended.

"You're the daughter of a very important man. Why, then, do you spend most of your days in the slums?"

The question was a familiar one. When she was younger and still not altogether certain as to exactly what was expected of a Farmington, Sara had occasionally been very wicked, affecting the frivolous, somewhat addlepated behavior people seemed to expect from the idle rich. She had given that up as soon as she'd realized that her feigned foolishness was exactly what they approved of.

These days, she no longer played such games. She was not at all impressed about her station in life, but on the other hand she didn't take it for granted. Most of the time, she was glad to be the daughter of the wealthy, influential Lewis Farmington. It gave her the means to do many of the things she believed needed doing.

Besides, she liked her family. Father was a wonderful man, if a bit eccentric—eccentric by society's standards, that is. He loved to work with his hands, and he didn't care nearly so much for the money he made as he did for the fine ships that made the money. He was always generous in helping to fund Sara's "projects," and wasn't above harassing his friends and associates to do likewise.

Her brother, Gordie, was also a dear, though his wife, Doris, was a terrible bore. Doris *was* impressed with their station in life, and determined that everybody else should be as well. Poor Gordie had to sneak *his* contributions to Sara's "projects" out from under his wife's avaricious eye.

"Miss Farmington? I'm sorry, I had no right to ask you such a question."

Apparently she'd been silent so long he was worried he might have insulted her. Sara shook her head, smiling to reassure him. "It's a perfectly natural question, Sergeant," she said honestly. They turned now and headed back toward the hackney. "I just don't happen to have a very good answer for it. I suppose I do what I do because I think it's what Jesus would have done if *He* had been born wealthy instead of poor."

Sergeant Burke slowed his pace and shot her a surprised look.

"I promised Him when I was still a little girl that I would be as much like Him as I possibly could be," Sara tried to explain. "I didn't realize until I began to grow up how difficult it was going to be to keep that promise, mostly because of my father's money."

By now they had reached the cab, and the driver was eyeing them curiously. Still holding the baby, the sergeant continued to watch Sara with a half smile. His close scrutiny made her feel awkward, but the obvious approval in his gaze also made her feel...good.

"If I may venture my opinion, Miss Farmington," he finally said, his voice quiet but warm, "I think you have kept your promise in a grand way." He paused. This time when he smiled it was broad and friendly. "Now then, I believe you mentioned something about needing an escort for another excursion into Five Points next week?"

Sara stared at him, then grinned. "I did indeed, Sergeant."

He helped her into the cab before handing over the infant, now wide awake and beginning to make more insistent threats. "Would next Tuesday suit you, then, Miss Farmington?" the sergeant asked, leaning close as she adjusted the baby on her shoulder. "About two o'clock, say?"

Bouncing the infant gently up and down to soothe him, Sara returned his smile. "It would suit me just fine, Sergeant Burke."

As the cab pulled away, Sara looked down at the baby in her arms and sighed deeply. She was almost twenty-six-years old and had already faced the likelihood that she would remain a spinster. She wouldn't have trusted a single one of the eligible suitors in her own crowd. In the first place, most of them were terrible bores who couldn't carry on a conversation about anything but making more money and gambling it away. In the second place, she was quite sure they were more attracted to her father's fortune than to her.

Then, too, there was the matter of her being lame. It didn't bother *her* all that much, except for those times when the aching in her leg kept her awake most of the night, but she supposed many men were put off by it.

It seemed the few really interesting men she met—and they *were* few—were already married, or at least about to be. Like Sergeant Burke.

Again she sighed. After a moment, however, her mouth twitched. She put a hand to her lips to catch the giggle rising in her throat. How *would* the cream of New York's society react to the idea of Lewis Farmington's only daughter being smitten with an Irish "copper"?

Sara glanced down at the baby. He had stopped his complaining and now lay quiet, staring up at her with a miniature frown and wide eyes.

Impulsively, Sara drew him as close as she dared, taking care not to squeeze him too tightly. During the remainder of the ride to the hospital, she cuddled the warm little bundle to her heart, pretending he was her own.

Half an hour later, Michael was walking south on Elm, his step somewhat lighter than it had been earlier in the day. Miss Sara Farmington seemed to have a cheering effect on a person, she did.

Again today he had noted that something about the young woman reminded him of Nora. That, of course, was why his heartbeat increased a bit when she was close by.

Still, she was a wonder on her own. Certainly she set aside the idea that all wealthy young women were vapid and foolish. She was as sharp-witted as any man Michael had ever met, and seemed to have the purpose of her life well in focus.

Glancing around his surroundings, he frowned in exasperation. The street was ankle-deep in mud and refuse, its stench sickening in the warm temperatures. The rotting smell of garbage, the clamor of children playing in the street, and the barking dogs darting wildly in and out between heaps of rubbish intruded into Michael's thoughts of Sara Farmington. It seemed wrong, even disrespectful, to be thinking of her in the midst of these surroundings. Perhaps he was being foolish, but he deliberately put the thought of her out of his mind.

He had reached the corner of Elm and Duane when he heard the barking of a horde of wild dogs, then gunshots.

His stomach knotted. Whipping around the corner onto Duane, he spotted a middle-aged Negro, pistol in hand, shooting randomly into the midst of a pack of dogs.

One after another fell into a bloody heap in the mud, while those still alive darted back and forth, yelping and barking as if caught in a net. Others, wounded but not quite dead, lay whimpering helplessly in their pain.

In an instant Michael grasped the fact that this was apparently one of the Negroes paid two dollars a day by the city to rid the streets of wild dogs. He froze, his hand going to his gun even as he took in the grisly scene.

Across the street, he spied three little boys, the smallest scarcely out of didies, all huddled together, watching wide-eyed as the Negro took aim at a bedraggled black-and-white pup. The little mutt was racing around in circles as if it had gone berserk from all the commotion.

A cry went up from the frightened little boys across the street when they saw the Negro's intent.

What Michael saw was the likelihood of a bullet hitting one of the children.

With a cry, he lunged forward, raising his gun and taking aim at the black man. *"Drop your gun! Throw it down!"*

Slowing his stride as he approached the man, he again warned him off the dogs. "I said, get rid of the gun!"

The man was either deaf or an idiot. Waving the gun at the pup, he ignored Michael entirely.

At the same time a big, mean-looking black dog bared his fangs and planted his feet in the mud in direct challenge to the Negro.

Heart pounding, Michael yelled once more. This time the man turned, bringing the gun around with him.

Michael's eyes swept the scene, taking in the black dog, the Negro's gun now trained on *him*, and the panicked little boys. He turned his own gun on the black dog.

Suddenly the dog leaped from the ground, hitting the Negro full force.

The man screamed as the dog slammed into him with a roar. The Negro's eyes were stunned and panic-stricken. His arm went up, and the gun went off.

Michael's chest exploded into a fireball, and the afternoon sun fell to earth.

38

A Clashing of Swords

In that spectralest hour, in that Valley of Gloom,
Fell a Voice on mine ear, like a wail from the tomb...
For here were my cords of Sleep suddenly broken,
The bell booming Three;
But there seemed in mine ears, as I started up, woken,
A noise like fierce cheers, blent with clashings of swords,
And the roar of the sea!

JAMES CLARENCE MANGAN (1803–1849)

The rumor circulating steerage claimed they would see America within days, perhaps as early as next week. Each time she heard the word being passed among the aisles, Nora was struck by a new wave of anxiety.

Folding the blankets from the girls' bunk, she stood holding them in her arms, staring across the room at the children. Except for Katie, who was too weak and wrung out to be petulant, they were bored, and growing more and more restless in their confinement. They had all lost weight and looked unhealthy. The sparse remainder of the few provisions they had carried on board was now entirely ruined, invaded by weevils and rats. They were subsisting on their ship allowance, which was scarcely enough to keep them from starving.

They were all weak, Nora included, all ill to some extent. Even those who thus far had managed to escape the typhus still suffered the effects of stale air, insufficient food and fresh water, not to mention the deadly fumes of sickness they were forced to endure day and night.

Still, the children had their rare moments of cheerfulness, and Daniel John was one of the reasons. Tonight he had a group of a dozen or more in the corner, entertaining them with his harp, he and an elderly man with a squeeze box.

Nora tried not to think about the squalid floor where the children had flopped to listen. Katie, wee Tom, and at least a dozen others had made a ring around the musicians and sat, nodding their heads and patting their knees in time to the music. Even the deaf Johanna, taking her cue from the others, rocked to and fro in her silent world to a rhythm only she could hear.

Thank the Lord for the children, Nora thought, watching them. At times they almost managed to make life's madness and troubles bearable.

But what would become of the children once they reached America? Apprehension twisted like a rope around her heart. Starting over in a new land all alone would be frightening enough in itself, but starting over with a son and three young children in tow was enough to make her quake with terror. She had absolutely nobody to depend on except herself—and they had nobody to depend on except her.

Why…oh, why had she thrown Michael's letter away? He was their only link to this new land. He would have helped them—indeed, had wanted to help them!

Foolish! So foolish! In her mindless pride, she had thrown away their best hope. Why hadn't she thought of the young ones instead of herself? Now they would be completely alone, with nobody who would care— who would even *know*—they had arrived! In her selfish disregard for the consequences, she had tossed away the address of the one person who might have made a difference for them!

What in the name of heaven would she do with these children? She could not fail them; she must not. She and Catherine had promised each other years ago to look after each other's children should it ever become necessary.

In addition, there was Evan Whittaker to think about. Obviously, they could not abandon him, not after all he had done for them.

What worried her most was the question of where they would live, once they arrived. The money from Morgan would not last long, not with so many to house and feed. She would have to arrange affordable lodging until she could find a job.

A job. *God have mercy, what kind of job could a widow with a houseful of children hope to find?*

Angry with herself, she turned and began making up the bunk. She *must* not do this, she *would* not give in to her old fears! Worry over the terrors of the lurking unknown would defeat her before she ever stepped off the ship. She must think things through, stay calm, try to plan.

It helped to remember that she had a son who was no longer a child. Daniel John was smart and strong and always eager to do what was asked of him, and then some. He must go to school, of course, but that didn't mean he couldn't work part-time.

They would manage. They *had* to manage.

But on the heels of her resolve came a fresh stab of regret at her thoughtless haste in destroying Michael's letter. If Morgan knew what she had done, he would be livid with her!

On the other hand, if Morgan knew what *he* had done to *them,* he would be devastated.

Morgan. She must not think of Morgan. It only made things harder than they already were.

Evan was trying to wake up. He thought he heard music…a harp… the bright sound of children. He wanted to listen, but the sounds swelled and died away into silence.

He fought to open his eyes, but they were too heavy, and he was too weak. It didn't matter. Whether he was awake or asleep, the days and nights remained the same.

He passed the time in a twilight world induced by the laudanum, drifting through the slow-rolling hours in a haze of pain and macabre dreams. He never quite slept, but simply hung suspended in a drug-induced web, where his nightmares were the only reality.

Tonight was no different. He was awake, yet not awake, aware but without any real sensations—except for the pain. Even that was easier now, almost bearable. He was healing, that much was certain. Even the sullen Dr. Leary had made a grudging snarl of approval the last time he'd examined his…

Stump. Say the word. Say it!

He tried to force the word from leaden lips, but it remained only a hateful thought.

You no longer have an arm. You have a stump...

For days now, he had struggled to face the reality of his circumstances. Between the ebb and flow of an opium stupor, he tried out a number of words and descriptions, searching for one that did not sound quite so grisly.

He was a man with one arm. A one-armed man. He'd had an arm surgically removed. Amputated.

He was a cripple...he had a stump. He would never be whole again...

There. That was further than he had gone before. And as far as he would ever need to go. There was nothing else to be said.

Lord...oh, Lord, why did You allow this to happen to me? Didn't I do what You asked? Didn't I go where You sent me? I was obedient, I even managed to put aside my cowardice, to trust Your guidance, Your power...Why, Lord?

The pain that seized him now was far worse than all the physical agony he had endured so far, a pain that went beyond bodily suffering. Indeed, the distress of body was nothing compared to the anguish of soul that now closed over him, weighing him down like a sodden grave blanket.

From somewhere...a dark, shadowy place he had not known existed within him...came a whispering, an ugly hiss of accusation:

God betrayed you, didn't He? He let you down completely, after everything you went through to obey Him! He let you down...He failed you...failed you...

Evan shuddered, stiffened in horrified denial. Again the dark pit in his spirit gaped open, and the whisper grew more insistent:

You trusted Him...you've always trusted Him. Well, just see how He's rewarded your trust. Look at yourself...look at your ugly self...

His Bible...where had he put his Bible? Desperate, he pushed himself up on his right arm, looked around, but all was a blur. Where were his eyeglasses? His heart thudding madly with the effort, he patted the bunk around him, stretching to peer down at the floor. There was no sign of the eyeglasses or the Bible.

He tried to squirm to the edge of the bunk to feel beneath it, but was overwhelmed by a dizzying surge of nausea.

Sinking back onto the bunk, he threw his arm over his eyes and waited for his head to stop spinning.

Why did God allow this to happen? You were only doing what was expected of you, just as you always have. You've always done your best, you've been a good man, a decent man, lived an honorable life. But does God care about any of that? Does He care about what you're going through right now, at this moment...does He even know?

Something cold and depraved was breathing on Evan's soul, struggling to suffocate his faith.

"Jesus...Savior...Jesus..."

Over and over he mumbled his Shepherd's name, clinging to it like a shield.

Finally, out of his memory, the words came, light exploding in the darkness:

"The Lord gave, and the Lord has taken away; blessed be the name of the Lord."

He has failed you...

"Shall we receive good from the hand of God and not trouble?"

He allowed it to happen...

"He wounds, but He binds up...He smites, but He also heals."

If He's really as powerful as you seem to believe, why didn't He keep you from this dread thing? Why didn't He save your arm? Where was His power when you needed it? Where was He then?

"In his hand is the life of every living thing and the breath of all mankind."

He took your arm...He made you ugly and repulsive...He made you a joke, a caricature of a man...

"But the Lord sees not as man sees...He looks on the heart."

He has deserted you, you fool! Why shouldn't you deny Him and start anew?

"I know that my Redeemer lives...though He slay me, yet will I trust in Him..."

"Mr. Whittaker? *Mr. Whittaker!* Are you all right? Is there something you need?"

Evan opened his eyes. It was the boy, Daniel, peering down at him with worried eyes. "What is it, Mr. Whittaker? Can I get you anything?"

"Oh...no...I...I'm all right." As if coming out of a fog, Evan's mind began to clear slowly.

"Do you need the laudanum, Mr. Whittaker?"

"No! No," he said again, this time more quietly. "No more laudanum.

I'm...I b-believe I'm feeling somewhat better...I don't want any more laudanum. But perhaps...one thing..."

"Aye, sir, what is it?"

"My B-Bible...do you think you could find it for me? I, ah, I like to
k-keep it handy. And my eyeglasses...I can't seem to find them either..."

"They're under here." The boy reached into a small box at the foot of
the berth and handed Evan his eyeglasses, then his Bible. "I put them away
until you were ready to read again."

Fumbling, Evan set his eyeglasses in place, noting grimly that even
such a simple task was awkward for a man with only one hand. Then he
held the Bible to his chest for a moment.

Frowning with concern, Daniel bent over him. "Are you quite sure
you're feeling better, Mr. Whittaker?"

Nodding, Evan lay the Bible beside him. "I am now, yes," he said,
managing a weak smile. "There is something else you could do for m-me,
though, Daniel—if you don't m-mind."

"Of course. Anything at all, sir."

"I want you to g-get rid of the laudanum. Right away. All of it."

The boy's gaze was skeptical. "*All* of it, Mr. Whittaker? Are you sure?"

Evan reached to grip the boy's forearm. "Yes, I'm *very* sure! I...I don't
b-believe I'll have any further use for it, and it...it makes me sleep too
much." He paused, then added, "Tomorrow, once my head clears a b-bit
more, perhaps you would help me get up, walk around a little. I must start
b-building up my strength."

Daniel nodded, his eyes still uncertain. "I'll be glad to do that. If you're
sure you feel strong enough."

Evan put a hand to his cheek, grimacing at the feel of a full growth of
beard at his fingertips. "Oh, my. Do you suppose you could help m-me
get rid of this as well? I must look dreadful."

The boy studied him soberly. "I'll help you shave, of course, if that's
what you want, Mr. Whittaker. But I believe Mother's right—you look
right snappy with the beard."

Evan blinked. "Snappy? Your mother said that?"

Daniel nodded, smiling. "We were going to try to convince you to
leave it, once you felt more yourself."

"Oh." Evan blinked again. "Well, I—*snappy*, you say? Perhaps I'll wait
a bit...just for a while, before I d-decide."

"I'm truly glad you're feeling better," Daniel said quietly. "I've missed our talks."

Evan studied the boy's thin, strongly molded face, the fine, noble head, the genuine goodness in the deep blue eyes. "As have I, Daniel. I'll tell you what," he said briskly, patting the opposite side of the bunk, "why don't you sit down right n-now and k-keep me company?"

The boy looked at him, then sank down onto the bunk beside him. After a second or two, he wet his lips and said, his tone hesitant, "Mr. Whittaker, are you truly feeling stronger now? Strong enough that I could confide in you about something—something that's been a fierce worry to me? There's been no one else I could tell, and I need to know what you think about it."

"Why, of course, Daniel." Immediately curious and concerned, Evan twisted to prop himself up, finally waiting to allow Daniel to help by plumping a coat beneath his head like a pillow.

"All right, now," he said, feeling more comfortable than he had since the surgery. "What seems to be bothering you? Tell me everything."

As Daniel talked, he felt a wonderful sense of relief settle over him. He hadn't realized just how much he had come to depend on Whittaker's precise, matter-of-fact way of putting things in order. Being able to confide his suspicions and fears about Captain Schell and the ship went a long way in relieving the anxiety he'd been carrying around for days.

His relief was short-lived, however. Reaching the end of his tale, he caught his breath and sat, waiting. When Whittaker remained silent, Daniel could stand it no longer. "So, then, Mr. Whittaker, what can we do? How can we find out what's going on?"

Whittaker regarded him with a solemn, worried expression, still delaying his reply. After another long silence, he drew a deep sigh and began to rub his right temple as if his head ached. "Well...I d-don't know that there's anything we *can* do, Daniel, at least until we're off the ship."

"But we *must*! If we wait until we leave the ship, it may be too late for—for whoever is in the cabins! Besides, what difference will it make, our leaving the ship? We'll be total strangers in New York—we won't know how to help ourselves, much less anyone else!"

Still massaging his head, Whittaker closed his eyes. Only when Daniel saw how weary and pale he looked did he realize he'd been talking far too long.

"I'm sorry, I've tired you out," he murmured, sliding down from the bunk. "I'll go so you can rest."

"Wait." Whittaker opened his eyes, put his hand to Daniel's arm. "Before you go, there's something I think we should pray about. Here," he said, indicating that Daniel should kneel beside his bunk.

"I want us to pray that God will p-put some p-people in the city for us."

Daniel looked at him. "I don't understand."

Propping himself up a bit more, Whittaker explained. "When the apostle Paul was in Corinth, the Lord appeared to him in a vision one night and told him to g-go right on doing what he'd been sent to do—proclaiming the gospel—and not to be afraid, because God had many people in the city."

Whittaker paused, sinking back onto the berth. "God does that for us, I believe. When we're in His will and facing the unknown, He puts some of His people in 'our city.' In other words, He sends His own to help protect His own. Let us pray that He'll put some of His people in New York City for us, Daniel."

Daniel sank down to his knees. Whittaker did the praying for both of them, but when he was done, Daniel added his own silent petition: *Lord, there are many of us, so if You have plenty to spare, would You please put a great number of people in the city, enough to go around?*

It had already occurred to Evan that it might not be only the mysterious occupants of the cabins who were in jeopardy. The more he mulled things over—Schell's vicious explosion of temper the night Daniel had gone above in search of the doctor, the boy's suspicion that Leary was hiding something, either about the captain or the ship itself, and the recent confrontation between Schell and the sailor—the more apprehensive he became about the captain's character. Who could tell what kind of perfidy the man might be involved in, might have involved the entire ship in?

As to the unseen passengers in the cabins—he had read enough about white slavery during recent years to suspect the *Green Flag* was involved in something of that nature—perhaps in other illegal cargo as well. Where prostitution flourished, opium could often be found in partnership. Indeed, the drug was becoming as much a plague in American and European cities as it had been in the Orient for centuries. Thanks to the fast-sailing packet ships and the burgeoning populations in cities like New York and London, running opium and foreign prostitutes from one country to another had become a highly profitable activity.

Eyes closed, a hand to his head, Evan fretted over the fact that Daniel was disappointed in him. The boy was obviously hoping for some sort of plan as to how they might help whoever was hidden in the passenger cabins.

But as far as Evan could see, the best plan at the moment—the *safest* plan—was to pretend they knew nothing, had noticed nothing at all out of the ordinary, at least until he could attempt to find out more about the dark-natured Captain Schell and his drunken surgeon.

When the surgeon came to examine him and others in steerage later that night, Evan was ready for him.

He was somewhat relieved to see that the man was, as usual, in his cups. A drunken tongue wagged far more freely than a sober one.

Leary was putting the finishing touches on a fresh bandage. "You're looking feistier than I've seen you for a time," he said thickly. "Must be feeling more yourself."

"Yes, I b-believe I am. I'm actually beginning to get used to the idea of having...only one arm."

"Might as well," slurred the surgeon. "You'll not be changing things."

Compassionate soul...

"That's true," Evan agreed through clenched teeth.

"There are artificial limbs, you know," Leary said, straightening. "You might want to see about one later, after you're entirely healed."

Evan swallowed, thinking of all the hook-handed pirates in his adventure novels. "Perhaps," he managed to say. "I've heard rumors that we'll see N-New York soon. How much longer, do you think?"

Leary scratched his grizzled cheek, obviously groping for a lucid thought in the blur of his brain.

"A week, ten days, says the captain. If the weather holds."

"That soon?" A mixture of relief and apprehension washed over Evan.

Leary fumbled with rewrapping a roll of bandages. Without looking up, he simply grunted a neutral reply.

"I say," Evan ventured, watching the man closely, "what sort of cargo does this ship carry? I don't believe I remember hearing anything about cargo."

The doctor paused in his fumbling to look at him. "I'm the surgeon, not a sailor. I wouldn't know about cargo."

"I see." *What accounted for the guilt plastered over the man's face?*

"Well, perhaps you'd be willing to advise me of the procedures once we arrive in New York," Evan continued, trying another tack. "What can we expect, once we're ready to leave the ship?"

The surgeon's eyes seemed glued on the roll of bandages. "There'll be people there to help you. The captain has seen to all the arrangements, I'm sure."

Evan sensed the man was sidestepping. "Yes. Well, ah…what k-kind of…arrangements, exactly?"

The surgeon seemed to resent every syllable he uttered. "You'll need to pass through quarantine, have a medical examination." He paused, then uttered a nasty laugh. "Which will be anything but thorough, you need not worry."

"My…surgery? It won't prevent m-me from leaving the ship, will it?" Evan asked, his concern genuine.

Again the doctor laughed. "Nothing much prevents you from passing quarantine unless you are black with the typhus or already dead."

Evan stared at the man. "Yes. And…where do we actually g-go, once we're permitted to leave the harbor?"

Averting his gaze, the surgeon closed his medical case. "I told you," he said, half under his breath, "the captain has arranged for people to be there. Guides for the lot of you. You needn't worry."

Something in the man's furtive demeanor—in spite of his drunken vagueness—sent a warning directly to Evan's brain.

He suddenly knew that they *did* have something to worry about, perhaps more than he'd first feared.

39

A Tale of Deception

And the world went on between folly and reason
With gladness and sorrow by turns in season.

JOHN DE JEAN FRAZER (1809–1852)

In Bellevue Hospital late the following Tuesday afternoon, Sara Farmington sat by the bedside of the sleeping Sergeant Burke, thinking about how different the day was to have been.

Instead of venturing into Five Points with the Irish policeman as her escort, she had ended up in this dreary hospital ward, feeling unsettled and vaguely ill at ease.

A curtain had been drawn around the cubicle for privacy. The sergeant had been sleeping ever since she arrived—almost two hours ago, she realized with surprise. It was an oddly disturbing sensation, seeing such a big, vigorous man lying vulnerable and silent in a hospital bed. Shirtless, his entire chest was swathed in thick bandages, stained in two or three places with dried blood.

To Sara's eyes he looked gray and drawn and ill. As she watched, he stirred slightly, muttering something in his sleep Sara couldn't catch. Instantly, she tensed, perching forward on her chair. But after another second or two, he groaned, threw a hand up over his eyes, and quieted.

She sighed, leaning back as her mind reviewed the last few hours that had led her to Bellevue. She had arrived early at the Hall of Justice, expecting him to meet her there, only to be told by the desk officer that the sergeant had been shot just last week—the very day they had last been together!—and was now recuperating in the hospital from a serious chest wound.

Thank heaven she had asked Uriah to drive her carriage today, rather than depending on a hackney! The elderly Negro driver had frightened half a dozen other teams off the streets as he followed her bidding to take her to Bellevue at once.

Framing her face between her hands for a moment, she deliberately avoided thinking of the weakness that had seized her upon learning Sergeant Burke had been shot. Nor did she dwell on the overwhelming tide of relief that had swept through her the moment she heard he would be all right. For now, it was enough to sit here beside him, pretending that when he woke up he would be glad to see her.

Immediately, another discomforting thought thrust itself into her mind, forcing out her feelings of relief. Did she dare tell him of her father's response to her queries about the *Green Flag?*

She glanced over at him, wondering just how much he really cared for his...Nora.

Stop it, you ninny! she silently reprimanded herself. *The man is as good as engaged, with a sweetheart sailing the Atlantic to be with him. All you can hope for is to be his friend, to be of help to him if there's any way you can. Now, for heaven's sake, stop behaving like a giddy schoolgirl!*

"They did not tell me I was dying, those rascally surgeons. But what else could it mean, finding an angel at my side?"

Sara shot bolt upright on the chair, her eyes snapping open. "Sergeant Burke! Oh—I must have dozed—"

He was lying with his head turned toward her, watching her with a mischievous, if feeble, grin.

Flustered, Sara stammered out an apology, feeling decidedly foolish to think he'd been lying there staring at her, even as she sat thinking of *him.* "Gracious, here I am, waiting for *you* to wake up, and *I'm* the one who falls asleep!"

"Well, I must say, Miss Farmington, it's grand to wake up to the sight of you instead of that prune-faced old Harrison."

"Harrison?"

"'Harrison the Harridan,' I affectionately call her," he explained sourly. "She fancies herself a nurse, but between you and me I'm convinced she's actually a British spy they've turned loose in the States to get rid of all the Irish coppers."

"I'm relieved to see that you're feeling better," Sara remarked dryly. "I heard you very nearly died, but you seem to be making a remarkable recovery." That was an exaggeration, of course, but the glint of amusement in his eyes was reassuring.

His smile turned to a scowl. "No, and I did not 'very nearly die!'" he groused, waving one hand in exasperation. "I could have left this chamber of horrors long before now if I could only find somebody to give me my trousers!"

Immediately his face flamed. "Sorry, Miss Farmington. It's little time that I spend with proper young ladies—I'm afraid I tend to forget my manners." Glancing down at himself, he gave the blanket a tug to cover his torso.

Suppressing a smile, Sara looked down at the floor, but not before noting that his hand trembled slightly on the bedding. Obviously, he was weaker than he wanted anyone to know.

"I *am* glad you're doing so well, Sergeant Burke. Your surgeon and the nurses seem delighted with your progress."

"That's because they can't wait to be rid of me," he muttered. "Harrison claims I am the most provoking patient she's ever encountered."

"Somehow I'm inclined to believe her," Sara said. "I can't imagine how this could have happened and I didn't hear of it. I'm certain there was nothing in the papers."

One dark brow lifted cynically. "They'd not be advertising the fact that a policeman got shot by another city employee."

"A city employee? But I thought the desk officer said it was a man shooting dogs in the street!"

"It was. Those boyos are paid by the city to do just that—rid the streets of wild dogs. This fellow, however, had fortified himself with a bit of the rye before he went on duty. Both his aim and his brain may have been somewhat unsteady," he concluded with a grim smile.

Sara shuddered. "That's horrible."

"My getting shot or the dogs?"

Her mouth twitched. "Both."

His expression sobered. "Well, it's done, and I'm alive, for which I'm thankful. I mean to be gone from this place by the end of the week, though. I *must*—the ship may be in the harbor by then, and I intend to be there when she docks."

Sara frowned as she considered him. "You can't be serious, Sergeant! You'll be in no condition to leave the hospital by then. Besides," she added, "you don't actually have a specific arrival date for the ship, do you?"

He shook his head. "Not yet," he admitted. "I don't suppose you remembered to ask your father if he knew anything of the *Green Flag?*"

Sara swallowed, wishing she could avoid answering his question. "As a matter of fact, I did."

The sergeant's eyes widened with interest. "Did you now? *And?*"

Taking a deep breath, Sara turned on the chair to face him more fully. "Well, at first he wasn't able to tell me very much at all. The name of the ship wasn't familiar to him."

Disappointment clouded his expression, and Sara quickly added, "He did get the name of the captain, however."

"The captain?"

"Yes. Father had one of the men at the yards do some checking on the ships scheduled to arrive during the coming weeks. Apparently the *Green Flag* isn't listed, but it's commanded by a Captain Schell. Abidas Schell."

"Peculiar name," he commented. When Sara said nothing more, he rubbed a hand down the side of his face, frowning, and went on. "Will knowing the captain's name make it possible to find out when the ship is due to arrive?"

"Well...possibly," Sara replied, wringing her hands in her lap. "Sergeant Burke, as it happens, this Captain Schell...is a familiar name to my father." She hesitated, and caught a deep breath before going on. "Apparently, he's not a—a reputable person."

The sergeant's eyes darkened. "What does that mean, exactly? What makes a ship captain disreputable?"

She sighed. "I suppose I might just as well tell you exactly what Father told me," she said reluctantly. "It would seem that this...Abidas Schell... is nothing more than a common criminal. Most likely he's only managed to avoid prison by never staying in any one port long enough to be caught. He's a known smuggler—opium, munitions, and other...other illegal cargoes. Father said he's been involved in slaving and almost every other criminal act covered by maritime law."

Michael pushed himself up on one arm, staring at her. Sara flinched when she saw the sharp flash of pain that crossed his face with the effort.

"That's not...quite all," she said tersely.

His eyes narrowed.

"It seems that on a number of occasions Schell has also been known to sell his entire list of steerage passengers to some of the larger, more sophisticated runners."

Sara shrank at the thunderous look that now settled over his face. Of course, a police sergeant would know only too well what that meant.

Until recently, it had been common practice for a certain despicable kind of thief to board a ship as soon as it appeared in the harbor with the sole purpose of bilking the bewildered, frightened immigrants out of their money and belongings, all to the profit of the runner's employer, usually a tavern owner or a company.

Preying on their fear and confusion, the runner could easily wheedle his way into their trust because he was of their own kind—Irish runners plundered the Irish, Italians the Italians, and so on. The poor aliens were completely ignorant of the practice. Within moments, the unscrupulous parasite would be on his way out of the harbor with an entire family, or families, in tow, leading them to a "respectable boardinghouse they could afford, where they would enjoy the companionship of other souls from the auld sod while planning for their future."

The swindler would take the unsuspecting family to his employer's boardinghouse—most often a squalid tavern or tenement. There they would be charged an exorbitant rent for holing up with several other families in the same filthy, often unfurnished room. During their stay, their funds would swiftly disappear, along with most of their possessions.

These days, a new, more vicious practice was springing up, according to Lewis Farmington. Now unprincipled captains were selling their entire steerage lists to the runners of highly organized brokers. With this prepaid arrangement, all the steerage immigrants were turned over to one runner, who met the ship when it arrived and then proceeded to make a killing with a minimum of effort.

Apparently, the captain of the *Green Flag* was one of the innovators of this merciless brand of thievery.

"I must get out of here!" Pushing himself up as far as he could, the ser-geant turned white with the effort and immediately collapsed onto his pillows.

With a cry, Sara shot up off the chair. "Don't be foolish! You see how weak you still are—why, you'd fall on your face before you made it past the door! The surgeon said you'll have to stay here for at least another week, perhaps longer."

"I will not!" he bit out, his voice shaking with rage and weakness. "I *can't!* I can't just lie here, knowing Nora and the others are at the mercy of that—*pirate!"* Even as he spoke, he balled one large hand into a fist, grind-ing his jaw against an obvious onslaught of pain.

"Sergeant, there is absolutely nothing you can do until the ship actu-ally arrives."

"But there's no knowing when that will *be."* His face was pinched, his eyes burning with frustration at his own helplessness.

"I'll find out," Sara assured him. "I promise you, I'll find out."

"How?"

"Father will know a way, I'm sure. I'll talk with him the moment I get home. But *you* must promise *me* in the meantime you'll not try anything foolish. You're not nearly strong enough to be up, and you'll be of little help to—to your friend, Nora, if you injure yourself and have to lie abed for *weeks."*

He was furious. Furious and grieved. Sara knew instinctively that this man had never in his life had to depend upon anyone other than himself. And here he was, flat on his back, almost wholly dependent on a crotch-ety nurse and a lame society spinster.

Watching him, Sara breathed a prayer that God would enable her to help Sergeant Burke. Otherwise, she had no doubt at all that he would ultimately risk his life to save the woman Sara was trying her utmost not to envy.

"I do not understand how Morgan could do such a thing," he muttered, staring at the ceiling with hard eyes.

Sara strained to hear. "Morgan?"

"My best friend in Ireland," he said. "He arranged the passages for Nora and the others, or at least *had* things arranged." Shaking his head in disbe-lief, he said, "He could not have known. He would never have put Nora aboard if he had any knowledge of Schell's reputation. He was deceived;

he *must* have been!" Breaking off, he looked at Sara again. "God help the man who betrayed him. He will rue the day, and that's certain."

Sara stepped closer to the bed. "Sergeant, I must leave, but I'm asking you to promise me that you will do exactly as your surgeon and your nurses say."

When he remained stubbornly silent, she pressed. *"Sergeant?"*

He glared at her, his wide upper lip curled down in a terrible scowl.

Sara drew herself up. "Sergeant Burke, I will agree to gather your information for you only if *you* agree to take proper care of yourself! It's entirely your choice."

The glare heated to a boil, and Sara recalled rumors she had heard about the Irish temper. Still, she held his gaze with a frigid stare of her own.

"All right, all right, then!" he snarled, again trying to haul himself up on one arm, this time succeeding. "But you'll let me know right away once you learn the arrival date, mind! I intend to be there when that ship enters the harbor, and neither you nor anybody else will be stopping me!"

Sara rolled her eyes, entirely unintimidated by his masculine bluster.

A thought struck her, and she felt she should ask. "Your son—is there anything you'd like me to do for—Tierney, is it—while you're in the hospital?"

A look of surprise crossed his face. "That's kind of you," he said somewhat grudgingly, "but I'm sure he's fine. He comes every day that he can, and he seems to be getting on well enough. Tierney's almost a man—he can manage."

"Yes, of course," Sara said dryly. "Men always...manage."

She turned and did her best to flounce out of the room. Flouncing was difficult, of course, when one was lame, but Sara thought she managed it rather well, under the circumstances—until she heard his deep voice, laced with amusement, at her back.

"Did you know, Miss Farmington, that you are really quite lovely when you're fussed?"

Sara managed not to stumble as she flounced through the door.

40

How Far the Shore

Our feet on the torrent's brink,
Our eyes on the cloud afar,
We fear the things we think,
Instead of the things that are.

WILLIAM B. MCBURNEY (1855–1892)

It took three days for Lewis Farmington to ferret out the information Sara had requested regarding the arrival of the *Green Flag*. Throughout the entire period, Sara routinely cajoled and nagged him to do all he could on behalf of Sergeant Burke.

They had dinner alone Friday evening, just the two of them, in the long, narrow dining room of their home on Fifth Avenue. As was his custom, whether entertaining guests or simply enjoying his daughter's company, Lewis Farmington was attired in his black dress coat and silk neck cloth.

Bending to kiss him on top of the head before seating herself, Sara noted his appearance with approval. "You're looking very elegant tonight, Father."

She wasn't flattering him. In her estimation, Lewis Farmington was a fine-looking gentleman. His hair had gone entirely to silver, but had thinned very little. His almost black eyes usually danced with fun; his figure was trim, his skin ruddy from all the hours spent outside in the yards rather than inside his office.

Glancing up from his newspaper, he watched Sara closely as she sat down and rang for Ginger to begin serving.

"And you look harried," he said, regarding her with a speculative expression. "Just as you have all week."

Sara smiled sweetly at him. "Please ask the blessing, Father."

After he prayed, her father transferred his critical eye to Ginger as she set a silver soup tureen in front of him.

"How many years," he said with deliberate emphasis, "is it going to take before you stop trying to foist that seasoned dishwater off on me, woman? Must I tell you again? *Take away the soup! I do not like soup.*"

The striking, middle-aged black woman slanted an unconcerned look at him. "Soup is a part of your meal," she replied, making no move to take away the tureen. "Polite gentlemen eat their soup."

"Polite gentlemen have polite housekeepers."

Ginger smiled, all pearly teeth and flashing dark eyes beneath her white turban.

Sara grinned into her own soup as she lifted her spoon. Her father and Ginger had been engaged in an ongoing argument for almost as long as she could remember. When it wasn't soup, it was something else. They loved to argue, and both were extremely creative in their efforts. How many times had she enjoyed the stunned reactions of dinner guests who happened to witness a session of informal banter between Lewis Farmington and his British West Indies housekeeper? Close family friends knew, of course, that Ginger would lay down her life for Lewis Farmington or any member of his family, just as they were aware that Father held *her* in high respect, with an almost brotherly affection.

Sara waited until Ginger brought her father's serving of pot roast and set it down in front of him with a pointed thud—alongside the soup tureen—before asking her daily question.

"*Well,* Father?"

He forked a generous bite of meat into his mouth. "Well, what?" he finally said.

"Father—"

"I want you to answer a question for *me,* my dear. I would like to know," he said solemnly, pausing to take a sip of water, "the exact nature of your interest in this…Irish policeman."

"Sergeant Burke."

"What?"

"He's a police sergeant, and his name is Burke," Sara said matter-of-factly.

"Yes. Well, is this...*Sergeant Burke* simply another one of your projects, or is there more to this than you're telling me?"

"No, Sergeant Burke is *not* another one of my projects, and, no, there is no more to this than I've told you," Sara said patiently. "As for the nature of my interest, I've already explained that to you: The man was shot in the line of duty and is presently incapacitated. I'm trying to do him a simple favor, that's all."

"Why?"

Sara looked at him blankly. "Why?"

Swallowing a bite of potato, he glanced over at her. "Why would you want to do a favor for a man you scarcely know?"

"Because he needs help," Sara answered easily, meeting his gaze. "And because I like him."

He appraised her for another moment, then resumed eating. "Very odd behavior, a girl of your background becoming friends with an Irish copper."

"My behavior has always been odd for a girl of my background, just as yours is frequently considered odd for a man of your position. Indeed, we are probably the only two people among our circle of acquaintances who aren't shocked by our odd behavior. That doesn't bother me in the least. Does it bother you, Father?"

"Not at all!" he said with a grin, lifting his fork in an unmannerly fashion. "I rather enjoy myself, don't you?" Without waiting for an answer, he went on cheerfully, "All right, then, since you assure me there's nothing improper about this, ah, concern for the sergeant, I will tell you what I've learned."

Sara replaced her spoon, beaming at him excitedly. "Then you *do* have news! Tell me."

"It's nothing definite, you understand," he cautioned as he went on devouring his meal, "but I should think it's fairly reliable. Poston at the yards did some investigating for me, and in the process he talked with the captain of the *Yorkshire*, one of the Black Ball packets. They just came in today, and he thinks they may have overtaken this *Green Flag* two days ago. The *Yorkshire* is supposed to be the fastest ship built, you know," he explained rather petulantly, "although I think we have one nearly ready to launch that is far superior. At any rate, if he's right—if it was the *Green Flag* they passed—she should be coming into the harbor as early as tomorrow or Sunday, I'd say."

Tomorrow or Sunday! Sara's mind raced. There was so much to do and scarcely any time in which to do it! If this awful Captain Schell was the scoundrel his reputation touted him to be, the people on that ship could be in dreadful danger.

Of course, she reminded herself, Sergeant Burke didn't even know for certain his friends were actually *aboard* the *Green Flag.* Was she being altogether foolish, intending to rush to the rescue of a ship filled with immigrants who might be strangers to both her *and* Sergeant Burke?

But they were human beings, whether they were known to her or Sergeant Burke or not. That in itself was reason enough to try to help them.

Turning to her father, she studied him for a moment.

When he raised an inquiring eyebrow, Sara ran a finger around the rim of her porcelain teacup, thinking.

"Father, I wonder if I might enlist your help?"

He pursed his lips. "I suppose you're referring to this ship thing."

Sara nodded. "Knowing what we know, I really think we at least have to make an effort to help those people."

"Would it do any good to remind you that we don't know for certain those people need our help?"

"I'm afraid not."

Lewis Farmington sighed and pushed his plate away. "I thought not," he said mildly. "Very well, then. What, exactly, are you going to drag me into *this* time?"

꩜

On Friday evening, the steerage passengers were given extra water rations. Nora used hers to launder a change of clothing for all of them, including Whittaker.

She used one of their precious last scraps of soap, scrubbing as many items as she could until the water was no longer clean enough to make a difference. With the help of Katie and Johanna, Daniel John strung a line from the iron plate on the hull where his bunk was secured to the next bunk across the aisle. Nothing would really dry, of course. Steerage was too damp and very cold, plus the fact that the damage incurred during the storm allowed continuous leakage of the sea. But Nora felt better—less like a squatter—just to have made the effort.

While the children hung up the laundry, she applied salve to the sores on Little Tom's knees, rubbed raw from playing on the rough floor of the deck. She was as gentle as she could possibly be with the tyke, but he whimpered, trying to push her hand away. "Hurts!" he chanted accusingly.

Poor wee wane. Just that morning he had asked for his "mum" again. Most of the time he seemed to have accepted Catherine's death, but on occasion, when he was sleepy or fretful, he still called for her. It nearly broke Nora's heart.

"You're very close to the F-Fitzgerald children, aren't you?" Evan Whittaker stood beside her, dangling a piece of rope in an effort to distract the little boy so Nora could tend to him.

"Aye, I am. We were more family than friends, always popping in and out of one another's houses and the like." Memories flooded her mind, making it impossible for her to go on.

"Have you thought about what you'll d-do once we reach America? With the children, I mean?"

Nora squeezed her eyes shut for a moment. When she opened them, she set wee Tom to the floor, and he went at a run toward his sisters and Daniel John.

"I think about it all the time," she answered truthfully. "But there are only questions, never answers."

"Mrs. K-Kavanagh, I will help you—and the children—however I can."

Nora turned, lifting her face to look at the Englishman. He had been staying up, walking around the deck, for longer periods of time each day. But one glance revealed the frailty and weakness of the man. He had a long way to go before he would be able to help himself again, much less anyone else.

"You are kind, Mr. Whittaker. I do not know how I will ever repay you for your kindness to us."

Pulling up a stool across from her, he braced himself on the rim of the bunk until he'd managed to sit down. Nora instinctively reached to help the man, then withdrew her hand, sensing her gesture would not be welcome.

"Friends d-don't concern themselves with repayment, Mrs. Kavanagh,"

Whittaker said, his face pale from even this small exertion. "And I *would* like to think that, after all we have g-gone through together by now, we are friends."

Nora regarded him with genuine liking. "Mr. Whittaker, no soul ever had a better friend than yourself."

He flushed a bit, but looked extremely pleased. "In that case, d-do you suppose you could stop c-calling me 'Mr. Whittaker'? Just plain 'Whittaker' or 'Evan' will do between friends, don't you think?"

"I do, yes." She paused, then added, "And I think you should call me 'Nora,' if you please."

"Thank you...*Nora.*"

Nora liked the way he said her name, so soft and carefully that he made it sound like music.

"Are you excited, now that we're nearing New York?" Whittaker asked.

Nora turned to replace the tube of salve in the box beside her. "Excited?" She shook her head. "Frightened is what I am."

"Yes. I confess that I share your f-fear. Still, I'm sure the Lord understands and considers our anxiety. I'm d-doing my best to trust Him in this."

She looked at him. Of course he would be frightened. What would become of an ill, one-armed man in a foreign country? *What would become of them all?*

She wished she could share his belief that God was aware of and concerned about their circumstances. But these past weeks of hell aboard the *Green Flag* had convinced her of what she'd only suspected back in Killala: God had withdrawn His blessing from them all. Apparently, He had judged them and found them guilty and was now meting out His punishment on a rebellious people, herself included. Not a soul on this evil ship had managed to escape His wrath.

After a long silence, Evan cleared his throat and looked away from her. "Are you still missing your son...Tahg...very much, Nora? I know losing him...in addition to your other losses...m-must have made all this even harder for you."

She looked at Whittaker, saw his gentle frown of concern as he asked the question.

"Aye, I will always miss him," she answered quietly. The image of Tahg's white face, his pain-filled eyes flashed before her. Instinctively, she put a hand to her throat, touching the wooden cross that lay next to her skin, the cross carved by Owen and worn by Tahg up until his death.

"It isn't likely I will ever stop missing him," she said softly, "Tahg and the others. So many gone, so much lost—"

Her voice broke, and she stopped for a moment until she could regain her composure. "But I would not wish them back. Not now, not knowing the torment they would have had to endure if they had lived. My sorrow for them all will go on, but I am grateful they were spared…all this."

Their eyes met, and Whittaker gave a slow nod of understanding.

Later that night, Abidas Schell sat at his desk, writing in his journal, making what would be one of the final entries for this voyage:

Light winds, NE by E. Weather pleasant, but some fog. Saw two land birds, much weed. Should spot a pilot boat by morning.

Should enter the Narrows late tomorrow night or early Sunday….

In his cabin, William Leary, the ship's surgeon, sat hunched over his desk, half drunk, but still sober enough to handle a pen.

Smoothing the paper with a trembling hand, he held the pen suspended as his thoughts wandered.

He was writing the letter now, rather than later. Later tonight he would be too drunk, and tomorrow he would be too busy with preparations for arrival. After tomorrow…

He would not think beyond tomorrow.

With any luck, he would sleep tonight, once the letter was completed. By tomorrow night, they should be sighting New York. Finally, this latest nightmare would end.

For him, the nightmares were about to end altogether. He would make no more voyages with Abidas Schell.

The pistol was safe in his medical case, hidden beneath the bandages. He had not yet decided whether to use it on himself alone or on the both of them. Either way, he would be free of his demon.

At least in this life.

Shaking off any thought of the future, he began to write, penning the only address he could think of: *The New York Police Department....*

"We'll need to go to Sergeant Burke first thing in the morning," Sara said to her father, "and at least get a description of his intended. I don't imagine he can help us much beyond that, unless he happens to know exactly how many are traveling in her party."

"How long has it been since he's seen this woman?" asked her father, finishing his custard.

"Almost seventeen years or thereabouts, I believe. Let's hope she still looks somewhat like he remembers her. We need at least one person we can identify rather quickly."

Lewis Farmington met his daughter's eyes over his teacup. "He's going to marry a woman he hasn't seen in seventeen years?"

Sara shrugged, toying idly with her custard. "He's a very unusual man, Father."

"Mmm. Either that or a perfect fool."

"He's no fool," Sara said quietly, but with marked emphasis.

He darted a sharp look at her. "Sara, are you quite sure you're not taken with this man yourself?"

Jabbing the custard with her spoon, Sara answered bluntly, "I could be, I imagine, if he weren't committed to somebody else." She looked up at him, saw the mixture of doubt and worry in his eyes, and added, "But I am no fool either, Father. You needn't concern yourself."

She glanced up to find him still searching her face. "Very well," he said, blotting his lips with his dinner napkin. "We will have Uriah drive us to Bellevue in the morning."

41

A Meeting in Dublin

And sweet our life's decline for it hath left us
A nearer Good to cure an older Ill:
And sweet are all things, when we learn to prize them
Not for their sake, but His who grants them or denies them.

AUBREY DE VERE (1814–1902)

N elson Hall was a great rambling structure, a vast entanglement of Georgian dignities, sprawling palisades, and endless wings that seemed to have sprung up at will, with no real pattern or purpose in mind.

Not quite a castle but more than a mansion, it reigned to the north of Dublin, near the coast and almost directly below Drogheda. Its uniformly gray landscape was relieved in the distance by deep emerald hills, soaring gulls, and pearl-white clouds swirling in from the coast.

Morgan thought it the most hideous affront to architecture he had ever seen.

He had noticed it before, of course, during his roamings—indeed, had stopped to study it from a distance any number of times.

Until today, however, he had never viewed it as the palatial home of his own grandfather.

Richard Avery Nelson. Retired member of Parliament, philanthropist, art collector, descendant of a Cromwellian toady whose reward was this valley of fertile land and rolling hillside.

Early on Saturday morning, Morgan hitched Pilgrim to a fence post, then went strolling up to the immense front door. He had deliberately decked himself out in his tattered blanket-cloak, muddy boots, and worn frieze trousers.

An aristocratic looking footman, clothed entirely in black except for his frosty linen, appeared in the doorway before Morgan could lift a hand to the brass knocker. The man took him in from head to toe in one scathing glance, but to his credit he did not so much as blink an eye at the sight of this rabble who had the audacity to appear at the front door, rather than the back.

As the elderly servant chose not to dignify the shabby caller with even a glint of acknowledgment, Morgan bluntly announced his business.

"I am here to see Richard Nelson."

The man's face was a stone as their eyes met and held. "For what purpose?"

"Ah, that would be personal, I'm afraid."

The footman lifted his eyes upward a fraction, an indictment of this ragman's impertinence. "Sir Richard does not receive. He is indisposed."

Morgan regarded him with lively amusement. "The thing is, you see, I am invited."

"Invited?" A blinking of eyes, a lifting of brows, a clearing of throat. "By whom?"

"By himself."

Silence. Finally, "And you are…?"

"His grandson," Morgan said with a nasty grin. "Would you be announcing me now?"

Nelson's library was everything Joseph Mahon had proclaimed it to be. Thousands of books, hundreds of them rare and carefully preserved, filled a cavernous room that smelled of aged leather, rich wood, and years of lemon oil.

Morgan's first surprise came when the old man behind the desk stood for the first time. This, then, was the source of his ungainly height and wide shoulders. Odd; he'd always assumed his and Thomas's long legs had been passed down to them from the Fitzgerald clan.

Richard Avery Nelson looked to be well into his eighties. His hair was white, his face a map of years. But his back was still straight, his shoulders broad, and his eyes clear and discerning.

Bracing both hands palms down on top of the desk, he surveyed his grandson with a keen, discerning gaze. In his prime, Morgan thought, the man across from him must have presented an imposing sight.

Nelson stood waiting, almost as if he half expected Morgan to approach him with an outstretched hand.

Morgan stopped several feet short of the desk, meeting the old man's appraisal with one of his own.

"You are Morgan Fitzgerald."

"I am."

"My grandson."

"So you say." Morgan's eyes went to the old man's hands splayed widely on the polished desktop. They were trembling.

"The fact that you are a free man confirms it."

Morgan stood, legs apart, hands behind his back. If this was about obligation, he would not be staying long.

The old man beckoned to a comfortable-looking leather chair near the desk. "Please, sit down."

"I believe I will stand, thank you."

"As you wish." With stiff movements, Nelson sank down onto his own chair. "I assume you have read my letter by now."

Morgan nodded. "It was very informative." Hesitating, he added, "I suppose I should be thanking you for my pardon, though I wonder why you bothered."

"You're of my blood."

"No doubt I am as grieved over that fact as yourself."

The old man nodded, as if he had expected this. "You are very bitter. I rather imagined you would be."

Morgan uttered a short laugh. "Now, why would I be bitter? You disowned my mother, ruined my father, and chose to ignore every drop of the harm done until you heard I was about to wear a noose. Sure, and there is nothing in that to make a man bitter."

In spite of his diatribe, Morgan was beginning to feel a bit uncomfortable under the old gentleman's calm, almost sorrowful scrutiny. He wasn't sure what he had expected to find here—self-righteousness, perhaps, certainly arrogance and condescension—but not the serenity emanating from this mild-mannered old patriarch.

"You may say whatever you wish to me, young man. I probably deserve the worst of it. But we can save each other a great deal of time if you'll simply listen to me first, and listen with an open mind."

Morgan stared silently at him.

"I wanted to see you," Nelson said, ignoring Morgan's sullenness, "to tell you I am sorry for whatever pain I caused your father, as well as you and your brother."

Morgan found himself wondering if the old man was dying and this was his idea of a deathbed confession. But he did not look to be dying, and he did not seem the type to make superficial confessions even if he were. He remained silent, waiting.

"As I explained in my letter, I was a pompous fool when I was a younger man, but to be fair you must realize I was a victim of my own upbringing and environment. I thought my daughter's love for your father was irresponsible and foolish. I handled it miserably and then was too proud to do anything about it. One thing you must believe," he said, looking up from his hands, "your grandmother and I would have been good to you and your brother had Aidan not run off with you. Our willingness to raise you both was quite genuine."

Morgan spoke for the first time since the old man had begun. "A magnanimous gesture, I am sure. You hoped to save us from our Irishness, from Rome—and at the same time, from the devil," he bit out resentfully. "All by separating us from our father."

To his surprise, the old man did not argue. "That was a part of it, I imagine. And, of course, I simply lost my head altogether when Aidan ran off with the two of you and the money we'd given him—"

"Aye," Morgan broke in roughly, "thanks to you, we all went on the road like animals."

"Yes. And that was shameful." Nelson stopped and looked away for a moment before turning back to face Morgan. "I will tell you once more, just as I told you in my letter—I am deeply sorry. I was a fool, and I realize I caused a great deal of pain for you, for *all* of you. I shall go to my grave regretting any hurt I brought upon you and your brother."

"My brother is dead," Morgan said flatly. "As is my father."

The old man's expression grew even more pained. "I know."

"You wrote all this in your letter," Morgan said impatiently. "Why, then, did you demand I come here?"

Nelson folded his hands, his eyes going over Morgan's face as if to measure what he saw there. "I know before I answer that you will not believe me. But I swear to you that I am telling you the truth, and I mean every word of it with all my heart. Promise me you will listen and say nothing until I am done."

Shifting from one foot to the other, Morgan gave a grudging nod of assent.

For a moment the old man's eyes took on a distant, haunted expression, as if his thoughts had temporarily wandered past this room to a faraway place. "I have spent most of my life in this country. Indeed, it has become *my* country, in a way I cannot explain. It means far more to me than England ever did. I have grown to love the land, and, believe it or not, the people."

He leaned forward, regarding Morgan with frank directness. "At the same time," he went on, "I have come to know great sorrow over what the country of my birth—England—has done to this land. Out of old prejudices and ignorance and indifference, England has run roughshod over this small and ancient island, trampling an entire noble race into the dirt."

The old gentleman now had Morgan's undivided attention, if not his trust.

"I am nearing the end of my years, and over the last half dozen of them I've become much better acquainted with the God to whom I once gave only lip service. Much to my surprise, I've found great joy in becoming His friend, as well as trying to be an obedient son. Perhaps that's why He's gradually, over the past few months, chosen to show me at least a small part of His concern and love for this island."

Morgan drew his hands into white-knuckled fists at his sides.

Nelson nodded, as if sensing the younger man's cynicism. "I know," he said, smiling sadly. "It's difficult for you to believe that God would reveal His love for Ireland to an Englishman. Still, it's true. He has shown me, during my times alone with Him, that the tragedy of Ireland grieves His heart. I long to do whatever I can to make a difference on this island, but I'm afraid there's very little I *can* do, with my health failing as it is. Therefore, I need to look to someone else, someone with the youth and energy to accomplish what I cannot."

He paused, then with a sweep of one hand, said, "Morgan, please—won't you at least sit down? I won't keep you much longer if you choose to go."

Morgan hesitated, but finally dropped down onto the chair the old man indicated.

"I want you to know that I've made you my heir. My only heir."

Morgan gripped both arms of the chair, half rising. "You—*no*! I don't want a shilling from you!"

Again came a wan smile. "I understand. But it's not entirely for you. That's why I asked you to come, so I can explain."

Morgan frowned skeptically, but relaxed into the seat again.

"I have been reading your writings," said the old man with a look that conveyed genuine admiration and interest. "In fact, once I learned who you were, I made it my business to read everything you've written—your poems, your essays, your songs—everything I could put my hands to. Actually, that was what motivated me to demand that you refrain from your…illegal activities. I could not bear the thought that such a valiant heart and a mighty pen would be silenced on the gallows."

Still, Morgan waited, trying to steel himself against the power of the old man's words.

"Morgan, we both know there is a planned rising, a rebellion that many of your friends are trying to foist upon the people. And we both know just as certainly that, if it comes, it will fail—and very possibly destroy any future Ireland might have as a free country."

Morgan softened enough to nod his agreement.

Encouraged, the old man continued. "I am making you my heir because I believe with all my heart that you possess the wisdom, the genius—and the *love* for this suffering island—to make a difference. Men like you can speak to the hatred that has been the root of Ireland's struggles for centuries."

When Morgan would have interrupted, Nelson put up a restraining hand. "It has been given many names, many guises, but at the heart of all the conflict and the anguish is *hatred*. It has *always* been hatred!" The old man leaned forward, his eyes burning. "Hatred between the English and the Irish. Between Protestant and Catholic. Between tenant and landlord. Hatred that repeats itself and feeds on itself from one generation after another."

Knotting his hands together, Morgan bent his head to them for a moment, as if deeply grieved. He was unable to deny the man's sincerity any longer. Nelson's love and sorrow for the land laced his every word.

"Great evil has been done to this ancient, beautiful island," the old man continued. "And great evil has been done *by* her. But in the end, no matter how righteous, how just, each side believes its cause to be, *hatred* is still the wall that holds any hope of compromise, any chance of resolution, beyond reach."

He appeared to be tiring suddenly, and Morgan felt an unexpected sting of concern for the old man as he went on speaking in a weary, somewhat tremulous voice.

"I happen to believe that men like you, Morgan—men who have a gift for seeking and finding God's truth and then communicating it with vigor and power—may well be the only hope of saving Ireland from total destruction. All I can do is provide you with the security, the funds, to make it possible for you to devote yourself to your writing on behalf of your country.

"I foresee a day, unless these foolish prejudices and ungodly hatreds can finally be destroyed, when this island will run red with the blood of brother against brother, father against son, even mother against daughter."

Suddenly he leaned back in his chair, his shoulders sagging as if he had exhausted himself. "I am asking you to stay with me a while, Morgan, to get to know me—and allow me to get to know you. I yearn to know your heart, your whole heart, and to share mine with you."

Straightening slightly in his chair, he turned a look of appeal on Morgan. "You are my *grandson*! My blood runs through your veins! I am asking for only a few days, a few weeks, if you would. In the meantime, whether you agree or refuse, I want you to know that I've already drawn up the papers, amended my will. My estate will make it possible for you to dedicate the rest of your life—if you are willing—to saving this land you love so much.

"Morgan…Morgan," he said softly, his eyes beseeching, "your words stir a man's heart as no drumbeat ever will. They pierce the human spirit as no sword ever could! You speak with the voice of Ireland's heart, the voice of truth and hope and the promise of freedom. *Morgan…son of my son…please, forgive this old fool! Allow me to at least be your friend, if not your family.*"

Morgan's hands tightened still more on the chair arms. His gaze locked with the old man's, and what he saw there shook him to his very soul.

He might have been gazing into his own face, fifty years from now, with all the grief and shattered dreams of one who has never known the enduring love of a family. In Richard Nelson's stricken eyes, he saw his own lonely heart.

On the heels of that revelation came the thought, not without its own touch of irony, that twice now his neck had been saved—and both times by an Englishman!

And last came the reminder that he himself had been forgiven, and his offenses had no doubt grieved the Lord more than those of the old man seated across from him.

Who, then, was he to withhold forgiveness from Richard Nelson?

"Many in the movement are counting on me to speak out on behalf of the rising," he said hesitantly.

The old man nodded. "Smith O'Brien being one of them."

"He is a good friend. I respect him."

"But he has been drawn into something he can no longer control."

When Morgan remained silent, Nelson pressed, "Do you deny it?"

Reluctantly, Morgan shook his head. "But that doesn't change the fact that he is counting on my help."

The old man studied him for a long moment. "Do you believe in this rising? Do you believe it's best for your people?"

Morgan met his eyes. "No," he said, again shaking his head. "I believe it could finish them."

"Then why not do what you can for *all* Ireland, rather than for only a few? That is the opportunity I am trying to afford you, son."

Morgan looked down at his hands, then at the old man's face. And he knew what he must do. What *God* would have him do.

"Aye...Grandfather," he said quietly, testing the name on his lips and finding it far easier to say than he would have guessed. "Aye, I will stay with you a while, and we will talk of Ireland."

42

Survivors in a Strange Land

Wail no more, lonely one, mother of exiles, wail no More,
Banshee of the world!—no more! Thy sorrows are the
world's, thou art no more alone; Thy wrongs, the world's.

JOHN TODHUNTER (1839–1916)

Hundreds of emigrant vessels put into New York City every year, sometimes as many as thirty or forty a day, bringing hundreds of thousands of steerage passengers from their respective countries—the majority
of them from Ireland and Germany. Thousands died before they reached
New York, but new babies were born every day aboard ship.

Some of the vessels brought opium into the city, along with whiskey
and prostitutes. Others carried typhus, smallpox, and cholera. Hundreds
of cases of disease managed to slip by the cursory quarantine examinations,
escaping into the city to contaminate entire neighborhoods.

New York had become a refuge for the homeless, the destitute, the
suffering. In return for her open door, she inherited disease, labor dilemmas, and some of the worst slums in the world. Within the city, among
her tenements and revival brownstones, inside the mansions along Fifth
Avenue and the shanties on Vinegar Hill, resentment and rebellion had
begun to breed.

But to the immigrant in search of hope and a new life, the city still
loomed as the Promised Land, the Golden Shore, the American Dream.

Aboard the *Green Flag* this Saturday morning, hearts had begun to stir
and hopes had begun to rise.

They would soon be in New York City.

≈✒

The directive came down from the mate on the foredeck to begin the final scrubdown. With it came the shocking order that all mattresses, pillows, and bed covers were to be tossed overboard with the refuse and leftover food.

Finally, they were given the heartening news that their captain had arranged for them to be met by reputable guides who would lead them to clean, respectable, and affordable lodgings. They were sternly warned to take no heed of other individuals who might try to lure them away from the ship, for these despicable characters preyed on helpless foreigners, robbing them of their valuables and taking advantage of their women.

This information brought exclamations of "Thanks be to God!" and whispers of horror at what might have become of them had it not been for the captain's foresight. The voyage had been a dreadful experience, but perhaps they had judged Captain Schell a bit too harshly. He had been looking out for their welfare, after all.

The order to throw their mattresses and bed covers overboard, however, was met with a great general outcry. To many of the destitute in steerage, their bedding represented the sum total of their personal belongings, virtually all they had to bring with them into the new world other than the rags on their back. But when the mate warned that to disobey could mean weeks spent in quarantine, they rushed to do as they were told.

Soon, the sea around them was mucked with mattress ticking, blankets, and baskets of rotten food. At the last, and against the heartrending pleas of their loved ones, the bodies of three recent typhus victims were thrown callously into the sea, along with the other castoffs.

≈✒

Nora and the children worked in a frenzy alongside the others, scrubbing the walls and floor with sand, then sluicing them down, even drying the timbers with hot coals the crew provided from the galley. Within a few hours, the former hellhole had taken on a tidy, almost comfortable appearance. Certainly any inspector appraising the *Green Flag's* steerage would now have only marks of approval for what he saw.

Once they were done with the cleaning, Nora scrutinized first the children, then herself, with a choked exclamation of despair. They looked like filthy squatters!

Appalled at her own condition—her dress was in tatters, her hands grimy, and she smelled of seawater and sweat—she was equally dismayed at the appearance of the children.

"We cannot go ashore looking like tinkers!" she declared. "We will use a bit of the water to wash ourselves before changing into fresh clothes."

"Don't fret so, Mother," Daniel John told her, already stripping Little Tom out of his raggedy shirt. "Your friend, Sergeant Burke, will understand. He made the voyage himself, remember?"

Physical pain shot through Nora at his words, immediately followed by an even stronger surge of guilt. From the beginning, she had told no one, not even her son, of Michael Burke's questionable proposal of marriage. As far as the others knew, he was simply an old friend standing by in New York to help them get settled.

Nor did they know she had selfishly torn up his letter and address. All of them—Daniel John, the children, even Whittaker—had hopes that there would be at least one friendly face waiting for them in this city of strangers. Why, only the day before, Daniel John had repeated to her a conversation he'd had with Whittaker about this very thing, explaining how they had prayed that God would put some "people in the city" for them!

What if Michael Burke's proposal had been God's way of doing just that—and she had gone and ruined things for them all?

Now they were entirely on their own. Ashamed and dismayed, she realized she would have to tell them the truth, and soon.

But not now. There was no time. For now, the truth would have to wait.

The most recent announcement from the mate on the foredeck brought shouts of joy and relieved weeping below.

"Steerage passengers are now allowed above decks!" he proclaimed through a megaphone. *"The captain hopes you will enjoy your first sight of America! You should be able to see Staten Island within an hour or so, perhaps sooner."*

The ladder almost collapsed with the rolling weight of groping hands and shoving bodies as those who had survived the nightmare of steerage clambered up to the hatch in pursuit of freedom.

William Leary had carried the letter in his shirt pocket ever since he'd written it, along with the key to the cabins, waiting for the right time and a trustworthy messenger. In the pocket of his seaman's jacket he fingered the pistol.

When he saw the Kavanagh boy help the Englishman through the hatch, he cornered them, hauling them both to one side.

The boy, in a fever to get to the rail, shot Leary an impatient glare.

"Here, now, listen to me!" the surgeon muttered, glancing furtively around to see that no one nearby was paying any heed to them. "I have only a moment, and there's something I need to ask of you!"

Pretending to make a cursory examination of the Englishman's surgery, he spoke in a harsh, frenzied whisper. "Take this letter to a policeman as soon as you get off the ship!" he urged. "It is vital! Promise me you will give it to nobody else—only a policeman!"

The Englishman and the boy looked at each other, obviously bewildered.

"Promise me!"

"Yes…all right!" the Englishman agreed, regarding Leary with a measuring stare as the surgeon pressed the letter into his hand. "B-But what—"

"No time for questions! Just guard the letter!" Leary paused, adding, "All you need know is that it will help to put Abidas Schell where he belongs— and perhaps save a number of future victims at the same time!"

Turning abruptly to the boy, he snapped, "Are you a lad to be trusted?"

The youth shot him an indignant look, followed by a grudging nod.

"Take these keys, then," Leary told him, pressing them into the boy's hand. "They open the first two cabins. A pilot will be coming aboard to guide the ship into South Street, to tie up. You must unlock the doors and take the children who are inside the cabins to the pilot. Only to the *pilot*, mind—*not* the medical officer! Do you understand me, lad?"

The boy stared at the keys in his hand as if they would set his palm ablaze. "Children? What children?"

"Little girls!" The words ripped from Leary like a wailing on the wind. "Little girls who have been sold for evil use! You must get them out of those cabins while the pilot is still on board! Can you do this, lad?"

The boy's head came up slowly, and Leary saw understanding begin to dawn in his eyes. "Aye," he said, his voice hard. "I will do it, you can be sure."

"One thing more," Leary said, his words spilling out in a ragged stream. "Whatever you do, be sure you do not go with the captain's 'representative'! Plead illness—" He returned his gaze to the Englishman. "Say you think you have the typhus, say whatever you must. Just don't let yourselves be taken!"

Leaning toward them, he hurried on. "Even quarantine is to be preferred over the place where he would take you. You think you have known hell aboard this ship, but you have known no hell at all until you've seen Five Points!"

Several members of the crew were beginning to close in around them now, herding the immigrants already on deck out of the way to make room for others pouring through the hatch.

The blood pounding wildly in his ears, Leary locked gazes with the Englishman. "Once you are free of this ship, tell others the truth about what you have been through. It is happening on other vessels as well, a growing number of them. People should know."

Feeling the man's hand on his arm, Leary glanced down.

"How did this happen?" Whittaker rasped. "Morgan Fitzgerald would never have booked passage for his family on a coffin ship like this had he known!"

"I have no knowledge of any Fitzgerald!" Leary said, his eyes sweeping the crowd pressing in on them. "It's all done through brokers. Sometimes I act as a go-between for Schell, when the brokers are booking for Irish immigrants."

The contempt blazing out from the Englishman's eyes seared Leary's skin. "In other words, you sell your own countrymen to the devil! *Why?* What could possibly make it worth your while to betray your own people—and with most of them already half dead at that?"

Leary averted his gaze from the disgust that filled Whittaker's countenance. "There is no more time," he said gruffly. "Just guard the letter and the keys if you want to save some lives."

Before the Englishman could hurl any further questions at him, the surgeon turned and began to push his way through the mass of confused immigrants that now filled the main deck. Consumed by his need for the bottle as much as his resolve to be done with his final voyage aboard the

Green Flag, he pushed a number of bewildered passengers aside and stumbled almost blindly toward his cabin.

In New York that Saturday morning, Michael Burke was lying in his hospital bed, talking somewhat glumly with his son, Tierney, when Sara Farmington and her father walked in.

Stunned but pleased, he managed a stammering introduction to Tierney, who immediately gave up his chair to Miss Farmington. Stuck for words, Michael could only stare at his unexpected visitors with amazement, especially when they explained the reason for their visit and what they planned to do after they left.

"If it *was* the *Green Flag* that the *Yorkshire* passed just two days ago, Sergeant Burke," Sara Farmington was saying, "the ship should be coming into the harbor at any hour now. It would be a great help if we at least knew what your friend Nora looks like. We need you to describe her for us as best as you can remember."

Michael was surprised at how vivid his memories had remained. Describing Nora to the Farmingtons was no trouble at all—he could see her in his mind almost as clearly as he had the day he had kissed her good-bye and sailed for America.

"She's just a wee thing, a slip of a lass," he told them. "Back then she had hair the color of a raven's wings and the loveliest gray eyes—huge eyes, like a little girl's—but sad. Nora always had such sorrowful eyes…" He spoke softly, his words drifting off to join his memories.

Preoccupied with her own troubled thoughts, Sara said little to her father as they drove away from the hospital.

Sergeant Burke had appeared so weak this morning, he almost seemed to be losing ground instead of getting better. Stopping in the hallway on the way out of his room, Sara had voiced her concern to the ward nurse—Harrison—but received nothing more than an impatient mumble about a "punctured lung taking time to heal."

Sara wasn't so sure the sergeant's condition was entirely due to his injury. She thought she'd sensed an uncommon moroseness about the policeman, a dulling of the spirit that wasn't at all like him.

Ninny! Listen to yourself, you'd think you knew the man well! He's little more than a stranger to you!

Still, his frustration at being incapacitated might be slowing down his recovery. More than likely, the sergeant was used to being in control and was finding it difficult to deal with his present helplessness.

She could not shake the memory of the look that had settled over his face as he described his Nora.

How she wished for the day when a man would speak of her in the same lovely way! And with such a look in his eyes!

She sighed deeply. That man would not be Sergeant Burke. He was still in love with his Nora, no matter how many years lay between them.

Abruptly, she turned to look at her father, only to find him studying her with a troubled gaze. "Did you see his face when he spoke of her, Father? We must help him! We must help Sergeant Burke find his Nora with the raven hair and sorrowful eyes."

Taking her hand, her father squeezed it gently. "And we shall, dear," he said, still searching her face. "We shall. We'll stop at the Hall of Justice on the way and enlist the help of some of Sergeant Burke's fellow officers." He paused. "Sara—are you all right, my dear?"

Sara met his gaze with a level one of her own. "Yes, Father, I'm quite all right. I'm simply feeling anxious about a friend. You understand that, don't you?"

Her father put an arm around her shoulders. "Yes, my dear. I understand very well. And I'm extremely proud of you."

⌒

A thought kept nagging at Michael, worrying him, refusing to let go.

"Tierney?" He turned to look at his son, again seated on the chair next to his bed.

"Aye, Da?" The boy leaned forward.

Studying Tierney's lean, intent face, Michael silently questioned his judgment, yet felt the urgency inside him peak. "You used to haunt the docks regularly. You know them well, do you not?"

Frowning, Tierney nodded. "Sure, I do."

His decision made, Michael pushed himself up a bit. "I want you to go after the Farmingtons, go with them to the harbor. I don't know why exactly, but I'd feel better if you went along."

His son stared at him for a moment, then leaped off the chair and bolted from the room.

Long after Tierney had gone, Michael lay staring at the bleak ceiling of the ward. *He* should have been the one to go to the harbor, not his son. It seemed that everybody else was looking after *his* responsibilities these days.

As much as the thought rankled, and as worried as he was about Nora and the others, the knowledge that Tierney was standing in for him at the harbor gave Michael a certain amount of reassurance.

Why it should be so, he hadn't the faintest idea.

People in the City

I turned my back
On the dream I had shaped,
And to this road before me
My face I turned.

PADRAIC PEARSE (1879–1916)

The uniformed officer designated to pilot the *Green Flag* into port stood facing the wide-eyed immigrants, giving them their first glimpse of a real American.

Smart and wiry in his white uniform and peaked hat, he dazzled them with his smile and air of authority. Then, with the crew's assistance and Captain Schell's dark, hovering presence, he proceeded to pilot the ship expertly through the Narrows, the channel between Staten Island and Brooklyn.

This was his favorite part of the job.

Trying to look everywhere at once, Daniel craned his neck to take in the placid bay, the green hills, the fine houses in the distance. All around them in the water were other boats and ships: medical boats darting from one ship to another, longboats, anchored clippers. Hundreds of people thronged the dock, some dressed in odd, foreign-looking clothing, others decked out in fine apparel.

It nearly took his breath away! He was determined to commit to memory every splendid detail, for he intended to remember this day when he was a very old man!

He turned to his mother, who stood with Little Tom in her arms, tears coursing down her face. "We will be fine, Mother," he said, raising his voice above the noise on deck. "God will put some people in the city for us, just as Mr. Whittaker and I asked. You will see."

His mother dragged her eyes away from the harbor scene to study his face. "Do you truly believe that, Daniel John?" she asked in a choked voice. "That we will be all right, at last?"

"Aye, I do, Mother." Even as he said the words, Daniel realized he *did* believe so. He had no idea what lay ahead, but somehow over the past hours an unshakable conviction had seized his heart, an assurance that the Kavanaghs and the Fitzgeralds—yes, and Evan Whittaker, too—had a future here in New York City.

"A future and a hope," he said firmly to his mother. "That's what God is giving us. I believe that with all my heart, Mother, and you must believe it, too."

Still she wept, and Daniel promised himself at that moment that he would do whatever he could in the days and weeks ahead to wipe away her tears, to make her smile again.

"Don't be afraid, Mother."

She shook her head. "'Tis not fear. I was thinking of Tahg. And Thomas. Wishing they had made it this far, that they could have seen—" Her voice broke, and she made no attempt to finish her thought.

Daniel nodded to let her know he understood, but beyond that, he had no means of comforting her. Her loss was his as well, her sorrow his to share. What was to be said, after all? No words could make a difference. There was no changing the reality that Tahg was gone; Thomas, too. And the both of them would be sorely missed.

But those who remained must somehow go on, and going on, do more than simply survive. They must *live*.

Over his mother's head, he met Evan Whittaker's eyes. Standing between Katie and Johanna, the Englishman looked frail and weak, his expression a blend of both hope and sadness.

"Well, then, Mr. Whittaker—we made it. We survived to see America! Whittaker managed a smile. "We did indeed, Daniel. We survived."

"Thanks be to God..."

Surprised, Daniel realized the soft words of praise had come from his mother.

Again his gaze locked with Whittaker's, and the Englishman nodded slightly, still smiling as he turned to Daniel's mother and echoed her words. "Yes, thanks be to God."

The harbor rang with the sounds from the ship—familiar sounds heard every day, yet somehow unique to each vessel. Dozens of immigrants fell to the deck and prayed. Others wept for the land and the loved ones left behind. Children shouted and laughed with excitement.

They *had* survived. They were here at last, in America. It was time to commit the past to yesterday, with all its suffering and sorrow and shattered dreams. It was time to go in search of new dreams, new hopes, new beginnings. Time to look forward, to start over.

In the confusion and noise blowing over the deck, nobody heard the gunshot that came from the direction of the surgeon's cabin.

Engulfed by excitement and his own turbulent emotions, Daniel very nearly forgot the keys he had tucked down inside his jacket pocket. Turning to shoot a meaningful look at Evan Whittaker, then assuring his mother and the Fitzgerald girls he would return straightaway, he quickly slipped backward into the crowd.

The deck was all chaos and clamor as he melted into the throng of immigrants lining the deck. His heart was pounding, his hands clammy, but nobody seemed to take notice of him.

He half expected a flock of children to come pouring out onto the deck the instant he turned the key in the first lock. When no one appeared after a moment, he stuck his head cautiously inside the door. With sick amazement, he saw half a dozen young Chinese girls huddled together in the corner, staring at him with terrified eyes.

Daniel motioned that they should follow him, but they didn't move. Frowning, he made his voice as urgent as he could, again gesturing frantically that they should leave the cabin. At last, one of the bigger girls got to her feet, taking a tentative step forward.

Daniel smiled at her, nodding encouragement.

Immediately, she stopped dead-still, her dark almond eyes measuring him with fear and distrust. Daniel made no move, no gesture whatsoever. Finally, the girl once more began to creep toward him, her eyes never leaving his face. At last the others got to their feet and followed behind her.

Gulping in a huge breath of relief, Daniel waited until they passed by him, then went to unlock the other cabin. He went through the same gesturing and posturing as before until another group of frightened young girls slipped silently past him, out the door.

After a number of awkward attempts to reassure them that he meant only to help, he started down the deck in search of the pilot, twelve girls trailing behind him.

By the time they came in sight of the white-uniformed American, it was too late for the dumbfounded Captain Schell at his side to do anything more than stare at Daniel with murder in his eyes.

Tierney had caught up with the Farmingtons not long after they drove away from the hospital. He rode in their stylish carriage only as far as the Hall of Justice. From there, he continued on to the harbor in a Black Maria, one of the horse-drawn patrol wagons used for transporting prisoners. Five policemen recruited by Lewis Farmington accompanied them.

Near the dock, a cluster of dandified runners quickly parted and scattered as the Black Maria pulled into their midst. Tierney and the five policemen jumped from the patrol wagon before it stopped, falling in behind Mr. Farmington and his daughter as they headed toward the gangplank.

Lewis Farmington was probably one of only half a dozen men in New York City who wielded enough power to board an immigrant vessel over the objections of two medical officers and an entire crew of sailors.

Board it he did, and, although he attempted to dissuade Sara, she was at his side. Behind them came Tierney Burke with an entourage of New York's finest.

The men headed directly for the quarterdeck. Sara fell back, immediately beginning to search the crowd for a small woman with black hair and enormous gray eyes.

As they converged on the pilot, Lewis Farmington's gaze went to the hard-looking, scar-faced man standing stiffly beside the white-uniformed navigator. A fury bordering on madness burned in the man's gaze. That and his cap identified him as the degenerate captain of the *Green Flag,* Abidas Schell.

As the policemen descended on the captain in a wave, Lewis Farmington and the Burke boy stopped just inside the ring of curious onlookers. Close to the American pilot, an immigrant boy stood like a sentry in front of a group of terrified Oriental girls. The lad was almost shouting, trying to make himself heard over all the commotion.

Two of the policemen moved to take charge of the frightened girls, at the same time ordering the immigrant boy to identify himself.

Both Lewis Farmington and the Burke lad started when the youth gave his name.

Sergeant Burke's son hesitated only an instant before lunging forward, thrusting himself into the melee, shouting the boy's name. *"Daniel! Daniel Kavanagh!"*

The tall, curly-headed Irish boy whirled around, searching the sea of faces, his eyes quickly coming to rest on Tierney Burke, who had stopped only a few feet away.

The two youths stood staring at each other for a moment, then Tierney moved forward. The grin he shot at the Kavanagh lad brought a smile to Lewis Farmington's face as well, especially when he heard the boy's greeting.

"Pleased to meet you, Daniel Kavanagh! I'm your new bunk mate, Tierney Burke! Welcome to America!"

He paused for a moment, cocking his head. "Say, it's a relief to see all those girls aren't your sisters!"

Lewis Farmington wished he could have captured the gaping look of astonishment, then relief, that washed over Daniel Kavanagh's face. "You're Michael Burke's son? You came…to *meet* us?"

Tierney Burke nodded, and the Kavanagh lad looked for all the world as if he'd just been presented with the gift of a new brother!

Sara was beginning to panic. Her lame leg hindered her progress through the throng of pressing bodies, and only now was she beginning to realize the utter futility of trying to find one vague face among hundreds.

She decided she'd best thread her way out of the crowd and go in search of her father. She was really quite vexed with both him and the Burke boy—it would have been nice if at least one of them had stayed with *her*.

Edging sideways, inward of the ship, her eyes skimmed over a heavy-jowled man wearing a crumpled cap who stood shouting angrily at an entire horde of confused-looking immigrants. At the front of the crowd stood a woman, holding a small boy in her arms, with two obviously frightened little girls just behind her. At her side stood a thin, somewhat ill-looking man with glasses, a beard...and an empty sleeve.

The woman appeared to be arguing violently with the nasty-looking man, with considerable input from the one-armed fellow at her side. Sara glanced away for a moment, peering closely into the ranks of the mob of immigrants milling around the deck.

Suddenly, a man whose badge identified him as a medical inspector parted the crowd. He wore an angry, authoritative expression, and Sara began to push forward to hear what he was saying. Seeing one of the city policemen now heading directly toward the inspector, Sara looked back to the woman with the child in her arms.

Her heart stopped, then skipped and raced.

A slip of a lass...hair the color of raven's wings...and huge sad eyes... This woman looked faded and worn, not at all like the girl Michael Burke had described. Her dark hair, graying at the temples, was pulled back, and her cheekbones protruded from a drawn and sunken face. *Yet, she was the right size, and her eyes...*

"*Nora!* Nora Kavanagh?"

The woman's head snapped around, and enormous gray eyes anxiously searched the crowd. The one-armed man at her side pointed toward Sara.

Sara again called out to her, pushing strangers out of her way. Shoving forward, she ignored the pain in her leg as she attempted to close the distance between them.

Finally, she reached the dark-haired woman, who stood staring at her with a thoroughly stunned expression.

"You are Nora Kavanagh, aren't you?" Sara asked breathlessly.

The huge eyes studied Sara.

"Aye...aye, I am Nora Kavanagh," she said in a soft, wondering voice. "But how is it you know—"

Hesitating only an instant, Sara put a hand to the woman's arm, wincing at the fragile bones beneath her fingers. She had no idea who the haggard-looking man with the empty sleeve might be, but he was obviously with Nora Kavanagh. Nodding briefly to him, Sara then turned back to the woman.

"Sergeant Burke gave me a wonderful description of you! My name is Sara Farmington, and I'm a friend of the sergeant's. I've come to take you to him."

Nearly an hour later, with the entire Kavanagh family and the Fitzgerald children finally gathered together on the dock, along with the weary-looking Englishman called Whittaker, the Farmingtons stood watching the bizarre procession coming down the gangplank.

Three grim-faced policemen led Abidas Schell and the medical inspector onto the dock, while two others took charge of the little Chinese girls.

Last came two crew members with a stretcher, bearing the body of the surgeon, found dead by his own hand in his cabin.

Nobody spoke until the entire procession had disappeared into the crowd on the dock.

The Englishman finally broke the silence. "Miss Farmington?"

When Sara turned to him, she felt an instant's surprise at the kindness and the warmth she encountered in the man's eyes. She found herself wondering what the story was with this Evan Whittaker. Nora's introduction had been most peculiar, identifying him only as "our good friend, to whom we owe our lives."

He was fumbling to pull something from his pocket as he spoke. "I've already showed this letter to one of the policemen who came with you. He said Sergeant Burke would want to read it also. If you and Nora would see that he gets it..."

Sara reached for the letter then stopped. "You take it, Nora."

Nora looked at her, hesitated, then took the letter from Evan Whittaker, who turned and began talking with the boy, Daniel, and Tierney Burke.

When Sara felt Nora's hand on her arm, she turned, smiling at her.

"You *did* say that Michael will be all right?" Nora asked softly, her eyes still worried and fearful. "You are sure?"

"He's going to be just fine!" Sara assured her. Impulsively, she took the woman's thin hand and squeezed it gently. "Especially now that he has someone to help look after him. He's a stubborn man, your Sergeant Burke."

Nora studied her with a searching gaze. "Yes," she said uncertainly. "Yes, Michael was always...stubborn." Hesitating, she ventured, "You— you are a good friend of Michael's, then?"

Their eyes met and held. "Yes, I am," Sara answered quietly. "And I'd like very much to be your friend as well, Nora."

44

A Reunion

But one man loved the pilgrim soul in you,
And loved the sorrows of your changing face.

W. B. YEATS (1865–1939)

Tierney Burke was determined to beat the others to the hospital.

The voyagers were on their way to the Farmington mansion to "freshen up" before going on to Bellevue, but Tierney had declined the invitation to accompany them. Instead, he set off at a dead run from the harbor. Leaping fences, ignoring the mud, he didn't slow down until he reached the hospital grounds.

Nora was pretty! She actually was! He couldn't wait to see Da's face when he got a look at her. Of course, she *did* look a bit older than he had pictured her—but little wonder, what with the famine and the long voyage.

And, of course, she would still be grieving for her eldest son, who had died before they ever set sail. Of all Nora's children, it seemed only Daniel was left.

At least *he* appeared to be fine. And he was sharp as a tack, that was certain! They were going to get along swell! Daniel Kavanagh must have dozens of tales to tell of Ireland and their trip across the Atlantic—and Tierney planned to hear them all!

Approaching the hospital entrance now, he slowed down to a trot. As soon as he cleared the door, though, he took off at a run down the hall, ignoring the angry squawk of a long-faced nurse who had to duck out of his way.

He started talking even before he was all the way into the room.

Nora glanced down over the clean gingham dress Sara Farmington was hastily adapting to the newcomer's thin frame.

She was still dazed from the incredible kindness of the Farmingtons. After rescuing Nora and the others at the dock, both Mr. Farmington and this fine-looking daughter had insisted on taking them all home for a bit before going to the hospital.

Home? The place was a *castle!* Nora had never even seen the *outside* of such a house, could not possibly have imagined the luxury she encountered within. And now she stood in the middle of this sumptuous bedroom, staring at herself in a full-length looking glass while Sara Farmington pinned and tucked her own gingham dress to fit Nora. She had even helped Nora wrap her hair in a neat twist at the back of her neck.

While Nora was being readied for her meeting with Michael, the children were downstairs in the kitchen, being fed.

"They can stay here while you're at the hospital," said Sara, standing at Nora's shoulder as she appraised the Irish lass in the mirror. "Father thinks your British friend, Mr. Whittaker, needs medical attention right away. He's sent for our physician."

Nora turned, studying the young woman next to her. "How can we ever be thanking you for—"

"You can't," Sara interrupted firmly, taking Nora by the arm and leading her from the bedroom. "Come along now. You look wonderful. We mustn't keep Sergeant Burke waiting any longer."

Sara took her at once to the library, where they were met by another surprise. Sara's father had offered Whittaker a job.

Lewis Farmington stood in front of the elegantly carved mantel, his hands tucked inside his waistcoat pockets. "You'll never imagine, Sara!" he announced cheerfully as soon as they entered. "It seems I've found myself a personal secretary at last. Mr. Whittaker here has had years of experience in just that capacity. With an English lord, no less!"

"Why, that's wonderful, Father. But does Mr. Whittaker know how terribly disorganized you are?"

Farmington beamed. "He says he likes a challenge."

Nora looked at Evan Whittaker, whose pale countenance was flushed with obvious pleasure. He met her gaze with a nod and a smile, and Nora could almost read his thoughts: God had, indeed, placed some of His people in this city.

Lewis Farmington had not quite finished taking charge. "As for you, Mrs. Kavanagh—"

"Nora—please call me Nora."

"Nora," he continued, "Sara and I would like it very much if you and the children would consent to stay with us for now. We've more than enough room, and our housekeeper desperately needs someone to share the responsibility of running this household." He paused, smiling at his daughter, who was still holding on to Nora's arm. "Sara, you see, is entirely too busy with her projects to be of any use to Ginger. We need a dependable, capable woman like you around the place."

Dumbfounded, Nora could only gape at the man as he went on. "Ginger—that's our housekeeper—will continue her duties, of course. What we'd like you to do, Nora, is to oversee some of the things she doesn't have time for. You might even want to help Sara with some of her projects, if you've a mind to interfere with other people's business."

Unexpectedly, Nora felt her eyes fill with tears. "You're so kind…I…I don't know what to say…"

"Well, you can say *yes*, of course!" boomed Mr. Farmington.

"Father," Sara said, turning to Nora, "it's a wonderful idea—"

"I thought so—"

"—but Nora and Sergeant Burke…well, I believe that he's hoping…"

Nora stared at the young woman beside her. Had Michael *confided* in her, then, about his proposal?

Again, Lewis Farmington took the situation in hand. "If Nora decides to make other plans later, we'll understand, of course. But that will take time; meanwhile, she and the children can visit with us. What do you think, Nora?"

The man's dark eyes were warm with a kind of…*knowing*, almost as if he understood Nora's confusion and inward conflict. Lewis Farmington was offering her shelter, Nora suddenly realized. A safe place…a resting place…until she could get on with her life.

Ignoring the tears that now spilled over from her eyes, Nora moistened her lips and said, "I…am most grateful, Mr. Farmington. The children and I would be happy to stay here. And I would like very much, I'm sure, to work for you."

"Nora?"

Sara's soft voice helped Nora check her tears.

"I'll take you to Sergeant Burke now. I'm sure he's getting very anxious."

Nora nodded, swallowing hard against a new surge of panic.

The Lord had been good...so good. He had affirmed His love in immeasurable ways this day, meeting their every question, their every fear, their every need, with infinite caring. Indeed, He had not abandoned them, after all, as Nora had feared. Today He had proven to her the reality of His presence in ways she could never have imagined.

But now...now, Michael was waiting. And Nora was suddenly frightened again.

⌘

Nora's legs quaked beneath her as she approached Michael's hospital room. She was certain she would fall on her face before she got through the door.

Glancing down over the dress Sara had loaned her, she knew an instant of dismay. She was nothing but bones! He would think her ugly...

"You look *lovely*, Nora."

She turned wild eyes on Sara, who was very nearly holding her up.

"Everything's going to be all right," Sara said quietly, smiling. "You'll see. Go on now. He's waiting."

Just outside the door, she hesitated again, swallowing down the taste of her terror, fighting for a deep breath. Her stomach was knotted, her heart hammering like a wild thing. For a moment she did believe she was going to be ill!

Thank the dear Lord the others had not come with them. At least if she disgraced herself, there would be no one to see.

No one except Sara Farmington. And Michael.

Nora had never felt so foolish, so...vulnerable as she did at that moment. She had survived the Hunger and a nightmare ocean voyage, but she was suddenly quite certain she would not survive this meeting.

Sara Farmington pushed her through the doorway, then disappeared.

Michael sat on the edge of the bed, his hands braced at his sides.

He appeared to be having a serious discussion with his son in the chair across from him.

The boy shot to his feet at the sight of Nora.

She stood waiting, just inside the room, staring at the two of them with anxious eyes.

In his American clothes, a blue woolen shirt and dark blue trousers, this man seemed a stranger.

Then he looked up, and Nora's heart leaped to her throat.

He was older, but still Michael. The dark eyes had lost a bit of their mischief, perhaps, but they were just as kind. His thick hair was still the color of chestnuts, with touches of silver here and there. The chin was still arrogant, as if he would take on the world. And win.

Leaning on the arm of his son, he got to his feet. The broad shoulders were stooped as he stood there, watching her, and for an instant pain crossed his features.

The boy stayed in the room only long enough to look from one to the other, then again. Then, shooting Nora an encouraging grin, he slipped past her, through the door.

Nora dragged her eyes back to Michael. Seventeen years hung suspended between them. It seemed a lifetime.

Finally Michael reached out a hand to her. "So, Nora Ellen," he said in a strangled voice, "you are here at last."

Nora bit her lip, searched his eyes.

This was no stranger...

"Aye, Michael," she said, taking a step toward him. "I am here at last."

Later, they sat on the side of his bed—he was unable to stand yet for any length of time—and talked.

She told him about Tahg and wee Ellie and Owen, then about Thomas Fitzgerald and Morgan.

He told her about his wife and Tierney and his job.

She told him about Evan Whittaker, how he had saved them and looked after them so faithfully. She told him about the voyage, the evil captain, the poor little Chinese girls, and about the tragic surgeon who had shot himself.

She gave him the surgeon's letter, and he read it aloud, pausing in places when Nora would make a strangled cry of dismay.

"He murdered his own *wife?*" she cried, once Michael finished reading.

He nodded. "She was dying in agony. He couldn't bear to see her suffer, so he got drunk and gave her an injection to end the pain—to end her *life*—not knowing her brother saw the whole thing."

"And the captain…Schell. He was her brother?"

Again Michael nodded, folding the letter and laying it on the table beside the bed. "Schell was already involved in white slaving and opium running. He started blackmailing the doctor then and there, and it never stopped. Threatened to tell the medical authorities, the surgeon's son—"

"And after all those years the son died, too!" Nora cried. "Oh, that poor, doomed man!"

"Don't feel too sorry for him," Michael said grimly. "He was the one who acted as go-between for Schell and a number of brokers, selling out entire steerage lists. Apparently that's what happened when Morgan's men arranged your passage. They thought they were dealing through a reliable Irish surgeon!"

They both remained silent for a long time. At last, clearing his throat, Michael took her hand.

Nora looked down, then glanced back at his face. "Can we talk about a more cheerful letter now?" he said with just the ghost of a smile.

"Michael—you needn't say anything more," Nora put in quickly. "I know this was Morgan's idea, that he arranged everything—"

Frowning, he lifted a hand to quiet her. "I don't know what you *think* you know, Nora Ellen, but I can tell you I only wrote the truth in my letter. I want to marry you, lass. I want that very much."

Averting her eyes Nora shook her head. "Michael, you don't want to marry me! We haven't seen each other in all these years, why—you can't possibly take on such a responsibility!"

He stared at her for a moment, then reached for her other hand, holding both firmly in his. "Listen to me, Nora. Listen to the truth. I *do* want to marry you. It's all I've thought about for weeks now."

He paused, still gripping her hands. "Nora, I am a lonely man. I want you in my life. I want to make a home with you. I know we have much to learn about each other, that it will take time. If you're not ready to be a wife to me in the…intimate…sense, I will wait. Even if you never want anything more than friendship and companionship from our marriage, I will accept that. But you must know the truth, lass, and the truth is that I want your presence in my life.

"We were good friends once—we still are, I hope." He paused. "Can you think of a better foundation for a good marriage?"

"Michael—"

"Say yes, Nora. This is what is best for both of us, for our children."

"How can you be sure of that, Michael? After all these years—"

"Nora," he interrupted, "you once told me, when you were still a wee, scrawny thing, that I had a way of always making things come out right. Do you remember?"

She did.

"Nora…don't you see, lass? Some things simply don't change."

She stared at him, watching the old confident grin spread across his good-natured face.

"Now, Nora, before you say anthing more, I have a favor to ask," he said, still smiling.

"What sort of a favor would that be, Michael?"

"Seventeen years ago I asked you to marry me and come to America. You turned me down, and I kissed you goodbye with a great sorrow."

She nodded, acknowledging the memory.

His eyes went soft as he moved to pull her into his arms. "Now, lass, seventeen years later, you are in America, and I am again asking you to marry me. I would also like to kiss you hello."

Nora made no protest when he leaned toward her. His lips touched hers, gently…so gently. A brief, unsettling memory flashed across Nora's mind—a memory of Morgan Fitzgerald, his fierce embrace, his urgent last kiss, his eyes filled with love…

"Nora?" Michael's voice called her back, and she shuddered.

His eyes probed hers, questioning. "Is something wrong?"

"No—no, Michael, of course not," she stammered. And then another memory invaded her mind: Evan Whittaker, hovering over her in the midst of his own terrible pain, offering to be her protector during the horrifying voyage to America.

And suddenly, in the deepest part of Nora's spirit, a light began to dawn. Hadn't she prayed, while still aboard the *Green Flag*, that God would give her the strength to be dependent only on *Him*? Hadn't she pleaded with Him to change her, to make her adequate for whatever might lie ahead?

She turned her eyes on Michael's face. There was a nobility there, a goodness and strength of character. This man would never renege on his promises, never leave her, as Morgan had. This man would remain true to his word. She could *trust* him, and he was waiting.

But there was another who would always be true to His Word. He would never leave her either. She could trust Him. And He was waiting...

At that moment, a strange, unfamiliar warmth rose up inside Nora, and she knew the Lord's presence as she had never known it before. He was waiting...waiting to answer her prayer...but waiting for her to take one step of faith before He answered...

And suddenly Nora knew what that step had to be. Before she could ever place her trust in, or offer her heart to, another man, she must first learn to lean on her Savior. She must learn to trust His love, His will for her life.

Perhaps she *would* marry Michael...someday. But not now, not so soon. Not yet.

"Michael," she said softly, her eyes brimming with unshed tears, "I cannot marry you."

"Now, Nora, just—"

She hushed his protests by touching a finger to his lips. "Listen to me, Michael," she urged him. "I want you to understand. I *need* you to understand."

And so he listened as Nora revealed her heart. She confessed her shame and her terror, her doubt and her despair. She admitted her need for healing, explained her need to learn to trust, to try on this new strength she believed the Lord wanted to give to her.

Little by little, as she spoke, Michael's expression began to change. Confusion gave place to understanding, frustration to acceptance. Friendship deepened, made room for respect.

"Michael," she finished, "I *do* love you. I have always loved you...in a very special way...and I do not doubt that I always will. But before I can love you—or any other man—with the fullness of a woman's heart, I have another journey to make."

He frowned, and she hurried to reassure him. "Oh, this is a different kind of journey, Michael. It's a journey...of faith. And today right now, at this moment...I'm taking the first step."

Before Nora left the hospital, Michael asked another favor...and a promise.

"If he's willing...let your son come and stay with Tierney and me for a while," he urged her. "Just for a time. Until you're settled. I'd like the boys to become friends, and Tierney was so looking forward to having another lad about the house. I'll make sure he gets good schooling, and you'll see him often, whenever you want. Would you think about it, at least, Nora? For me, and for my son?"

The promise was more a puzzle, and yet Nora was inclined to grant it.

"I want your word," Michael said, gripping both her hands in his and searching her gaze, "that you will obey your heart. When the time comes that your heart sings love for a man, Nora, promise me you'll not let it be silenced by uncertainty or foolish pride. Promise me, lass, that, whether the song is for me...or for another...that you will give love's song a voice."

After a long silence, Nora leaned to kiss him gently on the cheek. "Aye, Michael...dear friend...I do promise."

Epilogue

Dublin
Late June

Morgan Fitzgerald had located this fine shop during his first month's stay at his grandfather's estate. The blind shopkeeper was a reputed master at fixing broken instruments, especially fiddles and harps.

While he waited for Mr. Higgins, the shopkeeper, to go in the back and have the wife tally his bill, Morgan pulled out one of the letters he'd been carrying in his shirt pocket more than a week now.

Unfolding it, it occurred to him that he was even able to smile a bit when he read the words these days. There was still some pain behind the smile, but it was not nearly so sharp as it had once been.

Daniel John had penned a message of his own, tucking it in with a more detailed letter from Michael. They had posted the letters to Joseph Mahon, in hopes the priest would see that they reached Morgan, if indeed he still lived.

He read them both regularly, but it was the lad's to which he most often returned. Leaning up against a broad, double-door cabinet, his eyes again scanned the last page, which was mostly about Whittaker.

The enterprising Englishman seemed to have landed himself a job with Lewis Farmington, the wealthy shipbuilder who had not only helped to rescue them all, but had even taken Nora and the children into his home for the time being.

> *...Whittaker says his new position is a great improvement over his old job, because Mr. Farmington is such a fine man. He also says he is thankful that he is right-handed.*

I like Tierney a lot, and although I miss being with Mother and the Fitzgeralds every day, I have to admit it was a better idea, my staying with Uncle Mike and Tierney for now. There is no room here for all of us, and the Fitzgerald children need Mother with them.

Johanna is like a shadow to Tierney when we're all together; can you imagine that? It's odd, how he seems to understand exactly what she means, though she can't speak a word. He's more than kind to her, and very patient.

Sure, and you were right about Uncle Mike, Morgan—he is a grand fellow! He is very kind to all of us and treats Mother with great gentleness and consideration...

Morgan glanced up, rubbing a hand over his eyes. How long would it be before the thought of Nora would no longer wring his heart dry?

"Well, then, sir, here is your instrument."

The shopkeeper's voice brought Morgan back to his surroundings. "I hope you will be pleased with it."

Returning the letter to his shirt pocket, Morgan turned and smiled at the man before remembering Higgins' blindness. "I've no doubt but what I will."

"That is a fine harp, sir," said the shopkeeper, "a very fine harp, indeed. I was pleased to repair one of such antiquity. You play it often, do you?"

Morgan laid the requested sum and an extra sovereign on top of the counter. "Aye, she has been a grand friend to me," he replied, examining the harp before tucking it under his arm.

With a word of thanks to the shopkeeper, he turned to go.

"Is it a minstrel boy you are then, sir?"

Morgan stopped, glancing back over his shoulder as he considered the question.

At last he nodded and smiled. "Aye, Mr. Higgins. That is exactly what I am. A minstrel boy."

Caressing the harp with a reassuring touch, he flung open the door and walked outside.

It was a fine afternoon in Dublin, and the Irish sunshine set the big man's copper hair ablaze as he slung his harp over his back and stepped into the street.

> *The minstrel boy to the war is gone,*
> *In the ranks of death you'll find him,*
> *His father's sword he has girded on,*
> *And his wild harp slung behind him.*
> *"Land of song!" said the warrior bard,*
> *"Though all the world betrays thee,*
> *One sword, at least, thy rights shall guard,*
> *One faithful harp shall praise thee!"*

Discussion Questions for Song of the Silent Harp

Book One of The Emerald Ballad series

1. People blamed various factors for the devastation that ravaged Ireland in the 1840s, but Morgan Fitzgerald was convinced the great destroyer was "the Hunger." What do *you* think?

2. What is the icon—the article that's passed down from one generation to another in the Kavanagh family throughout the Emerald Ballad series? What does it represent?

3. When Daniel John questions Morgan about the unfairness of what's happening to Ireland and to his family, Morgan cautions him not to compare God with life, telling him that life will never be fair but God is never *less* than fair. Do you believe that? Can you think of any particular incident in your own life or in the life of someone you know that clearly demonstrates Morgan's words?

4. Even in America, the immigrant Irish met with much resistance and rejection. Why do you think that was? Yet many people had compassion for the poverty-stricken immigrants and took steps to help them settle in their new country. What were some of the measures undertaken to help the Irish?

5. What is the main source of conflict between Michael Burke and his son, Tierney? Do you see any way in which their differences could be resolved to improve the father–son relationship?

6. Who is the "Red Wolf?" Why does Evan Whittaker refer to him as an "Irish Robin Hood?"

7. Who's another unlikely hero in *Song of the Silent Harp*? What accounts for him being considered unlikely?

8. Before the escape ship leaves Ireland, Evan Whittaker makes one request of Morgan Fitzgerald—and at the same time issues a warning to him. What was that request, and what was the warning?

9. How did you feel when you made your first "visit" to the Five Points slum? Have you ever experienced an area similar to this? How did it affect you?

10. All throughout the different stories that make up *Song of the Silent Harp*, we see God putting people—sometimes unlikely people—in just the right places at the right times to rescue or help those in need or desperate circumstances. Do you believe God does this in real life? Examples?

RACHEL'S SECRET

Bestselling author BJ Hoff delights with her compelling series *The Riverhaven Years*. With the first book, *Rachel's Secret*, you'll discover a community of unforgettable characters, a tender love story, the faith journeys of people you'll grow to know and love, and enough suspense to keep the pages turning quickly.

When wounded Irish American riverboat captain Jeremiah Gant bursts into the rural Amish setting of Riverhaven, he brings chaos and conflict to the community—especially for young widow Rachel Brenneman. The unwelcome "outsider" needs a safe place to recuperate before continuing his secret role as an Underground Railroad conductor. Neither he nor Rachel is prepared for the forbidden love that threatens to endanger a man's mission, a woman's heart, and a way of life for an entire people.

WHERE GRACE ABIDES

In this compelling second book in the The Riverhaven Years series, you'll get an even closer look at the Amish community of Riverhaven and the people who live and love and work there. Secrets, treachery, and persecution are a few of the challenges that test Rachel's faith and her love for the forbidden "outsider," while Gant's own hopes and dreams are dealt a life–changing blow, rendering the vow he made to Rachel seemingly impossible to honor.

The Amish community finds their gentle, unassuming lives of faith jeopardized by a malicious outside influence. At the same time, those striving to help runaway slaves escape to freedom through the Underground Railroad face deception and the danger of discovery.

SONG OF ERIN

The mysteries of the past confront the secrets of the present in bestselling author BJ Hoff's magnificent Song of Erin saga.

You'll be intrigued by this panoramic story that crosses the ocean from Ireland to America. In this tale of struggle and love and uncompromising faith, Jack Kane, the always charming but sometimes ruthless titan of New York's most powerful publishing empire, is torn between the conflict of his own heart and the grace and light of Samantha Harte, the woman he loves, whose troubled past continues to haunt her.

AMERICAN ANTHEM

At the entrance to the city, an Irish governess climbs into a carriage and sets out to confront the man who destroyed her sister's life—a blind musician who hears music no one else can hear ...

On a congested city street, a lonely Scot physician with a devastating secret meets a woman doctor with the capacity to heal not only the sick ... but also his heart...

In a tumbledown shack among hundreds of others like it, an immigrant family struggles to survive, and a ragged street singer old beyond her years appoints herself an unlikely guardian...

So begins American Anthem, a story set in 1870s New York that lets you step into another time to share the hopes and dreams and triumphant faith of a people you'll grow to love.

> "An eloquently told story that weaves
> history, music, faith and intrigue...
> an absolute pleasure."
> CHRISTIAN RETAILING

> "The story gently unfolds with intriguing characters,
> and the sound of music, which Hoff manages to make fly off
> the pages with her glorious and passionate descriptions."
> —CHRISTIAN LIBRARY JOURNAL

BOOK ONE, *A DISTANT MUSIC*

"BJ Hoff always delights readers with her warm stories and characters who become part of your 'circle of special friends.'"

JANETTE OKE,
BESTSELLING AUTHOR OF *LOVE COMES SOFTLY*

"For this Kentucky woman, reading *A Distant Music* was like driving through the eastern hills and hollers on a perfect autumn day, with the scent of wood smoke in the air and the trees ablaze with color. BJ Hoff's lyrical prose brings to life this gentle, moving story of a beloved teacher and his students, who learn far more than the three Rs. I brushed away tears at several tender points in the story and held my breath when it seemed all might be lost. Yet, even in the darkest moments, hope shines on every page. A lovely novel by one of historical fiction's finest wordsmiths."

LIZ CURTIS HIGGS, BESTSELLING AUTHOR OF *THORN IN MY HEART*

"As always when I open BJ's books I'm drawn into a place that is both distant and at home...as I tell my husband, I wish I could create the kinds of characters BJ does because I fall in love with them and want them always as my friends."

JANE KIRKPATRICK, AUTHOR OF *LOOK FOR A CLEARING IN THE WILD*

"In some ways, *A Distant Music* is reminiscent of the Little House series. Each chapter recalls the details of an event or some character's dilemma. Eventually, though, Hoff connects all the threads into a solid story whose ending will deeply touch readers. *A Distant Music* should find an eager audience."

ASPIRING RETAIL MAGAZINE

BOOK TWO, *THE WIND HARP*

BJ always does a great job of drawing her readers into the lives of her characters. I'm sure that there will be many who will be eagerly pleading to know 'what happens next.' I will be among them."

JANETTE OKE, *LOVE COMES SOFTLY*

"BJ Hoff continues the story of Maggie and Jonathan, who must endure their share of trials before reaping their reward. Though this novel is historical, BJ Hoff deals with issues that are completely contemporary...Kudos to the author for charming us again!"

ANGELA HUNT, BESTSELLING AUTHOR OF *THE NOVELIST*

BOOK THREE, *THE SONG WEAVER*

"Like a warm visit with a good friend over a hot cup of tea, *The Song Weaver* offers comfort and satisfaction... and you don't want the visit to come to an end."

CINDY SWANSON

"BJ Hoff is a master at characterization, and her stories are rich with insight. I love the historical setting and learned something new about the role of women in that society."

JILL E. SMITH

"*The Song Weaver* is the last book in the Mountain Song Legacy story, and I hate to see it end. I'll miss Maggie and Jonathan and all the others...A very satisfying end to a special series. She never disappoints."

BARBARA WARREN

The Writer's Presence
A Pool of Readings

The Writer's Presence

A Pool of Readings
Third Edition

EDITED BY

Donald McQuade
University of California, Berkeley

Robert Atwan
Series Editor, The Best American Essays

Bedford / St. Martin's   Boston   ◆   New York

For Bedford/St. Martin's

Developmental Editor: Alanya Harter
Production Editor: Ara Salibian
Production Supervisor: Catherine Hetmansky
Marketing Manager: Karen Melton
Editorial Assistants: Ellen Thibault, Amy Thomas
Production Assistant: Amy Lawless
Copyeditor: Susan Zorn
Cover Design: Hannus Design Associates
Cover Art: Richard Shaffer, *Still-life with Black Package,* 1979–80, oil on canvas
Composition: Pine Tree Composition, Inc.
Printing and Binding: Haddon Craftsmen, Inc.

President: Charles H. Christensen
Editorial Director: Joan E. Feinberg
Director of Editing, Design, and Production: Marcia Cohen
Managing Editor: Elizabeth M. Schaaf

Library of Congress Catalog Card Number: 99–65150

For information, write: Bedford/St. Martin's, 75 Arlington Street, Boston, MA 02116 (617-399-4000)

ISBN: 0–312–19767–5

Acknowledgments

Dorothy Allison. "This Is Our World," *DoubleTake* 13, Summer 1998. Copyright © 1998 by Dorothy Allison. Reprinted by permission of the author.
Maya Angelou. "What's Your Name, Girl?" from *I Know Why the Caged Bird Sings* by Maya Angelou. Copyright © 1969 and renewed 1997 by Maya Angelou. Reprinted by permission of Random House, Inc.
Gloria Anzaldúa. "How to Tame a Wild Tongue" from *Borderlands/La Frontera: The New Mestiza* by Gloria Anzaldúa. Copyright © 1987 by Gloria Anzaldúa. Reprinted by permission.

Preface
for Instructors _____

This new — and greatly expanded—edition of *The Writer's Presence* was designed to achieve three fundamental objectives: to allow writing instructors maximum flexibility in assigning reading materials and writing models; to introduce students to a wide range of prose genres emphasizing a strong authorial presence and voice; and to support composition teachers and students as effectively as possible with helpful, though unobtrusive, editorial and pedagogical features. We are confident that the reading material we have selected, the ways we have chosen to arrange that material, and the instructional resources we have provided both within the book and in the extensive instructor's manual will make this a uniquely useful collection that will satisfy the requirements of most first-year writing programs.

NEW TO THIS EDITION

The third edition represents a major revision of the length, scope, and overall content of *The Writer's Presence*. Although we have retained the book's key features (its flexible format and its emphasis on authorial presence and cultural diversity), we have made a number of substantive changes that we believe will greatly enhance the book's appeal and utility. We have:

- **significantly expanded the book's contents,** bringing the total number of selections from 84 to 141.

- **added two new sections.** The new opening chapter, "The Private Voice: Diaries, Journals, Notebooks," collects vivid entries by such well-known diarists as Anne Frank and Virginia Woolf and

introduces such rarely reprinted works as the notes a Hiroshima
physician recorded immediately after his city endured the atomic
bomb and the rushed journal entries of an American infantryman
at the massacre at My Lai. The new concluding chapter, "The
Voices of Fiction: Eight Modern Short Stories," features classics
by such widely known American writers as Alice Walker, John
Updike, Joyce Carol Oates, and Raymond Carver.

- **provided new alternate arrangements of material.** The main alphabetical table of contents is now followed by a thematic organization that arranges the selections in fourteen broad categories
  representing commonly taught topics and areas of study, among
  them Childhood and Family, Psychology and Human Behavior,
  History and Biography, Popular Culture and Mass Media, and
  The Sciences. Readers will also discover in the back of the book
  three other options for arranging the selections: a rhetorical table
  of contents that outlines the major patterns of narration and exposition and pinpoints many types of argumentative writing; a
  table of contents that lists appropriate selections according to
  their coverage of important contemporary issues; and finally a
  table of contents that arranges selections according to research
  techniques and various ways of reporting information.

- **added a new feature, "The Writer at Work."** In addition to the
  book's 128 numbered selections, we have included 13 informative
  passages from essays or interviews that show writers talking about
  their beliefs, backgrounds, literary standards, motives, or writing
  processes. Each of these passages is separately introduced and follows a selection by that author. The passages—featuring such
  prominent writers as Langston Hughes, George Orwell, Annie
  Dillard, and Flannery O'Connor—are intended to shed light on
  the author's own work as well as to illuminate compositional
  methods in general.

- **introduced a number of emerging authors** who are relatively new
  to anthologies. In addition to many established and frequently an-
  thologized authors, this edition features the work of many
  younger or emerging writers who are just now finding their way
  into major collections, for example Frank McCourt, Edwidge
  Danticat, Kathleen Norris, Chang-rae Lee, Luc Sante, Kathryn
  Harrison, Barbara Katz Rothman, and Debra Dickerson. We hope
  that readers will be as delighted as we are with the selections from
  these outstanding authors. We have also made an effort to include
  figures who, though more established, are not often included in
  composition readers; in this edition, we are pleased to introduce
  essays by such well-known novelists as Jane Smiley and John
  Grisham; the satirist Garry Trudeau; two prominent historians,
  William Cronon and Howard Zinn; and two bestselling physicians, the late Benjamin Spock and Andrew Weil.

FLEXIBLE ORGANIZATION

We organized *The Writer's Presence* to display a broad range of private, personal, expository, argumentative, and creative writing without imposing an order or specifying an instructional context in which to work with individual selections. In that sense, the contents of *The Writer's Presence* can truly be called "A Pool of Readings." The nonfiction selections that comprise the first four chapters are roughly divided into the four most commonly taught types of nonfiction—informal writing, personal essays, exposition, and argumentation. But that is the extent of the book's schematization. Within each of the chapters, the writers are presented in alphabetical order and the selections are numbered consecutively. This loose arrangement frees the instructor from an overly engineered text that locks its readers into a particular compositional pedagogy. The selections are easy to retrieve, assign, and interpret regardless of instructional emphasis. To make it even easier to explore different approaches, this edition includes a series of alternate tables of contents in the front and back of the book. Embedded within the collection is a variety of organizational options: *The Writer's Presence* was carefully designed to be used as a thematic reader, a rhetorical reader, a contemporary argument reader, and a research/interdisciplinary reader. Each selection was scrupulously chosen to play multiple roles.

DIVERSE SELECTIONS WITH A STRONG WRITER'S PRESENCE

All of the selections in *The Writer's Presence* display the distinctive signature that characterizes memorable prose: the presence of a lively individual imagination attempting to explore the self, shape information into meaning, or contend with issues through discussion and debate. Ranging widely across subjects, methods of development, and stylistic patterns, the selections illustrate the expectations as well as the uncertainties that surface when a writer attempts to create a memorable presence in prose. We have built the book—as in previous editions—around first-rate teaching material, much of it proven to work in the writing classroom. We continue to feature a large number of authors whose works instructors have repeatedly enjoyed teaching over the years. These classroom favorites include essays and other nonfiction selections from such respected writers as Maya Angelou, James Baldwin, Joan Didion, Annie Dillard, Loren Eiseley, Edward Hoagland, Langston Hughes, Zora Neale Hurston, Jamaica Kincaid, N. Scott Momaday, George Orwell, Adrienne Rich, Scott Russell Sanders, Jonathan Swift, Henry David Thoreau, Mark Twain, Virginia Woolf, Alice Walker, and E. B. White. In fact, as this list of writers clearly indicates, *The Writer's Presence* could be conveniently used as an introduction to the essay or to literary nonfiction in general. For instructors with even more literary ambitions, we have included paired selections so that certain writers can be shown working in two different genres. These writers are Virginia Woolf, Raymond Carver, Jamaica Kincaid, Amy Tan, and Alice Walker (who is represented by two essays and a short story).

HELPFUL AND UNOBTRUSIVE APPARATUS

As in previous editions, we have kept instructional apparatus to a minimum, though we prudently tried to find a middle ground between "too much" and "too little." In our opinion, student readers profit from brief headnotes that provide useful and accessible information about a particular writer's background, relevant publications, and compositional practices and goals. Many selections possess interesting stories in themselves, and many readers understandably want to know when a piece was written and how and where it originally appeared. We try in our headnotes to be as attentive as possible to a selection's original source. We don't want readers to mistakenly conclude that an excerpt is actually an essay. This distorts one's approach to the selection and is often unfair to the author. For example, we want readers to know at the outset that Maya Angelou's well-known selection, "What's Your Name, Girl?" is taken from her award-winning autobiography, *I Know Why the Caged Bird Sings,* and was never intended to be an essay in itself. The selection requires a certain amount of preliminary context (and a few notes) to fully understand the dramatic situation she so vividly describes.

It is our experience, too, that many students can be guided in their assessment or rereading of a selection by carefully constructed follow-up questions. In this edition we have retained "The Reader's Presence," the small clusters of questions after every numbered selection. These questions can be used privately by student readers and writers in their attempt to come to terms with the selection, or in the classroom to stimulate group discussion and evaluation. As discussion-starters, the questions are designed to cover some of the dominant features of the selection and refer to matters of content, style, and structure. As their title indicates, the questions will often draw attention to the specific ways in which readers are also present in a piece of writing—either as an implied reader (the reader imagined by the writer) or as an actual reader (oneself). The concept of *presence*—both the writer's and the reader's—is covered more fully in the "Introduction for Students."

RESOURCES FOR TEACHING *The Writer's Presence*

Carefully managing the amount of instructional apparatus in *The Writer's Presence* does not weaken our commitment to provide you with a wealth of specific instructional activities. In 300 spiral-bound pages,

Resources for Teaching THE WRITER'S PRESENCE is the most extensive instructor's manual available for any composition reader.

This resource-full guide to *The Writer's Presence* includes the following four parts in each entry:

- "Approaching the Essay" provides a thorough overview of the pedagogical prospects of working with the essay in the classroom.

- "Additional Activities" offers imaginative classroom activities, including write-before-reading exercises, connections to other essays in the book, and collaborative projects.

- "Generating Writing" includes a range of writing exercises — from suggestions for informal writing to essay assignments and ideas for research papers.

- "The Reader's Presence" addresses the questions that follow each selection in the text, pointing to illuminating passages in the selection and anticipating possible responses from students.

ACKNOWLEDGMENTS

Revisions of *The Writer's Presence* have grown out of correspondence and conversation — on the phone, in person, in letters, and on the Internet — with the many teachers and an appreciable number of students who have worked with *The Writer's Presence* in their writing classes. We continue to learn a great deal from these discussions, and we are grateful to the colleagues and friends who graciously have allowed us into their already crowded lives to seek advice and encouragement. As it has been since its inception, *The Writer's Presence* continues to be a truly collaborative enterprise.

Much in the manner of our plan to develop *The Writer's Presence*, this revision has emerged from spirited discussions with instructors who prefer to pick and choose — at their own discretion and with their own instructional purposes — from among a wide range of eminently readable and teachable essays. We are grateful to these colleagues across the country who took the time to tell us about what did — and did not — work well when they used the second edition: Linda Baker, Portland Community College; Jennifer Buckley, John Carroll University; Eileen Donovan-Kranz, Boston College; Susan M. Eisenthal, University of Massachusetts — Boston; Jack Jacobs, Auburn University; Michael M. Walker, Palomar College; Genoveva Llosa, Boston College; Lolly Ockerstrom, Virginia Commonwealth University; Jean Pace, Emerson College; Jan Zlotnick Schmidt, State University of New York, New Paltz; Joanne Sibicky, Virginia Commonwealth University; Robert Singleton, State University of New York, New Paltz; Robert L. Stapleton, Long Beach City College; and Chad R. Stockton, Emerson College.

We would also like to acknowledge those instructors who gave us feedback about the first edition: Lisa Altomari, Vermont Technical

College; Maurice H. Barr, Spokane Community College; Todd W. Bersley, California State University—Northridge; Gerri Black, Stockton State College; Scott Brookman, Virginia Commonwealth University; Larry Brunt, Highline Community College; Irene Burgess, SUC Cortland; Dolores M. Burton, Boston University; Diane Challis, Virginia Commonwealth University; Jimmy Cheshire, Wright State University; Chet Childress, Virginia Commonwealth University; Alice Cleveland, College of Mareu; Michel S. Connell, University of Iowa; Chase Crossingham, University of South Carolina; Ruth Y. Davidson, Pennsylvania State University—Schuylkill Campus; Michael G. Davros, University of Illinois at Chicago; Peggy C. de Broux, Peninsula College; Jessica Deforest, Michigan State University; Mary Devaney, Rutgers University—Newark Campus; Debra DiPiazza, Bernard M. Baruch College (CUNY); Maria Rowena P. Dolorico, Bristol Community College; Alex Fagan, Virginia Commonwealth University; Grace Farrell, Butler University; Joan Gabriele, University of Colorado; Christie Anderson Garcia, Spokane Falls Community College; Jane Gatewood, Mary Washington College; Rae Greiner, Radford University; Brian Hale, University of South Carolina; Sarah Hanselman, Tufts University; Dave Hendrickson, Virginia Commonwealth University; Curtis W. Herr, Kutztown University; Professor Goldie Johnson, Winona State University; Nancy B. Johnson, Pace University; Ronald L. King, Virginia Commonwealth University; Harriet Malinowitz, Hunter College (CUNY); Barbara Mallonee, Loyola College; Denice Martone, New York University; Ilene Miele, Moorpark College; Andrew Mossin, Temple University; Cathryn A. Myers, Virginia Commonwealth University; Cheryl Pallant, Virginia Commonwealth University; Marty Patton, University of Missouri—Columbia; Gary D. Pratt, Brandeis University; Catherine S. Quick, University of Missouri—Columbia; Larry Rodgers, Kansas State University; Colleen Richmond, George Fox College; Lissa Schneider, University of Miami; Marilyn S. Scott, California State University—Hayward; Constance Fletcher Smith, Mary Washington College; Roger Sorkin, University of Massachusetts—Dartmouth; J. F. Stenerson, Pace University; Steven Strang, Massachusetts Institute of Technology; Pamela Topping, Long Island University—Southampton Campus; Mary Turnbull, University of Puget Sound; Donna M. Turner, University of North Dakota; Sandra Urban, Loyola University of Chicago; Jennifer Lynne Von Ammon, Florida State University; and Ed Wiltse, Tufts University.

We would especially like to acknowledge our colleagues in the Expository Writing Program at New York University — Alfred Guy, Lisa Altomari, Karen Boiko, Darlene Forrest, Mary Helen Kolisnyk, Jim Marcall, Denice Martone, and Will McCormack — for taking the time to talk with us and for sharing their ideas during the planning stages.

We also extend our thanks to all the people at Bedford/St. Martin's for their innumerable contributions to this revision. We deeply appreciate the continuous support and intelligent suggestions we received from our editor, Alanya Harter—she helped make this a better book in every conceivable way. We are also grateful to Ellen Thibault, who supplied invaluable research contributions during the early stages of the project, and to Amy Thomas, who helped bring together all the inevitable loose ends as we neared the conclusion. Many thanks, too, to Ara Salibian for deftly moving an enormous and complex manuscript through production and to Elizabeth Schaaf for managing the entire process with her usual attentiveness.

As ever, Chuck Christensen, the president of Bedford/St. Martin's, offered us spirited encouragement, first-rate and rigorous advice, as well as numerous suggestions for improving the project. He never hesitated to urge us to venture with an idea or to explore an instructional feature of the book if it might make our purposes clearer and more useful to teachers and students. And when our conversations veered occasionally toward uncertainty, we relied on the steady editorial presence of Editorial Director Joan Feinberg, who invariably helped us convert pedagogical principle into sound instructional practice.

The comprehensive instructional guide that accompanies this collection, *Resources for Teaching THE WRITER'S PRESENCE,* was prepared this year by Shelley Salamensky of the University of Albany, State University of New York. Shelley also supplied many of "The Reader's Presence" questions and has linked these closely to the entries in the manual. We appreciate her intelligent contributions and her remarkable ability to assess the classroom potential of so wide a variety of texts. We continue to be grateful to Alfred Guy (New York University), Jon Roberts (St. Thomas Aquinas College), and Alix Schwartz (University of California, Berkeley) for their work in previous editions; their very helpful suggestions are still amply evident in the instructor's guide. We also continue to appreciate the help received from Greg Mullins, who provided a good deal of the biographical and compositional information contained in the headnotes to selections carried over from previous editions. The new headnote research and writing for this edition was expertly handled by Donna Ashley; we are enormously grateful to her for all of her efforts. We extend our thanks, too, to Arthur Johnson, who adroitly assembled the hundreds of moving parts that go into securing reprint permissions.

Finally, we hope that Hélène, Gregory, and Emily Atwan, along with Susanne, Christine, and Marc McQuade, will once again share our satisfaction in seeing this project in print and our pleasure in continuing our productive collaboration.

Donald McQuade
Robert Atwan

Contents _____

"We stood in the street, uncertain and afraid, until a house across from us began to sway and then with a rending motion fell almost at our feet. Our own house began to sway, and in a minute it, too, collapsed in a cloud of dust."

"Happiness in this world, when it comes, comes incidentally. Make it the object of pursuit, and it leads us a wild-goose chase, and is never attained."

"We started to move slowly through the village shooting everything in sight children men and women and animals. Some was sickening."

"Future years will never know the seething hell and the black infernal background of countless minor scenes and interiors . . . of the Secession war; and it is best they should not—the real war will never get in the books."

"What sort of diary should I like mine to be? Something loose knit and yet not slovenly, so elastic that it will embrace anything, solemn, slight or beautiful that comes into my mind. I should like it to resemble some deep old desk, or capacious hold-all, in which one flings a mass of odds and ends without looking them through."

II. PERSONAL WRITING: Exploring Our Own Lives   55

"Every person I knew had a hellish horror of being 'called out of his name.' It was a dangerous practice to call a Negro anything that could be loosely construed as insulting because of the centuries of their having been called niggers, jigs, dinges, blackbirds, crows, boots, and spooks."

"I had never met a writer, had shown no previous urge to write, and hadn't a notion how to become a writer, but I loved stories and thought that making up stories must surely be almost as much fun as reading them."

"Memory teaches me what I know of these matters. The boy reminds the adult. I was a bilingual child, but of a certain kind: 'socially disadvantaged,' the son of working-class parents, both Mexican immigrants."

THE WRITER AT WORK:
Richard Rodriguez on a Writer's Identity   239
"The notion of the writer as a kind of sociological sample of a community is ludicrous. Even worse is the notion that writers should provide an example of how to live."

"My brother calls. He's always envied me, my woman's body. The same body I live in and have cursed for its softness. He asks me how I feel about myself. He says, "You know, you are really our father's first-born son.'"

"We lived on rolls and hot dogs. My mother made me sleep wrapped in a chiffon scarf to protect me from the cockroaches. My father took his watch, of a decent but undistinguished Swiss make, to a pawnshop, where he was given five dollars in return."

"Mother said that Jesus had been a good man, and he wanted peace and harmony in the hearts of all men. She said this while I looked at Jesus on his cross, poor Jesus who had nails and blood all over him. If they did that to someone who was so good I wondered what they would do to me. You see, I was turning out bad."

"She cast back a worried glance. To her, the youngish black man—a broad six feet two inches with a beard and billowing hair, both hands shoved into the pockets of a bulky military jacket—seemed menacingly close. After a few more quick glimpses, she picked up her pace and was soon running in earnest."

THE WRITER AT WORK:
Another Version of "Just Walk on By"   269
"She looked back at me once, then again, and picked up her pace. She looked back again and started to run. I stopped where I was and looked up at the surrounding windows. What did this look like to people peeking out through their blinds?"

inspired images do most brilliantly. Art should provoke more questions than answers and, most of all, should make us think about what we rarely want to think about at all."

the day. I can kill and clean a hog as mercilessly as a man. My fat keeps me hot in zero weather."

Selections Arranged by Theme ──────

PSYCHOLOGY AND HUMAN BEHAVIOR

ETHICS AND MORALITY

PHILOSOPHY, SPIRITUALITY, AND RELIGION

POPULAR CULTURE AND MASS MEDIA

LANGUAGE AND LITERATURE

GENDER ROLES

The Writer's Presence
A Pool of Readings

Introduction for Students:
The Writer's Presence

Presence is a word—like *charisma*—that we reserve for people who create powerful and memorable impressions. Many public figures and political leaders are said to "have presence" (John F. Kennedy and Martin Luther King Jr., were two superb examples) as well as many athletes, dancers, and musicians. In fact, the quality of presence is found abundantly in the performing arts; think of Michael Jackson or Madonna, two entertainers who have self-consciously fashioned—through style, costume, and gesture—an instantly recognizable public presence. Clearly, people with presence are able to command our attention. How do they do it?

Presence is far easier to identify than it is to define. We recognize it when we see it, but how do we capture it in words? Virtually everyone would agree, for example, that when Michael Jordan stepped onto a basketball court, he displayed an exceptional degree of presence; we acknowledge this whether or not we are basketball fans. But what is it about such individuals that commands our attention? How can we begin to understand this elusive characteristic known as presence?

On one level, *presence* simply means "being present." But the word is more complex than that; it suggests much more than the mere fact of being physically present. Most dictionaries define *presence* as an ability to project a sense of self-assurance, poise, ease, or dignity. We thus speak of someone's "stage presence" or "presence of mind." But the word is also used today to suggest an impressive personality, an individual who can make his or her presence felt. As every college student knows, to be present in a classroom is not the same thing as *having a presence* there. We may be present in body, but not in spirit. In that sense, presence is also a matter of individual energy and exertion, of putting something of ourselves into whatever it is we do.

Presence is especially important in writing, which is what this book is about. Just as we notice individual presence in sports, or music, or conversation, so too we discover it in good writing. If what we read seems dreary, dull, or dead, it's usually because the writer forgot to include an

1

important ingredient: *personal presence*. That doesn't mean that your essays should be written *in* the first-person singular (this book contains many exceptional essays that aren't), but that your essays should be written *by* the first-person singular — by *you*. Interesting essays are produced by a real and distinct person, not an automaton following a set of mechanical rules and abstract principles.

PRESENCE IN WRITING

How can someone be present in writing? How can you project yourself into an essay so that it seems that you're personally there, even though all your reader sees are words on a piece of paper?

The Writer's Presence shows you how this is done. It shows how a wide variety of talented writers establish a distinct presence in many different kinds of writing and for many different purposes and audiences. Though the book offers numerous examples of how presence is compositionally established, there are several methods that nearly all experienced writers observe and that are worth pointing out at the start. Let's examine four of the chief ways a writer can be present in an essay.

1. Personal Experience. One of the most straightforward ways of making your presence felt in an essay is to include appropriate personal experiences. Of course, many assignments may call for a personal essay, and in those cases you will naturally be putting episodes from your own life at the center of your writing. But writers also find ways to build their personal experiences into essays that are basically informative or argumentative, essays on topics other than the self. They do this to show their close connection with a subject, to offer testimony, or to establish their personal authority on a subject. Many of the essays in this collection offer clear illustrations of how writers incorporate personal experience into an essay on a specific topic or issue.

Look, for example, at the essay by Amy Cunningham, "Why Women Smile" (page 342). This essay is primarily an explanation of a cultural phenomenon — the way women are socially conditioned to maintain a smiling attitude. But note that Cunningham begins the essay not with a general observation but with a personal anecdote: "After smiling brilliantly for nearly four decades, I now find myself trying to quit." Though her essay is not "personal," her opening sentence, besides establishing her own connection with the topic, provides readers with a personal motive for her writing.

One of the first places to look for the writer's presence is in the motive, the purpose, for putting pen to paper. Virginia Woolf calls this a "fierce attachment to an idea." The extent of our success in making clear our motive for writing will largely depend on our interest both in our subject as well as in our idea about the subject. It will prove extremely difficult for any writer to establish a presence when he or she is either bored with—or simply uninterested in—the subject at hand. Investing in a clearly articulated purpose will yield an attractive return in reader attention.

2. *Voice.* Another way a writer makes his or her presence felt is through creating a distinctive and identifiable *voice*. All words are composed of sounds, and language itself is something nearly all of us originally learned through *hearing*. Any piece of writing can be read aloud, though many readers have developed such ingrained habits of silent reading that they no longer *hear* the writing. Good writers, however, want their words to be heard. They want their sentences to have rhythm, cadence, and balance. Experienced authors revise a great deal of their writing just to make sure the sentences *sound* right. They're writing for the reader's ear as well as the reader's mind.

In many respects, voice is the writer's "signature," what finally distinguishes the work of one writer from another. Consider how quickly we recognize voice. We only *hear* the opening lines of a humorous sketch on television, yet we instantly recognize the comedian. So, too, whenever we read a piece of writing, we ought to think of it as an experience similar to listening to someone speak aloud. Doing so adds drama to writing and reading. Here is what the poet Robert Frost has to say on the subject:

> Everything written is as good as it is dramatic. . . . A dramatic necessity goes deep into the nature of the sentence. Sentences are not different enough to hold the attention unless they are dramatic. No ingenuity of varying structure will do. All that can save them is the speaking tone of voice somehow entangled in the words and fastened to the page for the ear of the imagination. That is all that can save poetry from singing, all that can save prose from itself. (Preface to *A Way Out,* in *Selected Prose of Robert Frost,* 1)

Frost spent a good portion of his celebrated public life encouraging people to cultivate what he called "the hearing imagination."

A writer's voice is usually fairly consistent from essay to essay and can be detected quickly by an experienced reader who pays attention to "the hearing imagination." To be distinctive and effective, a writer's voice need not be strange, artificial, or self-consciously literary. Many essayists develop a casual, familiar, flexible tone of voice that allows them to range easily from the intimate to the intellectual. Sentence rhythm and word choice play a large part in determining a writer's tone of voice. Observe how Raymond Carver begins an essay about his father (page 69):

> My dad's name was Clevie Raymond Carver. His family called him Raymond and friends called him C.R. I was named Raymond Clevie Carver, Jr. I hated the "Junior" part. When I was little my dad called me Frog, which was okay. . . .

Carver's voice here is casual and almost childlike, a quality he is striving for in an essay intended to be candid, intimate, and low-key.

Throughout the essay, for example, he rarely uses the word *father* but always the more colloquial *dad.* If you read this passage aloud, you will get the feeling that someone is speaking directly to you.

A more specific dimension of voice is *tone,* which refers not only to the implied social relationship of the writer to the reader, but also to the manner the writer adopts in addressing the reader. When considering tone as a feature of the writer's presence, it is useful to remember that tone addresses the ways in which writers convey attitudes. In this respect, tone does not speak to the attitudes themselves but to the manner in which those attitudes are revealed. In either projecting or analyzing the writer's tone, writers and readers ought to consider its intensity, the force with which the writer's attitudes are expressed. The strength of the writer's tone depends on such factors as the seriousness of the situation, the nature and extent of the writer's involvement in the situation, and the control the writer exercises over expression. In practical terms, tone is usually a matter of diction and individual word choice.

3. Point of View. Another sure way to establish presence is in the point of view we adopt toward a subject. In this sense, point of view comprises the "whereness" of the writer's presence. Sometimes a point of view can be a literal reality, an actual place or situation in which we physically locate ourselves as writers. This occurs most frequently in autobiographical essays in which the writer is present both as the narrator and as a character. For example, in "A Clack of Tiny Sparks: Remembrances of a Gay Boyhood" (page 85), Bernard Cooper is always meticulous about telling us his actual location at any given moment in his writing. The essay begins: "Theresa Sanchez sat behind me in ninth-grade algebra."

Note, too, how extremely important point of view is to another essayist in the volume, Brent Staples, in "Just Walk on By: A Black Man Ponders His Power to Alter Public Space" (page 265). Here is how Staples opens his essay:

> My first victim was a woman—white, well dressed, probably in her early twenties. I came upon her late one evening on a deserted street in Hyde Park, a relatively affluent neighborhood in an otherwise mean, impoverished section of Chicago. As I swung onto the avenue behind her, there seemed to be a discreet, uninflammatory distance between us. Not so. She cast back a worried glance. To her, the youngish black man—a broad six feet two inches with a beard and billowing hair, both hands shoved into the pockets of a bulky military jacket—seemed menacingly close. After a few more quick glimpses, she picked up her pace and was soon running in earnest. Within seconds she disappeared into a cross street.

Point of view in this essay is crucial to Staples, since, in order to see why he frightens people, he needs to see himself in the stereotypical ways that others see him. Thus, by the middle of this opening para-

graph (in the sentence beginning "To her"), he literally switches the point
of view from his own perspective to that of the young and terrified white
woman, describing his appearance as she would perceive it.

Point of view is not always a matter of a specific location or position.
Writers are not always present in their essays as dramatic characters. In
many reflective, informative, or argumentative essays, the point of view is
determined more by a writer's intellectual attitude or opinions—an angle
of vision—than by a precise physical perspective. As an example of how a
writer establishes a personal perspective without introducing a first-person
narrator or a characterized self, note the following passage from June
Jordan's "Nobody Mean More to Me Than You and the Future Life of
Willie Jordan." The author prefaces her personal experiences as a teacher
with a clear presentation of her position on the subject of Black English, arguing that "white standards of English persist, supreme and unquestioned,
in these United States." She goes on to show why this could be considered
from an international perspective an odd state of affairs:

> Nonetheless, white standards of English persist, supreme and un-
> questioned, in these United States. Despite our multilingual population,
> and despite the deepening Black and white cleavage within that con-
> glomerate, white standards control our official and popular judgments
> of verbal proficiency and correct, or incorrect, language skills, including
> speech. In contrast to India, where at least fourteen languages co-exist as
> legitimate Indian languages, in contrast to Nicaragua, where all citizens
> are legally entitled to formal school instruction in their regional or tribal
> languages, compulsory education in America compels accommodation
> to exclusively white forms of "English." White English, in America, is
> "Standard English" (page 714).

There is no first person singular here, nor a dramatically rendered self.
Yet this passage conveys a very distinct point of view.

4. Patterns. A writer can also be present in an essay as a *writer*—that
is, a person consciously crafting and shaping his or her work. This artistic
presence is not always obvious. Yet when we begin to detect in our reading certain kinds of repeated elements—a metaphor or an image, a twist
on an earlier episode, a conclusion that echoes the opening—we become
aware that someone is deliberately shaping experience or ideas in a special manner. We often find this type of presence in imaginative literature—especially in novels and poems—as well as in essays that possess a
distinct literary flavor.

As an example of creating a presence through patterns, look at the
opening paragraph of E. B. White's now-classic essay, "Once More to the
Lake" (page 292).

> One summer, along about 1904, my father rented a camp on a lake in
> Maine and took us all there for the month of August. We all got ring-
> worm from some kittens and had to rub Pond's Extract on our arms and
> legs night and morning, and my father rolled over in a canoe with all his

clothes on; but outside of that the vacation was a success and from then on none of us ever thought there was any place in the world like that lake in Maine. We returned summer after summer—always on August 1st for one month. I have since become a salt-water man, but sometimes in summer there are days when the restlessness of the tides and the fearful cold of the sea water and the incessant wind that blows across the afternoon and into the evening make me wish for the placidity of a lake in the woods. A few weeks ago this feeling got so strong I bought myself a couple of bass hooks and a spinner and returned to the lake where we used to go, for a week's fishing and to revisit old haunts.

If in rereading this opening, you circle every use of the word *and,* you will clearly see a pattern of repetition. *And,* of course, is a very unobtrusive word, and you may not notice right off how White keeps it present throughout the passage. This repetition alone may strike you at first as of no special importance, but as you read through the essay and see how much of White's central theme depends on the idea of return and repetition, you will get a better sense of why the little word *and*—a word that subtly reinforces the idea of repetition itself—is so significant.

E. B. White is present in his essay in more obvious ways—he is both telling us the story and he appears in it as a character. But he is also present to us as a writer, someone consciously shaping the language and form of his essay. We are dealing here with three levels of presence (which might also be described as three levels of "I"). If this sounds confusing, just think of a movie in which a single person directs the film, writes the script, and plays a leading role. It's not the uncommon. If you watch the 1987 film *Hannah and Her Sisters,* for example, you can observe the three presences of Woody Allen. Allen is not only visibly present in the film as one of the chief characters, but we also can detect his creative and shaping presence as the author of the screenplay (for which he won an Oscar) and as the director. The audience can directly see him on the screen as an actor; but the audience can also infer his presence as a scriptwriter and especially as a director—presences that, though less directly observable, are still original and powerful.

THE SELECTIONS IN THIS BOOK

Many of the selections in this book feature the first-person point of view directly. These selections appear mostly in the first two chapters, "The Private Voice: Diaries, Journals, Notebooks" and "Personal Writing: Exploring Our Own Lives." In most of these journal entries and essays, the writer will appear as both narrator and main character, and the writer's presence will be quite observable.

But private and personal writing provide only a fraction of the different types of nonfiction that appear regularly in books, newspapers, and magazines. Many essays are written on specific topics and deal with specific issues. Most of the essays appearing in America's dominant periodicals, for example, are intended to be either informative or persuasive; the author wants to convey information about a particular subject (a Civil War battle) or wants to express an opinion about a particular issue (how to deal with the homeless). The book's third and fourth parts, "Expository Writing: Shaping Information" and "Argumentative Writing: Contending with Issues," contain a large number of selections that illustrate writing intended to inform, argue, and persuade.

You'll notice, however, a strong writer's presence in many of the informative and persuasive essays. This is deliberate. To write informatively or persuasively about subjects other than yourself doesn't mean that you have to disappear as a writer. Sometimes you will want to insert your own experiences and testimony into an argumentative essay; at other times you will want to assume a distinct viewpoint concerning a piece of information; and at still other times—though you may not introduce the first-person singular—you will make your presence strongly felt in your tone of voice or simply in the way you arrange your facts and juxtapose details. At the heart of the word *information* is *form*. Writers don't passively receive facts and information in a totally finished format; they need to shape their information, to give it form. This shaping or patterning is something the writer *contributes*. A large part of the instructional purpose of this collection is to encourage you to pay more attention to the different ways writers are present in their work.

An individual writer's presence and voice are perhaps more easily discerned in nonfiction than in fiction. The reason for this is that a novelist or short story writer invents and gives voices to numerous characters who should not be confused with the author. Sometimes, a story is told by an invented character who also should not be closely identified with his or her author. A good example of this technique can be found in John Updike's "A & P" (see page 922), in which a story is narrated in the distinctive voice of its main character, Sammy, a teenager who is working at a small suburban supermarket. Although the story is written in the first-person singular—exactly like most personal essays—the character and voice are fictional and do not correspond to any real person. Sammy is not John Updike nor does he necessarily speak like John Updike would if we met him.

To further complicate matters, this biographical gap between narrator and author remains even when a story that is told in the third person appears to be written in the voice of the author. The third-person narrator is also invented and the narrative voice and presence may have little to do with the life of the author who created it. So in what ways can the writer's presence be observed in a story if we cannot attach to its teller any biographical connection with its author? In fiction, we often find a writer's presence in a distinctive style of writing, in certain repeated patterns, in the dynamics of structure and plot, and of course in the ethical, spiritual, or intellectual values a story may be intended to illustrate. In certain stories, to be sure, a particular character may clearly represent the author's own values, and in those cases we might argue that the writer becomes "present" in that character. As can be seen in Part V, "The Voices of Fiction: Eight Modern Short Stories," an author may refuse to locate his or her moral and psychological values within a particular character but will expect instead that the reader will derive these values from the overall perspective of the story itself. Unlike essayists, short story writers rarely state their ethical or aesthetic values directly and explicitly. As the novelist D. H. Lawrence aptly put it, in fiction we must trust the tale and not the teller. We have included in *The Writer's Presence* several examples of fiction and nonfiction by the same author (e.g., Raymond Carver, Jamaica Kincaid, Amy Tan, and Alice Walker) so that readers can explore the different ways a writer's values are conveyed in different genres.

THE READER'S PRESENCE

Because almost all writing (and *all* published writing) is intended to be read, we can't dismiss the importance of the reader. Just as we find different levels of a writer's presence in a given piece of writing, so too can we detect different ways in which a reader can be present.

An author writes a short essay offering an opinion about gun control. The author herself has been the victim of a shooting, and her piece, though it includes her personal experiences, is largely made up of a concrete plan to eliminate all guns—even hunting rifles—from American life. She would like lawmakers to adopt her plan. Yet, in writing her essay, she imagines a great deal of resistance to her argument. In other words, she imagines a reader who will most likely disagree with her and who needs to be won over. Let's imagine she gets her essay published in *Newsweek*.

Now imagine three people in a dentist's office who within the same afternoon pick up this issue of *Newsweek* and read the essay. One of them has also been victimized by guns (her son was accidentally wounded by a hunter), and she reads the essay with great sympathy and conviction. She understands perfectly what this woman has gone through and believes in her plan completely. The next reader, a man who has never once in his life committed a crime and has no tolerance for criminals, is outraged by the essay. He was practically brought up in the woods and loves to hunt. He could never adopt a gun control plan that would in effect criminalize hunting. He's ready to fire off a letter attacking this woman's plan. The third reader also enjoys hunting and has always felt that hunting rifles should be exempt from any government regulation of firearms. But he finds the woman's plan convincing and feasible. He spends the rest of the day trying to think of counterarguments.

Obviously, these are only three of many possibilities. But you should be able to see from this example the differences between the reader imagined by the writer and some actual readers. The one person who completely agreed with the writer was not the kind of reader the author had originally imagined or was trying to persuade; she was already persuaded. And though the other two readers were part of her intended audience, one of them could never be persuaded to her point of view, whereas the other one might.

The differences briefly outlined here are distinctions between what can be called implied readers and actual readers. The implied reader is the reader imagined by the writer for a particular piece of writing. In constructing arguments, for example, it is usually effective to imagine readers we are *trying* to win over to our views. Otherwise, we are simply asking people who already agree with us to agree with us—what's commonly known as "preaching to the converted."

In informative or critical essays, a writer also needs to be careful about the implied reader. For example, it's always important to ask how much your intended audience may already know about your subject. Here's a practical illustration. If you were asked to write a review of a recent film for your college newspaper, you would assume your readers had not yet seen it (or else you might annoy them by giving away some surprises). On the other hand, if you were asked to write a critical essay about the same movie for a film course, you could assume your readers had seen it. It's the same movie, and you have the same opinions about it, but your two essays had two different purposes, and in the process of writing them you imagined readers with two different levels of knowledge about the film.

Actual readers, of course, differ from implied readers in that they are real people who read the writing—not readers intended or imagined by the writer. As you read the essays in this collection, you should be aware of at least two readers—(1) the reader you think the writer imagines for the essay, and (2) the reader you are in actuality. Sometimes you will seem very close to the kind of reader the writer is imagining. In those cases, you might say that you "identify" with a particular writer, essay, or point of view. At other times, however, you will notice a great deal of distance between the reader the author imagines and you as an actual reader. For example, you may feel excluded by the author on the basis of race, gender, class, or expected knowledge and educational level. Or you may feel you know more than the author does about a particular topic.

To help you get accustomed to your role as a reader, each selection in the book is followed by a set of questions, "The Reader's Presence." These questions are designed to orient you to the various levels of reading suggested by the selection. Some of the questions will ask you to identify the kind of reader you think the author imagines; other questions will prompt you to think about specific ways you may differ from the author's intended reader. In general, the questions are intended to make you more deeply aware of your *presence* as a reader.

In this brief introduction, we covered only two levels of readers (imagined and actual), but some literary essays demand more complex consideration. Whenever we think more than these two types of readers need to be identified in an essay, we will introduce this information in the questions.

We hope you will find *The Writer's Presence* a stimulating book to read and think about. To make our presence felt as writers is as much a matter of self-empowerment as it is of faith. It requires the confidence that we can affect others, or determine a course of action, or even surprise ourselves by new ideas or by acquiring new powers of articulation. Part of the enduring pleasure of writing is precisely that element of surprise, of originality—that lifelong pleasure of discovering new resources of language, finding new means of knowing ourselves, and inventing new ways to be present in the world.

Part I

The Private Voice: Diaries, Journals, Notebooks

1

Rachel Carson
From *Field Notebooks*

Silent Spring, the book on pesticides that launched the modern environmental movement and became an international best-seller in 1962, was written by a courageous and dedicated woman who would die of cancer within two years of its publication. Its author, Rachel Carson (1907–1964), had early ambitions of becoming a poet but as a student at Pennsylvania College for Women fell in love with the biological sciences. After taking a master's degree in zoology at Johns Hopkins, Carson worked for a few years as a teacher and later as an aquatic biologist with the U.S. Bureau of Fisheries. In the 1930s, she began turning her scientific fascination with the sea into a series of elegant essays that eventually led to several nonfiction books on marine life, including Under the Sea-Wind *(1941) and the award-winning* The Sea Around Us *(1952).* The Edge of the Sea *(1954) completed her "sea trilogy." In preparing research for that book, Carson made meticulous observations of life along the Atlantic coast. The following two fragments from her notebooks are reprinted from* Lost Woods: The Discovered Writings of Rachel Carson *(Beacon Press, 1998); they offer a fine indication of a remarkable naturalist who clearly never lost her childhood passion for poetry.*

SATURDAY

Hiked north on beach. Very windy, a quick shower or two, much froth. Saw a little one-legged sanderling hopping along hunting food. Without my glasses I couldn't be sure whether the injured leg was cut off or drawn up under the body, but it was completely useless. Still he ran and probed, not venturing as near the surf as they usually do. When I came near he wheeled out over the water, his sharp "pit, pil" quickly lost in the sound of the waves. I thought of the long miles of travel ahead of him and wondered how long he would last. As I came back down the beach I saw him again still hopping along bravely.

A very few ghost crabs were out, but scuttled back quickly into their holes. I sat down on a box to wait for one to come out, feeling like a cat watching a mouse hole, but soon it began to rain and I moved on.

Saw tracks of a shore bird—probably a sanderling, and followed them a little, then they turned toward the water and were soon obliterated by the sea. How much it washes away, and makes as though it had never been. Time itself is like the sea, containing all that came before us, sooner or later sweeping us away on its flood and washing over and obliterating the traces of our presence, as the sea this morning erased the footprints of the bird.

On the way back I met the little one-legged sanderling again, the one I had seen Saturday afternoon. Remembering how the legs of the normal ones twinkle as they dash up and down the beach, it was amazing to see how fast this little fellow got about just hopping, hopping on his good right leg. This time I could see that his left leg is only a short stump less than an inch long. I wondered if some animal, maybe a fox, had caught it in the Arctic, or whether it had gotten into a trap. Their way of feeding being what it is, one would say he would have been eliminated before this as "unfit"—yet he must be even tougher than his two-legged comrades. That last word is a misnomer, he had no companions—either time I saw him—just hunting alone, he would hop, hop, hop, toward the surf; probing and jabbing busily with opened bill, turn and hop away from the advancing foam. Only twice did I see him have to take to his wings to escape a wetting. It made my heart ache to think how tired his little leg must be, but his whole manner suggested a cheerfulness of spirit and a gameness which must mean that the God of fallen sparrows has not forgotten him.

DUNES

What peculiar brand of magic is inherent in that combination of sand   5
and sky and water it is hard to say. It is bleak and stark. But somehow it is not forbidding. Its bleakness is part of its quiet, calm strength.
The dune land is a place of overwhelming silence, or so it seems at first. But soon you realize that what you take for silence is an absence of human created sound. For the dunes have a voice of their own, which you may hear if you will but sit down and listen to it. It is compounded of many natural sounds which are never heard in the roar of a city or even in the stir of a small town. A soft, confused, hollow rustling fills the air. In part it is the sound of surf on the beach half a mile away—a wide sand valley and another ridge of sand hills between us—the deep thunder of the surf reduced to a sigh by the intervening distance. In part it is the confused whisperings of the wind, which seems to be never wholly still there, but always to be exploring the contours of the land it made, roaming down into the valleys and leaping in little, unexpected gusts over the crests of the sand hills. And there are the smaller voices, the voices of the sand and the dune grass. The soft swish of the grass as it dips and bends

in the wind to trace its idle arcs and circles in the sand at its feet. Arcs, especially on the southeast side of the grass, mean unsettled weather, so they say; whole circles foretell fair weather because they show the wind to be blowing alternately from different quarters. I cannot say as to that; but the scribblings of the dune grass always enchant me, though I cannot read their meaning.

I knew the history of that land, and there, under the wind and beside the surf that had carved it, I recalled the story—

I stood where a new land was being built out of the sea, and I came away deeply moved. Although our intelligence forbids the idea, I believe our deeply rooted attitude toward the creation of the earth and the evolution of living things is a feeling that it all took place in a time infinitely remote. Now I understood. Here, as if for the benefit of my puny human understanding, the processes of creation—of earth building—had been speeded up so that I could trace the change within the life of my own contemporaries. The changes that were going on before my eyes were part and parcel of the same processes that brought the first dry land emerging out of the ancient and primitive ocean; or that led the first living creatures step by step out of the sea into the perilous new world of earth.

Water and wind and sand were the builders, and only the gulls and I were there to witness this act of creation.

Strange thoughts come to a man or woman who stands alone in that   10
bleak and barren world. It is a world stripped of the gracious softness of the trees, the concealing mercies of abundant vegetation, the refreshment of a quiet lake, the beguilement of shade. It is a world stripped to the naked elements of life. And it is, after all, so newly born of the sea that it could hardly be otherwise. And then there is the voice of the sand itself— the quick sharp sibilance of a gust of sand blown over a dune crest by a sudden shift of the breeze, the all but silent sound of the never ending, restless shifting of the individual grains, one over another.

I am not sure that I can recommend the dunes as a tonic for all souls, nor for all moods. But I can say that anyone who will go alone into the dune lands for a day, or even for an hour, will never forget what he has seen and felt there.

The Reader's Presence

1. In what ways does Carson "personalize" her experiences of nature? Can you think of other ways she might have described the one-legged shore bird? What does her description of the bird indicate about her own personality?

2. What features of Carson's notebooks indicate a mind in process? How is her interest in "process" also reflected in the things she observes? As you read her notes on the dunes, can you hear her developing an image that helps her understand the natural world?

2

Toi Derricotte

From *The Black Notebooks*

In the 1970s Toi Derricotte, a well-known and award-winning African American poet, moved with her husband and young son to an upscale, all-white New Jersey suburb. She soon began keeping a sketchy yet intimate journal of her experiences with friends, neighbors, and family as complex and unpleasant tensions developed. As she wrote, she realized that her disclosures were bringing her face to face with her own shame, her own "internalized racism." She worked at the notebooks for twenty-five years, slowly revising them until they captured "the language of self-hate, the pain of re-emerging thought and buried memory and consciousness." The Black Notebooks: An Interior Journey, *from which the following selections were extracted, was published in 1997. "October" recounts an episode that took place while Derricotte and her husband were house-hunting in New Jersey; the incident in "July" occurred after they had moved to the all-white community.*

Born in Detroit, Michigan, in 1941, Derricotte is also the author of four collections of poetry: Natural Birth, The Empress of the Death House, Captivity, *and* Tender. *She currently teaches at the University of Pittsburgh.*

OCTOBER

It's the overriding reality I must get through. Each time I drive down the streets and see only whites, each time I notice no blacks in the local supermarket or walking on the streets, I think, *I'm not supposed to be here.* When I go into real estate agents' offices, I put on a mask. At first they hope you are in for a quick sell. They show you houses they want to get rid of. But if you stick around, and if you are the "right kind," they show you ones just newly listed, and sometimes not even on the market.

There are neighborhoods that even most white people are not supposed to be in.

I make myself likable, optimistic. I am married, a woman who belongs to a man. Sometimes I reveal I am Catholic, if it might add a feeling of connection. It is not entirely that I am acting. I am myself but slightly strained, like you might strain slightly in order to hear something whispered.

Yesterday an agent took me into the most lily-white neighborhood imaginable, took me right into the spotless kitchen, the dishwasher rumbling, full of the children's dishes. I opened the closets as if I were a thief, as if I were filthying them, as if I believe about myself what they believe: that I'm "passing," that my silence is a crime.

The first woman I knew about who "passed" was the bronze-haired daughter of insurance money, one of the wealthiest black families in the United States. I remember my mother telling me stories of her white roadster, how she wrote plays and opened a theater. She had directed several of the plays in which my mother and father had acted. She went to New York to "make it" and was published in the *New York Times*. I was seven when my father went down to meet the midnight train that brought her home: people said she had confessed to her rich fiancé that she was black and he had jilted her. They dressed her in a long bronze dress, a darkened tone of her long auburn hair. She looked like Sleeping Beauty in a casket made especially for her with a glass top.

My mother told me how, when she was young, her mother used to   5
get great pleasure when she would seat her daughter in the white part of the train and then depart, as if she were her servant. She said her mother would stand alongside the train and wave good-bye with a smile on her face, like a kid who has gotten away with the cookies. And my father told how, during the Detroit riots of 1943, when black men were being pulled off the buses and beaten to death, he used to walk down East Grand Boulevard as a dare.

Of course, we are never caught; it is absolutely inconceivable that we could go unrecognized, that we are that much like them. In fact, we are the same.

When Bruce and I first got married, I had been looking for an apartment for months. Finally, I found a building in a nice neighborhood with a playground nearby, and a school that was integrated. I rang the bell and was relieved when the supervisor who came to the door was black. I loved the apartment. Then I became terrified. Should I tell *him* we're black? Would that make my chances of getting the apartment greater? I wondered if he would be glad to have another black family in the building, or if maybe his job was dependent on his keeping us out. I decided to be silent, to take the chance that he liked me.

When I left, sailing over the George Washington Bridge, I had my first panic attack. I thought I might drive my car right over the edge. I felt so high up there, so disconnected, so completely at my own mercy. Some part of me doesn't give a fuck about boundaries—in fact, sees the boundaries and is determined to dance over them no matter what the consequences are. I am so precarious, strung out between two precipices, that even when I get to the other side, I am still not down, still not so low I can't harm myself.

I could hardly control my car, my heart pounding, my hands sweaty on the wheel. I had to pull off the West Side Highway as soon as I could, and I went into the first place I could find, a meat-packing house. The kind white man let me use the phone to call Bruce before he took me in a big meat truck to the nearest hospital. The doctor said it was anxiety, and I should just go home and rest. For days I was afraid to come out of my house, and even now, though I push myself to do it, every time I go over a high place, or am in a strange territory, I fear I will lose control, that something horrible and destructive will come out of me.

Each night Bruce and I don't talk about it, as if there were no cost to   10
what I'm doing, or as if whatever the cost is I've got to pay.

JULY

This morning I put my car in the shop. The neighborhood shop. When I went to pick it up I had a conversation with the man who had worked on it. I told him I had been afraid to leave the car there at night with the keys in it. "Don't worry," he said. "You don't have to worry about stealing as long as the niggers don't move in." I couldn't believe it. I hoped I had heard him wrong. "What did you say?" I asked. He repeated the same thing without hesitation.

In the past, my anger would have swelled quickly. I would have blurted out something, hotly demanded he take my car down off the rack immediately, though he had not finished working on it, and taken off in a blaze. I love that reaction. The only feeling of power one can possibly have in a situation in which there is such a sudden feeling of powerlessness is to "do" something, handle the situation. When you "do" something, everything is clear. But this is the only repair shop in the city. Might I have to come back here someday in an emergency?

Blowing off steam is supposed to make you feel better. But in this situation it *doesn't!* After responding in anger, I often feel sad, guilty, frightened, and confused. Perhaps my anger isn't just about race. Perhaps it's like those rapid-fire responses to Bruce—a way of dulling the edge of feelings that lie even deeper.

I let the tension stay in my body. I go home and sit with myself for an hour, trying to grasp the feeling—the odor of self-hatred, the biting stench of shame.

The Reader's Presence

1. In what ways does Derricotte try to fit into a white community? What features of an all-white community does she appear to find desirable? What features worry her? What does she mean by "passing"? How does she feel about the act of "passing"?

2. Why doesn't Derricotte express her anger to the auto mechanic? What explanations does she offer? What feelings does her silence lead to?

3

Joan Didion

On Keeping a Notebook

The author of novels, short stories, screenplays, and essays, Joan Didion (b. 1934) began her career in 1956 as a staff writer at Vogue *magazine in New York. In 1963 she published her first novel,* Run River, *and the following year returned to her native California. Didion's essays have appeared in periodicals ranging from* Mademoiselle *to the* National Review. *Her essay "On Keeping a Notebook" can be found in her collection of essays,* Slouching Towards Bethlehem *(1968). Didion's other nonfiction publications include* The White Album *(1979),* Salvador *(1983),* Miami *(1987), and* After Henry *(1992).*

Didion has defined a writer as "a person whose most absorbed and passionate hours are spent arranging words on pieces of paper. I write entirely to find out what's on my mind, what I'm thinking, what I'm looking at, what I'm seeing and what it means, what I want and what I'm afraid of." She has also said that "all writing is an attempt to find out what matters, to find the pattern in disorder, to find the grammar in the shimmer. Actually I don't know whether you find the grammar in the shimmer or you impose a grammar on the shimmer, but I am quite specific about the grammar—I mean it literally. The scene that you see in your mind finds its own structure; the structure dictates the arrangement of the words. . . . All the writer has to do really is to find the words." However, she warns, "You have to be alone to do this."

"'That woman Estelle,'" the note reads, "'is partly the reason why George Sharp and I are separated today.' *Dirty crepe-de-Chine wrapper, hotel bar, Wilmington RR, 9:45 a.m. August Monday morning.*"

Since the note is in my notebook, it presumably has some meaning to me. I study it for a long while. At first I have only the most general notion of what I was doing on an August Monday morning in the bar of the hotel across from the Pennsylvania Railroad station in Wilmington, Delaware (waiting for a train? missing one? 1960? 1961? why Wilmington?), but I do remember being there. The woman in the dirty crepe-de-Chine wrapper had come down from her room for a beer, and the bartender had heard before the reason why George Sharp and she were separated today. "Sure," he said, and went on mopping the floor. "You told me." At the other end of the bar is a girl. She is talking, pointedly, not to the man beside her but to a cat lying in the triangle of sunlight cast through the open door. She is wearing a plaid silk dress from Peck & Peck, and the hem is coming down.

Here is what it is: The girl has been on the Eastern Shore, and now she is going back to the city, leaving the man beside her, and all she can see ahead are the viscous summer sidewalks and the 3 A.M. long-distance calls that will make her lie awake and then sleep drugged through all the steaming mornings left in August (1960? 1961?). Because she must go directly from the train to lunch in New York, she wishes that she had a safety pin for the hem of the plaid silk dress, and she also wishes that she could forget about the hem and the lunch and stay in the cool bar that smells of disinfectant and malt and make friends with the woman in the crepe-de-Chine wrapper. She is afflicted by a little self-pity, and she wants to compare Estelles. That is what that was all about.

Why did I write it down? In order to remember, of course, but exactly what was it I wanted to remember? How much of it actually happened? Did any of it? Why do I keep a notebook at all? It is easy to deceive oneself on all those scores. The impulse to write things down is a peculiarly compulsive one, inexplicable to those who do not share it, useful only accidentally, only secondarily, in the way that any compulsion tries to justify itself. I suppose that it begins or does not begin in the cradle. Although I have felt compelled to write things down since I was five years old, I doubt that my daughter ever will, for she is a singularly blessed and accepting child, delighted with life exactly as life presents itself to her, unafraid to go to sleep and unafraid to wake up. Keepers of private notebooks are a different breed altogether, lonely and resistant rearrangers of things, anxious malcontents, children afflicted apparently at birth with some presentiment of loss.

My first notebook was a Big Five tablet, given to me by my mother with the sensible suggestion that I stop whining and learn to amuse myself by writing down my thoughts. She returned the tablet to me a few years ago; the first entry is an account of a woman who believed herself to be freezing to death in the Arctic night, only to find, when day broke, that she had stumbled onto the Sahara Desert, where she would die of the heat before lunch. I have no idea what turn of a five-year-old's mind could have prompted so insistently "ironic" and exotic a story, but it

5

does reveal a certain predilection for the extreme which has dogged me into adult life; perhaps if I were analytically inclined I would find it a truer story than any I might have told about Donald Johnson's birthday party or the day my cousin Brenda put Kitty Litter in the aquarium.

So the point of my keeping a notebook has never been, nor is it now, to have an accurate factual record of what I have been doing or thinking. That would be a different impulse entirely, an instinct for reality which I sometimes envy but do not possess. At no point have I ever been able successfully to keep a diary; my approach to daily life ranges from the grossly negligent to the merely absent, and on those few occasions when I have tried dutifully to record a day's events, boredom has so overcome me that the results are mysterious at best. What is this business about "shopping, typing piece, dinner with E, depressed"? Shopping for what? Typing what piece? Who is E? Was this "E" depressed, or was I depressed? Who cares?

In fact I have abandoned altogether that kind of pointless entry; instead I tell what some would call lies. "That's simply not true," the members of my family frequently tell me when they come up against my memory of a shared event. "The party was *not* for you, the spider was *not* a black widow, *it wasn't that way at all.*" Very likely they are right, for not only have I always had trouble distinguishing between what happened and what merely might have happened, but I remain unconvinced that the distinction, for my purposes, matters. The cracked crab that I recall having for lunch the day my father came home from Detroit in 1945 must certainly be embroidery, worked into the day's pattern to lend verisimilitude; I was ten years old and would not now remember the cracked crab. The day's events did not turn on cracked crab. And yet it is precisely that fictitious crab that makes me see the afternoon all over again, a home movie run all too often, the father bearing gifts, the child weeping, an exercise in family love and guilt. Or that is what it was to me. Similarly, perhaps it never did snow that August in Vermont; perhaps there never were flurries in the night wind, and maybe no one else felt the ground hardening and summer already dead even as we pretended to bask in it, but that was how it felt to me, and it might as well have snowed, could have snowed, did snow.

How it felt to me: that is getting closer to the truth about a notebook. I sometimes delude myself about why I keep a notebook, imagine that some thrifty virtue derives from preserving everything observed. See enough and write it down, I tell myself, and then some morning when the world seems drained of wonder, some day when I am only going through the motions of doing what I am supposed to do, which is write—on that bankrupt morning I will simply open my notebook and there it will all be, a forgotten account with accumulated interest, paid passage back to the world out there: dialogue overheard in hotels and elevators and at the hatcheck counter in Pavillon (one middle-aged man shows his hat check

to another and says, "That's my old football number"); impressions of
Bettina Aptheker and Benjamin Sonnenberg and Teddy ("Mr. Acapulco")
Stauffer; careful *aperçus*[1] about tennis bums and failed fashion models
and Greek shipping heiresses, one of whom taught me a significant lesson
(a lesson I could have learned from F. Scott Fitzgerald, but perhaps we all
must meet the very rich for ourselves) by asking, when I arrived to interview her in her orchid-filled sitting room on the second day of a paralyzing New York blizzard, whether it was snowing outside.

I imagine, in other words, that the notebook is about other people.
But of course it is not. I have no real business with what one stranger said
to another at the hatcheck counter in Pavillon; in fact I suspect that the
line "That's my old football number" touched not my own imagination
at all, but merely some memory of something once read, probably "The
Eighty-Yard Run."[2] Nor is my concern with a woman in a dirty crepe-de-
Chine wrapper in a Wilmington bar. My stake is always, of course, in the
unmentioned girl in the plaid silk dress. *Remember what it was to be me:*
that is always the point.

It is a difficult point to admit. We are brought up in the ethic that   10
others, any others, all others, are by definition more interesting than ourselves; taught to be diffident, just this side of self-effacing. ("You're the
least important person in the room and don't forget it," Jessica Mitford's[3]
governess would hiss in her ear on the advent of any social occasion; I
copied that into my notebook because it is only recently that I have been
able to enter a room without hearing some such phrase in my inner ear.)
Only the very young and the very old may recount their dreams at breakfast, dwell upon self, interrupt with memories of beach picnics and favorite Liberty lawn dresses and the rainbow trout in a creek near Colorado Springs. The rest of us are expected, rightly, to affect absorption in
other people's favorite dresses, other people's trout.

And so we do. But our notebooks give us away, for however dutifully
we record what we see around us, the common denominator of all we
see is always, transparently, shamelessly, the implacable "I." We are not
talking here about the kind of notebook that is patently for public consumption, a structural conceit for binding together a series of graceful
pensées;[4] we are talking about something private, about bits of the mind's
string too short to use, an indiscriminate and erratic assemblage with
meaning only for its maker.

And sometimes even the maker has difficulty with the meaning.
There does not seem to be, for example, any point in my knowing for the
rest of my life that, during 1964, 720 tons of soot fell on every square

---

[1] *aperçus:* Summarizing glimpse or insight (French). — EDS.
[2] *"The Eighty-Yard Run":* Popular short story by Irwin Shaw. — EDS.
[3] *Jessica Mitford* (b. 1917): British satirical writer. — EDS.
[4] *pensées:* Thoughts or reflections (French). — EDS.

mile of New York City, yet there it is in my notebook, labeled "FACT."
Nor do I really need to remember that Ambrose Bierce liked to spell
Leland Stanford's[5] name "£eland $tanford" or that "smart women al-
most always wear black in Cuba," a fashion hint without much potential
for practical application. And does not the relevance of these notes seem
marginal at best?:

> In the basement museum of the Inyo County Courthouse in Indepen-
> dence, California, sign pinned to a mandarin coat: "This MANDARIN
> COAT was often worn by Mrs. Minnie S. Brooks when giving lectures on
> her TEAPOT COLLECTION."

> Redhead getting out of car in front of Beverly Wilshire Hotel, chinchilla
> stole, Vuitton bags with tags reading:

> MRS. LOU FOX
> HOTEL SAHARA
> VEGAS

Well, perhaps not entirely marginal. As a matter of fact, Mrs. Minnie
S. Brooks and her MANDARIN COAT pull me back into my own childhood,
for although I never knew Mrs. Brooks and did not visit Inyo County
until I was thirty, I grew up in just such a world, in houses cluttered with
Indian relics and bits of gold ore and ambergris and the souvenirs my
Aunt Mercy Farnsworth brought back from the Orient. It is a long way
from that world to Mrs. Lou Fox's world, where we all live now, and is it
not just as well to remember that? Might not Mrs. Minnie S. Brooks help
me to remember what I am? Might not Mrs. Lou Fox help me to remember what I am not?

But sometimes the point is harder to discern. What exactly did I have in
mind when I noted down that it cost the father of someone I know $650 a
month to light the place on the Hudson in which he lived before the Crash?
What use was I planning to make of this line by Jimmy Hoffa:[6] "I may have
my faults, but being wrong ain't one of them"? And although I think it interesting to know where the girls who travel with the Syndicate have their
hair done when they find themselves on the West Coast, will I ever make
suitable use of it? Might I not be better off just passing it on to John
O'Hara?[7] What is a recipe for sauerkraut doing in my notebook? What
kind of magpie keeps this notebook? "*He was born the night the* Titanic
went down." That seems a nice enough line, and I even recall who said it,
but is it not really a better line in life than it could ever be in fiction?

---

[5]*Bierce . . . Stanford's:* Ambrose Bierce (1842–1914?), American journalist and short
story writer known for his savage wit; Leland Stanford (1824–1893), wealthy railroad
builder who was a governor of California and the founder of Stanford University.—EDS.

[6]*Jimmy Hoffa* (1913–1975?): Controversial leader of the Teamsters Union who disappeared in the mid-seventies.—EDS.

[7]*John O'Hara* (1905–1970): American novelist who wrote several books about gangsters.—EDS.

But of course that is exactly it: not that I should ever use the line, but 15
that I should remember the woman who said it and the afternoon I heard
it. We were on her terrace by the sea, and we were finishing the wine left
from lunch, trying to get what sun there was, a California winter sun.
The woman whose husband was born the night the *Titanic* went down
wanted to rent her house, wanted to go back to her children in Paris. I remember wishing that I could afford the house, which cost $1,000 a
month. "Someday you will," she said lazily. "Someday it all comes."
There in the sun on her terrace it seemed easy to believe in someday, but
later I had a low-grade afternoon hangover and ran over a black snake on
the way to the supermarket and was flooded with inexplicable fear when
I heard the checkout clerk explaining to the man ahead of me why she
was finally divorcing her husband. "He left me no choice," she said over
and over as she punched the register. "He has a little seven-month-old
baby by her, he left me no choice." I would like to believe that my dread
then was for the human condition, but of course it was for me, because I
wanted a baby and did not then have one and because I wanted to own
the house that cost $1,000 a month to rent and because I had a hangover.

It all comes back. Perhaps it is difficult to see the value in having
one's self back in that kind of mood, but I do see it; I think we are well
advised to keep on nodding terms with the people we used to be whether
we find them attractive company or not. Otherwise they turn up unan-
nounced and surprise us, come hammering on the mind's door at 4 A.M.
of a bad night and demand to know who deserted them, who betrayed
them, who is going to make amends. We forget all too soon the things we
thought we could never forget. We forget the loves and the betrayals
alike, forget what we whispered and what we screamed, forget who we
were. I have already lost touch with a couple of people I used to be; one
of them, a seventeen-year-old, presents little threat, although it would be
of some interest to me to know again what it feels like to sit on a river
levee drinking vodka-and-orange-juice and listening to Les Paul and
Mary Ford[8] and their echoes sing "How High the Moon" on the car
radio. (You see I still have the scenes, but I no longer perceive myself
among those present, no longer could even improvise the dialogue.) The
other one, a twenty-three-year-old, bothers me more. She was always a
good deal of trouble, and I suspect she will reappear when I least want to
see her, skirts too long, shy to the point of aggravation, always the injured party, full of recriminations and little hurts and stories I do not
want to hear again, at once saddening me and angering me with her vulnerability and ignorance, an apparition all the more insistent for being so
long banished.

It is a good idea, then, to keep in touch, and I suppose that keeping in
touch is what notebooks are all about. And we are all on our own when it

---

[8]*Les Paul and Mary Ford:* Husband-and-wife musical team of the forties and fifties
who had many hit records. — EDS.

comes to keeping those lines open to ourselves: your notebook will never help me, nor mine you. "*So what's new in the whiskey business?*" What could that possibly mean to you? To me it means a blonde in a Pucci bathing suit sitting with a couple of fat men by the pool at the Beverly Hills Hotel. Another man approaches, and they all regard one another in silence for a while. "So what's new in the whiskey business?" one of the fat men finally says by way of welcome, and the blonde stands up, arches one foot and dips it in the pool, looking all the while at the cabaña where Baby Pignatari is talking on the telephone. That is all there is to that, except that several years later I saw the blonde coming out of Saks Fifth Avenue in New York with her California complexion and a voluminous mink coat. In the harsh wind that day she looked old and irrevocably tired to me, and even the skins in the mink coat were not worked the way they were doing them that year, not the way she would have wanted them done, and there is the point of the story. For a while after that I did not like to look in the mirror, and my eyes would skim the newspapers and pick out only the deaths, the cancer victims, the premature coronaries, the suicides, and I stopped riding the Lexington Avenue IRT because I noticed for the first time that all the strangers I had seen for years — the man with the seeing-eye dog, the spinster who read the classified pages every day, the fat girl who always got off with me at Grand Central — looked older than they once had.

It all comes back. Even that recipe for sauerkraut: even that brings it back. I was on Fire Island when I first made that sauerkraut, and it was raining, and we drank a lot of bourbon and ate the sauerkraut and went to bed at ten, and I listened to the rain and the Atlantic and felt safe. I made the sauerkraut again last night and it did not make me feel any safer, but that is, as they say, another story.

The Reader's Presence

1. Notice that Didion begins her essay not with a general comment about notebooks but with an actual notebook entry. What does the entry sound like at first? What effect do you think Didion wants it to have on you as a reader?

2. Consider the comparison Didion makes in paragraph 6 between a notebook and a diary. How do they differ? Why is she fond of one and not the other? How does her example of a diary entry support her distinction?

3. Didion's notebook entries were never intended to have an audience. How is that apparent from the entries themselves? In what sense is Didion now the audience for her own writing? Where do you fit in as a reader? How has she now created a public audience for her private writing?

4

Anne Frank

From *The Diary of a Young Girl*

While hiding from the Nazis in Amsterdam, Holland, during World War II and living in a cramped attic, Anne Frank started a diary on her thirteenth birthday. She soon began calling her diary "Kitty," addressing it in the form of letters that candidly and freely expressed her most personal thoughts and feelings. Living in conditions that allowed for little privacy, she cherished the secrecy her diary provided: "Who besides me will ever read these letters?" she writes, never dreaming that after her death her intimate diary would be found, published, and read by millions throughout the world.

In August 1944 the Frank family's hiding place was discovered by the Nazis and in March 1945, three months before her sixteenth birthday, Anne died in the concentration camp at Bergen-Belsen. As they searched the attic for valuables and important documents, the Nazis left behind on the floor an insignificant-looking little red-checkered cloth book. Anne Frank: The Diary of a Young Girl *was first published in 1952.*

THINGS THAT LIE BURIED DEEP IN MY HEART

Saturday, June 20, 1942

I haven't written for a few days, because I wanted first of all to think about my diary. It's an odd idea for someone like me to keep a diary; not only because I have never done so before, but because it seems to me that neither I—nor for that matter anyone else—will be interested in the unbosomings of a thirteen-year-old schoolgirl. Still, what does that matter? I want to write, but more than that, I want to bring out all kinds of things that lie buried deep in my heart.

There is a saying that "paper is more patient than man"; it came back to me on one of my slightly melancholy days, while I sat chin in hand, feeling too bored and limp even to make up my mind whether to go out or stay at home. Yes, there is no doubt that paper is patient and as I don't intend to show this cardboard-covered notebook, bearing the proud name of "diary," to anyone, unless I find a real friend, boy or girl, probably nobody cares. And now I come to the root of the matter, the reason for my starting a diary: it is that I have no such real friend.

Let me put it more clearly, since no one will believe that a girl of thirteen feels herself quite alone in the world, nor is it so. I have darling parents and a sister of sixteen. I know about thirty people whom one might call friends—I have strings of boy friends, anxious to catch a glimpse of me and who, failing that, peep at me through mirrors in class. I have relations, aunts and uncles, who are darlings too, a good home, no—I don't seem to lack anything. But it's the same with all my friends, just fun and joking, nothing more. I can never bring myself to talk of anything outside the common round. We don't seem to be able to get any closer, that is the root of the trouble. Perhaps I lack confidence, but anyway, there it is, a stubborn fact and I don't seem to be able to do anything about it.

Hence, this diary. In order to enhance in my mind's eye the picture of the friend for whom I have waited so long, I don't want to set down a series of bald facts in a diary like most people do, but I want this diary itself to be my friend, and I shall call my friend Kitty. No one will grasp what I'm talking about if I begin my letters to Kitty just out of the blue, so albeit unwillingly, I will start by sketching in brief the story of my life.

My father was thirty-six when he married my mother, who was then   5
twenty-five. My sister Margot was born in 1926 in Frankfort-on-Main, I followed on June 12, 1929, and, as we are Jewish, we emigrated to Holland in 1933, where my father was appointed Managing Director of Travies N.V. This firm is in close relationship with the firm of Kolen & Co. in the same building, of which my father is a partner.

The rest of our family, however, felt the full impact of Hitler's anti-Jewish laws, so life was filled with anxiety. In 1938 after the pogroms, my two uncles (my mother's brothers) escaped to the U.S.A. My old grandmother came to us, she was then seventy-three. After May 1940 good times rapidly fled: first the war, then the capitulation, followed by the arrival of the Germans, which is when the sufferings of us Jews really began. Anti-Jewish decrees followed each other in quick succession. Jews must wear a yellow star,[1] Jews must hand in their bicycles, Jews are banned from trains and are forbidden to drive. Jews are only allowed to do their shopping between three and five o'clock and then only in shops which bear the placard "Jewish shop." Jews must be indoors by eight o'clock and cannot even sit in their own gardens after that hour. Jews are forbidden to visit theaters, cinemas, and other places of entertainment. Jews may not take part in public sports. Swimming baths, tennis courts, hockey fields, and other sports grounds are all prohibited to them. Jews

---

[1]All Jews were ordered to wear a yellow six-pointed star. — EDS.

may not visit Christians. Jews must go to Jewish schools, and many more restrictions of a similar kind.

So we could not do this and were forbidden to do that. But life went on in spite of it all. Jopie[2] used to say to me, "You're scared to do anything, because it may be forbidden." Our freedom was strictly limited. Yet things were still bearable.

Granny died in January 1942; no one will ever know how much she is present in my thoughts and how much I love her still.

In 1934 I went to school at the Montessori Kindergarten and continued there. It was at the end of the school year, I was in form 6B, when I had to say good-by to Mrs. K. We both wept, it was very sad. In 1941 I went, with my sister Margot, to the Jewish Secondary School, she into the fourth form and I into the first.

So far everything is all right with the four of us and here I come to the   10
present day.

I ALWAYS COME BACK TO MY DIARY

Saturday, November 7, 1942

Dear Kitty,

Mummy is frightfully irritable and that always seems to herald unpleasantness for me. Is it just chance that Daddy and Mummy never rebuke Margot and that they always drop on me for everything? Yesterday evening, for instance: Margot was reading a book with lovely drawings in it; she got up and went upstairs, put the book down ready to go on with it later. I wasn't doing anything, so picked up the book and started looking at the pictures. Margot came back, saw "her" book in my hands, wrinkled her forehead and asked for the book back. Just because I wanted to look a little further on, Margot got more and more angry. Then Mummy joined in: "Give the book to Margot; she was reading it," she said. Daddy came into the room. He didn't even know what it was all about, but saw the injured look on Margot's face and promptly dropped on me: "I'd like to see what you'd say if Margot ever started looking at one of your books!" I gave way at once, laid the book down, and left the room — offended, as they thought. It so happened I was neither offended nor cross, just miserable. It wasn't right of Daddy to judge without knowing what the squabble was about. I would have given Margot the book myself, and much more quickly, if Mummy and Daddy hadn't interfered. They took Margot's part at once, as though she were the victim of some great injustice.

It's obvious that Mummy would stick up for Margot; she and Margot always do back each other up. I'm so used to that that I'm utterly indifferent to both Mummy's jawing and Margot's moods.

[2]*Jopie:* A girlfriend. — EDS.

I love them; but only because they are Mummy and Margot. With Daddy it's different. If he holds Margot up as an example, approves of what she does, praises and caresses her, then something gnaws at me inside, because I adore Daddy. He is the one I look up to. I don't love anyone in the world but him. He doesn't notice that he treats Margot differently from me. Now Margot is just the prettiest, sweetest, most beautiful girl in the world. But all the same I feel I have some right to be taken seriously too. I have always been the dunce, the ne'er-do-well of the family, I've always had to pay double for my deeds, first with the scolding and then again because of the way my feelings are hurt. Now I'm not satisfied with this apparent favoritism any more. I want something from Daddy that he is not able to give me.

I'm not jealous of Margot, never have been. I don't envy her good looks or her beauty. It is only that I long for Daddy's real love: not only as his child, but for me — Anne, myself.

I cling to Daddy because it is only through him that I am able to retain the remnant of family feeling. Daddy doesn't understand that I need to give vent to my feelings over Mummy sometimes. He doesn't want to talk about it; he simply avoids anything which might lead to remarks about Mummy's failings. Just the same, Mummy and her failings are something I find harder to bear than anything else. I don't know how to keep it all to myself. I can't always be drawing attention to her untidiness, her sarcasm, and her lack of sweetness, neither can I believe that I'm always in the wrong.

We are exact opposites in everything; so naturally we are bound to run up against each other. I don't pronounce judgment on Mummy's character, for that is something I can't judge. I only look at her as a mother, and she just doesn't succeed in being that to me; I have to be my own mother. I've drawn myself apart from them all; I am my own skipper and later on I shall see where I come to land. All this comes about particularly because I have in my mind's eye an image of what a perfect mother and wife should be; and in her whom I must call "Mother" I find no trace of that image.

I am always making resolutions not to notice Mummy's bad example. I want to see only the good side of her and to seek in myself what I cannot find in her. But it doesn't work; and the worst of it is that neither Daddy nor Mummy understands this gap in my life, and I blame them for it. I wonder if anyone can ever succeed in making their children absolutely content.

Sometimes I believe that God wants to try me, both now and later on; I must become good through my own efforts, without examples and without good advice. Then later on I shall be all the stronger. Who besides me will ever read these letters? From whom but myself shall I get comfort? As I need comforting often, I frequently feel weak, and dissatisfied with myself; my shortcomings are too great. I know this, and every day I try to improve myself, again and again.

₁₅

My treatment varies so much. One day Anne is so sensible and is allowed to know everything; and the next day I hear that Anne is just a silly little goat who doesn't know anything at all and imagines that she's learned a wonderful lot from books. I'm not a baby or a spoiled darling any more, to be laughed at, whatever she does. I have my own views, plans, and ideas, though I can't put them into words yet. Oh, so many things bubble up inside me as I lie in bed, having to put up with people I'm fed up with, who always misinterpret my intentions. That's why in the end I always come back to my diary. That is where I start and finish, because Kitty is always patient. I'll promise her that I shall persevere, in spite of everything, and find my own way through it all, and swallow my tears. I only wish I could see the results already or occasionally receive encouragement from someone who loves me.

Don't condemn me; remember rather that sometimes I too can reach   20
the bursting point.

Yours, Anne

A SWEET SECRET

Wednesday, January 5, 1944

Dear Kitty,

I have two things to confess to you today, which will take a long time. But I must tell someone and you are the best one to tell, as I know that, come what may, you always keep a secret.

The first is about Mummy. You know that I've grumbled a lot about Mummy, yet still tried to be nice to her again. Now it is suddenly clear to me what she lacks. Mummy herself has told us that she looked upon us more as her friends than her daughters. Now that is all very fine, but still, a friend can't take a mother's place. I need my mother as an example which I can follow, I want to be able to respect her. I have the feeling that Margot thinks differently about these things and would never be able to understand what I've just told you. And Daddy avoids all arguments about Mummy.

I imagine a mother as a woman who, in the first place, shows great tact, especially towards her children when they reach our age, and who does not laugh at me if I cry about something—not pain, but other things—like "Mums" does.

One thing, which perhaps may seem rather fatuous, I have never forgiven her. It was on a day that I had to go to the dentist. Mummy and Margot were going to come with me, and agreed that I should take my bicycle. When we had finished at the dentist, and were outside again, Margot and Mummy told me that they were going into the town to look at something or buy something—I don't remember exactly what. I wanted to go, too, but was not allowed to, as I had my bicycle with me. Tears of rage sprang into my eyes, and Mummy and Margot began laughing at me. Then I became so furious that I stuck my tongue out at them in the street just as an old woman happened to pass by, who looked very shocked! I rode home on my bicycle, and I know I cried for a long time.

It is queer that the wound that Mummy made then still burns, when I think of how angry I was that afternoon.

The second is something that is very difficult to tell you, because it is about myself.

Yesterday I read an article about blushing by Sis Heyster. This article might have been addressed to me personally. Although I don't blush very easily, the other things in it certainly all fit me. She writes roughly something like this—that a girl in the years of puberty becomes quiet within and begins to think about the wonders that are happening to her body.

I experience that, too, and that is why I get the feeling lately of being embarrassed about Margot, Mummy, and Daddy. Funnily enough, Margot, who is much more shy than I am, isn't at all embarrassed.

I think what is happening to me is so wonderful, and not only what can be seen on my body, but all that is taking place inside. I never discuss myself or any of these things with anybody; that is why I have to talk to myself about them.

Each time I have a period—and that has only been three times—I have the feeling that in spite of all the pain, unpleasantness, and nastiness, I have a sweet secret, and that is why, although it is nothing but a nuisance to me in a way, I always long for the time that I shall feel that secret within me again.

Sis Heyster also writes that girls of this age don't feel quite certain of themselves, and discover that they themselves are individuals with ideas, thoughts, and habits. After I came here, when I was just fourteen, I began to think about myself sooner than most girls, and to know that I am a "person." Sometimes, when I lie in bed at night, I have a terrible desire to feel my breasts and to listen to the quiet rhythmic beat of my heart.

I already had these kinds of feelings subconsciously before I came here, because I remember that once when I slept with a girl friend I had a strong desire to kiss her, and that I did do so. I could not help being terribly inquisitive over her body, for she had always kept it hidden from me. I asked her whether, as proof of our friendship, we should feel one another's breasts, but she refused. I go into ecstasies every time I see the naked figure of a woman, such as Venus, for example. It strikes me as so wonderful and exquisite that I have difficulty in stopping the tears rolling down my cheeks.

If only I had a girl friend!

Yours, Anne

The Reader's Presence

1. Why do you think the thirteen-year-old Frank feels compelled to write? Does she have a purpose for keeping a diary?

2. Speculate why her diary is addressed to "Kitty." What is the effect of personalizing her diary in this way? What does that personalization allow her to do as a person and as a writer?

3. How would you characterize Anne's relationship with her family and friends? Do they seem abnormal to you or do you think they represent the normal feelings of a young teenage girl? Explain why you feel one way or another.

5

Michihiko Hachiya

From *Hiroshima Diary*

On August 6, 1945, the United States dropped an atomic bomb on the Japanese city of Hiroshima and introduced a new, devastating weapon into modern war. Two days later, the military dropped another bomb on Nagasaki, forcing the Japanese government into an unconditional surrender. For years, the Japanese survivors of the blasts suffered from unhealing burns, radiation poisoning, cancers, and a score of other illnesses. At first, the Japanese had no idea what had hit them, though rumors of a new secret weapon circulated rapidly. Most Americans today know of the bombing mainly through repeated images of the mushroom cloud itself; rarely do they see photographs or footage of the destruction and casualties. One of the most vivid accounts of the bombing and its immediate aftermath can be found in a diary kept by a Hiroshima physician, Michihiko Hachiya, who, though severely injured himself, miraculously found the time to record both his professional observations of a medical nightmare and his human impressions of an utterly destroyed community. The diary runs only for some two months, from the moment of the blast on the sunny morning of August 6 to the end of September, when the American occupation was well under way.

WHAT HAD HAPPENED?
August 6, 1945

Badly injured from the blast, Dr. Hachiya managed to make his way to the hospital where he served as director and which, fortunately, was quite near his house. He spent several days in bed and did not begin writing his diary until August 8. As we can see from the following passage, however, the events were still fresh in his mind.

The hour was early; the morning still, warm, and beautiful. Shimmering leaves, reflecting sunlight from a cloudless sky, made a pleasant contrast with shadows in my garden as I gazed absently through wide-flung doors opening to the south.

Clad in drawers and undershirt, I was sprawled on the living room floor exhausted because I had just spent a sleepless night on duty as an air warden in my hospital.

Suddenly, a strong flash of light startled me — and then another. So well does one recall little things that I remember vividly how a stone lantern in the garden became brilliantly lit and I debated whether this light was caused by a magnesium flare or sparks from a passing trolley.

Garden shadows disappeared. The view where a moment before all had been so bright and sunny was now dark and hazy. Through swirling dust I could barely discern a wooden column that had supported one corner of my house. It was leaning crazily and the roof sagged dangerously.

Moving instinctively, I tried to escape, but rubble and fallen timbers   5
barred the way. By picking my way cautiously I managed to reach the *rōka*[1] and stepped down into my garden. A profound weakness overcame me, so I stopped to regain my strength. To my surprise I discovered that I was completely naked. How odd! Where were my drawers and undershirt?

What had happened?

All over the right side of my body I was cut and bleeding. A large splinter was protruding from a mangled wound in my thigh, and something warm trickled into my mouth. My cheek was torn, I discovered as I felt it gingerly, with the lower lip laid wide open. Embedded in my neck was a sizable fragment of glass which I matter-of-factly dislodged, and with the detachment of one stunned and shocked I studied it and my blood-stained hand.

Where was my wife?

Suddenly thoroughly alarmed, I began to yell for her: "Yaeko-san! Yaeko-san! Where are you?"

Blood began to spurt. Had my carotid artery been cut? Would I bleed   10
to death? Frightened and irrational, I called out again: "It's a five-hundred-ton bomb! Yaeko-san, where are you? A five-hundred-ton bomb has fallen!"

Yaeko-san, pale and frightened, her clothes torn and blood-stained, emerged from the ruins of our house holding her elbow. Seeing her, I was reassured. My own panic assuaged, I tried to reassure her.

"We'll be all right," I exclaimed. "Only let's get out of here as fast as we can."

She nodded, and I motioned for her to follow me.

The shortest path to the street lay through the house next door so through the house we went — running, stumbling, falling, and then

---

[1] *rōka:* A narrow outside hall. — EDS.

running again until in headlong flight we tripped over something and fell sprawling into the street. Getting to my feet, I discovered that I had tripped over a man's head.

"Excuse me! Excuse me, please!" I cried hysterically.   15

There was no answer. The man was dead. The head had belonged to a young officer whose body was crushed beneath a massive gate.

We stood in the street, uncertain and afraid, until a house across from us began to sway and then with a rending motion fell almost at our feet. Our own house began to sway, and in a minute it, too, collapsed in a cloud of dust. Other buildings caved in or toppled. Fires sprang up and whipped by a vicious wind began to spread.

It finally dawned on us that we could not stay there in the street, so we turned our steps towards the hospital. Our home was gone; we were wounded and needed treatment; and after all, it was my duty to be with my staff. This latter was an irrational thought—what good could I be to anyone, hurt as I was.

We started out, but after twenty or thirty steps I had to stop. My breath became short, my heart pounded, and my legs gave way under me. An overpowering thirst seized me and I begged Yaeko-san to find me some water. But there was no water to be found. After a little my strength somewhat returned and we were able to go on.

I was still naked, and although I did not feel the least bit of shame, I   20
was disturbed to realize that modesty had deserted me. On rounding a corner we came upon a soldier standing idly in the street. He had a towel draped across his shoulder, and I asked if he would give it to me to cover my nakedness. The soldier surrendered the towel quite willingly but said not a word. A little later I lost the towel, and Yaeko-san took off her apron and tied it around my loins.

Our progress towards the hospital was interminably slow, until finally, my legs, stiff from drying blood, refused to carry me farther. The strength, even the will, to go on deserted me, so I told my wife, who was almost as badly hurt as I, to go on alone. This she objected to, but there was no choice. She had to go ahead and try to find someone to come back for me.

Yaeko-san looked into my face for a moment, and then, without saying a word, turned away and began running towards the hospital. Once, she looked back and waved and in a moment she was swallowed up in the gloom. It was quite dark now, and with my wife gone, a feeling of dreadful loneliness overcame me.

I must have gone out of my head lying there in the road because the next thing I recall was discovering that the clot on my thigh had been dislodged and blood was again spurting from the wound. I pressed my hand to the bleeding area and after a while the bleeding stopped and I felt better.

Could I go on?

I tried. It was all a nightmare—my wounds, the darkness, the road   25
ahead. My movements were ever so slow; only my mind was running at
top speed.

In time I came to an open space where the houses had been removed
to make a fire lane. Through the dim light I could make out ahead of me
the hazy outlines of the Communications Bureau's big concrete building,
and beyond it the hospital. My spirits rose because I knew that now
someone would find me; and if I should die, at least my body would be
found.

I paused to rest. Gradually things around me came into focus. There
were the shadowy forms of people, some of whom looked like walking
ghosts. Others moved as though in pain, like scarecrows, their arms held
out from their bodies with forearms and hands dangling. These people
puzzled me until I suddenly realized that they had been burned and were
holding their arms out to prevent the painful friction of raw surfaces rubbing together. A naked woman carrying a naked baby came into view. I
averted my gaze. Perhaps they had been in the bath. But then I saw a
naked man, and it occurred to me that, like myself, some strange thing
had deprived them of their clothes. An old woman lay near me with an
expression of suffering on her face; but she made no sound. Indeed, one
thing was common to everyone I saw—complete silence. . . .

PIKADON
August 9, 1945

*As the wounded poured into Dr. Hachiya's hospital, the physicians
tried to make sense of the symptoms and injuries, which did not resemble
those of ordinary bombings. Because many of the patients with horrible
symptoms showed no obvious signs of injuries, Dr. Hachiya could only
speculate about what might have occurred. He had no idea as yet what
type of weapon had been used against them.*

Today, Dr. Hanaoka's[2] report on the patients was more detailed.
One observation particularly impressed me. Regardless of the type of injury, nearly everybody had the same symptoms. All had a poor appetite,
the majority had nausea and gaseous indigestion, and over half had
vomiting.

Not a few had shown improvement since yesterday. Diarrhea,
though, continued to be a problem and actually appeared to be increasing. Distinctly alarming was the appearance of blood in the stools of patients who earlier had only diarrhea. The isolation of these people was becoming increasingly difficult.

[2]*Dr. Hanaoka:* Head of Internal Medicine.—EDS.

One seriously ill man complained of a sore mouth yesterday, and 30 today, numerous small hemorrhages began to appear in his mouth and under his skin. His case was the more puzzling because he came to the hospital complaining of weakness and nausea and did not appear to have been injured at all.

This morning, other patients were beginning to show small subcutaneous hemorrhages, and not a few were coughing and vomiting blood in addition to passing it in their stools. One poor woman was bleeding from her privates. Among these patients there was not one with symptoms typical of anything we knew, unless you could excuse those who developed signs of severe brain disease before they died.

Dr. Hanaoka believed the patients could be divided into three groups:

1. Those with nausea, vomiting, and diarrhea who were improving.

2. Those with nausea, vomiting, and diarrhea who were remaining stationary.

3. Those with nausea, vomiting, and diarrhea who were developing 35 hemorrhage under the skin or elsewhere.

Had these patients been burned or otherwise injured, we might have tried to stretch the logic of cause and effect and assume that their bizarre symptoms were related to injury, but so many patients appeared to have received no injury whatsoever that we were obliged to postulate an insult heretofore unknown.

The only other possible cause for the weird symptoms observed was a sudden change in atmospheric pressure. I had read somewhere about bleeding that follows ascent to high altitudes and about bleeding in deep sea divers who ascend too rapidly from the depths. Having never seen such injury I could not give much credence to my thoughts.

Still, it was impossible to dismiss the thought that atmospheric pressure had had something to do with the symptoms of our patients. During my student days at Okayama University, I had seen experiments conducted in a pressure chamber. Sudden, temporary deafness was one symptom everyone complained of if pressure in the chamber was abruptly altered.

Now, I could state positively that I heard nothing like an explosion when we were bombed the other morning, nor did I remember any sound during my walk to the hospital as houses collapsed around me. It was as though I walked through a gloomy, silent motion picture. Others whom I questioned had had the same experience.

Those who experienced the bombing from the outskirts of the city 40 characterized it by the word: *pikadon*.[3]

---

[3]*Pika* means a glitter, sparkle, or bright flash of light, like a flash of lightning. *Don* means a boom! or loud sound. Together, the words came to mean to the people of Hiroshima an explosion characterized by a flash and a boom. Hence: "flash-boom!" Those who remember the flash only speak of the "*pika*"; those who were far enough from the hypocenter to experience both speak of the "*pikadon*." —HACHIYA'S NOTE.

How then could one account for my failure and the failure of others to hear an explosion except on the premise that a sudden change in atmospheric pressure had rendered those nearby temporarily deaf: Could the bleeding we were beginning to observe be explained on the same basis?

Since all books and journals had been destroyed, there was no way to corroborate my theories except by further appeal to the patients. To that end Dr. Katsube[4] was asked to discover what else he could when he made ward rounds.

It was pleasing to note my scientific curiosity was reviving, and I lost no opportunity to question everyone who visited me about the bombing of Hiroshima. Their answers were vague and ambiguous, and on one point only were they in agreement: a new weapon had been used. *What* the new weapon was became a burning question. Not only had our books been destroyed, but our newspapers, telephones, and radios as well. . . .

The Reader's Presence

1. In many ways it is fortunate that one of the diaries kept immediately after the atomic blast was written by a medical doctor. Why? How does it contribute to the diary's historical value? Could this be a disadvantage? Would you have preferred to read a patient's diary instead? If so, why?

2. Dr. Hachiya's first entry on August 6 was written a few days after the events it depicts. What indications do you receive from the writing that the entry was predated? Can you detect any differences from the second entry (August 9), which was apparently composed on the stated day?

---

[4]*Dr. Katsube:* Chief of Surgery. — EDS.

6

Nathaniel Hawthorne
From His *Journals*

Throughout his career, the great American novelist Nathaniel Hawthorne (1804–1864) kept copious notebooks, jotting down observations of his daily life, ideas for stories, travel incidents, conversations with friends, and encounters with celebrated figures. Many of Hawthorne's famous short stories had their origins in concepts he had carefully recorded in his notebooks. Although most of these concepts were never turned into stories, they are interesting in themselves and help us see an enormously creative mind in process. When he died, Hawthorne left fifteen manuscript volumes of notebooks. In the following entries, taken from The Heart of Hawthorne's Journals, *edited by Newton Arvin (1929), we can sample his intelligence and imagination at work.*

A WRITER'S NOTEBOOK

October 25, 1835

A person to be writing a tale, and to find that it shapes itself against his intentions; that the characters act otherwise than he thought; that unforeseen events occur; and a catastrophe comes which he strives in vain to avert. It might shadow forth his own fate—he having made himself one of the personages. . . .

October 25, 1836

Two persons to be expecting some occurrence, and watching for the two principal actors in it, and to find that the occurrence is even then passing, and that they themselves are the two actors. . . .

August 22, 1837

A young man and girl meet together, each in search of a person to be known by some particular sign. They watch and wait a great while for that person to pass. At last some casual circumstance discloses that each is the one that the other is waiting for. Moral—that what we need for our happiness is often close at hand, if we knew but how to seek for it.

A blind man to set forth on a walk through ways unknown to him, and to trust to the guidance of anybody who will take the trouble; the different characters who would undertake it: some mischievous, some well-meaning, but incapable; perhaps one blind man undertakes to lead another. At last, possibly, he rejects all guidance, and blunders on by himself. . . .

October 14, 1837

A person to be in the possession of something as perfect as mortal man has a right to demand; he tries to make it better, and ruins it entirely.[1] . . .

5

January 4, 1839

A person to be the death of his beloved in trying to raise her to more than mortal perfection; yet this should be a comfort to him of having aimed so highly and holily.[2] . . .

1842

Bees are sometimes drowned in the honey which they collect—so some writers lost in their collected learning.

1844

A dream, the other night, that the world had become dissatisfied with the inaccurate manner in which facts are reported, and had employed me, with a salary of a thousand dollars, to relate things of public importance exactly as they happen.

The search of an investigator for the Unpardonable Sin—he at last finds it in his own heart and practice.

[1] "The Birthmark." —EDS.
[2] "The Birthmark." —EDS.

The Unpardonable Sin might consist in a want of love and reverence   10
for the Human Soul; in consequence of which, the investigator pried into
its dark depths, not with a hope or purpose of making it better, but
from a cold philosophical curiosity—content that it should be wicked in
whatever kind or degree, and only desiring to study it out. Would
not this, in other words, be the separation of the intellect from the
heart? . . .

October 21, 1851

Happiness in this world, when it comes, comes incidentally. Make it
the object of pursuit, and it leads us a wild-goose chase, and is never attained. Follow some other object, and very possibly we may find that we
have caught happiness without dreaming of it; but likely enough it is gone
the moment we say to ourselves, "Here it is!" like the chest of gold that
treasure-seekers find. . . .

ON MUSEUMS

March 27, 1856

Yesterday, I went out at about twelve, and visited the British Museum; an exceedingly tiresome affair. It quite crushes a person to see so
much at once; and I wandered from hall to hall with a weary and heavy
heart, wishing (Heaven forgive me!) that the Elgin marbles and the frieze
of the Parthenon were all burnt into lime, and that the granite Egyptian
statues were hewn and squared into building-stones, and that the mum-
mies had all turned to dust, two thousand years ago; and, in fine, that all
the material relics of so many successive ages had disappeared with the
generations that produced them. The present is burthened too much with
the past. We have not time, in our earthly existence, to appreciate what is
warm with life, and immediately around us; yet we heap up all these old
shells, out of which human life has long emerged, casting them off
forever. I do not see how future ages are to stagger onward under all
this dead weight, with the additions that will be continually made
to it. . . .

A VISIT TO STONEHENGE

June 17, 1856

As we drove over the plain (my seat was beside the driver), I saw, at a
distance, a cluster of large gray stones, mostly standing upright, and some
of them slightly inclined towards each other—very irregular, and, so far

off, forming no very picturesque or noteworthy spectacle. Of course I knew at once that this was Stonehenge, and also knew that the reality was going to dwindle wofully within my ideal, as almost everything else does. When we reached the spot, we found a picnic-party just finishing their dinner, on one of the overthrown stones of the druidical temple; and within the sacred circle, an artist was painting a wretched daub of the scene; and an old shepherd (I suppose, the very Shepherd of Salisbury Plain) sat erect in the centre of the ruin.

There never was a ruder thing than Stonehenge made by mortal hands; it is so very rude, that it seems as if Nature and man had worked upon it with one consent, and so it is all the stranger and more impressive from its rudeness. The spectator wonders to see art and contrivance, and a regular and even somewhat intricate plan, beneath all the uncouth simplicity of this arrangement of rough stones; and, certainly, whatever was the intellectual and scientific advancement of the people who built Stonehenge, no succeeding architects will ever have a right to triumph over them; for nobody's work, in after times, is likely to endure till it becomes a mystery who built it, and how, and for what purpose. Apart from the moral considerations suggested by it, Stonehenge is not very well worth seeing. Materially, it is one of the poorest of spectacles; and when complete, it must have been even less picturesque than now—a few huge, rough stones, very imperfectly squared, standing on end, and each group of two supporting a third huge stone on their two tops; other stones, of the same pattern, overthrown, and tumbled one upon another; and the whole comprised within a circuit of about a hundred feet diameter; the short, sheep-cropped grass of Salisbury Plain growing among all these uncouth boulders. I am not sure that a misty, lowering day would not have better suited Stonehenge, as the dreary midpoint of the great, desolate, trackless plain; not literally trackless, however, for the London and Exeter Road passes within fifty yards of the ruins, and another road intersects it. . . .

THE DREAD OF CORPSES

May 8, 1858

The Italians have a terrible dread of corpses, and never meddle with those of their nearest and dearest relatives. They have a horror of death, too, especially of sudden death, and most particularly of apoplexy; and no wonder, as it gives no time for the last rites of the Church, and so exposes them to a fearful risk of perdition forever. On the whole, the ancient practice was perhaps the preferable one; but Nature has made it very difficult for us to do anything pleasant and satisfactory with a dead body. God knows best; but I wish he had so ordered it that our mortal bodies, when we have done with them, might vanish out of sight and sense, like bubbles. A person of delicacy hates to think of leaving such a burthen as his decaying mortality, to be disposed of by his friends; but, I say again, how delightful it would be, and how helpful towards our faith in a blessed futurity, if the dying could disappear like vanishing bubbles, leaving perhaps a sweet fragrance, diffused for a minute or two throughout the death-chamber. This would be the odor of sanctity! And if sometimes the evaporation of a sinful soul should leave a smell not so delightful, a breeze through the open windows would soon waft it quite away.

Apropos of the various methods of disposing of dead bodies, William Story recalled a newspaper paragraph respecting a ring, with a stone of a new species in it, which a widower was observed to wear upon his finger. Being questioned as to what the gem was, he answered, "It is my wife." He had procured her body to be chemically resolved into this stone. I think I could make a story on this idea; the ring should be one of the widower's bridal gifts to a second wife; and, of course, it should have wondrous and terrible qualities, symbolizing all that disturbs the quiet of a second marriage—on the husband's part, remorse for his inconstancy, and the constant comparison between the dead wife of his youth, now idealized, and this grosser reality which he had now adopted into his bed and hers; while, on the new wife's finger, it should give pressures, shooting pangs into her heart, jealousies of the past, and all such miserable emotions. . . .

The Reader's Presence

1. Choose one of Hawthorne's story ideas and imagine how you would write the story. How would it develop? What point would it make? Do you find any pattern to Hawthorne's ideas, any psychological preoccupations that link them to the same imagination?

2. What do Hawthorne's visit to the British Museum and to Stonehenge have in common? What do we learn about Hawthorne from these observations?

7

Thomas R. Partsch

From *Vietnam Journal: The My Lai Massacre*

On the morning of March 16, 1968, Charlie Company, led by Captain Ernest L. Medina, attacked the Vietnamese village of My Lai in the expectation of confronting a particularly troublesome Viet Cong battalion. When they hit the village, which the soldiers also referred to as "Pinkville," they experienced no enemy resistance and discovered only civilians. What happened in the next four hours proved to be one of the most horrible and disgraceful episodes in American military history. Between four and five hundred civilians were killed, most of them women, children, and the elderly. Many women and girls were raped and then murdered; at one point, according to an eyewitness, five soldiers raped a teenage girl and afterwards shot her beyond recognition. Babies were shot in their mothers' arms. Some of the men, however, refused to participate in what they quickly realized was the mass murder of civilians. A few helicopter pilots tried to stop the massacre and even held guns on their own troops as they attempted to rescue a few wounded children. Though the army attempted to cover up the incident, word leaked out and an official investigation was launched in November 1969. Then, in December, Life magazine shocked the public—and confirmed its worst suspicions—with several pages of grisly color photographs that had been taken by an army photographer at the scene. Yet, after investigations, indictments, and trials, only one officer was found guilty of war crimes—Lt. William Calley, a platoon leader, who never denied the accusation but claimed he had acted under express orders. Convicted in March 1971 of multiple murders, Calley was sentenced to life imprisonment, but within months the sentence was reduced to twenty years. In November 1974, he was pardoned and released.

Several men in Charlie Company kept journals. The following entries were made by Thomas R. Partsch. Written under extreme pressure and in a combat zone, they are understandably rough. The misspellings and lapses in punctuation, however, enhance the document's immediacy and authenticity.

MARCH 15, 1968

Mar 15 Fri: got up at 5 a.m. ate chow had police call after that. Had garbage detail sure get a kick out of that. Brought mess garbage down and they even ate that. Just sitting around now cleaning weapons and took another bath at the stream. Had meeting [w]hole company said we are going to really hit something tomorrow going to hit 4 places its a hot place.

MARCH 16–18, 1968

Mar 16 Sat: got up at 5:30 left at 7:15 we had 9 choppers. 2 lifts first landed had mortar team with us. We started to move slowly through the village shooting everything in sight children men and women and animals. Some was sickening. There legs were shot off and they were still moving it was just hanging there. I think there bodies were made of rubber. I didn't fire a round yet and didn't kill anybody not even a chicken I couldn't. We are know suppose to push through 2 more it is about 10 A.M. and we are taken a rest before going in. We also got 2 weapons M1 and a carbine our final desti[na]tion is the Pinkville suppose to be cement bunkers we killed about 100 people after a while they said not to kill women and children. Stopped for chow about 1 P.M. we didn't do much after that. We are know setting up for the night 2 companies B and someone else we are set up in part of a village and rice patties had to dig foxhole area is pretty level are mortars are out with us. Are serving hot chow tonite I looked in my pack for dry socks and found out they were stolen from the time we were out in the field the name of the villages are My Lai 4, 5, and 6. I am know pulling my guard for night. 1½ hours I am with the 1st squad had pop and beer. Sky is a little cloudy but it is warm out.

Mar 17 Sun: got up at 6:30 foggy out. We didn't go to Pinkville went to My Lai 2, 3, and 4 no one was there we burned as we pushed. We got 4 VC[1] and a nurse. Had documents on them yesterday we took 14 VC. We pushed as far as the coast to the South China Sea there was a village along the coast also a lot of sailboats we stayed there for about an hour we went back about 2 kilometers to set up camp its in a graveyard actually we didn't pull guard but awake most of the night.

Mar 18 Mon: moved back to another area 1 VC said he would take us to a tunnel he took us all over didn't find any after that we met with other platoons as we were going 2 guys hit mines there flack jackets saved them not hurt bad Trevino and Gonzalez. . . . [T]here is a lot of fuss on what happened at the village a Gen was asking questions. There is going

---

[1]VC: Viet Cong. — EDS.

to be an investigation on Medina. We are not supposed to say anything. I didn't think it was right but we did it but we did it at least I can say I didn't kill anybody. I think I wanted to but in another way I didn't.

The Reader's Presence

1. What details in Partsch's entries do you personally find shocking? What makes you think he is reporting what actually occurred? Does he seem shocked by the incident he describes? Explain your response.

2. If you were part of the committee investigating the My Lai massacre, which details of Partsch's journal entries would be of special interest? If you were defending the men charged with multiple murders, how might you discredit the journal entries?

3. Compare Partsch's entries from My Lai with the journal notes Walt Whitman took during the Civil War (see page below). How do they differ? Are there any features you find similar?

8

Walt Whitman

From *Specimen Days: Civil War Diary*

If the United States can be said to have a national poet, it would be Walt Whitman. No other American poet has represented the national experience more fully and has had a deeper influence on the shape of our literature. His major work, Leaves of Grass, *is almost universally considered a world masterpiece, though when it first appeared in 1855, it was loudly condemned as incoherent and obscene. Born into a working-class family near Huntington, Long Island, in 1819, Whitman grew up in Brooklyn, New York, where he attended public schools until he dropped out at the age of eleven to start work as an office boy and later as a printer's apprentice. Whitman enjoyed a successful career in newspaper journalism but by the late 1840s decided to concentrate on more literary endeavors, while supporting himself with various jobs and freelance writing. In 1862, as the Civil War intensified, Whitman visited the front in Virginia, where his brother had been wounded. Feeling great sympathy for the average soldier, he settled in Washington, D.C., to perform volunteer work nursing the wounded in*

military hospitals. He kept notes of this experience and years later included them
(with some slight revision) in a volume of reminiscence, Specimen Days *(1882),*
from which the following few passages have been taken. Whitman died in Cam-
den, New Jersey, in 1892.

DOWN AT THE FRONT
Falmouth, Va., opposite Fredericksburgh, December 21, 1862

Whitman kept a diary of his Civil War experiences among the sick
and wounded. It now represents one of our literature's most moving on-
the-spot accounts of the war's human devastation. Whitman, however,
did not intend to be composing a literary work when he recorded his en-
tries, which were often written in a hurry and during a pause from emer-
gency duties. When he returned to this diary years later, he sometimes
added information in parentheses (his titles, too, are later additions), as
you will note in the passages below, but he never allowed himself to edit
out the immediacy of his observations and feelings of the moment.

Begin my visits among the camp hospitals in the army of the Po-
tomac. Spend a good part of the day in a large brick mansion on the
banks of the Rappahannock, used as a hospital since the battle — seems
to have receiv'd only the worst cases. Out doors, at the foot of a tree,
within ten yards of the front of the house, I notice a heap of amputated
feet, legs, arms, hands, &c., a full load for a one-horse cart. Several dead
bodies lie near, each cover'd with its brown woolen blanket. In the dooryard, towards the river, are fresh graves, mostly of officers, their names
on pieces of barrel-staves or broken boards, stuck in the dirt. (Most of
these bodies were subsequently taken up and transported north to their
friends.) The large mansion is quite crowded upstairs and down, everything impromptu, no system, all bad enough, but I have no doubt the
best that can be done; all the wounds pretty bad, some frightful, the men
in their old clothes, unclean and bloody. Some of the wounded are rebel
soldiers and officers, prisoners. One, a Mississippian, a captain, hit badly
in leg, I talk'd with some time; he ask'd me for papers, which I gave him.
(I saw him three months afterward in Washington, with his leg amputated, doing well.) I went through the rooms, downstairs and up. Some of
the men were dying. I had nothing to give at that visit, but wrote a few
letters to folks home, mothers, &c. Also talk'd to three or four, who
seem'd most susceptible to it, and needing it.

FIFTY HOURS LEFT WOUNDED ON THE FIELD
[undated; most likely late January 1863]

One of the horrors of the war that especially disturbed Whitman was
the army's inability to rescue wounded soldiers quickly. Many died un-

necessarily in the field on both sides because of inadequate first aid. Whit-
man noted the following example shortly after he went to the front.
Though Whitman was fiercely committed to the Union cause, the entry
shows his unwillingness to demonize the Confederate soldier, whom he
frequently refers to in his diary as a "secesh" (secessionist).

Here is a case of a soldier I found among the crowded cots in the
Patent-office. He likes to have some one to talk to, and we will listen to
him. He got badly hit in his leg and side at Fredericksburgh that eventful
Saturday, 13th of December. He lay the succeeding two days and nights
helpless on the field, between the city and those grim terraces of batteries;
his company and regiment had been compell'd to leave him to his fate. To
make matters worse, it happen'd he lay with his head slightly down hill,
and could not help himself. At the end of some fifty hours he was brought
off, with other wounded, under a flag of truce. I ask him how the rebels
treated him as he lay during those two days and nights within reach of
them—whether they came to him—whether they abused him? He answers that several of the rebels, soldiers and others, came to him at one
time and another. A couple of them, who were together, spoke roughly
and sarcastically, but nothing worse. One middle-aged man, however,
who seem'd to be moving around the field, among the dead and
wounded, for benevolent purposes, came to him in a way he will never
forget; treated our soldier kindly, bound up his wounds, cheer'd him,
gave him a couple of biscuits and a drink of whiskey and water; asked
him if he could eat some beef. This good secesh, however, did not change
our soldier's position, for it might have caused the blood to burst from
the wounds, clotted and stagnated. Our soldier is from Pennsylvania; has
had a pretty severe time; the wounds proved to be bad ones. But he re-
tains a good heart, and is at present on the gain. (It is not uncommon
for the men to remain on the field this way, one, two, or even four or
five days.)

Abraham Lincoln
August 12, 1863

Whitman was a fervent supporter and great admirer of Lincoln, and
throughout his later years often lectured on the assassinated president.
His poem on the assassination, "When Lilacs Last in the Dooryard
Bloom'd" remains one of America's finest elegies. While in Washington,
Whitman saw Lincoln on numerous occasions, though the two never met.
In this entry, Whitman obtains a close glimpse of a somber leader.

I see the President almost every day, as I happen to live where he
passes to or from his lodgings out of town. He never sleeps at the White
House during the hot season, but has quarters at a healthy location some
three miles north of the city, the Soldiers' home, a United States military

establishment. I saw him this morning about 8½ coming in to business, riding on Vermont avenue, near L street. He always has a company of twenty-five or thirty cavalry, with sabres drawn and held upright over their shoulders. They say this guard was against his personal wish, but he let his counselors have their way. The party makes no great show in uniform or horses. Mr. Lincoln on the saddle generally rides a good-sized, easy-going gray horse, is dress'd in plain black, somewhat rusty and dusty, wears a black stiff hat, and looks about as ordinary in attire, &c., as the commonest man. A lieutenant, with yellow straps, rides at his left, and following behind, two by two, come the cavalry men, in their yellow-striped jackets. They are generally going at a slow trot, as that is the pace set them by the one they wait upon. The sabres and accoutrements clank, and the entirely unornamental *cortège* as it trots towards Lafayette square arouses no sensation, only some curious stranger stops and gazes. I see very plainly Abraham Lincoln's dark brown face, with the deep-cut lines, the eyes, always to me with a deep latent sadness in the expression. We have got so that we exchange bows, and very cordial ones. Sometimes the President goes and comes in an open barouche. The cavalry always accompany him, with drawn sabres. Often I notice as he goes out evenings—and sometimes in the morning, when he returns early—he turns off and halts at the large and handsome residence of the Secretary of War, on K street, and holds conference there. If in his barouche, I can see from my window he does not alight, but sits in his vehicle, and Mr. Stanton comes out to attend him. Sometimes one of his sons, a boy of ten or twelve, accompanies him, riding at his right on a pony. Earlier in the summer I occasionally saw the President and his wife, toward the latter part of the afternoon, out in a barouche, on a pleasure ride through the city. Mrs. Lincoln was dress'd in complete black, with a long crape veil. The equipage is of the plainest kind, only two horses, and they nothing extra. They pass'd me once very close, and I saw the President in the face fully, as they were moving slowly, and his look, though abstracted, happen'd to be directed steadily in my eye. He bow'd and smiled, but far beneath his smile I noticed well the expression I have alluded to. None of the artists or pictures has caught the deep, though subtle and indirect expression of this man's face. There is something else there. One of the great portrait painters of two or three centuries ago is needed.

TWO BROTHERS, ONE SOUTH, ONE NORTH
May 28–29, 1865

Whitman stayed on to help with the wounded after the South surrendered. In the following entry he personally experiences one of the war's distressing incidents—the way it sometimes resulted in brother battling brother.

I staid to-night a long time by the bedside of a new patient, a young Baltimorean, aged about 19 years, W. S. P., (2d Maryland, southern,) very feeble, right leg amputated, can't sleep hardly at all—has taken a great deal of morphine, which, as usual, is costing more than it comes to. Evidently very intelligent and well bred—very affectionate—held on to my hand, and put it by his face, not willing to let me leave. As I was lingering, soothing him in his pain, he says to me suddenly, "I hardly think you know who I am—I don't wish to impose upon you—I am a rebel soldier." I said I did not know that, but it made no difference. Visiting him daily for about two weeks after that, while he lived, (death had mark'd him, and he was quite alone,) I loved him much, always kiss'd him, and he did me. In an adjoining ward I found his brother, an officer of rank, a Union soldier, a brave and religious man, (Col. Clifton K. Prentiss, sixth Maryland infantry, Sixth corps, wounded in one of the engagements at Petersburgh, April 2—linger'd, suffer'd much, died in Brooklyn, Aug. 20, '65.) It was in the same battle both were hit. One was a strong Unionist, the other Secesh; both fought on their respective sides, both badly wounded, and both brought together here after a separation of four years. Each died for his cause.

THE REAL WAR WILL NEVER GET IN THE BOOKS
[undated]

As he reviewed the page proofs of Specimen Days, *Whitman worried that his "diary would prove, at best, but a batch of convulsively written reminiscences." Yet he decided to leave it that way, for the notes "are but parts of the actual distraction, heat, smoke and excitement of those times." The war itself, he realized, could only be described by the word* convulsiveness. *In other words, the real war—as he suggests in this famous passage from* Specimen Days—*will never properly be seen by writers or historians in retrospect. It can perhaps best be conveyed by the spontaneous and fragmentary jottings of a diary.*

And so good-bye to the war. I know not how it may have been, or   5
may be, to others—to me the main interest I found, (and still, on recollection, find,) in the rank and file of the armies, both sides, and in those specimens amid the hospitals, and even the dead on the field. To me the points illustrating the latent personal character and eligibilities of these States, in the two or three millions of American young and middle-aged men, North and South, embodied in those armies—and especially the one-third or one-fourth of their number, stricken by wounds or disease at some time in the course of the contest—were of more significance even than the political interests involved. (As so much of a race depends on how it faces death, and how it stands personal anguish and sickness. As, in the glints of emotions under emergencies, and the indirect traits and

asides in Plutarch, we get far profounder clues to the antique world than all its more formal history.)

Future years will never know the seething hell and the black infernal background of countless minor scenes and interiors, (not the official surface-courteousness of the Generals, not the few great battles) of the Secession war; and it is best they should not—the real war will never get in the books. In the mushy influences of current times, too, the fervid atmosphere and typical events of those years are in danger of being totally forgotten. I have at night watch'd by the side of a sick man in the hospital, one who could not live many hours. I have seen his eyes flash and burn as he raised himself and recurr'd to the cruelties of his surrender'd brother, and mutilations of the corpse afterward. . . .

Such was the war. It was not a quadrille in a ball-room. Its interior history will not only never be written—its practicality, minutiæ of deeds and passions, will never be even suggested. The actual soldier of 1862-'65, North and South, with all his ways, his incredible dauntlessness, habits, practices, tastes, language, his fierce friendship, his appetite, rankness, his superb strength and animality, lawless gait, and a hundred unnamed lights and shades of camp, I say, will never be written—perhaps must not and should not be.

The preceding notes may furnish a few stray glimpses into that life, and into those lurid interiors, never to be fully convey'd to the future. The hospital part of the drama from '61 to '65, deserves indeed to be recorded. Of that many-threaded drama, with its sudden and strange surprises, its confounding of prophecies, its moments of despair, the dread of foreign interference, the interminable campaigns, the bloody battles, the mighty and cumbrous and green armies, the drafts and bounties—the immense money expenditure, like a heavy-pouring constant rain—with, over the whole land, the last three years of the struggle, an unending, universal mourning-wail of women, parents, orphans—the marrow of the tragedy concentrated in those Army Hospitals—(it seem'd sometimes as if the whole interest of the land, North and South, was one vast central hospital, and all the rest of the affair but flanges)—those forming the untold and unwritten history of the war—infinitely greater (like life's) than the few scraps and distortions that are ever told or written. Think how much, and of importance, will be—how much, civic and military, has already been—buried in the grave, in eternal darkness.

The Reader's Presence

1. In your opinion, what aspects of Whitman's Civil War diary help make the experience of the war vivid and realistic? How are these aspects captured in Whitman's writing?

2. Formulate in your own words what Whitman means by his expression "the real war will never get in the books." What sort of book is he thinking about? Do you think he means that it could never be conveyed in language at all?

9

Virginia Woolf
From *A Writer's Diary*

At the time of her death, Virginia Woolf (1882–1941), one of modern literature's outstanding creative voices, left twenty-six volumes of a handwritten diary that she had started in 1915. Her diary records her daily activities, social life, reading, and, most importantly, her thoughts about the writing process. In 1953, her husband, Leonard Woolf, extracted her remarks about writing and published them in a separate volume called A Writer's Diary. *The following diary entries are taken from this edition. They show Virginia Woolf struggling with creative doubts and aesthetic demands, as well as with social obligations, depression, and, with the onset of World War II, the Nazi bombing of England. For more information on Virginia Woolf, see page 610.*

THIS LOOSE, DRIFTING MATERIAL OF LIFE
Easter Sunday, April 20, 1919

One of the pleasures of keeping a diary is rereading what we've written. Here, just having completed a newspaper article on the novelist Daniel Defoe, Virginia Woolf decides to take a break and think about the different ways she composes when she writes in her diary as opposed to when she writes more formally for publication.

In the idleness which succeeds any long article, and Defoe is the second leader this month, I got out this diary and read, as one always does read one's own writing, with a kind of guilty intensity. I confess that the rough and random style of it, often so ungrammatical, and crying for a word altered, afflicted me somewhat. I am trying to tell whichever self it is that reads this hereafter that I can write very much better; and take no time over this; and forbid her to let the eye of man behold it. And now I may add my little compliment to the effect that it has a slapdash and vigour and sometimes hits an unexpected bull's eye. But what is more to the point is my belief that the habit of writing thus for my own eye only is good practice. It loosens the ligaments. Never mind the misses and the stumbles. Going at such a pace as I do I must make the most direct and instant shots at my object, and thus have to lay hands on words, choose them and shoot them with no more pause than is needed to put my pen in the ink. I believe that during the past year I can trace some increase of ease in my professional writing which I attribute to my casual half hours after tea. Moreover there looms ahead of me the shadow of some kind of form which a diary might attain to. I might in the course of time learn what it is that one can make of this loose, drifting material of life; finding another use for it than the use I put it to, so much more consciously and scrupulously, in fiction. What sort of diary should I like mine to be? Something loose knit and yet not slovenly, so elastic that it will embrace anything, solemn, slight or beautiful that comes into my mind. I should like it to resemble some deep old desk, or capacious hold-all, in which one flings a mass of odds and ends without looking them through. I should like to come back, after a year or two, and find that the collection had sorted itself and refined itself and coalesced, as such deposits so mysteriously do, into a mould, transparent enough to reflect the light of our life, and yet steady, tranquil compounds with the aloofness of a work of art. The main requisite, I think on re-reading my old volumes, is not to play the part of censor, but to write as the mood comes or of anything whatever; since I was curious to find how I went for things put in haphazard, and found the significance to lie where I never saw it at the time. But looseness quickly becomes slovenly. A little effort is needed to face a character or an incident which needs to be recorded. . . .

CHAINED TO MY ROCK
Thursday, August 18, 1921

In 1919, Virginia and Leonard (referred to throughout the diaries as L.) purchased a small country house in Sussex. For many years, they divided their time between there and London. In 1921, Virginia Woolf suffered a bout of nervous depression and was advised by a local doctor (who, she wrote, thought of her as a "chronic invalid") to rest and do nothing for a while. In an irritable state of mind, the day after the doctor's visit, she wrote the following entry in which she compares herself to Prometheus, the Greek mythic hero who was chained to a rock by Zeus as punishment for stealing fire from the gods and giving it to human beings.

Nothing to record; only an intolerable fit of the fidgets to write away. Here I am chained to my rock; forced to do nothing; doomed to let every worry, spite, irritation and obsession scratch and claw and come again.

This is a day that I may not walk and must not work. Whatever book I read bubbles up in my mind as part of an article I want to write. No one in the whole of Sussex is so miserable as I am; or so conscious of an infinite capacity of enjoyment hoarded in me, could I use it. The sun streams (no, never streams; floods rather) down upon all the yellow fields and the long low barns; and what wouldn't I give to be coming through Firle woods, dirty and hot, with my nose turned home, every muscle tired and the brain laid up in sweet lavender, so sane and cool, and ripe for the morrow's task. How I should notice everything—the phrase for it coming the moment after and fitting like a glove; and then on the dusty road, as I ground my pedals, so my story would begin telling itself; and then the sun would be down; and home, and some bout of poetry after dinner, half read, half lived, as if the flesh were dissolved and through it the flowers burst red and white. There! I've written out half my irritation. I hear poor L. driving the lawn mower up and down, for a wife like I am should have a latch to her cage. She bites! And he spent all yesterday running round London for me. Still if one is Prometheus, if the rock is hard and the gadflies pungent, gratitude, affection, none of the nobler feelings have sway. And so this August is wasted.

Only the thought of people suffering more than I do at all consoles; and that is an aberration of egotism, I suppose. I will now make out a time table if I can to get through these odious days. . . .

THEY GET CLOSER EVERY TIME
Wednesday, October 2, 1940

The Woolfs lost their London house during the Nazi bombing raids in 1940. But even in their Sussex house they experienced the incessant raids. They often witnessed air battles above their home. On one occasion, having watched an enemy plane being shot down, Woolf wrote that it "would have been a peaceful matter of fact death to be popped off on the terrace . . . this very fine cool sunny August evening." The thought of death returned during another bombing raid in October. Six months later, on March 28, 1941, she took her own life.

Ought I not to look at the sunset rather than write this? A flush of red in the blue; the haystack on the marsh catches the glow; behind me, the apples are red in the trees. L. is gathering them. Now a plume of smoke goes from the train under Caburn. And all the air a solemn stillness holds. Till 8:30 when the cadaverous twanging in the sky begins; the planes going to London. Well it's an hour still to that. Cows feeding. The elm tree sprinkling its little leaves against the sky. Our pear tree swagged with pears; and the weathercock above the triangular church tower above it. Why try again to make the familiar catalogue, from which something escapes. Should I think of death? Last night a great heavy plunge of bomb under the window. So near we both started. A plane had passed dropping this fruit. We went on to the terrace. Trinkets of stars sprinkled and glittering. All quiet. The bombs dropped on Itford Hill. There are two by the river, marked with white wooden crosses, still unburst. I said to L.: I don't want to die yet. The chances are against it. But they're aiming at the railway and the power works. They get closer every time. Caburn was crowned with what looked like a settled moth, wings extended—a Messerschmitt it was, shot down on Sunday. . . . Oh I try to imagine how one's killed by a bomb. I've got it fairly vivid—the sensation: but can't see anything but suffocating nonentity following after. I shall think—oh I wanted another 10 years—not this—and shan't, for once, be able to describe it. It—I mean death; no, the scrunching and scrambling, the crushing of my bone shade in on my very active eye and brain: the process of putting out the light—painful? Yes. Terrifying. I suppose so. Then a swoon; a drain; two or three gulps attempting consciousness—and then dot dot dot.

The Reader's Presence

1. In the first entry from Woolf's diaries, what positive qualities does she discover about her diary as she rereads it? Does she note any negative tendencies? In what ways does her diary offer her a means of self-discovery?

2. Woolf observed that one of the problems with diaries is that we usually turn to them only in certain moods (for example, loneliness, depression) and that therefore they provide only a limited view of someone's personality. Do you think, from the three excerpts reprinted here, that this observation would pertain to her own diaries? Can you apply her observation to some of the other diary entries in this chapter?

Part II

Personal Writing: Exploring Our Own Lives

10

Maya Angelou

"What's Your Name, Girl?"

Maya Angelou (b. 1928) grew up in St. Louis, Missouri, and in Stamps, Arkansas, a victim of poverty, discrimination, and abuse. Angelou courageously confronts the pain and injustice of her childhood in I Know Why the Caged Bird Sings *(1969), from which the selection "What's Your Name, Girl?" is taken. James Baldwin praised this book as the mark of the "beginning of a new era in the minds and hearts of all black men and women." Angelou is currently Reynolds Professor of American Studies at Wake Forest University. In addition to the several volumes of her autobiography, she is the author of articles, short stories, and poetry. Her most recent publications are a collection of essays,* Even the Stars Look Lonesome *(1997), and a children's book,* Kofi and His Magic *(1996). She has also directed her first feature-length film,* Down in the Delta, *released in 1998.*

Angelou describes a typical day in her life as a writer in this way: "When I'm writing, everything shuts down. I get up about five. . . . I get in my car and drive off to a hotel room: I can't write in my house, I take a hotel room and ask them to take everything off the walls so there's me, the Bible, Roget's Thesaurus, *and some good, dry sherry and I'm at work by 6:30. I write on the bed lying down— one elbow is darker than the other, really black from leaning on it— and I write in longhand on yellow pads. Once into it, all disbelief is suspended, it's beautiful. I hate to go, but I've set for myself 12:30 as the time to leave, because after that it's an indulgence, it becomes stuff I am going to edit out anyway. . . . After dinner I re-read what I have written . . . if April is the cruellest month, then 8:00 at night is the cruellest hour because that's when I start to edit and all that pretty stuff I've written gets axed out. So if I've written ten or twelve pages in six hours, it'll end up as three or four if I'm lucky."*

Recently a white woman from Texas, who would quickly describe herself as a liberal, asked me about my hometown. When I told her that in Stamps[1] my grandmother had owned the only Negro general merchandise store since the turn of the century, she exclaimed, "Why, you were a

---

[1]*Stamps:* A town in southwestern Arkansas. —EDS.

debutante." Ridiculous and even ludicrous. But Negro girls in small Southern towns, whether poverty-stricken or just munching along on a few of life's necessities, were given as extensive and irrelevant preparations for adulthood as rich white girls shown in magazines. Admittedly the training was not the same. While white girls learned to waltz and sit gracefully with a teacup balanced on their knees, we were lagging behind, learning the mid-Victorian values with very little money to indulge them. (Come and see Edna Lomax spending the money she made picking cotton on five balls of ecru tatting thread. Her fingers are bound to snag the work and she'll have to repeat the stitches time and time again. But she knows that when she buys the thread.)

We were required to embroider and I had trunkfuls of colorful dish-towels, pillowcases, runners, and handkerchiefs to my credit. I mastered the art of crocheting and tatting, and there was a lifetime's supply of dainty doilies that would never be used in sacheted dresser drawers. It went without saying that all girls could iron and wash, but the finer touches around the home, like setting a table with real silver, baking roasts, and cooking vegetables without meat, had to be learned else-where. Usually at the source of those habits. During my tenth year, a white woman's kitchen became my finishing school.

Mrs. Viola Cullinan was a plump woman who lived in a three-bedroom house somewhere behind the post office. She was singularly un-attractive until she smiled, and then the lines around her eyes and mouth which made her look perpetually dirty disappeared, and her face looked like the mask of an impish elf. She usually rested her smile until late after-noon when her women friends dropped in and Miss Glory, the cook, served them cold drinks on the closed-in porch.

The exactness of her house was inhuman. This glass went here and only here. That cup had its place and it was an act of impudent rebellion to place it anywhere else. At twelve o'clock the table was set. At 12:15 Mrs. Cullinan sat down to dinner (whether her husband had arrived or not). At 12:16 Miss Glory brought out the food.

It took me a week to learn the difference between a salad plate, a   5 bread plate, and a dessert plate.

Mrs. Cullinan kept up the tradition of her wealthy parents. She was from Virginia. Miss Glory, who was a descendant of slaves that had worked for the Cullinans, told me her history. She had married beneath her (according to Miss Glory). Her husband's family hadn't had their money very long and what they had "didn't 'mount to much."

As ugly as she was, I thought privately, she was lucky to get a husband above or beneath her station. But Miss Glory wouldn't let me say a thing against her mistress. She was very patient with me, however, over the housework. She explained the dishware, silverware, and servants' bells.

The large round bowl in which soup was served wasn't a soup bowl, it was a tureen. There were goblets, sherbet glasses, ice-cream glasses, wine glasses, green glass coffee cups with matching saucers, and water glasses. I had a glass to drink from, and it sat with Miss Glory's on a separate shelf from the others. Soup spoons, gravy boat, butter knives, salad forks, and carving platter were additions to my vocabulary and in fact almost represented a new language. I was fascinated with the novelty, with the fluttering Mrs. Cullinan and her Alice-in-Wonderland house.

Her husband remains, in my memory, undefined. I lumped him with all the other white men that I had ever seen and tried not to see.

On our way home one evening, Miss Glory told me that Mrs. Cullinan   10
couldn't have children. She said that she was too delicate-boned. It was hard to imagine bones at all under those layers of fat. Miss Glory went on to say that the doctor had taken out all her lady organs. I reasoned that a pig's organs included the lungs, heart, and liver, so if Mrs. Cullinan was walking around without these essentials, it explained why she drank alcohol out of unmarked bottles. She was keeping herself embalmed.

When I spoke to Bailey[2] about it, he agreed that I was right, but he also informed me that Mr. Cullinan had two daughters by a colored lady and that I knew them very well. He added that the girls were the spitting image of their father. I was unable to remember what he looked like, although I had just left him a few hours before, but I thought of the Coleman girls. They were very light-skinned and certainly didn't look very much like their mother (no one ever mentioned Mr. Coleman).

My pity for Mrs. Cullinan preceded me the next morning like the Cheshire cat's smile. Those girls, who could have been her daughters, were beautiful. They didn't have to straighten their hair. Even when they were caught in the rain, their braids still hung down straight like tamed snakes. Their mouths were pouty little cupid's bows. Mrs. Cullinan didn't know what she missed. Or maybe she did. Poor Mrs. Cullinan.

For weeks after, I arrived early, left late, and tried very hard to make up for her barrenness. If she had had her own children, she wouldn't have had to ask me to run a thousand errands from her back door to the back door of her friends. Poor old Mrs. Cullinan.

Then one evening Miss Glory told me to serve the ladies on the porch. After I set the tray down and turned toward the kitchen, one of the women asked, "What's your name, girl?" It was the speckled-face one. Mrs. Cullinan said, "She doesn't talk much. Her name's Margaret."

"Is she dumb?"   15

"No. As I understand it, she can talk when she wants to but she's usually quiet as a little mouse. Aren't you, Margaret?"

I smiled at her. Poor thing. No organs and couldn't even pronounce my name correctly.[3]

"She's a sweet little thing, though."

"Well, that may be, but the name's too long. I'd never bother myself. I'd call her Mary if I was you."

---

[2]***Bailey:*** Her brother. — EDS.
[3]Angelou's first name is actually Marguerite. — EDS.

I fumed into the kitchen. That horrible woman would never have the   20
chance to call me Mary because if I was starving I'd never work for her. I
decided I wouldn't pee on her if her heart was on fire. Giggles drifted in
off the porch and into Miss Glory's pots. I wondered what they could be
laughing about.

Whitefolks were so strange. Could they be talking about me? Everybody knew that they stuck together better than the Negroes did. It was
possible that Mrs. Cullinan had friends in St. Louis who heard about a
girl from Stamps being in court and wrote to tell her. Maybe she knew
about Mr. Freeman.[4]

My lunch was in my mouth a second time and I went outside and relieved myself on the bed of four-o'clocks. Miss Glory thought I might be
coming down with something and told me to go on home, that Momma
would give me some herb tea, and she'd explain to her mistress.

I realized how foolish I was being before I reached the pond. Of
course Mrs. Cullinan didn't know. Otherwise she wouldn't have given me
the two nice dresses that Momma cut down, and she certainly wouldn't
have called me a "sweet little thing." My stomach felt fine, and I didn't
mention anything to Momma.

That evening I decided to write a poem on being white, fat, old, and
without children. It was going to be a tragic ballad. I would have to
watch her carefully to capture the essence of her loneliness and pain.

The very next day, she called me by the wrong name. Miss Glory and   25
I were washing up the lunch dishes when Mrs. Cullinan came to the doorway. "Mary?"

Miss Glory asked, "Who?"

Mrs. Cullinan, sagging a little, knew and I knew. "I want Mary to go
down to Mrs. Randall's and take her some soup. She's not been feeling
well for a few days."

Miss Glory's face was a wonder to see. "You mean Margaret,
ma'am. Her name's Margaret."

"That's too long. She's Mary from now on. Heat that soup from last
night and put it in the china tureen and, Mary, I want you to carry it
carefully."

Every person I knew had a hellish horror of being "called out of his   30
name." It was a dangerous practice to call a Negro anything that could
be loosely construed as insulting because of the centuries of their
having been called niggers, jigs, dinges, blackbirds, crows, boots, and
spooks.

Miss Glory had a fleeting second of feeling sorry for me. Then as she
handed me the hot tureen she said, "Don't mind, don't pay that no mind.
Sticks and stones may break your bones, but words . . . You know, I been
working for her for twenty years."

---

[4]**Mr. Freeman:** A friend of Angelou's mother; he was convicted of raping Angelou
when she was a child. — EDS.

She held the back door open for me. "Twenty years; I wasn't much older than you. My name used to be Hallelujah. That's what Ma named me, but my mistress give me 'Glory,' and it stuck. I likes it better too."

I was in the little path that ran behind the houses when Miss Glory shouted. "It's shorter too."

For a few seconds it was a tossup over whether I would laugh (imagine being named Hallelujah) or cry (imagine letting some white woman rename you for her convenience). My anger saved me from either outburst. I had to quit the job, but the problem was going to be how to do it. Momma wouldn't allow me to quit for just any reason.

"She's a peach. That woman is a real peach." Mrs. Randall's maid   35 was talking as she took the soup from me, and I wondered what her name used to be and what she answered to now.

For a week I looked into Mrs. Cullinan's face as she called me Mary. She ignored my coming late and leaving early. Miss Glory was a little annoyed because I had begun to leave egg yolk on the dishes and wasn't putting much heart in polishing the silver. I hoped that she would complain to our boss, but she didn't.

Then Bailey solved my dilemma. He had me describe the contents of the cupboard and the particular plates she liked best. Her favorite piece was a casserole shaped like a fish and the green glass coffee cups. I kept his instructions in mind, so on the next day when Miss Glory was hanging out clothes and I had again been told to serve the old biddies on the porch, I dropped the empty serving tray. When I heard Mrs. Cullinan scream, "Mary!" I picked up the casserole and two of the green glass cups in readiness. As she rounded the kitchen door I let them fall on the tiled floor.

I could never absolutely describe to Bailey what happened next, because each time I got to the part where she fell on the floor and screwed up her ugly face to cry, we burst out laughing. She actually wobbled around on the floor and picked up shards of the cups and cried, "Oh, Momma. Oh, dear Gawd. It's Momma's china from Virginia. Oh, Momma, I sorry."

Miss Glory came running in from the yard and the women from the porch crowded around. Miss Glory was almost as broken up as her mistress. "You mean to say she broke our Virginia dishes? What we gone do?"

Mrs. Cullinan cried louder. "That clumsy nigger. Clumsy little black   40 nigger."

Old speckled-face leaned down and asked, "Who did it, Viola? Was it Mary? Who did it?"

Everything was happening so fast I can't remember whether her action preceded her words, but I know that Mrs. Cullinan said, "Her name's Margaret, goddamn it, her name's Margaret!" And she threw a wedge of the broken plate at me. It could have been the hysteria which put her aim off, but the flying crockery caught Miss Glory right over her ear and she started screaming.

I left the front door wide open so all the neighbors could hear.
Mrs. Cullinan was right about one thing. My name wasn't Mary.

The Reader's Presence

1. At the center of this autobiographical episode is the importance of people's names in African American culture. Where does Angelou make this point clear? If she hadn't explained the problem of names directly, how might your interpretation of the episode be different? To what extent do the names of things also play an important role in the essay?

2. After rereading the essay, try to describe the emotional attitudes of the characters to one another. What, for example, is Marguerite's attitude toward Mrs. Cullinan? Do you feel pity or sympathy at any point for Mrs. Cullinan? How does Marguerite's attitude toward her fluctuate throughout the episode? With whom do you sympathize most in the final scene, and why? For which character do you have the least sympathy?

3. Consider Marguerite's final act very carefully. Why does she respond by deliberately destroying Mrs. Cullinan's china? What else could she have done? Why was that act especially appropriate? What does the china represent?

11

Russell Baker

Gumption

From 1962 to 1998, Russell Baker (b. 1925) wrote the "Observer" column in the New York Times, *a column that is syndicated to over four hundred and fifty newspapers across the nation. Baker's articles on contemporary American politics, culture, and language are consistently funny and often sharply satiric. Collections of his articles have been published in several volumes, including* So This Is Depravity *(1980) and* There's a Country in My Cellar *(1990). He is also the author of fiction and children's literature. Since 1993, Baker has hosted* Masterpiece Theater *on public television.*

Among other professional honors, he has twice been awarded the Pulitzer Prize, in 1979 for commentary and in 1983 for his autobiography, Growing Up

(1982), from which the selection "Gumption" is taken, and was awarded the George Polk Career Award in 1998. Baker's second volume of memoirs, The Good Times, *was published in 1989. Baker engaged in extensive research efforts in preparation for writing these memoirs. After all, he explains, "I was writing about a world that seemed to exist 200 years ago. I had one foot back there in this primitive country life where the women did the laundry running their knuckles on scrub boards and heated irons on coal stoves."*

I began working in journalism when I was eight years old. It was my mother's idea. She wanted me to "make something" of myself and, after a levelheaded appraisal of my strengths, decided I had better start young if I was to have any chance of keeping up with the competition.

The flaw in my character which she had already spotted was the lack of "gumption." My idea of a perfect afternoon was lying in front of the radio rereading my favorite Big Little Book, *Dick Tracy Meets Stooge Viller*. My mother despised inactivity. Seeing me having a good time in repose, she was powerless to hide her disgust. "You've got no more gumption than a bump on a log," she said. "Get out in the kitchen and help Doris do those dirty dishes."

My sister Doris, though two years younger than I, had enough gumption for a dozen people. She positively enjoyed washing dishes, making beds, and cleaning the house. When she was only seven she could carry a piece of short-weighted cheese back to the A&P, threaten the manager with legal action, and come back triumphantly with the full quarter-pound we'd paid for and a few extra ounces thrown in for forgiveness. Doris could have made something of herself if she hadn't been a girl. Because of this defect, however, the best she could hope for was a career as a nurse or schoolteacher, the only work that capable females were considered up to in those days.

This must have saddened my mother, this twist of fate that had allocated all the gumption to the daughter and left her with a son who was content with Dick Tracy and Stooge Viller. If disappointed, though, she wasted no energy on self-pity. She would make me make something of myself whether I wanted to or not. "The Lord helps those who help themselves," she said. That was the way her mind worked.

She was realistic about the difficulty. Having sized up the material the 5 Lord had given her to mold, she didn't overestimate what she could do with it. She didn't insist that I grow up to be president of the United States.

Fifty years ago parents still asked boys if they wanted to grow up to be president, and asked it not jokingly but seriously. Many parents who were hardly more than paupers still believed their sons could do it. Abraham Lincoln had done it. We were only sixty-five years from Lincoln. Many a grandfather who walked among us could remember Lincoln's time. Men of grandfatherly age were the worst for asking if you wanted to grow up to be president. A surprising number of little boys said yes and meant it.

I was asked many times myself. No, I would say, I didn't want to grow up to be president. My mother was present during one of these interrogations. An elderly uncle, having posed the usual question and exposed my lack of interest in the presidency, asked, "Well, what *do* you want to be when you grow up?"

I loved to pick through trash piles and collect empty bottles, tin cans with pretty labels, and discarded magazines. The most desirable job on earth sprang instantly to mind. "I want to be a garbage man," I said.

My uncle smiled, but my mother had seen the first distressing evidence of a bump budding on a log. "Have a little gumption, Russell," she said. Her calling me Russell was a signal of unhappiness. When she approved of me I was always "Buddy."

When I turned eight years old she decided that the job of starting me   10
on the road toward making something of myself could no longer be safely delayed. "Buddy," she said one day, "I want you to come home right after school this afternoon. Somebody's coming and I want you to meet him."

When I burst in that afternoon she was in conference in the parlor with an executive of the Curtis Publishing Company. She introduced me. He bent low from the waist and shook my hand. Was it true as my mother had told him, he asked, that I longed for the opportunity to conquer the world of business?

My mother replied that I was blessed with a rare determination to make something of myself.

"That's right," I whispered.

"But have you got the grit, the character, the never-say-quit spirit it takes to succeed in business?"

My mother said I certainly did.   15

"That's right," I said.

He eyed me silently for a long pause, as though weighing whether I could be trusted to keep his confidence, then spoke man-to-man. Before taking a crucial step, he said, he wanted to advise me that working for the Curtis Publishing Company placed enormous responsibility on a young man. It was one of the great companies of America. Perhaps the greatest publishing house in the world. I had heard, no doubt, of the *Saturday Evening Post*?

Heard of it? My mother said that everyone in our house had heard of the *Saturday Post* and that I, in fact, read it with religious devotion.

Then doubtless, he said, we were also familiar with those two monthly pillars of the magazine world, the *Ladies Home Journal* and the *Country Gentleman*.

Indeed we were familiar with them, said my mother.   20

Representing the *Saturday Evening Post* was one of the weightiest honors that could be bestowed in the world of business, he said. He was personally proud of being a part of that great corporation.

My mother said he had every right to be.

Again he studied me as though debating whether I was worthy of a knighthood. Finally: "Are you trustworthy?"

My mother said I was the soul of honesty.

"That's right," I said.   25

The caller smiled for the first time. He told me I was a lucky young man. He admired my spunk. Too many young men thought life was all play. Those young men would not go far in this world. Only a young man willing to work and save and keep his face washed and his hair neatly combed could hope to come out on top in a world such as ours. Did I truly and sincerely believe that I was such a young man?

"He certainly does," said my mother.

"That's right," I said.

He said he had been so impressed by what he had seen of me that he was going to make me a representative of the Curtis Publishing Company. On the following Tuesday, he said, thirty freshly printed copies of the *Saturday Evening Post* would be delivered at our door. I would place these magazines, still damp with the ink of the presses, in a handsome canvas bag, sling it over my shoulder, and set forth through the streets to bring the best in journalism, fiction, and cartoons to the American public.

He had brought the canvas bag with him. He presented it with a reverence fit for a chasuble. He showed me how to drape the sling over my left shoulder and across the chest so that the pouch lay easily accessible to my right hand, allowing the best in journalism, fiction, and cartoons to be swiftly extracted and sold to a citizenry whose happiness and security depended upon us soldiers of the free press.   30

The following Tuesday I raced home from school, put the canvas bag over my shoulder, dumped the magazines in, and, tilting to the left to balance their weight on my right hip, embarked on the highway of journalism.

We lived in Belleville, New Jersey, a commuter town at the northern fringe of Newark. It was 1932, the bleakest year of the Depression. My father had died two years before, leaving us with a few pieces of Sears, Roebuck furniture and not much else, and my mother had taken Doris and me to live with one of her younger brothers. This was my Uncle Allen. Uncle Allen had made something of himself by 1932. As salesman for a soft-drink bottler in Newark, he had an income of $30 a week; wore pearl-gray spats, detachable collars, and a three-piece suit; was happily married; and took in threadbare relatives.

With my load of magazines I headed toward Belleville Avenue. That's where the people were. There were two filling stations at the intersection with Union Avenue, as well as an A&P, a fruit stand, a bakery, a barbershop, Zuccarelli's drugstore, and a diner shaped like a railroad car. For several hours I made myself highly visible, shifting position now and then from corner to corner, from shop window to shop window, to make sure

everyone could see the heavy black lettering on the canvas bag that said
THE SATURDAY EVENING POST. When the angle of the light indicated that
it was suppertime, I walked back to the house.

"How many did you sell, Buddy?" my mother asked.

"None." 35

"Where did you go?"

"The corner of Belleville and Union Avenues."

"What did you do?"

"Stood on the corner waiting for somebody to buy a *Saturday
Evening Post*."

"You just stood there?" 40

"Didn't sell a single one."

"For God's sake, Russell!"

Uncle Allen intervened. "I've been thinking about it for some time,"
he said, "and I've about decided to take the *Post* regularly. Put me down
as a regular customer." And I handed him a magazine and he paid me a
nickel. It was the first nickel I earned.

Afterwards my mother instructed me in salesmanship. I would have to
ring doorbells, address adults with charming self-confidence, and break
down resistance with a sales talk pointing out that no one, no matter how
poor, could afford to be without the *Saturday Evening Post* in the home.

I told my mother I'd changed my mind about wanting to succeed in 45
the magazine business.

"If you think I'm going to raise a good-for-nothing," she replied,
"you've got another think coming." She told me to hit the streets with the
canvas bag and start ringing doorbells the instant school was out the next
day. When I objected that I didn't feel any aptitude for salesmanship, she
asked how I'd like to lend her my leather belt so she could whack some
sense into me. I bowed to superior will and entered journalism with a
heavy heart.

My mother and I had fought this battle almost as long as I could remember. It probably started even before memory began, when I was a
country child in northern Virginia and my mother, dissatisfied with my
father's plain workman's life, determined that I would not grow up like
him and his people, with calluses on their hands, overalls on their backs,
and fourth-grade educations in their heads. She had fancier ideas of life's
possibilities. Introducing me to the *Saturday Evening Post*, she was trying
to wean me as early as possible from my father's world where men left
with their lunch pails at sunup, worked with their hands until the grime
ate into the pores, and died with a few sticks of mail-order furniture as
their legacy. In my mother's vision of the better life there were desks and
white collars, well-pressed suits, evenings of reading and lively talk, and
perhaps—if a man were very, very lucky and hit the jackpot, really made
something important of himself—perhaps there might be a fantastic
salary of $5,000 a year to support a big house and a Buick with a rumble
seat and a vacation in Atlantic City.

And so I set forth with my sack of magazines. I was afraid of the dogs that snarled behind the doors of potential buyers. I was timid about ringing the doorbells of strangers, relieved when no one came to the door, and scared when someone did. Despite my mother's instructions, I could not deliver an engaging sales pitch. When a door opened I simply asked, "Want to buy a *Saturday Evening Post?*" In Belleville few persons did. It was a town of thirty thousand people, and most weeks I rang a fair majority of its doorbells. But I rarely sold my thirty copies. Some weeks I canvassed the entire town for six days and still had four or five unsold magazines on Monday evening; then I dreaded the coming of Tuesday morning, when a batch of thirty fresh *Saturday Evening Post*s was due at the front door.

"Better get out there and sell the rest of those magazines tonight," my mother would say.

I usually posted myself then at a busy intersection where a traffic   50
light controlled commuter flow from Newark. When the light turned red I stood on the curb and shouted my sales pitch at the motorists.

"Want to buy a *Saturday Evening Post?*"

One rainy night when car windows were sealed against me I came back soaked and with not a single sale to report. My mother beckoned to Doris.

"Go back down there with Buddy and show him how to sell these magazines," she said.

Brimming with zest, Doris, who was then seven years old, returned with me to the corner. She took a magazine from the bag, and when the light turned red she strode to the nearest car and banged her small fist against the closed window. The driver, probably startled at what he took to be a midget assaulting his car, lowered the window to stare, and Doris thrust a *Saturday Evening Post* at him.

"You need this magazine," she piped, "and it only costs a nickel."   55

Her salesmanship was irresistible. Before the light changed half a dozen times she disposed of the entire batch. I didn't feel humiliated. To the contrary. I was so happy I decided to give her a treat. Leading her to the vegetable store on Belleville Avenue, I bought three apples, which cost a nickel, and gave her one.

"You shouldn't waste your money," she said.

"Eat your apple." I bit into mine.

"You shouldn't eat before supper," she said. "It'll spoil your appetite."

Back at the house that evening, she dutifully reported me for wasting   60
a nickel. Instead of a scolding, I was rewarded with a pat on the back for having the good sense to buy fruit instead of candy. My mother reached into her bottomless supply of maxims and told Doris, "An apple a day keeps the doctor away."

By the time I was ten I had learned all my mother's maxims by heart. Asking to stay up past normal bedtime, I knew the refusal would be explained with, "Early to bed and early to rise, makes a man healthy, wealthy, and wise." If I whimpered about having to get up early in the morning, I could depend on her to say, "The early bird gets the worm."

The one I most despised was, "If at first you don't succeed, try, try again." This was the battle cry with which she constantly sent me back into the hopeless struggle whenever I moaned that I had rung every door-bell in town and knew there wasn't a single potential buyer left in Belleville that week. After listening to my explanation, she handed me the canvas bag and said, "If at first you don't succeed . . ."

Three years in that job, which I would gladly have quit after the first day except for her insistence, produced at least one valuable result. My mother finally concluded that I would never make something of myself by pursuing a life in business and started considering careers that demanded less competitive zeal.

One evening when I was eleven I brought home a short "composition" on my summer vacation which the teacher had graded with an A. Reading it with her own schoolteacher's eye, my mother agreed that it was top-drawer seventh grade prose and complimented me. Nothing more was said about it immediately, but a new idea had taken life in her mind. Halfway through supper she suddenly interrupted the conversation.

"Buddy," she said, "maybe you could be a writer."   65

I clasped the idea to my heart. I had never met a writer, had shown no previous urge to write, and hadn't a notion how to become a writer, but I loved stories and thought that making up stories must surely be al-most as much fun as reading them. Best of all, though, and what really gladdened my heart, was the ease of a writer's life. Writers did not have to trudge through the town peddling from canvas bags, defending them-selves against angry dogs, being rejected by surly strangers. Writers did not have to ring doorbells. So far as I could make out, what writers did couldn't even be classified as work.

I was enchanted. Writers didn't have to have any gumption at all. I did not dare tell anybody for fear of being laughed at in the schoolyard, but se-cretly I decided that what I'd like to be when I grew up was a writer.

The Reader's Presence

1. Baker writes that his sister "could have made something of herself if she hadn't been a girl. Because of this defect, however, the best she could hope for was a career as a nurse or schoolteacher, the only work that capable females were considered up to in those days" (paragraph 3). How would you describe Baker's tone in this passage? Do you think he really believes his sister's gender is a "defect"?

2. Baker's autobiographical essay is sprinkled with maxims and clichés (for example, "an apple a day," "bump on a log"). Such language is

usually considered a flaw in writing; how can you tell that Baker is using these phrases intentionally? What effect on the reader do you think they are intended to have?

3. What sort of word is *gumption*? What synonyms can you think of for the term? How does Baker convey what his mother meant by the word without resorting to definitions? Do you believe Baker when he says in the final paragraph that writers don't need any gumption at all?

12

Raymond Carver

My Father's Life

Son of a laborer and a homemaker in Clatskanie, Oregon, Raymond Carver (1938–1988) resembled the characters in the short stories for which he is widely acclaimed. Once a manual laborer, a gas station attendant, and a janitor himself, Carver acquired his vision of the working class and the desperate lives of ordinary folk through direct experience. The Pacific Northwest of Carver's writing is peopled with types such as "the waitress, the bus driver, the mechanic, the hotel keeper"—people Carver feels are "good people." First published in Esquire *in 1984, "My Father's Life," Carver's account of his father's hardships during the Great Depression, puts a biographical spin on these "good people." Carver's short story collections,* Will You Please Be Quiet, Please? *(1976),* Cathedral *(1984), and* Where I'm Calling From *(1988), were all nominated for the National Book Critics Circle Award. The latter two collections were also nominated for the Pulitzer Prize for fiction in 1985 and 1989, respectively. Carver's poetry is collected in* Where Water Comes Together with Other Water *(1985), recipient of the 1986 Los Angeles Times Book Prize;* Ultramarine *(1986); and* A New Path to the Waterfall *(1989).*

In his essay "On Writing," Carver states, "Writers don't need tricks or gimmicks or even necessarily to be the smartest fellows on the block. At the risk of appearing foolish, a writer sometimes needs to be able to just stand and gape at this or that thing—a sunset or an old shoe—in absolute and simple amazement."

My dad's name was Clevie Raymond Carver. His family called him Raymond and friends called him C. R. I was named Raymond Clevie Carver, Jr. I hated the "Junior" part. When I was little my dad called me Frog, which was okay. But later, like everybody else in the family, he began calling me Junior. He went on calling me this until I was thirteen or fourteen and announced that I wouldn't answer to that name any longer. So he began calling me Doc. From then until his death, on June 17, 1967, he called me Doc, or else Son.

When he died, my mother telephoned my wife with the news. I was away from my family at the time, between lives, trying to enroll in the School of Library Science at the University of Iowa. When my wife answered the phone, my mother blurted out, "Raymond's dead!" For a moment, my wife thought my mother was telling her that I was dead. Then my mother made it clear *which* Raymond she was talking about and my wife said, "Thank God. I thought you meant *my* Raymond."

My dad walked, hitched rides, and rode in empty boxcars when he went from Arkansas to Washington State in 1934, looking for work. I don't know whether he was pursuing a dream when he went out to Washington. I doubt it. I don't think he dreamed much. I believe he was simply looking for steady work at decent pay. Steady work was meaningful work. He picked apples for a time and then landed a construction laborer's job on the Grand Coulee Dam. After he'd put aside a little money, he bought a car and drove back to Arkansas to help his folks, my grandparents, pack up for the move west. He said later that they were about to starve down there, and this wasn't meant as a figure of speech. It was during that short while in Arkansas, in a town called Leola, that my mother met my dad on the sidewalk as he came out of a tavern.

"He was drunk," she said. "I don't know why I let him talk to me. His eyes were glittery. I wish I'd had a crystal ball." They'd met once, a year or so before, at a dance. He'd had girlfriends before her, my mother told me. "Your dad always had a girlfriend, even after we married. He was my first and last. I never had another man. But I didn't miss anything."

They were married by a justice of the peace on the day they left   5
for Washington, this big, tall country girl and a farmhand-turned-construction worker. My mother spent her wedding night with my dad and his folks, all of them camped beside the road in Arkansas.

In Omak, Washington, my dad and mother lived in a little place not much bigger than a cabin. My grandparents lived next door. My dad was still working on the dam, and later, with the huge turbines producing electricity and the water backed up for a hundred miles into Canada, he stood in the crowd and heard Franklin D. Roosevelt when he spoke at the construction site. "He never mentioned those guys who died building that dam," my dad said. Some of his friends had died there, men from Arkansas, Oklahoma, and Missouri.

He then took a job in a sawmill in Clatskanie, Oregon, a little town alongside the Columbia River. I was born there, and my mother has a picture of my dad standing in front of the gate to the mill, proudly holding me up to face the camera. My bonnet is on crooked and about to come untied. His hat is pushed back on his forehead, and he's wearing a big grin. Was he going in to work or just finishing his shift? It doesn't matter. In either case, he had a job and a family. These were his salad days.

In 1941 we moved to Yakima, Washington, where my dad went to work as a saw filer, a skilled trade he'd learned in Clatskanie. When war broke out, he was given a deferment because his work was considered necessary to the war effort. Finished lumber was in demand by the armed services, and he kept his saws so sharp they could shave the hair off your arm.

After my dad had moved us to Yakima, he moved his folks into the same neighborhood. By the mid-1940s the rest of my dad's family—his brother, his sister, and her husband, as well as uncles, cousins, nephews, and most of their extended family and friends—had come out from Arkansas. All because my dad came out first. The men went to work at Boise Cascade, where my dad worked, and the women packed apples in the canneries. And in just a little while, it seemed—according to my mother—everybody was better off than my dad. "Your dad couldn't keep money," my mother said. "Money burned a hole in his pocket. He was always doing for others."

The first house I clearly remember living in, at 1515 South Fifteenth   10 Street, in Yakima, had an outdoor toilet. On Halloween night, or just any night, for the hell of it, neighbor kids, kids in their early teens, would carry our toilet away and leave it next to the road. My dad would have to get somebody to help him bring it home. Or these kids would take the toilet and stand it in somebody else's backyard. Once they actually set it on fire. But ours wasn't the only house that had an outdoor toilet. When I was old enough to know what I was doing, I threw rocks at the other toilets when I'd see someone go inside. This was called bombing the toilets. After a while, though, everyone went to indoor plumbing until, suddenly, our toilet was the last outdoor one in the neighborhood. I remember the shame I felt when my third-grade teacher, Mr. Wise, drove me home from school one day. I asked him to stop at the house just before ours, claiming I lived there.

I can recall what happened one night when my dad came home late to find that my mother had locked all the doors on him from the inside. He was drunk, and we could feel the house shudder as he rattled the door. When he'd managed to force open a window, she hit him between the eyes with a colander and knocked him out. We could see him down there on the grass. For years afterward, I used to pick up this colander—it was as heavy as a rolling pin—and imagine what it would feel like to be hit in the head with something like that.

It was during this period that I remember my dad taking me into the bedroom, sitting me down on the bed, and telling me that I might have to go live with my Aunt LaVon for a while. I couldn't understand what I'd done that meant I'd have to go away from home to live. But this, too—whatever prompted it—must have blown over, more or less, anyway, because we stayed together, and I didn't have to go live with her or anyone else.

I remember my mother pouring his whiskey down the sink. Sometimes she'd pour it all out and sometimes, if she was afraid of getting caught, she'd only pour half of it out and then add water to the rest. I tasted some of his whiskey once myself. It was terrible stuff, and I don't see how anybody could drink it.

After a long time without one, we finally got a car, in 1949 or 1950, a 1938 Ford. But it threw a rod the first week we had it, and my dad had to have the motor rebuilt.

"We drove the oldest car in town," my mother said. "We could have   15
had a Cadillac for all he spent on car repairs." One time she found someone else's tube of lipstick on the floorboard, along with a lacy handkerchief. "See this?" she said to me. "Some floozy left this in the car."

Once I saw her take a pan of warm water into the bedroom where my dad was sleeping. She took his hand from under the covers and held it in the water. I stood in the doorway and watched. I wanted to know what was going on. This would make him talk in his sleep, she told me. There were things she needed to know, things she was sure he was keeping from her.

Every year or so, when I was little, we would take the North Coast Limited across the Cascade Range from Yakima to Seattle and stay in the Vance Hotel and eat, I remember, at a place called the Dinner Bell Cafe. Once we went to Ivar's Acres of Clams and drank glasses of warm clam broth.

In 1956, the year I was to graduate from high school, my dad quit his job at the mill in Yakima and took a job in Chester, a little sawmill town in northern California. The reasons given at the time for his taking the job had to do with a higher hourly wage and the vague promise that he might, in a few years' time, succeed to the job of head filer in this new mill. But I think, in the main, that my dad had grown restless and simply wanted to try his luck elsewhere. Things had gotten a little too predictable for him in Yakima. Also, the year before, there had been the deaths, within six months of each other, of both his parents.

But just a few days after graduation, when my mother and I were packed to move to Chester, my dad penciled a letter to say he'd been sick for a while. He didn't want us to worry, he said, but he'd cut himself on a saw. Maybe he'd got a tiny sliver of steel in his blood. Anyway, something had happened and he'd had to miss work, he said. In the same mail was an unsigned postcard from somebody down there telling my mother that my dad was about to die and that he was drinking "raw whiskey."

When we arrived in Chester, my dad was living in a trailer that be-   20
longed to the company. I didn't recognize him immediately. I guess for a moment I didn't want to recognize him. He was skinny and pale and looked bewildered. His pants wouldn't stay up. He didn't look like my dad. My mother began to cry. My dad put his arm around her and patted her shoulder vaguely, like he didn't know what this was all about, either. The three of us took up life together in the trailer, and we looked after him as best we could. But my dad was sick, and he couldn't get any better. I worked with him in the mill that summer and part of the fall. We'd

get up in the mornings and eat eggs and toast while we listened to the radio, and then go out the door with our lunch pails. We'd pass through the gate together at eight in the morning, and I wouldn't see him again until quitting time. In November I went back to Yakima to be closer to my girlfriend, the girl I'd made up my mind I was going to marry.

He worked at the mill in Chester until the following February, when he collapsed on the job and was taken to the hospital. My mother asked if I would come down there and help. I caught a bus from Yakima to Chester, intending to drive them back to Yakima. But now, in addition to being physically sick, my dad was in the midst of a nervous breakdown, though none of us knew to call it that at the time. During the entire trip back to Yakima, he didn't speak, not even when asked a direct question. ("How do you feel, Raymond?" "You okay, Dad?") He'd communicate, if he communicated at all, by moving his head or by turning his palms up as if to say he didn't know or care. The only time he said anything on the trip, and for nearly a month afterward, was when I was speeding down a gravel road in Oregon and the car muffler came loose. "You were going too fast," he said.

Back in Yakima a doctor saw to it that my dad went to a psychiatrist. My mother and dad had to go on relief, as it was called, and the county paid for the psychiatrist. The psychiatrist asked my dad, "Who is the President?" He'd had a question put to him that he could answer. "Ike," my dad said. Nevertheless, they put him on the fifth floor of Valley Memorial Hospital and began giving him electroshock treatment. I was married by then and about to start my own family. My dad was still locked up when my wife went into this same hospital, just one floor down, to have our first baby. After she had delivered, I went upstairs to give my dad the news. They let me in through a steel door and showed me where I could find him. He was sitting on a couch with a blanket over his lap. *Hey,* I thought. *What in hell is happening to my dad?* I sat down next to him and told him he was a grandfather. He waited a minute and then he said, "I feel like a grandfather." That's all he said. He didn't smile or move. He was in a big room with a lot of other people. Then I hugged him, and he began to cry.

Somehow he got out of there. But now came the years when he couldn't work and just sat around the house trying to figure what next and what he'd done wrong in his life that he'd wound up like this. My mother went from job to crummy job. Much later she referred to that time he was in the hospital, and those years just afterward, as "when Raymond was sick." The word *sick* was never the same for me again. '

In 1964, through the help of a friend, he was lucky enough to be hired on at a mill in Klamath, California. He moved down there by himself to see if he could hack it. He lived not far from the mill, in a one-room cabin not much different from the place he and my mother had started out living in when they went west. He scrawled letters to my mother, and if I called she'd read them aloud to me over the phone. In the letters, he said it was touch and go. Every day that he went to work, he felt like it was the most important day of his life. But every day, he told her, made the next day that much easier. He said for her to tell me he said hello. If he couldn't sleep at night, he said, he thought about me and the good times we used to have. Finally, after a couple of months, he regained some of his confidence. He could do the work and didn't think he had to worry that he'd let anybody down ever again. When he was sure, he sent for my mother.

He'd been off from work for six years and had lost everything in that   25
time — home, car, furniture, and appliances, including the big freezer that had been my mother's pride and joy. He'd lost his good name too — Raymond Carver was someone who couldn't pay his bills — and his self-respect was gone. He'd even lost his virility. My mother told my wife, "All during that time Raymond was sick we slept together in the same bed, but we didn't have relations. He wanted to a few times, but nothing happened. I didn't miss it, but I think he wanted to, you know."

During those years I was trying to raise my own family and earn a living. But, one thing and another, we found ourselves having to move a lot. I couldn't keep track of what was going down in my dad's life. But I did have a chance one Christmas to tell him I wanted to be a writer. I might as well have told him I wanted to become a plastic surgeon. "What are you going to write about?" he wanted to know. Then, as if to help me out, he said, "Write about stuff you know about. Write about some of those fishing trips we took." I said I would, but I knew I wouldn't. "Send me what you write," he said. I said I'd do that, but then I didn't. I wasn't writing anything about fishing, and I didn't think he'd particularly care about, or even necessarily understand, what I was writing in those days. Besides, he wasn't a reader. Not the sort, anyway, I imagined I was writing for.

Then he died. I was a long way off, in Iowa City, with things still to say to him. I didn't have the chance to tell him goodbye, or that I thought he was doing great at his new job. That I was proud of him for making a comeback.

My mother said he came in from work that night and ate a big supper. Then he sat at the table by himself and finished what was left of a bottle of whiskey, a bottle she found hidden in the bottom of the garbage under some coffee grounds a day or so later. Then he got up and went to bed, where my mother joined him a little later. But in the night she had to get up and make a bed for herself on the couch. "He was snoring so loud I couldn't sleep," she said. The next morning when she looked in on him, he was on his back with his mouth open, his cheeks caved in. *Graylooking,* she said. She knew he was dead — she didn't need a doctor to tell her that. But she called one anyway, and then she called my wife.

Among the pictures my mother kept of my dad and herself during those early days in Washington was a photograph of him standing in front of a car, holding a beer and a stringer of fish. In the photograph he is wearing his hat back on his forehead and has this awkward grin on his face. I asked her for it and she gave it to me, along with some others. I put it up on my wall, and each time we moved, I took the picture along and put it up on another wall. I looked at it carefully from time to time, trying to figure out some things about my dad, and maybe myself in the process. But I couldn't. My dad just kept moving further and further away from me and back into time. Finally, in the course of another move, I lost the photograph. It was then that I tried to recall it, and at the same time make an attempt to say something about my dad, and how I thought that in some important ways we might be alike. I wrote the poem when I was living in an apartment house in an urban area south of San Francisco, at a time when I found myself, like my dad, having trouble with alcohol. The poem was a way of trying to connect up with him.

PHOTOGRAPH OF MY FATHER IN HIS TWENTY-SECOND YEAR

October. Here in this dank, unfamiliar kitchen
I study my father's embarrassed young man's face.
Sheepish grin, he holds in one hand a string
of spiny yellow perch, in the other
a bottle of Carlsberg beer.

In jeans and flannel shirt, he leans
against the front fender of a 1934 Ford.
He would like to pose brave and hearty for his posterity,
wear his old hat cocked over his ear.
All his life my father wanted to be bold.

But the eyes give him away, and the hands
that limply offer the string of dead perch
and the bottle of beer. Father, I love you,
yet how can I say thank you, I who can't hold my liquor either
and don't even know the places to fish.

The poem is true in its particulars, except that my dad died in June and not October, as the first word of the poem says. I wanted a word with more than one syllable to it to make it linger a little. But more than that, I wanted a month appropriate to what I felt at the time I wrote the poem—a month of short days and failing light, smoke in the air, things perishing. June was summer nights and days, graduations, my wedding anniversary, the birthday of one of my children. June wasn't a month your father died in.

After the service at the funeral home, after we had moved outside, a woman I didn't know came over to me and said, "He's happier where he is now." I stared at this woman until she moved away. I still remember the little knob of a hat she was wearing. Then one of my dad's cousins—I didn't know the man's name—reached out and took my hand. "We all miss him," he said, and I knew he wasn't saying it just to be polite.

I began to weep for the first time since receiving the news. I hadn't been able to before. I hadn't had the time, for one thing. Now, suddenly, I couldn't stop. I held my wife and wept while she said and did what she could do to comfort me there in the middle of that summer afternoon.

I listened to people say consoling things to my mother, and I was glad that my dad's family had turned up, had come to where he was. I thought I'd remember everything that was said and done that day and maybe find a way to tell it sometime. But I didn't. I forgot it all, or nearly. What I do remember is that I heard our name used a lot that afternoon, my dad's name and mine. But I knew they were talking about my dad. *Raymond,* these people kept saying in their beautiful voices out of my childhood. *Raymond.*

The Reader's Presence

1. You may have noticed that Carver begins and ends his essay with a reference to his and his father's name. Of what importance is this information at the opening? What do we learn about his relationship with his father through their names? How do names matter in the final paragraph?

2. Though the essay is titled "My Father's Life," Carver throughout uses the word *dad.* Why do you think he chose to do this? What difference does it make? Why do you think Carver used *father* instead of *dad* in the poem he wrote years earlier?

3. Try rereading the essay with particular attention to the conversations between father and son. How many reported conversations can you find? What do the conversations sound like? Can you find any pattern to them? To what extent do these conversations help you understand Carver's relationship with his father?

13

Judith Ortiz Cofer

Silent Dancing

Born in Puerto Rico in 1952, Judith Ortiz Cofer moved to the United States in 1960. Her poetry has appeared in numerous literary magazines, and several collections of her poems have been published. Her first novel, The Line of the Sun

(1989), was nominated for the Pulitzer Prize. "Silent Dancing" is from Cofer's 1990 essay collection, Silent Dancing: A Partial Remembrance of a Puerto Rican Childhood, *which won a PEN/Martha Albrand special citation for nonfiction. Her most recent books are* The Latin Deli: Prose and Poetry *(1993),* An Island Like You: Stories of the Barrio *(1995), and* The Year of Our Revolution *(1998).*

Reflecting on her life as a writer, Cofer has said, "The 'infinite variety' and power of language interest me. I never cease to experiment with it. As a native Puerto Rican, my first language was Spanish. It was a challenge, not only to learn English, but to master it enough to teach it and—the ultimate goal—to write poetry in it." Cofer is currently associate professor of English at the University of Georgia.

We have a home movie of this party. Several times my mother and I have watched it together, and I have asked questions about the silent revelers coming in and out of focus. It is grainy and of short duration, but it's a great visual aid to my memory of life at that time. And it is in color—the only complete scene in color I can recall from those years.

We lived in Puerto Rico until my brother was born in 1954. Soon after, because of economic pressures on our growing family, my father joined the United States Navy. He was assigned to duty on a ship in Brooklyn Yard—a place of cement and steel that was to be his home base in the States until his retirement more than twenty years later. He left the Island first, alone, going to New York City and tracking down his uncle who lived with his family across the Hudson River in Paterson, New Jersey. There my father found a tiny apartment in a huge tenement that had once housed Jewish families but was just being taken over and transformed by Puerto Ricans, overflowing from New York City. In 1955 he sent for us. My mother was only twenty years old, I was not quite three, and my brother was a toddler when we arrived at *El Building,* as the place had been christened by its newest residents.

My memories of life in Paterson during those first few years are all in shades of gray. Maybe I was too young to absorb vivid colors and details, or to discriminate between the slate blue of the winter sky and the darker hues of the snow-bearing clouds, but that single color washes over the whole period. The building we lived in was gray, as were the streets, filled with slush the first few months of my life there. The coat my father had bought for me was similar in color and too big; it sat heavily on my thin frame.

I do remember the way the heater pipes banged and rattled, startling all of us out of sleep until we got so used to the sound that we automatically shut it out or raised our voices above the racket. The hiss from the valve punctuated my sleep (which has always been fitful) like a nonhuman presence in the room—a dragon sleeping at the entrance of my childhood. But the pipes were also a connection to all the other lives being lived around us. Having come from a house designed for a single family back in Puerto Rico—my mother's extended-family home—it was curious to know that strangers lived under our floor and above our heads, and that the heater pipe went through everyone's apartments. (My first spanking in Paterson came as a result of playing tunes on the pipes in my room to see if there would be an answer.) My mother was as new to this concept of beehive life as I was, but she had been given strict orders by my father to keep the doors locked, the noise down, ourselves to ourselves.

It seems that Father had learned some painful lessons about prejudice   5
while searching for an apartment in Paterson. Not until years later did I hear how much resistance he had encountered with landlords who were panicking at the influx of Latinos into a neighborhood that had been Jewish for a couple of generations. It made no difference that it was the American phenomenon of ethnic turnover which was changing the urban core of Paterson, and that the human flood could not be held back with an accusing finger.

"You Cuban?" one man had asked my father, pointing at his name tag on the Navy uniform—even though my father had the fair skin and light-brown hair of his northern Spanish background, and the name Ortiz is as common in Puerto Rico as Johnson is in the United States.

"No," my father had answered, looking past the finger into his adversary's angry eyes. "I'm Puerto Rican."

"Same shit." And the door closed.

My father could have passed as European, but we couldn't. My brother and I both have our mother's black hair and olive skin, and so we lived in El Building and visited our great-uncle and his fair children on the next block. It was their private joke that they were the German branch of the family. Not many years later that area too would be mainly Puerto Rican. It was as if the heart of the city map were being gradually colored brown—*café con leche*[1] brown. Our color.

The movie opens with a sweep of the living room. It is "typical" im-   10
migrant Puerto Rican decor for the time: The sofa and chairs are square and hard-looking, upholstered in bright colors (blue and yellow in this instance), and covered with the transparent plastic that furniture salesmen then were so adept at convincing women to buy. The linoleum on the floor is light blue; if it had been subjected to spike heels (as it was in most places), there were dime-sized indentations all over it that cannot be seen in this movie. The room is full of people dressed up: dark suits for the men, red dresses for the women. When I have asked my mother why most of the women are in red that night, she has shrugged, "I don't remember. Just a coincidence." She doesn't have my obsession for assigning symbolism to everything.

The three women in red sitting on the couch are my mother, my eighteen-year-old cousin, and her brother's girlfriend. The novia *is just up*

---

[1] *café con leche:* Coffee with cream. In Puerto Rico it is sometimes prepared with boiled milk. — COFER'S NOTE.

from the Island, which is apparent in her body language. She sits up for-
mally, her dress pulled over her knees. She is a pretty girl, but her posture
makes her look insecure, lost in her full-skirted dress, which she has care-
fully tucked around her to make room for my gorgeous cousin, her future
sister-in-law. My cousin has grown up in Paterson and is in her last year
of high school. She doesn't have a trace of what Puerto Ricans call la
mancha (literally, the stain: the mark of the new immigrant—something
about the posture, the voice, or the humble demeanor that makes it obvi-
ous to everyone the person has just arrived on the mainland). My cousin
is wearing a tight, sequined, cocktail dress. Her brown hair has been
lightened with peroxide around the bangs, and she is holding a cigarette
expertly between her fingers, bringing it up to her mouth in a sensuous
arc of her arm as she talks animatedly. My mother, who has come up to
sit between the two women, both only a few years younger than herself,
is somewhere between the poles they represent in our culture.

It became my father's obsession to get out of the barrio, and thus we
were never permitted to form bonds with the place or with the people
who lived there. Yet El Building was a comfort to my mother, who never
got over yearning for *la isla*. She felt surrounded by her language: The
walls were thin, and voices speaking and arguing in Spanish could be
heard all day. *Salsas* blasted out of radios, turned on early in the morning
and left on for company. Women seemed to cook rice and beans perpetually—the strong aroma of boiling red kidney beans permeated the
hallways.

Though Father preferred that we do our grocery shopping at the supermarket when he came home on weekend leaves, my mother insisted
that she could cook only with products whose labels she could read. Consequently, during the week I accompanied her and my little brother to *La
Bodega*—a hole-in-the-wall grocery store across the street from El Building. There we squeezed down three narrow aisles jammed with various
products. Goya's and Libby's—those were the trademarks that were
trusted by *her mamá*, so my mother bought many cans of Goya beans,
soups, and condiments, as well as little cans of Libby's fruit juices for us.
And she also bought Colgate toothpaste and Palmolive soap. (The final *e*
is pronounced in both these products in Spanish, so for many years I believed that they were manufactured on the Island. I remember my surprise
at first hearing a commercial on television in which Colgate rhymed with
"ate.") We always lingered at La Bodega, for it was there that Mother
breathed best, taking in the familiar aromas of the foods she knew from
Mamá's kitchen. It was also there that she got to speak to the other
women of El Building without violating outright Father's dictates against
fraternizing with our neighbors.

Yet Father did his best to make our "assimilation" painless. I can still
see him carrying a real Christmas tree up several flights of stairs to our
apartment, leaving a trail of aromatic pine. He carried it formally, as if it

were a flag in a parade. We were the only ones in El Building that I knew
of who got presents on both Christmas day AND *dia de Reyes*, the day
when the Three Kings brought gifts to Christ and to Hispanic children.

Our supreme luxury in El Building was having our own television set.   15
It must have been a result of Father's guilt feelings over the isolation he
had imposed on us, but we were among the first in the barrio to have one.
My brother quickly became an avid watcher of Captain Kangaroo and
Jungle Jim, while I loved all the series showing families. By the time I
started first grade, I could have drawn a map of Middle America as exem-
plified by the lives of characters in "Father Knows Best," "The Donna
Reed Show," "Leave It to Beaver," "My Three Sons," and (my favorite)
"Bachelor Father," where John Forsythe treated his adopted teenage
daughter like a princess because he was rich and had a Chinese houseboy
to do everything for him. In truth, compared to our neighbors in El Building, *we* were rich. My father's Navy check provided us with financial security and a standard of life that the factory workers envied. The only
thing his money could not buy us was a place to live away from the barrio — his greatest wish, Mother's greatest fear.

*In the home movie the men are shown next, sitting around a card
table set up in one corner of the living room, playing dominoes. The clack
of the ivory pieces was a familiar sound. I heard it in many houses on the
Island and in many apartments in Paterson. In "Leave It to Beaver," the
Cleavers played bridge in every other episode; in my childhood, the men
started every social occasion with a hotly debated round of dominoes.
The women would sit around and watch, but they never participated in
the games.*

*Here and there you can see a small child. Children were always
brought to parties and, whenever they got sleepy, were put to bed in the
host's bedroom. Babysitting was a concept unrecognized by the Puerto
Rican women I knew: A responsible mother did not leave her children
with any stranger. And in a culture where children are not considered intrusive, there was no need to leave the children at home. We went where
our mother went.*

Of my preschool years I have only impressions: the sharp bite of the
wind in December as we walked with our parents toward the brightly lit
stores downtown; how I felt like a stuffed doll in my heavy coat, boots, and
mittens; how good it was to walk into the five-and-dime and sit at the
counter drinking hot chocolate. On Saturdays our whole family would
walk downtown to shop at the big department stores on Broadway.
Mother bought all our clothes at Penney's and Sears, and she liked to buy
her dresses at the women's specialty shops like Lerner's and Diana's. At
some point we'd go into Woolworth's and sit at the soda fountain to eat.

We never ran into other Latinos at these stores or when eating out,
and it became clear to me only years later that the women from El Build-

ing shopped mainly in other places—stores owned by other Puerto Ricans or by Jewish merchants who had philosophically accepted our presence in the city and decided to make us their good customers, if not real neighbors and friends. These establishments were located not downtown but in the blocks around our street, and they were referred to generically as *La Tienda, El Bazar, La Bodega, La Botánica.* Everyone knew what was meant. These were the stores where your face did not turn a clerk to stone, where your money was as green as anyone else's.

One New Year's Eve we were dressed up like child models in the   20
Sears catalogue: my brother in a miniature man's suit and bow tie, and I in black patent-leather shoes and a frilly dress with several layers of crinoline underneath. My mother wore a bright red dress that night, I remember, and spike heels; her long black hair hung to her waist. Father, who usually wore his Navy uniform during his short visits home, had put on a dark civilian suit for the occasion: We had been invited to his uncle's house for a big celebration. Everyone was excited because my mother's brother Hernan—a bachelor who could indulge himself with luxuries— had bought a home movie camera, which he would be trying out that night.

Even the home movie cannot fill in the sensory details such a gathering left imprinted in a child's brain. The thick sweetness of women's perfumes mixing with the ever-present smells of food cooking in the kitchen: meat and plantain *pasteles,* as well as the ubiquitous rice dish made special with pigeon peas—*gandules*—and seasoned with precious *sofrito*[2] sent up from the Island by somebody's mother or smuggled in by a recent traveler. *Sofrito* was one of the items that women hoarded, since it was hardly ever in stock at La Bodega. It was the flavor of Puerto Rico.

The men drank Palo Viejo rum, and some of the younger ones got weepy. The first time I saw a grown man cry was at a New Year's Eve party: He had been reminded of his mother by the smells in the kitchen. But what I remember most were the boiled *pasteles*—plantain or yucca rectangles stuffed with corned beef or other meats, olives, and many other savory ingredients, all wrapped in banana leaves. Everybody had to fish one out with a fork. There was always a "trick" pastel—one without stuffing—and whoever got that one was the "New Year's Fool."

There was also the music. Long-playing albums were treated like precious china in these homes. Mexican recordings were popular, but the songs that brought tears to my mother's eyes were sung by the melancholy Daniel Santos, whose life as a drug addict was the stuff of legend. Felipe Rodríguez was a particular favorite of couples, since he sang about faithless women and brokenhearted men. There is a snatch of one lyric that has stuck in my mind like a needle on a worn groove: *De piedra ha de ser mi*

---

[2]*sofrito:* A cooked condiment. A sauce composed of a mixture of fatback, ham, tomatoes, and many island spices and herbs. It is added to many typical Puerto Rican dishes for a distinctive flavor.—COFER'S NOTE.

cama, de piedra la cabezera . . . la mujer que a mi me quiera . . . ha de quererme de veras. Ay, Ay, Ay, corazón, porque no amas.[3] . . . I must have heard it a thousand times since the idea of a bed made of stone, and its connection to love, first troubled me with its disturbing images.

The five-minute home movie ends with people dancing in a circle — the creative filmmaker must have set it up, so that all of them could file past him. It is both comical and sad to watch silent dancing. Since there is no justification for the absurd movements that music provides for some of us, people appear frantic, their faces embarrassingly intense. It's as if you were watching sex. Yet for years I've had dreams in the form of this home movie. In a recurring scene, familiar faces push themselves forward into my mind's eyes, plastering their features into distorted close-ups. And I'm asking them: "Who is *she*? Who is the old woman I don't recognize? Is she an aunt? Somebody's wife? Tell me who she is."

"See the beauty mark on her cheek as big as a hill on the lunar landscape of her face — well, that runs in the family. The women on your father's side of the family wrinkle early; it's the price they pay for that fair skin. The young girl with the green stain on her wedding dress is *La Novia* — just up from the Island. See, she lowers her eyes when she approaches the camera, as she's supposed to. Decent girls never look at you directly in the face. *Humilde*, humble, a girl should express humility in all her actions. She will make a good wife for your cousin. He should consider himself lucky to have met her only weeks after she arrived here. If he marries her quickly, she will make him a good Puerto Rican–style wife; but if he waits too long, she will be corrupted by the city — just like your cousin there."

"She means me. I do what I want. This is not some primitive island I live on. Do they expect me to wear a black mantilla on my head and go to mass every day? Not me. I'm an American woman, and I will do as I please. I can type faster than anyone in my senior class at Central High, and I'm going to be a secretary to a lawyer when I graduate. I can pass for an American girl anywhere — I've tried it. At least for Italian, anyway — I never speak Spanish in public. I hate these parties, but I wanted the dress. I look better than any of these *humildes* here. *My* life is going to be different. I have an American boyfriend. He is older and has a car. My parents don't know it, but I sneak out of the house late at night sometimes to be with him. If I marry him, even my name will be American. I hate rice and beans — that's what makes these women fat."

"Your *prima*[4] is pregnant by that man she's been sneaking around with. Would I lie to you? I'm your *Tía Política*,[5] your great-uncle's

[3]*De piedra ha de ser . . . amas:* Lyrics from a popular romantic ballad (called a *bolero* in Puerto Rico). Freely translated: "My bed will be made of stone, of stone also my headrest (or pillow), the woman who (dares to) loves me, will have to love me for real. Ay, Ay, Ay, my heart, why can't you (let me) love. . . ." — COFER'S NOTE.

[4]*prima:* Female cousin. — COFER'S NOTE.

[5]*Tía Política:* Aunt by marriage. — COFER'S NOTE.

common-law wife — the one he abandoned on the Island to go marry your cousin's mother. *I* was not invited to this party, of course, but I came anyway. I came to tell you that story about your cousin that you've always wanted to hear. Do you remember the comment your mother made to a neighbor that has always haunted you? The only thing you heard was your cousin's name, and then you saw your mother pick up your doll from the couch and say: 'It was as big as this doll when they flushed it down the toilet.' This image has bothered you for years, hasn't it? You had nightmares about babies being flushed down the toilet, and you wondered why anyone would do such a horrible thing. You didn't dare ask your mother about it. She would only tell you that you had not heard her right, and yell at you for listening to adult conversations. But later, when you were old enough to know about abortions, you suspected.

"I am here to tell you that you were right. Your cousin was growing an *Americanito* in her belly when this movie was made. Soon after she put something long and pointy into her pretty self, thinking maybe she could get rid of the problem before breakfast and still make it to her first class at the high school. Well, *Niña*,[6] her screams could be heard downtown. Your aunt, her mamá, who had been a midwife on the Island, managed to pull the little thing out. Yes, they probably flushed it down the toilet. What else could they do with it — give it a Christian burial in a little white casket with blue bows and ribbons? Nobody wanted that baby — least of all the father, a teacher at her school with a house in West Paterson that he was filling with real children, and a wife who was a natural blonde.

"Girl, the scandal sent your uncle back to the bottle. And guess where your cousin ended up? Irony of ironies. She was sent to a village in Puerto Rico to live with a relative on her mother's side: a place so far away from civilization that you have to ride a mule to reach it. A real change in scenery. She found a man there — women like that cannot live without male company — but believe me, the men in Puerto Rico know how to put a saddle on a woman like her. *La Gringa*,[7] they call her. Ha, ha, ha. *La Gringa* is what she always wanted to be. . . ."

The old woman's mouth becomes a cavernous black hole I fall into. And as I fall, I can feel the reverberations of her laughter. I hear the echoes of her last mocking words: *La Gringa, La Gringa!* And the conga line keeps moving silently past me. There is no music in my dream for the dancers.

When Odysseus visits Hades to see the spirit of his mother, he makes 25 an offering of sacrificial blood, but since all the souls crave an audience with the living, he has to listen to many of them before he can ask questions. I, too, have to hear the dead and the forgotten speak in my dream. Those who are still part of my life remain silent, going around and around in their dance. The others keep pressing their faces forward to say things about the past.

[6]*Niña:* Girl. — COFER'S NOTE.
[7]*La Gringa:* Derogatory epithet used here to ridicule a Puerto Rican girl who wants to look like a blonde North American. — COFER'S NOTE.

My father's uncle is last in line. He is dying of alcoholism, shrunken and shriveled like a monkey, his face a mass of wrinkles and broken arteries. As he comes closer I realize that in his features I can see my whole family. If you were to stretch that rubbery flesh, you could find my father's face, and deep within *that* face — my own. I don't want to look into those eyes ringed in purple. In a few years he will retreat into silence, and take a long, long time to die. *Move back, Tio,* I tell him. *I don't want to hear what you have to say. Give the dancers room to move. Soon it will be midnight. Who is the New Year's Fool this time?*

The Reader's Presence

1. "Silent Dancing" explores the personal, familial, and communal transformations that resulted from moving in the 1950s to Paterson, New Jersey — to "a huge tenement that had once housed Jewish families," and to a new community that emerged from the sprawling barrio that Puerto Ricans "overflowing from New York City" called home. Reread the essay carefully, and summarize the transformations that occurred in the life of the narrator, her family, and their larger Puerto Rican community.

2. Cofer uses an account of a home movie to create a structure for her essay. Comment on the specific advantages and disadvantages of this strategy. How, for example, does the home movie serve as "a great visual aid" to recounting life in the barrio of Paterson, New Jersey? What effect does the fact that the home movie is in color have on what she notices? on how she writes?

3. Because Cofer's essay is built around the occasion of watching a home movie, the narrator assumes the position of an observer of the scenes and people she describes. What specific strategies as a writer does Cofer use to establish a presence for herself in this narrative and descriptive account of growing up?

14 _____

Bernard Cooper

A Clack of Tiny Sparks:
Remembrances of a Gay Boyhood

*Born (1951), raised, and still residing in Los Angeles, Bernard Cooper re-
ceived his B.F.A. and M.F.A. from the California Institute of the Arts. He has
taught at the Otis/Parsons Institute of Art and Design and Southern California
Institute of Architecture, Los Angeles, and at the UCLA writing program and
now teaches at Antioch/Los Angeles. His collection of essays,* Maps to Anywhere
*(1990), covers a wide range of topics as varying as the aging of his father, the ex-
tinction of the dinosaur, and the future of American life and culture. Cooper contributes to various periodicals such as* Harper's, *where "A Clack of Tiny Sparks:
Remembrances of a Gay Boyhood" first appeared in January 1991. He is currently working on a new collection of short stories,* Guess Again.*
   Commenting on his 1993 novel,* A Year of Rhymes, *Cooper notes, "One of
the reasons why there is so much detail in my work is that I'm a person that essentially shies away from abstractions, from Large Issues and Big Ideas. The
world only seems real and vivid and meaningful to me in the smaller details,
what's heard and felt and smelled and tasted."*

Theresa Sanchez sat behind me in ninth-grade algebra. When Mr.
Hubbley faced the blackboard, I'd turn around to see what she was reading; each week a new book was wedged inside her copy of *Today's Equations*. The deception worked; from Mr. Hubbley's point of view, Theresa
was engrossed in the value of X, but I knew otherwise. One week she pe-
rused *The Wisdom of the Orient*, and I could tell from Theresa's contemplative expression that the book contained exotic thoughts, guidelines
handed down from high. Another week it was a paperback novel whose
title, *Let Me Live My Life*, appeared in bold print atop every page, and
whose cover, a gauzy photograph of a woman biting a strand of pearls,
head thrown back in an attitude of ecstasy, confirmed my suspicion that
Theresa Sanchez was mature beyond her years. She was the tallest girl in
school. Her bouffant hairdo, streaked with blond, was higher than the
flaccid bouffants of other girls. Her smooth skin, plucked eyebrows, and

painted fingernails suggested hours of pampering, a worldly and sensual vanity that placed her within the domain of adults. Smiling dimly, steeped in daydreams, Theresa moved through the crowded halls with a languid, self-satisfied indifference to those around her. "You are merely children," her posture seemed to say. "I can't be bothered." The week Theresa hid *101 Ways to Cook Hamburger* behind her algebra book, I could stand it no longer and, after the bell rang, ventured a question.

"Because I'm having a dinner party," said Theresa. "Just a couple of intimate friends."

No fourteen-year-old I knew had ever given a dinner party, let alone used the word "intimate" in conversation. "Don't you have a mother?" I asked.

Theresa sighed a weary sigh, suffered my strange inquiry. "Don't be so naive," she said. "Everyone has a mother." She waved her hand to indicate the brick school buildings outside the window. "A higher education should have taught you that." Theresa draped an angora sweater over her shoulders, scooped her books from the graffiti-covered desk, and just as she was about to walk away, she turned and asked me, "Are you a fag?"

There wasn't the slightest hint of rancor or condescension in her   5
voice. The tone was direct, casual. Still I was stunned, giving a sidelong glance to make sure no one had heard. "No," I said. Blurted really, with too much defensiveness, too much transparent fear in my response. Octaves lower than usual, I tried a "Why?"

Theresa shrugged. "Oh, I don't know. I have lots of friends who are fags. You remind me of them." Seeing me bristle, Theresa added, "It was just a guess." I watched her erect, angora back as she sauntered out the classroom door.

She had made an incisive and timely guess. Only days before, I'd invited Grady Rogers to my house after school to go swimming. The instant Grady shot from the pool, shaking water from his orange hair, freckled shoulders shining, my attraction to members of my own sex became a matter I could no longer suppress or rationalize. Sturdy and boisterous and gap-toothed, Grady was an inveterate backslapper, a formidable arm wrestler, a wizard at basketball. Grady was a boy at home in his body.

My body was a marvel I hadn't gotten used to; my arms and legs would sometimes act of their own accord, knocking over a glass at dinner or flinching at an oncoming pitch. I was never singled out as a sissy, but I could have been just as easily as Bobby Keagan, a gentle, intelligent, and introverted boy reviled by my classmates. And although I had always been aware of a tacit rapport with Bobby, a suspicion that I might find with him a rich friendship, I stayed away. Instead, I emulated Grady in the belief that being seen with him, being like him, would somehow vanquish my self-doubt, would make me normal by association.

Apart from his athletic prowess, Grady had been gifted with all the trappings of what I imagined to be a charmed life: a fastidious, aproned mother who radiated calm, maternal concern; a ruddy, stoic father with a knack for home repairs. Even the Rogerses' small suburban house in Hollywood, with its spindly Colonial furniture and chintz curtains, was a testament to normalcy.

Grady and his family bore little resemblance to my clan of Eastern European Jews, a dark and vociferous people who ate with abandon — matzo and halvah and gefilte fish; foods the goyim couldn't pronounce — who cajoled one another during endless games of canasta, making the simplest remark about the weather into a lengthy philosophical discourse on the sun and the seasons and the passage of time. My mother was a chain-smoker, a dervish in a frowsy housedress. She showed her love in the most peculiar and obsessive ways, like spending hours extracting every seed from a watermelon before she served it in perfectly bite-sized, geometric pieces. Preoccupied and perpetually frantic, my mother succumbed to bouts of absentmindedness so profound she'd forget what she was saying midsentence, smile and blush and walk away. A divorce attorney, my father wore roomy, iridescent suits, and the intricacies, the deceits inherent in his profession, had the effect of making him forever tense and vigilant. He was "all wound up," as my mother put it. But when he relaxed, his laughter was explosive, his disposition prankish: "Walk this way," a waitress would say, leading us to our table, and my father would mimic the way she walked, arms akimbo, hips liquid, while my mother and I were wracked with laughter. Buoyant or brooding, my parents' moods were unpredictable, and in a household fraught with extravagant emotion it was odd and awful to keep my longing secret.

One day I made the mistake of asking my mother what a "fag" was. I knew exactly what Theresa had meant but hoped against hope it was not what I thought; maybe "fag" was some French word, a harmless term like "naive." My mother turned from the stove, flew at me, and grabbed me by the shoulders. "Did someone call you that?" she cried.

"Not me," I said. "Bobby Keagan."

"Oh," she said, loosening her grip. She was visibly relieved. And didn't answer. The answer was unthinkable.

For weeks after, I shook with the reverberations from that afternoon in the kitchen with my mother, pained by the memory of her shocked expression and, most of all, her silence. My longing was wrong in the eyes of my mother, whose hazel eyes were the eyes of the world, and if that longing continued unchecked, the unwieldy shape of my fate would be cast, and I'd be subjected to a lifetime of scorn.

During the remainder of the semester, I became the scientist of my own desire, plotting ways to change my yearning for boys into a yearning for girls. I had enough evidence to believe that any habit, regardless of how compulsive, how deeply ingrained, could be broken once and for all: The plastic cigarette my mother purchased at the Thrifty pharmacy — one end was red to approximate an ember, the other tan like a filtered tip —

10

15

was designed to wean her from the real thing. To change a behavior required self-analysis, cold resolve, and the substitution of one thing for another: plastic, say, for tobacco. Could I also find a substitute for Grady? What I needed to do, I figured, was kiss a girl and learn to like it.

This conclusion was affirmed one Sunday morning when my father, seeing me wrinkle my nose at the pink slabs of lox he layered on a bagel, tried to convince me of its salty appeal. "You should try some," he said. "You don't know what you're missing."

"It's loaded with protein," added my mother, slapping a platter of sliced onions onto the dinette table. She hovered above us, cinching her housedress, eyes wet from onion fumes, the mock cigarette dangling from her lips.

My father sat there chomping with gusto, emitting a couple of hearty grunts to dramatize his satisfaction. And still I was not convinced. After a loud and labored swallow, he told me I may not be fond of lox today, but sooner or later I'd learn to like it. One's tastes, he assured me, are destined to change.

"Live," shouted my mother over the rumble of the Mixmaster. "Expand your horizons. Try new things." And the room grew fragrant with the batter of a spice cake.

The opportunity to put their advice into practice, and try out my plan   20
to adapt to girls, came the following week when Debbie Coburn, a member of Mr. Hubbley's algebra class, invited me to a party. She cornered me in the hall, furtive as a spy, telling me her parents would be gone for the evening and slipping into my palm a wrinkled sheet of notebook paper. On it were her address and telephone number, the lavender ink in a tidy cursive. "Wear cologne," she advised, wary eyes darting back and forth. "It's a make-out party. Anything can happen."

The Santa Ana wind blew relentlessly the night of Debbie's party, careening down the slopes of the Hollywood hills, shaking the road signs and stoplights in its path. As I walked down Beachwood Avenue, trees thrashed, surrendered their leaves, and carob pods bombarded the pavement. The sky was a deep but luminous blue, the air hot, abrasive, electric. I had to squint in order to check the number of the Coburns' apartment, a three-story building with glitter embedded in its stucco walls. Above the honeycombed balconies was a sign that read BEACHWOOD TERRACE in lavender script resembling Debbie's.

From down the hall, I could hear the plaintive strains of Little Anthony's "I Think I'm Going Out of My Head." Debbie answered the door bedecked in an Empire dress, the bodice blue and orange polka dots, the rest a sheath of black and white stripes. "Op art," proclaimed Debbie. She turned in a circle, then proudly announced that she'd rolled her hair in orange juice cans. She patted the huge unmoving curls and dragged me inside. Reflections from the swimming pool in the courtyard, its surface ruffled by wind, shuddered over the ceiling and walls. A dozen of my classmates were seated on the sofa or huddled together in corners, their whispers full of excited imminence, their bodies barely discernible in the dim light. Drapes flanking the sliding glass doors bowed out with every gust of wind, and it seemed that the room might lurch from its foundations and sail with its cargo of silhouettes into the hot October night.

Grady was the last to arrive. He tossed a six-pack of beer into Debbie's arms, barreled toward me, and slapped my back. His hair was slicked back with Vitalis, lacquered furrows left by the comb. The wind hadn't shifted a single hair. "Ya ready?" he asked, flashing the gap between his front teeth and leering into the darkened room. "You bet," I lied.

Once the beers had been passed around, Debbie provoked everyone's attention by flicking on the overhead light. "Okay," she called. "Find a partner." This was the blunt command of a hostess determined to have her guests aroused in an orderly fashion. Everyone blinked, shuffled about, and grabbed a member of the opposite sex. Sheila Garabedian landed beside me — entirely at random, though I wanted to believe she was driven by passion — her timid smile giving way to plain fear as the light went out. Nothing for a moment but the heave of the wind and the distant banter of dogs. I caught a whiff of Sheila's perfume, tangy and sweet as Hawaiian Punch. I probed her face with my own, grazing the small scallop of an ear, a velvety temple, and though Sheila's trembling made me want to stop, I persisted with my mission until I found her lips, tightly sealed as a private letter. I held my mouth over hers and gathered her shoulders closer, resigned to the possibility that, no matter how long we stood there, Sheila would be too scared to kiss me back. Still, she exhaled through her nose, and I listened to the squeak of every breath as though it were a sigh of inordinate pleasure. Diving within myself, I monitored my heartbeat and respiration, trying to will stimulation into being, and all the while an image intruded, an image of Grady erupting from our pool, rivulets of water sliding down his chest. "Change," shouted Debbie, switching on the light. Sheila thanked me, pulled away, and continued her routine of gracious terror with every boy throughout the evening. It didn't matter whom I held — Margaret Sims, Betty Vernon, Elizabeth Lee — my experiment was a failure; I continued to picture Grady's wet chest, and Debbie would bellow "change" with such fervor, it could have been my own voice, my own incessant reprimand.

Our hostess commandeered the light switch for nearly half an hour.   25 Whenever the light came on, I watched Grady pivot his head toward the newest prospect, his eyebrows arched in expectation, his neck blooming with hickeys, his hair, at last, in disarray. All that shuffling across the carpet charged everyone's arms and lips with static, and eventually, between low moans and soft osculations, I could hear the clack of tiny sparks and see them flare here and there in the dark like meager, short-lived stars.

I saw Theresa, sultry and aloof as ever, read three more books — *North American Reptiles, Bonjour Tristesse,* and *MGM: A Pictorial History* — before she vanished early in December. Rumors of her fate abounded. Debbie Coburn swore that Theresa had been "knocked up" by an older man, a traffic cop, she thought, or a grocer. Nearly quivering with relish, Debbie told me and Grady about the home for unwed mothers in the San Fernando Valley, a compound teeming with pregnant girls who had nothing to do but touch their stomachs and contemplate their mistake. Even Bobby Keagan, who took Theresa's place behind me in algebra, had a theory regarding her disappearance colored by his own wish for escape; he imagined that Theresa, disillusioned with society, booked passage to a tropical island, there to live out the rest of her days without restrictions or ridicule. "No wonder she flunked out of school," I overheard Mr. Hubbley tell a fellow teacher one afternoon. "Her head was always in a book."

Along with Theresa went my secret, or at least the dread that she might divulge it, and I felt, for a while, exempt from suspicion. I was, however, to run across Theresa one last time. It happened during a period of torrential rain that, according to reports on the six o'clock news, washed houses from the hillsides and flooded the downtown streets. The halls of Joseph Le Conte Junior High were festooned with Christmas decorations: crepe-paper garlands, wreaths studded with plastic berries, and one requisite Star of David twirling above the attendance desk. In Arts and Crafts, our teacher, Gerald (he was the only teacher who allowed us—*required* us—to call him by his first name), handed out blocks of balsa wood and instructed us to carve them into bugs. We would paint eyes and antennae with tempera and hang them on a Christmas tree he'd made the previous night. "Voilà," he crooned, unveiling his creation from a burlap sack. Before us sat a tortured scrub, a wardrobe-worth of wire hangers that were bent like branches and soldered together. Gerald credited his inspiration to a Charles Addams cartoon he's seen in which Morticia, grimly preparing for the holidays, hangs vampire bats on a withered pine. "All that red and green," said Gerald. "So predictable. So *boring*."

As I chiseled a beetle and listened to rain pummel the earth, Gerald handed me an envelope and asked me to take it to Mr. Kendrick, the drama teacher. I would have thought nothing of his request if I hadn't seen Theresa on my way down the hall. She was cleaning out her locker, blithely dropping the sum of its contents—pens and textbooks and mimeographs—into a trash can. "Have a nice life," she sang as I passed. I mustered the courage to ask her what had happened. We stood alone in the silent hall, the reflections of wreaths and garlands submerged in brown linoleum.

"I transferred to another school. They don't have grades or bells, and you get to study whatever you want." Theresa was quick to sense my incredulity. "Honest," she said. "The school is progressive." She gazed into a glass cabinet that held the trophies of track meets and intramural spelling bees. "God," she sighed, "this place is so . . . barbaric." I was still trying to decide whether or not to believe her story when she asked me where I was headed. "Dear," she said, her exclamation pooling in the silence, "that's no ordinary note, if you catch my drift." The envelope was blank and white; I looked up at Theresa, baffled. "Don't be so naive," she muttered, tossing an empty bottle of nail polish into the trash can. It struck bottom with a resolute thud. "Well," she said, closing her locker and breathing deeply, "bon voyage." Theresa swept through the double doors and in seconds her figure was obscured by rain.

As I walked toward Mr. Kendrick's room, I could feel Theresa's in-   30
sinuation burrow in. I stood for a moment and watched Mr. Kendrick through the pane in the door. He paced intently in front of the class, handsome in his shirt and tie, reading from a thick book. Chalked on the blackboard behind him was THE ODYSSEY BY HOMER. I have no recollection of how Mr. Kendrick reacted to the note, whether he accepted it with pleasure or embarrassment, slipped it into his desk drawer or the pocket of his shirt. I have scavenged that day in retrospect, trying to see Mr. Kendrick's expression, wondering if he acknowledged me in any way as his liaison. All I recall is the sight of his mime through a pane of glass, a lone man mouthing an epic, his gestures ardent in empty air.

Had I delivered a declaration of love? I was haunted by the need to know. In fantasy, a kettle shot steam, the glue released its grip, and I read the letter with impunity. But how would such a letter begin? Did the common endearments apply? This was a message between two men, a message for which I had no precedent, and when I tried to envision the contents, apart from a hasty, impassioned scrawl, my imagination faltered.

Once or twice I witnessed Gerald and Mr. Kendrick walk together into the faculty lounge or say hello at the water fountain, but there was nothing especially clandestine or flirtatious in their manner. Besides, no matter how acute my scrutiny, I wasn't sure, short of a kiss, exactly what to look for—what semaphore of gesture, what encoded word. I suspected there were signs, covert signs that would give them away, just as I'd unwittingly given myself away to Theresa.

In the school library, a *Webster's* unabridged dictionary lay on a wooden podium, and I padded toward it with apprehension; along with clues to the bond between my teachers, I risked discovering information that might incriminate me as well. I had decided to consult the dictionary during lunch period, when most of the students would be on the playground. I clutched my notebook, moving in such a way as to appear both studious and nonchalant, actually believing that, unless I took precautions, someone would see me and guess what I was up to. The closer I came to the podium, the more obvious, I thought, was my endeavor; I felt like the model of The Visible Man in our science class, my heart's undulations, my overwrought nerves legible through transparent skin. A couple of kids riffled through the card catalogue. The librarian, a skinny woman whose perpetual whisper and rubber-soled shoes caused her to drift through the room like a phantom, didn't seem to register my presence. Though I'd looked up dozens of words before, the pages felt strange beneath my fingers. *Homer* was the first word I saw. *Hominid. Homogenize.* I feigned interest and skirted other words before I found the word I was after. Under the heading HO•MO•SEX•U•AL was the terse definition: *adj. Pertaining to, characteristic of, or exhibiting homosexuality. — n. A homosexual person.* I read the definition again and again, hoping the words would yield more than they could. I shut the dictionary, swallowed hard, and, none the wiser, hurried away.

As for Gerald and Mr. Kendrick, I never discovered evidence to prove or dispute Theresa's claim. By the following summer, however, I had overheard from my peers a confounding amount about homosexuals: They wore green on Thursday, couldn't whistle, hypnotized boys with a piercing glance. To this lore, Grady added a surefire test to ferret them out.

"A test?" I said.   35

"You ask a guy to look at his fingernails, and if he looks at them like this" — Grady closed his fingers into a fist and examined his nails with manly detachment— "then he's okay. But if he does this" — he held out his hands at arm's length, splayed his fingers, and coyly cocked his head— "you'd better watch out." Once he'd completed his demonstration, Grady peeled off his shirt and plunged into our pool. I dove in after. It was early June, the sky immense, glassy, placid. My father was cooking spareribs on the barbecue, an artist with a basting brush. His apron bore the caricature of a frazzled French chef. Mother curled on a chaise lounge, plumes of smoke wafting from her nostrils. In a stupor of contentment she took another drag, closed her eyes, and arched her face toward the sun.

Grady dog-paddled through the deep end, spouting a fountain of chlorinated water. Despite shame and confusion, my longing for him hadn't diminished; it continued to thrive without air and light, like a luminous fish in the dregs of the sea. In the name of play, I swam up behind him, encircled his shoulders, astonished by his taut flesh. The two of us flailed, pretended to drown. Beneath the heavy press of water, Grady's orange hair wavered, a flame that couldn't be doused.

I've lived with a man for seven years. Some nights, when I'm half-asleep and the room is suffused with blue light, I reach out to touch the expanse of his back, and it seems as if my fingers sink into his skin, and I feel the pleasure a diver feels the instant he enters a body of water.

I have few regrets. But one is that I hadn't said to Theresa, "Of course I'm a fag." Maybe I'd have met her friends. Or become friends with her. Imagine the meals we might have concocted: hamburger Stroganoff, Swedish meatballs in a sweet translucent sauce, steaming slabs of Salisbury steak.

The Reader's Presence

1. Cooper's essay begins and ends with references to a sophisticated classmate, Theresa Sanchez. Of what importance is she to the essay? Why does Cooper like her? What information does she provide the reader?

2. Cooper's first stirrings of attraction for his friend Grady occur in a swimming pool. What importance does swimming play in Cooper's essay? How does it provide him with a cluster of images for sexual experience?

3. Why does Cooper attend the "make-out party"? What does he hope will happen? Why do you think he ends his description of the party with the observation of the "clack of tiny sparks"? Why do you think he used that image for his title?

15

Frederick Douglass

Learning to Read and Write

Born into slavery, Frederick Douglass (1817?–1895) was taken from his mother as an infant and denied any knowledge of his father's identity. He escaped to the north at the age of twenty-one and created a new identity for himself as a free man. He educated himself and went on to become one of the most eloquent orators and persuasive writers of the nineteenth century. He was a national leader in the abolition movement and, among other activities, founded and edited the North Star *and* Douglass' Monthly. *His public service included appointments as United States marshal and consul general to the Republic of Haiti. His most lasting literary accomplishment was his memoirs, which he revised several times before they were published as the* Life and Times of Frederick Douglass *(1881 and 1892). "Learning to Read and Write" is taken from these memoirs.*

Douglass overcame his initial reluctance to write his memoirs because, as he put it, "not only is slavery on trial, but unfortunately, the enslaved people are also on trial. It is alleged that they are, naturally, inferior; that they are so low in the scale of humanity, and so utterly stupid, that they are unconscious of their wrongs, and do not apprehend their rights." Therefore, wishing to put his talents to work "to the benefit of my afflicted people," Douglass agreed to write the story of his life.

I lived in Master Hugh's family about seven years. During this time, I succeeded in learning to read and write. In accomplishing this, I was compelled to resort to various stratagems. I had no regular teacher. My mistress, who had kindly commenced to instruct me, had, in compliance with the advice and direction of her husband, not only ceased to instruct, but had set her face against my being instructed by anyone else. It is due, however, to my mistress to say of her, that she did not adopt this course of treatment immediately. She at first lacked the depravity indispensable to shutting me up in mental darkness. It was at least necessary for her to have some training in the exercise of irresponsible power, to make her equal to the task of treating me as though I were a brute.

My mistress was, as I have said, a kind and tender-hearted woman; and in the simplicity of her soul she commenced, when I first went to live with her, to treat me as she supposed one human being ought to treat another. In entering upon the duties of a slaveholder, she did not seem to perceive that I sustained to her the relation of a mere chattel, and that for her to treat me as a human being was not only wrong, but dangerously so. Slavery proved as injurious to her as it did to me. When I went there, she was a pious, warm, and tender-hearted woman. There was no sorrow or suffering for which she had not a tear. She had bread for the hungry, clothes for the naked, and comfort for every mourner that came within her reach. Slavery soon proved its ability to divest her of these heavenly qualities. Under its influence, the tender heart became stone, and the lamb-like disposition gave way to one of tiger-like fierceness. The first step in her downward course was in her ceasing to instruct me. She now commenced to practice her husband's precepts. She finally became even more violent in her opposition than her husband himself. She was not satisfied with simply doing as well as he had commanded; she seemed anxious to do better. Nothing seemed to make her more angry than to see me with a newspaper. She seemed to think that here lay the danger. I have had her rush at me with a face made all up of fury, and snatch from me a newspaper, in a manner that fully revealed her apprehension. She was an apt woman; and a little experience soon demonstrated, to her satisfaction, that education and slavery were incompatible with each other.

From this time I was most narrowly watched. If I was in a separate room any considerable length of time, I was sure to be suspected of having a book, and was at once called to give an account of myself. All this, however, was too late. The first step had been taken. Mistress, in teaching me the alphabet, had given me the *inch,* and no precaution could prevent me from taking the *ell.*

The plan which I adopted, and the one by which I was most successful, was that of making friends of all the little white boys whom I met in the street. As many of these as I could, I converted into teachers. With their kindly aid, obtained at different times and in different places, I finally succeeded in learning to read. When I was sent to errands, I always took my book with me, and by doing one part of my errand quickly, I found time to get a lesson before my return. I used also to carry bread with me, enough of which was always in the house, and to which I was always welcome; for I was much better off in this regard than many of the poor white children in our neighborhood. This bread I used to bestow upon the hungry little urchins, who, in return, would give me that more valuable bread of knowledge. I am strongly tempted to give the names of two or three of those little boys, as a testimonial of the gratitude and affection I bear them; but prudence forbids—not that it would injure me, but it might embarrass them; for it is almost an unpardonable offense to teach slaves to read in this Christian country. It is enough to say of the dear little fellows, that they lived on Philpot Street, very near Durgin and Bailey's ship-yard. I used to talk this matter of slavery over with them. I would sometimes say to them, I wished I could be as free as they would be when they got to be men. "You will be free as soon as you are twenty-one, *but I am a slave for life!* Have not I as good a right to be free as you have?" These words used to trouble them; they would express for me the liveliest sympathy, and console me with the hope that something would occur by which I might be free.

I was now about twelve-years-old, and the thought of being *a slave*   5
for life began to bear heavily upon my heart. Just about this time, I got hold of a book entitled "The Columbian Orator." Every opportunity I got, I used to read this book. Among much of other interesting matter, I found in it a dialogue between a master and his slave. The slave was represented as having run away from his master three times. The dialogue represented the conversation which took place between them, when the slave was retaken the third time. In this dialogue, the whole argument in behalf of slavery was brought forward by the master, all of which was disposed of by the slave. The slave was made to say some very smart as well as impressive things in reply to his master—things which had the desired though unexpected effect; for the conversation resulted in the voluntary emancipation of the slave on the part of the master.

In the same book, I met with one of Sheridan's[1] mighty speeches on and in behalf of Catholic emancipation. These were choice documents to me. I read them over and over again with unabated interest. They gave tongue to interesting thoughts of my own soul, which had frequently flashed through my mind, and died away for want of utterance. The moral which I gained from the dialogue was the power of truth over the conscience of even a slaveholder. What I got from Sheridan was a bold denunciation of slavery, and a powerful vindication of human rights. The reading of these documents enabled me to utter my thoughts, and to meet the arguments brought forward to sustain slavery; but while they relieved me of one difficulty, they brought on another even more painful than the one of which I was relieved. The more I read, the more I was led to abhor and detest my enslavers. I could regard them in no other light than a band of successful robbers, who had left their homes, and gone to Africa, and stolen us from our homes, and in a strange land reduced us to slavery. I loathed them as being the meanest as well as the most wicked of men. As I read and contemplated the subject, behold! that very discontentment which Master Hugh had predicted would follow my learning to read had already come, to torment and sting my soul to unutterable anguish. As I

[1]*Sheridan's:* Richard Brinsley Butler Sheridan (1751–1816), Irish dramatist and orator.—EDS.

writhed under it, I would at times feel that learning to read had been a curse rather than a blessing. It had given me a view of my wretched condition, without the remedy. It opened my eyes to the horrible pit, but to no ladder upon which to get out. In moments of agony, I envied my fellow-slaves for their stupidity. I have often wished myself a beast. I preferred the condition of the meanest reptile to my own. Anything, no matter what, to get rid of thinking! It was this everlasting thinking of my condition that tormented me. There was no getting rid of it. It was pressed upon me by every object within sight or hearing, animate or inanimate. The silver trump of freedom had roused my soul to eternal wakefulness. Freedom now appeared, to disappear no more forever. It was heard in every sound, and seen in every thing. It was ever present to torment me with a sense of my wretched condition. I saw nothing without seeing it, I heard nothing without hearing it, and felt nothing without feeling it. It looked from every star, it smiled in every calm, breathed in every wind, and moved in every storm.

I often found myself regretting my own existence, and wishing myself dead; and but for the hope of being free, I have no doubt but that I should have killed myself, or done something for which I should have been killed. While in this state of mind, I was eager to hear anyone speak of slavery. I was a ready listener. Every little while, I could hear something about the abolitionists. It was some time before I found what the word meant. It was always used in such connections as to make it an interesting word to me. If a slave ran away and succeeded in getting clear, or if a slave killed his master, set fire to a barn, or did anything very wrong in the mind of a slaveholder, it was spoken of as the fruit of *abolition*. Hearing the word in this connection very often, I set about learning what it meant. The dictionary afforded me little or no help. I found it was "the act of abolishing"; but then I did not know what was to be abolished. Here I was perplexed. I did not dare to ask anyone about its meaning, for I was satisfied that it was something they wanted me to know very little about. After a patient waiting, I got one of our city papers, containing an account of the number of petitions from the North, praying for the abolition of slavery in the District of Columbia, and of the slave trade between the States. From this time I understood the words *abolition* and *abolitionist,* and always drew near when that word was spoken, expecting to hear something of importance to myself and fellow-slaves. The light broke in upon me by degrees. I went one day down on the wharf of Mr. Waters; and seeing two Irishmen unloading a scow of stone, I went, unasked, and helped them. When we had finished, one of them came to me and asked me if I were a slave. I told him I was. He asked, "Are ye a slave for life?" I told him that I was. The good Irishman seemed to be deeply affected by the statement. He said to the other that it was a pity so fine a little fellow as myself should be a slave for life. He said it was a shame to hold me. They both advised me to run away to the North; that I should find friends there, and that I should be free. I pretended not to be interested in what they said, and treated them as if I did not understand them; for I feared they might be treacherous. White men have been known to encourage slaves to escape, and then, to get the reward, catch them and return them to their masters. I was afraid that these seemingly good men might use me so; but I nevertheless remembered their advice, and from that time I resolved to run away. I looked forward to a time at which it would be safe for me to escape. I was too young to think of doing so immediately; besides, I wished to learn how to write, as I might have occasion to write my own pass. I consoled myself with the hope that I should one day find a good chance. Meanwhile, I would learn to write.

The idea as to how I might learn to write was suggested to me by being in Durgin and Bailey's ship-yard, and frequently seeing the ship carpenters, after hewing, and getting a piece of timber ready for use, write on the timber the name of that part of the ship for which it was intended. When a piece of timber was intended for the larboard side, it would be marked thus—"L." When a piece was for the starboard side, it would be marked thus—"S." A piece for the larboard side forward, would be marked thus—"L.F." When a piece was for starboard side forward, it would be marked thus—"S.F." For larboard aft, it would be marked thus—"L.A." For starboard aft, it would be marked thus—"S.A." I soon learned the names of these letters, and for what they were intended when placed upon a piece of timber in the shipyard. I immediately commenced copying them, and in a short time was able to make the four letters named. After that, when I met with any boy who I knew could write, I would tell him I could write as well as he. The next word would be, "I don't believe you. Let me see you try it." I would then make the letters which I had been so fortunate as to learn, and ask him to beat that. In this way I got a good many lessons in writing, which it is quite possible I should never have gotten in any other way. During this time, my copy-book was the board fence, brick wall, and pavement; my pen and ink was a lump of chalk. With these, I learned mainly how to write. I then commenced and continued copying the Italics in *Webster's Spelling Book,* until I could make them all without looking in the book. By this time, my little Master Thomas had gone to school, and learned how to write, and had written over a number of copy-books. These had been brought home, and shown to some of our near neighbors, and then laid aside. My mistress used to go to class meeting at the Wilk Street meeting-house every Monday afternoon, and leave me to take care of the house. When left thus, I used to spend the time in writing in the spaces left in master Thomas's copy-book, copying what he had written. I continued to do this until I could write a hand very similar to that of Master Thomas. Thus, after a long, tedious effort for years, I finally succeeded in learning how to write.

The Reader's Presence

1. What sort of audience does Douglass anticipate for his reminiscence? How much does he assume his readers know about the conditions of slavery?

2. What kind of book seems to interest Douglass the most? What lessons does he learn from his reading? Why does he say that learning to read was more of a curse than a blessing? In general, what are his motives for wanting to read and write?

3. Notice that Douglass learns to read *before* he learns to write. Is that the way you learned? What other ways are possible? What method seems best to you? While rereading the essay, try making a chart of Douglass's educational progress. Having already learned to read, why does he need the letters used by ship carpenters in order to learn how to write?

16

Nora Ephron

A Few Words about Breasts

Nora Ephron (b. 1941) started her writing career as a reporter for the New York Post, *and since then has written for numerous magazines, including* New York, McCall's, *and* Cosmopolitan. *Ephron has published four collections of essays on popular culture, including* Crazy Salad *(1975), from which the essay "A Few Words about Breasts" is taken. She also wrote the screenplays for* Silkwood *(with Alice Arlen),* When Harry Met Sally, *and* Sleepless in Seattle. *In 1992 she directed her first movie,* This Is My Life, *written with her sister Delia Ephron; since then she has directed the films* Michael *(1996) and* You've Got Mail *(1998). Her most recent books are* Heartburn *(1983), and* Nora Ephron Collected *(1991).*

Ephron relies heavily on events from her own life to inspire her writing. She told an interviewer, "I've always written about my life. That's how I grew up. 'Take notes. Everything is copy.' All that stuff my mother said to us." As you read the essay that follows, notice the way that Ephron draws on her personal experience.

I have to begin with a few words about androgyny. In grammar school, in the fifth and sixth grades, we were all tyrannized by a rigid set of rules that supposedly determined whether we were boys or girls. The episode in *Huckleberry Finn* where Huck is disguised as a girl and gives himself away by the way he threads a needle and catches a ball — that kind of thing. We learned that the way you sat, crossed your legs, held a cigarette, and looked at your nails — the way you did these things instinctively was absolute proof of your sex. Now obviously most children did not take this literally, but I did. I thought that just one slip, just one incorrect cross of my legs or flick of an imaginary cigarette ash would turn me from whatever I was into the other thing; that would be all it took, really. Even though I was outwardly a girl and had many of the trappings generally associated with girldom — a girl's name, for example, and dresses, my own telephone, an autograph book — I spent the early years of my adolescence absolutely certain that I might at any point gum it up. I did not feel at all like a girl. I was boyish. I was athletic, ambitious, outspoken, competitive, noisy, rambunctious. I had scabs on my knees and my socks slid into my loafers and I could throw a football. I wanted desperately not to be that way, not to be a mixture of both things, but instead just one, a girl, a definite indisputable girl. As soft and as pink as a nursery. And nothing would do that for me, I felt, but breasts.

I was about six months younger than everyone else in my class, and so for about six months after it began, for six months after my friends had begun to develop (that was the word we used, develop), I was not particularly worried. I would sit in the bathtub and look down at my breasts and know that any day now, any second now, they would start growing like everyone else's. They didn't. "I want to buy a bra," I said to my mother one night. "What for?" she said. My mother was really hateful about bras, and by the time my third sister had gotten to the point where she was ready to want one, my mother had worked the whole business into a comedy routine. "Why not use a Band-Aid instead?" she would say. It was a source of great pride to my mother that she had never even had to wear a brassiere until she had her fourth child, and then only because her gynecologist made her. It was incomprehensible to me that anyone could ever be proud of something like that. It was the 1950s, for God's sake. Jane Russell. Cashmere sweaters. Couldn't my mother see that? *"I am too old to wear an undershirt."* Screaming. Weeping. Shouting. "Then don't wear an undershirt," said my mother. "But I want to buy a bra." "What for?"

I suppose that for most girls, breasts, brassieres, that entire thing, has more trauma, more to do with the coming of adolescence, with becoming a woman, than anything else. Certainly more than getting your period, although that, too, was traumatic, symbolic. But you could see breasts; they were there; they were visible. Whereas a girl could claim to have her period for months before she actually got it and nobody would ever know the difference. Which is exactly what I did. All you had to do was make a great fuss over having enough nickels for the Kotex machine and walk around clutching your stomach and moaning for three to five days a month about The Curse and you could convince anybody. There is a school of thought somewhere in the women's lib/women's mag/ gynecology establishment that claims that menstrual cramps are purely psychological, and I lean toward it. Not that I didn't have them finally. Agonizing cramps, heating-pad cramps, go-down-to-the-school-nurse-and-lie-on-the-cot cramps. But unlike any pain I had ever suffered, I adored the pain of cramps, welcomed it, wallowed in it, bragged about it. "I can't go. I have cramps." "I can't do that. I have cramps." And most of all, gigglingly, blushingly: "I can't swim. I have cramps." Nobody ever used the hard-core word. Menstruation. God, what an awful word. Never that. "I have cramps."

The morning I first got my period, I went into my mother's bedroom to tell her. And my mother, my utterly-hateful-about-bras mother, burst into tears. It was really a lovely moment, and I remember it so clearly not just because it was one of the two times I ever saw my mother cry on my account (the other was when I was caught being a six-year-old kleptomaniac), but also because the incident did not mean to me what it meant to her. Her little girl, her firstborn, had finally become a woman. That was what she was crying about. My reaction to the event, however, was that I might well be a woman in some scientific, textbook sense (and could at least stop faking every month and stop wasting all those nickels). But in another sense—in a visible sense—I was as androgynous and as liable to tip over into boyhood as ever.

I started with a 28 AA bra. I don't think they made them any smaller   5 in those days, although I gather that now you can buy bras for five-year-olds that don't have any cups whatsoever in them; trainer bras they are called. My first brassiere came from Robinson's Department Store in Beverly Hills. I went there alone, shaking, positive they would look me over and smile and tell me to come back next year. An actual fitter took me into the dressing room and stood over me while I took off my blouse and tried the first one on. The little puffs stood out on my chest. "Lean over," said the fitter. (To this day, I am not sure what fitters in bra departments do except to tell you to lean over.) I leaned over, with the fleeting hope that my breasts would miraculously fall out of my body and into the puffs. Nothing.

"Don't worry about it," said my friend Libby some months later, when things had not improved. "You'll get them after you're married."

"What are you talking about?" I said.

"When you get married," Libby explained, "your husband will touch your breasts and rub them and kiss them and they'll grow."

That was the killer. Necking I could deal with. Intercourse I could deal with. But it had never crossed by mind that a man was going to touch my breasts, that breasts had something to do with all that, petting, my God, they never mentioned petting in my little sex manual about the fertilization of the ovum. I became dizzy. For I knew instantly—as naïve as I had been only a moment before—that only part of what she was saying was true: the touching, rubbing, kissing part, not the growing part. And I knew that no one would ever want to marry me. I had no breasts. I would never have breasts.

My best friend in school was Diana Raskob. She lived a block from   10
me in a house full of wonders. English muffins, for instance. The Raskobs were the first people in Beverly Hills to have English muffins for breakfast. They also had an apricot tree in the back, and a badminton court, and a subscription to *Seventeen* magazine, and hundreds of games, like Sorry and Parcheesi and Treasure Hunt and Anagrams. Diana and I spent three or four afternoons a week in their den reading and playing and eating. Diana's mother's kitchen was full of the most colossal assortment of junk food I have ever been exposed to. My house was full of apples and peaches and milk and homemade chocolate-chip cookies—which were nice, and good for you, but-not-right-before-dinner-or-you'll-spoil-your-appetite. Diana's house had nothing in it that was good for you, and what's more, you could stuff it in right up until dinner and nobody cared. Bar-B-Q potato chips (they were the first in them, too), giant bottles of ginger ale, fresh popcorn with melted butter, hot fudge sauce on Baskin-Robbins jamoca ice cream, powdered-sugar doughnuts from Van de Kamp's. Diana and I had been best friends since we were seven; we were about equally popular in school (which is to say, not particularly), we had about the same success with boys (extremely intermittent), and we looked much the same. Dark. Tall. Gangly.

It is September, just before school begins. I am eleven years old, about to enter the seventh grade, and Diana and I have not seen each other all summer. I have been to camp and she has been somewhere like Banff with her parents. We are meeting, as we often do, on the street midway between our two houses, and we will walk back to Diana's and eat junk and talk about what has happened to each of us that summer. I am walking down Walden Drive in my jeans and my father's shirt hanging out and my old red loafers with the socks falling into them and coming toward me is . . . I take a deep breath . . . a young woman. Diana. Her hair is curled and she has a waist and hips and a bust and she is wearing a straight skirt, an article of clothing I have been repeatedly told I will be unable to wear until I have the hips to hold it up. My jaw drops, and suddenly I am crying, crying hysterically, can't catch my breath sobbing. My best friend has betrayed me. She has gone ahead without me and done it. She has shaped up.

Here are some things I did to help:
Bought a Mark Eden Bust Developer.
Slept on my back for four years.
Splashed cold water on them every night because some French ac-   15
tress said in *Life* magazine that that was what *she* did for her perfect bustline.

Ultimately, I resigned myself to a bad toss and began to wear padded bras. I think about them now, think about all those years in high school that I went around in them, my three padded bras, every single one of them with different-sized breasts. Each time I changed bras I changed sizes: one week nice perky but not too obtrusive breasts, the next medium-sized slightly pointy ones, the next week knockers, true knockers; all the time, whatever size I was, carrying around this rubberized appendage on my chest that occasionally crashed into a wall and was poked inward and had to be poked outward—I think about all that and wonder how anyone kept a straight face through it. My parents, who normally had no restraints about needling me—why did they say nothing as they watched my chest go up and down? My friends, who would periodically inspect my breasts for signs of growth and reassure me—why didn't they at least counsel consistency?

And the bathing suits. I die when I think about the bathing suits. That was the era when you could lay an uninhabited bathing suit on the beach and someone would make a pass at it. I would put one on, an absurd swimsuit with its enormous bust built into it, the bones from the suit stabbing me in the rib cage and leaving little red welts on my body, and there I would be, my chest plunging straight downward absolutely vertically from my collarbone to the top of my suit and then suddenly, wham, out came all that padding and material and wiring absolutely horizontally.

Buster Klepper was the first boy who ever touched them. He was my boyfriend my senior year of high school. There is a picture of him in my high-school yearbook that makes him look quite attractive in a Jewish, horn-rimmed-glasses sort of way, but the picture does not show the pimples, which were air-brushed out, or the dumbness. Well, that isn't really fair. He wasn't dumb. He just wasn't terribly bright. His mother refused to accept it, refused to accept the relentlessly average report cards, refused to deal with her son's inevitable destiny in some junior college or other. "He was tested," she would say to me, apropos of nothing, "and it came out a hundred and forty-five. That's near-genius." Had the word "underachiever" been coined, she probably would have lobbed that one at me, too. Anyway, Buster was really very sweet—which is, I know, damning with faint praise, but there it is. I was the editor of the front page of the high-school newspaper and he was editor of the back page; we had to work together, side by side, in the print shop, and that was how it started. On our first date, we went to see *April Love,* starring Pat Boone. Then we started going together. Buster had a green coupe, a 1950 Ford with an engine he had hand-chromed until it shone, dazzled, reflected the image of anyone who looked into it, anyone usually being Buster polishing it or the gas-station attendants he constantly asked to check the oil in order for them to be overwhelmed by the sparkle on the valves. The car also had a boot stretched over the back seat for reasons I never understood; hanging from the rearview mirror, as was the custom, was a pair of angora dice. A previous girlfriend named Solange, who was famous throughout Beverly Hills High School for having no pigment in her right eyebrow, had knitted them for him. Buster and I would ride around town, the two of us seated to the left of the steering wheel. I would shift gears. It was nice.

There was necking. Terrific necking. First in the car, overlooking Los Angeles from what is now the Trousdale Estates. Then on the bed of his parents' cabana at Ocean House. Incredibly wonderful, frustrating necking, I loved it, really, but no further than necking, please don't, please, because there I was absolutely terrified of the general implications of going-a-step-further with a near-dummy and also terrified of his finding out there was next to nothing there (which he knew, of course; he wasn't that dumb).

I broke up with him at one point. I think we were apart for about   20 two weeks. At the end of that time, I drove down to see a friend at a boarding school in Palos Verdes Estates and a disc jockey played "April Love" on the radio four times during the trip. I took it as a sign. I drove straight back to Griffith Park to a golf tournament Buster was playing in (he was the sixth-seeded teenage golf player in southern California) and presented myself back to him on the green of the eighteenth hole. It was all very dramatic. That night we went to a drive-in and I let him get his hand under my protuberances and onto my breasts. He really didn't seem to mind at all.

> "Do you want to marry my son?" the woman asked me.
> "Yes," I said.
> I was nineteen years old, a virgin, going with this woman's son, this big strange woman who was married to a Lutheran minister in New Hampshire and pretended she was gentile and had this son, by her first husband, this total fool of a son who ran the hero-sandwich concession at Harvard Business School and whom for one moment one December in New Hampshire I said — as much out of politeness as anything else — that I wanted to marry.
> "Fine," she said. "Now, here's what you do. Always make sure you're on top of him so you won't seem so small. My bust is very large, you see, so I always lie on my back to make it look smaller, but you'll have to be on top most of the time."
> I nodded. "Thank you," I said.
> "I have a book for you to read," she went on. "Take it with you when you leave. Keep it." She went to the bookshelf, found it, and gave it to me. It was a book on frigidity.
> "Thank you," I said.

That is a true story. Everything in this article is a true story, but I feel I have to point out that that story in particular is true. It happened on December 30, 1960. I think about it often. When it first happened, I naturally assumed that the woman's son, my boyfriend, was responsible. I invented a scenario where he had had a little heart-to-heart with his mother and had confessed that his only objection to me was that my breasts were small; his mother then took it upon herself to help out. Now I think I was wrong about the incident. The mother was acting on her own, I think: That was her way of being cruel and competitive under the guise of being helpful and maternal. You have small breasts, she was saying; therefore you will never make him as happy as I have. Or you have small breasts; therefore you will doubtless have sexual problems. Or you have small breasts; therefore you are less woman than I am. She was, as it happens, only the first of what seems to me to be a never-ending string of women who have made competitive remarks to me about breast size. "I would love to wear a dress like that," my friend Emily says to me, "but my bust is too big." Like that. Why do women say these things to me? Do I attract these remarks the way other women attract married men or alcoholics or homosexuals? This summer, for example. I am at a party in East Hampton and I am introduced to a woman from Washington. She is a minor celebrity, very pretty and Southern and blond and outspoken, and I am flattered because she has read something I have written. We are talking animatedly, we have been talking no more than five minutes, when a man comes up to join us. "Look at the two of us," the woman says to the man, indicating me and her. "The two of us together couldn't fill an A cup." Why does she say that? It isn't even true, dammit, so why? Is she even more addled than I am on this subject? Does she honestly believe there is something wrong with her size breasts, which, it seems to me, now that I look hard at them, are just right? Do I unconsciously bring out competitiveness in women? In that form? What did I do to deserve it?

As for men.

There were men who minded and let me know that they minded. There were men who did not mind. In any case, *I* always minded.

And even now, now that I have been countlessly reassured that my figure is a good one, now that I am grown-up enough to understand that most of my feelings have very little to do with the reality of my shape, I am nonetheless obsessed by breasts. I cannot help it. I grew up in the terrible fifties—with rigid stereotypical sex roles, the insistence that men be men and dress like men and women be women and dress like women, the intolerance of androgyny—and I cannot shake it, cannot shake my feelings of inadequacy. Well, that time is gone, right? All those exaggerated examples of breast worship are gone, right? Those women were freaks, right? I know all that. And yet here I am, stuck with the psychological remains of it all, stuck with my own peculiar version of breast worship. You probably think I am crazy to go on like this: Here I have set out to write a confession that is meant to hit you with the shock of recognition, and instead you are sitting there thinking I am thoroughly warped. Well, what can I tell you? If I had had them, I would have been a completely different person. I honestly believe that.

After I went into therapy, a process that made it possible for me to   25
tell total strangers at cocktail parties that breasts were the hang-up of my life, I was often told that I was insane to have been bothered by my condi-

tion. I was also frequently told, by close friends, that I was extremely boring on the subject. And my girlfriends, the ones with nice big breasts, would go on endlessly about how their lives had been far more miserable than mine. Their bra straps were snapped in class. They couldn't sleep on their stomachs. They were stared at whenever the word "mountain" cropped up in geography. And *Evangeline,* good God what they went through every time someone had to stand up and recite the Prologue to Longfellow's *Evangeline:* ". . . stand like druids of eld . . . / With beards that rest on their bosoms." It was much worse for them, they tell me. They had a terrible time of it, they assure me. I don't know how lucky I was, they say.

I have thought about their remarks, tried to put myself in their place, considered their point of view. I think they are full of shit.

The Reader's Presence

1. How does Ephron make small breasts a matter of identity as well as appearance? Do you agree with her? Do you think her reasons for this are well founded? Are they based only on her personal experience?

2. "That is a true story. Everything in this article is a true story, . . ." Ephron maintains in paragraph 21. Why does she feel she must say this? What attitude does she anticipate in her reader? Why might she think her readers would doubt her story? Do you?

3. In paragraph 24, Ephron addresses her readers directly: "You probably think I am crazy to go on like this: Here I have set out to write a confession that is meant to hit you with the shock of recognition, and instead you are sitting there thinking I am thoroughly warped." What are her assumptions about her readers at this point? What does she seem worried about? What is your response as a reader? How closely do you fit into the role she is assigning for her readers?

17

Louise Erdrich

Skunk Dreams

Poet, novelist, and short story writer Louise Erdrich (b. 1954) was raised near the Turtle Mountain Chippewa Reservation in North Dakota. Her mother was a Chippewa, and her German-born father taught on the reservation. Her first novel, Love Medicine *(1984), won the National Book Critics Circle Award and the American Academy and Institute of Arts and Letters award for the best first work of fiction. Her other novels are* The Beet Queen *(1986),* Tracks *(1988),* The Bingo Palace *(1994),* The Crown of Columbus *(1991), and* Tales of Burning Love *(1996). Her poetry is collected in* Jacklight *(1984) and* Baptism of Desire *(1989). Erdrich has also written children's books:* Grandmother's Pigeon *(1996) and* The Birchbark House *(1999). "Skunk Dreams" appears in her recent essay collection,* The Blue Jay's Dance *(1995). Erdrich's most recent novel is* The Antelope Wife *(1998).*

Erdrich got a very early start as a writer; she recalls the encouragement of her parents during her childhood: "My father used to give me a nickel for every story I wrote, and my mother wove strips of construction paper together and stapled them into book covers. So at an early age, I felt myself to be a published author earning substantial royalties."

When I was fourteen, I slept alone on a North Dakota football field under cold stars on an early September night. Fall progresses swiftly in the Red River Valley, and I happened to hit a night when frost formed in the grass. A skunk trailed a plume of steam across the forty-yard line near moonrise. I tucked the top of my sleeping bag over my head and was just dozing off when the skunk walked onto me with simple authority.

Its ripe odor must have dissipated in the heavy summer grass and ditch weeds, because it didn't smell all that bad, or perhaps it was just that I took shallow breaths in numb surprise. I felt him, her, whatever, pause on the side of my hip and turn around twice before evidently deciding I was a good place to sleep. At the back of my knees, on the quilting of my sleeping bag, it trod out a spot for itself and then, with a serene little groan, curled up and lay perfectly still. That made two of us. I was wildly awake, trying to forget the sharpness and number of skunk teeth, trying not to think of the high percentage of skunks with rabies, or the reason that on camping trips my father always kept a hatchet under his pillow.

Inside the bag, I felt as if I might smother. Carefully, making only the slightest of rustles, I drew the bag away from my face and took a deep breath of the night air, enriched with skunk, but clear and watery and cold. It wasn't so bad, and the skunk didn't stir at all, so I watched the moon—caught that night in an envelope of silk, a mist—pass over my sleeping field of teenage guts and glory. The grass harbored a sere dust both old and fresh. I smelled the heat of spent growth beneath the rank tone of my bag-mate—the stiff fragrance of damp earth and the thick pungency of newly manured fields a mile or two away—along with my sleeping bag's smell, slightly mildewed, forever smoky. The skunk settled even closer and began to breathe rapidly; its feet jerked a little like a dog's. I sank against the earth, and fell asleep too.

Of what easily tipped cans, what molten sludge, what dogs in yards on chains, what leftover macaroni casseroles, what cellar holes, crawl spaces, burrows taken from meek woodchucks, of what miracles of garbage did my skunk dream? Or did it, since we can't be sure, dream the plot of *Moby-Dick,* how to properly age Parmesan, or how to restore the brick-walled tumble-down creamery that was its home? We don't know about the dreams of any other biota, and even much about our own. If dreams are an actual dimension, as some assert, then the usual rules of life by which we abide do not apply. In that place, skunks may certainly dream themselves into the vests of stockbrokers. Perhaps that night the skunk and I dreamed each other's thoughts or are still dreaming them. To paraphrase the problem of the Taoist philosopher Chuang Tzu, I may be a woman who has dreamed herself a skunk, or a skunk still dreaming that she is a woman.

In a book called *Death and Consciousness,* David H. Lund—who wants very much to believe in life after death—describes human dream life as a possible model for a disembodied existence.   5

"Many of one's dreams," he says, "are such that they involve the activities of an apparently embodied person whom one takes to be oneself as long as one dreams. . . . Whatever is the source of the imagery . . . apparently has the capacity to bring about the images of a human body and to impart the feeling that the body is mine. It is, of course, just an image body, but it serves as a perfectly good body for the dream experience. I regard it as mine, I act on the dream environment by means of it, and it constitutes the center of the perpetual world of my dream."

Over the years I have acquired and reshuffled my beliefs and doubts about whether we live on after death—in any shape or form, that is, besides the molecular level at which I am to be absorbed by the taproots of cemetery elms or pines and the tangled mats of fearfully poisoned, too green lawn grass. I want something of the self on whom I have worked so hard to survive the loss of the body (which, incidentally, the self has done a fairly decent job of looking after, excepting spells of too much cabernet and a few idiotic years of rolling my own cigarettes out of Virginia Blond tobacco.) I am put out with the marvelous discoveries of the intricate bio-chemical configuration of our brains, though I realize that the processes themselves are quite miraculous. I understand that I should be self-proud, content to gee-whiz at the fact that I am the world's only mechanism that can admire itself. I should be grateful that life is here today, though gone tomorrow, but I can't help it. I want more.

Skunks don't mind each other's vile perfume. Obviously, they find each other more than tolerable. And even I, who have been in the pres-ence of a direct skunk hit, wouldn't classify their weapon as mere smell. It is more on the order of a reality-enhancing experience. It's not so pleasant as standing in a grove of old-growth cedars, or on a lyrical moonshed plain, or watching trout rise to the shadow of your hand on the placid surface of Alpine lake. When the skunk lets go, you're surrounded by skunk presence: inhabited, owned, involved with something that you can only describe as powerfully *there*.

I woke at dawn, stunned into that sprayed sense of being. The dog that had approached me was rolling in the grass, half addled, sprayed too. My skunk was gone. I abandoned my sleeping bag and started home. Up Eighth Street, past the tiny blue and pink houses, past my grade school, past all the addresses where I baby-sat, I walked in my own strange wind. The streets were wide and empty; I met no one — not a dog, not a squirrel, not even an early robin. Perhaps they had all scattered be-fore me, blocks away. I had gone out to sleep on the football field be-cause I was afflicted with a sadness I had to dramatize. Mood swings had begun, hormones, feverish and raw. They were nothing to me now. My emotions had seemed vast, dark, and sickeningly private. But they were minor, mere wisps, compared to skunk.

A SHORT PERSONAL DREAM HISTORY.
THE FENCE.

I have found that my best dreams come to me in cheap motels. One such dream about an especially haunting place occurred in a rattling room in Valley City, North Dakota. There, in the home of the Winter Show, in the old Rudolph Hotel, I was to spend a week-long residency as a poet-in-the-schools. I was supporting myself, at the time, by teaching poetry to children, convicts, rehabilitation patients, high school hoods, and recovering alcoholics. What a marvelous job it was, and what oppor-tunities I had to dream, since I paid my own lodging and lived low, some-times taking rooms for less than ten dollars a night in motels that had al-ready been closed by local health departments.

The images that assailed me in Valley City came about because the bedspread was so thin and worn — a mere brown tissuey curtain — that I had to sleep beneath my faux-fur Salvation Army coat, wearing all of my clothing, even a scarf. Cold often brings on the most spectacular of dreams, as though the brain has been incited to fevered activity. On that particular frigid night, the cold somehow seemed to snap boundaries, shift my time continuum, and perhaps even allow me to visit my own life in a future moment. After waking once, transferring the contents of my entire suitcase onto my person, and shivering to sleep again, I dreamed of a vast, dark, fenced place. The fencing was chain-link in places, chicken wire, sagging X wire, barbed wire on top, jerry-built with tipped-out poles and uncertain corners nailed to log posts and growing trees. And yet, it was quite impermeable and solid, as time-tested, broken-looking things so often are.

Behind it, trees ran for miles — large trees, grown trees, big pines the likes of which do not exist on the Great Plains. In my dream I walked up to the fence, looked within, and saw tawny, humpbacked elk move among the great trunks and slashing green arms. Suave, imponderable, magnificently dumb, they lurched and floated through the dim-complexioned air. One turned, however, before they all vanished, and from either side of that flimsy-looking barrier there passed between us a look, a communion, a long measureless regard that left me, on waking, with a sensation of penetrating sorrow.

THE WOMAN PINE. THE DREAM FENCE.

I don't think about my dream for many years, until after I move to New Hampshire. I have become civilized and sedentary since the days when I slept with skunks, and I've turned inward. Unused to walking in the woods, at first I do not even realize that trees drop branches — often large ones — or that there is any possible danger in going out on windy days, drawn by the natural drama. There is a white pine I love, a tree of the size foresters call overgrown, a waste, a thing made of long-since harvestable material. The tree is so big that three people can barely reach around it. Standing at the bottom, craning back, fingers clenched in grooves of bark, I hold on as the crown of the tree roars and beats the air a hundred feet above. The movement is frantic, the soft-needled branches long and supple, I think of a woman tossing, anchored in passion: calm one instant, full-throated the next, hair vast and dark, shedding the piercing, fresh oil of broken needles. I go to visit her often, and walk onward, farther, though it is not so far at all, and then one day I reach the fence.

Chain-link in places, chicken wire, sagging X wire, barbed wire on top, jerry-built with tipped-out poles and uncertain corners nailed to log posts and growing trees, still it seems impermeable and solid. Behind it, there are trees for miles: large trees, grown trees, big pines. I walk up to the fence, look within, and can see elk moving. Suave, imponderable, magnificently dumb, they lurch and float through the dim air.

I am on the edge of a game park, a rich man's huge wilderness, prob-   15
ably the largest parcel of protected land in western New Hampshire, certainly the largest privately owned piece I know about. At forty square miles—more than 25,000 acres—it is bigger than my mother's home reservation. And it has the oddest fence around it that I've ever seen, the longest and the tackiest. Though partially electrified, the side closest to our house is so piddling that an elk could easily toss it apart. Certainly a half-ton wild boar, the condensed and living version of a tank, could stroll right through. But then animals, much like most humans, don't charge through fences unless they have sound reasons. As I soon find out, because I naturally grow fascinated with the place, there are many more animals trying to get into the park than out, and they couldn't care less about ending up in a hunter's stew pot.

These are not wild animals, the elk—since they are grained at feeding stations, how can they be? They are not domesticated either, however, for beyond the no-hunt boundaries they flee and vanish. They are game. Since there is no sport in shooting feedlot steers, these animals—still harboring wild traits and therefore more challenging to kill—are maintained to provide blood pleasure for the members of the Blue Mountain Forest Association.

As I walk away from the fence that day, I am of two minds about the place—and I am still. Shooting animals inside fences, no matter how big the area they have to hide in, seems abominable and silly. And yet, I am glad for that wilderness. Though secretly managed and off limits to me, it is the source of flocks of evening grosbeaks and pine siskins, of wild turkeys, ravens, pileated woodpeckers, and grouse, vireo, of Eastern coyotes, oxygen-rich air, foxes, goldfinches, skunks, and bears that tunnel in and out.

I dreamed of this place in Valley City, or it dreamed me. There is an affinity here, beyond any explanation I can offer, so I don't try. I continue to visit the tracts of big trees, and on deep nights—windy nights, especially when it storms—I like to fall asleep imagining details. I see the great crowns touching, hearing the raving sound of wind and thriving, knocking cries as the blackest of ravens fling themselves across acres upon indifferent acres of tossing, old-growth pine. I fall asleep picturing how, below that dark air, taproots thrust into a deeper blankness, drinking the powerful rain.

Or is it so only in my dreams? The park, known locally as Corbin's Park, after its founder Austin Corbin, is knit together of land and farmsteads he bought in the late nineteenth century from 275 individuals. Among the first animals released there, before the place became a hunting club, were thirty buffalo, remnants of the vast western herds. Their presence piqued the interest of Ernest Harold Bayne, a conservation-minded local journalist, who attempted to break a pair of buffalo calves to the yoke. He exhibited them at county fairs and even knit mittens out of buffalo wool, hoping to persuade the skeptical of their usefulness. His work inspired sympathy, if not a trend for buffalo yarn, and collective zeal for the salvation of the buffalo grew so that by 1915 the American Bison Society, of which Bayne was secretary, had helped form government reserves that eventually more than doubled the herd that remained.

The buffalo dream seems to have been the park's most noble hour.   20
Since that time it has been the haunt of wealthy hunting enthusiasts. The owner of Ruger Arms currently inhabits the stunning, butter yellow original Corbin mansion and would like to buy the whole park for his exclusive use, or so local gossip has it.

OBSTACLES AND DESIRE

For some months I walk the boundary admiring the tangled landscape, at least all that I, or baby and I, can see. She comes with me most days in her blue backpack with the aluminum frame. The walking lulls her. I feel her head settle on my back, her weight go from lively to inert. After my first apprehension and discovery, I ignore the fence. I walk along it as if it simply does not exist, as if I really am part of that place just beyond my reach. The British psychotherapist Adam Phillips has examined obstacles from several different angles, attempting to define their emotional use. "It is impossible to imagine desire without obstacles," he writes, "and wherever we find something to be an obstacle we are at the same time desiring something. It is part of the fascination of the Oedipus story in particular, and perhaps narrative in general, that we and the heroes and heroines of our fiction never know whether obstacles create desire or desire creates obstacles." He goes on to characterize the unconscious, our dream world, as a place without obstacles: "A good question to ask of a dream is: What are the obstacles that have been removed to make this extraordinary scene possible?"

My current dream, however, is about obstacles still in place. The fence is the main component, the defining characteristic of the forbidden territory that I watch but cannot enter or experience. The obstacles that we overcome define us. We are composed of hurdles we set up to pace our headlong needs, to control our desires, or against which to measure our growth. "Without obstacles," Phillips writes, "the notion of development is inconceivable. There would be nothing to master."

Walking along the boundary of the park no longer satisfies me. The preciousness and deceptive stability of that fence begins to rankle. Longing fills me. I want to brush against the old pine bark and pass beyond the ridge, to see specifically what is there: what blue mountain, what empty views, what lavender hillside, what old cellar holes, what unlikely animals. I am filled with poacher's lust, except I want only to smell the air. The linked web restraining me begins to grate, and I start to look for weak spots, holes, places where the rough wire sags. From the moment I begin to see the fence as permeable, it is no longer a fence. I return time after time — partly to see if I can spot anyone on the other side, partly because I know I must trespass.

Then, one clear morning, while Michael is taking care of our baby, I walk alone. I travel along the fence until I come to a place that looks shaky — and is. I go through. There are no trails that I can see, and I know I need to stay away from any perimeter roads or snowmobile paths, as well as from the feeding stations where the animals congregate. I want to see the animals, but only from a distance. Of course, as I walk on, leaving a trail easily backtracked, I encounter no animals at all. Still, the terrain is beautiful, the columns of pine tall, virgin, and second growth, the patches of oak and elderly maple from an occasional farmstead knotted and patient. I am satisfied and I decide to turn back and head toward the fence again. Skirting a low, boggy area that teems with wild turkey tracks, heading toward the edge of a deadfall of trashed branches and brush, I stare too hard into the sun, and stumble.

In a half crouch, I look straight into the face of a boar, massive as a   25
boulder. Corn-fed, razor-tusked, alert, sensitive ears pricked, it edges slightly backward into the convening shadows. Two ice picks of light gleam from its shrouded, tiny eyes, impossible to read. Beyond the rock of its shoulder, I see more: a sow and three well-grown cinnamon brown farrows crossing a small field lit by dazzling sun. The young skitter along, lumps of muscled fat on tiny hooves. They remind me of snowsuited toddlers on new skates. When they are out of sight the boar melts through the brush after them, leaving not a snapped twig or crushed leaf in his wake.

I almost don't breathe in the silence, letting the fact of that presence settle before I retrace my own tracks.

Next time, I go to the game park via front gates, driven by a friend down the avenues of tough old trees. I see herds of wild pigs and elk meandering past the residence of the gamekeeper. A no-hunting zone exists around the house, where the animals are almost tame. But I've been told by privileged hunters that just beyond that invisible boundary they vanish, becoming suddenly and preternaturally elusive.

So what is wild? What is wilderness? What are dreams but an internal wilderness and what is desire but a wilderness of the soul?

There is something in me that resists the notion of fair use of this land if the only alternative is to have it cut up, sold off in lots, condominiumized. I like to have it *there*. Yet the dumb fervor of the place depresses me — the wilderness locked up and managed but not for its sake, the animals imported and cultivated to give pleasure through their deaths. All animals, that is, except for skunks.

Not worth hunting, inedible except to old trappers like my uncle Ben 30 Gourneau, who boiled his skunk with onions and three changes of water, skunks pass in and out of Corbin's Park without hindrance, without concern. They live off the corn in the feeding cribs (or the mice it draws), off the garbage of my rural neighbors, off bugs and frogs and grubs. They nudge their way onto our back porch for cat food, and even when disturbed they do not, ever, hurry. It's easy to get near a skunk, even to capture one. When skunks become a nuisance, people either shoot them or catch them in crates, cardboard boxes, Havahart traps, plastic garbage barrels.

Natives of the upper Connecticut River Valley have neatly solved the problem of what to do with such catches. They hoist their trapped mustelid into the back of a pickup truck and cart the animal across the river to the neighboring state — New Hampshire to Vermont, Vermont to New Hampshire — before releasing it. The skunk population is estimated as about even on both sides.

If I were an animal, I'd choose to be a skunk: live fearlessly, eat anything, gestate my young in just two months, and fall into a state of dreaming torpor when the cold bit hard. Wherever I went, I'd leave my sloppy tracks. I wouldn't walk so much as putter, destinationless, in a serene belligerence — past hunters, past death overhead, past death all around.

The Reader's Presence

1. Although Erdrich bases most of her observations on personal experience, she also quotes two authors on the subject of dreams. What effect does Erdrich's citation of external sources have? Does it make you trust her authority more or less?

2. Erdrich describes a dream she had about a fence during one freezing night in a North Dakota motel. Several pages later she repeats the same passage, this time as a description of an actual place in New Hampshire. What do you think Erdrich is saying about the connection between dreams and reality?

3. One of the key images in the essay is that of a "boundary." Why is this image important to Erdrich? In what ways are boundaries related to the processes of her thinking and writing?

18

Henry Louis Gates Jr.

In the Kitchen

The critic, educator, writer, and activist Henry Louis Gates Jr. (b. 1950) is perhaps the most recent in a long line of African American intellectuals who are also public figures. In 1979 he became the first African American to earn a Ph.D. from Cambridge University in its eight-hundred-year history. He has been the recipient of countless honors, including a Carnegie Foundation Fellowship, a Mellon Fellowship, a MacArthur "genius" grant for his work in literary theory, and the 1998 National Medal for the Humanities. Gates is currently the W. E. B. Du Bois Professor of the Humanities at Harvard University, where he also chairs the department of Afro-American Studies. He has been at the forefront of the movement to expand the literary canon that is studied in American schools to include the works of non-European authors. He is also known for his work as a "literary archaeologist," uncovering literally thousands of previously unknown stories, poems, and reviews written by African American authors between 1829 and 1940, and making those texts available to modern readers. Much of his writing, in particular for publications such as the New York Times, Newsweek, *and* Sports Illustrated, *is accessible to general audiences. His testimony on behalf of the rap group 2 Live Crew helped earn them an acquittal in their trial for obscenity, because he was able to bring his understanding of the history of black culture—specifically the language game known as "signifying"—to bear on their contemporary lyrics.*

Gates's publications include Figures in Black: Words, Signs, and the "Racial" Self *(1987),* The Signifying Monkey: A Theory of African-American Literary Criticism *(1988),* Loose Canons: Notes on the Culture Wars *(1992), and* Colored People: A Memoir *(1994), from which "In the Kitchen" is taken. About this book, Gates says, "I'm trying to recollect a lost era, what I can call a sepia time, a whole world that simply no longer exists." His most recent book is* Wonders of the African World *(1999).*

We always had a gas stove in the kitchen, though electric cooking became fashionable in Piedmont, like using Crest toothpaste rather than Colgate, or watching Huntley and Brinkley rather than Walter Cronkite. But for us it was gas, Colgate, and good ole Walter Cronkite, come what may. We used gas partly out of loyalty to Big Mom, Mama's mama, because she was mostly blind and still loved to cook, and she could feel her way better with gas than with electric.

But the most important thing about our gas-equipped kitchen was that Mama used to do hair there. She had a "hot comb" — a fine-tooth iron instrument with a long wooden handle — and a pair of iron curlers that opened and closed like scissors: Mama would put them into the gas fire until they glowed. You could smell those prongs heating up.

I liked what that smell meant for the shape of my day. There was an intimate warmth in the women's tones as they talked with my mama while she did their hair. I knew what the women had been through to get their hair ready to be "done," because I would watch Mama do it herself. How that scorched kink could be transformed though grease and fire into a magnificent head of wavy hair was a miracle to me. Still is.

Mama would wash her hair over the sink, a towel wrapped round her shoulders, wearing just her half-slip and her white bra. (We had no shower until we moved down Rat Tail Road into Doc Wolverton's house, in 1954.) After she had dried it, she would grease her scalp thoroughly with blue Bergamot hair grease, which came in a short, fat jar with a picture of a beautiful colored lady on it. It's important to grease your scalp real good, my mama would explain, to keep from burning yourself.

Of course, her hair would return to its natural kink almost as soon as   5
the hot water and shampoo hit it. To me, it was another miracle how hair so "straight" would so quickly become kinky again once it even approached some water.

My mama had only a "few" clients whose heads she "did" — and did, I think, because she enjoyed it, rather than for the few dollars it brought in. They would sit on one of our red plastic kitchen chairs, the kind with the shiny metal legs, and brace themselves for the process. Mama would stroke that red-hot iron, which by this time had been in the gas fire for a half hour or more, slowly but firmly through their hair, from scalp to strand's end. It made a scorching, crinkly sound, the hot iron did, as it burned its way though the damp kink, leaving in its wake the straightest of hair strands, each of them standing up long and tall but drooping at the end, like the top of a heavy willow tree. Slowly, steadily, with deftness and grace, Mama's hands would transform a round mound of Odetta kink[1] into a darkened swamp of everglades. The Bergamot made the hair shiny; the heat of the hot iron gave it a brownish-red cast. Once all the hair was as straight as God allows kink to get, Mama would take the well-heated curling iron and twirl the straightened strands into more or less loosely wrapped curls. She claimed that she owed her strength and skill as a hairdresser to her wrists, and her little finger would poke out the way it did when she sipped tea. Mama was a southpaw,

---

[1] *Odetta kink:* A reference to Odetta Holmes Felious Gorden, a popular African American folk singer of the 1960s who helped popularize the hairstyle known as the "afro." — EDS.

who wrote upside down and backwards to produce the cleanest, roundest letters you've ever seen.

The "kitchen" she would all but remove from sight with a pair of shears bought for this purpose. Now, the *kitchen* was the room in which we were sitting, the room where Mama did hair and washed clothes, and where each of us bathed in a galvanized tub. But the word has another meaning, and the "kitchen" I'm speaking of now is the very kinky bit of hair at the back of the head, where our neck meets the shirt collar. If there ever was one part of our African past that resisted assimilation, it was the kitchen. No matter how hot the iron, no matter how powerful the chemical, no matter how stringent the mashed-potatoes-and-lye formula of a man's "process," neither God nor woman nor Sammy Davis, Jr., could straighten the kitchen. The kitchen was permanent, irredeemable, invincible kink. Unassimilably African. No matter what you did, no matter how hard you tried, nothing could dekink a person's kitchen. So you trimmed it off as best you could.

When hair had begun to "turn," as they'd say, or return to its natural kinky glory, it was the kitchen that turned first. When the kitchen started creeping up the back of the neck, it was time to get your hair done again. The kitchen around the back, and nappy edges at the temples.

Sometimes, after dark, Mr. Charlie Carroll would come to have his hair done. Mr. Charlie Carroll was very light-complected and had a ruddy nose, the kind of nose that made me think of Edmund Gwenn playing Kris Kringle in *Miracle on 34th Street*. At the beginning, they did it after Rocky and I had gone to sleep. It was only later that we found out he had come to our house so Mama could iron his hair — not with a comb and curling iron but with our very own Proctor-Silex steam iron. For some reason, Mr. Charlie would conceal his Frederick Douglass mane[2] under a big white Stetson hat, which I never saw him take off. Except when he came to our house, late at night, to have his hair pressed.

(Later, Daddy would tell us about Mr. Charlie's most prized piece of knowledge, which the man would confide only after his hair had been pressed, as a token of intimacy. "Not many people know this," he'd say in a tone of circumspection, "but George Washington was Abraham Lincoln's daddy." Nodding solemnly, he'd add the clincher: "A white man told me." Though he was in dead earnest, this became a humorous refrain around the house — "a white man told me" — used to punctuate especially preposterous assertions.)   10

My mother furtively examined my daughters' kitchens whenever we went home for a visit in the early eighties. It became a game between us. I had told her not to do it, because I didn't like the politics it suggested of "good" and "bad" hair. "Good" hair was straight. "Bad" hair was

---

[2]***Frederick Douglass mane:*** Frederick Douglass (1817?–1895), an escaped slave who became a prominent African American writer, abolitionist, and orator. His photographs reveal an impressive head of hair. — EDS.

kinky. Even in the late sixties, at the height of Black Power, most people could not bring themselves to say "bad" for "good" and "good" for "bad." They still said that hair like white hair was "good," even if they encapsulated it in a disclaimer like "what we used to call 'good.'"

Maggie would be seated in her high chair, throwing food this way and that, and Mama would be cooing about how cute it all was, remembering how I used to do the same thing, and wondering whether Maggie's flinging her food with her left hand meant that she was going to be a southpaw too. When my daughter was just about covered with Franco-American SpaghettiOs, Mama would seize the opportunity and wipe her clean, dipping her head, tilted to one side, down under the back of Maggie's neck. Sometimes, if she could get away with it, she'd even rub a curl between her fingers, just to make sure that her bifocals had not deceived her. Then she'd sigh with satisfaction and relief, thankful that her prayers had been answered. No kink . . . yet. "Mama!" I'd shout, pretending to be angry. (Every once in a while, if no one was looking, I'd peek too.)

I say "yet" because most black babies are born with soft, silken hair. Then, sooner or later, it begins to "turn," as inevitably as do the seasons or the leaves turn on a tree. And if it's meant to turn, it *turns,* no matter how hard you try to stop it. People once thought baby oil would stop it. They were wrong.

Everybody I knew as a child wanted to have good hair. You could be as ugly as homemade sin dipped in misery and still be thought attractive if you had good hair. Jesus Moss was what the girls at Camp Lee, Virginia, had called Daddy's hair during World War II. I know he played that thick head of hair for all it was worth, too. Still would, if he could.

My own hair was "not a bad grade," as barbers would tell me when they cut my head for the first time. It's like a doctor reporting the overall results of the first full physical that he had given you. "You're in good shape" or "Blood pressure's kind of high; better cut down on salt."

I spent much of my childhood and adolescence messing with my hair. I definitely wanted straight hair. Like Pop's.

When I was about three, I tried to stick a wad of Bazooka bubble gum to that straight hair of his. I suppose what fixed that memory for me is the spanking I got for doing so: he turned me upside down, holding me by the feet, the better to paddle my behind. Little *nigger,* he shouted, walloping away. I started to laugh about it two days later, when my behind stopped hurting.

When black people say "straight," of course, they don't usually mean "straight" literally, like, say, the hair of Peggy Lipton (the white girl on *The Mod Squad*) or Mary of Peter, Paul and Mary fame; black people call that "stringy" hair. No, "straight" just means not kinky, no matter what contours the curl might take. Because Daddy had straight hair, I would have done *anything* to have straight hair — and I used to try everything to make it straight, short of getting a process, which only riffraff were dumb enough to do.

Of the wide variety of techniques and methods I came to master in the great and challenging follicle prestidigitation, almost all had two things in common: a heavy, oil-based grease and evenly applied pressure. It's no accident that many of the biggest black companies in the fifties and sixties made hair products. Indeed, we do have a vast array of hair grease. And I have tried it all, in search of that certain silky touch, one that leaves neither the hand nor the pillow sullied by grease.

I always wondered what Frederick Douglass put on *his* hair, or Phillis   20
Wheatley.[3] Or why Wheatley has that rag on her head in the little engraving in the frontispiece of her book. One thing is for sure: you can bet that when Wheatley went to England to see the Countess of Huntington, she did not stop by the Queen's Coiffeur on the way. So many black people still get their hair straightened that it's a wonder we don't have a national holiday for Madame C. J. Walker, who invented the process for straightening kinky hair, rather than for Dr. King. Jheri-curled or "relaxed" — it's still fried hair.

I used all the greases, from sea-blue Bergamot, to creamy vanilla Duke (in its orange-and-white jar), to the godfather of grease, the formidable Murray's. Now, Murray's was some *serious* grease. Whereas Bergamot was like oily Jell-O and Duke was viscous and sickly sweet, Murray's was light brown and *hard*. Hard as lard and twice as greasy, Daddy used to say whenever the subject of Murray's came up. Murray's came in an orange can with a screw-on top. It was so hard that some people would put a match to the can, just to soften it and make it more manageable. In the late sixties, when Afros came into style, I'd use Afro-Sheen. From Murray's to Duke to Afro-Sheen: that was my progression in black consciousness.

We started putting hot towels or washrags over our greased-down Murray's-coated heads, in order to melt the wax into the scalp and follicles. Unfortunately, the wax had a curious habit of running down your neck, ears, and forehead. Not to mention your pillowcase.

Another problem was that if you put two palmfuls of Murray's on your head, your hair turned white. Duke did the same thing. It was a challenge: if you got rid of the white stuff, you had a magnificent head of wavy hair. Murray's turned kink into waves. Lots of waves. Frozen waves. A hurricane couldn't have blown those waves around.

That was the beauty of it. Murray's was so hard that it froze your hair into the wavy style you brushed it into. It looked really good if you wore a part. A lot of guys had parts *cut* into their hair by a barber, with clippers or a straight-edge razor. Especially if you had kinky hair — in which case you'd generally wear a short razor cut, or what we called a Quo Vadis.

Being obsessed with our hair, we tried to be as innovative as possible.   25
Everyone knew about using a stocking cap, because your father or your uncle or the older guys wore them whenever something really big was about to happen, secular or sacred, a funeral or a dance, a wedding or a trip

---

[3]*Phillis Wheatley* (1753?–1784): An African-born slave who became America's first major black poet. — EDS.

in which you confronted official white people, or when you were trying to look really sharp. When it was time to be clean, you wore a stocking cap. If the event was really a big one, you made a new cap for the occasion.

A stocking cap was made by asking your mother for one of her hose, cutting it with a pair of scissors about six inches or so from the open end, where the elastic goes to the top of the thigh. Then you'd knot the cut end, and behold—a conical-shaped hat or cap, with an elastic band that you pulled down low on your forehead and down around your neck in the back. A good stocking cap, to work well, had to fit tight and snug, like a press. And it had to fit that tightly because it *was* a press: it pressed your hair with the force of the hose's elastic. If you greased your hair down real good and left the stocking cap on long enough—*voilà:* you got a head of pressed-against-the-scalp waves. If you used Murray's, and if you wore a stocking cap to sleep, you got a *whole lot* of waves. (You also got a ring around your forehead when you woke up, but eventually that disappeared.)

And then you could enjoy your concrete 'do. Swore we were bad, too, with all that grease and those flat heads. My brother and I would brush it out a bit in the morning so it would look—ahem—"natural."

Grown men still wear stocking caps, especially older men, who generally keep their caps in their top drawer, along with their cuff links and their see-through silk socks, their Maverick tie, their silk handkerchief, and whatever else they prize most.

A Murrayed-down stocking cap was the respectable version of the process, which, by contrast, was most definitely not a cool thing to have, at least if you weren't an entertainer by trade.

Zeke and Keith and Poochie and a few other stars of the basketball team all used to get a process once or twice a year. It was expensive, and to get one you had to go to Pittsburgh or D.C. or Uniontown, someplace where there were enough colored people to support a business. They'd disappear, then reappear a day or two later, strutting like peacocks, their hair burned slightly red from the chemical lye base. They'd also wear "rags" or cloths or handkerchiefs around it when they slept or played basketball. Do-rags, they were called. But the result was *straight* hair with a hint of wave. No curl. Do-it-yourselfers took their chances at home with a concoction of mashed potatoes and lye.

The most famous process, outside of what Malcolm X describes in his *Autobiography* and maybe that of Sammy Davis, Jr., was Nat King Cole's. Nat King Cole had patent-leather hair.

"That man's got the finest process money can buy." That's what Daddy said the night Cole's TV show aired on NBC, November 5, 1956. I remember the date because everyone came to our house to watch it and to celebrate one of Daddy's buddies' birthdays. Yeah, Uncle Joe chimed in, they can do shit to his hair that the average Negro can't even *think* about—secret shit.

Nat King Cole was *clean.* I've had an ongoing argument with a Nigerian friend about Nat King Cole for twenty years now. Not whether or not he could sing; any fool knows that he could sing. But whether or not he was a handkerchief-head for wearing that patent-leather process.

Sammy Davis's process I detested. It didn't look good on him. Worse still, he liked to have a fried strand dangling down the middle of his forehead, shaking it out from the crown when he sang. But Nat King Cole's hair was a thing unto itself, a beautifully sculpted work of art that he and he alone should have had the right to wear.

The only difference between a process and a stocking cap, really, was   35 taste; yet Nat King Cole—unlike, say, Michael Jackson—looked *good* in his process. His head looked like Rudolph Valentino's in the twenties, and some say it was Valentino that the process imitated. But Nat King Cole wore a process because it suited his face, his demeanor, his name, his style. He was as clean as he wanted to be.

I had forgotten all about Nat King Cole and that patent-leather look until the day in 1971 when I was sitting in an Arab restaurant on the island of Zanzibar, surrounded by men in fezzes and white caftans, trying to learn how to eat curried goat and rice with the fingers of my right hand, feeling two million miles from home, when all of a sudden the old transistor radio sitting on top of a china cupboard stopped blaring out its Swahili music to play "Fly Me to the Moon" by Nat King Cole. The restaurant's din was not affected at all, not even by half a decibel. But in my mind's eye, I saw it: the King's sleek black magnificent tiara. I managed, barely, to blink back the tears.

The Reader's Presence

1. At what point in the essay do you, as a reader, begin to become aware of the social or political significance of the hair-straightening process? At what point in his own development does Gates begin to ascribe a political significance to hair? How would you describe his attitude toward the "kitchen"? toward "the process"? toward the prominent black Americans whom he names in the essay?

2. Reread the essay carefully, and mark any references to nature, including the word *natural* and any metaphors drawn from nature. What conclusions might you draw from their use and placement in the essay? How do they help complicate the meaning of the hairstyle choices available to the characters?

3. How would you characterize the author's voice in this essay? Which words and phrases hark back to the language of his home and family? How does Gates integrate these words and phrases into the text? What difference, if any, does it make to you as a reader when he puts certain words, such as *kitchen* or *good,* in quotation marks, as opposed to the passages in which phrases (such as "ugly as homemade sin dipped in misery" [paragraph 14]) are not set off in the text in this way?

THE WRITER AT WORK

Henry Louis Gates Jr. on the Writer's Voice

Skilled at critical and academic writing, the Harvard English professor Henry Louis Gates Jr. hoped to find ways to tell stories about his growing up in a small West Virginia community. In writing his memoir, Colored People, *from which "In the Kitchen" is taken, Gates found the voice he wanted. The following comments appeared in a collection,* Swing Low: Black Men Writing, *edited by Rebecca Carroll in 1995.*

My father told stories all the time when I was growing up. My mother used to call them "lies." I didn't know that "lies" was the name for stories in the black vernacular, I just thought it was her own word that she had made up. I was inspired by those "lies," though, and knew that I wanted to tell some too one day.

When I was ten or twelve, I had a baseball column in the local newspaper. I was the scorekeeper for the minor-league games in my town—I would compile all of the facts, and then the editor and I would put together a narrative. I did that every week during the summer. The best part was seeing my name in print. After that, I was hooked—hooked to seeing my name in black and white on paper.

At fourteen or fifteen, I read James Baldwin's work and became fascinated with the idea of writing. When I started reading about black people through the writings of black people, suddenly I was seized by the desire to write. I was in awe of how writers were able to take words and create an illusion of the world that people could step into—a world where people opened doors and shut doors, fell in love and out of love, where people lived and died. I wanted to be able to create those worlds too. I knew I had a voice even before I knew what a "writer's voice" meant. I didn't know what it was, but I could hear it, and I knew when my rhythm was on—it was almost as if I could hear myself write. I thought I had a unique take on the world and trusted my sensibility. It struck me that perhaps it would be a good thing to share it with other people. . . .

I don't think that the prime reason for writing is to save the world, or to save black people. I do it because it makes me feel good. I want to record my vision and to entertain people. When I was writing reviews, although it was an intriguing way to discuss literature, I would have a lot of black people say to me, "I'm having a hard time understanding you, brother." I've always had two conflicting voices within me, one that wants to be outrageous and on the edge, always breaking new ground, and another that wants to be loved by the community for that outrageousness. It is very difficult to expect that people will let you have it both ways like that. Those who really care about a community are the ones who push the boundaries and create new definitions, but generally they get killed for doing that, which is what I mean when I refer to myself as a griot in the black community — the one who makes the wake-up call, who loves his people enough to truly examine the status quo.

The wonderful thing about *Colored People* is that everybody gets it   5
and can appreciate it because it is a universal story. It is my segue from non-fiction to fiction. I wrote it to preserve a world that has passed away, and to reveal some secrets — not for the shock value, but because I want to re-create a voice that black people use when there are no white people around. Oftentimes in black literature, black authors get all lockjawed in their writing because they are doing it for a white audience, and not for themselves. You don't hear the voice of black people when it's just us in the kitchen, talking out the door and down the road, and that is the voice that I am trying to capture in *Colored People*. Integration may have cost us that voice. We cannot take it for granted and must preserve it whenever possible. I don't know what kind of positive language and linguistic rituals are being passed down in the fragmented, dispossessed black underclass. I think it's very different from when and where I was raised, when there was a stronger sense of community, and that language was everywhere I turned.

19

Langston Hughes

Salvation

One of the leading figures of the Harlem Renaissance, Langston Hughes (1902–1967) was a prolific writer. He started his career as a poet, but also wrote fiction, autobiography, biography, history, plays, and worked at various times as a journalist. One of his most famous poems, "The Negro Speaks of Rivers," was written while he was a high school student. Although Langston Hughes traveled widely, most of his writings are concerned with the lives of urban working-class African Americans.

Hughes used the rhythms of blues and jazz to bring to his writing a distinctive expression of black culture and experience. His work continues to be popular today, especially collections of short stories such as The Ways of White Folks *(1934), volumes of poetry such as* Montage of a Dream Deferred *(1951), and his series of vignettes on the character Jesse B. Simple, collected and published from 1950 to 1965. Hughes published two volumes of autobiography; "Salvation" is taken from the first of these,* The Big Sea *(1940).*

Throughout his work, Hughes refused to idealize his subject. "Certainly," he said, "I personally knew very few people anywhere who were wholly beautiful and wholly good. Besides I felt that the masses of our people had as much in their lives to put into books as did those more fortunate ones who had been born with some means and the ability to work up to a master's degree at a Northern college." Expressing the writer's truism about writing about what one knows best, he continued, "Anyway, I didn't know the upper-class Negroes well enough to write much about them. I only knew the people I had grown up with, and they weren't the people whose shoes were always shined, who had been to Harvard, or who had heard of Bach. But they seemed to me good people too."

I was saved from sin when I was going on thirteen. But not really saved. It happened like this. There was a big revival at my Auntie Reed's church. Every night for weeks there had been much preaching, singing, praying, and shouting, and some very hardened sinners had been brought to Christ, and the membership of the church had grown by leaps and bounds. Then just before the revival ended, they held a special meeting for children, "to bring the young lambs to the fold." My aunt spoke of it for days ahead. That night I was escorted to the front row and placed on the mourners' bench with all the other young sinners, who had not yet been brought to Jesus.

My aunt told me that when you were saved you saw a light, and something happened to you inside! And Jesus came into your life! And God was with you from then on! She said you could see and hear and feel Jesus in your soul. I believed her. I had heard a great many old people say the same thing and it seemed to me they ought to know. So I sat there calmly in the hot, crowded church, waiting for Jesus to come to me.

The preacher preached a wonderful rhythmical sermon, all moans and shouts and lonely cries and dire pictures of hell, and then he sang a song about the ninety and nine safe in the fold, but one little lamb was left out in the cold. Then he said: "Won't you come? Won't you come to Jesus? Young lambs, won't you come?" And he held out his arms to all us young sinners there on the mourners' bench. And the little girls cried. And some of them jumped up and went to Jesus right away. But most of us just sat there.

A great many old people came and knelt around us and prayed, old women with jet-black faces and braided hair, old men with work-gnarled hands. And the church sang a song about the lower lights are burning, some poor sinners to be saved. And the whole building rocked with prayer and song.

Still I kept waiting to *see* Jesus.   5

Finally all the young people had gone to the altar and were saved, but one boy and me. He was a rounder's son named Westley. Westley and I were surrounded by sisters and deacons praying. It was very hot in the church, and getting late now. Finally Westley said to me in a whisper: "God damn! I'm tired o' sitting here. Let's get up and be saved." So he got up and was saved.

Then I was left all alone on the mourners' bench. My aunt came and knelt at my knees and cried, while prayers and song swirled all around me in the little church. The whole congregation prayed for me alone, in a mighty wail of moans and voices. And I kept waiting serenely for Jesus, waiting, waiting—but he didn't come. I wanted to see him, but nothing happened to me. Nothing! I wanted something to happen to me, but nothing happened.

I heard the songs and the minister saying: "Why don't you come? My dear child, why don't you come to Jesus? Jesus is waiting for you. He wants you. Why don't you come? Sister Reed, what is this child's name?"

"Langston," my aunt sobbed.

"Langston, why don't you come? Why don't you come and be saved?   10
Oh, Lamb of God! Why don't you come?"

Now it was really getting late. I began to be ashamed of myself, holding everything up so long. I began to wonder what God thought about Westley, who certainly hadn't seen Jesus either, but who was now sitting proudly on the platform, swinging his knickerbockered legs and grinning down at me, surrounded by deacons and old women on their knees praying. God had not struck Westley dead for taking his name in vain or for lying in the temple. So I decided that maybe to save further trouble, I'd better lie, too, and say that Jesus had come, and get up and be saved.

So I got up.

Suddenly the whole room broke into a sea of shouting, as they saw me rise. Waves of rejoicing swept the place. Women leaped in the air. My aunt threw her arms around me. The minister took me by the hand and led me to the platform.

When things quieted down, in a hushed silence, punctuated by a few ecstatic "Amens," all the new young lambs were blessed in the name of God. Then joyous singing filled the room.

That night, for the last time in my life but one—for I was a big boy   15
twelve years old—I cried. I cried, in bed alone, and couldn't stop. I buried my head under the quilts, but my aunt heard me. She woke up and told my uncle I was crying because the Holy Ghost had come into my life, and because I had seen Jesus. But I was really crying because I couldn't bear to tell her that I had lied, that I had deceived everybody in the church, that I hadn't seen Jesus, and that now I didn't believe there was a Jesus anymore, since he didn't come to help me.

The Reader's Presence

1. Pay close attention to Hughes's two opening sentences. How would you describe their tone? How do they suggest the underlying pattern of the essay? How do they introduce the idea of deception right from the start? Who is being deceived in the essay? Is it the congregation? God? Hughes's aunt? the reader?

2. Consider the character of Westley. Why is he important to Hughes's narrative? What would happen to the essay if Westley were not introduced and described?

3. In many ways this is an essay about belief. What is it that Hughes has been asked to believe? What does he expect to see? Reread the essay and consider the word *come*. Hughes waits for Jesus to come to him. Yet the preacher invites the children to come to Jesus. How does an awareness of this difference affect your reading of the essay?

THE WRITER AT WORK

Langston Hughes on "How to Be a Bad Writer (In Ten Easy Lessons)"

Established authors are frequently asked for tips on writing. Here Langston Hughes reverses the practice and offers young writers some memorable advice on how to write poorly. "How to Be a Bad Writer" first appeared in The Harlem Quarterly *(Spring 1950). Some of his suggestions no longer seem applicable today, thanks in part to his own literary efforts. But which lessons do you think are still worth paying attention to?*

1. Use all the clichés possible, such as "He had a gleam in his eye," or "Her teeth were white as pearls."

2. If you are a Negro, try very hard to write with an eye dead on the white market—use modern stereotypes of older stereotypes—big burly Negroes, criminals, low-lifers, and prostitutes.

3. Put in a lot of profanity and as many pages as possible of near-pornography and you will be so modern you pre-date Pompei in your lonely crusade toward the best seller lists. By all means be misunderstood, unappreciated, and ahead of your time in print and out, then you can be felt-sorry-for by your own self, if not the public.

4. Never characterize characters. Just name them and then let them go for themselves. Let all of them talk the same way. If the reader hasn't imagination enough to make something out of cardboard cut-outs, shame on him!

5. Write about China, Greece, Tibet, or the Argentine pampas—any-place you've never seen and know nothing about. Never write about anything you know, your home town, or your home folks, or yourself.   5

6. Have nothing to say, but use a great many words, particularly high-sounding words, to say it.

7. If a playwright, put into your script a lot of hand-waving and spirituals, preferably the ones everybody has heard a thousand times from Marion Anderson to the Golden Gates.

8. If a poet, rhyme June with moon as often and in as many ways as possible. Also use *thee's* and *thou's* and *'tis* and *o'er,* and invert your sentences all the time. Never say, "The sun rose, bright and shining." But, rather, "Bright and shining rose the sun."

9. Pay no attention to spelling or grammar or the neatness of the

manuscript. And in writing letters, never sign your name so anyone can read it. A rapid scrawl will better indicate how important and how busy you are.

10. Drink as much liquor as possible and always write under the in-   10
fluence of alcohol. When you can't afford alcohol yourself, or even if you can, drink on your friends, fans, and the general public.

If you are white, there are many more things I can advise in order to be a bad writer, but since this piece is for colored writers, there are some things I know a Negro just will not do, not even for writing's sake, so there is no use mentioning them.

20

Zora Neale Hurston

How It Feels to Be Colored Me

Born in Eatonville, Florida, in a year that she never remembered the same way twice, Zora Neale Hurston (1901?–1960) entered Howard University in 1923. In 1926 she won a scholarship to Barnard College, where she was the first black woman to be admitted. There Hurston developed an interest in anthropology, which was cultivated by Columbia University's distinguished anthropologist, Frank Boas. From 1928 to 1931 she collected voodoo folklore in the South and published her findings in Mules and Men *(1935). Two successive Guggenheim Fellowships allowed her to do field work in the Caribbean, resulting in another anthropological study,* Tell My Horse *(1938). She also collected folklore about Florida for the Works Progress Administration and published the two novels for which she is justly famous,* Jonah's Gourd Vine *(1934), and* Their Eyes Were Watching God *(1937).*

Langston Hughes said that "she was always getting scholarships and things from wealthy white people." But when the economy collapsed and brought the famous Harlem Renaissance down with it, Hurston's patrons all but disappeared. She managed to publish two more books, Moses, Man of the Mountain *(1939) and* Seraph on the Suwanee *(1948), and her autobiography,* Dust Tracks on a Road *(1942), before her reputation suffered a serious decline during the 1950s. After working as a librarian, part-time teacher, and maid near the end of her life, Hurston died in a county welfare home in Florida in virtual obscurity. The rediscovery of her work is largely attributed to Alice Walker, who edited a collection of Hurston's writings,* I Love Myself When I'm Laughing *(1975). "How It Feels to Be Colored Me" originally appeared in* The World Tomorrow *in 1928.*

Hurston said, "I regret all my books. It is one of the tragedies of life that one cannot have all the wisdom one is ever to possess in the beginning. Perhaps, it is just as well to be rash and foolish for a while. If writers were too wise, perhaps no books would be written at all. It might be better to ask yourself 'Why?' afterwards than before. Anyway, the force from somewhere in Space which commands you to write in the first place, gives you no choice. You take up the pen when you are told, and write what is commanded. There is no agony like bearing an untold story inside you."

I am colored but I offer nothing in the way of extenuating circumstances except the fact that I am the only Negro in the United States whose grandfather on the mother's side was *not* an Indian chief.

I remember the very day that I became colored. Up to my thirteenth year I lived in the little Negro town of Eatonville, Florida. It is exclusively a colored town. The only white people I knew passed through the town going to or coming from Orlando. The native whites rode dusty horses, the Northern tourists chugged down the sandy village road in automobiles. The town knew the Southerners and never stopped cane chewing[1] when they passed. But the Northerners were something else again. They were peered at cautiously from behind curtains by the timid. The more venturesome would come out on the porch to watch them go past and got just as much pleasure out of the tourists as the tourists got out of the village.

The front porch might seem a daring place for the rest of the town, but it was a gallery seat for me. My favorite place was atop the gate-post. Proscenium box for a born first-nighter. Not only did I enjoy the show, but I didn't mind the actors knowing that I liked it. I usually spoke to them in passing. I'd wave at them and when they returned my salute, I would say something like this: "Howdy-do-well-I-thank-you-where-you-goin'?" Usually automobile or the horse paused at this, and after a queer exchange of compliments, I would probably "go a piece of the way" with them, as we say in farthest Florida. If one of my family happened to come to the front in time to see me, of course negotiations would be rudely broken off. But even so, it is clear that I was the first "welcome-to-our-state" Floridian, and I hope the Miami Chamber of Commerce will please take notice.

During this period, white people differed from colored to me only in that they rode through town and never lived there. They liked to hear me "speak pieces" and sing and wanted to see me dance the parse-me-la,[2] and gave me generously of their small silver for doing these things, which seemed strange to me for I wanted to do them so much that I needed bribing to stop. Only they didn't know it. The colored people gave no dimes. They deplored any joyful tendencies in me, but I was their Zora nevertheless. I belonged to them, to the nearby hotels, to the county—everybody's Zora.

[1]*cane chewing:* Chewing on sugar cane. — EDS.
[2]*parse-me-la:* Probably an old dance song. — EDS.

But changes came in the family when I was thirteen, and I was sent to   5
school in Jacksonville. I left Eatonville, the town of the oleanders, as Zora.
When I disembarked from the river-boat at Jacksonville, she was no more.
It seemed that I had suffered a sea change. I was not Zora of Orange
County any more, I was now a little colored girl. I found it out in certain
ways. In my heart as well as in the mirror, I became a fast brown — war-
ranted not to rub nor run.

But I am not tragically colored. There is no great sorrow dammed up
in my soul, nor lurking behind my eyes. I do not mind at all. I do not belong to the sobbing school of Negrohood who hold that nature somehow
has given them a lowdown dirty deal and whose feelings are all hurt
about it. Even in the helter-skelter skirmish that is my life, I have seen
that the world is to the strong regardless of a little pigmentation more
or less. No, I do not weep at the world — I am too busy sharpening my
oyster knife.

Someone is always at my elbow reminding me that I am the grand-
daughter of slaves. It fails to register depression with me. Slavery is sixty
years in the past. The operation was successful and the patient is doing
well, thank you. The terrible struggle that made me an American out of a
potential slave said "On the line!" The Reconstruction[3] said "Get set!";
and the generation before said "Go!" I am off to a flying start and I must
not halt in the stretch to look behind and weep. Slavery is the price I paid
for civilization, and the choice was not with me. It is a bully adventure
and worth all that I have paid through my ancestors for it. No one on
earth ever had a greater chance for glory. The world to be won and nothing to be lost. It is thrilling to think — to know that for any act of mine, I
shall get twice as much praise or twice as much blame. It is quite exciting
to hold the center of the national stage, with the spectators not knowing
whether to laugh or to weep.

The position of my white neighbor is much more difficult. No brown
specter pulls up a chair beside me when I sit down to eat. No dark ghost
thrusts its leg against mine in bed. The game of keeping what one has is
never so exciting as the game of getting.

I do not always feel colored. Even now I often achieve the unconscious Zora of Eatonville before the Hegira.[4] I feel most colored when I
am thrown against a sharp white background.

For instance at Barnard. "Beside the waters of the Hudson" I feel my   10
race. Among the thousand white persons, I am a dark rock surged upon,
and overswept, but through it all, I remain myself. When covered by the
waters, I am; and the ebb but reveals me again.

---

[3]***Reconstruction:*** The period of rebuilding and reorganizing immediately following the
Civil War. —Eds.
  [4]***Hegira:*** A journey to safety. Historically it refers to Mohammed's flight from Mecca
in A.D. 622. —Eds.

Sometimes it is the other way around. A white person is set down in our midst, but the contrast is just as sharp for me. For instance, when I sit in the drafty basement that is The New World Cabaret with a white person, my color comes. We enter chatting about any little nothing that we have in common and are seated by the jazz waiters. In the abrupt way that jazz orchestras have, this one plunges into a number. It loses no time in circumlocutions, but gets right down to business. It constricts the thorax and splits the heart with its tempo and narcotic harmonies. This orchestra grows rambunctious, rears on its hind legs and attacks the tonal veil with primitive fury, rending it, clawing it until it breaks through to the jungle beyond. I follow those heathen—follow them exultingly. I dance wildly inside myself; I yell within, I whoop; I shake my assegai[5] above my head, I hurl it true to the mark *yeeeeooww!* I am in the jungle and living in the jungle way. My face is painted red and yellow and my body is painted blue. My pulse is throbbing like a war drum. I want to slaughter something—give pain, give death to what, I do not know. But the piece ends. The men of the orchestra wipe their lips and rest their fingers. I creep back slowly to the veneer we call civilization with the last tone and find the white friend sitting motionless in his seat, smoking calmly.

"Good music they have here," he remarks, drumming the table with his fingertips.

Music. The great blobs of purple and red emotion have not touched him. He has only heard what I felt. He is far away and I see him but dimly across the ocean and the continent that have fallen between us. He is so pale with his whiteness then and I am *so* colored.

At certain times I have no race, I am *me.* When I set my hat at a certain angle and saunter down Seventh Avenue, Harlem City, feeling as snooty as the lions in front of the Forty-Second Street Library, for instance. So far as my feelings are concerned, Peggy Hopkins Joyce[6] on the Boule Mich[7] with her gorgeous raiment, stately carriage, knees knocking together in a most aristocratic manner, has nothing on me. The cosmic Zora emerges. I belong to no race nor time. I am the eternal feminine with its string of beads.

I have no separate feeling about being an American citizen and colored. I am merely a fragment of the Great Soul that surges within the boundaries. My country, right or wrong.   15

Sometimes, I feel discriminated against, but it does not make me angry. It merely astonishes me. How *can* any deny themselves the pleasure of my company? It's beyond me.

---

[5] *assegai:* A hunting spear.—EDS.
[6] *Peggy Hopkins Joyce:* A fashionable American who was a celebrity in the 1920s. —EDS.
[7] *Boule Mich:* The Boulevard Saint-Michel in Paris.—EDS.

But in the main, I feel like a brown bag of miscellany propped against a wall. Against a wall in company with other bags, white, red, and yellow. Pour out the contents, and there is discovered a jumble of small things priceless and worthless. A first-water diamond, an empty spool, bits of broken glass, lengths of string, a key to a door long since crumbled away, a rusty knife-blade, old shoes saved for a road that never was and never will be, a nail bent under the weight of things too heavy for any nail, a dried flower or two still a little fragrant. In your hand is the brown bag. On the ground before you is the jumble it held—so much like the jumble in the bags, could they be emptied, that all might be dumped in a single heap and the bags refilled without altering the content of any greatly. A bit of colored glass more or less would not matter. Perhaps that is how the Great Stuffer of Bags filled them in the first place—who knows?

The Reader's Presence

1. Hurston's essay is divided into four sections. Do you find this division significant? What relationships can you detect among the separate parts?

2. How much does being "colored" inform Hurston's identity? Does it seem to matter throughout the essay? At what points does color seem deeply important to Hurston? When does it seem less important? What do you think the reasons are for these differences?

3. Consider Hurston's startling image in the final paragraph: "But in the main, I feel like a brown bag of miscellany propped against a wall." Try rereading the essay with this image in mind. In what ways does it help you understand Hurston's sense of personal identity? In what ways can it be said to describe the form and style of the essay itself?

21

Jamaica Kincaid

Biography of a Dress

Jamaica Kincaid was born in Antigua in 1949 and came to the United States at the age of seventeen to work for a New York family as an au pair. Her novel Lucy *(1990) is an imaginative account of her experience of coming into adult-*

hood in a foreign country and continues the narrative of her personal history begun in the novel Annie John *(1985). She has also published a collection of short stories,* At the Bottom of the River *(1983), a collection of essays,* A Small Place *(1988), and a third novel,* The Autobiography of My Mother *(1995). Her most recent publications include* My Brother *(1997), which was a National Book Award Finalist for Nonfiction, and* My Favorite Plant: Writers and Gardeners on the Plants They Love *(1998), which she edited. Her writing also appears in national magazines, especially the* New Yorker, *where she worked as a staff writer until 1995.*

"I'm someone who writes to save her life," *Kincaid says,* "I mean, I can't imagine what I would do if I didn't write. I would be dead or I would be in jail because—what else could I do? I can't really do anything but write. All the things that were available to someone in my position involved being a subject person. And I'm very bad at being a subject person."

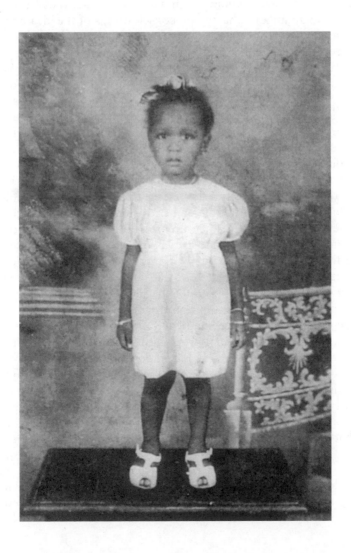

The dress I am wearing in this black-and-white photograph, taken when I was two years old, was a yellow dress made of cotton poplin (a fabric with a slightly unsmooth texture first manufactured in the French town of Avignon and brought to England by the Huguenots, but I could not have known that at the time), and it was made for me by my mother. This shade of yellow, the color of my dress that I am wearing when I was two years old, was the same shade of yellow as boiled cornmeal, a food that my mother was always eager for me to eat in one form (as a porridge) or another (as fongie, the starchy part of my midday meal) because it was cheap and therefore easily available (but I did not know that at the time), and because she thought that foods bearing the colors yellow, green or orange were particularly rich in vitamins and so boiled cornmeal would be particularly good for me. But I was then (not so now) extremely particular about what I would eat, not knowing then (but I do now) of shortages and abundance, having no consciousness of the idea of rich and poor (but I know now that we were poor then), and would eat only boiled beef (which I required my mother to chew for me first and, after she had made it soft, remove it from her mouth and place it in mine), certain kinds of boiled fish (doctor or angel), hard-boiled eggs (from hens, not ducks), poached calf's liver and the milk from cows, and so would not even look at the boiled cornmeal (porridge or fongie). There was not one single thing that I could isolate and say I did not like about the boiled cornmeal (porridge or fongie) because I could not isolate parts of things then (though I can and do now), but whenever I saw this bowl of trembling yellow substance before me I would grow still and silent, I did not cry, that did not make me cry. My mother told me this then (she does not tell me this now, she does not remember this now, she does not remember telling me this now): she knew of a man who had eaten boiled cornmeal at least once a day from the time he was my age then, two years old, and he lived for a very long time, finally dying when he was almost one hundred years old, and when he died he had looked rosy and new, with the springy wrinkles of the newborn, not the slack pleats of skin of the aged; as he lay dead his stomach was cut open, and all his insides were a beautiful shade of yellow, the same shade of yellow as boiled cornmeal. I was powerless then (though not so now) to like or dislike this story; it was beyond me then (though not so now) to understand the span of my lifetime then, two years old, and it was beyond me then (though not so now), the span of time called almost one hundred years old; I did not know then (though I do now) that there was such a thing as an inside to anybody, and that this inside would have a color, and that if the insides were the same shade of yellow as the yellow of boiled cornmeal my mother would want me to know about it.

On a day when it was not raining (that would have been unusual, that would have been out of the ordinary, ruining the fixed form of the day), my mother walked to one of the Harneys stores (there were many Harneys who owned stores, and they sold the same things, but I did not know then and I do not know now if they were all of the same people) and bought one-and-a-half yards of this yellow cotton poplin to make a dress for me, a dress I would wear to have my picture taken on the day I turned two years old. Inside, the store was cool and dark, and this was a good thing because outside was hot and overly bright. Someone named Harney did not wait on my mother, but someone named Miss Verna did and she was very nice still, so nice that she tickled my cheek as she spoke to my mother, and I reached forward as if to kiss her, but when her cheek met my lips I opened my mouth and bit her hard with my small child's teeth. Her cry of surprise did not pierce the air, but she looked at me hard, as if she knew me very, very well; and later, much later, when I was about twelve years old or so and she was always in and out of the crazy house, I would pass her on the street and throw stones at her, and she would turn and look at me hard, but she did not know who I was, she did not know who anyone was at all, not at all. Miss Verna showed my mother five flat thick bolts of cloth, white, blue (sea), blue (sky), yellow and pink, and my mother chose the yellow after holding it up against the rich copper color that my hair was then (it is not so now); she paid for it with a one-pound note that had an engraving of the king George Fifth on it (an ugly man with a cruel, sharp, bony nose, not the kind, soft, fleshy noses I was then used to), and she received change that included crowns, shillings, florins and farthings.

My mother, carrying me and the just-bought piece of yellow poplin wrapped in coarse brown paper in her arms, walked out of Mr. Harney's store, up the street a few doors away, and into a store called Murdoch's (because the family who owned it were the Murdochs), and there my mother bought two skeins of yellow thread, the kind used for embroidering and a shade of yellow almost identical to the yellow poplin. My mother not only took me with her everywhere she went, she carried me, sometimes in her arms, sometimes on her back; for this errand she carried me in her arms; she did not complain, she never complained (but later she refused to do it anymore and never gave an explanation, at least not one that I can remember now); as usual, she spoke to me and sang to me in French patois (but I did not understand French patois then and I do not now and so I can never know what exactly she said to me then). She walked back to our house on Dickenson Bay Street, stopping often to hold conversations with people (men and women) she knew, speaking to them sometimes in English, sometimes in French; and if after they said how beautiful I was (for people would often say that about me then but they do not say that about me now), she would laugh and say that I did not liked to be kissed (and I don't know if that was really true then but it is not so now). And that night after we had eaten our supper (boiled fish in a butter-and-lemon-juice sauce) and her husband (who was not my father but I did not know that at the time, I know that now) had gone for a walk (to the jetty), she removed her yellow poplin from its brown wrapper and folded and made creases in it and with scissors made holes (for the arms and neck) and slashes (for an opening in the back and the shoulders); she then placed it along with some ordinary thread (yellow), the thread for embroidering, the scissors and a needle in a basket that she had brought with her from her home in Dominica when she first left it at sixteen years of age.

For days afterward, my mother, after she had finished her usual chores (clothes washing, dish washing, floor scrubbing, bathing me, her only child, feeding me a teaspoon of cod-liver-oil), sat on the sill of the doorway, half in the sun, half out of the sun, and sewed together the various parts that would make up altogether my dress of yellow poplin; she gathered and hemmed and made tucks; she was just in the early stages of teaching herself how to make smocking and so was confined to making straight stitches (up-cable, down-cable, outline, stem, chain); the bodice of the dress appeared simple, plain, and the detail and pattern can only be seen close up and in real life, not from far away and not in a photograph; and much later, when she grew in confidence with this craft, the bodice of my dresses became overburdened with the stitches, chevron, trellis, diamonds, Vandyke, and species of birds she had never seen (swan) and species of flowers she had never seen (tulip) and species of animals she had never seen (bear) in real life, only in a picture in a book.

My skin was not the color of cream in the process of spoiling, my   5
hair was not the texture of silk and the color of flax, my eyes did not gleam like blue jewels in a crown, the afternoons in which I sat watching my mother make me this dress were not cool, and verdant lawns and pastures and hills and dales did not stretch out before me; but it was the picture of such a girl at two years old — a girl whose skin was the color of cream in the process of spoiling, whose hair was the texture of silk and the color of flax, a girl whose eyes gleamed like blue jewels in a crown, a girl whose afternoons (and mornings and nights) were cool, and before whom stretched verdant lawns and pastures and hills and dales — that my mother saw, a picture on an almanac advertising a particularly fine and scented soap (a soap she could not afford to buy then but I can now), and this picture of this girl wearing a yellow dress with smocking on the front bodice perhaps created in my mother the desire to have a daughter who looked like that or perhaps created the desire in my mother to try and make the daughter she already had look like that. I do not know now and I did not know then. And who was that girl really? (I did not ask then because I could not ask then but I ask now.) And who made her dress? And this girl would have had a mother; did the mother then have some friends, other women, did they sit together under a tree (or sit somewhere else) and compare strengths of potions used to throw away a child, or weigh the satisfactions to be had from the chaos of revenge or the smooth order of forgiveness; and this girl with skin of cream on its way to spoiling and hair the color of flax, what did her insides look like, what did she eat? (I did not ask then because I could not ask then and I ask now but no one can answer me, really answer me.)

My second birthday was not a major event in anyone's life, certainly not my own (it was not my first and it was not my last, I am now forty-three years old), but my mother, perhaps because of circumstances (I would not have known then and to know now is not a help), perhaps only because of an established custom (but only in her family, other people didn't do this), to mark the occasion of my turning two years old had my ears pierced. One day, at dusk (I would not have called it that then), I was taken to someone's house (a woman from Dominica, a woman who was as dark as my mother was fair, and yet they were so similar that I am sure now as I was then that they shared the same tongue), and two thorns that had been heated in a fire were pierced through my earlobes. I do not now know (and could not have known then) if the pain I experienced resembled in any way the pain my mother experienced while giving birth to me or even if my mother, in having my ears bored in that way, at that time, meant to express hostility or aggression toward me (but without meaning to and without knowing that it was possible to mean to). For days afterward my earlobes were swollen and covered with a golden crust (which might have glistened in the harsh sunlight, but I can only imagine that now), and the pain of my earlobes must have filled up all that made up my entire being then and the pain of my earlobes must have been unbearable, because it was then that was the first time that I separated myself from myself, and I became two people (two small children then, I was two years old), one having the experience, the other observing the one having the experience. And the observer, perhaps because it was an act of my own will (strong then, but stronger now), my first and only real act of self-invention, is the one of the two I most rely on, the one of the two whose voice I believe to be the true voice; and of course it is the observer who cannot be relied on as the final truth to be believed, for the observer has woven between myself and the person who is having an experience a protective membrane, which allows me to see but only feel as much as I can handle at any given moment. And so . . .

. . . On the day I turned two years old, the twenty-fifth of May 1951, a pair of earrings, small hoops made of gold from British Guiana (it was called that then, it is not called that now), were placed in the bored holes in my earlobes (which by then had healed); a pair of bracelets made of silver from someplace other than British Guiana (and that place too was called one thing then, something else now) was placed one on each wrist; a pair of new shoes bought from Bata's was placed on my feet. That afternoon, I was bathed and powdered, and the dress of yellow poplin, completed, its seams all stitched together with a certainty found only in the natural world (I now realize), was placed over my head, and it is quite possible that this entire act had about it the feeling of being draped in a shroud. My mother, carrying me in her arms (as usual), took me to the studio of a photographer, a man named Mr. Walker, to have my picture taken. As she walked along with me in her arms (not complaining), with the heat of the sun still so overwhelming that it, not gravity, seemed to be the force that kept us pinned to the earth's surface, I placed my lips against one side of her head (the temple) and could feel the rhythm of the blood pulsing through her body; I placed my lips against her throat and could hear her swallow saliva that had collected in her mouth; I placed my face against her neck and inhaled deeply a scent that I could not identify then (how could I, there was nothing to compare it to) and cannot now, because it is not of animal or place or thing, it was (and is) a scent unique to her, and it left a mark of such depth that it eventually became a part of my other senses, and even now (yes, now) that scent is also taste, touch, sight and sound.

And Mr. Walker lived on Church Street in a house that was mysterious to me (then, not now) because it had a veranda (unlike my own house) and it had many rooms (unlike my own house, but really Mr. Walker's house had only four rooms, my own house had one) and the windows were closed (the windows in my house were always open). He spoke to my mother, I did not understand what they said, they did not share the same tongue. I knew Mr. Walker was a man, but how I knew that I cannot say (now, then, sometime to come). It is possible that because he touched his hair often, smoothing down, caressing, the forcibly straightened strands, and because he admired and said that he admired my dress of yellow poplin with its simple smocking (giving to me a false air of delicacy), and because he admired and said that he admired the plaid taffeta ribbon in my hair, I thought that he perhaps wasn't a man at all, I had never seen a man do or say any of those things, I had then only seen a woman do or say those things. He (Mr. Walker) stood next to a black box which had a curtain at its back (this was his camera but I did not know that at the time, I only know it now) and he asked my mother to stand me on a table, a small table, a table that made me taller, because the scene in the background, against which I was to be photographed, was so vast, it overwhelmed my two-year-old frame, making me seem a mere figurine, not a child at all; and when my mother picked me up, holding my by the armpits with her hands, her thumb accidentally (it could have been deliberate, how could someone who loved me inflict so much pain just in passing?) pressed deeply into my shoulder, and I cried out and then (and still now) looked up at her face and couldn't find any reason in it, and could find no malice in it, only that her eyes were full of something, a feeling that I thought then (and am convinced now) had nothing to do with me; and of course it is possible that just at that moment she had realized that she was exhausted, not physically, but just exhausted by this whole process, celebrating my second birthday, commemorating an event, my birth, that she may not have wished to occur in the first place and may have tried repeatedly to prevent, and then, finally, in trying to find some beauty in it, ended up with a yard and a half of yellow poplin being shaped into a dress, teaching herself smocking and purchasing gold hoops from places whose names never remained the same and silver bracelets from places whose names never remained the same. And Mr. Walker, who was not at all interested in my mother's ups and downs and would never have dreamed of taking in the haphazard mess of her life (but there was nothing so unusual about that, every life, I now know, is a haphazard mess), looked on for a moment as my mother, belying the look in her eyes, said kind and loving words to me in a kind and loving voice, and he then walked over to a looking glass that hung on a wall and squeezed with two of his fingers a lump the size of a pinch of sand that was on his cheek; the lump had a shiny white surface and it broke, emitting a tiny plap sound, and from it came a long ribbon of thick, yellow pus that curled on Mr. Walker's cheek imitating, almost, the decoration on the birthday cake that awaited me at home, and my birthday cake was decorated with a series of species of flora and fauna my mother had never seen (and still has not seen to this day, she is seventy-three years old).

After that day I never again wore my yellow poplin dress with the smocking my mother had just taught herself to make. It was carefully put aside, saved for me to wear to another special occasion; but by the time another special occasion came (I could say quite clearly then what the special occasion was and can say quite clearly now what the special occasion was but I do not want to), the dress could no longer fit me, I had grown too big for it.

The Reader's Presence

1. The visit to Mr. Walker seems a turning point in the narrative, yet Kincaid leaves its greater meaning unexplained. What do you make of Mr. Walker and the events surrounding the photograph? What might Mr. Walker's seemingly insignificant behavior indicate? Why might Kincaid have chosen to end the story with the visit rather than the birthday party?

2. The writer's early surroundings are evoked through objects and sensations; she never identifies the locale nor explicitly describes it. The reader is forced to absorb potentially unfamiliar background material in the course of following the plot. How might this experience parallel that of the young Kincaid, navigating a world full of alien images? How might Kincaid's stylistic approach serve to challenge traditional colonial hierarchies?

3. Kincaid interrupts her primary story, set in the past, with parenthetical references to the present. Is your experience of the childhood account impoverished or enriched by the adult perspective, and in what ways? Do these interjections interpret the earlier story, or simply add a second layer of narrative? Compare Kincaid's writing style in this piece to that in the story "Girl" (see page 873).

22

Chang-rae Lee

The Faintest Echo of Our Language

Born in Seoul, South Korea, in 1965, Chang-rae Lee came to the United States with his family when he was three and grew up outside of New York City. After graduating from Exeter, Lee received a B.A. from Yale and an M.F.A. from the University of Oregon in 1993. He won the prestigious PEN/Hemingway Award for his first novel, Native Speaker *(1995). His writing has appeared in the* New Yorker, the New York Times, *and in various anthologies, including* The Best American Essays 1996. *His new novel is* A Gesture Life. *The following selection, first published in the* New England Review, *is one of a series of autobiographical essays Lee has been writing about his family. After teaching in the creative writing program at the University of Oregon, Lee returned to the New York area, where he is currently director of the M.F.A. Program in Creative Writing at Hunter College.*

My mother died on a bare January morning in our family room, the room all of us favored. She died upon the floor-bed I had made up for her, on the old twin mattress from the basement that I slept on during my childhood. She died with her husband kneeling like a penitent boy at her ear, her daughter tightly grasping the soles of her feet, and her son vacantly kissing the narrow, brittle fingers of her hand. She died with her best friend weeping quietly above her, and with her doctor unmoving and silent. She died with no accompaniment of music or poetry or prayer. She died with her eyes and mouth open. She died blind and speechless. She died, as I knew she would, hearing the faintest echo of our language at the last moment of her mind.

That, I think, must be the most ardent of moments.

I keep considering it, her almost-ending time, ruminating the nameless, impossible mood of its ground, toiling over it like some desperate topographer whose final charge is to survey only the very earth beneath his own shifting feet. It is an improbable task. But I am continually traveling through that terrible province, into its dark region where I see again and again the strangely vast scene of her demise.

138

I see.

Here before me (as I now enter my narrative moment), the dying- 5
room, our family room. It has changed all of a sudden — it is as if there
has been a shift in its proportion, the scale horribly off. The room seems
to open up too fast, as though the walls were shrinking back and giving
way to the wood flooring that seems to unfurl before us like runaway carpet. And there, perched on this crest somehow high above us, her body so
flat and quiet in the bed, so resident, so immovable, caught beneath the
somber light of these unwinking lamps, deep among the rolls of thick
blankets, her furniture pushed to the walls without scheme, crowded in
by the medicines, syringes, clear tubing, machines, shot through with the
full false hopes of the living and the fearsome calls of the dead, my
mother resides at an unfathomable center where the time of my family
will commence once again.

No one is speaking. Except for the babble of her machines the will of
silence reigns in this house. There is no sound, no word or noise, that we
might offer up to fill this place. She sleeps for a period, then reveals her
live eyes. For twelve or eighteen hours we have watched her like this, our
legs and feet deadened from our squatting, going numb with tired blood.
We sometimes move fitfully about, sighing and breathing low, but no one
strays too far. The living room seems too far, the upstairs impossible.
There is nothing, nothing at all outside of the house. I think perhaps it is
snowing but it is already night and there is nothing left but this room and
its light and its life.

People are here earlier (when?), a group from the church, the minister
and some others. I leave her only then, going through the hallway to the
kitchen. They say prayers and sing hymns. I do not know the high Korean
words (I do not know many at all), and the music of their songs does not
comfort me. Their one broad voice seems to be calling, beckoning something, bared in some kind of sad invitation. It is an acknowledgment.
These people, some of them complete strangers, have come in from the
outside to sing and pray over my mother, their overcoats still bearing the
chill of the world.

I am glad when they are finished. They seem to sing too loud; I think
they are hurting her ears — at least, disturbing her fragile state. I keep
thinking, as if in her mind: *I'm finally going to get my sleep, my sleep
after all this raw and painful waking, but I'm not meant to have it. But
sing, sing.*

When the singers finally leave the room and quickly put on their
coats I see that the minister's wife has tears in her eyes: so it is that clear.
She looks at me; she wants to say something to me but I can see from her
stunted expression that the words will not come. Though I wanted them
earlier to cease I know already how quiet and empty it will feel when they
are gone. But we are all close together now in the foyer, touching hands
and hugging each other, our faces flushed, not talking but assenting to
what we know, moving our lips in a silent, communal speech. For what

we know, at least individually, is still unutterable, dwelling peacefully in the next room as the unnameable, lying there and waiting beside her, and yet the feeling among us is somehow so formidable and full of hope, and I think if I could hear our thoughts going round the room they would speak like the distant report of ten thousand monks droning the song of the long life of the earth.

Long, long life. Sure life. It had always seemed that way with us, with our square family of four, our destiny clear to me and my sister when we would sometimes speak of ourselves, not unlucky like those friends of ours whose families were wracked with ruinous divorce or drinking or disease — we were untouched, maybe untouchable, we'd been safe so far in our isolation in this country, in the country of our own house smelling so thickly of crushed garlic and seaweed and red chili pepper, as if that piquant wreath of scent from our mother's kitchen protected us and our house, kept at bay the persistent ghosts of the land who seemed to visit everyone else.

Of course, we weren't perfectly happy or healthy. Eunei and I were sometimes trouble to my parents, we were a little lazy and spoiled (myself more than my sister), we didn't study hard enough in school (though we always received the highest marks), we chose questionable friends, some from broken families, and my father, who worked fourteen hour days as a young psychiatrist, already suffered from mild hypertension and high cholesterol.

If something happened to him, my mother would warn me, if he were to die, we'd lose everything and have to move back to Korea where the living was hard and crowded and where all young men spent long years in the military. Besides, our family in Korea — the whole rest of it still there (for we were the lone emigrees) — so longed for us, missed us terribly, and the one day each year when we phoned they would plead for our return. What we could do, my mother said, to aid our father and his struggle in this country, was to relieve his worry over us, release him from that awful burden through our own hard work which would give him ease of mind and help him not to die.

My mother's given name was Inja, although I never once called her that, nor ever heard my sister or even my father address her so. I knew from a young age that her name was Japanese in style and origin, from the time of Japan's military occupation of Korea, and I've wondered since why she chose never to change it to an authentic Korean name, why her mother or father didn't change the names of all their daughters after the liberation. My mother often showed open enmity for the Japanese, her face seeming to ash over when she spoke of her memories, that picture of the platoon of lean-faced soldiers burning books and scrolls in the center of her village still aglow in my head (but from her or where else I don't know), and how they tried to erase what was Korean by criminalizing the home language and history by shipping slave labor, draftees, and young Korean women back to Japan and its other Pacific colonies. How they taught her to speak in Japanese. And as she would speak of her childhood, of the pretty, stern-lipped girl (that I only now see in tattered rust-edged photos) who could only whisper to her sisters in the midnight safety of their house the Korean words folding inside her all day like mortal secrets, I felt the same burning, troubling lode of utter pride and utter shame still jabbing at the sweet belly of her life, that awful gem, about who she was and where her mother tongue and her land had gone.

She worried all the time that I was losing my Korean. When I was in my teens, she'd get attacks of despair and urgency and say she was going to send me back to Korea for the next few summers to learn the language again. What she didn't know was that it had been whole years since I had lost the language, had left it somewhere for good, perhaps from the time I won a prize in the first grade for reading the most books in my class. I must have read fifty books. She had helped me then, pushed me to read and then read more to exhaustion until I fell asleep, because she warned me that if I didn't learn English I wouldn't be anybody and couldn't really live here like a true American. *Look at me,* she'd say, offering herself as a sad example, *look how hard it is for me to shop for food or speak to your teachers, look how shameful I am, how embarrassing.*

Her words frightened me. But I was so proud of myself and my prolific   15
reading, particularly since the whole year before in kindergarten I could barely speak a word of English. I simply listened. We played mostly anyway, or drew pictures. When the class sang songs I'd hum along with the melody and silently mouth the strange and difficult words. My best friend was another boy in the class who also knew no English, a boy named Tommy. He was Japanese. Of course, we couldn't speak to each other but it didn't matter; somehow we found a way to communicate through gestures and funny faces and laughter, and we became friends. I think we both sensed we were the smartest kids in the class. We'd sit off by ourselves with this one American girl who liked us best and play house around a wooden toy oven. I've forgotten her name. She'd hug us when we "came home from work," her two mute husbands, and she would sit us down at the little table and work a pan at the stove and bring it over and feed us. We pretended to eat her food until we were full and then she'd pull the two of us sheepish and cackling over to the shaggy remnants of carpet that she'd laid down, and we'd all go to sleep, the girl nestled snuggly between Tommy and me, hotly whispering in our ears the tones of a night music she must have heard echoing through her own house.

Later that year, after a parents' visiting day at school, my mother told me that Tommy and his family were moving away. I didn't know how she'd found that out, but we went to his house one day, and Tommy and his mother greeted us at the door. They had already begun packing, and there were neatly stacked boxes and piles of newspapers pushed to a corner of their living room. Tommy immediately led me outside to his swing set and we horsed about for an hour before coming back in, and I looked at my mother and Tommy's mother sitting upright and formally in the living room, a tea set and plate of rice cookies between them on the coffee table. The two of them weren't really talking, more smiling and waiting for us.

And then from Tommy's room full of toys, I began to hear a conversation, half of it in profoundly broken English, the other half in what must have been Japanese, at once breathy and staccato, my mother's version of it in such shreds and remnants that the odd sounds she made seemed to hurt her throat as they were called up. After we said goodbye and drove away in the car, I thought she seemed quiet and sad for me, and so I felt sadder still, though now I think that it was she who was moved and saddened by the visit, perhaps by her own act. For the momentary sake of her only son and his departing friend, she was willing to endure those two tongues of her shame, one present, one past. Language, sacrifice, the story never ends.

Inside our house (wherever it was, for we moved several times when I was young) she was strong and decisive and proud; even my father deferred to her in most matters, and when he didn't it seemed that she'd arranged it that way. Her commandments were stiff, direct. When I didn't listen to her, I understood that the disagreement was my burden, my problem. But outside, in the land of always-talking strangers and other Americans, my mother would lower her steadfast eyes, she'd grow mute, even her supremely solemn and sometimes severe face would dwindle with uncertainty; I would have to speak to a mechanic for her, I had to call the school myself when I was sick, I would write out notes to neighbors, the postman, the paper carrier. Do the work of voice. Negotiate *us*, with this here, now. I remember often fuming because of it, this one of the recurring pangs of my adolescence, feeling frustrated with her inabilities, her misplacement, and when she asked me one morning to call up the bank for her I told her I wouldn't do it and suggested that she needed "to practice" the language anyway.

Gracious god. I wished right then for her to slap me. She didn't. Couldn't. She wanted to scream something, I could tell, but bit down on her lip as she did and hurried upstairs to my parents' bedroom where I knew she found none of this trouble with her words. There she could not fail, nor could I. In that land, her words sang for her, they did good work, they pleaded for my life, shouted entreaties, ecstasies, they could draw blood if they wanted, and they could offer grace, and they could kiss.

But now — and I think, *right now* (I am discovering several present tenses) — she is barely conscious, silent.

Her eyes are very small and black. They are only half-opened. I can-   20
not call up their former kind shade of brown. Not because I am forgetting, but because it is impossible to remember. I think I cannot remember the first thing about her. I am not amnesiac because despite all this *I know everything about her*. But the memories are like words I cannot call up, the hidden vocabularies of our life together. I cannot remember, as I will in a later narrative time, her bright red woolen dress with the looming black buttons that rub knobbly and rough against my infant face; I cannot remember, as I will soon dream it, the way her dark clean hair falls on me like a cloak when she lifts me from the ground; I cannot remember — if I could ever truly forget — the look of those soft Korean

words as they play on her face when she speaks to me of honor and respect and devotion.

This is a maddening state, maybe even horrifying, mostly because I think I must do anything but reside in this very place and time and moment, that to be able to remember her now—something of her, anything—would be to forget the present collection of memories, this inexorable gathering of future remembrances. I want to disband this accumulation, break it apart before its bonds become forever certain.

She wears only a striped pajama top. Her catheter tube snakes out from between the top buttons. We know she is slipping away, going fast now, so someone, not me, disconnects the line to her food and water. The tube is in her way. These last moments will not depend on it. Her line to the morphine, though, is kept open and clear and running.

This comforts me. I have always feared her pain and I will to the end. Before she received the automatic pump that gives her a regular dosage of the drug I would shoot her with a needle at least five times a day.

For some reason I wish I could do it now:

I will have turned her over gently. She will moan. Every movement   25
except the one mimicking death is painful. I fit the narrow white syringe with a small needle, twisting it on tight. I then pull off the needle's protective plastic sheath. (Once, I will accidently jab myself deep in the ring finger and while I hold gauze to the bloody wound she begins to cry. I am more careful after that.) Now I fill the syringe to the prescribed line, and then I go several lines past it; I always give her a little more than what the doctors tell us, and she knows of this transgression, my little gift to her, to myself. I say I am ready and then she lifts her hips so I can pull down her underwear to reveal her buttocks.

I know her body. The cancer in her stomach is draining her, hungrily sucking the life out of her, but the liquid food she gets through the tube has so many calories that it bloats her, giving her figure the appearance of a young girl who likes sweets too well. Her rump is full, fleshy, almost healthy-looking except for the hundreds of needlemarks. There is almost no space left. I do not think it strange anymore that I see her naked like this. Even the sight of her pubic hair, darkly coursing out from under her, is now, if anything, of a certain more universal reminiscence, a kind of metonymic reminder that not long before she was truly in the world, one of its own, a woman, fully alive, historical, a mother, a bearer of life.

I feel around for unseeable bruises until I find a spot we can both agree on.

"Are you ready?" I say. "I'm going to poke."

"*Gu-rhach,*" she answers, which, in this context, means some cross between "That's right" and "Go ahead, damn it."

I jab and she sucks in air between her teeth, wincing.   30

"*Ay, ah-po.*" It hurts.

"A lot?" I ask, pulling the needle out as straight as I can, to avoid brushing her. We have the same exchange each time; but each time there arises a renewed urgency, and then I know I know nothing of her pains.

I never dreamed of them. Imagined them. I remember writing short stories in high school with narrators or chief characters of unidentified race and ethnicity. Of course this meant they were white, everything in my stories was some kind of white, though I always avoided physical descriptions of them or passages on their lineage and they always had cryptic first names like Garlo or Kram.

Mostly, though, they were figures who (I thought) could appear in an *authentic* short story, *belong* to one, that no reader would notice anything amiss in them, as if they'd inhabited forever those visionary landscapes of tales and telling, where a snow still falls faintly and faintly falls over all of Joyce's Ireland, that great muting descent, all over Hemingway's Spain, and Cheever's Suburbia, and Bellow's City of Big Shoulders.

I was to breach that various land, become its finest citizen and furiously speak its dialects. And it was only with one story that I wrote back then, in which the character is still unidentified but his *mother* is Asian (maybe even Korean), that a cleaving happened. That the land broke open at my feet. At the end of the story, the protagonist returns to his parents' home after a long journey; he is ill, feverish, and his mother tends to him, offers him cool drink, compresses, and she doesn't care where he's been in the strange wide country. They do not speak; she simply knows that he is home.

> Now I dab the pinpoint of blood. I'm trying to be careful.
> "*Gaen-cha-na,*" she says. *It is fine.*
> "Do you need anything?"
> "*Ggah,*" she says, flitting her hand, "*kul suh.*" *Go, go and write.*
> "What do you want? Anything, anything."
> "*In-jeh na jal-leh.*" *Now I want to sleep.*
> "Okay, sleep. Rest. What?"
> "*Boep-bo.*" *Kiss.*
> "Kiss."
> *Kiss.*

This will be our language always. To me she speaks in a child's Korean, and for her I speak that same child's English. We use only the simplest words. I think it strange that throughout this dire period we necessarily speak like this. Neither of us has ever grown up or out of this language; by virtue of speech I am forever her perfect little boy, she my eternal righteous guide. We are locked in a time. I love her, and I cannot grow up. And if all mothers and sons converse this way I think the communication must remain for the most part unconscious; for us, however, this speaking is everything we possess. And although I wonder if our union is handicapped by it I see also the minute discoveries in the mining of the words. I will say to her as naturally as I can — as I could speak only years before as a child — *I love you, Mother,* and then this thing will happen, the diction will take us back, bridge this moment with the others, remake this time so full and real. And in our life together, our strange language is the bridge and all that surrounds it; language is the brook streaming through it; it is the mossy stones, the bank, the blooming canopy above, the ceaseless sound, the sky. It is the last earthly thing we have.

My mother, no longer connected to her machine, lies on the bed on the floor. Over the last few hours she suffers brief fits and spasms as if she is chilled. She stirs when we try to cover her with the blanket. She kicks her legs to get it off. Something in her desires to be liberated. Finally we take it away. Let her be, we think. And now, too, you can begin to hear the indelicate sound of her breathing; it is audible, strangely demonstrative. Her breath resonates in this house, begins its final cadence. She sounds as though she were inhaling and exhaling for the very first time. Her body shudders with that breath. My sister tries to comfort her by stroking her arms. My mother groans something unintelligible, though strangely I say to myself for her, *Leave me alone, all of you. I am dying. At last I am dying.* But then I stroke her, too. She keeps shuddering, but it is right.

What am I thinking? Yes. It is that clear. The closer she slips away, down into the core of her being, what I think of as an origin, a once-starting point, the more her body begins to protest the happening, to try to hold down, as I am, the burgeoning, blooming truth of the moment.

For we think we know how this moment will be. Each of us in this room has been elaborating upon it from the very moment we gained knowledge of her illness. This is the way it comes to me, but I think we have written, each of us, the somber epic novel of her death. It has taken two and one-half years and we are all nearly done. I do not exactly know of the others' endings. Eunei, my sister (if I may take this liberty), perhaps envisioning her mother gently falling asleep, never really leaving us, simply dreams of us and her life for the rest of ever. I like that one.

My father, a physician, may write that he finally saves her, that he 50 spreads his hands on her belly where the cancer is mighty and lifts it out from her with one ultimate, sovereign effort. Sometimes (and this ought not be attributed to him) I think that his entire life has come down to this struggle against the palpable fear growing inside of his wife. And after she dies, he will cry out in a register I have never heard from his throat as he pounds his hand on the hardwood above her colorless head, *"Eeh-guh-moy-yah? Eeh-guh-moy-yah?"* *What is this? What is this?* It—the cancer, the fear—spites him, mocks him, this doctor who is afraid of blood. It—this cancer, this happening, this time—is the shape of our tragedy, the cruel sculpture of our life and family.

In the ending to my own story, my mother and I are alone. We are always alone. And one thing is certain; she needs to say something only to me. That is why I am there. Then she speaks to me, secretly. What she says exactly is unclear; it is enough, somehow, that she and I are together, alone, apart from everything else, while we share this as yet unborn and momentary speech. The words are neither in Korean nor in English, languages which in the end we cannot understand. I hear her anyway. But now we can smile and weep and laugh. We can say goodbye to each other. We can kiss, unflinching, on our mouths.

Then she asks if I might carry her to the window that she might see the new blossoms of our cherry tree. I lift her. She is amazingly light, barely there, barely physical, and while I hold her up she reaches around my neck and leans her head against my shoulder. I walk with her to the window and then turn so that she faces the tree. I gaze longingly at it myself, marveling at the gaudy flowers, and then I turn back upon her face, where the light is shining, and I can see that her eyes have now shut, and she is gone.

But here in this room we are not alone. I think she is probably glad for this, as am I. Her breathing, the doctor says, is becoming labored. He kneels and listens to her heart. "I think we should be ready," he says. "Your mother is close." He steps back. He is a good doctor, a good friend. I think he can see the whole picture of the time. And I think about what he is saying: *Your mother is close.* Yes. Close to us, close to life, close to death. She is close to everything, I think; she is attaining an irrevocable nearness of being, a proximity to everything that has been spoken or written or thought, in every land and language on earth. How did we get to this place? Why are we here in this room, assembled as we are, as if arrayed in some ancient haunted painting whose grave semblance must be known in every mind and heart of man?

I count a full five between her breaths. The color is leaving her face. The mask is forming. Her hand in mine is cold, already dead. I think it is now that I must speak to her. I understand that I am not here to listen; that must be for another narrative. I am not here to bear her in my arms towards bright windows. I am not here to be strong. I am not here to exchange goodbyes. I am not here to recount old stories. I am not here to acknowledge the dead.

I am here to speak. Say the words. Her nearness has delivered   55
me to this moment, an ever-lengthening moment between her breaths, that I might finally speak the words turning inward, for the first time, in my own beginning and lonely language: Do not be afraid. It is all right, so do not be afraid. You are not really alone. You may die, but you will have been heard. Keep speaking—it is real. You have a voice.

The Reader's Presence

1. Language plays an important role in Lee's conception of cultural identity. Language, however, can be considered both literally and figuratively. What does Japanese symbolize for Lee's mother? What "languages" other than Korean do Lee and his mother fail

to share? What "languages" do they learn through her illness? In what ways does Lee function as a "translator"?

2. Lee's young pretend-wife seems unaware of cultural expectations. To what extent does her behavior upset traditional social roles? Why might Lee have chosen to include this anecdote in his account of his relationship with his mother? Where else in the essay are such confusions evident?

3. Lee's essay abounds with unresolved conflicts. What is the effect of this irresolution upon the reader? Which sort of essay do you feel is stronger: one in which the author has determined his or her conclusion in advance, or one in which the writer is actively working through a problem in the process of writing? Why?

23

Nancy Mairs

On Being a Cripple

Nancy Mairs (b. 1943) has contributed poetry, short stories, articles, and essays to numerous journals. "On Being a Cripple" comes from, Plaintext, *which was published in 1986. More recent publications include* Remembering the Bone House: An Erotics of Time and Space *(1989),* Carnal Acts: Essays *(1990),* Ordinary Time: Cycles in Marriage, Faith, and Renewal *(1993), and* Waist High in the World: A Life Among the Nondisabled *(1996). From 1983 to 1985 she served as assistant director of the Southwest Institute for Research on Women, and has also taught at the University of Arizona and at UCLA.*

In Voice Lessons: On Becoming a (Woman) Writer *(1994), she writes, "I want a prose that is allusive and translucent, that eases you into me and embraces you, not one that baffles you or bounces you around so that you can't even tell where I am. And so I have chosen to work, very, very carefully, with the language we share, faults and all, choosing each word for its capacity, its ambiguity, the space it provides for me to live my life within it, relating rather than opposing each word to the next, each sentence to the next, 'starting on all sides at once . . . twenty times, thirty times, over': the stuttering adventure of the essay."*

To escape is nothing. Not to escape is nothing.

—Louise Bogan

The other day I was thinking of writing an essay on being a cripple. I was thinking hard in one of the stalls of the women's room in my office building, as I was shoving my shirt into my jeans and tugging up my zipper. Preoccupied, I flushed, picked up my book bag, took my cane down from the hook, and unlatched the door. So many movements unbalanced me, and as I pulled the door open I fell over backward, landing fully clothed on the toilet seat with my legs splayed in front of me: the old beetle-on-its-back routine. Saturday afternoon, the building deserted, I was free to laugh aloud as I wriggled back to my feet, my voice bouncing off the yellowish tiles from all directions. Had anyone been there with me, I'd have been still and faint and hot with chagrin. I decided that it was high time to write the essay.

First, the matter of semantics. I am a cripple. I choose this word to name me. I choose from among several possibilities, the most common of which are "handicapped" and "disabled." I made the choice a number of years ago, without thinking, unaware of my motives for doing so. Even now, I'm not sure what those motives are, but I recognize that they are complex and not entirely flattering. People—crippled or not—wince at the word "cripple," as they do not at "handicapped" or "disabled." Perhaps I want them to wince. I want them to see me as a tough customer, one to whom the fates/gods/viruses have not been kind, but who can face the brutal truth of her existence squarely. As a cripple, I swagger.

But, to be fair to myself, a certain amount of honesty underlies my choice. "Cripple" seems to me a clean word, straightforward and precise. It has an honorable history, having made its first appearance in the Lindisfarne Gospel in the tenth century. As a lover of words, I like the accuracy with which it describes my condition: I have lost the full use of my limbs. "Disabled," by contrast, suggests any incapacity, physical or mental. And I certainly don't like "handicapped," which implies that I have deliberately been put at a disadvantage, by whom I can't imagine (my God is not a Handicapper General), in order to equalize chances in the great race of life. These words seem to me to be moving away from my condition, to be widening the gap between word and reality. Most remote is the recently coined euphemism "differently abled," which partakes of the same semantic hopefulness that transformed countries from "undeveloped" to "underdeveloped," then to "less developed," and finally to "developing" nations. People have continued to starve in those countries during the shift. Some realities do not obey the dictates of language.

Mine is one of them. Whatever you call me, I remain crippled. But I don't care what you call me, so long as it isn't "differently abled," which strikes me as pure verbal garbage designed, by its ability to describe anyone, to describe no one. I subscribe to George Orwell's thesis that "the slovenliness of our language makes it easier for us to have foolish thoughts."[1] And I refuse to participate in the degeneration of the language to the extent that I deny that I have lost anything in the course of

---

[1] *Orwell:* From his essay "Politics and The English Language" (see page 498). —EDS.

this calamitous disease; I refuse to pretend that the only difference between you and me are the various ordinary ones that distinguish any one person from another. But call me "disabled" or "handicapped" if you like. I have long since grown accustomed to them; and if they are vague, at least they hint at the truth. Moreover, I use them myself. Society is no readier to accept crippledness than to accept death, war, sex, sweat, or wrinkles. I would never refer to another person as a cripple. It is the word I use to name only myself.

I haven't always been crippled, a fact for which I am soundly grateful. To be whole of limb is, I know from experience, infinitely more pleasant and useful than to be crippled: and if that knowledge leaves me open to bitterness at my loss, the physical soundness I once enjoyed (though I did not enjoy it half enough) is well worth the occasional stab of regret. Though never any good at sports, I was a normally active child and young adult. I climbed trees, played hopscotch, jumped rope, skated, swam, rode my bicycle, sailed. I despised team sports, spending some of the wretchedest afternoons of my life, sweaty and humiliated, behind a field-hockey stick and under a basketball hoop. I tramped alone for miles along the bridle paths that webbed the woods behind the house I grew up in. I swayed through countless dim hours in the arms of one man or another under the scattered shot of light from mirrored balls, and gyrated through countless more as Tab Hunter and Johnny Mathis gave way to the Rolling Stones, Creedance Clearwater Revival, Cream. I walked down the aisle. I pushed baby carriages, changed tires in the rain, marched for peace.

When I was twenty-eight I started to trip and drop things. What at first seemed my natural clumsiness soon became too pronounced to shrug off. I consulted a neurologist, who told me that I had a brain tumor. A battery of tests, increasingly disagreeable, revealed no tumor. About a year and a half later I developed a blurred spot in one eye. I had, at last, the episodes "disseminated in space and time" requisite for a diagnosis: multiple sclerosis. I have never been sorry for the doctor's initial misdiagnosis, however. For almost a week, until the negative results of the tests were in, I thought that I was going to die right away. Every day for the past nearly ten years, then, has been a kind of gift. I accept all gifts.

Multiple sclerosis is a chronic degenerative disease of the central nervous system, in which the myelin that sheathes the nerves is somehow eaten away and scar tissue forms in its place, interrupting the nerves' signals. During its course, which is unpredictable and uncontrollable, one may lose vision, hearing, speech, the ability to walk, control of bladder and/or bowels, strength in any or all extremities, sensitivity to touch, vibration, and/or pain, potency, coordination of movements — the list of possibilities is lengthy and, yes, horrifying. One may also lose one's sense of humor. That's the easiest to lose and the hardest to survive without.

In the past ten years, I have sustained some of these losses. Characteristic of MS are sudden attacks, called exacerbations, followed by remissions, and these I have not had. Instead, my disease has been slowly progressive. My left leg is now so weak that I walk with the aid of a brace and a cane; and for distances I use an Amigo, a variation on the electric wheelchair that looks rather like an electrified kiddie car. I no longer have much use of my left hand. Now my right side is weakening as well. I still have the blurred spot in my right eye. Overall, though, I've been lucky so far. My world has, of necessity, been circumscribed by my losses, but the terrain left me has been ample enough for me to continue many of the activities that absorb me: writing, teaching, raising children and cats and plants and snakes, reading, speaking publicly about MS and depression, even playing bridge with people patient and honorable enough to let me scatter cards every which way without sneaking a peek.

Lest I begin to sound like Pollyanna, however, let me say that I don't like having MS. I hate it. My life holds realities—harsh ones, some of them—that no right-minded human being ought to accept without grumbling. One of them is fatigue. I know of no one with MS who does not complain of bone-weariness; in a disease that presents an astonishing variety of symptoms, fatigue seems to be a common factor. I wake up in the morning feeling the way most people do at the end of a bad day, and I take it from there. As a result, I spend a lot of time *in extremis* and, impatient with limitation, I tend to ignore my fatigue until my body breaks down in some way and forces rest. Then I miss picnics, dinner parties, poetry readings, the brief visits of old friends from out of town. The offspring of a puritanical tradition of exceptional venerability, I cannot view these lapses without shame. My life often seems a series of small failures to do as I ought.

I lead, on the whole, an ordinary life, probably rather like the one I   10 would have led had I not had MS. I am lucky that my predilections were already solitary, sedentary, and bookish—unlike the world-famous French cellist I have read about, or the young woman I talked with one long afternoon who wanted only to be a jockey. I had just begun graduate school when I found out something was wrong with me, and I have remained, interminably, a graduate student. Perhaps I would not have if I'd thought I had the stamina to return to a full-time job as a technical editor; but I've enjoyed my studies.

In addition to studying, I teach writing courses. I also teach medical students how to give neurological examinations. I pick up freelance editing jobs here and there. I have raised a foster son and sent him into the world, where he has made me two grandbabies, and I am still escorting my daughter and son through adolescence. I go to Mass every Saturday. I am a superb, if messy, cook. I am also an enthusiastic laundress, capable of sorting a hamper full of clothes into five subtly differentiated piles, but a terrible housekeeper. I can do italic writing and, in an emergency, bathe an oil-soaked cat. I play a fiendish game of Scrabble. When I have the time and the money, I'd like to sit on my front steps with my husband, drinking Amaretto and smoking a cigar, as we imagine our counterparts in Leningrad and make sure that the sun gets down once more behind the sharp childish scrawl of the Tucson Mountains.

This lively plenty has its bleak complement, of course, in all the things I can no longer do. I will never run again, except in dreams, and one day I may have to write that I will never walk again. I like to go camping, but I can't follow George and the children along the trails that wander out of a campsite through the desert or into the mountains. In fact, even on the level I've learned never to check the weather or try to hold a coherent conversation: I need all my attention for my wayward feet. Of late, I have begun to catch myself wondering how people can propel themselves without canes. With only one usable hand, I have to select my clothing with care not so much for style as for ease of ingress and egress, and even so, dressing can be laborious. I can no longer do fine stitchery, pick up babies, play the piano, braid my hair. I am immobilized by acute attacks of depression, which may or may not be physiologically related to MS but are certainly its logical concomitant.

These two elements, the plenty and the privation, are never pure, nor are the delight and wretchedness that accompany them. Almost every pickle that I get into as a result of my weakness and clumsiness—and I get into plenty—is funny as well as maddening and sometimes painful. I recall one May afternoon when a friend and I were going out for a drink after finishing up at school. As we were climbing into opposite sides of my car, chatting, I tripped and fell, flat and hard, onto the asphalt parking lot, my abrupt departure interrupting him in mid-sentence. "Where'd you go?" he called as he came around the back of the car to find me hauling myself up by the door frame. "Are you all right?" Yes, I told him, I was fine, just a bit rattly, and we drove off to find a shady patio and some beer. When I got home an hour or so later, my daughter greeted me with "What have you done to yourself?" I looked down. One elbow of my white turtleneck with the green froggies, one knee of my white trousers, one white kneesock were blood-soaked. We peeled off the clothes and inspected the damage, which was nasty enough but not alarming. That part wasn't funny: The abrasions took a long time to heal, and one got a little infected. Even so, when I think of my friend talking earnestly, suddenly, to the hot thin air while I dropped from his view as though through a trap door, I find the image as silly as something from a Marx Brothers movie.

I may find it easier than other cripples to amuse myself because I live propped by the acceptance and the assistance and, sometimes, the amusement of those around me. Grocery clerks tear my checks out of my checkbook for me, and sales clerks find chairs to put into dressing rooms when I want to try on clothes. The people I work with make sure I teach at times when I am least likely to be fatigued, in places I can get to, with the materials I need. My students, with one anonymous exception (in an end-of-the-semester evaluation), have been unperturbed by my disability. Some even like it. One was immensely cheered by the information that I paint my own fingernails; she decided, she told me, that if I could go to such trouble over fine details, she could keep on writing essays. I suppose I became some sort of bright-fingered muse. She wrote good essays, too.

The most important struts in the framework of my existence, of course, are my husband and children. Dismayingly few marriages survive the MS test, and why should they? Most twenty-two- and nineteen-year-olds, like George and me, can vow in clear conscience, after a childhood of chicken pox and summer colds, to keep one another in sickness and in health so long as they both shall live. Not many are equipped for catastrophe: the dismay, the depression, the extra work, the boredom that a degenerative disease can insinuate into a relationship. And our society, with its emphasis on fun and its association of fun with physical performance, offers little encouragement for a whole spouse to stay with a crippled partner. Children experience similar stresses when faced with a crippled parent, and they are more helpless, since parents and children can't usually get divorced. They hate, of course, to be different from their peers, and the child whose mother is tacking down the aisle of a school auditorium packed with proud parents like a Cape Cod dinghy in a stiff breeze jolly well stands out in a crowd. Deprived of legal divorce, the child can at least deny the mother's disability, even her existence, forgetting to tell here about recitals and PTA meetings, refusing to accompany her to stores or church or the movies, never inviting friends to the house. Many do.

But I've been limping along for ten years now, and so far George and the children are still at my left elbow, holding tight. Anne and Matthew vacuum floors and dust furniture and haul trash and rake up dog droppings and button my cuffs and bake lasagna and Toll House cookies with just enough grumbling so I know that they don't have brain fever. And far from hiding me, they're forever dragging me by racks of fancy clothes or through teeming school corridors, or welcoming gaggles of friends while I'm wandering through the house in Anne's filmy pink babydoll pajamas. George generally calls before he brings someone home, but he does just as many dumb thankless chores as the children. And they all yell at me, laugh at some of my jokes, write me funny letters when we're apart—in short, treat me as an ordinary human being for whom they have some use. I think they like me. Unless they're faking. . . .

Faking. There's the rub. Tugging at the fringes of my consciousness always is the terror that people are kind to me only because I'm a cripple. My mother almost shattered me once, with that instinct mothers have—blind, I think, in this case, but unerring nonetheless—for striking blows along the fault-lines of their children's hearts, by telling me, in an attack on my selfishness, "We all have to make allowances for you, of course, because of the way you are." From the distance of a couple of years, I have to admit that I haven't any idea just what she meant, and I'm not sure that she knew either. She was awfully angry. But at the time, as the words thudded home, I felt my worst fear, suddenly realized. I could bear being called selfish: I am. But I couldn't bear the corroboration that those around me were doing in fact what I'd always suspected them of doing, professing fondness while silently putting up with me because of the way I am. A cripple. I've been a little cracked ever since.

Along with this fear that people are secretly accepting shoddy goods comes a relentless pressure to please—to prove myself worth the burdens I impose, I guess, or to build a substantial account of good will against which I may write drafts in times of need. Part of the pressure arises from social expectations. In our society, anyone who deviates from the norm had better find some way to compensate. Like fat people, who are expected to be jolly, cripples must bear their lot meekly and cheerfully. A grumpy cripple isn't playing by the rules. And much of the pressure is self-generated. Early on I vowed that, if I had to have MS, by God I was going to do it well. This is a class act, ladies and gentlemen. No tears, no recriminations, no faint-heartedness.

One way and another, then, I wind up feeling like Tiny Tim,[2] peering over the edge of the table at the Christmas goose, waving my crutch, piping down God's blessing on us all. Only sometimes I don't want to play Tiny Tim, I'd rather be Caliban,[3] a most scurvy monster. Fortunately, at home no one much cares whether I'm a good cripple or a bad cripple as long as I make vichyssoise with fair regularity. One evening several years ago, Anne was reading at the dining-room table while I cooked dinner. As I opened a can of tomatoes, the can slipped in my left hand and juice spattered me and the counter with bloody spots. Fatigued and infuriated, I bellowed, "I'm so sick of being crippled!" Anne glanced at me over the top of her book. "There now," she said, "do you feel better?" "Yes," I said, "yes, I do." She went back to her reading. I felt better. That's about all the attention my scurviness ever gets.

Because I hate being crippled, I sometimes hate myself for being a cripple. Over the years I have come to expect—even accept—attacks of violent self-loathing. Luckily, in general our society no longer connects deformity and disease directly with evil (though a charismatic once told me that I have MS because a devil is in me) and so I'm allowed to move largely at will, even among small children. But I'm not sure that this revision of attitude has been particularly helpful. Physical imperfection, even freed of moral disapprobation, still defies and violates the ideal, especially for women, whose confinement in their bodies as objects of desire is far from over. Each age, of course, has its ideal, and I doubt that ours is any better or worse than any other. Today's ideal woman, who lives on the glossy pages of dozens of magazines, seems to be between the ages of eighteen and twenty-five; her hair has body, her teeth flash white, her breath smells minty, her underarms are dry; she has a career but is still a fabulous cook, especially of meals that take less than twenty minutes to prepare; she does not ordinarily appear to have a husband or children; she is trim and deeply tanned; she jogs, swims, plays tennis, rides a bicycle, sails, but does not bowl; she travels widely, even to out-of-the-way places like Finland and Samoa, always in the company of the ideal man,

20

[2]**Tiny Tim:** Crippled boy in Charles Dickens's *A Christmas Carol.*—EDS.
[3]**Caliban:** A character in Shakespeare's play, *The Tempest.*—EDS.

who possesses a nearly identical set of characteristics. There are a few exceptions. Though usually white and often blonde, she may be black, Hispanic, Asian, or Native American, so long as she is unusually sleek. She may be old, provided she is selling a laxative or is Lauren Bacall. If she is selling a detergent, she may be married and have a flock of strikingly messy children. But she is never a cripple.

Like many women I know, I have always had an uneasy relationship with my body. I was not a popular child, largely, I think now, because I was peculiar: intelligent, intense, moody, shy, given to unexpected actions and inexplicable notions and emotions. But as I entered adolescence, I believed myself unpopular because I was homely; my breasts too flat, my mouth too wide, my hips too narrow, my clothing never quite right in fit or style. I was not, in fact, particularly ugly, old photographs inform me, though I was well off the ideal; but I carried this sense of self-alienation with me into adulthood, where it regenerated in response to the depredations of MS. Even with my brace I walk with a limp so pronounced that, seeing myself on the videotape of a television program on the disabled, I couldn't believe that anything but an inchworm could make progress humping along like that. My shoulders droop and my pelvis thrusts forward as I try to balance myself upright, throwing my frame into a bony S. As a result of contractures, one shoulder is higher than the other and I carry one arm bent in front of me, the fingers curled into a claw. My left arm and leg have wasted into pipe-stems, and I try always to keep them covered. When I think about how my body must look to others, especially to men, to whom I have been trained to display myself, I feel ludicrous, even loathsome.

At my age, however, I don't spend much time thinking about my appearance. The burning egocentricity of adolescence, which assures one that all the world is looking all the time, has passed, thank God, and I'm generally too caught up in what I'm doing to step back, as I used to, and watch myself as though upon a stage. I'm also too old to believe in the accuracy of self-image. I know that I'm not a hideous crone, that in fact, when I'm rested, well dressed, and well made up, I look fine. The self-loathing I feel is neither physically nor intellectually substantial. What I hate is not me but a disease.

I am not a disease.

And a disease is not—at least not singlehandedly—going to determine who I am, though at first it seemed to be going to. Adjusting to a chronic incurable illness, I have moved through a process similar to that outlined by Elizabeth Kübler-Ross in *On Death and Dying*. The major difference—and it is far more significant than most people recognize—is that I can't be sure of the outcome, as the terminally ill cancer patient can. Research studies indicate that, with proper medical care, I may achieve a "normal" life span. And in our society, with its vision of death as the ultimate evil, worse even than decrepitude, the response to such news is, "Oh well, at least you're not going to *die,*" Are there worse things than dying? I think that there may be.

I think of two women I know, both with MS, both enough older than   25
I to have served me as models. One took to her bed several years ago and
has been there ever since. Although she can sit in a high-backed wheelchair, because she is incontinent she refuses to go out at all, even though
incontinence pants, which are readily available at any pharmacy, could
protect her from embarrassment. Instead, she stays at home and insists
that her husband, a small quiet man, a retired civil servant, stay there
with her except for a quick weekly foray to the supermarket. The other
woman, whose illness was diagnosed when she was eighteen, a nursing
student engaged to a young doctor, finished her training, married her
doctor, accompanied him to Germany when he was in the service, bore
three sons and a daughter, now grown and gone. When she can, she travels with her husband; she plays bridge, embroiders, swims regularly; she
works, like me, as a symptomatic-patient instructor of medical students in
neurology. Guess which woman I hope to be.

At the beginning, I thought about having MS almost incessantly. And
because of the unpredictable course of the disease, my thoughts were always terrified. Each night I'd get into bed wondering whether I'd get out
again the next morning, whether I'd be able to see, to speak, to hold a
pen between my fingers. Knowing that the day might come when I'd be
physically incapable of killing myself, I thought perhaps I ought to do so
right away, while I still had the strength. Gradually I came to understand
that the Nancy who might one day lie inert under a bedsheet, arms and
legs paralyzed, unable to feed or bathe herself, unable to reach out for a
gun, a bottle of pills, was not the Nancy I was at present, and that I could
not presume to make decisions for that future Nancy, who might well not
want in the least to die. Now the only provision I've made for the future
Nancy is that when the time comes—and it is likely to come in the form
of pneumonia, friend to the weak and the old—I am not to be treated
with machines and medications. If she is unable to communicate by then.
I hope she will be satisfied with these terms.

Thinking all the time about having MS grew tiresome and intrusive,
especially in the large and tragic mode in which I was accustomed to considering my plight. Months and even years went by without catastrophe
(at least without one related to MS), and really I was awfully busy, what
with George and children and snakes and students and poems, and I
hadn't the time, let alone the inclination, to devote myself to being a disease. Too, the richer my life became, the funnier it seemed, as though
there were some connection between largesse and laughter, and so my
tragic stance began to waver until, even with the aid of a brace and a
cane, I couldn't hold it for very long at a time.

After several years I was satisfied with my adjustment. I had suffered
my grief and fury and terror, I thought, but now I was at ease with my
lot. Then one summer day I set out with George and the children across
the desert for a vacation in California. Part way to Yuma I became aware
that my right leg felt funny. "I think I've had an exacerbation," I told

George. "What shall we do?" he asked. "I think we'd better get the hell to California," I said, "because I don't know whether I'll ever make it again." So we went on to San Diego and then to Orange, up the Pacific Coast Highway to Santa Cruz, across to Yosemite, down to Sequoia and Joshua Tree, and so back over the desert to home. It was a fine two-week trip, filled with friends and fair weather, and I wouldn't have missed it for the world, though I did in fact make it back to California two years later. Nor would there have been any point in missing it, since in MS, once the symptoms have appeared, the neurological damage has been done, and there's no way to predict or prevent that damage.

The incident spoiled my self-satisfaction, however. It renewed my grief and fury and terror, and I learned that one never finishes adjusting to MS. I don't know now why I thought one would. One does not, after all, finish adjusting to life, and MS is simply a fact of my life—not my favorite fact, of course—but as ordinary as my nose and my tropical fish and my yellow Mazda station wagon. It may at any time get worse, but no amount of worry or anticipation can prepare me for a new loss. My life is a lesson in losses. I learn one at a time.

And I had best be patient in the learning, since I'll have to do it like it   30
or not. As any rock fan knows, you can't always get what you want. Particularly when you have MS. You can't, for example, get cured. In recent years researchers and the organizations that fund research have started to pay MS some attention even though it isn't fatal; perhaps they have begun to see that life is something other than a quantitative phenomenon, that one may be very much alive for a very long time in a life that isn't worth living. The researchers have made some progress toward understanding the mechanism of the disease: It may well be an autoimmune reaction triggered by a slow-acting virus. But they are nowhere near its prevention, control, or cure. And most of us want to be cured. Some, unable to accept incurability, grasp at one treatment after another, no matter how bizarre: megavitamin therapy, gluten-free diet, injections of cobra venom, hypothermal suits, lymphocytopharesis, hyperbaric chambers. Many treatments are probably harmless enough, but none are curative.

The absence of a cure often makes MS patients bitter toward their doctors. Doctors are, after all, the priests of modern society, the new shamans, whose business is to heal, and many an MS patient roves from one to another, searching for the "good" doctor who will make him well. Doctors too think of themselves as healers, and for this reason many have trouble dealing with MS patients, whose disease in its intransigence defeats their aims and mocks their skills. Too few doctors, it is true, treat their patients as whole human beings, but the reverse is also true. I have always tried to be gentle with my doctors, who often have more at stake in terms of ego than I do. I may be frustrated, maddened, depressed by the incurability of my disease, but I am not diminished by it, and they are. When I push myself up from my seat in the waiting room and stumble toward them, I incarnate the limitation of their powers. The least I can do is refuse to press on their tenderest spots.

This gentleness is part of the reason that I'm not sorry to be a cripple. I didn't have it before. Perhaps I'd have developed it anyway — how could I know such a thing? — and I wish I had more of it, but I'm glad of what I have. It has opened and enriched my life enormously, this sense that my frailty and need must be mirrored in others, that in searching for and shaping a stable core in a life wrenched by change and loss, change and loss, I must recognize the same process, under individual conditions, in the lives around me. I do not deprecate such knowledge, however I've come by it.

All the same, if a cure were found, would I take it? In a minute. I may be a cripple, but I'm only occasionally a loony and never a saint. Anyway, in my brand of theology God doesn't give bonus points for a limp. I'd take a cure; I just don't need one. A friend who also has MS startled me once by asking, "Do you ever say to yourself, 'Why me, Lord?'" "No, Michael, I don't," I told him, "because whenever I try, the only response I can think of is 'Why not?'" If I could make a cosmic deal, who would I put in my place? What in my life would I give up in exchange for sound limbs and a thrilling rush of energy? No one. Nothing. I might as well do the job myself. Now that I'm getting the hang of it."

The Reader's Presence

1. What does the epigraph from Louise Bogan mean to you? What might it signify in relation to Mairs's essay? What is "escape," in Mairs's context? What meanings might the word *nothing* have?

2. Mairs frequently makes allusions to literature. How many can you find? What effect do they have on your reading experience? What purpose might they serve, for the reader or the writer?

3. Mairs's approach to her difficulties may come across as ironic, jaunty, or tough. What position does the essay attempt to persuade the reader to take toward Mairs and her illness? Is this approach identical to the one she takes? Do you think it would be acceptable for a person without her illness to address Mairs's condition in a tone similar to her own?

THE WRITER AT WORK

Nancy Mairs on Finding a Voice

In writing workshops and lectures, the essayist Nancy Mairs is often asked what appears to be a simple question: How did you find your voice as a writer? Yet is the question truly an easy one? In the following passage from her book "on becoming a (woman) writer," Voice Lessons, *Mairs closely examines the question*

and suggests a way it might be answered. You might want to compare her con-
cern about finding a voice to that of Henry Louis Gates Jr. on page 121.

The question I am most often asked when I speak to students and others interested in writing is, How did you find your voice? I have some trouble with this locution because "find" always suggests to me the discovery, generally fortuitous, of some lack or loss. I have found an occasional four-leaf clover. I have found a mate. I have, more than once, found my way home. But is a voice susceptible of the same sort of revelation or retrieval? Hasn't mine simply always been there, from my earliest lallation to the "I love you" I called after my husband on his way to school several hours ago?

But of course, I remind myself, the question doesn't concern *my* voice at all but the voice of another woman (also named Nancy Mairs, confusingly enough) whose "utterances" are, except for the occasional public reading, literally inaudible: not, strictly speaking, a voice at all, but a fabrication, a device. And when I look again at the dictionary, I see that "find" can indeed also mean "devise." The voice in question, like the woman called into being to explain its existence, is an invention.

But of whom? For simplicity's sake, we assume that the voice in a work is that of the writer (in the case of nonfiction) or one invented by her (in the case of fiction). This assumption describes the relationship between writer (the woman in front of a luminous screen) and persona (whoever you hear speaking to you right now) adequately for most readers. And maybe for most writers, too. Until that earnest student in the second row waves a gnawed pencil over her head and asks, timidly as a rule because hers is the first question, "How did you find your voice?"

As though "you" were a coherent entity already existing at some original point, who had only to open her mouth and agitate her vocal chords—or, to be precise, pick up her fingers and diddle the keys—to call the world she had in mind into being. Not just a writer, an Author. But I've examined this process over and over in myself, and the direction of this authorial plot simply doesn't ring true. In the beginning, remember, was the *Word*. Not me. And the question, properly phrased, should probably be asked of my voice: How did you find (devise, invent, contrive) your Nancy?

24

Malcolm X

Homeboy

Malcolm X (1925–1965) is regarded as one of the most influential figures in the struggle for racial equality. Born Malcolm Little in Omaha, Nebraska, his family was frequently the target of racist violence: white supremacists burned their home, and his father, a Baptist minister, was horribly murdered. After his father's death, his mother was hospitalized for mental illness, and he and his seven brothers and sisters were placed in foster homes. Although a gifted student, Malcolm was discouraged by a racist teacher and quit high school. He later moved to Boston, where he engaged in various illegal activities, became addicted to narcotics, and was imprisoned for robbery. While in jail Malcolm made extensive use of the prison library and studied philosophy, politics, and the teachings of the Black Muslims' Nation of Islam. After his release from prison, Malcolm worked with Elijah Muhammad, founder and leader of the Nation of Islam, and changed his name to Malcolm X. He became known as an outspoken and articulate minister, championing racial separatism, faith in Allah, and rejection of white society, and quickly rose to a position of prominence within the organization. While on a pilgrimage to Mecca in 1964, Malcolm X became an orthodox Muslim, adopted the name El-Hajj Malik El-Shabazz, and formed his own religious organization. Hostilities grew between his followers and the Black Muslims, and in 1965 Malcolm X was assassinated in a Harlem ballroom. The Autobiography of Malcolm X (1965), from which "Homeboy" is taken, was written with Alex Haley and was published posthumously.

I looked like Li'l Abner. Mason, Michigan, was written all over me. My kinky, reddish hair was cut hick style, and I didn't even use grease in it. My green suit's coat sleeves stopped above my wrists, the pants legs showed three inches of socks. Just a shade lighter green than the suit was my narrow-collared, three-quarter length Lansing department store topcoat. My appearance was too much for even Ella.[1] But she told me later

---

[1] *Ella:* Malcolm's older sister. He left Lansing, Michigan, and moved to her house in the Roxbury section of Boston in 1948. — EDS.

she had seen countrified members of the Little family come up from Georgia in even worse shape than I was.

Ella had fixed up a nice little upstairs room for me. And she was truly a Georgia Negro woman when she got into the kitchen with her pots and pans. She was the kind of cook who would heap up your plate with such as ham hock, greens, black-eyed peas, fried fish, cabbage, sweet potatoes, grits and gravy, and cornbread. And the more you put away, the better she felt. I worked out at Ella's kitchen table like there was no tomorrow.

Ella still seemed to be as big, black, outspoken and impressive a woman as she had been in Mason and Lansing. Only about two weeks before I arrived, she had split up with her second husband—the soldier, Frank, whom I had met there the previous summer; but she was taking it right in stride. I could see, though I didn't say, how any average man would find it almost impossible to live for very long with a woman whose every instinct was to run everything and everybody she had anything to do with—including me. About my second day there in Roxbury, Ella told me that she didn't want me to start hunting for a job right away, like most newcomer Negroes did. She said that she had told all those she'd brought North to take their time, to walk around, to travel the buses and the subway, and get the feel of Boston, before they tied themselves down working somewhere, because they would never again have the time to really see and get to know anything about the city they were living in. Ella said she'd help me find a job when it was time for me to go to work.

So I went gawking around the neighborhood—the Waumbeck and Humboldt Avenue Hill section of Roxbury, which is something like Harlem's Sugar Hill, where I'd later live. I saw those Roxbury Negroes acting and living differently from any black people I'd ever dreamed of in my life. This was the snooty-black neighborhood; they called themselves the "Four Hundred," and looked down their noses at the Negroes of the black ghetto, or so-called "town" section where Mary, my other half-sister, lived.

What I thought I was seeing there in Roxbury were high-class, edu-   5
cated, important Negroes, living well, working in big jobs and positions. Their quiet homes sat back in their mowed yards. These Negroes walked along the sidewalks looking haughty and dignified, on their way to work, to shop, to visit, to church. I know now, of course, that what I was really seeing was only a big-city version of those "successful" Negro bootblacks and janitors back in Lansing. The only difference was that the ones in Boston had been brainwashed even more thoroughly. They prided themselves on being incomparably more "cultured," "cultivated," "dignified," and better off than their black brethren down in the ghetto, which was no further away than you could throw a rock. Under the pitiful misapprehension that it would make them "better," these Hill Negroes were breaking their backs trying to imitate white people.

Any black family that had been around Boston long enough to own the home they lived in was considered among the Hill elite. It didn't make any difference that they had to rent out rooms to make ends meet. Then the native-born New Englanders among them looked down upon recently migrated Southern home-owners who lived next door, like Ella. And a big percentage of the Hill dwellers were in Ella's category—Southern strivers and scramblers, and West Indian Negroes, whom both the New Englanders and the Southerners called "Black Jews." Usually it was the Southerners and the West Indians who not only managed to own the places where they lived, but also at least one other house which they rented as income property. The snooty New Englanders usually owned less than they.

In those days on the Hill, any who could claim "professional" status—teachers, preachers, practical nurses—also considered themselves superior. Foreign diplomats could have modeled their conduct on the way the Negro postmen, Pullman porters, and dining car waiters of Roxbury acted, striding around as if they were wearing top hats and cutaways.

I'd guess that eight out of ten of the Hill Negroes of Roxbury, despite the impressive-sounding job titles they affected, actually worked as menials and servants. "He's in banking," or "He's in securities." It sounded as though they were discussing a Rockefeller or a Mellon—and not some grayheaded, dignity-posturing bank janitor, or bond-house messenger. "I'm with an old family" was the euphemism used to dignify the professions of white folks' cooks and maids who talked so affectedly among their own kind in Roxbury that you couldn't even understand them. I don't know how many forty- and fifty-year-old errand boys went down the Hill dressed like ambassadors in black suits and white collars, to downtown jobs "in government," "in finance," or "in law." It has never ceased to amaze me how so many Negroes, then and now, could stand the indignity of that kind of self-delusion.

Soon I ranged out of Roxbury and began to explore Boston proper. Historic buildings everywhere I turned, and plaques and markers and statues for famous events and men. One statue in the Boston Commons astonished me: a Negro named Crispus Attucks, who had been the first man to fall in the Boston Massacre. I had never known anything like that.

I roamed everywhere. In one direction, I walked as far as Boston University. Another day, I took my first subway ride. When most of the people got off, I followed. It was Cambridge, and I circled all around in the Harvard University campus. Somewhere, I had already heard of Harvard—though I didn't know much more about it. Nobody that day could have told me I would give an address before the Harvard Law School Forum some twenty years later.

I also did a lot of exploring downtown. Why a city would have *two* big railroad stations—North Station and South Station—I couldn't understand. At both of the stations, I stood around and watched people arrive and leave. And I did the same thing at the bus station where Ella had met me. My wanderings even led me down along the piers and docks where I read plaques telling about the old sailing ships that used to put into port there.

In a letter to Wilfred, Hilda, Philbert, and Reginald back in Lansing, I told them about all this, and about the winding, narrow, cobblestoned streets, and the houses that jammed up against each other. Downtown Boston, I wrote them, had the biggest stores I'd ever seen, and white people's restaurants and hotels. I made up my mind that I was going to see every movie that came to the fine, air-conditioned theaters.

On Massachusetts Avenue, next door to one of them, the Loew's State Theater, was the huge, exciting Roseland State Ballroom. Big posters out in front advertised the nationally famous bands, white and Negro, that had played there. "COMING NEXT WEEK," when I went by that first time, was Glenn Miller.[2] I remember thinking how nearly the whole evening's music at Mason High School dances had been Glenn Miller's records. What wouldn't that crowd have given, I wondered, to be standing where Glenn Miller's band was actually going to play? I didn't know how familiar with Roseland I was going to become.

Ella began to grow concerned, because even when I had finally had enough sight-seeing, I didn't stick around very much on the Hill. She kept dropping hints that I ought to mingle with the "nice young people my age" who were to be seen in the Townsend Drugstore two blocks from her house, and a couple of other places. But even before I came to Boston, I had always felt and acted toward anyone my age as if they were in the "kid" class, like my younger brother Reginald. They had always looked up to me as if I were considerably older. On weekends back in Lansing where I'd go to get away from the white people in Mason, I'd hung around in the Negro part of town with Wilfred's and Philbert's set. Though all of them were several years older than me, I was bigger, and I actually looked older than most of them.

I didn't want to disappoint or upset Ella, but despite her advice, I began going down into the town ghetto section. That world of grocery stores, walk-up flats, cheap restaurants, poolrooms, bars, storefront churches, and pawnshops seemed to hold a natural lure for me.   15

Not only was this part of Roxbury much more exciting, but I felt more relaxed among Negroes who were being their natural selves and not putting on airs. Even though I did live on the Hill, my instincts were never—and still aren't—to feel myself any better than any other Negro.

I spent my first month in town with my mouth hanging open. The sharp-dressed young "cats" who hung on the corners and in the poolrooms, bars and restaurants, and who obviously didn't work anywhere, completely entranced me. I couldn't get over marveling at how their hair was straight and shiny like white men's hair; Ella told me this was called a "conk." I had never tasted a sip of liquor, never even smoked a cigarette, and here I saw little black children, ten and twelve years old, shooting craps, playing cards, fighting, getting grown-ups to put a penny or a nickel on their number for them, things like that. And these children

[2]***Miller:*** One of America's most popular band leaders of the 1940s.—EDS.

threw around swear words I'd never heard before, even, and slang expressions that were just as new to me, such as "stud" and "cat" and "chick" and "cool" and "hip." Every night as I lay in bed I turned these new words over in my mind. It was shocking to me that in town, especially after dark, you'd occasionally see a white girl and a Negro man strolling arm in arm along the sidewalk, and mixed couples drinking in the neon-lighted bars — not slipping off to some dark corner, as in Lansing. I wrote Wilfred and Philbert about that, too.

I wanted to find a job myself, to surprise Ella. One afternoon, something told me to go inside a poolroom whose window I was looking through. I had looked through that window many times. I wasn't yearning to play pool; in fact, I had never held a cue stick. But I was drawn by the sight of the cool-looking "cats" standing around inside, bending over the big, green, felt-topped tables, making bets and shooting the bright-colored balls into the holes. As I stared through the window this particular afternoon, something made me decide to venture inside and talk to a dark, stubby, conk-headed fellow who racked up balls for the pool-players, whom I'd heard called "Shorty." One day he had come outside and seen me standing there and said "Hi, Red," so that made me figure he was friendly.

As inconspicuously as I could, I slipped inside the door and around the side of the poolroom, avoiding people, and on to the back, where Shorty was filling an aluminum can with the powder that pool players dust on their hands. He looked up at me. Later on, Shorty would enjoy teasing me about how with that first glance he knew my whole story. "Man, that cat still *smelled* country!" he'd say, laughing. "Cat's legs was so long and his pants so short his knees showed — an' his head looked like a briar patch!"

But that afternoon Shorty didn't let it show in his face how "country" I appeared when I told him I'd appreciate it if he'd tell me how could somebody go about getting a job like his.   20

"If you mean racking up balls," said Shorty, "I don't know of no pool joints around here needing anybody. You mean you just want any slave you can find?" A "slave" meant work, a job.

He asked what kind of work I had done. I told him that I'd washed restaurant dishes in Mason, Michigan. He nearly dropped the powder can. "My homeboy! Man, gimme some skin! I'm from Lansing!"

I never told Shorty — and he never suspected — that he was about ten years older than I. He took us to be about the same age. At first I would have been embarrassed to tell him, later I just never bothered. Shorty had dropped out of first-year high school in Lansing, lived a while with an uncle and aunt in Detroit, and had spent the last six years living with his cousin in Roxbury. But when I mentioned the names of Lansing people and places, he remembered many, and pretty soon we sounded as if we had been raised in the same block. I could sense Shorty's genuine gladness, and I don't have to say how lucky I felt to find a friend as hip as he obviously was.

"Man, this is a swinging town if you dig it," Shorty said. "You're my homeboy—I'm going to school you to the happenings." I stood there and grinned like a fool. "You got to go anywhere now? Well, stick around until I get off."

One thing I liked immediately about Shorty was his frankness. When I told him where I lived, he said what I already knew—that nobody in town could stand the Hill Negroes. But he thought a sister who gave me a "pad," not charging me rent, not even running me out to find "some slave," couldn't be all bad. Shorty's slave in the poolroom, he said, was just to keep ends together while he learned his horn. A couple of years before, he'd hit the numbers and bought a saxophone. "Got it right in there in the closet now, for my lesson tonight." Shorty was taking lessons "with some other studs," and he intended one day to organize his own small band. "There's a lot of bread to be made gigging right around here in Roxbury," Shorty explained to me. "I don't dig joining some big band, one-nighting all over just to say I played with Count or Duke or somebody." I thought that was smart. I wished I had studied a horn; but I never had been exposed to one.

All afternoon, between trips up front to rack balls, Shorty talked to me out of the corner of his mouth: which hustlers—standing around, or playing at this or that table—sold "reefers," or had just come out of prison, or were "second-story men." Shorty told me that he played at least a dollar a day on the numbers. He said as soon as he hit a number, he would use the winnings to organize his band.

I was ashamed to have to admit that I had never played the numbers. "Well, you ain't never had nothing to play with," he said, excusing me, "but you start when you get a slave, and if you hit, you got a stake for something."

He pointed out some gamblers and some pimps. Some of them had white whores, he whispered. "I ain't going to lie—I dig them two-dollar white chicks," Shorty said. "There's a lot of that action around here, nights: you'll see it." I said I already had seen some. "You ever had one?" he asked.

My embarrassment at my inexperience showed. "Hell, man," he said, "don't be ashamed. I had a few before I left Lansing—them Polack chicks that used to come over the bridge. Here, they're mostly Italians and Irish. But it don't matter what kind, they're something else! Ain't no different nowhere—there's nothing they love better than a black stud."

Through the afternoon, Shorty introduced me to players and loungers. "My homeboy," he'd say, "he's looking for a slave if you hear anything." They all said they'd look out.

At seven o'clock, when the night ball-racker came on, Shorty told me he had to hurry to his saxophone lesson. But before he left, he held out to me the six or seven dollars he had collected that day in nickel and dime tips. "You got enough bread, homeboy?"

I was okay, I told him—I had two dollars. But Shorty made me take three more. "Little fattening for your pocket," he said. Before we went out, he opened his saxophone case and showed me the horn. It was gleaming brass against the green velvet, an alto sax. He said, "Keep cool, homeboy, and come back tomorrow. Some of the cats will turn you up a slave."

When I got home, Ella said there had been a telephone call from somebody named Shorty. He had left a message that over at the Roseland State Ballroom, the shoeshine boy was quitting that night, and Shorty had told him to hold the job for me.

"Malcolm, you haven't had any experience shining shoes," Ella said. Her expression and tone of voice told me she wasn't happy about my taking that job. I didn't particularly care, because I was already speechless thinking about being somewhere close to the greatest bands in the world. I didn't even wait to eat any dinner.

The ballroom was all lighted when I got there. A man at the front   35
door was letting in members of Benny Goodman's band. I told him I wanted to see the shoeshine boy, Freddie.

"You're going to be the new one?" he asked. I said I thought I was, and he laughed, "Well, maybe you'll hit the numbers and get a Cadillac, too." He told me that I'd find Freddie upstairs in the men's room on the second floor.

But downstairs before I went up, I stepped over and snatched a glimpse inside the ballroom. I just couldn't believe the size of that waxed floor! At the far end, under the soft, rose-colored lights, was the bandstand with the Benny Goodman musicians moving around, laughing and talking, arranging their horns and stands.

A wiry, brown-skinned, conked fellow upstairs in the men's room greeted me. "You Shorty's homeboy?" I said I was, and he said he was Freddie. "Good old boy," he said. "He called me, he just heard I hit the big number, and he figured right I'd be quitting." I told Freddie what the man at the front door had said about a Cadillac. He laughed and said, "Burns them white cats up when you get yourself something. Yeah, I told them I was going to get me one—just to bug them."

Freddie then said for me to pay close attention, that he was going to be busy and for me to watch but not get in the way, and he'd try to get me ready to take over at the next dance, a couple of night later.

As Freddie busied himself setting up the shoeshine stand, he told me,   40
"Get here early . . . your shoeshine rags and brushes by this footstand . . . your polish bottles, paste wax, suede brushes over here . . . everything in place, you get rushed, you never need to waste motion. . . ."

While you shined shoes, I learned, you also kept watch on customers inside, leaving the urinals. You darted over and offered a small white hand towel. "A lot of cats who ain't planning to wash their hands, sometimes you can run up with a towel and shame them. Your towels are really your best hustle in here. Cost you a penny apiece to launder—you always get at least a nickel tip."

The shoeshine customers, and any from the inside rest room who took a towel, you whiskbroomed a couple of licks. "A nickel or a dime tip, just give 'em that," Freddie said. "But for two bits, Uncle Tom a little—white cats especially like that. I've had them to come back two, three times a dance."

From down below, the sound of the music had begun floating up. I guess I stood transfixed. "You never seen a big dance?" asked Freddie. "Run on awhile, and watch."

There were a few couples already dancing under the rose-colored lights. But even more exciting to me was the crowd thronging in. The most glamorous-looking white women I'd ever seen—young ones, old ones, white cats buying tickets at the window, sticking big wads of green bills back into their pockets, checking the women's coats, and taking their arms and squiring them inside.

Freddie had some early customers when I got back upstairs. Between   45
the shoeshine stand and thrusting towels to me just as they approached the wash basin, Freddie seemed to be doing four things at once. "Here, you can take over the whiskbroom," he said, "just two or three licks—but let 'em feel it."

When things slowed a little, he said, "You ain't seen nothing tonight. You wait until you see a spooks' dance! Man, our own people carry *on!*" Whenever he had a moment, he kept schooling me. "Shoelaces, this drawer here. You just starting out, I'm going to make these to you as a present. Buy them for a nickel a pair, tell cats they need laces if they do, and charge two bits."

Every Benny Goodman record I'd ever heard in my life, it seemed, was filtering faintly into where we were. During another customer lull, Freddie let me slip back outside again to listen. Peggy Lee was at the mike singing. Beautiful! She had just joined the band and she was from North Dakota and had been singing with a group in Chicago when Mrs. Benny Goodman discovered her, we had heard some customers say. She finished the song and the crowd burst into applause. She was a big hit.

"It knocked me out, too, when I first broke in here," Freddie said, grinning, when I went back in there. "But, look, you ever shined any shoes?" He laughed when I said I hadn't excepting my own. "Well, let's go to work. I never had neither." Freddie got on the stand and went to work on his own shoes. Brush, liquid polish, brush, paste wax, shine rag, lacquer sole dressing . . . step by step, Freddie showed me what to do.

"But you got to get a whole lot faster. You can't waste time!" Freddie showed me how fast on my own shoes. Then, because business was tapering off, he had time to give me a demonstration of how to make the shine rag pop like a firecracker. "Dig the action?" he asked. He did it in slow motion. I got down and tried it on his shoes. I had the principle of it. "Just got to do it faster," Freddie said. "It's a jive noise, that's all. Cats tip better, they figure you're knocking yourself out!"

By the end of the dance, Freddie had let me shine the shoes of three   50
or four stray drunks he talking into having shines, and I had practiced picking up my speed on Freddie's shoes until they looked like mirrors.

After we had helped the janitors to clean up the ballroom after the dance, throwing out all the paper and cigarette butts and empty liquor bottles, Freddie was nice enough to drive me all the way home to Ella's on the Hill in the second-hand maroon Buick he said he was going to trade in on his Cadillac. He talked to me all the way. "I guess it's all right if I tell you, pick up a couple of dozen packs of rubbers, two-bits apiece. You notice some of those cats that came up to me around the end of the dance? Well, when some have new chicks going right, they'll come asking you for rubbers. Charge a dollar, generally you'll get an extra tip."

He looked across at me. "Some hustles you're too new for. Cats will ask you for liquor, some will want reefers. But you don't need to have nothing except rubbers—until you can dig who's a cop.

"You can make ten, twelve dollars a dance for yourself if you work everything right," Freddie said, before I got out of the car in front of Ella's. "The main thing you got to remember is that everything in the world is a hustle. So long, Red."

The next time I ran into Freddie I was downtown one night a few weeks later. He was parked in his pearl gray Cadillac, sharp as a tack, "cooling it."

"Man, you sure schooled me!" I said, and he laughed; he knew what I meant. It hadn't taken me long on the job to find out that Freddie had done less shoeshining and towel-hustling than selling liquor and reefers, and putting white "Johns" in touch with Negro whores. I also learned that white girls always flocked to the Negro dances—some of them whores whose pimps brought them to mix business and pleasure, others who came with their black boy friends, and some who came in alone, for a little freelance lusting among a plentiful availability of enthusiastic Negro men.

At the white dances, of course, nothing black was allowed, and that's where the black whores' pimps soon showed a new shoeshine boy what he could pick up on the side by slipping a phone number or address to the white Johns who came around the end of the dance looking for "black chicks."

Most of Roseland's dances were for whites only, and they had white bands only. But the only white band ever to play there at a Negro dance to my recollection, was Charlie Barnet's. The fact is that very few white bands could have satisfied the Negro dancers. But I know that Charlie Barnet's "Cherokee" and his "Redskin Rhumba" drove those Negroes wild. They'd jampack that ballroom, the black girls in way-out silk and satin dresses and shoes, their hair done in all kinds of styles, the men sharp in their zoot suits and crazy conks, and everybody grinning and greased and gassed.

Some of the bandsmen would come up to the men's room at about eight o'clock and get shoeshines before they went to work. Duke Ellington, Count Basie, Lionel Hampton, Cootie Williams, Jimmie Lunceford were just a few of those who sat in my chair. I would really make my shine rag sound like someone had set off Chinese firecrackers. Duke's great alto saxman, Johnny Hodges—he was Shorty's idol—still owes me for a shoeshine I gave him. He was in the chair one night, having a friendly argument with the drummer, Sonny Greer, who was standing there, when I tapped the bottom of his shoes to signal that I was finished. Hodges stepped down, reaching his hand in his pocket to pay me, but then snatched his hand out to gesture, and just forgot me, and walked away. I wouldn't have dared to bother the man who could do what he did with "Daydream" by asking him for fifteen cents.

I remember that I struck up a little shoeshine-stand conversation with Count Basie's great blues singer, Jimmie Rushing. (He's the one famous for "Sent For You Yesterday, Here You Come Today" and things like that.) Rushing's feet, I remember, were big and funny-shaped—not long like most big feet, but they were round and roly-poly like Rushing. Anyhow, he even introduced me to some of the other Basie cats, like Lester Young, Harry Edison, Buddy Tate, Don Byas, Dickie Wells, and Buck Clayton. They'd walk in the rest room later, by themselves. "Hi, Red." They'd be up there in my chair, and my shine rag was popping to the beat of all of their records, spinning in my head. Musicians never have had, anywhere, a greater shoeshine-boy fan than I was. I would write to Wilfred and Hilda and Philbert and Reginald back in Lansing, trying to describe it.

I never got any decent tips until the middle of the Negro dances, which is when the dancers started feeling good and getting generous. After the white dances, when I helped to clean out the ballroom, we would throw out perhaps a dozen empty liquor bottles. But after the Negro dances, we would have to throw out cartons full of empty fifth bottles—not rotgut, either, but the best brands, and especially Scotch.

During lulls up there in the men's room, sometimes I'd get in five   60
minutes of watching the dancing. The white people danced as though somebody had trained them—left, one, two; right, three, four—the same steps and patterns over and over, as though somebody had wound them up. But those Negroes—nobody in the world could have choreographed the way they did whatever they felt—just grabbing partners, even the white chicks who came to the Negro dances. And my black brethren today may hate me for saying it, but a lot of black girls nearly got run over by some of those Negro males scrambling to get at those white women; you would have thought God had lowered some of his angels. Times have sure changed; if it happened today, those same black girls would go after those Negro men—and the white women, too.

Anyway, some couples were so abandoned—flinging high and wide, improvising steps and movements—that you couldn't believe it. I could feel the beat in my bones, even though I had never danced.

"*Showtime!*" people would start hollering about the last hour of the dance. Then a couple of dozen really wild couples would stay on the floor, the girls changing to low white sneakers. The band now would really be blasting, and all the other dancers would form a clapping, shouting circle to watch that wild competition as it began, covering only a quarter or so of the ballroom floor. The band, the spectators and the dancers, would be making the Roseland Ballroom feel like a big rocking ship. The spotlight would be turning, pink, yellow, green, and blue, picking up the couples lindy-hopping as if they had gone mad. "*Wail, man, wail!*" people would be shouting at the band; and it *would* be wailing, until first one and then another couple just ran out of strength and stumbled off toward the crowd, exhausted and soaked with sweat. Sometimes I would be down there standing inside the door jumping up and down in my gray jacket with the whiskbroom in the pocket, and the manager would have to come and shout at me that I had customers upstairs.

The first liquor I drank, my first cigarettes, even my first reefers, I can't specifically remember. But I know they were all mixed together with my first shooting craps, playing cards, and betting my dollar a day on the numbers, as I started hanging out at night with Shorty and his friends. Shorty's jokes about how country I had been made us all laugh. I still was country, I know now, but it all felt so great because I was accepted. All of us would be in somebody's place, usually one of the girls', and we'd be turning on, the reefers making everybody's head light, or the whiskey aglow in our middles. Everybody understood that my head had to stay kinky a while longer, to grow long enough for Shorty to conk it for me. One of these nights, I remarked that I had saved about half enough to get a zoot.

"*Save?*" Shorty couldn't believe it. "Homeboy, you never heard of credit?" He told me he'd call a neighborhood clothing store the first thing in the morning, and that I should be there early.

A salesman, a young Jew, met me when I came in. "You're Shorty's friend?" I said I was; it amazed me—all of Shorty's contacts. The salesman wrote my name on a form, and the Roseland as where I worked, and Ella's address as where I lived. Shorty's name was put down as recommending me. The salesman said, "Shorty's one of our best customers."   65

I was measured, and the young salesman picked off a rack a zoot suit that was just wild: sky-blue pants thirty inches in the knee and angle-narrowed down to twelve inches at the bottom, and a long coat that pinched my waist and flared out below my knees.

As a gift, the salesman said, the store would give me a narrow leather belt with my initial "L" on it. Then he said I ought to also buy a hat, and I did—blue, with a feather in the four-inch brim. Then the store gave me another present: a long, thick-lined, gold-plated chain that swung down lower than my coat hem. I was sold forever on credit.

When I modeled the zoot for Ella, she took a long look and said, "Well, I guess it had to happen." I took three of those twenty-five-cent sepia-toned, while-you-wait pictures of myself, posed the way "hipsters" wearing their zoots would "cool it"—hat dangled, knees drawn close together, feet wide apart, both index fingers jabbed toward the floor. The long coat and swinging chain and the Punjab pants were much more dramatic if you stood that way. One picture, I autographed and airmailed to my brothers and sisters in Lansing, to let them see how well I was doing. I gave another one to Ella, and the third to Shorty, who was really moved: I could tell by the way he said, "Thanks, homeboy." It was part of our "hip" code not to show that kind of affection.

Shorty soon decided that my hair was finally long enough to be conked. He had promised to school me in how to beat the barbershops' three- and four-dollar price by making up congolene, and then conking ourselves.

I took the little list of ingredients he had printed out for me, and went to a grocery store, where I got a can of Red Devil lye, two eggs, and two medium-sized white potatoes. Then at a drugstore near the poolroom, I asked for a large jar of vaseline, a large bar of soap, a large-toothed comb and a fine-toothed comb, one of those rubber hoses with a metal spray-head, a rubber apron and a pair of gloves.

"Going to lay on that first conk?" the drugstore man asked me. I proudly told him, grinning, "Right!"

Shorty paid six dollars a week for a room in his cousin's shabby apartment. His cousin wasn't at home. "It's like the pad's mine, he spends so much time with his woman," Shorty said. "Now, you watch me —"

He peeled the potatoes and thin-sliced them into a quart-sized Mason fruit jar, then started stirring them with a wooden spoon as he gradually poured in a little over half the can of lye. "Never use a metal spoon; the lye will turn it black," he told me.

A jelly-like, starchy-looking glop resulted from the lye and potatoes, and Shorty broke in the two eggs, stirring real fast — his own conk and dark face bent down close. The congolene turned pale-yellowish. "Feel the jar," Shorty said. I cupped my hand against the outside, and snatched it away. "Damn right, it's hot, that's the lye," he said. "So you know it's going to burn when I comb it in — it burns *bad*. But the longer you can stand it, the straighter the hair."

He made me sit down, and he tied the string of a new rubber apron tightly around my neck, and combed up my bush of hair. Then, from the big vaseline jar, he took a handful and massaged it hard all through my hair and into the scalp. He also thickly vaselined my neck, ears and forehead. "When I get to washing out your head, be sure to tell me anywhere you feel any little stinging," Shorty warned me, washing his hands, then pulling on the rubber gloves, and tying on his own rubber apron. "You always got to remember that any congolene left in burns a sore into your head."

The congolene just felt warm when Shorty started combing it in. But then my head caught fire.

I gritted my teeth and tried to pull the sides of the kitchen table together. The comb felt as if it was raking my skin off.

My eyes watered, my nose was running. I couldn't stand it any longer; I bolted to the washbasin. I was cursing Shorty with every name I could think of when he got the spray going and started soap-lathering my head.

He lathered and spray-rinsed, lathered and spray-rinsed, maybe ten or twelve times, each time gradually closing the hot-water faucet, until the rinse was cold, and that helped some.

"You feel any stinging spots?"   80

"No," I managed to say. My knees were trembling.

"Sit back down, then. I think we got it all out okay."

The flame came back as Shorty, with a thick towel, started drying my head, rubbing hard. *"Easy, man, easy!"* I kept shouting.

"The first time's always worst. You get used to it better before long. You took it real good, homeboy. You got a good conk."

When Shorty let me stand up and see in the mirror, my hair hung   85
down in limp, damp strings. My scalp still flamed, but not as badly; I could bear it. He draped the towel around my shoulders, over my rubber apron, and began again vaselining my hair.

I could feel him combing, straight back, first the big comb, then the fine-tooth one.

Then, he was using a razor, very delicately, on the back of my neck. Then, finally, shaping the sideburns.

My first view in the mirror blotted out the hurting. I'd seen some pretty conks, but when it's the first time, on your *own* head, the transformation, after the lifetime of kinks, is staggering.

The mirror reflected Shorty behind me. We both were grinning and sweating. And on top of my head was this thick, smooth sheen of shining red hair—real red—as straight as any white man's.

How ridiculous I was! Stupid enough to stand there simply lost in ad- 90
miration of my hair now looking "white," reflected in the mirror in Shorty's room. I vowed that I'd never again be without a conk, and I never was for many years.

This was my first really big step toward self-degradation: when I endured all of that pain, literally burning my flesh to have it look like a white man's hair. I had joined that multitude of Negro men and women in America who are brainwashed into believing that the black people are "inferior"—and white people "superior"—that they will even violate and mutilate their God-created bodies to try to look "pretty" by white standards.

Look around today, in every small town and big city, from two-bit catfish and soda-pop joints into the "integrated" lobby of the Waldorf-Astoria, and you'll see conks on black men. And you'll see black women wearing these green and pink and purple and red and platinum-blond wigs. They're all more ridiculous than a slapstick comedy. It makes you wonder if the Negro has completely lost his sense of identity, lost touch with himself.

You'll see the conk worn by many, many so-called "upper class" Negroes, and, as much as I hate to say it about them, on all too many Negro entertainers. One of the reasons that I've especially admired some of them, like Lionel Hampton and Sidney Poitier, among others, is that they have kept their natural hair and fought to the top. I admire any Negro man who has never had himself conked, or who has had the sense to get rid of it—as I finally did.

I don't know which kind of self-defacing conk is the greater shame—the one you'll see on the heads of the black so-called "middle class" and "upper class," who ought to know better, or the one you'll see on the heads of the poorest, most downtrodden, ignorant black men. I mean the legal-minimum-wage ghetto-dwelling kind of Negro, as I was when I got my first one. It's generally among these poor fools that you'll see a black kerchief over the man's head, like Aunt Jemima; he's trying to make his conk last longer, between trips to the barbershop. Only for special occasions is this kerchief-protected conk exposed—to show off how "sharp" and "hip" its owner is. The ironic thing is that I have never heard any woman, white or black, express any admiration for a conk. Of course, any white woman with a black man isn't thinking about his hair. But I don't see how on earth a black woman with any race pride could walk down the street with any black man wearing a conk—the emblem of his shame that he is black.

To my own shame, when I say all of this I'm talking first of all about 95 myself—because you can't show me any Negro who ever conked more faithfully than I did. I'm speaking from personal experience when I say of any black man who conks today, or any white-wigged black woman, that if they gave the brains in their heads just half as much attention as they do their hair, they would be a thousand times better off.

The Reader's Presence

1. The young Malcolm resists Ella's pressure to imitate white lifestyles in order to get ahead. Instead, he chooses lower-class jobs and friends. What might this resistance signify politically? What relation might it bear to his later name change from "Little" to "X"? What elements of African American identity appeal to the young Malcolm X?

2. The writer, of course, was a courageous African American leader who was assassinated in his prime. How does this knowledge affect your reading of this account of his early years? How does Malcolm himself indicate the difference in time between the events he is relating and the time at which he is writing? Suppose his autobiography went on to detail a long and uneventful life? Would the piece ring differently? Why?

3. Despite his awareness of the horrors of injustice and inequality, Malcolm X describes the events of his politically naïve youth with gentleness and a degree of nostalgia. Compare this to Richard Wright's approach to similar issues in "The Ethics of Living Jim Crow" (see page 298).

25

David Mamet

The Rake: A Few Scenes from My Childhood

David Mamet (b. 1947) is a playwright, screenwriter, and director whose work is appreciated for the attention he pays to language as it is spoken by ordinary people in the contemporary world. His Pulitzer Prize–winning play, Glengarry Glen Ross, *explores the psychology of ambition, competition, failure, and despair among a group of Chicago real estate agents who are driven to sell worthless property to unsuspecting customers. He has recently written and directed two films:* The Spanish Prisoner *(1998) and* The Winslow Boy *(1999), adapted from Terence Ratigan's play. Mamet lives in Cambridge, Massachusetts, and Vermont.*

Mamet has said that "playwriting is simply showing how words influence actions and vice versa. All my plays attempt to bring out the poetry in the plain, everyday language people use. That's the only way to put art back in the theater." Mamet's sensitivity to working-class language and experience is due in part to his own work experience in factories, at a real estate agency, and as a window washer, office cleaner, and taxi driver. More recently, he has taught theater at several leading universities and has published two collections of essays. His most recent publications include a play, The Old Neighborhood *(1997), a collection of essays,* Jafsie and John Henry *(1999), and two nonfiction books,* True and False: Heresy and Common Sense for the Actor *(1997) and* Three Uses of the Knife *(1998). "The Rake: A Few Scenes from My Childhood" appeared in* Harper's *in 1992.*

There was the incident of the rake and there was the incident of the school play, and it seems to me that they both took place at the round kitchen table.

The table was not in the kitchen proper but in an area called "the nook," which held its claim to that small measure of charm by dint of a waist-high wall separating it from an adjacent area known as the living room.

All family meals were eaten in the nook. There was a dining room to the right, but, as in most rooms of that name at the time and in those surroundings, it was never used.

The round table was of wrought iron and topped with glass; it was noteworthy for that glass, for it was more than once and rather more than several times, I am inclined to think, that my stepfather would grow so angry as to bring some object down on the glass top, shattering it, thus giving us to know how we had forced him out of control.

And it seems that most times when he would shatter the table, as   5
often as that might have been, he would cut some portion of himself on the glass, or that he or his wife, our mother, would cut their hands on picking up the glass afterward, and that we children were to understand, and did understand, that these wounds were our fault.

So the table was associated in our minds with the notion of blood.

The house was in a brand-new housing development in the southern suburbs. The new community was built upon, and now bordered, the remains of what had once been a cornfield. When our new family moved in, there were but a few homes in the development completed, and a few more under construction. Most streets were mud, and boasted a house here or there, and many empty lots marked out by white stakes.

The house we lived in was the development's Model Home. The first time we had seen it, it had signs plastered on the front and throughout the interior telling of the various conveniences it contained. And it had a lawn, and was one of the only homes in the new community that did.

My stepfather was fond of the lawn, and he detailed me and my sister to care for it, and one fall afternoon we found ourselves assigned to rake the leaves.

Why this chore should have been so hated I cannot say, except that   10
we children, and I especially, felt ourselves less than full members of this new, cobbled-together family, and disliked being assigned to the beautification of a home that we found unbeautiful in all respects, and for which we had neither natural affection nor a sense of proprietary interest.

We went to the new high school. We walked the mile down the open two-lane road on one side of which was the just-begun suburban community and on the other side of which was the cornfield.

The school was as new as the community, and still under construction for the first three years of its occupancy. One of its innovations was the notion that honesty would be engendered by the absence of security, and so the lockers were designed and built both without locks and without the possibility of attaching locks. And there was the corresponding rash of thievery and many lectures about the same from the school administration, but it was difficult to point with pride to any scholastic or community tradition supporting the suggestion that we, the students, pull together in this new, utopian way. We were, in school, in an uncompleted building in the midst of a mud field in the midst of a cornfield. Our various sports teams were called The Spartans; and I played on those teams, which were of a wretchedness consistent with their novelty.

Meanwhile my sister interested herself in the drama society. The year after I had left the school she obtained the lead in the school play. It called for acting and singing, both of which she had talent for, and it looked to be a signal triumph for her in her otherwise unremarkable and unenjoyed school career.

On the night of the play's opening, she sat down to dinner with our mother and our stepfather. It may be that they ate a trifle early to allow her to get to the school to enjoy the excitement of opening night. But however it was, my sister had no appetite, and she nibbled a bit at her food, and then she got up from the table to carry her plate back to scrape it in the sink, when my mother suggested that she sit down, as she had not finished her food. My sister said she really had no appetite, but my mother insisted that, as the meal had been prepared, it would be good form to sit and eat it.

My sister sat down with the plate and pecked at her food and she   15
tried to eat a bit, and told my mother that, no, really, she possessed no appetite whatever, and that was due, no doubt, not to the food, but to her nervousness and excitement at the prospect of opening night.

My mother, again, said that, as the food had been cooked, it had to be eaten, and my sister tried and said that she could not; at which my mother nodded. She then got up from the table and went to the telephone and looked the number up and called the school and got the drama teacher and identified herself and told him that her daughter wouldn't be coming to school that night, that, no, she was not ill, but that she would not be coming in. Yes, yes, she said, she knew her daughter had the lead in the play, and, yes, she was aware that many children and teachers had worked hard for it, et cetera, and so my sister did not play the lead in her school play. But I was long gone, out of the house by that time, and well out of it. I heard that story, and others like, at the distance of twenty-five years.

In the model house our rooms were separated from their room, the master bedroom, by a bathroom and a study. On some weekends I would go alone to visit my father in the city and my sister would stay and sometimes grow frightened or lonely in her part of the house. And once, in the period when my grandfather, then in his sixties, was living with us, she became alarmed at a noise she had heard in the night; or perhaps she just became lonely, and she went out of her room and down the hall, calling for my mother, or my stepfather, or my grandfather, but the house was dark, and no one answered.

And, as she went farther down the hall, toward the living room, she heard voices, and she turned the corner, and saw a light coming from under the closed door in the master bedroom, and heard my stepfather crying, and the sound of my mother weeping. So my sister went up to the door, and she heard my stepfather talking to my grandfather and saying, "Jack. Say the words. Just say the words . . ." And my grandfather in his Eastern European accent, saying with obvious pain and difficulty, "No. No. I can't. Why are you making me do this? Why?" And the sound of my mother crying convulsively.

My sister opened the door, and she saw my grandfather sitting on the bed, and my stepfather standing by the closet and gesturing. On the floor of the closet she saw my mother, curled in a fetal position, moaning and crying and hugging herself. My stepfather was saying, "Say the words. Just say the words." And my grandfather was breathing fast and repeating, "I can't. She knows how I feel about her. I can't." And my stepfather said, "Say the words, Jack. Please. Just say you love her." At which my mother would moan louder. And my grandfather said, "I can't."

My sister pushed the door open farther and said—I don't know what   20
she said, but she asked, I'm sure, for some reassurance, or some explanation, and my stepfather turned around and saw her and picked up a hairbrush from a dresser that he passed as he walked toward her, and he hit her in the face and slammed the door on her. And she continued to hear "Jack, say the words."

She told me that on weekends when I was gone my stepfather ended every Sunday evening by hitting or beating her for some reason or other. He would come home from depositing his own kids back at their mother's house after their weekend visitation, and would settle down tired and angry, and, as a regular matter on those evenings, would find out some intolerable behavior on my sister's part and slap or hit or beat her.

Years later, at my mother's funeral, my sister spoke to our aunt, my mother's sister, who gave a footnote to this behavior. She said when they were young, my mother and my aunt, they and their parents lived in a small flat on the West Side. My grandfather was a salesman on the road from dawn on Monday until Friday night. Their family had a fiction, and that fiction, that article of faith, was that my mother was a naughty child. And each Friday, when he came home, his first question as he climbed the stairs was, "What has she done this week . . . ?" At which my grandmother would tell him the terrible things that my mother had done, after which she, my mother, was beaten.

This was general knowledge in my family. The footnote concerned my grandfather's behavior later in the night. My aunt had a room of her own, and it adjoined her parents' room. And she related that each Friday, when the house had gone to bed, she, through the thin wall, heard my grandfather pleading for sex. "Cookie, please." And my grandmother responding, "No, Jack." "Cookie, please." "No, Jack." "Cookie, please."

And once, my grandfather came home and asked, "What has she done this week?" and I do not know, but I imagine that the response was not completed, and perhaps hardly begun; in any case, he reached and grabbed my mother by the back of the neck and hurled her down the stairs.

And once, in our house in the suburbs there had been an outburst by   25
my stepfather directed at my sister. And she had, somehow, prevailed. It
was, I think, that he had the facts of the case wrong, and had accused her of
the commission of something for which she had demonstrably had no opportunity, and she pointed this out to him with what I can imagine, given
the circumstances, was an understandable, and, given my prejudice, a com-
mendable degree of freedom. Thinking the incident closed she went back to
her room to study, and, a few moments later, saw him throw open her
door, bat the book out of her hands, and pick her up and throw her against
the far wall, where she struck the back of her neck on the shelf.

She was told, the next morning, that her pain, real or pretended, held
no weight, and that she would have to go to school. She protested that
she could not walk, or, if at all, only with the greatest of difficulty and in
great pain; but she was dressed and did walk to school, where she fainted,
and was brought home. For years she suffered various headaches; an
X ray taken twenty years later for an unrelated problem revealed that
when he threw her against the shelf he had cracked her vertebrae.

When we left the house we left in good spirits. When we went out to
dinner, it was an adventure, which was strange to me, looking back, because many of these dinners ended with my sister or myself being banished, sullen or in tears, from the restaurant, and told to wait in the car,
as we were in disgrace.

These were the excursions that had ended, due to her or my intolerable arrogance, as it was explained to us.

The happy trips were celebrated and capped with a joke. Here is the
joke: My stepfather, my mother, my sister, and I would exit the restaurant, my stepfather and mother would walk to the car, telling us that they
would pick us up. We children would stand by the restaurant entrance.
They would drive up in the car, open the passenger door, and wait until
my sister and I had started to get in. They would then drive away.

They would drive ten or fifteen feet, and open the door again, and we   30
would walk up again, and they would drive away again. They sometimes
would drive around the block. But they would always come back, and by
that time the four of us would be laughing in camaraderie and appreciation of what, I believe, was our only family joke.

We were raking the lawn, my sister and I. I was raking, and she was
stuffing the leaves into a bag. I loathed the job, and my muscles and my
mind rebelled, and I was viciously angry, and my sister said something,
and I turned and threw the rake at her and hit her in the face.

The rake was split bamboo and metal, and a piece of metal caught
her lip and cut her badly.

We were both terrified, and I was sick with guilt, and we ran into the
house, my sister holding her hand to her mouth, and her mouth and her
hand and the front of her dress covered in blood.

We ran into the kitchen where my mother was cooking dinner, and
my mother asked what happened.

Neither of us, myself out of guilt, of course, and my sister out of a de-   35
sire to avert the terrible punishment she knew I would receive, neither of
us would say what occurred.

My mother pressed us, and neither of us would answer. She said that
until one or the other answered, we would not go to the hospital; and so
the family sat down to dinner where my sister clutched a napkin to her
face and the blood soaked the napkin and ran down onto her food, which
she had to eat; and I also ate my food and we cleared the table and went
to the hospital.

I remember the walks home from school in the frigid winter, along
the cornfield that was, for all its proximity to the city, part of the prairie.
The winters were viciously cold. From the remove of years, I can see how
the area might and may have been beautiful. One could have walked in
the stubble of the cornfields, or hunted birds, or enjoyed any of a number
of pleasures naturally occurring.

The Reader's Presence

1. Mamet relates that he and his sister hated doing chores, in part
   because they "had neither natural affection nor a sense of proprietary interest" (paragraph 10) toward their house. How does
   Mamet's choice of words and details in the essay's opening paragraphs echo this? Why does he emphasize that his was a "Model
   Home"?

2. Near the end of the essay, Mamet recalls a "joke" that his family
   shared. How does he present the joke to the reader? Do you think
   Mamet wants the reader to think the joke is funny? Would the
   joke seem different if Mamet had told it at the beginning of the
   essay?

3. Why do you think that the incident of the rake plays such a significant role in the essay? Mamet introduces the rake in his opening
   sentence but does not describe the incident itself until near the
   end. Why? Do you think the rake has a symbolic value? If so,
   what does it represent?

26

Frank McCourt

First Communion Day

Frank McCourt was born in Brooklyn, New York, in 1930, shortly after his parents had immigrated from Ireland. His alcoholic father was often unemployed, and when he was a young child the family returned to Ireland, where they faced even harsher circumstances. McCourt lived in Limerick until, at the age of nineteen, he and his brother returned to the United States, supporting themselves by performing their own vaudeville show. A high school teacher for twenty-seven years, McCourt did not seriously begin his writing career until he was in his sixties and had retired. "First Communion Day" is a chapter of his first book, Angela's Ashes *(1996), an autobiographical account of his poverty-stricken childhood, which received a national Book Critics Circle Award and a Pulitzer Prize. His most recent book,* 'Tis: A Memoir *(1999), is a sequel to* Angela's Ashes.

The master says it's time to prepare for First Confession and First Communion, to know and remember all the questions and answers in the catechism, to become good Catholics, to know the difference between right and wrong, to die for the Faith if called on.

The master says it's a glorious thing to die for the Faith and Dad says it's a glorious thing to die for Ireland and I wonder if there's anyone in the world who would like us to live. My brothers are dead and my sister is dead and I wonder if they died for Ireland or the Faith. Dad says they were too young to die for anything. Mam says it was disease and starvation and him never having a job. Dad says, Och, Angela, puts on his cap and goes for a long walk.

The master says we're each to bring threepence for the First Communion catechism with the green cover. The catechism has all the questions and answers we have to know by heart before we can receive First Communion. Older boys in the fifth class have the thick Confirmation catechism with the red cover and that costs sixpence. I'd love to be big and important and parade around with the red Confirmation catechism but I don't think I'll live that long the way I'm expected to die for this or that. I want to ask why there are so many big people who haven't died for

Ireland or the Faith but I know if you ask a question like that you get you the thump on the head or you're told go out and play.

It's very handy to have Mikey Molloy living around the corner from me. He's eleven, he has fits and behind his back we call him Molloy the Fit. People in the lane say the fit is an affliction and now I know what affliction means. Mikey knows everything because he has visions in his fits and he reads books. He's the expert in the lane on Girls' Bodies and Dirty Things in General and he promises, I'll tell you everything, Frankie, when you're eleven like me and you're not so thick and ignorant.

It's a good thing he says Frankie so I'll know he's talking to me be-   5
cause he has crossed eyes and you never know who he's looking at. If he's talking to Malachy[1] and I think he's talking to me he might go into a rage and have a fit that will carry him off. He says it's a gift to have crossed eyes because you're like a god looking two ways at once and if you had crossed eyes in the ancient Roman times you had no problem getting a good job. If you look at pictures of Roman emperors you'll see there's always a great hint of crossed eyes. When he's not having the fit he sits on the ground at the top of the lane reading the books his father brings home from the Carnegie Library. His mother says books books books, he's ruining his eyes with the reading, he needs an operation to straighten them but who'll pay for it. She tells him if he keeps on straining his eyes they'll float together till he has one eye in the middle of his head. Ever after his father calls him Cyclops, who is in a Greek story.

Nora Molloy knows my mother from the queues at the St. Vincent de Paul Society. She tells Mam that Mikey has more sense than twelve men drinking pints in a pub. He knows the names of all the Popes from St. Peter to Pius the Eleventh. He's only eleven but he's a man, oh, a man indeed. Many a week he saves the family from pure starvation. He borrows a handcart from Aidan Farrell and knocks on doors all over Limerick to see if there are people who want coal or turf delivered, and down the Dock Road he'll go to haul back great bags a hundredweight or more. He'll run messages for old people who can't walk and if they don't have a penny to give him a prayer will do.

If he earns a little money he hands it over to his mother, who loves her Mikey. He is her world, her heart's blood, her pulse, and if anything ever happened to him they might as well stick her in the lunatic asylum and throw away the key.

Mikey's father, Peter, is a great champion. He wins bets in the pubs by drinking more pints than anyone. All he has to do is go out to the jakes, stick his finger down his throat and bring it all up so that he can start another round. Peter is such a champion he can stand in the jakes and throw up without using his finger. He's such a champion they could chop off his fingers and he'd carry on regardless. He wins all that money

---

[1]*Malachy:* His younger brother. — EDS.

but doesn't bring it home. Sometimes he's like my father and drinks the dole itself and that's why Nora Molloy is often carted off to the lunatic asylum demented with worry over her hungry famishing family. She knows as long as you're in the asylum you're safe from the world and its torments, there's nothing you can do, you're protected, and what's the use of worrying. It's well known that all the lunatics in the asylum have to be dragged in but she's the only one that has to be dragged out, back to her five children and the champion of all pint drinkers.

You can tell when Nora Molloy is ready for the asylum when you see her children running around white with flour from poll to toe. That happens when Peter drinks the dole money and leaves her desperate and she knows the men will come to take her away. You know she's inside frantic with the baking. She wants to make sure the children won't starve while she's gone and she roams Limerick begging for flour. She goes to priests, nuns, Protestants, Quakers. She goes to Rank's Flour Mills and begs for the sweepings from the floor. She bakes day and night. Peter begs her to stop but she screams, This is what comes of drinking the dole. He tells her the bread will only go stale. There's no use talking to her. Bake bake bake. If she had the money she'd bake all the flour in Limerick and regions beyond. If the men didn't come from the lunatic asylum to take her away she'd bake till she fell to the floor.

The children stuff themselves with so much bread people in the lane say they're looking like loaves. Still the bread goes stale and Mikey is so bothered by the waste he talks to a rich woman with a cookbook and she tells him make bread pudding. He boils the hard bread in water and sour milk and throws in a cup of sugar and his brother loves it even if that's all they have the fortnight their mother is in the lunatic asylum.

My father says, Do they take her away because she's gone mad baking bread or does she go mad baking bread because they're taking her away?

Nora comes home calm as if she had been at the seaside. She always says, Where's Mikey? Is he alive? She worries over Mikey because he's not a proper Catholic and if he had a fit and died who knows where he might wind up in the next life. He's not a proper Catholic because he could never receive his First Communion for fear of getting anything on his tongue that might cause a fit and choke him. The master tried over and over with bits of the *Limerick Leader* but Mikey kept spitting them out till the master got into a state and sent him to the priest, who wrote to the bishop, who said, Don't bother me, handle it yourself. The master sent a note home saying Mikey was to practice receiving Communion with his father or mother but even they couldn't get him to swallow a piece of the *Limerick Leader* in the shape of a wafer. They even tried a piece of bread shaped like the wafer with bread and jam and it was no use. The priest tells Mrs. Molloy not to worry. God moves in mysterious ways His wonders to perform and surely He has a special purpose for Mikey, fits and all. She says, Isn't it remarkable he can swally all kinds of sweets and buns but if he has to swally the body of Our Lord he goes into a fit? Isn't that remarkable? She worries Mikey might have the fit and die and go to hell if he has any class of a sin on his soul though everyone knows he's an angel out of heaven. Mikey tells her God is not going to afflict you with the fit and then boot you into hell on top of it. What kind of a God would do a thing like that?

Are you sure, Mikey?

I am. I read it in a book.

He sits under the lamppost at the top of the lane and laughs over his   15
First Communion day, which was all a cod. He couldn't swallow the wafer but did that stop his mother from parading him around Limerick in his little black suit for The Collection? She said to Mikey, Well, I'm not lying so I'm not. I'm only saying to the neighbors, Here's Mikey in his First Communion suit. That's all I'm saying, mind you. Here's Mikey. If they think you swallied your First Communion who am I to contradict them and disappoint them? Mikey's father said, "Don't worry, Cyclops. You have loads of time. Jesus didn't become a proper Catholic till he took the bread and wine at the Last Supper and He was thirty-three years of age. Nora Molloy said, Will you stop calling him Cyclops? He has two eyes in his head and he's not a Greek. But Mikey's father, champion of all pint drinkers, is like my uncle Pa Keating, he doesn't give a fiddler's fart what the world says and that's the way I'd like to be myself.

Mikey tells me the best thing about First Communion is The Collection. Your mother has to get you a new suit somehow so she can show you off to the neighbors and relations and they give you sweets and money and you can go to the Lyric Cinema to see Charlie Chaplin.

What about James Cagney?

Never mind James Cagney. Lots of blather. Charlie Chaplin is your only man. but you have to be with your mother on The Collection. The grown-up people of Limerick are not going to be handing out money to every little Tom Dick and Mick with a First Communion suit that doesn't have his mother with him.

Mikey got over five shillings on his First Communion day and ate so many sweets and buns he threw up in the Lyric Cinema and Frank Goggin, the ticket man, kicked him out. He says he didn't care because he had money left over and went to the Savoy Cinema the same day for a pirate film and ate Cadbury chocolate and drank lemonade till his stomach stuck out a mile. He can't wait for Confirmation day because you're older, there's another collection and that brings more money than First Communion. He'll go to the cinema the rest of his life, sit next to girls from lanes and do dirty things like an expert. He loves his mother but he'll never get married for fear he might have a wife in and out of the lunatic asylum. What's the use of getting married when you can sit in cinemas and do dirty things with girls from lanes who don't care what they do because they already did it with their brothers. If you don't get married you won't have any children at home bawling for tea and bread and gasping with the fit and looking in every direction with their eyes. When he's older he'll go to the pub like his father, drink pints galore, stick the finger down the throat to bring it all up, drink more pints, win the bets and bring the money home to his mother to keep her from going demented. He says he's not a proper Catholic which means he's doomed so he can do anything he bloody well likes.

He says, I'll tell you more when you grow up, Frankie. You're too young now and you don't know your arse from your elbow.

The master, Mr. Benson, is very old. He roars and spits all over us every day. The boys in the front row hope he has no diseases for it's the spit that carries all the diseases and he might be spreading consumption right and left. He tells us we have to know the catechism backwards, forwards and sideways. We have to know the Ten Commandments, the Seven Virtues, Divine and Moral, the Seven Sacraments, the Seven Deadly Sins. We have to know by heart all the prayers, the Hail Mary, the Our Father, the Confiteor, the Apostles' Creed, the Act of Contrition, the Litany of the Blessed Virgin Mary. We have to know them in Irish and English and if we forget an Irish word and use English he goes into a rage and goes at us with the stick. If he had his way we'd be learning our religion in Latin, the language of the saints who communed intimately with God and His Holy Mother, the language of the early Christians, who huddled in the catacombs and went forth to die on rack and sword, who expired in the foaming jaws of the ravenous lion. Irish is fine for patriots, English for traitors and informers, but it's the Latin that gains us entrance to heaven itself. It's the Latin the martyrs prayed in when the barbarians pulled out their nails and cut their skin off inch by inch. He tells us we'd be better off in Africa praying to bush or tree. He tells us we're hopeless, the worst class he ever had for First Communion but as sure as God made little apples he'll make Catholics of us, he'll beat the idler out of us and the Sanctifying Grace into us.

Brendan Quigley raises his hand. We call him Question Quigley because he's always asking questions. He can't help himself. Sir, he says, what's Sanctifying Grace?

The master rolls his eyes to heaven. He's going to kill Quigley. Instead he barks at him, Never mind what's Sanctifying Grace, Quigley. That's none of your business. You're here to learn the catechism and do what you're told. You're not here to be asking questions. There are too many people wandering the world asking questions and that's what has us in the state we're in and if I find any boy in this class asking questions I won't be responsible for what happens. Do you hear me, Quigley?

I do.

I do what?

I do, sir.

He goes on with his speech, There are boys in this class who will never know the Sanctifying Grace. And why? Because of the greed. I have heard them abroad in the schoolyard talking about First Communion day, the happiest day of your life. Are they talking about receiving the body and blood of Our Lord? Oh, no. Those greedy little blaguards are talking about the money they'll get, The Collection. They'll go from house to house in their little suits like beggars for The Collection. And will they take any of that money and send it to the little black babies in Africa? Will they think of those little pagans doomed forever for lack of baptism and knowledge of the True Faith? Little black babies denied knowledge of the Mystical Body of Christ? Limbo is packed with little black babies flying around and crying for their mothers because they'll never be admitted to the ineffable presence of Our Lord and the glorious company of saints, martyrs, virgins. Oh, no. It's off to the cinemas, our First Communion boys run to wallow in the filth spewed across the world by the devil's henchmen in Hollywood. Isn't that right, McCourt?

'Tis, sir.

Question Quigley raises his hand again. There are looks around the room and we wonder if it's suicide he's after.

What's henchmen, sir?   30

The master's face goes white, then red. His mouth tightens and opens and spit flies everywhere. He walks to Question and drags him from his seat. He snorts and stutters and his spit flies around the room. He flogs Question across the shoulders, the bottom, the legs. He grabs him by the collar and drags him to the front of the room.

Look at this specimen, he roars.

Question is shaking and crying. I'm sorry, sir.

The master mocks him. I'm sorry, sir. What are you sorry for?

I'm sorry I asked the question. I'll never ask a question again, sir.   35

The day you do, Quigley, will be the day you wish God would take you to His bosom. What will you wish, Quigley?

That God will take me to His bosom, sir.

Go back to your seat, you omadhaun,[2] you poltroon, you thing from the far dark corner of a bog.

He sits down with the stick before him on the desk. He tells Question to stop the whimpering and be a man. If he hears a single boy in this class asking foolish questions or talking about The Collection again he'll flog that boy till the blood spurts.

What will I do, boys?   40

Flog the boy, sir.

Till?

Till the blood spurts, sir.

Now, Clohessy, what is the Sixth Commandment?

Thou shalt not commit adultery.   45

Thou shalt not commit adultery what?

Thou shalt not commit adultery, sir.

---

[2]*Omadhaun:* A stupid, idle, foolish fellow; fool. — EDS.

And what is adultery, Clohessy?

Impure thoughts, impure words, impure deeds, sir.

Good, Clohessy. You're a good boy. You may be slow and forgetful 50 in the sir department and you may not have a shoe to your foot but you're powerful with the Sixth Commandment and that will keep you pure.

Paddy Clohessy has no shoe to his foot, his mother shaves his head to keep the lice away, his eyes are red, his nose always snotty. The sores on his kneecaps never heal because he picks at the scabs and puts them in his mouth. His clothes are rags he has to share with his six brothers and a sister and when he comes to school with a bloody nose or a black eye you know he had a fight over the clothes that morning. He hates school. He's seven going on eight, the biggest and oldest boy in the class, and he can't wait to grow up and be fourteen so that he can run away and pass for seventeen and join the English army and go to India where it's nice and warm and he'll live in a tent with a dark girl with the red dot on her forehead and he'll be lying there eating figs, that's what they eat in India, figs, and she'll cook the curry day and night and plonk on a ukulele and when he has enough money he'll send for the whole family and they'll all live in the tent especially his poor father who's at home coughing up great gobs of blood because of the consumption. When my mother sees Paddy on the street she says, Wisha, look at that poor child. He's a skeleton with rags and if they were making a film about the famine he'd surely be put in the middle of it.

I think Paddy likes me because of the raisin and I feel a bit guilty because I wasn't that generous in the first place. The master, Mr. Benson, said the government was going to give us the free lunch so we wouldn't have to be going home in the freezing weather. He led us down to a cold room in the dungeons of Leamy's School where the charwoman, Nellie Ahearn, was handing out the half pint of milk and the raisin bun. The milk was frozen in the bottles and we had to melt it between our thighs. The boys joked and said the bottles would freeze our things off and the master roared, Any more of that talk and I'll warm the bottles on the backs of yeer heads. We all searched our raisin buns for a raisin but Nellie said they must have forgotten to put them in and she'd inquire from the man who delivered. We searched again every day till at last I found a raisin in my bun and held it up. The boys started grousing and said they wanted a raisin and Nellie said it wasn't her fault. She'd ask the man again. Now the boys were begging me for the raisin and offering me everything, a slug of their milk, a pencil, a comic book. Toby Mackey said I could have his sister and Mr. Benson heard him and took him out to the hallway and knocked him around till he howled. I wanted the raisin for myself but I saw Paddy Clohessy standing in the corner with no shoes and the room was freezing and he was shivering like a dog that had been kicked and I always felt sad over kicked dogs so I walked over and gave Paddy the raisin because I didn't know what else to do and all the boys yelled that I was a fool and a feckin' eejit and I'd regret the day and after I handed the raisin to Paddy I longed for it but it was too late now because he pushed it right into his mouth and gulped it and looked at me and said nothing and I said in my head what kind of an eejit are you to be giving away your raisin.

Mr. Benson gave me a look and said nothing and Nellie Ahearn said, You're a great oul'Yankee, Frankie.

The priest will come soon to examine us on the catechism and everything else. The master himself has to show us how to receive Holy Communion. He tells us gather round him. He fills his hat with the *Limerick Leader* torn into little bits. He gives Paddy Clohessy the hat, kneels on the floor, tells Paddy to take one bit of paper and place it on his tongue. He shows us how to stick out the tongue, receive the bit of paper, hold it a moment, draw in the tongue, fold your hands in prayer, look toward heaven, close your eyes in adoration, wait for the paper to melt in your mouth, swallow it, and thank God for the gift, the Sanctifying Grace wafting in on the odor of sanctity. When he sticks out his tongue we have to hold in the laugh because we never saw a big purple tongue before. He opens his eyes to catch the boys who are giggling but he can't say anything because he still has God on his tongue and it's a holy moment. He gets off his knees and tells us kneel around the classroom for the Holy Communion practice. He goes around the room placing bits of paper on our tongues and mumbling in Latin. Some boys giggle and he roars at them that if the giggling doesn't stop it's not Holy Communion they'll be getting but the Last Rites and what is that sacrament called, McCourt?

Extreme Unction, sir.

That's right, McCourt. Not bad for a yank from the sinful shores of Amerikay.

He tells us we have to be careful to stick out our tongues far enough so that the Communion wafer won't fall to the floor. He says, That's the worst thing that can happen to a priest. If the wafer slides off your tongue that poor priest has to get down on his two knees, pick it up with his own tongue and lick the floor around it in case it bounced from one spot to another. The priest could get a splinter that would make his tongue swell to the size of a turnip and that's enough to choke you and kill you entirely.

He tells us that next to a relic of the True Cross the Communion wafer is the holiest thing in the world and our First Communion is the holiest moment in our lives. Talking about First Communion makes the master all excited. He paces back and forth, waves his stick, tells us we must never forget that the moment the Holy Communion is placed on our tongues we become members of that most glorious congregation, the One, Holy, Roman, Catholic and Apostolic Church, that for two thousand years men, women and children have died for the Faith, that the Irish have nothing to be ashamed of in the martyr department. Haven't

55

we provided martyrs galore? Haven't we bared our necks to the Protestant ax? Haven't we mounted the scaffold, singing, as if embarking on a picnic, haven't we, boys?

We have, sir.

What have we done boys?   60

Bared our necks to the Protestant ax, sir.

And?

Mounted the scaffold singing, sir.

As if?

Embarking on a picnic, sir.   65

He says that, perhaps, in this class there is a future priest or a martyr for the Faith, though he doubts it very much for we are the laziest gang of ignoramuses it has ever been his misfortune to teach.

But it takes all kinds, he says, and surely God had some purpose when He sent the likes of ye to infest this earth. Surely God had a purpose when among us He sent Clohessy with no shoes, Quigley with his damnable questions and McCourt heavy with sin from America. And remember this, boys, God did not send His only begotten Son to hang on the cross so that ye can go around on yeer First Communion day with the paws clutching for The Collection. Our Lord died so that ye might be redeemed. It is enough to receive the gift of Faith. Are ye listening to me?

We are, sir.

And what's enough?

The gift of Faith, sir.   70

Good. Go home.

At night three of us sit under the light pole at the top of the lane reading, Mikey, Malachy and I. The Molloys are like us with their father drinking the dole money or the wages and leaving no money for candles or paraffin oil for the lamp. Mikey reads books and the rest of us read comic books. His father, Peter, brings books from the Carnegie Library so that he'll have something to do when he's not drinking pints or when he's looking after the family anytime Mrs. Molloy is in the lunatic asylum. He lets Mikey read any book he likes and now Mikey is reading this book about Cuchulain[3] and talking as if he knows everything about him. I want to tell him I knew all about Cuchulain when I was three going on four, that I saw Cuchulain in Dublin, that Cuchulain thinks nothing of dropping into my dreams. I want to tell him stop talking about Cuchulain, he's mine, he was mine years ago when I was young, but I can't because Mikey reads us a story I never heard of before, a dirty story about Cuchulain which I can never tell my father or mother, the story of how Emer became Cuchulain's wife.

Cuchulain was getting to be an old man of twenty-one. He was lonely and wanted to get married, which made him weak, says Mikey, and got him

---

[3]***Cuchulain:*** Celtic folk hero whose precocity as a child and bravery as a man are the subjects of many Irish legends. — EDS.

killed in the end. All the women in Ireland were mad about Cuchulain and they wanted to marry him. He said that would be grand, he wouldn't mind marrying all the women of Ireland. If he could fight all the men of Ireland why couldn't he marry all the women? But the King, Conor MacNessa, said, That's all very well for you, Cu, but the men of Ireland don't want to be lonely in the far reaches of the night. The King decided there would have to be a contest to see who would marry Cuchulain and it would be a pissing contest. All the women of Ireland assembled on the plains of Muirthemne to see who could piss the longest and it was Emer. She was the champion woman pisser of Ireland and married Cuchulain and that's why to this day she is called Great Bladdered Emer.

Mikey and Malachy laugh over this story though I don't think Malachy understands it. He's young and far from his First Communion and he's only laughing over the piss word. Then Mikey tells me I've committed a sin by listening to a story that has that word in it and when I go to my First Confession I'll have to tell the priest. Malachy says, That's right. Piss is a bad word and you have to tell the priest because 'tis a sin word.

I don't know what to do. How can I go to the priest and tell him this   75
terrible thing in my First Confession? All the boys know what sins they're going to tell so that they'll get the First Communion and make The Collection and go to see James Cagney and eat sweets and cakes at the Lyric Cinema. The master helped us with our sins and everyone has the same sins. I hit my brother. I told a lie. I stole a penny from my mother's purse. I disobeyed my parents, I ate a sausage on Friday.

But now I have a sin no one else has and the priest is going to be shocked and drag me out of the confession box into the aisle and out into the street where everyone will know I listened to a story about Cuchulain's wife being the champion woman pisser in all Ireland. I'll never be able to make my First Communion and mothers will hold their small children up and point at me and say, Look at him. He's like Mikey Molloy, never made his First Communion, wandering around in a state of sin, never made The Collection, never saw James Cagney.

I'm sorry I ever heard of First Communion and The Collection. I'm sick and I don't want any tea or bread or anything. Mam tells Dad it's a strange thing when a child won't have his bread and tea and Dad says, Och, he's just nervous over the First Communion. I want to go over to him and sit on his lap and tell him what Mikey Molloy did to me but I'm too big to be sitting on laps and if I did Malachy would go out in the lane and tell everyone I was a big baby. I'd like to tell my troubles to the Angel on the Seventh Step but he's busy bringing babies to mothers all over the world. Still, I'll ask Dad.

Dad, does the Angel on the Seventh Step have other jobs besides bringing babies?

He does.

Would the Angel on the Seventh Step tell you what to do if you didn't   80
know what to do?

Och, he would, son, he would. That's the job of an angel, even the one on the seventh step.

Dad goes for a long walk, Mam takes Michael and goes to see Grandma, Malachy plays in the lane, and I have the house to myself so that I can sit on the seventh step and talk to the angel. I know he's there because the seventh step feels warmer than the other steps and there's a light in my head. I tell him my troubles and I hear a voice. Fear not, says the voice.

He's talking backward and I tell him I don't know what he's talking about.

Do not fear, says the voice. Tell the priest your sin and you'll be forgiven.

Next morning I'm up early and drinking tea with Dad and telling him   85
about the Angel on the Seventh Step. He places his hand on my forehead to see if I'm feeling all right. He asks if I'm sure I had a light in my head and heard a voice and what did the voice say?

I tell him the voice said Fear not and that means Do not fear.

Dad tells me the angel is right, I shouldn't be afraid, and I tell him what Mikey Molloy did to me. I tell him all about Great Bladdered Emer and I even use the piss word because the angel said, Fear not. Dad puts down his jam jar of tea and pats the back of my hand. Och, och, och, he says, and I wonder if he's going demented like Mrs. Molloy, in and out of the lunatic asylum, but he says, Is that what you were worried about last night?

I tell him it is and he says it's not a sin and I don't have to tell the priest.

But the Angel on the Seventh Step said I should.

All right. Tell the priest if you like but the Angel on the Seventh Step   90
said that only because you didn't tell me first. Isn't it better to be able to tell your father your troubles rather than an angel who is a light and a voice in your head?

'Tis, Dad.

The day before First Communion the master leads us to St. Joseph's Church for First Confession. We march in pairs and if we so much as move a lip on the streets of Limerick he'll kill us on the spot and send us to hell bloated with sin. That doesn't stop the bragging about the big sins. Willie Harold is whispering about his big sin, that he looked at his sister's naked body. Paddy Hartigan says he stole ten shillings from his aunt's purse and made himself sick with ice cream and chips. Question Quigley says he ran away from home and spent half the night in a ditch with four goats. I try to tell them about Cuchulain and Emer but the master catches me talking and gives me a thump on the head.

We kneel in the pews by the confession box and I wonder if my Emer sin is as bad as looking at your sister's naked body because I know now that some things in the world are worse than others. That's why they have different sins, the sacrilege, the mortal sin, the venial sin. Then the masters and grown-up people in general talk about the unforgivable sin, which is a great mystery. No one knows what it is and you wonder how you can know if you've committed it if you don't know what it is. If I tell a priest about Great Bladdered Emer and the pissing contest he might say that's the unforgivable sin and kick me out of the confession box and I'll be disgraced all over Limerick and doomed to hell tormented forever by devils who have nothing else to do but stab me with hot pitchforks till I'm worn out.

I try to listen to Willie's confession when he goes in but all I can hear is a hissing from the priest and when Willie comes out he's crying.

It's my turn. The confession box is dark and there's a big crucifix   95
hanging over my head. I can hear a boy mumbling his confession on the other side. I wonder if there's any use trying to talk to the Angel on the Seventh Step. I know he's not supposed to be hanging around confession boxes but I feel the light in my head and the voice is telling me, Fear not.

The panel slides back before my face and the priest says, Yes, my child?

Bless me, Father, for I have sinned. This is my First Confession.

Yes, my child, and what sins have you committed?

I told a lie. I hit my brother. I took a penny from my mother's purse. I said a curse.

Yes, my child. Anything else?   100

I, I listened to a story about Cuchulain and Emer.

Surely that's not a sin, my child. After all we are assured by certain writers that Cuchulain turned Catholic in his last moments as did his King, Conor MacNessa.

'Tis about Emer, Father, and how she married him.

How was that, my child?

She won him in a pissing contest.   105

There is heavy breathing. The priest has his hand over his mouth and he's making choking sounds and talking to himself, Mother o'God.

Who, who told you that story, my child?

Mikey Molloy, Father.

And where did he hear it?

He read it in a book, Father.   110

Ah, a book. Books can be dangerous for children, my child. Turn your mind from those silly stories and think of the lives of the saints. Think of St. Joseph, the Little Flower, the sweet and gentle St. Francis of Assisi, who loved the birds of the air and the beasts of the field. Will you do that, my child?

I will, Father.

Are there any other sins, my child?

No, Father.

For your penance say three Hail Marys, three Our Fathers, and say a   115
special prayer for me.

I will. Father, was that the worst sin?

What do you mean?

Am I the worst of all the boys, Father?

No, my child, you have a long way to go. Now say an Act of Contrition and remember Our Lord watches you every minute. God bless you, my child.

First Communion day is the happiest day of your life because of The   120
Collection and James Cagney at the Lyric Cinema. The night before I was so excited I couldn't sleep till dawn. I'd still be sleeping if my grandmother hadn't come banging at the door.

Get up! Get up! Get that child outa the bed. Happiest day of his life an' him snorin' above in the bed.

I ran to the kitchen. Take off that shirt, she said. I took off the shirt and she pushed me into a tin tub of icy cold water. My mother scrubbed me, my grandmother scrubbed me. I was raw, I was red.

They dried me. They dressed me in my black velvet First Communion suit with the white frilly shirt, the short pants, the white stockings, the black patent leather shoes. Around my arm they tied a white satin bow and on my lapel they pinned the Sacred Heart of Jesus, a picture of the Sacred Heart, with blood dripping from it, flames erupting all around it and on top a nasty-looking crown of thorns.

Come here till I comb your hair, said Grandma. Look at that mop, it won't lie down. You didn't get that hair from my side of the family. That's that North of Ireland hair you got from your father. That's the kind of hair you see on Presbyterians. If your mother had married a proper decent Limerickman you wouldn't have this standing up, North of Ireland, Presbyterian hair.

She spat twice on my head.   125

Grandma, will you please stop spitting on my head.

If you have anything to say, shut up. A little spit won't kill you. Come on, we'll be late for the Mass.

We ran to the church. My mother panted along behind with Michael in her arms. We arrived at the church just in time to see the last of the boys leaving the altar rail where the priest stood with the chalice and the host glaring at me. Then he placed on my tongue the wafer, the body and blood of Jesus. At last, at last.

It's on my tongue. I draw it back.

It stuck.   130

I had God glued to the roof of my mouth. I could hear the master's voice, Don't let that host touch your teeth for if you bite God in two you'll roast in hell for eternity.

I tried to get God down with my tongue but the priest hissed at me, Stop that clucking and get back to your seat.

God was good. He melted and I swallowed Him and now, at last, I was a member of the True Church, an official sinner.

When the Mass ended there they were at the door of the church, my mother with Michael in her arms, my grandmother. They each hugged me to their bosoms. They each told me it was the happiest day of my life. They each cried all over my head and after my grandmother's contribution that morning my head was a swamp.

Mam, can I go now and make The Collection?   135

She said, After you have a little breakfast.

No, said Grandma. You're not making no collection till you've had a proper First Communion breakfast at my house. Come on.

We followed her. She banged pots and rattled pans and complained that the whole world expected her to be at their beck and call. I ate the egg, I ate the sausage, and when I reached for more sugar for my tea she slapped my hand away.

Go aisy with that sugar. Is it a millionaire you think I am? An American? Is it bedecked in glitterin' jewelry you think I am? Smothered in fancy furs?

The food churned in my stomach. I gagged. I ran to her backyard and   140 threw it all up. Out she came.

Look at what he did. Thrun up his First Communion breakfast. Thrun up the body and blood of Jesus. I have God in me backyard. What am I goin' to do? I'll take him to the Jesuits for they know the sins of the Pope himself.

She dragged through the streets of Limerick. She told the neighbors and passing strangers about God in her backyard. She pushed me into the confession box.

In the name of the Father, the Son, the Holy Ghost. Bless me, Father, for I have sinned. It's a day since my last confession.

A day? And what sins have you committed in a day, my child?

I overslept. I nearly missed my First Communion. My grandmother   145 said I have standing up, North of Ireland, Presbyterian hair. I threw up my First Communion breakfast. Now Grandma says she has God in her backyard and what should she do.

The priest is like the First Confession priest. He has the heavy breathing and the choking sounds.

Ah . . . ah . . . tell your grandmother to wash God away with a little water and for your penance say one Hail Mary and one Our Father. Say a prayer for me and God bless you, my child.

Grandma and Mam were waiting close to the confession box. Grandma said, Were you telling jokes to that priest in the confession box? If 'tis a thing I ever find out you were telling jokes to Jesuits I'll tear the bloody kidneys outa you. Now what did he say about God in me backyard?

He said wash Him away with a little water, Grandma.

Holy water or ordinary water?   150

He didn't say, Grandma.

Well, go back and ask him.

But, Grandma . . .

She pushed me back into the confessional.

Bless me, Father, for I have sinned, it's a minute since my last con-   155
fession.

A minute! Are you the boy that was just here?

I am, Father.

What is it now?

My grandma says, Holy water or ordinary water?

Ordinary water, and tell your grandmother not to be bothering me   160
again.

I told her, Ordinary water, Grandma, and he said don't be bothering
him again.

Don't be bothering him again. That bloody ignorant bogtrotter.

I asked Mam, Can I go now and make The Collection? I want to see
James Cagney.

Grandma said, You can forget about The Collection and James
Cagney because you're not a proper Catholic the way you left God on the
ground. Come on, go home.

Mam said, Wait a minute. That's my son. That's my son on his First   165
Communion day. He's going to see James Cagney.

No he's not.

Yes he is.

Grandma said, Take him then to James Cagney and see if that will
save his Presbyterian North of Ireland American soul. Go ahead.

She pulled her shawl around her and walked away.

Mam said, God, it's getting very late for The Collection and you'll   170
never see James Cagney. We'll go the Lyric Cinema and see if they'll let
you in anyway in your First Communion suit.

We met Mikey Molloy on Barrington Street. He asked if I was going
to the Lyric and I said I was trying. Trying? He said. You don't have
money?

I was ashamed to say no but I had to and he said, That's all right. I'll
get you in. I'll create a diversion.

What's a diversion?

I have the money to go and when I get in I'll pretend to have the fit
and the ticket man will be out of his mind and you can slip in when I let
out the big scream. I'll be watching the door and when I see you in I'll
have a miraculous recovery. That's a diversion. That's what I do to get
my brothers in all the time.

Mam said, Oh, I don't know about that, Mikey. Wouldn't that be a   175
sin and surely you wouldn't want Frank to commit a sin on his First
Communion day.

Mikey said if there was a sin it would be on his soul and he wasn't a
proper Catholic anyway so it didn't matter. He let out his scream and I
slipped in and sat next to Question Quigley and the ticket man, Frank
Goggin, was so worried over Mikey he never noticed. It was a thrilling

film but sad in the end because James Cagney was a public enemy[4] and when they shot him they wrapped him in bandages and threw him in the door, shocking his poor old Irish mother, and that was the end of my First Communion day.

The Reader's Presence

1. The writer often describes painful facts of his early life in a casual, humorous tone. Is the power of McCourt's narrative weakened or strengthened by this treatment, and in what ways? In what ways does McCourt's manner of writing resemble the structure of jokes?

2. McCourt renders his characters' dialogue free of quotation marks. What effect does that have for the reader? Why might the writer have chosen this style?

3. The account proceeds through indirect and circuitous routes. The reader is forced to do the work of assembling the narrative into a cohesive whole. Which feels to you more "natural" — chronological or "nonlinear" narrative? Why? Which style seems closer to that of conventional storytelling? Which seems closer to the structure of lived experience?

27

N. Scott Momaday

The Way to Rainy Mountain

N. Scott Momaday (b. 1934) was born on a Kiowa Indian reservation in Oklahoma and grew up surrounded by the cultural traditions of his people. Since 1982, he has been professor of English at the University of Arizona. His first novel, House Made of Dawn *(1968), won a Pulitzer Prize. The author of poetry and autobiography, Momaday has edited a collection of Kiowa oral literature. His most recent publications include* In the Bear's House *(1999),* The Man Made of Words: Essays, Stories, Passages *(1997),* Ancestral Voice: Conversations with N. Scott Momaday *(1989),* The Ancient Child *(1989),* In the Presence of the Sun:

---

[4]*public enemy:* The Public Enemy, *a motion picture released in 1931, was actor James Cagney's first major role.* — EDS.

Stories and Poems *(1991), and* Circle of Wonder: A Native American Christmas Story *(1994). "The Way to Rainy Mountain" appears as the introduction to the book of that name, published in 1969.*

Momaday thinks of himself as a storyteller. When asked to compare his written voice with his speaking voice, he replied, "My physical voice is something that bears on my writing in an important way. I listen to what I write. I work with it until it is what I want it to be in my hearing. I think that the voice of my writing is very much like the voice of my speaking. And I think in both cases it's distinctive. At least, I mean for it to be. I think that most good writers have individual voices, and that the best writers are those whose voices are most distinctive— most recognizably individual."

A single knoll rises out of the plain in Oklahoma, north and west of the Wichita Range. For my people, the Kiowas, it is an old landmark, and they gave it the name Rainy Mountain. The hardest winter in the world is there. Winter brings blizzards, hot tornadic winds arise in the spring, and in summer the prairie is an anvil's edge. The grass turns brittle and brown, and it cracks beneath your feet. There are green belts along the rivers and creeks, linear groves of hickory and pecan, willow and witch hazel. At a distance in July or August, the steaming foliage seems almost to writhe in fire. Great green and yellow grasshoppers are everywhere in the tall grass, popping up like corn to sting the flesh, and tortoises crawl about on the red earth, going nowhere in the plenty of time. Loneliness is an aspect of the land. All things in the plain are isolate; there is no confusion of objects in the eye, but *one* hill or *one* tree or *one* man. To look upon that landscape in the early morning, with the sun at your back, is to lose the sense of proportion. Your imagination comes to life, and this, you think, is where Creation was begun.

I returned to Rainy Mountain in July. My grandmother had died in the spring, and I wanted to be at her grave. She had lived to be very old and at last infirm. Her only living daughter was with her when she died, and I was told that in death her face was that of a child.

I like to think of her as a child. When she was born, the Kiowas were living the last great moment of their history. For more than a hundred years they had controlled the open range from the Smoky Hill River to the Red, from the headwaters of the Canadian to the fork of the Arkansas and Cimarron. In alliance with the Comanches, they had ruled the whole of the southern Plains. War was their sacred business, and they were among the finest horsemen the world has ever known. But warfare for the Kiowas was pre-eminently a matter of disposition rather than of survival, and they never understood the grim, unrelenting advance of the U.S. Cavalry. When at last, divided and ill-provisioned, they were driven onto the Staked Plains in the cold rains of autumn, they fell into panic. In Palo Duro Canyon they abandoned their crucial stores to pillage and had nothing then but their lives. In order to save themselves, they surrendered to the soldiers of Fort Sill and were imprisoned in the old stone corral that now stands as a military museum. My grandmother was spared the humiliation of those high gray walls by eight or ten years, but she must have known from birth the affliction of defeat, the dark brooding of old warriors.

Her name was Aho, and she belonged to the last culture to evolve in North America. Her forebears came down from the high country in western Montana nearly three centuries ago. They were a mountain people, a mysterious tribe of hunters whose language has never been positively classified in any major group. In the late seventeenth century they began a long migration to the south and east. It was a journey toward the dawn, and it led to a golden age. Along the way the Kiowas were befriended by the Crows, who gave them the culture and religion of the Plains. They acquired horses, and their ancient nomadic spirit was suddenly free of the ground. They acquired Tai-me, the sacred Sun Dance doll, from that moment the object and symbol of their worship, and so shared in the divinity of the sun. Not least, they acquired the sense of destiny, therefore courage and pride. When they entered upon the southern Plains they had been transformed. No longer were they slaves to the simple necessity of survival; they were a lordly and dangerous society of fighters and thieves, hunters and priests of the sun. According to their origin myth, they entered the world through a hollow log. From one point of view, their migration was the fruit of an old prophecy, for indeed they emerged from a sunless world.

Although my grandmother lived out her long life in the shadow of Rainy Mountain, the immense landscape of the continental interior lay like memory in her blood. She could tell of the Crows, whom she had never seen, and of the Black Hills, where she had never been. I wanted to see in reality what she had seen more perfectly in the mind's eye, and traveled fifteen hundred miles to begin my pilgrimage.   5

Yellowstone, it seemed to me, was the top of the world, a region of deep lakes and dark timber, canyons and waterfalls. But, beautiful as it is, one might have the sense of confinement there. The skyline in all directions is close at hand, the high wall of the woods and deep cleavages of shade. There is a perfect freedom in the mountains, but it belongs to the eagle and the elk, the badger and the bear. The Kiowas reckoned their stature by the distance they could see, and they were bent and blind in the wilderness.

Descending eastward, the highland meadows are a stairway to the plain. In July the inland slope of the Rockies is luxuriant with flax and buckwheat, stonecrop and larkspur. The earth unfolds and the limit of the land recedes. Clusters of trees, and animals grazing far in the distance, cause the vision to reach away and wonder to build upon the mind. The sun follows a longer course in the day, and the sky is immense beyond all comparison. The great billowing clouds that sail upon it are shadows that move upon the grain like water, dividing light. Farther down, in the land of the Crows and Blackfeet, the plain is yellow. Sweet clover takes hold of the hills and bends upon itself to cover and seal the soil. There the

Kiowas paused on their way; they had come to the place where they must change their lives. The sun is at home on the plains. Precisely there does it have the certain character of a god. When the Kiowas came to the land of the Crows, they could see the dark lees of the hills at dawn across the Bighorn River, the profusion of light on the grain shelves, the oldest deity ranging after the solstices. Not yet would they veer southward to the caldron of the land that lay below; they must wean their blood from the northern winter and hold the mountains a while longer in their view. They bore Tai-me in procession to the east.

A dark mist lay over the Black Hills, and the land was like iron. At the top of the ridge I caught sight of Devil's Tower upthrust against the gray sky as if in the birth of time the core of the earth had broken through its crust and the motion of the world was begun. There are things in nature that engender an awful quiet in the heart of man; Devil's Tower is one of them. Two centuries ago, because they could not do otherwise, the Kiowas made a legend at the base of the rock. My grandmother said:

> Eight children were there at play, seven sisters and their brother. Suddenly the boy was struck dumb; he trembled and began to run upon his hands and feet. His fingers became claws, and his body was covered with fur. Directly there was a bear where the boy had been. The sisters were terrified; they ran, and the bear ran after them. They came to the stump of a great tree, and the tree spoke to them. It bade them climb upon it, and as they did so it began to rise into the air. The bear came to kill them, but they were just beyond its reach. It reared against the tree and scored the bark all around with its claws. The seven sisters were borne into the sky, and they became the stars of the Big Dipper.

From that moment, and so long as the legend lives, the Kiowas have kinsmen in the night sky. Whatever they were in the mountains, they could be no more. However tenuous their well-being, however much they had suffered and would suffer again, they had found a way out of the wilderness.

My grandmother had a reverence for the sun, a holy regard that now is all but gone out of mankind. There was a wariness in her, and an ancient awe. She was a Christian in her later years, but she had come a long way about, and she never forgot her birthright. As a child she had been to the Sun Dances; she had taken part in those annual rites, and by them she had learned the restoration of her people in the presence of Tai-me. She was about seven when the last Kiowa Sun Dance was held in 1887 in the Washita River above Rainy Mountain Creek. The buffalo were gone. In order to consummate the ancient sacrifice — to impale the head of a buffalo bull upon the medicine tree — a delegation of old men journeyed into Texas, there to beg and barter for an animal from the Goodnight herd. She was ten when the Kiowas came together for the last time as a living Sun Dance culture. They could find no buffalo; they had to hang an old hide from the sacred tree. Before the dance could begin, a company of soldiers rode out from Fort Sill under orders to disperse the tribe. Forbidden without cause the essential act of their faith, having seen the wild herds slaughtered and left to rot upon the ground, the Kiowas backed away forever from the medicine tree. That was July 20, 1890, at the great bend of the Washita. My grandmother was there. Without bitterness, and for as long as she lived, she bore a vision of deicide.

Now that I can have her only in memory, I see my grandmother in   10 the several postures that were peculiar to her: standing at the wood stove on a winter morning and turning meat in a great iron skillet; sitting at the south window, bent above her beadwork, and afterwards, when her vision failed, looking down for a long time into the fold of her hands; going out upon a cane, very slowly as she did when the weight of age came upon her; praying. I remember her most often at prayer. She made long, rambling prayers out of suffering and hope, having seen many things. I was never sure that I had the right to hear, so exclusive were they of all mere custom and company. The last time I saw her she prayed standing by the side of her bed at night, naked to the waist, the light of a kerosene lamp moving upon her dark skin. Her long, black hair, always drawn and braided in the day, lay upon her shoulders and against her breasts like a shawl. I do not speak Kiowa, and I never understood her prayers, but there was something inherently sad in the sound, some merest hesitation upon the syllables of sorrow. She began in a high and descending pitch, exhausting her breath to silence; then again and again—and always the same intensity of effort, of something that is, and is not, like urgency in the human voice. Transported so in the dancing light among the shadows of her room, she seemed beyond the reach of time. But that was illusion; I think I knew then that I should not see her again.

Houses are like sentinels in the plain, old keepers of the weather watch. There, in a very little while, wood takes on the appearance of great age. All colors wear soon away in the wind and rain, and then the wood is burned gray and the grain appears and the nails turn red with rust. The windowpanes are black and opaque; you imagine there is nothing within, and indeed there are many ghosts, bones given up to the land. They stand here and there against the sky, and you approach them for a longer time than you expect. They belong in the distance; it is their domain.

Once there was a lot of sound in my grandmother's house, a lot of coming and going, feasting and talk. The summers there were full of excitement and reunion. The Kiowas are a summer people; they abide the cold and keep to themselves, but when the season turns and the land becomes warm and vital they cannot hold still; an old love of going returns upon them. The aged visitors who came to my grandmother's house when I was a child were made of lean and leather, and they bore themselves upright. They wore great black hats and bright ample shirts that shook in the wind. They rubbed fat upon their hair and wound their braids with strips of colored cloth. Some of them painted their faces and carried the scars of old and cherished enmities. They were an old council of war-lords, come to remind and be reminded of who they were. Their wives and daughters served them well. The women might indulge themselves; gossip was at once the mark and compensation of their servitude. They made loud and elaborate talk among themselves, full of jest and gesture, fright and false alarm. They went abroad in fringed and flowered shawls, bright beadwork and German silver. They were at home in the kitchen, and they prepared meals that were banquets.

There were frequent prayer meetings, and great nocturnal feasts. When I was a child I played with my cousins outside, where the lamplight fell upon the ground and the singing of the old people rose up around us and carried away into the darkness. There were a lot of good things to eat, a lot of laughter and surprise. And afterwards, when the quiet returned, I lay down with my grandmother and could hear the frogs away by the river and feel the motion of the air.

Now there is a funeral silence in the rooms, the endless wake of some final word. The walls have closed in upon my grandmother's house. When I returned to it in mourning, I saw for the first time in my life how small it was. It was late at night, and there was a white moon, nearly full. I sat for a long time on the stone steps by the kitchen door. From there I could see out across the land; I could see the long row of trees by the creek, the low light upon the rolling plains, and the stars of the big dipper. Once I looked at the moon and caught sight of a strange thing. A cricket had perched upon the handrail, only a few inches away from me. My line of vision was such that the creature filled the moon like a fossil. It had gone there, I thought, to live and die, for there, of all places, was its small definition made whole and eternal. A warm wind rose up and purled like the longing within me.

The next morning I awoke at dawn and went out on the dirt road to 15 Rainy Mountain. It was already hot, and the grasshoppers began to fill the air. Still, it was early in the morning, and the birds sang out of the shadows. The long yellow grass on the mountain shone in the bright light, and a scissortail hied above the land. There, where it ought to be, at the end of a long and legendary way, was my grandmother's grave. Here and there on the dark stones were ancestral names. Looking back once, I saw the mountain and came away.

The Reader's Presence

1. In the interview quoted in the introductory note to this selection, Momaday talks about capturing his speaking voice in his writing. What are some of the phrases and passages that make you hear his distinctive voice as you read? Point to—and analyze—specific words and phrases to discuss how the effect of each is created.

2. Momaday tells several stories in this selection, including the history of the Kiowa people, the story of his grandmother's life and death, the story of his homecoming, and the legend of Devil's Tower. How does each story overlap and intertwine with the others? What forces compel the telling or creation of each story? What needs do the stories satisfy? Look, for example, at the legend related in paragraph 8. The Kiowas made this legend "because they could not do otherwise." Why could they have not done otherwise? What does the legend explain for them? How does this embedded legend enhance and complicate the other stories Momaday tells here?

3. From the beginning of this essay, Momaday sets his remarks very firmly in space and then in time. Discuss the importance of physical space in this essay. Why does Momaday take the journey to Rainy Mountain, and the fifteen-hundred-mile "pilgrimage" (paragraph 5)? Why does he say that his grandmother's vision of this landscape is more perfect than his, even though she has never actually seen the landscape he travels? Consider the many remarks about perspective, and change of perspective, that he includes, as well as remarks on proportion. What significance does he attach to these remarks? Where, literally and figuratively, does his grandmother's grave lie? More generally, consider the temporal journeys that run parallel to the spatial journeys: the Kiowas' "journey toward the dawn [that] led to a golden age" (paragraph 4) and Momaday's own journeys that he relates in the essay. How would you characterize the sense of space and time and the relation between the two that are conveyed in this essay?

28

George Orwell

Shooting an Elephant

George Orwell (1903–1950) was born Eric Arthur Blair in Bengal, India, the son of a colonial administrator. He was sent to England for his education and attended Eton on a scholarship, but rather than go on to university in 1922 he returned to the East and served with the Indian Imperial Police in Burma. Orwell hated his work and the colonial system; published posthumously, the essay "Shooting an Elephant" was based on his experience in Burma and is found in

Shooting an Elephant and Other Essays *(1950). In 1927 Orwell returned to England and began a career as a professional writer. He served briefly in the Spanish Civil War until he was wounded and then settled in Hertfordshire. Best remembered for his novels* Animal Farm *(1945) and* Nineteen Eighty-Four *(1949), Orwell also wrote articles, essays, and reviews, usually with a political point in mind. In 1969 Irving Howe honored Orwell as "the best English essayist since Hazlitt, perhaps since Dr. Johnson. He was the greatest moral force in English letters during the last several decades: craggy, fiercely polemical, sometimes mistaken, but an utterly free man."*

In his 1946 essay "Why I Write," Orwell said that from a very early age "I knew that when I grew up I should be a writer." At first he saw writing as a remedy for loneliness, but as he grew up his reasons for writing expanded: "Looking back through my work, I see it is invariably when I lacked a political purpose that I wrote lifeless books." In his mature work, he relied on simple, clear prose to express his political and social convictions: "Good prose," he once wrote, "is like a windowpane."

In Moulmein, in Lower Burma, I was hated by large numbers of people—the only time in my life that I have been important enough for this to happen to me. I was subdivisional police officer of the town, and in an aimless, petty kind of way anti-European feeling was very bitter. No one had the guts to raise a riot, but if a European woman went through the bazaars alone somebody would probably spit betel juice over her dress. As a police officer I was an obvious target and was baited whenever it seemed safe to do so. When a nimble Burman tripped me up on the football field and the referee (another Burman) looked the other way, the crowd yelled with hideous laughter. This happened more than once. In the end the sneering yellow faces of young men that met me everywhere, the insults hooted after me when I was at a safe distance, got badly on my nerves. The young Buddhist priests were the worst of all. There were several thousands of them in the town and none of them seemed to have anything to do except stand on street corners and jeer at Europeans.

All this was perplexing and upsetting. For at that time I had already made up my mind that imperialism was an evil thing and the sooner I chucked up my job and got out of it the better. Theoretically—and secretly, of course—I was all for the Burmese and all against the oppressors, the British. As for the job I was doing, I hated it more bitterly than I can perhaps make clear. In a job like that you see the dirty work of Empire at close quarters. The wretched prisoners huddling in the stinking cages of the lockups, the grey, cowed faces of the long-term convicts, the scarred buttocks of the men who had been flogged with bamboos—all these oppressed me with an intolerable sense of guilt. But I could get nothing into perspective. I was young and ill-educated and I had had to think out my problems in the utter silence that is imposed on every Englishman in the East. I did not even know that the British Empire is dying, still less did I know that it is a great deal better than the younger empires that are going to supplant it. All I knew was that I was stuck between my hatred of the empire I served and my rage against the evil-spirited little beasts who tried to make my job impossible. With one part of my mind I thought of the British Raj[1] as an unbreakable tyranny, as something clamped down, in *saecula saeculorum*,[2] upon the will of prostrate peoples; with another part I thought that the greatest joy in the world would be to drive a bayonet into a Buddhist priest's guts. Feelings like these are the normal by-products of imperialism; ask any Anglo-Indian official, if you can catch him off duty.

One day something happened which in a roundabout way was enlightening. It was a tiny incident in itself, but it gave me a better glimpse than I had had before of the real nature of imperialism—the real motives for which despotic governments act. Early one morning the subinspector at a police station the other end of town rang me up on the phone and said that an elephant was ravaging the bazaar. Would I please come and do something about it? I did not know what I could do, but I wanted to see what was happening and I got on to a pony and started out. I took my rifle, an old .44 Winchester and much too small to kill an elephant, but I thought the noise might be useful *in terrorem*.[3] Various Burmans stopped me on the way and told me about the elephant's doings. It was not, of course, a wild elephant, but a tame one which had gone "must."[4] It had been chained up, as tame elephants always are when their attack of "must" is due, but on the previous night it had broken its chain and escaped. Its mahout,[5] the only person who could manage it when it was in that state, had set out in pursuit, but had taken the wrong direction and was now twelve hours' journey away, and in the morning the elephant had suddenly reappeared in the town. The Burmese population had no weapons and were quite helpless against it. It had already destroyed somebody's bamboo hut, killed a cow, and raided some fruit stalls and devoured the stock; also it had met the municipal rubbish van and, when the driver jumped out and took to his heels, had turned the van over and inflicted violences upon it.

The Burmese subinspector and some Indian constables were waiting for me in the quarter where the elephant had been seen. It was a very poor quarter, a labyrinth of squalid bamboo huts, thatched with palm-leaf, winding all over a steep hillside. I remember that it was a cloudy, stuffy morning at the beginning of the rains. We began questioning the people as to where the elephant had gone and, as usual, failed to get any definite information. That is invariably the case in the East; a story always sounds clear enough at a distance, but the nearer you get to the scene of events the vaguer it becomes. Some of the people said that the elephant had gone in one direction, some said that he had gone in an-

---

[1] *Raj:* The British administration. — EDS.
[2] *saecula saeculorum:* Forever and ever (Latin). — EDS.
[3] *in terrorem:* As a warning (Latin). — EDS.
[4] *"must":* Sexual arousal. — EDS.
[5] *mahout:* Keeper (Hindi). — EDS.

other, some professed not even to have heard of any elephant. I had almost made up my mind that the whole story was a pack of lies, when we heard yells a little distance away. There was a loud, scandalized cry of "Go away, child! Go away this instant!" and an old woman with a switch in her hand came round the corner of a hut, violently shooing away a crowd of naked children. Some more women followed, clicking their tongues and exclaiming; evidently there was something that the children ought not to have seen. I rounded the hut and saw a man's dead body sprawling in the mud. He was an Indian, a black Dravidian[6] coolie, almost naked, and he could not have been dead many minutes. The people said that the elephant had come suddenly upon him round the corner of the hut, caught him with its trunk, put its foot on his back, and ground him into the earth. This was the rainy season and the ground was soft, and his face had scored a trench a foot deep and a couple of yards long. He was lying on his belly with arms crucified and head sharply twisted to one side. His face was coated with mud, the eyes wide open, the teeth bared and grinning with an expression of unendurable agony. (Never tell me, by the way, that the dead look peaceful. Most of the corpses I have seen looked devilish.) The friction of the great beast's foot had stripped the skin from his back as neatly as one skins a rabbit. As soon as I saw the dead man I sent an orderly to a friend's house nearby to borrow an elephant rifle. I had already sent back the pony, not wanting it to go mad with fright and throw me if it smelled the elephant.

The orderly came back in a few minutes with a rifle and five cartridges, and meanwhile some Burmans had arrived and told us that the elephant was in the paddy fields below, only a few hundred yards away. As I started forward practically the whole population of the quarter flocked out of the houses and followed me. They had seen the rifle and were all shouting excitedly that I was going to shoot the elephant. They had not shown much interest in the elephant when he was merely ravaging their homes, but it was different now that he was going to be shot. It was a bit of fun to them, as it would be to an English crowd; besides they wanted the meat. It made me vaguely uneasy. I had no intention of shooting the elephant—I had merely sent for the rifle to defend myself if necessary—and it is always unnerving to have a crowd following you. I marched down the hill, looking and feeling a fool, with the rifle over my shoulder and an ever-growing army of people jostling at my heels. At the bottom, when you got away from the huts, there was a metalled road and beyond that a miry waste of paddy fields a thousand yards across, not yet ploughed but soggy from the first rains and dotted with coarse grass. The elephant was standing eight yards from the road, his left side towards us. He took not the slightest notice of the crowd's approach. He was tearing up bunches of grass, beating them against his knees to clean them and stuffing them into his mouth.

[6]**Dravidian:** A populous Indian group. — EDS.

I had halted on the road. As soon as I saw the elephant I knew with perfect certainty that I ought not to shoot him. It is a serious matter to shoot a working elephant—it is comparable to destroying a huge and costly piece of machinery—and obviously one ought not to do it if it can possibly be avoided. And at that distance, peacefully eating, the elephant looked no more dangerous than a cow. I thought then and I think now that his attack of "must" was already passing off; in which case he would merely wander harmlessly about until the mahout came back and caught him. Moreover, I did not in the least want to shoot him. I decided that I would watch him for a little while to make sure that he did not turn savage again, and then go home.

But at that moment, I glanced round at the crowd that had followed me. It was an immense crowd, two thousand at the least and growing every minute. It blocked the road for a long distance on either side. I looked at the sea of yellow faces above the garish clothes—faces all happy and excited over this bit of fun, all certain that the elephant was going to be shot. They were watching me as they would watch a conjuror about to perform a trick. They did not like me, but with the magical rifle in my hands I was momentarily worth watching. And suddenly I realized that I should have to shoot the elephant after all: The people expected it of me and I had got to do it; I could feel their two thousand wills pressing me forward, irresistibly. And it was at this moment, as I stood there with the rifle in my hands, that I first grasped the hollowness, the futility of the white man's dominion in the East. Here was I, the white man with his gun, standing in front of the unarmed native crowd—seemingly the leading actor of the piece; but in reality I was only an absurd puppet pushed to and fro by the will of those yellow faces behind. I perceived in this moment that when the white man turns tyrant it is his own freedom that he destroys. He becomes a sort of hollow, posing dummy, the conventionalized figure of a sahib. For it is the condition of his rule that he shall spend his life in trying to impress the "natives," and so in every crisis he has got to do what the "natives" expect of him. He wears a mask, and his face grows to fit it. I had got to shoot the elephant. I had committed myself to doing it when I sent for the rifle. A sahib has got to act like a sahib; he has got to appear resolute, to know his own mind and do definite things. To come all that way, rifle in hand, with two thousand people marching at my heels, and then to trail feebly away, having done nothing—no, that was impossible. The crowd would laugh at me. And my whole life, every white man's life in the East, was one long struggle not to be laughed at.

But I did not want to shoot the elephant. I watched him beating his bunch of grass against his knees, with that preoccupied grandmotherly air that elephants have. It seemed to me that it would be murder to shoot him. At that age I was not squeamish about killing animals, but I had never shot an elephant and never wanted to. (Somehow it always seems worse to kill a *large* animal.) Besides, there was the beast's owner to be considered. Alive, the elephant was worth at least a hundred pounds; dead, he would only be worth the value of his tusks, five pounds, possibly. But I had got to act quickly. I turned to some experienced-looking Burmans who had been there when we arrived, and asked them how the elephant had been behaving. They all said the same thing: He took no notice of you if you left him alone, but he might charge if you went too close to him.

It was perfectly clear to me what I ought to do. I ought to walk up to within, say, twenty-five yards of the elephant and test his behavior. If he charged, I could shoot; if he took no notice of me, it would be safe to leave him until the mahout came back. But also I knew that I was going to do no such thing. I was a poor shot with a rifle and the ground was soft mud into which one would sink at every step. If the elephant charged and I missed him, I should have about as much chance as a toad under a steamroller. But even then I was not thinking particularly of my own skin, only of the watchful yellow faces behind. For at that moment, with the crowd watching me, I was not afraid in the ordinary sense, as I would have been if I had been alone. A white man mustn't be frightened in front of "natives"; and so, in general, he isn't frightened. The sole thought in my mind was that if anything went wrong those two thousand Burmans would see me pursued, caught, trampled on, and reduced to a grinning corpse like that Indian up the hill. And if that happened it was quite probable that some of them would laugh. That would never do. There was only one alternative. I shoved the cartridges into the magazine and lay down on the road to get a better aim.

The crowd grew very still, and a deep, low, happy sigh, as of people   10
who see the theatre curtain go up at last, breathed from innumerable throats. They were going to have their bit of fun after all. The rifle was a beautiful German thing with cross-hair sights. I did not then know that in shooting an elephant one would shoot to cut an imaginary bar running from ear-hole to ear-hole. I ought, therefore, as the elephant was sideways on, to have aimed straight at his ear-hole; actually I aimed several inches in front of this, thinking the brain would be further forward.

When I pulled the trigger I did not hear the bang or feel the kick—one never does when a shot goes home—but I heard the devilish roar of glee that went up from the crowd. In that instant, in too short a time, one would have thought, even for the bullet to get there, a mysterious, terrible change had come over the elephant. He neither stirred nor fell, but every line of his body had altered. He looked suddenly stricken, shrunken, immensely old, as though the frightful impact of the bullet had paralyzed him without knocking him down. At last, after what seemed a long time—it might have been five seconds, I dare say—he sagged flabbily to his knees. His mouth slobbered. An enormous senility seemed to have settled upon him. One could have imagined him thousands of years old. I fired again into the same spot. At the second shot he did not collapse but climbed with desperate slowness to his feet and stood weakly upright, with legs sagging and head drooping. I fired a third time. That was the shot that did for him. You could see the agony of it jolt his whole body and knock the last remnant of strength from his legs. But in falling he seemed for a moment to rise, for as his hind legs collapsed beneath him he seemed to tower upward like a huge rock toppling, his trunk reaching skywards like a tree. He trumpeted, for the first and only time. And then down he came, his belly towards me, with a crash that seemed to shake the ground even where I lay.

I got up. The Burmans were already racing past me across the mud. It was obvious that the elephant would never rise again, but he was not dead. He was breathing very rhythmically with long rattling gasps, his great mound of a side painfully rising and falling. His mouth was wide open. I could see far down into caverns of pale pink throat. I waited a long time for him to die, but his breathing did not weaken. Finally, I fired my two remaining shots into the spot where I thought his heart must be. The thick blood welled out of him like red velvet, but still he did not die. His body did not even jerk when the shots hit him, the tortured breathing continued without a pause. He was dying, very slowly and in great agony, but in some world remote from me where not even a bullet could damage him further. I felt I had got to put an end to that dreadful noise. It seemed dreadful to see the great beast lying there, powerless to move and yet powerless to die, and not even to be able to finish him. I sent back for my small rifle and poured shot after shot into his heart, and down his throat. They seemed to make no impression. The tortured gasps continued as steadily as the ticking of a clock.

In the end I could not stand it any longer and went away. I heard later that it took him half an hour to die. Burmans were bringing dahs[7] and baskets even before I left, and I was told they had stripped his body almost to the bones by the afternoon.

Afterwards, of course, there were endless discussions about the shooting of the elephant. The owner was furious, but he was only an Indian and could do nothing. Besides, legally I had done the right thing, for a mad elephant has to be killed, like a mad dog, if its owner fails to control it. Among the Europeans opinion was divided. The older men said I was right, the younger men said it was a damn shame to shoot an elephant for killing a coolie, because the elephant was worth more than any damn Coringhee coolie. And afterwards I was very glad that the coolie had been killed; it put me legally in the right and it gave me sufficient pretext for shooting the elephant. I often wondered whether any of the others grasped that I had done it solely to avoid looking a fool.

The Reader's Presence

1. Discuss Orwell's dilemma. How would you react in his situation? Is he recommending that readers see his behavior as a model of what to do in such a conflict?

---

[7]*dahs:* Large knives. — EDS.

2. Do you find Orwell's final sentence believable? Do you think that Orwell shot the elephant solely to avoid looking like a fool? In what sense would he have looked like a fool if he had refused to kill the creature? Why do you think he makes this claim, and how does it affect your reading of the entire essay?

3. Some literary critics doubt that Orwell really did shoot an elephant in Burma. No external historical documentation has ever been found to corroborate Orwell's account. Yet what *internal* elements in the essay—what details or features—help persuade you that the episode is fact and not fiction? In other words, what makes you think that you are reading an essay and not a short story?

29

Adrienne Rich

Split at the Root: An Essay on Jewish Identity

Adrienne Rich (b. 1929) has published numerous volumes of poetry and her work has appeared in many anthologies. She received her first award for poetry, a Yale Series of Younger Poets Award, while a student at Radcliffe College in 1951. Since then Rich has received many other professional honors, including a National Institute of Art and Letters Award (1961), a National Book Award (1974), a Fund for Human Dignity Award from the National Gay Task Force (1981), and the Lenore Marshall Nation Poetry Prize for her 1991 book, An Atlas of the Difficult World. *Her most recent book of poems is* Midnight Salvage *(1999). Adrienne Rich's poetics are informed by her political work against the oppression of women and against homophobia.*

Besides poetry, Rich has published four prose collections, including Blood, Bread and Poetry: Selected Prose *(1986), from which "Split at the Root" is excerpted, and* What Is Found There: Notebooks on Poetry and Politics *(1993). She has taught at many colleges and universities, most recently as a professor of English and feminist studies at Stanford University, and as the Marjorie Kouler visiting fellow at the University of Chicago.*

Rich has written about a pivotal moment in her life as a writer: "To write directly and overtly as a woman, out of a woman's body and experience, to take women's existence seriously as theme and source for art, was something I had been hungering to do, needing to do, all my writing life. It placed me nakedly face to face with both terror and anger; it did indeed imply the breakdown of the world as I had always known it, the end of safety, *to paraphrase Baldwin. . . . But it released tremendous energy in me, as in many other women, to have that way*

*of writing affirmed and validated in a growing political community. I felt for the
first time the closing of the gap between poet and woman."*

For about fifteen minutes I have been sitting chin in hand in front of
the typewriter, staring out at the snow. Trying to be honest with myself,
trying to figure out why writing this seems to be so dangerous an act,
filled with fear and shame, and why it seems so necessary. It comes to me
that in order to write this I have to be willing to do two things: I have to
claim my father, for I have my Jewishness from him and not from my
gentile mother, and I have to break his silence, his taboos; in order to
claim him I have in a sense to expose him.

And there is, of course, the third thing: I have to face the sources and
the flickering presence of my own ambivalence as a Jew; the daily, mundane anti-Semitisms of my entire life.

These are stories I have never tried to tell before. Why now? Why, I
asked myself sometime last year, does this question of Jewish identity
float so impalpably, so ungraspably around me, a cloud I can't quite see
the outlines of, which feels to me to be without definition?

And yet I've been on the track of this longer than I think.

In a long poem written in 1960, when I was thirty-one years old, I de-   5
scribed myself as "Split at the root, neither Gentile nor Jew, / Yankee nor
Rebel."[1] I was still trying to have it both ways: to be neither/nor, trying to
live (with my Jewish husband and three children more Jewish in ancestry
than I) in the predominantly gentile Yankee academic world of Cambridge, Massachusetts.

But this begins, for me, in Baltimore, where I was born in my father's
workplace, a hospital in the black ghetto, whose lobby contained an immense white marble statue of Christ.

My father was then a young teacher and researcher in the department
of pathology at the Johns Hopkins Medical School, one of the very few
Jews to attend or teach at that institution. He was from Birmingham, Alabama; his father, Samuel, was Ashkenazic,[2] an immigrant from Austria-
Hungary and his mother, Hattie Rice, a Sephardic[3] Jew from Vicksburg,
Mississippi. My grandfather had had a shoe store in Birmingham, which
did well enough to allow him to retire comfortably and to leave my
grandmother income on his death. The only souvenirs of my grandfather,
Samuel Rich, were his ivory flute, which lay on our living-room mantel
and was not to be played with; his thin gold pocket watch, which my fa-

---

[1]Adrienne Rich, "Readings of History," in *Snapshots of a Daughter-in-Law* (New
York: W. W. Norton, 1967), pp. 36–40. — RICH'S NOTE.
[2]*Ashkenazic:* Descendants of the Jews, generally Yiddish-speaking, who settled in
middle and northern Europe. — EDS.
[3]*Sephardic:* Descendants of the Jews who settled for the most part in Spain, Portugal,
and northern Africa. — EDS.

ther wore; and his Hebrew prayer book, which I discovered among my father's books in the course of reading my way through his library. In this prayer book there was a newspaper clipping about my grandparents' wedding, which took place in a synagogue.

My father, Arnold, was sent in adolescence to a military school in the North Carolina mountains, a place for training white southern Christian gentlemen. I suspect that there were few, if any, other Jewish boys at Colonel Bingham's, or at "Mr. Jefferson's university" in Charlottesville, where he studied as an undergraduate. With whatever conscious fore-thought, Samuel and Hattie sent their son into the dominant southern WASP culture to become an "exception," to enter the professional class. Never, in describing these experiences, did he speak of having suffered — from loneliness, cultural alienation, or outsiderhood. Never did I hear him use the word *anti-Semitism*.

It was only in college, when I read a poem by Karl Shapiro beginning "To hate the Negro and avoid the Jew / is the curriculum," that it flashed on me that there was an untold side to my father's story of his student years. He looked recognizably Jewish, was short and slender in build with dark wiry hair and deep-set eyes, high forehead, and curved nose.

My mother is a gentile. In Jewish law I cannot count myself a Jew. If it is true that "we think back through our mothers if we are women" (Virginia Woolf) — and I myself have affirmed this — then even according to lesbian theory, I cannot (or need not?) count myself a Jew. 10

The white southern Protestant woman, the gentile, has always been there for me to peel back into. That's a whole piece of history in itself, for my gentile grandmother and my mother were also frustrated artists and intellectuals, a lost writer and a lost composer between them. Readers and annotators of books, note takers, my mother a good pianist still, in her eighties. But there was also the obsession with ancestry, with "back-ground," the southern talk of family, not as people you would necessarily know and depend on, but as heritage, the guarantee of "good breeding." There was the inveterate romantic heterosexual fantasy, the mother telling the daughter how to attract men (my mother often used the word "fascinate"); the assumption that relations between the sexes could only be romantic, that it was in the woman's interest to cultivate "mystery," conceal her actual feelings. Survival tactics of a kind, I think today, knowing what I know about the white woman's sexual role in the south-ern racist scenario. Heterosexuality as protection, but also drawing white women deeper into collusion with white men.

It would be easy to push away and deny the gentile in me — that white southern woman, that social christian. At different times in my life I have wanted to push away one or the other burden of inheritance, to say merely *I am a woman; I am a lesbian.* If I call myself a Jewish lesbian, do I thereby try to shed some of my southern gentile white woman's culpability? If I call myself only through my mother, is it because I pass more easily through a world where being a lesbian often seems like outsiderhood enough?

According to Nazi logic, my two Jewish grandparents would have made me a *Mischling, first-degree*—nonexempt from the Final Solution.[4]

The social world in which I grew up was christian virtually without needing to say so—christian imagery, music, language, symbols, assumptions everywhere. It was also a genteel, white, middle-class world in which "common" was a term of deep opprobrium. "Common" white people might speak of "niggers"; *we* were taught never to use that word—*we* said "Negroes" (even as we accepted segregation, the eating taboo, the assumption that black people were simply of a separate species). Our language was more polite, distinguishing us from the "rednecks" or the lynch-mob mentality. But so charged with negative meaning was even the word "Negro" that as children we were taught never to use it in front of black people. We were taught that any mention of skin color in the presence of colored people was treacherous, forbidden ground. In a parallel way, the word *Jew* was not used by polite gentiles. I sometimes heard my best friend's father, a Presbyterian minister, allude to "the Hebrew people" or "people of the Jewish faith." The world of acceptable folk was white, gentile (christian, really), and had "ideals" (which colored people, white "common" people, were not supposed to have). "Ideals" and "manners" included not hurting someone's feelings by calling her or him a Negro or a Jew—naming the hated identity. This is the mental framework of the 1930s and 1940s in which I was raised.

(Writing this, I feel dimly like the betrayer: of my father, who did not   15
speak the word; of my mother, who must have trained me in the messages; of my caste and class; of my whiteness itself.)

Two memories: I am in a play reading at school of *The Merchant of Venice.* Whatever Jewish law says, I am quite sure I was *seen* as Jewish (with a reassuringly gentile mother) in that double vision that bigotry allows. I am the only Jewish girl in the class, and I am playing Portia. As always, I read my part aloud for my father the night before, and he tells me to convey, with my voice, more scorn and contempt with the word *Jew:* "Therefore, Jew . . ." I have to say the word out, and say it loudly. I was encouraged to pretend to be a non-Jewish child acting a non-Jewish character who has to speak the word *Jew* emphatically. Such a child would not have had trouble with the part. But *I* must have had trouble with the part, if only because the word itself was really taboo. I can see that there was a kind of terrible, bitter bravado about my father's way of handling this. And who would not dissociate from Shylock in order to identify with Portia? As a Jewish child who was also a female, I loved Portia—and, like every other Shakespearean heroine, she proved a treacherous role model.

A year or so later I am in another play, *The School for Scandal,* in which a notorious spendthrift is described as having "many excellent friends . . . among the Jews." In neither case was anything explained,

---

[4]***Final Solution:*** The Nazi plan to exterminate the Jews. — EDS.

either to me or to the class at large, about this scorn for Jews and the disgust surrounding Jews and money. Money, when Jews wanted it, had it, or lent it to others, seemed to take on a peculiar nastiness; Jews and money had some peculiar and unspeakable relation.

At the same school—in which we had Episcopalian hymns and prayers, and read aloud through the Bible morning after morning—I gained the impression that Jews were in the Bible and mentioned in English literature, that they had been persecuted centuries ago by the wicked Inquisition, but that they seemed not to exist in everyday life. These were the 1940s, and we were told a great deal about the Battle of Britain, the noble French Resistance fighters, the brave, starving Dutch—but I did not learn of the resistance of the Warsaw ghetto until I left home.

I was sent to the Episcopal church, baptized and confirmed, and attended it for about five years, though without belief. That religion seemed to have little to do with belief or commitment; it was liturgy that mattered, not spiritual passion. Neither of my parents ever entered that church, and my father would not enter *any* church for any reason—wedding or funeral. Nor did I enter a synagogue until I left Baltimore. When I came home from church, for a while, my father insisted on reading aloud to me from Thomas Paine's *The Age of Reason*—a diatribe against institutional religion. Thus, he explained, I would have a balanced view of these things, a choice. He—they—did not give me the choice to be a Jew. My mother explained to me when I was filling out forms for college that if any question was asked about "religion," I should put down "Episcopalian" rather than "none"—to seem to have no religion was, she implied, dangerous.

But it was white social christianity, rather than any particular christian sect, that the world was founded on. The very word *Christian* was used as a synonym for virtuous, just, peace-loving, generous, etc., etc.[5] The norm was christian: "Religion: none" was indeed not acceptable. Anti-Semitism was so intrinsic as not to have a name. I don't recall exactly being taught that the Jews killed Jesus—"Christ killer" seems too strong a term for the bland Episcopal vocabulary—but certainly we got the impression that the Jews had been caught out in a terrible mistake, failing to recognize the true Messiah, and were thereby less advanced in moral and spiritual sensibility. The Jews had actually allowed *money-lenders in the Temple* (again, the unexplained obsession with Jews and money). They were of the past, archaic, primitive, as older (and darker) cultures are supposed to be primitive; christianity was lightness, fairness, peace on earth, and combined the feminine appeal of "The meek shall inherit the earth" with the masculine stride of "Onward, Christian Soldiers."

20

---

[5]In a similar way the phrase *That's white of you* implied that you were behaving with the superior decency and morality expected of white but not of black people.—RICH'S NOTE.

Sometime in 1946, while still in high school, I read in the newspaper that a theater in Baltimore was showing films of the Allied liberation of the Nazi concentration camps. Alone, I went downtown after school one afternoon and watched the stark, blurry, but unmistakable newsreels. When I try to go back and touch the pulse of that girl of sixteen, growing up in many ways so precocious and so ignorant, I am overwhelmed by a memory of despair, a sense of inevitability more enveloping than any I had ever known. Anne Frank's diary and many other personal narratives of the Holocaust were still unknown or unwritten. But it came to me that every one of those piles of corpses, mountains of shoes and clothing had contained, simply, individuals, who had believed, as I now believed of myself, that they were intended to live out a life of some kind of meaning, that the world possessed some kind of sense and order; yet *this* had happened to them. And I, who believed my life was intended to be so interesting and meaningful, was connected to those dead by something — not just mortality but a taboo name, a hated identity. Or was I — did I really have to be? Writing this now, I feel belated rage that I was so impoverished by the family and social worlds I lived in, that I had to try to figure out by myself what this did indeed mean for me. That I had never been taught about resistance, only about passing. That I had no language for anti-Semitism itself.

When I went home and told my parents where I had been, they were not pleased. I felt accused of being morbidly curious, not healthy, sniffing around death for the thrill of it. And since, at sixteen, I was often not sure of the sources of my feelings or of my motives for doing what I did, I probably accused myself as well. One thing was clear: There was nobody in my world with whom I could discuss those films. Probably at the same time, I was reading accounts of the camps in magazines and newspapers; what I remember were the films and having questions that I could not even phrase, such as *Are those men and women "them" or "us"?*

To be able to ask even the child's astonished question *Why do they hate us so?* means knowing how to say "we." The guilt of not knowing, the guilt of perhaps having betrayed my parents or even those victims, those survivors, through mere curiosity — these also froze in me for years the impulse to find out more about the Holocaust.

1947: I left Baltimore to go to college in Cambridge, Massachusetts, left (I thought) the backward, enervating South for the intellectual, vital North. New England also had for me some vibration of higher moral rectitude, of moral passion even, with its seventeenth-century Puritan self-scrutiny, its nineteenth-century literary "flowering," its abolitionist righteousness, Colonel Shaw and his black Civil War regiment depicted in granite on Boston Common. At the same time, I found myself, at Radcliffe, among Jewish women. I used to sit for hours over coffee with what I thought of as the "real" Jewish students, who told me about middle-class Jewish culture in America. I described my background — for the first

time to strangers—and they took me on, some with amusement at my illiteracy, some arguing that I could never marry into a strict Jewish family,
some convinced I didn't "look Jewish," others that I did. I learned the
names of holidays and foods, which surnames are Jewish and which are
"changed names"; about girls who had had their noses "fixed," their hair
straightened. For these young Jewish women, students in the late 1940s,
it was acceptable, perhaps even necessary, to strive to look as gentile as
possible; but they stuck proudly to being Jewish, expected to marry a
Jew, have children, keep the holidays, carry on the culture.

I felt I was testing a forbidden current, that there was danger in these   25
revelations. I bought a reproduction of a Chagall portrait of a rabbi in
striped prayer shawl and hung it on the wall of my room. I was admittedly young and trying to educate myself, but I was also doing something
that *is* dangerous: I was flirting with identity.

One day that year I was in a small shop where I had bought a dress
with a too-long skirt. The shop employed a seamstress who did alterations, and she came in to pin up the skirt on me. I am sure that she was a
recent immigrant, a survivor. I remember a short, dark woman wearing
heavy glasses, with an accent so foreign I could not understand her
words. Something about her presence was very powerful and disturbing
to me. After marking and pinning up the skirt, she sat back on her knees,
looked up at me, and asked in a hurried whisper: "You Jewish?" Eighteen
years of training in assimilation sprang into the reflex by which I shook
my head, rejecting her, and muttered, "No."

What was I actually saying "no" to? She was poor, older, struggling
with a foreign tongue, anxious; she had escaped the death that had been
intended for her, but I had no imagination of her possible courage and
foresight, her resistance—I did not see in her a heroine who had perhaps
saved many lives, including her own. I saw the frightened immigrant, the
seamstress hemming the skirts of college girls, the wandering Jew. But I
was an American college girl having her skirt hemmed. And I was frightened myself, I think, because she had recognized me ("It takes one to
know one," my friend Edie at Radcliffe had said) even if I refused to recognize myself or her, even if her recognition was sharpened by loneliness
or the need to feel safe with me.

But why should she have felt safe with me? I myself was living with a
false sense of safety.

There are betrayals in my life that I have known at the very moment
were betrayals: this was one of them. There are other betrayals committed so repeatedly, so mundanely, that they leave no memory trace behind,
only a growing residue of misery, of dull, accreted self-hatred. Often these
take the form not of words but of silence. Silence before the joke at which
everyone is laughing: the anti-woman joke, the racist joke, the anti-
Semitic joke. Silence and then amnesia. Blocking it out when the oppressor's language starts coming from the lips of one we admire, whose

courage and eloquence have touched us: *She didn't really mean that; he didn't really say that.* But the accretions build up out of sight, like scale inside a kettle.

1948: I come home from my freshman year at college, flaming with   30
new insights, new information. I am the daughter who has gone out into the world, to the pinnacle of intellectual prestige, Harvard, fulfilling my father's hopes for me, but also exposed to dangerous influences. I have already been reproved for attending a rally for Henry Wallace[6] and the Progressive party. I challenge my father: "Why haven't you told me that I am Jewish? Why do you never talk about being a Jew?" He answers measuredly, "You know that I have never denied that I am a Jew. But it's not important to me. I am a scientist, a deist. I have no use for organized religion. I choose to live in a world of many kinds of people. There are Jews I admire and others whom I despise. I am a person, not simply a Jew." The words are as I remember them, not perhaps exactly as spoken. But that was the message. And it contained enough truth—as all denial drugs itself on partial truth—so that it remained for the time being unanswerable, leaving me high and dry, split at the root, gasping for clarity, for air.

At that time Arnold Rich was living in suspension, waiting to be appointed to the professorship of pathology at Johns Hopkins. The appointment was delayed for years, no Jew ever having held a professional chair in that medical school. And he wanted it badly. It must have been a very bitter time for him, since he had believed so greatly in the redeeming power of excellence, of being the most brilliant, inspired man for the job. With enough excellence, you could presumably make it stop mattering that you were Jewish; you could become the *only* Jew in the gentile world, a Jew so "civilized," so far from "common," so attractively combining southern gentility with European cultural values that no one would ever confuse you with the raw, "pushy" Jews of New York, the "loud, hysterical" refugees from eastern Europe, the "overdressed" Jews of the urban South.

We—my sister, mother, and I—were constantly urged to speak quietly in public, to dress without ostentation, to repress all vividness or spontaneity, to assimilate with a world which might see us as too flamboyant. I suppose that my mother, pure gentile though she was, could be seen as acting "common" or "Jewish" if she laughed too loudly or spoke aggressively. My father's mother, who lived with us half the year, was a model of circumspect behavior, dressed in dark blue or lavender, retiring in company, ladylike to an extreme, wearing no jewelry except a good gold chain, a narrow brooch, or a string of pearls. A few times, within the family, I saw her anger flare, felt the passion she was repressing. But when Arnold took us out to a restaurant or on a trip, the Rich women

---

[6]*Henry Wallace* (1888–1965): American journalist, agriculturist, and politician, as well as the 1948 Progressive party's candidate for the presidency. — EDS.

were always tuned down to some WASP level my father believed, surely, would protect us all—maybe also make us unrecognizable to the "real Jews" who wanted to seize us, drag us back to the *shtetl,* the ghetto, in its many manifestations.

For, yes, that *was* a message—that some Jews would be after you, once they "knew," to rejoin them, to re-enter a world that was messy, noisy, unpredictable, maybe poor—"even though," as my mother once wrote me, criticizing my largely Jewish choice of friends in college, "some of them will be the most brilliant, fascinating people you'll ever meet." I wonder if that isn't one message of assimilation—of America—that the unlucky or the unachieving want to pull you backward, that to identify with them is to court downward mobility, lose the precious chance of passing, of token existence. There was always within this sense of Jewish identity a strong class discrimination. Jews might be "fascinating" as in-dividuals but came with huge unruly families who "poured chicken soup over everyone's head" (in the phrase of a white southern male poet). Anti-Semitism could thus be justified by the bad behavior of certain Jews; and if you did not effectively deny family and community, there would al-ways be a remote cousin claiming kinship with you who was the "wrong kind" of Jew.

I have always believed his attitude toward other Jews depended on who they were. . . . It was my impression that Jews of this background looked down on Eastern European Jews, including Polish Jews and Rus-sian Jews, who generally were not as well educated. This from a letter written to me recently by a gentile who had worked in my father's depart-ment, whom I had asked about anti-Semitism there and in particular re-garding my father. This informant also wrote me that it was hard to per-ceive anti-Semitism in Baltimore because the racism made so much more intense an impression: *I would almost have to think that blacks went to a different heaven than the whites, because the bodies were kept in a sepa-rate morgue, and some white persons did not even want blood transfu-sions from black donors.* My father's mind was predictably racist and misogynist; yet as a medical student he noted in his journal that southern male chivalry stopped at the point of any white man in a streetcar giving his seat to an old, weary black woman standing in the aisle. Was this a Jewish insight—an outsider's insight, even though the outsider was striv-ing to be on the inside?

Because what isn't named is often more permeating than what is, I   35
believe that my father's Jewishness profoundly shaped my own iden-tity and our family existence. They were shaped both by external anti-Semitism and my father's self-hatred, and by his Jewish pride. What Arnold did, I think, was call his Jewish pride something else: achieve-ment, aspiration, genius, idealism. Whatever was unacceptable got left back under the rubric of Jewishness or the "wrong kind" of Jews—uned-ucated, aggressive, loud. The message I got was that we were really supe-rior: Nobody else's father had collected so many books, had traveled so

far, knew so many languages. Baltimore was a musical city, but for the most part, in the families of my school friends, culture was for women. My father was an amateur musician, read poetry, adored encyclopedic knowledge. He prowled and pounced over my school papers, insisting I use "grown-up" sources; he criticized my poems for faulty technique and gave me books on rhyme and meter and form. His investment in my intellect and talent was egotistical, tyrannical, opinionated, and terribly wearing. He taught me, nevertheless, to believe in hard work, to mistrust easy inspiration, to write and rewrite; to feel that I *was* a person of the book, even though a woman; to take ideas seriously. He made me feel, at a very young age, the power of language and that I could share in it.

The Riches were proud, but we also had to be very careful. Our behavior had to be more impeccable than other people's. Strangers were not to be trusted, nor even friends; family issues must never go beyond the family; the world was full of potential slanderers, betrayers, *people who could not understand.* Even within the family, I realize that I never in my whole life knew what my father was really feeling. Yet he spoke—monologued—with driving intensity. You could grow up in such a house mesmerized by the local electricity, the crucial meanings assumed by the merest things. This used to seem to me a sign that we were all living on some high emotional plane. It was a difficult force field for a favored daughter to disengage from.

Easy to call that intensity Jewish; and I have no doubt that passion is one of the qualities required for survival over generations of persecution. But what happens when passion is rent from its original base, when the white gentile world is softly saying "Be more like us and you can be almost one of us"? What happens when survival seems to mean closing off one emotional artery after another? His forebears in Europe had been forbidden to travel or expelled from one country after another, had special taxes levied on them if they left the city walls, had been forced to wear special clothes and badges, restricted to the poorest neighborhoods. He had wanted to be a "free spirit," to travel widely, among "all kinds of people." Yet in his prime of life he lived in an increasingly withdrawn world, in his house up on a hill in a neighborhood where Jews were not supposed to be able to buy property, depending almost exclusively on interactions with his wife and daughters to provide emotional connectedness. In his home, he created a private defense system so elaborate that even as he was dying, my mother felt unable to talk freely with his colleagues or others who might have helped her. Of course, she acquiesced in this.

The loneliness of the "only," the token, often doesn't feel like loneliness but like a kind of dead echo chamber. Certain things that ought to don't resonate. Somewhere Beverly Smith writes of women of color "inspiring the behavior" in each other. When there's nobody to "inspire the behavior," act out of the culture, there is an atrophy, a dwindling, which is partly invisible....

Sometimes I feel I have seen too long from too many disconnected angles: white, Jewish, anti-Semite, racist, anti-racist, once-married, lesbian, middle-class, feminist, exmatriate southerner, *split at the root*— that I will never bring them whole. I would have liked, in this essay, to bring together the meanings of anti-Semitism and racism as I have experienced them and as I believe they intersect in the world beyond my life. But I'm not able to do this yet. I feel the tension as I think, make notes: *If you really look at the one reality, the other will waver and disperse.* Trying in one week to read Angela Davis and Lucy Davidowicz,[7] trying to hold throughout to a feminist, a lesbian, perspective—what does this mean? Nothing has trained me for this. And sometimes I feel inadequate to make any statement as a Jew; I feel the history of denial within me like an injury, a scar. For assimilation has affected *my* perceptions; those early lapses in meaning, those blanks, are with me still. My ignorance can be dangerous to me and to others.

Yet we can't wait for the undamaged to make our connections for us;   40 we can't wait to speak until we are perfectly clear and righteous. There is no purity and, in our lifetimes, no end to this process.

This essay, then, has no conclusions: It is another beginning for me. Not just a way of saying, in 1982 Right Wing America, *I, too, will wear the yellow star.* It's a moving into accountability, enlarging the range of accountability. I know that in the rest of my life, the next half century or so, every aspect of my identity will have to be engaged. The middle-class white girl taught to trade obedience for privilege. The Jewish lesbian raised to be a heterosexual gentile. The woman who first heard oppression named and analyzed in the black Civil Rights struggle. The woman with three sons, the feminist who hates male violence. The woman limping with a cane, the woman who has stopped bleeding are also accountable. The poet who knows that beautiful language can lie, that the oppressor's language sometimes sounds beautiful. The woman trying, as part of her resistance, to clean up her act.

The Reader's Presence

1. Why does Rich feel she needs to "claim" her father in order to come to terms with her identity? What does she mean by "claim"? How do we make such claims? Why is her father so closely tied to her sense of identity?

2. Rich doesn't begin with a statement about her personal history but with a reference to her act of writing at the moment. What is the effect of beginning this way? How does writing figure

[7]Angela Y. Davis, *Women, Race and Class* (New York: Random House, 1981); Lucy S. Davidowicz, *The War against the Jews 1933–1945* (New York: Bantam, 1979).—RICH'S NOTE.

throughout the essay? What connection can you see between writing and identity?

3. In rereading Rich's essay, pay close attention to her use of time. Try to construct a chronology for the essay. How does she organize that chronology in the essay itself? Can you think of some explanations for why Rich does not proceed in an orderly and straightforward manner? Can you discover any patterns in the procedure she chose to follow?

30

Alberto Alvaro Ríos

Green Cards

Alberto Alvaro Ríos (b. 1952) is a first-generation American; his father was born in Mexico, and his mother in England. His writing reflects this double heritage and the experience of living in the borderlands between languages and cultures. Ríos was raised and educated in Arizona, where he now teaches in the English department at Arizona State University. He has received, among other honors, a fellowship from the National Endowment for the Arts. He has published several collections of poetry, including Whispering to Fool the Wind *(1982) and* The Warrington Poems *(1989), and fiction, including* The Iguana Killer: Twelve Stories of the Heart *(1984) and* Pig Cookies and Other Stories *(1995). His most recent collection of fiction is* The Curtain of Trees: Stories *(1999). "Green Cards" appeared in* Indiana Review *in 1995.*

Reflecting on his relationship to language, writing, and translation, Ríos talks "about the duality of language using the metaphor of binoculars, how by using two lenses one might see something better, closer, with more detail. The apparatus, the binoculars, are of course physically clumsy — as is the learning of two languages . . . but once put to the eyes a new world in that moment opens up to us. And it's not a new world at all — it's the same world, but simply better seen, and therefore better understood."

All colors exist to satisfy the longing for blue.

There's a folk saying in Spanish, *el que quiera azul que le cueste.* One must pay for what one wants; it's a variation of the older Spanish proverb, "Take what you want and pay for it, says God." But the phrase means, more literally, *he who wants blue, let it cost him.*

A green card is what you get if you are a citizen of another country but you find yourself in, or cross over to, the United States. The card is a first step toward applying for citizenship. My wife, who was born in Mexico, had one. My mother, who was born in England, had one. My father, who was born in Mexico, didn't have one. But that's another story, involving some curious papers and shady explanations. My mother-in-law, after more than forty years here, still has one. She's never been quite sure what to do next. But she's learned well that you don't raise your hand to ask the Immigration Service anything. They notice you then. Everybody knows that.

They notice you, and then they do something. And they're everywhere, maybe. So you don't speak loudly, you don't ask questions, you don't make trouble. Run away when you have to. Don't sign anything. Get a job only where everybody else is getting one, where it's safe.

There were all kinds of stories. The one my mother-in-law lived with the longest was how, her sister in Guaymas told her, they had heard that when you become a citizen of the United States, you have to spit on the flag of Mexico. And they would all shake their heads in a *no*.

My mother, when she became a citizen, recalls a curious moment. After the ceremony, the high-school band came in to the courtroom and, because she was special—which is to say, in this border town with Mexico, she was not Mexican—they played the British national anthem. Someone thought it was a good idea. At that moment, though, she says she felt a little funny. She never forgot.

None of this is easy, and nobody knows what will happen when you come, and everybody is not treated the same. And things do happen. I think, finally, they were right.

Crossing over from Mexico, for example, was more than just being there and then being here. It was a change in how one walked, and a change in color. Over there, the ground moved one way, coiled and trailed and offered itself. Here was not there, and the coiling and trailing and offering were to the left and to the right, but never the same. To this, the legs and the body had to adjust. It was not the same ground.

And in Mexico, the color was green. Here, it is blue. And that Latin-American green is not the green of here, in the way that this blue is not the same blue in Mexico. The eyes, like the legs, have to learn over.

It is more than the music and the food and the clothing. It is the walk, and the color. And smell—not of food, but of things. And if one walked this other walk, and smells were new so the nose had to accommodate itself, one then began to look different. The body and the mirror made their changes.

I remember something from the middle of all this, from the middle of color and the middle of the century. During the '50s, I remember driving through town and seeing pickup trucks full of men dressed in white. They were *braceros*, the workers imported specifically from Mexico for a brief time, sometimes only a day, just to work. After work, either at the end of the day or the end of the growing season, they had to go back to Mexico. What that meant was taking the pickup truck to the border and dropping them all off.

Arizona was the last state to hold out against minimum wage, championing the *laissez-faire* system of government oversight: in this case, let the growers pay what the workers will accept and don't get in the way. And these workers worked for almost nothing. It seemed, for a while, like a good idea to the growers and to the government, whose program this was.

As a kid, I remember only all these men dressed in white. It was a color that meant they didn't belong anywhere.

Crossing over from Mexico to the United States is not a small thing, but not large either. This is an incorrect vocabulary. To cross over was big, but that part was easy. The big is like that. It was the small that was difficult.

To cross the border was made up of these smaller things, then. It was lived as these more difficult-to-explain changes in color, more like that, more something of the body than one might suspect. It was the different way of walking because the ground was new, in all things. A different way of walking or a different way of hiding. More surprise, or more dullness, dullness or quiet. Something.

It is a movement from green, but who would know it? How to explain it? This is what I've heard all my life. It is a movement like the planet's, a movement that is there absolute, but who can feel it? A movement from green, from green to what is next.   15

For my family, crossing over was crossing over from green, not from Mexico. Green from before, but sorted out, from all the moments of green in a life, sorted and lifted out and then assembled together, into a big green, into green only. Fresh from the inhuman jungles of Chiapas and farther still, somewhere middle on the Western-hemisphere map, into the green day, into the green night, into the in-between—the light and the dark greens, the green that is brown and the green that is white—but green, and inside green, green incarnate, from the back and from the front, from the shoulders and the feet, green from yesterday and green from before yesterday, all of it ocean-like, all of it water, all of it moving as claws and tendrils and tongues, as eyes, as webs, and as base and rough flight, so that to navigate upon it one needed to ride above it to move through it, and even then to be careful and to look around. One needed to paddle and to chart, the paddle as a half-weapon and a half-tool, remembering never to dangle foolishly—for the one moment green takes—an arm into it.

From green utterly and in whispers, green eyes and green tongue, green taste and green sound; green from tea, but then from coffee; from bitter, but then from sweet; green from garden, and a little then from bean and root and tuber, but then from sky and from air, and from light.

But at light, and in dream, sound and strong, four-square and, yet, in that moment of pellucid strength, in that moment also inexplicably tinged with rue, there it is that green wavers and is for a moment inconstant, is for a moment green that is hollowed, or absent; is, for a moment, blue. There is the pivotal point, the narrows in this repeating hourglass of colors, in this life. There for a second, but there absolutely: green shifts to blue, and it is done.

It is Blue. Only and just blue. It is the log sawed and in its moment of breaking. It is the yawn pushed fully and then fully engaged. It is a blue. Blue and not green. Only blue. Only blue and the memory of green. Not a desire yet—green is too close—but a memory.

So much was the green.   20

On the far other side of green was a yellow, somewhere out there, somewhere only in imagination perhaps, yellow and red and some other colors on the other side of memory. Yellow, then the green, but now blue. It was the end at last, or the beginning. It was not the middle. But it was the discovery of the middle.

In this way, the green stayed, the way the Virgin Mary was painted, and in the shades of the hillside houses. It stayed in the Chinese teas, in the *yerba buena*,[1] how that green was a cure for things, and in the afternoons, in talk. Green stayed, and had a place in my family, but always as a memory. It stayed as a sadness for something.

It stayed as what used to be.

The Reader's Presence

1. How does Ríos use color as a metaphor in this essay? In what ways does he suggest that the border between Mexico and the United States is like the border between blue and green? What do you think Ríos is saying in general about boundaries and divisions?

2. Ríos begins his essay with a Spanish phrase that he translates in several different ways. How does this opening amplify the essay's central themes? What difference would it make if Ríos were to give the phrase only in its English version?

3. How does Ríos's account of the immigrant experience compare to the images we often see of immigrants in the media? Do you think he is pro- or anti-immigration? Do you think that Ríos's use of literary and poetic language diminishes the political elements of the essay, or enhances them?

---

[1] *yerba buena:* A mint tea. — EDS.

31

Richard Rodriguez

Aria: A Memoir of a Bilingual Childhood

Richard Rodriguez (b. 1944) has contributed articles to many magazines and newspapers, including Harper's, American Scholar, *the* Los Angeles Times, *and the* New York Times. *He is an editor at Pacific News Service, and a contributing editor for* Harper's, U.S. News & World Report, *and the* Los Angeles Times. *He is also a regular essayist for the News Hour with Jim Lehrer, for which he received the 1997 George Foster Peabody Award. His most sensational literary accomplishment, however, is his autobiography,* Hunger of Memory: The Education of Richard Rodriguez *(1982). In it, Rodriguez outlines his positions on issues such as bilingualism, affirmative action, and assimilation, and concludes that current policies in these areas are misguided and only serve to reinforce current social inequalities. His most recent book is* Days of Obligations: An Argument with My Mexican Father *(1992), and a book called* The Color Brown *is forthcoming. Rodriguez lives in San Francisco.*

About the experience of writing his autobiography, Rodriguez comments, "By finding public words to describe one's feelings, one can describe oneself to oneself. . . . I have come to think of myself as engaged in writing graffiti."

The following essay originally appeared in The American Scholar *(winter 1980/81) and later served as the opening chapter in his intellectual autobiography* Hunger of Memory *(1982).*

I remember, to start with, that day in Sacramento, in a California now nearly thirty years past, when I first entered a classroom—able to understand about fifty stray English words. The third of four children, I had been preceded by my older brother and sister to a neighborhood Roman Catholic school. But neither of them had revealed very much about their classroom experiences. They left each morning and returned each afternoon, always together, speaking Spanish as they climbed the five steps to the porch. And their mysterious books, wrapped in brown shopping-bag paper, remained on the table next to the door, closed firmly behind them.

An accident of geography sent me to a school where all my class-mates were white and many were the children of doctors and lawyers and business executives. On that first day of school, my classmates must cer-tainly have been uneasy to find themselves apart from their families, in the first institution of their lives. But I was astonished. I was fated to be the "problem student" in class.

The nun said, in a friendly but oddly impersonal voice: "Boys and girls, this is Richard Rodriguez." (I heard her sound it out: *Rich-heard Road-ree-guess.*) It was the first time I had heard anyone say my name in English. "Richard," the nun repeated more slowly, writing my name down in her book. Quickly I turned to see my mother's face dissolve in a watery blur behind the pebbled-glass door.

Now, many years later, I hear of something called "bilingual educa-tion" — a scheme proposed in the late 1960s by Hispanic-American social activists, later endorsed by a congressional vote. It is a program that seeks to permit non-English-speaking children (many from lower class homes) to use their "family language" as the language of school. Such, at least, is the aim its supporters announce. I hear them, and am forced to say no: It is not possible for a child, any child, ever to use his family's language in school. Not to understand this is to misunderstand the public uses of schooling and to trivialize the nature of intimate life.

Memory teaches me what I know of these matters. The boy reminds the adult. I was a bilingual child, but of a certain kind: "socially disad-vantaged," the son of working-class parents, both Mexican immigrants.   5

In the early years of my boyhood, my parents coped very well in America. My father had steady work. My mother managed at home. They were nobody's victims. When we moved to a house many blocks from the Mexican-American section of town, they were not intimidated by those two or three neighbors who initially tried to make us unwel-come. ("Keep your brats away from my sidewalk!") But despite all they achieved, or perhaps because they had so much to achieve, they lacked any deep feeling of ease, of belonging in public. They regarded the people at work or in crowds as being very distant from us. Those were the oth-ers, *los gringos.* That term was interchangeable in their speech with an-other, even more telling: *los americanos.*

I grew up in a house where the only regular guests were my relations. On a certain day, enormous families of relatives would visit us, and there would be so many people that the noise and the bodies would spill out to the backyard and onto the front porch. Then for weeks no one would come. (If the doorbell rang, it was usually a salesman.) Our house stood apart — gaudy yellow in a row of white bungalows. We were the people with the noisy dog, the people who raised chickens. We were the foreign-ers on the block. A few neighbors would smile and wave at us. We waved back. But until I was seven years old, I did not know the name of the old couple living next door or the names of the kids living across the street.

In public, my father and mother spoke a hesitant, accented, and not always grammatical English. And then they would have to strain, their bodies tense, to catch the sense of what was rapidly said by *los gringos.* At home, they returned to Spanish. The language of their Mexican past sounded in counterpoint to the English spoken in public. The words would come quickly, with ease. Conveyed through those sounds was the pleasing, soothing, consoling reminder that one was at home.

During those years when I was first learning to speak, my mother and father addressed me only in Spanish; in Spanish I learned to reply. By contrast, English (*inglés*) was the language I came to associate with gringos, rarely heard in the house. I learned my first words of English overhearing my parents speaking to strangers. At six years of age, I knew just enough words for my mother to trust me on errands to stores one block away — but no more.

I was then a listening child, careful to hear the very different sounds of Spanish and English. Wide-eyed with hearing, I'd listen to sounds more than to words. First, there were English (gringo) sounds. So many words still were unknown to me that when the butcher or the lady at the drugstore said something, exotic polysyllabic sounds would bloom in the midst of their sentences. Often the speech of people in public seemed to me very loud, booming with confidence. The man behind the counter would literally ask, "What can I do for you?" But by being so firm and clear, the sound of his voice said that he was a gringo; he belonged in public society. There were also the high, nasal notes of middle-class American speech — which I rarely am conscious of hearing today because I hear them so often, but could not stop hearing when I was a boy. Crowds at Safeway or at bus stops were noisy with the birdlike sounds of *los gringos.* I'd move away from them all — all the chirping chatter above me.

My own sounds I was unable to hear, but I knew that I spoke English poorly. My words could not extend to form complete thoughts. And the words I did speak I didn't know well enough to make distinct sounds. (Listeners would usually lower their heads to hear better what I was trying to say.) But it was one thing for *me* to speak English with difficulty; it was more troubling to hear my parents speaking in public: their high-whining vowels and guttural consonants; their sentences that got stuck with "eh" and "ah" sounds; the confused syntax; the hesitant rhythm of sounds so different from the way gringos spoke. I'd notice, moreover, that my parents' voices were softer than those of gringos we would meet.

I am tempted to say now that none of this mattered. (In adulthood I am embarrassed by childhood fears.) And, in a way, it didn't matter very much that my parents could not speak English with ease. Their linguistic difficulties had no serious consequences. My mother and father made themselves understood at the county hospital clinic and at government offices. And yet, in another way, it mattered very much. It was unsettling to hear my parents struggle with English. Hearing them, I'd grow nervous, and my clutching trust in their protection and power would be weakened.

There were many times like the night at a brightly lit gasoline station (a blaring white memory) when I stood uneasily hearing my father talk to a teenage attendant. I do not recall what they were saying, but I cannot forget the sounds my father made as he spoke. At one point his words slid together to form one long word—sounds as confused as the threads of blue and green oil in the puddle next to my shoes. His voice rushed through what he had left to say. Toward the end, he reached falsetto notes, appealing to his listener's understanding. I looked away at the lights of passing automobiles. I tried not to hear any more. But I heard only too well the attendant's reply, his calm, easy tones. Shortly afterward, headed for home, I shivered when my father put his hand on my shoulder. The very first chance that I got, I evaded his grasp and ran on ahead into the dark, skipping with feigned boyish exuberance.

But then there was Spanish: *español,* the language rarely heard away from the house; *español,* the language which seemed to me therefore a private language, my family's language. To hear its sounds was to feel myself specially recognized as one of the family, apart from *los otros.* A simple remark, an inconsequential comment could convey that assurance. My parents would say something to me and I would feel embraced by the sounds of their words. Those sounds said: *I am speaking with ease in Spanish. I am addressing you in words I never use with* los gringos. *I recognize you as someone special, close, like no one outside. You belong with us. In the family. Ricardo.*

At the age of six, well past the time when most middle-class children   15
no longer notice the difference between sounds uttered at home and words spoken in public, I had a different experience. I lived in a world compounded of sounds. I was a child longer than most. I lived in a magical world, surrounded by sounds both pleasing and fearful. I shared with my family a language enchantingly private—different from that used in the city around us.

Just opening or closing the screen door behind me was an important experience. I'd rarely leave home all alone or without feeling reluctance. Walking down the sidewalk, under the canopy of tall trees, I'd warily notice the (suddenly) silent neighborhood kids who stood warily watching me. Nervously, I'd arrive at the grocery store to hear there the sounds of the gringo, reminding me that in this so-big world I was a foreigner. But if leaving home was never routine, neither was coming back. Walking toward our house, climbing the steps from the sidewalk, in summer when the front door was open, I'd hear voices beyond the screen door talking in Spanish. For a second or two I'd stay, linger there listening. Smiling, I'd hear my mother call out, saying in Spanish, "Is that you, Richard?" Those were her words, but all the while her sounds would assure me: *You are home now. Come closer inside. With us.* "*Sí,*" I'd reply.

Once more inside the house, I would resume my place in the family. The sounds would grow harder to hear. Once more at home, I would grow less conscious of them. It required, however, no more than the blurt of the doorbell to alert me all over again to listen to sounds. The house would turn instantly quiet while my mother went to the door. I'd hear her hard English sounds. I'd wait to hear her voice turn to soft-sounding Spanish, which assured me, as surely as did the clicking tongue of the lock on the door, that the stranger was gone.

Plainly it is not healthy to hear such sounds so often. It is not healthy to distinguish public from private sounds so easily. I remained cloistered by sounds, timid and shy in public, too dependent on the voices at home. And yet I was a very happy child when I was at home. I remember many nights when my father would come back from work, and I'd hear him call out to my mother in Spanish, sounding relieved. In Spanish, his voice would sound the light and free notes that he never could manage in English. Some nights I'd jump up just hearing his voice. My brother and I would come running into the room where he was with our mother. Our laughing (so deep was the pleasure!) became screaming. Like others who feel the pain of public alienation, we transformed the knowledge of our public separateness into a consoling reminder of our intimacy. Excited, our voices joined in a celebration of sounds. *We are speaking now the way we never speak out in public—we are together,* the sounds told me. Some nights no one seemed willing to loosen the hold that sounds had on us. At dinner we invented new words that sounded Spanish, but made sense only to us. We pieced together new words by taking, say, an English verb and giving it Spanish endings. My mother's instructions at bedtime would be lacquered with mock-urgent tones. Or a word like *sí*, sounded in several notes, would convey added measures of feeling. Tongues lingered around the edges of words, especially fat vowels. And we happily sounded that military drum roll, the twirling roar of the Spanish *r*. Family language, my family's sounds: the voices of my parents and sisters and brother. Their voices insisting: *You belong here. We are family members. Related. Special to one another. Listen!* Voices singing and sighing, rising and straining, then surging, teeming with pleasure which burst syllables into fragments of laughter. At times it seemed there was steady quiet only when, from another room, the rustling whispers of my parents faded and I edged closer to sleep.

Supporters of bilingual education imply today that students like me miss a great deal by not being taught in their family's language. What they seem not to recognize is that, as a socially disadvantaged child, I regarded Spanish as a private language. It was a ghetto language that deepened and strengthened my feeling of public separateness. What I needed to learn in school was that I had the right, and the obligation, to speak the public language. The odd truth is that my first-grade classmates could have become bilingual, in the conventional sense of the word, more easily than I. Had they been taught early (as upper middle-class children often are taught) a "second language" like Spanish or French, they could have regarded it simply as another public language. In my case, such bilingualism could not have been so quickly achieved. What I did not believe was that I could speak a single public language.

Without question, it would have pleased me to have heard my teach- 20
ers address me in Spanish when I entered the classroom. I would have felt much less afraid. I would have imagined that my instructors were some-how "related" to me; I would indeed have heard their Spanish as my fam-ily's language. I would have trusted them and responded with ease. But I would have delayed—postponed for how long?—having to learn the language of public society. I would have evaded—and for how long?—learning the great lesson of school: that I had a public identity.

Fortunately, my teachers were unsentimental about their responsibil-ity. What they understood was that I needed to speak public English. So their voices would search me out, asking me questions. Each time I heard them I'd look up in surprise to see a nun's face frowning at me. I'd mumble, not really meaning to answer. The nun would persist. "Richard, stand up. Don't look at the floor. Speak up. Speak to the entire class, not just to me!" But I couldn't believe English could be my language to use. (In part, I did not want to believe it.) I continued to mumble. I resisted the teacher's demands. (Did I somehow suspect that once I learned this public language my family life would be changed?) Silent, waiting for the bell to sound, I remained dazed, diffident, afraid.

Because I wrongly imagined that English was intrinsically a public lan-guage and Spanish was intrinsically private, I easily noted the difference be-tween classroom language and the language of home. At school, words were directed to a general audience of listeners. ("Boys and girls . . .") Words were meaningfully ordered. And the point was not self-expression alone, but to make oneself understood by many others. The teacher quizzed: "Boys and girls, why do we use that word in this sentence? Could we think of a better word to use there? Would the sentence change its meaning if the words were differently arranged? Isn't there a better way of saying much the same thing?" (I couldn't say. I wouldn't try to say.)

Three months passed. Five. A half year. Unsmiling, ever watchful, my teachers noted my silence. They began to connect my behavior with the slow progress my brother and sisters were making. Until, one Saturday morning, three nuns arrived at the house to talk to our parents. Stiffly they sat on the blue living-room sofa. From the doorway of another room, spying on the visitors, I noted the incongruity, the clash of two worlds, the faces and voices of school intruding upon the familiar setting of home. I overheard one voice gently wondering, "Do your children speak only Spanish at home, Mrs. Rodriguez?" While another voice added, "That Richard especially seems so timid and shy."

That Rich-heard!

With great tact, the visitors continued, "Is it possible for you and 25
your husband to encourage your children to practice their English when they are home?" Of course my parents complied. What would they not do for their children's well-being? And how could they question the

Church's authority which those women represented? In an instant they agreed to give up the language (the sounds) which had revealed and accentuated our family's closeness. The moment after the visitors left, the change was observed. "*Ahora,* speak to us only *en inglés,*" my father and mother told us.

At first, it seemed a kind of game. After dinner each night, the family gathered together to practice "our" English. It was still then *inglés,* a language foreign to us, so we felt drawn to it as strangers. Laughing, we would try to define words we could not pronounce. We played with strange English sounds, often over-anglicizing our pronunciations. And we filled the smiling gaps of our sentences with familiar Spanish sounds. But that was cheating, somebody shouted, and everyone laughed.

In school, meanwhile, like my brother and sisters, I required to attend a daily tutoring session. I needed a full year of this special work. I also needed my teachers to keep my attention from straying in class by calling out, "*Rich-heard!*"—their English voices slowly loosening the ties to my other name, with its three notes, *Ri-car-do.* Most of all, I needed to hear my mother and father speak to me in a moment of seriousness in "broken"—suddenly heartbreaking—English. This scene was inevitable. One Saturday morning I entered the kitchen where my parents were talking, but I did not realize that they were talking in Spanish until, the moment they saw me, their voices changed and they began speaking English. The gringo sounds they uttered startled me. Pushed me away. In that moment of trivial misunderstanding and profound insight, I felt my throat twisted by unsounded grief. I simply turned and left the room. But I had no place to escape to where I could grieve in Spanish. My brother and sisters were speaking English in another part of the house.

Again and again in the days following, as I grew increasingly angry, I was obliged to hear my mother and father encouraging me: "Speak to us *en inglés.*" Only then did I determine to learn classroom English. Thus, sometime afterward it happened: one day in school, I raised my hand to volunteer an answer to a question. I spoke out in a loud voice and I did not think it remarkable when the entire class understood. That day I moved very far from being the disadvantaged child I had been only days earlier. Taken hold at last was the belief, the calming assurance, that I *belonged* in public.

Shortly after, I stopped hearing the high, troubling sounds of *los gringos.* A more and more confident speaker of English, I didn't listen to how strangers sounded when they talked to me. With so many English-speaking people around me, I no longer heard American accents. Conversations quickened. Listening to persons whose voices sounded eccentrically pitched, I might note their sounds for a few seconds, but then I'd concentrate on what they were saying. Now when I heard someone's tone of voice—angry or questioning or sarcastic or happy or sad—I didn't distinguish it from the words it expressed. Sound and word were thus tightly wedded. At the end of each day I was often bemused, and always relieved, to realize how "soundless," though crowded with words, my day in public had been. An eight-year-old boy, I finally came to accept what had been technically true since my birth: I was an American citizen.

But diminished by then was the special feeling of closeness at home.   30
Gone was the desperate, urgent, intense feeling of being at home among those with whom I felt intimate. Our family remained a loving family, but one greatly changed. We were no longer so close, no longer bound tightly together by the knowledge of our separateness from *los gringos*. Neither my older brother nor my sisters rushed home after school any more. Nor did I. When I arrived home, often there would be neighborhood kids in the house. Or the house would be empty of sounds.

Following the dramatic Americanization of their children, even my parents grew more publicly confident—especially my mother. First she learned the names of all the people on the block. Then she decided we needed to have a telephone in our house. My father, for his part, continued to use the word gringo, but it was no longer charged with bitterness or distrust. Stripped of any emotional content, the word simply became a name for those Americans not of Hispanic descent. Hearing him, sometimes, I wasn't sure if he was pronouncing the Spanish word *gringo,* or saying gringo in English.

There was a new silence at home. As we children learned more and more English, we shared fewer and fewer words with our parents. Sentences needed to be spoken slowly when one of us addressed our mother or father. Often the parent wouldn't understand. The child would need to repeat himself. Still the parent misunderstood. The young voice, frustrated, would end up saying, "Never mind"—the subject was closed. Dinners would be noisy with the clinking of knives and forks against dishes. My mother would smile softly between her remarks; my father, at the other end of the table, would chew and chew his food while he stared over the heads of his children.

My mother! My father! After English became my primary language, I no longer knew what words to use in addressing my parents. The old Spanish words (those tender accents of sound) I had earlier used—*mamá* and *papá*—I couldn't use any more. They would have been all-too-painful reminders of how much had changed in my life. On the other hand, the words I heard neighborhood kids call their parents seemed equally unsatisfactory. "Mother" and "father," "ma," "papa," "pa," "dad," "pop" (how I hated the all-American sound of that last word)— all these I felt were unsuitable terms of address for *my* parents. As a result, I never used them at home. Whenever I'd speak to my parents, I would try to get their attention by looking at them. In public conversations, I'd refer to them as my "parents" or my "mother" and "father."

My mother and father, for their part, responded differently, as their children spoke to them less. My mother grew restless, seemed troubled and anxious at the scarceness of words exchanged in the house. She would question me about my day when I came home from school. She smiled at my small talk. She pried at the edges of my sentences to get me to say something more. ("What . . . ?") She'd join conversations she overheard, but her intrusions often stopped her children's talking. By contrast, my father seemed to grow reconciled to the new quiet. Though his English somewhat improved, he tended more and more to retire into silence. At dinner he spoke very little. One night his children and even his wife helplessly giggled at his garbled English pronunciation of the Catholic "Grace Before Meals." Thereafter he made his wife recite the prayer at the start of each meal, even on formal occasions when there were guests in the house.

Hers became the public voice of the family. On official business it   35 was she, not my father, who would usually talk to strangers on the phone or in stores. We children grew so accustomed to his silence that years later we would routinely refer to his "shyness." (My mother often tried to explain: Both of his parents died when he was eight. He was raised by an uncle who treated him as little more than a menial servant. He was never encouraged to speak. He grew up alone—a man of few words.) But I realized my father was not shy whenever I'd watch him speaking Spanish with relatives. Using Spanish, he was quickly effusive. Especially when talking with other men, his voice would spark, flicker, flare alive with varied sounds. In Spanish he expressed ideas and feelings he rarely revealed when speaking English. With firm Spanish sounds he conveyed a confidence and authority that English would never allow him.

The silence at home, however, was not simply the result of fewer words passing between parents and children. More profound for me was the silence created by my inattention to sounds. At about the time I no longer bothered to listen with care to the sounds of English in public, I grew careless about listening to the sounds made by the family when they spoke. Most of the time I would hear someone speaking at home and didn't distinguish his sounds from the words people uttered in public. I didn't even pay much attention to my parents' accented and ungrammatical speech—at least not at home. Only when I was with them in public would I become alert to their accents. But even then their sounds caused me less and less concern. For I was growing increasingly confident of my own public identity.

I would have been happier about my public success had I not recalled, sometimes, what it had been like earlier, when my family conveyed its intimacy through a set of conveniently private sounds. Sometimes in public, hearing a stranger, I'd hark back to my lost past. A Mexican farm worker approached me one day downtown. He wanted directions to some place. "*Hijito,* . . ." he said. And his voice stirred old longings. Another time I was standing beside my mother in the visiting room of a Carmelite convent, before the dense screen which rendered the nuns shadowy figures. I heard several of them speaking Spanish in their busy, singsong, overlapping voices, assuring my mother that, yes, yes, we were remembered, all our family was remembered, in their prayers. Those voiccs echoed faraway family sounds. Another day a dark-faced old woman touched my shoulder lightly to steady herself as she boarded a bus. She murmured something to me I couldn't quite comprehend. Her Spanish voice came near, like the face of a never-before-seen relative in the instant before I was kissed. That voice, like so many of the Spanish voices I'd hear in public, recalled the golden age of my childhood.

Bilingual educators say today that children lose a degree of "individuality" by becoming assimilated into public society. (Bilingual schooling is a program popularized in the seventies, that decade when middle-class "ethnics" began to resist the process of assimilation — the "American melting pot.") But the bilingualists oversimplify when they scorn the value and necessity of assimilation. They do not seem to realize that a person is individualized in two ways. So they do not realize that, while one suffers a diminished sense of *private* individuality by being assimilated into public society, such assimilation makes possible the achievement of *public* individuality.

Simplistically again, the bilingualists insist that a student should be reminded of his difference from others in mass society, of his "heritage." But they equate mere separateness with individuality. The fact is that only in private — with intimates — is separateness from the crowd a prerequisite for individuality; an intimate "tells" me that I am unique, unlike all others, apart from the crowd. In public, by contrast, full individuality is achieved, paradoxically, by those who are able to consider themselves members of the crowd. Thus it happened for me. Only when I was able to think of myself as an American, no longer an alien in gringo society, could I seek the rights and opportunities necessary for full public individuality. The social and political advantages I enjoy as a man began on the day I came to believe that my name is indeed *Rich-heard Road-ree-guess*. It is true that my public society today is often impersonal; in fact, my public society is usually mass society. But despite the anonymity of the crowd, and despite the fact that the individuality I achieve in public is often tenuous — because it depends on my being one in a crowd — I celebrate the day I acquired my new name. Those middle-class ethnics who scorn assimilation seem to me filled with decadent self-pity, obsessed by the burden of public life. Dangerously, they romanticize public separateness and trivialize the dilemma of those who are truly socially disadvantaged.

If I rehearse here the changes in my private life after my Americanization, it is finally to emphasize a public gain. The loss implies the gain. The house I returned to each afternoon was quiet. Intimate sounds no longer greeted me at the door. Inside there were other noises. The telephone rang. Neighborhood kids ran past the door of the bedroom where I was reading my schoolbooks — covered with brown shopping-bag paper. Once I learned the public language, it would never again be easy for me to hear intimate family voices. More and more of my day was spent

40

hearing words, not sounds. But that may only be a way of saying that on the day I raised my hand in class and spoke loudly to an entire roomful of faces, my childhood started to end.

I grew up the victim of a disconcerting confusion. As I became fluent in English, I could no longer speak Spanish with confidence. I continued to understand spoken Spanish, and in high school I learned how to read and write Spanish. But for many years I could not pronounce it. A powerful guilt blocked my spoken words; an essential glue was missing whenever I would try to connect words to form sentences. I would be unable to break a barrier of sound, to speak freely. I would speak, or try to speak, Spanish, and I would manage to utter halting, hiccuping sounds which betrayed my unease. (Even today I speak Spanish very slowly, at best.)

When relatives and Spanish-speaking friends of my parents came to the house, my brother and sisters would usually manage to say a few words before being excused. I never managed so gracefully. Each time I'd hear myself addressed in Spanish, I couldn't respond with any success. I'd know the words I wanted to say, but I couldn't say them. I would try to speak, but everything I said seemed to me horribly anglicized. My mouth wouldn't form the sounds right. My jaw would tremble. After a phrase or two, I'd stutter, cough up a warm, silvery sound, and stop.

My listeners were surprised to hear me. They'd lower their heads to grasp better what I was trying to say. They would repeat their questions in gentle, affectionate voices. But then I would answer in English. No, no, they would say, we want you to speak to us in Spanish ("*en español*"). But I couldn't do it. Then they would call me *Pocho*. Sometimes playfully, teasing, using the tender diminutive—*mi pochito*. Sometimes not so playfully but mockingly, *pocho*. (A Spanish dictionary defines that word as an adjective meaning "colorless" or "bland." But I heard it as a noun, naming the Mexican-American who, in becoming an American, forgets his native society.) "*¡Pocho!*" my mother's best friend muttered, shaking her head. And my mother laughed, somewhere behind me. She said that her children didn't want to practice "our Spanish" after they started going to school. My mother's smiling voice made me suspect that the lady who faced me was not really angry at me. But searching her face, I couldn't find the hint of a smile.

Embarrassed, my parents would often need to explain their children's inability to speak fluent Spanish during those years. My mother encountered the wrath of her brother, her only brother, when he came up from Mexico one summer with his family and saw his nieces and nephews for the very first time. After listening to me, he looked away and said what a disgrace it was that my siblings and I couldn't speak Spanish, "*su propria idioma.*" He made that remark to my mother, but I noticed that he stared at my father.

One other visitor from those years I clearly remember: a long-time friend of my father from San Francisco who came to stay with us for sev-   45 eral days in late August. He took great interest in me after he realized that I couldn't answer his questions in Spanish. He would grab me, as I started to leave the kitchen. He would ask me something. Usually he wouldn't bother to wait for my mumbled response. Knowingly, he'd murmur, *"¿Ay pocho, pocho, donde vas?"* And he would press his thumbs into the upper part of my arms, making me squirm with pain. Dumbly I'd stand there, waiting for his wife to notice us and call him off with a benign smile. I'd giggle, hoping to deflate the tension between us, pretending that I hadn't seen the glittering scorn in his glance.

I recount such incidents only because they suggest the fierce power that Spanish had over many people I met at home, how strongly Spanish was associated with closeness. Most of those people who called me a *pocho* could have spoken English to me, but many wouldn't. They seemed to think that Spanish was the only language we could use among ourselves, that Spanish alone permitted our association. (Such persons are always vulnerable to the ghetto merchant and the politician who have learned the value of speaking their clients' "family language" so as to gain immediate trust.) For my part, I felt that by learning English I had somehow committed a sin of betrayal. But betrayal against whom? Not exactly against the visitors to the house. Rather, I felt I had betrayed my immediate family. I knew that my parents had encouraged me to learn English. I knew that I had turned to English with angry reluctance. But once I spoke English with ease, I came to feel guilty. I sensed that I had broken the spell of intimacy which had once held the family so close together. It was this original sin against my family that I recalled whenever anyone addressed me in Spanish and I responded, confounded.

Yet even during those years of guilt, I was coming to grasp certain consoling truths about language and intimacy—truths that I learned gradually. Once, I remember playing with a friend in the backyard when my grandmother appeared at the window. Her face was stern with suspicion when she saw the boy (the *gringo* boy) I was with. She called out to me in Spanish, sounding the whistle of her ancient breath. My companion looked up and watched her intently as she lowered the window and moved (still visible) behind the light curtain, watching us both. He wanted to know what she had said. I started to tell him, to translate her Spanish words into English. The problem was, however, that though I knew how to translate exactly what she had told me, I realized that any translation would distort the deepest meaning of her message: it had been directed only to me. This message of intimacy could never be translated because it did not lie in the actual words she had used but passed through them. So any translation would have seemed wrong; the words would have been stripped of an essential meaning. Finally I decided not to tell my friend anything—just that I didn't hear all she had said.

This insight was unfolded in time. As I made more and more friends outside my house, I began to recognize intimate messages spoken in English in a close friend's confidential tone or secretive whisper. Even more remarkable were those instances when, apparently for no special reason, I'd become conscious of the fact that my companion was speaking *only to me*. I'd marvel then, just hearing his voice. It was a stunning event to be able to break through the barrier of public silence, to be able to hear the voice of the other, to realize that it was directed just to me. After such moments of intimacy outside the house, I began to trust what I heard intimately conveyed through my family's English. Voices at home at last punctured sad confusion. I'd hear myself addressed as an intimate—in English. Such moments were never as raucous with sound as in past times, when we had used our "private" Spanish. (Our English-sounding house was never to be as noisy as our Spanish-sounding house had been.) Intimate moments were usually moments of soft sound. My mother would be ironing in the dining room while I did my homework nearby. She would look over at me, smile, and her voice sounded to tell me that I was her son. *Richard.*

Intimacy thus continued at home; intimacy was not stilled by English. Though there were fewer occasions for it—a change in my life that I would never forget—there were also times when I sensed the deep truth about language and intimacy: *Intimacy is not created by a particular language; it is created by intimates*. Thus the great change in my life was not linguistic but social. If, after becoming a successful student, I no longer heard intimate voices as often as I had earlier, it was not because I spoke English instead of Spanish. It was because I spoke public language for most of my day. I moved easily at last, a citizen in a crowded city of words.

As a man I spend most of my day in public, in a world largely devoid of speech sounds. So I am quickly attracted by the glamorous quality of certain alien voices. I still am gripped with excitement when someone passes me on the street, speaking in Spanish. I have not moved beyond the range of the nostalgic pull of those sounds. And there is something very compelling about the sounds of lower-class blacks. Of all the accented versions of English that I hear in public, I hear theirs most intently. The Japanese tourist stops me downtown to ask me a question and I inch my way past his accent to concentrate on what he is saying. The eastern European immigrant in the neighborhood delicatessen speaks to me and, again, I do not pay much attention to his sounds, nor to the Texas accent of one of my neighbors or the Chicago accent of the woman who lives in the apartment below me. But when the ghetto black teenagers get on the city bus, I hear them. Their sounds in my society are the sounds of the outsider. Their voices annoy me for being so loud—so self-sufficient and unconcerned by my presence, but for the same reason they are glamorous: a romantic gesture against public acceptance. And as I listen to their shouted laughter, I realize my own quietness. I feel envious of them—envious of their brazen intimacy.

I warn myself away from such envy, however. Overhearing those teenagers, I think of the black political activists who lately have argued in favor of using black English in public schools—an argument that varies only slightly from that of foreign-language bilingualists. I have heard "radical" linguists make the point that black English is a complex and intricate version of English. And I do not doubt it. But neither do I think that black English should be a language of public instruction. What makes it inappropriate in classrooms is not something in the language itself but, rather, what lower-class speakers make of it. Just as Spanish would have been a dangerous language for me to have used at the start of my education, so black English would be a dangerous language to use in the schooling of teenagers for whom it reinforces feelings of public separateness.

This seems to me an obvious point to make, and yet it must be said. In recent years there have been many attempts to make the language of the alien a public language. "Bilingual education, two ways to understand . . ." television and radio commercials glibly announce. Proponents of bilingual education are careful to say that above all they want every student to acquire a good education. Their argument goes something like this: Children permitted to use their family language will not be so alienated and will be better able to match the progress of English-speaking students in the crucial first months of schooling. Increasingly confident of their ability, such children will be more inclined to apply themselves to their studies in the future. But then the bilingualists also claim another very different goal. They say that children who use their family language in school will retain a sense of their ethnic heritage and their family ties. Thus the supporters of bilingual education want it both ways. They propose bilingual schooling as a way of helping students acquire the classroom skills crucial for public success. But they likewise insist that bilingual instruction will give students a sense of their identity apart from the English-speaking public.

Behind this scheme gleams a bright promise for the alien child: One can become a public person while still remaining a private person. Who would not want to believe such an appealing idea? Who can be surprised that the scheme has the support of so many middle-class ethnic Americans? If the barrio or ghetto child can retain his separateness even while being publicly educated, then it is almost possible to believe that no private cost need be paid for public success. This is the consolation offered by any of the number of current bilingual programs. Consider, for example, the bilingual voter's ballot. In some American cities one can cast a ballot printed in several languages. Such a document implies that it is possible for one to exercise that most public of rights—the right to vote—while still keeping oneself apart, unassimilated in public life.

It is not enough to say that such schemes are foolish and certainly doomed. Middle-class supporters of public bilingualism toy with the confusion of those Americans who cannot speak standard English as well as they do. Moreover, bilingual enthusiasts sin against intimacy. A Hispanic-American tells me, "I will never give up my family language," and he clutches a group of words as though they were the source of his family ties. He credits to language what he should credit to family members. This is a convenient mistake, for as long as he holds on to certain familiar words, he can ignore how much else has actually changed in his life.

It has happened before. In earlier decades, persons ambitious for so- 55
cial mobility, and newly successful, similarly seized upon certain "family words." Workingmen attempting to gain political power, for example, took to calling one another "brother." The word as they used it, how-ever, could never resemble the word (the sound) "brother" exchanged by two people in intimate greeting. The context of its public delivery made it at best a metaphor; with repetition it was only a vague echo of the inti-mate sound. Context forced the change. Context could not be overruled. Context will always protect the realm of the intimate from public misuse. Today middle-class white Americans continue to prove the importance of context as they try to ignore it. They seize upon idioms of the black ghetto, but their attempt to appropriate such expressions invariably changes the meaning. As it becomes a public expression, the ghetto idiom loses its sound, its message of public separateness and strident intimacy. With public repetition it becomes a series of words, increasingly lifeless.

The mystery of intimate utterance remains. The communication of in-timacy passes through the word and enlivens its sound, but it cannot be held by the word. It cannot be retained or ever quoted because it is too fluid. It depends not on words but on persons.

My grandmother! She stood among my other relations mocking me when I no longer spoke Spanish. *Pocho,* she said. But then it made no dif-ference. She'd laugh, and our relationship continued because language was never its source. She was a woman in her eighties during the first decade of my life—a mysterious woman to me, my only living grandpar-ent, a woman of Mexico in a long black dress that reached down to her shoes. She was the one relative of mine who spoke no word of English. She had no interest in gringo society and remained completely aloof from the public. She was protected by her daughters, protected even by me when we went to Safeway together and I needed to act as her translator. An eccentric woman. Hard. Soft.

When my family visited my aunt's house in San Francisco, my grand-mother would search for me among my many cousins. When she found me, she'd chase them away. Pinching her granddaughters, she would warn them away from me. Then she'd take me to her room, where she had prepared for my coming. There would be a chair next to the bed, a dusty jellied candy nearby, and a copy of *Life en Español* for me to examine. "There," she'd say. And I'd sit content, a boy of eight. *Pocho,* her favorite. I'd sift through the pictures of earthquake-destroyed Latin-American cities and blonde-wigged Mexican movie stars. And all the while I'd listen to the sound of my grandmother's voice. She'd pace around the room, telling me stories of her life. Her past. They were sto-ries so familiar that I couldn't remember when I'd heard them for the first time. I'd look up sometimes to listen. Other times she'd look over at me, but she never expected a response. Sometimes I'd smile or nod. (I understood exactly what she was saying.) But it never seemed to matter to her one way or the other. It was enough that I was there. The words she spoke were almost irrelevant to that fact. We were content. And the great mystery remained: intimate utterance.

I learn nothing about language and intimacy listening to those social activists who propose using one's family language in public life. I learn much more simply by listening to songs on a radio, or hearing a great voice at the opera, or overhearing the woman downstairs at an open window singing to herself. Singers celebrate the human voice. Their lyrics are words, but, animated by voice, those words are subsumed into sounds. (This suggests a central truth about language: All words are capable of becoming sounds as we fill them with the "music" of our life.) With excitement I hear the words yielding their enormous power to sound, even though their meaning is never totally obliterated. In most songs, the drama or tension results from the way that the singer moves between words (sense) and notes (song). At one moment the song simply "says" something; at another moment the voice stretches out the words and moves to the realm of pure sound. Most songs are about love: lost love, celebrations of loving, pleas. By simply being occasions when sounds soar through words, however, songs put me in mind of the most intimate moments of life.

Finally, among all types of music, I find songs created by lyric poets   60
most compelling. On no other public occasion is sound so important for me. Written poems on a page seem at first glance a mere collection of words. And yet, without musical accompaniment, the poet leads me to hear the sounds of the words that I read. As song, a poem moves between the levels of sound and sense, never limited to one realm or the other. As a public artifact, the poem can never offer truly intimate sound, but it helps me to recall the intimate times of my life. As I read in my room, I grow deeply conscious of being alone, sounding my voice in search of another. The poem serves, then, as a memory device; it forces remembrance. And it refreshes; it reminds me of the possibility of escaping public words, the possibility that awaits me in intimate meetings.

The child reminds the adult: To seek intimate sounds is to seek the company of intimates. I do not expect to hear those sounds in public. I would dishonor those I have loved, and those I love now, to claim anything else. I would dishonor our intimacy by holding on to a particular language and calling it my family language. Intimacy cannot be trapped within words; it passes through words. It passes. Intimates leave the room. Doors close. Faces move away from the window. Time passes, and voices recede into the dark. Death finally quiets the voice. There is no way to deny it, no way to stand in the crowd claiming to utter one's family language.

The last time I saw my grandmother I was nine years old. I can tell you some of the things she said to me as I stood by her bed, but I cannot quote the message of intimacy she conveyed with her voice. She laughed, holding my hand. Her voice illumined disjointed memories as it passed them again. She remembered her husband—his green eyes, his magic name of Narcissio, his early death. She remembered the farm in Mexico, the eucalyptus trees nearby (their scent, she remembered, like incense). She remembered the family cow, the bell around its neck heard miles away. A dog. She remembered working as a seamstress, how she'd leave her daughters and son for long hours to go into Guadalajara to work. And how my mother would come running toward her in the sun—in her bright yellow dress—on her return. "MMMAAAAMMMMÁÁÁÁÁ," the old lady mimicked her daughter (my mother) to her daughter's son. She laughed. There was the snap of a cough. An aunt came into the room and told me it was time I should leave. "You can see her tomorrow," she promised. So I kissed my grandmother's cracked face. And the last thing I saw was her thin, oddly youthful thigh, as my aunt rearranged the sheet on the bed.

At the funeral parlor a few days after, I remember kneeling with my relatives during the rosary. Among their voices I traced, then lost, the sounds of individual aunts in the surge of the common prayer. And I heard at that moment what since I have heard very often—the sound the women in my family make when they are praying in sadness. When I went up to look at my grandmother, I saw her through the haze of a veil draped over the open lid of the casket. Her face looked calm—but distant and unyielding to love. It was not the face I remembered seeing most often. It was the face she made in public when the clerk at Safeway asked her some question and I would need to respond. It was her public face that the mortician had designed with his dubious art.

The Reader's Presence

1. The writer blames the intrusion of English into his family's private language, Spanish, for a breakdown of communication, and even of caring. How does the Spanish language appear in the essay? What associations does it have for the author?

2. Rodriguez's rhetorical style alternates between persuasive argumentation and personal drama. Do these divergent tactics undercut or reinforce each other? Why?

3. Rodriguez opposes proposals to teach bilingual children in their native languages, wishing to keep native language "private" and fearing it will further contribute to the marginalization of minorities. In contrast, Gloria Anzaldúa, in "How to Tame a Wild Tongue" (see page 311), considers Spanish one of America's na-

tive languages and wishes to see it publicly accepted and promoted. Whose argument do you find more persuasive, and why?

THE WRITER AT WORK

Richard Rodriguez on a Writer's Identity

How important is cultural or ethnic identity to a writer? Some writers clearly draw creative strength from their allegiances and affiliations, whereas others prefer to remain independent of groups, even those they are undeniably part of. In the following passage from a recent interview published in Sun Magazine, *Scott London asks Richard Rodriguez some tough questions about his various "identities." Could you have anticipated his responses based on his essay, "Aria: A Memoir of a Bilingual Childhood"?*

London: Many people feel that the call for diversity and multiculturalism is one reason the American educational system is collapsing.

Rodriguez: It's no surprise that at the same time that American universities have engaged in a serious commitment to diversity, they have been thought-prisons. We are not talking about diversity in any real way. We are talking about brown, black, and white versions of the same political ideology. It is very curious that the United States and Canada both assume that diversity means only race and ethnicity. They never assume it might mean more Nazis, or more Southern Baptists. That's diversity, too, you know.

London: What do *you* mean by diversity?

Rodriguez: For me, diversity is not a value. Diversity is what you find in Northern Ireland. Diversity is Beirut. Diversity is brother killing brother. Where diversity is *shared*—where I share with you my difference—that can be valuable. But the simple fact that we are unlike each other is a terrifying notion. I have often found myself in foreign settings where I became suddenly aware that I was not like the people around me. That, to me, is not a pleasant discovery.

London: You've said that it's tough in America to lead an intellectual   5
life outside the universities. Yet you made a very conscious decision to leave academia.

Rodriguez: My decision was sparked by affirmative action. There was a point in my life when affirmative action would have meant something to me—when my family was working-class, and we were struggling. But very early in life I became part of the majority culture and now don't think of myself as a minority. Yet the university said I was one. Anybody who has met a real minority—in the economic sense, not the numerical sense—would understand how ridiculous it is to describe a young man who is already at the university, already well into his studies in Italian and English Renaissance literature, as a minority. Affirmative

action ignores our society's real minorities—members of the disadvantaged classes, no matter what their race. We have this ludicrous, bureaucratic sense that certain racial groups, regardless of class, are minorities.
So what happens is those "minorities" at the very top of the ladder get
chosen for everything.

London: Is that what happened to you?

Rodriguez: Well, when it came time for me to look for jobs, the jobs
came looking for me. I had teaching offers from the best universities in
the country. I was about to accept one from Yale when the whole thing
collapsed on me.

London: What do you mean?

Rodriguez: I had all this anxiety about what it meant to be a minor-   10
ity. My professors—these same men who taught me the intricacies of language—just shied away from the issue. They didn't want to talk about it,
other than to suggest I could be a "role model" to other Hispanics—
when I went back to my barrio, I suppose. I came from a white, middle-
class neighborhood. Was I expected to go back there and teach the
woman next door about Renaissance sonnets? The embarrassing truth of
the matter was that I was being chosen because Yale University had some
peculiar idea about what my skin color or ethnicity signified. Who knows
what Yale thought it was getting when it hired Richard Rodriguez? The
people who offered me the job thought there was nothing wrong with
that. I thought there was something very wrong. I still do. I think race-
based affirmative action is crude and absolutely mistaken.

London: I noticed that some university students put up a poster outside the lecture hall where you spoke the other night. It said, "Richard
Rodriguez is a disgrace to the Chicano community."

Rodriguez: I sort of like that. I don't think writers should be convenient examples. I don't think we should make people feel settled. I don't
try to be a gadfly, but I do think that real ideas are troublesome. There
should be something about my work that leaves the reader unsettled. I intend that. The notion of the writer as a kind of sociological sample of a
community is ludicrous. Even worse is the notion that writers should provide an example of how to live. Virginia Woolf ended her life by putting a
rock in her sweater one day and walking into a lake. She is not a model
for how I want to live my life. On the other hand, the bravery of her syntax, of her sentences, written during her deepest depression, is a kind of
example for me. But I do not want to become Virginia Woolf. That is not
why I read her.

London: What's wrong with being a role model?

Rodriguez: The popular idea of a role model implies that an adult's
influence on a child is primarily occupational, that all a black child needs
is to see a black doctor, and then this child will think, "Oh, I can become
a doctor, too." I have a good black friend who is a doctor, but he didn't
become a doctor because he saw other black men who were doctors. He
became a doctor because his mother cleaned office buildings at night, and

because she loved her children. She grew bowlegged from cleaning office buildings at night, and in the process she taught him something about courage and bravery and dedication to others. I became a writer not because my father was one — my father made false teeth for a living. I became a writer because the Irish nuns who educated me taught me something about bravery with their willingness to give so much to me.

London: There used to be a category for writers and thinkers and intellectuals — "the intelligentsia." But not anymore.   15

Rodriguez: No, I think the universities have co-opted the intellectual, by and large. But there is an emerging intellectual set coming out of Washington think tanks now. There are people who are leaving the universities and working for the government or in think tanks, simply looking for freedom. The university has become so stultified since the sixties. There is so much you can't do at the university. You can't say this, you can't do that, you can't think this, and so forth. In many ways, I'm free to range as widely as I do intellectually precisely because I'm not at a university. The tiresome Chicanos would be after me all the time. You know: "We saw your piece yesterday, and we didn't like what you said," or, "You didn't sound happy enough," or, "You didn't sound proud enough."

London: You've drawn similar responses from the gay community, I understand.

Rodriguez: Yes, I've recently gotten in trouble with certain gay activists because I'm not gay enough! I am a morose homosexual. I'm melancholy. *Gay* is the last adjective I would use to describe myself. The idea of being gay, like a little sparkler, never occurs to me. So if you ask me if I'm gay, I say no.

After the second chapter of *Days of Obligation,* which is about the death of a friend of mine from AIDS, was published in *Harper's,* I got this rather angry letter from a gay-and-lesbian group that was organizing a protest against the magazine. It was the same old problem: political groups have almost no sense of irony. For them, language has to say exactly what it means. "Why aren't you proud of being gay?" they wanted to know. "Why are you so dark? Why are you so morbid? Why are you so sad? Don't you realize, we're all OK? Let's celebrate that fact." But that is not what writers do. We don't celebrate being "OK." If you want to be OK, take an aspirin.

London: Do you consider yourself more Mexican, or more American?   20

Rodriguez: In some ways I consider myself more Chinese, because I live in San Francisco, which is becoming a predominantly Asian city. I avoid falling into the black-and-white dialectic in which most of America still seems trapped. I have always recognized that, as an American, I am in relationship with other parts of the world; that I have to measure myself against the Pacific, against Asia. Having to think of myself in relationship to that horizon has liberated me from the black-and-white checkerboard.

32

Judy Ruiz

Oranges and Sweet Sister Boy

Judy Ruiz (b. 1944) earned an M.F.A. in poetry from the University of Arkansas in 1988 and has taught writing at Southwest Missouri State University in Springfield, Missouri. Her poems have been widely published in various literary journals and have been collected in her book, Talking Razzmatazz *(1991). "Oranges and Sweet Sister Boy," which originally appeared in* Iowa Woman *in 1988, was selected for* The Best American Essays 1989. *Her nonfiction writing has most recently been included in the anthologies* Surviving Crisis *(1997) and* Connecting *(1998).*

I am sleeping, hard, when the telephone rings. It's my brother, and he's calling to say that he is now my sister. I feel something fry a little, deep behind my eyes. Knowing how sometimes dreams get mixed up with not-dreams, I decide to do a reality test at once. "Let me get a cigarette," I say, knowing that if I reach for a Marlboro and it turns into a trombone or a snake or anything else on the way to my lips that I'm still out in the large world of dreams.

The cigarette stays a cigarette. I light it. I ask my brother to run that stuff by me again.

It is the Texas Zephyr[1] at midnight—the woman in a white suit, the man in a blue uniform; she carries flowers—I know they are flowers. The petals spill and spill into the aisle, and a child goes past this couple who have just come from their own wedding—goes past them and past them, going always to the toilet but really just going past them; and the child could be a horse or she could be the police and they'd not notice her any more than they do, which is not at all—the man's hands high up on the woman's legs, her skirt up, her stockings and garters, the petals and finally all the flowers spilling out into the aisle and his mouth open on her. My mother. My father. I am conceived near Dallas in the

---

[1]*Texas Zephyr:* A passenger train. — EDS.

dark while a child passes, a young girl who knows and doesn't know, who witnesses, in glimpses, the creation of the universe, who feels an odd hurt as her own mother, fat and empty, snores with her mouth open, her false teeth slipping down, snores and snores just two seats behind the Creators.

News can make a person stupid. It can make you think you can do something. So I ask The Blade question, thinking that if he hasn't had the operation yet that I can fly to him, rent a cabin out on Puget Sound. That we can talk. That I can get him to touch base with reality.

"Begin with an orange," I would tell him. "Because oranges are mildly intrusive by nature, put the orange somewhere so that it will not bother you—in the cupboard, in a drawer, even a pocket or a handbag will do. The orange, being a patient fruit, will wait for you much longer than say a banana or a peach."

I would hold an orange out to him. I would say, "This is the one that will save your life." And I would tell him about the woman I saw in a bus station who bit right into her orange like it was an apple. She was wild looking, as if she'd been outside for too long in a wind that blew the same way all the time. One of the dregs of humanity, our mother would have called her, the same mother who never brought fruit into the house except in cans. My children used to ask me to "start" their oranges for them. That meant to make a hole in the orange so they could peel the rind away, and their small hands weren't equipped with fingernails that were long enough or strong enough to do the job. Sometimes they would suck the juice out of the hole my thumbnail had made, leaving the orange flat and sad.

The earrings are as big as dessert plates, filigree gold-plated with thin dangles hanging down that touch her bare shoulders. She stands in front of the Alamo while a bald man takes her picture. The sun is absorbed by the earrings so quickly that by the time she feels the heat, it is too late. The hanging dangles make small blisters on her shoulders, as if a centipede had traveled there. She takes the famous river walk in spiked heels, rides in a boat, eats some Italian noodles, returns to the motel room, soaks her feet, and applies small band-aids to her toes. She is briefly concerned about the gun on the nightstand. The toilet flushes. She pretends to be sleeping. The gun is just large and heavy. A .45? A .357 magnum? She's never been good with names. She hopes he doesn't try to. Or that if he does, that it's not loaded. But he'll say it's loaded just for fun. Or he'll pull the trigger and the bullet will lodge in her medulla oblongata, ripping through her womb first, taking everything else vital on the way.

In the magazine articles, you don't see this: "Well, yes. The testicles have to come out. And yes. The penis is cut off." What you get is tonsils. So-and-so has had a "sex change" operation. A sex change operation. How precious. How benign. Doctor, just what do you people do with those penises?

News can make a person a little crazy also. News like, "We regret to inform you that you have failed your sanity hearing."

The bracelet on my wrist bears the necessary information about me, but there is one small error. The receptionist typing the information asked me my religious preference. I said, "None." She typed, "Neon."

> Pearl doesn't have any teeth and her tongue looks weird. She says "Pumpkin pie." That's all she says. Sometimes she runs her hands over my bed sheets and says pumpkin pie. Sometimes I am under the sheets. Marsha got stabbed in the chest, but she tells everyone she fell on a knife. Elizabeth—she's the one who thinks her shoe is a baby—hit me in the back with a tray right after one of the cooks gave me extra toast. There's a note on the bulletin board about a class for the nurses: "How Putting A Towel On Someone's Face Makes Them Stop Banging Their Spoon/OR Reduction of Disruptive Mealtime Behavior By Facial Screening—7 P.M.—Conference Room." Another note announces the topic for remotivation class: "COWS." All the paranoid schizophrenics will be there.
>
> Here, in the place for the permanently bewildered, I fit right in. Not because I stood at the window that first night and listened to the trains. Not because I imagined those trains were bracelets, the jewelry of earth. Not even because I imagined that one of those bracelets was on my own arm and was the Texas Zephyr where a young couple made love and conceived me. I am eighteen and beautiful and committed to the state hospital by a district court judge for a period of one day to life. Because I am a paranoid schizophrenic.
>
> I will learn about cows.

So I'm being very quiet in the back of the classroom, and I'm peeling an orange. It's the smell that makes the others begin to turn around, that mildly intrusive nature. The course is called "Women and Modern Literature," and the diaries of Virginia Woolf are up for discussion except nobody has anything to say. I, of course, am making a mess with the orange; and I'm wanting to say that my brother is now my sister.

Later, with my hands still orangey, I wander in to leave something on   10
a desk in a professor's office, and he's reading so I'm being very quiet, and then he says, sort of out of nowhere, "Emily Dickinson up there in her room making poems while her brother was making love to her best friend right downstairs on the dining room table. A regular thing. Think of it. And Walt Whitman out sniffing around the boys. Our two great American poets." And I want to grab this professor's arm and say, "Listen. My brother called me and now he's my sister, and I'm having trouble making sense out of my life right now, so would you mind not telling me any more stuff about sex." And I want my knuckles to turn white while the pressure of my fingers leaves imprints right through his jacket, little indentations he can interpret as urgent. But I don't say anything. And I don't grab his arm. I go read a magazine. I find this:

"I've never found an explanation for why the human race has so many languages. When the brain became a language brain, it obviously needed to develop an intense degree of plasticity. Such plasticity allows languages to be logical, coherent systems and yet be extremely variable. The same brain that thinks in words and symbols is also a brain that has to be freed up with regard to sexual turn-on and partnering. God knows why sex attitudes have not been subject to the corresponding degrees of modification and variety as language. I suspect there's a close parallel between the two. The brain doesn't seem incredibly efficient with regard to sex."

John Money said that. The same John Money who, with surgeon Howard W. Jones, performed the first sex change operation in the United States in 1965 at Johns Hopkins University and Hospital in Baltimore.

Money also tells about the *hijra* of India who disgrace their families because they are too effeminate: "The ultimate stage of the *hijra* is to get up the courage to go through the amputation of penis and testicles. They had no anesthetic." Money also answers anyone who might think that "heartless members of the medical profession are forcing these poor darlings to go and get themselves cut up and mutilated," or who think the medical profession should leave them alone. "You'd have lots of patients willing to get a gun and blow off their own genitals if you don't do it. I've had several who got knives and cut themselves trying to get rid of their sex organs. That's their obsession!"

Perhaps better than all else, I understand obsession. It is of the mind. And it is language-bound. Sex is of the body. It has no words. I am stunned to learn that someone with an obsession of the mind can have parts of the body surgically removed. This is my brother I speak of. This is not some lunatic named Carl who becomes Carlene. This is my brother.

So while we're out in that cabin on Puget Sound, I'll tell him about LuAnn. She is the sort of woman who orders the in-season fruit and a little cottage cheese. I am the sort of woman who orders a double cheeseburger and fries. LuAnn and I are sitting in her car. She has a huge orange, and she peels it so the peel falls off in one neat strip. I have a sack of oranges, the small ones. The peel of my orange comes off in hunks about the size of a baby's nail. "Oh, you bought the *juice* oranges," LuAnn says to me. Her emphasis on the word "juice" makes me want to die or something. I lack the courage to admit my ignorance, so I smile and breathe "yes," as if I know some secret, when I'm wanting to scream at her about how my mother didn't teach me about fruit and my own blood pounds in my head wanting out, out.

There is a pattern to this thought as there is a pattern for a jumpsuit. Sew the sleeve to the leg, sew the leg to the collar. Put the garment on. Sew the mouth shut. This is how I tell about being quiet because I am bad, and because I cannot stand it when he beats me or my brother.

"The first time I got caught in your clothes was when I was four years old and you were over at Sarah what's-her-name's babysitting. Dad beat me so hard I thought I was going to die. I really thought I was going to die. That was the day I made up my mind I would *never* get caught again. And I never got caught again." My brother goes on to say he continued to go through my things until I was hospitalized. A mystery is solved.

He wore my clothes. He played in my makeup. I kept saying, back   15
then, that someone was going through my stuff. I kept saying it and saying it. I told the counselor at school. "Someone goes in my room when I'm not there, and I *know* it—goes in there and wears my clothes and goes through my stuff." I was assured by the counselor that this was not so. I was assured by my mother that this was not so. I thought my mother was doing it, snooping around for clues like mothers do. It made me a little crazy, so I started deliberately leaving things in a certain order so that I would be able to prove to myself that someone, indeed, was going through my belongings. No one, not one person, ever believed that my room was being ransacked; I was accused of just making it up. A paranoid fixation.

And all the time it was old Goldilocks.

So I tell my brother to promise me he'll see someone who counsels adult children from dysfunctional families. I tell him he needs to deal with the fact that he was physically abused on a daily basis. He tells me he doesn't remember being beaten except on three occasions. He wants me to get into a support group for families of people who are having a sex change. Support groups are people who are in the same boat. Except no one has any oars in the water.

I tell him I know how it feels to think you are in the wrong body. I tell him how I wanted my boyfriend to put a gun up inside me and blow the woman out, how I thought wearing spiked heels and low-cut dresses would somehow help my crisis, that putting on an ultrafeminine outside would mask the maleness I felt needed hiding. I tell him it's the rule, rather than the exception, that people from families like ours have very spooky sexual identity problems. He tells me that his sexuality is a birth defect. I recognize the lingo. It's support-group-for-transsexuals lingo. He tells me he sits down to pee. He told his therapist that he used to wet all over the floor. His therapist said, "You can't aim the bullets if you don't touch the gun." Lingo. My brother is hell-bent for castration, the castration that started before he had language: the castration of abuse. He will simply finish what was set in motion long ago.

I will tell my brother about the time I took ten sacks of oranges into a school so that I could teach metaphor. The school was for special students—those who were socially or intellectually impaired. I had planned to have them peel the oranges as I spoke about how much the world is like the orange. I handed out the oranges. The students refused to peel them, not because they wanted to make life difficult for me—they were enchanted with the gift. One child asked if he could have an orange to take home to his little brother. Another said he would bring me ten dollars the next day if I would give him a sack of oranges. And I knew I was at home, that these children and I shared something that *makes* the leap of mind the metaphor attempts. And something in me healed.

A neighbor of mine takes pantyhose and cuts them up and sews them   20
up after stuffing them. Then she puts these things into Mason jars and sells them, you know, to put out on the mantel for conversation. They are little penises and little scrotums, complete with hair. She calls them "Pickled Peters."

A friend of mine had a sister who had a sex change operation. This young woman had her breasts removed and ran around the house with no shirt on before the stitches were taken out. She answered the door one evening. A young man had come to call on my friend. The sex-changed sister invited him in and offered him some black bean soup as if she were perfectly normal with her red surgical wounds and her black stitches. The young man left and never went back. A couple years later, my friend's sister/brother died when s/he ran a car into a concrete bridge railing. I hope for a happier ending. For my brother, for myself, for all of us.

My brother calls. He's done his toenails: Shimmering Cinnamon. And he's left his wife and children and purchased some nightgowns at a yard sale. His hair is getting longer. He wears a special bra. Most of the people he works with know about the changes in his life. His voice is not the same voice I've heard for years; he sounds happy.

My brother calls. He's always envied me, my woman's body. The same body I live in and have cursed for its softness. He asks me how I feel about myself. He says, "You know, you are really our father's first-born son." He tells me he used to want to be me because I was the only person our father almost loved.

The drama of life. After I saw that woman in the bus station eat an orange as if it were an apple, I went out into the street and smoked a joint with some guy I'd met on the bus. Then I hailed a cab and went to a tattoo parlor. The tattoo artist tried to talk me into getting a nice bird or butterfly design; I had chosen a design on his wall that appealed to me— a symbol I didn't know the meaning of. It is the Yin-Yang, and it's tattooed above my right ankle bone. I supposed my drugged, crazed consciousness knew more than I knew: that yin combines with yang to produce all that comes to be. I am drawn to androgyny.

Of course there is the nagging possibility that my brother's dilemma is   25
genetic. Our father used to dress in drag on Halloween, and he made a beautiful woman. One year, the year my mother cut my brother's blond curls off, my father taped those curls to his own head and tied a silk scarf over the

tape. Even his close friends didn't know it was him. And my youngest daughter was a body builder for a while, her lean body as muscular as a man's. And my sons are beautiful, not handsome: they look androgynous.

Then there's my grandson. I saw him when he was less than an hour old. He was naked and had hiccups. I watched as he had his first bath, and I heard him cry. He had not been named yet, but his little crib had a blue card affixed to it with tape. And on the card were the words "Baby Boy." There was no doubt in me that the words were true.

When my brother was born, my father was off flying jets in Korea. I went to the hospital with my grandfather to get my mother and this new brother. I remember how I wanted a sister, and I remember looking at him as my mother held him in the front seat of the car. I was certain he was a sister, certain that my mother was joking. She removed his diaper to show me that he was a boy. I still didn't believe her. Considering what has happened lately, I wonder if my child-skewed consciousness knew more than the anatomical proof suggested.

I try to make peace with myself. I try to understand his decision to alter himself. I try to think of him as her. I write his woman name, and I feel like I'm betraying myself. I try to be open-minded, but something in me shuts down. I think we humans are in big trouble, that many of us don't really have a clue as to what acceptable human behavior is. Something in me says no to all this, that this surgery business is the ultimate betrayal of the self. And yet, I want my brother to be happy.

It was in the city of San Antonio that my father had his surgery. I rode the bus from Kansas to Texas, and arrived at the hospital two days after the operation to find my father sitting in the solarium playing solitaire. He had a type of cancer that particularly thrived on testosterone. And so he was castrated in order to ease his pain and to stop the growth of tumors. He died six months later.

Back in the sleep of the large world of dreams, I have done surgeries 30 under water in which I float my father's testicles back into him, and he— the brutal man he was—emerges from the pool a tan and smiling man, parting the surface of the water with his perfect head. He loves all the grief away.

I will tell my brother all I know of oranges, that if you squeeze the orange peel into a flame, small fires happen because of the volatile oil in the peel. Also, if you squeeze the peel and it gets into your cat's eyes, the cat will blink and blink. I will tell him there is no perfect rhyme for the word "orange," and that if we can just make up a good word we can be immortal. We will become obsessed with finding the right word, and I will be joyous at our legitimate pursuit.

I have purchased a black camisole with lace to send to my new sister. And a card. On the outside of the card there's a drawing of a woman sitting by a pond and a zebra is off to the left. Inside are these words: "The past is ended. Be happy." And I have asked my companions to hold me and I have cried. My self is wet and small. But it is not dark. Sometimes, if no one touches me, I will die.

Sister, you are the best craziness of the family. Brother, love what you love.

The Reader's Presence

1. The essay opens with the author asleep. How do sleep and dreams figure throughout the essay? How might they help account for the odd jumps and connections that sometimes make the essay hard to follow?

2. Note the moments in the essay where Ruiz inserts paragraphs in smaller type. What are these moments? What have they to do with the main body of the essay? What do those moments have in common? How are you intended to read them?

3. In rereading the essay, make a note of all references to the body. In what ways is the human body present? According to Ruiz, how does the body differ from the mind? (See paragraph 12.) How is that difference dramatized by the essay itself?

33

Luc Sante

Résumé

As a child, Luc Sante (b. 1954) moved back and forth between Belgium and the United States several times until his family settled in New Jersey. When in his early twenties, Sante got a job at a bookstore and began reading obscure stories about New York City's seedy history from the late 1800s to the early 1900s. These accounts of prostitutes, corrupt police officers, thieves, gamblers, and drug dealers provided rich material for his first two books, Low Life: Lures and Snares of Old New York *(1991) and* Evidence *(1992). "Résumé" is the opening chapter of Sante's most recent book, a memoir entitled* The Factory of Facts *(1998).*

I was born on May 25, 1954, in Verviers, Belgium, the only child of Lucien Mathieu Amélie Sante and Denise Lambertine Alberte Marie Ghislaine Nandrin. Following the bankruptcy of my father's employer, an iron foundry that manufactured wool-carding machinery, and at the suggestion of friends who had emigrated earlier, my parents decided to move to the United States in search of work. We arrived at Idlewild Airport[1] in February 1959, and moved in with my parents' friends in Summit, New Jersey. Prospects were not as bright as they had been depicted, and that November we sailed back to Belgium, but the situation there was no better, and early in 1960 we re-emigrated. Several more such trips occurred over the next few years, spurred by momentary hopes, by the Cuban Missile Crisis, by the illnesses and deaths of my maternal grandparents. At length my parents decided to remain in America, at least until the time came when they could retire to Belgium.

I was born in 1954 in Verviers, Belgium, the only child of Lucien and Denise Sante. Following the bankruptcy of my father's employer, an iron foundry that manufactured wool-carding machinery, and at the suggestion of my mother's brother, René Nandrin, my parents decided to move to the Belgian Congo, where my father would take up a position as local field director for a palm-oil concern. In February 1959, we arrived in Coquilhatville, on the banks of the Congo River, and moved into a company-owned villa in the European district. Suddenly we had servants and a chauffeured car. On the other hand, I came down with a succession of ailments aggravated by the climate and spent most of my time in bed. Barely a year later the Belgian government announced that the Congo would be granted its independence that June, and my parents' friends and colleagues began to show signs of alarm, sending prized possessions, for example, back to their families in Belgium. Emotions had risen to a point of panic by late May, when the first general elections were held. My parents and their friends dismissed their servants, fearing treachery. My father barricaded my mother and me and would himself not leave the house without a loaded revolver on his hip. Violent incidents began occurring, most of them in the south of the country, but some close enough that my father, over my mother's protests, sent us home. He followed a little over a month later, when fighting had become widespread; his employer turned over local control to native African managers. Connections made in the Congo led my father to a job with the Ministry of Commerce, and we moved to Berchem-Ste. Agathe, a suburb of Brussels, where I recovered and later found I had a surprising aptitude for competitive cycling.

I was born in 1954 in Verviers, Belgium, the only child of Lucien and Denise Sante. Following the bankruptcy of his employer, an iron foundry that manufactured wool-carding machinery, my father tried to find another

---

[1]*Idlewild Airport:* Renamed John F. Kennedy International in 1963. — EDS.

job, but without success. After depleting their savings and selling our house in Pepinster, as well as most of the major household possessions, my parents moved into a succession of progressively smaller and dingier apartments, finally winding up in a single room in Seraing, an industrial suburb of Liège, where my father got a barely remunerative stint as nightwatchman in a warehouse. We endured two years of this as a family. My mother became chronically ill, probably due to stress as much as to bad food and lack of heat, and consequently I was taken in by my Remacle cousins in the country. They, too, were feeling the pinch of the economy, however, and palmed me off on other relatives, who in turn passed me along after a while. I spent three years being thus shunted around, until the Christian Brothers admitted me as a hardship case at their boarding school in Liège in the winter of 1964. By then my mother had been hospitalized full-time and my father had retreated into a vigilant and apparently unbreakable silence. At the school I was constantly victimized by the other pupils, most of them offspring of well-to-do families. Finally, at thirteen, I snapped. I set a fire that consumed the dormitory and took the lives of five boys.

I was born in 1954 in Verviers, Belgium, the only child of Lucien and Denise Sante. My father's employer, an iron foundry that manufactured wool-carding machinery, miraculously escaped the effects of the recession of 1958 and the collapse of Verviers's textile industry by a rapid and timely change to the manufacture of radiators. My father, who had worked his way up to junior management from the labor ranks, devised a streamlined method of cooling molds that earned him a succession of promotions, ultimately to the top seat. By 1968 we had sold our row house in Pepinster and moved into a villa in a parklike setting on the heights of the "boulevard" district of Verviers. I grew up fast, and was quickly bored by the provincial life around me. I barely maintained passing grades at St. François-Xavier, the local Jesuit *collège,* and would surely have failed and been expelled had it not been for my parents' social and political prominence. As it was, I was taking clandestine excursions— longer and longer ones—out into the world: to Amsterdam, to Paris, to London, to Majorca. I took every drug I could get my hands on, and I was possibly a father several times over; I was adept at vanishing when matters came to a head. My parents' threats to cut off my allowance became steadily more credible until, in the spring of 1971, I bribed the manager of the Place Verte branch of the Générale de Banque and withdrew my entire trust fund in cash—or nearly entire; I left a token five hundred francs. I flew to Marrakech, where I lived for eight months in a hotel frequented by members of British rock groups, until a run-in with one of the Berber chieftains who controlled the hashish traffic from the Rif caused me to fear for my life. I snared a series of van rides that took me to Goa, on the Indian Ocean, where I dwelt in a permanent cloud of dope in a waterfront flat. When my money ran out, I relocated to the beach. I contracted scabies and syphilis, but I didn't care.

I was born in 1954 in Verviers, Belgium, the only child of Lucien and   5
Denise Sante. Following the bankruptcy of my father's employer, an iron
foundry that manufactured wool-carding machinery, my parents decided
to emigrate to the United States. We arrived at Idlewild Airport in February 1959, with eight suitcases and an address in Johnsonburg, Pennsylvania. The address belonged to a family whose son had died near Henri-
Chapelle in the terrible winter of 1944, and whose grave my mother
had maintained as part of a program in which young Belgian women
"adopted" the remains of American servicemen. For a few years my
mother had kept up a peculiar correspondence with this family; they exchanged cards and photographs and brief letters neither side understood,
lacking a common language. Upon deciding to come to America she had
dug out the address, writing this time in laborious, dictionary-assisted
English, but had not received a reply. She maintained, however, that they
must have gotten her address wrong, misreading her Belgian script; their
return letter surely lay in some bin in Brussels. She was determined to call
on them upon our arrival, but, after many halting inquiries, discovered
that there was no public transport that went anywhere near Johnsonburg,
Pennsylvania. My parents were directed by Travelers' Aid to an agency
that helped them find an apartment in Ozone Park, Queens, and after a
time my father found work as custodian at a doughnut franchise in Long
Island City. My parents were miserable, impoverished and isolated and
increasingly without hope, but lacked the means to return to Belgium; all
their savings went into a fund that eventually enabled them to send me to
boarding school with the Christian Brothers in Liège. I languished there,
dreaming only of returning to America.

I was born in 1954 in Verviers, Belgium, the only child of Lucien and
Denise Sante. Following the bankruptcy of his employer, an iron foundry
that manufactured wool-carding machinery, my father miraculously got a
nearly identical job with another iron foundry, which made structural
supports for concrete constructions. I grew up in Pepinster, attending the
Catholic primary school and then St. François-Xavier, the Jesuit *collège*
in Verviers, with money my grandmother had provided for this purpose
in her will. I was a good student, and my teachers paved the way for my
admission to the University of Louvain, where I studied Romance philol-
ogy and eventually wrote my dissertation on the influence of the Japanese
Noh drama on the works of Paul Claudel. In the course of my studies
there it occurred to me one day that I had a calling, that I had in fact long
had this calling but had been inattentive to it. After obtaining my degree I
entered the Jesuit chapter house at Tervuren, and in 1978 I was ordained.
I celebrated my first Mass at St. Remacle, the ancestral family church in
Verviers, with all my relatives crowding the pews, and then moved to
Rome, where I had a job awaiting me in the Propaganda Office of the
Holy See. Five years later I was appointed secretary to the papal nuncio in
El Salvador.

I was born in 1954 in Verviers, Belgium, the only child of Lucien and Denise Sante. Following the bankruptcy of my father's employer, an iron foundry that manufactured wool-carding machinery, my parents decided to emigrate to the United States, on no more firm a basis than a visit to the U.S. pavilion at the 1958 Brussels World's Fair. We arrived at Idlewild Airport in February 1959, with eight suitcases, my father's pre-war memories of high-school English, and the name of someone's cousin who apparently lived in Long Island, New York, which my parents thought was a town. A taxi driver who knew some French took us to a hotel in Manhattan, which turned out to be a clip joint. We lost three of our suitcases before fleeing to another hotel, respectable enough but commensurately expensive. My parents combed telephone books in search of the cousin, but to no avail. They applied for help from the Belgian consulate, and were turned away with frosty finality. They spent days on complex and indeterminate errands, looking for chimeric friends of relatives of friends, my father trying to look for jobs in his field without much idea of where to start. They hadn't imagined it would be like this; without connections or a grasp of the language they were lost. The money was rapidly dwindling, too; already there was not enough left for passage back to Europe, and soon they would no longer be able to foot the hotel bill. On the advice of the chambermaid, a kind woman from Puerto Rico—communication between her and my parents, conducted around a tongue none of them possessed, was comically histrionic—my parents relocated to a dank hostelry near Herald Square where the rooms were lit by fluorescent tubes. We lived on rolls and hot dogs. My mother made me sleep wrapped in a chiffon scarf to protect me from the cockroaches. My father took his watch, of a decent but undistinguished Swiss make, to a pawnshop, where he was given five dollars in return. Our suitcases, minus their contents, followed, and soon my parents' overcoats and their extra pairs of shoes went as well. They were beginning to consider applying to a church for assistance, but were hindered by their pride. One day, when it seemed no other option remained, a man who lived down the hall from us offered my father a job. He was to deliver a manila envelope to an address in Newark; he would be paid fifty dollars. He accepted with alacrity and set off. That night, after I had fallen asleep, while my mother wept with fear at having heard nothing from him, two men in dark suits came to our room and took us away. They were FBI agents. My father had been arraigned for interstate traffic in narcotics; the house to which he made his delivery had been under surveillance for several weeks. My mother was held as a material witness in the Essex County Women's Correctional Facility. I was kept in a wing of Juvenile Hall for four days, in the course of which I repeatedly wet my bed and was punished by being deprived of food. Then I was sent to a foster home, with a large and strict Irish-American family in Irvington. My inability to speak English enraged the father, who would take me into the vest-pocket backyard and beat me with a razor strop. I was moved to another foster home, and then another and another—I lost count. I had no news from my parents. After a while I couldn't remember their faces.

I was born in 1954 in Verviers, Belgium, the only child of Lucien and Denise Sante. Following the bankruptcy of my father's employer, an iron foundry that manufactured wool-carding machinery, and with the knowledge that there were no other jobs to be had, a combined result of the collapse of the centuries-old Verviers textile industry and of the recession of 1958, my parents decided to go for broke. They sold our row house in Pepinster and the bulk of its contents, and we set off by train for Biarritz, the beautiful city in France fronting on the Bay of Biscay and backed against the Pyrenees. The trip was glorious; we laughed and sang songs and pointed out the window at the spectacular scenery. When we got there my parents checked into a modest hotel, left me with sandwiches and a pile of comics, and went to the casino. My father's plan was to parlay the stake amassed from selling off their possessions into a small fortune at the baccarat table. It didn't work.

I was born in 1954 in Verviers, Belgium, the only child of Lucien and Denise Sante. Following the bankruptcy of my father's employer, an iron foundry that manufactured wool-carding machinery, my parents sat on the floor. Dust accumulated. Things fell and were not picked up. Mold grew on the potatoes in the cellar. The milk solidified. The electricity was cut off. Neighboring boys threw stones that broke the windows, and cold air blew in. First insects, then rodents, and eventually birds arrived to make their homes with us. Soon snow covered the dust, and then soot covered the snow. We grew increasingly warm as we slept.

The Reader's Presence

1. Sante's first version of his life story may seem convincing until you read the second, and then the third, and so on. What effect does each successive tale have in terms of those previous to it?

2. This essay parodies standard conventions of autobiography. What elements does he challenge or lampoon? Can you find a more serious side to the piece? Why do you think he titled the essay "Résumé"? What does that word mean to you? Does his essay resemble any résumé you've ever seen?

3. Sante's essay leads the reader to question its own truth. What other sorts of conventional truth might it call into doubt? How does Sante highlight the means by which our experience of "reality" is constructed through language?

34

Gary Soto

The Childhood Worries, or Why I Became a Writer

Gary Soto (b. 1952) grew up in Fresno, California, and he currently lives in Berkeley, California. He has published several collections of poetry, including The Elements of San Joaquin *(1977), which won the United States Award of the International Poetry Forum, and* New and Selected Poems *(1995), which was nominated for both the Los Angeles Times Book Award and the National Book Award. His* New and Selected Poems *and* Canto Familiar/Familiar Song *were published in 1995. Soto has also written and edited several collections of essays and short stories, the most recent of which is* Jesse *(1994). His work has appeared in many literary magazines, including the* Nation, Ploughshares, Ontario Review, *and* Poetry. *"The Childhood Worries, or Why I Became a Writer" appeared in the* Iowa Review *in 1995.*

Soto writes fiction for children as well; his books include Too Many Tamales *(1993),* Chato's Kitchen *(1995),* Old Man and His Door *(1996),* Buried Onions *(1997),* Petty Crimes *(1998), and* Big Bushy Mustache *(1998). He has also produced three films for television, recently published a play,* Novio Boy *(1996), and has written the libretto for an opera entitled* Nerd-Landia *for The Los Angeles Opera. In an interview, Soto said, "I like writing. I'm fairly prolific; it's a daily activity for me. And that keeps the youth and the imagination going. If I were to stop, I'd be in serious trouble."*

As a boy growing up in Fresno I knew that disease lurked just beneath the skin, that it was possible to wake up in the morning unable to move your legs or arms or even your head, that stone on a pillow. Your eyeballs might still swim in their own liquids as they searched the ceiling, or beyond, toward heaven and whatever savage god did this to you. Frail and whimpering, you could lie in your rickety bed. You could hear the siren blast at the Sun-Maid Raisin plant, and answer that blast with your own chirp-like cry. But that was it for you, a boy now reduced to the dull activity of blinking. In the adjoining rooms, a chair scraped against the linoleum floor, the kitchen faucet ran over frozen chicken parts, the toilet flushed, the radio sputtered something in Spanish. But you were not involved. You lay useless in bed while your family prepared for the day.

Disease startled Uncle Johnnie first, a mole on his forearm having turned cancerous and bright as a red berry. He was living in Texas when he wrote my mother about his illness. We took him in in spring. He lived with us the last three months of his life, mostly lying ill on the couch, a space meant for my brother Rick and me. Before our uncle arrived, we jumped on that couch, me with a flea-like leap and my brother with the heavier bounce of a frog. Now he had the couch to himself, this uncle who was as tender as a pony.

I didn't have much memory to go on. At age six, I didn't lie in bed at night, arms folded behind my head, and savor the time when I was four and a half, a sprout of orneriness. I was too busy in my young body to consider my trail of footprints, all wiped out at the end of a day. But I recall Uncle Johnnie and the apple pie he bought me at Charlie's Market. My greed for sweetness grinned from my sticky mouth, and we devoured the pie as we strolled home, I walking backwards and looking at the market. Later I would return to that market and let my hands settle like small crabs on two candy bars. They opened and closed around them as I decided whether to take them, thus steal, thus let my mouth lather itself with the creamy taste of chocolate. Charlie was probably looking at me, wagging his large Armenian head at my stupidity. But that wasn't the point: I was deciding for myself whether I should sin and then worry about this sin, the wings of my bony shoulder blades less holy.

I recall also when our television was broken and my father pulled the tube out and took it to a repair shop. The TV was eyeless, just sprouts of wires and a smothering scent of dust. While Uncle Johnnie lay on the couch, I climbed into the back of the television set and pretended to be someone funny, one of the Three Stooges, and then someone scary, like Rodan[1] with his monstrous roar. My uncle watched me with a weary smile but no joy. I told him that I could be funny or scary, but in such a small space I couldn't play a horse or an Indian shot by the calvary. He died that spring, all because of a cancerous mole, died after the tube was once again fitted into the television set. Then the couch returned to us.

For one summer disease scared me. My whiskery neighbor, whose   5
name I have forgotten, was a talker and addressed every growing plant, chicken, and dog in his dirt yard. When he got sick, his talk increased, as if he needed to get out all the words that he had intended to use in his old age. He had to use them then or never. One afternoon he came into our yard and showed me his fingernails, yellow and hard. He held them out quivering, as if he were going to do a hocus-pocus magic trick, and when he said it was cancer, I flinched. When I looked up into his face, pale as a fistful of straw, I saw that his eyes were large and bluish, his face already sinking in disease. I was eating grapes, feeding them into my

---

[1] **Rodan:** A flying monster of science fiction films. — EDS.

mouth, and I didn't know what to do about his dying except to offer him some of my grapes. He laughed at this. He walked away, straight as any other man, and returned to his yard where he talked to himself and revved up a boat engine clamped to a barrel. A scarf of smoke unfurled from the engine, and the blackish water boiled. He didn't seem to be getting anywhere.

That summer we did our rough living on the street, and our dogs did too. When my Uncle Junior's collie got hit by a car on Van Ness Avenue, I watched my uncle, a teenager with a flattop haircut, gather his dog into his arms. He was the bravest person I knew, for he hugged to his chest what he loved best. A few of the kids from Braly Street milled around; the barber came out of his shop, snapped his sheet as if in surrender, and stared at the commotion for a moment, his eyes the color of twilight itself.

Uncle Junior yelled at us to get away, but I shadowed him for a while, barefoot and pagan. He walked up the alley that ran along our dusty-white house. I didn't know then that he intended to wait out the last breaths and then bury his dog. I didn't know that months later at the end of this same alley we were walking down, a car would roll, its wheels in the air, the man inside dead and his hat as flat as cardboard. I would be excited. Like my uncle's collie, I panted, except from exhilaration, when the police asked if we knew the person. I pointed and said that he lived near the man with the motorboat engine and cancer.

This was the summer I began to worry about disease. My father was in road camp with my uncle Shorty. They'd gotten drunk and stolen a car, but I was behaving. I drank my milk, ate my Graham Crackers, and dutifully picked slivers from my palm, but despite my hygiene, I was involved in disease. One morning my brother woke with his throat pinched with a clot that made it difficult for him to swallow. He opened his mouth in the backyard light and, along with my mother, I looked in, worried that I would have to wallow in the same bedroom and, in time, the same disease. His mouth was like any other mouth, wet with a push of milky air. But our mother knew better: The tonsils would have to come out. Mine would have to come out, too, no matter how many times I swallowed, cried, and said, "See, Mom, I'm OK." She figured that if you do one son you might as well do two.

That night I stood by the window in our bedroom and ate M & M candies and wondered about Father and Uncle Shorty. They were in a sort of a prison camp, I knew. We had gone to see them, and father had shown his hands, which were speckled white with paint. I rode on his knee, a camel ride of excitement because I was chewing gum and sunflower seeds at the same time. I asked him when he was coming home. Pretty soon, he answered. I didn't know that he and my uncle were painting rocks along the rural Kearny Boulevard and hoisting railroad ties that became bumpers in the gravel parking lots of Kearny Park.

I thought about them as I ate my M & Ms and touched my throat   10
when I swallowed the candy. Father wasn't there to help me. He was far

away, it seemed, and I peered out the window toward the junkyard, with its silhouette of pipes, plumbing, and jagged sheet metal, the playground of my childhood. The summer wind picked up the metallic scent and whipped it about. When a sweep of headlights from the cars that turned from Van Ness onto Braly Street frisked the junkyard, the eyes of its German Shepherd watchdog glowed orange and stared at me. I ate my candy, one last taste of sweetness on the eve of blood and gagging.

When we arrived at the community hospital, I hugged my pajamas and coloring book. I glanced nervously down the corridor. I looked at the old people's yellow fingernails, clear signs of cancer, and I peeked in a lab where I knew that blood was drawn. My brother and I walked on each side of our mother. We were led to a room where there was another child sitting up in a crib-like bed, mute as a teddy bear. He spit red into a bowl, and I immediately knew this was a scary place.

After we settled into our room, I worried not about dying, but about the filthy act of baring my bottom to a bedpan. I was in a hospital gown, not my pajamas. I held out for hours, but when I couldn't stand it anymore, I told the nurse I had to use the bathroom. She wouldn't allow me to get up from bed. I started to cry, but she scolded me, and I knew better than to carry on because she had the instruments of pain. I told my brother not to laugh, but he was too scared to entertain the thought. I squatted on the bedpan and was letting my water flow when a blind, teenage girl walked past our open door, a ghost-like figure blowing down the corridor. A nurse was helping her along, step by hesitant step. I wanted to ask the nurse if she was blind forever, or would she one day peel off that bandage and smile at every bloodshot color in the precious world. I did my number and then looked over at the boy, now asleep and pale as an angel.

I don't recall my brother and me talking much at the hospital. I lay in bed, touching the plastic wrist band with my typed name. I closed my eyes. I tried to shut out the image of the "thing" they would take out of my throat, a kidney-bean sac no longer needed. I knew that my baby teeth would eventually loosen and come out, possibly when I was biting into a peach or an apple, but I was terrified that someone behind a white mask would probe my mouth.

A few hours later, my brother was wheeled away with tears brimming in his eyes. If my big brother had dime-sized tears in his eyes, than I, his little brother with just baby teeth, would have silver dollars rolling down my cheeks. I considered crying and sobbing as pitifully as I could manage, but who would listen? My mother was gone, a tiny egg of memory living inside my head. Now my brother was gone. I looked over to where the other boy was, but his parents had come and rescued him. I didn't have anything to do except thumb through my animal coloring book and imagine what crayons I would use on the deer, elephant, giraffe, and grinning hyena. This diversion helped. But then I was wheeled away.

This was the late '50s when almost every child's tonsils were routinely clipped from his throat. I remember the room where a nurse in a   15 mask lowered a disk-like mask onto my nose and mouth. She lowered it three times and each time said, "breathe in" as they basted my face with ether. I did what I was told until my consciousness receded like a wave, and I was in a room full of testing patterns, something like television when it was still too early for cartoons. They operated, and I bled into a bowl all night, it seemed, but happily drank 7-Up with no ice, a treat that didn't cost me anything except for hoarse speech for three days.

When Rick and I got home, we were pampered with ice cream and 7-Up, a lovely blast of carbonation which singed my nostrils. I believed that we might continue to live our remaining childhood that way with mounds of ice cream, 7-Up, and cooing words from our mother. But too soon that stopped, and we were back to the usual plates of *frijoles* and tortillas. At that time, while my father and uncle were in jail, my mother worked at Readi-Spud, peeling potatoes that scurried down troughs of icy water. She would give us over to Mrs. Moreno, the mother of at least nine children and the jolliest woman in the western world. She laughed more than she spoke, and she spoke a lot. While in Mrs. Moreno's care, I became even more worried about disease because I knew roaches made a princely living in her cupboards.

Mrs. Moreno worked at a Chinese noodle factory and came to get Rick and me after work. One day, when we climbed into the back seat of her station wagon, her son Donald was standing in a cardboard tub of noodles. His feet pumped up and down and emitted a sucking sound with each marching step. When I asked Mrs. Moreno about dinner she was laughing because the baby on the front seat was crawling toward her breast. She giggled, "You like chow mein?" I slowly lowered my gaze to Donald's bare feet and felt sick.

They ate noodles right after we arrived, slurped them down so that the ends wiggled like worms into their suctioning mouths. My brother and I ate grapes and drank water. Later, all of us—eleven kids—played our version of "The Old Woman Who Lived in a Shoe." We climbed onto the roof and jumped off, a cargo of unkillable kids hitting the ground like sacks of flour. It may not have been that same evening, but I recall three babies at the end of a long, dirty hallway and some of the kids, the older ones, trying to knock them over with a real bowling ball. There was squealing and crying, but it was mostly laughter that cut through the cloistered air of a dank hallway, laughter coming even from Mrs. Moreno when one of the babies went down.

One untroubled afternoon Lloyd showed me a toy rifle, the kind that you had to crack in half to cock and which shot arrows tipped with red suction cups. He took one suction cup off, cocked the rifle, and shot the arrow into the flat spatula of his palm. "It doesn't hurt," he told me, and let me shoot the arrow repeatedly into my palm, the pressure of the arrow no more than a push. He recocked the rifle and fit the arrow into one of his nostrils. I automatically stepped back even though Lloyd was smiling. He was smiling just a moment before he pulled the trigger, before blood suddenly streamed from his nose and his eyes grew huge as two white moons and full of fright. He started crying and running around the house with the arrow in his nose, and I ran after him, almost crying. When his mother caught him by the arm, I raced out of the house, not wanting to get involved, and returned home, scared as I touched my own nose. I imagined the arrow in my own nose. I imagined blood spilling on the back porch. Later, just after I had finished dinner, I returned to Lloyd's house. He was at the table, with the threads of cotton balls hanging from his nostrils. The family was eating chow mein, piled like worms and wiggling down their throats.

The house was a poor, curled shoe, and it scared me because in its   20
carelessness lurked disease and calamity. I recall standing at their stove and asking a teenage boy who had drifted inside the house, "What's that you're making?" I looked at a large, dented kettle containing a grayish soup which Arnold was stirring with a pencil. I peeked into the soup, sipped it with a large spoon, and saw small things wheeling in the water as he stirred them—a merry-go-round of meats, I thought. When he said, "pigeons," I looked closely and could see the plucked birds bob and rise, bob and rise, and with each rise I could see the slits of their closed eyes.

The Moreno place, however, was not nearly as scary as the hospital. There were no instruments of pain, unless you counted the hive of tapeworms that showed up later because I ate raw bacon, white strips we peeled like Band-Aids from the wrapper. The Morenos taught me this too; they said it was good, and I ate my share while sitting on the roof, the sunset a stain the color of bright, bright medicine. How I would need that sun! How I would need a cure for my worry, and a cure for my brother, who was sporting on the bottom of his foot a sliver the size of a chopstick.

At age six disease scared me, and so did Grandpa, who lived just down the alley from our house on Braly Street. When I went over to eat lunch—yet another pile of *frijoles* wrapped in a diaper-sized tortilla—he was at the kitchen table playing solitaire with a big chunk of his head missing. I backed out of the house, bristling with fear, because the only thing left was his face. He looked like the poker-face card in front of him: Jack of Bad Luck, or King of Almighty Mistakes? While I backed out of the screen door, Uncle Junior caught me from behind and nudged me into the kitchen. He told me that Grandpa was wearing a nylon stocking on his head, trying to grow his hair back. A stinky concoction of *yerba buena*[2] and earthly fuels smothered his crown and temples. I sat down and ate my beans while watching Grandpa eat from his plate. I asked him if his head would grow back; he was chewing a huge amount of food like a camel. I thought I would turn seven by the time he cleared his throat and heard his answer, which was, "*Mi'jo,*[3] you got beans on your shirt. Shaddup."

---

[2] *yerba buena:* A mint tea.—EDS.
[3] *Mi'jo:* My son (*mi hijo*).—EDS.

Two kittens died from distemper and then Pete, our canary, was de-voured by mama cat. A stray dog showed up outside our yard with a piece of wood in its watery eye. I touched my own eye, pulling at a tiny string of sleep. Everything seemed ill and ominous. Even our house began to slip on its foundation, which excited me because the bathroom was now at a slant. The water in the tub slouched now that one side was higher. With a scoop of my hands, it was easy to force a tidal wave on the line of ants scurrying along the baseboard.

I looked around at family and friends who were hurt or dying, but I didn't know that a year later my father would die, his neck broken in an industrial accident. This would be in August, when we were settled in a new house the color of cement. He didn't live in that house more than a week, and then he was gone. The funeral didn't mean much to me. It was the scent of flowers and the wash of tears; it was a sympathetic squeeze of my shoulders and candies slipped into the pockets of my tweed coat, which was too small because it was borrowed. After his burial I recall eating donuts at my grandparents' house. When a doctor was called be-cause Grandma was in hysterics, I didn't stop eating. I took what was rightly mine and devoured it in the dark, near the ugly claw-like crowns of a rose bush.

I didn't know what to think except that Father was out of prison and   25
now in the earth forever. Because he wasn't returning, I began to play with his squeaky hand drill, boring into trees and fences. I liked the smell of the blond shavings and liked to think that maybe Father used the drill in prison. He mostly painted rocks, this much I was told, but I fantasized about how he might have used it in prison to get away. I saw him poking holes in a cement wall and then pushing over that wall to get Uncle Shorty in the adjacent cell. Uncle Johnnie was there, too, a ghost-like bundle of flesh on the cot. My father was going to save not only the both of them, but in the end himself as well.

Occasionally, we would visit my father's grave, where my mother cried and set flowers, half-shadowing the oval photo on his grave. What worried me was not his death, but the gold-painted cannon on a hill that pointed at our Chevy when we drove through the cement gates. The can-non scared me because my vision of death was that when you died an angel would pick you up, place your head in the cannon, and give your neck a little twist. I was spooked by this cannon and wanted to ask my mother about it, but she was too busy in her sorrow for a straight an-swer. I kept quiet on the matter. I figured there was one cannon, like one God, and all graves rolled on a hill. In time, you were asked to put your head in a cannon and die as well.

I didn't realize that I was probably ill. Neither did I realize how I used my time when my mother would send me off to school. For weeks, I didn't go there. I stayed in an alley, kicking though the garbage and bore-dom, and returned home only after I assumed my classmates had finished with whatever the teacher had asked them to do. Sometimes I would take the drill and make holes, occasionally even in the lawn. But I had grown bored with this. I had discovered how I could make a huge noise. In the empty bedroom, the one my father and mother would have used, I spent hours with fistfuls of marbles. I bounced them off the baseboard, a rico-chetting clatter that I imagined were soldiers getting their fill of death. The clatter of noise busied my mind with something like hate. If I had looked into a mirror, I would have seen this hate pleated on my forehead. If anyone, including my sister or brother, had smarted off to me, I had plans to get even. I would let them go to sleep and then blast them with marbles at close range as they inhaled a simple dream.

My mother was alone, and in her loneliness she often piled us into our Chevy and drove us over to my *nina's* house on the west side of Fresno, a place that was so scary that even the blacks were afraid. My *nina*—godmother—took in identical twin boys, same age as me but filthier. Their dirty hair was like the hair Woody Woodpecker wore. They were orphans. They were sadly nicknamed "Caca" and "Peepee," and for a while they made me feel good because I knew they were poorer than me. "Peepee, is your dad dead?" I would ask. "Caca, what grade are you in?" I would inquire. They shrugged their shoulders a lot and ran when they saw my *nina,* a woman you dared not play with. Every time we vis-ited, I took a toy to show them—plastic plane, steel car, sock of marbles, and even my brother's glow-in-the-dark statue of Jesus. I wanted them to know that even though my father was dead, I still owned things. After a few visits I didn't have anything left to share, just a ten-foot link of rub-ber bands. This lack made me mad, and I began to pick on them, even beat them up, in a kind of Punch-and-Judy show in the dirt driveway. When we found out that the twins were scared of ghosts, my brother and Rachel, my *nina's* daughter, told them to sit and wait in the living room because their mother and father were going to pick them up. We gave them fistfuls of raisins. Rick and Rachel then ran outside, where they scraped a bamboo rake against the window. The twins looked at me, then the curtain that was dancing like ghosts from the blast of the window cooler. Their mouths stopped churning on those raisins and the gray light of the TV flashed briefly in their eyes. When I yelled, "*La llorona*[4] is out-side," they jumped and ran from the house, poor, terrified "Caca" and "Peepee" living up to their names that early evening.

I often attended church, a place that was scarier than the hospital or the Moreno's house or grandfather's head. Mother said that Jesus had been a good man, and he wanted peace and harmony in the hearts of all men. She said this while I looked at Jesus on his cross, poor Jesus who had nails and blood all over him. If they did that to someone who was so good I wondered what they might do to me. You see, I was turning out bad. I was so angry from having to worry all the time that I had become violent. Once I stuck a broken shaft of bottle in my brother's leg for

---

[4]*La llorona:* The weeping woman; a ghost in a Mexican folk tale.—EDS.

going swimming without me. Blood ran down my knuckles, and I ran away amazed that it was so calming to hurt someone who was bigger. My mother beat me with a hanger for my violence and then made me eat dinner in the bathroom. I put my bowl first on the hamper, then moved it to my knees, because I wanted a better view of the faucet dripping water. In the bathroom, then, I began to worry about our wasting water. I counted the drips to a hundred. I swallowed and pictured in my mind a pagan baby sucking a rock for moisture. Later, after I was allowed out of the bathroom, I took a pair of pliers and tried to tighten the faucet. I managed only to scratch the chrome plating on the faucets, and I went to bed worrying that my mother would conclude that it was me. I closed my eyes and let the pagan baby swallow the rock.

I asked my mother if you ever had to stop worrying, or if you had to   30
continue until you were old. I was already tired of having to learn about Jesus and the more important apostles. She answered yes and mumbled something about life not being easy. This was when I began to look at pictures in the medical dictionary: ringworms, rickets, TB, tongues with canker sores, and elephantiasis. With elephantiasis, the scariest disease, your legs swelled fat as water balloons and, I suspected, sloshed some evil liquids. I looked down at my own legs, those reeds of bone and marrow. They were skinny, but still I worried that my legs could swell and the rest of me, arms mainly, would stay thin, possibly from rickets which had made headway at school. I would be the second deformed kid on this street, the other being an older boy with one small arm that was shaped like a banana.

I knew the face of the boy in the iron lung. His hair was black and his eyes flat. He was motherless, for who could wrap a loving hug around a machine large as a barrel. I could hardly look at this boy. He might have shared my name, or my brother's name, or been related to the kid at school who had one leg shrunken from polio. I didn't like the idea of lying down for what might be forever. Still, I practiced what he lived by lying still on the couch until I fell asleep. When I woke I didn't know if I was at the new house or the old house, or if an angel had already picked me up and fit my head in the gold-painted cannon.

Then I worried about air and radiation and religious equations like the Trinity and, finally, the march of communists against our country. The hollowness in my face concerned my mother. She studied me when I did my homework at the kitchen table. She suspected that I might have ringworm because there were pale splotches on my face. It was only dirt, though, a film of dirt you could rub off with spit and a thumb.

My worry lessened when I began to understand that nothing could really hurt me. It was another summer and the beginning of the '60s. On our new street, which was green with lawns and squeaky with new trikes, I discovered my invincibility when I was running with new friends, barefoot, and with no shirt. I was particularly proud because I had hooked a screwdriver in a belt loop on my pants. I tripped and fell, and as I fell I worried for a moment, wondering if the screwdriver would drive its point into my belly. The fall was slow, like the build-up to my seven years, and the result would either be yes or no to my living.

The screwdriver kicked up sparks when it cut across the sidewalk. They were wonderful, these sparks that lasted no longer than a blink. Right then, with gravel pitted in my palm and my belly spanked by the fall, I rolled onto my back, cried, and knew that hurt and disease were way off, in another country, one that thanks to Jesus Almighty, I would never think to visit.

The Reader's Presence

1. Consider the alternate title of the essay: "Why I Became a Writer." What do the narrator's many worries about disease and encounters with death have to do with his decision to become a writer? What is the effect on the reader of the barrage of deaths — from the uncle to the neighbor to the dog, kittens, canary, ants, and the boy's own father — narrated in this essay? Identify specific passages to support your response. Which details bring home the seriousness of the losses the boy has suffered?

2. In paragraph 3, Soto writes, "I didn't have much memory to go on." He speaks of his young life as a "trail of footprints all wiped out at the end of a day." Still, this avowedly ephemeral life has left a trail of memories that informs the essay and provides its richness and texture. Discuss the role of memory in this essay. Which details are most memorable for you? Why? Which memories turn out to be touchstones for the author? How does memory transform events into prose?

3. In the child's mind, what are the causes of death and disease? What role does sin play? To what extent does the boy hold himself responsible for the calamities he faces? What role do his parents and the other adults in his life play? What lessons does he learn, directly and indirectly, from each of them? What causes the transition from his state of continuous worry to his feeling of invincibility?

35

Brent Staples

Just Walk on By: A Black Man Ponders His Power to Alter Public Space

As he describes in Parallel Time: Growing Up in Black and White *(1994), Brent Staples (b. 1951) escaped a childhood of urban poverty through success in school and his determination to be a writer. Although Staples earned a Ph.D. in psychology from the University of Chicago in 1982, his love of journalism led him to leave the field of psychology and start a career that has taken him to his current position on the editorial board of the* New York Times. *Staples contributes to several national magazines, including* Harper's, *the* New York Times Magazine, *and* Ms., *in which "Just Walk on By" appeared in 1986.*

In his autobiography, Staples remembers how in Chicago he prepared for his writing career by keeping a journal. "I wrote on buses on the Jackson Park el—though only at the stops to keep the writing legible. I traveled to distant neighborhoods, sat on their curbs, and sketched what I saw in words. Thursdays meant free admission at the Art Institute. All day I attributed motives to people in paintings, especially people in Rembrandts. At closing time I went to a nightclub in The Loop and spied on patrons, copied their conversations and speculated about their lives. The journal was more than 'a record of my inner transactions.' It was a collection of stolen souls from which I would one day construct a book."

My first victim was a woman—white, well dressed, probably in her early twenties. I came upon her late one evening on a deserted street in Hyde Park, a relatively affluent neighborhood in an otherwise mean, impoverished section of Chicago. As I swung onto the avenue behind her, there seemed to be a discreet, uninflammatory distance between us. Not so. She cast back a worried glance. To her, the youngish black man—a broad six feet two inches with a beard and billowing hair, both hands shoved into the pockets of a bulky military jacket—seemed menacingly close. After a few more quick glimpses, she picked up her pace and was soon running in earnest. Within seconds she disappeared into a cross street.

That was more than a decade ago. I was twenty-two years old, a graduate student newly arrived at the University of Chicago. It was in the echo of that terrified woman's footfalls that I first began to know the un-wieldy inheritance I'd come into—the ability to alter public space in ugly ways. It was clear that she thought herself the quarry of a mugger, a rapist, or worse. Suffering a bout of insomnia, however, I was stalking sleep, not defenseless wayfarers. As a softy who is scarcely able to take a knife to a raw chicken—let alone hold it to a person's throat—I was sur-prised, embarrassed, and dismayed all at once. Her flight made me feel like an accomplice in tyranny. It also made it clear that I was indistin-guishable from the muggers who occasionally seeped into the area from the surrounding ghetto. That first encounter, and those that followed, sig-nified that a vast, unnerving gulf lay between nighttime pedestrians—particularly women—and me. And I soon gathered that being perceived as dangerous is a hazard in itself. I only needed to turn a corner into a dicey situation, or crowd some frightened, armed person in a foyer some-where, or make an errant move after being pulled over by a policeman. Where fear and weapons meet—and they often do in urban America—there is always the possibility of death.

In that first year, my first away from my hometown, I was to become thoroughly familiar with the language of fear. At dark, shadowy intersec-tions in Chicago, I could cross in front of a car stopped at a traffic light and elicit the *thunk, thunk, thunk, thunk* of the driver—black, white, male, or female—hammering down the door locks. On less traveled streets after dark, I grew accustomed to but never comfortable with people who crossed to the other side of the street rather than pass me. Then there were the standard unpleasantries with police, doormen, bouncers, cabdrivers, and others whose business is to screen out trouble-some individuals *before* there is any nastiness.

I moved to New York nearly two years ago and I have remained an avid night walker. In central Manhattan, the near-constant crowd cover minimizes tense one-on-one street encounters. Elsewhere—visiting friends in SoHo,[1] where sidewalks are narrow and tightly spaced build-ings shut out the sky—things can get very taut indeed.

Black men have a firm place in New York mugging literature. Norman   5
Podhoretz[2] in his famed (or infamous) 1963 essay, "My Negro Problem—And Ours," recalls growing up in terror of black males; they "were tougher than we were, more ruthless," he writes—and as an adult on the Upper West Side of Manhattan, he continues, he cannot constrain his nervousness when he meets black men on certain streets. Similarly, a decade later, the essayist and novelist Edward Hoagland extols a New York where once "Negro bitterness bore down mainly on other Negroes." Where some see mere panhandlers, Hoagland sees "a mugger who is clearly screwing up his nerve to do more than just *ask* for money." But Hoagland has "the New Yorker's quick-hunch posture for broken-field maneuvering," and the bad guy swerves away.

---

[1]*Soho:* A district of lower Manhattan known for its art galleries. —EDS.
[2]*Norman Podhoretz:* A well-known literary critic and editor of *Commentary* maga-zine. —Eds.

I often witness that "hunch posture," from women after dark on the warrenlike streets of Brooklyn where I live. They seem to set their faces on neutral and, with their purse straps strung across their chests bandolier style, they forge ahead as though bracing themselves against being tackled. I understand, of course, that the danger they perceive is not a hallucination. Women are particularly vulnerable to street violence, and young black males are drastically overrepresented among the perpetrators of that violence. Yet these truths are no solace against the kind of alienation that comes of being ever the suspect, against being set apart, a fearsome entity with whom pedestrians avoid making eye contact.

It is not altogether clear to me how I reached the ripe old age of twenty-two without being conscious of the lethality nighttime pedestrians attributed to me. Perhaps it was because in Chester, Pennsylvania, the small, angry industrial town where I came of age in the 1960s, I was scarcely noticeable against a backdrop of gang warfare, street knifings, and murders. I grew up one of the good boys, had perhaps a half-dozen fistfights. In retrospect, my shyness of combat has clear sources.

Many things go into the making of a young thug. One of those things is the consummation of the male romance with the power to intimidate. An infant discovers that random flailings send the baby bottle flying out of the crib and crashing to the floor. Delighted, the joyful babe repeats those motions again and again, seeking to duplicate the feat. Just so, I recall the points at which some of my boyhood friends were finally seduced by the perception of themselves as tough guys. When a mark cowered and surrendered his money without resistance, myth and reality merged — and paid off. It is, after all, only manly to embrace the power to frighten and intimidate. We, as men, are not supposed to give an inch of our lane on the highway; we are to seize the fighter's edge in work and in play and even in love; we are to be valiant in the face of hostile forces.

Unfortunately, poor and powerless young men seem to take all this nonsense literally. As a boy, I saw countless tough guys locked away; I have since buried several, too. They were babies, really — a teenage cousin, a brother of twenty-two, a childhood friend in his midtwenties — all gone down in episodes of bravado played out in the streets. I came to doubt the virtues of intimidation early on. I chose, perhaps even unconsciously, to remain a shadow — timid, but a survivor.

The fearsomeness mistakenly attributed to me in public places often 10 has a perilous flavor. The most frightening of these confusions occurred in the late 1970s and early 1980s when I worked as a journalist in Chicago. One day, rushing into the office of a magazine I was writing for with a deadline story in hand, I was mistaken for a burglar. The office manager called security and, with an ad hoc posse, pursued me through the labyrinthine halls, nearly to my editor's door. I had no way of proving who I was. I could only move briskly toward the company of someone who knew me.

Another time I was on assignment for a local paper and killing time before an interview. I entered a jewelry store on the city's affluent Near

North Side. The proprietor excused herself and returned with an enormous red Doberman pinscher straining at the end of a leash. She stood, the dog extended toward me, silent to my questions, her eyes bulging nearly out of her head. I took a cursory look around, nodded, and bade her good night. Relatively speaking, however, I never fared as badly as another black male journalist. He went to nearby Waukegan, Illinois, a couple of summers ago to work on a story about a murderer who was born there. Mistaking the reporter for the killer, police hauled him from his car at gunpoint and but for his press credentials would probably have tried to book him. Such episodes are not uncommon. Black men trade tales like this all the time.

In "My Negro Problem—And Ours," Podhoretz writes that the hatred he feels for blacks makes itself known to him through a variety of avenues—one being his discomfort with that "special brand of paranoid touchiness" to which he says blacks are prone. No doubt he is speaking here of black men. In time, I learned to smother the rage I felt at so often being taken for a criminal. Not to do so would surely have led to madness—via that special "paranoid touchiness" that so annoyed Podhoretz at the time he wrote the essay.

I began to take precautions to make myself less threatening. I move about with care, particularly late in the evening. I give a wide berth to nervous people on subway platforms during the wee hours, particularly when I have exchanged business clothes for jeans. If I happen to be entering a building behind some people who appear skittish, I may walk by, letting them clear the lobby before I return, so as not to seem to be following them. I have been calm and extremely congenial on those rare occasions when I've been pulled over by the police.

And on late-evening constitutionals along streets less traveled by, I employ what has proved to be an excellent tension-reducing measure: I whistle melodies from Beethoven and Vivaldi and the more popular classical composers. Even steely New Yorkers hunching toward nighttime destinations seem to relax, and occasionally they even join in the tune. Virtually everybody seems to sense that a mugger wouldn't be warbling bright, sunny selections from Vivaldi's *Four Seasons*. It is my equivalent of the cowbell that hikers wear when they know they are in bear country.

The Reader's Presence

1. Why does Staples use the word *victim* in his opening sentence? In what sense is the white woman a "victim"? How is he using the term? As readers, how might we interpret the opening sentence upon first reading? How does the meaning of the term change in rereading?

2. Does Staples blame the woman for being afraid of him? How does he deal with her anxiety? How does Staples behave on the street? How has he "altered" his own public behavior? In what ways is his behavior on the street similar to his "behavior" as a writer?

3. In rereading the essay, pay close attention to the way Staples handles point of view. When does he shift viewpoints or perspectives? What is his purpose in doing so? What are some of the connections Staples makes in this essay between the point of view one chooses and one's identity?

THE WRITER AT WORK

Another Version of "Just Walk on By"

When he published his memoir, Parallel Time, *in 1994, Brent Staples decided to incorporate his earlier essay into the book. He also decided to revise it substantially. As you compare the two versions, note the passages Staples retained and those he chose not to carry forward into book form. Do you agree with his changes? Why in general do you think he made them? If you had been his book editor, what revision strategy would you have suggested?*

At night, I walked to the lakefront whenever the weather permitted. I was headed home from the lake when I took my first victim. It was late fall, and the wind was cutting. I was wearing my navy pea jacket, the collar turned up, my hands snug in the pockets. Dead leaves scuttled in shoals along the streets. I turned out of Blackstone Avenue and headed west on 57th Street, and there she was, a few yards ahead of me, dressed in business clothes and carrying a briefcase. She looked back at me once, then again, and picked up her pace. She looked back again and started to run. I stopped where I was and looked up at the surrounding windows. What did this look like to people peeking out through their blinds? I was out walking. But what if someone had thought they'd seen something they hadn't and called the police. I held back the urge to run. Instead, I walked south to The Midway, plunged into its darkness, and remained on The Midway until I reached the foot of my street.

I'd been a fool. I'd been walking the streets grinning good evening at people who were frightened to death of me. I did violence to them by just being. How had I missed this? I kept walking at night, but from then on I paid attention.

I became expert in the language of fear. Couples locked arms or reached for each other's hand when they saw me. Some crossed to the other side of the street. People who were carrying on conversations went mute and stared straight ahead, as though avoiding my eyes would save them. This reminded me of an old wives' tale: that rabid dogs didn't bite if you avoided their eyes. The determination to avoid my eyes made me invisible to classmates and professors whom I passed on the street.

It occurred to me for the first time that I was big. I was 6 feet 1 ½ inches tall, and my long hair made me look bigger. I weighed only 170 pounds. But the navy pea jacket that Brian had given me was broad at the shoulders, high at the collar, making me look bigger and more fearsome that I was.

I tried to be innocuous but didn't know how. The more I thought   5
about how I moved, the less my body belonged to me; I became a false
character riding along inside it. I began to avoid people. I turned out of
my way into side streets to spare them the sense that they were being
stalked. I let them clear the lobbies of buildings before I entered, so they
wouldn't feel trapped. Out of nervousness I began to whistle and discovered I was good at it. My whistle was pure and sweet—and also in tune.
On the street at night I whistled popular tunes from the Beatles and Vivaldi's *Four Seasons*. The tension drained from people's bodies when they
heard me. A few even smiled as they passed me in the dark.

Then I changed. I don't know why, but I remember when. I was walking west on 57th Street, after dark, coming home from the lake. The man
and the woman walking toward me were laughing and talking but
clammed up when they saw me. The man touched the woman's elbow,
guiding her toward the curb. Normally I'd have given way and begun to
whistle, but not this time. This time I veered toward them and aimed myself
so that they'd have to part to avoid walking into me. The man stiffened,
threw back his head and assumed the stare: eyes dead ahead, mouth open.
His face took on a bluish hue under the sodium vapor streetlamps. I suppressed the urge to scream into his face. Instead I glided between them, my
shoulder nearly brushing his. A few steps beyond them I stopped and
howled with laughter. I called this game Scatter the Pigeons.

Fifty-seventh Street was too well lit for the game to be much fun;
people didn't feel quite vulnerable enough. Along The Midway were
heart-stopping strips of dark sidewalk, but these were so frightening that
few people traveled them. The stretch of Blackstone between 57th and
55th provided better hunting. The block was long and lined with young
trees that blocked out the streetlight and obscured the heads of people
coming toward you.

One night I stooped beneath the branches and came up on the other
side, just as a couple was stepping from their car into their town house.
The woman pulled her purse close with one hand and reached for her
husband with the other. The two of them stood frozen as I bore down
on them. I felt a surge of power: these people were mine; I could do with
them as I wished. If I'd been younger, with less to lose, I'd have robbed
them, and it would have been easy. All I'd have to do was stand silently
before them until they surrendered their money. I thundered, "Good
evening!" into their bleached-out faces and cruised away laughing.

I held a special contempt for people who cowered in their cars as they
waited for the light to change at 57th and Woodlawn. The intersection
was always deserted at night, except for a car or two stuck at the red.
Thunk! Thunk! Thunk! they hammered down the door locks when I
came into view. Once I had hustled across the street, head down, trying
to seem harmless. Now I turned brazenly into the headlights and laughed.
Once across, I paced the sidewalk, glaring until the light changed. They'd
made me terrifying. Now I'd show them how terrifying I could be.

36

Amy Tan

Mother Tongue

Amy Tan (b. 1952) was born in California shortly after her parents immigrated to the United States from China. She started writing as a child and won a writing contest at age eight. As an adult, Tan made her living as a free-lance business writer for many years, but started to write fiction in 1985. In 1987, Tan traveled to China for the first time, an experience that helped shape her consciousness of both her American and Chinese identities. In 1989 she published her best-selling first novel, The Joy Luck Club, *followed by* The Kitchen God's Wife *(1991), the children's books* The Moon Lady *(1992) and* The Chinese Siamese Cat *(1994), and* The Hundred Secret Senses *(1995). "Mother Tongue" originally appeared in the* Threepenny Review *in 1990.*

Commenting on the art of writing, Tan has said, "I had a very unliterary background, but I had a determination to write for myself." She believes that the goal of every serious writer of literature is "to try to find your voice and your art, because it comes from your own experiences, your own pain."

I am not a scholar of English or literature. I cannot give you much more than personal opinions on the English language and its variations in this country or others.

I am a writer. And by that definition, I am someone who has always loved language. I am fascinated by language in daily life. I spend a great deal of my time thinking about the power of language—the way it can evoke an emotion, a visual image, a complex idea, or a simple truth. Language is the tool of my trade. And I use them all—all the Englishes I grew up with.

Recently, I was made keenly aware of the different Englishes I do use. I was giving a talk to a large group of people, the same talk I had already given to half a dozen other groups. The nature of the talk was about my writing, my life, and my book, *The Joy Luck Club*. The talk was going along well enough, until I remembered one major difference that made the whole talk sound wrong. My mother was in the room. And it was perhaps the first time she had heard me give a lengthy speech, using the kind of English I have never used with her. I was saying things like "The intersection of memory upon imagination" and "There is an aspect of my fiction that relates to thus-and-thus"—a speech filled with carefully wrought grammatical phrases, burdened, it suddenly seemed to me, with nominalized forms, past perfect tenses, conditional phrases, all the forms of standard English that I had learned in school and through books, the forms of English I did not use at home with my mother.

Just last week, I was walking down the street with my mother, and I again found myself conscious of the English I was using, the English I do use with her. We were talking about the price of new and used furniture and I heard myself saying this: "Not waste money that way." My husband was with us as well, and he didn't notice any switch in my English. And then I realized why. It's because over the twenty years we've been together I've often used that same kind of English with him, and sometimes he even uses it with me. It has become our language of intimacy, a different sort of English that relates to family talk, the language I grew up with.

So you'll have some idea of what this family talk I heard sounds like,   5
I'll quote what my mother said during a recent conversation which I videotaped and then transcribed. During this conversation, my mother was talking about a political gangster in Shanghai who had the same last name as her family's, Du, and how the gangster in his early years wanted to be adopted by her family, which was rich by comparison. Later, the gangster became more powerful, far richer than my mother's family, and one day showed up at my mother's wedding to pay his respects. Here's what she said in part:

"Du Yusong having business like fruit stand. Like off the street kind. He is Du like Du Zong—but not Tsung-ming Island people. The local people call putong, the river east side, he belong to that side local people. That man want to ask Du Zong father take him in like become own family. Du Zong father wasn't look down on him, but didn't take seriously, until that man big like become a mafia. Now important person, very hard to inviting him. Chinese way, came only to show respect, don't stay for dinner. Respect for making big celebration, he shows up. Mean gives lots of respect. Chinese custom. Chinese social life that way. If too important won't have to stay too long. He come to my wedding. I didn't see, I heard it. I gone to boy's side, they have YMCA dinner. Chinese age I was nineteen."

You should know that my mother's expressive command of English belies how much she actually understands. She reads the *Forbes* report, listens to *Wall Street Week*, converses daily with her stockbroker, reads all of Shirley MacLaine's books with ease—all kinds of things I can't begin to understand. Yet some of my friends tell me they understand 50 percent of what my mother says. Some say they understand 80 to 90 percent. Some say they understand none of it, as if she were speaking pure Chinese. But to me, my mother's English is perfectly clear, perfectly natural. It's my mother tongue. Her language, as I hear it, is vivid, direct, full of observation and imagery. That was the language that helped shape the way I saw things, expressed things, made sense of the world.

Lately, I've been giving more thought to the kind of English my mother speaks. Like others, I have described it to people as "broken" or "fractured" English. But I wince when I say that. It has always bothered me that I can think of no other way to describe it other than "broken," as if it were damaged and needed to be fixed, as if it lacked a certain wholeness and soundness. I've heard other terms used, "limited English," for example. But they seem just as bad, as if everything is limited, including people's perceptions of the limited English speaker.

I know this for a fact, because when I was growing up, my mother's "limited" English limited *my* perception of her. I was ashamed of her English. I believed that her English reflected the quality of what she had to say. That is, because she expressed them imperfectly her thoughts were imperfect. And I had plenty of empirical evidence to support me: the fact that people in department stores, at banks, and at restaurants did not take her seriously, did not give her good service, pretended not to understand her, or even acted as if they did not hear her.

My mother has long realized the limitations of her English as well. When I was fifteen, she used to have me call people on the phone to pretend I was she. In this guise, I was forced to ask for information or even to complain and yell at people who had been rude to her. One time it was a call to her stockbroker in New York. She had cashed out her small portfolio and it just so happened we were going to go to New York the next week, our very first trip outside California. I had to get on the phone and say in an adolescent voice that was not very convincing, "This is Mrs. Tan." 10

And my mother was standing in the back whispering loudly, "Why he don't send me check, already two weeks late. So mad he lie to me, losing me money."

And then I said in perfect English, "Yes, I'm getting rather concerned. You had agreed to send the check two weeks ago, but it hasn't arrived."

Then she began to talk more loudly. "What he want, I come to New York tell him front of his boss, you cheating me?" And I was trying to calm her down, make her be quiet, while telling the stockbroker, "I can't tolerate any more excuses. If I don't receive the check immediately, I am going to have to speak to your manager when I'm in New York next week." And sure enough, the following week there we were in front of this astonished stockbroker, and I was sitting there red-faced and quiet, and my mother, the real Mrs. Tan, was shouting at his boss in her impeccable broken English.

We used a similar routine just five days ago, for a situation that was far less humorous. My mother had gone to the hospital for an appointment, to find out about a benign brain tumor a CAT scan had revealed a month ago. She said she had spoken very good English, her best English, no mistakes. Still, she said, the hospital did not apologize when they said they had lost the CAT scan and she had come for nothing. She said they did not seem to have any sympathy when she told them she was anxious to know the exact diagnosis, since her husband and son had both died of brain tumors. She said they would not give her any more information until the next time and she would have to make another appointment for that. So she said she would not leave until the doctor called her daughter. She wouldn't budge. And when the doctor finally called her daughter, me, who spoke in perfect English—lo and behold—we had assurances the CAT scan would be found, promises that a conference call on Monday would be held, and apologies for any suffering my mother had gone through for a most regrettable mistake.

I think my mother's English almost had an effect on limiting my pos-   15
sibilities in life as well. Sociologists and linguists probably will tell you that a person's developing language skills are more influenced by peers. But I do think that the language spoken in the family, especially in immigrant families which are more insular, plays a large role in shaping the language of the child. And I believe that it affected my results on achievement tests, IQ tests, and the SAT. While my English skills were never judged as poor, compared to math, English could not be considered my strong suit. In grade school I did moderately well, getting perhaps B's, sometimes B-pluses, in English and scoring perhaps in the sixtieth or seventieth percentile on achievement tests. But those scores were not good enough to override the opinion that my true abilities lay in math and science, because in those areas I achieved A's and scored in the ninetieth percentile or higher.

This was understandable. Math is precise; there is only one correct answer. Whereas, for me at least, the answers on English tests were always a judgment call, a matter of opinion and personal experience. Those tests were constructed around items like fill-in-the-blank sentence completion, such as "Even though Tom was _____, Mary thought he was _____." And the correct answer always seemed to be the most bland combinations of thoughts, for example, "Even though Tom was shy, Mary thought he was charming," with the grammatical structure "even though" limiting the correct answer to some sort of semantic opposites, so you wouldn't get answers like, "Even though Tom was foolish, Mary thought he was ridiculous." Well, according to my mother, there were very few limitations as to what Tom could have been and what Mary might have thought of him. So I never did well on tests like that.

The same was true with word analogies, pairs of words in which you were supposed to find some sort of logical, semantic relationship—for example, "*Sunset* is to *nightfall* as _____ is to _____." And here you would be presented with a list of four possible pairs, one of which showed the same kind of relationship: *red* is to *stoplight*, *bus* is to *arrival*, *chills* is to *fever*, *yawn* is to *boring*. Well, I could never think that way. I knew what the tests were asking, but I could not block out of my mind the images already created by the first pair, "*sunset* is to *nightfall*" — and I would see a burst of colors against a darkening sky, the moon rising, the lowering of a curtain of stars. And all the other pairs of words — red, bus, stoplight, boring — just threw up a mass of confusing images, making it impossible for me to sort out something as logical as saying: "A sunset precedes nightfall" is the same as "a chill precedes a fever." The only way I would have gotten that answer right would have been to imagine an associative situation, for example, my being disobedient and staying out past sunset, catching a chill at night, which turns into feverish pneumonia as punishment, which indeed did happen to me.

I have been thinking about all this lately, about my mother's English, about achievement tests. Because lately I've been asked, as a writer, why there are not more Asian Americans represented in American literature. Why are there few Asian Americans enrolled in creative writing programs? Why do so many Chinese students go into engineering? Well, these are broad sociological questions I can't begin to answer. But I have noticed in surveys — in fact, just last week — that Asian students, as a whole, always do significantly better on math achievement tests than in English. And this makes me think that there are other Asian-American students whose English spoken in the home might also be described as "broken" or "limited." And perhaps they also have teachers who are steering them away from writing and into math and science, which is what happened to me.

Fortunately, I happen to be rebellious in nature and enjoy the challenge of disproving assumptions made about me. I became an English major my first year in college, after being enrolled as pre-med. I started writing nonfiction as a freelancer the week after I was told by my former boss that writing was my worst skill and I should hone my talents toward account management.

But it wasn't until 1985 that I finally began to write fiction. And at 20 first I wrote using what I thought to be wittily crafted sentences, sentences that would finally prove I had mastery over the English language. Here's an example from the first draft of a story that later made its way into *The Joy Luck Club*, but without this line: "That was my mental quandary in its nascent state." A terrible line, which I can barely pronounce.

Fortunately, for reasons I won't get into today, I later decided I should envision a reader for the stories I would write. And the reader I decided upon was my mother, because these were stories about mothers. So with this reader in mind — and in fact she did read my early drafts — I began to write stories using all the Englishes I grew up with: the English I spoke to my mother, which for lack of a better term might be described as "simple": the English she used with me, which for lack of a better term might be described as "broken"; my translation of her Chinese, which could certainly be described as "watered down"; and what I imagined to be her translation of her Chinese if she could speak in perfect English, her internal language, and for that I sought to preserve the essence, but neither an English nor a Chinese structure. I wanted to capture what language ability tests can never reveal: her intent, her passion, her imagery, the rhythms of her speech, and the nature of her thoughts.

Apart from what any critic had to say about my writing, I knew I had succeeded where it counted when my mother finished reading my book and gave me her verdict: "So easy to read."

The Reader's Presence

1. In her second paragraph, Tan mentions "all the Englishes" she grew up with. What were those "Englishes"? What is odd about the term? How does the oddity of the word reinforce the point of her essay?

2. What exactly is Tan's "mother tongue"? What does the phrase usually mean? How is Tan using it? How would you describe this language? Would you call it "broken English"? What does that phrase imply?

3. In paragraph 20, Tan gives an example of a sentence that she once thought showed her "mastery" of English. What does she now find wrong with that sentence? What do you think of it? What would her mother have thought of it? What sort of reader does that sentence anticipate?

37 _____

James Thurber

University Days

A short story writer, essayist, author of children's books, and cartoonist, James Thurber (1894–1961), is known for his outlandish and humorous characterizations of both urban and domestic life. Thurber, proclaimed by Alistair Cooke as "one of the world's greatest humorists," worked for the New Yorker *for most of his career and helped establish its urbane tone. While at the* New Yorker, *Thurber worked with E. B. White (see page 292), and together they wrote* Is Sex Necessary? *(1929), a spoof on sex manuals. One of Thurber's most famous short stories, "The Secret Life of Walter Mitty," depicts a man whose heroic daydreams help him escape from a dull job and a domineering wife. His publications include a collection of pieces from the* New Yorker, The Owl in the Attic and Other Perplexities *(1931); a book of drawings,* The Seal in the Bedroom and Other Predicaments *(1931); short stories,* My World—and Welcome to It *(1942); and an account of his days at the* New Yorker, The Years with Ross *(1959).* "University Days" *appeared in* The Thurber Carnival *(1931).*

I passed all the other courses that I took at my University, but I could never pass botany. This was because all botany students had to spend several hours a week in a laboratory looking through a microscope at plant cells, and I could never see through a microscope. I never once saw a cell through a microscope. This used to enrage my instructor. He would wander around the laboratory pleased with the progress all the students were making in drawing the involved and, so I am told, interesting structure of flower cells, until he came to me. I would just be standing there. "I can't see anything," I would say. He would begin patiently enough, explaining how anybody can see through a microscope, but he would always end up in a fury, claiming that I could *too* see through a microscope but just pretended that I couldn't. "It takes away from the beauty of flowers anyway," I used to tell him. "We are not concerned with beauty in this course," he would say. "We are concerned solely with what I may call the *mechanics* of flars." "Well," I'd say, "I can't see anything." "Try it just once again," he'd say, and I would put my eye to the microscope and see nothing at all, except now and again a nebulous milky substance—a phenomenon of maladjustment. You were supposed to see a vivid, restless clockwork of sharply defined plant cells. "I see what looks like a lot of milk," I would tell him. This, he claimed, was the result of my not having adjusted the microscope properly, so he would readjust it for me, or rather, for himself. And I would look again and see milk.

I finally took a deferred pass, as they called it, and waited a year and tried again. (You had to pass one of the biological sciences or you couldn't graduate.) The professor had come back from vacation brown as a berry, bright-eyed, and eager to explain cell-structure again to his classes. "Well," he said to me, cheerily, when we met in the first laboratory hour of the semester, "we're going to see cells this time, aren't we?" "Yes, sir," I said. Students to right of me and to left of me and in front of me were seeing cells; what's more, they were quietly drawing pictures of them in their notebooks. Of course, I didn't see anything.

"We'll try it," the professor said to me, grimly, "with every adjustment of the microscope known to man. As God is my witness, I'll arrange this glass so that you see cells through it or I'll give up teaching. In twenty-two years of botany, I—" He cut off abruptly for he was beginning to quiver all over, like Lionel Barrymore, and he genuinely wished to hold onto his temper; his scenes with me had taken a great deal out of him.

So we tried it with every adjustment of the microscope known to man. With only one of them did I see anything but blackness or the familiar lacteal opacity, and that time I saw, to my pleasure and amazement, a variegated constellation of flecks, specks, and dots. These I hastily drew. The instructor, noting my activity, came back from an adjoining desk, a smile on his lips and his eyebrows high in hope. He looked at my cell drawing. "What's that?" he demanded, with a hint of a squeal in his voice. "That's what I saw," I said. "You didn't, you didn't, you *did*n't!" he screamed, losing control of his temper instantly, and he bent over and squinted into the microscope. His head snapped up. "That's your eye!" he shouted. "You've fixed the lens so that it reflects! You've drawn your eye!"

Another course that I didn't like, but somehow managed to pass, was   5 economics. I went to that class straight from the botany class, which didn't help me any in understanding either subject. I used to get them mixed up. But not as mixed up as another student in my economics class who came there direct from a physics laboratory. He was a tackle on the football team, named Bolenciecwcz. At that time Ohio State University had one of the best football teams in the country, and Bolenciecwcz was one of its outstanding stars. In order to be eligible to play it was necessary for him to keep up in his studies, a very difficult matter, for while he was not dumber than an ox he was not any smarter. Most of his professors were lenient and helped him along. None gave him more hints, in answering questions, or asked him simpler ones than the economics professor, a thin, timid man named Bassum. One day when we were on the subject of transportation and distribution, it came Bolenciecwcz's turn to answer a question. "Name one means of transportation," the professor said to him. No light came into the big tackle's eyes. "Just any means of transportation," said the professor. Bolenciecwcz sat staring at him. "That is," pursued the professor, "any medium, agency, or method of going from one place to another." Bolenciecwcz had the look of a man who is being led into a trap. "You may choose among steam, horse-drawn, or electrically propelled vehicles," said the instructor. "I might suggest the one which we commonly take in making long journeys across land." There was a profound silence in which everybody stirred uneasily, including Bolenciecwcz and Mr. Bassum. Mr. Bassum abruptly broke this silence in an amazing manner. "Choo-choo-choo," he said, in a low voice, and turned instantly scarlet. He glanced appealingly around the room. All of us, of course, shared Mr. Bassum's desire that Bolenciecwcz should stay abreast of the class in economics, for the Illinois game, one of the hardest and most important of the season, was only a week off. "Toot, toot, too-tooooooot!" some student with a deep voice moaned, and we all looked encouragingly at Bolenciecwcz. Somebody else gave a fine imitation of a locomotive letting off steam. Mr. Bassum himself rounded off the little show. "Ding, dong, ding, dong," he said, hopefully. Bolenciecwcz was staring at the floor now, trying to think, his great brow furrowed, his huge hands rubbing together, his face red.

"How did you come to college this year, Mr. Bolenciecwcz?" asked the professor. "*Chuff*a chuffa, *chuff*a chuffa."

"M'father sent me," said the football player.

"What on?" asked Bassum.

"I git an 'lowance," said the tackle, in a low, husky voice, obviously embarrassed.

"No, no," said Bassum. "Name a means of transportation. What did   10 you *ride* here on?"

"Train," said Bolenciecwcz.

"Quite right," said the professor. "Now, Mr. Nugent, will you tell us——"

If I went through anguish in botany and economics—for different reasons—gymnasium work was even worse. I don't even like to think about it. They wouldn't let you play games or join in the exercises with your glasses on and I couldn't see with mine off. I bumped into professors, horizontal bars, agricultural students, and swinging iron rings. Not being able to see, I could take it but I couldn't dish it out. Also, in order to pass gymnasium (and you had to pass it to graduate) you had to learn to swim if you didn't know how. I didn't like the swimming pool, I didn't like swimming, and I didn't like the swimming instructor, and after all these years I still don't. I never swam but I passed my gym work anyway, by having another student give my gymnasium number (978) and swim across the pool in my place. He was a quiet, amiable blond youth, number 473, and he would have seen through a microscope for me if we could have got away with it, but we couldn't get away with it. Another thing I didn't like about gymnasium work was that they made you strip the day you registered. It is impossible for me to be happy when I am stripped and being asked a lot of questions. Still, I did better than a lanky agricultural student who was cross-examined just before I was. They asked each student what college he was in—that is, whether Arts, Engineering, Commerce, or Agriculture. "What college are you in?" the instructor snapped at the youth in front of me. "Ohio State University," he said promptly.

It wasn't that agricultural student but it was another a whole lot like him who decided to take up journalism, possibly on the ground that when farming went to hell he could fall back on newspaper work. He didn't realize, of course, that that would be very much like falling back full-length on a kit of carpenter's tools. Haskins didn't seem cut out for journalism, being too embarrassed to talk to anybody and unable to use a typewriter, but the editor of the college paper assigned him to the cow barns, the sheep house, the horse pavilion, and the animal husbandry department generally. This was a genuinely big "beat," for it took up five times as much ground and got ten times as great a legislative appropriation as the College of Liberal Arts. The agricultural student knew animals, but nevertheless his stories were dull and colorlessly written. He took all afternoon on each of them, on account of having to hunt for each letter on the typewriter. Once in a while he had to ask somebody to help him hunt. "C" and "L," in particular, were hard letters for him to find. His editor finally got pretty much annoyed at the farmer-journalist because his pieces were so uninteresting. "See here, Haskins," he snapped at him one day, "why is it we never have anything hot from you on the horse pavilion? Here we have two hundred head of horses on this campus—more than any other university in the Western Conference except Purdue—and yet you never get any real low down on them. Now shoot over to the horse barns and dig up something lively." Haskins shambled out and came back in about an hour; he said he had something. "Well, start it off snappily," said the editor. "Something people will read." Haskins set to work and in a couple of hours brought a sheet of typewritten paper to the desk; it was a two-hundred word story about some disease that had broken out among the horses. Its opening sentence was simple but arresting. It read: "Who has noticed the sores on the tops of the horses in the animal husbandry building?"

Ohio State was a land grant university and therefore two years of   15
military drill was compulsory. We drilled with old Springfield rifles and studied the tactics of the Civil War even though the World War was going on at the time. At 11 o'clock each morning thousands of freshmen and sophomores used to deploy over the campus, moodily creeping up on the old chemistry building. It was good training for the kind of warfare that was waged at Shiloh but it had no connection with what was going on in Europe. Some people used to think there was German money behind it, but they didn't dare say so or they would have been thrown in jail as German spies. It was a period of muddy thought and marked, I believe, the decline of higher education in the Middle West.

As a soldier I was never any good at all. Most of the cadets were glumly indifferent soldiers, but I was no good at all. Once General Littlefield, who was commandant of the cadet corps, popped up in front of me during regimental drill and snapped, "You are the main trouble with this university!" I think he meant that my type was the main trouble with the university but he may have meant me individually. I was mediocre at drill, certainly—that is, until my senior year. By that time I had drilled longer than anybody else in the Western Conference, having failed at military at the end of each preceding year so that I had to do it all over again. I was the only senior still in uniform. The uniform which, when new, had made me look like an interurban railway conductor, now that it had become faded and too tight made me look like Bert Williams in his bellboy act. This had a definitely bad effect on my morale. Even so, I had become by sheer practice little short of wonderful at squad maneuvers.

One day General Littlefield picked our company out of the whole regiment and tried to get it mixed up by putting it through one movement after another as fast as we could execute them: squads right, squads left, squads on right into line, squads right about, squads left front into line etc. In about three minutes one hundred and nine men were marching in one direction and I was marching away from them at an angle of forty degrees, all alone. "Company, halt!" shouted General Littlefield, "That man is the only man who has it right!" I was made a corporal for my achievement.

The next day General Littlefield summoned me to his office. He was swatting flies when I went in. I was silent and he was silent too, for a long time. I don't think he remembered me or why he had sent for me, but he didn't want to admit it. He swatted some more flies, keeping his eyes on them narrowly before he let go with the swatter. "Button up your coat!" he snapped. Looking back on it now I can see that he meant me although he was looking at a fly, but I just stood there. Another fly came to rest on a paper in front of the general and began rubbing its hind legs together. The General lifted the swatter cautiously. I moved restlessly and the fly flew away. "You startled him!" barked General Littlefield, looking at me severely. I said I was sorry. "That won't help the situation!" snapped the General, with cold military logic. I didn't see what I could do except offer to chase some more flies toward his desk, but I didn't say anything. He stared out the window at the faraway figures of co-eds crossing the campus toward the library. Finally, he told me I could go. So I went. He either didn't know which cadet I was or else he forgot what he wanted to see me about. It may have been that he wished to apologize for having called me the main trouble with the university; or maybe he had decided to compliment me on my brilliant drilling of the day before and then at the last minute decided not to. I don't know. I don't think about it much any more.

The Reader's Presence

1. How does Thurber's depiction of his college life contrast with common expectations of the educational experience? What does he seem to have learned?

2. Thurber is able to render fairly ordinary events in a highly comedic manner. List the events of his "choo-choo" story as simply as possible and then determine what sorts of verbal tools he uses to build and maintain humor in the scene. To what extent is humor determined by form alone?

3. Compare this piece with Russell Baker's "Gumption" (see page 62). What similarities in comic style do the pieces share? How do they differ? Do you think the younger Russell Baker learned any humorous techniques from the popular Thurber?

38

Garry Trudeau

My Inner Shrimp

*Garry Trudeau (b. 1948), creator of the popular comic strip "Doonesbury,"
has also contributed articles to such publications as* Harper's, Rolling Stone, *the*
New Republic, *the* New Yorker, New York, *and the* Washington Post. *He received bachelor's and master's degrees from Yale University. Trudeau won a
Pulitzer Prize in 1975 and in 1994 received the award for best comic strip from
the National Cartoonists Society. For five years he was an occasional columnist
for the* New York Times *opinion and editorial page. Currently, he is a contributing essayist for* Time *magazine. He lives in New York City with his wife, Jane
Pauley, and their three children.*

For the rest of my days, I shall be a recovering short person. Even
from my lofty perch of something over six feet (as if I don't know within
a micron), I have the soul of a shrimp. I feel the pain of the diminutive, ir-
respective of whether they feel it themselves, because my visit to the
planet of the teenage midgets was harrowing, humiliating, and extended.
I even perceive my last-minute escape to have been flukish, somehow unearned—as if the Commissioner of Growth Spurts had been an old classmate of my father.

My most recent reminder of all this came the afternoon I went hunting for a new office. I had noticed a building under construction in my
neighborhood—a brick warren of duplexes, with wide, westerly-facing
windows, promising ideal light for a working studio. When I was ushered
into the model unit, my pulse quickened: The soaring, twenty-two-foot
living room walls were gloriously aglow with the remains of the day. I
bonded immediately.

Almost as an afterthought, I ascended the staircase to inspect the loft,
ducking as I entered the bedroom. To my great surprise, I stayed ducked:
The room was a little more than six feet in height. While my head technically cleared the ceiling, the effect was excruciatingly oppressive. This certainly wasn't a space I wanted to spend any time in, much less take out a
mortgage on.

Puzzled, I wandered down to the sales office and asked if there were any other units to look at. No, replied a resolutely unpleasant receptionist, it was the last one. Besides, they were all exactly alike.

"Are you aware of how low the bedroom ceilings are?" I asked. 5

She shot me an evil look. "Of course we are," she snapped. "There were some problems with the building codes. The architect knows all about the ceilings.

"He's not an idiot, you know," she added, perfectly anticipating my next question.

She abruptly turned away, but it was too late. She'd just confirmed that a major New York developer, working with a fully licensed architect, had knowingly created an entire twelve-story apartment building virtually uninhabitable by anyone of even average height. It was an exclusive high-rise for shorties.

Once I knew that, of course, I couldn't stay away. For days thereafter, as I walked to work, some perverse, unreasoning force would draw me back to the building. But it wasn't just the absurdity, the stone silliness of its design that had me in its grip; it was something far more compelling. Like some haunted veteran come again to an ancient battlefield, I was revisiting my perilous past.

When I was fourteen, I was the third-smallest in a high school class of 10 one hundred boys, routinely mistaken for a sixth grader. My first week of school, I was drafted into a contingent of students ignominiously dubbed the "Midgets," so grouped by taller boys presumably so they could taunt us with more perfect efficiency. Inexplicably, some of my fellow Midgets refused to be diminished by the experience, but I retreated into self-pity. I sent away for a book on how to grow tall, and committed to memory its tips on overcoming one's genetic destiny—or at least making the most of a regrettable situation. The book cited historical figures who had gone the latter route—Alexander the Great, Caesar, Napoleon (the mind involuntarily added Hitler). Strategies for stretching the limbs were suggested—hanging from door frames, sleeping on your back, doing assorted floor exercises—all of which I incorporated into my daily routine (get up, brush teeth, hang from door frame). I also learned the importance of meeting girls early in the day, when, the book assured me, my rested spine rendered me perceptibly taller.

For six years, my condition persisted; I grew, but at nowhere near the rate of my peers. I perceived other problems as ancillary, and loaded up the stature issue with freight shipped in daily from every corner of my life. Lack of athletic success, all absence of a social life, the inevitable run-ins with bullies—all could be attributed to the missing inches. The night I found myself sobbing in my father's arms was the low point; we both knew it was one problem he couldn't fix.

Of course what we couldn't have known was that he and my mother already had. They had given me a delayed developmental timetable. In my seventeenth year, I miraculously shot up six inches, just in time for graduation and a fresh start. I was, in the space of a few months, reborn—and I made the most of it. Which is to say that thereafter, all of life's disappointments, reversals, and calamities still arrived on schedule—but blissfully free of subtext.

Once you stop being the butt, of course, any problem recedes, if only to give way to a new one. And yet the impact of being literally looked down on, of being *made* to feel small, is forever. It teaches you how to stretch, how to survive the scorn of others for things that are beyond your control. Not growing forces you to grow up fast.

Sometimes I think I'd like to return to a high-school reunion to surprise my classmates. Not that they didn't know me when I finally started catching up. They did, but I doubt they'd remember. Adolescent hierarchies have a way of enduring; I'm sure I am still recalled as the Midget I myself have never really left behind.

Of course, if I'm going to show up, it'll have to be soon. I'm starting   15
to shrink.

The Reader's Presence

1. It is said that "beauty is in the eye of the beholder"; Trudeau's testimony challenges this old saw. Does Trudeau's piece convince you that imagined shortcomings are nearly as ruinous as those apparent to others? Why or why not?

2. Locate examples in the essay of exaggeration or hyperbole. Does this descriptive technique support or weaken Trudeau's case, and why? What phrase does Trudeau's title intentionally echo? Why?

3. Trudeau speaks as a formerly diminutive person, but he is now quite tall. Do you think that to be short is a negative physical feature? Is it only negative in males? Would Trudeau have written the same essay if he had never grown taller? Why or why not?

39

Alice Walker

Beauty: When the Other Dancer Is the Self

Alice Walker (b. 1944) was awarded the Pulitzer Prize and the American Book Award for her second novel, The Color Purple *(1982), which was made into a popular film. This novel helped establish Walker's reputation as one of America's most important contemporary writers. In both her fiction and nonfiction, she shares her compassion for the black women of America whose lives have long been largely excluded from or distorted in literary representation. Walker is also the author of other novels, short stories, several volumes of poetry, a children's biography of Langston Hughes, essays, and criticism. Her most recent books are* Anything We Love Can Be Saved: A Writer's Activism *(1997),* By the Light of My Father's Smile: A Novel *(1998), and* The Same River Twice *(1996). "Beauty: When the Other Dancer Is the Self" comes from her 1983 collection,* In Search of Our Mothers' Gardens.*

When asked by an interviewer about her writing habits, Walker replied, "Generally speaking I work in the morning and then I garden—I do watering. Writing is just a part of my life. I don't like to emphasize it so much it becomes a distortion. I think it was Hemingway who said that each day that you write, you don't try to write to the absolute end of what you feel and think. You leave a little, you know, so that the next day you have something else to go on. And I would take it a little further—the thing is being able to create out of fullness, and that in order to create out of fullness, you have to let it well up. You cannot do what is done so much in this culture and the world. You know, the image of what has happened to the planet is of a man and mankind just grabbing the earth by the throat and shaking it and saying 'give, give, give,' and just squeezing it until the last drop of life leaves it. That, needless to say, is very uncreative. It can only lead to death. . . . In creation you must always leave something. You have to go to the bottom of the well with creativity. You have to give it everything you've got, but at the same time you have to leave that last drop for the creative spirit or for the earth itself."

It is a bright summer day in 1947. My father, a fat, funny man with beautiful eyes and a subversive wit, is trying to decide which of his eight children he will take with him to the county fair. My mother, of course,

285

will not go. She is knocked out from getting most of us ready: I hold my neck stiff against the pressure of her knuckles as she hastily completes the braiding and the beribboning of my hair.

My father is the driver for the rich old white lady up the road. Her name is Miss Mey. She owns all the land for miles around, as well as the house in which we live. All I remember about her is that she once offered to pay my mother thirty-five cents for cleaning her house, raking up piles of her magnolia leaves, and washing her family's clothes, and that my mother—she of no money, eight children, and a chronic earache—refused it. But I do not think of this in 1947. I am two-and-a-half years old. I want to go everywhere my daddy goes. I am excited at the prospect of riding in a car. Someone has told me fairs are fun. That there is room in the car for only three of us doesn't faze me at all. Whirling happily in my starchy frock, showing off my biscuit-polished patent-leather shoes and lavender socks, tossing my head in a way that makes my ribbons bounce, I stand, hands on hips, before my father. "Take me, Daddy," I say with assurance; "I'm the prettiest!"

Later, it does not surprise me to find myself in Miss Mey's shiny black car, sharing the back seat with the other lucky ones. Does not surprise me that I thoroughly enjoy the fair. At home that night I tell the unlucky ones all I can remember about the merry-go-round, the man who eats live chickens, and the teddy bears, until they say: that's enough, baby Alice. Shut up now, and go to sleep.

It is Easter Sunday, 1950. I am dressed in a green, flocked, scalloped-hem dress (handmade by my adoring sister, Ruth) that has its own smooth satin petticoat and tiny hot-pink roses tucked into each scallop. My shoes, new T-strap patent leather, again highly biscuit-polished. I am six years old and have learned one of the longest Easter speeches to be heard that day, totally unlike the speech I said when I was two: "Easter lilies / pure and white / blossom in / the morning light." When I rise to give my speech I do so on a great wave of love and pride and expectation. People in the church stop rustling their new crinolines. They seem to hold their breath. I can tell they admire my dress, but it is my spirit, bordering on sassiness (womanishness), they secretly applaud.

"That girl's a little *mess*," they whisper to each other, pleased.   5

Naturally I say my speech without stammer or pause, unlike those who stutter, stammer, or, worst of all, forget. This is before the word "beautiful" exists in people's vocabulary, but "Oh, isn't she the *cutest* thing!" frequently floats my way. "And got so much sense!" they gratefully add . . . for which thoughtful addition I thank them to this day.

It was great fun being cute. But then, one day, it ended.

I am eight years old and a tomboy. I have a cowboy hat, cowboy boots, checkered shirt and pants, all red. My playmates are my brothers, two and four years older than I. Their colors are black and green, the only difference in the way we are dressed. On Saturday nights we all go to the picture show, even my mother; Westerns are her favorite kind of movie. Back home, "on the ranch," we pretend we are Tom Mix, Hopalong Cassidy, Lash LaRue (we've even named one of our dogs Lash LaRue); we chase each other for hours rustling cattle, being outlaws, delivering damsels from distress. Then my parents decide to buy my brothers guns. These are not "real" guns. They shoot BBs, copper pellets my brothers say will kill birds. Because I am a girl, I do not get a gun. Instantly I am relegated to the position of Indian. Now there appears a great distance between us. They shoot and shoot at everything with their new guns. I try to keep up with my bow and arrows.

One day while I am standing on top of our makeshift "garage"— pieces of tin nailed across some poles—holding my bow and arrow and looking out toward the fields, I feel an incredible blow in my right eye. I look down just in time to see my brother lower his gun.

Both brothers rush to my side. My eye stings, and I cover it with my   10
hand. "If you tell," they say, "we will get a whipping. You don't want that to happen, do you?" I do not. "Here is a piece of wire," says the older brother, picking it up from the roof; "say you stepped on one end of it and the other flew up and hit you." The pain is beginning to start. "Yes," I say. "Yes, I will say that is what happened." If I do not say this is what happened, I know my brothers will find ways to make me wish I had. But now I will say anything that gets me to my mother.

Confronted by our parents we stick to the lie agreed upon. They place me on a bench on the porch and I close my left eye while they examine the right. There is a tree growing from underneath the porch that climbs past the railing to the roof. It is the last thing my right eye sees. I watch as its trunk, its branches, and then its leaves are blotted out by the rising blood.

I am in shock. First there is intense fever, which my father tries to break using lily leaves bound around my head. Then there are chills: my mother tries to get me to eat soup. Eventually, I do not know how, my parents learn what has happened. A week after the "accident" they take me to see a doctor. "Why did you wait so long to come?" he asks, looking into my eye and shaking his head. "Eyes are sympathetic," he says. "If one is blind, the other will likely become blind too."

This comment of the doctor's terrifies me. But it is really how I look that bothers me most. Where the BB pellet struck there is a glob of whitish scar tissue, a hideous cataract, on my eye. Now when I stare at people—a favorite pastime, up to now—they will stare back. Not at the "cute" little girl, but at her scar. For six years I do not stare at anyone, because I do not raise my head.

Years later, in the throes of a mid-life crisis, I ask my mother and sister whether I changed after the "accident." "No," they say, puzzled. "What do you mean?"

What do I mean?   15

I am eight, and, for the first time, doing poorly in school, where I have been something of a whiz since I was four. We have just moved to the place where the "accident" occurred. We do not know any of the people around us because this is a different county. The only time I see the friends I knew is when we go back to our old church. The new school is the former state penitentiary. It is a large stone building, cold and drafty, crammed to over-flowing with boisterous, ill-disciplined children. On the third floor there is a huge circular imprint of some partition that has been torn out.

"What used to be here?" I ask a sullen girl next to me on our way past it to lunch.

"The electric chair," says she.

At night I have nightmares about the electric chair, and about all the people reputedly "fried" in it. I am afraid of the school, where all the students seem to be budding criminals.

"What's the matter with your eye?" they ask, critically.   20

When I don't answer (I cannot decide whether it was an "accident" or not), they shove me, insist on a fight.

My brother, the one who created the story about the wire, comes to my rescue. But then brags so much about "protecting" me, I become sick.

After months of torture at the school, my parents decide to send me back to our old community, to my old school. I live with my grandparents and the teacher they board. But there is no room for Phoebe, my cat. By the time my grandparents decide there *is* room, and I ask for my cat, she cannot be found. Miss Yarborough, the boarding teacher, takes me under her wing, and begins to teach me to play the piano. But soon she marries an African—a "prince," she says—and is whisked away to his continent.

At my old school there is at least one teacher who loves me. She is the teacher who "knew me before I was born" and bought my first baby clothes. It is she who makes life bearable. It is her presence that finally helps me turn on the one child at the school who continually calls me "one-eyed bitch." One day I simply grab him by his coat and beat him until I am satisfied. It is my teacher who tells me my mother is ill.

My mother is lying in bed in the middle of the day, something I have   25
never seen. She is in too much pain to speak. She has an abscess in her ear. I stand looking down on her, knowing that if she dies, I cannot live. She is being treated with warm oils and hot bricks held against her cheek. Finally a doctor comes. But I must go back to my grandparents' house. The weeks pass but I am hardly aware of it. All I know is that my mother might die, my father is not so jolly, my brothers still have their guns, and I am the one sent away from home.

"You did not change," they say.

Did I imagine the anguish of never looking up?

I am twelve. When relatives come to visit I hide in my room. My cousin Brenda, just my age, whose father works in the post office and whose mother is a nurse, comes to find me. "Hello," she says. And then she asks, looking at my recent school picture, which I did not want taken, and on which the "glob," as I think of it, is clearly visible, "You still can't see out of that eye?"

"No," I say, and flop back on the bed over my book.

That night, as I do almost every night, I abuse my eye. I rant and rave   30
at it, in front of the mirror. I plead with it to clear up before morning. I tell it I hate and despise it. I do not pray for sight. I pray for beauty.

"You did not change," they say.

I am fourteen and baby-sitting for my brother Bill, who lives in Boston. He is my favorite brother and there is a strong bond between us. Understanding my feelings of shame and ugliness he and his wife take me to a local hospital, where the "glob" is removed by a doctor named O. Henry. There is still a small bluish crater where the scar tissue was, but the ugly white stuff is gone. Almost immediately I become a different person from the girl who does not raise her head. Or so I think. Now that I've raised my head I win the boyfriend of my dreams. Now that I've raised my head I have plenty of friends. Now that I've raised my head classwork comes from my lips as faultlessly as Easter speeches did, and I leave high school as valedictorian, most popular student, and *queen*, hardly believing my luck. Ironically, the girl who was voted most beautiful in our class (and was) was later shot twice through the chest by a male companion, using a "real" gun, while she was pregnant. But that's another story in itself. Or is it?

"You did not change," they say.

It is now thirty years since the "accident." A beautiful journalist comes to visit and to interview me. She is going to write a cover story for her magazine that focuses on my latest book. "Decide how you want to look on the cover," she says. "Glamorous, or whatever."

Never mind "glamorous," it is the "whatever" that I hear. Suddenly   35
all I can think of is whether I will get enough sleep the night before the photography session: If I don't, my eye will be tired and wander, as blind eyes will.

At night in bed with my lover I think up reasons why I should not appear on the cover of a magazine. "My meanest critics will say I've sold out," I say. "My family will now realize I write scandalous books."

"But what's the real reason you don't want to do this?" he asks.

"Because in all probability," I say in a rush, "my eye won't be straight."

"It will be straight enough," he says. Then, "Besides, I thought you'd made your peace with that."

And I suddenly remember that I have.   40

I remember:

I am talking to my brother Jimmy, asking if he remembers anything unusual about the day I was shot. He does not know I consider that day the last time my father, with his sweet home remedy of cool lily leaves, chose me, and that I suffered and raged inside because of this. "Well," he says, "all I remember is standing by the side of the highway with Daddy, trying to flag down a car. A white man stopped, but when Daddy said he needed somebody to take his little girl to the doctor, he drove off."

I remember:

I am in the desert for the first time. I fall totally in love with it. I am so overwhelmed by its beauty, I confront for the first time, consciously, the meaning of the doctor's words years ago: "Eyes are sympathetic. If one is blind, the other will likely become blind too." I realize I have dashed about the world madly, looking at this, looking at that, storing up images against the fading of the light. *But I might have missed seeing the desert!* The shock of that possibility—and gratitude for over twenty-five years of sight—sends me literally to my knees. Poem after poem comes—which is perhaps how poets pray.

ON SIGHT

I am so thankful I have seen
The Desert
And the creatures in the desert
And the desert Itself.

The desert has its own moon
Which I have seen
With my own eye.
There is no flag on it.

Trees of the desert have arms
All of which are always up
That is because the moon is up
The sun is up
Also the sky
The Stars
Clouds
None with flags.

If there were flags, I doubt
the trees would point.
Would you?

But mostly, I remember this: 45

I am twenty-seven, and my baby daughter is almost three. Since her birth I have worried about her discovery that her mother's eyes are different from other people's. Will she be embarrassed? I think. What will she say? Every day she watches a television program called *Big Blue Marble*. It begins with a picture of the earth as it appears from the moon. It is bluish, a little battered-looking, but full of light, with whitish clouds swirling around it. Every time I see it I weep with love, as if it is a picture of Grandma's house. One day when I am putting Rebecca down for her nap, she suddenly focuses on my eye. Something inside me cringes, gets ready to try to protect myself. All children are cruel about physical differences, I know from experience, and that they don't always mean to be is another matter. I assume Rebecca will be the same.

But no-o-o-o. She studies my face intently as we stand, her inside and me outside her crib. She even holds my face maternally between her dimpled little hands. Then, looking every bit as serious and lawyerlike as her father, she says, as if it may just possibly have slipped my attention: "Mommy, there's a *world* in your eye." (As in, "Don't be alarmed, or do anything crazy.") And then, gently, but with great interest: "Mommy, where did you *get* that world in your eye?"

For the most part, the pain left then. (So what, if my brothers grew up to buy even more powerful pellet guns for their sons and to carry real guns themselves. So what, if a young "Morehouse[1] man" once nearly fell off the steps of Trevor Arnett Library because he thought my eyes were blue.) Crying and laughing I ran to the bathroom, while Rebecca mumbled and sang herself to sleep. Yes indeed, I realized, looking into the mirror. There *was* a world in my eye. And I saw that it was possible to love it: that in fact, for all it had taught me of shame and anger and inner vision, I *did* love it. Even to see it drifting out of orbit in boredom, or rolling up out of fatigue, not to mention floating back at attention in excitement (bearing witness, a friend has called it), deeply suitable to my personality, and even characteristic of me.

That night I dream I am dancing to Stevie Wonder's song "Always" (the name of the song is really "As," but I hear it as "Always"). As I dance, whirling and joyous, happier than I've ever been in my life, another bright-faced dancer joins me. We dance and kiss each other and hold each other through the night. The other dancer has obviously come through all right, as I have done. She is beautiful, whole, and free. And she is also me.

The Reader's Presence

1. In her opening paragraph, Walker refers to her father's "beautiful eyes." How does that phrase take on more significance in rereading? Can you find other words, phrases, or images that do the same? For example, why might Walker have mentioned the pain of having her hair combed?

2. Note that Walker uses the present tense throughout the essay. Why might this be unusual, given her subject? What effect does it have for both writer and reader? Try rewriting the opening paragraph in the past tense. What difference do you think it makes?

---

[1]*Morehouse:* Morehouse College, a black men's college in Atlanta, Georgia. —EDS.

3. What is the meaning of Walker's occasional italicized comments? What do they have in common? Whose comments are they? To whom do they seem addressed? What time frame do they seem to be in? What purpose do you think they serve?

40

E. B. White

Once More to the Lake

Elwyn Brooks White (1899–1985) started contributing to the New Yorker *soon after the magazine began publication in 1925, and in the "Talk of the Town" and other columns helped establish the magazine's reputation for precise and brilliant prose. Collections of his contributions can be found in* Every Day Is Saturday *(1934),* Quo Vadimus? *(1939), and* The Wild Flag *(1946). He also wrote essays for* Harper's *on a regular basis; these essays include "Once More to the Lake" and are collected in* One Man's Meat *(1941). In his comments on this work, the critic Jonathan Yardley observed that White is "one of the few writers of this or any century who has succeeded in transforming the ephemera of journalism into something that demands to be called literature."*

Capable of brilliant satire, White could also be sad and serious, as in his compilation of forty years of writing, Essays *(1977). Among his numerous awards and honors, White received the American Academy of Arts and Letters Gold Medal (1960), a Presidential Medal of Freedom (1963), and a National Medal for Literature (1971). He made a lasting contribution to children's literature with* Stuart Little *(1945),* Charlotte's Web *(1952), and* The Trumpet of the Swan *(1970).*

White has written, "I have always felt that the first duty of a writer was to ascend—to make flights, carrying others along if he could manage it." According to White, the writer needs not only courage, but also hope and faith to accomplish this goal: "Writing itself is an act of faith, nothing else. And it must be the writer, above all others, who keeps it alive—choked with laughter, or with pain."

One summer, along about 1904, my father rented a camp on a lake in Maine and took us all there for the month of August. We all got ringworm from some kittens and had to rub Pond's Extract on our arms and legs night and morning, and my father rolled over in a canoe with all his clothes on; but outside of that the vacation was a success and from then on none of us ever thought there was any place in the world like that lake in Maine. We returned summer after summer—always on August 1st for one month. I have since become a salt-water man, but sometimes in sum-

mer there are days when the restlessness of the tides and the fearful cold
of the sea water and the incessant wind that blows across the afternoon
and into the evening make me wish for the placidity of a lake in the
woods. A few weeks ago this feeling got so strong I bought myself a
couple of bass hooks and a spinner and returned to the lake where we
used to go, for a week's fishing and to revisit old haunts.

I took along my son, who had never had any fresh water up his nose
and who had seen lily pads only from train windows. On the journey
over to the lake I began to wonder what it would be like. I wondered how
time would have marred this unique, this holy spot—the coves and
streams, the hills that the sun set behind, the camps and the paths behind
the camps. I was sure that the tarred road would have found it out and I
wondered in what other ways it would be desolated. It is strange how
much you can remember about places like that once you allow your mind
to return into the grooves that lead back. You remember one thing, and
that suddenly reminds you of another thing. I guess I remembered clearest
of all the early mornings, when the lake was cool and motionless, remembered how the bedroom smelled of the lumber it was made of and the wet
woods whose scent entered through the screen. The partitions in the
camp were thin and did not extend clear to the top of the rooms, and as I
was always the first up I would dress softly so as not to wake the others,
and sneak out into the sweet outdoors and start out in the canoe, keeping
close along the shore in the long shadows of the pines. I remembered
being very careful never to rub my paddle against the gunwale for fear of
disturbing the stillness of the cathedral.

The lake had never been what you would call a wild lake. There were
cottages sprinkled about the shores, and it was in farming country although
the shores of the lake were quite heavily wooded. Some of the cottages were
owned by nearby farmers, and you would live at the shore and eat your
meals at the farmhouse. That's what our family did. But although it wasn't
wild, it was a fairly large and undisturbed lake and there were places in it
which, to a child at least, seemed infinitely remote and primeval.

I was right about the tar: It led to within half a mile of the shore. But
when I got back there, with my boy, and we settled into a camp near a
farmhouse and into the kind of summertime I had known, I could tell
that it was going to be pretty much the same as it had been before—I
knew it, lying in bed the first morning, smelling the bedroom, and hearing
the boy sneak quietly out and go off along the shore in a boat. I began to
sustain the illusion that he was I, and therefore, by simple transposition,
that I was my father. This sensation persisted, kept cropping up all the
time we were there. It was not an entirely new feeling, but in this setting it
grew much stronger. I seemed to be living a dual existence. I would be in
the middle of some simple act, I would be picking up a bait box or laying
down a table fork, or I would be saying something, and suddenly it
would be not I but my father who was saying the words or making the
gesture. It gave me a creepy sensation.

We went fishing the first morning. I felt the same damp moss cover-   5
ing the worms in the bait can, and saw the dragonfly alight on the tip of
my rod as it hovered a few inches from the surface of the water. It was
the arrival of this fly that convinced me beyond any doubt that everything
was as it always had been, that the years were a mirage and there had
been no years. The small waves were the same, chucking the rowboat
under the chin as we fished at anchor, and the boat was the same boat,
the same color green and the ribs broken in the same places, and under
the floor-boards the same fresh-water leavings and debris—the dead hell-
grammite, the wisps of moss, the rusty discarded fishhook, the dried
blood from yesterday's catch. We stared silently at the tips of our rods, at
the dragonflies that came and went. I lowered the tip of mine into the
water, tentatively, pensively dislodging the fly, which darted two feet
away, poised, darted two feet back, and came to rest again a little farther
up the rod. There had been no years between the ducking of this dragonfly and the other one—the one that was part of memory. I looked at the
boy, who was silently watching his fly, and it was my hands that held his
rod, my eyes watching. I felt dizzy and didn't know which rod I was at
the end of.

We caught two bass, hauling them in briskly as though they were
mackerel, pulling them over the side of the boat in a businesslike manner
without any landing net, and stunning them with a blow on the back of
the head. When we got back for a swim before lunch, the lake was exactly where we had left it, the same number of inches from the dock, and
there was only the merest suggestion of a breeze. This seemed an utterly
enchanted sea, this lake you could leave to its own devices for a few
hours and come back to, and find that it had not stirred, this constant
and trustworthy body of water. In the shallows, the dark, watersoaked
sticks and twigs, smooth and old, were undulating in clusters on the bottom against the clean ribbed sand, and the track of the mussel was plain.
A school of minnows swam by, each minnow with its small individual
shadow, doubling the attendance, so clear and sharp in the sunlight.
Some of the other campers were in swimming, along the shore, one of
them with a cake of soap, and the water felt thin and clear and unsub-
stantial. Over the years there had been this person with the cake of soap,
this cultist, and here he was. There had been no years.

Up to the farmhouse to dinner through the teeming, dusty field, the
road under our sneakers was only a two-track road. The middle track
was missing, the one with the marks of the hooves and splotches of dried,
flaky manure. There had always been three tracks to choose from in
choosing which track to walk in; now the choice was narrowed down to
two. For a moment I missed terribly the middle alternative. But the way
led past the tennis court, and something about the way it lay there in the
sun reassured me; the tape had loosened along the backline, the alleys
were green with plantains and other weeds, and the net (installed in June

and removed in September) sagged in the dry noon, and the whole place steamed with midday heat and hunger and emptiness. There was a choice of pie for dessert, and one was blueberry and one was apple, and the waitresses were the same country girls, there having been no passage of time, only the illusion of it as in a dropped curtain—the waitresses were still fifteen; their hair had been washed, that was the only difference—they had been to the movies and seen the pretty girls with the clean hair.

Summertime, oh summertime, pattern of life indelible, the fade-proof lake, the woods unshatterable, the pasture with the sweetfern and the juniper forever and ever, summer without end; this was the background, and the life along the shore was the design, the cottages with their innocent and tranquil design, their tiny docks with the flagpole and the American flag floating against the white clouds in the blue sky, the little paths over the roots of the trees leading from camp to camp and the paths leading back to the outhouses and the can of lime for sprinkling, and at the souvenir counters at the store the miniature birch-bark canoes and the post cards that showed things looking a little better than they looked. This was the American family at play, escaping the city heat, wondering whether the newcomers in the camp at the head of the cove were "common" or "nice," wondering whether it was true that the people who drove up for Sunday dinner at the farmhouse were turned away because there wasn't enough chicken.

It seemed to me, as I kept remembering all this, that those times and those summers had been infinitely precious and worth saving. There had been jollity and peace and goodness. The arriving (at the beginning of August) had been so big a business in itself, at the railway station the farm wagon drawn up, the first smell of the pine-laden air, the first glimpse of the smiling farmer, and the great importance of the trunks and your father's enormous authority in such matters, and the feel of the wagon under you for the long ten-mile haul, and at the top of the last long hill catching the first view of the lake after eleven months of not seeing this cherished body of water. The shouts and cries of the other campers when they saw you, and the trunks to be unpacked, to give up their rich burden. (Arriving was less exciting nowadays, when you sneaked up in your car and parked it under a tree near the camp and took out the bags and in five minutes it was all over, no fuss, no loud wonderful fuss about trunks).

Peace and goodness and jollity. The only thing that was wrong now, 10 really, was the sound of the place, an unfamiliar nervous sound of the outboard motors. This was the note that jarred, the one thing that would sometimes break the illusion and set the years moving. In those other summertimes all motors were inboard; and when they were at a little distance, the noise they made was a sedative, an ingredient of summer sleep. They were one-cylinder and two-cylinder engines, and some were make-and-break and some were jump-spark, but they all made a sleepy sound across the lake. The one-lungers throbbed and fluttered, and the twin-cylinder ones purred and purred, and that was a quiet sound too. But now the campers all had outboards. In the daytime, in the hot mornings, these motors made a petulant, irritable sound; at night, in the still evening when the afterglow lit the water, they whined about one's ears like mosquitoes. My boy loved our rented outboard, and his great desire was to achieve singlehanded mastery over it, and authority, and he soon learned the trick of choking it a little (but not too much), and the adjustment of the needle valve. Watching him I would remember the things you could do with the old one-cylinder engines with the heavy flywheel, how you could have it eating out of your hand if you got really close to it spiritually. Motor boats in those days didn't have clutches, and you would make a landing by shutting off the motor at the proper time and coasting in with a dead rudder. But there was a way of reversing them, if you learned the trick, by cutting the switch and putting it on again exactly on the final dying revolution of the flywheel, so that it would kick back against compression and begin reversing. Approaching a dock in a strong following breeze, it was difficult to slow up sufficiently by the ordinary coasting method, and if a boy felt he had complete mastery over his motor, he was tempted to keep it running beyond its time and then reverse it a few feet from the dock. It took a cool nerve, because if you threw the switch a twentieth of a second too soon you could catch the flywheel when it still had speed enough to go up past center, and the boat would leap ahead, charging bull-fashion at the dock.

We had a good week at the camp. The bass were biting well and the sun shone endlessly, day after day. We would be tired at night and lie down in the accumulated heat of the little bedrooms after the long hot day and the breeze would stir almost imperceptibly outside and the smell of the swamp drift in through the rusty screens. Sleep would come easily and in the morning the red squirrel would be on the roof, tapping out his gay routine. I kept remembering everything, lying in bed in the mornings—the small steamboat that had a long rounded stern like the lip of a Ubangi, and how quietly she ran on the moonlight sails, when the older boys played their mandolins and the girls sang and we ate doughnuts dipped in sugar, and how sweet the music was on the water in the shining night, and what it had felt like to think about girls then. After breakfast we would go up to the store and the things were in the same place—the minnows in a bottle, the plugs and spinners disarranged and pawed over by the youngsters from the boys' camp, the Fig Newtons and the Beeman's gum. Outside, the road was tarred and cars stood in front of the store. Inside, all was just as it had always been, except there was more Coca-Cola and not so much Moxie and root beer and birch beer and sarsaparilla. We would walk out with a bottle of pop apiece and sometimes the pop would backfire up our noses and hurt. We explored the streams, quietly, where the turtles slid off the sunny logs and dug their way into the soft bottom; and we lay on the town wharf and fed worms to the tame bass.

Everywhere we went I had trouble making out which was I, the one walking at my side, the one walking in my pants.

One afternoon while we were there at that lake a thunderstorm came up. It was like the revival of an old melodrama that I had seen long ago with childish awe. The second-act climax of the drama of the electrical disturbance over a lake in America had not changed in any important respect. This was the big scene, still the big scene. The whole thing was so familiar, the first feeling of oppression and heat and a general air around camp of not wanting to go very far away. In midafternoon (it was all the same) a curious darkening of the sky, and a lull in everything that had made life tick; and then the way the boats suddenly swung the other way at their moorings with the coming of a breeze out of the new quarter, and the premonitory rumble. Then the kettle drum, then the snare, then the bass drum and cymbals, then crackling light against the dark, and the gods grinning and licking their chops in the hills. Afterward the calm, the rain steadily rustling in the calm lake, the return of light and hope and spirits, and the campers running out in joy and relief to go swimming in the rain, their bright cries perpetuating the deathless joke about how they were getting simply drenched, and the children screaming with delight at the new sensation of bathing in the rain, and the joke about getting drenched linking the generations in a strong indestructible chain. And the comedian who waded in carrying an umbrella.

When the others went swimming my son said he was going in too. He pulled his dripping trunks from the line where they had hung all through the shower, and wrung them out. Languidly, and with no thought of going in, I watched him, his hard little body, skinny and bare, saw him wince slightly as he pulled up around his vitals the small, soggy, icy garment. As he buckled the swollen belt suddenly my groin felt the chill of death.

The Reader's Presence

1. In this essay, almost every word is deliberately chosen and intended to contribute to the meaning. Even the little words are important. For example, in paragraph 5, why does White say "*the* dragonfly" rather than "*a* dragonfly"? What difference does this word choice make?

2. In paragraph 4, White refers to a "creepy sensation." What is the basis of that sensation? Why is it "creepy"? In rereading the essay, pay close attention to other examples of fear and anxiety. What connection do these have to White's main theme?

3. Go through the essay and identify words and images having to do with the sensory details of seeing, hearing, touching, and so on. How do these details contribute to the overall effect of the essay? How do they anticipate White's final paragraph?

41

Richard Wright

The Ethics of Living Jim Crow

Richard Wright (1908–1960) experienced the life of poor black share-croppers in Mississippi as a child and the life of the urban poor in Chicago and New York as an adult. A novelist, short story writer, poet, and essayist, he spent his writing career coming to terms with poverty, violence, and racism. During the 1930s Wright wrote for communist newspapers and was active in the Communist party; he eventually became disillusioned with communism and severed his ties in 1944. In 1947 Wright moved to Paris and lived there until his death. Wright first gained critical acclaim with his depiction of the dehumanization of blacks in a racist society in his novel Native Son *(1940). "The Ethics of Living Jim Crow" is the introduction to* Uncle Tom's Children: Five Long Stories *1938.*

I

My first lesson in how to live as a Negro came when I was quite small. We were living in Arkansas. Our house stood behind the railroad tracks. Its skimpy yard was paved with black cinders. Nothing green ever grew in that yard. The only touch of green we could see was far away, beyond the tracks, over where the white folks lived. But cinders were good enough for me and I never missed the green growing things. And anyhow cinders were fine weapons. You could always have a nice hot war with huge black cinders. All you had to do was crouch behind the brick pillars of a house with your hands full of gritty ammunition. And the first woolly black head you saw pop out from behind another row of pillars was your target. You tried your very best to knock it off. It was great fun.

I never fully realized the appalling disadvantages of a cinder environ-ment till one day the gang to which I belonged found itself engaged in a war with the white boys who lived beyond the tracks. As usual we laid down our cinder barrage, thinking that this would wipe the white boys out. But they replied with a steady bombardment of broken bottles. We doubled our cinder barrage, but they hid behind trees, hedges, and the sloping embankments of their lawns. Having no such fortifications, we retreated to the brick pillars of our homes. During the retreat a broken milk bottle caught me behind the ear, opening a deep gash which bled profusely. The sight of blood pouring over my face completely demoralized our ranks. My fellow-combatants left me standing paralyzed in the center of the yard, and scurried for their homes. A kind neighbor saw me and rushed me to a doctor, who took three stitches in my neck.

I sat brooding on my front steps, nursing my wound and waiting for my mother to come from work. I felt that a grave injustice had been done me. It was all right to throw cinders. The greatest harm a cinder could do was leave a bruise. But broken bottles were dangerous; they left you cut, bleeding, and helpless.

When night fell, my mother came from the white folks' kitchen. I raced down the street to meet her. I could just feel in my bones that she would understand. I knew she would tell me exactly what to do next time. I grabbed her hand and babbled out the whole story. She examined my wound, then slapped me.

"How come yuh didn't hide?" she asked me. "How come yuh awways fightin'?"   5

I was outraged, and bawled. Between sobs I told her that I didn't have any trees or hedges to hide behind. There wasn't a thing I could have used as a trench. And you couldn't throw very far when you were hiding behind the brick pillars of a house. She grabbed a barrel stave, dragged me home, stripped me naked, and beat me till I had a fever of one hundred and two. She would smack my rump with the stave, and, while the skin was still smarting, impart to me gems of Jim Crow wisdom. I was never to throw cinders any more. I was never to fight any more wars. I was never, never, under any conditions, to fight *white* folks again. And they were absolutely right in clouting me with the broken milk bottle. Didn't I know she was working hard every day in the hot kitchens of the white folks to make money to take care of me? When was I ever going to learn to be a good boy? She couldn't be bothered with my fights. She finished by telling me that I ought to be thankful to God as long as I lived that they didn't kill me.

All that night I was delirious and could not sleep. Each time I closed my eyes I saw monstrous white faces suspended from the ceiling, leering at me.

From that time on, the charm of my cinder yard was gone. The green trees, the trimmed hedges, the cropped lawns grew very meaningful, became a symbol. Even today when I think of white folks, the hard, sharp outlines of white houses surrounded by trees, lawns, and hedges are present somewhere in the background of my mind. Through the years they grew into an overreaching symbol of fear.

It was a long time before I came in close contact with white folks again. We moved from Arkansas to Mississippi. Here we had the good fortune not to live behind the railroad tracks, or close to white neighborhoods. We lived in the very heart of the local Black Belt. There were black churches and black preachers; there were black schools and black teachers; black groceries and black clerks. In fact, everything was so solidly black that for a long time I did not even think of white folks, save in remote and vague terms. But this could not last forever. As one grows older one eats more. One's clothing costs more. When I finished grammar school I had to go to work. My mother could no longer feed and clothe me on her cooking job.

There is but one place where a black boy who knows no trade can get   10
a job, and that's where the houses and faces are white, where the trees, lawns, and hedges are green. My first job was with an optical company in Jackson, Mississippi. The morning I applied I stood straight and neat before the boss, answering all his questions with sharp yessirs and nosirs. I was very careful to pronounce my *sirs* distinctly, in order that he might know that I was polite, that I knew where I was, and that I knew he was a *white* man. I wanted that job badly.

He looked me over as though he were examining a prize poodle. He questioned me closely about my schooling, being particularly insistent about how much mathematics I had had. He seemed very pleased when I told him I had had two years of algebra.

"Boy, how would you like to try to learn something around here?" he asked me.

"I'd like it fine, sir," I said, happy. I had visions of "working my way up." Even Negroes have those visions.

"All right," he said. "Come on."

I followed him to the small factory.   15

"Pease," he said to a white man of about thirty-five, "this is Richard. He's going to work for us."

Pease looked at me and nodded.

I was then taken to a white boy of about seventeen.

"Morrie, this is Richard, who's going to work for us."

"Whut yuh sayin' there, boy!" Morrie boomed at me.   20

"Fine!" I answered.

The boss instructed these two to help me, teach me, give me jobs to do, and let me learn what I could in my spare time.

My wages were five dollars a week.

I worked hard, trying to please. For the first month I got along O.K. Both Pease and Morrie seemed to like me. But one thing was missing. And I kept thinking about it. I was not learning anything and nobody was volunteering to help me. Thinking they had forgotten that I was to learn something about the mechanics of grinding lenses, I asked Morrie one day to tell me about the work. He grew red.

"Whut yuh tryin' t' do, nigger, get smart?" he asked.   25

"Naw; I ain' tryin' t' git smart," I said.

"Well, don't, if yuh know whut's good for yuh!"

I was puzzled. Maybe he just doesn't want to help me, I thought. I went to Pease.

"Say, are yuh crazy, you black bastard?" Pease asked me, his gray eyes growing hard.

I spoke out, reminding him that the boss had said I was to be given a   30
chance to learn something.

"Nigger, you think you're *white,* don't you?"

"Naw, sir!"

"Well, you're acting mighty like it!"

"But, Mr. Pease, the boss said . . ."

Pease shook his fist in my face.   35

"This is a *white* man's work around here, and you better watch your-self!"

From then on they changed toward me. They said good-morning no more. When I was just a bit slow in performing some duty, I was called a lazy black son-of-a-bitch.

Once I thought of reporting all this to the boss. But the mere idea of what would happen to me if Pease and Morrie should learn that I had "snitched" stopped me. And after all the boss was a white man, too. What was the use?

The climax came at noon one summer day. Pease called me to his work-bench. To get to him I had to go between two narrow benches and stand with my back against a wall.

"Yes, sir," I said.   40

"Richard, I want to ask you something," Pease began pleasantly, not looking up from his work.

"Yes, sir," I said again.

Morrie came over, blocking the narrow passage between the benches. He folded his arms, staring at me solemnly.

I looked from one to the other, sensing that something was coming.

"Yes, sir," I said for the third time.   45

Pease looked up and spoke very slowly.

"Richard, *Mr.* Morrie here tells me you called me *Pease.*"

I stiffened. A void seemed to open up in me. I knew this was the show-down.

He meant that I had failed to call him Mr. Pease. I looked at Morrie. He was gripping a steel bar in his hands. I opened my mouth to speak, to protest, to assure Pease that I had never called him simply *Pease,* and that I had never had my intentions of doing so, when Morrie grabbed me by the collar, ramming my head against the wall.

"Now, be careful, nigger!" snarled Morrie, baring his teeth. "*I* heard   50
yuh call 'im *Pease!* 'N' if yuh say yuh didn't, yuh're callin' me a *lie,* see?"
He waved the steel bar threateningly.

If I had said: No, sir, Mr. Pease, I never called you *Pease,* I would have been automatically calling Morrie a liar. And if I had said: Yes, sir, Mr. Pease, I called you Pease, I would have been pleading guilty to having uttered the worst insult that a Negro can utter to a southern white man. I stood hesitating, trying to frame a neutral reply.

"Richard, I asked you a question!" said Pease. Anger was creeping into his voice.

"I don't remember calling you *Pease*, Mr. Pease," I said cautiously. "And if I did, I sure didn't mean . . ."

"You black son-of-a-bitch! You called me *Pease*, then!" he spat, slapping me till I bent sideways over a bench. Morrie was on top of me, demanding:

"Didn't yuh call 'im *Pease*? If yuh say yuh didn't, I'll rip yo' gut   55
string loose with this bar, yuh black granny dodger! Yuh can't call a white man a lie 'n' git erway with it, you black son-of-a-bitch!"

I wilted. I begged them not to bother me. I knew what they wanted. They wanted me to leave.

"I'll leave," I promised. I'll leave right *now*."

They gave me a minute to get out of the factory. I was warned not to show up again, or tell the boss.

I went.

When I told the folks at home what had happened, they called me a   60
fool. They told me that I must never again attempt to exceed my boundaries. When you are working for white folks, they said, you got to "stay in your place" if you want to keep working.

II

My Jim Crow education continued on my next job, which was portering in a clothing store. One morning, while polishing brass out front, the boss and his twenty-year-old son got out of their car and half dragged and half kicked a Negro woman into the store. A policeman standing at the corner looked on, twirling his night-stick. I watched out of the corner of my eye, never slackening the strokes of my chamois upon the brass. After a few minutes, I heard shrill screams coming from the rear of the store. Later the woman stumbled out, bleeding, crying, and holding her stomach. When she reached the end of the block, the policeman grabbed her and accused her of being drunk. Silently, I watched him throw her into a patrol wagon.

When I went to the rear of the store, the boss and his son were washing their hands at the sink. They were chuckling. The floor was bloody and strewn with wisps of hair and clothing. No doubt I must have appeared pretty shocked, for the boss slapped me reassuringly on the back.

"Boy, that's what we do to niggers when they don't want to pay their bills," he said, laughing.

His son looked at me and grinned.

"Here, hava cigarette," he said.   65

Not knowing what to do, I took it. He lit his and held the match for me. This was a gesture of kindness, indicating that even if they had beaten the poor old woman, they would not beat me if I knew enough to keep my mouth shut.

"Yes, sir," I said, and asked no questions.

After they had gone, I sat on the edge of a packing box and stared at the bloody floor till the cigarette went out.

That day at noon, while eating in a hamburger joint, I told my fellow Negro porters what had happened. No one seemed surprised. One fellow, after swallowing a huge bite, turned to me and asked:

"Huh! Is tha' all they did t' her?"   70

"Yeah. Wasn't tha' enough?" I asked.

"Shucks! Man, she's a lucky bitch!" he said, burying his lips deep into a juicy hamburger. "Hell, it's a wonder they didn't lay her when they got through."

III

I was learning fast, but not quite fast enough. One day, while I was delivering packages in the suburbs, my bicycle tire was punctured. I walked along the hot, dusty road, sweating and leading my bicycle by the handle-bars.

A car slowed at my side.

"What's the matter, boy?" a white man called.   75

I told him my bicycle was broken and I was walking back to town.

"That's too bad," he said. "Hop on the running board."

He stopped the car. I clutched hard at my bicycle with one hand and clung to the side of the car with the other.

"All set?"

"Yes, sir." I answered. The car started.   80

It was full of young white men. They were drinking. I watched the flask pass from mouth to mouth.

"Wanna drink, boy?" one asked.

I laughed as the wind whipped my face. Instinctively obeying the freshly planted precepts of my mother, I said:

"Oh, no!"

The words were hardly out of my mouth before I felt something hard   85
and cold smash me between the eyes. It was an empty whisky bottle. I saw stars, and fell backwards from the speeding car into the dust of the road, my feet becoming entangled in the steel spokes of my bicycle. The white men piled out and stood over me.

"Nigger, ain' yuh learned no better sense'n tha' yet?" asked the man who hit me. "Ain' yuh learned t' say *sir* t' a white man yet?"

Dazed, I pulled to my feet. My elbows and legs were bleeding. Fists doubled, the white man advanced, kicking my bicycle out of the way.

"Aw, leave the bastard alone. He's got enough," said one.

They stood looking at me. I rubbed my shins, trying to stop the flow of blood. No doubt they felt a sort of contemptuous pity, for one asked:

"Yuh wanna ride t' town now, nigger? Yuh reckon yuh know enough   90
t' ride now?"

"I wanna walk," I said, simply.

Maybe it sounded funny. They laughed.

"Well, walk, yuh black son-of-a-bitch!"

When they left they comforted me with:

"Nigger, yuh sho better be damn glad it wuz us yuh talked t' tha'   95
way. Yuh're a lucky bastard, 'cause if yuh'd said tha' t' somebody else,
yuh might've been a dead nigger now."

IV

Negroes who have lived South know the dread of being caught alone
upon the streets in white neighborhoods after the sun has set. In such a
simple situation as this the plight of the Negro in America is graphically
symbolized. While white strangers may be in these neighborhoods trying
to get home, they can pass unmolested. But the color of a Negro's skin
makes him easily recognizable, makes him suspect, converts him into a
defenseless target.

Late one Saturday night I made some deliveries in a white neighborhood. I was pedaling my bicycle back to the store as fast as I could, when
a police car, swerving toward me, jammed me into the curbing.

"Get down and put up your hands!" the policemen ordered.

I did. They climbed out of the car, guns drawn, faces set, and advanced slowly.

"Keep still!" they ordered.   100

I reached my hands higher. They searched my pockets and packages.
They seemed dissatisfied when they could find nothing incriminating. Finally, one of them said:

"Boy, tell your boss not to send you out in white neighborhoods after
sundown."

As usual, I said:

"Yes, sir."

V

My next job was as hall-boy in a hotel. Here my Jim Crow education   105
broadened and deepened. When the bell-boys were busy, I was often
called to assist them. As many of the rooms in the hotel were occupied by
prostitutes, I was constantly called to carry them liquor and cigarettes.
These women were nude most of the time. They did not bother about
clothing, even for bell-boys. When you went into their rooms, you were
supposed to take their nakedness for granted, as though it startled you no
more than a blue vase or a red rug. Your presence awoke in them no
sense of shame, for you were not regarded as human. If they were alone,
you could steal sidelong glimpses at them. But if they were receiving men,
not a flicker of your eyelids could show. I remember one incident vividly.

A new woman, a huge, snowy-skinned blonde, took a room on my floor. I was sent to wait upon her. She was in bed with a thick-set man; both were nude and uncovered. She said she wanted some liquor and slid out of bed and waddled across the floor to get her money from a dresser drawer. I watched her.

"Nigger, what in hell you looking at?" the white man asked me, raising himself upon his elbows.

"Nothing," I answered, looking miles deep into the blank wall of the room.

"Keep your eyes where they belong, if you want to be healthy!" he said.

"Yes, sir."

VI

One of the bell-boys I knew in this hotel was keeping steady company 110 with one of the Negro maids. Out of a clear sky the police descended upon his home and arrested him, accusing him of bastardy. The poor boy swore he had had no intimate relations with the girl. Nevertheless, they forced him to marry her. When the child arrived, it was found to be much lighter in complexion than either of the two supposedly legal parents. The white men around the hotel made a great joke of it. They spread the rumor that some white cow must have scared the poor girl while she was carrying the baby. If you were in their presence when this explanation was offered, you were supposed to laugh.

VII

One of the bell-boys was caught in bed with a white prostitute. He was castrated and run out of town. Immediately after this all the bell-boys and hall-boys were called together and warned. We were given to understand that the boy who had been castrated was a "mighty, mighty lucky bastard." We were impressed with the fact that next time the management of the hotel would not be responsible for the lives of "trouble-makin' niggers." We were silent.

VIII

One night, just as I was about to go home, I met one of the Negro maids. She lived in my direction, and we fell in to walk part of the way home together. As we passed the white night-watchman, he slapped the maid on her buttock. I turned around, amazed. The watchman looked at me with a long, hard, fixed-under state. Suddenly he pulled his gun and asked:

"Nigger, don't yuh like it?"

I hesitated.

"I asked yuh don't yuh like it?" he asked again, stepping forward.   115

"Yes, sir," I mumbled.

"Talk like it, then!"

"Oh, yes, sir!" I said with as much heartiness as I could muster.

Outside, I walked ahead of the girl, ashamed to face her. She caught up with me and said:

"Don't be a fool! Yuh couldn't help it!"   120

This watchman boasted of having killed two Negroes in self-defense.

Yes, in spite of all this, the life of the hotel ran with an amazing smoothness. It would have been impossible for a stranger to detect anything. The maids, the hall-boys, and the bell-boys were all smiles. They had to be.

IX

I had learned my Jim Crow lessons so thoroughly that I kept the hotel job till I left Jackson for Memphis. It so happened that while in Memphis I applied for a job at a branch of the optical company. I was hired. And for some reason, as long as I worked there, they never brought my past against me.

Here my Jim Crow education assumed quite a different form. It was no longer brutally cruel, but subtly cruel. Here I learned to lie, to steal, to dissemble. I learned to play that dual role which every Negro must play if he wants to eat and live.

For example, it was almost impossible to get a book to read. It was   125
assumed that after a Negro had imbibed what scanty schooling the state furnished he had no further need for books. I was always borrowing books from men on the job. One day I mustered enough courage to ask one of the men to let me get books from the library in his name. Surprisingly, he consented. I cannot help but think that he consented because he was a Roman Catholic and felt a vague sympathy for Negroes, being himself an object of hatred. Armed with a library card, I obtained books in the following manner: I would write a note to the librarian, saying: "Please let this nigger boy have the following books." I would then sign it with the white man's name.

When I went to the library, I would stand at the desk, hat in hand, looking as unbookish as possible. When I received the books desired I would take them home. If the books listed in the note happened to be out, I would sneak into the lobby and forge a new one. I never took any chances guessing with the white librarian about what the fictitious white man would want to read. No doubt if any of the white patrons had suspected that some of the volumes they enjoyed had been in the home of a Negro, they would not have tolerated it for an instant.

The factory force of the optical company in Memphis was much larger than that in Jackson, and more urbanized. At least they liked to talk, and would engage the Negro help in conversation whenever possible. By this means I found that many subjects were taboo from the white man's point of view. Among the topics they did not like to discuss with Negroes were the following: American white women; the Ku Klux Klan; France, and how Negro soldiers fared while there; French women; Jack Johnson; the entire northern part of the United States; the Civil War; Abraham Lincoln; U.S. Grant; General Sherman; Catholics; the Pope; Jews; the Republican Party; slavery; social equality; Communism; Socialism; the 13th and 14th Amendments to the Constitution; or any topic calling for positive knowledge or manly self-assertion on the part of the Negro. The most accepted topics were sex and religion.

There were many times when I had to exercise a great deal of ingenuity to keep out of trouble. It is a southern custom that all men must take off their hats when they enter an elevator. And especially did this apply to us blacks with rigid force. One day I stepped into an elevator with my arms full of packages. I was forced to ride with my hat on. Two white men stared at me coldly. Then one of them very kindly lifted my hat and placed it upon my armful of packages. Now the most accepted response for a Negro to make under such circumstances is to look at the white man out of the corner of his eye and grin. To have said: "Thank you!" would have made the white man *think* that you *thought* you were receiving from him a personal service. For such an act I have seen Negroes take a blow in the mouth. Finding the first alternative distasteful, and the second dangerous, I hit upon an acceptable course of action which fell safely between these two poles. I immediately — no sooner than my hat was lifted — pretended that my packages were about to spill, and appeared deeply distressed with keeping them in my arms. In this fashion I evaded having to acknowledge his service, and, in spite of adverse circumstances, salvaged a slender shred of personal pride.

How do Negroes feel about the way they have to live? How do they discuss it when alone among themselves? I think this question can be answered in a single sentence. A friend of mine who ran an elevator once told me:

"Lawd, man! Ef it wuzn't fer them polices 'n' them ol' lynch-mobs,   130 there wouldn't be nothin' but uproar down here!"

The Reader's Presence

1. Wright is a highly accomplished writer, yet his style is outwardly straightforward and colloquial. Why might he have chosen to tell his story in an "everyday" rather than in a more "literary" language?

2. The writer relates his experiences in patient, vivid scenes. How does the reader's "education" parallel Wright's own? How might Wright's essay compare to a third-person, historical, or purely statistical account? Which approach would you find most convincing, and why?

3. Compare this piece to Malcolm X's "Homeboy" (page 159). How does Wright's "education" resemble Malcolm X's? How does it differ? How do the writers' stylistic renderings of this "education" differ? You might also compare Wright's essay to Maya Angelou's account of growing up in a racist environment (see page 57). How does the sensitive issue of names arise in both Wright's and Angelou's experiences?

Part III

Expository Writing: Shaping Information

42

Gloria Anzaldúa

How to Tame a Wild Tongue

Gloria Anzaldúa, born in south Texas in 1942, is a poet, cultural theorist, essayist, and editor who uses her writings to explore issues such as racism, Chicano culture, lesbianism, and feminism. In addition to writing and editing, Anzaldúa has taught creative writing, literature, and feminist studies at San Francisco State University, Oakes College at the University of California in Santa Cruz, and Norwich University. She is coeditor of This Bridge Called My Back: Writings by Radical Women of Color *(1981), which received the Before Columbus Foundation American Book Award. She is also the editor of* Making Face, Making Soul/ Haciendo Caras: Creative and Critical Perspectives by Women of Color *(1990), and, most recently, coeditor of* Cassell's Encyclopedia of Queer Myth, Symbol, and Spirit: Gay, Lesbian, Bisexual, and Transgender Lore *(1997). She is the author of two bilingual children's books,* Friends from the Other Side/Amigos del Otro Lado *(1993) and* Prietita and the Ghost Woman/Prietita y la Ilorona *(1995). Her first book,* Borderlands/La Frontera: The New Mestiza *(1987), from which "How to Tame a Wild Tongue" is taken, is a blend of poetry, memoir, and historical analysis. Anzaldúa lives in Santa Cruz, California, and frequently participates in panel discussions, teaches workshops, and gives lectures.*

"We're going to have to control your tongue," the dentist says, pulling out all the metal from my mouth. Silver bits plop and tinkle into the basin. My mouth is a motherlode.

The dentist is cleaning out my roots. I get a whiff of the stench when I gasp. "I can't cap that tooth yet, you're still draining," he says.

"We're going to have to do something about your tongue," I hear the anger rising in his voice. My tongue keeps pushing out the wads of cotton, pushing back the drills, the long thin needles. "I've never seen anything as strong or as stubborn," he says. And I think how do you tame a wild tongue, train it to be quiet, how do you bridle and saddle it? How do you make it lie down?

"Who is to say that robbing a people of its language is less violent than war?"

—Ray Gwyn Smith[1]

I remember being caught speaking Spanish at recess—that was good for three licks on the knuckles with a sharp ruler. I remember being sent to the corner of the classroom for "talking back" to the Anglo teacher when all I was trying to do was tell her how to pronounce my name. "If you want to be American, speak 'American.' If you don't like it, go back to Mexico where you belong."

"I want you to speak English. *Pa' hallar buen trabajo tienes que*   5
saber hablar el inglés bien. Qué vale toda tu educación si todavía hablas inglés con un 'accent,'" my mother would say, mortified that I spoke English like a Mexican. At Pan American University, I, and all Chicano students were required to take two speech classes. Their purpose: to get rid of our accents.

Attacks on one's form of expression with the intent to censor are a violation of the First Amendment. *El Anglo con cara de inocente nos arrancó la lengua.* Wild tongues can't be tamed, they can only be cut out.

OVERCOMING THE TRADITION OF SILENCE

> *Ahogadas, escupimos el oscuro.*
> *Peleando con nuestra propia sombra*
> *el silencio nos sepulta.*

En boca cerrada no entran moscas. "Flies don't enter a closed mouth" is a saying I kept hearing when I was a child. *Ser habladora* was to be a gossip and a liar, to talk too much. *Muchachitas bien criadas,* well-bred girls don't answer back. *Es una falta de respeto* to talk back to one's mother or father. I remember one of the sins I'd recite to the priest in the confession box the few times I went to confession: talking back to my mother, *hablar pa' 'tras, repelar. Hocicona, repelona, chismosa,* having a big mouth, questioning, carrying tales are all signs of being *mal criada.* In my culture they are all words that are derogatory if applied to women—I've never heard them applied to men.

The first time I heard two women, a Puerto Rican and a Cuban, say the word *"nosotras,"* I was shocked. I had not known the word existed. Chicanas use *nosotros* whether we're male or female. We are robbed of our female being by the masculine plural. Language is a male discourse.

And our tongues have become
dry   the wilderness has

[1]Ray Gwyn Smith, *Moorland is Cold Country,* unpublished book.

dried out our tongues   and
we have forgotten speech.

> —Irena Klepfisz[2]

Even our own people, other Spanish speakers *nos quieren poner candados en la boca.* They would hold us back with their bag of *reglas de academia.*

OYÉ COMO LADRA: EL LENGUAJE DE LA FRONTERA

Quien tiene boca se equivoca.

> —Mexican saying

"*Pocho,* cultural traitor, you're speaking the oppressor's language by   10
speaking English, you're ruining the Spanish language," I have been accused by various Latinos and Latinas. Chicano Spanish is considered by the purist and by most Latinos deficient, a mutilation of Spanish.

But Chicano Spanish is a border tongue which developed naturally. Change, *evolución, enriquecimiento de palabras nuevas por invención o adopción* have created variants of Chicano Spanish, *un nuevo lenguaje. Un lenguaje que corresponde a un modo de vivir.* Chicano Spanish is not incorrect, it is a living language.

For people who are neither Spanish nor live in a country in which Spanish is the first language; for a people who live in a country in which English is the reigning tongue but who are not Anglo; for a people who cannot entirely identify with either standard (formal, Castillian) Spanish nor standard English, what recourse is left to them but to create their own language? A language which they can connect their identity to, one capable of communicating the realities and values true to themselves—a language with terms that are neither *español ni inglés,* but both. We speak a patois, a forked tongue, a variation of two languages.

Chicano Spanish sprang out of the Chicanos' need to identify ourselves as a distinct people. We needed a language with which we could communicate with ourselves, a secret language. For some of us, language is a homeland closer than the Southwest—for many Chicanos today live in the Midwest and the East. And because we are a complex, heterogeneous people, we speak many languages. Some of the languages we speak are:

1. Standard English
2. Working class and slang English

---

[2]Irena Klepfisz, "*Di rayze aheym*/The Journey Home," in *The Tribe of Dina: A Jewish Women's Anthology,* Melanie Kaye/Kantrowitz and Irena Klepfisz, eds. (Montpelier, VT: Sinister Wisdom Books, 1986), 49.

3. Standard Spanish
4. Standard Mexican Spanish
5. North Mexican Spanish dialect
6. Chicano Spanish (Texas, New Mexico, Arizona and California have regional variations)
7. Tex-Mex
8. *Pachuco* (called *caló*)

My "home" tongues are the languages I speak with my sister and brothers, with my friends. They are the last five listed, with 6 and 7 being closest to my heart. From school, the media and job situations, I've picked up standard and working class English. From Mamagrande Locha and from reading Spanish and Mexican literature, I've picked up Standard Spanish and Standard Mexican Spanish. From *los recién llegados,* Mexican immigrants, and *braceros,* I learned the North Mexican dialect. With Mexicans I'll try to speak either Standard Mexican Spanish or the North Mexican dialect. From my parents and Chicanos living in the Valley, I picked up Chicano Texas Spanish, and I speak it with my mom, younger brother (who married a Mexican and who rarely mixes Spanish with English), aunts and older relatives.

With Chicanas from *Nuevo México* or *Arizona* I will speak Chicano   15
Spanish a little, but often they don't understand what I'm saying. With most California Chicanas I speak entirely in English (unless I forget). When I first moved to San Francisco, I'd rattle off something in Spanish, unintentionally embarrassing them. Often it is only with another Chicana *tejana* that I can talk freely.

Words distorted by English are known as anglicisms or *pochismos.* The *pocho* is an anglicized Mexican or American of Mexican origin who speaks Spanish with an accent characteristic of North Americans and who distorts and reconstructs the language according to the influence of English.[3] Tex-Mex, or Spanglish, comes most naturally to me. I may switch back and forth from English to Spanish in the same sentence or in the same word. With my sister and my brother Nune and with Chicano *tejano* contemporaries I speak in Tex-Mex.

From kids and people my own age I picked up *Pachuco. Pachuco* (the language of the zoot suiters) is a language of rebellion, both against Standard Spanish and Standard English. It is a secret language. Adults of the culture and outsiders cannot understand it. It is made up of slang words from both English and Spanish. *Ruca* means girl or woman, *vato* means guy or dude, *chale* means no, *simón* means yes, *churro* is sure, talk is *periquiar, pigionear* means petting, *que gacho* means how nerdy, *ponte águila* means

---

[3]R. C. Ortega, *Dialectología Del Barrio,* trans. Hortencia S. Alwan (Los Angeles, CA: R. C. Ortega Publisher & Bookseller, 1977), 132.

watch out, death is called *la pelona*. Through lack of practice and not having others who can speak it, I've lost most of the *Pachuco* tongue.

CHICANO SPANISH

Chicanos, after 250 years of Spanish/Anglo colonization have developed significant differences in the Spanish we speak. We collapse two adjacent vowels into a single syllable and sometimes shift the stress in certain words such as *maíz/maiz, cohete/cuete*. We leave out certain consonants when they appear between vowels: *lado/lao, mojado/majao*. Chicanos from South Texas pronounce *f* as *j* as in *jue (fue)*. Chicanos use "archaisms," words that are no longer in the Spanish language, words that have been evolved out. We say *semos, truje, haiga, ansina,* and *naiden*. We retain the "archaic" *j*, as in *jalar*, that derives from an earlier *h*, (the French *halar* or the Germanic *halon* which was lost to standard Spanish in the 16th century), but which is still found in several regional dialects such as the one spoken in South Texas. (Due to geography, Chicanos from the Valley of South Texas were cut off linguistically from other Spanish speakers. We tend to use words that the Spaniards brought over from Medieval Spain. The majority of the Spanish colonizers in Mexico and the Southwest came from Extremadura—Hernán Cortés was one of them—and Andalucía. Andalucians pronounce *ll* like a *y*, and their *d*'s tend to be absorbed by adjacent vowels: *tirado* becomes *tirao*. They brought *el lenguaje popular, dialectos y regionalismos*.[4])

Chicanos and other Spanish speakers also shift *ll* to *y* and *z* to *s*.[5] We leave out initial syllables, saying *tar* for *estar, toy* for *estoy, hora* for *ahora* (*cubanos* and *puertorriqueños* also leave out initial letters of some words.) We also leave out the final syllable such as *pa* for para. The intervocalic *y*, the *ll* as in *tortilla, ella, botella*, gets replaced by *tortia* or *tortiya, ea, botea*. We add an additional syllable at the beginning of certain words: *atocar* for *tocar, agastar* for *gastar*. Sometimes we'll say *lavaste las vacijas*, other times *lavates* (substituting the *ates* verb endings for the *aste*).

We use anglicisms, words borrowed from English: *bola* from ball, *carpeta* from carpet, *máchina de lavar* (instead of *lavadora*) from washing machine. Tex-Mex argot, created by adding a Spanish sound at the beginning or end of an English word such as *cookiar* for cook, *watchar* for watch, *parkiar* for park, and *rapiar* for rape, is the result of the pressures on Spanish speakers to adapt to English.

We don't use the word *vosotros/as* or its accompanying verb form. We don't say *claro* (to mean yes), *imagínate,* or *me emociona,* unless we

20

---

[4] Eduardo Hernández-Chávez, Andrew D. Cohen, and Anthony F. Beltramo, *El Lenguaje de los Chicanos: Regional and Social Characteristics of Language Used By Mexican Americans* (Arlington, VA: Center for Applied Linguistics, 1975), 39.
[5] Hernández-Chávez, xvii.

picked up Spanish from Latinas, out of a book, or in a classroom. Other Spanish-speaking groups are going through the same, or similar, development in their Spanish.

LINGUISTIC TERRORISM

> *Deslenguadas. Somos los del español deficiente.* We are your lingistic nightmare, your linguistic aberration, your linguistic *mestisaje,* the subject of your *burla.* Because we speak with tongues of fire we are culturally crucified. Racially, culturally and linguistically *somos huérfanos*—we speak an orphan tongue.

Chicanas who grew up speaking Chicano Spanish have internalized the belief that we speak poor Spanish. It is illegitimate, a bastard language. And because we internalize how our language has been used against us by the dominant culture, we use our language differences against each other.

Chicana feminists often skirt around each other with suspicion and hesitation. For the longest time I couldn't figure it out. Then it dawned on me. To be close to another Chicana is like looking into the mirror. We are afraid of what we'll see there. *Pena.* Shame. Low estimation of self. In childhood we are told that our language is wrong. Repeated attacks on our native tongue diminish our sense of self. The attacks continue throughout our lives.

Chicanas feel uncomfortable talking in Spanish to Latinas, afraid of their censure. Their language was not outlawed in their countries. They had a whole lifetime of being immersed in their native tongue; generations, centuries in which Spanish was a first language, taught in school, heard on radio and TV, and read in the newspaper.

If a person, Chicana or Latina, has a low estimation of my native   25
tongue, she also has a low estimation of me. Often with *mexicanas y latinas* we'll speak English as a neutral language. Even among Chicanas we tend to speak English at parties or conferences. Yet, at the same time, we're afraid the other will think we're *agringadas* because we don't speak Chicano Spanish. We oppress each other trying to out-Chicano each other, vying to be the "real" Chicanas, to speak like Chicanos. There is no one Chicano language just as there is no one Chicano experience. A monolingual Chicana whose first language is English or Spanish is just as much a Chicana as one who speaks several variants of Spanish. A Chicana from Michigan or Chicago or Detroit is just as much a Chicana as one from the southwest. Chicano Spanish is as diverse linguistically as it is regionally.

By the end of this century, Spanish speakers will comprise the biggest minority group in the U.S., a country where students in high schools and colleges are encouraged to take French classes because French is considered more "cultured." But for a language to remain alive it must be used.[6]

---

[6]Irena Klepfisz, "Secular Jewish Identity: Yidishkayt in America," in *The Tribe of Dina,* Kaye/Kantrowitz and Klepfisz, eds., 43.

By the end of this century English, and not Spanish, will be the mother tongue of most Chicanos and Latinos.

So, if you want to really hurt me, talk badly about my language. Ethnic identity is twin skin to linguistic identity—I am my language. Until I can take pride in my language, I cannot take pride in myself. Until I can accept as legitimate Chicano Texas Spanish, Tex-Mex and all the other languages I speak, I cannot accept the legitimacy of myself. Until I am free to write bilingually and to switch codes without having always to translate, while I still have to speak English or Spanish when I would rather speak Spanglish, and as long as I have to accommodate the English speakers rather than having them accommodate me, my tongue will be illegitimate.

I will no longer be made to feel ashamed of existing. I will have my voice: Indian, Spanish, white. I will have my serpent's tongue—my woman's voice, my sexual voice, my poet's voice. I will overcome the tradition of silence.

> My fingers
> move sly against your palm
> Like women everywhere, we speak in code. . . .
>
> —Melanie Kaye/Kantrowitz[7]

"VISTAS," CORRIDOS, Y COMIDA: MY NATIVE TONGUE

In the 1960s, I read my first Chicano novel. It was *City of Night* by John Rechy, a gay Texan, son of a Scottish father and a Mexican mother. For days I walked around in stunned amazement that a Chicano could write and could get published. When I read *I Am Joaquín*[8] I was surprised to see a bilingual book by a Chicano in print. When I saw poetry written in Tex-Mex for the first time, a feeling of pure joy flashed through me. I felt like we really existed as a people. In 1971, when I started teaching High School English to Chicano students, I tried to supplement the required texts with works by Chicanos, only to be reprimanded and forbidden to do so by the principal. He claimed that I was supposed to teach "American" and English literature. At the risk of being fired, I swore my students to secrecy and slipped in Chicano short stories, poems, a play. In graduate school, while working toward a Ph.D., I had to "argue" with one advisor after the other, semester after semester, before I was allowed to make Chicano literature an area of focus.

---

[7]Melanie Kaye/Kantrowitz, "Sign," in *We Speak In Code: Poems and Other Writings* (Pittsburgh, PA: Motheroot Publications, Inc., 1980), 85.

[8] Rodolfo Gonzales, *I Am Joaquín/Yo Soy Joaquín* (New York, NY: Bantam Books, 1972). It was first published in 1967.

Even before I read books by Chicanos or Mexicans, it was the Mexican movies I saw at the drive-in—the Thursday night special of $1.00 a carload—that gave me a sense of belonging. *"Vámonos a las vistas,"* my mother would call out and we'd all—grandmother, brothers, sister and cousins—squeeze into the car. We'd wolf down cheese and bologna white bread sandwiches while watching Pedro Infante in melodramatic tear-jerkers like *Nosotros los pobres,* the first "real" Mexican movie (that was not an imitation of European movies). I remember seeing *Cuando los hijos se van* and surmising that all Mexican movies played up the love a mother has for her children and what ungrateful sons and daughters suffer when they are not devoted to their mothers. I remember the singing-type "westerns" of Jorge Negrete and Miquel Aceves Mejía. When watching Mexican movies, I felt a sense of homecoming as well as alienation. People who were to amount to something didn't go to Mexican movies, or *bailes* or tune their radios to *bolero, rancherita,* and *corrido* music.

The whole time I was growing up, there was *norteño* music sometimes called North Mexican border music, or Tex-Mex music, or Chicano music, or *cantina* (bar) music. I grew up listening to *conjuntos,* three- or four-piece bands made up of folk musicians playing guitar, *bajo sexto,* drums and button accordion, which Chicanos had borrowed from the German immigrants who had come to Central Texas and Mexico to farm and build breweries. In the Rio Grande Valley, Steve Jordan and Little Joe Hernández were popular, and Flaco Jiménez was the accordian king. The rhythms of Tex-Mex music are those of the polka, also adapted from the Germans, who in turn had borrowed the polka from the Czechs and Bohemians.

I remember the hot, sultry evenings when *corridos*—songs of love and death on the Texas-Mexican borderlands—reverberated out of cheap amplifiers from the local *cantinas* and wafted in through my bedroom window.

Corridos first became widely used along the South Texas/Mexican border during the early conflict between Chicanos and Anglos. The *corridos* are usually about Mexican heroes who do valiant deeds against the Anglo oppressors. Pancho Villa's song, *"La cucaracha,"* is the most famous one. *Corridos* of John F. Kennedy and his death are still very popular in the Valley. Older Chicanos remember Lydia Mendoza, one of the great border *corrido* singers who was called *la Gloria de Tejas.* Her *"El tango negro,"* sung during the Great Depression, made her a singer of the people. The everpresent *corridos* narrated one hundred years of border history, bringing news of events as well as entertaining. These folk musicians and folk songs are our chief cultural myth-makers, and they made our hard lives seem bearable.

I grew up feeling ambivalent about our music. Country-western and rock-and-roll had more status. In the 50s and 60s, for the slightly educated and *agringado* Chicanos, there existed a sense of shame at being caught listening to our music. Yet I couldn't stop my feet from thumping to the music, could not stop humming the words, nor hide from myself the exhilaration I felt when I heard it.

There are more subtle ways that we internalize identification, espe-   35
cially in the forms of images and emotions. For me food and certain smells are tied to my identity, to my homeland. Woodsmoke curling up to an immense blue sky; woodsmoke perfuming my grandmother's clothes, her skin. The stench of cow manure and the yellow patches on the ground; the crack of a .22 rifle and the reek of cordite. Homemade white cheese sizzling in a pan, melting inside a folded *tortilla*. My sister Hilda's hot, spicy *menudo, chile colorado* making it deep red, pieces of *panza* and hominy floating on top. My brother Carito barbequing *fajitas* in the backyard. Even now and 3,000 miles away, I can see my mother spicing the ground beef, pork and venison with *chile*. My mouth salivates at the thought of the hot steaming *tamales* I would be eating if I were home.

SI LE PREGUNTAS A MI MAMÁ, "¿QUÉ ERES?"

> "Identity is the essential core of who
> we are as individuals, the conscious
> experience of the self inside."
>
> —Kaufman[9]

Nosotros los Chicanos straddle the borderlands. On one side of us, we are constantly exposed to the Spanish of the Mexicans, on the other side we hear the Anglos' incessant clamoring so that we forget our language. Among ourselves we don't say *nosotros los americanos, o nosotros los españoles, o nosotros los hispanos*. We say *nosotros los mexicanos* (by *mexicanos* we do not mean citizens of Mexico; we do not mean a national identity, but a racial one). We distinguish between *mexicanos del otro lado* and *mexicanos de este lado*. Deep in our hearts we believe that being Mexican has nothing to do with which country one lives in. Being Mexican is a state of soul—not one of mind, not one of citizenship. Neither eagle nor serpent, but both. And like the ocean, neither animal respects borders.

> *Dime con quien andas y te diré quien eres.*
> (Tell me who your friends are and I'll tell you who you are.)
>
> —Mexican saying

Si le preguntas a mi mamá, "¿Qué eres?" te dirá, "Soy mexicana." My brothers and sister say the same. I sometimes will answer "*soy mexi-*

[9]Kaufman, 68.

cana" and at others will say *"soy Chicana" o "soy tejana."* But I identified as "Raza" before I ever identified as *"mexicana"* or "Chicana."

As a culture, we call ourselves Spanish when referring to ourselves as a linguistic group and when copping out. It is then that we forget our predominant Indian genes. We are 70–80% Indian.[10] We call ourselves Hispanic[11] or Spanish-American or Latin American or Latin when linking ourselves to other Spanish-speaking peoples of the Western hemisphere and when copping out. We call ourselves Mexican-American[12] to signify we are neither Mexican nor American, but more the noun "American" than the adjective "Mexican" (and when copping out).

Chicanos and other people of color suffer economically for not acculturating. This voluntary (yet forced) alienation makes for psychological conflict, a kind of dual identity—we don't identify with the Anglo-American cultural values and we don't totally identify with the Mexican cultural values. We are a synergy of two cultures with various degrees of Mexicanness or Angloness. I have so internalized the borderland conflict that sometimes I feel like one cancels out the other and we are zero, nothing, no one. *A veces no soy nada ni nadie. Pero hasta cuando no lo soy, lo soy.*

When not copping out, when we know we are more than nothing, we   40
call ourselves Mexican, referring to race and ancestry; *mestizo* when affirming both our Indian and Spanish (but we hardly ever own our Black ancestry); Chicano when referring to a politically aware people born and/or raised in the U.S.; *Raza* when referring to Chicanos; *tejanos* when we are Chicanos from Texas.

Chicanos did not know we were a people until 1965 when Ceasar Chavez and the farmworkers united and *I Am Joaquín* was published and *la Raza Unida* party was formed in Texas. With that recognition, we became a distinct people. Something momentous happened to the Chicano soul—we became aware of our reality and acquired a name and a language (Chicano Spanish) that reflected that reality. Now that we had a name, some of the fragmented pieces began to fall together—who we were, what we were, how we had evolved. We began to get glimpses of what we might eventually become.

Yet the struggle of identities continues, the struggle of borders is our reality still. One day the inner struggle will cease and a true integration take place. In the meantime, *tenémos que hacer la lucha. ¿Quién está protegiendo los ranchos de mi gente? ¿Quién está tratando de cerrar la fisura entre la india y el blanco en nuestra sangre? El Chicano, si, el Chicano que anda como un ladrón en su propia casa.*

---

[10]Chávez, 88–90.

[11]"Hispanic" is derived from *Hispanis* (*España*, a name given to the Iberian Peninsula in ancient times when it was a part of the Roman Empire) and is a term designated by the U.S. government to make it easier to handle us on paper.

[12]The Treaty of Guadalupe Hidalgo created the Mexican-American in 1848.

Los Chicanos, how patient we seem, how very patient. There is the quiet of the Indian about us.[13] We know how to survive. When other races have given up their tongue, we've kept ours. We know what it is to live under the hammer blow of the dominant *norteamericano* culture. But more than we count the blows, we count the days the weeks the years the centuries the eons until the white laws and commerce and customs will rot in the deserts they've created, lie bleached. *Humildes* yet proud, *quietos* yet wild, *nosotros los mexicanos-Chicanos* will walk by the crumbling ashes as we go about our business. Stubborn, persevering, impenetrable as stone, yet possessing a malleability that renders us unbreakable, we, the *mestizas* and *mestizos,* will remain.

The Reader's Presence

1. The writer links her dentist's literal use of the word *tongue* to a metaphorical meaning. What connotations do the two senses of the word share? How does the tongue-as-organ/tongue-as-language pun relate to the quotation from Ray Gwyn Smith and questions of cultural silencing?

2. Anzaldúa peppers her English prose with untranslated Spanish words and phrases. How does this formal innovation influence the reader's experience of the text? How does the reader's experience mirror Anzaldúa's own in English-speaking America? In what ways might this technique underline the writer's insistence on the importance of keeping different languages active and alive?

3. Anzaldúa champions Spanish as the language of Mexican Americans. Spanish, of course, was brought to native Mexicans by colonizing conquistadors. The writer also distinguishes numerous dialects of Spanish and "Spanglish" as tongues in their own right. Cultural identity, in Anzaldúa's formulation, seems at once a unified and divided entity. How does this condition compare to the one suggested by Richard Rodriguez's "Aria: A Memoir of a Bilingual Childhood" (see page 222)?

[13]Anglos, in order to alleviate their guilt for dispossessing the Chicano, stressed the Spanish part of us and perpetrated the myth of the Spanish Southwest. We have accepted the fiction that we are Hispanic, that is Spanish, in order to accommodate ourselves to the dominant culture and its abhorrence of Indians. Chávez, 88–91.

43

Robert Bly

Men's Initiation Rites

Robert Bly (b. 1926) is a highly regarded poet, translator, editor, and leading figure of the men's movement. Avoiding an academic career, Bly lives in rural Minnesota and teaches writing workshops, gives frequent lectures and readings, and conducts seminars about the men's movement throughout the country. He has published dozens of books and received the National Book Award for his collection of poems, The Light around the Body *(1967). Other books of poetry include* Silence in the Snowy Fields *(1962),* Loving a Woman in Two Worlds *(1987),* Morning Poems *(1997), and* Eating the Honey of Words *(1999).* Iron John *(1990), his book about men's rituals, ancient myths, and the cultural constraints of manhood, became a best-seller. "Men's Initiation Rites" was originally published in the* Utne Reader *in 1986.*

The ancient rites of male initiation were complicated and subtle experiences which could be imagined better as a continual spiral than as a walk down a road. The spiral could be described as a year which repeats itself in seasons. The four seasons of male development amount to four stages, four steps, and four events, though we all know that seasons run into each other, and repeat.

The four seasons, or stages, I'll discuss here are bonding with and separation from the mother; bonding with and separation from the father; finding of the male mother; and the interior marriage or marriage with the Hidden Woman.

BONDING WITH AND SEPARATION FROM MOTHER

The first event is bonding with the mother and separation from the mother. Bonding of the son with the mother usually goes quite well in this country, though we could distinguish between instantaneous birth-bonding and a later, slower emotional bonding. The medical profession has adopted birth practices involving harsh lights, steel tables, painful medicines, and, most harmful of all, the infant's isolation for long periods, all of which damage the birth bond. Joseph Chilton Pearce has written of that movingly in *The Magical Child* (Dell). Mothers can sometimes repair that bonding later by careful attention to their sons' needs, by praise, carrying, talking, protecting, comforting—and many mothers do exactly that. Most American men achieve a successful bonding with the mother. It is the *separation* from the mother that doesn't go well.

When the world of men is submerged in the world of technology and business, it seems to the boy that cool excitement lies there, and warm excitement with the mother; money with the father, food with the mother; anxiety with the father, assurance with the mother; conditional love with the father, and unconditional love with the mother. All over the United States we meet women whose thirty-five-year-old sons are still living at home. One such woman told me that her divorce brought her freedom from the possessiveness of her husband, who wanted her home every night, etc. But she had noticed last week that her son said, "Why are you going out so much in the evenings?" In recent years the percentage of adult sons still living at home has increased; and we can see much other evidence of the difficulty the male feels in breaking with the mother: the guilt often felt toward the mother; the constant attempt, usually unconscious, to be a nice boy; lack of male friends; absorption in boyish flirtation with women; attempts to carry women's pain, and be their comforters; efforts to change a wife into a mother; abandonment of discipline for "softness and gentleness"; a general confusion about maleness. These qualities are all simple human characteristics, and yet when they, or a number of them, appear together, they point toward a failure in the very first stage of initiation. Ancient initiation practices, still going on in many parts of the world, solve this problem decisively through active intervention by the older males. Typically, when three or four boys in a tribe get to be eight to twelve years old, a group of older men simply appears at the houses one night, and takes them from their mothers, with whom the boys never live again. They may return, but often with faces covered with ash, to indicate that they are now "dead" to their mothers, who in their part return this play by crying out in mourning when they see their sons again, and acting out rituals otherwise done for the dead.

BONDING WITH AND SEPARATION FROM FATHER

The second season of initiation is bonding with the father and separation from the father. Before the Industrial Revolution this event took place with most sons. But this bonding requires many hours in which the bodies of the father and son sit, stand, or work close to each other, within a foot or two. The average father in the United States talks to his son less   5 than ten minutes a day. And that talk may be talk from a distance, such as "Is your room cleaned up?" or "Are you on drugs?" As we know, the psyche of the child interprets the death of a parent personally; that is, the psyche regards it as a failure on the child's part: "If I had been worthy, my parent would not have died." So the psyche of the small son interprets without question the father's absence from the house for hours and hours each day as evidence of the same unworthiness. The German psychiatrist Alexander Mitscherlich in his book *Society Without the Father* (Tavistock Publications) gives an image still more startling. He declares that when a son does not witness his father at work through the day and through the year, a hole develops in the son's psyche, and that hole fills with demons. Dustin Hoffman played such a son in *Marathon Man:* The son does not bond with the father then, but on the contrary a magnetic repulsion takes place, for by secret processes the father becomes associated in the son's mind with demonic energy, cold evil, Nazis, concentration camp guards, evil capitalists, agents of the CIA, powers of world conspiracy. Some of the fear felt in the sixties by young leftist men ("Never trust anyone over thirty") came from that well of demons.

The severance that the Norwegian immigrant male, for example, experienced when he lost his old language in which feelings naturally expressed themselves—and the Polish immigrant, and the German immigrant—affected the ability of these men to talk to their sons, and their sons to their sons. We might add to that the frontier mentality, whose pressure of weather, new land, building, plowing, etc. left almost all feeling activities—music appreciation, novel reading, poetry recital—to women. This request to women that they carry on "feeling" activities obviously deepened the crisis, because the boy then learns cultural feeling, verbal feeling, discrimination of feeling almost entirely from his mother. Bonding requires physical closeness, a sense of protection, approval of one's very being, conversation in which feelings and longings can step out, and some attention which the young male can feel as *care for the soul.* The boy in the United States receives almost all of these qualities, if he receives them at all, from the mother, and so his bonding takes place with her, not with the father. If bonding with the father does not take place, how can separation from the father take place? There are many exceptions to this generalization, of course, but most of the exceptions I met were in men who worked in some physical way with their fathers, as carpenters, woodcutters, musicians, farmers, etc.

American men in general cannot achieve separation from the father because they have not achieved bonding with the father; or more exactly, our bonding with the father goes on slowly, bit by bit, often beginning again, after the remoteness of adolescence, at the age of thirty-five or so; and of course this gradual bonding over many years slows up the separation as well, so that the American man is often forty or forty-five before the first two events of initiation have taken place completely enough to be felt as events. The constant attempt by young males working in popular music to play a music their fathers never played or heard suggests an inability to bond with their fathers. The fathers in their turn feel puzzled, rejected inadequate, and defeated. So many American fathers if they answer the phone when a son or daughter calls will usually say after a moment: "Here is your mother."

MALE MOTHER

A third event in the ancient male initiation was the appearance of the male mother, and we'll call that the essential event. John Layard, who gained much of his knowledge of male initiation from his years with the Stone-Age tribes of Malekula, declares in his study called *The Celtic Quest* (Spring Publications) that Arthur was a male mother. "Arthur" may have been the name traditionally given to such an initiator centuries before he became King Arthur. In the ancient Mabinogion[1] story "Culhwch and Olwen," Arthur is the keeper of a castle to which the young male initiate gains entry. Though male, Arthur's kingdom, Layard says, "has to be 'entered' as though it were a woman." Layard continues: "This entry into the male world which is a 'second mother' is what all initiation rites are concerned with." When Arthur has accepted the invader, he details the things he will not give to the young man, which are ship, cloak, sword, shield, dagger, and Guinevere, his wife. He then asks the boy, "What do you want?" Culhwch says, "I want my hair trimmed." Then "Arthur took a golden comb and shears with loops of silver, and combed his head." The younger male places his head, or his consciousness, into the hands of an older man he trusts, and by that act he is symbolically freed from his bonds both to his mother and to his father.

Our culture lacks the institution of the male mother: The memory of it seems to have dropped into forgetfulness. We receive only one birth, from the mother, even though Jesus insisted on the importance of a second birth. We lose the meaning of his metaphor by interpreting it as a conversion experience. It was a new birth from the male, and it is possible that Jesus himself provided this second birth to young men. The Australian aborigines to this day arrange an experience of male birth that the sons do not forget: They construct a sort of tunnel of sticks and brush twenty to thirty feet long, and at the proper moment put the boys in at one end, and receive them, surrounded by the tremendous male noise of the bullroarers, at the other end, and immediately declare them to be born out of the male body for once and for all—a new boy, a new body, a new spirit, a man at last.

This experience, of course, implies the willingness of the older males to become male mothers, and so exhibit the protectiveness, self-sacrificing generosity and soul-caring that the female mother traditionally shows. In 10

---

[1]*Mabinogion:* Welsh prose narrative. —EDS.

Africa, males of the Kikuyu tribe take boys who are hungry and terrified, after a day's fasting, and sit them down among adult males around a fire late at night. Each adult male then cuts his arm with a knife and lets his blood flow into a gourd which is passed on to the young boys to drink, so that they can see and taste the depth of the older males' love for them. By this single ceremony, the boy is asked to shift from female milk to male blood.

It is Arthur's kindness, savvy, spiritual energy, his store of psychic knowledge, his willingness to lead, guide, and welcome the young male which we lack in American ritual, when, for example, the initiating power is held by sergeants, priests, or corporate executives. The qualities I've mentioned above cannot appear together, or only rarely, in those three roles because we have forgotten the male mother role. We need to rethink the purpose of a male mother and how he achieves that purpose. The old apprentice system in crafts and arts through the Middle Ages and Renaissance accomplished initiation for some young men, but the mass university lectures of today cannot provide it—nor can workshop classes of twenty. Pablo Casals was a male mother to some young men; William Carlos Williams to others, and there are always a few marvelous teachers or woodsmen here and there who understand the concept and embody it. By and large, however, one would say that if the American male does achieve the first two events—bonding with and separation from the mother, bonding with and separation from the father—he will come up short on this third step. A man needs to look decisively for a male mother, but he cannot look if the culture has not even retained the concept in its storehouse of possibilities. The men around Arthur were healthy because he nourished them, and they expected it.

THE INVISIBLE CZARINA

We notice that the male mother, or primary initiator, is not one's personal father; so by this third step, the male passes beyond the realm of his personal mother and father. He also expands his conception of women beyond the roles of wife, girlfriend, mistress, chick, movie actress, model. The predominant figure in the fourth stage is the Invisible Czarina, or Elena the Wise, as some Russian fairy tales call her, and in the fourth season it is the man's task to marry her. Edward Schieffel, in *Rituals of Manhood,* writing about contemporary male rituals in New Guinea, reports that in the Kaluli tribe the young boys sometimes find in the pool below a waterfall during ceremonies a "stone bride," which they can identify because it moves on its own. We see here again a connection being made with a secret, powerful, and usually helpful woman who is not a living woman. The fourth step does not aim then at a hardening or intensification of maleness, but rather at a deepening of feeling toward the religious life. We can immediately see the connection with the worship of the woman in Arthurian legend, the image of Mona Lisa in Italy, "Diotima" in Socrates' Greece, and lunar substance that contributes to the creation of "gold" that is the aim of alchemy. The "woman by the well" preserves in many European fairy tales and in the New Testament the memory of the Hidden Woman. In Celtic initiation, Arthur guides the young male toward the marriage with her; she is in fact the Olwen ("white trace" or "track of the moon") mentioned in the title of the Celtic story, "Culhwch and Olwen."

The fourth season therefore represents an astonishing leap into the other world and a love for a radiance of the yin. Initiation results in less dependence on living women or "strong" women, less fear of the feminine and creation of the more balanced older man that Zen and Tibetan traditions, to name only these two, aim at. Western culture has retained a dim memory of this fourth stage; and when most men today imagine initiation, a fourth stage like this is probably not a part of their imaginative scenario, even though the Wild Man story or "Iron Hans" ends like so many Grimm Brothers tales, in a marriage. The twentieth-century Spanish poet Antonio Machado retained a very lively memory of Elena or the Hidden Woman, about whom he wrote a number of poems. This poem he wrote around 1900:

> Close to the road we sit down one day,
> our whole life now amounts to time, and our sole concern
> the attitudes of despair that we adopt
> while we wait. But She will not fail to arrive.

I want to emphasize that the ancient view of male development implies a spiral movement rather than a linear passage through clearly defined stages, with a given stage finished once and for all. As men, we go through all stages in a shallow way, then go back, live in several stages at once, go through them all with slightly less shallowness, return again to our parents, bond and separate once more, find a new male mother, and so on and so on. The old initiation systems having been destroyed, and their initiators gone, no step is ever done cleanly, just as we don't achieve at twelve a clean break with our mothers. So a quality of male initiation as we live it in the culture is a continual returning. Gradually and messily over many years a man achieves this complicated or subtle experience; it is very slow.

The Reader's Presence

1. The writer proposes a highly unusual approach to men's gender formation. What are the stages of development he outlines? What effect might the writer hope his words will have upon adult men's lives and parents' attitudes toward raising male children?

2. Some feminists have argued that Bly's approach reinforces dangerous masculine traits and male privilege. For instance, Bly's insistence on the importance of male role models for boys has been
read as derogating single mothers, and his all-male workshops
have been called exclusionary. Others say that gender differences
are an outworn notion. How do you think Bly might argue, based
on this piece?

3. Bly is interested in restoring mythical structures to the modern
world. What sorts of tales, traditions, and myths does he call
upon in this piece? How does he propose men of the present time
reintegrate these lost elements? "Myth," of course, also means "illusion." How does Bly try to persuade us that illusion — generally
viewed negatively in our culture — will enrich our lives? How does
his writing style reinforce this perspective?

44

Stephen L. Carter

The Insufficiency of Honesty

*Law professor and writer Stephen L. Carter (b. 1954) is an insightful and inci-
sive critic of contemporary cultural politics. His first book,* Reflections of an Affirmative Action Baby *(1992), criticizes affirmative action policies that reinforce racial
stereotypes rather than break down structures of discrimination. Carter's critique
emerges from his own experience as an African American student at Stanford University and at Yale University Law School. After graduating from Yale, he served as
a law clerk for Supreme Court justice Thurgood Marshall and eventually joined the
faculty at Yale as professor of law, where he has served since 1991 as the Cromwell
Professor of Law. Carter has published widely on legal and social topics, including
his books* The Culture of Disbelief: How American Law and Politics Trivialize Religious Devotion *(1993),* The Confirmation Mess: Cleaning Up the Federal Appointments Process *(1994),* Civility: Manners, Morals, and the Etiquette of Democracy,
(1998), and The Dissent of the Governed: A Meditation on Law, Religion, and Loyalty *(1998). "The Insufficiency of Honesty" appears in* Integrity *(1996).*

A couple of years ago I began a university commencement address by
telling the audience that I was going to talk about integrity. The crowd broke
into applause. Applause! Just because they had heard the word "integrity":
that's how starved for it they were. They had no idea how I was using the

word, or what I was going to say about integrity, or, indeed, whether I was for it or against it. But they knew they liked the idea of talking about it.

Very well, let us consider this word "integrity." Integrity is like the weather: everybody talks about it but nobody knows what to do about it. Integrity is that stuff that we always want more of. Some say that we need to return to the good old days when we had a lot more of it. Others say that we as a nation have never really had enough of it. Hardly anybody stops to explain exactly what we mean by it, or how we know it is a good thing, or why everybody needs to have the same amount of it. Indeed, the only trouble with integrity is that everybody who uses the word seems to mean something slightly different.

For instance, when I refer to integrity, do I mean simply "honesty"? The answer is no; although honesty is a virtue of importance, it is a different virtue from integrity. Let us, for simplicity, think of honesty as not lying; and let us further accept Sissela Bok's definition of a lie: "any intentionally deceptive message which is *stated*." Plainly, one cannot have integrity without being honest (although, as we shall see, the matter gets complicated), but one can certainly be honest and yet have little integrity.

When I refer to integrity, I have something very specific in mind. Integrity, as I will use the term, requires three steps: discerning what is right and what is wrong; acting on what you have discerned, even at personal cost; and saying openly that you are acting on your understanding of right and wrong. The first criterion captures the idea that integrity requires a degree of moral reflectiveness. The second brings in the ideal of a person of integrity as steadfast, a quality that includes keeping one's commitments. The third reminds us that a person of integrity can be trusted.

The first point to understand about the difference between honesty and integrity is that a peson may be entirely honest without ever engaging in the hard work of discernment that integrity requires; she may tell us quite truthfully what she believes without ever taking the time to figure out whether what she believes is good and right and true. The problem may be as simple as someone's foolishly saying something that hurts a friend's feelings; a few moments of thought would have revealed the likelihood of the hurt and the lack of necessity for the comment. Or the problem may be more complex, as when a man who was raised from birth in a society that preaches racism states his belief in one race's inferiority as a fact, without ever really considering that perhaps this deeply held view is wrong. Certainly the racist is being honest—he is telling us what he actually thinks—but his honesty does not add up to integrity.

TELLING EVERYTHING YOU KNOW

A wonderful epigram sometimes attributed to the filmmaker Sam Goldwyn goes like this: "The most important thing in acting is honesty; once you learn to fake that, you're in." The point is that honesty can be something one *seems* to have. Without integrity, what passes for honesty often is nothing of the kind; it is fake honesty — or it is honest but irrelevant and perhaps even immoral.

Consider an example. A man who has been married for fifty years confesses to his wife on his deathbed that he was unfaithful thirty-five years earlier. The dishonesty was killing his spirit, he says. Now he has cleared his conscience and is able to die in peace.

The husband has been honest — sort of. He has certainly unburdened himself. And he has probably made his wife (soon to be his widow) quite miserable in the process, because even if she forgives him, she will not be able to remember him with quite the vivid image of love and loyalty that she had hoped for. Arranging his own emotional affairs to ease his transition to death, he has shifted to his wife the burden of confusion and pain, perhaps for the rest of her life. Moreover, he has attempted his honesty at the one time in his life when it carries no risk; acting in accordance with what you think is right and risking no loss in the process is a rather thin and unadmirable form of honesty.

Besides, even though the husband has been honest in a sense, he has now twice been unfaithful to his wife: once thirty-five years ago, when he had his affair, and again when, nearing death, he decided that his own peace of mind was more important than hers. In trying to be honest he has violated his marriage vow by acting toward his wife not with love but with naked and perhaps even cruel self-interest.

As my mother used to say, you don't have to tell people everything you know. Lying and nondisclosure, as the law often recognizes, are not the same thing. Sometimes it is actually illegal to tell what you know, as, for example, in the disclosure of certain financial information by market insiders. Or it may be unethical, as when a lawyer reveals a confidence entrusted to her by a client. It may be simple bad manners, as in the case of a gratuitous comment to a colleague on his or her attire. And it may be subject to religious punishment, as when a Roman Catholic priest breaks the seal of the confessional — an offense that carries automatic excommunication.

In all the cases just mentioned, the problem with telling everything you know is that somebody else is harmed. Harm may not be the intention, but it is certainly the effect. Honesty is most laudable when we risk harm to ourselves; it becomes a good deal less so if we instead risk harm to others when there is no gain to anyone other than ourselves. Integrity may counsel keeping our secrets in order to spare the feelings of others. Sometimes, as in the example of the wayward husband, the reason we want to tell what we know is precisely to shift our pain onto somebody else — a course of action dictated less by integrity than by self-interest. Fortunately, integrity and self-interest often coincide, as when a politician of integrity is rewarded with our votes. But often they do not, and it is at those moments that our integrity is truly tested.

ERROR

Another reason that honesty alone is no substitute for integrity is that if forthrightness is not preceded by discernment, it may result in the expression of an incorrect moral judgment. In other words, I may be honest about what I believe, but if I have never tested my beliefs, I may be wrong. And here I mean "wrong" in a particular sense: the proposition in question is wrong if I would change my mind about it after hard moral reflection.

Consider this example. Having been taught all his life that women are not as smart as men, a manager gives the women on his staff less-challenging assignments than he gives the men. He does this, he believes, for their own benefit: he does not want them to fail, and he believes that they will if he gives them tougher assignments. Moreover, when one of the women on his staff does poor work, he does not berate her as harshly as he would a man, because he expects nothing more. And he claims to be acting with integrity because he is acting according to his own deepest beliefs.

The manager fails the most basic test of integrity. The question is not whether his actions are consistent with what he most deeply believes but whether he has done the hard work of discerning whether what he most deeply believes is right. The manager has not taken this harder step.

Moreover, even within the universe that the manager has constructed for himself, he is not acting with integrity. Although he is obviously wrong to think that the women on his staff are not as good as the men, even were he right, that would not justify applying different standards to their work. By so doing he betrays both his obligation to the institution that employs him and his duty as a manger to evaluate his employees. 15

The problem that the manager faces is an enormous one in our practical politics, where having the dialogue that makes democracy work can seem impossible because of our tendency to cling to our views even when we have not examined them. As Jean Bethke Elshtain has said, borrowing from John Courtney Murray, our politics are so fractured and contentious that we often cannot reach *disagreement*. Our refusal to look closely at our own most cherished principles is surely a large part of the reason. Socrates thought the unexamined life not worth living. But the unhappy truth is that few of us actually have the time for constant reflection on our views—on public or private morality. Examine them we must, however, or we will never know whether we might be wrong.

None of this should be taken to mean that integrity as I have described it presupposes a single correct truth. If, for example, your integrity-guided search tells you that affirmative action is wrong, and my integrity-guided search tells me that affirmative action is right, we need not conclude that one of us lacks integrity. As it happens, I believe—both as a Christian and as a secular citizen who struggles toward moral understanding—that we *can* find true and sound answers to our moral questions. But I do not pretend to have found very many of them, nor is an exposition of them my purpose here.

It is the case not that there aren't any right answers but that, given human fallibility, we need to be careful in assuming that we have found them. However, today's political talk about how it is wrong for the government to impose one person's morality on somebody else is just mindless chatter. *Every* law imposes one person's morality on somebody else, because law has only two functions: to tell people to do what they would rather not or to forbid them to do what they would.

And if the surveys can be believed, there is far more moral agreement in America than we sometimes allow ourselves to think. One of the reasons that character education for young people makes so much sense to so many people is precisely that there seems to be a core set of moral understandings—we might call them the American Core—that most of us accept. Some of the virtues in this American Core are, one hopes, relatively noncontroversial. About 500 American communities have signed on to Michael Josephson's program to emphasize the "six pillars" of good character: trustworthiness, respect, responsibility, caring, fairness, and citizenship. These virtues might lead to a similarly noncontroversial set of political values: having an honest regard for ourselves and others, protecting freedom of thought and religious belief, and refusing to steal or murder.

HONESTY AND COMPETING RESPONSIBILITIES

A further problem with too great an exaltation of honesty is that it may allow us to escape responsibilities that morality bids us bear. If honesty is substituted for integrity, one might think that if I say I am not planning to fulfill a duty, I need not fulfill it. But it would be a peculiar morality indeed that granted us the right to avoid our moral responsibilities simply by stating our intention to ignore them. Integrity does not permit such an easy escape. 20

Consider an example. Before engaging in sex with a woman, her lover tells her that if she gets pregnant, it is her problem, not his. She says that she understands. In due course she does wind up pregnant. If we believe, as I hope we do, that the man would ordinarily have a moral responsibility toward both the child he will have helped to bring into the world and the child's mother, then his honest statement of what he intends does not spare him that responsibility.

This vision of responsibility assumes that not all moral obligations stem from consent or from a stated intention. The linking of obligations to promises is a rather modern and perhaps uniquely Western way of looking at life, and perhaps a luxury that the well-to-do can afford. As Fred and Shulamit Korn (a philosopher and an anthropologist) have pointed out, "If one looks at ethnographic accounts of other societies, one finds that, while obligations everywhere play a crucial role in social life, promising is not preeminent among the sources of obligation and is not even mentioned by most anthropologists." The Korns have made a study of Tonga, where promises are virtually unknown but the social order is remarkably stable. If life without any promises seems extreme, we Americans sometimes go too far the other way, parsing not only our contracts but even out marriage vows in order to discover the absolute minimum obligation that we have to others as a result of our promises.

That some societies in the world have worked out evidently functional structures of obligation without the need for promise or consent does not tell us what *we* should do. But it serves as a reminder of the basic proposition that our existence in civil society creates a set of mutual responsibilities that philosophers used to capture in the fiction of the social contract. Nowadays, here in America, people seem to spend their time thinking of even cleverer ways to avoid their obligations, instead of doing what integrity commands and fulfilling them. And all too often honesty is their excuse.

The Reader's Presence

1. If Carter intends his essay to be a discussion of honesty, why does he begin with a consideration of the concept of integrity? How are the terms related? In what important ways are they different? What does integrity involve that honesty doesn't?

2. Notice that in this essay Carter never once offers a dictionary definition of the words *honesty* or *integrity*. Look up each term in a standard dictionary. As a reader, do you think such definitions would have made Carter's distinctions more clear? Why do you think he chose not to define the words according to their common dictionary meanings? How does he define them?

3. Though honesty and integrity may seem to be individual, moral virtues, Carter concludes his essay with a discussion of practical American politics. How are his earlier considerations of honesty and integrity related to his conclusion? Explain why, in his terms, integrity leads to a better society than does honesty. Abraham Lincoln liked to say that "honesty is the best policy." Was he wrong?

45

K. C. Cole

Calculated Risks

K. C. Cole (b. 1946) is a highly regarded science writer for the Los Angeles Times. *Born in Detroit, Michigan, she received a B. A. from Columbia University and began writing about science while affiliated with the Exploratorium in San Francisco in the 1970s. Using vivid examples and a clear writing style, Cole makes science accessible to a broad audience and is a frequent contributor to periodicals such as* Smithsonian, Omni, *and* Discover. *She has published a number of books, including* Vision: In the Eye of the Beholder *(1978),* What Only a Mother Can Tell You about Having a Baby *(1980), and* Sympathetic Vibrations: Reflections on Physics as a Way of Life *(1985). In* The Universe and the Teacup: The Mathematics of Truth and Beauty *(1998), in which "Calculated Risks" appears, Cole explains exponential growth, quantum theory, optics, astrophysics, and the influence of mathematics on everyday life.*

Newsweek magazine plunged American women into a state of near panic some years ago when it announced that the chances of a college-educated thirty-five-year-old woman finding a husband was less than her chance of being killed by a terrorist. Although Susan Faludi made mincemeat of this so-called statistic in her book *Backlash*, the notion that we can precisely quantify risk has a strong hold on the Western psyche. Scientists, statisticians, and policy makers attach numbers to the risk of getting breast cancer or AIDS, to flying and food additives, to getting hit by lightning or falling in the bathtub.

Yes despite (or perhaps because of) all the numbers floating around, most people are quite properly confused about risk. I know people who live happily on the San Andreas Fault and yet are afraid to ride the New York subways (and vice versa). I've known smokers who can't stand to be in the same room with a fatty steak, and women afraid of the side effects of birth control pills who have unprotected sex with strangers. Risk assessment is rarely based on purely rational considerations—even if people could agree on what those considerations were. We worry about negligible quantities of Alar in apples, yet shrug off the much higher probability of dying from smoking. We worry about flying, but not driving. We worry about getting brain cancer from cellular phones, although the link is quite tenuous. In fact, it's easy to make a statistical argument — albeit a fallacious one — that cellular phones prevent cancer, because the proportion of people with brain tumors is smaller among cell phone users than among the general population.[1]

Even simple pleasures such as eating and breathing have become suspect. Love has always been risky, and AIDS has made intimacy more perilous than ever. On the other hand, not having relationships may be riskier still. According to at least one study, the average male faces three times the threat of early death associated with not being married as he does from cancer.

Of course, risk isn't all bad. Without knowingly taking risks, no one would ever walk out the door, much less go to school, drive a car, have a baby, submit a proposal for a research grant, fall in love, or swim in the ocean. It's hard to have any fun, accomplish anything productive, or experience life without taking on risks — sometimes substantial ones. Life, after all, is a fatal disease, and the mortality rate for humans, at the end of the day, is 100 percent.

Yet, people are notoriously bad at risk assessment. I couldn't get over   5
this feeling watching the aftermath of the crash of TWA Flight 800 and the horror it spread about flying, with the long lines at airports, the increased security measures, the stories about grieving families day after day in the newspaper, the ongoing attempt to figure out why and who and what could be done to prevent such a tragedy from happening again.

Meanwhile, tens of thousands of children die every day around the world from common causes such as malnutrition and disease. That's roughly the same as a hundred exploding jumbo jets full of children every single day. People who care more about the victims of Flight 800 aren't callous or ignorant. It's just the way our minds work. Certain kinds of tragedies make an impact; others don't. Our perceptual apparatus is geared toward threats that are exotic, personal, erratic, and dramatic. This doesn't mean we're ignorant; just human.

This skewed perception of risk has serious social consequences, however. We aim our resources at phantoms, while real hazards are ignored. Parents, for example, tend to rate drug abuse and abduction by strangers as the greatest threats to their children. Yet hundreds of times more children die each year from choking, burns, falls, drowning, and other accidents that public safety efforts generally ignore.

We spend millions to fight international terrorism and wear combat fatigues for a morning walk to protect against Lyme disease. At the same time, "we see several very major problems that have received relatively

---

[1]John Allen Paulos was the first person I know of to make this calculation; it is probably related to the fact that people who use cellular phones are on average richer, and therefore healthier, than people who don't.

little attention," write Bernard Cohen and I-Sing Lee in *Health Physics*. The physicists suggest—not entirely tongue in cheek—that resources might be far more efficiently spent on programs such as government-organized computer dating services. "Favorable publicity on the advantages of marriage might be encouraged."

It's as if we incarcerated every petty criminal with zeal, while inviting mass murderers into our bedrooms. If we wanted to put the money on the real killers, we'd go after suicide, not asbestos.

Even in terms of simple dollars, our policies don't make any sense. It's   10
well known, for example, that prenatal care for pregnant women saves enormous amounts of money—in terms of care infants need in the first year of life—and costs a pittance. Yet millions of low-income women don't get it.

Numbers are clearly not enough to make sense of risk assessment. Context counts, too. Take cancer statistics. It's always frightening to hear that cancer is on the rise. However, at least one reason for the increase is simply that people are living longer—long enough to get the disease.

Certain conclusions we draw from statistics are downright silly. Physicist Hal Lewis writes in *Technological Risk* that per mile traveled a person is more likely to be killed by a car as a pedestrian than as a driver or passenger. Should we conclude that driving is safer than walking and therefore that all pedestrians should be forced into cars?

Charles Dickens made a point about the absurdity of misunderstanding numbers associated with risk by refusing to ride the train. One day late in December, the story goes, Dickens announced that he couldn't travel by train any more that year, "on the grounds that the average annual quota of railroad accidents in Britain had not been filled and therefore further disasters were obviously imminent."

Purely numerical comparisons also may be socially unacceptable. When the state of Oregon decided to rank its medical services according to benefit-cost ratios, some results had to be thrown out—despite their statistical validity. Treatment for thumb sucking, crooked teeth, and headaches, for example, came out on the priorities list ahead of therapy for cystic fibrosis and AIDS.

What you consider risky, after all, depends somewhat on the circum-   15
stances of your life and lifestyle. People who don't have enough to eat don't worry about apples contaminated with Alar. People who face daily violence at their front door don't worry about hijackings on flights to the Bahamas. Attitudes toward risk evolve in cultural contexts and are influenced by everything from psychology to ethics to beliefs about personal responsibility.

In addition to context, another factor needed to see through the maze of conflicting messages about risk is human psychology. For example, imminent risks strike much more fear in our hearts than distant ones; it's much harder to get a teenager than an older person to take long-term dangers like smoking seriously.

Smoking is also a habit people believe they can control, which makes the risk far more acceptable. (People seem to get more upset about the effects of passive smoking than smoking itself—at least in part because smokers get to choose, and breathers don't.)

As a general principle, people tend to grossly exaggerate the risk of any danger perceived to be beyond their control, while shrugging off risks they think they can manage. Thus, we go skiing and skydiving, but fear asbestos. We resent and fear the idea that anonymous chemical companies are putting additives into our food; yet the additives we load onto our own food—salt, sugar, butter—are millions of times more dangerous.

This is one reason that airline accidents seem so unacceptable—because strapped into our seats in the cabin, what happens is completely beyond our control. In a poll taken soon after the TWA Flight 800 crash, an overwhelming majority of people said they'd be willing to pay up to fifty dollars more for a round-trip ticket if it increased airline safety. Yet the same people resist moves to improve automobile safety, for example, especially if it costs money.

The idea that we can control what happens also influences who we   20
blame when things go wrong. Most people don't like to pay the costs for treating people injured by cigarettes or riding motorcycles because we think they brought these things on themselves. Some people also hold these attitudes toward victims of AIDS, or mental illness, because they think the illness results from lack of character or personal morals.

In another curious perceptual twist, risks associated with losing something and gaining something appear to be calculated in our minds according to quite different scales. In a now-classic series of studies, Stanford psychologist Amos Tversky and colleague Daniel Kahneman concluded that most people will bend over backward to avoid small risks, even if that means sacrificing great potential rewards. "The threat of a loss has a greater impact on a decision than the possibility of an equivalent gain," they concluded.

In one of their tests, Tversky and Kahneman asked physicians to choose between two strategies for combating a rare disease, expected to kill 600 people. Strategy A promised to save 200 people (the rest would die), while Strategy B offered a one-third probability that everyone would be saved, and a two-thirds probability that no one would be saved. Betting on a sure thing, the physicians choose A. But presented with the identical choice, stated differently, they choose B. The difference in language was simply this: Instead of stating that Strategy A would guarantee 200 out of 600 saved lives, it stated that Strategy A would mean 400 sure deaths.

People will risk a lot to prevent a loss, in other words, but risk very little for possible gain. Running into a burning house to save a pet or fighting back when a mugger asks for your wallet are both high-risk gambles that people take repeatedly in order to hang on to something they care about. The same people might not risk the hassle of, say, fastening a seat belt in a car even though the potential gain might be much higher.

The bird in the hand always seems more attractive than the two in the bush. Even if holding on to the one in your hand comes at a higher risk and the two in the bush are gold-plated.

The reverse situation comes into play when we judge risks of com-   25
mission versus risks of omission. A risk that you assume by actually doing something seems far more risky than a risk you take by not doing something, even though the risk of doing nothing may be greater.

Death from natural causes, like cancer, are more readily acceptable than deaths from accidents or murder. That's probably one reason it's so much easier to accept thousands of starving children than the death of one in a drive-by shooting. The former is an act of omission — a failure to step in and help, send food or medicine. The latter is the commission of a crime — somebody pulled the trigger.

In the same way, the Food and Drug Administration is far more likely to withhold a drug that might help a great number of people if it threatens to harm a few; better to hurt a lot of people by failing to do something than act with the deliberate knowledge that some people will be hurt. Or as the doctors' credo puts it: First do no harm.

For obvious reasons, dramatic or exotic risks seem far more dangerous than more familiar ones. Plane crashes and AIDS are risks associated with ambulances and flashing lights, sex and drugs. While red dye #2 strikes terror in our hearts, that great glob of butter melting into our baked potato is accepted as an old friend. "A woman drives down the street with her child romping around in the front seat," says John Allen Paulos. "Then they arrive at the shopping mall, and she grabs the child's hand so hard it hurts, because she's afraid he'll be kidnapped."

Children who are kidnapped are far more likely to be whisked away by relatives than strangers, just as most people are murdered by people they know.

Familiar risks creep up on us like age and are often difficult to see until   30
it's too late to take action. Mathematician Sam C. Saunders of Washington State University reminds us that a frog placed in hot water will struggle to escape, but the same frog placed in cool water that's slowly warmed up will sit peacefully until it's cooked. "One cannot anticipate what one does not perceive," he says, which is why gradual accumulations of risk due to lifestyle choices (like smoking or eating) are so often ignored. We're in hot water, but it's gotten hot so slowly that no one notices.

To bring home his point, Saunders asks us to imagine that cigarettes are not harmful — with the exception of an occasional one that has been packed with explosives instead of tobacco. These dynamite-stuffed cigarettes look just like normal ones. There's only one hidden away in every 18,250 packs—not a grave risk, you might say. The only catch is, if you smoke one of those explosive cigarettes, it might blow your head off.

The mathematician speculates, I think correctly, that given such a situation, cigarettes would surely be banned outright. After all, if 30 million packs of cigarettes are sold each day, an average of 1,600 people a day would die in gruesome explosions. Yet the number of deaths is the same to be expected from normal smoking. "The total expected loss of life or health to smokers using dynamite-loaded (but otherwise harmless) cigarettes over forty years would not be as great as with ordinary filtered cigarettes," says Saunders.

We can accept getting cooked like a frog, in other words, but not getting blown up like a firecracker.

It won't come as a great surprise to anyone that ego also plays a role in the way we assess risks. Psychological self-protection leads us to draw consistently wrong conclusions. In general, we overestimate the risks of bad things happening to others, while vastly underrating the possibility that they will happen to ourselves. Indeed, the lengths people go to minimize their own perceived risks can be downright "ingenious," according to Rutgers psychologist Neil Weinstein. For example, people asked about the risk of finding radon in their houses always rate their risk as "low" or "average," never "high." "If you ask them why," says Weinstein, "they take anything and twist it around in a way that reassures them. Some say their risk is low because the house is new; others, because the house is old. Some will say their risk is low because their house is at the top of a hill; others, because it's at the bottom of a hill."

Whatever the evidence to the contrary, we think: "It won't happen to   35
me." Weinstein and others speculate that this has something to do with preservation of self-esteem. We don't like to see ourselves as vulnerable. We like to think we've got some magical edge over the others. Ego gets involved especially in cases where being vulnerable to risk implies personal failure—for example, the risk of depression, suicide, alcoholism, drug addiction. "If you admit you're at risk," says Weinstein, "you're admitting that you can't handle stress. You're not as strong as the next person."

Average people, studies have shown, believe that they will enjoy longer lives, healthier lives, and longer marriages than the "average" person. Despite the obvious fact that they themselves are, well, average people, too. According to a recent poll, 3 out of 4 baby boomers (those born between 1946 and 1964) think they look younger than their peers, and 4 out of 5 say they have fewer wrinkles than other people their age—a statistical impossibility.

Kahneman and Tversky studied this phenomenon as well and found that people think they'll beat the odds because they're special. This is no doubt a necessary psychological defense mechanism, or no one would ever get married again without thinking seriously about the potential for divorce. A clear view of personal vulnerability, however, could go a long way toward preventing activities like drunken driving. But then again, most people think they are better than average drivers—even when intoxicated.

We also seem to believe it won't happen to us if it hasn't happened yet. That is, we extrapolate from the past to the future. "I've been taking that highway at eighty miles per hour for ten years and I haven't crashed yet," we tell ourselves. This is rather like reasoning that flipping a coin ten times that comes up heads guarantees that heads will continue to come up indefinitely.

Curiously, one advertising campaign against drunken driving that was quite successful featured the faces of children killed by drunken drivers. These children looked real to us. We could identify with them. In the same way as we could identify with the people on TWA Flight 800. It's much easier to empathize with someone who has a name and a face than a statistic.

That explains in part why we go to great expense to rescue children who fall down mine shafts, but not children dying from preventable diseases. Economists call this the "rule of rescue." If you know that someone is in danger and you know that you can help, you have a moral obligation to do so. If you don't know about it, however, you have no obligation. Columnist Roger Simon speculates that's one reason the National Rifle Association lobbied successfully to eliminate the program at the Centers for Disease Control that keeps track of gun deaths. If we don't have to face what's happening, we won't feel obligated to do anything about it.

Even without the complication of all these psychological factors, however, calculating risks can be tricky because not everything is known about every situation. "We have to concede that a single neglected or unrecognized risk can invalidate all the reliability calculations, which are based on known risk," writes Ivar Ekeland. There is always a risk, in other words, that the risk assessment itself is wrong.

Genetic screening, like tests for HIV infection, has a certain probability of being wrong. If your results come back positive, how much should you worry? If they come back negative, how safe should you feel?

The more factors involved, the more complicated the risk assessment becomes. When you get to truly complex systems like nationwide telephone networks and power grids, worldwide computer networks and hugely complex machines like space shuttles, the risk of disaster becomes infinitely harder to pin down. No one knows when a minor glitch will set off a chain reaction of events that will culminate in disaster. Potential risk in complex systems, in other words, are subject to the same kinds of exponential amplification discussed in the previous chapter.

Needless to say, the way a society assesses risk is very different from the way an individual views the same choices. Whether or not you wish to ride a motorcycle is your own business. Whether society pays the bills for the thousands of people maimed by cycle accidents, however, is everybody's business. Any one of us might view our own survival on a transatlantic flight as more important than the needs of the nation's children. Governments, one presumes, ought to have a somewhat different agenda.

But how far does society want to go in strictly numerical accounting? It certainly hasn't helped much in the all-important issue of health care, where an ounce of prevention has been proven again and again to be worth many pounds of cures. Most experts agree that we should be spending much more money preventing common diseases and accidents, especially in children. But no one wants to take health dollars away from precarious newborns or the elderly — where most of it goes. These are decisions that ultimately will not be made by numbers alone. Calculating risk only helps us to see more clearly what exactly is going on.

45

According to anthropologist Melvin Konner, author of *Why the Reckless Survive,* our poor judgment about potential risks may well be the legacy of evolution. Early peoples lived at constant risk from predators, disease, accidents. They died young. And in evolutionary terms, "winning" means not longevity, but merely sticking around long enough to pass on your genes to the next generation. Taking risk was therefore a "winning" strategy, especially if it meant a chance to mate before dying. Besides, decisions had to be made quickly. If going for a meal of ripe berries meant risking an attack from a saber-toothed tiger, you dove for the berries. For a half-starved cave dweller, this was a relatively simple choice. Perhaps our brains are simply not wired, speculates Konner, for the careful calculations presented by the risks of modern life.

Indeed, some of our optimistic biases toward personal risk may still serve important psychological purposes. In times of stress and danger, they help us to put one foot in front of the other; they help us to get on with our lives, and out the door.

In the end, Konner, the cautious professor, ruminates somewhat wistfully bout his risk-taking friends — who smoke, and ride motorcycles, and drive with their seat belts fastened behind them. Beside them, he feels "safe and virtuous," yet somehow uneasy. "I sometimes think," he muses, "that the more reckless among us may have something to teach the careful about the sort of immortality that comes from living fully every day."

The Reader's Presence

1. Cole posits the notion of risk as relative. For example, she argues that suicide takes more lives than asbestos poisoning and that people without food do not worry about contaminants. What

rhetorical techniques does Cole use to support her argument? Do you find them convincing? Why or why not?

2. What does Cole see as the difference between individual risks versus those taken by society as a whole? Which risks receive more attention and why?

3. The essay raises many questions, yet rarely answers them directly. How does Cole propose we handle risk? What risks does she advise we take, and why? Cole concludes her essay by discussing a book by Melvin Konner called *Why the Reckless Survive*. What ideas does Cole echo? Does Konner's argument enhance or undercut Cole's, and why?

46

Amy Cunningham
Why Women Smile

Amy Cunningham (b. 1955) has been writing on psychological issues and modern life for magazines such as Redbook, Glamour, *and the* Washington Post Magazine *since she graduated from the University of Virginia in 1977 with a bachelor's degree in English. Cunningham says that the essay reprinted here grew out of her own experience as an "easy to get along with person" who was raised by Southerners in the suburbs of Chicago. She also recalls that when writing it, "I was unhappy with myself for taking too long, for not being efficient the way I thought a professional writer should be—but the work paid off and now I think it is one of the best essays I've written." "Why Women Smile" originally appeared in* Lear's *in 1993.*

Looking back on her writing career, Cunningham notes, "When I was younger I thought if you had talent you would make it as a writer. I'm surprised to realize now that good writing has less to do with talent and more to do with the discipline of staying seated in the chair, by yourself, in front of the computer and getting the work done."

After smiling brilliantly for nearly four decades, I now find myself trying to quit. Or, at the very least, seeking to lower the wattage a bit.

Not everyone I know is keen on this. My smile has gleamed like a cheap plastic night-light so long and so reliably that certain friends and relatives worry that my mood will darken the moment my smile dims.

"Gee," one says, "I associate you with your smile. It's the essence of you. I should think you'd want to smile more!" But the people who love me best agree that my smile—which springs forth no matter where I am or how I feel—hasn't been serving me well. Said my husband recently, "Your smiling face and unthreatening demeanor make people like you in a fuzzy way, but that doesn't seem to be what you're after these days."

Smiles are not the small and innocuous things they appear to be: Too many of us smile in lieu of showing what's really on our minds. Indeed, the success of the women's movement might be measured by the sincerity—and lack of it—in our smiles. Despite all the work we American women have done to get and maintain full legal control of our bodies, not to mention our destinies, we still don't seem to be fully in charge of a couple of small muscle groups in our faces.

We smile so often and so promiscuously—when we're angry, when we're tense, when we're with children, when we're being photographed, when we're interviewing for a job, when we're meeting candidates to employ—that the Smiling Woman has become a peculiarly American archetype. This isn't entirely a bad thing, of course. A smile lightens the load, diffuses unpleasantness, redistributes nervous tension. Women doctors smile more than their male counterparts, studies show, and are better liked by their patients.

Oscar Wilde's old saw that "a woman's face is her work of fiction" is often quoted to remind us that what's on the surface may have little connection to what we're feeling. What is it in our culture that keeps our smiles on automatic pilot? The behavior seems to be an equal blend of nature and nurture. Research has demonstrated that since females often mature earlier than males and are less irritable, girls smile more than boys from the very beginning. But by adolescence, the differences in the smiling rates of boys and girls are so robust that it's clear the culture has done more than its share of the dirty work. Just think of the mothers who painstakingly embroidered the words ENTER SMILING on little samplers, and then hung their handiwork on doors by golden chains. Translation: "Your real emotions aren't welcome here."

Clearly, our instincts are another factor. Our smiles have their roots in the greetings of monkeys, who pull their lips up and back to show their fear of attack, as well as their reluctance to vie for a position of dominance. And like the opossum caught in the light by the clattering garbage cans, we, too, flash toothy grimaces when we make major mistakes. By declaring ourselves nonthreatening, our smiles provide an extremely versatile means of protection.

Our earliest baby smiles are involuntary reflexes having only the vaguest connection to contentment or comfort. In short, we're genetically wired to pull on our parents' heartstrings. As Desmond Morris explains in *Babywatching*, this is our way of attaching ourselves to our caretakers, as truly as baby chimps clench their mothers' fur. Even as babies we're capable of projecting onto others (in this case, our parents) the feelings we know we need to get back in return.

Bona fide social smiles occur at two-and-a-half to three months of age, usually a few weeks after we first start gazing with intense interest into the faces of our parents. By the time we are six months old, we are smiling and laughing regularly in reaction to tickling, feedings, blown raspberries, hugs, and peekaboo games. Even babies who are born blind intuitively know how to react to pleasurable changes with a smile, though their first smiles start later than those of sighted children.

Psychologists and psychiatrists have noted that babies also smile and laugh with relief when they realize that something they thought might be dangerous is not dangerous after all. Kids begin to invite their parents to indulge them with "scary" approach-avoidance games; they love to be chased or tossed up into the air. (It's interesting to note that as adults, we go through the same gosh-that's-shocking-and-dangerous-but-it's-okay-to-laugh-and-smile cycles when we listen to raunchy stand-up comics.)

From the wilds of New Guinea to the sidewalks of New York, smiles   10 are associated with joy, relief, and amusement. But smiles are by no means limited to the expression of positive emotions: People of many different cultures smile when they are frightened, embarrassed, angry, or miserable. In Japan, for instance, a smile is often used to hide pain or sorrow.

Psychologist Paul Ekman, the head of the University of California's Human Interaction Lab in San Francisco, has identified 18 distinct types of smiles, including those that show misery, compliance, fear, and contempt. The smile of true merriment, which Dr. Ekman calls the Duchenne Smile, after the nineteenth-century French doctor who first studied it, is characterized by heightened circulation, a feeling of exhilaration, and the employment of two major facial muscles: the zygomaticus major of the lower face, and the orbicularis oculi, which crinkles the skin around the eyes. But since the average American woman's smile often has less to do with her actual state of happiness than it does with the social pressure to smile no matter what, her baseline social smile isn't apt to be a felt expression that engages the eyes like this. Ekman insists that if people learned to read smiles, they could see the sadness, misery, or pain lurking there, plain as day.

Evidently, a woman's happy, willing deference is something the world wants visibly demonstrated. Woe to the waitress, the personal assistant or receptionist, the flight attendant, or any other woman in the line of public service whose smile is not offered up to the boss or client as proof that there are no storm clouds—no kids to support, no sleep that's been missed—rolling into the sunny workplace landscape. Women are expected to smile no matter where they line up on the social, cultural, or economic ladder: College professors are criticized for not smiling, political spouses are pilloried for being too serious, and women's roles in films have historically been smiling ones. It's little wonder that men on the street still call out, "Hey, baby, smile! Life's not *that* bad, is it?" to women passing by, lost in thought.

A friend remembers being pulled aside by a teacher after class and asked, "What is wrong, dear? You sat there for the whole hour looking so sad!" "All I could figure," my friend says now, "is that I wasn't smiling. And the fact that *she* felt sorry for me for looking normal made me feel horrible."

Ironically, the social laws that govern our smiles have completely reversed themselves over the last two thousand years. Women weren't always expected to seem animated and responsive; in fact, immoderate laughter was once considered one of the more conspicuous vices a woman could have, and mirth was downright sinful. Women were kept apart, in some cultures even veiled, so that they couldn't perpetuate Eve's seductive, evil work. The only smile deemed appropriate on a privileged woman's face was the serene, inward smile of the Virgin Mary at Christ's birth, and even that expression was best directed exclusively at young children. Cackling laughter and wicked glee were the kinds of sounds heard only in hell.

What we know of women's facial expressions in other centuries   15
comes mostly from religious writings, codes of etiquette, and portrait paintings. In fifteenth century Italy, it was customary for artists to paint lovely, blank-faced women in profile. A viewer could stare endlessly at such a woman, but she could not gaze back. By the Renaissance, male artists were taking some pleasure in depicting women with a semblance of complexity, Leonardo da Vinci's Mona Lisa, with her veiled enigmatic smile, being the most famous example.

The Golden Age of the Dutch Republic marks a fascinating period for studying women's facial expressions. While we might expect the drunken young whores of Amsterdam to smile devilishly (unbridled sexuality and lasciviousness were *supposed* to addle the brain), it's the faces of the Dutch women from fine families that surprise us. Considered socially more free, these women demonstrate a fuller range of facial expressions than their European sisters. Frans Hals's 1622 portrait of Stephanus Geraerdt and Isabella Coymans, a married couple, is remarkable not just for the full, friendly smiles on each face, but for the frank and mutual pleasure the couple take in each other.

In the 1800s, sprightly, pretty women began appearing in advertisements for everything from beverages to those newfangled Kodak Land cameras. Women's faces were no longer impassive, and their willingness to bestow status, to offer, proffer, and yield, was most definitely promoted by their smiling images. The culture appeared to have turned the smile, originally a bond shared between intimates, into a socially required display that sold capitalist ideology as well as kitchen appliances. And female viewers soon began to emulate these highly idealized pictures. Many longed to be more like her, that perpetually smiling female. She seemed so beautiful. So content. So whole.

By the middle of the nineteenth century, the bulk of America's smile burden was falling primarily to women and African-American slaves, providing a very portable means of protection, a way of saying, "I'm harmless. I won't assert myself here." It reassured those in power to see signs of gratitude and contentment in the faces of subordinates. As long ago as 1963, adman David Ogilvy declared the image of a woman smiling approvingly at a product clichéd, but we've yet to get the message. Cheerful Americans still appear in ads today, smiling somewhat less disingenuously than they smiled during the middle of the century, but smiling broadly nonetheless.

Other countries have been somewhat reluctant to import our "Don't worry, be happy" American smiles. When McDonald's opened in Moscow not long ago and when EuroDisney debuted in France last year, the Americans involved in both business ventures complained that they couldn't get the natives they'd employed to smile worth a damn.

Europeans visiting the United States for the first time are often sur-   20
prised at just how often Americans smile. But when you look at our history, the relentless good humor (or, at any rate, the pretense of it) falls into perspective. The American wilderness was developed on the assumption that this country had a shortage of people in relation to its possibilities. In countries with a more rigid class structure or caste system, fewer people are as captivated by the idea of quickly winning friends and influencing people. Here in the States, however, every stranger is a potential associate. Our smiles bring new people on board. The American smile is a democratic version of a curtsy or doffed hat, since, in this land of free equals, we're not especially formal about the ways we greet social superiors.

The civil rights movement never addressed the smile burden by name, but activists worked on their own to set new facial norms. African-American males stopped smiling on the streets in the 1960s, happily aware of the unsettling effect this action had on the white population. The image of the simpleminded, smiling, white-toothed black was rejected as blatantly racist, and it gradually retreated into the distance. However, like the women of Sparta and the wives of samurai, who were expected to look happy upon learning their sons or husbands had died in battle, contemporary American women have yet to unilaterally declare their faces their own property.

For instance, imagine a woman at a morning business meeting being asked if she could make a spontaneous and concise summation of a complicated project she's been struggling to get under control for months. She might draw the end of her mouth back and clench her teeth—Eek!—in a protective response, a polite, restrained expression of her surprise, not unlike the expression of a conscientious young schoolgirl being told to get out paper and pencil for a pop quiz. At the same time, the woman might be feeling resentful of the supervisor who sprang the request, but she fears taking that person on. So she holds back a comment. The whole performance resolves in a weird grin collapsing into a nervous smile that conveys discomfort and unpreparedness. A pointed remark by way of explanation or self-defense might've worked better for her—but her mouth was otherwise engaged.

We'd do well to realize just how much our smiles misrepresent us, and swear off for good the self-deprecating grins and ritual displays of deference. Real smiles have beneficial physiological effects, according to Paul Ekman. False ones do nothing for us at all.

"Smiles are as important as sound bites on television," insists producer and media coach Heidi Berenson, who has worked with many of Washington's most famous faces. "And women have always been better at understanding this than men. But the smile I'm talking about is not a cutesy smile. It's an authoritative smile. A genuine smile. Properly timed, it's tremendously powerful."

To limit a woman to one expression is like editing down an orchestra to one instrument. And the search for more authentic means of expression isn't easy in a culture in which women are still expected to be magnanimous smilers, helpmates in crisis, and curators of everybody else's morale. But change is already floating in the high winds. We see a boon in assertive female comedians who are proving that women can *dish out* smiles, not just wear them. Actress Demi Moore has stated that she doesn't like to take smiling roles. Nike is running ads that show unsmiling women athletes sweating, reaching, pushing themselves. These women aren't overly concerned with issues of rapport; they're not being "nice" girls—they're working out.

If a woman's smile were truly her own, to be smiled or not, according to how the *woman* felt, rather than according to what someone else needed, she would smile more spontaneously, without ulterior, hidden motives. As Rainer Maria Rilke wrote in *The Journal of My Other Self,* "Her smile was not meant to be seen by anyone and served its whole purpose in being smiled."

That smile is my long-term aim. In the meantime, I hope to stabilize on the smile continuum somewhere between the eliciting grin of Farrah Fawcett and the haughty smirk of Jeane Kirkpatrick.

The Reader's Presence

1. Cunningham presents an informative précis of the causes and effects of smiling in Western culture. Consider the points of view from which she addresses this subject. Summarize and evaluate her treatment of smiling from a psychological, physiological,

sociological, and historical point of view. Which do you find most incisive? Why? What other points of view does she introduce into her discussion of smiling? What effects do they create? What does she identify as the benefits (and the disadvantages) of smiling?

2. At what point in this essay does Cunningham address the issue of gender? Characterize the language she uses to introduce this issue. She distinguishes between the different patterns—and the consequences—experienced by men and women who smile. Summarize these differences and assess the nature and the extent of the evidence she provides for each of her points. What more general distinctions does she make about various kinds of smiles? What are their different purposes and degrees of intensity? What information does she provide about smiling as an issue of nationality and race? What is the overall purpose of this essay? Where—and how—does Cunningham create and sustain a sense of her own presence in this essay? What does she set as her personal goal in relation to smiling?

3. Cunningham presents an explanation of the causes of an activity that few of her readers think of in either scientific or historical terms. How does her audience's knowledgeability affect the nature of the metaphors and diction she uses? Point to specific words and phrases to support and develop your point. What principles of organization does she rely on to create a sequence and structure for her essay? Comment on her use of surprise in her essay—in terms of the structure, metaphors, and diction she uses to make her points.

47

Lars Eighner

On Dumpster Diving

Lars Eigner (b. 1948) was born in Texas and attended the University of Texas at Austin. An essayist and fiction writer, he contributes regularly to the Threepenny Review, Advocate Men, The Guide, *and* Inches. *He has published several collections of short stories, essays, and gay erotica. His most recent publications include a camp novel,* Pawnto Queen Four *(1995); a collection of essays,* Gay Cosmos *(1995); an erotic short story collection,* Whispered in the Dark *(1995); and* WANK: The Tapes *(1998).*

Eighner became homeless in 1988, when he lost his job as a mental-hospital attendant. "On Dumpster Diving" is Eigner's prize-winning essay based on this experience, later reprinted as part of his full-length book about homelessness, Travels with Lizbeth: Three Years on the Road and on the Streets *(1993). Eighner and Lizbeth, Eighner's dog, became homeless again in 1996. Friends organized a fund under the auspices of the* Texas Observer *and obtained an apartment for Eighner and Lizbeth in Austin. Lizbeth recently passed away.*

On what is required to find success as a writer, Eighner has said, "I was not making enough money to support myself as a housed person, but I was writing well before I became homeless. . . . A writer needs talent, luck, and persistence. You can make do with two out of three, and the more you have of one, the less you need of the others."

Long before I began Dumpster diving I was impressed with Dumpsters, enough so that I wrote the Merriam-Webster research service to discover what I could about the word "Dumpster." I learned from them that "Dumpster" is a proprietary word belonging to the Dempster Dumpster company.

Since then I have dutifully capitalized the word although it was lowercased in almost all of the citations Merriam-Webster photocopied for me. Dempster's word is too apt. I have never heard these things called anything but Dumpsters. I do not know anyone who knows the generic name for these objects. From time to time, however, I hear a wino or hobo give some corrupted credit to the original and call them Dipsy Dumpsters.

I began Dumpster diving about a year before I became homeless.

I prefer the term "scavenging" and use the word "scrounging" when I mean to be obscure. I have heard people, evidently meaning to be polite, using the word "foraging," but I prefer to reserve that word for gathering nuts and berries and such which I do also according to the season and the opportunity. "Dumpster diving" seems to me to be a little too cute and, in my case, inaccurate because I lack the athletic ability to lower myself into the Dumpsters as the true divers do, much to their increased profit.

I like the frankness of the word "scavenging," which I can hardly think of without picturing a big black snail on an aquarium wall. I live from the refuse of others. I am a scavenger. I think it a sound and honorable niche, although if I could I would naturally prefer to live the comfortable consumer life, perhaps—and only perhaps—as a slightly less wasteful consumer owing to what I have learned as a scavenger.

While my dog Lizbeth and I were still living in the house on Avenue B in Austin, as my savings ran out, I put almost all my sporadic income into rent. The necessities of daily life I began to extract from Dumpsters. Yes, we ate from Dumpsters. Except for jeans, all my clothes came from Dumpsters. Boom boxes, candles, bedding, toilet paper, medicine, books, a typewriter, a virgin male love doll, change sometimes amounting to many dollars: I acquired many things from the Dumpsters.

5

I have learned much as a scavenger. I mean to put some of what I have learned down here, beginning with the practical art of Dumpster diving and proceeding to the abstract.

What is safe to eat?

After all, the finding of objects is becoming something of an urban art. Even respectable employed people will sometimes find something tempting sticking out of a Dumpster or standing beside one. Quite a number of people, not all of them of the bohemian type, are willing to brag that they found this or that piece in the trash. But eating from Dumpsters is the thing that separates the dilettanti from the professionals.

Eating safely from the Dumpsters involves three principles: using the   10
senses and common sense to evaluate the condition of the found materials, knowing the Dumpsters of a given area and checking them regularly, and seeking always to answer the question "Why was this discarded?"

Perhaps everyone who has a kitchen and a regular supply of groceries has, at one time or another, made a sandwich and eaten half of it before discovering mold on the bread or got a mouthful of milk before realizing the milk had turned. Nothing of the sort is likely to happen to a Dumpster diver because he is constantly reminded that most food is discarded for a reason. Yet a lot of perfectly good food can be found in Dumpsters.

Canned goods, for example, turn up fairly often in the Dumpsters I frequent. All except the most phobic people would be willing to eat from a can even if it came from a Dumpster. Canned goods are among the safest of foods to be found in Dumpsters, but are not utterly foolproof.

Although very rare with modern canning methods, botulism is a possibility. Most other forms of food poisoning seldom do lasting harm to a healthy person. But botulism is almost certainly fatal and often the first symptom is death. Except for carbonated beverages, all canned goods should contain a slight vacuum and suck air when first punctured. Bulging, rusty, dented cans and cans that spew when punctured should be avoided, especially when the contents are not very acidic or syrupy.

Heat can break down the botulin, but this requires much more cooking than most people do to canned goods. To the extent that botulism occurs at all, of course, it can occur in cans on pantry shelves as well as in cans from Dumpsters. Need I say that home-canned goods found in Dumpsters are simply too risky to be recommended.

From time to time one of my companions, aware of the source of my   15
provisions, will ask, "Do you think these crackers are really safe to eat?" For some reason it is most often the crackers they ask about.

This question always makes me angry. Of course I would not offer my companion anything I had doubts about. But more than that I wonder why he cannot evaluate the condition of the crackers for himself. I have no special knowledge and I have been wrong before. Since he knows where the food comes from, it seems to me he ought to assume some of the responsibility for deciding what he will put in his mouth.

For myself I have few qualms about dry foods such as crackers, cookies, cereal, chips, and pasta if they are free of visible contaminates and still dry and crisp. Most often such things are found in the original packaging, which is not so much a positive sign as it is the absence of a negative one.

Raw fruits and vegetables with intact skins seem perfectly safe to me, excluding of course the obviously rotten. Many are discarded for minor imperfections which can be pared away. Leafy vegetables, grapes, cauliflower, broccoli, and similar things may be contaminated by liquids and may be impractical to wash.

Candy, especially hard candy, is usually safe if it has not drawn ants. Chocolate is often discarded only because it has become discolored as the cocoa butter de-emulsified. Candying after all is one method of food preservation because pathogens do not like very sugary substances.

All of these foods might be found in any Dumpster and can be evaluated with some confidence largely on the basis of appearance. Beyond these are foods which cannot be correctly evaluated without additional information. 20

I began scavenging by pulling pizzas out of the Dumpster behind a pizza delivery shop. In general prepared food requires caution, but in this case I knew when the shop closed and went to the Dumpster as soon as the last of the help left.

Such shops often get prank orders, called "bogus." Because help seldom stays long at these places pizzas are often made with the wrong topping, refused on delivery for being cold, or baked incorrectly. The products to be discarded are boxed up because inventory is kept by counting boxes: A boxed pizza can be written off; an unboxed pizza does not exist.

I never placed a bogus order to increase the supply of pizzas and I believe no one else was scavenging in this Dumpster. But the people in the shop became suspicious and began to retain their garbage in the shop overnight.

While it lasted I had a steady supply of fresh, sometimes warm pizza. Because I knew the Dumpster I knew the source of the pizza, and because I visited the Dumpster regularly I knew what was fresh and what was yesterday's.

The area I frequent is inhabited by many affluent college students. I am not here by chance; the Dumpsters in this area are very rich. Students throw out many good things, including food. In particular they tend to throw everything out when they move at the end of a semester, before and after breaks, and around midterm when many of them despair of college. So I find it advantageous to keep an eye on the academic calendar. 25

The students throw food away around the breaks because they do not know whether it has spoiled or will spoil before they return. A typical discard is a half jar of peanut butter. In fact nonorganic peanut butter does not require refrigeration and is unlikely to spoil in any reasonable time. The student does not know that, and since it is Daddy's money, the student decides not to take a chance.

Opened containers require caution and some attention to the question "Why was this discarded?" But in the case of discards from student apartments, the answer may be that the item was discarded through carelessness, ignorance, or wastefulness. This can sometimes be deduced when the item is found with many others, including some that are obviously perfectly good.

Some students, and others, approach defrosting a freezer by chucking out the whole lot. Not only do the circumstances of such a find tell the story, but also the mass of frozen goods stays cold for a long time and items may be found still frozen or freshly thawed.

Yogurt, cheese, and sour cream are items that are often thrown out while they are still good. Occasionally I find a cheese with a spot of mold, which of course I just pare off, and because it is obvious why such a cheese was discarded, I treat it with less suspicion than an apparently perfect cheese found in similar circumstances. Yogurt is often discarded, still sealed, only because the expiration date on the carton had passed. This is one of my favorite finds because yogurt will keep for several days, even in warm weather.

Students throw out canned goods and staples at the end of semesters   30
and when they give up college at midterm. Drugs, pornography, spirits, and the like are often discarded when parents are expected—Dad's day, for example. And spirits also turn up after big party weekends, presumably discarded by the newly reformed. Wine and spirits, of course, keep perfectly well even once opened.

My test for carbonated soft drinks is whether they still fizz vigorously. Many juices or other beverages are too acid or too syrupy to cause much concern provided they are not visibly contaminated. Liquids, however, require some care.

One hot day I found a large jug of Pat O'Brien's Hurricane mix. The jug had been opened, but it was still ice cold. I drank three large glasses before it became apparent to me that someone had added the rum to the mix, and not a little rum. I never tasted the rum and by the time I began to feel the effects I had already ingested a very large quantity of the beverage. Some divers would have considered this a boon, but being suddenly and thoroughly intoxicated in a public place in the early afternoon is not my idea of a good time.

I have heard of people maliciously contaminating discarded food and even handouts, but mostly I have heard of this from people with vivid imaginations who have had no experience with the Dumpsters themselves. Just before the pizza shop stopped discarding its garbage at night, jalapeños began showing up on most of the discarded pizzas. If indeed this was meant to discourage me it was a wasted effort because I am native Texan.

For myself, I avoid game, poultry, pork, and egg-based foods whether I find them raw or cooked. I seldom have the means to cook what I find, but when I do I avail myself of plentiful supplies of beef which is often in very good condition. I suppose fish becomes disagreeable before it becomes dangerous. The dog is happy to have any such thing that is past its prime and, in fact, does not recognize fish as food until it is quite strong.

Home leftovers, as opposed to surpluses from restaurants, are very 35 often bad. Evidently, especially among students, there is a common type of personality that carefully wraps up even the smallest leftover and shoves it into the back of the refrigerator for six months or so before discarding it. Characteristic of this type are the reused jars and margarine tubs which house the remains.

I avoid ethnic foods I am unfamiliar with. If I do not know what it is supposed to look like when it is good, I cannot be certain I will be able to tell if it is bad.

No, matter how careful I am I still get dysentery at least once a month, oftener in warm weather. I do not want to paint too romantic a picture. Dumpster diving has serious drawbacks as a way of life.

I learned to scavenge gradually, on my own. Since then I have initiated several companions into the trade. I have learned that there is a predictable series of stages a person goes through in learning to scavenge.

At first the new scavenger is filled with disgust and self-loathing. He is ashamed of being seen and may lurk around, trying to duck behind things, or he may try to dive at night.

(In fact, most people instinctively look away from a scavenger. By 40 skulking around, the novice calls attention to himself and arouses suspicion. Diving at night is ineffective and needlessly messy.)

Every grain of rice seems to be a maggot. Everything seems to stink. He can wipe the egg yolk off the found can, but he cannot erase the stigma of eating garbage out of his mind.

That stage passes with experience. The scavenger finds a pair of running shoes that fit and look and smell brand new. He finds a pocket calculator in perfect working order. He finds pristine ice cream, still frozen, more than he can eat or keep. He begins to understand: People do throw away perfectly good stuff, a lot of perfectly good stuff.

At this stage, Dumpster shyness begins to dissipate. The diver, after all, has the last laugh. He is finding all manner of good things which are his for the taking. Those who disparage his profession are the fools, not he.

He may begin to hang onto some perfectly good things for which he has neither a use nor a market. Then he begins to take note of the things which are not perfectly good but are nearly so. He mates a Walkman with broken earphones and one that is missing a battery cover. He picks up things which he can repair.

At this stage he may become lost and never recover. Dumpsters are   45
full of things of some potential value to someone and also of things which
never have much intrinsic value but are interesting. All the Dumpster
divers I have known come to the point of trying to acquire everything
they touch. Why not take it, they reason, since it is all free.

This is, of course, hopeless. Most divers come to realize that they
must restrict themselves to items of relatively immediate utility. But in
some cases the diver simply cannot control himself. I have met several of
these pack-rat types. Their ideas of the values of various pieces of junk
verge on the psychotic. Every bit of glass may be a diamond, they think,
and all that glistens, gold.

I tend to gain weight when I am scavenging. Partly this is because I
always find far more pizza and doughnuts than water-packed tuna, non-
fat yogurt, and fresh vegetables. Also I have not developed much faith in
the reliability of Dumpsters as a food source, although it has been proven
to me many times. I tend to eat as if I have no idea where my next meal is
coming from. But mostly I just hate to see food go to waste and so I eat
much more than I should. Something like this drives the obsession to collect junk.

As for collecting objects, I usually restrict myself to collecting one
kind of small object at a time, such as pocket calculators, sunglasses, or
campaign buttons. To live on the street I must anticipate my needs to a
certain extent: I must pick up and save warm bedding I find in August because it will not be found in Dumpsters in November. But even if I had a
home with extensive storage space I could not save everything that might
be valuable in some contingency.

I have proprietary feelings about my Dumpsters. As I have suggested,
it is no accident that I scavenge from Dumpsters where good finds are
common. But my limited experience with Dumpsters in other areas suggests to me that it is the population of competitors rather than the afflu-
ence of the dumpers that most affects the feasibility of survival by scavenging. The large number of competitors is what puts me off the idea of
trying to scavenge in places like Los Angeles.

Curiously, I do not mind my direct competition, other scavengers, so   50
much as I hate the can scroungers.

People scrounge cans because they have to have a little cash. I have
tried scrounging cans with an able-bodied companion. Afoot a can
scrounger simply cannot make more than a few dollars a day. One can
extract the necessities of life from the Dumpsters directly with far less effort than would be required to accumulate the equivalent value in cans.

Can scroungers, then, are people who *must* have small amounts of
cash. These are drug addicts and winos, mostly the latter because the
amounts of cash are so small.

Spirits and drugs do, like all other commodities, turn up in Dumpsters and the scavenger will from time to time have a half bottle of a
rather good wine with his dinner. But the wino cannot survive on these

occasional finds; he must have his daily dose to stave off the DTs. All the cans he can carry will buy about three bottles of Wild Irish Rose.

I do not begrudge them the cans, but can scroungers tend to tear up the Dumpsters, mixing the contents and littering the area. They become so specialized that they can see only cans. They earn my contempt by passing up change, canned goods, and readily hockable items.

There are precious few courtesies among scavengers. But it is a com- 55 mon practice to set aside surplus items: pairs of shoes, clothing, canned goods, and such. A true scavenger hates to see good stuff go to waste and what he cannot use he leaves in good condition in plain sight.

Can scroungers lay waste to everything in their path and will stir one of a pair of good shoes to the bottom of a Dumpster, to be lost or ruined in the muck. Can scroungers will even go through individual garbage cans, something I have never seen a scavenger do.

Individual garbage cans are set out on the public easement only on garbage days. On other days going through them requires trespassing close to a dwelling. Going through individual garbage cans without scattering litter is almost impossible. Litter is likely to reduce the public's tolerance of scavenging. Individual garbage cans are simply not as productive as Dumpsters; people in houses and duplexes do not move as often and for some reason do not tend to discard as much useful material. Moreover, the time required to go through one garbage can that serves one household is not much less than the time required to go through a Dumpster that contains the refuse of twenty apartments.

But my strongest reservation about going through individual garbage cans is that this seems to me a very personal kind of invasion to which I would object if I were a householder. Although many things in Dumpsters are obviously meant never to come to light, a Dumpster is somehow less personal.

I avoid trying to draw conclusions about the people who dump in the Dumpsters I frequent. I think it would be unethical to do so, although I know many people will find the idea of scavenger ethics too funny for words.

Dumpsters contain bank statements, bills, correspondence, and other 60 documents, just as anyone might expect. But there are also less obvious sources of information. Pill bottles, for example. The labels on pill bottles contain the name of the patient, the name of the doctor, and the name of the drug. AIDS drugs and antipsychotic medicines, to name but two groups, are specific and are seldom prescribed for any other disorders. The plastic compacts for birth control pills usually have complete label information.

Despite all of this sensitive information, I have had only one apartment resident object to my going through the Dumpster. In that case it turned out the resident was a university athlete who was taking bets and who was afraid I would turn up his wager slips.

Occasionally a find tells a story. I once found a small paper bag containing some unused condoms, several partial tubes of flavored sexual lubricant, a partially used compact of birth control pills, and the torn pieces of a picture of a young man. Clearly she was through with him and planning to give up sex altogether.

Dumpster things are often sad—abandoned teddy bears, shredded wedding books, despaired-of sales kits. I find many pets lying in state in Dumpsters. Although I hope to get off the streets so that Lizbeth can have a long and comfortable old age, I know this hope is not very realistic. So I suppose when her time comes she too will go into a Dumpster. I will have no better place for her. And after all, for most of her life her livelihood has come from the Dumpster. When she finds something I think is safe that has been spilled from the Dumpster I let her have it. She already knows the route around the best Dumpsters. I like to think that if she survives me she will have a chance of evading the dog catcher and of finding her sustenance on the route.

Silly vanities also come to rest in the Dumpsters. I am a rather accomplished needleworker. I get a lot of materials from the Dumpsters. Evidently sorority girls, hoping to impress someone, perhaps themselves, with their mastery of a womanly art, buy a lot of embroider-by-number kits, work a few stitches horribly, and eventually discard the whole mess. I pull out their stitches, turn the canvas over, and work an original design. Do not think I refrain from chuckling as I make original gifts from these kits.

I find diaries and journals. I have often thought of compiling a book   65
of literary found objects. And perhaps I will one day. But what I find is hopelessly commonplace and bad without being, even unconsciously, camp. College students also discard their papers. I am horrified to discover the kind of paper which now merits an A in an undergraduate course. I am grateful, however, for the number of good books and magazines the students throw out.

In the area I know best I have never discovered vermin in the Dumpsters, but there are two kinds of kitty surprise. One is alley cats which I meet as they leap, claws first, out of Dumpsters. This is especially thrilling when I have Lizbeth in tow. The other kind of kitty surprise is a plastic garbage bag filled with some ponderous, amorphous mass. This always proves to be used cat litter.

City bees harvest doughnut glaze and this makes the Dumpster at the doughnut shop more interesting. My faith in the instinctive wisdom of animals is always shaken whenever I see Lizbeth attempt to catch a bee in her mouth, which she does whenever bees are present. Evidently some birds find Dumpsters profitable, for birdie surprise is almost as common as kitty surprise of the first kind. In hunting season all kinds of small game turn up in Dumpsters, some of it, sadly, not entirely dead. Curiously, summer and winter, maggots are uncommon.

The worst of the living and near-living hazards of the Dumpsters are the fire ants. The food that they claim is not much of a loss, but they are vicious and aggressive. It is very easy to brush against some surface of the Dumpster and pick up half a dozen or more fire ants, usually in some sensitive area such as the underarm. One advantage of bringing Lizbeth along as I make Dumpster rounds is that, for obvious reasons, she is very alert to ground-based fire ants. When Lizbeth recognizes the signs of fire ant infestation around our feet she does the Dance of the Zillion Fire Ants. I have learned not to ignore this warning from Lizbeth, whether I perceive the tiny ants or not, but to remove ourselves at Lizbeth's first pas de bourrée.[1] All the more so because the ants are the worst in the months I wear flip-flops, if I have them.

(Perhaps someone will misunderstand the above. Lizbeth does the Dance of the Zillion Fire Ants when she recognizes more fire ants than she cares to eat, not when she is being bitten. Since I have learned to react promptly, she does not get bitten at all. It is the isolated patrol of fire ants that falls in Lizbeth's range that deserves pity. Lizbeth finds them quite tasty.)

By far the best way to go through a Dumpster is to lower yourself into it. Most of the good stuff tends to settle at the bottom because it is usually weightier than the rubbish. My more athletic companions have often demonstrated to me that they can extract much good material from a Dumpster I have already been over.   70

To those psychologically or physically unprepared to enter a Dumpster, I recommend a stout stick, preferably with some barb or hook at one end. The hook can be used to grab plastic garbage bags. When I find canned goods or other objects loose at the bottom of a Dumpster I usually can roll them into a small bag that I can then hoist up. Much Dumpster diving is a matter of experience for which nothing will do except practice.

Dumpster diving is outdoor work, often surprisingly pleasant. It is not entirely predictable; things of interest turn up every day and some days there are finds of great value. I am always very pleased when I can turn up exactly the thing I most wanted to find. Yet in spite of the element of change, scavenging more than most other pursuits tends to yield returns in some proportion to the effort and intelligence brought to bear. It is very sweet to turn up a few dollars in change from a Dumpster that has just been gone over by a wino.

The land is now covered with cities. The cities are full of Dumpsters. I think of scavenging as a modern form of self-reliance. In any event, after ten years of government service, where everything is geared to the lowest common denominator, I find work that rewards initiative and effort refreshing. Certainly I would be happy to have a sinecure again, but I am not heartbroken not to have one anymore.

I find from the experience of scavenging two rather deep lessons. The first is to take what I can use and let the rest go by. I have come to think

---

[1]*pas de bourrée:* A transitional ballet step. — EDS.

that there is no value in the abstract. A thing I cannot use or make useful, perhaps by trading, has no value however fine or rare it may be. I mean useful in a broad sense — so, for example, some art I would think useful and valuable, but other art might be otherwise for me.

I was shocked to realize that some things are not worth acquiring, but now I think it is so. Some material things are white elephants that eat up the possessor's substance.   75

The second lesson is of the transience of material being. This has not quite converted me to a dualist, but it has made some headway in that direction. I do not suppose that ideas are immortal, but certainly mental things are longer-lived than other material things.

Once I was the sort of person who invests material objects with sentimental value. Now I no longer have those things, but I have the sentiments yet.

Many times in my travels I have lost everything but the clothes I was wearing and Lizbeth. The things I find in Dumpsters, the love letters and ragdolls of so many lives, remind me of this lesson. Now I hardly pick up a thing without envisioning the time I will cast it away. This I think is a healthy state of mind. Almost everything I have now has already been cast out at least once, proving that what I own is valueless to someone.

Anyway, I find my desire to grab for the gaudy bauble has been largely sated. I think this is an attitude I share with the very wealthy — we both know there is plenty more where what we have came from. Between us are the rat-race millions who have confounded their selves with the objects they grasp and who nightly scavenge the cable channels looking for they know not what.

I am sorry for them.   80

The Reader's Presence

1. At the center of "On Dumpster Diving" is Lars Eighner's effort to bring out from the shadows of contemporary American life the lore and practices of scavenging, what he calls "a modern form of self-reliance." His essay also provides a compelling account of his self-education as he took to the streets for "the necessities of life." Outline the stages in this process, and summarize the ethical and moral issues and the questions of decorum that Eighner confronted along the way. Show how this process reflects the structure of his essay, "beginning with the practical art of Dumpster diving and proceeding to the abstract."

2. One of the most remarkable aspects of Eighner's essay is the tone (the attitude) he expresses toward his subject. Select a paragraph from Eighner's essay. Read it aloud. How would you characterize the sound of his voice? Does he sound, for example, tough-

minded? polite? strident? experienced? cynical? something else? Consider, for example, paragraph 34, where he notes: "For myself, I avoid game, poultry, pork, and egg-based foods whether I find them raw or cooked." Where have you heard talk like this before? Do you notice any changes as the essay develops, or does Eighner maintain the same tone in discussing his subject? What responses does he elicit from his readers when he speaks of scavenging as a "profession" and a "trade"?

3. Consider Eighner's relationship with his readers. Does he consider himself fundamentally different from or similar to his audience? In what specific ways? Consider, for example, the nature of the information Eighner provides in the essay. Does he expect his readers to be familiar with the information? How does he characterize his own knowledgeability about this often-noticed but rarely discussed activity in urban America? Comment on his use of irony in presenting information about Dumpster diving and in anticipating his readers' responses to the circumstances within which he does the work of his trade.

48

Loren Eiseley

How Flowers Changed the World

Loren Eiseley (1907–1977) taught at various universities and colleges, including the University of Pennsylvania, where he was Benjamin Franklin Professor of Anthropology and History of Science, and where he also served as provost and as curator. A versatile writer, Eiseley published fiction, essays, and poetry and was noted for his ability to make difficult science accessible to lay readers. He was a frequent contributor to both scientific journals such as American Anthropologist *and* Scientific Monthly *and to popular magazines such as* Harper's, Ladies' Home Journal, *the* Saturday Evening Post, *and the* Atlantic. *Among Eiseley's many acclaimed books are* Darwin's Century *(1958),* The Firmament of Time *(1960), and* The Star Thrower *(1978); the following essay, "How Flowers Changed the World," is from* The Immense Journey *(1957).*

If it had been possible to observe the Earth from the far side of the solar system over the long course of geological epochs, the watchers might have been able to discern a subtle change in the light emanating from our planet. That world of long ago would, like the red deserts of Mars, have reflected light from vast drifts of stone and gravel, the sands of wandering wastes, the blackness of naked basalt, the yellow dust of endlessly moving storms. Only the ceaseless marching of the clouds and the intermittent flashes from the restless surface of the sea would have told a different story, but still essentially a barren one. Then, as the millennia rolled away and age followed age, a new and greener light would, by degrees, have come to twinkle across those endless miles.

This is the only difference those far watchers, by the use of subtle instruments, might have perceived in the whole history of the planet Earth. Yet that slowly growing green twinkle would have contained the epic march of life from the tidal oozes upward across the raw and unclothed continents. Out of the vast chemical bath of the sea—not from the deeps, but from the element-rich, light-exposed platforms of the continental shelves—wandering fingers of green had crept upward along the meanderings of river systems and fringed the gravels of forgotten lakes.

In those first ages plants clung of necessity to swamps and watercourses. Their reproductive processes demanded direct access to water. Beyond the primitive ferns and mosses that enclosed the borders of swamps and streams the rocks still lay vast and bare, the winds still swirled the dust of a naked planet. The grass cover that holds our world secure in place was still millions of years in the future. The green marchers had gained a soggy foothold upon the land, but that was all. They did not reproduce by seeds but by microscopic swimming sperm that had to wriggle their way through water to fertilize the female cell. Such plants in their higher forms had clever adaptations for the use of rain water in their sexual phases, and survived with increasing success in a wet land environment. They now seem part of man's normal environment. The truth is, however, that there is nothing very "normal" about nature. Once upon a time there were no flowers at all.

A little while ago—about one hundred million years, as the geologist estimates time in the history of our four-billion-year-old planet—flowers were not to be found anywhere on the five continents. Wherever one might have looked, from the poles to the equator, one would have seen only the cold dark monotonous green of a world whose plant life possessed no other color.

Somewhere, just a short time before the close of the Age of Reptiles,   5 there occurred a soundless, violent explosion. It lasted millions of years, but it was an explosion, nevertheless. It marked the emergence of the angiosperms—the flowering plants. Even the great evolutionist, Charles Darwin, called them "an abominable mystery," because they appeared so suddenly and spread so fast.

Flowers changed the face of the planet. Without them, the world we know—even man himself—would never have existed. Francis Thompson, the English poet, once wrote that one could not pluck a flower without troubling a star. Intuitively he had sensed like a naturalist the enormous interlinked complexity of life. Today we know that the appearance of the flowers contained also the equally mystifying emergence of man.

If we were to go back into the Age of Reptiles, its drowned swamps and birdless forests would reveal to us a warmer but, on the whole, a sleepier world than that of today. Here and there, it is true, the serpent heads of bottom-feeding dinosaurs might be upreared in suspicion of their huge flesh-eating compatriots. Tyrannosaurs, enormous bipedal caricatures of men, would stalk mindlessly across the sites of future cities and go their slow way down into the dark of geologic time.

In all that world of living things nothing saw save with the intense concentration of the hunt, nothing moved except with the grave sleep-walking intentness of the instinct-driven brain. Judged by modern standards, it was a world in slow motion, a cold-blooded world whose occupants were most active at noonday but torpid on chill nights, their brains damped by a slower metabolism than any known to even the most primitive of warm-blooded animals today.

A high metabolic rate and the maintenance of a constant body temperature are supreme achievements in the evolution of life. They enable an animal to escape, within broad limits, from the overheating or the chilling of its immediate surroundings, and at the same time to maintain a peak mental efficiency. Creatures without a high metabolic rate are slaves to weather. Insects in the first frosts of autumn all run down like little clocks. Yet if you pick one up and breathe warmly upon it, it will begin to move about once more.

In a sheltered spot such creatures may sleep away the winter, but they are hopelessly immobilized. Though a few warm-blooded mammals, such as the woodchuck of our day, have evolved a way of reducing their metabolic rate in order to undergo winter hibernation, it is a survival mechanism with drawbacks, for it leaves the animal helplessly exposed if enemies discover him during his period of suspended animation. Thus bear or woodchuck, big animal or small, must seek, in this time of descending sleep, a safe refuge in some hidden den or burrow. Hibernation is, therefore, primarily a winter refuge of small, easily concealed animals rather than of large ones.

A high metabolic rate, however, means a heavy intake of energy in order to sustain body warmth and efficiency. It is for this reason that even some of these later warm-blooded mammals existing in our day have learned to descend into a slower, unconscious rate of living during the winter months when food may be difficult to obtain. On a slightly higher plane they are following the procedure of the cold-blooded frog sleeping in the mud at the bottom of a frozen pond.

The agile brain of the warm-blooded birds and mammals demands a high oxygen consumption and food in concentrated forms, or the creatures cannot long sustain themselves. It was the rise of the flowering

10

plants that provided that energy and changed the nature of the living world. Their appearance parallels in a quite surprising manner the rise of the birds and mammals.

Slowly, toward the dawn of the Age of Reptiles, something over two hundred and fifty million years ago, the little naked sperm cells wriggling their way through dew and raindrops had given way to a kind of pollen carried by the wind. Our present-day pine forests represent plants of a pollen-disseminating variety. Once fertilization was no longer dependent on exterior water, the march over drier regions could be extended. Instead of spores simple primitive seeds carrying some nourishment for the young plant had developed, but true flowers were still scores of millions of years away. After a long period of hesitant evolutionary groping, they exploded upon the world with truly revolutionary violence.

The event occurred in Cretaceous times in the close of the Age of Reptiles. Before the coming of the flowering plants our own ancestral stock, the warm-blooded mammals, consisted of a few mousy little creatures hidden in trees and underbrush. A few lizard-like birds with carnivorous teeth flapped awkwardly on ill-aimed flights among archaic shrubbery. None of these insignificant creatures gave evidence of any remarkable talents. The mammals in particular had been around for some millions of years, but had remained well lost in the shadow of the mighty reptiles. Truth to tell, man was still, like the genie in the bottle, encased in the body of a creature about the size of a rat.

As for the birds, their reptilian cousins the Pterodactyls, flew farther and better. There was just one thing about the birds that paralleled the physiology of the mammals. They, too, had evolved warm blood and its accompanying temperature control. Nevertheless, if one had been seen stripped of his feathers, he would still have seemed a slightly uncanny and unsightly lizard.   15

Neither the birds nor the mammals, however, were quite what they seemed. They were waiting for the Age of Flowers. They were waiting for what flowers, and with them the true encased seed, would bring. Fish-eating, gigantic leather-winged reptiles, twenty-eight feet from wing tip to wing tip, hovered over the coasts that one day would be swarming with gulls.

Inland the monotonous green of the pine and spruce forests with their primitive wooden cone flowers stretched everywhere. No grass hindered the fall of the naked seeds to earth. Great sequoias towered to the skies. The world of that time has a certain appeal but it is a giant's world, a world moving slowly like the reptiles who stalked magnificently among the boles of its trees.

The trees themselves are ancient, slow-growing and immense, like the redwood groves that have survived to our day on the California coast. All is stiff, formal upright and green, monotonously green. There is no grass as yet; there are no wide plains rolling in the sun, no tiny daisies dotting the meadows underfoot. There is little versatility about this scene; it is, in truth, a giant's world.

A few nights ago it was brought home vividly to me that the world has changed since that far epoch. I was awakened out of sleep by an unknown sound in my living room. Not a small sound—not a creaking timber or a mouse's scurry—but a sharp, rending explosion as though as unwary foot had been put down upon a wine glass. I had come instantly out of sleep and lay tense, unbreathing. I listened for another step. There was none.

Unable to stand the suspense any longer, I turned on the light and   20
passed from room to room glancing uneasily behind chairs and into closets. Nothing seemed disturbed, and I stood puzzled in the center of the living room floor. Then a small button-shaped object upon the rug caught my eye. It was hard and polished and glistening. Scattered over the length of the room were several more shining up at me like wary little eyes. A pine cone that had been lying in a dish had been blown the length of the coffee table. The dish itself could hardly have been the source of the explosion. Beside it I found two ribbon-like strips of a velvety-green. I tried to place the two strips together to make a pod. They twisted resolutely away from each other and would no longer fit.

I relaxed in a chair, then, for I had reached a solution of the midnight disturbance. The twisted strips were wistaria pods that I had brought in a day or two previously and placed in the dish. They had chosen midnight to explode and distribute their multiplying fund of life down the length of the room. A plant, a fixed, rooted thing, immobilized in a single spot, had devised a way of propelling its offspring across open space. Immediately there passed before my eyes the million airy troopers of the milkweed pod and the clutching hooks of the sandburs. Seeds on the coyote's tail, seeds on the hunter's coat, thistledown mounting on the winds—all were somehow triumphing over life's limitations. Yet the ability to do this had not been with them at the beginning. It was the product of endless effort and experiment.

The seeds on my carpet were not going to lie stiffly where they had dropped like their antiquated cousins, the naked seeds on the pine-cone scales. They were travelers. Struck by the thought, I went out next day and collected several other varieties. I line them up now in a row on my desk—so many little capsules of life, winged, hooked or spiked. Every one is an angiosperm, a product of the true flowering plants. Contained in these little boxes is the secret of that far-off Cretaceous explosion of a hundred million years ago that changed the face of the planet. And somewhere in here, I think, as I poke seriously at one particularly resistant seedcase of a wild grass, was once man himself.

When the first simple flower bloomed on some raw upland late in the Dinosaur Age, it was wind pollinated, just like its early pine-cone relatives. It was a very inconspicuous flower because it had not yet evolved the idea of using the surer attraction of birds and insects to achieve the transportation of pollen. It sowed its own pollen and received the pollen of other flowers by the simple vagaries of the wind. Many plants in regions where insect life is scant still follow this principle today. Nevertheless, the true flower—and the seed that it produced—was a profound innovation in the world of life.

In a way, this event parallels, in the plant world, what happened among animals. Consider the relative chance for survival of the exteriorly deposited egg of a fish in contrast with the fertilized egg of a mammal, carefully retained for months in the mother's body until the young animal (or human being) is developed to a point where it may survive. The biological wastage is less—and so it is with the flowering plants. The primitive spore, a single cell fertilized in the beginning by a swimming sperm, did not promote rapid distribution, and the young plant, moreover, had to struggle up from nothing. No one had left it any food except what it could get by its own unaided efforts.

By contrast, the true flowering plants (angiosperm itself means "encased seed") grew a seed in the heart of a flower, a seed whose development was initiated by a fertilizing pollen grain independent of outside moisture. But the seed, unlike the developing spore, is already a fully equipped *embryonic plant* packed in a little enclosed box stuffed full of nutritious food. Moreover, by featherdown attachments, as in dandelion or milkweed seed, it can be wafted upward on gusts and ride the wind for miles; or with hooks it can cling to a bear's or a rabbit's hide; or like some of the berries, it can be covered with a juicy, attractive fruit to lure birds, pass undigested through their intestinal tracts and be voided miles away.

The ramifications of this biological invention were endless. Plants traveled as they had never traveled before. They got into strange environments heretofore never entered by the old spore plants or stiff pine-cone-seed plants. The well-fed, carefully cherished little embryos raised their heads everywhere. Many of the older plants with more primitive reproductive mechanisms began to fade away under this unequal contest. They contracted their range into scheduled environments. Some, like the giant redwoods, lingered on as relics; many vanished entirely.

The world of the giants was a dying world. These fantastic little seeds skipping and hopping and flying about the woods and valleys brought with them an amazing adaptability. If our whole lives had not been spent in the midst of it, it would astound us. The old, stiff, sky-reaching wooden world had changed into something that glowed here and there with strange colors, put out queer, unheard-of fruits and little intricately carved seed cases, and, most important of all, produced concentrated foods in a way that the land had never seen before, or dreamed of back in the fish-eating, leaf-crunching days of the dinosaurs.

That food came from three sources, all produced by the reproductive system of the flowering plants. There were the tantalizing nectars and pollens intended to draw insects for pollenizing purposes, and which are responsible also for that wonderful jeweled creation, the hummingbird. There were the juicy and enticing fruits to attract larger animals, and in which tough-coated seeds were concealed, as in the tomato, for example. Then, as if this were not enough, there was the food in the actual seed itself, the food intended to nourish the embryo. All over the world, like hot corn in a popper, these incredible elaborations of the flowering plants kept exploding. In a movement that was almost instantaneous, geologically speaking, the angiosperms had taken over the world. Grass was beginning to cover the bare earth until, today, there are over six thousand species. All kinds of vines and bushes squirmed and writhed under new trees with flying seeds.

The explosion was having its effect on animal life also. Specialized groups of insects were arising to feed on the new sources of food and, incidentally and unknowingly, to pollinate the plant. The flowers bloomed and bloomed in ever larger and more spectacular varieties. Some were pale unearthly night flowers intended to lure months in the evening twilight, some among the orchids even took the shape of female spiders in order to attract wandering males, some flamed redly in the light of noon or twinkled modesty in the meadow grasses. Intricate mechanisms splashed pollen on the breasts of hummingbirds, or stamped it on the bellies of black, grumbling bees droning assiduously from blossom to blossom. Honey ran, insects multiplied, and even the descendants of that toothed and ancient lizard-bird had become strangely altered. Equipped with prodding beaks instead of biting teeth they pecked the seeds and gobbled the insects that were really converted nectar.

Across the planet grasslands were now spreading. A slow continental upthrust which had been a part of the early Age of Flowers had cooled the world's climates. The stalking reptiles and the leather-winged black imps of the seashore cliffs had vanished. Only birds roamed the air now, hot-blooded and high-speed metabolic machines.

The mammals, too, had survived and were venturing into new domains, staring about perhaps a bit bewildered at their sudden eminence now that the thunder lizards were gone. Many of them, beginning as small browsers upon leaves in the forest, began to venture out upon this new sunlit world of the grass. Grass has a high silica content and demands a new type of very tough and resistant tooth enamel, but the seeds taken incidentally in the cropping of the grass are highly nutritious. A new world had opened out for the warm-blooded mammals. Great herbivores like the mammoths, horses, and bisons appeared. Skulking about them had arisen savage flesh-feeding carnivores like the now extinct dire wolves and the saber-toothed tiger.

Flesh eaters though these creatures were, they were being sustained on nutritious grasses one step removed. Their fierce energy was being maintained on a high, effective level, through hot days and frosty nights, by the concentrated energy of the angiosperms. That energy, thirty percent or more of the weight of the entire plant among some of the cereal grasses, was being accumulated and concentrated in the rich proteins and fats of the enormous game herds of the grasslands.

On the edge of the forest, a strange, old-fashioned animal still hesitated. His body was the body of a tree dweller, and though tough and knotty by human standards, he was, in terms of that world into which he gazed, a weakling. His teeth, though strong for chewing on the tough fruits of the forest, or for crunching an occasional unwary bird caught with his prehensile hands, were not the tearing sabers of the great cats. He had a passion for lifting himself up to see about, in his restless, roving curiosity. He would run a little stiffly and uncertainly, perhaps, on his hind legs, but only in those rare moments when he ventured out upon the ground. All this was the legacy of his climbing days; he had a hand with flexible fingers and no fine specialized hoofs upon which to gallop like the wind.

If he had any idea of competing in that new world, he had better forget it; teeth or hooves, he was much too late for either. He was a ne'er-do-well, an in-betweener. Nature had not done well by him. It was as if she had hesitated and never quite made up her mind. Perhaps as a consequence he had a malicious gleam in his eye, the gleam of an outcast who has been left nothing and knows he is going to have to take what he gets. One day a little band of these odd apes — for apes they were — shambled out upon the grass; the human story had begun.

Apes were to become men, in the inscrutable wisdom of nature, because flowers had produced seeds and fruits in such tremendous quantities that a new and totally different store of energy had become available in concentrated form. Impressive as the slow-moving, dimbrained dinosaurs had been, it is doubtful if their age had supported anything like the diversity of life that now rioted across the planet or flashed in and out among the trees. Down on the grass by a streamside, one of those apes with inquisitive fingers turned over a stone and hefted it vaguely. The group clucked together in a throaty tongue and moved off through the tall grass foraging for seeds and insects. The one still held, sniffed, and hefted the stone he had found. He liked the feel of it in his fingers. The attack on the animal world was about to begin. ³⁵

If one could run the story of that first human group like a speeded-up motion picture through a million years of time, one might see the stone in the hand change to the flint ax and the torch. All that swarming grassland world with its giant bison and trumpeting mammoths would go down in ruin to feed the insatiable and growing numbers of a carnivore who, like the great cats before him, was taking his energy indirectly from the grass. Later he found fire and it altered the tough meats and drained their energy even faster into a stomach ill adapted for the ferocious turn man's habits had taken.

His limbs grew longer, he strode more purposefully over the grass. The stolen energy that would take man across the continents would fail him at last. The great Ice Age herds were destined to vanish. When they did so, another hand like the hand that grasped the stone by the river long ago would pluck a handful of grass seed and hold it contemplatively.

In that moment, the golden towers of man, his swarming millions, his turning wheels, the vast learning of his packed libraries, would glimmer dimly there in the ancestor of wheat, a few seeds held in a muddy hand. Without the gift of flowers and the infinite diversity of their fruits, man and bird, if they had continued to exist at all, would be today unrecognizable. Archaeopteryx, the lizard-bird, might still be snapping at beetles on a sequoia limb; man might still be a nocturnal insectivore gnawing a roach in the dark. The weight of a petal has changed the face of the world and made it ours.

The Reader's Presence

1. Eiseley's appreciation of flowers appears more than scientific. Where do the scientific and the aesthetic meet in the essay? Where is the aesthetic represented as basically scientific? Where does the scientific become aesthetic? What is the effect of this blurring of categories upon the reader?

2. Eiseley is an unusual prose stylist. Choose a short passage and note where information is conveyed through poetic imagery. What sorts of images does Eiseley choose? How does form influence content in the piece? Which do you think is more effective: a straightforward, factual argument, or a lyrical evocation like this one? Why?

3. Briefly trace the essay's development of its theme from beginning to end. What do you notice in terms of the essay's direction and breadth of focus? How does Eiseley link disparate periods, items, and perspectives? Do Eiseley's extended connections enhance or detract from his message? In what ways?

49

Ralph Ellison

What America Would Be Like without Blacks

Ralph Ellison (1914–1994), one of the most influential writers of the twentieth century, wrote novels, short stories, essays, and social criticisms. His novel about a black man's struggle for identity, Invisible Man *(1952), received the National Book Award and is considered to be a landmark of modern fiction. Ellison was born in Oklahoma City and in his twenties moved to New York City, where he met Langston Hughes (see page 122) and Richard Wright (see page 298). He began writing his second novel in 1954, but a large portion of the manuscript was destroyed in a fire in 1967. For the last forty years of his life, he rewrote hundreds and hundreds of pages in an effort to complete this second novel. With the help of editor John Callahan, this long-awaited book,* Juneteenth, *was finally published in 1999. "What America Would Be Like without Blacks" first appeared in* Time *in 1970.*

The fantasy of an America free of blacks is at least as old as the dream of creating a truly democratic society. While we are aware that there is something inescapably tragic about the cost of achieving our democratic ideals, we keep such tragic awareness segregated to the rear of our minds. We allow it to come to the fore only during moments of great national crisis.

On the other hand, there is something so embarrassingly absurd about the notion of purging the nation of blacks that it seems hardly a product of thought at all. It is more like a primitive reflex, a throwback to the dim past of tribal experience, which we rationalize and try to make respectable by dressing it up in the gaudy and highly questionable trappings of what we call the "concept of race." Yet, despite its absurdity, the fantasy of a blackless America continues to turn up. It is a fantasy born not merely of racism but of petulance, of exasperation, of moral fatigue. It is like a boil bursting forth from impurities in the bloodstream of democracy.

In its benign manifestations, it can be outrageously comic — as in the picaresque adventures of Percival Brownlee who appears in William Faulkner's story "The Bear." Exasperating to his white masters because his aspirations and talents are for preaching and conducting choirs rather than for farming, Brownlee is "freed" after much resistance and ends up as the prosperous proprietor of a New Orleans brothel. In Faulkner's hands, the uncomprehending drive of Brownlee's owners to "get shut" of him is comically instructive. Indeed, the story resonates certain abiding, tragic themes of American history with which it is interwoven, and which are causing great turbulence in the social atmosphere today. I refer to the exasperation and bemusement of the white American with the black, the black American's ceaseless (and swiftly accelerating) struggle to escape the misconceptions of whites, and the continual confusing of the black American's racial background with his individual culture. Most of all, I refer to the recurring fantasy of solving one basic problem of American democracy by "getting shut" of the blacks through various wishful schemes that would banish them from the nation's bloodstream, from its social structure, and from its conscience and historical consciousness.

This fantastic vision of a lily-white America appeared as early as 1713, with the suggestion of a white "native American," thought to be from New Jersey, that all the Negroes be given their freedom and returned to Africa. In 1777, Thomas Jefferson, while serving in the Virginia legislature, began drafting a plan for the gradual emancipation and exportation of the slaves. Nor were Negroes themselves immune to the fantasy. In 1815, Paul Cuffe, a wealthy merchant, shipbuilder, and landowner from the New Bedford area, shipped and settled at his own expense thirty-eight of his fellow Negroes in Africa. It was perhaps his example that led in the following year to the creation of the American Colonization Society, which was to establish in 1821 the colony of Liberia. Great amounts of cash and a perplexing mixture of motives went into the venture. The slave owners and many Border-state politicians wanted to use it as a scheme to rid the country not of slaves but of the militant free Negroes who were agitating against the "peculiar institution." The abolitionists, until they took a lead from free Negro leaders and began attacking the scheme, also participated as a means of righting a great historical injustice. Many blacks went along with it simply because they were sick of the black and white American mess and hoped to prosper in the quiet peace of the old ancestral home.

Such conflicting motives doomed the Colonization Society to failure, but what amazes one even more than the notion tht anyone could have believed in its success is the fact that it was attempted during a period when the blacks, slave and free, made up eighteen percent of the total population. When we consider how long blacks had been in the New World and had been transforming it and being Americanized by it, the scheme appears not only fantastic, but the product of a free-floating irrationality. Indeed, a national pathology.   5

Nevertheless, some of the noblest of Americans were bemused. Not only Jefferson but later Abraham Lincoln was to give the scheme credence. According to historian John Hope Franklin, Negro colonization seemed as important to Lincoln as emancipation. In 1862, Franklin notes, Lincoln called a group of prominent free Negroes to the White House and urged them to support colonization, telling them, "Your race suffers greatly, many of them by living among us, while ours suffers from your presence. If this is admitted, it affords a reason why we should be separated."

In spite of his unquestioned greatness, Abraham Lincoln was a man of his times and limited by some of the less worthy thinking of his times. This is demonstrated both by his reliance upon the concept of race in his analysis of the American dilemma and by his involvement in a plan of purging the nation of blacks as a means of healing the badly shattered ideals of democratic federalism. Although benign, his motive was no less a product of fantasy. It envisaged an attempt to relieve an inevitable suffering that marked the growing pains of the youthful body politic by an operation which would have amounted to the severing of a healthy and indispensable member.

Yet, like its twin, the illusion of secession, the fantasy of a benign amputation that would rid the country of black men to the benefit of a nation's health not only persists; today, in the form of neo-Garveyism, it fascinates black men no less than it once hypnotized whites. Both fantasies become operative whenever the nation grows weary of the struggle toward the ideal of American democratic equality. Both would use the black man as a scapegoat to achieve a national catharsis, and both would, by way of curing the patient, destroy him.

What is ultimately intriguing about the fantasy of "getting shut" of the Negro American is the fact that no one who entertains it seems ever to have considered what the nation would have become had Africans *not* been brought to the New World, and had their descendants not played such a complex and confounding role in the creation of American history and culture. Nor do they appear to have considered with any seriousness the effect upon the nation of having any of the schemes for exporting blacks succeed beyond settling some fifteen thousand or so in Liberia.

We are reminded that Daniel Patrick Moynihan,[1] who has recently aggravated our social confusion over the racial issue while allegedly attempting to clarify it, is co-author of a work which insists that the American melting pot didn't melt because our white ethnic groups have resisted all assimilative forces that appear to threaten their identities. The problem here is that few Americans know who and what they really are. That is why few of these groups — or at least few of the children of these groups — have been able to resist the movies, television, baseball, jazz, football, drum-majoretting, rock, comic strips, radio commercials, soap operas, book clubs, slang, or any of a thousand other expressions and carriers of our pluralistic and easily available popular culture. And it is here precisely that ethnic resistance is least effective. On this level the melting pot did indeed melt, creating such deceptive metamorphoses and blending of identities, values, and life-styles that most American whites are culturally part Negro American without even realizing it.

If we can resist for a moment the temptation to view everything having to do with Negro Americans in terms of their racially imposed status, we become aware of the fact that for all the harsh reality of the social and economic injustices visited upon them, these injustices have failed to keep Negroes clear of the cultural mainstream; Negro Americans are in fact one of its major tributaries. If we can cease approaching American social reality in terms of such false concepts as white and nonwhite, black culture and white culture, and think of these apparently unthinkable matters in the realistic manner of Western pioneers confronting the unknown prairie, perhaps we can begin to imagine what the United States would have been, or not been, had there been no blacks to give it — if I may be so bold as to say — color.

For one thing, the American nation is in a sense the product of the American language, a colloquial speech that began emerging long before

10

---

[1]*Moynihan:* Moynihan wrote extensively on issues of poverty and welfare; he will retire as senator of New York in 2000. — EDS.

the British colonials and Africans were transformed into Americans. It is a language that evolved from the king's English but, basing itself upon the realities of the American land and colonial institutions—or lack of institutions, began quite early as a vernacular revolt against the signs, symbols, manners, and authority of the mother country. It is a language that began by merging the sounds of many tongues, brought together in the struggle of diverse regions. And whether it is admitted or not, much of the sound of that language is derived from the timbre of the African voice and the listening habits of the African ear. So there is a *de'z* and *do'z* of slave speech sounding beneath our most polished Harvard accents, and if there is such a thing as a Yale accent, there is a Negro wail in it— doubtlessly introduced there by Old Yalie John C. Calhoun, who probably got it from his mammy.

Whitman viewed the spoken idiom of Negro Americans as a source for a native grand opera. Its flexibility, its musicality, its rhythms, free-wheeling diction, and metaphors, as projected in Negro American folklore, were absorbed by the creators of our great nineteenth-century literature even when the majority of blacks were still enslaved. Mark Twain celebrated it in the prose of *Huckleberry Finn;* without the presence of blacks, the book could not have been written. No Huck and Jim, no American novel as we know it. For not only is the black man a co-creator of the language that Mark Twain raised to the level of literary eloquence, but Jim's condition as American and Huck's commitment to freedom are at the moral center of the novel.[2]

In other words, had there been no blacks, certain creative tensions arising from the cross-purposes of whites and blacks would also not have existed. Not only would there have been no Faulkner; there would have been no Stephen Crane, who found certain basic themes of his writing in the Civil War. Thus, also, there would have been no Hemingway, who took Crane as a source and guide. Without the presence of Negro American style, our jokes, our tall tales, even our sports would be lacking in the sudden turns, the shocks, the swift changes of pace (all jazz-shaped) that serve to remind us that the world is ever unexplored, and that while a complete mastery of life is mere illusion, the real secret of the game is to make life swing. It is its ability to articulate this tragic-comic attitude toward life that explains much of the mysterious power and attractiveness of that quality of Negro American style known as "soul." An expression of American diversity within unity, of blackness with whiteness, soul announces the presence of a creative struggle against the realities of existence.

Without the presence of blacks, our political history would have been   15
otherwise. No slave economy, no Civil War; no violent destruction of the Reconstruction; no K.K.K. and no Jim Crow system. And without the

---

[2]Ellison's observations on *Huckleberry Finn* became the basis of much subsequent literary criticism. — EDS.

disenfranchisement of black Americans and the manipulation of racial fears and prejudices, the disproportionate impact of white Southern politicians upon our domestic and foreign policies would have been impossible. Indeed, it is almost impossible to conceive of what our political system would have become without the snarl of forces—cultural, racial, religious—that make our nation what it is today.

Absent, too, would be the need for that tragic knowledge which we try ceaselessly to evade: that the true subject of democracy is not simply material well-being but the extension of the democratic process in the direction of perfecting itself. And that the most obvious test and clue to that perfection is the inclusion—*not* assimilation—of the black man.

Since the beginning of the nation, white Americans have suffered from a deep inner uncertainty as to who they really are. One of the ways that has been used to simplify the answer has been to seize upon the presence of black Americans and use them as a marker, a symbol of limits, a metaphor for the "outsider." Many whites could look at the social position of blacks and feel that color formed an easy and reliable gauge for determining to what extent one was or was not American. Perhaps that is why one of the first epithets that many European immigrants learned when they got off the boat was the term "nigger"—it made them feel instantly American. But this is tricky magic. Despite his racial difference and social status, something indisputably American about Negroes not only raised doubts about the white man's value system but aroused the troubling suspicion that whatever else the true American is, he is also somehow black.

Materially, psychologically, and culturally, part of the nation's heritage is Negro American, and whatever it becomes will be shaped in part by the Negro's presence. Which is fortunate, for today it is the black American who puts pressure upon the nation to live up to its ideals. It is he who gives creative tension to our struggle for justice and for the elimination of those factors, social and psychological, which make for slums and shaky suburban communities. It is he who insists that we purify the American language by demanding that there be a closer correlation between the meaning of words and reality, between ideal and conduct, our assertions and our actions. Without the black American, something irrepressibly hopeful and creative would go out of the American spirit, and the nation might well succumb to the moral slobbism that has ever threatened its existence from within.

When we look objectively at how the dry bones of the nation were hung together, it seems obvious that some one of the many groups that compose the United States had to suffer the fate of being allowed no easy escape from experiencing the harsh realities of the human condition as they were to exist under even so fortunate a democracy as ours. It would seem that some one group had to be stripped of the possibility of escaping such tragic knowledge by taking sanctuary in moral equivocation, racial chauvinism, or the advantage of superior social status. There is no point in complaining over the past or apologizing for one's fate. But for blacks, there are no hiding places down here, not in suburbia or in penthouse, neither in country nor in city. They are an American people who are geared to what *is* and who yet are driven by a sense of what it is possible for human life to be in this society. The nation could not survive being deprived of their presence because, by the irony implicit in the dynamics of American democracy, they symbolize both its most stringent testing and the possibility of its greatest human freedom.

The Reader's Presence

1. Ellison recounts little known information about Abraham Lincoln. What might Ellison's purpose be in challenging the common view of history? How might he hope to influence the future by uncovering unsettling aspects of the past? He also argues that white people in America are culturally part black. Why might this notion have seemed radical at the time of this essay's writing?

2. What does Ellison mean by describing certain aspects of mainstream American culture as "jazz-shaped"? Where else does Ellison's writing venture from the literal to the figurative? Are Ellison's metaphors more or less effective than his straightforward statements in advancing his argument? Why? Where does Ellison write from a basis of cool reason, and where does emotion seem to arise? Which style of expression do you find more effective? Why?

3. What connections can you find in the essay between cultural difference and invisibility? By what means, according to Ellison, do African American lives and their contributions to mainstream culture become and remain hidden? Does Ellison represent America's notion of itself as a great "melting-pot"? Why or why not? Compare this essay to Mary Gordon's "The Ghosts of Ellis Island" (see page 391).

50

Kai Erikson

The Witches of Salem Village

Kai Erikson (b. 1931), son of renowned psychoanalyst Erik Erikson, has been a professor of sociology and American studies at Yale University since 1966. A noted scholar, Erikson has published several books and received numerous professional awards. His interests in communities and the effects of human disasters are reflected in Everything in Its Path: Destruction of Community in the Buffalo Creek Flood *(1976) and* A New Species of Trouble: Explorations in Disaster, Trauma, and Community *(1994). Most recently, Erikson edited* Sociological Vision *(1997), a collection of writings on social problems. "The Witches of Salem Village" is from his study of Puritan New England,* Wayward Puritans: A Study in the Sociology of Deviance *(1966).*

No one really knows how the witchcraft hysteria began, but it originated in the home of the Reverend Samuel Parris, minister of the local church. In early 1692, several girls from the neighborhood began to spend their afternoons in the Parris' kitchen with a slave named Tituba, and it was not long before a mysterious sorority of girls, aged between nine and twenty, became regular visitors to the parsonage. We can only speculate what was going on behind the kitchen door, but we know that Tituba had been brought to Massachusetts from Barbados and enjoyed a reputation in the neighborhood for her skills in the magic arts. As the girls grew closer together, a remarkable change seemed to come over them: perhaps it is not true, as someone later reported, that they went out into the forest to celebrate their own version of a black mass, but it is apparent that they began to live in a state of high tension and shared secrets with one another which were hardly becoming to quiet Puritan maidens.

Before the end of winter, the two youngest girls in the group succumbed to the shrill pitch of their amusements and began to exhibit a most unusual malady. They would scream unaccountably, fall into grotesque convulsions, and sometimes scamper along on their hands and knees making noises like the barking of a dog. No sooner had word gone around about this extraordinary affliction than it began to spread like a contagious disease. All over the community young girls were groveling on the ground in a panic of fear and excitement, and while some of the less credulous townspeople were tempted to reach for their belts in the hopes of strapping a little modesty into them, the rest could only stand by in helpless horror as the girls suffered their torments.

The town's one physician did what he could to stem the epidemic, but he soon exhausted his meagre store of remedies and was forced to conclude that the problem lay outside the province of medicine. The Devil had come to Salem Village, he announced; the girls were bewitched. At this disturbing news, ministers from many of the neighboring parishes came to consult with their colleague and offer what advice they might. Among the first to arrive was a thoughtful clergyman named Deodat Lawson, and he had been in town no more than a few hours when he happened upon a frightening exhibition of the devil's handiwork. "In the beginning of the evening," he later recounted of his first day in the village,

> I went to give Mr. Parris a visit. When I was there, his kinswoman, Abigail Williams, (about 12 years of age,) had a grievous fit; she was at first hurried with violence to and fro in the room, (though Mrs. Ingersoll endeavored to hold her,) sometimes making as if she would fly, stretching up her arms as high as she could, and crying "whish, whish, whish!" several times. . . . After that, she run to the fire, and began to throw fire brands about the house; and run against the back, as if she would run up the chimney, and, as they said, she had attempted to go into the fire in other fits.[1]

Faced by such clear-cut evidence, the ministers quickly agreed that Satan's new challenge would have to be met with vigorous action, and this meant that the afflicted girls would have to identify the witches who were harassing them.

It is hard to guess what the girls were experiencing during those early days of the commotion. They attracted attention everywhere they went and exercised a degree of power over the adult community which would have been exhilarating under the sanest of circumstances. But whatever else was going on in those young minds, the thought seems to have gradually occurred to the girls that they were indeed bewitched, and after they had been coaxed over and over again to name their tormentors, they finally singled out three women in the village and accused them of witchcraft.

Three better candidates could not have been found if all the gossips in New England had met to make the nominations. The first, understandably, was Tituba herself, a woman who had grown up among the rich colors and imaginative legends of Barbados and who was probably

5

---

[1]Deodat Lawson, "A Brief and True Narrative of Witchcraft at Salem Village," 1692, in *Narratives of the Witchcraft Cases, 1648–1706,* edited by George Lincoln Burr (New York: Scribner's, 1914), p. 154.

acquainted with some form of voodoo. The second, Sarah Good, was a proper hag of a witch if Salem Village had ever seen one. With a pipe clenched in her leathery face she wandered around the countryside neglecting her children and begging from others, and on more than one occasion the old crone had been overheard muttering threats against her neighbors when she was in an unusually sour humor. Sarah Osburne, the third suspect, had a higher social standing than either of her alleged accomplices, but she had been involved in a local scandal a year or two earlier when a man moved into her house some months before becoming her husband.

A preliminary hearing was set at once to decide whether the three accused women should be held for trial. The girls were ushered to the front row of the meeting house, where they took full advantage of the space afforded them by rolling around in apparent agony whenever some personal fancy (or the invisible agents of the devil) provoked them to it. It was a remarkable show. Strange creatures flew about the room pecking at the girls or taunting them from the rafters, and it was immediately obvious to everyone that the women on trial were responsible for all the disorder and suffering. When Sarah Good and Sarah Osburne were called to the stand and asked why they sent these spectres to torment the girls, they were too appalled to say much in their defense. But when Tituba took the stand she had a ready answer. A lifetime spent in bondage is poor training for standing up before a bench of magistrates, and anyway Tituba was an excitable woman who had breathed the warmer winds of the Caribbean and knew things about magic her crusty old judges would never learn. Whatever the reason, Tituba gave her audience one of the most exuberant confessions ever recorded in a New England courtroom. She spoke of the creatures who inhabit the invisible world, the dark rituals which bind them together in the service of Satan; and before she had ended her astonishing recital she had convinced everyone in Salem Village that the problem was far worse than they had dared imagine. For Tituba not only implicated Sarah Good and Sarah Osburne in her own confession but announced that many other people in the colony were engaged in the devil's conspiracy against the Bay.

So the hearing that was supposed to bring a speedy end to the affair only stirred up a hidden hornet's nest, and now the girls were urged to identify other suspects and locate new sources of trouble. Already the girls had become more than unfortunate victims: in the eyes of the community they were diviners, prophets, oracles, mediums, for only they could see the terrible spectres swarming over the countryside and tell what persons had sent them on their evil errands. As they became caught up in the enthusiasm of their new work, then, the girls began to reach into every corner of the community in a search for likely suspects. Martha Corey was an upstanding woman in the village whose main mistake was to snort incredulously at the girls' behavior. Dorcas Good, five years old, was a daughter of the accused Sarah. Rebecca Nurse was a saintly old woman who had been bedridden at the time of the earlier hearings. Mary Esty and Sarah Cloyce were Rebecca's younger sisters, themselves accused when they rose in energetic defense of the older woman. And so it went — John Proctor, Giles Corey, Abigail Hobbs, Bridgit Bishop, Sarah Wild, Susanna Martin, Dorcas Hoar, the Reverend George Burroughs: as winter turned into spring the list of suspects grew to enormous length and the Salem jail was choked with people awaiting trial. We know nothing about conditions of life in prison, but it is easy to imagine the tensions which must have echoed within those grey walls. Some of the prisoners had cried out against their relatives and friends in a desperate effort to divert attention from themselves, others were witless persons with scarcely a clue as to what had happened to them, and a few (very few, as it turned out) were accepting their lot with quiet dignity. If we imagine Sarah Good sitting next to Rebecca Nurse and lighting her rancid pipe or Tituba sharing views on supernatural phenomena with the Reverend George Burroughs, we may have a rough picture of life in those crowded quarters.

By this time the hysteria had spread well beyond the confines of Salem Village, and as it grew in scope so did the appetites of the young girls. They now began to accuse persons they had never seen from places they had never visited (in the course of which some absurd mistakes were made),[2] yet their word was so little questioned that it was ordinarily warrant enough to put respected people in chains.

From as far away as Charlestown, Nathaniel Cary heard that his wife had been accused of witchcraft and immediately traveled with her to Salem "to see if the afflicted did now her." The two of them sat through an entire day of hearings, after which Cary reported:

> I observed that the afflicted were two girls of about ten years old, and about two or three others, of about eighteen. . . . The prisoners were called in one by one, and as they came in were cried out of [at]. . . . The prisoner was placed about seven or eight feet from the Justices, and the accusers between the Justices and them; the prisoner was ordered to stand right before the Justices, with an officer appointed to hold each hand, lest they should therewith afflict them, and the prisoner's eyes must be constantly on the Justices; for if they looked on the afflicted, they would either fall into their fits, or cry out of being hurt by them. . . . Then the Justices said to the accusers, "which of you will go and touch the prisoner at the bar?" Then the most courageous would adventure, but before they had made three steps would ordinarily fall down as in a fit. The Justices ordered that they should be taken up and carried to the prisoner, that she might touch them; and as soon as they were touched by the accused, the Justices would say "they are well," before I could discern any alteration. . . . Thus far I was only as a

---

[2]John Alden later reported in his account of the affair that the girls pointed their fingers at the wrong man when they first accused him of witchcraft and only realized their mistake when an obliging passer-by corrected them. See Robert Calef, "More Wonders of the Invisible World," Boston, 1701, in Burr, *Narratives*, p. 353.

spectator, my wife also was there part of the time, but no notice taken of her by the afflicted, except once or twice they came to her and asked her name.

After this sorry performance the Carys retired to the local inn for   10
dinner, but no sooner had they taken seats than a group of afflicted girls burst into the room and "began to tumble about like swine" at Mrs. Cary's feet, accusing her of being the cause of their miseries. Remarkably, the magistrates happened to be sitting in the adjoining room— "waiting for this," Cary later decided—and an impromptu hearing took place on the spot.

> Being brought before the Justices, her chief accusers were two girls. My wife declared to the Justices that she never had any knowledge of them before that day; she was forced to stand with her arms stretched out. I did request that I might hold one of her hands, but it was denied me; then she desired me to wipe the tears from her eyes, and the sweat from her face, which I did; then she desired she might lean herself on me, saying she should faint. Justice Hathorne replied, she had strength enough to torment those persons, and she should have strength enough to stand I speaking something against their cruel proceedings, they commanded me to be silent, or else I should be turned out of the room. An Indian . . . was also brought in to be one of her accusers: being come in, he now (when before the Justices) fell down and tumbled about like a hog, but said nothing. The Justices asked the girls, "who afflicted the Indian?", they answered "she" (meaning my wife). . . . The Justices ordered her to touch him, in order of his cure . . . but the Indian took hold of her in a barbarous manner; then his hand was taken off, and her hand put on his, and the cure was quickly wrought. . . . Then her mittimus was writ.[3]

For another example of how the hearings were going, we might listen for a moment to the examination of Mrs. John Proctor. This record was taken down by the Reverend Samuel Parris himself, and the notes in parentheses are his. Ann Putnam and Abigail Williams were two of the most energetic of the young accusers.

> Justice: Ann Putnam, doth this woman hurt you?
> Putnam: Yes, sir, a good many times. (Then the accused looked upon them and they fell into fits.)
> Justice: She does not bring the book to you, does she?[4]
> Putnam: Yes, sir, often, and saith she hath made her maid set her hand to it.
> Justice: Abigail Williams, does this woman hurt you?
> Williams: Yes, sir, often.

---

[3]Reproduced in Calef, "More Wonders," in Burr, *Narratives*, pp. 350–352.
[4]The "book" refers to the Devil's registry. The girls were presumably being tormented because they refused to sign the book and ally themselves with Satan.

Justice: Does she bring the book to you?

Williams: Yes.

Justice: What would she have you do with it?

Williams: To write in it and I shall be well.

Putnam to Mrs. Proctor: Did you not tell me that your maid had written?

Mrs. Proctor: Dear child, it is not so. There is another judgment, dear child. (Then Abigail and Ann had fits. By and by they cried out, "look you, there is Goody Proctor upon the beam." By and by both of them cried out of Goodman Proctor himself, and said he was a wizard. Immediately, many, if not all of the bewitched, had grievous fits.)

Justice: Ann Putnam, who hurt you?

Putnam: Goodman Proctor and his wife too. (Some of the afflicted cried, "there is Proctor going to take up Mrs. Pope's feet" — and her feet were immediately taken up.)

Justice: What do you say Goodman Proctor to these things?

Proctor: I know not. I am innocent.

Williams: There is Goodman Proctor going to Mrs. Pope (and immediately said Pope fell into a fit).

Justice: You see, the Devil will deceive you. The children could see what you was going to do before the woman was hurt. I would advise you to repentance, for the devil is bringing you out.[5]

This was the kind of evidence the magistrates were collecting in readiness for the trials; and it was none too soon, for the prisons were crowded with suspects. In June the newly arrived Governor of the Bay, Sir William Phips, appointed a special court of Oyer and Terminer to hear the growing number of witchcraft cases pending, and the new bench went immediately to work. Before the month was over, six women had been hanged from the gallows in Salem. And still the accused poured in.

As the court settled down to business, however, a note of uncertainty began to flicker across the minds of several thoughtful persons in the colony. To begin with, the net of accusation was beginning to spread out in wider arcs, reaching not only across the surface of the country but up the social ladder as well, so that a number of influential people were now among those in the overflowing prisons. Nathaniel Cary was an important citizen of Charlestown, and other men of equal rank (including the almost legendary Captain John Alden) were being caught up in the widening circle of panic and fear. Slowly but surely, a faint glimmer of skepticism was introduced into the situation; and while it was not to assert a modifying influence on the behavior of the court for some time to come, this new voice had become a part of the turbulent New England climate of 1692.

Meantime, the girls continued to exercise their extraordinary powers. Between sessions of the court, they were invited to visit the town of Andover and help the local inhabitants flush out whatever witches might still

[5]Hutchinson, *History*, II, pp. 27–28.

remain at large among them. Handicapped as they were by not knowing anyone in town, the girls nonetheless managed to identify more than fifty witches in the space of a few hours. Forty warrants were signed on the spot, and the arrest total only stopped at that number because the local Justice of the Peace simply laid down his pen and refused to go on with the frightening charade any longer—at which point, predictably, he became a suspect himself.

Yet the judges worked hard to keep pace with their young representatives in the field. In early August five persons went to the gallows in Salem. A month later fifteen more were tried and condemned, of which eight were hung promptly and the others spared because they were presumably ready to confess their sins and turn state's evidence. Nineteen people had been executed, seven more condemned, and one pressed to death under a pile of rocks for standing mute at his trial. At least two more persons had died in prison, bringing the number of deaths to twenty-two. And in all that time, not one suspect brought before the court had been acquitted.

At the end of this strenuous period of justice, the whole witchcraft mania began to fade. For one thing, the people of the Bay had been shocked into a mood of sober reflection by the deaths of so many persons. For another, the afflicted girls had obviously not learned very much from their experience in Andover and were beginning to display an ambition which far exceeded their credit. It was bad enough that they should accuse the likes of John Alden and Nathaniel Cary, but when they brought up the name of Samuel Willard, who doubled as pastor of Boston's First Church and President of Harvard College, the magistrates flatly told them they were mistaken. Not long afterwards, a brazen finger was pointed directly at the executive mansion in Boston, where Lady Phips awaited her husband's return from an expedition to Canada, and one tradition even has it that Cotton Mather's mother was eventually accused.[6]

This was enough to stretch even a Puritan's boundless credulity. One by one the leading men of the Bay began to reconsider the whole question and ask aloud whether the evidence accepted in witchcraft hearings was really suited to the emergency at hand. It was obvious that people were being condemned on the testimony of a few excited girls, and responsible minds in the community were troubled by the thought that the girls' excitement may have been poorly diagnosed in the first place. Suppose the girls were directly possessed by the devil and not touched by intermediate witches? Suppose they were simply out of their wits altogether? Suppose, in fact, they were lying? In any of these events the rules of evidence used in court would have to be reviewed—and quickly.

Deciding what kinds of evidence were admissible in witchcraft cases was a thorny business at best. When the court of Oyer and Terminer had first met, a few ground rules had been established to govern the unusual sit-

[6]Burr, *Narratives*, p. 377.

uation which did not entirely conform to ordinary Puritan standards of trial procedure. In the first place, the scriptural rule that two eye-witnesses were necessary for conviction in capital cases was modified to read that any two witnesses were sufficient even if they were testifying about different events—on the interesting ground that witchcraft was a "habitual" crime. That is, if one witness testified that he had seen Susanna Martin bewitch a horse in 1660 and another testified that she had broken uninvited into his dreams twenty years later, then both were witnesses to the same general offense. More important, however, the court accepted as an operating principle the old idea that Satan could not assume the shape of an innocent person, which meant in effect that any spectres floating into view which resembled one of the defendants must be acting under his direct instruction. If an afflicted young girl "saw" John Proctor's image crouched on the window sill with a wicked expression on his face, for example, there could be no question that Proctor himself had placed it there, for the devil could not borrow that disguise without the permission of its owner. During an early hearing, one of the defendants had been asked: "How comes your appearance to hurt these [girls]?" "How do I know," she had answered testily, "He that appeared in the shape of Samuel, a glorified saint, may appear in anyone's shape."[7] Now this was no idle retort, for every man who read his Bible knew that the Witch of Endor had once caused the image of Samuel to appear before Saul, and this scriptural evidence that the devil might indeed be able to impersonate an innocent person proved a difficult matter for the court to handle. Had the defendant been able to win her point, the whole machinery of the court might have fallen in pieces at the magistrates' feet; for if the dreadful spectres haunting the girls were no more than free-lance apparitions sent out by the devil, then the court would have no prosecution case at all.

All in all, five separate kinds of evidence had been admitted by the court during its first round of hearings. First were trials by test, of which repeating the Lord's Prayer, a feat presumed impossible for witches to perform, and curing fits by touch were the most often used. Second was the testimony of persons who attributed their own misfortunes to the sorcery of a neighbor on trial. Third were physical marks like warts, moles, scars, or any other imperfection through which the devil might have sucked his gruesome quota of blood. Fourth was spectral evidence, of the sort just noted; and fifth were the confessions of the accused themselves.

Now it was completely obvious to the men who began to review the court's proceedings that the first three types of evidence were quite inconclusive. After all, anyone might make a mistake reciting the Lord's Prayer, particularly if the floor was covered with screaming, convulsive girls, and it did not make much sense to execute a person because he had spiteful neighbors or a mark upon his body. By those standards, half the people in Massachusetts might qualify for the gallows. This left spectral evidence and

20

---

[7]Cotton Mather, "Wonders of the Invisible World," in Drake, *The Witchcraft Delusion*, p. 176.

confessions. As for the latter, the court could hardly maintain that any real attention had been given to that form of evidence, since none of the executed witches had confessed and none of the many confessors had been executed. Far from establishing guilt, a well-phrased and tearfully delivered confession was clearly the best guarantee against hanging. So the case lay with spectral evidence, and legal opinion in the Bay was slowly leaning toward the theory that this form of evidence, too, was worthless.

In October, Governor Phips took note of the growing doubts by dismissing the special court of Oyer and Terminer and releasing several suspects from prison. The tide had begun to turn, but still there were 150 persons in custody and some 200 others who had been accused.

In December, finally, Phips appointed a new session of the Superior Court of Judicature to try the remaining suspects, and this time the magistrates were agreed that spectral evidence would be admitted only in marginal cases. Fifty-two persons were brought to trial during the next month, and of these, forty-nine were immediately acquitted. Three others were condemned ("two of which," a contemporary observer noted, "were the most senseless and ignorant creatures that could be found"),[8] and in addition death warrants were signed for five persons who had been condemned earlier. Governor Phips responded to these carefully reasoned judgments by signing reprieves for all eight of the defendants anyway, and at this, the court began to empty the jails as fast as it could hear cases. Finally Phips ended the costly procedure by discharging every prisoner in the colony and issuing a general pardon to all persons still under suspicion.

The witchcraft hysteria had been completely checked within a year of the day it first appeared in Salem Village.

The Reader's Presence

1. This essay appears in a larger work on social deviance. What is social deviance, in Erickson's perspective? How has it been perceived and controlled? Why might Erickson view the long-past historical events of Salem as relevant to questions of deviance today?

2. Erickson retells a familiar American story in a deceptively straightforward manner. Does his tone endorse or undercut the surface meaning of his tale? What position toward the events does the essay appear to encourage in the reader? By what means?

3. The writer often quotes from original sources without further comment upon them. What is the effect of this rhetorical technique? Can a writer safely assume that a reader will derive the intended meaning of a quotation without assistance? Why might a writer refrain from explicitly spelling out a quotation's significance?

[8]Calef, "More Wonders," in Burr, *Narratives*, p. 382.

51

James Fallows

Throwing Like a Girl

James Fallows (b. 1949) is a defense reporter, economic theorist, and media critic. He attended Harvard University and received a diploma in economic development from Queen's College, Oxford. He has been editor of the Washington Monthly, Texas Monthly, *the* Atlantic Monthly, *and, most recently,* U.S. News and World Report. *In addition to* National Defense, *which won the National Book Award, he has written* Looking at the Sun *(1995) and* Breaking the News: How the Media Undermines American Democracy *(1996). The following article first appeared in the* Atlantic Monthly *for August 1996.*

Most people remember the 1994 baseball season for the way it ended — with a strike rather than a World Series. I keep thinking about the way it began. On opening day, April 4, Bill Clinton went to Cleveland and, like many Presidents before him, threw out a ceremonial first pitch. That same day Hillary Rodham Clinton went to Chicago and, like no First Lady before her, also threw out a first ball, at a Cubs game in Wrigley Field.

The next day photos of the Clintons in action appeared in newspapers around the country. Many papers, including the *New York Times* and the *Washington Post,* chose the same two photos to run. The one of Bill Clinton showed him wearing an Indians cap and warm-up jacket. The President throwing lefty, had turned his shoulders sideways to the plate in preparation for delivery. He was bringing the ball forward from behind his head in a clean-looking throwing action as the photo was snapped. Hillary Clinton was pictured wearing a dark jacket, a scarf, and an oversized Cubs hat. In preparation for her throw she was standing directly facing the plate. A right-hander, she had the elbow of her throwing arm pointed out in front of her. Her forearm was tilted back, toward her shoulder. The ball rested on her upturned palm. As the picture was taken, she was in the middle of an action that can only be described as throwing like a girl.

The phrase "throwing like a girl" has become an embattled and offensive one. Feminists smart at its implication that to do something "like a girl" is to do it the wrong way. Recently, on the heels of the O. J. Simpson case, a book appeared in which the phrase was used to help explain why male athletes, especially football players, were involved in so many assaults against women. Having been trained (like most American boys) to dread the accusation of doing anything "like a girl," athletes were said to grow into the assumption that women were valueless, and natural prey.

I grant the justice of such complaints. I am attuned to the hurt caused by similar broad-brush stereotypes when they apply to groups I belong to — "dancing like a white man," for instance, or "speaking foreign languages like an American," or "thinking like a Washingtonian."

Still, whatever we want to call it, the difference between the two Clintons in what they were doing that day is real, and it is instantly recognizable. And since seeing those photos I have been wondering, Why, exactly, do so many women throw "like a girl"? If the motion were easy to change, presumably a woman as motivated and self-possessed as Hillary Clinton would have changed it. (According to her press secretary, Lisa Caputo, Mrs. Clinton spent the weekend before opening day tossing a ball in the Rose Garden with her husband, for practice.) Presumably, too, the answer to the question cannot be anything quite as simple as, because they *are* girls.

A surprising number of people think that there is a structural difference between male and female arms or shoulders — in the famous "rotator cuff," perhaps — that dictates different throwing motions. "It's in the shoulder joint," a well-educated woman told me recently. "They're hinged differently." Someday researchers may find evidence to support a biological theory of throwing actions. For now, what you'll hear if you ask an orthopedist, an anatomist, or (especially) the coach of a women's softball team is that there is no structural reason why men and women should throw in different ways. This point will be obvious to any male who grew up around girls who liked to play baseball and became good at it. It should be obvious on a larger scale this summer, in broadcasts of the Olympic Games. This year, for the first time, women's fast-pitch softball teams will compete in the Olympics. Although the pitchers in these games will deliver the ball underhand, viewers will see female shortstops, center fielders, catchers, and so on pegging the ball to one another at speeds few male viewers could match.

Even women's tennis is a constant if indirect reminder that men's and women's shoulders are "hinged" the same way. The serving motion in tennis is like a throw — but more difficult, because it must be coordinated with the toss of the tennis ball. The men in professional tennis serve harder than the women, because they are bigger and stronger. But women pros serve harder than most male amateurs have ever done, and the service motion for good players is the same for men and women alike. There is no expectation in college or pro tennis that because of their anatomy female players must "serve like a girl." "I know many women who can throw a lot harder and better than the normal male," says Linda Wells, the coach of the highly successful women's softball team at Arizona State University. "It's not gender that makes the difference in how they throw."

So what is it, then? Since Hillary Clinton's ceremonial visit to Wrigley Field, I have asked men and women how they learned to throw, or didn't. Why did I care? My impetus was the knowledge that eventually my sons would be grown and gone. If my wife, in all other ways a talented athlete, could learn how to throw, I would still have someone to play catch with. My research left some women, including my wife, thinking that I am some kind of obsessed lout, but it has led me to the solution to the mystery. First let's be clear about what there is to be explained.

At a superficial level it's easy to tick off the traits of an awkward-looking throw. The fundamental mistake is the one Mrs. Clinton appeared to be making in the photo: trying to throw a ball with your body facing the target, rather than rotating your shoulders and hips ninety degrees away from the target and then swinging them around in order to accelerate the ball. A throw looks bad if your elbow is lower than your shoulder as your arm comes forward (unless you're throwing sidearm). A throw looks really bad if, as the ball leaves your hand, your wrist is "inside your elbow" — that is, your elbow joint is bent in such a way that your forearm angles back toward your body and your wrist is closer to your head than your elbow is. Slow-motion film of big-league pitchers shows that when they release the ball, the throwing arm is fully extended and straight from shoulder to wrist. The combination of these three elements — head-on stance, dropped elbow, and wrist inside the elbow — mechanically dictates a pushing rather than a hurling motion, creating the familiar pattern of "throwing like a girl."

It is surprisingly hard to find in the literature of baseball a deeper explanation of the mechanics of good and bad throws. Tom Seaver's pitching for the Mets and the White Sox got him into the Hall of Fame, but his book *The Art of Pitching* is full of bromides that hardly clarify the process of throwing, even if they might mean something to accomplished pitchers. His chapter "The Absolutes of Pitching Mechanics," for instance, lays out these four unhelpful principles: "Keep the Front Leg Flexible!" "Rub Up the Baseball." "Hide the Baseball!" "Get it Out, Get it Up!" (The fourth refers to the need to get the ball out of the glove and into the throwing hand in a quick motion.)

A variety of other instructional documents, from *Little League's Official How-to-Play Baseball Book* to *Softball for Girls & Women,* mainly reveal the difficulty of finding words to describe a simple motor activity that everyone can recognize. The challenge, I suppose, is like that of writing a manual on how to ride a bike, or how to kiss. Indeed, the most useful description I've found of the mechanics of throwing comes from a

10

man whose specialty is another sport: Vic Braden made his name as a tennis coach, but he has attempted to analyze the physics of a wide variety of sports so that they all will be easier to teach.

Braden says that an effective throw involves connecting a series of links in a "kinetic chain." The kinetic chain, which is Braden's tool for analyzing most sporting activity, operates on a principle like that of crack-the-whip. Momentum builds up in one part of the body. When that part is suddenly stopped, as the end of the "whip" is stopped in crack-the-whip, the momentum is transferred to and concentrated in the next link in the chain. A good throw uses six links of chain, Braden says. The first two links involve the lower body, from feet to waist. The first motion of a throw (after the body has been rotated away from the target) is to rotate the legs and hips back in the direction of the throw, building up momentum as large muscles move body mass. Then those links stop—a pitcher stops turning his hips once they face the plate—and the momentum is transferred to the next link. This is the torso, from waist to shoulders, and since its mass is less than that of the legs, momentum makes it rotate faster than the hips and legs did. The torso stops when it is facing the plate, and the momentum is transferred to the next link—the upper arm. As the upper arm comes past the head, it stops moving forward, and the momentum goes into the final links—the forearm and wrist, which snap forward at tremendous speed.

This may sound arcane and jerkily mechanical, but it makes perfect sense when one sees Braden's slow-mo movies of pitchers in action. And it explains why people do, or don't, learn how to throw. The implication of Braden's analysis is that throwing is a perfectly natural action (millions and millions of people can do it) but not at all innate. A successful throw involves an intricate series of actions coordinated among muscle groups, as each link of the chain is timed to interact with the next. Like bike riding or skating, it can be learned by anyone—male or female. No one starts out knowing how to ride a bike or throw a ball. Everyone has to learn.

Readers who are happy with their throwing skills can prove this to themselves in about two seconds. If you are right-handed, pick up a ball with your left hand and throw it. Unless you are ambidextrous or have some other odd advantage, you will throw it "like a girl." The problem is not that your left shoulder is hinged strangely or that you don't know what a good throw looks like. It is that you have not spent time training your leg, hip, shoulder, and arm muscles on that side to work together as required for a throw. The actor John Goodman, who played football seriously and baseball casually when he was in high school, is right-handed. When cast in the 1992 movie *The Babe,* he had to learn to bat and throw left-handed, for realism in the role of Babe Ruth. For weeks before the filming began, he would arrive an hour early at the set of his TV show, *Roseanne,* so that he could practice throwing a tennis ball against a wall left-handed. "I made damn sure no one could see me," Goodman told me recently. "I'm hard enough on myself without the derisive laughter of my so-called friends." When *The Babe* was released, Goodman told a news-paper interviewer, "I'll never say something like 'He throws like a girl' again. It's not easy to learn how to throw."

What Goodman discovered is what most men have forgotten: that if   15
they know how to throw now, it is because they spent time learning at some point long ago. (Goodman says that he can remember learning to ride a bi-cycle but not learning to throw with his right hand.) This brings us back to the roots of the "throwing like a girl" phenomenon. The crucial factor is not that males and females are put together differently but that they typi-cally spend their early years in different ways. Little boys often learn how to throw without noticing that they are learning. Little girls are more rarely in environments that encourage them to learn in the same way. A boy who wonders why a girl throws the way she does is like a Frenchman who won-ders why so many Americans speak French "with an accent."

"For young boys it is culturally acceptable and politically correct to develop these skills," says Linda Wells, of the Arizona State softball team. "They are mentored and networked. Usually girls are not coached at all, or are coached by Mom—or if it's by Dad, he may not be much of an athlete. Girls are often stuck with the bottom of the male talent pool as examples. I would argue that rather than learning to 'throw like a girl,' they learn to throw like poor male athletes. I say that a bad throw is 'throwing like an old man.' This is not gender, its acculturation."

Almost any motor skill, from doing handstands to dribbling a basket-ball, is easier to learn if you start young, which is why John Goodman did not realize that learning to throw is difficult until he attempted it as an adult. Many girls reach adulthood having missed the chance to learn to throw when that would have been easiest to do. And as adults they have neither John Goodman's incentive to teach their muscles a new set of skills nor his confidence that the feat is possible. Five years ago, Joseph Russo, long a baseball coach at St. John's University, gave athletic-talent tests to actresses who were trying out for roles in *A League of Their Own,* a movie about women's baseball. Most of them were "well coordi-nated in general, like for dancing," he says. But those who had not hap-pened to play baseball or softball when they were young had a problem: "It sounds silly to say it, but they kept throwing like girls." (The best ball-field talents, by the way, were Madonna, Demi Moore, and the rock singer Joan Jett, who according to Russo "can really hit it hard." Careful viewers of *A League of Their Own* will note that only in a fleeting instant in one scene is the star, Geena Davis, shown actually throwing a ball.)

I'm not sure that I buy Linda Well's theory that most boys are "mentored" or "networked" into developing ball skills. Those who make the baseball team, maybe. But for a far larger number the decisive ingredi-ent seems to be the hundreds of idle hours spent throwing balls, sticks, rocks, and so on in the playground or the back yard. Children on the play-ground, I think, demonstrate the moment when the kinetic chain begins to work. It is when a little boy tries to throw a rock farther than his friend can or to throw a stick over a telephone wire thirty feet up. A toddler's first, instinctive throw is a push from the shoulder, showing the essential traits of "throwing like a girl." But when a child is really trying to put some oomph into the throw, his natural instinct is to wind up his body and let fly with the links of the chain. Little girls who do the same thing—compete with each other in distance throwing—learn the same way, but whereas many boys do this, few girls do. Tammy Richards, a woman who was raised on a farm in central California, says that she learned to throw by trying to heave dried cow chips farther than her brother could. It may have helped that her father, Bob Richards, was a former Olympic competitor in the decathlon (and two-time Olympic champion in the pole vault) and that he taught all his sons and daughters to throw not only the ball but also the discus, the shotput, and the javelin.

Is there a way to make up for lost time if you failed to invest those long hours on the playground years ago? Of course. Adults may not be able to learn to speak unaccented French, but they can learn to ride a bike, or skate, or throw. All that is required for developing any of these motor skills is time for practice—and spending that time requires overcoming the sense of embarrassment and futility that adults often have when attempting something new. Here are two tips that may help.

One is a surprisingly valuable drill suggested by the Little League's 20 *How-to-Play* handbook. Play catch with a partner who is ten or fifteen feet away—but do so while squatting with the knee of your throwing side touching the ground. When you start out this low, you have to keep the throw high to get the ball to your partner without bouncing it. This encourages a throw with the elbow held well above the shoulder, where it belongs.

The other is to play catch with a person who can throw like an athlete but is using his or her off hand. The typical adult woman hates to play catch with the typical adult man. She is well aware that she's not looking graceful and reacts murderously to the condescending tone in his voice ("That's more like it, honey!"). Forcing a right-handed man to throw left-handed is the great equalizer. He suddenly concentrates his attention on what it takes to get hips, shoulder, and elbow working together. He is suddenly aware of the strength of character needed to ignore the snickers of onlookers while learning new motor skills. He can no longer be condescending. He may even be nervous, wondering what he'll do if his partner makes the breakthrough first and he's the one still throwing like a girl.

The Reader's Presence

1. Fallows acknowledges the objections of feminists to the phrase "throwing like a girl." What other activities are linked to one gender or the other? Which gender gathers more negative associa-

tions? Why might feminists challenge the phrase? In your opinion, does Fallows satisfactorily answer such objections?

2. As a reporter, Fallows has covered many serious issues. Where does his use of language indicate that this essay is a lighter piece? Where does Fallows use an exaggerated or self-mocking tone? How does his use of humor affect the reader's reception of his message?

3. How does the writer attempt to communicate a sense of the joy he feels in movement? Is this successful? Why or why not? Reread Fallow's description of the "kinetic chain" movement in paragraphs 12–14. Is it well described? Is it possible to understand the motion without imitating it, or must the reader also enact it? In terms of explanation, why is it important to break the movement down into separate elements?

52

Ian Frazier

Pride

The journalist and essayist Ian Frazier (b. 1951) started his career on the staff of the New Yorker, *writing "Talk of the Town" pieces as well as signed essays. Many of these essays can be found in his first two books:* Dating Your Mom *(1986) and* Nobody Better, Better than Nobody *(1987). In the mid-1980s Frazier left his job in New York and embarked on a journey across the North American prairies from Texas to Montana. The book that emerged after several years spent exploring this region,* Great Plains *(1989), was a huge success with both critics and readers. In* Family *(1994), Frazier turns to a subject closer to home and tells the story of twelve generations of his family. His most recent collection is of comic essays,* Coyote v. Acme *(1996); his next book* On the Rez, *will be released in 2000.*

In all of his writing Frazier pays close attention to detail and location. "If you know something about a place it can save your sanity," he says, and a writer can find that knowledge through observation. "With a lot of writing, what you see is the top, the pinnacle, and the rest is invisible—all of these observations are ways of keeping yourself from flying off into space."

One time I stopped on an icy road in Montana in my van and then couldn't get going again. The road was so slippery and my tires so bald that I had no traction either in forward or reverse. All I needed was a push, but unfortunately I was alone. I sat there spinning. Nobody came along. When I got out to take another look, I forgot I had left the car in drive. That made no difference, because the wheels continued spinning as before. Experimentally, I gave the van a shove from the rear. I could see it would be easy to rock it out of the rut. The idle on that van was set so that even with no foot on the gas it went about eight miles an hour. I opened the driver's side door, went back to the rear of the vehicle, checked again for traffic, and pushed. One heave, another, and the van was off and heading down the road. I ran after it, slipped, and fell. When I got up the van had a 50-foot lead. I ran at top speed, caught up, jumped in, and drove away.

No one but me saw me do that. The exclusivity of this feat made me think even more highly of myself as I tooled on into town. I was the top celebrity in that van. Of course, I was also an idiot.

What I'm trying to describe here is the fine line between pride and stupidity. Actually, there's a fine line between stupidity and lots of things (bravery, love, being funny), so many that the line probably should be re-drawn as a circle, with those important accessories of humanity in the middle, and a vast parade ground of stupidity all around. Of those accessories, none will fraternize with stupidity as readily as pride. Pride and stupidity are thick. Except for the part that keeps you from going on *The Ricki Lake Show*, pride almost is stupidity. This is revealed most comically and horribly in what we do outdoors.

Going down a flooded creek in a boat we'd found, me bailing and my friend Kent fending off obstacles with a surveyor's stake, both of us about 13; up ahead, unexpectedly, a large deadfall lying clear across the creek; and Kent said, "Don't worry, I've got everything under control." I used to tell the rest of that story, but now I understand that I don't have to. Certain prideful declarations — "I know this road like the back of my hand" — seem to exist mainly as preludes to the inevitable disaster. We Americans like to think of ourselves as thumbs-up, can-do types. More recently, we have begun to suspect that the cocky, grinning bush pilot who flies twice a week across the Arctic Circle and back carrying no emergency supplies but a Clark Bar may actually be insane. That we took on the alteration of this continent in the first place now looks more and more like hubris on a gigantic scale. "Manifest Destiny" may be a fancy, nineteenth-century way of saying "I know this road like the back of my hand."

But what the heck. We're here. For better or worse, our pride/stupidity has a lot to do with bringing us this far. Pride, the deadliest sin, is a crime of attitude — of overweening ambition, of imagining ourselves equal to powers beyond our range. Oddly, though, it's a sin whose punishment equals its failure: We approach too near the sun, the wax melts, the wings fall off, and we plunge into the sea. Yet once in a while we don't fail, miraculously, and instantly the sin is erased, and all is glory. In the town where I live — Missoula, Montana — someone recently climbed the tallest building on the campus of the University of Montana and impaled a pumpkin on the spire atop the uppermost tower. In the night, the perpetrator or perpetrators scaled several steeply pitched tile roofs, ascended the tower, carried or hoisted an extra-large pumpkin, and left it there for the school to see when the sun rose in the morning. The administration grumbled about the irresponsibility of this act, and about how expensive it would be to take the pumpkin down. But they didn't take it down, and it's been there ever since. I've looked at it from many angles, wondering how the feat was managed, admiring the mountaineering skill it took, and in the process noticing the architecture of this estimable old building much more closely than I ever would have otherwise. If the pumpkin-impalers had fallen and hurt or killed themselves, public opinion would rightly have regarded them as worse than stupid. But fate turned out better, and the lofty pumpkin remains, making us proud to live in the same town as the idiot or idiots who put it there.

The Reader's Presence

1. This essay is lighthearted, yet also hints at more serious issues. How does Frazier make a serious point through humor? Would the essay be more effective without it, or less? Why?

2. What commentary does Frazier's essay make on heroism and nationalism? How does he challenge commonly held historical notions?

3. Frazier tells stories of misguided pride from his own first-person perspective. Would the reader's experience of the same essay written from a third-person, general, or statistical perspective differ? How and why? What is the effect of Frazier's self-mocking, confessional mode?

53

Mary Gordon

The Ghosts of Ellis Island

Mary Gordon (b. 1949) is a professor of English at Barnard College and frequently contributes articles and short stories to Harper's, Ladies' Home Journal, Virginia Quarterly Review, *and the* Atlantic Monthly. *Since her first novel,* Final

Payments *(1978), earned her critical success, Gordon has published numerous books, including* The Company of Women *(1981),* The Other Side *(1989),* The Shadow Man *(1996), and, most recently,* Spending: A Utopian Divertimento *(1998). A collection of essays,* Seeing through Places, *is forthcoming. "The Ghosts of Ellis Island" originally appeared in the* New York Times *in 1985.*

I once sat in a hotel in Bloomsbury trying to have breakfast alone. A Russian with a habit of compulsively licking his lips asked if he could join me. I was afraid to say no; I thought it might be bad for détente. He explained to me that he was a linguist, and that he always liked to talk to Americans to see if he could make any connection between their speech and their ethnic background. When I told him about my mixed ancestry — my mother is Irish and Italian, my father a Lithuanian Jew — he began jumping up and down in his seat, rubbing his hands together, and licking his lips even more frantically:

"Ah," he said, "so you are really somebody who comes from what is called the boiling pot of America." Yes, I told him, yes I was, but I quickly rose to leave. I thought it would be too hard to explain to him the relation of the boiling potters to the main course, and I wanted to get to the British Museum. I told him that the only thing I could think of that united people whose backgrounds, histories, and points of view were utterly diverse was that their people had landed at a place called Ellis Island.

I didn't tell him that Ellis Island was the only American landmark I'd ever visited. How could I describe to him the estrangement I'd always felt from the kind of traveler who visits shrines to America's past greatness, those rebuilt forts with muskets behind glass and sabers mounted on the walls and gift shops selling maple sugar candy in the shape of Indian headdresses, those reconstructed villages with tables set for fifty and the Paul Revere silver gleaming? All that Americana — Plymouth Rock, Gettysburg, Mount Vernon, Valley Forge — it all inhabits for me a zone of blurred abstraction with far less hold on my imagination than the Bastille or Hampton Court. I suppose I've always known that my uninterest in it contains a large component of the willed: I am American, and those places purport to be my history. But they are not mine.

Ellis Island is, though; it's the one place I can be sure my people are connected to. And so I made a journey there to find my history, like any Rotarian traveling in his Winnebago to Antietam to find his. I had become part of that humbling democracy of people looking in some site for a past that has grown unreal. The monument I traveled to was not, however, a tribute to some old glory. The minute I set foot upon the island I could feel all that it stood for: insecurity, obedience, anxiety, dehumanization, the terrified and careful deference of the displaced. I hadn't traveled to the Battery and boarded a ferry across from the Statue of Liberty to raise flags or breathe a richer, more triumphant air. I wanted to do homage to the ghosts.

I felt them everywhere, from the moment I disembarked and saw the   5
building with its high-minded brick, its hopeful little lawn, its ornamental

cornices. The place was derelict when I arrived; it had not functioned for more than thirty years—almost as long as the time it had operated at full capacity as a major immigration center. I was surprised to learn what a small part of history Ellis Island had occupied. The main building was constructed in 1892, then rebuilt between 1898 and 1900 after a fire. Most of the immigrants who arrived during the latter half of the nineteenth century, mainly northern and western Europeans, landed not at Ellis Island but on the western tip of the Battery at Castle Garden, which had opened as a receiving center for immigrants in 1855.

By the 1880s the facilities at Castle Garden had grown scandalously inadequate. Officials looked for an island on which to build a new immigration center because they thought that on an island immigrants could be more easily protected from swindlers and quickly transported to railroad terminals in New Jersey. Bedloe's Island was considered, but New Yorkers were aghast at the idea of a "Babel" ruining their beautiful new treasure, "Liberty Enlightening the World." The statue's sculptor, Frédéric Auguste Bartholdi, reacted to the prospect of immigrants landing near his masterpiece in horror; he called it a "monstrous plan." So much for Emma Lazarus.

Ellis Island was finally chosen because the citizens of New Jersey petitioned the federal government to remove from the island an old naval powder magazine that they thought dangerously close to the Jersey shore. The explosives were removed; no one wanted the island for anything. It was the perfect place to build an immigration center.

I thought about the island's history as I walked into the building and made my way to the room that was the center in my imagination of the Ellis Island experience: the Great Hall. It had been made real for me in the stark, accusing photographs of Louis Hine and others who took those pictures to make a point. It was in the Great Hall that everyone had waited—waiting, always, the great vocation of the dispossessed. The room was empty, except for me and a handful of other visitors and the park ranger who showed us around. I felt myself grow insignificant in that room, with its huge semicircular windows, its air, even in dereliction, of solid and official probity.

I walked in the deathlike expansiveness of the room's disuse and tried to think of what it might have been like, filled and swarming. More than sixteen million immigrants came through that room; approximately 250,000 were rejected. Not really a large proportion, but the implications for the rejected were dreadful. For some, there was nothing to go back to, or there was certain death; for others, who left as adventurers, to return would be to adopt in local memory the fool's role, and the failure's. No wonder that the island's history includes reports of three thousand suicides.

Sometimes immigrants could pass through Ellis Island in mere hours, 10
though for some the process took days. The particulars of the experience

in the Great Hall were often influenced by the political events and attitudes on the mainland. In the 1890s and the first years of the new century, when cheap labor was needed, the newly built receiving center took in its immigrants with comparatively little question. But as the century progressed, the economy worsened, eugenics became both scientifically respectable and popular, and World War I made American xenophobia seem rooted in fact.

Immigration acts were passed; newcomers had to prove, besides moral correctness and financial solvency, their ability to read. Quota laws came into effect, limiting the number of immigrants from southern and eastern Europe to less than 14 percent of the total quota. Intelligence tests were biased against all non-English-speaking persons and medical examinations became increasingly strict, until the machinery of immigration nearly collapsed under its own weight. The Second Quota Law of 1924 provided that all immigrants be inspected and issued visas at American consular offices in Europe, rendering the center almost obsolete.

On the day of my visit, my mind fastened upon the medical inspections, which had always seemed to me most emblematic of the ignominy and terror the immigrants endured. The medical inspectors, sometimes dressed in uniforms like soldiers, were particularly obsessed with a disease of the eyes called trachoma, which they checked for by flipping back the immigrants' top eyelids with a hook used for buttoning gloves — a method that sometimes resulted in the transmission of the disease to healthy people. Mothers feared that if their children cried too much, their red eyes would be mistaken for a symptom of the disease and the whole family would be sent home. Those immigrants suspected of some physical disability had initials chalked on their coats. I remembered the photographs I'd seen of people standing, dumbstruck and innocent as cattle, with their manifest numbers hung around their necks and initials marked in chalk upon their coats: "E" for eye trouble, "K" for hernia, "L" for lameness, "X" for mental defects, "H" for heart disease.

I thought of my grandparents as I stood in the room; my seventeen-year-old grandmother, coming alone from Ireland in 1896, vouched for by a stranger who had found her a place as a domestic servant to some Irish who had done well. I tried to imagine the assault it all must have been for her; I've been to her hometown, a collection of farms with a main street — smaller than the athletic field of my local public school. She must have watched the New York skyline as the first- and second-class passengers were whisked off the gangplank with the most cursory of inspections while she was made to board a ferry to the new immigration center.

What could she have made of it — this buff-painted wooden structure with its towers and its blue slate roof, a place *Harper's Weekly* described as "a latter-day watering place hotel"? It would have been the first time she'd have heard people speaking something other than English. She would have mingled with people carrying baskets on their heads and eating foods unlike any she had ever seen — dark-eyed people, like the Sicilian she would marry ten years later, who came over with his family, re-sponsible even then for his mother and sister. I don't know what they thought, my grandparents, for they were not expansive people, nor ro-mantic; they didn't like to think of what they called "the hard times," and their trip across the ocean was the single adventurous act of lives devoted after landing to security, respectability, and fitting in.

What is the potency of Ellis Island for someone like me—an Ameri- 15 can, obviously, but one who has always felt that the country really be-longed to the early settlers, that, as J. F. Powers wrote in "Morte D'Ur-ban," it had been "handed down to them by the Pilgrims, George Washington and others, and that they were taking a risk in letting you live in it." I have never been the victim of overt discrimination; nothing I have wanted has been denied me because of the accidents of blood. But I suppose it is part of being an American to be engaged in a somewhat tire-some but always self-absorbing process of national definition. And in this process, I have found in traveling to Ellis Island an important piece of evi-dence that could remind me I was right to feel my differentness. Some-thing had happened to my people on that island, a result of the eternal wrongheadedness of American protectionism and the predictabilities of simple greed. I came to the island, too, so I could tell the ghosts that I was one of them, and that I honored them—their stoicism, and their inno-cence, the fear that turned them inward, and their pride. I wanted to tell them that I liked them better than the Americans who made them pass through the Great Hall and stole their names and chalked their weak-nesses in public on their clothing. And to tell the ghosts what I have al-ways thought: that American history was a very classy party that was not much fun until they arrived, brought the good food, turned up the music, and taught everyone to dance.

The Reader's Presence

1. Gordon contrasts immigrant and mainstream American experi-ences, although nearly all present-day Americans have immigrant ancestry. How does she define *immigrant*? What imagery does she attach to the immigrant experience? How is this imagery made vivid for the reader? How do you think Gordon would wish a reader like herself to experience the essay? How do you think she would wish a mainstream American to experience the essay?

2. Gordon reveals little-known facts about the Statue of Liberty and Ellis Island. What symbolic meaning do these facts convey in terms of America's reception of immigrants? Ellis Island has since been refashioned into an impressive museum celebrating the his-tory of immigrants in America. Does this development undercut or reinforce Gordon's opposition of official and hidden history?

3. Gordon's description of immigrants' contributions to American culture recalls Ralph Ellison's essay "What America Would Be Like without Blacks" (page 367). What sorts of contributions does Gordon credit immigrants with? In what ways are the two writers' visions of America as a "melting pot" similar? How do they differ?

54

Stephen Jay Gould

Sex, Drugs, Disasters, and the Extinction of Dinosaurs

Stephen Jay Gould (b. 1941) is professor of geology and zoology at Harvard and curator of invertebrate paleontology at Harvard's Museum of Comparative Zoology. He has published widely on evolution and other topics and has earned a reputation for making technical subjects readily comprehensible to lay readers without trivializing the material. His The Panda's Thumb *(1980) won the American Book Award, and* The Mismeasure of Man *(1981) won the National Book Critics Circle Award. Gould has published over one hundred articles in scientific journals, and contributes to national magazines as well. "Sex, Drugs, Disasters, and the Extinction of Dinosaurs" appeared in* Discover *magazine in 1984. More recently, Gould has written* Questioning the Millennium: A Rationalists Guide to a Precisely Arbitrary Countdown *(1997),* Leonardo's Mountain of Clams and the Diet of Worms: Essays on Natural History *(1998), and* Rocks of Ages: Science & Religion in the Fullness of Life *(1999). Among many other honors and awards, he has been a fellow of the National Science Foundation and the MacArthur Foundation. In 1999 Gould became president of the American Association for the Advancement of Science. John Updike comments that "Gould, in his scrupulous explication of [other scientists'] carefully wrought half-truths, abolishes the unnecessary distinction between the humanities and science, and honors the latter as a branch of humanistic thought, fallible and poetic."*

When asked if he finds it difficult to write about complex scientific concepts in language that is accessible to general readers, Gould replied, "I don't see why it should be that difficult. . . . Every field has its jargon. I think scientists hide behind theirs perhaps more than people in other professions do—it's part of our mythology—but I don't think the concepts of science are intrinsically more difficult than the professional notions in any other field."

Science, in its most fundamental definition, is a fruitful mode of inquiry, not a list of enticing conclusions. The conclusions are the consequence, not the essence.

My greatest unhappiness with most popular presentations of science concerns their failure to separate fascinating claims from the methods that scientists use to establish the facts of nature. Journalists, and the public, thrive on controversial and stunning statements. But science is, basically, a way of knowing—in P. B. Medawar's apt words, "the art of the soluble." If the growing corps of popular science writers would focus on *how* scientists develop and defend those fascinating claims, they would make their greatest possible contribution to public understanding.

Consider three ideas, proposed in perfect seriousness to explain that greatest of all titillating puzzles—the extinction of dinosaurs. Since these three notions invoke the primally fascinating themes of our culture—sex, drugs, and violence—they surely reside in the category of fascinating claims. I want to show why two of them rank as silly speculation, while the other represents science at its grandest and most useful.

Science works with the testable proposals. If, after much compilation and scrutiny of data, new information continues to affirm a hypothesis, we may accept it provisionally and gain confidence as further evidence mounts. We can never be completely sure that a hypothesis is right, though we may be able to show with confidence that it is wrong. The best scientific hypotheses are also generous and expansive: They suggest extensions and implications that enlighten related, and even far distant, subjects. Simply consider how the idea of evolution has influenced virtually every intellectual field.

Useless speculation, on the other hand, is restrictive. It generates no testable hypothesis, and offers no way to obtain potentially refuting evidence. Please note that I am not speaking of truth or falsity. The speculation may well be true; still, if it provides, in principle, no material for affirmation or rejection, we can make nothing of it. It must simply stand forever as an intriguing idea. Useless speculation turns in on itself and leads nowhere; good science, containing both seeds for its potential refutation and implications for more and different testable knowledge, reaches out. But, enough preaching. Let's move on to dinosaurs, and the three proposals for their extinction.

1. *Sex:* Testes function only in a narrow range of temperature (those of mammals hang externally in a scrotal sac because internal body temperatures are too high for their proper function). A worldwide rise in temperature at the close of the Cretaceous period caused the testes of dinosaurs to stop functioning and led to their extinction by sterilization of males.

2. *Drugs:* Angiosperms (flowering plants) first evolved toward the end of the dinosaurs' reign. Many of these plants contain psychoactive agents, avoided by mammals today as a result of their bitter

taste. Dinosaurs had neither means to taste the bitterness nor livers effective enough to detoxify the substances. They died of massive overdoses.

3. *Disasters:* A large comet or asteroid struck the earth some 65 million years ago, lofting a cloud of dust into the sky and blocking sunlight, thereby suppressing photosynthesis and so drastically lowering world temperatures that dinosaurs and hosts of other creatures became extinct.

Before analyzing these three tantalizing statements, we must establish a basic ground rule often violated in proposals for the dinosaurs' demise. *There is no separate problem of the extinction of dinosaurs.* Too often we divorce specific events from their wider contexts and systems of cause and effect. The fundamental fact of dinosaur extinction is its synchrony with the demise of so many other groups across a wide range of habitats, from terrestrial to marine.

The history of life has been punctuated by brief episodes of mass extinction. A recent analysis by University of Chicago paleontologists Jack Sepkoski and Dave Raup, based on the best and most exhaustive tabulation of data ever assembled, shows clearly that five episodes of mass dying stand well above the "background" extinctions of normal times (when we consider all mass extinctions, large and small, they seem to fall in a regular 26-million-year cycle). The Cretaceous debacle, occurring 65 million years ago and separating the Mesozoic and Cenozoic eras of our geological time scale, ranks prominently among the five. Nearly all the marine plankton (single-celled floating creatures) died with geological suddenness; among marine invertebrates, nearly 15 percent of all families perished, including many previously dominant groups, especially the ammonites (relatives of squids in coiled shells). On land, the dinosaurs disappeared after more than 100 million years of unchallenged domination.

In this context, speculations limited to dinosaurs alone ignore the larger phenomenon. We need a coordinated explanation for a system of events that includes the extinction of dinosaurs as one component. Thus it makes little sense, though it may fuel our desire to view mammals as inevitable inheritors of the earth, to guess that dinosaurs died because small mammals ate their eggs (a perennial favorite among untestable speculations). It seems most unlikely that some disaster peculiar to dinosaurs befell these massive beasts—and that the debacle happened to strike just when one of history's five great dyings had enveloped the earth for completely different reasons.

The testicular theory, an old favorite from the 1940s, had its root in an interesting and thoroughly respectable study of temperature tolerances in the American alligator, published in the staid *Bulletin of the American Museum of Natural History* in 1946 by three experts on living and fossil reptiles—E. H. Colbert, my own first teacher in paleontology; R. B. Cowles; and C. M. Bogert.

The first sentence of their summary reveals a purpose beyond alliga-   10
tors: "This report describes an attempt to infer the reactions of extinct reptiles, especially the dinosaurs, to high temperatures as based upon reactions observed in the modern alligator." They studied, by rectal thermometry, the body temperatures of alligators under changing conditions of heating and cooling. (Well, let's face it, you wouldn't want to try sticking a thermometer under a 'gator's tongue.) The predictions under test go way back to an old theory first stated by Galileo in the 1630s—the unequal scaling of surfaces and volumes. As an animal, or an object, grows (provided its shape doesn't change), surface areas must increase more slowly than volumes—since surfaces gets larger as length squared, while volumes increase much more rapidly, as length cubed. Therefore, small animals have high ratios of surface to volume, while large animals cover themselves with relatively little surface.

Among cold-blooded animals lacking any physiological mechanism for keeping their temperatures constant, small creatures have a hell of a time keeping warm—because they lose so much heat through their relatively large surfaces. On the other hand, large animals, with their relatively small surfaces, may lose heat so slowly that, once warm, they may maintain effectively constant temperatures against ordinary fluctuations of climate. (In fact, the resolution of the "hot-blooded dinosaur" controversy that burned so brightly a few years back may simply be that, while large dinosaurs possessed no physiological mechanism for constant temperature, and were not therefore warm-blooded in the technical sense, their large size and relatively small surface area kept them warm.)

Colbert, Cowles, and Bogert compared the warming rates of small and large alligators. As predicted, the small fellows heated up (and cooled down) more quickly. When exposed to a warm sun, a tiny 50-gram (1.76-ounce) alligator heated up one degree Celsius every minute and a half, while a large alligator, 260 times bigger at 13,000 grams (28.7 pounds), took seven and a half minutes to gain a degree. Extrapolating up to an adult 10-ton dinosaur, they concluded that a one-degree rise in body temperature would take eighty-six hours. If large animals absorb heat so slowly (through their relatively small surfaces), they will also be unable to shed any excess heat gained when temperatures rise above a favorable level.

The authors then guessed that large dinosaurs lived at or near their optimum temperatures; Cowles suggested that a rise in global temperatures just before the Cretaceous extinction caused the dinosaurs to heat up beyond their optimal tolerance—and, being so large, they couldn't shed the unwanted heat. (In a most unusual statement within a scientific paper, Colbert and Bogert then explicitly disavowed this speculative extension of their empirical work on alligators.) Cowles conceded that this excess heat probably wasn't enough to kill or even to enervate the great beasts, but since testes often function only within narrow range of temperature, he proposed that this global rise might have sterilized all the males, causing extinction by natural contraception.

The overdose theory has recently been supported by UCLA psychiatrist Ronald K. Siegel. Siegel has gathered, he claims, more than 2,000 records of animals who, when given access, administer various drugs to themselves—from a mere swig of alcohol to massive doses of the big H. Elephants will swill the equivalent of twenty beers at a time, but do not like alcohol in concentrations greater than 7 percent. In a silly bit of anthropocentric speculation, Siegel states that "elephants drink, perhaps, to forget . . . the anxiety produced by shrinking rangeland and the competition for food."

Since fertile imaginations can apply almost any hot idea to the extinc- 15
tion of dinosaurs, Siegel found a way. Flowering plants did not evolve until late in the dinosaurs' reign. These plants also produced an array of aromatic, amino-acid-based alkaloids—the major group of psychoactive agents. Most mammals are "smart" enough to avoid these potential poisons. The alkaloids simply don't taste good (they are bitter); in any case, we mammals have livers happily supplied with the capacity to detoxify them. But, Siegel speculates, perhaps dinosaurs could neither taste the bitterness nor detoxify the substances once ingested. He recently told members of the American Psychological Association: "I'm not suggesting that all dinosaurs OD'd on plant drugs, but it certainly was a factor." He also argued that death by overdose may help explain why so many dinosaur fossils are found in contorted positions. (Do not go gentle into that good night.)

Extraterrestrial catastrophes have long pedigrees in the popular literature of extinction, but the subject exploded again in 1979, after a long lull, when the father-son, physicist-geologist team of Luis and Walter Alvarez proposed that an asteroid, some 10 km in diameter, struck the earth 65 million years ago (comets, rather than asteroids, have since gained favor. Good science is self-corrective).

The force of such a collision would be immense, greater by far than the megatonnage of all the world's nuclear weapons. In trying to reconstruct a scenario that would explain the simultaneous dying of dinosaurs on land and so many creatures in the sea, the Alvarezes proposed that a gigantic dust cloud, generated by particles blown aloft in the impact, would so darken the earth that photosynthesis would cease and temperatures drop precipitously. (Rage, rage against the dying of the light.) The single-celled photosynthetic oceanic plankton, with life cycles measured in weeks, would perish outright, but land plants might survive through the dormancy of their seeds (land plants were not much affected by the Cretaceous extinction, and any adequate theory must account for the curious pattern of differential survival). Dinosaurs would die by starvation and freezing; small, warm-blooded mammals, with more modest requirements for food and better regulation of body temperature, would squeak through. "Let the bastards freeze in the dark," as bumper stickers of our chauvinistic neighbors in sunbelt states proclaimed several years ago during the Northeast's winter oil crisis.

All three theories, testicular malfunction, psychoactive overdosing, and asteroidal zapping, grab our attention mightily. As pure phenomenology, they rank about equally high on any hit parade of primal fascination. Yet one represents expansive science, the others restrictive and untestable speculation. The proper criterion lies in evidence and methodology; we must probe behind the superficial fascination of particular claims.

How could we possibly decide whether the hypothesis of testicular frying is right or wrong? We would have to know things that the fossil record cannot provide. What temperatures were optimal for dinosaurs? Could they avoid the absorption of excess heat by staying in the shade, or in caves? At what temperatures did their testicles cease to function? Were late Cretaceous climates ever warm enough to drive the internal temperatures of dinosaurs close to this ceiling? Testicles simply don't fossilize, and how could we infer their temperature tolerances even if they did? In short, Cowles's hypothesis is only an intriguing speculation leading nowhere. The most damning statement against it appeared right in the conclusion of Colbert, Cowles, and Bogert's paper, when they admitted: "It is difficult to advance any definite arguments against the hypothesis." My statement may seem paradoxical—isn't a hypothesis really good if you can't devise any arguments against it? Quite the contrary. It is simply untestable and unusable.

Siegel's overdosing has even less going for it. At least Cowles extrapolated his conclusion from some good data on alligators. And he didn't completely violate the primary guideline of siting dinosaur extinction in the context of a general mass dying—for rise in temperature could be the root cause of a general catastrophe, zapping dinosaurs by testicular malfunction and different groups for other reasons. But Siegel's speculation cannot touch the extinction of ammonites or oceanic plankton (diatoms make their own food with good sweet sunlight; they don't OD on the chemicals of terrestrial plants). It is simply a gratuitous, attention-grabbing guess. It cannot be tested, for how can we know what dinosaurs tasted and what their livers could do? Livers don't fossilize any better than testicles.

The hypothesis doesn't even make any sense in its own context. Angiosperms were in full flower ten million years before dinosaurs went the way of all flesh. Why did it take so long? As for the pains of a chemical death recorded in contortions of fossils, I regret to say (or rather I'm pleased to note for the dinosaurs' sake) that Siegel's knowledge of geology must be a bit deficient: muscles contract after death and geological strata rise and fall with motions of the earth's crust after burial—more than enough reason to distort a fossil's pristine appearance.

The impact story, on the other hand, has a sound basis in evidence. It can be tested, extended, refined, and, if wrong, disproved. The Alvarezes

20

did not just construct an arresting guess for public consumption. They proposed their hypothesis after laborious geochemical studies with Frank Asaro and Helen Michael had revealed a massive increase of iridium in rocks deposited right at the time of extinction. Iridium, a rare metal of the platinum group, is virtually absent from indigenous rocks of the earth's crust; most of our iridium arrives on extraterrestrial objects that strike the earth.

The Alverez hypothesis bore immediate fruit. Based originally on evidence from two European localities, it led geochemists throughout the world to examine other sediments of the same age. They found abnormally high amounts of iridium everywhere — from continental rocks of the western United States to deep sea cores from the South Atlantic.

Cowles proposed his testicular hypothesis in the mid-1940s. Where has it gone since then? Absolutely nowhere, because scientists can do nothing with it. The hypothesis must stand as a curious appendage to a solid study of alligators. Siegel's overdose scenario will also win a few press notices and fade into oblivion. The Alverezes' asteroid falls into a different category altogether, and much of the popular commentary has missed this essential distinction by focusing on the impact and its attendant results, and forgetting what really matters to a scientist — the iridium. If you talk just about asteroids, dust, and darkness, you tell stories no better and no more entertaining than fried testicles or terminal trips. It is the iridium — the source of testable evidence — that counts and forges the crucial distinction between speculation and science.

The proof, to twist a phrase, lies in the doing. Cowles's hypothesis has generated nothing in thirty-five years. Since its proposal in 1979, the Alvarez hypothesis has spawned hundreds of studies, a major conference, and attendant publications. Geologists are fired up. They are looking for iridium at all other extinction boundaries. Every week exposes a new wrinkle in the scientific press. Further evidence that the Cretaceous iridium represents extraterrestrial impact and not indigenous volcanism continues to accumulate. As I revise this essay in November 1984 (this paragraph will be out of date when the book is published),[1] new data include chemical "signatures" of other isotopes indicating unearthly provenance, glass spherules of a size and sort produced by impact and not by volcanic eruptions, and high-pressure varieties of silica formed (so far as we know) only under the tremendous shock of impact.

My point is simply this: Whatever the eventual outcome (I suspect it will be positive), the Alvarez hypothesis is exciting, fruitful science because it generates tests, provides us with things to do, and expands outward. We are having fun, battling back and forth, moving toward a resolution, and extending the hypothesis beyond its original scope.

As just one example of the unexpected, distant cross-fertilization that good science engenders, the Alvarez hypothesis made a major contribu-

25

---

[1] **The Flamingo's Smile** (1985), in which Gould collected this essay. — EDS.

tion to a theme that has riveted public attention in the past few months—so-called nuclear winter. In a speech delivered in April 1982, Luis Alvarez calculated the energy that a ten-kilometer asteroid would release on impact. He compared such an explosion with a full nuclear exchange and implied that all-out atomic war might unleash similar consequences.

This theme of impact leading to massive dust clouds and falling temperatures formed an important input to the decision of Carl Sagan and a group of colleagues to model the climatic consequences of nuclear holocaust. Full nuclear exchange would probably generate the same kind of dust cloud and darkening that may have wiped out the dinosaurs. Temperatures would drop precipitously and agriculture might become impossible. Avoidance of nuclear war is fundamentally an ethical and political imperative, but we must know the factual consequences to make firm judgments. I am heartened by a final link across disciplines and deep concerns—another criterion, by the way, of science at its best.[2] A recognition of the very phenomenon that made our evolution possible by exterminating the previously dominant dinosaurs and clearing a way for the evolution of large mammals, including us, might actually help to save us from joining those magnificent beasts in contorted poses among the strata of the earth.

The Reader's Presence

1. Although the title of Gould's essay focuses on the extinction of dinosaurs, his overriding interest is in demonstrating the way science works, and his purpose is to make that process fully accessible and understandable to the general public. Where does he lay out this central claim, and how does he demonstrate, clarify, and complicate it as his essay proceeds?

2. What distinctions does Gould draw among "testable proposals," "intriguing ideas," and "useless speculation"? What features of each does he identify? Reread his summary of the three proposals for the extinction of dinosaurs. Which of the three terms cited above would you use to characterize this summary? In what specific ways does Gould use them to demonstrate the limitations of popular presentations of scientific theory? What crucial piece of evidence does he omit from the summary? With what effect?

3. Reread Gould's essay, with special attention to his use of tone, diction, syntax, and metaphor. How does he use these compositional strategies to make information accessible to his readers? Point to passages where Gould uses the diction and syntax of a

---

[2]This quirky connection so tickles my fancy that I break my own strict rule about eliminating redundancies from [this essay]. . . . —GOULD'S NOTE.

serious scientist. When—and with what effects—does his prose sound more colloquial? Does his tone remain consistent throughout the essay? If not, when and how does it change? With what effects?

55

Kathryn Harrison

What Remains

Kathryn Harrison was born in Los Angeles in 1961 and attended Stanford University and the University of Iowa Writers' Workshop. A former editor at Viking Publishers, Harrison is a frequent contributor to the New York Times Book Review, Harper's, Vogue, *and the* New Yorker. *She is the author of three novels,* Thicker Than Water *(1991),* Exposure *(1993), and* Poison *(1995). In her controversial memoir* The Kiss *(1997), she confesses to an incestuous relationship with her father while she was in her twenties. "What Remains" appeared in* Harper's *in December 1995.*

Earlier this year Guernsey's, a New York City auction house, sponsored an event advertised as "the greatest rock and roll auction of all time." Among the 4,000 items consigned for sale were electric guitars played by Jimi Hendrix and Paul McCartney; previously unseen photographs of Janis Joplin, Mick Jagger, and Patti Smith; rare acetate recordings by Elvis Presley and personal effects including clothing, jewelry, drawings, lyrics scrawled on notebook paper, even old bath towels. I am not a collector of rock memorabilia, but I attended the auction's preview in Manhattan's Puck Building because I wanted to look at three items mentioned on the local news the previous evening.

As it turned out, the three things I wanted to see were the same requested over and over by successive TV crews that I watched enter the Puck Building's ballroom and consult the young woman with the clipboard who was handling public relations. She smiled extravagantly as she pointed out potential objects of interest, but the eyes of the reporters glanced off all but the three, as described by the auction catalogue: B34A, "Washbasin from the apartment of John Lennon, the Dakota (72nd and Central Park West), New York City"; E257E, "Elvis Presley owned and used rechargeable Remington Razor . . . in original box"; and G126A, the "left-handed sunburst Stratocaster . . . smashed on stage by [Kurt]

Cobain" and bearing "remnants of blood from Cobain's fingers on the pickguard."

Waiting my turn behind the television crews, I watched as one and then another cameraman stepped up to the late Mr. Lennon's sink and, balancing unsteadily on a box or stool, contrived to point the lens of his video camera into the sink's drain. Then I got my chance to examine the sink; a Kohler wall-mount with two stainless-steel legs and shiny clean faucet and knobs, it was unremarkable.

But wait, what was that? Between the hygienically smooth white porcelain and the polished stainless-steel collar that circled the orifice of the drain was a narrow but definite band of brown crud. This residue, dug out with a fingernail or pin, would not have filled a teaspoon. What of John Lennon might have been preserved in the crevice encircling his washbasin's drain? What fragment of hair or skin, what molecule of saliva, mucus, possibly even blood, vomit, or piss? Anyone considering the purchase was assured that the plumbing was accompanied by an "affidavit verifying the circumstances" from the "gentleman who did the repairs and retained the sink offered herein."

Perhaps whoever bought the sink, the opening bid for which was set   5 at $6,000, has now collected and swallowed the dried sink scum, just as visitors to Goa, on the west coast of India, have bitten off two of the toes of Saint Francis Xavier, who died in 1552 and whose body, subsequently enshrined in the Portuguese colony, continues to draw crowds of pilgrims and miracle seekers. It is not an implausible idea. Who we consider holy changes over the centuries; what we want from them has not.

After her cremation, my own grandmother's ashes were returned to me by the Dunn Funeral Home in a white cardboard box bearing a yellow label whose return address was that of Brooklyn's Green-Wood Cemetery. Inside the white box was a thick black plastic one whose lid I pried at with a knife until it opened with a loud crack to reveal a polyurethane bag closed with a red twist tie, the kind that bakeries use. I took the bag out and held it in my lap. An average-sized human is said to yield seven pounds of cremated remains, about the weight of a cat, a number of which my grandmother had raised and pampered. The ashes felt as heavy as one of her pets but were cool. A certificate of cremation accompanying the bag bore this rubber-stamped message: VANDALISM FEE COLLECTED. This struck me as somewhat cryptic, but I guessed it was one of several supposed assurances that the ashes I held were indeed those of my grandmother, whose corpse was assigned a serial number by Green-Wood Cemetery, C 27594, that was inscribed on the boxes and all pertinent documents and stamped onto a coin I found among the ashes themselves when I opened the bag.

Ashes aren't so much ashes as fragments of burned bone, some large enough that I could observe the elegant tracery of the marrow's canals. These looked like lace, some white, others the color of rust; the rest was a fine gray dust that adhered to my fingers as I sifted through the remains. I withdrew my hand from the bag, sucked one finger, and felt the grit between my teeth. I licked the other fingers and my palm as well. Tasting what was left of my grandmother—a woman made holy to me by love and by blood—was something I did alone, behind the closed door to my study. The privacy of the act was not born of shame but of its being sacred: a last intimacy between two women who, in turn, had diapered each other. The following week, I poured the rest of her ashes into the sea; some were thrown back at me by the wind so that they stung my eyes and dusted my arms. I kept the bag within its two boxes and have occasionally pressed my face into it and inhaled.

What did I want from my grandmother's ashes? I have her temperament, I bear her features. Taking a little of her inside of me was not so much a superstitious reflex as it was a kind of communion: a private Eucharist, albeit one many might judge profane.

The acquisition and veneration of relics reflect a primitive longing, one that has been carried forward from prehistory and has taken forms as various as cannibalism and Buddhism. Among cannibals, some are selective to the point that they eat a bit of brain for wisdom or heart for courage, supplements they hope will help them overcome their enemies in much the same way we expect iron supplements to defend us from anemia.

Even religions that are generally understood to eschew connection to the material world and to the body venerate the remains of the dead. In Yangon, Myanmar (formerly Burma), construction of a great pagoda is under way. The building will enshrine one of the four teeth plucked from the Lord Buddha's cremation pyre in 483 B.C.; on some weekends thousands line up at the construction site to offer the gift of their labor. During the Middle Ages, Christian pilgrimages to shrines such as Spain's Santiago de Compostela (where, legend holds, the Apostle James was buried after Herod executed him in 42 A.D.) were undertaken as journeys whose destinations were more spiritual than geographic. Such pilgrimages had their precedent in a long-standing classical tradition of travel to the site of important shrines, those housing either first-class, or corporeal, remains or what are called second-class, or representative, relics, personal items such as Achilles' spear, which is kept in the temple of Athena at Phaselis. 10

If we no longer expect the tomb of a hero to guarantee a town heavenly protection, it still offers economic solace. Graceland in Memphis, Tennessee, on whose grounds Elvis is buried, draws 700,000 tourists each year, 40,000 on the anniversary of his death. Cooperstown, New York, lures crowds to the National Baseball Hall of Fame, which enshrines Babe Ruth's glove, Ty Cobb's sliding pads, and the bat used by Mickey Mantle to hit a 565-foot home run. The New York Public Library owns pieces of Percy Shelley's skull. Yale's Beinecke Collection includes a chamber pot used by FDR when he visited the university to receive an honorary degree. Americans who visit such reliquaries are doing what humans have always done: attempting to draw close to the sacred.

All of us persist against reason in believing that some manifestation of the dead's personality or spirit remains in his or her corpse, and our faith extends to include the dead's possessions, especially those objects that routinely come into direct contact with the body: clothing and tools used for eating or for grooming. At the auction preview, Elvis Presley's "Selektronic" razor, displayed in its original box lined with ersatz red velvet, and valued in the catalogue at $4,000, did indeed appear to have been used. The shaving head was dusted with what looked like skin and hair particles, and the corners of the box were gray with the same fine accumulation. Three days after I saw Presley's Remington, late-night talk show host Conan O'Brien taped a segment at the auction and was quoted by the *New York Times* as having said, "Maybe I'll buy Elvis's electric shaver. I'll open it up and look for stubble and then auction it off, hair by hair." It was a joke, but a serious one. Just as the Catholic Church attempts to protect the corpses of saints from the kind of worshipful abuses visited on Francis Xavier's feet, displaying holy remains behind iron grilles or under glass, so Elvis's razor was locked in a case, the glass door of which was smeared with greasy handprints and fogged with breath; one cameraman wiped it off before he began videotaping.

A few miles uptown from the Puck Building, New York City's Mother Cabrini shrine houses what is described in one guidebook as the "mummy" of Saint Frances Xavier Cabrini, the first United States citizen to have been canonized. The shrine is in a chapel on the campus of Mother Cabrini High School. A religious gift shop serves as an antechamber and carries an assortment of pious trash familiar to those who frequent such concessions: tiny plastic squirt bottles filled with holy water, rosaries and laminated felt scapulars made in the Philippines, statuettes, pocket prayer books, votive candles. But the Cabrini gift shop also functions as a mini-museum, its walls lined with the kind of display cases that elsewhere in the high school might hold team trophies or biology specimens. Through their glass doors visitors can examine Frances Cabrini's personal articles, among them a tightly coiled gold spring, approximately two inches long. Presented with it is a Xerox copy of a handwritten letter that begins, "My father, Hugo Ragaini, felt gravely honored to have been fortunate enough to make dentures for Mother Cabrini. When she came to him in 1914 to have new dentures made, she told him to keep the gold spring which came from the original dentures she had made in France. . . ." (Before dentures were fixed in place by adhesive cream, springs were used to keep uppers from falling closed onto lowers.) The letter goes on to describe a miracle of healing attributed to Mother Cabrini's denture spring, which the signer, Victor Ragaini, hereby bequeaths to the saint's shrine as a token of his gratitude.

Cabrini's physical remains are laid in a glass coffin that forms the base for the main altar of her chapel. The top is marble, but you can see the saint through the coffin's sides. If you've seen the Disney version of *Snow White,* the casket looks very much like the one in which the dwarfs preserve their beloved housekeeper until her prince can come to wake her.

This iconographic resemblance may be disturbing, but it is not accidental, for it is in anticipation of the Prince of Peace's resurrecting kiss that Frances Cabrini waits in preternatural sleep. The Church's use of symbols is determined by their potency, not their source, and many elements of fairy tales have been appropriated into hagiography. Saint Cabrini wears a gold crown; her face and hands project from a deflated, seemingly empty black habit. Below its hem, her shoes stick up and eerily recall another fantasy image. You suspect that were you to remove them, the saint's toes would shrivel, curl, and draw up under her habit.

Crouched by the casket on my hands and knees, I examined Mother   15
Frances's hands and face. I wasn't prepared to accept her remains as being supernaturally incorrupt, but what I could see of her looked to be a remarkable embalming job. The side of the coffin was fogged with my nervous breath. Clearly, visitors were not expected to approach the saint so intimately, and, afraid of being found prostrated next to Frances with nothing but a pane of glass between us, I returned to the gift shop, presided over by a taciturn nun.

"Is the body under the altar really Mother Cabrini?" I asked, beginning my question boldly but swallowing its last words. The nun made no response. She was one of those people who blink less frequently than the rest of us.

"What I mean to say is—" I paused. "Is what I see in the casket really Saint Cabrini?"

"Yes," said the nun. From behind the cash register, she crossed her arms over her habit.

"So the, uh, face and the hands, they aren't, uh—?" I was thinking *wax,* but the nun's impassive expression didn't allow me to utter the word.

"That's her," said the nun. I found it impossible to look her in the   20
eye. My gaze ascended only as far as the obligatory spinster's mustache that softened the hard set of her lips. The phone in the gift shop rang, and when she turned to answer it I left. Later, I learned that the saint's remains, exhumed in 1933 for examination by a papal commission, had been placed within a wax effigy five years later.

In the early Church, the Eucharist was commonly celebrated over the remains of a saint. The cult of martyrs was dropped—not unlike Dorothy's Kansas farmhouse—right onto the Greek worship of heroes. The subjects of veneration were replaced, but the custom of honoring the dead persisted, with one difference. The Greeks, who did not believe in an afterlife (the shades in the underworld were just that: dim memories of the lives that preceded them), buried corpses intact and did not disturb their graves, whereas early Christians were soon tearing up knuckles and gristle and hair. The relics trade, which would be condemned by leaders of the Reformation, reached its peak in the Middle Ages, when relics served a number of important functions for the dissemination of Catholicism. For a faith that is founded upon the idea of resurrection of body as well as soul, the literal creation of altar from tomb is an important symbolic act, and Rome required the presence of a martyr's relic for the official consecration of an altar. The Holy Office tried to control the establishment of new churches by dictating what was and was not a martyr's bona fide remains, but, not surprisingly, relics proliferated as quickly as Elvis sightings.

Every sainted excrescence and fluid was discovered and produced. The Virgin's milk was stored in vials all over Christendom—so much of it that Calvin remarked wryly that even if Mary had been a cow she could not have produced such a quantity in a mere lifetime. No one who could afford it was without some fleshly talisman, at the least a thread of someone's shroud or veil. For the common masses, the third-class, or substitute, relic was invented and persists today in such commercial pilgrimage centers as Lourdes. There, a bit of cloth that has supposedly touched a first- or second-class relic of Saint Bernadette is attached to an image of the saint and sold for an affordable price.

The contemplation of relics, Catholic or secular, has not encouraged my faith in resurrection any more than pressing the bag that once held my grandmother's ashes to my lips allows me to believe in her continued life. I am drawn to artifacts of the dead because through them I can approach death. Thus I was fascinated by a number of Frances Cabrini's garments hanging in the gift shop. Made of white linen or cotton, they were thin enough to appear as underclothes or nightgowns, and bore traces of the body that once filled them, including a mesmerizing, ghostly yellow stain in the lap of one. Did the saint spill her tea? Did she once lose control of some more intimate fluid? Whatever happened, the stain offered proof that a life passed through the fabric's embrace. The same proof rings the collars of shirts once worn by Elvis, stained their venerated armpits. Among Elvis's garments to be auctioned were a pristine white cardigan sweater (pressed flat under the glass of a frame) and a yellow silk shirt, shoulders drooping disconsolately off the hanger, cuffs in disrepair, stained at the neck. The dirty shirt was valued at $25,000 more than the clean sweater.

If we do not fancy ourselves as prone to superstition and magic thinking as medieval Christians, if we do not generally carry relics on our bodies in lockets and purses, in special rings, bracelets, and chokers, in order that they might deliver us from temptation and sin in this life and from hell in the next, still we fear what we have always feared—our own deaths. Afraid and therefore fascinated by the unthinkable end of ourselves, we need help in approaching a notion so alien and impossible that our society judges its clinical evidences obscene, something to be masked by the embalmer's art. For those of us who do not invest them with miraculous power, relics of the dead offer more pragmatic and humble gifts. They help us toward the challenging task of thinking about not being. And they comfort us through their mute witness, their not allowing mortality to mean erasure: the dead, they testify, *were*.

Is it because I have had more occasions to consider death than most women my age that I find the remains of the dead, both their bodies and their possessions, so compelling? I was raised by elderly grandparents and by my mother, all of whom died within the same few years. I saved relics of all these people I loved: locks of hair, photographs, jewelry, letters. And, as if that were not enough mourning, in the time between and surrounding their deaths I visited other graves and other shrines. In Los Angeles, where I grew up, I saw DiMaggio's rose, replaced daily outside Marilyn Monroe's tomb. In the reliquary at Madrid's Monasterio de la Encarnación, I saw a tiny gold-stoppered bottle of the dried blood of Saint Pantaléon, which is said to be 1,600 years old and is believed to liquefy every twenty-seventh of July, on the saint's feast day.

It is blood that I've looked at with the greatest fascination: stains and smears and crumbs of a substance both humble and mysterious. In the wake of the chemotherapy that destroyed her marrow, my mother received a number of transfusions, and I watched their startling testimony to blood's life and power, saw their blush infuse her white cheeks. The reprieves were brief, only as long as blood lives: two months, no more, for whole blood includes newborn cells that may expect to live for up to 120 days as well as cells that die even as they enter the recipient's bloodstream.

Seduced long ago by Catholic iconography's eroticized images of stigmata, of martyrdoms, of Christ's opening his robes and his breast to reveal his bleeding heart, I cannot help but associate blood with expiation and with grief. After my grandmother's death, I compulsively donated my own blood every eight weeks, as often as the Red Cross would take it, in what I've only recently understood as my acting out a controlled mourning. At the donor center, a technician whom I too easily confused with an acolyte would relieve me of only so much of my grief: one pint. The act was my assertion that I would contrive to have grief stanched long before I died of it.

At the auction preview, I saved Kurt Cobain's bloodstained guitar for last and stood before it longest, while the white plate under the strings of the smashed Stratocaster shined silver under the portable klieg lights of successive TV crews. One of the guitar's metal strings, perhaps the one on which the dead singer had cut his fingers, was broken; it zigzagged crazily away from the tight rank of its neighbors, making, no doubt, a little silver shiver for the camera's eye to record. As advertised, the white pick guard did bear visible traces of blood. Without that stain, would the guitar have been valued at $15,000? Would someone have paid, as he or she did, $19,500?

Like the martyrs of the early Church, Kurt Cobain is famous for having died. His name was unknown to many, me included, before he killed himself. And though I could not name a single song or lyric by Kurt Cobain, I was moved by the sight of his blood spilled on his guitar. I found it impossible not to read it as a foreshadowing of his taking his own life. Because most of us fear suffering so intensely, we are awed by evidence of it. And in order to help us accept its inevitability, we invest pain with meaning: we revere sufferers and sentimentally imagine that misery is universally (rather than rarely) ennobling, that it sanctifies. For fifty cents you can purchase a prayer by Mother Cabrini inscribed on a laminated card: "The knowledge of suffering is the knowledge of the saints. He who does not know what Christian suffering is, what can he know of greatness and wonder in his days?" Do these words make an exclusively Catholic prayer? Can you not remove the word "Christian" and any limiting definition of the word "saint" and read it as a general human confession?

Abraham Lincoln was not a Catholic, but in American terms he is a saint. He has earned that status as much for his statesmanship as for his suffering, which we believe we can see in his very face: lean, ascetic, as long and lugubrious as an El Greco. Man of sorrows, martyr, champion of the persecuted, Lincoln could not be anyone who enjoyed his life as much as well-heeled Jefferson or piggy-jowled Franklin. To be worthy of a reliquary, he would have to have been a man whose log-cabin birth was as humble as an arrival in a manger, whose childhood was doubly blighted by poverty and the death of his mother.

The National Museum of Health and Medicine, run by the Armed Forces Institute of Pathology and located on the grounds of the Walter Reed Army Medical Center in Washington, D.C., began its collecting activities during the Civil War. It greets visitors with a large, artfully lit glass case containing souvenirs of the autopsy performed on President Lincoln, as well as some from the autopsy of his assassin, John Wilkes Booth, including two bloodstained shirt cuffs once worn by army assistant surgeon Edward Curtis. In 1865, Curtis participated in Lincoln's autopsy, during which his shirt was splashed with the dead president's blood. There is an illicit quality to the relic, in part conferred by brown stains on yellowed cotton, which remind even the most reverent viewer of dirty underwear. But this humble aspect is part of what moves us, because we half expect that the blood of Lincoln would be different from our own, would have a luminosity, a molecular shiver. Because it is brown and dull and faded—utterly unremarkable—it witnesses to the grace of God or of fate, to whatever force can lift a poor boy from obscurity and make him our president.

I consider myself less a patriot than a Catholic, but the blood of Abraham Lincoln, along with the gray curls shorn from around his wound, brought unexpected tears to my eyes. Why? In part because I consider locks of hair as baby's mementos, all of which have an inherent melancholy: the reminder that time passes, that all babies age and die. But Lincoln's hair was forced right up against evil and violence, and it is the

30

knowledge of what was bought with those curls that strikes us so viscerally. In Lisieux, France, there is a shrine to Saint Therese that includes her hair in a resplendent gold frame.

The luxury of those long lustrous curls, shorn when she entered the Carmelite order at fifteen and saved by her father, together with an understanding of what austerity and suffering they bought, cannot fail to move visitors. Just as pilgrims to Lisieux are likely to believe that Therese's renunciation of the earthly pleasures symbolized by her frankly sexual tresses paid her way through gates of unimaginable splendor, so does the pilgrim to the Lincoln shrine accept his grizzled curls, lost in the wake of an assassin's bullet, as part of the price of admission to a different pantheon. Perhaps this is why Indiana University's Lilly Library bought Sylvia Plath's childhood curls in 1978, fifteen years after her suicide; their arrested innocence is made all the more powerful by what would follow in the poet's life—and vice versa.

The Lincoln exhibit includes one of several probes used to locate the bullet in Lincoln's brain, skull fragments removed from the wound, and the bullet itself, all of which keep close company with sections of spinal cord and vertebrae from John Wilkes Booth. I find the choice to enshrine the assassin's relics with those of the martyr surprising, and even a casual visitor is disturbed by this conjugal juxtaposition of sacred and profane. I watched several people pass by the lit case. "I don't like that," said one old woman in a wheelchair, pushed by her grandson. "Don't like what?" he asked. "Sticking his things in with the others," she said, pointing at Booth's vertebrae.

Had the nuns who arranged Mother Cabrini's relics been given curatorial privilege over the Lincoln artifacts, they would have created a more agreeable display. Their sophistication, probably intuitive—nothing that could have been stipulated in a manual—was such that they divided the woman into her divine and earthly tendencies. Her belt of nails and the knotted scourge are in a separate cabinet from her silver hairbrush and buttonhook. All are sensual artifacts, but tools for grooming the soul are different from those intended for the pleasure of the body.

Gowns and hair and hairbrushes. Shavers, guitars, washbasins. Things that once belonged to people we did not ever touch or speak with, people whose fame allows them the immortality of their stories but cannot halt the decay of their bodies or the inevitable denouements of their private, real lives. If Abraham Lincoln, Elvis, Babe Ruth, and all the saints are not endowed with powers enabling them to escape death, then who is? In the *Iliad*, Homer tells us that Achilles was given the choice of a short heroic life or a long unremarkable one. He chose to die a hero. Later, when Odysseus encounters him in the *Odyssey*, Achilles' shade bitterly laments such folly. Poetic license allows the dead Achilles to know what he could not and we cannot yet fully understand: life ends.

My grandfather, who raised me as his daughter, was the first member of my immediate family to die. I was twenty-three. He took long enough to die that, as I anticipated my loss, I had time to break down my fear into its parts. I was afraid of the pain I would feel at losing the companionship and protection of the man who was for me a father. But I was also afraid of death—not my grandfather's particular death but the unapproachable and unavoidable fact of human mortality. What if my grandfather should die in my presence? I worried that I might have to witness his turning from living to dead flesh. I had never before seen a corpse.

A cool, previously hidden pragmatism led me to prepare myself. I looked up funeral notices in the *Los Angeles Times,* picked out the nearest mortuary that advertised a "viewing" of a man of advanced years, and went to look at the embalmed corpse of someone I didn't know. I had the good fortune of an uninterrupted visit—there were no legitimate mourners to see as I leaned into the casket and brushed the corpse's cheek, touched its immobile, cool lips. How straightforward death was! I nearly laughed in relief. A month later, when I kissed my grandfather goodbye, I hugged his body in unabashed affection. Here was what had supported, given form and substance, to the person I had loved all my life. I brought scissors to the hospital morgue and cut a curl, which I still have, as well as his glasses and a pair of his wooden shoe trees.

Among what I have of my dead mother are two of her baby teeth, saved by my grandmother in a tiny glass-stoppered vial of rubbing alcohol. The teeth, in the sentimental vernacular of baby mementos, recall pearls, but in each a brown root cavity bears traces of her blood. They are a double relic because, beyond my mother, they attest to her own mother's love, which counted them of value, saved and bottled them. And they exist within generations of my family's baby teeth, generations that include my own and my daughter's. Holding the little bottle, I cannot not consider my little girl and boy, and what, after I am dead, they might keep of me and hold in their hands.

In the last months of my grandmother's life, she kept a mohair scarf   40
wrapped around her waist, hidden under the blankets of her bed. She was not cold but afraid. Without this security object she could not rest, and she allowed no one to take it from her, not even long enough to launder it. In the end, it was blood-stained from a wound I caused while bathing her one morning. She had sat hunched over for so long that the fold of skin at her waist grew together, and when I washed it I tore the adhesion open; it began to bleed and never healed. After my grandmother died, I never considered washing the scarf any more than whoever bought Elvis's dirty shirt did, or the curator who guards the stained cuffs of Lincoln's autopsy surgeon. Clean, it would tell me nothing.

When I hold the scarf I hold both my grandmother's and my own death in my hands. The scarf and I inform each other. Only I can tell the story it bears; only such an object can tell me what my helpless trips to the donor center belied: one day blood, and grief, will flow unchecked.

The Reader's Presence

1. What sorts of adjectives and imagery does Harrison use to describe icons of modern popular culture? How does she equate them with more traditionally "sacred" items? Does she describe the relics of Saint Cabrini with conventional reverence? How does she seem to define the sacred? How does her definition diverge from the norm?

2. Harrison relates an exchange she had with a nun at the shrine of Saint Cabrini. How is the nun's attitude toward the relics conveyed? How is Harrison's attitude conveyed? What does the interjection of this detailed scene contribute to the overall essay?

3. The essay covers a vast array of historical moments, experiences, and emotions. Does this broadness of scope, in your opinion, weaken or strengthen the piece? In what ways? The writer is driven by impulses toward the realms of both life and death. How is this conflict mirrored in the essay's form?

56

Linda M. Hasselstrom

Why One Peaceful Woman Carries a Pistol

Linda M. Hasselstrom (b. 1943) is a rancher and writer who splits her time between her home in Cheyenne, Wyoming, and her ranch in western South Dakota. She has written about her experiences as a rancher in Windbreak: A Woman Rancher on the Northern Plains *(1987) and* Going over East: Reflections of a Woman Rancher *(1987). Hasselstrom's poetry can be found in* Dakota Bones *(1992) and in a collection of poems and essays,* Land Circle: Writings Collected from the Land *(1991), in which "Why One Peaceful Woman Carries a Pistol" appears. She continues to write essays on ranching and the environment, and recently published* Roadside History of South Dakota *(1994). Her other recent projects include acting as coeditor of* Leaning into the Wind: Women Write from the Heart of the West *(1997) and providing the text for a collection of photographs,* Bison: Monarch of the Plains *(1998). She also teaches writing workshops to writers of all ages and from diverse backgrounds.*

Hasselstrom's writing is strongly connected to the natural environment in which she lives. "All parts of life need to come together, and I have tried to make my life into a circle," she says. "I write, do ranch work, garden, and they all fit together. I take care of the land and it takes care of me. It provides me with inspiration for my writing on many topics: on people, on animals, on the environment—and of course you can't separate them. It is important for me to be connected to country, to place, in order to keep writing.

I'm a peace-loving woman. I also carry a pistol. For years, I've written about my decision in an effort to help other women make intelligent choices about gun ownership, but editors rejected the articles. Between 1983 and 1986, however, when gun sales to men held steady, gun ownership among women rose fifty-three percent, to more than twelve million.

We learned that any female over the age of twelve can expect to be criminally assaulted some time in her life, that women aged thirty have a fifty-fifty chance of being raped, robbed, or attacked, and that many police officials say flatly that they cannot protect citizens from crime. During the same period, the number of women considering gun ownership quadrupled to nearly two million. Manufacturers began showing lightweight weapons with small grips, and purses with built-in holsters. A new magazine is called *Guns and Women,* and more than eight thousand copies of the video *A Woman's Guide to Firearms* were sold by 1988. Experts say female gun buyers are not limited to any particular age group, profession, social class, or area of the country, and most are buying guns to protect themselves. Shooting instructors say women view guns with more caution than do men, and may make better shots.

I decided to buy a handgun for several reasons. During one four-year period, I drove more than a hundred thousand miles alone, giving speeches, readings, and workshops. A woman is advised, usually by men, to protect herself by avoiding bars, by approaching her car like an Indian scout, by locking doors and windows. But these precautions aren't always enough. And the logic angers me: *Because* I am female, it is my responsibility to be extra careful.

As a responsible environmentalist, I choose to recycle, avoid chemicals on my land, minimize waste. As an informed woman alone, I choose to be as responsible for my own safety as possible: I keep my car running well, use caution in where I go and what I do. And I learned about self-protection—not an easy or quick decision. I developed a strategy of protection that includes handgun possession. The following incidents, chosen from a larger number because I think they could happen to anyone, helped make up my mind.

When I camped with another woman for several weeks, she didn't want to carry a pistol, and police told us Mace was illegal. We tucked spray deodorant into our sleeping bags, theorizing that any man crawling into our tent at night would be nervous anyway; anything sprayed in his face would slow him down until we could hit him with a frying pan, or escape. We never used our improvised weapon, because we were lucky

5

enough to camp beside people who came to our aid when we needed them. I returned from that trip determined to reconsider.

At that time, I lived alone and taught night classes in town. Along a city street I often traveled, a woman had a flat tire, called for help on her CB, and got a rapist; he didn't fix the tire either. She was afraid to call for help again and stayed in her car until morning. Also, CBs work best along line-of-sight; I ruled them out.

As I drove home one night, a car followed me, lights bright. It passed on a narrow bridge, while a passenger flashed a spotlight in my face, blinding me. I braked sharply. The car stopped, angled across the bridge, and four men jumped out. I realized the locked doors were useless if the broke my car windows. I started forward, hoping to knock their car aside so I could pass. Just then, another car appeared, and the men got back in their car, but continued to follow me, passing and repassing. I dared not go home. I passed no lighted houses. Finally, they pulled to the roadside, and I decided to use their tactic: fear. I roared past them inches away, horn blaring. It worked; they turned off the highway. But it was desperate and foolish, and I was frightened and angry. Even in my vehicle I was too vulnerable.

Other incidents followed. One day I saw a man in the field near my house, carrying a shotgun and heading for a pond full of ducks. I drove to meet him, and politely explained that the land was posted. He stared at me, and the muzzle of his shotgun rose. I realized that if he simply shot me and drove away, I would be a statistic. The moment passed; the man left.

One night, I returned home from class to find deep tire ruts on the lawn, a large gas tank empty, garbage in the driveway. A light shone in the house; I couldn't remember leaving it on. I was too embarrassed to wake the neighbors. An hour of cautious exploration convinced me the house was safe, but once inside, with the doors locked, I was still afraid. I put a .22 rifle by my bed, but I kept thinking of how naked I felt, prowling around my own house in the dark.

It was time to consider self-defense. I took a kung fu class and   10
learned to define the distance to maintain between myself and a stranger. Once someone enters that space without permission, kung fu teaches appropriate evasive or protective action. I learned to move confidently, scanning for possible attack. I learned how to assess danger, and techniques for avoiding it without combat.

I also learned that one must practice several hours every day to be good at kung fu. By that time I had married George; when I practiced with him, I learned how *close* you must be to your attacker to use martial arts, and decided a 120-pound woman dare not let a six-foot, 220-pound attacker get that close unless she is very, very good at self-defense. Some women who are well trained in martial arts have been raped and beaten anyway.

Reluctantly I decided to carry a pistol. George helped me practice with his .357 and .22. I disliked the .357's recoil, though I later became comfortable with it. I bought a .22 at a pawn shop. A standard .22 bullet, fired at close range, can kill, but news reports tell of attackers advancing with five such bullets in them. I bought magnum shells, with more power, and practiced until I could hit someone close enough to endanger me. Then I bought a license making it legal for me to carry the gun concealed.

George taught me that the most important preparation was mental: convincing myself I could shoot someone. Few of us really wish to hurt or kill another human being. But there is no point in having a gun—in fact, gun possession might increase your danger—unless you know you can use it against another human being. A good training course includes mental preparation, as well as training in safety. As I drive or walk, I often rehearse the conditions which would cause me to shoot. Men grow up handling firearms, and learn controlled violence in contact sports, but women grow up learning to be subservient and vulnerable. To make ourselves comfortable with the idea that we are capable of protecting ourselves requires effort. But it need not turn us into macho, gun-fighting broads. We must simply learn to do as men do from an early age: believe in, and rely on, *ourselves* for protection. The pistol only adds an extra edge, an attention-getter; it is a weapon of last resort.

Because shooting at another person means shooting to kill. It's impossible even for seasoned police officers to be sure of only wounding an assailant. If I shot an attacking man, I would aim at the largest target, the chest. This is not an easy choice, but for me it would be better than rape.

In my car, my pistol is within instant reach. When I enter a deserted   15
rest stop at night, it's in my purse, my hand on the grip. When I walk from a dark parking lot into a motel, it's in my hand, under a coat. When I walk my dog in the deserted lots around most motels, the pistol is in a shoulder holster, and I am always aware of my surroundings. In my motel room, it lies on the bedside table. At home, it's on the headboard.

Just carrying a pistol is not protection. Avoidance is still the best approach to trouble; watch for danger signs, and practice avoiding them. Develop your instinct for danger.

One day while driving to the highway mailbox, I saw a vehicle parked about halfway to the house. Several men were standing in the ditch, relieving themselves. I have no objection to emergency urination; we always need moisture. But they'd also dumped several dozen beer cans, which blow into pastures and can slash a cow's legs or stomach.

As I slowly drove closer, the men zipped their trousers ostentatiously while walking toward me. Four men gathered around my small foreign car, making remarks they wouldn't make to their mothers, and one of them demanded what the hell I wanted.

"This is private land; I'd like you to pick up the beer cans."

"What beer cans?" said the belligerent one, putting both hands on   20
the car door, and leaning in my window. His face was inches from mine, the beer fumes were strong, and he looked angry. The others laughed. One tried the passenger door, locked; another put his foot on the hood

and rocked the car. They circled, lightly thumping the roof, discussing my good fortune in meeting them, and the benefits they were likely to bestow upon me. I felt small and trapped; they knew it.

"The ones you just threw out," I said politely.

"I don't see no beer cans. Why don't you get out here and show them to me, honey?" said the belligerent one, reaching for the handle inside my door.

"Right over there," I said, still being polite, "there and over there." I pointed with the pistol, which had been under my thigh. Within one minute the cans and the men were back in the car, and headed down the road.

I believe this small incident illustrates several principles. The men were trespassing and knew it; their judgment may have been impaired by alcohol. Their response to the polite request of a woman alone was to use their size and numbers to inspire fear. The pistol was a response in the same language. Politeness didn't work; I couldn't intimidate them. Out of the car, I'd have been more vulnerable. The pistol just changed the balance of power.

My husband, George, asked one question when I told him. "What   25
would you have done if he'd grabbed for the pistol?"

"I had the car in reverse; I'd have hit the accelerator, and backed up; if he'd kept coming, I'd have fired straight at him." He nodded.

In fact, the sight of the pistol made the man straighten up; he cracked his head on the door frame. He and the two in front of the car stepped backward, catching the attention of the fourth, who joined them. They were all in front of me then, and as the car was still running and in reverse gear, my options had multiplied. If they'd advanced again, I'd have backed away, turning to keep the open window toward them. Given time, I'd have put the first shot into the ground in front of them, the second into the belligerent leader. It might have been better to wait until they were gone, pick up the beer cans, and avoid confrontation, but I believed it was reasonable and my right to make a polite request to strangers littering my property. Showing the pistol worked on another occasion when I was driving in a desolate part of Wyoming. A man played cat-and-mouse with me for thirty miles, ultimately trying to run my car off the road. When his car was only two inches from mine, I pointed my pistol at him, and he disappeared.

I believe that a handgun is like a car; both are tools for specific purposes; both can be lethal if used improperly. Both require a license, training, and alertness. Both require you to be aware of what is happening before and behind you. Driving becomes almost instinctive; so does handgun use. When I've drawn my gun for protection, I simply found it in my hand. Instinct told me a situation was dangerous before my conscious mind reacted; I've felt the same while driving. Most good drivers react to emergencies by instinct.

Knives are another useful tool often misunderstood and misused; some people acquire knives mostly for display, either on a wall or on a belt, and such knives are often so large as to serve no useful purpose. My pocket knives are always razor sharp, because a small, sharp knife will do most jobs. Skinning blades serve for cutting meat and splitting small kindling in camp. A *sgian dubh,* a four-inch flat blade in a wooden sheath, was easily concealed inside a Scotsman's high socks, and slips into my dress or work boots as well. Some buckskinners keep what they call a "grace knife" on a thong around their necks; the name may derive from *coup de grâce,* the welcome throat-slash a wounded knight asked from his closest friend, to keep him from falling alive into the hands of his enemies. I also have a push dagger, with a blade only three inches long, attached to a handle that fits into the fist so well that the knife would be hard to lose even in hand-to-hand combat. When I first showed it, without explanation, to an older woman who would never consider carrying a knife, she took one look and said, "Why, you could push that right into someone's stomach," and demonstrated with a flourish. That's what it's for. I wear it for decoration, because it was handmade by Jerry and fits my hand perfectly, but I am intently aware of its purpose. I like my knives, not because they are weapons, but because they are well designed, and beautiful, and because each is a tool with a specific purpose.

Women didn't always have jobs, or drive cars or heavy equipment,   30
though western women did many of those things almost as soon as they arrived here. Men in authority argued that their attempt to do so would unravel the fabric of society. Women, they said, would become less feminine; they hadn't the intelligence to cope with the mechanics of a car, or the judgment to cope with emergencies. Since these ideas were so wrong, perhaps it is time women brought a new dimension to the wise use of handguns as well.

We can and should educate ourselves in how to travel safely, take self-defense courses, reason, plead, or avoid trouble in other ways. But some men cannot be stopped by those methods; they understand only power. A man who is committing an attack already knows he's breaking laws; he has no concern for someone else's rights. A pistol is a woman's answer to his greater power. It makes her equally frightening. I have thought of revising the old Colt slogan: "God made man, but Sam Colt made them equal" to read "God made men *and women* but Sam Colt made them equal." Recently I have seen an ad for a popular gunmaker with a similar sentiment; perhaps this is an idea whose time has come, though the pacifist inside me will be saddened if the only way women can achieve equality is by carrying a weapon.

As a society, we were shocked in early 1989 when a female jogger in New York's Central Park was beaten and raped savagely and left in a coma. I was even more shocked when reporters interviewed children who lived near the victim and quoted a twelve-year-old as saying, "She had nothing to guard herself; she didn't have no man with her; she didn't have no Mace." And another sixth-grader said, "It is like she committed suicide." Surely this is not a majority opinion, but I think it is not so unusual, either, even in this liberated age. Yet there is no city or county in the nation where law officers can relax because all the criminals are in jail. Some authorities say citizens armed with handguns stop almost as many crimes annually as armed criminals succeed in committing, and that people defending themselves kill three times more attackers and robbers than police do. I don't suggest all criminals should be killed, but some can be stopped only by death or permanent incarceration. Law enforcement officials can't prevent crimes; later punishment may be of little comfort to the victim. A society so controlled that no crime existed would probably be too confined for most of us, and is not likely to exist any time soon. Therefore, many of us should be ready and able to protect ourselves, and the intelligent use of firearms is one way.

We must treat a firearm's power with caution. "Power tends to corrupt, and absolute power corrupts absolutely," as a man (Lord Acton) once said. A pistol is not the only way to avoid being raped or murdered in today's world, but a firearm, intelligently wielded, can shift the balance and provide a measure of safety.

The Reader's Presence

1. The title of Hasselstrom's essay announces her purpose. Outline each of the points she highlights in her defense of carrying a firearm. What alternatives to a handgun does she consider, and why does she reject each? How does she anticipate objections to her explanation? What kinds of preparation does she think necessary in order to "ready" herself to carry a pistol? What, finally, does she see as the most effective form of protection against trouble?

2. In what specific ways does Hasselstrom address the conventional perception that men are more likely to bear arms than women? When — and in what terms — does she make gender an issue in carrying a firearm? What specific words and phrases does she repeat to emphasize her own vulnerability and that of other women?

3. In the opening paragraphs of her detailed explanation of why she carries a gun, Hasselstrom announces to her readers the point of view from which she speaks: a "peace-loving woman," a freelance writer who lives on a ranch in western South Dakota. Recognizing that "handgun possession is a controversial subject," she immediately expresses her overall aim in writing: "perhaps my reasoning will interest others." Who might be included in the "others" she mentions here? Is there any evidence to suggest, for example, that she has women primarily in mind as her audience? If so, what evidence validates your reading? If, however, you believe that gender is not an important factor in determining who might be included in her audience for this article, what factors in her explanation might help you to identify her intended audience?

57

Edward Hoagland

The Courage of Turtles

Edward Hoagland, born in New York City in 1932, is an essayist, nature writer, and novelist. Before his graduation from Harvard University, his first novel, Cat Man *(1956), was accepted for publication and won the Houghton-Mifflin Literary Fellowship Award. He has received several other honors, including a Guggenheim Fellowship, an O. Henry Award, an award from the American Academy of Arts and Letters, and a Lannan Foundation Award. Hoagland's essays cover a wide range of topics, such as personal experiences, wild animals, travels to other countries, and ecological crisis. Among his many highly regarded books are* Walking the Dead Diamond River *(1973),* African Calliope: A Journey to the Sudan *(1979), and* Balancing Acts *(1992). In his most recent publication,* Tigers and Ice: Essays on Life and Nature *(1999), Hoagland discusses such issues as his three years of legal blindness, the possible extinction of tigers in India, and his love of ponds. He teaches at Bennington College in Vermont.*

Turtles are a kind of bird with the governor turned low. With the same attitude of removal, they cock a glance at what is going on, as if they need only to fly away. Until recently they were also a case of virtue rewarded, at least in the town where I grew up, because, being humble creatures, there were plenty of them. Even when we still had a few bobcats in the woods the local snapping turtles, growing up to forty pounds, were the largest carnivores. You would see them through the amber water, as big as greeny wash basins at the bottom of the pond, until they faded into the inscrutable mud as if they hadn't existed at all.

When I was ten I went to Dr. Green's Pond, a two-acre pond across the road. When I was twelve I walked a mile or so to Taggart's Pond, which was lusher, had big water snakes and a waterfall; and shortly after that I was bicycling way up to the adventuresome vastness of Mud Pond, a lake-sized body of water in the reservoir system of a Connecticut city, possessed of cat-backed little islands and empty shacks and a forest of pines and hardwoods along the shore. Otters, foxes and mink left their prints on the bank; there were pike and perch. As I got older, the estates and forgotten back lots in town were parceled out and sold for nice prices, yet, though the woods had shrunk, it seemed that fewer people walked in the woods. The new residents didn't know how to find them. Eventually, exploring, they did find them, and it required some ingenuity and doubling around on my part to go for eight miles without meeting someone. I was grown by now, I lived in New York, and that's what I wanted on the occasional weekends when I came out.

Since Mud Pond contained drinking water I had felt confident nothing untoward would happen there. For a long while the developers stayed away, until the drought of the mid-1960s. This event, squeezing the edges in, convinced the local water company that the pond really wasn't a necessity as a catch basin, however; so they bulldozed a hole in the earthen dam, bulldozed the banks to fill in the bottom, and landscaped the flow of water that remained to wind like an English brook and provide a domestic view for the houses which were planned. Most of the painted turtles of Mud Pond, who had been inaccessible as they sunned on their rocks wound up in boxes in boy's closets within a matter of days. Their footsteps in the dry leaves gave them away as they wandered forlornly. The snappers and the little musk turtles, neither of whom leave the water except once a year to lay their eggs, dug into the drying mud for another siege of hot weather, which they were accustomed to doing whenever the pond got low. But this time it was low for good; the mud baked over them and slowly entombed them. As for the ducks, I couldn't stroll in the woods and not feel guilty, because they were crouched beside every stagnant pothole, or were slinking between the bushes with their heads tucked into their shoulders so that I wouldn't see them. If they decided I had, they beat their way through the screen of trees, striking their wings dangerously, and wheeled about with that headlong, magnificent velocity to locate another poor puddle.

I used to catch possums and black snakes as well as turtles, and I kept dogs and goats. Some summers I worked in a menagerie with the big personalities of the animal kingdom, like elephants and rhinoceroses. I was twenty before these enthusiasms began to wane, and it was then that I picked turtles as the particular animal I wanted to keep in touch with. I was allergic to fur, for one thing, and turtles need minimal care and not much in the way of quarters. They're personable beasts. They see the same colors we do and they seem to see just as well, as one discovers in trying to sneak up on them. In the laboratory they unravel the twists of a maze with the hot-blooded rapidity of a mammal. Though they can't run as fast as a rat, they improve on their errors just as quickly, pausing at each crossroads to look left and right. And they rock rhythmically in place, as we often do, although they are hatched from eggs, not the womb. (A common explanation psychologists give for our pleasure in rocking quietly is that it recapitulates our mother's heartbeat *in utero*.)

Snakes, by contrast, are dryly silent and priapic. They are smooth movers, legalistic, unblinking, and they afford the humor which the humorless do. But they make challenging captives; sometimes they don't eat for months on a point of order—if the light isn't right, for instance. Alligators are sticklers too. They're like war-horses, or German shepherds, and with their bar-shaped, vertical pupils adding emphasis, they have the *idée fixe* of eating, eating, even when they choose to refuse all food and stubbornly die. They delight in tossing a salamander up towards the sky and grabbing him in their long mouths as he comes down. They're so eager that they get the jitters, and they're too much of a proposition for a casual aquarium like mine. Frogs are depressingly defenseless: that moist, extensive back, with the bones almost sticking through. Hold a frog and you're holding its skeleton. Frogs' tasty legs are the staff of life to many animals—herons, raccoons, ribbon snakes—though they themselves are hard to feed. It's not an enviable role to be the staff of life, and after frogs you descend down the evolutionary ladder a big step to fish.

Turtles cough, burp, whistle, grunt and hiss, and produce social judgments. They put their heads together amicably enough, but then one drives the other back with the suddenness of two dogs who have been conversing in tones too low for an onlooker to hear. They pee in fear when they're first caught, but exercise both pluck and optimism in trying to escape, walking for hundreds of yards within the confines of their pen, carrying the weight of that cumbersome box on legs which are cruelly positioned for walking. They don't feel that the contest is unfair; they keep plugging, rolling like sailorly souls—a bobbing, infirm gait, a brave, sea-legged momentum—stopping occasionally to study the lay of the land. For me, anyway, they manage to contain the rest of the animal world. They can stretch out their necks like a giraffe, or loom underwater like an apocryphal hippo. They browse on lettuce thrown on the water like a cow moose which is partly submerged. They have a penguin's alertness, combined with a build like a Brontosaurus when they rise up on tiptoe. Then they hunch and ponderously lunge like a grizzly going forward.

Baby turtles in a turtle bowl are a puzzle in geometrics. They're as decorative as pansy petals, but they are also self-directed building blocks, propping themselves on one another in different arrangements, before up-ending the tower. The timid individuals turn fearless, or vice versa. If one gets a bit arrogant he will push the others off the rock and afterwards climb down into the water and cling to the back of one of those he has bullied, tickling him with his hind feet until he bucks like a bronco. On the other hand, when this same milder-mannered fellow isn't exerting himself, he will stare right into the face of the sun for hours. What could be more lionlike? And he's at home in or out of the water and does lots of metaphysical tilting. He sinks and rises, with an infinity of levels to choose from; or, elongating himself, he climbs out on the land again to perambulate, sits boxed in his box, and finally slides back in the water, submerging into dreams.

I have five of these babies in a kidney-shaped bowl. The hatchling, who is a painted turtle, is not as large as the top joint of my thumb. He eats chicken gladly. Other foods he will attempt to eat but not with sufficient perseverance to succeed because he's so little. The yellow-bellied terrapin is probably a yearling, and he eats salad voraciously, but not meat, fish, or fowl. The Cumberland terrapin won't touch salad or chicken but eats fish and all of the meats except bacon. The little snapper, with a black crenelated shell, feasts on any kind of meat, but rejects greens and fish. The fifth of the turtles is African. I acquired him only recently and don't know him well. A mottled brown, he unnerves the green turtles, dragging their food off to his lairs. He doesn't seem to want to be green—he bites the algae off his shell, hanging meanwhile at daring, steep, head-first angles.

The snapper was a Ferdinand until I provided him with deeper water. Now he snaps at my pencil with his downturned and fearsome mouth, his swollen face like a napalm victim's. The Cumberland has an elliptical red mark on the side of his green-and-yellow head. He is benign by nature and ought to be as elegant as his scientific name (*Pseudemys scripta elegans*), except he has contracted a disease of the air bladder which has permanently inflated it; he floats high in the water at an undignified slant and can't go under. There may have been internal bleeding, too, because his carapace is stained along its ridge. Unfortunately, like flowers, baby turtles often die. Their mouths fill up with a white fungus and their lungs with pneumonia. Their organs clog up from the rust in the water, or diet troubles, and, like a dying man's, their eyes and heads become too prominent. Toward the end, the edge of the shell becomes flabby as felt and folds around them like a shroud.

While they live they're like puppies. Although they're vivacious, they would be a bore to be with all the time, so I also have an adult wood turtle about six inches long. Her shell is the equal of any seashell for sculpturing, even a Cellini shell; it's like an old, dusty, richly engraved medallion dug out of a hillside. Her legs are salmon-orange bordered with black and protected by canted, heroic scales. Her plastron—the bottom shell—is splotched like a margay cat's coat, with black ocelli on a yellow background. It is convex to make room for the female organs inside, whereas a male's would be concave to help him fit tightly on top of her. Altogether, she exhibits every camouflage color on her limbs and shells. She has a turtleneck, a tail like an elephant's, wise old pachydermous hind legs and the face of a turkey—except that when I carry her she gazes at the passing ground with a hawk's eyes and mouth. Her feet fit to the fingers of my hand, one to each one, and she rides looking down. She can walk on the floor in perfect silence, but usually she lets her shell knock portentously, like a footstep, so that she resembles some grand, concise, slow-moving id. But if an earthworm is presented, she jerks swiftly ahead, poises above it and strikes like a mongoose, consuming it with wild vigor. Yet she will climb on my lap to eat bread or boiled eggs.

10

If put into a creek, she swims like a cutter, nosing forward to inter-
cept a strange turtle and smell him. She drifts with the current to go
downstream, maneuvering behind a rock when she wants to take stock,
or sinking to the nether levels, while bubbles float up. Getting out, choosing her path, she will proceed a distance and dig into a pile of humus,
thrusting herself to the coolest layer at the bottom. The hole closes over
her until it's as small as a mouse's hole. She's not as aquatic as a musk
turtle, not quite as terrestrial as the box turtles in the same woods, but because of her versatility she's marvelous, she's everywhere. And though she
breathes the way we breathe, with scarcely perceptible movements of her
chest, sometimes instead she pumps her throat ruminatively, like a pipe
smoker sucking and puffing. She waits and blinks, pumping her throat,
turning her head, then sets off like a loping tiger in slow motion, hurdling
the jungly lumber, the pea vine and twigs. She estimates angles so well
that when she rides over the rocks, sliding down a drop-off with her
rugged front legs extended, she has the grace of a rodeo mare.

But she's well off to be with me rather than at Mud Pond. The other
turtles have fled—those that aren't baked into the bottom. Creeping up
the brooks to sad, constricted marshes, burdened as they are with that
box on their backs, they're walking into a setup where all their enemies
move thirty times faster than they. It's like the nightmare most of us have
whimpered through, where we are weighted down disastrously while trying to flee; fleeing our home ground, we try to run.

I've seen turtles in still worse straits. On Broadway, in New York,
there is a penny arcade which used to sell baby terrapins that were
scrawled with bon mots in enamel paint, such as KISS ME BABY. The
manager turned out to be a wholesaler as well, and once I asked him
whether he had any larger turtles to sell. He took me upstairs to a loft
room devoted to the turtle business. There were desks for the paper work
and a series of racks that held shallow tin bins atop one another, each
with several hundred babies crawling around in it. He was a smudgy-
complexioned, serious fellow and he did have a few adult terrapins, but I
was going to school and wasn't planning to buy; I'd only wanted to see
them. They were aquatic turtles, but here they went without water, presumably for weeks, lurching about in those dry bins like handicapped citizens, living on gumption. An easel where the artist worked stood in the
middle of the floor. She had a palette and a clip attachment for fastening
the babies in place. She wore a smock and beret, and was homely, short
and eccentric-looking, with funny black hair, like some of the ladies who
show their paintings in Washington Square in May. She had a cold, she
was smoking, and her hand wasn't very steady, although she worked
quickly enough. The smile that she produced for me would have looked
giddy if she had been happier, or drunk. Of course the turtles' doom was
sealed when she painted them, because their bodies inside would continue
to grow but their shells would not. Gradually, invisibly, they would be

crushed. Around us their bellies—two thousand belly shells—rubbed on the bins with a mournful, momentous hiss.

Somehow there were so many of them I didn't rescue one. Years later, however, I was walking on First Avenue when I noticed a basket of living turtles in front of a fish store. They were as dry as a heap of old bones in the sun; nevertheless, they were creeping over one another gimpily, doing their best to escape. I looked and was touched to discover that they appeared to be wood turtles, my favorites, so I bought one. In my apartment I looked closer and realized that in fact this was a diamond-back terrapin, which was bad news. Diamondbacks are tide-water turtles from brackish estuaries, and I had no sea water to keep him in. He spent his days thumping interminably against the baseboards, pushing for an opening through the wall. He drank thirstily but would not eat and had none of the hearty, accepting qualities of wood turtles. He was morose, paler in color, sleeker and more Oriental in the carved ridges and rings that formed his shell. Though I felt sorry for him, finally I found his unrelenting presence exasperating. I carried him, struggling in a paper bag, across town to the Morton Street Pier on the Hudson. It was August but gray and windy. He was very surprised when I tossed him in; for the first time in our association, I think, he was afraid. He looked afraid as he bobbed about on top of the water, looking up at me from ten feet below. Though we were both accustomed to his resistance and rigidity, seeing him still pitiful, I recognized that I must have done the wrong thing. At least the river was salty, but it was also bottomless; the waves were too rough for him, and the tide was coming in, bumping him against the pilings underneath the pier. Too late, I realized that he wouldn't be able to swim to a peaceful inlet in New Jersey, even if he could figure out which way to swim. But since, short of diving in after him, there was nothing I could do, I walked away.

The Reader's Presence

1. How does the selection relate turtles to the rest of the animal kingdom? to humans? Why does Hoagland seem to value turtles? What is the "courage" to which he refers?

2. Though his ostensible focus is turtles, the writer reveals a great deal about himself. What techniques does Hoagland use to discuss one subject through another? Why might he choose this indirect style?

3. The essay meanders through a number of locations and scenarios before arriving at its final anecdote: Hoagland's release of a turtle into the Hudson River. Why might the writer have chosen this structure? Suppose the events of the essay appeared in reverse. Would it affect your reception of the final anecdote?

58

Linda Hogan

Dwellings

The writer and educator Linda Hogan was born in Colorado in 1947. A member of the Chickasaw tribe, she is active in Native American communities and in environmental politics. Hogan has published essays, plays, short stories, and many volumes of poetry, including most recently The Book of Medicines *(1993). Her novels* Mean Spirit *(1990) and* Solar Storms *(1995) have been celebrated for their complex and compelling representation of Native Americans. Hogan's interest in narrative and the natural environment are represented in the essay included here, which appears in her book* Dwellings: Reflections on the Natural World *(1995). Her most recent publications include a novel,* Power *(1998), and* Intimate Nature: The Bond between Women and Animals *(1998), which she coedited. She has taught at the University of Minnesota and is currently professor of English at the University of Colorado at Boulder.*

Hogan has said, "My writing comes from and goes back to the community, both the human and the global community. I am interested in the deepest questions, those of spirit, of shelter, of growth and movement toward peace and liberation, inner and outer."

Not far from where I live is a hill that was cut into by the moving water of a creek. Eroded this way, all that's left of it is a broken wall of earth that contains old roots and pebbles woven together and exposed. Seen from a distance, it is only a rise of raw earth. But up close it is something wonderful, a small cliff dwelling that looks almost as intricate and well made as those the Anasazi left behind when they vanished mysteriously centuries ago. This hill is a place that could be the starry skies at night turned inward into the thousand round holes where solitary bees have lived and died. It is a hill of tunneling rooms. At the mouths of some of the excavations, half-circles of clay beetle out like awnings shading a doorway. It is earth that was turned to clay in the mouths of the bees and spit out as they mined deeper into their dwelling places.

This place is where the bees reside at an angle safe from rain. It faces the southern sun. It is a warm and intelligent architecture of memory, learned by whatever memory lives in the blood. Many of the holes still contain gold husks of dead bees, their faces dry and gone, their flat eyes gazing out from death's land toward the other uninhabited half of the hill that is across the creek from the catacombs.

The first time I found the residence of the bees, it was dusty summer. The sun was hot, and land was the dry color of rust. Now and then a car rumbled along the dirt road and dust rose up behind it before settling back down on older dust. In the silence, the bees made a soft droning hum. They were alive then, and working the hill, going out and returning with pollen, in and out through the holes, back and forth between daylight and the cooler, darker regions of the inner earth. They were flying an invisible map through air, a map charted by landmarks, the slant of light, and a circling story they told one another about the direction of food held inside the center of yellow flowers.

Sitting in the hot sun, watching the small bees fly in and out around the hill, hearing the summer birds, the light breeze, I felt right in the world. I belonged there. I thought of my own dwelling places, those real and those imagined. Once I lived in a town called Manitou, which means "Great Spirit," and where hot mineral springwater gurgled beneath the streets and rose into open wells. I felt safe there. With the underground movement of water and heat a constant reminder of other life, of what lives beneath us, it seemed to be the center of the world.

A few years after that, I wanted silence. My daydreams were full of   5 places I longed to be, shelters and solitudes. I wanted a room apart from others, a hidden cabin to rest in. I wanted to be in a redwood forest with trees so tall the owls called out in the daytime. I daydreamed of living in a vapor cave a few hours away from here. Underground, warm, and moist, I thought it would be the perfect world for staying out of cold winter, for escaping the noise of living.

And how often I've wanted to escape to a wilderness where a human hand has not been in everything. But those were only dreams of peace, of comfort, of a nest inside stone or woods, a sanctuary where a dream or life wouldn't be invaded.

Years ago, in the next canyon west of here, there was a man who followed one of those dreams and moved into a cave that could only be reached by climbing down a rope. For years he lived there in comfort, like a troglodite. The inner weather was stable, never too hot, too cold, too wet, or too dry. But then he felt lonely. His utopia needed a woman. He went to town until he found a wife. For a while after the marriage, his wife climbed down the rope along with him, but before long she didn't want the mice scurrying about in the cave, or the untidy bats that wanted to hang from the stones of the ceiling. So they built a door. Because of the closed entryway, the temperature changed. They had to put in heat. Then the inner moisture of earth warped the door, so they had to have air-conditioning, and after that the earth wanted to go about life in its own way and it didn't give in to the people.

In other days and places, people paid more attention to the strong-headed will of earth. Once homes were built of wood that had been felled from a single region in a forest. That way, it was thought, the house would hold together more harmoniously, and the family of walls would not fall or lend themselves to the unhappiness or arguments of the inhabitants.

An Italian immigrant to Chicago, Aldo Piacenzi, built birdhouses that were dwellings of harmony and peace. They were the incredible spired shapes of cathedrals in Italy. They housed not only the birds, but also his memories, his own past. He painted them the watery blue of his Mediterranean, the wild rose of flowers in a summer field. Inside them was straw and the droppings of lives that layed eggs, fledglings who grew there. What places to inhabit, the bright and sunny birdhouses in dreary alleyways of the city.

One beautiful afternoon, cool and moist, with the kind of yellow   10
light that falls on earth in these arid regions, I waited for barn swallows to return from their daily work of food gathering. Inside the tunnel where they live, hundreds of swallows had mixed their saliva with mud and clay, much like the solitary bees, and formed nests that were perfect as a potter's bowl. At five in the evening, they returned all at once, a dark, flying shadow. Despite their enormous numbers and the crowding together of nests, they didn't pause for even a moment before entering the nests, nor did they crowd one another. Instantly they vanished into the nests. The tunnel went silent. It held no outward signs of life.
But I knew they were there, filled with the fire of living. And what a marriage of elements was in those nests. Not only mud's earth and water, the fire of sun and dry air, but even the elements contained one another. The bodies of prophets and crazy men were broken down in that soil.

I've noticed often how when a house is abandoned, it begins to sag. Without a tenant, it has no need to go on. If it were a person, we'd say it is depressed or lonely. The roof settles in, the paint cracks, the walls and floorboards warp and slope downward in their own natural ways, telling us that life must stay in everything as the world whirls and tilts and moves through boundless space.

One summer day, cleaning up after long-eared owls where I work at a rehabilitation facility for birds of prey, I was raking the gravel floor of a flight cage. Down on the ground, something looked like it was moving. I bent over to look into the pile of bones and pellets I'd just raked together. There, close to the ground, were two fetal mice. They were new to the planet, pink and hairless. They were so tenderly young. Their faces had swollen blue-veined eyes. They were nestled in a mound of feathers, soft as velvet, each one curled up smaller than an infant's ear, listening to the first sounds of earth. But the ants were biting them. They turned in agony, unable to pull away, not yet having the arms or legs to move, but feeling, twisting away from, the pain of the bites. I was horrified to see them bitten out of life that way. I dipped them in water, as if to take away the sting, and let the ants fall in the bucket. Then I held the tiny mice in the palm of my hand. Some of ants were drowning in the water. I was trading one life for another, exchanging the lives of the ants for those of mice, but I hated their suffering, and hated even more that they had not yet grown to a life, and already they inhabited the miserable world of pain. Death and life feed each other. I know that.

Inside these rooms where birds are healed, there are other lives besides those of mice. There are fine gray globes the wasps have woven together, the white cocoons of spiders in a corner, the downward tunneling anthills. All these dwellings are inside one small walled space, but I think most about the mice. Sometimes the downy nests fall out of the walls where their mothers have placed them out of the way of their enemies. When one of the nests falls, they are so well made and soft, woven mostly from the chest feathers of birds. Sometimes the leg of a small quail holds the nest together like a slender cornerstone with dry, bent claws. The mice have adapted to life in the presence of their enemies, adapted to living in the thin wall between beak and beak, claw and claw. They move their nests often, as if a new rafter or wall will protect them from the inevitable fate of all our returns home to the deeper, wider nests of earth that houses us all.

One August at Zia Pueblo during the corn dance I noticed tourists 15 picking up shards of all the old pottery that had been made and broken there. The residents of Zia know not to take the bowls and pots left behind by the older ones. They know that the fragments of those earlier lives need to be smoothed back to earth, but younger nations, travelers from continents across the world who have come to inhabit this land, have little of their own to grow on. The pieces of earth that were formed into bowls, even on their way home to dust, provide the new people a lifeline to an unknown land, help them remember that they live in the old nest of earth.

It was in early February, during the mating season of the great horned owl. It was dusk, and I hiked up the back of a mountain to where I'd heard the owls a year before. I wanted to hear them again, the voices so tender, so deep, like a memory of comfort. I was halfway up the trail when I found a soft, round nest. It had fallen from one of the bare-branched trees. It was a delicate nest, woven together of feathers, sage, and strands of wild grass. Holding it in my hand in the rosy twilight, I noticed that a blue thread was entwined with the other gatherings there. I pulled at the thread a little, and then I recognized it. It was a thread from one of my skirts. It was blue cotton. It was the unmistakable color and shape of a pattern I knew. I liked it, that a thread of my life was in an abandoned nest, one that had held eggs and new life. I took the nest home. At home, I held it to the light and looked more closely. There, to my surprise, nestled into the gray-green sage, was a gnarl of black hair. It was also unmistakable. It was my daughter's hair, cleaned from a brush and picked up out in the sun beneath the maple tree, or the pit cherry where the birds eat from the overladen, fertile branches until only the seeds remain on the trees.

I didn't know what kind of nest it was, or who had lived there. It didn't matter. I thought of the remnants of our lives carried up the hill that way and turned into shelter. That night, resting inside the walls of our home, the world outside weighed so heavily against the thin wood of the house. The sloped roof was the only thing between us and the universe. Everything outside of our wooden boundaries seemed so large. Filled with the night's citizens, it all came alive. The world opened in the thickets of the dark. The wild grapes would soon ripen on the vines. The burrowing ones were emerging. Horned owls sat in treetops. Mice scurried here and there. Skunks, fox, the slow and holy porcupine, all were passing by this way. The young of the solitary bees were feeding on the pollen in the dark. The whole world was a nest on its humble tilt, in the maze of the universe, holding us.

The Reader's Presence

1. In each of the vignettes that make up this essay, Hogan contemplates the meaning of various dwellings. What are the specific characteristics of a dwelling place for Hogan? Who lives there? How does each dwelling suit and serve its inhabitants? Why does Hogan describe dwellings for animals as well as dwellings for humans? With what effect(s)? To what extent and in what ways do the two overlap? What are the advantages — and the disadvantages — of Hogan's having chosen to contemplate death as well as life in this essay about where we live? How would you characterize the vision of life, death, and the universe that emerges from this essay?

2. Reread carefully the story about the cave dweller and his wife told in paragraph 7. To what extent does Hogan encourage her readers to take the story literally? At what point does it begin to take on the qualities of myth or fable? Compare and contrast this story with the biblical story of Adam and Eve, and their fall from the Garden of Eden. To whom, or to what impulse(s), can each fall be attributed? How are women characterized in the respective stories? How are the endings similar, and where do they diverge?

Based on your comparative analysis of these stories, what inferences might you draw about the Native American and Judeo-Christian worldviews?

3. Identify and discuss the various analogies Hogan draws throughout the essay. Where does she compare dwellings made by animals to human-made artifacts? human-made dwellings to natural phenomena? the animate to the inanimate? With what effects? Where are analogies between the various vignettes implied, and what do you infer from those implied analogies? For example, how do the narrator's own actions in paragraph 16 echo the actions of the tourists in paragraph 15, and how do these echoes contribute to the overall effect of the essay? Examine, too, the remarkable shifts in scale, from the very small tunnels dug by the bees to the starry skies (paragraph 1), that Hogan weaves into this essay. How do these analogies between the very large and the very small contribute to the sense of a palpable universe, "the whole world" as "a nest on its humble tilt" (paragraph 16)?

59

John Hollander

Mess

John Hollander (b. 1929) is one of the leading poets in the United States today. His poems and prose appear regularly in the New Yorker, *the* Partisan Review, Esquire, *and other popular and scholarly magazines. The essay "Mess" appeared in the* Yale Review *in 1995. Hollander is the Sterling Professor of English at Yale University, and he has written and edited numerous scholarly works and anthologies. Hollander's most recent collection of literary criticism is* The Work of Poetry *(1997), which won the Robert Penn Warren-Cleanth Brooks award. He has published over twenty volumes of poetry, including* Selected Poetry *(1993),* Animal Poems *(1994), and* Figurehead and Other Poems *(1999).*

Commenting on the experience of writing both poetry and prose, Hollander notes, "Ordinarily, the prose I write is critical or scholarly, where there is some occasion (a lecture to be given, a longish review to be done, etc.) to elicit the piece of writing. My most important writing is my poetry, which is not occasional in these ways. . . . This brief essay was generated more from within, like a poem, than most other prose of mine—nobody asked me to write it, but I felt impelled to observe something about one aspect of life that tends to get swept under the rug, as it were."

Mess is a state of mind. Or rather, messiness is a particular relation between the state of arrangement of a collection of things and a state of mind that contemplates it in its containing space. For example, X's mess may be Y's delight—sheer profusion, uncompromised by any apparent structure even in the representation of it. Or there may be some inner order or logic to A's mess that B cannot possibly perceive. Consider: someone—Alpha—rearranges all the books on Beta's library shelf, which have been piled or stacked, sometimes properly, sometimes not, but all in relevant sequence (by author and, within that, by date of publication), and rearranges them neatly, by size and color. Beta surveys the result, and can only feel, if not blurt out, "WHAT A MESS!" This situation often occurs with respect to messes of the workplace generally.

For there are many kinds of mess, both within walls and outside them: neglected gardens and the aftermath of tropical storms, and the indoor kinds of disorder peculiar to specific areas of our life with, and in and among, *things*. There are messes of one's own making, messes not even of one's own person, places or things. There are personal states of mind about common areas of messiness—those of the kitchen, the bedroom, the bathroom, the salon (of whatever sort, from half a bed-sitter[1] to some grand public parlor), or those of personal appearance (clothes, hair, etc.). Then, for all those who are in any way self-employed or whose avocations are practiced in some private space—a workshop, a darkroom, a study or a studio—there is a mess of the workplace. It's not the most common kind of mess, but it's exemplary: the eye surveying it is sickened by the rollercoaster of scanning the scene. And, alas, it's the one I'm most afflicted with.

I know that things are really in a mess when—as about ninety seconds ago—I reach for the mouse on my Macintosh and find instead a thick layer of old envelopes, manuscript notes consulted three weeks ago, favorite pens and inoperative ones, folders used hastily and not replaced, and so forth. In order to start working, I brush these accumulated impedimenta aside, thus creating a new mess. But this is, worse yet, absorbed by the general condition of my study: piles of thin books and thick books, green volumes of the Loeb Classical Library and slimy paperbacks of ephemeral spy-thrillers, mostly used notebooks, bills paid and unpaid, immortal letters from beloved friends, unopened and untrashed folders stuffed with things that should be in various other folders, book-mailing envelopes, unanswered mail whose cries for help and attention are muffled by three months' worth of bank statements enshrouding them in the gloom of continued neglect. Even this fairly orderly inventory seems to simplify the confusion: in actuality, searching for a letter or a page of manuscript in this state of things involves crouching down with my head on one side and searching vertically along the outside of a teetering pile for what may be a thin, hidden layer of it.

---

[1]*bed-sitter:* A combined bedroom and sitting room.—EDS.

Displacement, and lack of design, are obscured in the origins of our very word *mess*. The famous biblical "mess of red pottage" (lentil mush or dal) for which Esau sold his birthright wasn't "messy" in our sense (unless, of course, in the not very interesting case of Esau having dribbled it on his clothing). The word meant a serving of food, or a course in a meal: something *placed* in front of you (from the Latin *missis*, put or placed), hence "messmates" (dining companions) and ultimately "officers' mess" and the like. It also came to mean a dish of prepared mixed food—like an *olla podrida* or a minestrone—then by extension (but only from the early nineteenth century on) any hodge-podge: inedible, and outside the neat confines of a bowl or pot, and thus unpleasant, confusing, and agitating or depressing to contemplate. But for us, the association with food perhaps remains only in how much the state of mind of being messy is like that of being fat: for example, X says, "God, I'm getting gross! I'll have to diet!" Y, *really* fat, cringes on hearing this, and feels that for the slender X to talk that way is an obscenity. Similarly, X: "God, this place is a pigsty!" Y: (ditto). For a person prone to messiness, Cyril Connolly's celebrated observation about fat people is projected onto the world itself: inside every neat arrangement is a mess struggling to break out, like some kind of statue of chaos lying implicit in the marble of apparent organization.

In Paradise, there was no such thing as messiness. This was partly because unfallen, ideal life needed no supplemental *things*—objects of use and artifice, elements of any sort of technology. Thus there was nothing to leave lying around, messily or even neatly, by Adam and Eve—according to Milton—"at their savory dinner set / Of herbs and other country messes." But it was also because order, hence orderliness, was itself so natural that whatever bit of nature Adam and Eve might have been occupied with, or even using in a momentary tool-like way, flew or leapt or crept into place in some sort of reasonable arrangement, even as in our unparadised state things *fall* under the joyless tug of gravity. But messiness may seem to be an inevitable state of the condition of having so many *things*, precious or disposable, in one's life.

As I observed before, even to describe a mess is to impose order on it. The ancient Greek vision of primal chaos, even, was not *messy* in that it was pre-messy: there weren't any categories by which to define order, so that there could be no disorder—no nextness or betweenness, no above, below, here, there, and so forth. "*Let there be light*" meant "Let there be perception of something," and it was then that order became possible, and mess possibly implied. Now, a list or inventory is in itself an orderly literary form, and even incoherent assemblages of items fall too easily into some other kind of order: in *Through the Looking-Glass*, the Walrus's "Of shoes and ships, and sealing wax, / Of cabbages, and kings," is given a harmonious structure by the pairs of alliterating words, and even by the half-punning association of "ships, [sailing] sealing wax." The wonderful catalogue in *Tom Sawyer* of the elements of what must have been, pocketed or piled on the ground, a mess of splendid proportions, is a poem of its own. The objects of barter for a stint of fence whitewashing (Tom, it will be remembered, turns *having* to do a chore into *getting* to do it by sheer con-man's insouciance) comprise

> twelve marbles, part of a jewsharp, a piece of blue bottle-glass to look through, a spool cannon, a key that wouldn't unlock anything, a fragment of chalk, a glass stopper of a decanter, a tin soldier, a couple of tadpoles, six fire-crackers, a kitten with only one eye, a brass door-knob, a dog collar—but no dog—the handle of a knife, four pieces of orange peel, and a dilapidated old window sash.

Thus such representations of disorder as lists, paintings, photos, etc., all compromise the purity of true messiness by the verbal or visual order they impose on the confusion. To get at the mess in my study, for example, a movie might serve best, alternately mixing mid-shot and zoom on a particular portion of the disaster, which would, in an almost fractal way, seem to be a mini-disaster of its own. There are even neatly conventionalized emblems of messiness that are, after all, all too neat: thus, whenever a movie wants to show an apartment or office that has been ransacked by Baddies (cop Baddies or baddy Baddies or whatever) in search of the Thing They Want, the designer is always careful to show at least one picture on the wall hanging carefully askew. All this could possibly tell us about a degree of messiness is that the searchers were so messy (at another level of application of the term) in their technique that they violated their search agenda to run over to the wall and tilt the picture (very messy procedure indeed), or that, hastily leaving the scene to avoid detection, they nonetheless took a final revenge against the Occupant for not having the Thing on his or her premises, and tilted the picture in a fit of pique. And yet a tilted picture gives good cueing mileage: it can present a good bit of disorder at the expense of a minimum of misalignment, after all.

A meditation on mess could be endless. As I struggle to conclude this one, one of my cats regards me from her nest in and among one of the disaster areas that all surfaces in my study soon become. Cats disdain messes in several ways. First, they are proverbially neat about their shit and the condition of their fur. Second, they pick their way so elegantly among my piles of books, papers, and ancillary objects (dishes of paper clips, scissors, functional and dried-out pens, crumpled envelopes, outmoded postage stamps, boxes of slides and disks, staplers, glue bottles, tape dispensers— *you* know) that they cannot even be said to acknowledge the mess's existence. The gray familiar creature currently making her own order out of a region of mess on my desk—carefully disposing herself around and over and among piles and bunches and stacks and crazily oblique layers and thereby reinterpreting it as natural landscape—makes me further despair until I realize that what she does with her body, I must do with my perception of this inevitable disorder—shaping its forms to the disorder and thereby shaping the disorder to its forms. She has taught me resignation.

The Reader's Presence

1. In the second sentence of his essay, Hollander defines "mess" as "a particular relation between the state of arrangement of a collection of things and a state of mind that contemplates it in its containing space." How would you paraphrase Hollander's definition? To what extent does his definition echo proverbs and traditional sayings such as "beauty is in the eye of the beholder"? What does Hollander's definition add to this kind of general insight about the observer? What role do the "things" play in messiness, and what role is played by the person who contemplates them? Examine carefully the many observers mentioned in this essay, from the hypothetical X and Y in the first paragraph to the real cat in the final paragraph. What are their various reactions to the seeming disorder around them?

2. Hollander traces the origins of the word *mess* in paragraph 4. What is the connection between its original meaning and the meaning it took on "by extension" in the nineteenth century? According to Hollander, how does the state of mind of being messy correspond to the state of mind of being fat? He follows this association with yet another: the sculpture lying latent within the marble. Examine carefully—and then comment on—the way each analogy leads by association into the next and the effect of this series of associations.

3. Hollander's project is complicated by the fact that he has chosen a word to define that is enmeshed in his own writing process and product. How does the act of describing the "mess" on his desk (paragraph 3) alter the nature of the scene he describes? Is it, according to the author, even possible to do justice to a mess in written terms? Consider the fluctuation between control and lack of control manifested not only in the subject of the essay but in the essay itself. Where, for example, does the moment of his writing erupt into the text itself? Why does Hollander find himself struggling to conclude the essay (paragraph 8)? How would you characterize the overall structure of Hollander's essay? Based on your analysis, how would you compare and contrast the degree of order in his study and in his writing? In what specific ways might there be a cause-and-effect relationship between the two?

60

Helen Keller

Living Words

Helen Keller (1880–1968) was an author, lecturer, and social advocate for the deaf and blind. Born in Tuscumbia, Alabama, Keller suffered the loss of her sight and hearing because of an acute illness when she was nineteen months old. Mute and unable to adequately communicate with others, Keller became a frustrated, willful, and angry child. When she was six years old, her parents sought help from Dr. Alexander Graham Bell, who recommended hiring a teacher from the Perkins Institute for the Blind. Her parents followed his advice and hired Anne Sullivan, Keller's lifelong teacher and friend. With Sullivan's help, Keller learned to read and write in Braille, understood hand symbols, and gained a college degree from Radcliffe. She devoted her life to educating the public about the need for social reform for people with disabilities and received numerous awards for her humanitarian efforts. Keller wrote a number of books, including The Story of My Life *(1902), in which "Living Words" appears as a chapter, and* Helen Keller's Journal *(1938).*

The most important day I remember in all my life is the one on which my teacher, Anne Mansfield Sullivan, came to me. I am filled with wonder when I consider the immeasurable contrasts between the two lives which it connects. It was the third of March, 1887, three months before I was seven years old.

On the afternoon of that eventful day, I stood on the porch, dumb, expectant. I guessed vaguely from my mother's signs and from the hurrying to and fro in the house that something unusual was about to happen, so I went to the door and waited on the steps. The afternoon sun penetrated the mass of honeysuckle that covered the porch, and fell on my upturned face. My fingers lingered almost unconsciously on the familiar leaves and blossoms which had just come forth to greet the sweet southern spring. I did not know what the future held of marvel or surprise for me. Anger and bitterness had preyed upon me continually for weeks and a deep languor had succeeded this passionate struggle.

Have you ever been at sea in a dense fog, when it seemed as if a tangible white darkness shut you in, and the great ship, tense and anxious, groped her way toward the shore with plummet and sounding-line, and you waited with beating heart for something to happen? I was like that ship before my education began, only I was without compass or sounding-line, and had no way of knowing how near the harbour was. "Light! give me light!" was the wordless cry of my soul, and the light of love shone on me in that very hour.

I felt approaching footsteps. I stretched out my hand as I supposed to my mother. Someone took it, and I was caught up and held close in the arms of her who had come to reveal all things to me, and, more than all things else, to love me.

The morning after my teacher came she led me into her room and   5
gave me a doll. The little blind children at the Perkins Institution had sent it and Laura Bridgman[1] had dressed it; but I did not know this until afterward. When I had played with it a little while, Miss Sullivan slowly spelled into my hand the word "d-o-l-l." I was at once interested in this finger play and tried to imitate it. When I finally succeeded in making the letters correctly I was flushed with childish pleasure and pride. Running downstairs to my mother I held up my hand and made the letters for doll. I did not know that I was spelling a word or even that words existed; I was simply making my fingers go in monkey-like imitation. In the days that followed I learned to spell in this uncomprehending way a great many words, among them *pin, hat, cup* and a few verbs like *sit, stand* and *walk.* But my teacher had been with me several weeks before I understood that everything has a name.

One day, while I was playing with my new doll, Miss Sullivan put my big rag doll into my lap also, spelled, "d-o-l-l" and tried to make me understand that "d-o-l-l" applied to both. Earlier in the day we had had a tussle over the words "m-u-g" and "w-a-t-e-r." Miss Sullivan had tried to impress upon me that "m-u-g" is *mug* and that "w-a-t-e-r" is *water,* but I persisted in confounding the two. In despair she had dropped the subject for the time, only to renew it at the first opportunity. I became impatient at her repeated attempts and, seizing the new doll, I dashed it upon the floor. I was keenly delighted when I felt the fragments of the broken doll at my feet. Neither sorrow nor regret followed my passionate outburst. I had not loved the doll. In the still, dark world in which I lived there was no strong sentiment or tenderness. I felt my teacher sweep the fragments to one side of the hearth and I had a sense of satisfaction that the cause of my discomfort was removed. She brought me my hat, and I knew I was going out into the warm sunshine. This thought, if a wordless sensation may be called a thought, made me hop and skip with pleasure.

---

[1]*Bridgman*: Laura Dewey Bridgman (1829–1889) was the first deaf-blind child to be successfully educated at the now famous Perkins School for the Blind in Boston. Charles Dickens visited her in 1842 and wrote a moving description of her progress. She became internationally celebrated. — EDS.

We walked down the path to the well-house, attracted by the fragrance of the honeysuckle with which it was covered. Someone was drawing water and my teacher placed my hand under the spout. As the cool stream gushed over one hand she spelled into the other the word *water*, first slowly, then rapidly. I stood still, my whole attention fixed upon the motions of her fingers. Suddenly I felt a misty consciousness as of something forgotten—a thrill of returning thought; and somehow the mystery of language was revealed to me. I knew then that "w-a-t-e-r" meant the wonderful cool something that was flowing over my hand. That living word awakened my soul, gave it light, hope, joy, set it free! There were barriers still, it is true, but barriers that could in time be swept away.

I left the well-house eager to learn. Everything had a name, and each name gave birth to a new thought. As we returned to the house every object which I touched seemed to quiver with life. That was because I saw everything with the strange, new sight that had come to me. On entering the door I remembered the doll I had broken. I felt my way to the hearth and picked up the pieces. I tried vainly to put them together. Then my eyes filled with tears; for I realized what I had done, and for the first time I felt repentance and sorrow.

I learned a great many new words that day. I do not remember what they all were; but I do know that *mother, father, sister, teacher* were among them—words that were to make the world blossom for me, "like Aaron's rod, with flowers." It would have been difficult to find a happier child than I was as I lay in my crib at the close of that eventful day and lived over the joys it had brought me, and for the first time longed for a new day to come.

The Reader's Presence

1. The writer treats what for most of us are everyday perceptions and sensations as bizarre and wonderful. How does her narrative style make us aware of experiences we might otherwise take for granted?

2. Keller's experiences are foreign to most of us, yet her account is highly moving. How does the narrative evoke shifts of emotion? How does Keller gain the reader's empathy?

3. Keller makes analogies to visual and auditory elements she could not have experienced directly. To what extent do Keller's descriptions seem drawn from other literature? How does she use terms from the reader's world to help the reader understand her own? Note that Helen Keller's learning in this chapter is dependent on understanding nouns. Could she learn verbs, adjectives, and pronouns through Sullivan's method? Explain how this might be done.

61

Maxine Hong Kingston

No Name Woman

Maxine Hong Kingston (b. 1940) won the National Book Critics Circle Award for nonfiction with her first book, The Woman Warrior: Memoirs of a Girlhood among Ghosts *(1976). "No Name Woman" is the opening chapter of this book, which* Time *magazine named one of the top ten nonfiction works of the 1970s. Her second book,* China Men *(1980), won the American Book Award and is also considered nonfiction, though Kingston's writing often blurs the distinction between fiction and nonfiction. Her narratives blend autobiography, history, myth, and legend, drawing on the stories she remembers from her childhood in the Chinese American community of Stockton, California. Kingston's essays, stories, and poems also appear in numerous magazines, and she received the 1997 National Medal for the Humanities. She currently teaches at the University of California, Berkeley.*

Kingston has said that before writing The Woman Warrior, *"My life as a writer had been a long struggle with pronouns. For 30 years I wrote in the first person singular. At a certain point I was thinking that I was self-centered and egotistical, solipsistic, and not very developed as a human being, nor as an artist, because I could only see from this one point of view." She began to write in the third person because "I thought I had to overcome this self-centeredness." As she wrote her third novel, Kingston experienced the disappearance of her authorial voice. "I feel that this is an artistic as well as psychological improvement on my part. Because I am now a much less selfish person."*

"You must not tell anyone," my mother said, "what I am about to tell you. In China your father had a sister who killed herself. She jumped into the family well. We say that your father has all brothers because it is as if she had never been born.

"In 1924 just a few days after our village celebrated seventeen hurry-up weddings—to make sure that every young man who went 'out on the road' would responsibly come home—your father and his brothers and your grandfather and his brothers and your aunt's new husband sailed for America, the Gold Mountain. It was your grandfather's last trip. Those lucky enough to get contracts waved good-bye from the decks. They fed and guarded the stowaways and helped them off in Cuba, New York, Bali, Hawaii. 'We'll meet in California next year,' they said. All of them sent money home.

"I remember looking at your aunt one day when she and I were dressing; I had not noticed before that she had such a protruding melon of a stomach. But I did not think, 'She's pregnant,' until she began to look like other pregnant women, her shirt pulling and the white tops of her black pants showing. She could not have been pregnant, you see, because her husband had been gone for years. No one said anything. We did not discuss it. In early summer she was ready to have the child, long after the time when it could have been possible.

"The village had also been counting. On the night the baby was to be born the villagers raided our house. Some were crying. Like a great saw, teeth strung with lights, files of people walked zigzag across our land, tearing the rice. Their lanterns doubled in the disturbed black water, which drained away through the broken bunds. As the villagers closed in, we could see that some of them, probably men and women we knew well, wore white masks. The people with long hair hung it over their faces. Women with short hair made it stand up on end. Some had tied white bands around their foreheads, arms, and legs.

"At first they threw mud and rocks at the house. Then they threw eggs and began slaughtering our stock. We could hear the animals scream their deaths—the roosters, the pigs, a last great roar from the ox. Familiar wild heads flared in our night windows; the villagers encircled us. Some of the faces stopped to peer at us, their eyes rushing like searchlights. The hands flattened against the panes, framed heads, and left red prints.

"The villagers broke in the front and the back doors at the same time, even though we had not locked the doors against them. Their knives dripped with the blood of our animals. They smeared blood on the doors and walls. One woman swung a chicken, whose throat she had slit, splattering blood in red arcs about her. We stood together in the middle of our house, in the family hall with the pictures and tables of the ancestors around us, and looked straight ahead.

"At that time the house had only two wings. When the men came back we would build two more to enclose our courtyard and a third one to begin a second courtyard. The villagers pushed through both wings, even your grandparents' rooms, to find your aunt's, which was also mine until the men returned. From this room a new wing for one of the younger families would grow. They ripped up her clothes and shoes and broke her combs, grinding them underfoot. They tore her work from the loom. They scattered the cooking fire and rolled the new weaving in it. We could hear them in the kitchen breaking our bowls and banging the pots. They overturned the great waist-high earthenware jugs; duck eggs, pickled fruits, vegetables burst out and mixed in acrid torrents. The old woman from the next field swept a broom through the air and loosed the

5

spirits-of-the-broom over our heads. 'Pig.' 'Ghost.' 'Pig,' they sobbed and scolded while they ruined our house.

"When they left, they took sugar and oranges to bless themselves. They cut pieces from the dead animals. Some of them took bowls that were not broken and clothes that were not torn. Afterward we swept up the rice and sewed it back up into sacks. But the smells from the spilled preserves lasted. Your aunt gave birth in the pigsty that night. The next morning when I went up for the water, I found her and the baby plugging up the family well.

"Don't let your father know that I told you. He denies her. Now that you have started to menstruate, what happened to her could happen to you. Don't humiliate us. You wouldn't like to be forgotten as if you had never been born. The villagers are watchful."

Whenever she had to warn us about life, my mother told stories that   10
ran like this one, a story to grow up on. She tested our strength to establish realities. Those in the emigrant generations who could not reassert
brute survival died young and far from home. Those of us in the first
American generations have had to figure out how the invisible world the
emigrants built around our childhoods fit in solid America.

The emigrants confused the gods by diverting their curses, misleading
them with crooked streets and false names. They must try to confuse their
offspring as well, who, I suppose, threaten them in similar ways—always
trying to get things straight, always trying to name the unspeakable. The
Chinese I know hide their names; sojourners take new names when their
lives change and guard their real names with silence.

Chinese-Americans, when you try to understand what things in you
are Chinese, how do you separate what is peculiar to childhood, to
poverty, insanities, one family, your mother who marked your growing
with stories, from what is Chinese? What is Chinese tradition and what is
the movies?

If I want to learn what clothes my aunt wore, whether flashy or ordinary, I would have to begin, "Remember Father's drowned-in-the-well
sister?" I cannot ask that. My mother has told me once and for all the
useful parts. She will add nothing unless powered by Necessity, a river-
bank that guides her life. She plants vegetable gardens rather than lawns;
she carries the odd-shaped tomatoes home from the fields and eats food
left for the gods.

Whenever we did frivolous things, we used up energy; we flew high
kites. We children came up off the ground over the melting cones our parents brought home from work and the American movie on New Years'
Day—*Oh, You Beautiful Doll* with Betty Grable one year, and *She Wore
a Yellow Ribbon* with John Wayne another year. After the one carnival
ride each, we paid in guilt; our tired father counted his change on the
dark walk home.

Adultery is extravagance. Could people who hatch their own chicks   15
and eat the embryos and the heads for delicacies and boil the feet in vinegar for party food, leaving only the gravel, eating even the gizzard lin-

ing—could such people engender a prodigal aunt? To be a woman, to have a daughter in starvation time was a waste enough. My aunt could not have been the lone romantic who gave up everything for sex. Women in the old China did not choose. Some man had commanded her to lie with him and be his secret evil. I wonder whether he masked himself when he joined the raid on her family.

Perhaps she encountered him in the fields or on the mountain where the daughters-in-law collected fuel. Or perhaps he first noticed her in the marketplace. He was not a stranger because the village housed no strangers. She had to have dealings with him other than sex. Perhaps he worked an adjoining field, or he sold her the cloth for the dress she sewed and wore. His demand must have surprised, then terrified her. She obeyed him; she always did as she was told.

When the family found a young man in the next village to be her husband, she stood tractably beside the best rooster, his proxy, and promised before they met that she would be his forever. She was lucky that he was her age and she would be the first wife, an advantage secure now. The night she first saw him, he had sex with her. Then he left for America. She had almost forgotten what he looked like. When she tried to envision him, she only saw the black and white face in the group photograph the men had had taken before leaving.

The other man was not, after all, much different from her husband. They both gave orders: she followed. "If you tell your family, I'll beat you. I'll kill you. Be here again next week." No one talked sex, ever. And she might have separated the rapes from the rest of living if only she did not have to buy her oil from him or gather wood in the same forest. I want her fear to have lasted just as long as rape lasted so that the fear could have been contained. No drawn-out fear. But women at sex hazarded birth and hence lifetimes. The fear did not stop but permeated everywhere. She told the man, "I think I'm pregnant." He organized the raid against her.

On nights when my mother and father talked about their life back home, sometimes they mentioned an "outcast table" whose business they still seemed to be settling, their voices tight. In a commensal tradition, where food is precious, the powerful older people made wrongdoers eat alone. Instead of letting them start separate new lives like the Japanese, who could become samurais and geishas, the Chinese family, faces averted but eyes glowering sideways, hung on to the offenders and fed them leftovers. My aunt must have lived in the same house as my parents and eaten at an outcast table. My mother spoke about the raid as if she had seen it, when she and my aunt, a daughter-in-law to a different household, should not have been living together at all. Daughters-in-law lived with their husbands' parents, not their own; a synonym for marriage in Chinese is "taking a daughter-in-law." Her husband's parents could have sold her, mortgaged her, stoned her. But they had sent her back to her own mother and father, a mysterious act hinting at disgraces not told me. Perhaps they had thrown her out to deflect the avengers.

She was the only daughter; her four brothers went with her father,   20
husband, and uncles "out on the road" and for some years became western men. When the goods were divided among the family, three of the
brothers took land, and the youngest, my father, chose an education.
After my grandparents gave their daughter away to her husband's family,
they had dispensed all the adventure and all the property. They expected
her alone to keep the traditional ways, which her brothers, now among
the barbarians, could fumble without detection. The heavy, deep-rooted
women were to maintain the past against the flood, safe for returning.
But the rare urge west had fixed upon our family, and so my aunt crossed
boundaries not delineated in space.

The work of preservation demands that the feelings playing about in
one's guts not be turned into action. Just watch their passing like cherry
blossoms. But perhaps my aunt, my forerunner, caught in a slow life, let
dreams grow and fade and after some months or years went toward what
persisted. Fear at the enormities of the forbidden kept her desires delicate,
wire and bone. She looked at a man because she liked the way the hair
was tucked behind his ears, or she liked the question-mark line of a long
torso curving at the shoulder and straight at the hip. For warm eyes or a
soft voice or a slow walk—that's all—a few hairs, a line, a brightness, a
sound, a pace, she gave up family. She offered us up for a charm that vanished with tiredness, a pigtail that didn't toss when the wind died. Why,
the wrong lighting could erase the dearest thing about him.

It could very well have been, however, that my aunt did not take
subtle enjoyment of her friend, but, a wild woman, kept rollicking company. Imagining her free with sex doesn't fit, though. I don't know any
women like that, or men either. Unless I see her life branching into mine,
she gives me no ancestral help.

To sustain her being in love, she often worked at herself in the mirror, guessing at the colors and shapes that would interest him, changing
them frequently in order to hit on the right combination. She wanted to
look back.

On a farm near the sea, a woman who tended her appearance reaped
a reputation for eccentricity. All the married women blunt-cut their hair
in flaps about their ears or pulled it back in tight buns. No nonsense.
Neither style blew easily into heart-catching tangles. And at their weddings they displayed themselves in their long hair for the last time. "It
brushed the back of my knees," my mother tells me. "It was braided, and
even so, it brushed the backs of my knees."

At the mirror my aunt combed individuality into her bob. A bun   25
could have been contrived to escape into black streamers blowing in the
wind or in quiet wisps about her face, but only the older women in our
picture album wear buns. She brushed her hair back from her forehead,
tucking the flaps behind her ears. She looped a piece of thread, knotted
into a circle between her index fingers and thumbs, and ran the double
strand across her forehead. When she closed her fingers as if she were
making a pair of shadow geese bite, the string twisted together catching

the little hairs. Then she pulled the thread away from her skin, ripping the hairs out neatly, her eyes watering from the needles of pain. Opening her fingers, she cleaned the thread, then rolled it along her hairline and the tops of the eyebrows. My mother did the same to me and my sisters and herself. I used to believe that the expression "caught by the short hairs" meant a captive held with a depilatory string. It especially hurt at the temples, but my mother said we were lucky we didn't have to have our feet bound when we were seven. Sisters used to sit on their beds and cry together, she said, as their mothers or their slave removed the bandages for a few minutes each night and let the blood gush back into their veins. I hope that the man my aunt loved appreciated a smooth brow, that he wasn't just a tits-and-ass man.

Once my aunt found a freckle on her chin, at a spot that the almanac said predestined her for unhappiness. She dug it out with a hot needle and washed the wound with peroxide.

More attention to her looks than these pullings of hairs and pickings at spots would have caused gossip among the villagers. They owned work clothes and good clothes, and they wore good clothes for feasting the new seasons. But since a woman combing her hair hexes beginnings, my aunt rarely found an occasion to look her best. Women looked like great sea snails—the corded wood, babies, and laundry they carried were the whorls on their backs. The Chinese did not admire a bent back; goddesses and warriors stood straight. Still there must have been a marvelous free-ing of beauty when a worker laid down her burden and stretched and arched.

Such commonplace loveliness, however, was not enough for my aunt. She dreamed of a lover for the fifteen days of New Year's, the time for families to exchange visits, money, and food. She plied her secret comb. And sure enough she cursed the year, the family, the village, and herself.

Even as her hair lured her imminent lover, many other men looked at her. Uncles, cousins, nephews, brothers would have looked, too, had they been home between journeys. Perhaps they had already been restraining their curiosity, and they left, fearful that their glances, like a field of nest-ing birds, might be startled and caught. Poverty hurt, and that was their first reason for leaving. But another, final reason for leaving the crowded house was the never-said.

She may have been unusually beloved, the precious only daughter,   30
spoiled and mirror-gazing because of the affection the family lavished on her. When her husband left, they welcomed the chance to take her back from the in-laws; she could live like the little daughter for just a while longer. There are stories that my grandfather was different from other people, "crazy ever since the little Jap bayoneted him in the head." He used to put his naked penis on the dinner table, laughing. And one day he brought home a baby girl, wrapped up inside his brown western-style greatcoat. He had traded one of his sons, probably my father, the youngest, for her. My grandmother made him trade back. When he fi-nally got a daughter of his own, he doted on her. They must have all

loved her, except perhaps my father, the only brother who never went back to China, having once been traded for a girl.

Brothers and sisters, newly men and women, had to efface their sexual color and present plain miens. Disturbing hair and eyes, a smile like no other, threatened the ideal of five generations living under one roof. To focus blurs, people shouted face to face and yelled from room to room. The immigrants I know have loud voices, unmodulated to American tones even after years away from the village where they called their friendships out across the fields. I have not been able to stop my mother's screams in public libraries or over telephones. Walking erect (knees straight, toes pointed forward, not pigeon-toed, which is Chinese-feminine) and speaking in an inaudible voice, I have tried to turn myself American-feminine. Chinese communication was loud, public. Only sick people had to whisper. But at the dinner table, where the family members came nearest one another, no one could talk, not the outcasts nor any eaters. Every word that falls from the mouth is a coin lost. Silently they gave and accepted food with both hands. A preoccupied child who took his bowl with one hand got a sideways glare. A complete moment of total attention is due everyone alike. Children and lovers have no singularity here, but my aunt used a secret voice, a separate attentiveness.

She kept the man's name to herself throughout her labor and dying; she did not accuse him that he be punished with her. To save her inseminator's name she gave silent birth.

He may have been somebody in her own household, but intercourse with a man outside the family would have been no less abhorrent. All the village were kinsmen, and the titles shouted in loud country voices never let kinship be forgotten. Any man within visiting distance would have been neutralized as a lover — "brother," "younger brother," "older brother" — 115 relationship titles. Parents researched birth charts probably not so much to assure good fortune as to circumvent incest in a population that has but one hundred surnames. Everybody has eight million relatives. How useless then sexual mannerisms, how dangerous.

As if it came from an atavism deeper than fear, I used to add "brother" silently to boys' names. It hexed the boys, who would or would not ask me to dance, and made them less scary and as familiar and deserving of benevolence as girls.

But, of course, I hexed myself also — no dates. I should have stood   35
up, both arms waving, and shouted out across libraries, "Hey, you! Love me back." I had no idea, though, how to make attraction selective, how to control its direction and magnitude. If I made myself American-pretty so that the five or six Chinese boys in the class fell in love with me, everyone else — the Caucasian, Negro, and Japanese boys — would too. Sisterliness, dignified and honorable, made much more sense.

Attraction eludes control so stubbornly that whole societies designed to organize relationships among people cannot keep order, not even when they bind people to one another from childhood and raise them together. Among the very poor and the wealthy, brothers married their adopted sisters, like doves. Our family allowed some romance, paying adult brides' prices and providing dowries so that their sons and daughters could marry strangers. Marriage promises to turn strangers into friendly relatives — a nation of siblings.

In the village structure, spirits shimmered among the live creatures, balanced and held in equilibrium by time and land. But one human being flaring up into violence could open up a black hole, a maelstrom that pulled in the sky. The frightened villagers, who depended on one another to maintain the real, went to my aunt to show her a personal, physical representation of the break she made in the "roundness." Misallying couples snapped off the future, which was to be embodied in true offspring. The villagers punished her for acting as if she could have a private life, secret and apart from them.

If my aunt had betrayed the family at a time of large grain yields and peace, when many boys were born, and wings were being built on many houses, perhaps she might have escaped such severe punishment. But the men — hungry, greedy, tired of planting in dry soil, cuckolded — had been forced to leave the village in order to send food-money home. There were ghost plagues, bandit plagues, wars with the Japanese, floods. My Chinese brother and sister had died of an unknown sickness. Adultery, perhaps only a mistake during good times, became a crime when the village needed food.

The round moon cakes and round doorways, the round tables of graduated size that fit one roundness inside another, round windows and rice bowls — these talismans had lost their power to warn this family of the law: A family must be whole, faithfully keeping the descent line by having sons to feed the old and the dead who in turn look after the family. The villagers came to show my aunt and lover-in-hiding a broken house. The villagers were speeding up the circling of events because she was too shortsighted to see that her infidelity had already harmed the village, that waves of consequences would return unpredictably, sometimes in disguise, as now, to hurt her. This roundness had to be made coin-sized so that she would see its circumference: Punish her at the birth of her baby. Awaken her to the inexorable. People who refused fatalism because they could invent small resources insisted on culpability. Deny accidents and wrest fault from the stars.

After the villagers left, their lanterns now scattering in various directions toward home, the family broke their silence and cursed her. "Aiaa, we're going to die. Death is coming. Death is coming. Look what you've done. You've killed us. Ghost! Dead Ghost! Ghost! You've never been born." She ran out into the fields, far enough from the house so that she could no longer hear their voices, and pressed herself against the earth, her own land no more. When she felt the birth coming, she thought that she had been hurt. Her body seized together. "They've hurt me too much," she thought. "This is gall, and it will kill me." With forehead and knees against the earth, her body convulsed and then relaxed. She turned on her back, lay on the ground. The black well of sky and stars went out and out forever; her body and her complexity seemed to disappear. She was one of the stars, a bright dot in blackness, without home, without a companion, in eternal cold and silence. An agoraphobia rose in her, speeding higher and higher, bigger and bigger; she would not be able to contain it; there would be no end to fear.

Flayed, unprotected against space, she felt pain return, focusing her body. This pain chilled her—a cold, steady kind of surface pain. Inside, spasmodically, the other pain, the pain of the child, heated her. For hours she lay on the ground, alternately body and space. Sometimes a vision of normal comfort obliterated reality: She saw the family in the evening gambling at the dinner table, the young people massaging their elders' backs. She saw them congratulating one another, high joy on the mornings the rice shoots came up. When these pictures burst, the stars drew yet further apart. Black space opened.

She got to her feet to fight better and remembered that old-fashioned women gave birth in their pigsties to fool the jealous, pain-dealing gods, who do not snatch piglets. Before the next spasms could stop her, she ran to the pigsty, each step a rushing out into emptiness. She climbed over the fence and knelt in the dirt. It was good to have a fence enclosing her, a tribal person alone.

Laboring, this woman who had carried her child as a foreign growth that sickened her every day, expelled it at last. She reached down to touch the hot, wet, moving mass, surely smaller than anything human, and could feel that it was human after all—fingers, toes, nails, nose. She pulled it up on to her belly, and it lay curled there, butt in the air, feet precisely tucked one under the other. She opened her loose shirt and buttoned the child inside. After resting, it squirmed and thrashed and she pushed it up to her breast. It turned its head this way and that until it found her nipple. There, it made little snuffling noises. She clenched her teeth at its preciousness, lovely as a young calf, a piglet, a little dog.

She may have gone to the pigsty as a last act of responsibility: She would protect this child as she had protected its father. It would look after her soul, leaving supplies on her grave. But how would this tiny child without family find her grave when there would be no marker for her anywhere, neither in the earth nor the family hall? No one would give her a family hall name. She had taken the child with her into the wastes. At its birth the two of them had felt the same raw pain of separation, a wound that only the family pressing tight could close. A child with no descent line would not soften her life but only trail after her, ghostlike, begging her to give it purpose. At dawn the villagers on their way to the fields would stand around the fence and look.

Full of milk, the little ghost slept. When it awoke, she hardened her breasts against the milk that crying loosens. Toward morning she picked up the baby and walked to the well.   45

Carrying the baby to the well shows loving. Otherwise abandon it. Turn its face into the mud. Mothers who love their children take them along. It was probably a girl; there is some hope of forgiveness for boys.

"Don't tell anyone you had an aunt. Your father does not want to hear her name. She has never been born." I have believed that sex was unspeakable and words so strong and fathers so frail that "aunt" would do my father mysterious harm. I have thought that my family, having settled among immigrants who had also been their neighbors in the ancestral land, needed to clean their name, and a wrong word would incite the kinspeople even here. But there is more to this silence: They want me to participate in her punishment. And I have.

In the twenty years since I heard this story I have not asked for details nor said my aunt's name; I do not know it. People who comfort the dead can also chase after them to hurt them further — a reverse ancestor worship. The real punishment was not the raid swiftly inflicted by the villagers, but the family's deliberately forgetting her. Her betrayal so maddened them, they saw to it that she would suffer forever, even after death. Always hungry, always needing, she would have to beg food from other ghosts, snatch and steal it from those whose living descendants give them gifts. She would have to fight the ghosts massed at crossroads for the buns a few thoughtful citizens leave to decoy her away from village and home so that the ancestral spirits could feast unharassed. At peace, they could act like gods, not ghosts, their descent lines providing them with paper suits and dresses, spirit money, paper houses, paper automobiles, chicken, meat, and rice into eternity — essences delivered up in smoke and flames, steam and incense rising from each rice bowl. In an attempt to make the Chinese care for people outside the family, Chairman Mao encourages us now to give our paper replicas to the spirits of outstanding soldiers and workers, no matter whose ancestors they may be. My aunt remains forever hungry. Goods are not distributed evenly among the dead.

My aunt haunts me — her ghost drawn to me because now, after fifty years of neglect, I alone devote pages of paper to her, though not origamied into houses and clothes. I do not think she always means me well. I am telling on her, and she was a spite suicide, drowning herself in the drinking water. The Chinese are always very frightened of the drowned one, whose weeping ghost, wet hair hanging and skin bloated, waits silently by the water to pull down a substitute.

The Reader's Presence

1. Kingston's account of her aunt's life and death is a remarkable blend of fact and speculation. Consider the overall structure of "No Name Woman." How many versions of the aunt's story do we hear? Where, for example, does the mother's story end? Where does the narrator's begin? Which version do you find more compelling? Why? What does the narrator mean when she says that her mother's stories "tested our strength to establish realities" (paragraph 10)?

2. The narrator's version of her aunt's story is replete with such words and phrases as *perhaps* and *It could very well have been.* The narrator seems far more speculative about her aunt's life than her mother is. At what point does the narrator raise doubts about the veracity of her mother's version of the aunt's story? What purpose does the mother espouse in telling the aunt's story? Is it meant primarily to express family lore? to issue a warning? Point to specific passages to verify your response. What is the proposed moral of the story? Is that moral the same for the mother as for the narrator? Explain.

3. What does the narrator mean when she says "They must try to confuse their offspring as well, who, I suppose, threaten them in similar ways—always trying to get things straight, always trying to name the unspeakable" (paragraph 11)? What line does Kingston draw between the two cultures represented in the story: between the mother, a superstitious, cautious Chinese woman, and the narrator, an American-born child trying to "straighten out" her mother's confusing story? How does the narrator resolve the issue by thinking of herself as neither Chinese or American, but as a Chinese American? How are these issues made matters of gender? Judging from the evidence in this story, how would you summarize—and characterize—Chinese expectations of men? of women? How much does the story depend on gender stereotypes, and how does the narrator explore the complexity of those roles in her version of her aunt's story?

THE WRITER AT WORK

Maxine Hong Kingston on Writing for Oneself

In the fire that raged through the Oakland, California, hills in 1991, Maxine Hong Kingston lost, along with her entire house, all her copies of a work in progress. In the following interview conducted by Diane Simmons at Kingston's new home in 1997, the writer discusses how the fire and the loss of her work have transformed her attitude toward her own writing. Confronted with a similar loss (whether the work was on paper or disk), most authors would try to recapture as best they could what they had originally written. Why do you think Kingston wants to avoid that sort of recovery? The following exchange is from the opening of that long interview, which appeared in a literary periodical, The Crab Orchard Review *(Spring/Summer 1998). Diane Simmons is the author of* Maxine Hong Kingston *(New York: Twayne Publishers, 1999).*

I began by asking Ms. Kingston to talk about the book that was lost, and where she was going with her recent work.

Kingston: In the book that I lost in the fire, I was working on an idea of finding the book of peace again. There was a myth that there were three lost books of peace and so I was going to find the book of peace for our time. I imagine that it has to do with how to wage peace on earth and that there would be tactics on how to wage peace and how to stop war. I see that the books of war are popular; they are taught in the military academies; they're translated into all different languages. They [are used to] help corporate executives succeed in business. And people don't even think about the books of peace; people don't even know about them. I'm the only one that knows about it.

And so I was writing this and that was what was burned in the fire. What I'm working on now I'm calling *The Fifth Book of Peace.* I'm not re-calling and remembering what I had written. To me it's the pleasure of writing to be constantly discovering, going into the new. To recall word by word what I had written before sounds like torture and agony for me. I know I can do it, I'm sure I can do it if I want to. One of my former students volunteered to hypnotize me so I could recall, but that seemed so wrong to me.

Simmons: How much was lost?

Kingston: About 200 written, rewritten pages, so it was very good. 5 But I had wanted to rewrite it again and I think to recall word by word would freeze me into a version and I didn't want to do that.

Simmons: Is the book you are working on now the same project, the same version?

Kingston: Yes, but it is not the same words. It's not the same story. It's the same idea that I want to work on peace. At one point I called it the global novel. But since then I've been thinking of it as a book of peace. And the one big difference is the Book of Peace was a work of fiction. I was imagining fictional characters. But after the fire I wanted to use writing for my personal self. I wanted to write directly what I was thinking and feeling, not imagining fictional other people. I wanted to write myself. I wanted to write in the way I wrote when I was a child which is to say my deepest feel-ings and thoughts as they could come out in a personal way and not for public consumption. It's not even for other people to read but for myself, to express myself, and it doesn't matter whether this would be published. I don't even want to think about publication or readers, but this is for my own expression of my own suffering or agony.

Simmons: You've said that that's how you wrote in the beginning.

Kingston: I always begin like that. I always have to begin like that. Getting back to the roots of language in myself. It's almost like diary writing which is not for others.

Simmons: You don't mean that you don't want other people to read 10 it necessarily.

Kingston: That's not a consideration. I don't want to think about any of that. I think of this as going back to a primitive state of what writing is for me which is that I am finding my own voice again.

Simmons: Was it lost?

Kingston: Well, I started not to think about it anymore. After a while I had such an effective public voice, from childhood to now, I had found it and I had created it.

Simmons: Where do we see that public voice?

Kingston: The public voice is the voice that's in all my books.   15

Simmons: Even *Woman Warrior?*

Kingston: Yes. All my works. That is a public voice. What I mean by the private, personal voice is what I write when I'm trying to figure out things, what I write that's just for me. I get to be the reader and nobody else gets to read this. For years now I have not written in that way. I usually don't write diaries as an adult and so after the fire I needed to get to that again. I had forgotten about it.

Simmons: You are going back to before *Woman Warrior,* to before being a writer.

Kingston: Yes. Before being a writer who publishes.

Simmons: Why do you think the fire caused you to turn away from   20 fiction?

Kingston: At the same time my father died; he died a few weeks before the fire. At that time I felt I'd lost a lot. So I wanted to say what I felt about all that, about all my losses. And I don't see that as writing for publication. I see that as writing for myself, to put into words my losses. And so I started there, and wrote and wrote and wrote. But as I was writing, it became some of the things I was thinking in the book that burned; those would come into the writing, and then of course I go back to that very *id* basic place. I'm old enough and civilized enough now so that the sentences and the words that come out are very elegant, very good, very crafted. I don't return to a place that's not crafted anymore. So all this stuff that I wrote down is going to be part of *The Fifth Book of Peace.*

62

Barry Lopez

A Passage of the Hands

Barry Lopez (b. 1945) writes on nature and the environment, using both fiction and nonfiction to convey the mystery and beauty of, for example, arctic wolves. Lopez is a frequent contributor to such newspapers and periodicals as the New York Times, *the* Washington Post, National Geographic, *and* Outside. *In addition to these publications, he is also the author of several books, including* Of Wolves and Men *(1978),* Winter Dreams *(1981),* Field Notes: The Grace Note of the Canyon Wren *(1994), and* About This Life: Journeys on the Threshold of Memory *(1998). He has received numerous awards and honors, such as the American Book Award for nonfiction for* Arctic Dreams *(1986), an award in literature from*

the American Academy and Institute of Arts and Letters, and a Lannan Foundation
Award for nonfiction in 1990. He is presently a contributing editor to Harper's *and*
North America Review. *The following essay originally appeared in* Men's Journal
for December 1996/January 1997 and was included in About This Life.

My hands were born breech in the winter of 1945, two hours before
sunrise. Sitting with them today, two thousand miles and more from that
spot, turning each one slowly in bright sunshine, watching the incisive
light raise short, pale lines from old cuts, and seeing the odd cant of the
left ring finger, I know they have a history, though I cannot remember
where it starts. As they began, they gripped whatever might hold me upright, surely caressed and kneaded my mother's breasts, yanked at the restrictions of pajamas. And then they learned to work buttons, to tie
shoelaces and lift the milk glass, to work together.

The pressure and friction of a pencil as I labored down the spelling of
words right-handed raised the oldest permanent mark, a callus on the
third joint of the middle finger. I remember no trying accident to either
hand in these early years, though there must have been glass cuts, thorn
punctures, spider bites, nails torn to the cuticle, scrapes from bicycle falls,
pin blisters from kitchen grease, splinters, nails blackened from door
pinches, pain lingering from having all four fingers forced backward at
once, and the first true weariness, coming from work with lumber and
stones, with tools made for larger hands.

It is from these first years, five and six and seven, that I am able to remember so well, or perhaps the hands themselves remember, a great range
of texture—the subtle corrugation of cardboard boxes, the slickness of the
oilcloth on the kitchen table, the shuddering bend of a horse's short-haired
belly, the even give in warm wax, the raised oak grain in my school-desk
top, the fuzziness of dead bumblebees, the coarseness of sheaves immediate
to the polished silk of unhusked corn, the burnish of rake handles and
bucket bails, the rigidness of the bony crest rising beneath the skin of a
dog's head, the tackiness of flypaper, the sharpness of saws and ice picks.

It is impossible to determine where in any such specific memory, of
course, texture gives way to heft, to shape, to temperature. The coolness
of a camellia petal seems inseparable from that texture, warmth from the
velvet rub of a horse's nose, heft from a brick's dry burr. And what can
be said, as the hand recalls the earliest touch and exploration, of how texture changes with depth? Not alone the press of the palm on a dog's head
or fingers boring to the roots of wool on a sheep's flank, but of, say, what
happens with an orange: the hands work in concert to disassemble the
fruit, running a thumb over the beaded surface of the skin, plying the soft
white flay of the interior, the string net of fiber clinging to the translucent
skin cases, dividing the yielding grain of the flesh beneath, with its hard,
wrinkled seeds. And, further, how is one to separate these textures from a
memory of the burst of fragrance as the skin is torn, or from the sound of
the sections being parted—to say nothing of the taste, juice dripping

from the chin, or the urge to devour, then, even the astringent skin, all
initiated by the curiosity of the hands?

Looking back, it's easy to see that the education of the hands (and so   5
the person) begins like a language: a gathering of simple words, the assembly of simple sentences, all this leading eventually to the forging of instructive metaphors. Afterward nothing can truly be separated, to stand
alone in the hands' tactile memory. Taking the lay of the dog's fur, the
slow petting of the loved dog is the increasingly complicated heart speaking with the hand.

Still, because of an occasional, surprising flair of the hands, the insistence of their scarred surfaces, it is possible for me to sustain the illusion
that they have a history independent of the mind's perception, the heart's
passion; a history of gathering what appeals, of expressing exasperation
with their own stupidity, of faith in the accrual of brute work. If my
hands began to explore complex knowledge by seeking and sorting texture — I am compelled to believe this — then the first names my memory
truly embraced came from the hands' differentiating among fruits and
woven fabrics.

Growing on farms and in orchards and truck gardens around our home
in rural California was a chaos of fruit: navel and Valencia oranges, tanger-
ines, red and yellow grapefruit, pomegranates, lemons, pomelos, greengage
and damson plums, freestone and cling peaches, apricots, figs, tangelos,
Concord and muscadine grapes. Nectarines, Crenshaw, casaba, and honeydew melons, watermelons, and cantaloupes. My boyish hands knew the
planting, the pruning, the picking, and the packing of some of these fruits,
the force and the touch required. I sought them all out for the resilience of
their ripeness and knew the different sensation of each — pips, radius,
cleavage. I ate even tart pomegranates with ardor, from melons I dug gobs
of succulent meat with mouth and fingers. Slicing open a cantaloupe or a
melon with a knife, I would hesitate always at the sight of the cleft fistula of
seeds. It unsettled me, as it if were the fruit's knowing brain.

The fabrics were my mother's. They were stacked in bolts catawam-
pus on open shelves and in a closet in a room in our small house where
she both slept and sewed, where she laid out skirts, suits, and dresses for
her customers. Lawn, organdy, batiste, and other fine cottons; cambric
and gingham; silks — moiré, crepe de chine, taffeta; handkerchief and
other weights of linen; light wools like gabardine; silk and cotton
damasks; silk and rayon satins; cotton and wool twills; velvet; netted
cloths like tulle. These fabrics differed not only in their texture and
weave, in the fineness of their threads, but in the way they passed or reflected light, in their drape, and, most obviously from a distance, in their
color and pattern.

I handled these fabrics as though they were animal skins, opening out
bolts on the couch when Mother was working, holding them against the
window light, raking them with my nails, crumpling them in my fist, then
furling them as neatly as I could. Decades later, reading "samite of Eth-

nise" and "uncut rolls of brocade of Tabronit" in a paperback translation of Wolfram von Eschenbach's *Parzival*, I watched my free hand rise up to welcome the touch of these cloths.

It embarrassed and confounded me that other boys knew so little of   10
cloth, and mocked the knowledge; but growing up with orchards and groves and vine fields, we shared a conventional, peculiar intimacy with fruit. We pelted one another with rotten plums and the green husks of walnuts. We flipped gourds and rolled melons into the paths of oncoming, unsuspecting cars. This prank of the hand—throwing, rolling, flipping—meant nothing without the close companionship of the eye. The eye measured the distance, the crossing or closing speed of the object, and then the hand—the wrist snapping, the fingers' tips guiding to the last—decided upon a single trajectory, measured force, and then a rotten plum hit someone square in the back or sailed wide, or the melon exploded beneath a tire or rolled cleanly to the far side of the road. And we clapped in glee and wiped out hands on our pants.

In these early years—eight and nine and ten—the hands became attuned to each other. They began to slide the hafts of pitchforks and pry bars smoothly, to be more aware of each other's placement for leverage and of the slight difference in strength. It would be three or four more years before, playing the infield in baseball, I would sense the spatial and temporal depth of awareness my hands had of each other, would feel, short-hopping a sharp grounder blind in front of third base, flicking the ball from gloved-left to bare-right hand, making the cross-body thrown, that balletic poise of the still fingers after the release, would sense how mindless the beauty of it was.

I do not remember the ascendancy of the right hand. It was the one I was forced to write with, though by that time the right hand could already have asserted itself, reaching always first for a hammer or a peach. As I began to be judged according to the performance of my right hand alone—how well it imitated the Palmer cursive, how legibly it totaled mathematical figures—perhaps here is where the hands first realized how complicated their relationship would become. I remember a furious nun grabbing my six-year-old hands in prayer and wrenching the right thumb from under the left. Right over left, she insisted. *Right over left.* Right over left in praying to God.

In these early years my hands were frequently folded in prayer. They, too, collected chickens' eggs, contended with the neat assembly of plastic fighter planes, picked knots from bale twine, clapped chalkboard erasers, took trout off baited hooks, and trenched flower beds. They harbored and applauded homing pigeons. When I was eleven, my mother married again and we moved east to New York. The same hands took on new city tasks, struggled more often with coins and with tying the full Windsor knot. Also, now, they pursued a more diligent and precise combing of my hair. And were in anxious anticipation of touching a girl. And that caress having been given, one hand confirmed the memory later with the other in exuberant disbelief. They overhauled and pulled at each other like puppies.

I remember from these years — fourteen and fifteen and sixteen — marveling at the dexterity of my hands. In games of catch, one hand tipped the falling ball to the other, to be seized firmly in the same instant the body crashed to the ground. Or the hands changed effortlessly on the dribble at the start of a fast break in basketball. I remember disassembling, cleaning, and reassembling a two-barrel carburetor, knowing the memory of where all the parts fit was within my hands. I can recall the baton reversal of a pencil as I wrote then erased, wrote then erased, composing sentences on a sheet of paper. And I remember how the hands, so clever with a ball, so deft with a pair of needle-nose pliers, fumbled attaching a cymbidium orchid so close to a girl's body, so near the mysterious breast.

By now, sixteen or so, my hands were as accustomed to books, to   15
magazines, newspapers, and typing paper, as they were to mechanic's tools and baseballs. A blade in my pocketknife was a shape my fingers had experienced years earlier as an oleander leaf. The shape of my fountain pen I knew first as a eucalyptus twig, drawing make-believe roads in wet ground. As my hands had once strained to bring small bluegills to shore, now they reeled striped bass from the Atlantic's surf. As they had once entwined horses' manes, now they twirled girls' ponytails. I had stripped them in those years of manure, paint, axle grease, animal gore, plaster, soap suds, and machine oil; I had cleaned them of sap and tar and putty, of pond scum and potting soil, of fish scales and grass stains. The gashes and cuts had healed smoothly. They were lithe, strenuous. The unimpeded reach of the fingers away from one another in three planes, their extreme effective span, was a subtle source of confidence and wonder. They showed succinctly the physical intelligence of the body. They expressed so unmistakably the vulnerability in sexual desire. They drew so deliberately the curtains of my privacy.

One July afternoon I stood at an ocean breakwater with a friend, firing stones one after another in long, beautiful arcs a hundred feet to the edge of the water. We threw for accuracy, aiming to hit small breaking waves with cutting *thwips*. My friend tired of the game and lay down on his towel. A few moments later I turned and threw in a single motion just as he leaped to his feet. The stone caught him full in the side of the head. He was in the hospital a month with a fractured skull, unable to speak clearly until he was operated on. The following summer we were playing baseball together again, but I could not throw hard or accurately for months after the accident, and I shied away completely from a growing desire to be a pitcher.

My hands lost innocence or gained humanity that day, as they had another day when I was pulled off my first dog, screaming, my hands grasping feebly in the air, after he'd been run over and killed in the road. Lying awake at night I sometimes remember throwing the near deadly stone, or punching a neighbor's horse with my adolescent fist, or heedlessly swinging a 16-gauge shotgun, leading quail — if I hadn't forgotten to switch off the trigger safety, I would have shot an uncle in the head. My hands lay silent at my sides those nights. No memory of their grace or benediction could change their melancholy stillness.

While I was in college I worked two summers at a ranch in Wyoming. My hands got the feel of new tools—foot nips, frog pick, fence pliers, skiving knife. I began to see that the invention, dexterity, and quickness of the hands could take many directions in a man's life; and that a man should be attentive to what his hands loved to do, and so learn not only what he might be good at for a long time but what would make him happy. It pleased me to smooth every wrinkle from a saddle blanket before I settled a saddle squarely on a horse's back. And I liked, too, to turn the thin pages of a Latin edition of the *Aeneid* as I slowly accomplished them that first summer, feeling the impression of the type. It was strengthening to work with my hands, with ropes and bridles and hay bales, with double-bitted axes and bow saws, currying horses, scooping grain, adding my hands' oil to wooden door latches in the barn, calming horses at the foot of a loading ramp, adjusting my hat against the sun, buckling my chaps on a frosty morning. I'd watch the same hand lay a book lovingly on a night table and reach for the lamp's pull cord.

I had never learned to type, but by that second summer, at nineteen, I was writing out the first few stories longhand in pencil. I liked the sound and the sight of the writing going on, the back pressure through my hand. When I had erased and crossed out and rewritten a story all the way through, I would type it out slowly with two or sometimes four fingers, my right thumb on the space bar, as I do to this day. Certain keys and a spot on the space bar are worn through to metal on my typewriters from the oblique angles at which my fingernails strike them.

Had I been able to grasp it during those summers in Wyoming, I 20 might have seen that I couldn't get far from writing stories and physical work, either activity, and remain happy. It proved true that in these two movements my hands found their chief joy, aside from the touching of other human beings. But I could not see it then. My hands only sought out and gave in to the pleasures.

I began to travel extensively while I was in college. Eventually I visited many places, staying with different sorts of people. Most worked some substantial part of the day with their hands. I gravitated toward the company of cowboys and farmers both, to the work of loggers and orchardists, but mostly toward the company of field biologists, college-educated men and women who worked long days open to the weather, studying the lives of wild animals. In their presence, sometimes for weeks at a time, occasionally in stupefying cold or under significant physical strain, I helped wherever I could and wrote in my journal what had happened and, sometimes, what I thought of what had happened. In this way my hands came to know the prick and compression of syringes, the wiring and soldering of radio collars, the arming of anesthetizing guns, the setting of traps and snares, the deployment of otter trawls and plankton tows, the operation of calipers and tripod scales, and the manipulation of various kinds of sieves and packages used to sort and store parts of dead animals, parts created with the use of skinning and butchering knives, with bone saws, teasing needles, tweezers, poultry shears, and hemostatic clamps. My hands were in a dozen kinds of blood, including my own.

Everywhere I journeyed I marveled at the hands of other creatures, at how their palms and digits revealed history, at how well they performed tasks, at the elegant and incontrovertible beauty of their design. I cradled the paws of wolves and polar bears, the hooves of caribou, the forefeet of marine iguanas, the foreflippers of ringed seals and sperm whales, the hands of wallabies, of deer mice. Palpating the tendons, muscles, and bones beneath the skin or fur, I gained a rough understanding of the range of ability, of expression. I could feel where a broken bone had healed and see from superficial scars something of what a life must have been like. Deeper down, with mammals during a necropsy, I could see how blood vessels and layers of fat in a paw or in a flipper were arranged to either rid the creature of its metabolic heat or hoard it. I could see the evidence of arthritis in its phalanges, how that could come to me.

I have never touched a dead human, nor do I wish to. The living hands of another person, however, draw me, as strongly as the eyes. What is their history? What are their emotions? What longing is there? I can follow a cabinetmaker's hands for hours as they verify and detect, shave, fit, and rub; or a chef's hands adroitly dicing vegetables or shaping pastry. And who has not known faintness at the sight of a lover's hand? What man has not wished to take up the hands of the woman he loves and pore over them with reverence and curiosity? Who has not in reverie wished to love the lover's hands?

Years after my mother died I visited her oldest living friend. We were doing dishes together and she said, "You have your mother's hands." Was that likeness a shade of love? And if now I say out of respect for my hands I would buy only the finest tools, is that, too, not love?

The hands evolve, of course. The creases deepen and the fingers begin   25
to move two or three together at a time. If the hands of a man are put to hard use, the fingers grow blunt. They lose dexterity and the skin calluses over like hide. Hardly a pair of man's hands known to me comes to mind without a broken or dislocated finger, a lost fingertip, a permanently crushed nail. Most women my age carry scars from kitchen and house-work, drawer pinches, scalds, knife and glass cuts. We hardly notice them. Sunlight, wind, and weather obscure many of these scars, but I believe the memory of their occurrence never leaves the hands. When I awaken in the night and sense my hands cupped together under the pillow, or when I sit somewhere on a porch, idly watching wind crossing a ripening field, and look down to see my hands nested in my lap as if asleep like two old dogs, it is not hard for me to believe they know. They remember all they have done, all that has happened to them, the ways in which they have been surprised or worked themselves free of desperate trouble, or lost their grip and so caused harm. It's not hard to believe they remember the heads patted, the hands shaken, the apples peeled, the hair braided, the wood split, the gears shifted, the flesh gripped and stroked, and that they convey their feelings to each other.

In recent years my hands have sometimes been very cold for long stretches. It takes little cold now to entirely numb thumbs and forefingers. They cease to speak what they know. When I was thirty-one, I accidentally cut the base of my left thumb, severing nerves, leaving the thumb confused about what was cold, what was hot, and whether or not it was touching something or only thought so. When I was thirty-six, I was helping a friend butcher a whale. We'd been up for many hours under twenty-four-hour arctic daylight and were tired. He glanced away and without thinking drove the knife into my wrist. It was a clean wound, easy to close, but with it I lost the nerves to the right thumb. Over the years each thumb has regained some sensitivity, and I believe the hands are more sympathetic to each other because of their similar wounds. The only obvious difference lies with the left hand. A broken metacarpal forced a rerouting of tendons to the middle and ring fingers as it healed and raised a boss of carpal bone tissue on the back of the hand.

At the base of the right thumb is a scar from a climbing accident. On the other thumb, a scar the same length from the jagged edge of a fuel-barrel pump. In strong sunlight, when there is a certain tension in the skin, as I have said, I can stare at my hands for a while, turning them slowly, and remember with them the days, the weather, the people present when some things happened that left scars behind. It brings forth affection for my hands. I recall how, long ago, they learned to differentiate between cotton and raw silk, between husks of the casaba and the honeydew melon, and how they thrilled to the wire bristle of a hog's back, how they clipped the water's surface in swimming-pool fights, how they painstakingly arranged bouquets, how they swung and lifted children. I have begun to wish they would speak to me, tell me stories I have forgotten.

I sit in a chair and look at the scars, the uneven cut of the nails, and reminisce. With them before me I grin as though we held something secret, remembering bad times that left no trace. I cut firewood for my parents once, winter in Alabama, swamping out dry, leafless vines to do so. Not until the next day did I realize the vines were poison ivy. The blisters grew so close and tight my hands straightened like paddles. I had to have them lanced to continue a cross-country trip, to dress and feed myself. And there have been days when my hands stiffened with cold so that I had to quit the work being done, sit it out and whimper with pain as they came slowly back to life. But these moments are inconsequential. I have looked at the pale, wrinkled hands of a drowned boy, and I have seen handless wrists.

If there were a way to speak directly to the hands, to allow them a language of their own, what I would most wish to hear is what they recall of human touch, of the first exploration of the body of another, the caresses, the cradling of breast, of head, of buttock. Does it seem to them as to me that we keep learning, even when the caressed body has been known for years? How do daydreams of an idealized body, one's own or another's, affect the hands' first tentative inquiry? Is the hand purely empirical? Does it apply an imagination? Does it retain a man's shyness, a boy's clumsiness? Do the hands anguish if there is no one to touch?

Tomorrow I shall pull blackberry vines and load a trailer with rotten   30
timber. I will call on my hands to help me dress, to turn the spigot for water
for coffee, to pull the newspaper from its tube. I will put my hands in the
river and lift water where the sunlight is brightest, a playing with fractured
light I never tire of. I will turn the pages of a book about the history of fire
in Australia. I will sit at the typewriter, working through a story about a
trip to Matagorda Island in Texas. I will ask my hands to undress me. Before I turn out the light, I will fold and set my reading glasses aside. Then I
will cup my hands, the left in the right, and slide them under the pillow beneath my head, where they will speculate, as will I, about what we shall
handle the next day and dream, a spooling of their time we might later remember together and I, so slightly separated from them, might recognize.

The Reader's Presence

1. The writer tells a larger story through what is known as a metonymic
    symbol: a part that stands for the whole. How does Lopez use his
    hands to represent his experience? Why might he have chosen this
    device? In what ways do his hands suggest a "language"?

2. The essay traces a number of episodes in Lopez's life. How does
    the narrative tie them together? Do they seem to form a compre-
    hensive meaning overall? Why or why not? What position does
    Lopez take toward his unusual life path? What position is the
    reader asked to take?

3. Lopez evokes different environments through rich imagery.
    Choose a passage and note words conveying sight, sound, smell,
    and so forth. Suppose the same passage were related in a strictly
    informational manner. How would that affect your reception of
    Lopez's experience?

63

Marvin Minsky

Will Robots Inherit the Earth?

*Toshiba Professor of Media Arts and Sciences and professor of electrical engi-
neering at the Massachusetts Institute of Technology, Marvin Minsky (b. 1927) is a
pioneer in the field of artificial intelligence. He defines this field as "research con-*

cerned with making machines do things that people consider to require intelligence," and in this field Minsky has had some notable success. In 1951, together with a colleague, he assembled four hundred vacuum tubes in the first neural network learning machine. In order to build a computer capable of thinking like a human mind, Minsky believes that it is first necessary to understand how the human mind works. He advances a theory about the processes of thought in his book The Society of Mind *(1988). Minsky has written numerous books and articles concerned with artificial intelligence, mathematics, electronics, and computing, and has also co-authored a science-fiction novel,* The Turing Option *(1992). He is currently at work on* The Emotion Machine, *a sequel to* The Society of Mind. *"Will Robots Inherit the Earth?" appeared in* Scientific American *in 1994.*

Concerning his own thought processes, Minsky has said, "It is largely during writing that I work out my ideas and theories. (I usually get the basic ideas themselves while giving deliberately unprepared lectures, or in arguing with people with whom I strongly disagree.) When I'm writing an essay it grows large, cluttered with fragments of theories and bits of text, which get rearranged, destroyed, and revised dozens of times. I envy writers who 'have the whole thing' planned out in their minds, and know where they're going at almost every step, but that's a different world to me. If I actually understand anything that well, it just seems too trivial to talk about."

Early to bed and early to rise,
Makes a man healthy, wealthy, and wise.
— Benjamin Franklin

Everyone wants wisdom and wealth. Nevertheless, our health often gives out before we achieve them. To lengthen our lives and improve our minds, we will need to change our bodies and brains. To that end, we first must consider how traditional Darwinian evolution brought us to where we are. Then we must imagine ways in which novel replacements for worn body parts might solve our problems of failing health. Next we must invent strategies to augment our brains and gain greater wisdom. Eventually, using nanotechnology, we will entirely replace our brains. Once delivered from the limitations of biology, we will decide the length of our lives—with the option of immortality—and choose among other, unimagined capabilities as well.

In such a future, attaining wealth will be easy; the trouble will be in controlling it. Obviously, such changes are difficult to envision, and many thinkers still argue that these advances are impossible, particularly in the domain of artificial intelligence. But the sciences needed to enact this transition are already in the making, and it is time to consider what this new world will be like.

Such a future cannot be realized through biology. In recent times we have learned much about health and how to maintain it. We have devised thousands of specific treatments for specific diseases and disabilities. Yet we do not seem to have increased the maximum length of our life span.

Benjamin Franklin lived for 84 years, and except in popular legends and myths no one has ever lived twice that long. According to the estimates of Roy L. Walford, professor of pathology at the University of California at Los Angeles School of Medicine, the average human lifetime was about 22 years in ancient Rome, was about 50 in the developed countries in 1900, and today stands at about 75 in the U.S. Despite this increase, each of those curves seems to terminate sharply near 115 years. Centuries of improvements in health care have had no effect on that maximum.

Why are our life spans so limited? The answer is simple: natural selection favors the genes of those with the most descendants. Those numbers tend to grow exponentially with the number of generations, and so natural selection prefers the genes of those who reproduce at earlier ages. Evolution does not usually preserve genes that lengthen lives beyond that amount adults need to care for their young. Indeed, it may even favor offspring who do not have to compete with living parents. Such competition could promote the accretion of genes that cause death. For example, after spawning, the Mediterranean octopus promptly stops eating and starves itself. If a certain gland is removed, the octopus continues to eat and lives twice as long. Many other animals are programmed to die soon after they cease reproducing. Exceptions to this phenomenon include animals such as ourselves and elephants, whose progeny learn a great deal from the social transmission of accumulated knowledge.

We humans appear to be the longest-lived warm-blooded animals.   5 What selective pressure might have led to our present longevity, which is almost twice that of our primate relatives? The answer is related to wisdom. Among all mammals our infants are the most poorly equipped to survive by themselves. Perhaps we need not only parents but grandparents, too, to care for us and to pass on precious survival tips.

Even with such advice there are many causes of mortality to which we might succumb. Some deaths result from infections. Our immune systems have evolved versatile ways to cope with most such diseases. Unhappily, those very same immune systems often injure us by treating various parts of ourselves as though they, too, were infectious invaders. This autoimmune blindness leads to diseases such as diabetes, multiple sclerosis, rheumatoid arthritis and many others.

We are also subject to injuries that our bodies cannot repair: accidents, dietary imbalances, chemical poisons, heat, radiation and sundry other influences can deform or chemically alter the molecules of our cells so that they are unable to function. Some of these errors get corrected by replacing defective molecules. Nevertheless, when the replacement rate is too low, errors build up. For example, when the proteins of the eyes' lenses lose their elasticity, we lose our ability to focus and need bifocal spectacles—a Franklin invention.

The major natural causes of death stem from the effects of inherited genes. These genes include those that seem to be largely responsible for heart disease and cancer, the two biggest causes of mortality, as well as countless other disorders, such as cystic fibrosis and sickle cell anemia.

New technologies should be able to prevent some of these disorders by replacing those genes.

Most likely, senescence is inevitable in all biological organisms. To be sure, certain species (including some varieties of fish, tortoises and lobster) do not appear to show any systematic increase in mortality as they age. These animals seem to die mainly from external causes, such as predators or starvation. All the same, we have no records of animals that have lived for as long as two hundred years—although this lack does not prove that none exist. Walford and many others believe a carefully designed diet, one seriously restricted in calories, can significantly increase a human's life span but cannot ultimately prevent death.

By learning more about our genes, we should be able to correct or at 10 least postpone many conditions that still plague our later years. Yet even if we found a cure for each specific disease, we would still have to face the general problem of "wearing out." The normal function of every cell involves thousands of chemical processes, each of which sometimes makes random mistakes. Our bodies use many kinds of correction techniques, each triggered by a specific type of mistake. But those random errors happen in so many different ways that no low-level scheme can correct them all.

The problem is that our genetic systems were not designed for very long term maintenance. The relation between genes and cells is exceedingly indirect; there are no blueprints or maps to guide our genes as they build or rebuild the body. To repair defects on larger scales, a body would need some kind of catalogue that specified which types of cells should be located where. In computer programs it is easy to install such redundancy. Many computers maintain unused copies of their most critical system programs and routinely check their integrity. No animals have evolved similar schemes, presumably because such algorithms cannot develop through natural selection. The trouble is that error correction would stop mutation, which would ultimately slow the rate of evolution of an animal's descendants so much that they would be unable to adapt to changes in their environments.

Could we live for several centuries simply by changing some number of genes? After all, we now differ from our relatives, the gorillas and chimpanzees, by only a few thousand genes—and yet we live almost twice as long. If we assume that only a small fraction of those new genes caused the increase in life span, then perhaps no more than one hundred or so of those genes were involved. Even if this turned out to be true, though, it would not guarantee that we could gain another century by changing another one hundred genes. We might need to change just a few of them—or we might have to change a good many more.

Making new genes and installing them are slowly becoming feasible. But we are already exploiting another approach to combat biological wear and tear: replacing each organ that threatens to fail with a biological or artificial substitute. Some replacements are already routine. Others are on the horizon. Hearts are merely clever pumps. Muscles and bones are motors and beams. Digestive systems are chemical reactors. Eventually, we will find ways to transplant or replace all these parts. But when it comes to the brain, a transplant will not work. You cannot simply exchange your brain for another and remain the same person. You would lose the knowledge and the processes that constitute your identity. Nevertheless, we might be able to replace certain worn-out parts of brains by transplanting tissue-cultured fetal cells. This procedure would not restore lost knowledge, but that might not matter as much as it seems. We probably store each fragment of knowledge in several different places, in different forms. New parts of the brain could be retrained and reintegrated with the rest, and some of that might even happen spontaneously.

Even before our bodies wear out, I suspect that we often run into limitations in our brain's abilities. As a species, we seem to have reached a plateau in our intellectual development. There is no sign that we are getting smarter. Was Albert Einstein a better scientist than Isaac Newton or Archimedes? Has any playwright in recent years topped William Shakespeare or Euripides? We have learned a lot in two thousand years, yet much ancient wisdom still seems sound, which makes me think we have not been making much progress. We still do not know how to resolve conflicts between individual goals and global interests. We are so bad at making important decisions that, whenever we can, we leave to chance what we are unsure about.

Why is our wisdom so limited? Is it because we do not have the time to   15
learn very much or that we lack enough capacity? Is it because, according to popular accounts, we use only a fraction of our brains? Could better education help? Of course, but only to a point. Even our best prodigies learn no more than twice as quickly as the rest. Everything takes us too long to learn because our brains are so terribly slow. It would certainly help to have more time, but longevity is not enough. The brain, like other finite things, must reach some limits to what it can learn. We do not know what those limits are; perhaps our brains could keep learning for several more centuries. But at some point, we will need to increase their capacity.

The more we learn about our brains, the more ways we will find to improve them. Each brain has hundreds of specialized regions. We only know a little about what each one does or how it does it, but as soon as we find out how any one part works, researchers will try to devise ways to extend that part's capacity. They will also conceive of entirely new abilities that biology has never provided. As these inventions grow ever more prevalent, we will try to connect them to our brains, perhaps though millions of microscopic electrodes inserted into the great nerve bundle called the corpus callosum, the largest databus in the brain. With further advances, no part of the brain will be out-of-bounds for attaching new accessories. In the end, we will find ways to replace every part of the body and brain and thus repair all the defects and injuries that make our lives so brief.

Needless to say, in doing so we will be making ourselves into machines. Does this mean machines will replace us? I do not feel that it makes much sense to think in terms of "us" and "them." I much prefer the attitude of Hans P. Moravec of Carnegie Mellon University, who suggests that we think of these future intelligent machines as our own "mind-children."

In the past we have tended to see ourselves as a final product of evolution, but our evolution has not ceased. Indeed, we are now evolving more rapidly, though not in the familiar, slow Darwinian way. It is time that we started to think about our new emerging identities. We can begin to design systems based on inventive kinds of "unnatural selection" that can advance explicit plans and goals and can also exploit the inheritance of acquired characteristics. It took a century for evolutionists to train themselves to avoid such ideas—biologists call them "teleological" and "Lamarckian"[1]—but now we may have to change those rules.

Almost all the knowledge we amass is embodied in various networks inside our brains. These networks consist of huge numbers of tiny nerve cells and smaller structures, called synapses, that control how signals jump from one nerve cell to another. To make a replacement of a human brain, we would need to know something about how each of these synapses relates to the two cells it joins. We would also have to know how each of those structures responds to the various electric fields, hormones, neurotransmitters, nutrients, and other chemicals that are active in its neighborhood. A human brain contains trillions of synapses, so this is no small requirement.

Fortunately, we would not need to know every minute detail. If details were important, our brains would not work in the first place. In biological organisms, each system has generally evolved to be insensitive to most of what goes on in the smaller subsystems on which it depends. Therefore, to copy a functional brain it should suffice to replicate just enough of the function of each part to produce its important effects on other parts.

20

Suppose we wanted to copy a machine, such as a brain, that contained a trillion components. Today we could not do such a thing (even with the necessary knowledge) if we had to build each component separately. But if we had a million construction machines that could each build one thousand parts per second, our task would take mere minutes. In the decades to come, new fabrication machines will make this possible. Most present-day manufacturing is based on shaping bulk materials. In contrast, nanotechnologists aim to build materials and machinery by placing each atom and molecule precisely where they want it.

By such methods we could make truly identical parts and thus escape from the randomness that hinders conventionally made machines. Today,

---

[1]*Lamarckian:* The early evolutionary theory of the French scientist Jean Baptiste Lamarck (1744–1829) held that acquired characteristics could be inherited.—Eds.

for example, when we try to etch very small circuits, the sizes of the wires
vary so much that we cannot predict their electrical properties. If we can locate each atom exactly, however, the behavior of those wires would be indistinguishable. This capability would lead to new kinds of materials that
current techniques could never make; we could endow them with enormous
strength or novel quantum properties. These products in turn could lead to
computers as small as synapses, having unparalleled speed and efficiency.

Once we can use these techniques to construct a general-purpose assembly machine that operates on atomic scales, further progress should
be swift. If it took one week for such a machine to make a copy of itself,
we could have a billion copies in less than a year. These devices would
transform our world. For example, we could program them to fabricate
efficient solar-energy collecting devices and attach these to nearby surfaces. Hence, the devices could power themselves. We would be able to
grow fields of microfactories in much the same way that we now grow
trees. In such a future we will have little trouble attaining wealth; our
trouble will be in learning how to control it. In particular, we must always take care to maintain control over those things (such as ourselves)
that might be able to reproduce themselves.

If we want to consider augmenting our brains, we might first ask how
much a person knows today. Thomas K. Landauer of Bellcore reviewed
many experiments in which people were asked to read text, look at pictures and listen to words, sentences, short passages of music and nonsense
syllables. They were later tested to see how much they remembered. In
none of these situations were people able to learn, and later remember for
any extended period, more than about two bits per second. If one could
maintain that rate for twelve hours every day for one hundred years, the
total would be about three billion bits—less than what we can currently
store on a regular five-inch compact disc. In a decade or so that amount
should fit on a single computer chip.

Although these experiments do not much resemble what we do in   25
real life, we do not have any hard evidence that people can learn more
quickly. Despite common reports about people with "photographic memories," no one seems to have mastered, word for word, the contents of as
few as one hundred books or of a single major encyclopedia. The complete works of Shakespeare come to about 130 million bits. Landauer's
limit implies that a person would need at least four years to memorize
them. We have no well-founded estimates of how much information we
require to perform skills such as painting or skiing, but I do not see any
reason why these activities should not be similarly limited.

The brain is believed to contain on the order of one hundred trillion
synapses, which should leave plenty of room for those few billion bits of
reproducible memories. Someday, using nanotechnology, it should be feasible to build that much storage space into a package as small as a pea.

Once we know what we need to do, our nanotechnologies should enable us to construct replacement bodies and brains that will not be constrained to work at the crawling pace of "real time." The events in our com-

puter chips already happen millions of times faster than those in brain cells. Hence, we could design our "mind-children" to think a million times faster than we do. To such a being, half a minute might seem as long as one of our years and each hour as long as an entire human lifetime.

But could such beings really exist? Many scholars from a variety of disciplines firmly maintain that machines will never have thoughts like ours, because no matter how we build them, they will always lack some vital ingredient. These thinkers refer to this missing essence by various names: sentience, consciousness, spirit or soul. Philosophers write entire books to prove that because of this deficiency, machines can never feel or understand the kinds of things that people do. Yet every proof in each of those books is flawed by assuming, in one way or another, what is purports to prove—the existence of some magical spark that has no detectable properties. I have no patience with such arguments. We should not be searching for any single missing part. Human thought has many ingredients, and every machine that we have ever built is missing dozens or hundreds of them! Compare what computers do today with what we call "thinking." Clearly, human thinking is far more flexible, resourceful and adaptable. When anything goes even slightly wrong within a present-day computer program, the machine will either come to a halt or generate worthless results. When a person thinks, things are constantly going wrong as well, yet such troubles rarely thwart us. Instead we simply try something else. We look at our problem differently and switch to another strategy. What empowers us to do this?

On my desk lies a textbook about the brain. Its index has approximately six thousand lines that refer to hundreds of specialized structures. If you happen to injure some of these components, you could lose your ability to remember the names of animals. Another injury might leave you unable to make long-range plans. Another impairment could render you prone to suddenly utter dirty words because of damage to the machinery that normally censors that type of expression. We know from thousands of similar facts that the brain contains diverse machinery. Thus, your knowledge is represented in various forms that are stored in different regions of the brain, to be used by different processes. What are those representations like? We do not yet know.

But in the field of artificial intelligence, researchers have found several 30 useful means to represent knowledge, each better suited to some purposes than to others. The most popular ones use collections of "if-then" rules. Other systems use structures called frames, which resemble forms that are to be filled out. Yet other programs use weblike networks or schemes that resemble trees or sequences of planlike scripts. Some systems store knowledge in languagelike sentences or in expressions of mathematical logic. A programmer starts any new job by trying to decide which representation will best accomplish the task at hand. Typically a computer program uses a single representation, which, should it fail, can cause the system to break down. This shortcoming justifies the common complaint that computers do not really "understand" what they are doing.

What does it mean to understand? Many philosophers have declared that understanding (or meaning or consciousness) must be a basic, elemental ability that only a living mind can possess. To me, this claim appears to be a symptom of "physics envy"—that is, they are jealous of how well physical science has explained so much in terms of so few principles. Physicists have done very well by rejecting all explanations that seem too complicated and then searching instead for simple ones. Still, this method does not work when we are addressing the full complexity of the brain. Here is an abridgment of what I said about the ability to understand in my book *The Society of Mind:*

> If you understand something in only one way, then you do not really understand it at all. This is because if something goes wrong you get stuck with a thought that just sits in your mind with nowhere to go. The secret of what anything means to us depends on how we have connected it to all the other things we know. This is why, when someone learns "by rote," we say that they do not really understand. However, if you have several different representations, when one approach fails you can try another. Of course, making too many indiscriminate connections will turn a mind to mush. But well-connected representations let you turn ideas around in your mind, to envision things from many perspectives, until you find one that works for you. And that is what we mean by thinking!

I think flexibility explains why, at the moment, thinking is easy for us and hard for computers. In *The Society of Mind,* I suggest that the brain rarely uses a single representation. Instead it always runs several scenarios in parallel so that multiple viewpoints are always available. Furthermore, each system is supervised by other, higher-level ones that keep track of their performance and reformulate problems when necessary. Because each part and process in the brain may have deficiencies, we should expect to find other parts that try to detect and correct such bugs.

In order to think effectively, you need multiple processes to help you describe, predict, explain, abstract and plan what your mind should do next. The reason we can think so well is not because we house mysterious sparklike talents and gifts but because we employ societies of agencies that work in concert to keep us from getting stuck. When we discover how these societies work, we can put them inside computers, too. Then if one procedure in a program gets stuck, another might suggest an alternative approach. If you saw a machine do things like that, you would certainly think it was conscious.

This article bears on our rights to have children, to change our genes and to die if we so wish. No popular ethical system yet, be it humanist or religion-based, has shown itself able to face the challenges that already confront us. How many people should occupy the earth? What sorts of people should they be? How should we share the available space? Clearly, we must change our ideas about making additional children. Individuals now are conceived by chance. Someday, instead, they could be "composed" in accord with considered desires and designs. Furthermore, when we build new brains, these need not start out the way ours do, with so little knowledge about the world. What kinds of things should our "mind-children" know? How many of them should we produce, and who should decide their attributes?

Traditional systems of ethical thought are focused mainly on individuals, as though they were the only entities of value. Obviously, we must also consider the rights and the roles of larger-scale beings — such as the superpersons we term cultures and the great, growing systems called sciences — that help us understand the world. How many such entities do we want? Which are the kinds that we most need? We ought to be wary of ones that get locked into forms that resist all further growth. Some future options have never been seen: imagine a scheme that could review both your mentality and mine and then compile a new, merged mind based on that shared experience. 35

Whatever the unknown future may bring, we are already changing the rules that made us. Most of us will fear change, but others will surely want to escape from our present limitations. When I decided to write this article, I tried these ideas out on several groups. I was amazed to find that at least three quarters of the individuals with whom I spoke seemed to feel our life-spans were already too long. "Why would any one want to live for five hundred years? Wouldn't it be boring? What if you outlived all your friends? What would you do with all that time?" they asked. It seemed as though they secretly feared that they did not deserve to live so long. I find it rather worrisome that so many people are resigned to die. Might not such people, who feel that they do not have much to lose, be dangerous?

My scientist friends showed few such concerns. "There are countless things that I want to find out and so many problems I want to solve that I could use many centuries," they said. Certainly immortality would seem unattractive if it means endless infirmity, debility and dependency on others, but we are assuming a state of perfect health. Some people expressed a sounder concern — that the old ones must die because young ones are needed to weed out their worn-out ideas. Yet if it is true, as I fear, that we are approaching our intellectual limits, then that response is not a good answer. We would still be cut off from the larger ideas in those oceans of wisdom beyond our grasp.

Will robots inherit the earth? Yes, but they will be our children. We owe our minds to the deaths and lives of all the creatures that were ever engaged in the struggle called evolution. Our job is to see that all this work shall not end up in meaningless waste.

The Reader's Presence

1. Throughout this essay, Minsky compares the human brain and the computer. What advantage does the brain have over the computer? What advantages does the computer have over the brain?

How does Minsky refute the "missing essence" theory proposed by some philosophers (paragraph 29)? How might those philosophers counter his argument?

2. Minsky provides an optimistic look into the future. If this were science fiction rather than an article in *Scientific American,* the author might have chosen a more negative set of predictions, if only to add an element of conflict to the narrative. Which of Minsky's predictions seem to have the most potential as the basis for a good disaster film or novel? What ideas does Minsky leave out in his attempt to paint a positive vision of the future? Where, for instance, does he address the question of who will maintain control of the scientific process he describes (paragraph 23)? Who does Minsky include in the "we" in paragraph 34? How might the "mind-children" and their parents get along? How does he answer the ethical questions he raises in paragraph 34?

3. Consider the intended audience for this article. What specific compositional strategies does Minsky use to make complex scientific concepts accessible to this audience? Point to specific rhetorical strategies as well as words and phrases that Minsky uses to aid his audience in comprehending the ideas he unfolds. How does Minsky help to shape the audience's reaction to his argument? Where did you position yourself when you read the closing paragraphs, in which he writes of the informal poll he took among his acquaintances? Did the reported results change your reaction?

64

Bharati Mukherjee

Two Ways to Belong in America

Bharati Mukherjee was born in Calcutta, India, in 1940 and came to the United States at the age of twenty-one to attend the Iowa Writers' Workshop. After she received her Ph. D. at the University of Iowa in 1969, Mukherjee moved to Canada with her husband, Clark Blaise, for several years. Tired of the racist attitudes Mukherjee encountered, she and Blaise eventually returned to the United States, where she has taught at various universities and colleges. She is the author of several novels, including Jasmine *(1989),* The Holder of the World *(1993), and* Leave It to Me *(1997). Her two collections of short stories are* Darkness *(1985) and* The Middleman and Other Stories *(1988), which won the National Book Critics' Circle Award. She currently teaches creative writing at the University of*

California at Berkeley. *"Two Ways to Belong in America"* originally appeared in the New York Times *in 1996.*

This is a tale of two sisters from Calcutta, Mira and Bharati, who have lived in the United States for some thirty-five years, but who find themselves on different sides in the current debate over the status of immigrants. I am an American citizen and she is not. I am moved that thousands of long-term residents are finally taking the oath of citizenship. She is not.

Mira arrived in Detroit in 1960 to study child psychology and pre-school education. I followed her a year later to study creative writing at the University of Iowa. When we left India, we were almost identical in appearance and attitude. We dressed alike, in saris; we expressed identical views on politics, social issues, love and marriage in the same Calcutta convent-school accent. We would endure our two years in America, secure our degrees, then return to India to marry the grooms of our father's choosing.

Instead, Mira married an Indian student in 1962 who was getting his business administration degree at Wayne State University. They soon acquired the labor certifications necessary for the green card of hassle-free residence and employment.

Mira still lives in Detroit, works in the Southfield, Mich., school system, and has become nationally recognized for her contributions in the fields of pre-school education and parent-teacher relationships. After 36 years as a legal immigrant in this country, she clings passionately to her Indian citizenship and hopes to go home to India when she retires.

In Iowa City in 1963, I married a fellow student, an American of Canadian parentage. Because of the accident of his North Dakota birth, I bypassed labor-certification requirements and the race-related "quota" system that favored the applicant's country of origin over his or her merit. I was prepared for (and even welcomed) the emotional strain that came with marrying outside my ethnic community. In thirty-three years of marriage, we have lived in every part of North America. By choosing a husband who was not my father's selection, I was opting for fluidity, self-invention, blue jeans and T-shirts, and renouncing three thousand years (at least) of caste-observant, "pure culture" marriage in the Mukherjee family. My books have often been read as unapologetic (and in some quarters overenthusiastic) texts for cultural and psychological "mongrelization." It's a word I celebrate.

Mira and I have stayed sisterly close by phone. In our regular Sunday morning conversations, we are unguardedly affectionate. I am her only blood relative on this continent. We expect to see each other through the looming crises of aging and ill health without being asked. Long before Vice President Gore's "Citizenship U.S.A." drive, we'd had our polite arguments over the ethics of retaining an overseas citizenship while expecting the permanent protection and economic benefits that come with living and working in America.

Like well-raised sisters, we never said what was really on our minds, but we probably pitied one another. She, for the lack of structure in my

5

life, the erasure of Indianness, the absence of an unvarying daily core. I, for the narrowness of her perspective, her uninvolvement with the mythic depths or the superficial pop culture of this society. But, now, with the scapegoating of "aliens" (documented or illegal) on the increase, and the targeting of long-term legal immigrants like Mira for new scrutiny and new self-consciousness, she and I find ourselves unable to maintain the same polite discretion. We were always unacknowledged adversaries, and we are now, more than ever, sisters.

"I feel used," Mira raged on the phone the other night. "I feel manipulated and discarded. This is such an unfair way to treat a person who was invited to stay and work here because of her talent. My employer went to the I.N.S. and petitioned for the labor certification. For over thirty years, I've invested my creativity and professional skills into the improvement of *this* country's pre-school system. I've obeyed all the rules, I've paid my taxes, I love my work, I love my students, I love the friends I've made. How dare America now change its rules in midstream? If America wants to make new rules curtailing benefits of legal immigrants, they should apply only to immigrants who arrive after those rules are already in place."

To my ears, it sounded like the description of a long-enduring, comfortable yet loveless marriage, without risk or recklessness. Have we the right to demand, and to expect, that we be loved? (That, to me is the subtext of the arguments by immigration advocates.) My sister is an expatriate, professionally generous and creative, socially courteous and gracious, and that's as far as her Americanization can go. She is here to maintain an identity, not to transform it.

I asked her if she would follow the example of others who have decided to become citizens because of the anti-immigration bills in Congress. And here, she surprised me. "If America wants to play the manipulative game, I'll play it too," she snapped. "I'll become a U.S. citizen for now, than change back to Indian when I'm ready to go home. I feel some kind of irrational attachment to India that I don't to America. Until all this hysteria against legal immigrants, I was totally happy. Having my green card meant I could visit any place in the world I wanted to and then come back to a job that's satisfying and that I do very well."

In one family, from two sisters alike as peas in a pod, there could not   10
be a wider divergence of immigrant experience. America spoke to me — I married it — I embraced the demotion from expatriate aristocrat to immigrant nobody, surrendering those thousands of years of "pure culture," the saris, the delightfully accented English. She retained them all. Which of us is the freak?

Mira's voice, I realize, is the voice not just of the immigrant South Asian community but of an immigrant community of the millions who have stayed rooted in one job, one city, one house, on ancestral culture, one cuisine, for the entirety of their productive years. She speaks for greater numbers than I possibly can. Only the fluency of her English and the anger, rather than fear, born of confidence from her education, differentiate her from the seamstresses, the domestics, the technicians, the shop owners, the millions of hard-working but effectively silenced documented immigrants as well as their less fortunate "illegal" brothers and sisters.

Nearly twenty years ago, when I was living in my husband's ancestral homeland of Canada, I was always well-employed but never allowed to feel part of the local Quebec or larger Canadian society. Then, through a Green Paper that invited a national referendum on the unwanted side effects of "nontraditional" immigration, the Government officially turned against its immigrant communities, particularly those from South Asia.

I felt then the same sense of betrayal that Mira feels now. I will never forget the pain of that sudden turning, and the casual racist outbursts the Green Paper elicited. That sense of betrayal had its desired effect and drove me, and thousands like me, from the country.

Mira and I differ, however, in the ways in which we hope to interact with the country that we have chosen to live in. She is happier to live in America as expatriate Indian than as an immigrant American. I need to feel like a part of the community I have adopted (as I tried to feel in Canada as well). I need to put roots down, to vote and make the difference that I can. The price that the immigrant willingly pays, and that the exile avoids, is the trauma of self-transformation.

The Reader's Presence

1. The writer champions "mongrelization." How does she conceive of community? identity? How do her conceptions differ from her sister's?

2. The essay primarily concerns immigrants and their choices. How are America itself and the citizenship drive portrayed? How does her piece challenge stereotypic views of immigrants as passive and fearful of asserting their rights? To whom does Mukherjee's argument seem directed? Why?

3. Mukherjee holds a strong opinion, yet strives to represent the opposing side. How is her sister's perspective portrayed? What images does the writer use to describe her sister's lifestyle? Might her sister describe her perspective differently? Does Mukherjee really offer the reader "two ways" of considering the conflict?

65

Gloria Naylor

A Question of Language

Gloria Naylor (b. 1950) won an American Book Award for her first novel,
The Women of Brewster Place *(1982); her most recent novel is a sequel,* The Men
of Brewster Place *(1998). Her other works of fiction include* Linden Hills *(1985),*
Mama Day *(1988), and* Bailey's Café *(1992), and her nonfiction has been pub-*
lished in Centennial *(1986). In addition to these books, Naylor contributes essays*
and articles to many periodicals, including Southern Review, Essence, Ms., Life,
Callaloo, *and the* Ontario Review. *Also, she recently founded One Way Produc-*
tions, an independent film company that she established to bring the novel Mama
Day *to the screen. Naylor has worked as the "Hers" columnist for the* New York
Times *and as a visiting professor and writer at Princeton University, New York*
University, the University of Pennsylvania, Boston University, and Brandeis Uni-
versity. In addition, Naylor was a cultural exchange lecturer in India in 1985 and a
senior fellow at the Society for the Humanities, Cornell University , in 1988. The
article "A Question of Language" first appeared in the New York Times *in 1986.*

Naylor credits her mother's inspiration for her love of books and writing:
"Realizing that I was a painfully shy child, she gave me my first diary and told me
to write my feeling down in there. Over the years that diary was followed by
reams and reams of paper that eventually culminated in The Women of Brewster
Place. *And I wrote that book as a tribute to her and other black women who, in*
spite of very limited personal circumstances, somehow manage to hold fierce be-
lief in the limitless possibilities of the human spirit."

Language is the subject. It is the written form with which I've managed to keep the wolf away from the door and, in diaries, to keep my sanity. In spite of this, I consider the written word inferior to the spoken, and
much of the frustration experienced by novelists is the awareness that
whatever we manage to capture in even the most transcendent passages
falls far short of the richness of life. Dialogue achieves its power in the
dynamics of a fleeting moment of sight, sound, smell, and touch.

I'm not going to enter the debate here about whether it is language
that shapes reality or vice versa. That battle is doomed to be waged
whenever we seek intermittent reprieve from the chicken and egg dispute.

I will simply take the position that the spoken word, like the written word, amounts to a nonsensical arrangement of sounds or letters without a consensus that assigns "meaning." And building from the meanings of what we hear, we order reality. Words themselves are innocuous; it is the consensus that gives them true power.

I remember the first time I heard the work *nigger*. In my third-grade class, our math tests were being passed down the rows, and as I handed the papers to a little boy in back of me, I remarked that once again he had received a much lower mark than I did. He snatched his test from me and spit out that word. Had he called me a nymphomaniac or a necrophiliac, I couldn't have been more puzzled. I didn't know what a nigger was, but I knew that whatever it meant, it was something he shouldn't have called me. This was verified when I raised my hand, and in a loud voice repeated what he had said and watched the teacher scold him for using a "bad" word. I was later to go home and ask the inevitable question that every black parent must face—"Mommy, what does 'nigger' mean?"

And what exactly did it mean? Thinking back, I realize that this could not have been the first time the word was used in my presence. I was part of a large extended family that had migrated from the rural South after World War II and formed a close-knit network that gravitated around my maternal grandparents. Their ground-floor apartment in one of the buildings they owned in Harlem was a weekend mecca for my immediate family, along with countless aunts, uncles, and cousins who brought along assorted friends. It was a bustling and open house with assorted neighbors and tenants popping in and out to exchange bits of gossip, pick up an old quarrel, or referee the ongoing checkers game in which my grandmother cheated shamelessly. They were all there to let down their hair and put up their feet after a week of labor in the factories, laundries, and shipyards of New York.

Amid the clamor, which could reach deafening proportions—two or three conversations going on simultaneously, punctuated by the sound of a baby's crying somewhere in the back rooms or out on the street—there was still a rigid set of rules about what was said and how. Older children were sent out of the living room when it was time to get into the juicy details about "you-know-who" up on the third floor who had gone and gotten herself "p-r-e-g-n-a-n-t!" But my parents, knowing that I could spell well beyond my years, always demanded that I follow the others out to play. Beyond sexual misconduct and death, everything else was considered harmless for our young ears. And so among the anecdotes of the triumphs and disappointments in the various workings of their lives, the word *nigger* was used in my presence, but it was set within contexts and inflections that caused it to register in my mind as something else.

In the singular, the word was always applied to a man who had distinguished himself in some situation that brought their approval for his strength, intelligence, or drive:

"Did Johnny really do that?"

"I'm telling you, that nigger pulled in $6,000 of overtime last year. Said he got enough for a down payment on a house."

When used with a possessive adjective by a woman—"my nigger"—it became a term of endearment for husband or boyfriend. But it could be more than just a term applied to a man. In their mouths it became the pure essence of manhood—a disembodied force that channeled their past history of struggle and present survival against the odds into a victorious statement of being: "Yeah, that old foreman found out quick enough—you don't mess with a nigger."

In the plural, it became a description of some group within the community that had overstepped the bounds of decency as my family defined it: Parents who neglected their children, a drunken couple who fought in public, people who simply refused to look for work, those with excessively dirty mouths or unkempt households were all "trifling niggers." This particular circle could forgive hard times, unemployment, the occasional bout of depression—they had gone through all of that themselves—but the unforgivable sin was lack of self-respect.

A woman could never be a *nigger* in the singular, with its connotation of confirming worth. The noun *girl* was its closest equivalent in that sense, but only when used in direct address and regardless of the gender doing the addressing. *Girl* was a token of respect for a woman. The one-syllable word was drawn out to sound like three in recognition of the extra ounce of wit, nerve, or daring that the woman had shown in the situation under discussion.

"G-i-r-l, stop. You mean you said that to his face?"

But if the word was used in a third-person reference or shortened so that it almost snapped out of the mouth, it always involved some element of communal disapproval. And age became an important factor in these exchanges. It was only between individuals of the same generation, or from an older person to a younger (but never the other way around), that "girl" would be considered a compliment.

I don't agree with the argument that use of the word *nigger* at this social stratum of the black community was an internalization of racism. The dynamics were the exact opposite: the people in my grandmother's living room took a word that whites used to signify worthlessness or degradation and rendered it impotent. Gathering there together, they transformed *nigger* to signify the varied and complex human beings they knew themselves to be. If the word was to disappear totally from the mouths of even the most liberal of white society, no one in that room was naïve enough to believe it would disappear from white minds. Meeting the word head-on, they proved it had absolutely nothing to do with the way they were determined to live their lives.

So there must have been dozens of times that the word *nigger* was spoken in front of me before I reached the third grade. But I didn't "hear" it until it was said by a small pair of lips that had already learned it could be a way to humiliate me. That was the word I went home and asked my mother about. And since she knew that I had to grow up in America, she took me in her lap and explained.

The Reader's Presence

1. Naylor analyzes the various meanings of the word *nigger,* meanings that are agreed to by consensus and that vary according to the speaker, the audience, and the context within which the word is spoken. Outline the different meanings of *nigger,* and evaluate the effectiveness of the example she provides to illustrate each definition. Do the same for her definitions of *girl.* Can you think of any other examples to reinforce the points she makes in each definition, or any examples that challenge her definitions?

2. Where — and how — does Naylor make her own point of view clear in this essay? How does she reveal her personal stake in the issues addressed in the essay? Consider her use of personal narrative. Comment, for example, on the effectiveness of paragraphs 4 and 5. What do they contribute to the overall point of her essay? What does this description of the circumstances of her extended family in Harlem add to the essay?

3. Naylor creates a two-part structure for her essay: two generalized, abstract opening paragraphs, followed by a series of extended illustrations of her definitions of the words *nigger* and *girl.* In the first paragraph she talks about the nature of language and its inadequacy in conveying the fullness and complexity of an experience. In the second she asserts the need for consensus in order to establish meaning. Where does she announce the overriding point of her essay? Review the different definitions she provides. What inferences can you draw from these definitions about the values of the communities she describes? What do these definitions tell us about what is important to these communities? about what kinds of behavior are to be avoided and censured?

66 —————————————————————————

Kathleen Norris

The Holy Use of Gossip

Kathleen Norris (b. 1947) is a poet, editor, and author who also manages her family's ranch in Lemmon, South Dakota. Norris has published several collections of poetry, including Falling Off *(1971),* The Middle of the World *(1981), and* Little Girls in Church *(1995). Although a poet throughout her writing career, she is most noted for her two spiritual memoirs. In* Dakota: A Spiritual Geography *(1993), which contains "The Holy Use of Gossip," Norris discusses how life in the Great Plains provides her with a source of inspiration and spiritual renewal. The* Cloister Walk *(1996), a follow-up, is a collection of personal meditations on organized religion, her experiences with monasticism, and the value of celibacy.*

It is the responsibility of writers to listen to gossip and pass it on. It is the way all storytellers learn about life.

—Grace Paley

If there's anything worth calling theology, it is listening to people's stories, listening to them and cherishing them.

—Mary Pellauer

I once scandalized a group of North Dakota teenagers who had been determined to scandalize me. Working as an artist-in-residence in their school for three weeks, I happened to hit prom weekend. Never much for proms in high school, I helped decorate, cutting swans out of posterboard and sprinkling them with purple glitter as the school gym was festooned with lavender and silver crepe paper streamers.

On Monday morning a group of the school outlaws was gossiping in the library, just loud enough for me to hear, about the drunken exploits that had taken place at a prairie party in the wee hours after the dance: kids meeting in some remote spot, drinking beer and listening to car stereos turned up loud, then, near dawn, going to one girl's house for breakfast. I finally spoke up and said, "See, it's like I told you: the party's

not over until you've told the stories. That's where all writing starts."
They looked up at me, pretending that it bothered them that I'd heard.

"And," I couldn't resist adding, "everyone knows you don't get piss-drunk and then eat scrambled eggs. If you didn't know it before, you know it now." "You're not going to write about *that,* are you?" one girl said, her eyes wide. "I don't know," I replied, "I might. It's all grist for the mill."

When my husband and I first moved to Dakota, people were quick to tell us about an eccentric young man who came from back East and gradually lost his grip on reality. He shared a house with his sheep until relatives came and took him away. "He was a college graduate," someone would always add, looking warily at us as if to say, we know what can happen to Easterners who are too well educated. This was one of the first tales to go into my West River treasure-house of stories. It was soon joined by the story of the man who shot himself to see what it felt like. He hit his lower leg and later said that while he didn't feel anything for a few seconds, after that it hurt like hell.

There was Rattlesnake Bill, a cowboy who used to carry rattlers in a paper sack in his pickup truck. If you didn't believe him, he's put his hand in without looking and take one out to show you. One night Bill limped into a downtown bar on crutches. A horse he was breaking had dragged him for about a mile, and he was probably lucky to be alive. He'd been knocked out, he didn't know for how long, and when he regained consciousness he had crawled to his house and changed clothes to come to town. Now Bill thought he'd drink a little whiskey for the pain. "Have you been to a doctor?" friends asked. "Nah, whiskey'll do." 5

Later that night at the steak house I managed to get Bill to eat something—most of my steak, as it turned out, but he needed it more than I. The steak was rare, and that didn't sit well with Bill. A real man eats his steak well done. But when I said, "What's the matter, are you too chicken to eat rare meat?" he gobbled it down. He slept in his pickup that night, and someone managed to get him to a doctor the next day. He had a broken pelvis.

There was another cowboy who had been mauled by a bobcat in a remote horse barn by the Grand River. The animal had leapt from a hayloft as he tied up a horse, and he had managed to grab a rifle and shoot her. He felt terrible afterwards, saying, "I should have realized the only reason she'd have attacked like that was because she was protecting young." He found her two young cubs, still blind, in the loft. In a desperate attempt to save them he called several veterinarians in the hope that they might know of a lactating cat who had aborted. Such a cat was found, but the cubs lived just a few more days.

There was a woman who nursed her husband through a long illness. A dutiful farm daughter and ranch wife, she had never experienced life on her own. When she was widowed, all the town spoke softly about "poor Ida." But when "poor Ida" kicked up her heels and, entering a delayed adolescence in her fifties, dyed her hair, dressed provocatively, and went dancing more than once a week at the steak house, the sympathetic cooing of the gossips turned to outrage. The woman at the center of the storm hadn't changed; she was still an innocent, bewildered by the calumny now directed at her. She lived it down and got herself a steady boyfriend, but she still dyes her hair and dresses flashy. I'm grateful for the color she adds to the town.

Sometimes it seems as if the whole world is fueled by gossip. Much of what passes for hard news today is the Hollywood fluff that was relegated to pulp movie magazines when I was a girl. From the Central Intelligence Agency to *Entertainment Tonight,* gossip is big business. But in small towns, gossip is still small-time. And as bad as it can be—venal, petty, mean—in the small town it also stays closer to the roots of the word. If you look up gossip in the *Oxford English Dictionary* you find that it is derived from the words for God and sibling, and originally meant "akin to God." It was used to describe one who has contracted spiritual kinship by acting as a sponsor at baptism; one who helps "give a name to." Eric Partridge's *Origins,* a dictionary of etymology, tells you simply to "see God," and there you find that the word's antecedents include gospel, godspell, *sippe* (or consanguinity) and "*sabha,* a village community—notoriously inter-related."

We are interrelated in a small town, whether or not we're related by   10
blood. We know without thinking about it who owns what car; inhabitants of a town as small as a monastery learn to recognize each other's footsteps in the hall. Story is a safety valve for people who live as intimately as that; and I would argue that gossip done well can be a holy thing. It can strengthen communal bonds.

Gossip provides comic relief for people under tension. Candidates at one monastery are told of a novice in the past who had such a hot temper that the others loved to bait him. Once when they were studying he closed a window and the other monks opened it; once, twice. When he got up to close the window for the third time, he yelled at them, "Why are you making me sin with this window?"

Gossip can help us give a name to ourselves. The most revealing section of the weekly *Lemmon Leader* is the personal column in the classified ads, where people express thanks to those who helped with the bloodmobile, a 4-H booth at the county fair, a Future Homemakers of America fashion show, a benefit for a family beset by huge medical bills. If you've been in the hospital or have suffered a death in the family, you take out an ad thanking the doctor, ambulance crew, and wellwishers who visited, sent cards, offered prayers, or brought gifts of food.

Often these ads are quite moving, written from the heart. The parents of a small boy recently thanked those who had remembered their son with

> prayers, cards, balloons, and gifts, and gave moral support to the rest of
> the family when Ty underwent surgery. . . . It's great to be home again
> in this caring community, and our biggest task now is to get Ty to eat

more often and larger amounts. Where else but Lemmon would we find people who would stop by and have a bedtime snack and milk with Ty or provide good snacks just to help increase his caloric intake, or a school system with staff that take the time to make sure he eats his extra snacks. May God Bless all of you for caring about our "special little" boy — who is going to gain weight!

No doubt it is the vast land surrounding us, brooding on the edge of our consciousness, that makes it necessary for us to call such attention to human activity. Publicly asserting, as do many of these ads, that we live in a caring community helps us keep our hopes up in a hard climate or hard times, and gives us a sense of identity.

Privacy takes on another meaning in such an environment, where you   15
are asked to share your life, humbling yourself before the common wisdom, such as it is. Like everyone else, you become public property and come to accept things that city people would consider rude. A young woman using the pay phone in a West River café is scrutinized by several older women who finally ask her, " Who are you, anyway?" On discovering that she is from a ranch some sixty miles south, they question her until, learning her mother's maiden name, they are satisfied. They know her grandparents by reputation; good ranchers, good people.

The *Leader* has correspondents in rural areas within some fifty miles of Lemmon — Bison, Chance, Duck Creek, Howe, Morristown, Rosebud (on the Grand River), Shadehill, Spring Butte, Thunder Hawk, White Butte — as well as at the local nursing home and in the town of Lemmon itself, who report on "doings." If you volunteer at the nursing home's weekly popcorn party and sing-along, your name appears. If you host a card party at your home, this is printed, along with the names of your guests. If you have guests from out of town, their names appear. Many notices would baffle an outsider, as they require an intimate knowledge of family relationships to decipher. One recent column from White Butte, headed "Neighbors Take Advantage of Mild Winter Weather to Visit Each Other," read in part: "Helen Johanssen spent several afternoons with Gaylene Francke; Mavis Merdahl was a Wednesday overnight guest at the Alvera Ellis home."

Allowing yourself to be a subject of gossip is one of the sacrifices you make, living in a small town. And the pain caused by the loose talk of ignorant people is undeniable. One couple I know, having lost their only child to a virulent pneumonia (a robust thirty-five year old, he was dead in a matter of days) had to endure rumors that he had died of suicide, AIDS, and even anthrax. But it's also true that the gossips don't know all that they think they know, and often misread things in a comical way. My husband was once told that he was having an affair with a woman he hadn't met, and I still treasure the day I was encountered by three people who said, "Have you sold your house yet?" "When's the baby due?" and, "I'm sorry to hear your mother died."

I could trace the sources of the first two rumors: we'd helped a friend move into a rented house, and I'd bought baby clothes downtown when I learned that I would soon become an aunt. The third rumor was easy enough to check; I called my mother on the phone. The flip side, the saving grace, is that despite the most diligent attentions of the die-hard gossips, it is possible to have secrets.

Of course the most important things can't be hidden: birth, sickness, death, divorce. But gossip is essentially democratic. It may be the plumber and his wife who had a screaming argument in a bar, or it could be the bank president's wife who moved out and rented a room in the motel; everyone is fair game. And although there are always those who take delight in the misfortunes of others, and relish a juicy story at the expense of truth and others' feelings, this may be the exception rather than the rule. Surprisingly often, gossip is the way small-town people express solidarity.

I recall a marriage that was on the rocks. The couple had split up,   20 and gossip ran wild. Much sympathy was expressed for the children, and one friend of the couple said to me, "The worst thing she could do is to take him back too soon. This will take time." Those were healing words, a kind of prayer. And when the family did reunite, the town breathed a collective sigh of relief.

My own parents' marriage was of great interest in Lemmon back in the 1930s. My mother, the town doctor's only child, eloped with another Northwestern University student; a musician, of all things. A poor preacher's kid. "This will bear watching," one matriarch said. My parents fooled her. As time went on, the watching grew dull. Now going on fifty-five years, their marriage has outlasted all the gossip.

Like the desert tales that monks have used for centuries as a basis for a theology and way of life, the tales of small-town gossip are often morally instructive, illustrating the ways ordinary people survive the worst that happens to them; or, conversely, the ways in which self-pity, anger, and despair can overwhelm and destroy them. Gossip is theology translated into experience. In it we hear great stories of conversion, like the drunk who turns his or her life around, as well as stories of failure. We can see that pride really does go before a fall, and that hope is essential. We watch closely those who retire, or who lose a spouse, lest they lose interest in living. When we gossip we are also praying, not only for them but for ourselves.

At its deepest level, small-town gossip is about how we face matters of life and death. We see the gossip of earlier times, the story immortalized in ballads such as "Barbara Allen," lived out before our eyes as a young man obsessively in love with a vain young woman nearly self-destructs. We also see how people heal themselves. One of the bravest people I know is a young mother who sewed and embroidered exquisite baptismal clothes for her church with the memorial money she received when her first baby died. When she gave birth to a healthy girl a few years later, the whole town rejoiced.

My favorite gossip takes note of the worst and the best that is in us. Two women I know were diagnosed with terminal cancer. One said, "If I

ever get out of this hospital, I'm going to look out for Number One."
And that's exactly what she did. Against overwhelming odds, she survived, and it made her mean. The other woman spoke about the blessings
of a life that had taken some hard blows: her mother had killed herself
when she was a girl, her husband had died young. I happened to visit her
just after she'd been told that she had less than a year to live. She was
dry-eyed, and had been reading the Psalms. She was entirely realistic
about her illness and said to me, "The one thing that scares me is the
pain. I hope I die before I turn into an old bitch." I told her family that
story after the funeral, and they loved it; they could hear in it their
mother's voice, the way she really was.

The Reader's Presence

1. How is gossip generally characterized? How does Norris characterize it? What positive possibilities does it offer? Why is the etymology of the word important to her point?

2. How does Norris describe the small town she lives in? What does
   she reveal about it through the anecdotes she tells? What is her attitude toward the town? What is her idea of a suitable community? What sort of audience does her description seem to be aimed
   at? Is she, for example, writing mainly for her own community?

3. This piece is drawn from a book called *Dakota: A Spiritual Biography*. Norris uses many religious terms in the piece and calls gossip "holy." How might her conceptions of the sacred differ from
   conventional ones? How does Norris evoke her sense of the sacred
   for the reader?

THE WRITER AT WORK

Kathleen Norris and the Vocabulary of Religion

Although Kathleen Norris was born and remains a Protestant, she has writ-
ten extensively of Catholic monasticism and has even become a lay member of the
Benedictine Order. In the following passages from an interview with Notre Dame
professor and poet Sonia Gernes which appeared in Notre Dame *magazine (Au-*
tumn 1998), Norris discusses how important ancestral and religious roots can be
to one's writing. Norris acknowledges that many people today are uncomfortable
with a religious vocabulary, but she believes that facing those discomforts directly
can be a source of creative strength. You might consider some of the religious
words you personally think carry (as Norris says) "negative charges." Are you
embarrassed to use a religious vocabulary? How does Norris herself use such
terms in the interview as well as in the preceding essay, "The Holy Use of
Gossip?"

Gernes: In the mid-1970s, you were a young poet in New York City with connections to the literary world—on the fringe of the Andy Warhol scene, I think you said in one of the books—and you decided to move to a very small town in the Dakotas. I know that your family inherited some property from your grandmother, but aside from that, why did you make that decision?

Norris: It really was largely a family decision. I was the only one of my brother and two sisters who had a job that I could give up. I was the one who could go out there and help manage the ranch and live in the house in town and do all of that. I also had this sneaking suspicion that it would be good for me as a writer to back away from the literary hot house. All my friends were other writers, which was very common in that world, so this was an opportunity for a dramatic change and I thought: Well, we'll see what sorts out here. I also thought [about] getting back to my ancestral roots in a sense, because I had three generations going back in that little town in South Dakota. Partly it was almost a writing experiment—I had a feeling that it would jog some things in my writing. Obviously I was right about that, but I had no idea how right I would be of course.

Gernes: Did you have any inkling that you were not only going back to your roots as a writer but also back to your religious roots?

Norris: Not terribly. What happened—and it was not conscious on my part—was [that] the little Presbyterian church was the church where I had gone to Sunday school every summer when I was a child, so I was familiar with the congregation and I had always known the ministers because of my grandmother. So there was a natural progression toward having the ministers as social friends. I got involved with the church very early on, back in '74, but then it was really a sort of exercise in nostalgia; it didn't really take hold until about ten years later.

Gernes: In *Dakota,* you talk about a "monster God" that was part of   5 your grandmother Norris' Protestant heritage. I grew up—and still am— Catholic and was a very scrupulous child. I spent a fair amount of my childhood fearing that I was in mortal sin and would go straight to hell. It was interesting to me to see you talking about that in terms of Protestantism also. Could you say any more about that?

Norris: I think the concept of the "monster God" was really very important because in both Catholic and Protestant religions you can certainly find this. Sometimes when I am on talk shows with people calling in—and of course when you go on talk shows talking about religion, you are really putting your life into your own hands and going where angels would fear to tread—but sometimes we will get these calls from people who are so angry that someone is saying anything good at all about the Christian religion. They will talk about their own bad experiences, and of course they make that the measure of everything. Their bottom line is sometimes: How could God let these things happen? And they might mention the Holocaust or the death of one child. I began to realize that they really think that God *is* a monster—that God is causing these horrible things to happen to punish us or just because God is capricious. It's incredible to listen to these calls and try to respond because you really can't get into the depths of it, but that is what I am often hearing from people who want to talk about God. I think too many people get raised in religions with that kind of attitude, and maybe as adults you need to shed some of that and try to figure out what is really going on there.

Gernes: You've said that for about twenty years you did not attend church and put "nothing" down in the blanks where it asked for religion. Do you think you would be where you are today in terms of spirituality if there hadn't been this fallow period that let you start over?

Norris: I think for me it was necessary; even that is hard to know for sure. It was also the typical baby boomer thing—drifting away from religion. I didn't really even think about it that much, I just drifted away in my late teens when I went to college. I went to Bennington, which is an extremely secular environment, so there really wasn't anything [religious] on that campus. Arts and psychiatry had replaced religion. But I think in terms of developmental stages with religion, adolescents do need to shed some of their childish faith and childish religion in order to mature into an adult religion, adult faith. I think that is really the progression in my three books, and I think in a sense that is really what I have been writing about. For myself, ironically, that twenty-year hiatus seems to have been a necessary part of the process. It was during that twenty years, of course, that I became a writer, and now I feel that I have sort of come full circle. I am joining all the parts together of this puzzle because it was becoming a writer that allowed me to tell this story.

Gernes: In *Dakota,* you make a statement about doctrinal language slamming doors in your face and "words obscuring the *Word.*" Was that a motive force behind this "vocabulary of faith" book?

Norris: Oh, yes. I think I really began writing this book the minute I crossed over and decided to go to church on my own. The Presbyterian worship service was like this bombardment with words that I had a very dim memory of, maybe having studied them when I was twelve years old, but never really getting an existential grasp, a deeper meaning of what this word could mean. It took me a long time to work out [an] adult accommodation of a lot of the vocabulary. I think poetry and religion are both taught rather badly in our culture. When I was twelve years old I memorized a lot of words, but they didn't have any real depth or any real meaning or significance in my life. Of course now they do, and of course I am still running into people my own age who just assume that the doctrinal language doesn't mean anything. I think it's a real problem, because to educate young people in the Christian tradition you have to use those words—you can't jettison them. When you do that you end up with something very murky. But how to teach it is really very difficult.

10

Gernes: I want to ask about the interplay between poetry and spirituality in your life. Does one help feed the other?

Norris: Oh sure. One of the most amazing things that has happened to me as a writer was that after I had finished *Dakota* and survived my book tour, I went back to [the Ecumenical Institute at] Saint John's in Minnesota. I hadn't really been writing any poetry; because of *Dakota* I had really been focusing on prose. I showed up there in fall of '93 and literally, as soon as I began going to the daily liturgy with the monks—morning prayer, noon prayer, evening prayer and usually the Mass—these poems just started coming. I ended up that fall writing almost a whole new book of poems. It was really inspiring and many of my poems that came out during that time really were like a dialogue with the liturgy, with the liturgical readings, with the Psalms, with the homilies sometimes; I mean everything sort of one fabric. It was just an amazing period for me. I have never had a period like that as a writer. I don't know that I ever will again.

Gernes: You mention in the new book that feminist theology became important, that you read a lot of it for a period of time. How did that influence the development of your thought?

Norris: It was very exciting. I read hundreds and hundreds of books on feminist scholarship and then I started reading anti-feminist things, because I wanted to read a whole spectrum of this incredible ferment. This would have been in the early '80s, so I had a lot of catching up to do, and I just immersed myself in reading theology and biblical scholarship for a couple of years. I don't think that anybody gets very good biblical studies, biblical scholarship in Sunday school; I certainly didn't. We learned how to do origami and sing a lot. The singing was very important, but the substantive look at biblical criticism wasn't allowed, you see, and the kind of questions that I might have been interested in weren't allowed to be raised.

All of a sudden I am in my early thirties and finding that I am able to read all of this wonderful biblical interpretation, all this exciting stuff, but ultimately it became a problem for me. I think there is a certain stage of feminist anger that everyone goes through when you look at the history. You get so depressed and angry about what is going on in the tradition but also I think for myself it was a very dangerous overintellectualizing of religion. The reason that I wrote the book was to just tell my experience in this little town where most people really don't care much about theology. They care about the church and they care about religion and their faith is really important to them, but they don't think about theology. The only people that I really had to talk it over with were the ministers. Sometimes, some of the feminist critique became an obstacle to simply enjoying the community of this little church and the worship there. I really had to try to figure out what matters more.

I felt a little scared about [writing the feminist chapter] because I am really writing about my experience only and not trying to make judgments on anybody—the conservative side, the liberal side, or feminist or

15

anti-feminist. I will be interested to see what kind of reaction I get. I have already had women come up to me and say, "You are describing exactly what happened to me," which is always good to hear.

Gernes: In redefining the childhood terms of religion, you started fresh because of your twenty years away from church. What about people for whom some of those old words still carry negative charges but who have never really left the tradition? Any advice for those of us?

Norris: If words carry negative charges that usually means that there's some significant relationship there, and I think one of the worst things we do in American culture with anything negative is try to deny it or shove it aside. I think one of the more profound spiritual insights that I've gathered from the Benedictine tradition [is] that if you are angry with someone or you feel sharp pain over something, that's a significant relationship that you need to look into. It isn't something that you just have to say "isn't that too bad" or "isn't that terrible" or you find someone to blame. In fact, this was one of the things that led me back to church: examining why, the few times that I did go to church, I had such uncomfortable emotional responses. I could have simply stayed away and said, "Well, that makes me uncomfortable and I don't want to go." I learned to say, "No, it makes me *so* uncomfortable I better find out why." I think with a lot of negative things that's really a much more fruitful approach than simply walking away or denying or stewing in anger. The Christian vocabulary still has a lot of pretty scary words in it and words that are used in scary ways in the culture. I am not trying to write it off. I think it is one of the things with active faith — you have to keep re-defining these words for yourself and adding to your knowledge of them. I really had to immerse myself in the tradition.

When I hear people just dismiss an ancient word like dogma, without really having any idea of what it means, I go, "Wait a minute! This word has some really interesting history and a derivation and there are reasons why you have dogmas." One of the things that I found out working with the words [was] this volatile mixture of strong emotional reaction with an alarming amount of ignorance on my part. The minute I would look at the way that the word had been interpreted in Christian history, not necessarily in the 1950s Sunday school I went to, but in the Christian tradition, there was so much there that was livable and usable and a whole richer understanding. This whole book in a sense was my way of educating myself, or reeducating myself.

Gernes: One last thing: In *Amazing Grace,* you quote an Anglican monk as saying, "Ambivalence is a sacred emotion." I found that statement consoling because of the scene in the Bible where Jesus talks about people being lukewarm and says, "Because you are neither hot nor cold I will vomit you out of my mouth." Can you say anything more about what you learned from this monk in terms of ambivalence?

Norris: Well, I just loved it when he said ambivalence is a sacred emotion; it was such a strong statement in his monastery newsletter that I really latched onto it. One of my favorite passages, really, in theology, is Emily Dickinson saying, "I believe and disbelieve one hundred times in an hour which keeps believing nimble." That contending with doubt and ambivalence is one of the things that evidently kept her faith alive. In that sort of nice Protestant upbringing, doubts were negative, like having dirty hands. So you didn't want to admit to having doubts, and you wanted everything to be clean and nice, and nice and nice, you see. It doesn't work that way with religious faith.

67

Susan Orlean

The American Man at Age Ten

The journalist and essayist Susan Orlean (b. 1955) began her career writing for the Willamette Week *in Portland, Oregon, before moving to the* Boston Phoenix *and then to the* Boston Globe. *Her first book,* Red Sox, Bluefish, and Other Things That Make New England New England *(1987), collects the columns she published at the* Globe. *From 1987 to 1991, Orlean was a contributing editor at* Rolling Stone *magazine, and since 1987 she has been a staff writer at the* New Yorker. *"The American Man at Age Ten" appeared in* Esquire *in 1992. Her other books include,* Saturday Night *(1990), which describes the various activities and entertainments pursued by all kinds of Americans on their Saturday nights; and her most recent,* The Orchid Thief *(1998), examines the obsession with orchid growing.*

"For me the biggest step in the writing process," says Orlean, "is to peel away all of the expectations I brought to the story—all of the preconceptions about the subject or the person I'm writing about—and to really find in my heart what I felt like in the moment of reporting. You need to dig into yourself to find your true emotions and thoughts and responses to what you have seen and felt and experienced. . . . Writing is a process of unlearning expectations and paying attention to the genuineness of the moment. How you do that is to reconsider, rethink, recollect, and talk about what you are trying to say. Eventually the writing will emerge out of that—the real thread of truth."

If Colin Duffy and I were to get married, we would have matching superhero notebooks. We would wear shorts, big sneakers, and long, baggy T-shirts depicting famous athletes every single day, even in the winter. We would sleep in our clothes. We would both be good at Nintendo Street Fighter II, but Colin would be better than me. We would have some homework, but it would not be too hard and we would always have just finished it. We would eat pizza and candy for all of our meals. We wouldn't have sex, but we would have crushes on each other and, magically, babies would appear in our home. We would win the lottery and then buy land in Wyoming, where we would have one of every kind of cute animal. All the while, Colin would be working in law enforcement — probably the FBI. Our favorite movie star, Morgan Freeman, would visit us occasionally. We would listen to the same Eurythmics song ("Here Comes the Rain Again") over and over again and watch two hours of television every Friday night. We would both be good at football, have best friends, and know how to drive; we would cure AIDS and the garbage problem and everything that hurts animals. We would hand out a lot with Colin's dad. For fun, we would load a slingshot with dog food and shoot it at my butt. We would have a very good life.

Here are the particulars about Colin Duffy: He is ten years old, on the nose. He is four feet eight inches high, weighs seventy-five pounds, and appears to be mostly leg and shoulder blade. He is a handsome kid. He has a broad forehead, dark eyes with dense lashes, and a sharp, dimply smile. I have rarely seen him without a baseball cap. He owns several, but favors a University of Michigan Wolverines model, on account of its pleasing colors. The hat styles his hair into wild disarray. If you ever managed to get the hat off his head, you would see a boy with a nimbus of golden-brown hair, dented in the back, where the hat hits him.

Colin lives with his mother, Elaine; his father, Jim; his older sister, Megan; and his little brother, Chris, in a pretty pale-blue Victorian house on a bosky street in Glen Ridge, New Jersey. Glen Ridge is a serene and civilized old town twenty miles west of New York City. It does not have much of a commercial district, but it is a town of amazing lawns. Most of the houses were built around the turn of the century and are set back a gracious, green distance from the street. The rest of the town seems to consist of parks and playing fields and sidewalks and backyards — in other words, it is a far cry from South-Central Los Angeles and from Bedford-Stuyvesant and other, grimmer parts of the country where a very different ten-year-old American man is growing up today.

There is a fine school system in Glen Ridge, but Elaine and Jim, who are both schoolteachers, choose to send their children to a parents' cooperative elementary school in Montclair, a neighboring suburb. Currently, Colin is in fifth grade. He is a good student. He plans to go to college, to a place he says is called Oklahoma City State College University. OCSCU satisfies his desire to live out west, to attend a small college, and to study law enforcement, which OCSCU apparently offers as a major. After four years at Oklahoma City State College University, he plans to work for the FBI. He says that getting to be a police officer involves tons of hard work, but working for the FBI will be a cinch, because all you have to do is fill out one form, which he has already gotten from the head FBI office.

Colin is quiet in class but loud on the playground. He has a great throwing arm, significant foot speed, and a lot of physical confidence. He is also brave. Huge wild cats with rabies and gross stuff dripping from their teeth, which he says run rampant throughout his neighborhood, do not scare him. Otherwise, he is slightly bashful. This combination of athletic grace and valor and personal reserve accounts for considerable popularity. He has a fluid relationship to many social groups, including the superbright nerds, the ultrajocks, the flashy kids who will someday become extremely popular and socially successful juvenile delinquents, and the kids who will be elected president of the student body. In his opinion, the most popular boy in his class is Christian, who happens to be black, and Colin's favorite television character is Steve Urkel on *Family Matters,* who is black, too, but otherwise he seems uninterested in or oblivious to race. Until this year, he was a Boy Scout. Now he is planning to begin karate lessons. His favorite schoolyard game is football, followed closely by prison dodge ball, blob tag, and bombardo. He's crazy about athletes, although sometimes it isn't clear if he is absolutely sure of the difference between human athletes and Marvel Comics action figures. His current athletic hero is Dave Meggett. His current best friend is named Japeth. He used to have another best friend named Ozzie. According to Colin, Ozzie was found on a doorstep, then changed his name to Michael and moved to Massachusetts, and then Colin never saw him or heard from his again.

He has had other losses in his life. His is old enough to know people 5
who have died and to know things about the world that are worrisome. When he dreams, he dreams about moving to Wyoming, which he has visited with his family. His plan is to buy land there and have some sort of ranch that would definitely include horses. Sometimes when he talks about this, it sounds as ordinary and hard-boiled as a real estate appraisal; other times it can sound fantastical and wifty and achingly naive, informed by the last inklings of childhood—the musings of a balmy real estate appraiser assaying a wonderful and magical landscape that erodes from memory a little bit every day. The collision in his mind of what he understands, what he hears, what he figures out, what popular culture pours into him, what he knows, what he pretends to know, and what he imagines, makes an interesting mess. The mess often has the form of what he will probably think like when he is a grown man, but the content of what he is like as a little boy.

He is old enough to begin imagining that he will someday get married, but at ten he is still convinced that the best thing about being married will be that he will be allowed to sleep in his clothes. His father once observed that living with Colin was like living with a Martian who had done some reading on American culture. As it happens, Colin is not especially sad or worried about the prospect of growing up, although he sometimes frets over whether he should be called a kid or a grown-up; he has settled on the word *kid-up.* Once I asked him what the biggest advantage to adulthood will be, and he said, "The best thing is that grown-ups can go wherever they want." I asked him what he meant, exactly, and he said, "Well, if you're grown-up, you'd have a car, and whenever you felt like it, you could get into your car and drive somewhere and get candy."

Colin loves recycling. He loves it even more than, say, playing with little birds. That ten-year-olds feel the weight of the world and consider it their mission to shoulder it came as a surprise to me. I had gone with Colin one Monday to his classroom at Montclair Cooperative School. The Coop is in a steep, old, sharp-angled brick building that had served for many years as a public school until a group of parents in the area took it over and made it into a private, progressive elementary school. The fifth-grade classroom is on the top floor, under the dormers, which gives the room the eccentric shape and closeness of an attic. It is a rather informal environment. There are computers lined up in an adjoining room and instructions spelled out on the chalkboard—BRING IN: 1) A CUBBY WITH YOUR NAME ON IT, 2) A TRAPPER WITH A 5-POCKET ENVELOPE LABELED SCIENCE, SOCIAL STUDIES, READING/LANGUAGE ARTS, MATH, MATH LAB/COMPUTER; WHITE LINED PAPER; A PLASTIC PENCIL BAG; A SMALL HOMEWORK PAD, 3) LARGE BROWN GROCERY BAGS—but there is also a couch in the center of the classroom, which the kids take turns occupying, a rocking chair, and three canaries in cages near the door.

It happened to be Colin's first day in fifth grade. Before class began, there was a lot of horsing around, but there were also a lot of conversations about whether Magic Johnson had AIDS or just HIV and whether someone falling in a pool of blood from a cut of his would get the disease. These jolts of sobriety in the midst of rank goofiness are a ten-year-old's specialty. Each one comes as a fresh, hard surprise, like finding a razor blade in a candy apple. One day, Colin and I had been discussing horses or dogs or something, and out of the blue he said, "What do you think is better, to dump garbage in the ocean, to dump it on land, or to burn it?" Another time, he asked me if I planned to have children. I had just spent an evening with him and his friend Japeth, during which they put every small, movable object in the house into Japeth's slingshot and fired it at me, so I told him I wanted children but that I hoped they would all be girls, and he said, "Will you have an abortion if you find out you have a boy?"

At school, after discussing summer vacation, the kids began choosing the jobs they would do to help out around the classroom. Most of the jobs are humdrum—putting the chairs up on the tables, washing the chalkboard, turning the computers off or on. Five of the most humdrum tasks are recycling chores—for example, taking bottles or stacks of paper down to the basement, where they would be sorted and prepared for pickup. Two children would be assigned to feed the birds and cover their cages at the end of the day.

I expected the bird jobs to be the first to go. Everyone loved the birds;   10
they'd spent an hour that morning voting on names for them (Tweetie, Montgomery, and Rose narrowly beating out Axl Rose, Bugs, Ol' Yeller, Fido, Slim, Lucy, and Chirpie). Instead, they all wanted to recycle. The

recycling jobs were claimed by the first five kids called by Suzanne Naka-mura, the fifth-grade teacher; each kid called after that responded by groaning, "Suzanne, aren't there any more recycling jobs?" Colin ended up with the job of taking down the chairs each morning. He accepted the task with a sort of resignation—this was just going to be a job rather than a mission.

On the way home that day, I was quizzing Colin about his world views.

"Who's the coolest person in the world?"

"Morgan Freeman."

"What's the best sport?"

"Football."

"Who's the coolest woman?"

"None. I don't know."

"What's the most important thing in the world?"

"Game Boy." Pause. "No, the world. The world is the most impor-tant thing in the world."

Danny's Pizzeria is a dark little shop next door to the Montclair Co-operative School. It is not much to look at. Outside, the brick facing is painted muddy brown. Inside, there are some saggy counters, a splintered bench, and enough room for either six teenagers or about a dozen ten-year-olds who happen to be getting along well. The light is low. The air is oily. At Danny's, you will find pizza, candy, Nintendo, and very few girls. To a ten-year-old boy, it is the most beautiful place in the world.

One afternoon, after class was dismissed, we went to Danny's with Colin's friend Japeth to play Nintendo. Danny's has only one game, Street Fighter II Champion Edition. Some teenage boys from a nearby middle school had gotten there first and were standing in a tall, impene-trable thicket around the machine.

"Next game," Colin said. The teenagers ignored him.

"Hey, we get next game," Japeth said. He is smaller than Colin, scrappy, and, as he explained to me once, famous for wearing his hat back-ward all the time and having a huge wristwatch and a huge bedroom. He stamped his foot and announced again, "Hey, we get next game."

One of the teenagers turned around and said, "Fuck you, *next game,*" and then turned back to the machine.

"Whoa," Japeth said.

He and Colin went outside, where they felt bigger.

"Which street fighter are you going to be?" Colin asked Japeth.

"Blanka," Japeth said. "I know how to do his head-butt."

"I hate that! I hate the head-butt," Colin said. He dropped his voice a little and growled, "I'm going to be Ken, and I will kill you with my dragon punch."

"Yeah, right, and monkeys will fly out of my butt," Japeth said.

Street Fighter II is a video game in which two characters have an ex-plosive brawl in a scenic international setting. It is currently the most popular video-arcade game in America. This is not an insignificant amount of popularity. Most arcade versions of video games, which end up in pizza parlors, malls, and arcades, sell about two thousand units. So far, some fifty thousand Street Fighter II and Street Fighter II Championship Edition arcade games have been sold. Not since Pac-Man, which was released the year before Colin was born, has there been a video game as popular as Street Fighter. The home version of Street Fighter is the most popular home video game in the country, and that, too, is not an insignificant thing. Thirty-two million Nintendo home systems have been sold since 1986, when it was introduced in this country. There is a Nintendo system in seven of every ten homes in America in which a child between the ages of eight and twelve resides. By the time a boy in America turns ten, he will almost certainly have been exposed to Nintendo home games, Nintendo arcade games, and Game Boy, the hand-held version. He will probably own a system and dozens of games. By ten, according to Nintendo studies, teachers, and psychologists, game prowess becomes a fundamental, essential male social marker and a schoolyard boast.

The Street Fighter characters are Dhalsim, Ken, Guile, Blanka, E. Honda, Ryu, Zangief, and Chun Li. Each represents a different country, and they each have their own special weapon. Chun Li, for instance, is from China and possesses a devastating whirlwind kick that is triggered if you push the control pad down for two seconds and them up for two seconds, and then you hit the kick button. Chun Li's kick is money in the bank, because most of the other fighters do not have a good defense against it. By the way, Chun Li happens to be a girl—the only female Street Fighter character.

I asked Colin if he was interested in being Chun Li. There was a long pause. "I'd rather be Ken," he said.

The girls in Colin's class at school are named Cortnerd, Terror, Spacey, Lizard, Maggot, and Diarrhea. "They do have other names, but that's what we call them," Colin told me. "The girls aren't very popular."

"They are about as popular as a piece of dirt," Japeth said. "Or, you know that couch in the classroom? That couch is more popular than any girl. A thousand times more." They talked for a minute about one of the girls in their class, a tall blonde with cheerleader genetic material, who they allowed was not quite as gross as some of the other girls. Japeth said that a chubby, awkward boy in their class was boasting that this girl liked him.

"No way," Colin said. "She would never like him. I mean, not that he's so . . . I don't know. I don't hate him because he's fat, anyway. I hate him because he's nasty."

"Well, she doesn't like him," Japeth said. "She's been really mean to me lately, so I'm pretty sure she likes me."

"Girls are different," Colin said. He hopped up and down on the balls of his feet, wrinkling his nose. "Girls are stupid and weird."

"I have a lot of girlfriends, about six or so," Japeth said, turning contemplative. "I don't exactly remember their names, though."

The teenagers came crashing out of Danny's and jostled past us, so we went inside. The man who runs Danny's, whose name is Tom, was leaning across the counter on his elbows, looking exhausted. Two little boys, holding Slush Puppies, shuffled toward the Nintendo, but Colin and Japeth elbowed them aside and slammed their quarters down on the machine. The little boys shuffled back toward the counter and stood gawking at them, sucking on their drinks.

"You want to know how to tell if a girl likes you?" Japeth said. "She'll act really mean to you. That's a sure sign. I don't know why they do it, but it's always a sure sign. It gets your attention. You know how I show a girl I like her? I steal something from her and then run away. I do it to get their attention, and it works."

They played four quarters' worth of games. During the last one, a teenager with a quilted leather jacket and a fade haircut came in, pushed his arm between them, and put a quarter down on the deck of the machine.

Japeth said, "Hey, what's that?"

The teenager said, "I get next game. I've marked it now. Everyone knows this secret sign for next game. It's a universal thing."

"So now we know," Japeth said. "Colin, let's get out of here and go   45
bother Maggie. I mean Maggot. Okay?" They picked up their backpacks and headed out the door.

Psychologists identify ten as roughly the age at which many boys experience the gender-linked normative developmental trauma that leaves them, as adult men, at risk for specific psychological sequelae often manifest as deficits in the arenas of intimacy, empathy, and struggles with commitment in relationships. In other words, this is around the age when guys get screwed up about girls. Elaine and Jim Duffy, and probably most of the parents who send their kids to Montclair Cooperative School, have done a lot of stuff to try to avoid this. They gave Colin dolls as well as guns. (He preferred guns.) Japeth's father has three motorcycles and two dirt bikes but does most of the cooking and cleaning in their home. Suzanne, Colin's teacher, is careful to avoid sexist references in her presentations. After school, the yard at Montclair Cooperative is filled with as many fathers as mothers — fathers who hug their kids when they come prancing out of the building and are dismayed when their sons clamor for Supersoaker water guns and war toys or take pleasure in beating up girls.

In a study of adolescents conducted by the Gesell Institute of Human Development, nearly half the ten-year-old boys questioned said they thought they had inadequate information about sex. Nevertheless, most ten-year-old boys across the country are subjected to a few months of sex education in school. Colin and his class will get their dose next spring. It is yet another installment in a plan to make them into new, improved men with reconstructed notions of sex and male-female relationships. One afternoon I asked Philip, a schoolmate of Colin's, whether he was looking forward to sex education, and he said, "No, because I think it'll probably make me really, really hyper. I have a feeling it's going to be just like what it was like when some television reporters came to school last year and filmed us in class and I got really hyper. They stood around with all these cameras and asked us questions. I think that's what sex education is probably like."

At a class meeting earlier in the day:

Suzanne: "Today was our first swimming class, and I have one observation to make. The girls went to their locker room, got dressed without a lot of fuss, and came into the pool area. The boys, on the other hand, the *boys* had some sort of problem doing that rather simple task. Can someone tell me exactly what went on in the locker room?"

Keith: "There was a lot of shouting." 50

Suzanne: "Okay, I hear you saying that people were being noisy and shouting. Anything else?"

Christian: "Some people were screaming so much that my ears were killing me. It gave me, like, a huge headache. Also, some of the boys were taking their towels, I mean, after they had taken their clothes off, they had their towels around their waists and then they would drop them really fast and then pull them back up, really fast."

Suzanne: "Okay, you're saying some people were being silly about their bodies."

Christian: "Well, yeah, but it was more like they were being silly about their pants."

Colin's bedroom is decorated simply. He has a cage with his pet parakeet, Dude, on his dresser, a lot of recently worn clothing piled haphazardly on the floor, and a husky brown teddy bear sitting upright in a chair near the foot of his bed. The walls are mostly bare, except for a Spiderman poster and a few ads torn out of magazines he has thumbtacked up. One of the ads is for a cologne, illustrated with several small photographs of cowboy hats; another, a feverish portrait of a woman on a horse, is an ad for blue jeans. These inspire him sometimes when he lies in bed and makes plans for the move to Wyoming. Also, he happens to like ads. He also likes television commercials. Generally speaking, he likes consumer products and popular culture. He partakes avidly but not indiscriminately. In fact, during the time we spent together, he provided a running commentary on merchandise, media, and entertainment: 55

"The only shoes anyone will wear are Reebok Pumps. Big T-shirts are cool, not the kind that are sticky and close to you, but big and baggy and long, not the kind that stop at your stomach."

"The best food is Chicken McNuggets and Life cereal and Frosted Flakes."

"Don't go to Blimpie's. They have the worst service."

"I'm not into Teenage Mutant Ninja Turtles anymore. I grew out of that. I like Donatello, but I'm not a fan. I don't buy the figures anymore."

"The best television shows are on Friday night on ABC. It's called 60 TGIF, and it's *Family Matters, Step by Step, Dinosaurs,* and *Perfect Strangers,* where the guy has a funny accent."

"The best candy is Skittles and Symphony bars and Crybabies and Warheads. Crybabies are great because if you eat a lot of them at once you feel so sour."

"Hyundais are Korean cars. It's the only Korean car. They're not that good because Koreans don't have a lot of experience building cars."

"The best movie is *City Slickers,* and the best part was when he saved his little cow in the river."

"The Giants really need to get rid of Ray Handley. They have to get somebody who has real coaching experience. He's just no good."

"My dog, Sally, costs seventy-two dollars. That sounds like a lot of   65
money but it's a really good price because you get a flea bath with your dog."

"The best magazines are *Nintendo Power,* because they tell you how to do the secret moves in the video games, and also *Mad* magazine and *Money Guide*—I really like that one."

"The best artist in the world is Jim Davis."

"The most beautiful woman in the world is not Madonna! Only Wayne and Garth think that! She looks like maybe a . . . a . . . slut or something. Cindy Crawford looks like she would look good, but if you see her on an awards program on TV she doesn't look that good. I think the most beautiful woman in the world probably is my mom."

Colin thinks a lot about money. This started when he was about nine and a half, which is when a lot of other things started—a new way of walking that has a little macho hitch and swagger, a decision about the Teenage Mutant Ninja Turtles (con) and Eurythmics (pro), and a persistent curiosity about a certain girl whose name he will not reveal. He knows the price of everything he encounters. He knows how much college costs and what someone might earn performing different jobs. Once, he asked me what my husband did; when I answered that he was a lawyer, he snapped, "You must be a rich family. Lawyers make $400,000 a year." His preoccupation with money baffles his family. They are not struggling, so this is not the anxiety of deprivation; they are not rich, so his is not responding to an elegant, advantaged world. His allowance is five dollars a week. It seems sufficient for his needs, which consist chiefly of quarters for Nintendo and candy money. The remainder is put into his Wyoming fund. His fascination is not just specific to needing money or having plans for money: It is as if money itself, and the way it makes the world work, and the realization that almost everything in the world can be assigned a price, has possessed him. "I just pay attention to things like that," Colin says. "It's really very interesting."

He is looking for a windfall. He tells me his mother has been notified   70
that she is in the fourth and final round of the Publisher's Clearinghouse Sweepstakes. This is not an ironic observation. He plays the New Jersey lottery every Thursday night. He knows the weekly jackpot; he knows the number to call to find out if he has won. I do not think this presages a future for Colin as a high-stakes gambler; I think it says more about the

powerful grasp that money has on imagination and what a large percent-age of a ten-year-old's mind is made up of imaginings. One Friday, we were at school together, and one of his friends was asking him about the lottery, and he said, "This week it was $4 million. That would be I forget how much every year for the rest of your life. It's a lot, I think. You should play. All it takes is a dollar and a dream."

Until the lottery comes through and he starts putting together the Wyoming land deal, Colin can be found most of the time in the backyard. Often, he will have friends come over. Regularly, children from the neigh-borhood will gravitate to the backyard, too. As a technical matter of real-property law, title to the house and yard belongs to Jim and Elaine Duffy, but Colin adversely possess the backyard, at least from 4:00 each after-noon until it gets dark. As yet, the fixtures of teenage life — malls, video arcades, friends' basements, automobiles — either hold little interest for him or are not his to have.

He is, at the moment, very content with his backyard. For most in-tents and purposes, it is as big as Wyoming. One day, certainly, he will grow and it will shrink, and it will become simply a suburban backyard and it won't be big enough for him anymore. This will happen so fast that one night he will be in the backyard, believing it a perfect place, and by the next night he will have changed and the yard as he imagined it will be gone, and this era of his life will be behind him forever.

Most days, he spends hours in the backyard building an Evil Spider-Web Trap. This entails running a spool of Jim's fishing line from every surface in the yard until it forms a huge web. Once a garbageman picking up the Duffy's trash got caught in the trap. Otherwise, the Evil Spider-Web Trap mostly has a deterrent effect, because the kids in the neighbor-hood who might roam over know that Colin builds it back there. "I do it all the time," he says. "First I plan who I'd like to catch in it, and then we get started. Trespassers have to beware."

One afternoon when I came over for a few rounds of Street Fighter at Danny's, Colin started building a trap. He selected a victim for inspira-tion — a boy in his class who had been pestering him — and began wrap-ping. He was entirely absorbed. He moved from tree to tree, wrapping; he laced fishing line through the railing of the deck and then back to the shed; he circled an old jungle gym, something he'd outgrown and aban-doned a few years ago, and then crossed over to a bush at the back of the yard. Briefly, he contemplated making his dog, Sally, part of the web. Dusk fell. He kept wrapping, paying out fishing line an inch at a time. We could hear mothers up and down the block hooting for their kids; two tiny children from next door stood transfixed at the edge of the yard, un-certain whether they would end up inside or outside the web. After a while, the spool spun around in Colin's hands one more time and then stopped; he was out of line.

It was almost too dark to see much of anything, although now and again the light from the deck would glance off a length of line, and it would glint and sparkle. "That's the point," he said. "You could do it with thread, but the fishing line is invisible. Now I have this perfect thing and the only one who knows about it is me." With that, he dropped the spool, skipped up the stairs of the deck, threw open the screen door, and then bounded into the house, leaving me and Sally the dog trapped in his web.

The Reader's Presence

1. Orlean begins the essay with a description of what life would be like if she and Colin Duffy got married. From whose perspective is she writing? How does this introduction set the tone for the rest of the essay?

2. Consider the role of gender in the essay. Do you think it makes any difference that the author is a woman? How might her tone and approach be different if Orlean had once been a ten-year-old boy? Why do you think she chose to title the essay "The American *Man* at Age Ten" rather than "The American *Boy* at Age Ten"? What is Orlean trying to say about the way that men learn cultural attitudes and beliefs?

3. By most standards, Colin Duffy's life is relatively privileged. How does Orlean acknowledge this fact? Is she presenting Colin as a representative ten-year-old boy? Which elements of his life do you see as universal, and which are specific to his situation?

68

George Orwell

Politics and the English Language

During his lifetime, George Orwell was well known for the political positions he laid out in his essays. The events that inspired Orwell to write his essays have long since passed, but his writing continues to be read and enjoyed. Orwell demonstrates that political writing need not be narrowly topical—it can speak to enduring issues and concerns. He suggested as much in 1946 when he wrote, "What I have most wanted to do throughout the past ten years is to make political writing into an art. My starting point is always a feeling of partisanship, a feeling of injustice. . . . But I could not do the work of writing a book, or even a long magazine article, if it were not also an aesthetic experience." "Politics and the English Language" appears in Shooting an Elephant and Other Essays *(1950).*

For more information about Orwell, see page 200.

Most people who bother with the matter at all would admit that the English language is in a bad way, but it is generally assumed that we cannot by conscious action do anything about it. Our civilization is decadent and our language—so that argument runs—must inevitably share in the general collapse. It follows that any struggle against the abuse of language is a sentimental archaism, like preferring candles to electric light or hansom cabs to airplanes. Underneath this lies the half-conscious belief that language is a natural growth and not an instrument which we shape for our own purposes.

Now, it is clear that the decline of a language must ultimately have political and economic causes: It is not due simply to the bad influence of this or that individual writer. But an effect can become a cause, reinforcing the original cause and producing the same effect in an intensified form, and so on indefinitely. A man may take to drink because he feels himself to be a failure, and then fail all the more completely because he drinks. It is rather the same thing that is happening to the English language. It becomes ugly and inaccurate because our thoughts are foolish, but the slovenliness of our language makes it easier for us to have foolish thoughts. The point is that the process is reversible. Modern English, especially written English, is full of bad habits which spread by imitation and which can be avoided if one is willing to take the necessary trouble. If one gets rid of these habits one can think more clearly, and to think clearly is a necessary first step towards political regeneration: so that the fight against bad English is not frivolous and is not the exclusive concern of professional writers. I will come back to this presently, and I hope that by that time the meaning of what I have said here will have become clearer. Meanwhile, here are five specimens of the English language as it is now habitually written.

These five passages have not been picked out because they are especially bad—I could have quoted far worse if I had chosen—but because they illustrate various of the mental vices from which we now suffer. They are a little below the average, but are fairly representative samples. I number them so that I can refer back to them when necessary:

(1) I am not, indeed, sure whether it is true to say that the Milton who once seemed not unlike a seventeenth-century Shelley had not become, out of an experience ever more bitter in each year, more alien [*sic*] to the founder of that Jesuit sect which nothing could induce him to tolerate.
Professor Harold Laski (Essay in *Freedom of Expression*).

(2) Above all, we cannot play ducks and drakes with a native battery of idioms which prescribes such egregious collections of vocals as the Basic *put up with* for *tolerate* or *put at a loss* for *bewilder*.
Professor Lancelot Hogben (*Interglossa*).

(3) On the one side we have the free personality: By definition it is not neurotic, for it has neither conflict nor dream. Its desires, such as they are, are transparent, for they are just what institutional approval keeps in the forefront of consciousness; another institutional pattern would

alter their number and intensity; there is little in them that is natural, ir-reducible, or culturally dangerous. But *on the other side,* the social bond itself is nothing but the mutual reflection of these self-secure intergities. Recall the definition of love. Is not this the very picture of a small acade-mic? Where is there a place in this hall of mirrors for either personality or fraternity?

> Essay on psychology in *Politics* (New York).

(4) All the "best people" from the gentlemen's clubs, and all the frantic fascist captains, united in common hatred of Socialism and bestial hor-ror of the rising tide of the mass revolutionary movement, have turned to acts of provocation, to foul incendiarism, to medieval legends of poi-soned wells, to legalize their own destruction of proletarian organiza-tions, and rouse the agitated petty-bourgeoisie to chauvinistic fervor on behalf of the fight against the revolutionary way out of the crisis.

> Communist pamphlet.

(5) If a new spirit *is* to be infused into this old country, there is one thorny and contentious reform which must be tackled, and that is the humanization and galvanization of the B.B.C. Timidity here will bespeak cancer and atrophy of the soul. The heart of Britain may be sound and of strong beat, for instance, but the British lion's roar at present is like that of Bottom in Shakespeare's *Midsummer Night's Dream*—as gentle as any sucking dove. A virile new Britain cannot continue indefinitely to be traduced in the eyes or rather ears, of the world by the effete languors of Langham Place, brazenly masquerading as "standard English." When the Voice of Britain is heard at nine o'clock, better far and infinitely less ludicrous to hear aitches honestly dropped than the present priggish, in-flated, inhibited, school-ma'amish arch braying of blameless bashful mewing maidens!

> Letter in *Tribune.*

Each of these passages has faults of its own, but, quite apart from avoidable ugliness, two qualities are common to all of them. The first is staleness of imagery: The other is lack of precision. The writer either has a meaning and cannot express it, or he inadvertently says something else, or he is almost indifferent as to whether his words mean anything or not. This mixture of vagueness and sheer incompetence is the most marked characteristic of modern English prose, and especially of any kind of po-litical writing. As soon as certain topics are raised, the concrete melts into the abstract and no one seems able to think of turns of speech that are not hackneyed: Prose consists less and less of *words* chosen for the sake of their meaning, and more and more of *phrases* tacked together like the sec-tions of a prefabricated hen-house. I list below, with notes and examples, various of the tricks by means of which the work of prose-construction is habitually dodged:

Dying Metaphors. A newly invented metaphor assists thought by   5
evoking a visual image, while on the other hand a metaphor which is technically "dead" (e.g., *iron resolution*) has in effect reverted to being an

ordinary word and can generally be used without loss of vividness. But in between these two classes there is a huge dump of worn-out metaphors which have lost all evocative power and are merely used because they save people the trouble of inventing phrases for themselves. Examples are: *Ring the changes on, take up the cudgels for, toe the line, ride roughshod over, stand shoulder to shoulder with, play into the hands of, no axe to grind, grist to the mill, fishing in troubled waters, rift within the lute, on the order of the day, Achilles' heel, swan song, hotbed.* Many of these are used without knowledge of their meaning (what is a "rift," for instance?), and incompatible metaphors are frequently mixed, a sure sign that the writer is not interested in what he is saying. Some metaphors now current have been twisted out of their original meaning without those who use them even being aware of the fact. For example, *toe the line* is sometimes written *tow the line.* Another example is *the hammer and the anvil,* now always used with the implication that the anvil gets the worst of it. In real life it is always the anvil that breaks the hammer, never the other way about: A writer who stopped to think what he was saying would be aware of this, and would avoid perverting the original phrase.

Operators or Verbal False Limbs. These save the trouble of picking out appropriate verbs and nouns, and at the same time pad each sentence with extra syllables which give it an appearance of symmetry. Characteristic phrases are *render inoperative, militate against, make contact with, be subjected to, give rise to, give grounds for, have the effect of, play a leading part (role) in, make itself felt, take effect, exhibit a tendency to, serve the purpose of, etc., etc.* The keynote is the elimination of simple verbs. Instead of being a single word, such as *break, stop, spoil, mend, kill,* a verb becomes a *phrase,* made up of a noun or adjective tacked on to some general-purpose verb such as *prove, serve, form, play, render.* In addition, the passive voice is wherever possible used in preference to the active, and noun constructions are used instead of gerunds (*by examination of* instead of *by examining*). The range of verbs is further cut down by means of the *-ize* and *de-* formation, and the banal statements are given an appearance of profundity by means of the *not un-* formation. Simple conjunctions and prepositions are replaced by such phrases as *with respect to, having regard to, the fact that, by dint of, in view of, in the interests of, on the hypothesis that;* and the ends of sentences are saved from anticlimax by such resounding commonplaces as *greatly to be desired, cannot be left out of account, a development to be expected in the near future, deserving of serious consideration, brought to a satisfactory conclusion,* and so on and so forth.

Pretentious Diction. Words like *phenomenon, element, individual* (as noun), *objective, categorical, effective, virtual, basic, primary, promote, constitute, exhibit, exploit, utilize, eliminate, liquidate,* are used to dress up simple statements and give an air of scientific impartiality to biased judgments. Adjectives like *epoch-making, epic, historic, unforgettable, triumphant, age-old, inevitable, inexorable, veritable,* are used to dignify the sordid processes of international politics, while writing that aims at glorifying war usually takes on an archaic color, its characteristic words being; *realm, throne, chariot, mailed fist, trident, sword, shield, buckler, banner, jackboot, clarion.* Foreign words and expressions such as *cul de sac, ancien régime, deus ex machina, mutatis mutandis, status quo, gleichschaltung, weltanschauung,* are used to give an air of culture and elegance. Except for the useful abbreviations *i.e., e.g.,* and *etc.,* there is no real need for any of the hundreds of foreign phrases now current in English. Bad writers, and especially scientific, political, and sociological writers, are nearly always haunted by the notion that Latin or Greek words are grander than Saxon ones, and unnecessary words like *expedite, ameliorate, predict, extraneous, deracinated, clandestine, subaqueous,* and hundreds of others constantly gain ground from their Anglo-Saxon opposite numbers.[1] The jargon peculiar to Marxist writing (*hyena, hangman, cannibal, petty bourgeois, these gentry, lackey, flunkey, mad dog, White Guard, etc.*) consists largely of words and phrases translated from Russian, German, or French; but the normal way of coining a new word is to use a Latin or Greek root with the appropriate affix and, where necessary, the *-ize* formation. It is often easier to make up words of this kind (*deregionalize, impermissible, extramarital, nonfragmentary,* and so forth) than to think up the English words that will cover one's meaning. The result, in general, is an increase in slovenliness and vagueness.

Meaningless Words. In certain kinds of writing, particularly in art criticism and literary criticism, it is normal to come across long passages which are almost completely lacking in meaning.[2] Words like *romantic, plastic, values, human, dead, sentimental, natural, vitality,* as used in art criticism, are strictly meaningless, in the sense that they not only do not point to any discoverable object, but are hardly ever expected to do so by the reader. When one critic writes, "The outstanding feature of Mr. X's work is its living quality," while another writes, "The immediately striking thing about Mr. X's work is its peculiar deadness," the reader accepts this as a simple difference of opinion. If words like *black* and *white* were involved, instead of the jargon words *dead* and *living,* he would see at once that language was being used in an improper way. Many political

---

[1] An interesting illustration of this is the way in which the English flower names which were in use till very recently are being ousted by Greek ones, *snapdragon* becoming *antirrhinum, forget-me-not* becoming *myosotis,* etc. It is hard to see any practical reason for this change of fashion: It is probably due to an instinctive turning away from the more homely word and a vague feeling that the Greek word is scientific. — ORWELL'S NOTE.

[2] Example: "Comfort's catholicity of perception and image, strangely Whitmanesque in range, almost the exact opposite in aesthetic compulsion, continues to evoke that trembling atmospheric accumulative hinting at a cruel, an inexorably serene timelessness. . . . Wrey Gardiner scores by aiming at simple bull's-eyes with precision. Only they are not so simple, and through this contented sadness runs more than the surface bitter-sweet of resignation." (*Poetry Quarterly.*) — ORWELL'S NOTE.

words are similarly abused. The word *Fascism* has now no meaning except in so far as it signifies "something not desirable." The words *democracy, socialism, freedom, patriotic, realistic, justice,* have each of them several different meanings which cannot be reconciled with one another. In the case of a word like *democracy,* not only is there no agreed definition, but the attempt to make one is resisted from all sides. It is almost universally felt that when we call a country democratic we are praising it: Consequently the defenders of every kind of regime claim that it is a democracy, and fear that they might have to stop using the word if it were tied down to any one meaning. Words of this kind are often used in a consciously dishonest way. That is, the person who uses them has his own private definition, but allows his hearer to think he means something quite different. Statements like *Marshal Pétain[3] was a true patriot, The Soviet Press is the freest in the world, The Catholic Church is opposed to persecution,* are almost always made with intent to deceive. Other words used in variable meanings, in most cases more or less dishonestly, are: *class, totalitarian, science, progressive, reactionary, bourgeois, equality.*

Now that I have made this catalogue of swindles and perversions, let me give another example of the kind of writing that they lead to. This time it must of its nature be an imaginary one. I am going to translate a passage of good English into modern English of the worst sort. Here is a well-known verse from *Ecclesiastes:*

> I returned and saw under the sun, that the race is not to the swift, nor the battle to the strong, neither yet bread to the wise, nor yet riches to men of understanding, nor yet favor to men of skill; but time and chance happeneth to them all.

Here it is in modern English:

> Objective consideration of contemporary phenomena compels the conclusion that success or failure in competitive activities exhibits no tendency to be commensurate with innate capacity, but that a considerable element of the unpredictable must invariably be taken into account.

This is a parody, but not a very gross one. Exhibit (3), above, for instance, contains several patches of the same kind of English. It will be seen that I have not made a full translation. The beginning and ending of the sentence follow the original meaning fairly closely, but in the middle the concrete illustrations—race, battle, bread—dissolve into the vague phrase "success or failure in competitive activities." This had to be so, because no modern writer of the kind I am discussing—no one capable of

10

---

[3]*Pétain:* Henry Philippe Pétain was a World War I French military hero who served as chief of state in France from 1940 to 1945, after France surrendered to Germany. A controversial figure, Pétain was regarded by some to be a patriot who had sacrificed himself for his country, while others considered him to be a traitor. He was sentenced to life imprisonment in 1945, the year before Orwell wrote his essay.—EDS.

using phrases like "objective consideration of contemporary phenomena"—would ever tabulate his thoughts in that precise and detailed way. The whole tendency of modern prose is away from concreteness. Now analyze these two sentences a little more closely. The first contains forty-nine words but only sixty syllables, and all its words are those of everyday life. The second contains thirty-eight words of ninety syllables: Eighteen of its words are from Latin roots, and one from Greek. The first sentence contains six vivid images, and only one phrase ("time and chance") that could be called vague. The second contains not a single fresh, arresting phrase, and in spite of its ninety syllables it gives only a shortened version of the meaning contained in the first. Yet without a doubt it is the second kind of sentence that is gaining ground in modern English. I do not want to exaggerate. This kind of writing is not yet universal, and outcrops of simplicity will occur here and there in the worst-written page. Still, if you or I were told to write a few lines on the uncertainty of human fortunes, we should probably come much nearer to my imaginary sentences than to the one from *Ecclesiastes*.

As I have tried to show, modern writing at its worst does not consist in picking out words for the sake of their meaning and inventing images in order to make the meaning clearer. It consists in gumming together long strips of words which have already been set in order by someone else, and making the results presentable by sheer humbug. The attraction of this way of writing is that it is easy. It is easier—even quicker once you have the habit—to say *In my opinion it is a not unjustifiable assumption that* than to say *I think*. If you use ready-made phrases, you not only don't have to hunt about for words; you also don't have to bother with the rhythms of your sentences, since these phrases are generally so arranged as to be more or less euphonious. When you are composing in a hurry—when you are dictating to a stenographer, for instance, or making a public speech—it is natural to fall into a pretentious, Latinized style. Tags like *a consideration which we should do well to bear in mind* or *a conclusion to which all of us would readily assent* will save many a sentence from coming down with a bump. By using stale metaphors, similes, and idioms, you save much mental effort, at the cost of leaving your meaning vague, not only for your reader but for yourself. This is the significance of mixed metaphors. The sole aim of a metaphor is to call up a visual image. When these images clash—as in *The Fascist octopus has sung its swan song, the jackboot is thrown into the melting pot*—it can be taken as certain that the writer is not seeing a mental image of the objects he is naming; in other words he is not really thinking. Look again at the examples I gave at the beginning of this essay. Professor Laski (1) uses five negatives in fifty-three words. One of these is superfluous, making nonsense of the whole passage, and in addition there is the slip—*alien* for akin—making further nonsense, and several avoidable pieces of clumsiness which increase the general vagueness. Professor Hogben (2) plays ducks and drakes with a battery which is able to write prescriptions, and, while disapproving of the everyday phrase *put up with,* is unwilling to look *egregious* up in the dictionary and see what it means; (3), if one takes an uncharitable attitude towards it, is simply meaningless: Probably one could work out its intended meaning by reading the whole of the article in which it occurs. In (4), the writer knows more or less what he wants to say, but an accumulation of stale phrases chokes him like tea leaves blocking a sink. In (5), words and meaning have almost parted company. People who write in this manner usually have a general emotional meaning—they dislike one thing and want to express solidarity with another—but they are not interested in the detail of what they are saying. A scrupulous writer, in every sentence that he writes, will ask himself at least four questions, thus: What am I trying to say? What words will express it? What image or idiom will make it clearer? Is this image fresh enough to have an effect? And he will probably ask himself two more: Could I put it more shortly? Have I said anything that is avoidably ugly? But you are not obliged to go to all this trouble. You can shirk it by simply throwing your mind open and letting the ready-made phrases come crowding in. They will construct your sentences for you—even think your thoughts for you, to a certain extent—and at need they will perform the important service of partially concealing your meaning even from yourself. It is at this point that the special connection between politics and the debasement of language becomes clear.

In our time it is broadly true that political writing is bad writing. Where it is not true, it will generally be found that the writer is some kind of rebel, expressing his private opinions and not a "party line." Orthodoxy, of whatever color, seems to demand a lifeless, imitative style. The political dialects to be found in pamphlets, leading articles, manifestos, White Papers, and the speeches of under-secretaries do, of course, vary from party to party, but they are all alike in that one almost never finds in them a fresh, vivid, home-made turn of speech. When one watches some tired hack on the platform mechanically repeating the familiar phrases— *bestial atrocities, iron heel, bloodstained tyranny, free peoples of the world, stand shoulder to shoulder*—one often has a curious feeling that one is not watching a live human being but some kind of dummy: a feeling which suddenly becomes stronger at moments when the light catches the speaker's spectacles and turns them into blank discs which seem to have no eyes behind them. And this is not altogether fanciful. A speaker who uses that kind of phraseology has gone some distance towards turning himself into a machine. The appropriate noises are coming out of his larynx, but his brain is not involved as it would be if he were choosing his words for himself. If the speech he is making is one that he is accustomed to make over and over again, he may be almost unconscious of what he is saying, as one is when one utters the responses in church. And this reduced state of consciousness, if not indispensable, is at any rate favorable to political conformity.

In our time, political speech and writing are largely the defense of the indefensible. Things like the continuance of British rule in India, the Russian purges and deportations, the dropping of the atom bombs on Japan, can indeed be defended, but only by arguments which are too brutal for most people to face, and which do not square with the professed aims of political parties. Thus political language has to consist largely of euphemism, question-begging, and sheer cloudy vagueness. Defenseless villages are bombarded from the air, the inhabitants driven out into the countryside, the cattle machine-gunned, the huts set on fire with incendiary bullets: This is called *pacification*. Millions of peasants are robbed of their farms and sent trudging along the roads with no more than they can carry: This is called *transfer of population* or *rectification of frontiers*. People are imprisoned for years without trial, or shot in the back of the neck or sent to die of scurvy in Arctic lumber camps:[4] This is called *elimination of unreliable elements*. Such phraseology is needed if one wants to name things without calling up mental pictures of them. Consider for instance some comfortable English professor defending Russian totalitarianism. He cannot say outright, "I believe in killing off your opponents when you get good results by doing so." Probably, therefore, he will say something like this:

"While freely conceding that the Soviet régime exhibits certain features which the humanitarian may be inclined to deplore, we must, I think, agree that a certain curtailment of the right to political opposition is an unavoidable concomitant of transitional periods, and that the rigors which the Russian people have been called upon to undergo have been amply justified in the sphere of concrete achievement."

The inflated style is itself a kind of euphemism. A mass of Latin   15
words falls upon the facts like soft snow, blurring the outlines and covering up all the details. The great enemy of clear language is insincerity. When there is a gap between one's real and one's declared aims, one turns as it were instinctively to long words and exhausted idioms, like a cuttlefish squirting out ink. In our age there is no such thing as "keeping out of politics." All issues are political issues, and politics itself is a mass of lies, evasions, folly, hatred, and schizophrenia. When the general atmosphere is bad, language must suffer. I should expect to find—this is a guess which I have not sufficient knowledge to verify—that the German, Russian, and Italian languages have all deteriorated in the last ten or fifteen years, as a result of dictatorship.

But if thought corrupts language, language can also corrupt thought. A bad usage can spread by tradition and imitation, even among people who should and do know better. The debased language that I have been discussing is in some ways very convenient. Phrases like *a not unjustifiable assumption, leaves much to be desired, would serve no good purpose, a consideration which we should do well to bear in mind,* are a continuous temptation, a packet of aspirins always at one's elbow. Look back through this essay, and for certain you will find that I have again

---

[4]*People . . . camps:* Though Orwell is decrying all totalitarian abuse of language, his examples are mainly pointed at the Soviet purges under Stalin.—EDS.

and again committed the very faults I am protesting against. By this morning's post I have received a pamphlet dealing with conditions in Germany. The author tells me that he "felt impelled" to write it. I open it at random, and here is almost the first sentence that I see: "(The Allies) have an opportunity not only of achieving a radical transformation of Germany's social and political structure in such a way as to avoid a nationalistic reaction in Germany itself, but at the same time of laying the foundations of a co-operative and unified Europe." You see, he "feels impelled" to write—feels, presumably, that he has something new to say—and yet his words, like cavalry horses answering the bugle, group themselves automatically into the familiar dreary pattern. The invasion of one's mind by ready-made phrases (*lay the foundations, achieve a radical transformation*) can only be prevented if one is constantly on guard against them, and every such phrase anaesthetizes a portion of one's brain.

I said earlier that the decadence of our language is probably curable. Those who deny this would argue, if they produced an argument at all, that language merely reflects existing social conditions, and that we cannot influence its development by any direct tinkering with words and constructions. So far as the general tone or spirit of a language goes, this may be true, but it is not true in detail. Silly words and expressions have often disappeared, not through any evolutionary process but owing to the conscious action of a minority. Two recent examples were *explore every avenue* and *leave no stone unturned,* which were killed by the jeers of a few journalists. There is a long list of flyblown metaphors which could similarly be got rid of if enough people would interest themselves in the jobs; and it should also be possible to laugh the *not un-* formation out of existence,[5] to reduce the amount of Latin and Greek in the average sentence, to drive out foreign phrases and strayed scientific words, and, in general, to make pretentiousness unfashionable. But all these are minor points. The defense of the English language implies more than this, and perhaps it is best to start by saying what it does *not* imply.

To begin with it has nothing to do with archaism, with the salvaging of obsolete words and turns of speech, or with the setting up of a "standard English" which must never be departed from. On the contrary, it is especially concerned with the scrapping of every word or idiom which has outworn its usefulness. It has nothing to do with correct grammar and syntax, which are of no importance so long as one makes one's meaning clear, or with the avoidance of Americanisms, or with having what is called a "good prose style." On the other hand it is not concerned with fake simplicity and the attempt to make written English colloquial. Nor does it even imply in every case preferring the Saxon word to the Latin one, though it does imply using the fewest and shortest words that will cover one's meaning. What is above all needed is to let the meaning

---

[5]One can cure oneself of the *not un-* formation by memorizing this sentence: *A not unblack dog was chasing a not unsmall rabbit across a not ungreen field.*—ORWELL'S NOTE.

choose the word, and not the other way about. In prose, the worst thing one can do with words is to surrender to them. When you think of a concrete object, you think wordlessly, and then, if you want to describe the thing you have been visualizing you probably hunt about till you find the exact words that seem to fit. When you think of something abstract you are more inclined to use words from the start, and unless you make a conscious effort to prevent it, the existing dialect will come rushing in and do the job for you, at the expense of blurring or even changing your meaning. Probably it is better to put off using words as long as possible and get one's meaning as clear as one can through pictures or sensations. Afterwards one can choose—not simply *accept*—the phrases that will best cover the meaning, and then switch round and decide what impression one's words are likely to make on another person. This last effort of the mind cuts out all stale or mixed images, all prefabricated phrases, needless repetitions, and humbug and vagueness generally. But one can often be in doubt about the effect of a word or a phrase, and one needs rules that one can rely on when instinct fails. I think the following rules will cover most cases:

(i)   Never use a metaphor, simile, or other figure of speech which you are used to seeing in print.

(ii) Never use a long word where a short one will do.

(iii) If it is possible to cut a word out, always cut it out.

(iv) Never use the passive where you can use the active.

(v)   Never use a foreign phrase, a scientific word, or a jargon word if you can think of an everyday English equivalent.

(vi) Break any of these rules sooner than say anything outright barbarous.

These rules sound elementary, and so they are, but they demand a deep change in attitude in anyone who has grown used to writing in the style now fashionable. One could keep all of them and still write bad English, but one could not write the kind of stuff that I quoted in those five specimens at the beginning of this article.

I have not here been considering the literary use of language, but merely language as an instrument for expressing and not for concealing or preventing thought. Stuart Chase and others have come near to claiming that all abstract words are meaningless, and have used this as a pretext for advocating a kind of political quietism. Since you don't know what Fascism is, how can you struggle against Fascism? One need not swallow such absurdities as these, but one ought to recognize that the present political chaos is connected with the decay of language, and the one can probably bring about some improvement by starting at the verbal end. If you simplify your English, you are freed from the worst follies of orthodoxy. You cannot speak any of the necessary dialects, and when you make a stupid remark its stupidity will be obvious, even to yourself.

Political language—and with variations this is true of all political parties, from Conservatives to Anarchists—is designed to make lies sound truthful and murder respectable, and to give an appearance of solidity to pure wind. One cannot change this all in a moment, but one can at least change one's own habits, and from time to time one can even, if one jeers loudly enough, send some worn-out and useless phrase—some *jackboot, Achilles' heel, hotbed, melting pot, acid test, veritable inferno,* or other lump of verbal refuse—into the dustbin where it belongs.

The Reader's Presence

1. Look carefully at Orwell's five examples of bad prose. Would you have identified this writing as "bad" writing if you had come across it in the course of your college reading? What do the examples remind you of?

2. What characteristics of Orwell's own writing demonstrate his six rules for writing good prose? Can you identify five examples in which Orwell practices what he preaches? Can you identify any moments when he seems to slip?

3. Note that Orwell does not provide *positive* examples of political expression. Why do you think this is so? Is Orwell implying that all political language—regardless of party or position—is corrupt? From this essay can you infer his political philosophy? Explain your answer.

THE WRITER AT WORK

George Orwell on the Four Reasons for Writing

As the preceding essay shows, George Orwell spent much time considering the art of writing. He believed it was of the utmost political importance to write clearly and accurately. In the following passage from another essay, "Why I Write," Orwell considers a more fundamental aspect of writing: the reasons behind why people write at all. You may observe that he doesn't list the reason most college students write—to respond to an assignment. Why do you think he omitted assigned writing? Can you think of other motives he doesn't take into account?

Putting aside the need to earn a living. I think there are four great motives for writing, at any rate for writing prose. They exist in different degrees in every writer, and in any one writer the proportions will vary from time to time, according to the atmosphere in which he is living. They are:

1. Sheer egoism. Desire to seem clever, to be talked about, to be remembered after death, to get your own back on grown-ups who snubbed

you in childhood, etc. etc. It is humbug to pretend that this is not a motive, and a strong one. Writers share this characteristic with scientists, artists, politicians, lawyers, soldiers, successful businessmen—in short, with the whole top crust of humanity. The great mass of human beings are not acutely selfish. After the age of about thirty they abandon individual ambition—in many cases, indeed, they almost abandon individual ambition—in many cases, indeed, they almost abandon the sense of being individuals at all—and live chiefly for others, or are simply smothered under drudgery. But there is also the minority of gifted, willful people who are determined to live their own lives to the end, and writers belong in this class. Serious writers, I should say, are on the whole more vain and self-centered than journalists, though less interested in money.

2. Aesthetic enthusiasm. Perception of beauty in the external world, or, on the other hand, in words and their right arrangement. Pleasure in the impact of one sound on another, in the firmness of good prose or the rhythm of a good story. Desire to share an experience which one feels is valuable and ought not to be missed. The aesthetic motive is very feeble in a lot of writers, but even a pamphleteer or a writer of textbooks will have pet words and phrases which appeal to him for non-utilitarian reasons; or he may feel strongly about typography, width of margins, etc. Above the level of a railway guide, no book is quite free from aesthetic considerations.

3. Historical impulse. Desire to see things as they are, to find out true facts and store them up for the use of posterity.

4. Political purpose—using the word "political" in the widest possible sense. Desire to push the world in a certain direction, to alter other people's idea of the kind of society that they should strive after. Once again, no book is genuinely free form political bias. The opinion that art should have nothing to do with politics is itself a political attitude.

5

69

Cynthia Ozick

The Seam of the Snail

A highly regarded novelist, short story writer, essayist, and critic, Cynthia Ozick (b. 1928) is best known for her fiction. She has received numerous honors for her writing, including a National Book Award nomination for her most recent novel, The Puttermesser Papers *(1997). Her essay collections include* Art & Ardor, Metaphor & Memory, *and* Fame & Folly. *Ozick also frequently con-*

tributes articles, reviews, and short stories to periodicals such as the New Yorker, *the* Atlantic Monthly, Commentary, *and the* New York Times Magazine. *In "The Seam of the Snail," Ozick provides a classic illustration of how a child perceives and defines herself in relation to her similarities and differences from a parent. This essay was entitled "Excellence" when it appeared in* Ms. *magazine in 1985.*

In my Depression childhood, whenever I had a new dress, my cousin Sarah would get suspicious. The nicer the dress was, and especially the more expensive it looked, the more suspicious she would get. Finally she would lift the hem and check the seams. This was to see if the dress had been bought or if my mother had sewed it. Sarah could always tell. My mother's sewing had elegant outsides, but there was something catch-as-catch-can about the insides. Sarah's sewing, by contrast, was as impeccably finished inside as out; not one stray thread dangled.

My Uncle Jake built meticulous grandfather clocks out of rosewood; he was a perfectionist, and sent to England for the clockworks. My mother built serviceable radiator covers and a serviceable cabinet, with hinged doors, for the pantry. She built a pair of bookcases for the living room. Once, after I was grown and in a house of my own, she fixed the sewer pipe. She painted ceilings, and also landscapes; she reupholstered chairs. One summer she planted a whole yard of tall corn. She thought herself capable of doing anything, and did everything she imagined. But nothing was perfect. There was always some clear flaw, never visible head-on. You had to look underneath, where the seams were. The corn thrived, though not in rows. The stalks elbowed one another like gossips in a dense little village.

"Miss Brrrroooobaker," my mother used to mock, rolling her Russian *r*'s, whenever I crossed a *t* she had left uncrossed, or corrected a word she had misspelled, or became impatient with a *v* that had tangled itself up with a *w* in her speech. ("Vwentriloquist," I would say, "Vwentriloquist," she would obediently repeat. And the next time it would come out "wiolinist.") Miss Brubaker was my high school English teacher, and my mother invoked her name as an emblem of raging finical obsession. "Miss Brrrroooobaker," my mother's voice hoots at me down the years, as I go on casting and recasting sentences in a tiny handwriting on monomaniacally uniform paper. The loops of my mother's handwriting—it was the Palmer Method[1]—were as big as soup bowls, spilling generous splashy ebullience. She could pull off, at five minutes' notice, a satisfying dinner for ten concocted out of nothing more than originality and panache. But the napkin would be folded a little off center, and the spoon might be on the wrong side of the knife. She was an optimist who ignored trifles; for her, God was not in the details but in the intent. And all these culinary and agricultural efflorescences were extracurricular, accomplished in the

[1]*Palmer Method:* A method of teaching handwriting that dominated American elementary schools for decades.—EDS.

crevices and niches of a fourteen-hour business day. When she scribbled out her family memoirs, in heaps of dog-eared notebooks, or on the backs of old bills, or on the margins of last year's calendar, I would resist typing them; in the speed of the chase she often omitted words like "the," "and," "will." The same flashing and bountiful hand fashioned and fired ceramic pots, and painted brilliant autumn views and vases of imaginary flowers and ferns, and decorated ordinary Woolworth platters with lavish enameled gardens. But bits of the painted petals would chip away.

Lavish: my mother was as lavish as nature. She woke early and saturated the hours with work and inventiveness, and read late into the night. She was all profusion, abundance, fabrication. Angry at her children, she would run after us whirling the cord of the electric iron, like a lasso or a whip; but she never caught us. When, in seventh grade, I was afraid of failing the Music Appreciation final exam because I could not tell the difference between "To a Wild Rose" and "Barcarole," she got the idea of sending me to school with a gauze sling rigged up on my writing arm, and an explanatory note that was purest fiction. But the sling kept slipping off. My mother gave advice like mad—she boiled over with so much passion for the predicaments of strangers that they turned into permanent cronies. She told intimate stories about people I had never heard of.

Despite the gargantuan Palmer loops (or possibly because of them), I   5 have always known that my mother's was a life of—intricately abashing word!—excellence: insofar as excellence means ripe generosity. She burgeoned, she proliferated; she was endlessly leafy and flowering. She wore red hats, and called herself a gypsy. In her girlhood she marched with the suffragettes and for Margaret Sanger[2] and called herself a Red. She made me laugh, she was so varied: like a tree on which lemons, pomegranates, and prickly pears absurdly all hang together. She had the comedy of prodigality.

My own way is a thousand times more confined. I am a pinched perfectionist, the ultimate fruition of Miss Brubaker; I attend to crabbed minutiae and am self-trammeled through taking pains. I am a kind of human snail, locked in and condemned by my own nature. The ancients believed that the moist track left by the snail as it crept was the snail's own essence, depleting its body little by little; the farther the snail toiled, the smaller it became, until it finally rubbed itself out. That is how perfectionists are. Say to us Excellence, and we will show you how we use up our substance and wear ourselves away, while making scarcely any progress at all. The fact that I am an exacting perfectionist in a narrow strait only, and nowhere else, is hardly to the point, since nothing matters to me so much as a comely and muscular sentence. It is my narrow strait,

---

[2]***Margaret Higgins Sanger*** (1883–1966): Public health reformer who began a famous crusade for birth control in 1912 and four years later established the first birth control clinic in the United States, which eventually developed into the Planned Parenthood Federation.—
EDS.

this snail's road; the track of the sentence I am writing now; and when I
have eked out the wet substance, ink or blood, that is its mark, I will
begin the next sentence. Only in treading out sentences am I perfectionist;
but then there is nothing else I know how to do, or take much interest in.
I miter every pair of abutting sentences as scrupulously as Uncle Jake fitted one strip of rosewood against another. My mother's worldly and
bountiful hand has escaped me. The sentence I am writing is my cabin
and my shell, compact, self-sufficient. It is the burnished horizon — a merciless planet where flawlessness is the single standard, where even the in-
most seams, however hidden from a laxer eye, must meet perfection. Here
"excellence" is not strewn casually from a tipped cornucopia, here disorder does not account for charm, here trifles rule like tyrants.

I measure my life in sentences pressed out, line by line, like the lustrous ooze on the underside of the snail, the snail's secret open seam, its
wound, leaking attar. My mother was too mettlesome to feel the force of
a comma. She scorned minutiae. She measured her life according to what
poured from the horn of plenty, which was her own seamless, ample, cas-
cading, elastic, susceptible, inexact heart. My narrower heart rides between the tiny twin horns of the snail, dwindling as it goes.

And out of this thinnest thread, this ink-wet line of words, must rise a
visionary fog, a mist, a smoke, forging cities, histories, sorrows, quag-
mires, entanglements, lives of sinners, even the life of my furnace-hearted
mother: so much wilderness, waywardness, plenitude on the head of the
precise and impeccable snail, between the horns. (Ah, if this could be!)

The Reader's Presence

1. Ozick contrasts her personality with her mother's. Which does she
   say she prefers? Which do you think she prefers, if either? What
   clues lead you to your conclusion?

2. Compare the images and rhythms of the sections in which Ozick
   describes her mother and herself. How do they differ? What do
   they convey? What effect do they have upon your reading experience?

3. What, as Ozick uses it, does the snail's "seam" signify? Where else
   is the word *seam* used? How might the different uses of *seam* be
   connected? What might the snail symbolize? What is Ozick's position on her own seams?

Katha Pollitt

Why Boys Don't Play with Dolls

Katha Pollitt was born in 1949 in New York City and is considered one of the leading poets of her generation. Her 1982 collection of poetry, Antarctic Traveller, *won a National Book Critics Circle Award. Her poetry has received many other honors and has appeared in the* Atlantic *and the* New Yorker. *Pollitt also writes essays, and she has gained a reputation for incisive analysis and persuasive argument. She contributes reviews and essays to many national magazines and is an associate editor and columnist for the* Nation. *Her column, "Subject to Debate," appears every other week. "Why Boys Don't Play with Dolls" appeared in the* New York Times Magazine *in 1995. Her essays can also be found in* Reasonable Creatures: Feminism and Society in American Culture at the End of the Twentieth Century *(1994).*

Pollitt thinks of writing poems and political essays as two distinct endeavors. "What I want in a poem—one that I read or one that I write—is not an argument, it's not a statement, it has to do with language. . . . There isn't that much political poetry that I find I even want to read once, and almost none that I would want to read again."

It's twenty-eight years since the founding of NOW, and boys still like trucks and girls still like dolls. Increasingly, we are told that the source of these robust preferences must lie outside society—in prenatal hormonal influences, brain chemistry, genes—and that feminism has reached its natural limits. What else could possibly explain the love of preschool girls for party dresses or the desire of toddler boys to own more guns than Mark from Michigan.[1]

True, recent studies claim to show small cognitive differences between the sexes: he gets around by orienting himself in space, she does it by remembering landmarks. Time will tell if any deserve the hoopla with which each is invariably greeted, over the protests of the researchers themselves. But even if the results hold up (and the history of such research is not en-

---

[1] *Mark from Michigan:* Mark Koernke, a former right-wing talk-show host who supports the militia movement's resistance to federal government.—EDS.

couraging), we don't need studies of sex-differentiated brain activity in reading, say, to understand why boys and girls still seem so unalike.

The feminist movement has done much for some women, and something for every woman, but it has hardly turned America into a playground free of sex roles. It hasn't even got women to stop dieting or men to stop interrupting them.

Instead of looking at kids to "prove" that differences in behavior by sex are innate, we can look at the ways we raise kids as an index to how unfinished the feminist revolution really is, and how tentatively it is embraced even by adults who fully expect their daughters to enter previously male-dominated professions and their sons to change diapers.

I'm at a children's birthday party. "I'm sorry," one mom silently   5
mouths to the mother of the birthday girl, who has just torn open her present—Tropical Splash Barbie. Now, you can love Barbie or you can hate Barbie, and there are feminists in both camps. But *apologize* for Barbie? Inflict Barbie, against your own convictions, on the child of a friend you know will be none too pleased?

Every mother in that room had spent years becoming a person who had to be taken seriously, not least by herself. Even the most attractive, I'm willing to bet, had suffered over her body's failure to fit the impossible American ideal. Given all that, it seems crazy to transmit Barbie to the next generation. Yet to reject her is to say that what Barbie represents—being sexy, thin, stylish—is unimportant, which is obviously not true, and children know it's not true.

Women's looks matter terribly in this society, and so Barbie, however ambivalently, must be passed along. After all, there are worse toys. The Cut and Style Barbie styling head, for example, a grotesque object intended to encourage "hair play." The grown-ups who give that probably apologize, too.

How happy would most parents be to have a child who flouted sex conventions? I know a lot of women, feminists, who complain in a comical, eyeball-rolling way about their sons' passion for sports: the ruined weekends, obnoxious coaches, macho values. But they would not think of discouraging their sons from participating in this activity they find so foolish. Or do they? Their husbands are sports fans, too, and they like their husbands a lot.

Could it be that even sports-resistant moms see athletics as part of manliness? That if their sons wanted to spend the weekend writing up their diaries, or reading, or baking, they'd find it disturbing? Too antisocial? Too lonely? Too gay?

Theories of innate differences in behavior are appealing. They let par-   10
ents off the hook—no small recommendation in a culture that holds moms, and sometimes even dads, responsible for their children's every misstep on the road to bliss and success.

They allow grown-ups to take the path of least resistance to the dominant culture, which always requires less psychic effort, even if it means more actual work: just ask the working mother who comes home exhausted and nonetheless finds it easier to pick up her son's socks than make him do it himself. They let families buy for their children, without *too* much guilt, the unbelievably sexist junk that the kids, who have been watching commercials since birth, understandably crave.

But the thing that theories do most of all is tell adults that the *adult* world—in which moms and dads still play by many of the old rules even as they question and fidget and chafe against them—is the way it's supposed to be. A girl with a doll and a boy with a truck "explain" why men are from Mars and women are from Venus, why wives do housework and husbands just don't understand.

The paradox is that the world of rigid and hierarchical sex roles evoked by determinist theories is already passing away. Three-year-olds may indeed insist that doctors are male and nurses female, even if their own mother is a physician. Six-year-olds know better. These days, something like half of all medical students are female, and male applications to nursing school are inching upward. When tomorrow's three-year-olds play doctor, who's to say how they'll assign the roles?

With sex roles, as in every area of life, people aspire to what is possible, and conform to what is necessary. But these are not fixed, especially today. Biological determinism may reassure some adults about their present, but it is feminism, the ideology of flexible and converging sex roles, that fits our children's future. And the kids, somehow, know this.

That's why, if you look carefully, you'll find that for every kid who   15
fits a stereotype, there's another who's breaking one down. Sometimes it's the same kid—the boy who skateboards *and* takes cooking in his after-school program; the girl who collects stuffed animals *and* A-pluses in science.

Feminists are often accused of imposing their "agenda" on children. Isn't that what adults always do, consciously and unconsciously? Kids aren't born religious, or polite, or kind, or able to remember where they put their sneakers. Inculcating these behaviors, and the values behind them, is a tremendous amount of work, involving many adults. We don't have a choice, really, about *whether* we should give our children messages about what it means to be male and female—they're bombarded with them from morning till night.

The question, as always, is what do we want those messages to be?

The Reader's Presence

1. Pollitt notes in her opening paragraph that "it's twenty-eight years since the founding of NOW, and boys still like trucks and girls still like dolls." What does Pollitt identify as the competing theories to

explain these differences between boys and girls? Which theory does Pollitt prefer, and how does she express her support of it?

2. How would you characterize Pollitt's stance toward today's parents? What are some of the reasons Pollitt gives to explain parents' choices and actions? What incentives does she offer, implicitly or explicitly, for them to alter those choices and behaviors?

3. As you reread the essay, consider carefully the role of the media in upholding the status quo with regard to differentiated roles for girls and boys. As you develop a response to this question, examine carefully both the media directed principally to children and the media targeted at adults. In the latter category, for instance, Pollitt refers to the media version of scientific research studies into gender differences (paragraph 2) and alludes to popular books that discuss the differences between men and women, such as *Men Are from Mars, Women Are from Venus,* and *You Just Don't Understand* (paragraph 12). Drawing on Pollitt's essay and on your own experience, identify—and discuss—the specific social responsibilities you would like to see America's mass media take more seriously.

71

Elayne Rapping

Daytime Inquiries

Elayne Rapping (b. 1938) is a professor of communications at Adelphi University in Garden City, New York. A media critic and analyst, Rapping has been writing about television, popular culture, and women's issues since the early 1970s, and she contributes regularly to the Nation, *the* Progressive, *the* Village Voice, *and the* Women's Review of Books. *Her publications include* The Looking Glass World of Nonfiction TV *(1987),* The Movie of the Week: Private Stories/Public Events *(1992),* Media-tions: Forays into the Culture and Gender Wars (1994), *and* The Culture of Recovery: Making Sense of the Self-Help Movement in Women's Lives *(1996). "Daytime Inquiries" appeared in 1991 in the* Progressive. *Although some of the talk shows she examines are no longer on the air, the cultural and social issues she raises are still highly relevant, perhaps more so than when the essay first appeared.*

"On *Oprah* today: women who sleep with their sisters' husbands!"
"Donahue talks to women married to bisexuals!"

"Today—Sally Jessy Raphael talks with black women who have bleached their hair blond!"

These are only three of my personal favorites of the past television season. Everyone's seen these promos and laughed at them. "What next?" we wonder to each other with raised eyebrows. And yet, these daytime talk shows are enormously popular and—more often than we like to admit—hard to stop watching once you start.

As with so much else about today's media, the knee-jerk response to   5
this state of affairs is to hold one's nose, distance oneself from those who actually watch this stuff, and moan about the degradation and sleaze with which we're bombarded. But this doesn't tell us much about what's really going on in America—and television's role in it. Worse, it blinds us to what's actually interesting about these shows, what they tell us about the way television maneuvers discussions of controversial and contested topics.

It's no secret that television has *become* the public sphere for Americans, the one central source of information and public debate on matters of national import. Ninety-eight percent of us live in homes in which the TV set is on, and therefore in one way or another being experienced and absorbed, an average of seven-and-a-half hours a day; 67 percent of us get *all* our information from TV. This is not a matter of laziness, stupidity, or even the seductive power of the tube. It is a tragic fact that illiteracy—actual and functional—is rampant. It is difficult if not impossible for more and more of us to read, even when we try. Television, in such cases, is a necessity, even a godsend.

In the early 1950s, when TV emerged as the dominant cultural form, it presented to us a middle-aged, middle-class, white-male image of authority. Network prime time *was* TV, and what it gave us, from dusk to bedtime, was a series of white middle-class fathers—Walter Cronkites and Ward Cleavers—assuring us night after night that they knew best, that all was in good hands, that we needn't worry about the many scary, confusing changes wrought by postwar capitalism.

Network prime time still plays that role, or tries to. The fathers sometimes are black now, the authority occasionally shared with mothers, a voice from the ideological fringes invited from time to time to be a "guest" (and behave appropriately or not get asked back). But prime time is still the home of Official, Authoritative Truth as presented by experts and institutional power brokers. Whatever oppositional voices are heard are always controlled by the Great White Fathers in charge, who get paid six- and seven-figure salaries for their trouble.

The money value of these guys to the media—the Koppels, the Jenningses—is so high because their jobs are increasingly difficult. TV, in a sense, was developed to put a reassuring, controlling facade over the structural fault lines of American life.

Ever since the 1960s, however, this has been harder and harder to   10
manage. The breakdown of the family, the crises in education, religion, and the credibility of the state, the growing visibility and vocality of mi-

nority groups and ideas—all these took the country and media by storm. The most recent dramatic proof of the impact of social crises and the progressive movements they spawned is the amazing media hullabaloo over "multiculturalism" and "political correctness" on campuses. The Left, people of color, women, gays, and lesbians are apparently making the old white men extremely nervous.

At night, all of this tumult is being handled more or less as it has always been handled. Things seem to be under control. *MacNeil/Lehrer* and *Nightline* have their panels of experts, which now often include women, blacks, and—on rare occasions—"leftists" who really are leftists. But the structure of these shows makes it impossible seriously to challenge the host and, therefore, seriously to challenge TV hegemony.

A much juicier and, in many ways, more encouraging kind of ideological battle rages before 5 P.M., however. Daytime, women's time, has always been delegated to "domestic matters." If Father Knew Best in the evening, on the soaps the women always ruled the roost and what mattered were family and relationship issues—sex, adultery, childbirth, marriage, and the negotiating of the social and domestic end of life in a class- and race-divided society.

This is still true on daytime. In fact, the soaps are more likely to treat such social issues as rape, incest, aging, and interracial relationships with depth and seriousness than any prime-time series. In the sexual division of labor, these matters of emotional and relational caretaking and socialization have always been seen as "women's domain." And so it goes in TV Land. Daytime equals women equals "soft" issues. Prime time equals men and the "hard" stuff.

Except that what used to be soft isn't so soft anymore. The social movements of the 1960s—especially feminism, with its insistence that "the personal is political"—changed all that. Everyone who isn't braindead knows—and feels with great intensity—that all the old rules for living one's life are up for grabs. Relations between the sexes, the generations, the races, among co-workers, neighbors, family members—all of these are matters of confusion and anxiety.

What is the line, in the workplace, between being friendly and sexual harassment? How do we deal with our children, who are increasingly media-savvy and street-savvy and whose social environments are radically different from ours? What about sex education? Drugs? Condoms? Interracial dating? How do we handle social interactions with gay men and lesbians, now that more and more people are out and proud?

These are just the obvious issues. But they grow out of changes in the larger political and economic environments and they resonate into every crevice of our lives in far stranger, more confusing ways. In the breakdown of accepted views about things, and of the ties that kept us on the straight and narrow in spite of ourselves, unconventional behavior is both more common and more visible.

Women do, in fact, sleep with their sisters' husbands or find themselves married to bisexuals. Or perhaps they always did these things but
never dreamed of discussing it, never saw it as a social topic, a matter for
debate and disagreement about right and wrong. The same is true of
something as seemingly trivial as one's choice of hair color. For black
women, such tensions are rife, reflecting divisions brought on by political
and cultural issues raised by black liberation movements.

The personal is ever more political, and inquiring minds not only
want to know, they need to know. Or at least they need to talk and listen
about these things. And so the coming of daytime talk shows, a financial
gold mine for the media and a sensationalized, trivialized "political"
event for confused and frightened people everywhere.

The political roots of this form are apparent. In structure, in process,
and in subject matter, they take their cues from an important political institution of the 1960s: the women's consciousness-raising movement. In
those small groups, through which hundreds of thousands of women
passed during a brief, highly charged four- or five-year period starting in
about 1968, we invented a democratic, emotionally safe way of bringing
out in the open things we never before spoke of. We found we were not
alone in our experiences and analyzed their meanings.

Of course, the purpose of these consciousness-raising groups was   20
empowerment, political empowerment. The idea that the personal was
political led to a strategy for social change. We hoped that when previously isolated and privatized women recognized common sources of our
unhappiness in the larger political world, we could organize to change
things.

The words "political" and "organize" do not, of course, occur on
daytime TV. The primary goal of talk shows as a television form is to lure
curious audiences and sell them products, not revolution. Thus the circus-
like atmosphere and the need for bizarre and giggle-inducing topics and
participants.

Still, the influence of feminism (and other social and cultural movements) is there, and the result is more interesting and contradictory because of it. Donahue, Oprah, and pals have reproduced, in a plasticized
format, the experience of being in a group and sharing deeply personal
and significant matters with others in the same boat. Consciousness-
raising, unfortunately, is long gone. But from 9 to 11 A.M. and from 3 to
5 P.M. on weekdays, there is a remarkable facsimile thereof.

One reason these shows appeal is because, in line with the democratic
thrust of 1960s feminism, their structure approaches the nonhierarchical.
The host is still the star, of course. But in terms of authority, she or he is
far from central. The physical set enforces this fact. Audiences and participants sit in a circular form and—this is the only TV format in which this
happens—speak out, sometimes without being called on. They yell at
each other and at the host, disagree with experts, and come to no authoritative conclusions. There is something exhilarating about watching

people who are usually invisible—because of class, race, gender, status—having their say and, often being wholly disrespectful to their "betters."

The discussion of black women with blond hair, for example, ignited a shouting match between those for whom such behavior meant a disavowal of one's "blackness," a desire to "be white," and those who insisted it was simply a matter of choosing how one wished to look, no different from the behavior of white women who dye their hair or tan their bodies. The audience, selected from the black community, took issue with everything that was said. Both participants and audience members attacked the "expert," a black writer committed to the natural—to BLACK IS BEAUTIFUL.

This is as close as television gets to open discourse on serious issues. 25
But it is only possible because the issues discussed are not taken seriously by those in power. And that is why the sensationalism of these shows is double-edged. If they were more respectable in their style and choice of issues, they'd be reined in more. By allowing themselves to seem frivolous and trashy, they manage to carry on often-serious discussions without being cut off the air or cleaned up.

This may seem contradictory, but it's not. The truth is that the fringy, emotional matters brought up on Oprah, Donahue, Sally, and the others are almost always related in some way to deep cultural and structural problems in our society. Most of us, obviously, wouldn't go on these shows and spill our guts or open ourselves to others' judgments. But the people on these shows are an emotional vanguard, blowing the lid off the idea that America is anything like the place Ronald Reagan pretended to live in.

A typical recent program, for instance, featured a predictably weird ratings lure as topic: FAMILIES WHO DATE PRISONERS. It featured a family of sisters, and some other women, who sought out relationships with convicts. The chance for humor at guests' expense was not spared; Procter & Gamble doesn't care if people watch just to feel superior, as long as they watch. But in the course of the program, important political points came out.

Two issues were of particular interest. The "expert," a psychologist, pushed the protofeminist line that these women had low self-esteem—"women who love too much." Some admitted to it. Others, however, refused to accept that analysis, at least in their own cases. They stressed the prejudice against prisoners in society and went on to discuss the injustices of the criminal-justice system and to insist that their men were good people who had either made a mistake or were treated unfairly by the courts.

Our discomfort on watching what seems to be gross exhibitionism is understandable. We are taught, as children, that we don't air our dirty laundry in public. We learn to be hypocritical and evasive, to keep secret our own tragedies and sorrows, to feign shock when a public official is exposed for his or hers. It is not easy, even today, for most of us to reveal difficulties to neighbors. We are rightly self-protective. But the result of this sense of decorum is to isolate us, to keep us frightened and alone, unwilling to seek out help or share problems.

And so we sit at home, from Omaha to Orlando, and watch Oprah in   30
order to get some sense of what it all means and how we might begin to
handle it, whatever it is. These talk shows are safe. They let it all hang
out. They don't judge anyone. They don't get shocked by anything. They
admit they don't know what's right or wrong for anyone else. They are,
for many people, a great relief.

Let me give one final example of how these shows operate as forums
for opposing views. A recent segment of *Donahue* concerned women and
eating disorders. This show was a gem. It seems Phil had not yet gotten
the word, or understood it, that eating disorders are serious matters from
which women suffer and die. Nor had he grasped that this is a feminist
issue, the result of highly sexist stereotypes imposed upon women who
want to succeed at work or love.

Donahue's approach was to make light of the topic. His guests were actresses from Henry Jaglom's film *Eating,* which concerns women, food,
and body image, and he teased them about their own bouts with food com-
pulsions. After all, they were all beautiful and thin; how bad could it be?

First the call-in audience, then the studio audience, and finally the actresses themselves, rebelled. Women called in to describe tearfully how
they had been suicidal because of their weight. Others rebuked the host's
frivolous attitude. Still others offered information about feminist counsel-
ing services and support groups. And finally, one by one, those down-
stage and then those on stage—the celebrities—rose to tell their stories
of bulimia, anorexia, self-loathing, many with tears streaming down their
faces.

Donahue was chastened and, I think, a bit scared. Ted Koppel would
never have allowed such a thing to happen. He would have several doctors, sociologists, or whatever, almost all of them white and male, answer
his questions about what medical and academic professionals know
about eating disorders. There would be no audience participation and
very little dialogue among guests. Certainly none would yell or cry or
show any other "excessive" emotional involvement in the matter. If they
did, Koppel, the smoothest of network journalists, would easily take control and redirect the show. For that matter, only when such a subject as
eating disorders is deemed nationally important by the media gatekeepers
will it ever get on *Nightline* anyway. Daytime is less cautious.

I have been stressing the positive side of these shows primarily be-   35
cause of their differences from their highbrow, prime-time counterparts,
which are far more reactionary in form and content. It is, in the grand
scheme of things as they are, a good thing to have these arenas of ideological interaction and open-endedness.

But, finally, these shows are a dead end, and they're meant to be.
They lead nowhere but to the drug store for more Excedrin. In fact,
what's most infuriating about them is not that they are sleazy or in bad
taste. It is that they work to co-opt and contain real political change.

What talk shows have done is take the best insights and traditions of a more politicized time and declaw them. They are all talk and no action. Unless someone yells something from the floor (as a feminist did during the eating discussion), there will be no hint that there is a world of political action, or of politics at all.

This makes perfect sense. It is the nature of the mass media in a contradictory social environment to take progressive ideas, once they gain strength, and contain them in the large, immobilizing structure of the political status quo.

We are allowed to voice our woes. We are allowed to argue, cry, shout, whatever. We are even allowed to hear about approved services and institutions that might help with this or that specific bruise or wound. But we are not allowed to rock the political or economic boat of television by suggesting that things could be different. That would rightly upset the sponsors and network heads. Who would buy their Excedrin if the headaches of American life went away?

The Reader's Presence

1. What is the conventional attitude toward daytime television, as Rapping characterizes it? How does Rapping challenge this characterization? What rhetorical techniques does she use in her attempt to demonstrate the value of the shows?

2. The writer draws many oppositions between male and female areas of power and speech. How are the different realms evoked? What images and issues pertain to each? She positions "politics" as occurring in the cultural rather than in the governmental arena. What are the characteristics of this politics? What does she believe can be accomplished in it? Is her argument convincing to you? Why or why not?

3. Rapping briefly traces the history of authority on TV. What evidence does she offer? Is this historical account believable? Why or why not? In what ways does her presentation of historical evidence reinforce her authority and predispose the reader to accept it?

72

Barbara Katz Rothman

On Authority

Barbara Katz Rothman (b. 1948) is a professor of sociology at the Baruch College of the City University of New York. A feminist, Rothman is noted for her books regarding issues relevant to women's reproductive health, especially pregnancy, childbirth, amniocentesis, and genetic screening. She is the author of a number of books that explore these topics, including The Tentative Pregnancy: Prenatal Diagnosis and the Future of Motherhood *(1986),* Recreating Motherhood: Ideology and Technology in a Patriarchal Society *(1989), and* Encyclopedia of Childbearing *(coeditor, 1993)."On Authority" is from her most recent collection of essays,* Genetic Maps and Human Imaginations: The Limits of Science in Understanding Who We Are *(1998).*

It is important to understand how far from perfect the predictive nature of genetic information is. And it is just as important to understand how far genetics is from control: in that way too, genetics is a lot like the weather reports.

But it is also important to recognize that genetic information, made available to us through genetic screening and testing, does offer some information, some predictability. Sometimes the prediction does approach the absolute: some versions of genes are lethal. If a baby inherits one of these forms of a gene, it simply won't survive. Most of the time the predictions are far more erratic, best expressed as probabilities: a 30 percent chance of type I diabetes; a 50 percent lifetime chance of ovarian cancer.

Genetic screening or testing starts with the gene, the genotype, and then makes predictions, however vague or specific, about the phenotype. These predictions—inaccurate, incomplete, uncertain as they are—open up the enormous quandaries of contemporary bioethics. But we also use genetics the other way around: this outcome, this phenotype, implies something about the genotype. This is most usually called "genetic determinism," saying that something—a physical trait, a characteristic, a skill, a disability—is caused by genes.

Genetics, as we use it, is a way of understanding life, "human nature," behavior, being in the world. But genetics is also a way of shutting our eyes to understanding. Genetics is also a way of avoiding explanations.

Saying "it's genetic" is like throwing your hands up in the air, it's a   5
fatalistic, deterministic "explanation" that is no explanation at all. When my oldest kid, Daniel, was in first grade, he came home all excited about a science experiment that they had done in school. He very carefully set it up for us in the kitchen, measuring baking soda and vinegar and creating quite a little flurry of activity in a glass jar. And when my husband and I admired all of this, and asked him, "So Danny, how does that work?" he answered, shrugging his shoulders, "I don't know—it's science!"

That is science-as-magic. Most of the time that kind of story presents a lesson about the necessity of understanding science better. We are continually told that if we understood science better, we wouldn't have foolish fears and superstitions. We wouldn't fear crazy science fiction scenarios because we would understand that science is no danger to us. For all of my working life in the sociology of biomedical technology, what I've heard continually from the scientists and the doctors and the technicians is that to know them is to love them: if only you understood what we are doing, you would appreciate our work.

But genetics itself has a science-as-magic quality. For all practical purposes the study of genetics often works like a surprisingly accurate and very sophisticated tea-leaf reading. One of my favorite cartoons shows a turbanned "Madame Rosa" replacing the "Fortune Teller" sign in her front window with one that says "Geneticist." For many of the "gene for" something-or-others that we've been hearing and reading so much about, they haven't even found the gene itself. They've found a marker, an indication that somewhere in that neighborhood on the chromosome there must be such a gene because people who share that marker share some illness, condition or phenomenon. It's a prediction, and it might work fairly well in some cases, but it is in no way an explanation.

In science as in life, prediction does not actually depend on explanation. Danny could predict a pretty good show in the jar for us, without any kind of explanation of why vinegar and baking soda would do that. All the livelong day we rely on predictions that we can't always explain. Part of that is because of the role of technology in our lives: nobody has the time or the energy to understand all of it. Some of it you just use, predicting that the alarm clock will work, the freezer will freeze the ice cubes yet again, the plane will stay up in the air. That is the appeal of those "how things work" books—we take an awful lot for granted in the world of technology. But there are other kinds of predictions we make, predictions that we cannot necessarily explain. Something happens that I know my sister will find funny and my mother will not. Can I explain that? Not in any meaningful way, just by saying it happened that way before and so it will happen that way again. It's the "kind of thing" my sister finds funny and my mother not. Why? What in their history, psyche, (genes?)?

Because the technology involved in the tea-leaf reading of genetics is so incredibly complicated, the essentially primitive nature of the predictions may elude us. This struck me forcefully some years back when I visited a lab where prenatal diagnosis was done. They worked with aspirated amniotic fluid, the water in the womb suctioned out with a needle. Cells from the fetus float in that water. Those cells were cultured, and then magnified and photographed. The next part of the process was cutting out the individual chromosomes and pasting them in size order on a piece of paper, counting how many pairs there were and seeing if there were any extras. Literally—cutting and pasting and counting. If there were three twenty-first chromosomes the fetus could be diagnosed as having Down syndrome. Three eighteenth chromosomes and the fetus had, by definition, the condition known as trisomy 18.

I'm not belittling how complicated it is to get to the cut-and-paste   10 portion of the diagnosis. Suffice it to say that up until the mid-1950s geneticists thought there were forty-eight rather than forty-six chromosomes. So it is a complicated technological feat to photograph, enlarge and count those chromosomes. But it is not an explanation. To diagnose, to predict Down syndrome is not to explain Down syndrome. And to predict the fact of Down syndrome is not to predict the experience of Down syndrome. One fetus so diagnosed is not strong enough to survive the pregnancy; another is born with grave physical and mental handicaps and dies very young; and another grows up well and strong and stars in a television show.

Even where genetics does offer understanding and explanation, that doesn't necessarily improve the predictions, a point I made earlier and will keep coming back to. Sickle-cell anemia is understood thoroughly, from the single misspelled base pair in the DNA through to the misshapen red blood cells clogging the capillaries, and still they cannot predict which person will be severely and which mildly affected by the disease.

So what genetics has to offer us is prediction, with greater or lesser accuracy and greater or lesser specificity. Prediction is a concept that you and I are familiar with. We can have ideas about predictions—legitimate ideas, backed by solid values we hold firmly and dearly—that are not dependent on the particular technology in use. Judgments about the worth, value and danger of genetic predictions do not require in understanding of the science underlying the prediction. Moral authority does not rest on technical authority.

A person might claim that this is not a good historical moment to predict the future sexual orientation of a male fetus. And that claim, that belief, that value judgment is not dependent on the technology. Tell me you can do it with a brain scan in utero, with fetal tells withdrawn from amniotic fluid, or by playing Judy Garland tapes at the pregnant belly.

One's judgment about whether or not this is a good kind of prediction to be making doesn't depend on the technology that does the predicting, and it certainly doesn't depend on one's ability to understand the technology.

This seems so obvious, so clear to me. And yet we permit ourselves, over and over again, to be intimidated by the technology, by the science of it all. I've attended countless conferences on genetics, biotechnology, ethical issues in genetics, and the like. And virtually every one of them starts with a scientist explaining the technology. The lights go down, the slides go up on the screen and the technological razzle-dazzle begins. Then, and only then, is the discussion opened up to "ethical" or "social" concerns.

The technical presentation is supposed to open up the discussion, but 15 what it does is silence people. People want to talk about the moral and ethical concerns they have, they want to talk about the consequences of these new technologies in their lives and the lives of their children. They want to talk about how this work might change the world, for better or for worse, and how we might control it. They want to talk about what the technology means in their lives, and instead they're told they have to understand the technology before they can judge it.

My family spends a couple of weeks each year in a cabin in the Adirondack Mountains, an interesting mix of primitive and modern. It's rather like a wooden tent—has a plank floor and wood walls and a roof that keeps out rain and a screened-over opening to the outside with a wood flap to close when it gets too cold. There's a pipe bringing water to a faucet outside the cabin. There's a two-burner propane stove inside, and a fire pit of stones outside. A refrigerator has been wired in but there is no other electricity—so you have the advantage of the storage and don't have to keep driving into town for ice. There are kerosene lanterns and we bring flashlights. Toilets and showers are up the hill.

When we're there we allow ourselves to be moved into a different kind of rhythm. We have leisurely breakfasts, spend long evenings play-ing games by kerosene lantern-light. The people who run this place have been encouraged to put electric lights in all the cabins, to save on their in-surance costs. There's been a big debate raging at the beach by the lake for years now. Some of us say that's nice, we will be able to see better at night. And some of us feel something is being lost. We know we don't have to turn on the lights, and can still use the lanterns, but. . . . Some-how you don't, or it doesn't feel the same, or something.

I enter into this debate, and having been there every year for over twenty years, feel qualified to have an opinion. I don't, when you come right down to it, actually understand how electricity works. I hesitate to come right out and say that. But after all of my own science courses, after god knows how many science fairs, projects and homeworks with my kids, I don't think I could build even the most primitive of generators without getting out a book and looking it up all over again. Let alone wire up the Adirondack Mountains. And I don't, I'm embarrassed to admit, actually know much about kerosene — do they manufacture that? Distill it? Out of what exactly? And matches — wood, sulfur and what?

And yet, in spite of all of that ignorance, I know what the consequences of electrifying the cabin might be and I know what the consequences of using kerosene lamps have been. Make a fool of me if you want to with a bunch of technical questions, but don't tell me I don't know what I am talking about.

I don't tell you this story in praise of ignorance, neither in matters   20 electrical nor in matters genetic. Rather I tell it to help place technical knowledge in the appropriate context. There are relevant technical questions to be asked and answered in the decision about wiring the cabin: the pollution caused by the kerosene compared to that caused by electricity; the actual fire risk; and so on. But if we on this hillside decided to have a big meeting on the beach to discuss it, should the meeting start with a presentation by an electrical engineer on how electricity works and how he would go about wiring our cabins? I'm sure he could tell us how it is done, and how safe and clean and cheap it is. And that would shape the discussion that followed.

When I go to a genetics conference to discuss the bioethical issues involved in, for example, finding the "gay gene," and the meeting starts with the geneticist explaining how he did his research, how he ran those gels, how the science and technology of it all works — that too shapes the discussion that follows. We don't discuss "Should you do this?"; we discuss "How did you do this?" We don't discuss "Do we want to know if there is a way of predicting sexual orientation?"; we discuss how well we can predict sexual orientation.

Is research into human genetics fundamentally a social, political and ethical concern, with some technological obstacles? Or is it fundamentally a technological concern, with some social, political and ethical obstacles? The official American version has been the latter: three billion dollars of funding goes to the technical work, and 3 percent is tithed for "ethical, legal and social implications (ELSI)." Arthur Caplan, a prominent bioethicist, has called ELSI the full-employment act for bioethicists. It came about as the response of James Watson, co-describer of the double helix and first director of the Human Genome Project, to the ethical questions being raised at a press conference. ELSI, the cash cow for ethics, stands in an inherently contradictory position: a statement that those concerns are being taken seriously, and a statement that they are not to be taken seriously enough to interfere with the project.

Bioethics generally, and ELSI specifically, ends up in the middle, between biomedical science and research on the one hand, and the concerns of the public on the other. But with all the power and the big money in the hands of the science, bioethics becomes a translator, sometimes an apologist, sometimes an enabler, of scientific "progress."

At bioethics committees and conferences and discussions people start off talking about moral wrongs and end up talking about regulatory oversight. They start off talking about playing God and end up talking about extra filters in the laboratory safety hoods. I never quite understood the process until John H. Evans, a graduate student in sociology at Princeton, introduced me to the idea of "moral Esperanto" in the bioethical discussions.

Esperanto was conceived as a shared language that a multitude of   25
ethnic and linguistic groups would develop and use in the market. Like bioethics, it would be its own world with its own language, a neutral place where competing moral and ethical considerations could play out. But Evans shows that Esperanto is a language learned from the colonizers, and that in framing the problems, in expressing them in a particular language, certain solutions come to be seen as inevitable.

The example Evans uses is the concern theologians raised about the prospects of human genetic engineering. They worried about "playing God," about people taking control over parts of life that people have no business controlling. They worried about doing wrong, about violating moral principles. Their concerns were raised in a joint letter to President Carter, and a presidential commission was established. Evans has done an analysis of that process, from the first letter through the committee working on five drafts, to the production of the final report, "Splicing Life." What Evans shows is the way the process of translation into a "common" tongue ends up leaving people speechless. At each point the theologians' concerns were translated, and lost everything in the translation. The commission objected to "vague" concepts, which meant just about everything the theologians might say. If your concerns are on the level of principles, values and morals, then they're vague. If you're worried about safety tolerances, you can be specific. To eliminate vagueness, "playing God" is translated as acting without knowing the consequences, taking risks. So controlling the risks becomes the solution. Bacteria are being genetically engineered and that creation of a new life form is playing God? Playing God is taking risks? Put more filters on the lab hoods and then you're not playing God? Somehow, that was not what the theologians intended.

Speculations weren't to be permitted, either: the theologians were worried about something that hadn't happened yet. Their greatest concern was about germ line therapy—genetic therapy that changes the cells that the treated individual will pass on to future generations. That was a central concern: scientists would do something to a person that would change future evolution. We would be, in a new, direct, intentional way, controlling our own evolution. The commission decided that since it hadn't happened yet, they couldn't evaluate germ line therapy, they couldn't judge the circumstances in the future in which people might want germ line therapy. That of course was precisely what worried the theologians: this was something they thought was wrong, and worried that it would come to pass. The commission said it couldn't address it until it had come to pass, that you cannot make judgments on speculation.

I've seen this technique used dozens of times: someone in the audience or on one of the panels at an open discussion of bioethical concerns raises some concern over something like human cloning, or parents doing selective abortion for gay fetuses. The scientists quickly speak up: that isn't possible, they reassure us, you don't understand the genetics involved. Five years later, of course, that *is* possible, and then it is too late to decide whether or not to do it: we wake up to find it done.

The theologians, whether or not you and I agree with them, are making a deontological argument: some things, they say, are wrong. Period. End of sentence. Germ line engineering, gene therapy that changes the gametes of the treated person, is wrong. The commission translated that, worked with that, massaged that, spun that. What came out was that people lack the knowledge of possible outcomes of genetic engineering, and thus genetic technology is not claimed to be wrong as such, but wrong because of its potential consequences. From the deontological position of absolute wrong, the issue had switched to the knowability of the consequences. As Evans summed it up, "God had become a consequentialist."

Bioethics has become its own kind of technical language, its own form of mystification. Mystification is a political tool: making something complicated is a way of disempowering people. I'm a sociology professor; I get paid to read. I can afford to take a couple of years and read in genetics and bioethics. Most people probably cannot do that; they have other things to do. But the conclusion that I have come to, from all of that technical reading in genetics and in bioethics, is that you don't need the technical understanding to make the moral judgments. 30

A group of sociologists in Scotland came to the same conclusion. They ran focus groups of lay people on ethical issues in genetics. They concluded, "Technical competence was neither relevant or important to the majority of participants in our study: they discussed issues without need to display technical competence. When technical issues were mentioned, the accuracy of the knowledge was irrelevant to the point being made." They gave an example of a group discussion in a working-class area of Edinburgh: "They are going a little far. If they want to go an' investigate the DNA system and find oot that OK somebody's gay because there is a little slip-up in the XY hormone, we can do an injection and fix that, or a kid's going to be born mongoloid, rather than abort we may be able to find a way that we can actually sort the gene oot. We are getting to the part with genetic engineering if somebody is going to get a deformed child then they just get rid of it and say 'right the next one that you produce will be.'"

This person is completely wrong on every technical point going. XY isn't a hormone; mongoloid isn't the current word and it's not a "gene" to be "sorted out." And so what? The question that the person is raising is about drawing moral lines, about drawing lines and going too far.

Again, you or I may or may not agree with him, just as we may or may not agree with the far more sophisticated language the theologians used. But moral authority does not rest on technical authority: the concerns that are being raised, including the concerns that you personally may feel, are in and of themselves worth discussing.

Genetics, as a science, as a practice and as an ideology, is offering us a great deal. But we have to decide if we want what it has to offer. Those decisions are not technical matters. The technology of it all *is* overwhelming. Keep bandying about terms like "alleles," "RFLPS," "clines," "22Qlocus," and most of us are left in the dust. Promise a cure for cancer, an end to human suffering, and it's hard to argue. As sociologist Troy Duster puts it, "Technical complexities of vanguard research in molecular biology and the promises of success incline us to go limp before such scientific know-how."

We cannot afford to go limp. We'll be carried off to places we might very well choose not to go.

Maps are being drawn, maps of the human genome, and with every map comes a claim to territory. I see three arenas in which genetics proceeds: evolutionary history; illness; and "genetic engineering," or controlling the future. For each of these concerns we need more than maps: we need an imagination. It's the kind of imagination C. Wright Mills wrote about, an imagination that can see the connections between our own personal troubles, our daily lives, our intimate concerns, and the world in which we live, the issues that face us collectively. We live a biography, a personal tale, but we live it in a moment of history, in a collective time, and it takes a leap of imagination to understand the connection.

The first area is evolutionary history, the story of how we came to be, the collective origins tale we can tell. Genetics promises to read us evolution, to map human history. In one way it is the promise of the new genetics that comes with the fewest strings attached: history can't be patented, evolution can't be marketed. There is no profit to be made. But in another way, it comes with the most strings: it comes in the tangled packaging of race. Race has been the only way we have had, for a long time, of talking about the differences and the relationships between the many and varied people of our world. And race was invented out of another moment of historical research and scientific exploration. Race is not, as I have often been reminded while working on this project, a system of classification; it is a system of oppression. There has never been, and I can't imagine how there ever could be, a way of classifying the peoples of the world that isn't also a way of controlling people. As the science and the technology get more impressive, the historical burdens of race get no less complex, no less impressive. We have no way to confront our history without standing in our history, no way to look back but from where we now stand. As the white mother of two white children and one black child, I stand in a particular place, as each of us does, and exercise my own imagination placed in my own map, and invite you to explore with me the implications of the new genetics for thinking about race.

The second area of work in the new genetics is illness: genetics promises to revolutionize medicine. Whether it can or cannot accomplish that, genetics is revolutionizing the way we think about the body. The solidity of the body is breaking down as we imagine activity at the cellular level. The wholeness of the self is fragmenting as we think about lists of instructions, the pages and pages of ATCGs that make up each gene and the three billion such letters that, we are told, make up each of us. Sickness defines wellness, as black defines white, as all things take their meanings from what we define as their opposites. It is cancer, when the instructions go "haywire," that increasingly defines normal for us, the body as it is supposed to be, taking its meanings from the body gone astray. And I stand here, amidst the cancer losses of my own life, in my middle-aged body, looking at the as-yet unscathed bodies of my children, and exercise my imagination as I explore this new map of the body that genetics is writing.

But most profoundly what the new genetics is offering us is what the clergy called "playing God." It offers us the possibility, the hope and the fear, that we can control the future. Genetics works as tea-leaf readings for the future, offering us predictions and, only sometimes, choices. We're being asked to think about what kinds of children we want to bring into the world, what kinds of people we want on our planet. We're being asked to look at all the bits and pieces of ourselves, and choose which ones to keep, which to discard in the generations to follow. And I stand here, on the brink of this future, and know there are no maps. There is only imagination.

The Reader's Presence

1. According to Rothman's account, how are genetics and fate linked in the public mind? Does she confirm or debunk common notions?

2. What devices does Rothman use to make science and scientific issues understandable to the average reader? What effect does her use of analogy, imagery, lyricism, and humor have on the reader's comprehension of her subject? Can you find examples of these four qualities in the essay?

3. How are scientists generally portrayed in popular culture? How does the conflict over lights in the Adirondack cabins symbolize

the writer's own professional and personal attitude toward science? What position does the essay seem to urge the reader to take? What might Rothman's inclusion of her personal experience accomplish? Suppose you eliminated from the essay all references to her personal experience. Would this make the essay more or less persuasive to you? Explain why or why not.

73

Richard Selzer

Room without Windows

Richard Selzer (b. 1928), like Anton Chekhov, W. Somerset Maugham, and William Carlos Williams, is that rare breed of doctor who is also a writer. Both careers cross-pollinated each other for a long time, and Selzer has said that "a doctor walks in and out of a dozen stories a day. It is irresistible to write them down." Before leaving medicine to write full-time, Richard Selzer spent fifteen years teaching surgery at the Yale School of Medicine and running a private surgical practice. Selzer has published several books, including Confessions of a Knife *(1979),* Letters to a Young Doctor *(1982), and* Raising the Dead *(Selzer's 1993 account of his near-death experience from Legionnaires' disease and his slow recovery). His most recent books include* Imagine a Woman and Other Tales *(1996) and* The Doctor Stories *(1998), which was nominated for the 1999 PEN/Faulkner Award for fiction. His essays have appeared in* Harper's, Esquire, Antaeus, *and many other magazines.*

In an interview, Selzer explained how he taught himself to write: "The way a surgeon would prepare himself for a new operation was exactly the way I approached the task of writing, and since words were to be my new instruments, I had to learn them, learn how to use them, put them down in order, suture them together, as it were." He continued by comparing the scalpel and the pen: "Since the new instrument I had picked up was a pen, I immediately felt at home with it. It's about the same size as a scalpel, has the same circumference, if you will. It sits differently in the hand; nevertheless it was an instrument so like the one I had used all my life that it was not a stranger, but a distant cousin of the knife. In the use of each, something is shed. When you use the scalpel, blood is shed; when you use the pen, ink is shed. I liked holding the instrument in my hand rather than typing because I was able to watch the word issuing from the end of my hand, as though it were a secretion from my own body, something that I had not only made, but done, as if it were coming out of me. And that intimacy with the word as it was being written became very important to me."

Not long ago, operating rooms had windows. It was a boon and a blessing in spite of the occasional fly that managed to strain through the screens and threaten our very sterility. For the adventurous insect drawn to such a ravishing spectacle, a quick swat and, Presto! The door to the next world sprang open. But for us who battled on, there was the benediction of the sky, the applause and reproach of thunder. A Divine consultation crackled in on the lightning! And at night, in Emergency, there was the pomp, the longevity of the stars to deflate a surgeon's ego. It did no patient a disservice to have Heaven looking over his doctor's shoulder. I very much fear that, having bricked up our windows, we have lost more than the breeze; we have severed a celestial connection.

Part of my surgical training was spent in a rural hospital in eastern Connecticut. The building was situated on the slope of a modest hill. Behind it, cows grazed in a pasture. The operating theater occupied the fourth, the ultimate floor, wherefrom huge windows looked down upon the scene. To glance up from our work and see the lovely cattle about theirs, calmed the frenzy of the most temperamental of prima donnas. Intuition tells me that our patients had fewer wound infections and made speedier recoveries than those operated upon in the airless sealed boxes where now we strive. Certainly the surgeons were of a gentler stripe.

I have spent too much time in these windowless rooms. Some part of me would avoid them if I could. Still, even here, in these bloody closets, sparks fly up from the dry husks of the human body. Most go unnoticed, burn out in an instant. But now and then, they coalesce into a fire which is an inflammation of the mind of him who watches.

Not in large cities is it likely to happen, but in towns the size of ours, that an undertaker will come to preside over the funeral of a close friend; a policeman will capture a burglar only to find that the miscreant is the uncle of his brother's wife. Say that a fire breaks out. The fire truck rushes to the scene; it proves to be the very house where one of the firemen was born, and the luckless man is now called on to complete, axe and hose, the destruction of his natal place. Hardly a civic landmark, you say, but for him who gulped first air within those walls, it is a hard destiny. So it is with a hospital, which is itself a community. Its citizens—orderlies, maids, nurses, x-ray technicians, doctors, a hundred others.

A man whom I knew has died. He was the hospital mailman. It was I   5 that presided over his death. A week ago I performed an exploratory operation upon him for acute surgical abdomen. That is the name given to an illness that is unknown, and for which there is no time to make a diagnosis with tests of the blood and urine, x-rays. I saw him writhing in pain, rolling from side to side, his knees drawn up, his breaths coming in short little draughts. The belly I lay the flat of my hand upon was hot to the touch. The slightest pressure of my fingers caused him to cry out—a great primitive howl of vowel and diphthong. This kind of pain owns no consonants. Only later, when the pain settles in, long and solid, only then does it grow a spine to sharpen the glottals and dentals a man can grip with his teeth, his throat. Fiercely then, to hide it from his wife, his children, for the pain shames him.

In the emergency room, fluid is given into the mailman's veins. Bags of blood are sent for, and poured in. Oxygen is piped into his nostrils, and a plastic tube is let down into his stomach. This, for suction. A dark tarry yield slides into a jar on the wall. In another moment, a second tube has sprouted from his penis, carrying away his urine. Such is the costume of acute surgical abdomen. In an hour, I know that nothing has helped him. At his wrist, a mouse skitters, stops, then darts away. His slaty lips insist upon still more oxygen. His blood pressure, they say, is falling. I place the earpieces of my stethoscope, this ever-asking Y, in my ears. Always, I am comforted a bit by this ungainly little hose. It is my oldest, my dearest friend. More, it is my lucky charm. I place the disc upon the tense mounding blue-tinted belly, gently, so as not to shock the viscera into commotion (those vowels!), and I listen for a long time. I hear nothing. The bowel sleeps. It plays possum in the presence of the catastrophe that engulfs it. We must go to the operating room.There must be an exploration. I tell this to the mailman. Narcotized, he nods and takes my fingers in his own, pressing. Thus has he given me all of his trust.

A woman speaks to me.

"Do your best for him, Doctor. Please."

My best? An anger rises toward her for the charge she has given. Still, I cover her hand with mine.

"Yes," I say, "my best."   10

An underground tunnel separates the buildings of our hospital. I accompany the stretcher that carries the mailman through that tunnel, cursing for the thousandth time the demonic architect that placed the emergency room in one building, and the operating room in the other.

Each tiny ridge in the cement floor is a rut from which rise and echo still more vowels of pain, new sounds that I have never heard before. Pain invents its own language. With this tongue, we others are not conversant. Never mind, we shall know it in our time.

We lift the mailman from the stretcher to the operating table. The anesthetist is ready with still another tube.

"Go to sleep, Pete," I say into his ear, my lips so close it is almost a kiss. "When you wake up, it will all be over, all behind you."

I should not have spoken his name aloud! No good will come of it.   15
The syllable has peeled from me something, a skin that I need. In a minute, the chest of the mailman is studded with electrodes. From his mouth a snorkel leads to tanks of gas. Each of these tanks is painted a different color. One is bright green. That is for oxygen.They group behind the anesthetist, hissing. I have never come to this place without seeing that dreadful headless choir of gas tanks.

Now red paint tracks across the bulging flanks of the mailman. It is a harbinger of the blood to come.

"May we go ahead?" I ask the anesthetist.

"Yes," he says. And I pull the scalpel across the framed skin, skirting the navel. There are arteries and veins to be clamped, cut, tied, and cauterized, fat and fascia to divide. The details of work engage a man, hold his terror at bay. Beneath us now, the peritoneum. A slit, and we are in. Hot fluid spouts through the small opening I have made. It is gray, with flecks of black. Pancreatitis! We all speak the word at once. We have seen it many times before. It is an old enemy. I open the peritoneum its full length. My fingers swim into the purse of the belly, against the tide of the issuing fluid. The pancreas is swollen, necrotic; a dead fish that has gotten tossed in, and now lies spoiling across the upper abdomen. I withdraw my hand.

"Feel," I invite the others. They do, and murmur against the disease. But they do not say anything that I have not heard many times. Unlike the mailman, who was rendered eloquent in its presence, we others are reduced to the commonplace at the touch of such stuff.

We suction away the fluid that has escaped from the sick pancreas. It   20
is rich in enzymes. If these enzymes remain free in the abdomen, they will digest the tissues there, the other organs. It is the pancreas alone that can contain them safely. This mailman and his pancreas—careful neighbors for fifty-two years until the night the one turned rampant and set fire to the house of the other. The digestion of tissues has already begun. Soap has formed here and there, from the compounding of the liberated calcium and the fat. It would be good to place a tube (still another tube) into the common bile duct, to siphon away the bile that is a stimulant to the pancreas. At least that. We try, but we cannot even see the approach to that duct, so swollen is the pancreas about it. And so we mop and suck and scour the floors and walls of this ruined place. Even as we do, the gutters run with new streams of the fluid. We lay in rubber drains and lead them to the outside. It is all that is left to us to do.

"Zero chromic on a Lukens," I say, and the nurse hands me the suture for closure.

I must not say too much at the operating table. There are new medical students here. I must take care what sparks I let fly toward such inflammable matter.

The mailman awakens in the recovery room. I speak his magic name once more.

"Pete." Again, "Pete," I call.

He sees me, gropes for my hand.   25

"What happens now?" he asks me.

"In a day or two, the pain will let up," I say. "You will get better."

"Was there any . . . ?"

"No," I say, knowing. "There was no cancer. You are clean as a whistle."

"Thank God," he whispers, and then, "Thank *you*, Doctor."   30

It took him a week to die in fever and pallor and pain.

It is the morning of the autopsy. It has been scheduled for eleven o'clock. Together, the students and I return from our coffee. I walk slowly. I do not want to arrive until the postmortem examination is well under way. It is twenty minutes past eleven when we enter the morgue. I pick the mailman out at once from the others. Damn! They have not even started. Anger swells in me, at being forced to face the *whole* patient again.

It isn't fair! Dismantled, he would at least be at some remove . . . a tube of flesh. But look! There is an aftertaste of life in him. In his fallen mouth a single canine tooth, perfectly embedded, gleams, a badge of better days.

The pathologist is a young resident who was once a student of mine. A tall lanky fellow with a bushy red beard. He wears the green pajamas of his trade. He pulls on rubber gloves, and turns to greet me.

"I've been waiting for you," he smiles. "Now we can start." 35

He steps to the table and picks up the large knife with which he will lay open the body from neck to pubis. All at once, he pauses, and, reaching with his left hand, he closes the lids of the mailman's eyes. When he removes his hand, one lid comes unstuck and slowly rises. Once more, he reaches up to press it down. This time it stays. The gesture stuns me. My heart is pounding, my head trembling. I think that the students are watching me. Perhaps my own heart has become visible, beating beneath this white laboratory coat.

The pathologist raises his knife.

"Wait," I say. "Do you always do that? Close the eyes?"

He is embarrassed. He smiles faintly. His face is beautiful, soft.

"No," he says, and shakes his head. "But just then, I remembered 40 that he brought the mail each morning . . . how his blue eyes used to twinkle."

Now he lifts the knife, and, like a vandal looting a gallery, carves open the body.

To work in windowless rooms is to live in a jungle where you cannot see the sky. Because there is no sky to see, there is no grand vision of God. Instead, there are the numberless fragmented spirits that lurk behind leaves, beneath streams. The one is no better than the other, no worse. Still, a man is entitled to the temple of his preference. Mine lies out on a prairie, wondering up at Heaven. Or in a many windowed operating room where, just outside the panes of glass, cows graze, and the stars shine down upon my carpentry.

The Reader's Presence

1. What are some of the more figurative meanings of "windows" in the essay? What do windows have to do with Selzer's central point? If he made his point more literally, do you think it would be more or less convincing? Why?

2. What metaphorical images can you find in the essay? What does Selzer mean when he writes "Pain invents its own language"? In what way does Selzer reinforce this image?

3. What does Selzer mean when he says sparks fly from a body? Why does Selzer regret having spoken the patient's name? Selzer often writes in heightened, nearly mystical tones. How many examples of this sort of writing can you find in the essay? Does this enhance his subject matter? Why or why not?

74

Jane Smiley

Reflections on a Lettuce Wedge

Jane Smiley (b. 1949) is the author of ten books of fiction and a frequent contributor of essays and short stories to many national periodicals, including the New York Times, Atlantic, Harper's, *and* U.S. News and World Report. *She received an M.A., M.F.A., and Ph.D. from the University of Iowa, where she taught from 1982 to 1996. Although her novels vary in subject and style, family dynamics is a predominant theme throughout much of her work. Her novels include* The Greenlanders *(1988), an epic set in fourteenth-century Greenland, and* Moo *(1995), a satiric comedy about academia. She received a Pulitzer Prize for* A Thousand Acres *(1991), a tragedy modeled on Shakespeare's* King Lear. *Her most recent novel is* The All-True Adventures of Lidie Newton *(1998). "Reflections on a Lettuce Wedge" first appeared in the fall 1993 issue of* Hungry Mind Review.

Some years ago, I went to a dinner party where the ideal midwestern repast was presented in its most extreme manifestation: baked potatoes the size of shoes, slices of beefsteak tomatoes as red as stoplights and nearly as large, mammoth rings of nacreous onion. If there was a leafy green vegetable other than lettuce, its memory does not linger, nor was it meant to. The show revolved around the phenomenal slab of beef, lapping the edges of the plate, visibly juicy, dangerously sizzling, borne to the table like a potentate on a litter, casting all around it into shadow. When the philosophy professor who cooked the meal committed suicide only two weeks later, I was not actually surprised. His manner at the table was personable though a bit edgy—I wasn't perspicacious enough to divine what was coming through the scrim of conviviality—but the menu, I always thought, was despair incarnate—five simple and distinct tastes, served in chokingly large pieces, everything juxtaposed but not allowed to mingle; nothing hidden, all conspicuous, raw materials mistaken for cuisine.

I was raised and have lived most of my life in the Midwest. Very little about the Midwest surprises me. The people are friendly, generous, and honest. The divisions of social class are minimal. Tact is a universally cherished virtue. Function is valued over style, the inner self over appearance. Nevertheless, it still astounds me, after forty years, that there is no good bread between Chicago and San Francisco.

Diners in the heartland, in fact, have been known to go for the white meal—pork chops and mashed potatoes in cream gravy, with a little cauliflower on the side and a dish of vanilla ice cream for dessert. I prefer recipes that begin with a head or two of garlic and go on to call for a packed cup of coriander and some chili peppers.

I do not ascribe the sorry state of midwestern cuisine to the northern European heritage of many of its denizens. In Northern Europe I've eaten plenty of scrumptious chow, from sauerbraten to liver pâté, from rye bread to pickled herring, not to mention towering cream cakes flavored with mysterious tasting liqueurs. If only you could get *that* in Galesburg, Illinois. Nor does the fault lie in scarcity. I understand that French *boulangers*[1] prefer hard wheat flour from our Midwest. Midwestern gardens abound with perfect tomatoes, peppers, broccoli, and sweet corn. The filet I get at my local supermarket compares with the best steaks at the best restaurants on either coast.

Quoting me back to myself, my daughter says, "De gustibus non est disputandum."[2] Okay, let them eat instant mashed potatoes dished up with an ice cream scoop, machine-formed turkey breast injected with artificially flavored turkey juice, string beans the color of army fatigues, and a pie-shaped wedge of cranberry jelly still bearing the imprint of its No. 42 can. Let them go out and eat it at a restaurant. Let them pay ten or fifteen real dollars for the privilege of eating it. It's neurotic of me to think that this is any of my business.   5

But I'm here! I'm hungry! And there isn't anything else on the menu! Here comes the salad. Is it a few simple leaves of spinach and romaine, dressed with the plainest vinaigrette—wine vinegar, olive oil, Dijon mustard, a crushed garlic clove, salt, and pepper? No! It is a wedge of flavorless and nutrient-free iceberg lettuce floating in bright orange "French" dressing, and sporting a tomato wedge that's been held near the freezing point ever since its embarkation in California. The clearest flavor note we have here is the potent taste of the sugar in the dressing. I'm the angriest person in the restaurant; I'm the only angry person in the restaurant. I consider this salad a spiritual assault. I ask for bread, and they give me, not a stone, but a white spongy thing called a "roll."

---

[1] *boulangers:* Bakers.—EDS.
[2] *De gustibus . . . :* Famous Latin saying that roughly means "There can be no arguments over taste."—EDS.

The spirit is inescapably connected to the body. The body, through the senses, seeks connection to the world. When a connection is made that is pleasurable, the spirit lifts. When the connection is routine, mundane, careless, the spirit sinks. What American commerce has done to bread, tomatoes, salad, turkey, the tartly sublime and healthful cranberry, the fresh and crunchy pole bean is to make them routine, mundane, and careless, multicolored fodder for merely biologic hunger, the hunger that sets in after five or six hours and craves only calories, not connection, delight, or even savor. That commerce alters all it touches is a truism, but why, of all Americans, do midwesterners most widely and passively accept the damage? Why do midwesterners hold their tastebuds in lower esteem than everyone else in the whole world, even the notorious British? (Five British delicacies worth making the trip: Devonshire cream, toasted Cheshire cheese, cider, ginger cake, and, since the Act of Union, shortbread.)

My husband says it all has to do with religion—militant Protestantism expressing itself as distaste for all the senses, including the least aggressive. Or perhaps the ubiquity of sugar, which serves as a pick-me-up through the light-deprived days of winter, has aborted the development of sharper, less easily learned preferences. In his more bitter moments, Garrison Keillor has commented that midwesterners are early taught the "Who do you think you are?" lesson—as in, "Who do you think you are to aspire to something more beautiful, more exotic, or more unusual than what is put before you?" The "Who do you think you are?" lesson is quickly internalized as the "Anything is good enough for me" attitude, an attitude that no one should ever bring to the table, considering the limitations placed on us all by appetite, physique, and the fact that no human life is long enough to sample more than a portion of the results of human imagination as it is applied to food.

Of course, I am told that there are those who care nothing for what they eat, but can a whole legion of eaters be so ascetic or, perhaps, such poor producers of endorphins?

I don't know what it is, myself. This is a diatribe, not a diagnosis. But   10
I do think that people tend to use the earth better if they take delight in its fruits. Eating is the one sensuous thing we do many times a day, day after day, year after year. Eating is our oftenest repeated connection to our agricultural roots. It seems to me that there are two choices: We can continue to process our food, as through a machine, from field to table, and continue to content ourselves with mechanically opening our jaws and processing it through our alimentary canals, or we can sow the seed, harvest the fruits, bring care and interest to the preparation of meals, and take our daily reward in the pleasures of aroma, flavor, and visceral satisfaction. We can decide that what doesn't taste good cannot be good for us. We can resist having our appetites dulled in the name of the countless mouths one single American farmer and all his machinery, petrochemi-

cals, and sacrificed topsoil are alleged to feed. The future begins at dinnertime. I hope mine contains a measure of very green, strong olive oil and a baguette of crusty, slightly sour, and perfectly fresh bread. A silky sauce with a flavor both rounded and tangy, enigmatic enough to deliberate over again and again. I hope my future contains ropes of garlic. And I hope it contains an Earth that is cherished, cared for, and abundant.

The Reader's Presence

1. Choose a passage from the essay describing food and note the writer's use of imagery. How does she evoke sensual experience through words?

2. How does Smiley link suicide to bad food? Why do you think she does this? Is this link meant humorously, sardonically, or seriously? What clues lead you to this conclusion? What rhetorical techniques does Smiley use to make this argument? Is it convincing? Why or why not?

3. In what ways does midwestern food represent midwestern culture in general? Why do you think the author chose the "lettuce wedge" as her representation of midwestern food? Could she have chosen any other types of food? What is the effect of this device?

75

Benjamin Spock

Should Children Play with Guns?

The pediatrician and Vietnam antiwar activist Dr. Benjamin Spock (1903–1998) became America's most respected expert on child care with the publication of The Common Sense Book of Baby and Child Care *in 1946. His book offered a new approach to the subject and challenged such previous views as Dr. John B. Watson's,* Psychological Care of Infant and Child *(1928), which advised parents to "never, never kiss your child. Never hold it on your lap. Never rock its carriage." Spock was both widely applauded and criticized for his relatively relaxed attitude toward childrearing, and he has even been blamed for fueling the countercultural youth movement of the 1960s. His publications include* Decent and Indecent: Our Personal and Political Behavior *(1970),* Raising Children in a Difficult Time *(1974)*, Spock on Spock: A Memoir of Growing Up with the Century *(1989)*, *and* A Better World for Our Children: Rebuilding American Family Values *(1994)*. *"Should Children Play with Guns?"* is taken from the 1976 edition of Baby and Child Care.

Is gun play good or bad for children? For many years I emphasized its harmlessness. When thoughtful parents expressed doubt about letting their children have pistols and other warlike toys, because they didn't want to encourage them in the slightest degree to become delinquents or militarists, I would explain how little connection there was. In the course of growing up, children have a natural tendency to bring their aggressiveness more and more under control provided their parents encourage this. One- to two-year-olds, when they're angry with another child, may bite the child's arm without hesitation. But by three or four they have already learned that crude aggression is not right. However, they like to pretend to shoot a pretend bad guy. They may pretend to shoot their mother or father, but grinning to assure them that the gun and the hostility aren't to be taken seriously.

In the six- to twelve-year-old period, children will play an earnest game of war, but it has lots of rules. There may be arguments and roughhousing, but real fights are relatively infrequent. At this age children don't shoot at their mother or father, even in fun. It's not that the parents have turned stricter; the children's own conscience has. They say, "Step on a crack; break your mother's back," which means that even the thought of wishing harm to their parents now makes them uncomfortable. In adolescence, aggressive feelings become much stronger, but well-brought-up children sublimate them into athletics and other competition or into kidding their pals.

In other words, I'd explain that playing at war is a natural step in the disciplining of the aggression of young children; that most clergymen and pacifists probably did the same thing; that an idealistic parent doesn't really need to worry about producing a scoundrel; that the aggressive delinquent was not distorted in personality by being allowed to play bandit at five or ten, he was neglected and abused in his first couple of years, when his character was beginning to take shape; that he was doomed before he had any toys worthy of the name.

But nowadays I'd give parents much more encouragement in their inclination to guide their child away from violence. A number of occurrences have convinced me of the importance of this.

One of the first things that made me change my mind, several years ago, was an observation that an experienced nursery school teacher told me about. Her children were crudely bopping each other much more than previously, without provocation. When she remonstrated with them, they would protest, "But that's what the Three Stooges do." (This was a children's TV program full of violence and buffoonery which had recently been introduced and which immediately became very popular.) This attitude of the children showed me that watching violence can lower a child's standards of behavior. Recent psychological experiments have shown that being shown brutality on film stimulates cruelty in adults, too.

What further shocked me into reconsidering my point of view was the assassination of President Kennedy, and the fact that some school-children cheered about this. (I didn't so much blame the children as I blamed the kind of parents who will say about a President they dislike, "I'd shoot him if I got the chance!")

These incidents made me think of other evidences that Americans have often been tolerant of harshness, lawlessness, and violence. We were ruthless in dealing with the Indians. In some frontier areas we slipped into the tradition of vigilante justice. We were hard on the later waves of immigrants. At times we've denied justice to groups with different religions or political views. We have crime rates way above those of other, comparable nations. A great proportion of our adult as well as our child population has been endlessly fascinated with dramas of Western violence and with brutal crime stories, in movies and on television. We have had a shameful history of racist lynchings and murders, as well as regular abuse and humiliation. In recent years it has been realized that infants and small children are being brought to hospitals with severe injuries caused by gross parental brutality.

Of course, some of these phenomena are characteristic of only a small percentage of the population. Even the others that apply to a majority of people don't necessarily mean that we Americans on the average have more aggressiveness inside us than the people of other nations. I think rather that the aggressiveness we have is less controlled, from childhood on.

To me it seems very clear that in order to have a more stable and civilized national life we should bring up the next generation of Americans with a greater respect for law and for other people's rights and sensibilities than in the past. There are many ways in which we could and should teach these attitudes. One simple opportunity we could utilize in the first half of childhood is to show our disapproval of lawlessness and violence in television programs and in children's gun play.

I also believe that the survival of the world now depends on a much   10
greater awareness of the need to avoid war and to actively seek peaceful agreements. There are enough nuclear arms to utterly destroy all civilization. One international incident in which belligerence or brinkmanship was carried a small step too far could escalate into annihilation within a few hours. This terrifying situation demands a much greater stability and self-restraint on the part of national leaders and citizens than they have ever shown in the past. We owe it to our children to prepare them very deliberately for this awesome responsibility. I see little evidence that this is being done now.

When we let people grow up feeling that cruelty is all right provided they know it is make-believe, or provided they sufficiently disapprove of certain individuals or groups, or provided the cruelty is in the service of their country (whether the country is right or wrong), we make it easier for them to go berserk when the provocation comes.

But can we imagine actually depriving American children of their guns or of watching their favorite Western or crime programs? I think we should consider it—to at least a partial degree.

I believe that parents should firmly stop children's war play or any other kind of play that degenerates into deliberate cruelty or meanness. (By this I don't mean they should interfere in every little quarrel or tussle.)

If I had a three- or four-year-old son who asked me to buy him a gun, I'd tell him—with a friendly smile, not a scowl—that I don't want to give him a gun for even pretend shooting because there is too much meanness and killing in the world, that we must all learn how to get along in a friendly way together. I'd ask him if he didn't want some other present instead.

If I saw him, soon afterward, using a stick for a pistol in order to join   15
a gang that was merrily going "bang-bang" at each other, I wouldn't rush out to remind him of my views. I'd let him have the fun of participating as long as there was no cruelty. If his uncle gave him a pistol or a soldier's helmet for his birthday, I myself wouldn't have the nerve to take it away from him. If when he was seven or eight he decided he wanted to spend his own money for battle equipment, I wouldn't forbid him. I'd remind him that I myself don't want to buy war toys or give them as presents; but from now on he will be playing more and more away from home and making more of his own decisions; he can make this decision for himself. I wouldn't give this talk in such a disapproving manner that he wouldn't dare decide against my policy. I would feel I'd made my point and that he had been inwardly influenced by my viewpoint as much as I could influence him. Even if he should buy weapons then, he would be likely to end up—in adolescence and adulthood—as thoughtful about the problems of peace as if I'd prohibited his buying them, perhaps more so.

One reason I keep backing away from a flat prohibition is that it would have its heaviest effect on the individuals who need it least. If all the parents of America became convinced and agreed on a toy-weapons ban on the first of next month, this would be ideal from my point of view. But this isn't going to happen for a long time, unless one nuclear missile goes off by accident and shocks the world into a banning of all weapons, real and pretend. A small percentage of parents—those most thoughtful and conscientious—will be the first ones who will want to dissuade their children from war toys; but their children will be most apt to be the sensitive, responsible children anyway. So I think it's carrying the issue unnecessarily far for those of us who are particularly concerned about peace and kindliness to insist that our young children demonstrate a total commitment to our cause while all their friends are gun toters. (It might be practical in a neighborhood where a majority of parents had the same conviction.) The main ideal is that children should grow up with a fond attitude toward all humanity. That will come about basically from the general atmosphere of our families. It will be strengthened by the attitude that we teach specifically toward other nations and groups. The elimination of war play would have some additional influence, but not as much as the two previous factors.

I feel less inclined to compromise on brutality on television and in movies. The sight of a real human face being apparently smashed by a fist has a lot more impact on children than what they imagine when they are making up their own stories. I believe that parents should flatly forbid programs that go in for violence. I don't think they are good for adults either. Young children can only partly distinguish between dramas and reality. Parents can explain, "It isn't right for people to hurt each other or kill each other and I don't want you to watch them do it."

Even if children cheat and watch such a program in secret, they'll know very well that their parents disapprove, and this will protect them to a degree from the coarsening effect of the scenes.

The Reader's Presence

1. Spock's advice on guns appears in his well-known book on baby and child care. Does building a more peaceable society count as a form of child care? Why or why not? Do you consider the doctor's political views valid in this context? Why or why not?

2. The essay includes personal reflections and detailed hypothetical scenarios. Suppose Spock offered only advice? How might the reader's approach to that advice differ?

3. The writer discusses his earlier opinions in depth before explicating his current views. What is the effect for the reader of learning his reasoning? Is the argument weakened or strengthened through the presentation of conflicting positions? Because of recent events in America's schools, the issue of children and guns is far more serious today than it was when Spock offered his opinion in 1976. Do you find Spock's position relevant today? Why or why not?

Brad Stroup

The Koans of Yogi Berra

Brad Stroup (b. 1929) received both a B.S. and an M.S. at the University of North Carolina in Chapel Hill. He worked as a manager at General Electric and Honeywell and was an executive at Data General Corporation until he retired in 1989. His publications consist of numerous annual reports, speeches, and articles on computers and jet engines that "nobody reads," according to Stroup. Writing about himself, Stroup said, "He lives in Tucson, Arizona, with his wife of forty-six years. . . . He has studied T'ai Chi for many years but still hasn't got it right, and teaches it in Tucson to others who may never get it right. . . . He came to Tucson in search of something he hasn't found. He and his wife retreat to the coast of Maine in the summer to look further. . . . He also helps Native Americans in Arizona start business enterprises, sometimes successfully. He has never met Yogi Berra."[1] "The Koans of Yogi Berra" was originally published in Tricycle: The Buddhist Review *in the 1998 fall issue.*

Discovered inside a catcher's mitt in the year 2087 by archaeologists while excavating rubble in the abandoned Yankee Stadium in the Bronx:

KOAN 1: "WHEN YOU COME TO A FORK
IN THE ROAD, TAKE IT."

Commentary: Yogi gave this mystifying advice to a young second baseman being sent down to the minors after popping out too many times with the Yankees. It caused the young man to stop in his tracks, freeze, and study the wall of the Yankee dugout for over an hour. He was last seen in Troy, New York, playing for the Mohawks, still carrying a frown

---

[1]**Berra:** According to the *Microsoft Complete Interactive Guide to Baseball,* Lawrence Peter Berra, the Hall of Fame Yankee catcher, received his nickname from a boyhood friend in St. Louis who thought Berra walked just like a yogi they had seen in a movie about an Indian snake charmer.

on his face. Hundreds of players have studied this koan as they have gone down to the minors. It sits like a boil on the forearm of pitchers—feverish, festering, a red circle surrounding a yellow mound. Once considered without spit or curves, the mind cannot escape the fork. The dust clears in the outfield.

KOAN 2: "IF I DIDN'T WAKE UP, I'D STILL BE SLEEPING."

Commentary: Similar to that in Koan 1, this absurd statement goes back on itself. Like the fork, it climbs on its own back and rides away in all directions at once. It forces the mind to focus on the fragile line between sleeping and waking. Yogi is thought to have made this statement to his wife one morning after a hard twilight doubleheader. His team had won one and lost one. Like so much in life, it was a draw. His wife is said to have looked at him for a moment, turned over and gone back to sleep without a word.

KOAN 3: YOGI (DURING A GAME OF TWENTY QUESTIONS): "IS HE LIVING?" TEAMMATE: "YES." YOGI: "IS HE LIVING NOW?"

Commentary: The teammate was reportedly to be Joe Garagiola, and the two families were playing the game in Joe's parlor in Hoboken in the early days. Garagiola was thinking of Dizzy Dean, then a radio commentator but formerly a pitcher. Already guessing who it was, Yogi was asking if he was living "now" because once you retired from baseball, like abandoning a koan, nobody could tell if you were alive. This koan penetrates to the core of what it is to live in the present moment and suggests the bardo to come.

KOAN 4: "NOBODY GOES THERE ANYMORE. IT'S TOO CROWDED."

Commentary: Where is "there"? The mind rebels at the idea of crowding if nobody goes there. Here Yogi encourages the person to become aware of spatial relationships among people—crowds and isolation. The paradoxes arise in the mind. If nobody goes there, then it can't be crowded, but it must be crowded to cause nobody to go there. The mind spins in circles, a runner caught between third and home, which is a necessary condition for the mind and body to fall away.

KOAN 5: "YOU CAN OBSERVE A LOT JUST BY WATCHING."

Commentary: A quiet, cool observation that relaxes the spirit while watching the sprinkler water the infield grass. Can we watch without waiting? The thought steals up behind you on soft, wet feet, just watching, just becoming aware.

5

KOAN 6: UMPIRE: "YOGI, WHAT TIME IS IT?" YOGI: "YOU MEAN RIGHT NOW?"

Commentary: One of the greatest koans in the Yogi tradition, Yogi's response to the umpire explodes in the mind like a pipe bomb. The umpire was blown away into outer Queens along with everyone else within earshot. He called a ten-minute recess after the comment. Fans threw tomatoes into the bull pen. Bedlam reigned. What is time? Is it right now? How can it be now if it is yet to come? If it be now, it's not to come. If it be not to come, it will be now. Readiness is all, says Hamlet.

KOAN 7: "NINETY PERCENT OF BASEBALL IS HALF MENTAL."

Commentary: Yogi here forces the mind into the mathematical relationships of mind and body. Where is the other ten percent if not mental? How much is the mind's work? How much is the body's work? Can they be shared? Can they be separated? Yogi suggests that they are so closely intertwined that numbers are meaningless, but there's more here in the head than in the arm.

KOAN 8: MAYOR JOHN LINDSAY TO YOGI AT GALA NEW YORK PARTY: "YOGI, YOU LOOK REAL COOL DRESSED UP IN A TUX." YOGI: "YOU DON'T LOOK SO HOT YOURSELF."

Commentary: This koan goes to the heart of the situation by stripping away the pretense of the Mayor treating Yogi as a separate being. It illustrates the danger of entering into a trivial social conversation with Yogi. If the Mayor had left Yogi alone, he would have looked cool himself. But once having introduced the idle compliment, he is hooked. There is no way out, and further response to Yogi is impossible.

KOAN 9: "A NICKEL AIN'T WORTH A DIME ANYMORE."

Commentary: While a profound understanding of inflation underlies this absurd remark, its real thrust is to reveal the illusion of money as a medium of exchange or measure of value. The operative word in this koan is "anymore," which strikes at the absurdity of time itself.

KOAN 10: "YOU'VE GOT TO BE CAREFUL IF YOU DON'T KNOW WHERE YOU'RE GOING BECAUSE YOU WON'T GET THERE."

Commentary: Note the warning "be careful," which suggests that you *can* get there if you don't know where you're going — which, of course, happens all the time in Rinzai Zen. But at a deeper level, the koan deals with the illusion of planning our lives and how fruitless it is to try to get anywhere.

10

KOAN 11: "I ALWAYS GO TO OTHER PEOPLE'S FUNERALS; OTHERWISE THEY WON'T COME TO YOURS."

Commentary: Here Yogi reveals the essence of karma, the inevitable connection between cause and effect. But again, more is implied — that cause and effect are one. All funerals are in the present, each attending the other, over and over. Life and death are one.

KOAN 12: YOGI (AS THE METS' COACH): "WE'RE NOT EXACTLY HITTING THE BALL OFF THE COVER."

Commentary: The casual misstatement of cliché contains the essence of living in the moment, forcing the mind to meditate on the confusion that results. Performance is not exactly the purpose of life. Winning is not exactly the purpose of games. Yet the koan implies a conventional assessment of playing the game: the batters are not exactly hitting the ball off the cover of the stadium, a feat unaccomplished in the history of the sport.

KOAN 13: YOGI (WITH A SCORE OF CHICAGO 12, METS 2, AT THE END OF THE THIRD INNING): "IT'S GETTING LATE EARLY."

Commentary: How can "late" be "early"? The baseball score is the reality but in a time-space continuum. For the Mets, time has swiftly passed by and opportunity has been lost. Yogi is saying "Take heed." He deftly hurls the two time concepts at each other and waits to see if we awaken.

KOAN 14: "I REALLY DIDN'T SAY EVERYTHING I SAID."

Commentary: This is Yogi's version of "The Tao that is known is not the eternal Tao." What is known is not known. You're on your own; there's nobody else out there. This final summary of Yogi's teachings parallel the truth of his spiritual slogan: "Light a candle to yourselves."

The Reader's Presence

1. The *Random House Webster's College Dictionary* offers the following definition of a koan: "A nonsensical or paradoxical question posed to a Zen student as a subject for meditation, intended to help the student break free of reason and develop intuition in order to achieve enlightenment." In what ways can the actual quotations of the great baseball catcher Lawrence ("Yogi") Berra be considered "koans"? Do you think the term is truly applicable or is the author simply being funny?

2. Can you find anything that Berra's quotations have in common? Are there any underlying verbal patterns that cause them to seem both ordinary and strange at the same time?

3. Choose your favorite Yogi Berra quotation and write your own explication.

77

Deborah Tannen

Listening to Men, Then and Now

Deborah Tannen (b. 1945) is University Professor of Linguistics at Georgetown University. She writes both for general and academic readers, and her many books and articles have been popular with both audiences. Her specialty is socio-

linguistics, and in her research Tannen focuses on the different ways men and women communicate—and on the difficulties of communicating across gender. Her 1990 book You Just Don't Understand: Women and Men in Conversation *was a best-seller and has been translated into twenty-four languages. In spite of the title, the book was written with the faith that men and women can understand each other better if they take the time to consider how gender influences communication styles. More recently she published* Gender and Conversational Interaction *(1993),* Gender and Discourse *(1994),* Talking from 9 to 5: Women and Men in the Workplace *(1995), and* The Argument Culture: Moving from Debate to Dialogue *(1998).* "Listening to Men, Then and Now" *first appeared in the* New York Times Magazine *for May 16, 1999.*

Reflecting on the experience of writing, Tannen says, "Writing is hard to begin—it's much easier to return a phone call or check E-mail for messages—but once underway, if it's going well, it's joy, exhilaration, intense pleasure."

A woman and a man meet at the end of the day. He asks how her day was, and she replies with a long report of what she did, whom she met, what they said and what that made her think and feel. Then she eagerly turns to him:

She: How was your day?

He: Same old rat race.

She: Didn't anything happen?

He: Nah, nothing much.   5

Her disappointment is deepened when that evening they go out to dinner with friends and suddenly he regales the group with an amusing account of something that happened at work. She is cut to the quick, crestfallen at hearing this story as part of an audience of strangers. "How could he have said nothing happened?" she wonders. "Why didn't he tell me this before? What am I? Chopped liver?"

The key to this frustration is that women and men typically have different ideas about what makes people friends. For many women, as for girls, talk is the glue of close relationships; your best friend is the one you tell your secrets to, the one you discuss your troubles with. For many men, as for boys, activities are central; your best friend is the one you do everything with (and the one who will stick up for you if there is a fight).

As the millennium approaches and commentators examine how our lives have changed in the last thousand years, I find myself wondering about the change in relations between the sexes. Clearly there has been a transformation. In the past, the woman was deferential, subordinate. Now we are not trying to be partners in a societal arrangement with a clearly defined separation of labor, but rather hoping to be each other's best friends. Yet at least two aspects of women's and men's relations have endured—our differing expectations about the importance of talk in intimacy, and the tendency of women to take the role of listener in conversation with men.

In the absence of tape recordings from earlier times, we can look to conversations in literature. For a glimpse of how a sixteenth-century couple might have talked to each other, I turned to Shakespeare—and my earliest memory of his plays. When I was at Ditmas Junior High in Brooklyn, my classmates were all atitter: our teacher had us reading "Julius Caesar" aloud, and, having read ahead, we knew that the next day some poor girl would have to stand and read a passage in which Brutus's wife uses the word "harlot." Susan Ehrlich had the bad luck to be chosen, and I can still see her, tall and brown-haired, reading, "Portia is Brutus's harlot, not his wife."

Revisiting those lines today, what strikes mc is how similar the senti-   10
ment is to what I hear from contemporary women. Portia wants to be Brutus's best friend—and her idea of what this means is very similar to ours. Waking up to discover that her husband has left their bed, she finds him pacing, and implores him to say what is worrying him. Like the modern woman who feels that best friends tell each other secrets, Portia pleads:

> Within the bond of marriage, tell me, Brutus,
> Is it excepted I should know no secrets
> That appertain to you?
>   Am I yourself
> But, as it were, in sort or limitation,
> To keep with you at meals, comfort your bed,
> And talk to you sometimes? Dwell I but in the suburbs
> Of your good pleasure? If it be no more,
> Portia is Brutus's harlot, not his wife.

A similar sentiment emerges in an even more distant conversation— in the Arabian romance of the Bedouin hero Antar, believed to have been written between 1080 and 1400. In one episode, a character named al-Minhal, escaping a king he has wronged, comes upon a ruined castle inhabited by a female demon named Dahiya. She gives him shelter, feeds him, falls in love with him and wins his love by her attentions, which include her conversation. Sounding rather like Portia, Dahiya says: "I want you to be my companion and to be my lord, and I will be your wife. Disclose to me what is in your heart. Do not believe that I will ever let you go. Open your mind to me for I have need to know your thoughts." They are married on the spot, and, we are told, "Long was their companionship, and they loved each other dearly."

I am not suggesting that relationships between women and men were the same then as now. But it's intriguing to think that what women regard as intimacy, talking about what's on your mind, has been a common thread right through the millennium. There's another, related pattern that seems to have endured. It, too, is evident in the case of the husband who can't think of anything to tell his wife but comes up with an amusing story to entertain a dinner gathering. To her, it's a failure of intimacy: if we're truly close, I should hear everything first. To him, I think, the situation of being home with someone he feels close to does not call for a story performance. This creates a paradox. Many women were drawn to the men they fell in love with because the men told captivating stories. After marriage, the women expect that the closer they get, the more the men will open up and tell. Instead, to their deep disappointment, after marriage the men clam up.

Once again, looking at how boys and girls are socialized provides a key. Boys' groups are hierarchical; low-status boys are pushed around. One way boys earn and keep status is to hold center stage by verbal performance—boasting, telling jokes or recounting mesmerizing stories. And this seems to work well in winning maidens as well.

This aspect of storytelling can be seen as far back as "Beowulf," that Anglo-Saxon saga, usually dated to the eighth century. The hero, a member of a Swedish tribe known as the Geats, wins the attention of Wealhtheow, queen of Hrothgar, who is serving beer to a gathering of men:

> *Beowulf spoke, the son of Ecgtheow: "I resolved, when I set out on the sea, sat down in the sea-boat with my band of men, that I should altogether fulfill the will of your people or else fall in slaughter, fast in the foe's grasp. I shall achieve a deed of manly courage or else have lived to see in the mead-hall my ending day." These words were well-pleasing to the woman, the boast of the Geat. Gold-adorned, the noble folk-queen went to sit by her lord.*

Boasting, my colleague Catherine Ball tells me, was a customary male   15
activity in the Anglo-Saxon mead-hall, so it is not surprising that Wealhtheow was well pleased, even though the exploits Beowulf boasts of have not yet taken place. (In fact, he sounds a little like Cassius Clay predicting what he will do to Sonny Liston.)

This scenario—a woman wooed by a man's boasts of exploits in battle—brings us back to Shakespearean icons: Desdemona and Othello. As Othello tells "how I did thrive in this fair lady's love," he explains that she became entranced when she heard him telling "the story of my life":

> *Wherein I spoke of most disastrous chances:*
> *Of moving accidents by flood and field,*
> *Of hair-breadth scapes i'th'imminent deadly breach;*
> *Of being taken by the insolent foe. . . .*

And so on, until:

> *My story being done,*
> *She gave me for my pains a world of kisses. . . .*
> *And bad me, if I had a friend that lov'd her,*
> *I should but teach him how to tell my story,*
> *And that would woo her.*

As we know, he wooed her himself with his own story.

In our era, the tactic of wooing by verbal performance takes a funny turn. Etiquette books of the fifties instructed young women to be good listeners if they wanted to win their men, and you need only look around a restaurant to see many women attentively listening to talking men. In place of battle yarns, what I hear, over and over, is that a woman fell in love because "he makes me laugh." That's why Michelle Pfeiffer said in 1992 she picked a particular boyfriend, and why Joanne Woodward fell for Paul Newman. I don't hear the same explanation from men as to why they fall in love. What I hear is the corresponding one, as for example when Woody Allen said of his relationship with Soon-Yi Previn: "She's a marvel. And she laughs at all my jokes."

We seem to have a situation of *plus ça change.*[1] Even as relationships   20
between men and women have changed, our contrasting expectations about the meaning of closeness still cause confusion and disappointment. And though the performance has shifted from heroic tales to amusing entertainment, more often than not the apportionment of roles has stayed the same: Women are the audience and men are the show.

The Reader's Presence

1. How does Tannen characterize most women's talk and need for talk? How does she characterize most men's talk and preference for silence with their partners? Does this reflect your own experience? Why or why not?

2. Tannen uses statistical evidence to back up her claims about current-day talk, but she must rely on works of literature to assemble a sense of talk in history. Does the latter methodology seem valid? reliable? Why or why not? What differences can you think of between the way Shakespeare's female characters speak and real-life women would have spoken at the time? In your opinion, how do these differences affect your evaluation of Tannen's historical argument?

3. Do you think Tannen values male and female speech behavior equally, or does she favor one over the other? How can you tell? Given the article's logic, does an understanding of the natural or societal basis of male or female behaviors lead one to accept either? Or does the article suggest that we need to work to change male or female behavior? Explain your conclusion.

[1]***Plus ça change:*** Tannen refers to the well-known French saying, *le plus ça change, le plus c'est la même chose,* meaning: "the more things change, the more they remain the same." — Eds.

Henry David Thoreau

From "*Where I Lived, and What I Lived For*"

Regarded today as one of the central literary figures of the nineteenth century, in his lifetime Henry David Thoreau (1817–1862) was for the most part viewed as a talented but largely unsuccessful disciple of Ralph Waldo Emerson. In fact, although the two men held many beliefs in common, Thoreau possessed a fiercely independent intellect together with political convictions that sometimes alienated Emerson. Despite the considerable impact of his writing on contemporary thought, it was not until the 1930s that Thoreau's masterpiece, Walden *(1845), began to be studied widely, and only more recently that the value of his other writings has been recognized.*

Walden *provides an account of the twenty-six months Thoreau lived alone in a small cabin he built by himself at the edge of Walden Pond in Concord, Massachusetts. In the following famous passage from the second chapter of* Walden, *"Where I Lived, and What I Lived For," Thoreau explains why a twenty-eight-year-old Harvard graduate decided to get away temporarily from the life of the town and retreat to the nearby woods. His book became a how-to manual for generations of Americans who followed in his footsteps.*

In his journal Thoreau once commented, "We cannot write well or truly but what we write with gusto. The body, the senses, must conspire with the mind. . . . Often I feel that my head stands out too dry, when it should be immersed. . . . Whatever things I perceive with my entire man, those let me record, and it will be poetry. The sounds which I hear with the consent and coincidence of all my senses, these are significant and musical; at least, they only are heard."

I went to the woods because I wished to live deliberately, to front only the essential facts of life, and see if I could not learn what it had to teach, and not, when I came to die, discover that I had not lived. I did not wish to live what was not life, living is so dear; nor did I wish to practice resignation, unless it was quite necessary. I wanted to live deep and suck out all the marrow of life, to live so sturdily and Spartan-like as to put to rout all that was not life, to cut a broad swath and shave close, to drive life into a corner, and reduce it to its lowest terms, and, if it proved to be mean, why then to get the whole and genuine meanness of it, and publish its meanness to the world; or if it were sublime, to know it by experience, and be able to give a true account of it in my next excursion. For most men, it appears to me, are in a strange uncertainty about it, whether it is of the devil or of God, and have *somewhat hastily* concluded that it is the chief end of man here to "glorify God and enjoy him forever."

Still we live meanly, like ants; though the fable tells us that we were long ago changed into men;[1] like pygmies we fight with cranes;[2] it is error upon error, and clout upon clout, and our best virtue has for its occasion a superfluous and evitable wretchedness. Our life is frittered away by detail. An honest man has hardly need to count more than his ten fingers, or in extreme cases he may add his ten toes, and lump the rest. Simplicity, simplicity, simplicity! I say, let your affairs be as two or three, and not a hundred or a thousand; instead of a million count half a dozen, and keep your accounts on your thumb nail. In the midst of this chopping sea of civilized life, such are the clouds and storms and quicksands and thousand-and-one items to be allowed for, that a man has to live, if he would not founder and go to the bottom and not make his port at all, by dead reckoning,[3] and he must be a great calculator indeed who succeeds. Simplify, simplify. Instead of three meals a day, if it be necessary eat but one; instead of a hundred dishes, five; and reduce other things in proportion. Our life is like a German Confederacy,[4] made up of petty states, with its boundary forever fluctuating, so that even a German cannot tell you how it is bounded at any moment. The nation itself, with all its so called internal improvements, which, by the way, are all external and superficial, is just such an unwieldy and overgrown establishment, cluttered with furniture and tripped up by its own traps, ruined by luxury and heedless expense, by want of calculation and a worthy aim, as the million households in the land; and the only cure for it as for them is in a rigid economy, a stern and more than Spartan simplicity of life and elevation of purpose. It lives too fast. Men think that it is essential that the *Nation* have commerce, and export ice, and talk through a telegraph, and ride thirty miles an hour, without a doubt, whether *they* do or not; but whether we should live like baboons or like men, is a little uncertain. If we do not get out sleepers,[5] and forge rails, and devote days and nights to the work, but go to tinkering upon our *lives* to improve *them,* who will build railroads? And if railroads are not built, how shall we get to heaven

---

[1]In a classic myth Zeus transformed ants into men for the purpose of repopulating a plague-devastated land. —EDS.

[2]The Trojans were likened to cranes that fought with pygmies in the *Iliad,* Book III. —EDS.

[3]A system for navigating a ship at sea without the aid of the sun and stars. —EDS.

[4]Germany, as Thoreau knew it during his lifetime, was an unstable grouping of states; only in 1871 was it brought together into a national unit by Bismarck. —EDS.

[5]Supports for railroad ties. —EDS.

in season? But if we stay at home and mind our business, who will want railroads? We do not ride on the railroad; it rides upon us. Did you ever think what those sleepers are that underlie the railroad? Each one is a man, an Irishman, or a Yankee man. The rails are laid on them, and they are covered with sand, and the cars run smoothly over them. They are sound sleepers, I assure you. And every few years a new lot is laid down and run over; so that, if some have the pleasure of riding on a rail, others have the misfortune to be ridden upon. And when they run over a man that is walking in his sleep, a supernumerary sleeper in the wrong position, and wake him up, they suddenly stop the cars, and make a hue and cry about it, as if this were an exception. I am glad to know that it takes a gang of men for every five miles to keep the sleepers down and level in their beds as it is, for this is a sign that they may sometime get up again.

Why should we live with such hurry and waste of life? We are determined to be starved before we are hungry. Men say that a stitch in time saves nine, and so they take a thousand stitches to-day to save nine to-morrow. As for *work*, we haven't any of any consequence. We have the Saint Vitus' dance, and cannot possibly keep our heads still. If I should only give a few pulls at the parish bell-rope, as for a fire, that is, without setting the bell,[6] there is hardly a man on his farm in the outskirts of Concord, notwithstanding that press of engagements which was his excuse so many times this morning, nor a boy, nor a woman, I might almost say, but would forsake all and follow that sound, not mainly to save property from the flames, but, if we will confess the truth, much more to see it burn, since burn it must, and we, be it known, did not set it on fire,—or to see it put out, and have a hand in it, if that is done as handsomely; yes, even if it were the parish church itself. Hardly a man takes a half hour's nap after dinner, but when he wakes he holds up his head and asks, "What's the news?" as if the rest of mankind had stood his sentinels. Some give directions to be waked every half hour, doubtless for no other purpose; and then, to pay for it, they tell what they have dreamed. After a night's sleep the news is as indispensable as the breakfast. "Pray tell me any thing new that has happened to a man any where on this globe,"— and he reads it over his coffee and rolls, that a man has had his eyes gouged out this morning on the Wachito River;[7] never dreaming the while that he lives in the dark unfathomed mammoth cave of this world, and has but the rudiment of an eye himself.

For my part, I could easily do without the post-office. I think that there are very few important communications made through it. To speak critically, I never received more than one or two letters in my life—I wrote this some years ago—that were worth the postage. The penny-post is, commonly, an institution through which you seriously offer a man that penny for his thoughts which is so often safely offered in jest. And I am

---

[6]Inverting the bell by pulling it too hard.—EDS.
[7]Tributary of the Red River in Arkansas.—EDS.

sure that I never read any memorable news in a newspaper. If we read of one man robbed, or murdered, or killed by accident, or one house burned, or one vessel wrecked, or one steamboat blown up, or one cow run over on the Western Railroad, or one mad dog killed, or one lot of grasshoppers in the winter, — we never read of another. One is enough. If you are acquainted with the principle, what do you care for a myriad instances and applications? To a philosopher all *news,* as it is called, is gossip, and they who edit and read it are old women over their tea. Yet not a few are greedy after this gossip. There was such a rush, as I hear, the other day at one of the offices to learn the foreign news by the last arrival, that several large squares of plate glass belonging to the establishment were broken by the pressure, — news which I seriously think a ready wit might write a twelve-month or twelve years beforehand with sufficient accuracy. As for Spain, for instance, if you know how to throw in Don Carlos and the Infanta, and Don Pedro[8] and Seville and Granada, from time to time in the right proportions, — they may have changed the names a little since I saw the papers, — and serve up a bull-fight when other entertainments fail, it will be true to the letter, and give us as good an idea of the exact state or ruin of things in Spain as the most succinct and lucid reports under this head in the newspapers: and as for England, almost the last significant scrap of news from that quarter was the revolution of 1649;[9] and if you have learned the history of her crops for an average year, you never need attend to that thing again, unless your speculations are of a merely pecuniary character. If one may judge who rarely looks into the newspapers, nothing new does ever happen in foreign parts, a French revolution not excepted.

What news! how much more important to know what that is which was never old! "Kieou-he-yu (great dignitary of the state of Wei) sent a man to Khoung-tseu[10] to know his news. Khoung-tseu caused the messenger to be seated near him, and questioned him in these terms: What is your master doing? The messenger answered with respect: My master desires to diminish the number of his faults, but he cannot come to the end of them. The messenger being gone, the philosopher remarked: What a worthy messenger! What a worthy messenger!" The preacher, instead of vexing the ears of drowsy farmers on their day of rest at the end of the week, — for Sunday is the fit conclusion of an ill-spent week, and not the fresh and brave beginning of a new one — with this one other draggle-tail of a sermon, should shout with thundering voice, — "Pause! Avast! Why so seeming fast, but deadly slow?"

Shams and delusions are esteemed for soundest truths, while reality is fabulous. If men would steadily observe realities only, and not allow

5

---

[8]Members of the Spanish nobility. — EDS.
[9]The end of the British monarchy at the hands of the Puritan Commonwealth. — EDS.
[10]Confucius. The incident is described in *The Analects,* XIV, 26. — EDS.

themselves to be deluded, life, to compare it with such things as we know, would be like a fairy tale and the Arabian Nights' Entertainments. If we respected only what is inevitable and has a right to be, music and poetry would resound along the streets. When we are unhurried and wise, we perceive that only great and worthy things have any permanent and absolute existence,—that petty fears and petty pleasures are but the shadow of the reality. This is always exhilarating and sublime. By closing the eyes and slumbering, and consenting to be deceived by shows, men establish and confirm their daily life of routine and habit every where, which still is built on purely illusory foundations. Children, who play life, discern its true law and relations more clearly than men, who fail to live it worthily, but who think that they are wiser by experience, that is, by failure. I have read in a Hindoo book, that "there was a king's son, who, being expelled in infancy from his native city, was brought up by a forester, and, growing up to maturity in that state, imagined himself to belong to the barbarous race with which he lived. One of his father's ministers having discovered him, revealed to him what he was, and the misconception of his character was removed, and he knew himself to be a prince. So soul," continues the Hindoo philosopher, "from the circumstances in which it is placed, mistakes its own character, until the truth is revealed to it by some holy teacher, and then it knows itself to be *Brahme*."[11] I perceive that we inhabitants of New England live this mean life that we do because our vision does not penetrate the surface of things. We think that that *is* which *appears* to be. If a man should walk through this town and see only the reality, where, think you, would the "Milldam"[12] go to? If he should give us an account of the realities he beheld there, we should not recognize the place in his description. Look at a meeting-house, or a court-house, or a jail, or a shop, or a dwelling-house, and say what that thing really is before a true gaze, and they would all go to pieces in your account of them. Men esteem truth remote, in the outskirts of the system, behind the farthest star, before Adam and after the last man. In eternity there is indeed something true and sublime. But all these times and places and occasions are now and here. God himself culminates in the present moment, and will never be more divine in the lapse of all the ages. And we are enabled to apprehend at all what is sublime and noble only by the perpetual instilling and drenching of the reality that surrounds us. The universe constantly and obediently answers to our conceptions; whether we travel fast or slow, the track is laid for us. Let us spend our lives in conceiving then. The poet or the artist never yet had so fair and noble a design but some of his posterity at least could accomplish it.

Let us spend one day as deliberately as Nature, and not be thrown off the track by every nutshell and mosquito's wing that falls on the rails. Let

[11]The foremost god in the Hindu hierarchy.—EDS.
[12]Concord's town center, meeting place for idle chatter.—EDS.

us rise early and fast, or break fast, gently and without perturbation; let company come and let company go, let the bells ring and the children cry,—determined to make a day of it. Why should we knock under and go with the stream? Let us not be upset and overwhelmed in that terrible rapid and whirlpool called a dinner, situated in the meridian shallows. Weather this danger and you are safe, for the rest of the way is down hill. With unrelaxed nerves, with morning vigor, sail by it, looking another way, tied to the mast like Ulysses.[13] If the engine whistles, let it whistle till it is hoarse for its pains. If the bell rings, why should we run? We will consider what kind of music they are like. Let us settle ourselves, and work and wedge our feet downward through the mud and slush of opinion, and prejudice, and tradition, and delusion, and appearance, that alluvion which covers the globe, through Paris and London, through New York and Boston and Concord, through church and state, through poetry and philosophy and religion, till we come to a hard bottom and rocks in place, which we can call *reality,* and say, This is, and no mistake; and then begin, having a *point d'appui,* below freshet and frost and fire, a place where you might found a wall or a state, or set a lamp-post safely, or perhaps a gauge, not a Nilometer, but a Realometer, that future ages might know how deep a freshet of shams and appearances had gathered from time to time. If you stand right fronting and face to face to a fact, you will see the sun glimmer on both its surfaces, as if it were a cimeter,[14] and feel its sweet edge dividing you through the heart and marrow, and so you will happily conclude your moral career. Be it life or death, we crave only reality. If we are really dying, let us hear the rattle in our throats and feel cold in the extremities; if we are alive, let us go about our business.

Time is but the stream I go a-fishing in. I drink at it; but while I drink I see the sandy bottom and detect how shallow it is. Its thin current slides away, but eternity remains. I would drink deeper; fish in the sky, whose bottom is pebbly with stars. I cannot count one. I know not the first letter of the alphabet. I have always been regretting that I was not as wise as the day I was born. The intellect is a cleaver; it discerns and rifts its way into the secret of things. I do not wish to be any more busy with my hands than is necessary. My head is hands and feet. I feel all my best faculties concentrated in it. My instinct tells me that my head is an organ for burrowing, as some creatures use their snout and fore-paws, and with it I would mine and burrow my way through these hills. I think that the richest vein is somewhere hereabouts; so by the divining rod and thin rising vapors I judge; and here I will begin to mine.

---

[13]I.e., be able to move past dangers in safety, like Ulysses in the *Odyssey*, who had himself bound to the ship's mast so that he could both listen to the Sirens' song and resist their fatal call.—EDS.

[14]Scimitar.—EDS.

The Reader's Presence

1. Thoreau's writing style is highly aphoristic; that is, it contains many well-put sentences and phrases that seem to embody general truths or pointed observations. Can you identify a few of these? What effect do they have?

2. Much of Thoreau's discontent is directed at what was for him "modern life" (i.e., America in the mid–1840s). What particular aspects of modern life concern him most? In what ways does moving to the woods help him escape modern life? Do you find any contemporary relevance to Thoreau's decision? For example, what might be some modern equivalents that Thoreau would find noxious if he were here today (do you think he would want to escape to the woods with a Jeep Cherokee and cellular phone)? What would he think of CNN?

3. Reread the selection's final paragraph. What do you think Thoreau is getting at? What image of him do you come away with? Try putting the main idea of this paragraph into your own words.

79

Sallie Tisdale

A Weight That Women Carry

Sallie Tisdale was born in 1957 in California and has lived in Oregon for many years. A nurse by profession, her medical training has shaped her career as a writer. Her first books, The Sorcerer's Apprentice: Tales of the Modern Hospital *(1986) and* Harvest Moon: Portrait of a Nursing Home *(1987), discuss the complex ethical issues that complicate the relationship between caregivers and patients. Tisdale takes up the subject of health from quite a different angle in her book* Lot's Wife: Salt and the Human Condition *(1988). This book uses the issue of salt consumption to reflect on the interconnections between people and the natural environment they inhabit. Tisdale's thoughts on these matters are further developed in* Stepping Westward: The Long Search for Home in the Pacific Northwest *(1991). More recently she has published* Talk Dirty to Me: An Intimate Philosophy of Sex *(1994), and her sixth book,* Pigs in Blankets, *is forthcoming. Tisdale has taught writing at the University of Portland and the University of California at Davis. "A Weight That Women Carry" appeared in* Harper's *in 1993,*

*where she is a contributing editor. She also writes a column, "Second Thoughts,"
for* Salon *magazine.*

    *Tisdale has said, "My love of writing is at its heart a love of language and
words, the joy of the successful search for the proper word, the joy of the process
of expression itself. . . . I have a particular love for the prose form, which can
contain everything we imagine."*

I don't know how much I weigh these days, though I can make a
good guess. For years I'd known that number, sometimes within a quarter
pound, known how it changed from day to day and hour to hour. I want
to weigh myself now; I lean toward the scale in the next room, imagine
standing there, lining up the balance. But I don't do it. Going this long,
starting to break the scale's spell — it's like waking up suddenly sober.

By the time I was sixteen years old I had reached my adult height of
five feet six inches and weighed 164 pounds. I weighed 164 pounds before and after a healthy pregnancy. I assume I weigh about the same now;
nothing significant seems to have happened to my body, this same old
body I've had all these years. I usually wear a size 14, a common clothing
size for American women. On bad days I think my body looks lumpy and
misshapen. On my good days, which are more frequent lately, I think I
look plush and strong; I think I look like a lot of women whose bodies
and lives I admire.

I'm not sure when the word "fat" first sounded pejorative to me, or
when I first applied it to myself. My grandmother was a petite woman, the
only one in my family. She stole food from other people's plates, and hid
the debris of her own meals so that no one would know how much she ate.
My mother was a size 14, like me, all her adult life; we shared clothes. She
fretted endlessly over food scales, calorie counters, and diet books. She
didn't want to quit smoking because she was afraid she would gain weight,
and she worried about her weight until she died of cancer five years ago. Dieting was always in my mother's way, always there in the conversations
above my head, the dialogue of stocky women. But I was strong and
healthy and didn't pay too much attention to my weight until I was grown.

It probably wouldn't have been possible for me to escape forever. It
doesn't matter that whole human epochs have celebrated big men and
women, because the brief period in which I live does not; since I was
born, even the voluptuous calendar girl has gone. Today's models, the
women whose pictures I see constantly, unavoidably, grow more minimal
by the day. When I berate myself for not looking like — whomever I think
I should look like that day, I don't really care that no one looks like that.
I don't care that Michelle Pfeiffer doesn't look like the photographs I see
of Michelle Pfeiffer, I want to look — think I should look — like the photographs. I want her little miracles; the makeup artists, photographers,
and computer imagers who can add a mole, remove a scar, lift the
breasts, widen the eyes, narrow the hips, flatten the curves. The final
product is what I see, have seen my whole adult life. And I've seen this:

Even when big people become celebrities, their weight is constantly re-marked upon and scrutinized; their successes seem always to be *in spite of* their weight. I thought my successes must be, too.

I feel myself expand and diminish from day to day, sometimes from hour to hour. If I tell someone my weight, I change in their eyes: I become bigger or smaller, better or worse, depending on what that number, my weight, means to them. I know many men and women, young and old, gay and straight, who look fine, whom I love to see and whose faces and forms I cherish, who despise themselves for their weight. For their ordi-nary, human bodies. They and I are simply bigger than we think we should be. We always talk about weight in terms of gains and losses, and don't wonder at the strangeness of the words. In trying always to lose weight, we've lost hope of simply being seen for ourselves.

My weight has never actually affected anything — it's never seemed to mean anything one way or the other to how I lived. Yet for the last ten years I've felt quite bad about it. After a time, the number on the scale be-came my totem, more important than my experience — it was layered, metaphorical, *metaphysical,* and it had bewitching power. I thought if I could change that number I could change my life.

In my mid-twenties I started secretly taking diet pills. They made me feel strange, half-crazed, vaguely nauseated. I lost about twenty-five pounds, dropped two sizes, and bought new clothes. I developed rituals and taboos around food, ate very little, and continued to lose weight. For a long time afterward I thought it only coincidental that with every pass-ing week I also grew more depressed and irritable.

I could recite the details, but they're remarkable only for being so common. I lost more weight until I was rather thin, and then I gained it all back. It came back slowly, pound by pound, in spite of erratic and melan-choly and sometimes frantic dieting, dieting I clung to even though being thin had changed nothing, had meant nothing to my life except that I was thin. Looking back, I remember blinding moments of shame and lightning-bright moments of clearheadedness, which inevitably gave way to rage at the time I'd wasted — rage that eventually would become, once again, self-disgust and the urge to lose weight. So it went, until I weighed exactly what I'd weighed when I began.

I used to be attracted to the sharp angles of the chronic dieter — the caffeine-wild, chain-smoking, skinny women I see sometimes. I consid-ered them a pinnacle not of beauty but of will. Even after I gained back my weight, I wanted to be like that, controlled and persevering, live that underfed life so unlike my own rather sensual and disorderly existence. I felt I should always be dieting, for the dieting of it; dieting had become a rule, a given, a constant. Every ordinary value is distorted in this lens. I felt guilty for not being completely absorbed in my diet, for getting dis-tracted, for not caring enough all the time. The fat person's character flaw is a lack of narcissism. She's let herself go.

So I would began again—and at first it would all seem so . . . easy.   10
Simple arithmetic. After all, 3,500 calories equal one pound of fat—so
the books and articles by the thousands say. I would calculate how long it
would take to achieve the magic number on the scale, to succeed, to win.
All past failures were suppressed. If 3,500 calories equal one pound, all I
needed to do was cut 3,500 calories out of my intake every week. The
first few days of a new diet would be colored with a sense of control—
organization and planning, power over the self. Then the basic futile misery took over.

I would weigh myself with foreboding, and my weight would determine how went the rest of my day, my week, my life. When 3,500 calories didn't equal one pound lost after all, I figured it was my body that
was flawed, not the theory. One friend, who had tried for years to lose
weight following prescribed diets, made what she called "an amazing discovery." The real secret to a diet, she said, was that you had to be willing
to be hungry *all the time.* You had to eat even less than the diet allowed.

I believed that being thin would make me happy. Such a pernicious,
enduring belief. I lost weight and wasn't happy and saw that elusive happiness disappear in a vanishing point, requiring more—more self-disgust,
more of the misery of dieting. Knowing all that I know now about the biology and anthropology of weight, knowing that people naturally come
in many shapes and sizes, knowing that diets are bad for me and won't
make me thin—sometimes none of this matters. I look in the mirror and
think: Who am I kidding? *I've got to do something about myself.* Only
then will this vague discontent disappear. Then I'll be loved.

For ages humans believed that the body helped create the personality,
from the humors of Galen to W. H. Sheldon's somatotypes. Sheldon distinguished between three templates—endomorph, mesomorph, and ecto-
morph—and combined them into hundreds of variations with physical,
emotional, and psychological characteristics. When I read about weight
now, I see the potent shift in the last few decades: The modern culture of
dieting is based on the idea that the personality creates the body. Our size
must be in some way voluntary, or else it wouldn't be subject to change.
A lot of my misery over my weight wasn't about how I looked at all. I
was miserable because I believed *I* was bad, not my body. I felt truly reduced then, reduced to being just a body and nothing more.

Fat is perceived as an *act* rather than a thing. It is antisocial, and curable through the application of social controls. Even the feminist revisions of dieting, so powerful in themselves, pick up the theme: the
hungry, empty heart; the woman seeking release from sexual assault, or
the man from the loss of the mother, through food and fat. Fat is now a
symbol not of the personality but of the soul—the cluttered, neurotic,
and immature soul.

Fat people eat for "mere gratification," I read, as though no one else   15
does. Their weight is *intentioned,* they simply eat "too much," their flesh

is lazy flesh. Whenever I went on a diet, eating became cheating. One pretzel was cheating. Two apples instead of one was cheating—a large potato instead of a small, carrots instead of broccoli. It didn't matter which diet I was on; diets have failure built in, failure is in the definition. Every substitution—even carrots for broccoli—was a triumph of desire over will. When I dieted, I didn't feel pious just for sticking to the rules. I felt condemned for the act of eating itself, as though my hunger were never normal. My penance was to not eat at all.

My attitude toward food became quite corrupt. I came, in fact, to subconsciously believe food itself was corrupt. Diet books often distinguish between "real" and "unreal" hunger, so that *correct* eating is hollowed out, unemotional. A friend of mine who thinks of herself as a compulsive eater says she feels bad only when she eats for pleasure. "Why?" I ask, and she says, "Because I'm eating food I don't need." A few years ago I might have admired that. Now I try to imagine a world where we eat only food we need, and it seems inhuman. I imagine a world devoid of holidays and wedding feasts, wakes and reunions, a unique shared joy. "What's wrong with eating a cookie because you like cookies?" I ask her, and she hasn't got an answer. These aren't rational beliefs, any more than the unnecessary pleasure of ice cream is rational. Dieting presumes pleasure to be an insignificant, or at least malleable, human motive.

I felt no joy in being thin—it was just work, something I had to do. But when I began to gain back the weight, I felt despair. I started reading about the "recidivism" of dieting. I wondered if I had myself to blame not only for needing to diet in the first place but for dieting itself, the weight inevitably regained. I joined organized weight-loss programs, spent a lot of money, listened to lectures I didn't believe on quack nutrition, ate awful, processed diet foods. I sat in groups and applauded people who'd lost a half pound, feeling smug because I'd lost a pound and a half. I felt ill much of the time, found exercise increasingly difficult, cried often. And I thought that if I could only lose a little weight, everything would be all right.

When I say to someone, "I'm fat," I hear, "Oh, no! You're not *fat!* You're just—" What? Plump? Big-boned? Rubenesque? I'm just *not thin*. That's crime enough. I began this story by stating my weight. I said it all at once, trying to forget it and take away its power; I said it to be done being scared. Doing so, saying it out loud like that, felt like confessing a mortal sin. I have to bite my tongue not to seek reassurance, not to defend myself, not to plead. I see an old friend for the first time in years, and she comments on how much my fourteen-year-old son looks like me—"except, of course, he's not chubby." "Look who's talking," I reply, through clenched teeth. This pettiness is never far away; concern with my weight evokes the smallest, meanest parts of me. I look at another woman passing on the street and think, "At least I'm not *that* fat."

Recently I was talking with a friend who is naturally slender about a mutual acquaintance who is quite large. To my surprise my friend reproached this woman because she had seen her eating a cookie at lunchtime. "How is she going to lose weight that way?" my friend wondered. When you are as fat as our acquaintance is, you are primarily, fundamentally, seen as fat. It is your essential characteristic. There are so many presumptions in my friend's casual, cruel remark. She assumes that this woman should diet all the time—and that she *can*. She pronounces whole categories of food to be denied her. She sees her unwillingness to behave in this externally prescribed way, even for a moment, as an act of rebellion. In his story "A Hunger Artist," Kafka writes that the guards of the fasting man were "usually butchers, strangely enough." Not so strange, I think.

I know that the world, even if it views me as overweight (and I'm not   20
sure it really does), clearly makes a distinction between me and this very big woman. I would rather stand with her and not against her, see her for all she is besides fat. But I know our experiences aren't the same. My thin friend assumes my fat friend is unhappy because she is fat: Therefore, if she loses weight she will be happy. My fat friend has a happy marriage and family and a good career, but insofar as her weight is a source of misery, I think she would be much happier if she could eat her cookie in peace, if people would shut up and leave her weight alone. But the world never lets up when you are her size; she cannot walk to the bank without risking insult. Her fat is seen as perverse bad manners. I have no doubt she would be rid of the fat if she could be. If my left-handedness invited the criticism her weight does, I would want to cut that hand off.

In these last several years I seem to have had an infinite number of conversations about dieting. They are really all the same conversation—weight is lost, then weight is gained back. This repetition finally began to sink in. Why did everyone sooner or later have the same experience? (My friend who had learned to be hungry all the time gained back all the weight she had lost and more, just like the rest of us.) Was it really our bodies that were flawed? I began reading the biology of weight more carefully, reading the fine print in the endless studies. There is, in fact, a preponderance of evidence disputing our commonly held assumptions about weight.

The predominant biological myth of weight is that thin people live longer than fat people. The truth is far more complicated. (Some deaths of fat people attributed to heart disease seem actually to have been the result of radical dieting.) If health were our real concern, it would be dieting we questioned, not weight. The current ideal of thinness has never been held before, except as a religious ideal; the underfed body is the martyr's body. Even if people can lose weight, maintaining an artificially low weight for any period of time requires a kind of starvation. Lots of people are naturally thin, but for those who are not, dieting is an unnatural act; biology rebels. The metabolism of the hungry body can change inalterably, making it ever harder and harder to stay thin. I think chronic dieting made me gain weight—not only pounds, but fat. This equation seemed so strange at first that I couldn't believe it. But the weight I put back on after losing was much more stubborn than the original weight. I had lost it by taking diet pills and not eating much of anything at all for quite a long time. I haven't touched the pills again, but not eating much of anything no longer works.

When Oprah Winfrey first revealed her lost weight, I didn't envy her. I thought, She's in trouble now. I knew, I was certain, she would gain it back; I believed she was biologically destined to do so. The tabloid headlines blamed it on a cheeseburger or mashed potatoes, they screamed OPRAH PASSES 200 POUNDS, and I cringed at her misery and how the world wouldn't let up, wouldn't leave her alone, wouldn't let her be anything else. How dare the world do this to anyone? I thought, and then realized I did it to myself.

The "Ideal Weight" charts my mother used were at their lowest acceptable-weight ranges in the 1950s, when I was a child. They were based on sketchy and often inaccurate actuarial evidence, using, for the most part, data on northern Europeans and allowing for the most minimal differences in size for a population of less than half a billion people. I never fit those weight charts, I was always just outside the pale. As an adult, when I would join an organized diet program, I accepted their version of my Weight Goal as gospel, knowing it would be virtually impossible to reach. But reach I tried; that's what one does with gospel. Only in the last few years have the weight tables begun to climb back into the world of the average human. The newest ones distinguish by gender, frame, and age. And suddenly I'm not off the charts anymore. I have a place.

A man who is attracted to fat women says, "I actually have less specific physical criteria than most men. I'm attracted to women who weigh 170 or 270 or 370. Most men are only attracted to women who weigh between 100 and 135. So who's got more of a fetish?" We look at fat as a problem of the fat person. Rarely do the tables get turned, rarely do we imagine that it might be the viewer, not the viewed, who is limited. What the hell is wrong with *them*, anyway? Do they believe everything they see on television?   25

My friend Phil, who is chronically and almost painfully thin, admitted that in his search for a partner he finds himself prejudiced against fat women. He seemed genuinely bewildered by this. I didn't jump to reassure him that such prejudice is hard to resist. What I did was bite my tongue at my urge to be reassured by him, to be told that I, at least, wasn't fat. That over the centuries humans have been inclined to prefer extra flesh rather than the other way around seems unimportant. All we see now tells us otherwise. Why does my kindhearted friend criticize another woman for eating a cookie when she would never dream of commenting in such a way on another person's race or sexual orientation or disability? Deprivation is the dystopian idea.

My mother called her endless diets "reducing plans." Reduction, the diminution of women, is the opposite of feminism, as Kim Chernin points out in *The Obsession*. Smallness is what feminism strives against, the smallness that women confront everywhere. All of women's spaces are smaller than those of men, often inadequate, without privacy. Furniture designers distinguish between a man's and a woman's chair, because women don't spread out like men. (A sprawling woman means only one thing.) Even our voices are kept down. By embracing dieting I was rejecting a lot I held dear, and the emotional dissonance that created just seemed like one more necessary evil.

A fashion magazine recently celebrated the return of the "well-fed" body; a particular model was said to be "the archetype of the new womanly woman . . . stately, powerful." She is a size 8. The images of women presented to us, images claiming so maliciously to be the images of women's whole lives, are not merely social fictions. They are *absolute* fictions; they can't exist. How would it feel, I began to wonder, to cultivate my own real womanliness rather than despise it? Because it was my fleshy curves I wanted to be rid of, after all. I dreamed of having a boy's body, smooth, hipless, lean. A body rapt with possibility, a receptive body suspended before the storms of maturity. A dear friend of mine, nursing her second child, weeps at her newly voluptuous body. She loves her children and hates her own motherliness, wanting to be unripened again, to be a bud and not a flower.

Recently I've started shopping occasionally at stores for "large women," where the smallest size is a 14. In department stores the size 12 and 14 and 16 clothes are kept in a ghetto called the Women's Department. (And who would want that, to be the size of a woman? We all dream of being "juniors" instead.) In the specialty stores the clerks are usually big women and the customers are big, too, big like a lot of women in my life—friends, my sister, my mother and aunts. Not long ago I bought a pair of jeans at Lane Bryant and then walked through the mall to the Gap, with its shelves of generic clothing. I flicked through the clearance rack and suddenly remembered the Lane Bryant shopping bag in my hand and its enormous weight, the sheer heaviness of that brand name shouting to the world. The shout is that I've let myself go. I still feel like crying out sometimes: Can't I feel *satisfied?* But I am not supposed to be satisfied, not allowed to be satisfied. My discontent fuels the market; I need to be afraid in order to fully participate.

American culture, which has produced our dieting mania, does more   30
then reward privation and acquisition at the same time: it actually associates them with each other. Read the ads: the virtuous runner's reward is a new pair of $180 running shoes. The fat person is thought to be impulsive, indulgent, but insufficiently or incorrectly greedy, greedy for the wrong thing. The fat person lacks ambition. The young executive is complimented for being "hungry"; he is "starved for success." We are teased with what we will *have* if we are willing to *have not* for a time. A dieting friend, avoiding the food on my table, says, "I'm just dying for a bite of that."

Dieters are the perfect consumers: They never get enough. The dieter wistfully imagines food without substance, food that is not food, that begs the definition of food, because food is the problem. Even the ways we *don't eat* are based in class. The middle class don't eat in support groups. The poor can't afford not to eat at all. The rich hire someone to not eat with them in private. Dieting is an emblem of capitalism. It has a venal heart.

The possibility of living another way, living without dieting, began to take root in my mind a few years ago, and finally my second trip through Weight Watchers ended dieting for me. This last time I just couldn't stand the details, the same kind of details I'd seen and despised in other programs, on other diets: the scent of resignation, the weighing-in by the quarter pound, the before and after photographs of group leaders prominently displayed. Jean Nidetch, the founder of Weight Watchers, says, "Most fat people need to be hurt badly before they do something about themselves." She mocks every aspect of our need for food, of a person's sense of entitlement to food, of daring to *eat what we want*. Weight Watchers refuses to release its own weight charts except to say they make no distinction for frame size; neither has the organization ever released statistics on how many people who lose weight on the program eventually gain it back. I hated the endlessness of it, the turning of food into portions and exchanges, everything measured out, permitted, denied. I hated the very idea of "maintenance." Finally I realized I didn't just hate the diet. I was sick of the way I acted on a diet, the way I whined, my niggardly, penny-pinching behavior. What I liked in myself seemed to shrivel and disappear when I dieted. Slowly, slowly I saw these things. I saw that my pain was cut from whole cloth, imaginary, my own invention. I saw how much time I'd spent on something ephemeral, something that simply wasn't important, didn't matter. I saw that the real point of dieting is dieting — to not be done with it, ever.

I looked in the mirror and saw a woman, with flesh, curves, muscles, a few stretch marks, the beginnings of wrinkles, with strength and softness in equal measure. My body is the one part of me that is always, undeniably, here. To like myself means to be, literally, shameless, to be wanton in the pleasures of being inside a body. I feel *loose* this way, a little abandoned, a little dangerous. That first feeling of liking my body — not being resigned to it or despairing of change, but actually *liking* it — was tentative and guilty and frightening. It was alarming, because it was the way I'd felt as a child, before the world had interfered. Because surely I was wrong; I knew, I'd known for so long, that my body wasn't all right this way. I was afraid even to act as though I were all right: I was afraid that by doing so I'd be acting a fool.

For a time I was thin, I remember — and what I remember is nothing special — strain, a kind of hollowness, the same troubles and fears, and no magic. So I imagine losing weight again. If the world applauded, would this comfort me? Or would it only compromise whatever approval the world gives me now? What else will be required of me besides thinness? What will happen to me if I get sick, or lose the use of a limb, or God forbid, grow old?

By fussing endlessly over my body, I've ceased to inhabit it. I'm trying   35
to reverse this equation now, to trust my body and enter it again with a whole heart. I know more now than I used to about what constitutes "happy" and "unhappy," what the depths and textures of contentment are like. By letting go of dieting, I free up mental and emotional room. I have more space, I can move. The pursuit of another, elusive body, the body someone else says I should have, is a terrible distraction, a side-tracking that might have lasted my whole life long. By letting myself go, I go places.

Each of us in this culture, this twisted, inchoate culture, has to choose between battles: one battle is against the cultural ideal, and the other is against ourselves. I've chosen to stop fighting myself. Maybe I'm tilting at windmills; the cultural ideal is ever-changing, out of my control. It's not a cerebral journey, except insofar as I have to remind myself to stop counting, to stop thinking in terms of numbers. I know, even now that I've quit dieting and eat what I want, how many calories I take in every day. If I eat as I please, I eat a lot one day and very little the next; I skip meals and snack at odd times. My nourishment is good—as far as nutrition is concerned. I'm in much better shape than when I was dieting. I know that the small losses and gains in my weight over a period of time aren't simply related to the number of calories I eat. Someone asked me not long ago how I could possibly know my calorie intake if I'm not dieting (the implication being, perhaps, that I'm dieting secretly). I know because calorie counts and grams of fat and fiber are embedded in me. I have to work to *not* think of them, and I have to learn to not think of them in order to really live without fear.

When I look, *really* look, at the people I see every day on the street, I see a jungle of bodies, a community of women and men growing every which way like lush plants, growing tall and short and slender and round, hairy and hairless, dark and pale and soft and hard and glorious. Do I look around at the multitudes and think all these people—all these people who are like me and not like me, who are various and different— are not loved or lovable? Lately, everyone's body interests me, every body is desirable in some way. I see how muscles and skin shift with movement; I sense a cornucopia of flesh in the world. In the midst of it I am a little capacious and unruly.

I repeat with Walt Whitman, "I dote on myself . . . there is that lot of me, and all so luscious." I'm eating better, exercising more, feeling fine— and then I catch myself thinking, *Maybe I'll lose some weight.* But my mood changes or my attention is caught by something else, something deeper, more lingering. Then I can catch a glimpse of myself by accident and think only: That's me. My face, my hips, my hands. Myself.

The Reader's Presence

1. Tisdale's essay on the compulsion to diet in American society offers a revealing look at the prejudices, standards, and values associated with being "fat" and "thin" in contemporary life. Summarize the stereotypes Tisdale presents about "fat" people. How are they characterized by others, and especially by thin people? What assumptions about their personalities are embedded in these stereotypes? For example, what does Tisdale mean when she says: "Fat is perceived as an *act* rather than a thing" (paragraph 14)? What, more generally, does she offer as the "preponderance of evidence disputing our commonly held assumptions about weight" (paragraph 21)?

2. What does Tisdale mean when, at the end of paragraph 5, she reminds her readers that "We always talk about weight in terms of gains and losses, and don't wonder at the strangeness of the words"? What is so "strange" about the language of dieting? What metaphors are most often used to talk about dieting? To what extent do irony and paradox play important roles in the ways in which Americans are encouraged to think and talk about dieting? Point to specific examples to support your response. At what point does Tisdale suggest that one's perspective on being fat is finally quite relative, a matter of point of view? How convincing do you find her analysis at this point and at related moments?

3. Tisdale shapes her information into a series of illustrative anecdotes about fat people and the American mania about dieting. What patterns do you notice in the sequence of examples she presents? Does the fact that Tisdale announces that she is five foot six inches and weighs 164 pounds make it easier—or more difficult—for you as a reader to be drawn to and convinced by her analysis of dieting, its mythology, and its social and individual consequences? What does she "gain" and "lose" by providing us with this information in the first paragraph? How persuasive do you find the alternatives to dieting that she presents in the conclusion of her essay? What, finally, is the overriding purpose of her essay?

80

Calvin Trillin

A Traditional Family

The journalist, critic, novelist, and humorist Calvin Trillin was born in Kansas City in 1935, but has lived in New York City for many years. He works as a staff writer at the New Yorker *and contributes to many other magazines, including the* Atlantic, Harper's, Life, *and the* Nation. *Trillin is especially well known for his nonfiction. His magazine columns are collected in* Uncivil Liberties *(1982),* With All Disrespect: More Uncivil Liberties *(1985),* If You Can't Say Something Nice *(1987), and* Enough's Enough *(1990). Trillin has also published a series of very popular books dealing with food and eating. In* American Fried *(1974) he paints a revealing portrait of American life through his discussion of regional and national eating habits. His love of traveling and eating in the company of his wife Alice also led him to write* Alice, Let's Eat *(1978),* Third Helpings *(1983), and* Travels with Alice *(1989). More recently Trillin has forsworn the temptation to eat for a living and has taken his keen sense of humor to the stage in one-man shows. "A Traditional Family" is excerpted from his book* Too Soon to Tell *(1995); his other recent publications include* Deadline Poet: My Life as a Doggerelist *(1994),* Messages from My Father *(1996), and* Family Man *(1998).*

When asked to describe the process he goes through when writing factual as opposed to imaginative columns, Trillin replied, "In a non-fiction piece . . . you really have to carry around a lot of baggage. You have what happened, your understanding of what happened, what you want to get across about what happened, all kinds of burdens of being fair to whatever sides there are. The facts are terribly restricting." Trillin typically writes at least four drafts of nonfiction articles, but finds that imaginative writing is less predictable. When writing his humor columns, for example, "it's a much less rigid system than that of writing non-fiction. Sometimes it only takes two drafts; sometimes it takes five."

I just found out that our family is no longer what the Census Bureau calls a traditional American family, and I want everyone to know that this is not our fault.

We now find ourselves included in the statistics that are used constantly to show the lamentable decline of the typical American household from something like Ozzie and Harriet and the kids to something like a bunch of kooks and hippies.

I want everyone to know right at the start that we are not kooks. Oh sure, we have our peculiarities, but we are not kooks. Also, we are not hippies. We have no children named Goodness. I am the first one to admit that reasonable people may differ on how to characterize a couple of my veteran sportcoats, and there may have been a remark or two passed in the neighborhood from time to time about the state of our front lawn. But no one has ever seriously suggested that we are hippies.

In fact, most people find us rather traditional. My wife and I have a marriage certificate, although I can't say I know exactly where to put my hands on it right at the moment. We have two children. We have a big meal on Christmas. We put on costumes at Halloween. (What about the fact that I always wear an ax murderer's mask on Halloween? That happens to be one of the peculiarities.) We make family decisions in the traditional American family way, which is to say the father is manipulated by the wife and the children. We lose a lot of socks in the wash. At our house, the dishes are done and the garbage is taken out regularly—after the glass and cans and other recyclable materials have been separated out. We're not talking about a commune here.

So why has the Census Bureau begun listing us with households that consist of, say, the ex-stepchild of someone's former marriage living with someone who is under the mistaken impression that she is the aunt of somebody or other? Because the official definition of a traditional American family is two parents and one or more children under age eighteen. Our younger daughter just turned nineteen. Is that our fault?

As it happens, I did everything in my power to keep her from turning nineteen. When our daughters were about two and five, I decided that they were the perfect age, and I looked around for some sort of freezing process that might keep them there. I discovered that there was no such freezing process on the market. Assuming, in the traditional American way, that the technology would come along by and by, I renewed my investigation several times during their childhoods—they always seemed to be at the perfect age—but the freezing process never surfaced. Meanwhile, they kept getting older at what seemed to me a constantly accelerating rate. Before you could say "Zip up your jacket," the baby turned nineteen. What's a parent to do?

Ask for an easement. That's what a parent's to do. When I learned about the Census Bureau's definition of a traditional family—it was mentioned in an Associated Press story about how the latest census shows the traditional family declining at a more moderate pace than "the rapid and destabilizing rate" at which it declined between 1970 and 1980—it occurred to me that we could simply explain the situation to the Census Bureau and ask that an exception be made in our case.

I realize that the Census Bureau would probably want to send out an inspector. I would acknowledge to him that our daughters are more or less away from home, but remind him that we have been assured by more experienced parents that we can absolutely count on their return. I would take the position, in other words, that we are just as traditional as any American family, just slightly undermanned at the moment—like a hockey team that has a couple of guys in the penalty box but is still a presence on the ice. We could show the official our Christmas tree decorations and our Halloween costumes and a lot of single socks. We might, in the traditional American way, offer him a cup of coffee and a small bribe.

I haven't decided for sure to approach the Census Bureau. For one thing, someone might whisper in the inspector's ear that I have been heard to refer to my older daughter's room—the room where we now keep the exercise bike—as "the gym," and that might take some explaining. Also, I haven't discussed the matter with my wife. I would, of course, abide by her wishes. It's traditional.

The Reader's Presence

1. According to Trillin, how does the Census Bureau define "a traditional American family"? How does Trillin discover that his family would no longer be included in the Census Bureau's statistical compilations about "traditional" American families? Why does his family no longer satisfy the Census Bureau's criteria? What does Trillin try to do about this "problem"?

2. What characteristics of his family's behavior does Trillin identify as "traditional"? Examine the effect(s) of Trillin's verb choices. What patterns do you notice? What other patterns do you notice that he has woven into his word choices? When—and how—does Trillin poke fun at himself and the members of his family? To what extent does his humor depend on irony? on wit? Point to specific words and phrases to support your response.

3. When—and how—does Trillin use gender and familial stereotypes to reinforce the points he makes? What significance do you attach to the attention to "fault" Trillin weaves into the essay? Identify—and then comment on the effectiveness of—how his examples subtly reinforce his concern about fault and responsibility.

81

Barbara Tuchman

"This Is the End of the World":
The Black Death

Barbara Tuchman (1912–1989) was an acclaimed historian who was noted for writing historical accounts in a literary style. Believing that most historians alienate their readers by including minute details and by ignoring the elements of well-written prose, Tuchman hoped to engage a broad audience with a well-told narrative. As she explained during a speech at the National Portrait Gallery in 1978, "I want the reader to turn the page and keep on turning to the end. . . . This is accomplished only when the narrative moves steadily ahead, not when it comes to a weary standstill, overloaded with every item uncovered in the research." Tuchman, a 1933 Radcliffe College graduate, never received formal training as a historian but developed an ability to document history early in her career while working as a research assistant for the Institute of Pacific Relations, a writer for the Nation, *a foreign correspondent during the Spanish Civil War, and as an editor for the Office of War Information during World War II. Tuchman earned critical attention when her third book,* The Zimmermann Telegram, *became a best-seller in 1958. She received a Pulitzer Prize for* The Guns of August *(1962), a description of the early days of World War I, and for* Stilwell and the American Experience in China, 1911–1945, *a biographical account of Joseph Warren Stilwell, an American military officer during China's shift from feudalism to communism. Other books include* The Proud Tower: A Portrait of the World before the War, 1890–1914 *(1966);* A Distant Mirror: The Calamitous Fourteenth Century *(1978), from which "This Is the End of the World": The Black Death is taken; and* The March of Folly: From Troy to Vietnam *(1984).*

In October 1347, two months after the fall of Calais,[1] Genoese trading ships put into the harbor of Messina in Sicily with dead and dying men at the oars. The ships had come from the Black Sea port of Caffa (now Feodosiya) in the Crimea, where the Genoese maintained a trading

---

[1]After a year-long siege, Calais surrendered to Edward III, king of England and self-declared king of France. — EDS.

post. The diseased sailors showed strange black swellings about the size of an egg or an apple in the armpits and groin. The swellings oozed blood and pus and were followed by spreading boils and black blotches on the skin from internal bleeding. The sick suffered severe pain and died quickly within five days of the first symptoms. As the disease spread, other symptoms of continuous fever and spitting of blood appeared instead of the swellings or buboes. These victims coughed and sweated heavily and died even more quickly, within three days or less, sometimes in twenty-four hours. In both types everything that issued from the body—breath, sweat, blood from the buboes and lungs, bloody urine, and blood-blackened excrement—smelled foul. Depression and despair accompanied the physical symptoms, and before the end "death is seen seated on the face."

The disease was bubonic plague, present in two forms: one that infected the bloodstream, causing the buboes and internal bleeding, and was spread by contact; and a second, more virulent pneumonic type that infected the lungs and was spread by respiratory infection. The presence of both at once cause the high mortality and speed of contagion. So lethal was the disease that cases were known of persons going to bed well and dying before they woke, of doctors catching the illness at a bedside and dying before the patient. So rapidly did it spread from one to another that to a French physician, Simon de Covino, it seemed as if one sick person "could infect the whole world." The malignity of the pestilence appeared more terrible because its victims knew no prevention and no remedy.

The physical suffering of the disease and its aspect of evil mystery were expressed in a strange Welsh lament which saw "death coming into our midst like black smoke, a plague which cuts off the young, a rootless phantom which has no mercy for fair countenance. Woe is me of the shilling in the armpit! It is seething, terrible . . . a head that gives pain and causes a loud cry . . . a painful angry knob . . . Great is its seething like a burning cinder . . . a grievous thing of ashy color." Its eruption is ugly like the "seeds of black peas, broken fragments of brittle sea-coal . . . the early ornaments of black death, cinders of the peelings of the cockle weed, a mixed multitude, a black plague like half-pence, like berries. . . ."

Rumors of a terrible plague supposedly arising in China and spreading through Tartary (Central Asia) to India and Persia, Mesopotamia, Syria, Egypt, and all of Asia Minor had reached Europe in 1346. They told of a death toll so devastating that all of India was said to be depopulated, whole territories covered by dead bodies, other areas with no one left alive. As added up by Pope Clement VI at Avignon, the total of reported dead reached 23,840,000. In the absence of a concept of contagion, no serious alarm was felt in Europe until the trading ships brought their black burden of pestilence into Messina while other infected ships from the Levant carried it to Genoa and Venice.

By January 1348 it penetrated France via Marseille, and North Africa via Tunis. Shipborne along coasts and navigable rivers, it spread west-

5

ward from Marseille through the ports of Languedoc to Spain and north-
ward up the Rhône to Avignon, where it arrived in March. It reached
Narbonne, Montpellier, Carcassonne, and Toulouse between February
and May, and at the same time in Italy spread to Rome and Florence and
their hinterlands. Between June and August it reached Bordeaux, Lyon,
and Paris, spread to Burgundy and Normandy, and crossed the Channel
from Normandy into southern England. From Italy during the same summer it crossed the Alps into Switzerland and reached eastward to Hungary.

In a given area the plague accomplished its kill within four to six
months and then faded, except in the larger cities, where, rooting into the
close-quartered population, it abated during the winter, only to reappear
in spring and rage for another six months.

In 1349 it resumed in Paris, spread to Picardy, Flanders, and the Low
Countries, and from England to Scotland and Ireland as well as to Nor-
way, where a ghost ship with a cargo of wool and a dead crew drifted off-
shore until it ran aground near Bergen. From there the plague passed into
Sweden, Denmark, Prussia, Iceland, and as far as Greenland. Leaving a
strange pocket of immunity in Bohemia, and Russia unattacked until
1351, it had passed from most of Europe by mid-1350. Although the
mortality rate was erratic, ranging from one fifth in some places to nine
tenths or almost total elimination in others, the overall estimate of modern demographers has settled—for the area extending from India to Iceland—around the same figure expressed in Froissart's casual words: "a
third of the world died." His estimate, the common one at the time, was
not an inspired guess but a borrowing of St. John's figure for mortality
from plague in Revelation, the favorite guide to human affairs of the
Middle Ages.

A third of Europe would have meant about 20 million deaths. No
one knows in truth how many died. Contemporary reports were an awed
impression, not an accurate count. In crowded Avignon, it was said, 400
died daily; (7,000 houses emptied by death were shut up; a single graveyard received 11,000 corpses in six weeks; half the city's inhabitants reportedly died, including 9 cardinals or one third of the total, and 70 lesser
prelates. Watching the endlessly passing death carts, chroniclers let normal exaggeration take wings and put the Avignon death toll at 62,000
and even at 120,000, although the city's total population was probably
less than 50,000.

When graveyards filled up, bodies at Avignon were thrown into the
Rhône until mass burial pits were dug for dumping the corpses. In London in such pits corpses piled up in layers until they overflowed. Everywhere reports speak of the sick dying too fast for the living to bury.
Corpses were dragged out of homes and left in front of doorways. Morning light revealed new piles of bodies. In Florence the dead were gathered
up by the Compagnia della Misericordia—founded in 1244 to care for
the sick—whose members wore red robes and hoods masking the face

except for the eyes. When their efforts failed, the dead lay putrid in the streets for days at a time. When no coffins were to be had, the bodies were laid on boards, two or three at once, to be carried to graveyards or common pits. Families dumped their own relatives into the pits, or buried them so hastily and thinly "that dogs dragged them forth and devoured their bodies."

Amid accumulating death and fear of contagion, people died without   10
last rites and were buried without prayers, a prospect that terrified the last hours of the stricken. A bishop in England gave permission to laymen to make confession to each other as was done by the Apostles, "or if no man is present then even to a woman," and if no priest could be found to administer extreme unction, "then faith must suffice." Clement VI found it necessary to grant remissions of sin to all who died of the plague because so many were unattended by priests. "And no bells tolled," wrote a chronicler of Siena, "and nobody wept no matter what his loss because almost everyone expected death. . . . And people said and believed, 'This is the end of the world.'"

In Paris, where the plague lasted through 1349, the reported death rate was 800 a day, in Pisa 500, in Vienna 500 to 600. The total dead in Paris numbered 50,000 or half the population. Florence, weakened by the famine of 1347, lost three to four fifths of its citizens, Venice two thirds, Hamburg and Bremen, though smaller in size, about the same proportion. Cities, as centers of transportation, were more likely to be affected than villages, although once a village was infected, its death rate was equally high. At Givry, a prosperous village in Burgundy of 1,200 to 1,500 people, the parish register records 615 deaths in the space of fourteen weeks, compared to an average of thirty deaths a year in the previous decade. In three villages of Cambridgeshire, manorial records show a death rate of 47 percent, 57 percent, and in one case 70 percent. When the last survivors, too few to carry on, moved away, a deserted village sank back into the wilderness and disappeared from the map altogether, leaving only a grass-covered ghostly outline to show where mortals once had lived.

In enclosed places such as monasteries and prisons, the infection of one person usually meant that of all, as happened in the Franciscan convents of Carcassonne and Marseille, where every inmate without exception died. Of the 140 Dominicans at Montpellier only seven survived. Petrarch's[2] brother Gherardo, member of a Carthusian monastery, buried the prior and 34 fellow monks one by one, sometimes three a day, until he was left alone with his dog and fled to look for a place that would take him in. Watching every comrade die, men in such places could not but wonder whether the strange peril that filled the air had not been sent to exterminate the human race. In Kilkenny, Ireland, Brother John Clyn of

---

[2]*Francesco Petrarch* (1304–1374): Italian writer whose sonnets influenced a tradition of European love poetry. — EDS.

the Friars Minor, another monk left alone among dead men, kept a record of what had happened lest "things which should be remembered perish with time and vanish from the memory of those who come after us." Sensing "the whole world, as it were, placed within the grasp of the Evil One," and waiting for death to visit him too, he wrote, "I leave parchment to continue this work, if perchance any man survive and any of the race of Adam escape this pestilence and carry on the work which I have begun." Brother John, as noted by another hand, died of the pestilence, but he foiled oblivion.

The largest cities of Europe, with populations of about 100,000, were Paris and Florence, Venice and Genoa. At the next level, with more than 50,000, were Ghent and Bruges in Flanders, Milan, Bologna, Rome, Naples, and Palermo, and Cologne. London hovered below 50,000, the only city in England except York with more than 10,000. At the level of 20,000 to 50,000 were Bordeaux, Toulouse, Montpellier, Marseille, and Lyon in France, Barcelona, Seville, and Toledo in Spain, Siena, Pisa, and other secondary cities in Italy, and the Hanseatic trading cities of the Empire. The plague raged through them all, killing anywhere from one third to two thirds of their inhabitants. Italy, with a total population of 10 to 11 million, probably suffered the heaviest toll. Following the Florentine bankruptcies, the crop failures and workers' riots of 1346–47, the revolt of Cola di Rienzi that plunged Rome into anarchy, the plague came as the peak of successive calamities. As if the world were indeed in the grasp of the Evil One, its first appearance on the European mainland in January 1348 coincided with a fearsome earthquake that carved a path of wreckage from Naples up to Venice. Houses collapsed, church towers toppled, villages were crushed, and the destruction reached as far as Germany and Greece. Emotional response, dulled by horrors, underwent a kind of atrophy epitomized by the chronicler who wrote "And in these days was burying without sorrow and wedding without friendschippe."

In Siena, where more than half the inhabitants died of the plague, work was abandoned on the great cathedral, planned to be the largest in the world, and never resumed, owing to loss of workers and master masons and "the melancholy and grief" of the survivors. The cathedral's truncated transept still stands in permanent witness to the sweep of death's scythe. Agnolo di Tura, a chronicler of Siena, recorded the fear of contagion that froze every other instinct. "Father abandoned child, wife husband, one brother another," he wrote, "for this plague seemed to strike through the breath and sight. And so they died. And no one could be found to bury the dead for money or friendship. . . . And I, Agnolo di Tura, called the Fat, buried my five children with my own hands, and so did many others likewise."

There were many to echo his account of inhumanity and few to balance it, for the plague was not the kind of calamity that inspired mutual help. Its loathsomeness and deadliness did not herd people together in mutual distress, but only prompted their desire to escape each other. 15

"Magistrates and notaries refused to come and make the wills of the dying," reported a Franciscan friar of Piazza in Sicily; what was worse, "even the priests did not come to hear their confessions." A clerk of the Archbishop of Canterbury reported the same of English priests who "turned away from the care of their benefices from fear of death." Cases of parents deserting children and children their parents were reported across Europe from Scotland to Russia. The calamity chilled the hearts of men, wrote Boccaccio[3] in his famous account of the plague in Florence that serves as introduction to the *Decameron.* "One man shunned another . . . kinsfolk held aloof, brother was forsaken by brother, often-times husband by wife; nay, what is more, and scarcely to be believed, fathers and mothers were found to abandon their own children to their fate, untended, unvisited as if they had been strangers." Exaggeration and literary pessimism were common in the fourteenth century, but the Pope's physician, Guy de Chauliac, was a sober, careful observer who reported the same phenomenon: "A father did not visit his son, nor the son his father. Charity was dead."

Yet not entirely. In Paris, according to the chronicler Jean de Venette, the nuns of the Hôtel Dieu or municipal hospital, "having no fear of death, tended the sick with all sweetness and humility." New nuns repeatedly took the places of those who died, until the majority "many times renewed by death now rest in peace with Christ as we may piously believe."

When the plague entered northern France in July 1348, it settled first in Normandy and, checked by winter, gave Picardy a deceptive interim until the next summer. Either in mourning or warning, black flags were flown from church towers of the worst-stricken villages of Normandy. "And in that time," wrote a monk of the abbey of Fourcarment, "the mortality was so great among the people of Normandy that those of Picardy mocked them." The same unneighborly reaction was reported of the Scots, separated by a winter's immunity from the English. Delighted to hear of the disease that was scourging the "southrons," they gathered forces for an invasion, "laughing at their enemies." Before they could move, the savage mortality fell upon them too, scattering some in death and the rest in panic to spread the infection as they fled.

In Picardy in the summer of 1349 the pestilence penetrated the castle of Coucy to kill Enguerrand's[4] mother, Catherine, and her new husband. Whether her nine-year-old son escaped by chance or was perhaps living elsewhere with one of his guardians is unrecorded. In nearby Amiens, tannery workers, responding quickly to losses in the labor force, combined to bargain for higher wages. In another place villagers were seen dancing

---

[3]*Giovanni Boccaccio* (1313–1375): Italian writer best known for his collection of stories about the Black Death, *The Decameron.* —EDS.

[4]Enguerrand de Coucy is the historical figure on which Tuchman focuses in her account of the fourteenth century. —EDS.

to drums and trumpets, and on being asked the reason, answered that, seeing their neighbors die day by day while their village remained immune, they believed they could keep the plague from entering "by the jollity that is in us. That is why we dance." Further north in Tournai on the border of Flanders, Gilles li Muisis, Abbot of St. Martin's, kept one of the epidemic's most vivid accounts. The passing bells rang all day and all night, he recorded, because sextons were anxious to obtain their fees while they could. Filled with the sound of mourning, the city became oppressed by fear, so that the authorities forbade the tolling of bells and the wearing of black and restricted funeral services to two mourners. The silencing of funeral bells and of criers' announcements of deaths was ordained by most cities. Siena imposed a fine on the wearing of mourning clothes by all except widows.

Flight was the chief recourse of those who could afford it or arrange it. The rich fled to their country places like Boccaccio's young patricians of Florence, who settled in a pastoral palace "removed on every side from the roads" with "wells of cool water and vaults of rare wines." The urban poor died in their burrows, "and only the stench of their bodies informed neighbors of their death." That the poor were more heavily afflicted than the rich was clearly remarked at the time, in the north as in the south. A Scottish chronicler, John of Fordun, stated flatly that the pest "attacked especially the meaner sort and common people — seldom the magnates." Simon de Covino of Montpellier made the same observation. He ascribed it to the misery and want and hard lives that made the poor more susceptible, which was half the truth. Close contact and lack of sanitation was the unrecognized other half. It was noticed too that the young died in greater proportion than the old; Simon de Covino compared the disappearance of youth to the withering of flowers in the fields.

In the countryside peasants dropped dead on the roads, in the fields, in their houses. Survivors in growing helplessness fell into apathy, leaving ripe wheat uncut and livestock untended. Oxen and asses, sheep and goats, pigs and chickens ran wild and they too, according to local reports, succumbed to the pest. English sheep, bearers of the precious wool, died throughout the country. The chronicler Henry Knighton, canon of Leicester Abbey, reported 5,000 dead in one field alone, "their bodies so corrupted by the plague that neither beast nor bird would touch them," and spreading an appalling stench. In the Austrian Alps wolves came down to prey upon sheep and then, "as if alarmed by some invisible warning, turned and fled back into the wilderness." In remote Dalmatia bolder wolves descended upon a plague-stricken city and attacked human survivors. For want of herdsmen, cattle strayed from place to place and died in hedgerows and ditches. Dogs and cats fell like the rest.

The dearth of labor held a fearful prospect because the fourteenth century lived close to the annual harvest both for food and for next year's seed "So few servants and laborers were left," wrote Knighton, "that no one knew where to turn for help." The sense of a vanishing future created a kind of dementia of despair. A Bavarian chronicler of Neuberg on the Danube recorded that "Men and women . . . wandered around as if mad" and let their cattle stray "because no one had any inclination to concern themselves about the future." Fields went uncultivated, spring seed unsown. Second growth with nature's awful energy crept back over cleared land, dikes crumbled, salt water reinvaded and soured the lowlands. With so few hands remaining to restore the work of centuries, people felt, in Walsingham's words, that "the world could never again regain its former prosperity."

Though the death rate was higher among the anonymous poor, the known and the great died too. King Alfonso XI of Castile was the only reigning monarch killed by the pest, but his neighbor King Pedro of Aragon lost his wife, Queen Leonora, his daughter Marie, and a niece in the space of six months. John Cantacuzene, Emperor of Byzantium, lost his son. In France the lame Queen Jeanne and her daughter-in-law Bonne de Luxemburg, wife of the Dauphin, both died in 1349 in the same phase that took the life of Enguerrand's mother. Jeanne, Queen of Navarre, daughter of Louis X, was another victim. Edward III's second daughter, Joanna, who was on her way to marry Pedro, the heir of Castile, died in Bordeaux. Women appear to have been more vulnerable than men, perhaps because, being more housebound, they were more exposed to fleas. Boccaccio's mistress Fiammetta, illegitimate daughter of the King of Naples, died, as did Laura, the beloved—whether real or fictional—of Petrarch. Reaching out to us in the future, Petrarch cried, "Oh happy posterity who will not experience such abysmal woe and will look upon our testimony as a fable."

In Florence Giovanni Villani, the great historian of his time, died at 68 in the midst of an unfinished sentence: *". . . e dure questo pistolenza fino a . . .* (in the midst of this pestilence there came to an end (. . .)." Siena's master painters, the brothers Ambrogio and Pietro Lorenzetti, whose names never appear after 1348, presumably perished in the plague, as did Andrea Pisano, architect and sculptor of Florence. William of Ockham and the English mystic Richard Rolle of Hampole both disappear from mention after 1349. Francisco Datini, merchant of Prato, lost both his parents and two siblings. Curious sweeps of mortality afflicted certain bodies of merchants in London. All eight wardens of the Company of Cutters, all six wardens of the Hatters, and four wardens of the Goldsmiths died before July 1350. Sir John Pulteney, master draper and four times Mayor of London, was a victim, likewise Sir John Montgomery, Governor of Calais.

Among the clergy and doctors the mortality was naturally high because of the nature of their professions. Out of 24 physicians in Venice, 20 were said to have lost their lives in the plague, although, according to another account, some were believed to have fled or to have shut themselves up in their houses. At Montpellier, site of the leading medieval medical school, the physician Simon de Covino reported that, despite the great number of doctors, "hardly one of them escaped." In Avignon, Guy de Chauliac confessed that he performed his medical visits only because he dared not stay away for fear of infamy, but "I was in continual fear." He claimed to have contracted the disease but to have cured himself by his own treatment; if so, he was one of the few who recovered.

Clerical mortality varied with rank. Although the one-third toll of   25
cardinals reflects the same proportion as the whole, this was probably due to their concentration in Avignon. In England, in strange and almost sinister procession, the Archbishop of Canterbury, John Stratford, died in August 1348, his appointed successor died in May 1349, and the next appointee three months later, all three within a year. Despite such weird vagaries, prelates in general managed to sustain a higher survival rate than the lesser clergy. Among bishops the deaths have been estimated at about one in twenty. The loss of priests, even if many avoided their fearful duty of attending the dying, was about the same as among the population as a whole.

Government officials, whose loss contributed to the general chaos, found, on the whole, no special shelter. In Siena four of the nine members of the governing oligarchy died, in France one third of the royal notaries, in Bristol 15 out of the 52 members of the Town Council or almost one third. Tax-collecting obviously suffered, with the result that Philip VI was unable to collect more than a fraction of the subsidy granted him by the Estates in the winter of 1347–48.

Lawlessness and debauchery accompanied the plague as they had during the great plague of Athens of 430 B.C., when according to Thucydides, men grew bold in the indulgence of pleasure: "For seeing how the rich died in a moment and those who had nothing immediately inherited their property, they reflected that life and riches were alike transitory and they resolved to enjoy themselves while they could." Human behavior is timeless. When St. John had his vision of plague in Revelation, he knew from some experience or race memory that those who survived "repented not of the work of their hands. . . . Neither repented they of their murders, nor of their sorceries, nor of their fornication, nor of their thefts."

Ignorance of the cause augmented the sense of horror. Of the real carriers, rats and fleas, the fourteenth century had no suspicion, perhaps because they were so familiar. Fleas, though a common household nuisance, are not once mentioned in contemporary plague writings, and rats only incidentally, although folklore commonly associated them with pestilence. The legend of the Pied Piper arose from an outbreak of 1284. The actual plague bacillus, *Pasturella pestis,* remained undiscovered for another 500 years. Living alternately in the stomach of the flea and the bloodstream of the rat who was the flea's host, the bacillus in its bubonic form was transferred to humans and animals by the bite of either rat or flea. It traveled by virtue of *Rattus rattus,* the small medieval black rat that lived on ships, as well as by the heavier brown or sewer rat. What precipitated the turn of the bacillus from innocuous to virulent form is unknown, but the occurrence is now believed to have taken place not in China but somewhere in central Asia and to have spread along the caravan routes. Chinese origin was a mistaken notion of the fourteenth century based on real but belated reports of huge death tolls in China from drought, famine, and pestilence which have since been traced to the 1330s, too soon to be responsible for the plague that appeared in India in 1346.

The phantom enemy had no name. Called the Black Death only in later recurrences, it was known during the first epidemic simply as the Pestilence or Great Mortality. Reports from the East, swollen by fearful imaginings, told of strange tempests and "sheets of fire" mingled with huge hailstones that "slew almost all," or a "vast rain of fire" that burned up men, beasts, stones, trees, villages, and cities. In another version, "foul blasts of wind" from the fires carried the infection to Europe "and now as some suspect it cometh round the seacoast." Accurate observation in this case could not make the mental jump to ships and rats because no idea of animal- or insect-borne contagion existed.

The earthquake was blamed for releasing sulfurous and foul fumes   30
from the earth's interior, or as evidence of a titanic struggle of planets and oceans causing waters to rise and vaporize until fish died in masses and corrupted the air. All these explanations had in common a factor of poisoned air, of miasmas and thick, stinking mists traced to every kind of natural or imagined agency from stagnant lakes to malign conjunction of the planets, from the hand of the Evil One to the wrath of God. Medical thinking, trapped in the theory of astral influences, stressed air as the communicator of disease, ignoring sanitation or visible carriers. The existence of two carriers confused the trail, the more so because the flea could live and travel independently of the rat for as long as a month and, if infected by the particularly virulent septicemic form of the bacillus, could infect humans without reinfecting itself from the rat. The simultaneous presence of the pneumonic form of the disease, which was indeed communicated through the air, blurred the problem further.

The mystery of the contagion was "the most terrible of all the terrors," as an anonymous Flemish cleric in Avignon wrote to a correspondent in Bruges. Plagues had been know before, from the plague of Athens (believed to have been typhus) to the prolonged epidemic of the sixth century A.D., to the recurrence of sporadic outbreaks in the twelfth and thirteenth centuries, but they had left no accumulated store of understanding. That the infection came from contact with the sick or with their houses, clothes, or corpses was quickly observed but not comprehended. Gentile da Foligno, renowned physician of Perugia and doctor of medicine at the universities of Bologna and Padua, came close to respiratory infection when he surmised that poisonous material was "communicated by means of air breathed out and in." Having no idea of microscopic carriers, he had to assume that the air was corrupted by planetary influences. Planets, however, could not explain the ongoing contagion. The agonized search for an answer gave rise to such theories as transference by sight. People fell ill, wrote Guy de Chauliac, not only by remaining with the sick but "even by looking at them." Three hundred years later Joshua Barnes, the seventeenth century biographer of Edward III, could write that the power of infection had entered into beams of light and "darted death from the eyes."

Doctors struggling with the evidence could not break away from the terms of astrology, to which they believed all human physiology was subject. Medicine was the one aspect of medieval life, perhaps because of its links with the Arabs, not shaped by Christian doctrine. Clerics detested astrology, but could not dislodge its influence. Guy de Chauliac, physician to three popes in succession, practiced in obedience to the zodiac. While his *Cirurgia* was the major treatise on surgery of its time, while he understood the use of anesthesia made from the juice of opium, mandrake, or hemlock, he nevertheless prescribed bleeding and purgatives by the planets and divided chronic from acute diseases on the basis of one being under the rule of the sun and the other of the moon.

In October 1348 Philip VI asked the medical faculty of the University of Paris for a report on the affliction that seemed to threaten human survival. With careful thesis, antithesis, and proofs, the doctors ascribed it to a triple conjunction of Saturn, Jupiter, and Mars in the 40th degree of Aquarius said to have occurred on March 20, 1345. They acknowledged, however, effects "whose cause is hidden from even the most highly trained intellects." The verdict of the masters of Paris became the official version. Borrowed, copied by scribes, carried abroad, translated from Latin into various vernaculars, it was everywhere accepted, even by the Arab physicians of Cordova and Granada, as the scientific if not the popular answer. Because of the terrible interest of the subject, the translations of the plague tracts stimulated use of national languages. In that one respect, life came from death.

To the people at large there could be but one explanation—the wrath of God. Planets might satisfy the learned doctors, but God was closer to the average man. A scourge so sweeping and unsparing without any visible cause could only be seen as Divine punishment upon mankind for its sins. It might even be God's terminal disappointment in his creature. Matteo Villani compared the plague to the Flood in ultimate purpose and believed he was recording "the extermination of mankind." Efforts to appease Divine wrath took many forms, as when the city of Rouen ordered that everything that could anger God, such as gambling, cursing, and drinking, must be stopped. More general were the penitent processions authorized at first by the Pope, some lasting as long as three days, some attended by as many as 2,000, which everywhere accompanied the plague and helped to spread it.

Barefoot in sackcloth, sprinkled with ashes, weeping, praying, tearing their hair, carrying candles and relics, sometimes with ropes around their

35

necks or beating themselves with whips, the penitents wound through the streets, imploring the mercy of the Virgin and saints at their shrines. In a vivid illustration for the *Très Riches Heures* of the Duc de Berry, the Pope is shown in a penitent procession attended by four cardinals in scarlet from hat to hem. He raises both arms in supplication to the angel on top of the Castel Sant'Angelo, while white-robed priests bearing banners and relics in golden cases turn to look as one of their number, stricken by the plague, falls to the ground, his face contorted with anxiety. In the rear, a gray-clad monk falls beside another victim already on the ground as the townspeople gaze in horror. (Nominally the illustration represents a 6th century plague in the time of Pope Gregory the Great, but as medieval artists made no distinction between past and present, the scene is shown as the artist would have seen it in the fourteenth century.) When it became evident that these processions were sources of infection, Clement VI had to prohibit them.

In Messina, where the plague first appeared, the people begged the Archbishop of neighboring Catania to lend them the relics of St. Agatha. When the Catanians refused to let the relics go, the Archbishop dipped them in holy water and took the water himself to Messina, where he carried it in a procession with prayers and litanies through the streets. The demonic, which shared the medieval cosmos with God, appeared as "demons in the shape of dogs" to terrify the people. "A black dog with a drawn sword in his paws appeared among them, gnashing his teeth and rushing upon them and breaking all the silver vessels and lamps and candlesticks on the altars and casting them hither and thither. . . . So the people of Messina, terrified by this prodigious vision, were all strangely overcome by fear."

The apparent absence of earthly cause gave the plague a supernatural and sinister quality. Scandinavians believed that a Pest Maiden emerged from the mouth of the dead in the form of a blue flame and flew through the air to infect the next house. In Lithuania the Maiden was said to wave a red scarf through the door or window to let in the pest. One brave man, according to legend, deliberately waited at his open window with drawn sword and, at the fluttering of the scarf, chopped off the hand. He died of his deed, but his village was spared and the scarf long preserved as a relic in the local church.

Beyond demons and superstition the final hand was God's. The Pope acknowledged it in a Bull[5] of September 1348, speaking of the "pestilence with which God is afflicting the Christian people." To the Emperor John Cantacuzene it was manifest that a malady of such horrors, stenches, and agonies, and especially one bringing the dismal despair that settled upon its victims before they died, was not a plague "natural" to mankind but "a chastisement from Heaven." To Piers Plowman "these pestilences were for pure sin."

---

[5]A bull is a formal papal document. —EDS.

The general acceptance of this view created an expanded sense of guilt, for if the plague were punishment there had to be terrible sin to have occasioned it. What sins were on the fourteenth century conscience? Primarily greed, the sin of avarice, followed by usury, worldliness, adultery, blasphemy, falsehood, luxury, irreligion. Giovanni Villani, attempting to account for the cascade of calamity that had fallen upon Florence, concluded that it was retribution for the sins of avarice and usury that oppressed the poor. Pity and anger about the condition of the poor, especially victimization of the peasantry in war, was often expressed by writers of the time and was certainly on the conscience of the century. Beneath it all was the daily condition of medieval life, in which hardly an act or thought, sexual, mercantile, or military, did not contravene the dictates of the Church. Mere failure to fast or attend mass was sin. The result was an underground lake of guilt in the soul that the plague now tapped.

That the mortality was accepted as God's punishment may explain in   40
part the vacuum of comment that followed the Black Death. An investigator has noticed that in the archives of Périgord references to the war are innumerable, to the plague few. Froissart mentions the great death but once, Chaucer gives it barely a glance. Divine anger so great that it contemplated the extermination of man did not bear close examination.

The Reader's Presence

1. History is a form of story. Which elements of Tuchman's account seem to pertain to pure fact, and which to storytelling? Events are related in an objective tone. Is the writer's approval or disapproval ever evident? If so, where and in what ways?

2. This piece is drawn from a book deliberately titled *A Distant Mirror: The Calamitous Fourteenth Century*. In what ways does Tuchman's account suggest that fourteenth-century behaviors reflect our behaviors today?

3. At times Tuchman recounts history in the aggregate; at times she traces history through a specific figure. Find a few instances of this technique. Why might she have chosen to augment the general with the particular and vice-versa? What is the effect of this technique on the reader?

82

Alice Walker

In Search of Our Mothers' Gardens

"In Search of Our Mothers' Gardens" is the title essay from the collection
Alice Walker published in 1983. Reflecting on what inspires her writing, Walker
once said, "If I spend a long time in silence, which I really love, that's very good
for my writing. The main thing is just to live intensely and to feel. If there's the
slightest little bubble from the spring coming up, I try to go with the bubble until
it gets to the top of the water and then try to be there for it so that I can begin to
understand what is happening down in the depths." For more information on
Walker, see page 285.

> I described her own nature and temperament. Told how they
> needed a larger life for their expression. . . . I pointed out that in lieu of
> proper channels, her emotions had overflowed into paths that dissipated
> them. I talked, beautifully I thought, about an art that would be born,
> an art that would open the way for women the likes of her. I asked her
> to hope, and build up an inner life against the coming of that day. . . . I
> sang, with a strange quiver in my voice, a promise song.
>
> — "Avey," JEAN TOOMER, CANE
>
> The poet speaking to a prostitute who
> falls asleep while he's talking.

When the poet Jean Toomer[1] walked through the South in the early
twenties, he discovered a curious thing: black women whose spirituality
were so intense, so deep, so *unconscious,* they were themselves unaware
of the richness they held. They stumbled blindly through their lives: creatures so abused and mutilated in body, so dimmed and confused by pain,
that they considered themselves unworthy even of hope. In the selfless abstractions their bodies became to the men who used them, they became
more than "sexual objects," more even than mere women: They became

---

[1]*Jean Toomer* (1894–1967): A black poet, novelist, and leading figure of the Harlem
Renaissance who wrote *Cane* in 1923. — EDS.

"Saints." Instead of being perceived as whole persons, their bodies became shrines: What was thought to be their minds became temples suitable for worship. These crazy Saints stared out at the world, wildly, like lunatics—or quietly, like suicides; and the "God" that was in their gaze was as mute as a great stone.

Who were these Saints? These crazy, loony, pitiful women?

Some of them, without a doubt, were our mothers and grandmothers.

In the still heat of the post-Reconstruction South, this is how they seemed to Jean Toomer: exquisite butterflies trapped in an evil honey, toiling away their lives in an era, a century, that did not acknowledge them, except as "the *mule* of the world." They dreamed dreams that no one knew—not even themselves, in any coherent fashion—and saw visions no one could understand. They wandered or sat about the countryside crooning lullabies to ghosts, and drawing the mother of Christ in charcoal on courthouse walls.

They forced their minds to desert their bodies and their striving spirits   5
sought to rise, like frail whirlwinds from the hard red clay. And when those frail whirlwinds fell, in scattered particles, upon the ground, no one mourned. Instead, men lit candles to celebrate the emptiness that remained, as people do who enter a beautiful but vacant space to resurrect a God.

Our mothers and grandmothers, some of them: moving to music not yet written. And they waited.

They waited for a day when the unknown thing that was in them would be made known; but guessed, somehow in their darkness, that on the day of their revelation they would be long dead. Therefore to Toomer they walked, and even ran, in slow motion. For they were going nowhere immediate, and the future was not yet within their grasp. And men took our mothers and grandmothers, "but got no pleasure from it." So complex was their passion and their calm.

To Toomer, they lay vacant and fallow as autumn fields, with harvest time never in sight: and he saw them enter loveless marriages, without joy; and become prostitutes, without resistance; and become mothers of children, without fulfillment.

For these grandmothers and mothers of ours were not Saints, but Artists; driven to a numb and bleeding madness by the springs of creativity in them for which there was no release. They were Creators, who lived lives of spiritual waste, because they were so rich in spirituality—which is the basis of Art—that the strain of enduring their unused and unwanted talent drove them insane. Throwing away this spirituality was their pathetic attempt to lighten the soul to a weight their work-worn, sexually abused bodies could bear.

What did it mean for a black woman to be an artist in our grand-   10
mothers' time? In our great-grandmothers' day? It is a question with an answer cruel enough to stop the blood.

Did you have a genius of a great-great-grandmother who died under some ignorant and depraved white overseer's lash? Or was she required to bake biscuits for a lazy backwater tramp, when she cried out in her soul to paint watercolors of sunsets, or the rain falling on the green and peaceful pasturelands? Or was her body broken and forced to bear children (who were more often than not sold away from her)—eight, ten, fifteen, twenty children—when her one joy was the thought of modeling heroic figures of rebellion, in stone or clay?

How was the creativity of the black woman kept alive, year after year and century after century, when for most of the years black people have been in America, it was a punishable crime for a black person to read or write? And the freedom to paint, to sculpt, to expand the mind with action did not exist. Consider, if you can bear to imagine it, what might have been the result if singing, too, had been forbidden by law. Listen to the voices of Bessie Smith, Billie Holiday, Nina Simone, Roberta Flack, and Aretha Franklin, among others and imagine those voices muzzled for life. Then you may begin to comprehend the lives of our "crazy," "Sainted" mothers and grandmothers. The agony of the lives of women who might have been Poets, Novelists, Essayists, and Short-Story Writers (over a period of centuries), who died with their real gifts stifled within them.

And, if this were the end of the story, we would have cause to cry out in my paraphrase of Okot p'Bitek's great poem:

> *O, my clanswomen*
> *Let us all cry together!*
> *Come,*
> *Let us mourn the death of our mother,*
> *The death of a Queen*
> *The ash that was produced*
> *By a great fire!*
> *O, this homestead is utterly dead*
> *Close the gates*
> *With* lacari *thorns,*
> *For our mother*
> *The creator of the Stool is lost!*
> *And all the young men*
> *Have perished in the wilderness!*

But this is not the end of the story, for all the young women—our mothers and grandmothers, *ourselves*—have not perished in the wilderness. And if we ask ourselves why, and search for and find the answer, we will know beyond all efforts to erase it from our minds, just exactly who, and of what, we black American women are.

One example, perhaps the most pathetic, most misunderstood one,   15 can provide a backdrop for our mothers' work: Phillis Wheatley,[2] a slave in the 1700s.

---

[2]***Phillis Wheatley*** (ca. 1754–1784): A slave in a prosperous Boston family; published her first poetry at the age of thirteen and enjoyed an international reputation, acclaimed by such figures as Voltaire, George Washington, and Benjamin Franklin. She died, however, in poverty and obscurity.—EDS.

Virginia Woolf, in her book *A Room of One's Own,* wrote that in order for a woman to write fiction she must have two things, certainly: a room of her own (with key and lock) and enough money to support herself.

What then are we to make of Phillis Wheatley, a slave, who owned not even herself? This sickly, frail black girl who required a servant of her own at times—her health was so precarious—and who, had she been white, would have been easily considered the intellectual superior of all the women and most of the men in the society of her day.

Virginia Woolf wrote further, speaking of course not of our Phillis, that "any woman born with a great gift in the sixteenth century [insert "eighteenth century," insert "black woman," insert "born or made a slave"] would certainly have gone crazed, shot herself, or ended her days in some lonely cottage outside the village, half witch, half wizard [insert "Saint"], feared and mocked at. For it needs little skill and psychology to be sure that a highly gifted girl who had tried to use her gift of poetry would have been so thwarted and hindered by contrary instincts [add "chains, guns, the lash, the ownership of one's body by someone else, submission to an alien religion"], that she must have lost her health and sanity to a certainty."

The key words, as they relate to Phillis, are "contrary instincts." For when we read the poetry of Phillis Wheatley—as when we read the novels of Nella Larsen or the oddly false-sounding autobiography of that freest of all black women writers, Zora Hurston—evidence of "contrary instincts" is everywhere. Her loyalties were completely divided, as was, without question, her mind.

But how could this be otherwise? Captured at seven, a slave of   20
wealthy, doting whites who instilled in her the "savagery" of the Africa they "rescued" her from . . . one wonders if she was even able to remember her homeland as she had known it, or as it really was.

Yet, because she did try to use her gift for poetry in a world that made her a slave, she was "so thwarted and hindered by . . . contrary instincts, that she . . . lost her health . . ." In the last years of her brief life, burdened not only with the need to express her gift but also with a penniless, friendless "freedom" and several small children for whom she was forced to do strenuous work to feed, she lost her health, certainly. Suffering from malnutrition and neglect and who knows what mental agonies, Phillis Wheatley died.

So torn by "contrary instincts" was black, kidnapped, enslaved Phillis that her description of "the Goddess"—as she poetically called the Liberty she did not have—is ironically, cruelly humorous. And, in fact, has held Phillis up to ridicule for more than a century. It is usually read prior to hanging Phillis's memory as that of a fool. She wrote:

The Goddess comes, she moves divinely fair,
Olive and laurel binds her golden hair.

Wherever shines this native of the skies,
Unnumber'd charms and recent graces rise. [My emphasis]

It is obvious that Phillis, the slave, combed the "Goddess's" hair every morning; prior, perhaps to bringing in the milk, or fixing her mistress's lunch. She took her imagery from the one thing she saw elevated above all others.

With the benefit of hindsight we ask, "How could she?"

But at last, Phillis, we understand. No more snickering when your stiff, 25 struggling, ambivalent lines are forced on us. We know now that you were not an idiot or a traitor; only a sickly little black girl, snatched from your home and country and made a slave; a woman who still struggled to sing the song that was your gift, although in a land of barbarians who praised you for your bewildered tongue. It is not so much what you sang, as that you kept alive, in so many of our ancestors, *the notion of song.*

Black women are called, in the folklore that so aptly identifies one's status in society, "the *mule* of the world," because we have been handed the burdens that everyone else—*everyone* else—refused to carry. We have also been called "Matriarchs," "Superwomen," and "Mean and Evil Bitches." Not to mention "Castrators" and "Sapphire's Mama." When we have pleaded for understanding, our character has been distorted; when we have asked for simple caring, we have been handed empty inspirational appellations, then stuck in the farthest corner. When we have asked for love, we have been given children. In short, even our plainer gifts, our labors of fidelity and love, have been knocked down our throats. To be an artist and a black woman, even today, lowers our status in many respects, rather than raises it: And yet, artists we will be.

Therefore we must fearlessly pull out of ourselves and look at and identify with our lives the living creativity some of our great-grandmothers were not allowed to know. I stress *some* of them because it is well known that the majority of our great-grandmothers knew, even without "knowing" it, the reality of their spirituality, even if they didn't recognize it beyond what happened in the singing at church—and they never had any intention of giving it up.

How they did it—those millions of black women who were not Phillis Wheatley, or Lucy Terry or Frances Harper or Zora Hurston or Nella Larsen or Bessie Smith; or Elizabeth Catlett, or Katherine Dunham, either—brings me to the title of this essay, "In Search of Our Mothers' Gardens," which is a personal account that is yet shared, in its theme and its meaning, by all of us. I found, while thinking about the far-reaching world of the creative black woman, that often the truest answer to a question that really matters can be found very close.

In the late 1920s my mother ran away from home to marry my father. Marriage, if not running away, was expected of seventeen-year-old girls. By the time she was twenty, she had two children and was pregnant with a third. Five children later, I was born. And this is how I came to know my mother: She seemed a large, soft, loving-eyed woman who was rarely impatient in our home. Her quick, violent temper was on view only a few times a year, when she battled with the white landlord who had the misfortune to suggest to her that her children did not need to go to school.

She made all the clothes we wore, even my brothers' overalls. She 30 made all the towels and sheets we used. She spent the summers canning vegetables and fruits. She spent the winter evenings making quilts enough to cover our beds.

During the "working" day, she labored beside—not behind—my father in the fields. Her day began before sunup, and did not end until late at night. There was never a moment for her to sit down, undisturbed, to unravel her own private thoughts; never a time free from interruption—by work or the noisy inquiries of her many children. And yet, it is to my mother—and all our mothers who were not famous—that I went in search of the secret of what has fed that muzzled and often mutilated, but vibrant, creative spirit that the black woman has inherited, and that pops out in wild and unlikely places to this day.

But when, you will ask, did my overworked mother have time to know or care about feeding the creative spirit?

The answer is to simple that many of us have spent years discovering it. We have constantly looked high, when we should have looked high—and low.

For example: In the Smithsonian Institution in Washington, D.C., there hangs a quilt unlike any other in the world. In fanciful, inspired, and yet simple and identifiable figures, it portrays the story of the Crucifixion. It is considered rare, beyond price. Though it follows no known pattern of quilt-making, and though it is made of bits and pieces of worthless rags, it is obviously the work of a person of powerful imagination and deep spiritual feeling. Below this quilt I saw a note that says it was made by "an anonymous Black woman in Alabama, a hundred years ago."

If we could locate this "anonymous" black woman from Alabama, 35 she would turn out to be one of our grandmothers—an artist who left her mark in the only materials she could afford, and in the only medium her position in society allowed her to use.

As Virginia Woolf wrote further, in *A Room of One's Own*:

> Yet genius of a sort must have existed among women as it must have existed among the working class. [Change this to "slaves" and "the wives and daughters of sharecroppers."] Now and again an Emily Brontë or a Robert Burns [change this to "a Zora Hurston or a Richard Wright"] blazes out and proves its presence. But certainly it never got itself on to paper. When, however, one reads of a witch being ducked, of a woman possessed by devils [or "Sainthood"], of a wise woman selling herbs [our root workers], or even a very remarkable man who had a mother, then I think we are on the track of a lost novelist, a suppressed poet, or some mute and inglorious Jane Austen. . . . Indeed, I would venture to guess that Anon, who wrote so many poems without signing them, was often a woman. . . .

And so our mothers and grandmothers have, more often than not anonymously, handed on the creative spark, the seed of the flower they themselves never hoped to see: or like a sealed letter they could not plainly read.

And so it is, certainly, with my own mother. Unlike "Ma" Rainey's songs, which retained their creator's name even while blasting forth from Bessie Smith's mouth, no song or poem will bear my mother's name. Yet so many of the stories that I write, that we all write, are my mother's stories. Only recently did I fully realize this: That through years of listening to my mother's stories of her life, I have absorbed not only the stories themselves, but something of the manner in which she spoke, something of the urgency that involves the knowledge that her stories — like her life — must be recorded. It is probably for this reason that so much of what I have written is about characters whose counterparts in real life are so much older than I am.

But the telling of these stories, which came from my mother's lips as naturally as breathing, was not the only way my mother showed herself as an artist. For stories, too, were subject to being distracted, to dying without conclusion. Dinners must be started, and cotton must be gathered before the big rains. The artist that was and is my mother showed itself to me only after many years. This is what I finally noticed:

Like Mem, a character in *The Third Life of Grange Copeland*,[3] my 40 mother adorned with flowers whatever shabby house we were forced to live in. And not just your typical straggly country stand of zinnias, either. She planted ambitious gardens — and still does — with over fifty different varieties of plants that bloom profusely from early March until late November. Before she left home for the fields, she watered her flowers, chopped up the grass, and laid out new beds. When she returned from the fields, she might divide clumps of bulbs, dig a cold pit, uproot and replant roses, or prune branches from her taller bushes or trees — until night came and it was too dark to see.

Whatever she planted grew as if by magic, and her fame as a grower of flowers spread over three counties. Because of her creativity with her flowers, even my memories of poverty are seen through a screen of blooms — sunflowers, petunias, roses, dahlias, forsythia, spirea, delphiniums, verbena . . . and on and on.

And I remember people coming to my mother's yard to be given cuttings from her flowers; I hear again the praise showered on her because whatever rocky soil she landed on, she turned into a garden. A garden so brilliant with colors, so original in its design, so magnificent with life and creativity, that to this day people drive by our house in Georgia — perfect strangers and imperfect strangers — and ask to stand or walk among my mother's art.

---

[3]*The Third Life of Grange Copeland:* Walker's first novel, published in 1970. — EDS.

I notice that it is only when my mother is working in her flowers that she is radiant, almost to the point of being invisible—except as Creator: hand and eye. She is involved in work her soul must have. Ordering the universe in the image of her personal conception of Beauty.

Her face, as she prepares the Art that is her gift, is a legacy of respect she leaves to me, for all that illuminates and cherishes life. She has handed down respect for the possibilities—and the will to grasp them.

For her, so hindered and intruded upon in so many ways, being an   45
artist has still been a daily part of her life. This ability to hold on, even in very simple ways, is work black women have done for a very long time.

This poem is not enough, but it is something, for the woman who literally covered the holes in our walls with sunflowers:

They were women then
My mamma's generation
Husky of voice—Stout of
Step
With fists as well as
Hands
How they battered down
Doors
And ironed
Starched white
Shirts
How they led
Armies
Headragged Generals
Across mined
Fields
Booby-trapped
Kitchens
To discover books
Desks
A place for us
How they knew what we
Must *know*
Without knowing a page
Of it
Themselves

Guided by my heritage of a love of beauty and a respect for strength— in search of my mother's garden, I found my own.

And perhaps in Africa over two hundred years ago, there was just such a mother; perhaps she painted vivid and daring decorations in oranges and yellows and greens on the walls of her hut; perhaps she sang— in a voice like Roberta Flack's—*sweetly* over the compounds of her village; perhaps she wove the most stunning mats or told the most ingenious stories of all the village storytellers. Perhaps she was herself a poet— though only her daughter's name is signed to the poems that we know.

Perhaps Phillis Wheatley's mother was also an artist.

Perhaps in more than Phillis Wheatley's biological life is her mother's   50
signature made clear.

The Reader's Presence

1. The *our* of the essay's title signals an identification of the author with an audience. Why didn't Walker title her essay "In Search of *My* Mother's Garden"? Does Walker's *our* include everyone who reads the essay—or is her audience more restricted? Explain your answer.

2. Consider carefully Walker's image of the garden. What does it mean both to her and to other women? What is the connection between gardens and a woman's "living creativity"? What other objects or activities in the essay are related to the idea of gardens?

3. In rereading the essay, note the many quotations throughout. Consider the way Walker uses quotation in general. Can you detect any patterns? What sort of "presence" do they convey? Why do you think she brought in so many quotations in an essay about silence? How does her use of quotations contribute to her overall theme?

83

Andrew Weil

Health as Wholeness; Wholeness as Balance

Andrew Weil (b. 1942) has an undergraduate degree in botany and a medical degree, both from Harvard University. A best-selling author and holistic practitioner, Weil is known for his promotion of alternatives to conventional medicine and for his faith in the power of the body to heal itself. His first three books, The Natural Mind: A New Way of Looking at Drugs and the Higher Consciousness *(1972),* The Marriage of the Sun and Moon: A Quest for Unity in Consciousness *(1980), and* Chocolate to Morphine: Understanding Mind-Active Drugs *(1983), assert his belief that the desire to alter one's consciousness is innate. His most recent book,* 8 Weeks to Optimum Health: A Proven Program for Taking Full Advantage of Your Body's Natural Healing Power *(1997), is a comprehensive self-help guide.* *"Health as Wholeness; Wholeness as Balance" appeared in Weil's handbook about alternative and conventional medicine,* Health and Healing *(1983).*

In an ideal whole, the components are not only all there, they are there in an arrangement of harmonious integration and balance. Balance is the other aspect of wholeness that enters into the meaning of health.

The word *balance,* comes from Latin *bilanx,* as it occurs in the compound *libra bilanx,* denoting a balance or scale (*libra*) for weighing, made of two (*bi-*) flat plates (*lanx*). The word *libra* will be familiar as a sign of the zodiac represented by such a balance, the only astrological sign associated with an inanimate object rather than an animal or human.

The sign of Libra is ruled by Venus, goddess of beauty and harmony, suggesting that beauty arises from the balanced arrangement of components. Saturn is said to be "exalted" in this sign, that is, to reach its highest expression. Since Saturn is known to astrologers as the Greater Evil or Greater Misfortune (Mars being the Lesser), representing everything inimical to life, that relationship bears scrutiny.

In the heavens, the planet Venus is the brightest object next to the moon. Its light is warm, soft, and radiant, easily stimulating associations of feminine beauty, love, and peace. By contrast, Saturn's light is pale and cold, and that planet moves ever so slowly, barely changing its position against the stars from month to month. It is the outermost of the visible planets known to the ancients; its great distance from us and the sun accounts for its apparent slowness in our sky. I can see how our ancestors came to associate it with time and old age, with skeletons and cold and other evils.

One image of Saturn is Father Time, holding an hourglass to measure out our allotted span of life. The Greek name for this old god who devoured his own children was Cronus; from it we get the combining form *chrono-,* meaning "time" (chronometer, chronic, synchronous, and so on). Another image of this same force is the Grim Reaper: Death as an animated skeleton who cuts down life with his scythe. In medical astrology, Saturn rules the bones—the most fixed, material components of our bodies, the skeletons we carry around beneath our living flesh and that will endure when all else has decomposed. Saturn is the force of limitation, that which cuts off all that grows and opposes all expansion. No wonder it earns the title of Greater Evil.   5

Yet this same force is said to be exalted in Libra, the sign of balance. The suggestion of that statement is that balance and harmony result from correct placement and use of limitation. To put the snakes of the caduceus into the mystic infinity pattern, you must oppose their tendency to stretch further outward when they have deviated just far enough from the midline.

If all this seems too abstract, consider a concrete example. I once lived in a country house in Virginia. On one side of the house was a huge, climbing rose, much overgrown, that did not flower. A professional gardener advised me to prune it. In late fall, when the plant was dormant, I cut it back extensively and with some regret, because I do not enjoy cutting living plants. From the point of view of the rose, the pruning was surely a dreadful experience, an assault by the Greater Evil. The next spring, however, it flowered magnificently, with a profusion of red blooms over many months. I think that story illustrates the practical meaning of the cryptical astrological statement of Saturn's exaltation in Libra. (It is especially fitting, incidentally, that red roses are one symbol of Venus.)

Properly aligned, the forces of expansion and limitation show us the place of balance, from which we can glimpse the perfection of a higher reality. Balance is truly a mystery. Learn to stand on your head or to walk a tightrope, and you will experience the mystery. The balance point is nondimensional but quite real. At first you overshoot it grossly, then overcorrect and miss it again in another direction. Your movements are exaggerated and jerky, anything but harmonious. Eventually, you become conscious of the special point, if only momentarily while falling through it. Soon you can stay in it for several moments, becoming familiar with the distinctive feeling of effortlessness it provides. Lose it even slightly, and you must put out tremendous effort to regain it, but when you are on target, there is no work to be done. You can just enjoy the grace of a magical zone where all external forces cancel out by virtue of precise arrangement, one against another. In balance there is stillness and beauty in the very midst of chaos.

This stillness and beauty at the heart of change is the magic of the hurricane's eye, of the moment of totality of a solar eclipse, and, indeed, of the very stability of the earth itself, whose motions on its axis, orbit, and path around the galaxy with the rest of the solar system are so complex that merely trying to imagine them makes one giddy. The equinoxes of the seasonal cycle are magical points, as are the moments of sunrise and sunset, the *equilibrated* times of day, when reflection and mediation are possible with least effort.

The word *equilibrium* contains that same Latin *libra*. It is the state an   10
analytical balance seeks as its two pans seesaw gracefully around the zero in harmonious motion. When the pans end their coupled dance and come to rest, they are in equilibrium, in this instance a static equilibrium, especially if the balance is enclosed in a protective glass case to screen out disturbing influences. In more complex systems, equilibriums are not static but dynamic, forged anew from moment to moment out of constantly changing conditions.

Dynamic equilibrium is a formal concept in chemistry, where it describes certain kinds of reactions. If table salt and sulfuric acid are mixed, they react to form hydrochloric acid and sodium sulfate. In addition, the newly formed substances react with each other to form more sodium chloride and sulfuric acid, because this is a reversible reaction. Eventually, the rate of the forward reaction and the rate of the reverse reaction become equal, and chemists say that a state of equilibrium exists.

The rates of such reactions and the time required to reach equilibrium depend on the nature of the substances, their molecular concentrations and physical states, as well as on temperature, pressure, and the presence or absence of catalysts. Once equilibrium is reached, the concentrations of the reacting substances remain constant, but this situation is not static. Rather, the forward reaction and the reverse reaction are taking place at equal velocities, with compounds breaking apart and re-forming continuously. The equilibrium is dynamic, giving the appearance of rest, while based on constant change.

The balance of health is also dynamic. The elements and forces making up a human being and the changing environmental stresses impinging on them constitute a system so elaborate as to be unimaginable in its complexity. We are islands of change in a sea of change, subject to cycles of rest and activity, of secretion of hormones, and of the rise and fall of powerful drives, subjected to noise, irritants, agents of disease, electrical and magnetic fields, the deteriorations of age, emotional tides. The variables are infinite, and all is in flux and motion. That equilibrium occurs even for an instant in such a system is miraculous, yet most of us are mostly healthy most of the time, our mind-bodies always trying to keep up the incredible balancing act demanded by all the stresses from inside and out. Moreover, they do it dynamically, since equilibrium is constantly destroyed and re-created.

The achievement of balance adds an extra quality to a whole. It makes the perfect whole greater than the sum of its parts, makes it beautiful and holy, and so connects it to a higher reality. Health is wholeness—wholeness in its most profound sense, with nothing left out and everything in just the right order to manifest the mystery of balance. Far from being simply the absence of disease, health is a dynamic and harmonious equilibrium of all the elements and forces making up and surrounding a human being.

The Reader's Presence

1. Weil uses an extended chain of metaphors to explain his concept of balance. How are traditional astrological figures and beliefs linked to his meaning? How are astrology, gardening, science, and athletic balance connected? By what logic is each image linked to the next? Can you detect any relation between Weil's praise of "balance" and the way he structures his essay?

2. Do you find Weil's notion of health convincing? compelling? Why or why not? Which parts are more, or less, convincing or

compelling? Why? How might a conventionally scientific medical practitioner debate Weil's points?

3. What does Weil mean by his notions of equilibrium within change and dynamism within a stationary body? What images does he use to convey his sense of balance as "magical," "beautiful," and "holy"?

84

Eudora Welty

The Little Store

One of America's most highly respected writers, Eudora Welty was born in 1909 in Jackson, Mississippi, and, except for attending college in Wisconsin and New York City, she has lived there her entire life. As she explains in One Writer's Beginnings *(1984), "I am a writer who came of a sheltered life. A sheltered life can be a daring life as well. For all serious daring starts from within." During the Depression, Welty worked for newspapers and a radio station in Jackson and traveled throughout Mississippi as a publicity agent for the state office of the Works Progress Administration (WPA). Welty documented small-town life while working at the WPA, interviewing and photographing hundreds of people from all social classes; these photographs were later published in* One Time, One Place: Mississippi in the Depression *(1971). She continued to portray everyday life in Mississippi in her novels, short stories, and nonfiction. Her writing has earned her many awards, including several O. Henry Awards, a Pulitzer for* The Optimist's Daughter *(1972), a National Medal for Literature (1980), and a National Medal of Arts (1987). Her works include* The Wide Net and Other Stories *(1943),* Delta Wedding *(1946),* The Ponder Heart *(1954), and* The Eye of the Story *(1978), in which the essay "The Little Store" appears.*

Two blocks away from the Mississippi State Capitol, and on the same street with it, where our house was when I was a child growing up in Jackson, it was possible to have a little pasture behind your backyard where you could keep a Jersey cow, which we did. My mother herself milked her. A thrifty homemaker, wife, mother of three, she also did all her own cooking. And as far as I can recall, she never set foot inside a grocery store. It wasn't necessary.

For her regular needs, she stood at the telephone in our front hall and consulted with Mr. Lemly, of Lemly's Market and Grocery downtown, who took her order and sent it out on his next delivery. And since Jackson at the heart of it was still within very near reach of the open country, the blackberry lady clanged on her bucket with a quart measure at your front door in June without fail, the watermelon man rolled up to your house exactly on time for the Fourth of July, and down through the summer, the quiet of the early-morning streets was pierced by the calls of farmers driving in with their plenty. One brought his with a song, so plaintive we would sing it with him:

"Milk, milk,
Buttermilk,
Snap beans — butterbeans —
Tender okra — fresh greens . . .
And buttermilk."

My mother considered herself pretty well prepared in her kitchen and pantry for any emergency that, in her words, might choose to present itself. But if she should, all of a sudden, need another lemon or find she was out of bread, all she had to do was call out, "Quick! Who'd like to run to the Little Store for me?"

I would.

She'd count out the change into my hand, and I was away. I'll bet the   5
nickel that would be left over that all over the country, for those of my day, the neighborhood grocery played a similar part in our growing up.

Our store had its name — it was that of the grocer who owned it, whom I'll call Mr. Sessions — but "the Little Store" is what we called it at home. It was a block down our street toward the capitol and a half a block further, around the corner, toward the cemetery. I knew even the sidewalk to it as well as I knew my own skin. I'd skipped my jumping-rope up and down it, hopped its length through mazes of hopscotch, played jacks in its island of shade, serpentined along it on my Princess bicycle, skated it backward and forward. In the twilight I had dragged my steamboat by its string (this was homemade out of every new shoebox, with candle in the bottom lighted and shinning through colored tissue paper pasted over windows scissored out in the shapes of the sun, moon and stars) across every crack of the walk without letting it bump or catch fire. I'd "played out" on that street after supper with my brothers and friends as long as "first-dark" lasted; I'd caught its lightning bugs. On the first Armistice Day[1] (and this will set the time I'm speaking of) we made our own parade down that walk on a single velocipede — my brother pedaling, our little brother riding the handlebars, and myself standing on the back, all with arms wide, flying flags in each hand. (My father snapped that picture as we raced by. It came out blurred.)

As I set forth for the Little Store, a tune would float toward me from the house where there lived three sisters, girls in their teens, who ratted their hair over their ears, wore headbands like gladiators, and were considered to be very popular. They practiced for this in the daytime; they'd wind up

[1]Veteran's Day; first celebrated to mark the end of World War I, November 11, 1918. — EDS.

the Victrola, leave the same record on they'd played before, and you'd see them bobbing past their dining room windows while they danced with each other. Being three, they could go all day, cutting in:

> "Everybody ought to know-oh
> How to do the Tickle-Toe
>   (how to do the Tickle-Toe)" —

they sang it and danced to it, and as I went by to the same song, I believed it.

A little further on, across the street, was the house where the principal of our grade school lived — lived on, even while we were having vacation. What if she would come out? She would halt me in my tracks — she had a very carrying and well-known voice in Jackson, where she'd taught almost everybody — saying "Eudora Alice Welty, spell OBLIGE." OBLIGE was the word that she of course knew had kept me from making 100 on my spelling exam. She'd make me miss it again now, by boring her eyes through me from across the street. This was my vacation fantasy, one good way to scare myself on the way to the store.

Down near the corner waited the house of a little boy named Lindsey. The sidewalk here was old brick, which the roots of a giant chinaberry tree had humped up and tilted this way and that. On skates, you took it fast, in a series of skittering hops, trying not to touch ground anywhere. If the chinaberries had fallen and rolled in the cracks, it was like skating through a whole shooting match of marbles. I crossed my fingers that Lindsey wouldn't be looking.

During the big flu epidemic he and I, as it happened, were being nursed through our sieges at the same time. I'd hear my father and mother murmuring to each other, at the end of a long day, "And I wonder how poor little *Lindsey* got along today?" Just as, down the street, he no doubt would have to hear his family saying, "And I wonder how is poor *Eudora* by now?" I got the idea that a choice was going to be made soon between poor little Lindsey and poor Eudora, and I came up with a funny poem. I wasn't prepared for it when my father told me it wasn't funny and my mother cried that if I couldn't be ashamed for myself, she'd have to be ashamed for me: 10

> There was a little boy and his name was Lindsey.
> He went to heaven with the influinzy.

He didn't, he survived it, poem and all, the same as I did. But his chinaberries could have brought me down in my skates in a flying act of contrition before his eyes, looking pretty funny myself, right in front of his house.

Setting out in this world, a child feels so indelible. He only comes to find out later that it's all the others along his way who are making themselves indelible to him.

Our Little Store rose right up from the sidewalk; standing in a street of family houses, it alone hadn't any yard in front, any tree or flowerbed.

It was a plain frame building covered over with brick. Above the door, a little railed porch ran across on an upstairs level and four windows with shades were looking out. But I didn't catch on to those.

Running in and out of the sun, you met what seemed total obscurity inside. There were almost tangible smells—licorice recently sucked in a child's cheek, dill-pickle brine that had leaked through a paper sack in a fresh trail across the wooden floor, ammonia-loaded ice that had been hoisted from wet croker sacks and slammed into the icebox with its sweet butter at the door, and perhaps the smell of still-untrapped mice.

Then through the motes of cracker dust, cornmeal dust, the Gold Dust of the Gold Dust Twins that the floor had been swept out with, the realities emerged. Shelves climbed to high reach all the way around, set out with not too much of any one thing but a lot of things—lard, molasses, vinegar, starch, matches, kerosene, Octagon soap (about a year's worth of octagon-shaped coupons cut out and saved brought a signet ring addressed to you in the mail. Furthermore, when the postman arrived at your door, he blew a whistle). It was up to you to remember what you came for, while your eye traveled from cans of sardines to ice cream salt to harmonicas to flypaper (over your head, batting around on a thread beneath the blades of the ceiling fan, stuck with its testimonial catch).

Its confusion may have been in the eye of its beholder. Enchantment is cast upon you by all those things you weren't supposed to have need for, it lures you close to wooden tops you'd outgrown, boy's marbles and agates in little net pouches, small rubber balls that wouldn't bounce straight, frazzly kite-string, clay bubble-pipes that would snap off in your teeth, the stiffest scissors. You could contemplate those long narrow boxes of sparklers gathering dust while you waited for it to be the Fourth of July or Christmas, and noisemakers in the shape of tin frogs for somebody's birthday party you hadn't been invited to yet, and see that they were all marvelous.

You might not have even looked for Mr. Sessions when he came around his store cheese (as big as a doll's house) and in front of the counter looking for you. When you'd finally asked him for, and received from him in its paper bag, whatever single thing it was that you had been sent for, the nickel that was left over was yours to spend.

Down at a child's eye level, inside those glass jars with mouths in their sides through which the grocer could run his scoop or a child's hand might be invited to reach for a choice, were wineballs, all-day suckers, gumdrops, peppermints. Making a row under the glass of a counter were the Tootsie Rolls, Hershey Bars, Goo-Goo Clusters, Baby Ruths. And whatever was the name of those pastilles that came stacked in a cardboard cylinder with a cardboard lid? They were thin and dry, about the size of tiddlywinks, and in the shape of twisted rosettes. A kind of chocolate dust came out with them when you shook them out in your hand. Were they chocolate? I'd say rather they were brown. They didn't taste of anything at all, unless it was wood. Their attraction was the number you got for a nickel.

Making up your mind, you circled the store around and around, around the pickle barrel, around the tower of Cracker Jack boxes; Mr. Sessions had built it for us himself on top of a packing case, like a house of cards.

If it seemed too hot for Cracker Jacks, I might get a cold drink. Mr. Sessions might have already stationed himself by the cold-drinks barrel, like a mind reader. Deep in ice water that looked black as ink, murky shapes that would come up as Coca-Colas, Orange Crushes, and various flavors of pop, were all swimming around together. When you gave the word, Mr. Sessions plunged his bare arm in to the elbow and fished out your choice, first try. I favored a locally bottled concoction called Lake's Celery. (What else could it be called? It was made by a Mr. Lake out of celery. It was a popular drink here for years but was not known universally, as I found out when I arrived in New York and ordered one in the Astor bar.) You drank on the premises, with feet set wide apart to miss the drip, and gave him back his bottle.

But he didn't hurry you off. A standing scales was by the door, with a   20
stack of iron weights and a brass slide on the balance arm, that would weigh you up to three hundred pounds. Mr. Sessions, whose hands were gentle and smelled of carbolic, would lift you up and set your feet on the platform, hold your loaf of bread for you, and taking his time while you stood still for him, he would make certain of what you weighed today. He could even remember what you weighed the last time, so you could subtract and announce how much you'd gained. That was goodbye.

Is there always a hard way to go home? From the Little Store, you could go partway through the sewer. If your brothers had called you a scarecat, then across the next street beyond the Little Store, it was possible to enter this sewer by passing through a privet hedge, climbing down into the bed of a creek, and going into its mouth on your knees. The sewer — it might have been no more than a "storm sewer" — came out and emptied here, where Town Creek, a sandy, most often shallow little stream that ambled through Jackson on its way to the Pearl River, ran along the edge of the cemetery. You could go in darkness through this tunnel to where you next saw light (if you ever did) and climb out through the culvert at your own street corner.

I was a scarecat, all right, but I was a reader with my own refuge in storybooks. Making my way under the sidewalk, under the street and the streetcar track, under the Little Store, down there in the wet dark by myself, I could be Persephone[2] entering into my six-month sojourn underground — though I didn't suppose Persephone had to crawl, hanging onto a loaf of bread, and come out through the teeth of an iron grating. Mother Ceres[3] would indeed be wondering where she could find me, and

---

[2]Greek mythological goddess, daughter of Zeus and Demeter, who was abducted by Pluto to rule the underworld every six months. — EDS.

[3]In Roman mythology, the mother of Persephone. — EDS.

mad when she knew. "Now am I going to have to start marching to the Little Store for *myself?*"

I couldn't picture it. Indeed I'm unable today to picture the Little Store with a grown person in it, except for Mr. Sessions and the lady who helped him, who belonged there. We children thought it was ours. The happiness of errands was in part that of running for the moment away from home, a free spirit. I believed the Little Store to be a center of the outside world, and hence of happiness — as If believed what I found in the Cracker Jack box to be a genuine prize, which was simply as I believed in the Golden Fleece.[4]

But a day came when I ran to the store to discover, sitting on the front step, a grown person, after all — more than a grown person. It was the Monkey Man, together with his monkey. His grinding-organ was lowered to the step beside him. In my whole life so far, I must have laid eyes on the monkey man no more than five or six times. An itinerant of rare and wayward appearances, he was not punctual like the Gipsies, who every year with the first cool days of fall showed up in the aisles of Woolworth's. You never knew when the Monkey Man might decide to favor Jackson, or which way he'd go. Sometimes you heard him as close as the next street, and then he didn't come up yours.

But now I saw the Monkey Man at the Little Store, where I'd never   25
seen him before. I'd never seen him sitting down. Low on that familiar doorstep, he was not the same any longer, and neither was his monkey. They looked just like an old man and an old friend of his that wore a fez, meeting quietly together, tired, and resting with their eyes fixed on some place far away, and not the same place. Yet their romance for me didn't have it in its power to waver. I wavered. I simply didn't know how to step around them, to proceed on into the Little Store for my mother's emergency as if nothing had happened. If I could have gone in there after it, whatever it was, I would have given it to them — putting it into the monkey's cool little fingers. I would have given them the Little Store itself.

In my memory they are still attached to the store — so are all the others. Everyone I saw on my way seemed to me then part of my errand, and in a way they were. As I myself, the free spirit, was part of it too.

All the years we lived in that house where we children were born, the same people lived in the other houses on our street too. People changed through the arithmetic of birth, marriage and death, but not by going away. So families just accrued stories, which through the fullness of time, in those times, their own lives made. And I grew up in those.

But I didn't know there'd ever been a story at the Little Store, one that was going on while I was there. Of course, all the time the Sessions family had been living right overhead there, in the upstairs rooms behind the little railed porch and the shaded windows; but I think we children never

[4]The mythological fleece of the golden ram, which was stolen by Jason and the Argonauts. — EDS.

thought of that. Did I fail to see them as a family because they weren't living in an ordinary house? Because I so seldom saw them close together, or having anything to say to each other? She sat in the back of the store, her pencil over a ledger, while he stood and waited on children to make up their minds. They worked in twin black eyeshades, held on their gray heads by elastic bands. It may be harder to recognize kindness—or unkindness either—in a face whose eyes are in shadow. His face underneath his shade was as round as the little wooden wheels in the Tinker Toy box. So was her face. I didn't know, perhaps didn't ever wonder: were they husband and wife or brother and sister? Were they father and mother? There were a few other persons, of various ages, wandering singly in by the back door and out. But none of their relationships could I imagine, when I'd never seen them sitting down together around their own table.

The possibility that they had any other life at all, anything beyond what we could see within the four walls of the Little Store, occurred to me only when tragedy struck their family. There was some act of violence. The shock to the neighborhood traveled to the children, of course; but I couldn't find out from my parents what had happened. They held it back from me, as they'd already held back many things, "until the time comes for you to know."

You could find out some of these things by looking in the unabridged   30
dictionary and the encyclopedia—kept to hand in our dining room—but you couldn't find out there what had happened to the family who for all the years of your life had lived upstairs over the Little Store, who had never been anything but patient and kind to you, who never once had sent you away. All I ever knew was its aftermath: they were the only people ever known to me who simply vanished. At the point where their life overlapped into ours, the story broke off.

We weren't being sent to the neighborhood grocery for facts of life, or death. But of course those are what we were on the track of, anyway. With the loaf of bread and the Cracker Jack prize, I was bringing home the intimations of pride and disgrace, and rumors and early news of people coming to hurt one another, while others practiced for joy—storing up a portion for myself of the human mystery.

The Reader's Presence

1. How is the world of childhood dramatized in the essay? What are its joys and wonders? its fears and terrors? Why is the author unable to visualize the store with a grown-up in it, except for Mr. Sessions and the lady helping him? What in general does the essay suggest about childhood memories?

2. When does the world of the little store begin to change? How does Welty describe her realization of this change? How does her

perception of people change as well, especially those of the Sessions and the Monkey Man?

3. The essay, like many myths and legends, contains the theme of a journey. How do Welty's classical allusions support this theme? How is the journey back home described? Why is it described as being "a hard way to go home"?

85

Marie Winn

TV Addiction

Born in 1936 in Prague, Czechoslovakia, Marie Winn came to the United States with her family in 1939. After receiving her education at Radcliffe College and Columbia University, Winn became a freelance writer specializing in children's literature. In addition to having written over a dozen books for children or for parents and teachers of children, she contributes regularly to the New York Times *and the* New York Times Book Review, *and writes a column on bird watching and nature for the* Wall Street Journal. *Her publications include* Children without Childhood *(1983),* Unplugging the Plug-In Drug *(1987), and* Redtails in Love: A Wildlife Drama in Central Park *(1998). "TV Addiction" is from* The Plug-In Drug: Television, Children and the Family *(1977).*

The word "addiction" is often used loosely and wryly in conversation. People will refer to themselves as "mystery book addicts" or "cookie addicts." E. B. White writes of his annual surge of interest in gardening: "We are hooked and are making an attempt to kick the habit." Yet nobody really believes that reading mysteries or ordering seeds by catalogue is serious enough to be compared with addictions to heroin or alcohol. The word "addiction" is here used jokingly to denote a tendency to overindulge in some pleasurable activity.

People often refer to being "hooked on TV." Does this, too, fall into the lighthearted category of cookie eating and other pleasures that people pursue with unusual intensity, or is there a kind of television viewing that falls into the more serious category of destructive addiction?

When we think about addiction to drugs or alcohol, we frequently focus on negative aspects, ignoring the pleasures that accompany drinking or drug-taking. And yet the essence of any serious addiction is a pursuit of pleasure, a search for a "high" that normal life does not supply. It is only the inability to function without the addictive substance that is dismaying, the dependence of the organism upon a certain experience and an increasing inability to function normally without it. Thus a person will take two or three drinks at the end of the day not merely for the pleasure drinking provides, but also because he "doesn't feel normal" without them.

An addict does not merely pursue a pleasurable experience and need to experience it in order to function normally. He needs to *repeat* it again and again. Something about that particular experience makes life without it less than complete. Other potentially pleasurable experiences are no longer possible, for under the spell of the addictive experience, his life is peculiarly distorted. The addict craves an experience and yet he is never really satisfied. The organism may be temporarily sated, but soon it begins to crave again.

Finally a serious addiction is distinguished from a harmless pursuit of pleasure by its distinctly destructive elements. A heroin addict, for instance, leads a damaged life: his increasing need for heroin in increasing doses prevents him from working, from maintaining relationships, from developing in human ways. Similarly an alcoholic's life is narrowed and dehumanized by his dependence on alcohol.

Let us consider television viewing in the light of the conditions that define serious addictions.

Not unlike drugs or alcohol, the television experience allows the participant to blot out the real world and enter into a pleasurable and passive mental state. The worries and anxieties of reality are as effectively deferred by becoming absorbed in a television program as by going on a "trip" induced by drugs or alcohol. And just as alcoholics are only inchoately aware of their addiction, feeling that they control their drinking more than they really do ("I can cut it out any time I want—I just like to have three or four drinks before dinner"), people similarly overestimate their control over television watching. Even as they put off other activities to spend hour after hour watching television, they feel they could easily resume living in a different, less passive style. But somehow or other while the television set is present in their homes, the click doesn't sound. With television pleasures available, those other experiences seem less attractive, more difficult somehow.

A heavy viewer (a college English instructor) observes: "I find television almost irresistible. When the set is on, I cannot ignore it. I can't turn it off. I feel sapped, will-less, enervated. As I reach out to turn off the set, the strength goes out of my arms. So I sit there for hours and hours."

The self-confessed television addict often feels he "ought" to do other things—but the fact that he doesn't read and doesn't plant his garden or sew or crochet or play games or have conversations means that those activities are no longer as desirable as television viewing. In a way a heavy viewer's life is as imbalanced by his television "habit" as a drug addict's or an alcoholic's. He is living in a holding pattern, as it were, passing up

5

the activities that lead to growth or development or a sense of accomplishment. This is one reason people talk about their television viewing so
ruefully, so apologetically. They are aware that it is an unproductive experience, that almost any other endeavor is more worthwhile by any
human measure.

Finally it is the adverse effect of television viewing on the lives of so   10
many people that defines it as a serious addiction. The television habit
distorts the sense of time. It renders other experiences vague and curiously unreal while taking on a greater reality for itself. It weakens relationships by reducing and sometimes eliminating normal opportunities
for talking, for communicating.

And yet television does not satisfy, else why would the viewer continue to watch hour after hour, day after day? "The measure of health,"
writes Lawrence Kubie, "is flexibility . . . and especially the freedom to
cease when sated." But the television viewer can never be sated with his
television experiences — they do not provide the true nourishment that sa-
tiation requires — and thus he finds that he cannot stop watching.

The Reader's Presence

1. How does Winn characterize addiction? How does she apply that
   characterization to television watching? Do you think watching
   television is a genuine addiction, similar to addiction to drugs, alcohol, or tobacco? Why or why not?

2. Does Winn rely more heavily on evidence or opinion for her argument? Is her methodology convincing? What evidence do you find
   most persuasive?

3. What other forms of addiction, legitimate and humorous, does
   Winn mention? How would mystery book reading or frequent
   telephone calling differ from TV watching? Do you know anyone
   who seems "addicted" to the phone? Winn's essay does not mention counterexamples. What arguments, if any, might be offered
   to class TV addiction with these lesser ills rather than with drug
   abuse and alcoholism?

86 _____

Virginia Woolf
The Death of the Moth

One of the most important writers of the twentieth century, Virginia Woolf (1882–1941) explored innovations in indirect narration and the impressionistic use of language that are now considered hallmarks of the modern novel and continue to influence novelists on both sides of the Atlantic. Together with her husband, Leonard Woolf, she founded the Hogarth Press, which published many experimental works that have now become classics, including her own. A central figure in the Bloomsbury group of writers, Woolf established her reputation with the novels Mrs. Dalloway *(1925),* To the Lighthouse *(1927), and* The Waves *(1931). The feminist movement has helped to focus attention on her work, and Woolf's nonfiction has provided the basis for several important lines of argument in contemporary feminist theory.* A Room of One's Own *(1929),* Three Guineas *(1938), and* The Common Reader *(1938) are the major works of nonfiction published in Woolf's lifetime; posthumously, her essays have been gathered together in* The Death of the Moth *(where the essay reprinted here appears) and in the four-volume* Collected Essays.*

Reflecting on her own writing life, Woolf wrote, "The novelist—it is his distinction and his danger—is terribly exposed to life. . . . He can no more cease to receive impressions than a fish in mid-ocean can cease to let the water rush through his gills." To turn those impressions into writing, Woolf maintained, requires solitude and the time for thoughtful selection. Given tranquility, a writer can, with effort, discover art in experience. "There emerges from the mist something stark, formidable and enduring, the bone and substance upon which our rush of indiscriminating emotion was founded."

For more on Virginia Woolf, see page 51.

Moths that fly by day are not properly to be called moths; they do not excite that pleasant sense of dark autumn nights and ivy-blossom which the commonest yellow-underwing asleep in the shadow of the curtain never fails to rouse in us. They are hybrid creatures, neither gay like butterflies nor somber like their own species. Nevertheless the present specimen, with his narrow hay-colored wings, fringed with a tassel of the same color, seemed to be content with life. It was a pleasant morning, mid-September, mild, benignant, yet with a keener breath than that of the summer months. The plough was already scoring the field opposite the window, and where the share had been, the earth was pressed flat and gleamed with moisture. Such vigor came rolling in from the fields and the down beyond that it was difficult to keep the eyes strictly turned upon the book. The rooks too were keeping one of their annual festivities; soaring round the tree tops until it looked as if a vast net with thousands of black knots in it had been cast up into the air; which, after a few moments sank slowly down upon the trees until every twig seemed to have a knot at the end of it. Then, suddenly, the net would be thrown into the air again in a wider circle this time, with the utmost clamor and vociferation, as though to be thrown into the air and settle slowly down upon the tree tops were a tremendously exciting experience.

The same energy which inspired the rooks, the ploughmen, the horses, and even, it seemed, the lean bare-backed downs, sent the moth fluttering from side to side of his square of the windowpane. One could not help watching him. One, was, indeed, conscious of a queer feeling of pity for him. The possibilities of pleasure seemed that morning so enormous and so various that to have only a moth's part in life, and a day moth's at that, appeared a hard fate, and his zest in enjoying his meager opportunities to the full, pathetic. He flew vigorously to one corner of his compartment, and after waiting there a second, flew across to the other. What remained for him but to fly to a third corner and then to a fourth? That was all he could do, in spite of the size of the downs, the width of the sky, the far-off smoke of houses, and the romantic voice, now and then, of a steamer out at sea. What he could do he did. Watching him, it seemed as if a fiber, very thin but pure, of the enormous energy of the world had been thrust into his frail and diminutive body. As often as he crossed the pane, I could fancy that a thread of vital light became visible. He was little or nothing but life.

Yet, because he was so small, and so simple a form of the energy that was rolling in at the open window and driving its way through so many narrow and intricate corridors in my own brain and in those of other human beings, there was something marvelous as well as pathetic about him. It was as if someone had taken a tiny bead of pure life and decking it as lightly as possible with down and feathers, had set it dancing and zigzagging to show us the true nature of life. Thus displayed one could not get over the strangeness of it. One is apt to forget all about life, seeing it humped and bossed and garnished and cumbered so that it has to move with the greatest circumspection and dignity. Again, the thought of all that life might have been had he been born in any other shape caused one to view his simple activities with a kind of pity.

After a time, tired by his dancing apparently, he settled on the window ledge in the sun, and, the queer spectacle being at an end, I forgot about him. Then, looking up, my eye was caught by him. He was trying to resume his dancing, but seemed either so stiff or so awkward that he could only flutter to the bottom of the windowpane; and when he tried to fly across it he failed. Being intent on other matters I watched these futile attempts for a time without thinking, unconsciously waiting for him to resume his flight, as one waits for a machine, that has stopped momentarily, to start again without considering the reason of its failure. After perhaps a seventh attempt he slipped from the wooden ledge and fell, fluttering his wings, on to his back on the windowsill. The helplessness of his attitude roused me. It flashed upon me that he was in difficulties; he could no longer raise himself; his legs struggled vainly. But, as I stretched out a pencil, meaning to help him to right himself, it came over me that the failure and awkwardness were the approach of death. I laid the pencil down again.

The legs agitated themselves once more. I looked as if for the enemy   5
against which he struggled. I looked out of doors. What had happened there? Presumably it was midday, and work in the fields had stopped. Stillness and quiet had replaced the previous animation. The birds had taken themselves off to feed in the brooks. The horses stood still. Yet the power was there all the same, massed outside, indifferent, impersonal, not attending to anything in particular. Somehow it was opposed to the little hay-colored moth. It was useless to try to do anything. One could only watch the extraordinary efforts made by those tiny legs against an oncoming doom which could, had it chosen, have submerged an entire city, not merely a city, but masses of human beings; nothing, I knew had any chance against death. Nevertheless after a pause of exhaustion the legs fluttered again. It was superb this last protest, and so frantic that he succeeded at last in righting himself. One's sympathies, of course, were all on the side of life. Also, when there was nobody to care or to know, this gigantic effort on the part of an insignificant little moth, against a power of such magnitude, to retain what no one else valued or desired to keep, moved one strangely. Again, somehow, one saw life, a pure bead. I lifted the pencil again, useless though I knew it to be. But even as I did so, the unmistakable tokens of death showed themselves. The body relaxed, and instantly grew stiff. The struggle was over. The insignificant little creature now knew death. As I looked at the dead moth, this minute wayside triumph of so great a force over so mean an antagonist filled me with wonder. Just as life had been strange a few minutes before, so death was now as strange. The moth having righted himself now lay most decently and uncomplainingly composed. O yes, he seemed to say, death is stronger than I am.

The Reader's Presence

1. Woolf calls her essay "The Death of *the* Moth" rather than "The Death of *a* Moth." Describe what difference this makes. What quality does the definite article add to the essay?

2. Can you find any connections between what happens to the moth and what happens outside the window? Why do you think Woolf brings in the outside world? Of what importance is it to the essay?

3. Reread the essay, paying special attention not to the moth but to the writer. What presence does Woolf establish for herself in the essay? How does the act of writing itself get introduced? Of what significance is the pencil? Can you discover any connection between the essay's subject and its composition? Can you find any connection between this essay and the author's ideas about the writing process in *A Writer's Diary* (see page 51)?

Part IV

Argumentative Writing: Contending with Issues

87

Dorothy Allison

This Is Our World

*Dorothy Allison (b. 1949) was born in Greenville, South Carolina, and re-
ceived an M.A. from the New School for Social Research in New York City. A
versatile writer, Allison has published poems, short stories, essays, and novels.
Her first collection of short stories,* Trash *(1988), won the Lambda Book Award
for the best work of lesbian fiction. She gained mainstream attention with her first
novel,* Bastard Out of Carolina *(1992), which was a finalist for the National
Book Award. Her most recent work,* Cavedweller *(1998), is an epic novel about
the lives of four women in a small town in Georgia. Allison also contributes to
many periodicals, including* Harper's, *the* New York Times, Village Voice, *and*
Southern Exposure. *"This Is Our World" first appeared in the summer 1998
issue of* DoubleTake, *a magazine featuring creative writing and photography.*

The first painting I ever saw up close was at a Baptist church when I
was seven years old. It was a few weeks before my mama was to be baptized. From it, I took the notion that art should surprise and astonish, and
hopefully make you think something you had not thought until you saw it.
The painting was a mural of Jesus at the Jordan River done on the wall behind the baptismal font. The font itself was a remarkable creation—a
swimming pool with one glass side set into the wall above and behind the
pulpit so that ordinarily you could not tell the font was there, seeing only
the painting of Jesus. When the tank was flooded with water, little lights
along the bottom came on, and anyone who stepped down the steps seemed
to be walking past Jesus himself and descending into the Jordan River.
Watching baptisms in that tank was like watching movies at the drive-in,
my cousins had told me. From the moment the deacon walked us around
the church, I knew what my cousin had meant. I could not take my eyes off
the painting or the glass-fronted tank. It looked every moment as if Jesus
were about to come alive, as if he were about to step out onto the water of
the river. I think the way I stared at the painting made the deacon nervous.

The deacon boasted to my mama that there was nothing like that
baptismal font in the whole state of South Carolina. It had been designed,

he told her, by a nephew of the minister—a boy who had gone on to build a shopping center out in New Mexico. My mama was not sure that someone who built shopping centers was the kind of person who should have been designing baptismal fonts, and she was even more uncertain about the steep steps by Jesus' left hip. She asked the man to let her practice going up and down, but he warned her it would be different once the water poured in.

"It's quite safe though," he told her. "The water will hold you up. You won't fall."

I kept my attention on the painting of Jesus. He was much larger than I was, a little bit more than life-size, but the thick layer of shellac applied to protect the image acted like a magnifying glass, making him seem larger still. It was Jesus himself that fascinated me, though. He was all rouged and pale and pouty as Elvis Presley. This was not my idea of the son of God, but I liked it. I liked it a lot.

"Jesus looks like a girl," I told my mama.   5

She looked up at the painted face. A little blush appeared on her cheekbones, and she looked as if she would have smiled if the deacon were not frowning so determinedly. "It's just the eyelashes," she said. The deacon nodded. They climbed back up the stairs. I stepped over close to Jesus and put my hand on the painted robe. The painting was sweaty and cool, slightly oily under my fingers.

"I liked that Jesus," I told my mama as we walked out of the church. "I wish we had something like that." To her credit, Mama did not laugh.

"If you want a picture of Jesus," she said, "we'll get you one. They have them in nice frames at Sears." I sighed. That was not what I had in mind. What I wanted was a life-size, sweaty painting, one in which Jesus looked as hopeful as a young girl—something other-worldly and peculiar, but kind of wonderful at the same time. After that, every time we went to church I asked to go up to see the painting, but the baptismal font was locked tight when not in use.

The Sunday Mama was to be baptized, I watched the minister step down into that pool past the Son of God. The preacher's gown was tailored with little weights carefully sewn into the hem to keep it from rising up in the water. The water pushed up at the fabric while the weights tugged it down. Once the minister was all the way down into the tank, the robe floated up a bit so that it seemed to have a shirred ruffle all along the bottom. That was almost enough to pull my eyes away from the face of Jesus, but not quite. With the lights on in the bottom of the tank, the eyes of the painting seemed to move and shine. I tried to point it out to my sisters, but they were uninterested. All they wanted to see was Mama.

Mama was to be baptized last, after three little boys, and their gowns   10 had not had any weights attached. The white robes floated up around their necks so that their skinny boy bodies and white cotton underwear were perfectly visible to the congregation. The water that came up above the hips of the minister lapped their shoulders, and the shortest of the boys seemed panicky at the prospect of gulping water, no matter how holy. He paddled furiously to keep above the water's surface. The water started to rock violently at his struggles, sweeping the other boys off their feet. All of them pumped their knees to stay upright and the minister, realizing how the scene must appear to the congregation below, speeded up the baptismal process, praying over and dunking the boys at high speed.

Around me the congregation shifted in their seats. My little sister slid forward off the pew, and I quickly grabbed her around the waist and barely stopped myself from laughing out loud. A titter from the back of the church indicated that other people were having the same difficulty keeping from laughing. Other people shifted irritably and glared at the noisemakers. It was clear that no matter the provocation, we were to pretend nothing funny was happening. The minister frowned more fiercely and prayed louder. My mama's friend Louise, sitting at our left, whispered a soft "Look at that" and we all looked up in awe. One of the hastily blessed boys had dog-paddled over to the glass and was staring out at us, eyes wide and his hands pressed flat to the glass. He looked as if he hoped someone would rescue him. It was too much for me. I began to giggle helplessly, and not a few of the people around me joined in. Impatiently the minister hooked the boy's robe, pulled him back, and pushed him toward the stairs.

My mama, just visible on the staircase, hesitated briefly as the sodden boy climbed up past her. Then she set her lips tightly together, and reached down and pressed her robe to her thighs. She came down the steps slowly, holding down the skirt as she did so, giving one stern glance to the two boys climbing past her up the steps, and then turning her face deliberately up to the painting of Jesus. Every move she made communicated resolution and faith, and the congregation stilled in respect. She was baptized looking up stubbornly, both hands holding down that cotton robe while below, I fought so hard not to giggle, tears spilled down my face.

Over the pool, the face of Jesus watched solemnly with his pink, painted cheeks and thick, dark lashes. For all the absurdity of the event, his face seemed to me startlingly compassionate and wise. That face understood fidgety boys and stubborn women. It made me want the painting even more, and to this day I remember it with longing. It had the weight of art, that face. It had what I am sure art is supposed to have — the power to provoke, the authority of a heartfelt vision.

I imagine the artist who painted the baptismal font in that Baptist church so long ago was a man who did not think himself much of an artist. I have seen paintings like his many times since, so perhaps he worked from a model. Maybe he traced that face off another he had seen in some other church. For a while, I tried to imagine him a character out of a Flannery O'Connor[1] short story, a man who traveled around the South in the fifties painting Jesus wherever he was needed, giving the Son of God the long lashes and pink cheeks of a young girl. He would be the kind of man who would see nothing blasphemous in painting eyes that followed the congregation as they moved up to the pulpit to receive a blessing and back to the pews to sit chastened and still for the benediction. Perhaps he had no sense of humor, or perhaps he had one too refined for intimidation. In my version of the story, he would have a case of whiskey in his van, right behind the gallon containers of shellac and buried notebooks of his own sketches. Sometimes, he would read thick journals of art criticism while sitting up late in cheap hotel rooms and then get roaring drunk and curse his fate.

"What I do is wallpaper," he would complain. "Just wallpaper." But   15 the work he so despised would grow more and more famous as time passed. After his death, one of those journals would publish a careful consideration of his murals, calling him a gifted primitive. Dealers would offer little churches large sums to take down his walls and sell them as installations to collectors. Maybe some of the churches would refuse to sell, but grow uncomfortable with the secular popularity of the paintings. Still, somewhere there would be a little girl like the girl I had been, a girl who would dream of putting her hand on the cool, sweaty painting while the Son of God blinked down at her in genuine sympathy. Is it a sin, she would wonder, to put together the sacred and the absurd? I would not answer her question, of course. I would leave it, like the art, to make everyone a little nervous and unsure.

I love black-and-white photographs, and I always have. I have cut photographs out of magazines to paste in books of my own, bought albums at yard sales, and kept collections that had one or two images I wanted near me always. Those pictures tell me stories—my own and others, scary stories sometimes, but more often simply everyday stories, what happened in that place at that time to those people. The pictures I collect leave me to puzzle out what I think about it later. Sometimes, I imagine my own life as a series of snapshots taken by some omniscient artist who is just keeping track—not interfering or saying anything, just capturing the moment for me to look back at it again later. The eye of God, as expressed in a Dorothea Lange or Wright Morris.[2] This is the way it is, the photograph says, and I nod my head in appreciation. The power of art is in that nod of appreciation, though sometimes I puzzle nothing out, and the nod is more a shrug. No, I do not understand this one, but I see it. I take it in. I will think about it. If I sit with this image long enough, this

---

[1]*O'Connor:* For an example of her fiction, see page 888. — EDS.

[2]*Dorothea Lange* (1895–1965) was an American photographer known for her depictions of rural poverty. *Wright Morris* (1910–1998) was a prominent midwestern novelist also known for his photography; he often published books that combined text and photographs. — EDS.

story, I have the hope of understanding something I did not understand before. And that, too, is art, the best art.

My friend Jackie used to call my photographs sentimental. I had pinned them up all over the walls of my apartment, and Jackie liked a few of them but thought on the whole they were better suited to being tucked away in a book. On her walls, she had half a dozen bright prints in bottle-cap metal frames, most of them bought from Puerto Rican artists at street sales when she was working as a taxi driver and always had cash in her pockets. I thought her prints garish and told her so when she made fun of my photographs.

"They remind me of my mama," she told me. I had only seen one photograph of Jackie's mother, a wide-faced Italian matron from Queens with thick, black eyebrows and a perpetual squint.

"She liked bright colors?" I asked.

Jackie nodded. "And stuff you could buy on the street. She was al-   20
ways buying stuff off tables on the street, saying that was the best stuff. Best prices. Cheap skirts that lost their dye after a couple of washes, shoes with cardboard insoles, those funky little icons, weeping saints and long-faced Madonnas. She liked stuff to be really colorful. She painted all the ceilings in our apartment red and white. Red-red and white-white. Like blood on bone."

I looked up at my ceiling. The high tin ceiling was uniformly bloody when I moved in, with paint put on so thick, I could chip it off in lumps. I had climbed on stacks of boxes to paint it all cream white and pale blue.

"The Virgin's colors," Jackie told me. "You should put gold roses on the door posts."

"I'm no artist," I told her.

"I am," Jackie laughed. She took out a pencil and sketched a leafy vine above two of my framed photographs. She was good. It looked as if the frames were pinned to the vine. "I'll do it all," she said, looking at me to see if I was upset.

"Do it," I told her.   25

Jackie drew lilies and potato vines up the hall while I made tea and admired the details. Around the front door she put the Virgin's roses and curious little circles with crosses entwined in the middle. "It's beautiful," I told her.

"A blessing," she told me. "Like a bit of magic. My mama magic." Her face was so serious, I brought back a dish of salt and water, and we blessed the entrance. "Now the devil will pass you by," she promised me.

I laughed, but almost believed.

For a few months last spring I kept seeing an ad in all the magazines that showed a small child high in the air dropping toward the upraised arms of a waiting figure below. The image was grainy and distant. I could not tell if the child was laughing or crying. The copy at the bottom of the page read: "Your father always caught you."

"Look at this," I insisted the first time I saw the ad. "Will you look at   30
this?"

A friend of mine took the magazine, looked at the ad, and then up into my shocked and horrified face.

"They don't mean it that way," she said.

I looked at the ad again. They didn't mean it that way? They meant it innocently? I shuddered. It was supposed to make you feel safe, maybe make you buy insurance or something. It did not make me feel safe. I dreamed about the picture, and it was not a good dream.

I wonder how many other people see that ad the way I do. I wonder how many other people look at the constant images of happy families and make wry faces at most of them. It's as if all the illustrators have television sitcom imaginations. I do not believe in those families. I believe in the exhausted mothers, frightened children, numb and stubborn men. I believe in hard-pressed families, the child huddled in fear with his face hidden, the father and mother confronting each other with their emotions hidden, dispassionate passionate faces, and the unsettling sense of risk in the baby held close to that man's chest. These images make sense to me. They are about the world I know, the stories I tell. When they are accompanied by wry titles or copy that is slightly absurd or unexpected, I grin and know that I will puzzle it out later, sometimes a lot later.

I think that using art to provoke uncertainty is what great writing   35
and inspired images do most brilliantly. Art should provoke more questions than answers and, most of all, should make us think about what we rarely want to think about at all. Sitting down to write a novel, I refuse to consider if my work is seen as difficult or inappropriate or provocative. I choose my subjects to force the congregation to look at what they try so stubbornly to pretend is not happening at all, deliberately combining the horribly serious with the absurd or funny, because I know that if I am to reach my audience I must first seduce their attention and draw them into the world of my imagination. I know that I have to lay out my stories, my difficult people, each story layering on top of the one before it with care and craft, until my audience sees something they had not expected. Frailty—stubborn, human frailty—that is what I work to showcase. The wonder and astonishment of the despised and ignored, that is what I hope to find in art and in the books I write—my secret self, my vulnerable and embattled heart, the child I was and the woman I have become, not Jesus at the Jordan but a woman with only her stubborn memories and passionate convictions to redeem her.

"You write such mean stories," a friend once told me. "Raped girls, brutal fathers, faithless mothers, and untrustworthy lovers—meaner than the world really is, don't you think?"

I just looked at her. Meaner than the world really is? No. I thought about showing her the box under my desk where I keep my clippings. Newspaper stories and black-and-white images—the woman who drowned her children, the man who shot first the babies in her arms and then his wife, the teenage boys who led the three-year-old away along the train track, the homeless family recovering from frostbite with their eyes glazed and indifferent while the doctor scowled over their shoulders. The world is meaner than we admit, larger and more astonishing. Strength appears in the most desperate figures, tragedy when we have no reason to expect it. Yes, some of my stories are fearful, but not as cruel as what I see in the world. I believe in redemption, just as I believe in the nobility of the despised, the dignity of the outcast, the intrinsic honor among misfits, pariahs, and queers. Artists—those of us who stand outside the city gates and look back at a society that tries to ignore us—we have an angle of vision denied to whole sectors of the sheltered and indifferent population within. It is our curse and our prize, and for everyone who will tell us our work is mean or fearful or unreal, there is another who will embrace us and say with tears in their eyes how wonderful it is to finally feel as if someone else has seen their truth and shown it in some part as it should be known.

"My story," they say. "You told my story. That is me, mine, us." And it is.

We are not the same. We are a nation of nations. Regions, social classes, economic circumstances, ethical systems, and political convictions—all separate us even as we pretend they do not. Art makes that plain. Those of us who have read the same books, eaten the same kinds of food as children, watched the same television shows, and listened to the same music, we believe ourselves part of the same nation—and we are continually startled to discover that our versions of reality do not match. If we were more the same, would we not see the same thing when we look at a painting? But what is it we see when we look at a work of art? What is it we fear will be revealed? The artist waits for us to say. It does not matter that each of us sees something slightly different. Most of us, confronted with the artist's creation, hesitate, stammer, or politely deflect the question of what it means to us. Even those of us from the same background, same region, same general economic and social class, come to "art" uncertain, suspicious, not wanting to embarrass ourselves by revealing what the work provokes in us. In fact, sometimes we are not sure. If we were to reveal what we see in each painting, sculpture, installation, or little book, we would run the risk of exposing our secret selves, what we know and what we fear we do not know, and of course incidentally what it is we truly fear. Art is the Rorschach test for all of us, the projective hologram of our secret lives. Our emotional and intellectual lives are laid bare. Do you like hologram roses? Big, bold, brightly painted canvases? Representational art? Little boxes with tiny figures posed precisely? Do you dare say what it is you like?

For those of us born into poor and working-class families, these are   40
not simple questions. For those of us who grew up hiding what our home
life was like, the fear is omnipresent—particularly when that home life
was scarred by physical and emotional violence. We know if we say anything about what we see in a work of art we will reveal more about ourselves than the artist. What do you see in this painting, in that one? I see a
little girl, terrified, holding together the torn remnants of her clothing. I
see a child, looking back at the mother for help and finding none. I see a
mother, bruised and exhausted, unable to look up for help, unable to believe anyone in the world will help her. I see a man with his fists raised,
hating himself but making those fists tighter all the time. I see a little girl,
uncertain and angry, looking down at her own body with hatred and contempt. I see that all the time, even when no one else sees what I see. I
know I am not supposed to mention what it is I see. Perhaps no one else
is seeing what I see. If they are, I am pretty sure there is some cryptic
covenant that requires that we will not say what we see. Even when looking at an image of a terrified child, we know that to mention why that
child might be so frightened would be a breach of social etiquette. The
world requires that such children not be mentioned, even when so many
of us are looking directly at her.

There seems to be a tacit agreement about what it is not polite to
mention, what it is not appropriate to portray. For some of us, that polite
behavior is set so deeply we truly do not see what seems outside that tacit
agreement. We have lost the imagination for what our real lives have
been or continue to be, what happens when we go home and close the
door on the outside world. Since so many would like us to never mention
anything unsettling anyway, the impulse to be quiet, the impulse to deny
and pretend, becomes very strong. But the artist knows all about that impulse. The artist knows that it must be resisted. Art is not meant to be polite, secret, coded, or timid. Art is the sphere in which that impulse to hide
and lie is the most dangerous. In art, transgression is holy, revelation a
sacrament, and pursuing one's personal truth the only sure validation.

Does it matter if our art is canonized, if we become rich and successful, lauded and admired? Does it make any difference if our pictures become popular, our books made into movies, our creations win awards?
What if we are the ones who wind up going from town to town with our
notebooks, our dusty boxes of prints or Xeroxed sheets of music, never
acknowledged, never paid for our work? As artists, we know how easily
we could become a Flannery O'Connor character, reading those journals
of criticism and burying our faces in our hands, staggering under the
weight of what we see that the world does not. As artists, we also know
that neither worldly praise not critical disdain will ultimately prove the
worth of our work.

Some nights I think of that sweating, girlish Jesus above my mother's
determined features, those hands outspread to cast benediction on those
giggling uncertain boys, me in the congregation struck full of wonder and

love and helpless laughter. If no one else ever wept at that image, I did. I wished the artist who painted that image knew how powerfully it touched me, that after all these years his art still lives inside me. If I can wish for anything for my art, that is what I want—to live in some child forever—and if I can demand anything of other artists, it is that they attempt as much.

The Reader's Presence

1. You may have heard the old writing advice to "say what you're going to say, say it, and then say what you've said." How does the structure of Allison's argument diverge from this rule? How does the essay begin? Where is her argument first explicitly stated? How is it developed?

2. What is the relation between the painting of Jesus and Allison's argument? Does the scene of her mother's baptism serve merely as an interesting anecdote, or can it be tied in some way to the questions she raises regarding the function and value of art? In your opinion, do Allison's personal stories contribute to or detract from her central argument? In what ways?

3. Allison argues that "art should provoke more questions than answers." Can you think of a story or novel you have read, or a play or a movie you have seen, that meets these stipulations? What issues did it raise? Which questions remained unanswered? What effect did this indeterminacy have on you? Does this essay meet Allison's own dictate? Why or why not?

88

James Baldwin

Stranger in the Village

James Baldwin (1924–1987) grew up in New York City but moved to France in 1948 because he felt personally and artistically stifled as a gay African American man in the United States. His first novels, Go Tell It on the Mountain *(1956) and* Giovanni's Room *(1956), and his first collection of essays,* Notes of a Native Son *(1955), were published during Baldwin's first stay abroad, where he was able to write critically about race, sexual identity, and social injustice in America. The essay "Stranger in the Village" appears in* Notes of a Native Son. *After nearly a decade in France, he returned to New York and became a national figure in the civil rights movement. Henry Louis Gates Jr. eulogized Baldwin as the conscience of the nation, for he "educated an entire generation of Americans about the civil-rights struggle and the sensibility of Afro-Americans as we faced and conquered the final barriers in our long quest for civil rights." Baldwin continues to educate through his essays, collected in* The Price of the Ticket: Collected Nonfiction *(1985).*

When asked if he approached the writing of fiction and nonfiction in different ways, Baldwin responded, "Every form is different, no one is easier than another. . . . An essay is not simpler, though it may seem so. An essay is clearly an argument. The writer's point of view in an essay is always absolutely clear. The writer is trying to make the readers see something, trying to convince them of something. In a novel or a play you're trying to show them something. The risks, in any case, are exactly the same."

From all available evidence no black man had ever set foot in this tiny Swiss village before I came. I was told before arriving that I would probably be a "sight" in the village; I took this to mean that people of my complexion were rarely seen in Switzerland, and also that city people are always something of a "sight" outside of the city. It did not occur to me — possibly because I am an American — that there could be people anywhere who had never seen a Negro.

It is a fact that cannot be explained on the basis of the inaccessibility of the village. The village is very high, but it is only four hours from Milan and three hours from Lausanne. It is true that it is virtually unknown. Few people making plans for a holiday would elect to come here. On the other hand, the villagers are able, presumably, to come and go as they please — which they do: to another town at the foot of the mountain, with a population of approximately five thousand, the nearest place to see a movie or go to the bank. In the village there is no movie house, no bank, no library, no theater; very few radios, one jeep, one station wagon; and, at the moment, one typewriter, mine, an invention which the woman next door to me here had never seen. There are about six hundred people living here, all Catholic — I conclude this from the fact that the Catholic church is open all year round, whereas the Protestant chapel, set off on a hill a little removed from the village, is open only in the summertime when the tourists arrive. There are four or five hotels, all closed now, and four or five bistros, of which, however, only two do any business during the winter. These two do not do a great deal, for life in the village seems to end around nine or ten o'clock. There are a few stores, butcher, baker, *épicerie*,[1] a hardware store, and a money-changer — who cannot change travelers' checks, but must send them down to the bank, an operation which takes two or three days. There is something called the *Ballet Haus*, closed in the winter and used for God knows what, certainly

---

[1]*épicerie:* A grocery store (French). — EDS.

not ballet, during the summer. There seems to be only one schoolhouse in the village, and this for the quite young children; I suppose this to mean that their older brothers and sisters at some point descend from these mountains in order to complete their education — possibly, again, to the town just below. The landscape is absolutely forbidding, mountains towering on all four sides, ice and snow as far as the eye can reach. In this white wilderness, men and women and children move all day, carrying washing, wood, buckets of milk or water, sometimes skiing on Sunday afternoons. All week long boys and young men are to be seen shoveling snow off the rooftops, or dragging wood down from the forest in sleds.

The village's only real attraction, which explains the tourist season, is the hot spring water. A disquietingly high proportion of these tourists are cripples, or semi-cripples, who come year after year — from other parts of Switzerland, usually — to take the waters. This lends the village, at the height of the season, a rather terrifying air of sanctity, as though it were a lesser Lourdes. There is often something beautiful, there is always something awful, in the spectacle of a person who has lost one of his faculties, a faculty he never questioned until it was gone, and who struggles to recover it. Yet people remain people, on crutches or indeed on deathbeds; and wherever I passed, the first summer I was here, among the native villagers or among the lame, a wind passed with me — of astonishment, curiosity, amusement, and outrage. That first summer I stayed two weeks and never intended to return. But I did return in the winter, to work; the village offers, obviously, no distractions whatever and has the further advantage of being extremely cheap. Now it is winter again, a year later, and I am here again. Everyone in the village knows my name, though they scarcely ever use it, knows that I come from America — though, this, apparently, they will never really believe: black men come from Africa — and everyone knows that I am the friend of the son of a woman who was born here, and that I am staying in their chalet. But I remain as much a stranger today as I was the first day I arrived, and the children shout *Neger! Neger!* as I walk along the streets.

It must be admitted that in the beginning I was far too shocked to have any real reaction. In so far as I reacted at all, I reacted by trying to be pleasant — it being a great part of the American Negro's education (long before he goes to school) that he must make people "like" him. This smile-and-the-world-smiles-with-you routine worked about as well in this situation as it had in the situation for which it was designed, which is to say that it did not work at all. No one, after all, can be liked whose human weight and complexity cannot be, or has not been, admitted. My smile was simply another unheard-of phenomenon which allowed them to see my teeth — they did not, really, see my smile and I began to think that, should I take to snarling, no one would notice any difference. All of the physical characteristics of the Negro which had caused me, in America, a very different and almost forgotten pain were nothing less than miraculous — or infernal — in the eyes of the village people. Some thought my hair was the color of tar, that it had the texture of wire, or the texture of cotton. It was jocularly suggested that I might let it all grow long and make myself a winter coat. If I sat in the sun for more than five minutes some daring creature was certain to come along and gingerly put his fingers on my hair, as though he were afraid of an electric shock, or put his hand on my hand, astonished that the color did not rub off. In all of this, in which it must be conceded there was the charm or genuine wonder and in which there was certainly no element of intentional unkindness, there was yet no suggestion that I was human: I was simply a living wonder.

I knew that they did not mean to be unkind, and I know it now; it is   5
necessary, nevertheless, for me to repeat this to myself each time I walk out of the chalet. The children who shout *Neger!* have no way of knowing the echoes this sound raises in me. They are brimming with good humor and the more daring swell with pride when I stop to speak with them. Just the same, there are days when I cannot pause and smile, when I have no heart to play with them; when, indeed, I mutter sourly to myself, exactly as I muttered on the streets of a city these children have never seen, when I was no bigger than these children are now: *Your* mother *was a nigger.* Joyce is right about history being a nightmare—but it may be the nightmare from which no one *can* awaken. People are trapped in history and history is trapped in them.

There is a custom in the village—I am told it is repeated in many villages—of "buying" African natives for the purpose of converting them to Christianity. There stands in the church all year round a small box with a slot for money, decorated with a black figurine, and into this box the villagers drop their francs. During the *carnaval* which precedes Lent, two village children have their faces blackened—out of which bloodless darkness their blue eyes shine like ice—and fantastic horsehair wigs are placed on their blond heads; thus disguised, they solicit among the villagers for money for the missionaries in Africa. Between the box in the church and the blackened children, the village "bought" last year six or eight African natives. This was reported to me with pride by the wife of one of the bistro owners and I was careful to express astonishment and pleasure at the solicitude shown by the village for the souls of black folk. The bistro owner's wife beamed with a pleasure far more genuine than my own and seemed to feel that I might now breathe more easily concerning the souls of at least six of my kinsmen.

I tried not to think of these so lately baptized kinsmen, of the price paid for them, or the peculiar price they themselves would pay, and said nothing about my father, who having taken his own conversion too literally never, at bottom, forgave the white world (which he described as heathen) for having saddled him with a Christ in whom, to judge at least from their treatment of him, they themselves no longer believed. I thought of white men arriving for the first time in an African village, strangers there, as I am a stranger here, and tried to imagine the astounded populace touching their hair and marveling at the color of their skin. But there is a great difference between being the first white man to be seen by Africans and being the first black man to be seen by whites. The white man takes the astonishment as tribute, for he arrives to conquer and to convert the natives, whose inferiority in relation to himself is not even to be questioned; whereas I, without a thought of conquest, find myself among a people whose culture controls me, has even, in a sense, created me, people who have cost me more in anguish and rage than they will ever know, who yet do not even know of my existence. The astonishment with which I might have greeted them, should they have stumbled into my African village a few hundred years ago, might have rejoiced their hearts. But the astonishmnt with which they greet me today can only poison mine.

And this is so despite everything I may do to feel differently, despite my friendly conversations with the bistro owner's wife, despite their three-year-old son who has at last become my friend, despite the *saluts* and *bonsoirs* which I exchange with people as I walk, despite the fact that I know that no individual can be taken to task for what history is doing, or has done. I say that the culture of these people controls me—but they can scarcely be held responsible for European culture. America comes out of Europe, but these people have never seen America, nor have most of them seen more of Europe than the hamlet at the foot of their mountain. Yet they move with an authority which I shall never have; and they regard me, quite rightly, not only as a stranger in their village but as a suspect latecomer, bearing no credentials, to everything they have—however unconsciously—inherited.

For this village, even were it incomparably more remote and incredibly more primitive, is the West, the West onto which I have been so strangely grafted. These people cannot be, from the point of view of power, strangers anywhere in the world; they have made the modern world, in effect, even if they do not know it. The most illiterate among them is related, in a way that I am not, to Dante, Shakespeare, Michelangelo, Aeschylus, Da Vinci, Rembrandt, and Racine; the cathedral at Chartres says something to them which it cannot say to me, as indeed would New York's Empire State Building, should anyone here ever see it. Out of their hymns and dances come Beethoven and Bach. Go back a few centuries and they are in their full glory—but I am in Africa, watching the conquerors arrive.

The rage of the disesteemed is personally fruitless, but it is also absolutely inevitable; this rage, so generally discounted, so little understood even among the people whose daily bread it is, is one of the things that makes history. Rage can only with difficulty, and never entirely, be brought under the domination of the intelligence and is therefore not susceptible to any arguments whatever. This is a fact which ordinary representatives of the *Herrenvolk*, having never felt this rage and being unable to imagine it, quite fail to understand. Also, rage cannot be hidden, it can only be dissembled. This dissembling deludes the thoughtless, and

10

strengthens rage, and adds, to rage, contempt. There are, no doubt, as many ways of coping with the resulting complex of tensions as there are black men in the world, but no black man can hope ever to be entirely liberated from this internal warfare—rage, dissembling, and contempt having inevitably accompanied his first realization of the power of white men. What is crucial here is that, since white men represent in the black man's world so heavy a weight, white men have for black men a reality which is far from being reciprocal; and hence all black men have toward all white men an attitude which is designed, really, either to rob the white man of the jewel of his naïveté, or else to make it cost him dear.

The black man insists, by whatever means he finds at his disposal, that the white man cease to regard him as an exotic rarity and recognize him as a human being. This is a very charged and difficult moment, for there is a great deal of will power involved in the white man's naïveté. Most people are not naturally reflective any more than they are naturally malicious, and the white man prefers to keep the black man at a certain human remove because it is easier for him thus to preserve his simplicity and avoid being called to account for crimes committed by his forefathers, or his neighbors. He is inescapably aware, nevertheless, that he is in a better position in the world than black men are, nor can he quite put to death the suspicion that he is hated by black men therefor. He does not wish to be hated, neither does he wish to change places, and at this point in his uneasiness he can scarcely avoid having recourse to those legends which white men have created about black men, the most usual effect of which is that the white man finds himself enmeshed, so to speak, in his own language which describes hell, as well as the attributes which lead one to hell, as being as black as night.

Every legend, moreover, contains its residuum of truth, and the root function of language is to control the universe by describing it. It is of quite considerable significance that black men remain, in the imagination, and in overwhelming numbers in fact, beyond the disciplines of salvation; and this despite the fact that the West has been "buying" African natives for centuries. There is, I should hazard, an instantaneous necessity to be divorced from this so visibly unsaved stranger, in whose heart, moreover, one cannot guess what dreams of vengeance are being nourished; and, at the same time, there are few things on earth more attractive than the idea of the unspeakable liberty which is allowed the unredeemed. When, beneath the black mask, a human being begins to make himself felt one cannot escape a certain awful wonder as to what kind of human being it is. What one's imagination makes of other people is dictated, of course, by the laws of one's own personality and it is one of the ironies of black-white relations that, by means of what the white man imagines the black man to be, the black man is enabled to know who the white man is.

I have said, for example, that I am as much a stranger in this village today as I was the first summer I arrived, but this is not quite true. The villagers wonder less about the texture of my hair than they did then, and wonder rather more about me. And the fact that their wonder now exists on another level is reflected in their attitudes and in their eyes. There are the children who make those delightful, hilarious, sometimes astonishing grave overtures of friendship in the unpredictable fashion of children; other children, having been taught that the devil is a black man, scream in genuine anguish as I approach. Some of the older women never pass without a friendly greeting, never pass, indeed, if it seems that they will be able to engage me in conversation; other women look down or look away or rather contemptuously smirk. Some of the men drink with me and suggest that I learn how to ski—partly, I gather, because they cannot imagine what I would look like on skis—and want to know if I am married, and ask questions about my métier. But some of the men have accused *le sale négre*—behind my back—of stealing wood and there is already in the eyes of some of them that peculiar intent, paranoiac malevolence which one sometimes surprises in the eyes of American white men when, out walking with their Sunday girl, they see a Negro male approach.

There is a dreadful abyss between the streets of this village and the streets of the city in which I was born, between the children who shout *Neger!* today and those who shouted *Nigger!* yesterday—the abyss is experience, the American experience. The syllable hurled behind me today expresses, above all, wonder: I am a stranger here. But I am not a stranger in America and the same syllable riding on the American air expresses the war my presence has occasioned in the American soul.

For this village brings home to me this fact: that there was a day, and   15
not really a very distant day, when Americans were scarcely Americans at all but discontented Europeans, facing a great unconquered continent and strolling, say, into a marketplace and seeing black men for the first time. The shock this spectacle afforded is suggested, surely, by the promptness with which they decided that these black men were not really men but cattle. It is true that the necessity on the part of the settlers of the New World of reconciling their moral assumptions with the fact—and the necessity—of slavery enhanced immensely the charm of this idea, and it is also true that this idea expresses, with a truly American bluntness, the attitude which to varying extents all masters have had toward all slaves.

But between all former slaves and slave-owners and the drama which begins for Americans over three hundred years ago at Jamestown, there are at least two differences to be observed. The American Negro slave could not suppose, for one thing, as slaves in past epochs had supposed and often done, that he would ever be able to wrest the power from his master's hands. This was a supposition which the modern era, which was to bring about such vast changes in the aims and dimensions of power, put to death; it only begins, in unprecedented fashion, and with dreadful implications, to be resurrected today. But even had this supposition persisted with undiminished force, the American Negro slave could not have used it to lend his condition dignity, for the reason that this supposition rests on another: that the slave in exile yet remains related to his past, has some means—if only in memory—of revering and sustaining the forms of his former life, is able, in short, to maintain his identity.

This was not the case with the American Negro slave. His is unique among the black men of the world in that his past was taken from him, almost literally, at one blow. One wonders what on earth the first slave found to say to the first dark child he bore. I am told that there are Haitians able to trace their ancestry back to African kings, but any American Negro wishing to go back so far will find his journey through time abruptly arrested by the signature on the bill of sale which served as the entrance paper for his ancestor. At the time—to say nothing of the circumstances—of the enslavement of the captive black man who was to become the American Negro, there was not the remotest possibility that he would ever take power from his master's hands. There was no reason to suppose that his situation would ever change, nor was there, shortly, anything to indicate that his situation had ever been different. It was his necessity, in the words of E. Franklin Frazier, to find a "motive for living under American culture or die." The identity of the American Negro comes out of this extreme situation, and the evolution of this identity was a source of the most intolerable anxiety in the minds and the lives of his masters.

For the history of the American Negro is unique also in this: that the question of his humanity, and of his rights therefore as a human being, became a burning one for several generations of Americans, so burning a question that it ultimately became one of those used to divide the nation. It is out of this argument that the venom of the epithet *Nigger!* is derived. It is an argument which Europe has never had, and hence Europe quite sincerely fails to understand how or why the argument arose in the first place, why its effects are so frequently disastrous and always so unpredictable, why it refuses until today to be entirely settled. Europe's black possessions remained—and do remain—in Europe's colonies, at which remove they represented no threat to European identity. If they posed any problem at all for the European conscience, it was a problem which remained comfortingly abstract: in effect, the black man, *as a man,* did not exist for Europe. But in America, even as a slave, he was an inescapable part of the general social fabric and no American could escape having an attitude toward him. Americans attempt until today to make an abstraction of the Negro, but the very nature of these abstractions reveals the tremendous effects the presence of the Negro has had on the American character.

When one considers the history of the Negro in America it is of the greatest importance to recognize that the moral beliefs of a person, or a people, are never really as tenuous as life—which is not moral—very often causes them to appear; these create for them a frame of reference and a necessary hope, the hope being that when life has done its worst they will be enabled to rise above themselves and to triumph over life. Life would scarcely be bearable if this hope did not exist. Again, even when the worst has been said, to betray a belief is not by any means to have put oneself beyond its power; the betrayal of a belief is not the same thing as ceasing to believe. If this were not so there would be no moral standards in the world at all. Yet one must also recognize that morality is based on ideas and that all ideas are dangerous—dangerous because ideas can only lead to action and where the action leads no man can say. And dangerous in this respect: that confronted with the impossibility of remaining faithful to one's beliefs, and the equal impossibility of becoming free of them, one can be driven to the most inhuman excesses. The ideas on which American beliefs are based are not, though Americans often seem to think so, ideas which originated in America. They came out of Europe. And the establishment of democracy on the American continent was scarcely as radical a break with the past as with the necessity, which Americans faced, of broadening this concept to include black men.

This was, literally, a hard necessity. It was impossible, for one thing, 20 for Americans to abandon their beliefs, not only because these beliefs alone seemed able to justify the sacrifices they had endured and the blood that they had spilled, but also because these beliefs afforded them their only bulwark against a moral chaos as absolute as the physical chaos of the continent it was their destiny to conquer. But in the situation in which Americans found themselves, these beliefs threatened an idea which, whether or not one likes to think so, is the very warp and woof of the heritage of the West, the idea of white supremacy.

Americans have made themselves notorious by the shrillness and the brutality with which they have insisted on this idea, but they did not invent it; and it has escaped the world's notice that those very excesses of which Americans have been guilty imply a certain, unprecedented uneasiness over the idea's life and power, if not, indeed, the idea's validity. The idea of white supremacy rests simply on the fact that white men are the creators of civilization (the present civilization, which is the only one that matters; all previous civilizations are simply "contributions" to our own) and are therefore civilization's guardians and defenders. Thus it was impossible for Americans to accept the black man as one of themselves, for to do so was to jeopardize their status as white men. But not so to accept him was to deny his human reality, his human weight and complexity, and the strain of denying the overwhelmingly undeniable forced Americans into rationalizations so fantastic that they approached the pathological.

At the root of the American Negro problem is the necessity of the American white man to find a way of living with the Negro in order to be able to live with himself. And the history of this problem can be reduced to the means used by Americans—lynch law and law, segregation and legal acceptance, terrorization and concession—either to come to terms with this necessity, or to find a way around it, or (most usually) to find a way of doing both these things at once. The resulting spectacle, at once foolish and dreadful, led someone to make the quite accurate observation that "the Negro-in-America is a form of insanity which overtakes white men."

In this long battle, a battle by no means finished, the unforseeable effects of which will be felt my many future generations, the white man's motive was the protection of his identity; the black man was motivated by the need to establish an identity. And despite the terrorization which the Negro in America endured and endures sporadically until today, despite the cruel and totally inescapable ambivalence of his status in his country, the battle for his identity has long ago been won. He is not a visitor to the West, but a citizen there, an American, as American as the Americans who despise him, the Americans who fear him, the Americans who love him—the Americans who became less than themselves, or rose to be greater than themselves by virtue of the fact that the challenge he represented was inescapable. He is perhaps the only black man in the world whose relationship to white men is more terrible, more subtle, and more meaningful than the relationship of bitter possessed to uncertain possessor. His survival depended, and his development depends, on his ability to turn his peculiar status in the Western world to his own advantage and, it may be, to the very great advantage of that world. It remains for him to fashion out of his experience that which will give him sustenance, and a voice.

The cathedral of Chartres, I have said, says something to the people of this village which it cannot say to me; but it is important to understand that this cathedral says something to me which it cannot say to them. Perhaps they are struck by the power of the spires, the glory of the windows; but they have known God, after all, longer than I have known him, and in a different way, and I am terrified by the slippery bottomless well to be found in the crypt, down which heretics were hurled to death, and by the obscene, inescapable gargoyles jutting out of the stone and seeming to say that God and the devil can never be divorced. I doubt that the villagers think of the devil when they face a cathedral because they have never been identified with the devil. But I must accept the status which myth, if nothing else, gives me in the West before I can hope to change the myth.

Yet, if the American Negro has arrived at his identity by virtue of the absoluteness of his estrangement from his past, American white men still nourish the illusion that there is some means of recovering the European innocence, of returning to a state in which black men do not exist. This is one of the greatest errors Americans can make. The identity they fought so hard to protect has, by virtue of that battle, undergone a change: Americans are as unlike any other white people in the world as it is possible to be. I do not think, for example, that it is too much to suggest that the American vision of the world—which allows so little reality, generally speaking, for any of the darker forces in human life, which tends until today to paint moral issues in glaring black and white—owes a great deal to the battle waged by Americans to maintain between themselves and black men a human separation which could not be bridged. It is only now beginning to be borne in on us—very faintly, it must be admitted, very slowly, and very much against our will—that this vision of the world is dangerously inaccurate, and perfectly useless. For it protects our moral high-mindedness at the terrible expense of weakening our grasp of reality. People who shut their eyes to reality simply invite their own destruction, and anyone who insists on remaining in a state of innocence long after that innocence is dead turns himself into a monster.

The time has come to realize that the interracial drama acted out on the American continent has not only created a new black man, it has created a new white man, too. No road whatever will lead Americans back to the simplicity of this European village where white men still have the luxury of looking on me as a stranger. I am not, really, a stranger any longer for any American alive. One of the things that distinguishes Americans from other people is that no other people has ever been so deeply involved in the lives of black men, and vice versa. This fact faced, with all its implications, it can be seen that the history of the American Negro problem is not merely shameful, it is also something of an achievement. For even when the worst has been said, it must also be added that the perpetual challenge posed by this problem was always, somehow, perpetually met. It is precisely this black-white experience which may prove of indispensable value to us in the world we face today. This world is white no longer, and it will never be white again.

The Reader's Presence

1. Baldwin opens the essay with an account of himself as a stranger in an actual Swiss village. But how do we begin to see him as a stranger in more general ways? What does the village come to represent? What is the relation of the Swiss village to Baldwin's America?

2. This is an essay that moves from autobiography to argument. In rereading it, can you find the place where Baldwin's autobiography begins to disappear and where his argument begins to take over? Try stating Baldwin's central argument in your own terms. To what extent is his argument historical?

3. In paragraph 21, Baldwin writes about the denial of "human weight and complexity." What role does such complexity play in this essay? In rereading the essay, locate several sentences in which you think Baldwin's ideas resist simplification. Study these sentences carefully. What do they have in common? How do they illustrate the kind of complexity that Baldwin sees as essentially human?

William Cronon

The Trouble with Wilderness

William Cronon (b. 1954) is a noted historian of the American environment and of the American West. Among many honors, Cronon has received a MacArthur Fellowship; the Francis Parkman Prize of the Society of American Historians for his first book, Changes in the Land: Indians, Colonists, and the Ecology of New England *(1983); and the Bancroft Prize for* Nature's Metropolis: Chicago and the Great West *(1991). After teaching for more than a decade at Yale University, Cronon became the Frederick Jackson Turner Professor of History, Geography, and Environmental Studies at the University of Wisconsin—Madison in 1992. In addition to being a professor, Cronon has served as president of the American Society for Environmental History and is general editor of the Weyerhaeuser Environmental Book Series. "The Trouble with Wilderness" appeared in the* New York Times Magazine *in 1995 and is a shorter version of an essay that was originally published in* Environmental History *also in that year.*

Preserving wilderness has for decades been a fundamental tenet—indeed, a passion—of the environmental movement, especially in the United States. For many Americans, wilderness stands as the last place where civilization, that all-too-human disease, has not fully infected the earth. It is an island in the polluted sea of urban-industrial modernity, a refuge we must somehow recover to save the planet. As Henry David Thoreau famously declared, "In Wilderness is the preservation of the World."

But is it? The more one knows of its peculiar history, the more one realizes that wilderness is not quite what it seems. Far from being the one place on earth that stands apart from humanity, it is quite profoundly a human creation—indeed, the creation of very particular human cultures at very particular moments in human history. It is not a pristine sanctuary where the last remnant of an endangered but still transcendent nature can be encountered without the contaminating taint of civilization. Instead, it is a product of that civilization. As we gaze into the mirror it holds up for us, we too easily imagine that what we behold is nature when in fact we see the reflection of our own longings and desires. Wilderness can hardly be the solution to our culture's problematic relationship with the nonhuman world, for wilderness is itself a part of the problem.

To assert the unnaturalness of so natural a place may seem perverse: we can all conjure up images and sensations that seem all the more hauntingly real for having engraved themselves so indelibly on our memories. Remember this? The torrents of mist shooting out from the base of a great waterfall in the depths of a Sierra Nevada canyon, the droplets cooling your face as you listen to the roar of the water and gaze toward the sky through a rainbow that hovers just out of reach. Or this: Looking out across a desert canyon in the evening air, the only sound a lone raven calling in the distance, the rock walls dropping away into a chasm so deep that its bottom all but vanishes as you squint into the amber light of the setting sun. Remember the feelings of such moments, and you will know as well as I do that you were in the presence of something irreducibly nonhuman, something profoundly Other than yourself. Wilderness is made of that too.

And yet: what brought each of us to the places where such memories became possible is entirely a cultural invention.

For the Americans who first celebrated it, wilderness was tied to the 5 myth of the frontier. The historian Frederick Jackson Turner wrote the classic academic statement of this myth in 1893, but it has been part of American thought for well over a century. As Turner described the process, Easterners and European immigrants, in moving to the wild lands of the frontier, shed the trappings of civilization and thereby gained an energy, an independence and a creativity that were the sources of American democracy and national character. Seen this way, wilderness became a place of religious redemption and national renewal, the quintessential location for experiencing what it meant to be an American.

Those who celebrate the frontier almost always look backward, mourning an older, simpler world that has disappeared forever. That world and all its attractions, Turner said, depended on free land—on wilderness. It is no accident that the movement to set aside national parks and wilderness areas gained real momentum just as laments about the vanishing frontier reached their peak. To protect wilderness was to protect the nation's most sacred myth of origin.

The decades following the civil war saw more and more of the nation's wealthiest citizens seeking out wilderness for themselves. The passion for wild land took many forms: enormous estates in the Adirondacks and elsewhere (disingenuously called "camps" despite their many servants and amenities); cattle ranches for would-be roughriders on the Great Plains; guided big-game hunting trips in the Rockies. Wilderness suddenly emerged as the landscape of choice for elite tourists. For them, it was a place of recreation.

In just this way, wilderness came to embody the frontier myth, standing for the wild freedom of America's past and seeming to represent a highly attractive natural alternative to the ugly artificiality of modern civilization. The irony, of course, was that in the process wilderness came to reflect the very civilization its devotees sought to escape. Ever since the nineteenth century, celebrating wilderness has been an activity mainly for well-to-do city folks. Country people generally know far too much about working the land to regard unworked land as their ideal.

There were other ironies as well. The movement to set aside national parks and wilderness areas followed hard on the heels of the final Indian wars, in which the prior human inhabitants of these regions were rounded up and moved onto reservations so that tourists could safely enjoy the illusion that they were seeing their nation in its pristine, original state — in the new morning of God's own creation. Meanwhile, its original inhabitants were kept out by dint of force, their earlier uses of the land redefined as inappropriate or even illegal. To this day, for instance, the Blackfeet continue to be accused of "poaching" on the lands of Glacier National Park, in Montana, that originally belonged to them and that were ceded by treaty only with the proviso that they be permitted to hunt there.

The removal of Indians to create an "uninhabited wilderness" reminds us just how invented and how constructed the American wilderness really is. One of the most striking proofs of the cultural invention of wilderness is its thoroughgoing erasure of the history from which it sprang. In virtually all its manifestations, wilderness represents a flight from history. Seen as the original garden, it is a place outside time, from which human beings had to be ejected before the fallen world of history could properly begin. Seen as the frontier, it is a savage world at the dawn of civilization, whose transformation represents the very beginning of the national historical epic. Seen as sacred nature, it is the home of a God who transcends history, untouched by time's arrow. No matter what the angle from which we regard it, wilderness offers us the illusion that we can escape the cares and troubles of the world in which our past has ensnared us. It is the natural, unfallen antithesis of an unnatural civilization that has lost its soul, the place where we can see the world as it really is, and so know ourselves as we really are — or ought to be.

10

The trouble with wilderness is that it reproduces the very values its devotees seek to reject. It offers the illusion that we can somehow wipe clean the slate of our past and return to the tabula rasa[1] that supposedly existed before we began to leave our marks on the world. The dream of an unworked natural landscape is very much the fantasy of people who have never themselves had to work the land to make a living — urban folk for whom food comes from a supermarket or a restaurant instead of a field, and for whom the wooden houses in which they live and work apparently have no meaningful connection to the forests in which trees grow and die. Only people whose relation to the land was already alienated could hold up wilderness as a model for human life in nature, for the

[1]*tabula rasa:* Latin for blank or empty slate. — EDS.

romantic ideology of wilderness leaves no place in which human beings can actually make their living from the land.

We live in an urban-industrial civilization, but too often pretend to ourselves that our real home is in the wilderness. We work our nine-to-five jobs, we drive our cars (not least to reach the wilderness), we benefit from the intricate and all too invisible networks with which society shelters us, all the while pretending that these things are not an essential part of who we are. By imagining that our true home is in the wilderness, we forgive ourselves for the homes we actually inhabit. In its flight from history, in its siren song of escape, in its reproduction of the dangerous dualism that sets human beings somehow outside nature—in all these ways, wilderness poses a threat to responsible environmentalism at the end of the twentieth century.

Do not misunderstand me. What I criticize here is not wild nature, but the alienated way we often think of ourselves in relation to it. Wilderness can still teach lessons that are hard to learn anywhere else. When we visit wild places, we find ourselves surrounded by plants and animals and landscapes whose otherness compels our attention. In forcing us to acknowledge that they are not of our making, that they have little or no need for humanity, they recall for us a creation far greater than our own. In wilderness, we need no reminder that a tree has its own reasons for being, quite apart from us—proof that ours is not the only presence in the universe.

We get into trouble only if we see the tree in the garden as wholly artificial and the tree in the wilderness as wholly natural. Both trees in some ultimate sense are wild; both in a practical sense now require our care. We need to reconcile them, to see a natural landscape that is also cultural, in which city, suburb, countryside and wilderness each has its own place. We need to discover a middle ground in which all these things, from city to wilderness, can somehow be encompassed in the word "home." Home, after all, is the place where we live. It is the place for which we take responsibility, the place we try to sustain so we can pass on what is best in it (and in ourselves) to our children.

Learning to honor the wild—learning to acknowledge the autonomy   15
of the other—means striving for critical self-consciousness in all our actions. It means that reflection and respect must accompany each act of use, and means we must always consider the possibility of nonuse. It means looking at the part of nature we intend to turn toward our own ends and asking whether we can use it again and again and again—sustainably— without diminishing it in the process. Most of all, it means practicing remembrance and gratitude for the nature, culture and history that have come together to make the world as we know it. If wildness can stop being (just) out there and start being (also) in here, if it can start being as humane as it is natural, then perhaps we can get on with the unending task of struggling to live rightly in the world—not just in the garden, not just in the wilderness, but in the home that encompasses them both.

The Reader's Presence

1. How is wilderness commonly defined, according to the writer? How does he define it? What is the "trouble" with the common view of nature, in his estimation? What practical effect, in his view, will a better understanding of the idea of wilderness have, if any?

2. Cronon argues that our national obsession with "uninhabited wilderness" and undeveloped land runs counter to the truth of history. What words does he choose to characterize our vision of unspoiled nature? What words does he choose to characterize our blindness and illusions? Are these words always negative? What tone are these words offered in, and how does the tone contribute to your sense of his argument?

3. Are you convinced by Cronon's argument that our notion of wilderness is incorrect and destructive? Why or why not? Can you propose some examples (known in argument as "counterexamples") to contradict Cronon's position? Can you propose a series of points to refute Cronon's (or what is called a "counterargument")?

90

Edwidge Danticat

We Are Ugly, but We Are Here

Edwidge Danticat was born in Port-au-Prince, Haiti, in 1969 and immigrated to Brooklyn, New York, when she was twelve years old. She received a B.A. from Barnard College and an M.F.A. from Brown University, where she wrote an earlier draft of her first novel, Breath, Eyes, Memory *(1994), as her thesis. She is regarded as one of the best young authors in the United States, and her book of short stories about the Haitian experience,* Krik? Krik! *(1995), was nominated for the National Book Award. Her most recent novel,* The Farming of Bones *(1998), is set on the Caribbean island of Hispaniola in 1937, when hostilities between Haiti and the Dominican Republic exploded into a bloody massacre. "We Are Ugly, but We Are Here" was originally published in the* Caribbean Writer *in 1996.*

One of the first people murdered on our land was a queen. Her name was Anacaona and she was an Arawak Indian. She was a poet, dancer, and even a painter. She ruled over the western part of an island so lush and green that the Arawaks called it Ayiti—land on high. When the Spaniards came from across the seas to look for gold, Anacaona was one of their first victims. She was raped and killed and her village pillaged. Anacaona's land is now the poorest country in the Western hemisphere, a place of continuous political unrest. Thus, for some, it is easy to forget that this land was the first Black Republic, home to the first people of African descent to uproot slavery and create an independent nation in 1804.

I was born under Haiti's dictatorial Duvalier regime. When I was four, my parents left Haiti to seek a better life in the United States. I must admit that their motives were more economic than political. But as anyone who knows Haiti will tell you, economics and politics are very intrinsically related in Haiti. Who is in power determines to a great extent whether or not people will eat.

I am twenty-six years old now and have spent more than half of my life in the United States. My most vivid memories of Haiti involve incidents that once represented the general situation there. In Haiti, there are a lot of "blackouts," sudden power failures. At those times, you can't read or study or watch TV, so you sit around a candle and listen to stories from the elders in the house. My grandmother was an old country woman who always felt displaced in the city of Port-au-Prince—where we lived—and had nothing but her patched-up quilts and her stories to console her. She was the one who told me about Anacaona. I used to share a room with her. I was in the room when she died. She was over a hundred years old. She died with her eyes wide open and I was the one who closed her eyes. I still miss the countless mystical stories that she told us. However, I accepted her death very easily because during my childhood death was always around us.

As a little girl, I attended more than my share of funerals. My uncle and legal guardian was a Baptist minister and his family was expected to attend every funeral he presided over. I went to all the funerals he presided over. I went to all the funerals in the same white lace dress. Perhaps it was because I attended so many funerals that I have such a strong feeling that death is not the end, that the people we bury are going off to live somewhere else. But at the same time, they will always be hovering around to watch over us and guide us through our journeys.

When I was eight, my uncle's brother-in-law went on a long journey to cut cane in the Dominican Republic. He came back, deathly ill. I remember his wife twirling feathers inside his nostrils and rubbing black pepper on his upper lip to make him sneeze. She strongly believed that if he sneezed, he would live. At night, it was my job to watch the sky above the house for signs of falling stars. In Haitian folklore, when a star falls out of the sky, it means someone will die. A star did fall out of the sky and he did die.

I have memories of Jean Claude "Baby Doc" Duvalier and his wife, racing by in their Mercedes Benz and throwing money out of the window

5

to the very poor children in our neighborhood. The children nearly killed each other trying to catch a coin or a glimpse of Baby Doc. One Christmas, they announced on the radio that the first lady, Baby Doc's wife, was giving away free toys at the palace. My cousins and I went and were nearly killed in the mob of children who flooded the palace lawns.

All of this now brings many questions buzzing to my head. Where was really my place in all of this? What was my grandmother's place? What is the legacy of the daughters of Anacaona? What do we all have left to remember, the daughters of Haiti?

Watching the news reports, it is often hard to tell whether there are real living and breathing women in conflict-stricken places like Haiti. The evening news broadcasts only allow us a brief glimpse of presidential coups, rejected boat people, and sabotaged elections. The women's stories never manage to make the front page. However they do exist.

Today, I know women who, when the soldiers came to their homes in Haiti, would tell their daughters to lie still and play dead. I once met a woman whose sister was shot in her pregnant stomach because she was wearing a t-shirt with an "anti-military image." I know a mother who was arrested and beaten for working with a pro-democracy group. Her body remains laced with scars where the soldiers put out their cigarettes on her flesh. At night, this woman still smells the ashes of the cigarette butts that were stuffed lit inside her nostrils. In the same jail cell, she watched as paramilitary "attachés" raped her fourteen-year-old daughter at gun point. When mother and daughter took a tiny boat to the United States, the mother had no idea that her daughter was pregnant. Nor did she know that the child had gotten the HIV virus from one of the paramilitary men who had raped her. The grandchild—the offspring of the rape—was named Anacaona, after the queen, because that family of women is from the same region where Anacaona was murdered. The infant Anacaona has a face which no longer shows any trace of indigenous blood; however, her story echoes back to the first flow of blood on a land that has seen much more than its share.

There is a Haitian saying which might upset the aesthetic images of   10
most women. *Nou led, Nou la,* it says. We are ugly, but we are here. This saying makes a deeper claim for poor Haitian women than maintaining beauty, be it skin deep or otherwise. For most of us, what is worth celebrating is the fact that we are here, that we—against all the odds—exist. To the women who might greet each other with this saying when they meet along the countryside, the very essence of life lies in survival. It is always worth reminding our sisters that we have lived yet another day to answer the roll call of an often painful and very difficult life. It is in this spirit that to this day a woman remembers to name her child Anacaona, a name which resonates both the splendor and agony of a past that haunts so many women.

When they were enslaved, our foremothers believed that when they died their spirits would return to Africa, most specifically to a peaceful land we call *Guinen,* where gods and goddesses live. The women who came before me were women who spoke half of one language and half another. They spoke the French and Spanish of their captors mixed in with their own African language. These women seemed to be speaking in tongues when they prayed to their old gods, the ancient African spirits. Even though they were afraid that their old deities would no longer understand them, they invented a new language—our Kreyòl—with which to describe their new surroundings, a language from which colorful phrases blossomed to fit the desperate circumstances. When these women greeted each other, they found themselves speaking in codes.

— How are we today, Sister?

— I am ugly, but I am here.

These days, many of my sisters are greeting each other away from the homelands where they first learned to speak in tongues. Many have made it to other shores, after traveling endless miles on the high seas, on rickety boats that almost took their lives. Two years ago, a mother jumped into the sea when she discovered that her baby daughter had died in her arms on a journey which they had hoped would take them to a brighter future. Mother and child, they sank to the bottom of an ocean which already holds millions of souls from the middle passage—the holocaust of the slave trade—that is our legacy. That woman's sacrifice moved then-deposed Haitian President Jean Bertrand Aristide to the brink of tears. However, like the rest of us, he took comfort in the past sacrifices that were made for all of us, so that we could be here.

The past is full of examples when our foremothers and forefathers   15 showed such deep trust in the sea that they would jump off slave ships and let the waves embrace them. They too believed that the sea was the beginning and the end of all things, the road to freedom and their entrance to *Guinen*. These women have been part of the very construction of my being ever since I was a little girl. Women like my grandmother who had taught me the story of Anacaona, the queen.

My grandmother believed that if a life is lost, then another one springs up replanted somewhere else, the next life even stronger than the last. She believed that no one really dies as long as someone remembers, someone who will acknowledge that this person had—in spite of everything—been here. We are part of an endless circle, the daughters of Anacaona. We have stumbled, but have not fallen. We are ill-favored, but we still endure. Every once in a while, we must scream this as far as the wind can carry our voices: We are ugly, but we are here! And here to stay.

The Reader's Presence

1. Danticat begins the essay with the story of Anacaona. How is Anacaona characterized? Where does this legend reappear in the essay? What relation does it bear to the essay's message of hope

and strength? What sort of hope and strength does the figure of Anacaona represent?

2. Danticat describes daily existence in Haiti: funerals, folk medicine, toys thrown from a palace. What tones does the writer use in evoking these scenes of her homeland? What moods do those tones convey? How might the essay's title tie into these everyday scenarios?

3. The events described in the essay are personal and anecdotal. How does Danticat use personal information to make a wider point? Suppose the essay were written from a more objective, political viewpoint — that is, in a style you might find in a news magazine? How would it be told? What would be lost? What would be gained? Would the plight of Haitian women seem more, or less, important? more, or less, affecting? Why?

THE WRITER AT WORK

Edwidge Danticat on Becoming a Writer

As the previous selection shows, Edwidge Danticat is a writer concerned deeply with Haitian legend and legacy. These concerns, especially when combined with her political ideals, have been the chief stimulus for her writing. In the following brief interview that appeared in Essence *magazine (May 1996), Danticat discusses how she became a writer and the motives that have inspired and guided her career. In an earlier "Writer at Work" selection, George Orwell (see page 509) outlines what he believes are the chief motives for why people write. How closely do you think Danticat's motives conform to Orwell's list? Does she offer any reasons for writing that you think should be added to Orwell's outline?*

While I was growing up, most of the writers I knew were either in hiding, missing, or dead. We were living under the brutal Duvalier dictatorship in Haiti, and silence was the law of the land. I learned that code of silence early on. It was as real as the earth beneath our feet, which was full of blood of martyrs, among them many novelists, poets, journalists, and playwrights who had criticized our government.

Writing was a dangerous activity. Perhaps it was that danger that attracted me, the feeling of doing a high-wire act between stretching the limits of silence and telling the whole truth.

Even though I now live in a country where people are not persecuted for their words, I still feel as though I am always balancing between the personal dangers of writing and the comfort and healing it offers me.

I write to communicate with my ancestors, to explore the truth of their lives and to link it to my own. When I write, I think of my foremothers, who as Zora Neale Hurston (see page 126) observed, were considered "the mules of the earth." I think of wives who were separated from their husbands by poverty and political violence, children who lived off other people's trash, mothers and daughters, fathers and sons, all linked by centuries of pillage and slaughter. These men and women sacrificed their own enjoyment and pleasures so that the next generation—my generation—would have a voice and a future.

I wrote my first short story when I was nine years old, on a few white pages folded to form a tiny notebook. The story was about a little girl who was visited every night by a clan of women just like the overburdened and underappreciated creatures who were part of my own lineage.

When I moved to the United States at age twelve, I was temporarily floating between languages—Creole and English—so I stopped writing for a while. At fourteen I was asked by a New York City–based newspaper, *New Youth Connections,* to write about my experiences as a new immigrant. I wrote a short essay about adapting to my new life in Brooklyn, and my public writing career began.

People often ask me, "How can I become a writer?" In response I tell them the story of a Haitian painter I know. He is a very poor man who often gives up food to buy materials to paint with. He lives in a worn-out house in a slum. He never shows his paintings, and you have to fight him to buy one from him.

One day while in his studio, pleading with him to sell me a piece, I asked him, "Why create anything if you won't put it out there for the world to see and enjoy?"

To that he replied, "I don't do this for the world. I do it because I have no choice. I do it to save my life."

Now when I write, I realize that I'm writing to save my life. I write to unearth all those things that scare me, to reach those places in my soul that may seem remote and dark to others. I write to preserve my sanity and to honor the sacrifices made by all those who came before me. The way I figure, it's a privilege just to be given a voice to speak and to be heard. God and the universe will take care of the rest.

91

Alan M. Dershowitz

Shouting "Fire!"

Outspoken and controversial, Alan Dershowitz (b. 1938) is regarded as one of the leading criminal defense and civil liberty lawyers in the country. His well-publicized cases have ranged from defending political dissidents to representing notorious murderers. He is the author of numerous books on legal matters, including The Best Defense *(1982),* Reasonable Doubts *(1996), and* Sexual McCarthyism *(1998). In both* Chutzpah *(1991) and* The Vanishing Jew *(1997), Dershowitz explores the various issues of Jewish life in America. Dershowitz is Felix Frankfurter Professor of Law at Harvard Law School, where he has taught since 1964. "Shouting 'Fire!' " originally appeared in the* Atlantic Monthly *and was selected for* The Best American Essays 1990.

When the Reverend Jerry Falwell learned that the Supreme Court had reversed his $200,000 judgment against *Hustler* magazine for the emotional distress that he had suffered from an outrageous parody, his response was typical of those who seek to censor speech: "Just as no person may scream 'Fire!' in a crowded theater when there is no fire, and find cover under the First Amendment, likewise, no sleazy merchant like Larry Flynt should be able to use the First Amendment as an excuse for maliciously and dishonestly attacking public figures, as he has so often done."

Justice Oliver Wendell Holmes's classic example of unprotected speech—falsely shouting "Fire!" in a crowded theater—has been invoked so often, by so many people, in such diverse contexts, that it has become part of our national folk language. It has even appeared—most appropriately—in the theater: in Tom Stoppard's play *Rosencrantz and Guildenstern Are Dead* a character shouts at the audience, "Fire!" He then quickly explains: "It's all right—I'm demonstrating the misuse of free speech." Shouting "Fire!" in the theater may well be the only jurisprudential analogy that has assumed the status of a folk argument. A prominent historian recently characterized it as "the most brilliantly persuasive expression that ever came from Holmes' pen." But in spite of its hallowed position in both the jurisprudence of the First Amendment and the arsenal of political discourse, it is and was an inapt analogy, even in the context in which it was originally offered. It has lately become—despite, perhaps even because of, the frequency and promiscuousness of its invocation—little more than a caricature of logical argumentation.

The case that gave rise to the "Fire!"-in-a-crowded-theater analogy, *Schenck* v. *United States,* involved the prosecution of Charles Schenck, who was the general secretary of the Socialist party in Philadelphia, and Elizabeth Baer, who was its recording secretary. In 1917 a jury found Schenck and Baer guilty of attempting to cause insubordination among soldiers who had been drafted to fight in the First World War. They and other party members had circulated leaflets urging draftees not to "submit to intimidation" by fighting in a war being conducted on behalf of "Wall Street's chosen few."

Schenck admitted, and the Court found, that the intent of the pamphlets' "impassioned language" was to "influence" draftees to resist the draft. Interestingly, however, Justice Holmes noted that nothing in the pamphlet suggested that the draftees should use unlawful or violent means to oppose conscription: "In form at least [the pamphlet] confined itself to peaceful measures, such as a petition for the repeal of the act" and an exhortation to exercise "your right to assert your opposition to the draft." Many of its most impassioned words were quoted directly from the Constitution.

Justice Holmes acknowledged that "in many places and in ordinary   5
times the defendants, in saying all that was said in the circular, would have been within their constitutional rights." "But," he added, "the character of every act depends upon the circumstances in which it is done." And to illustrate that truism he went on to say:

> The most stringent protection of free speech would not protect a man in falsely shouting fire in a theater, and causing a panic. It does not even protect a man from an injunction against uttering words that may have all the effect of force.

Justice Holmes then upheld the convictions in the context of a wartime draft, holding that the pamphlet created "a clear and present danger" of hindering the war effort while our soldiers were fighting for their lives and our liberty.

The example of shouting "Fire!" obviously bore little relationship to the facts of the Schenck case. The Schenck pamphlet contained a substantive political message. It urged its draftee readers to *think* about the message and then—if they so chose—to act on it in a lawful and nonviolent way. The man who shouts "Fire!" in a crowded theater is neither sending a political message nor inviting his listener to think about what he has said and decide what to do in a rational, calculated manner. On the contrary, the message is designed to force action *without* contemplation. The message "Fire!" is directed not to the mind and the conscience of the listener but, rather, to his adrenaline and his feet. It is a stimulus to immediate *action,* not thoughtful reflection. It is—as Justice Holmes recognized in his follow-up sentence—the functional equivalent of "uttering words that may have all the effect of force."

Indeed, in that respect the shout of "Fire!" is not even speech, in any meaningful sense of that term. It is a *clang* sound, the equivalent of setting off a nonverbal alarm. Had Justice Holmes been more honest about his example, he would have said that freedom of speech does not protect a kid who pulls a fire alarm in the absence of a fire. But that obviously would have been irrelevant to the case at hand. The proposition that pulling an alarm is not protected speech certainly leads to the conclusion that shouting the word "fire" is also not protected. But the core analogy is the nonverbal alarm, and the derivative example is the verbal shout. By cleverly substituting the derivative shout for the core alarm, Holmes made it possible to analogize one set of words to another—as he could not have done if he had begun with the self-evident proposition that setting off an alarm bell is not free speech.

The analogy is thus not only inapt but also insulting. Most Americans do not respond to political rhetoric with the same kind of automatic acceptance expected of schoolchildren responding to a fire drill. Not a single recipient of the Schenck pamphlet is known to have changed his mind after reading it. Indeed, one draftee, who appeared as a prosecution witness, was asked whether reading a pamphlet asserting that the draft law was unjust would make him "immediately decide that you must erase that law." Not surprisingly, he replied, "I do my own thinking." A theatergoer would probably not respond similarly if asked how he would react to a shout of "Fire!"

Another important reason why the analogy is inapt is that Holmes   10
emphasizes the factual falsity of the shout "Fire!" The Schenck pamphlet, however, was not factually false. It contained political opinions and ideas about the causes of the war and about appropriate and lawful responses to the draft. As the Supreme Court recently reaffirmed (in *Falwell* v. *Hustler*), "The First Amendment recognizes no such thing as a 'false' idea." Nor does it recognize false opinions about the causes of or cures for war.

A closer analogy to the facts of the Schenck case might have been provided by a person's standing outside a theater, offering the patrons a leaflet advising them that in his opinion the theater was structurally unsafe, and urging them not to enter but to complain to the building inspectors. That analogy, however, would not have served Holmes's argument for punishing Schenck. Holmes needed an analogy that would appear relevant to Schenck's political speech but that would invite the conclusion that censorship was appropriate.

Unsurprisingly, a war-weary nation—in the throes of a know-nothing hysteria over immigrant anarchists and socialists—welcomed the comparison between what was regarded as a seditious political pamphlet and a malicious shout of "Fire!" Ironically, the "Fire!" analogy is nearly all that survives from the Schenck case; the ruling itself is almost certainly not good law. Pamphlets of the kind that resulted in Schenck's imprisonment have been circulated with impunity during subsequent wars.

Over the past several years I have assembled a collection of instances—cases, speeches, arguments—in which proponents of censorship have maintained that the expression at issue is "just like" or "equivalent to" falsely shouting "Fire!" in a crowded theater and ought to be banned, "just as" shouting "Fire!" ought to be banned. The analogy is generally invoked, often with self-satisfaction, as an absolute argument-stopper. It does, after all, claim the high authority of the great Justice Oliver Wendell Holmes. I have rarely heard it invoked in a convincing, or even particularly relevant, way. But that, too, can claim lineage from the great Holmes.

Not unlike Falwell, with his silly comparison between shouting "Fire!" and publishing an offensive parody, courts and commentators have frequently invoked "Fire!" as an analogy to expression that is not an automatic stimulus to panic. A state supreme court held that "Holmes' aphorism . . . applies with equal force to pornography"—in particular to the exhibition of the movie *Carmen Baby* in a drive-in theater in close proximity to highways and homes. Another court analogized "picketing . . . in support of a secondary boycott" to shouting "Fire!" because in both instances "speech and conduct are brigaded." In the famous Skokie case one of the judges argued that allowing Nazis to march through a city where a large number of Holocaust survivors live "just might fall into the same category as one's 'right' to cry fire in a crowded theater."

Outside court the analogies become even more badly stretched. A   15
spokesperson for the New Jersey Sports and Exposition Authority complained that newspaper reports to the effect that a large number of football players had contracted cancer after playing in the Meadowlands—a stadium atop a landfill—were the "journalistic equivalent of shouting fire in a crowded theater." An insect researcher acknowledged that his prediction that a certain amusement park might become roach-infested "may be tantamount to shouting fire in a crowded theater." The philosopher Sidney Hook, in a letter to the *New York Times* bemoaning a Supreme Court decision that required a plaintiff in a defamation action to prove that the offending statement was actually false, argued that the First Amendment does not give the press carte blanche to accuse innocent persons "any more than the First Amendment protects the right of someone falsely to shout fire in a crowded theater."

Some close analogies to shouting "Fire!" or setting of an alarm are, of course, available: calling in a false bomb threat; dialing 911 and falsely describing an emergency; making a loud, gun-like sound in the presence of the President; setting off a voice-activated sprinkler system by falsely shouting "Fire!" In one case in which the "Fire!" analogy was directly to the point, a creative defendant tried to get around it. The case involved a man who calmly advised an airline clerk that he was "only here to hijack the plane." He was charged, in effect, with shouting "Fire!" in a crowded theater, and his rejected defense—as quoted by the court—was as follows: "If we built fire-proof theaters and let people know about this, then the shouting of 'Fire!' would not cause panic."

Here are some more-distant but still related examples: the recent incident of the police slaying in which some members of an onlooking crowd urged a mentally ill vagrant who had taken an officer's gun to shoot the officer; the screaming of racial epithets during a tense confrontation; shouting down a speaker and preventing him from continuing his speech.

Analogies are, by their nature, matters of degree. Some are closer to the core example than others. But any attempt to analogize political ideas in a pamphlet, ugly parody in a magazine, offensive movies in a theater, controversial newspaper articles, or any of the other expressions and actions catalogued above to the very different act of shouting "Fire!" in a crowded theater is either self-deceptive or self-serving.

The government does, of course, have some arguably legitimate bases for suppressing speech which bear no relationship to shouting "Fire!" It may ban the publication of nuclear-weapon codes, of information about troop movements, and of the identity of undercover agents. It may criminalize extortion threats and conspiratorial agreements. These expressions may lead directly to serious harm, but the mechanisms of causation are very different from that at work when an alarm is sounded. One may also argue—less persuasively, in my view—against protecting certain forms of public obscenity and defamatory statements. Here, too, the mechanisms of causation are very different. None of these exceptions to the First Amendment's exhortation that the government "shall make no law . . . abridging the freedom of speech, or of the press" is anything like falsely shouting "Fire!" in a crowded theater; they all must be justified on other grounds.

A comedian once told his audience, during a stand-up routine, about   20
the time he was standing around a fire with a crowd of people and got in trouble for yelling "Theater, theater!" That, I think, is about as clever and productive a use as anyone has ever made of Holmes's flawed analogy.

The Reader's Presence

1. Why does Dershowitz open his essay with several references to the use of falsely shouting "Fire!" in a crowded theater? How do these references help him prepare his argument? How does Dershowitz view the original "Fire!" ruling? Why does he think it was incorrect? How does he link it to questions of censorship?

2. Dershowitz cites a number of "close analogies to shouting 'Fire!' or setting off an alarm." Consider each example individually. Can you think of reasons why one might not fit the model? Can you think of additional or better examples?

3. Although Dershowitz is Jewish and opposed to racism, he has famously supported the rights of Nazi sympathizers and the Ku Klux Klan to free expression. In this way, he is more concerned with the logical process of argumentation itself than with the moral or emotional import of the case being argued. How does Dershowitz's emphasis on form over content manifest itself in this essay? How does his approach to these questions differ from that of Patricia Williams in "Hate Radio" (page 837)? Which approach do you prefer? Why?

Debra Dickerson

Who Shot Johnny?

Debra Dickerson (b. 1959) is a Harvard Law School graduate, a senior fellow at the New America Foundation, and a national correspondent for Salon *magazine. A well-established journalist, Dickerson served as senior editor at* U.S. News and World Report *and has written for many newspapers and magazines, such as the* Washington Post, *the* New Republic, Essence, *the* Nation, *and the* Village Voice. *Her political memoir,* A Whistling Woman, *is forthcoming. "Who Shot Johnny?" which first appeared in the* New Republic *in 1996, was included in* The Best American Essays 1997.

Given my level of political awareness, it was inevitable that I would come to view the everyday events of my life through the prism of politics and the national discourse. I read *The Washington Post, The New Republic, The New Yorker, Harper's, The Atlantic Monthly, The Nation, National Review, Black Enterprise,* and *Essence* and wrote a weekly column for the Harvard Law School *Record* during my three years just ended there. I do this because I know that those of us who are not well-fed white guys in suits must not yield the debate to them, however well-intentioned or well-informed they may be. Accordingly, I am unrepentant and vocal about having gained admittance to Harvard through affirmative action; I am a feminist, stoic about my marriage chances as a well-educated, thirty-six-year-old black woman who won't pretend to need help taking care of herself. My strength flags, though, in the face of the latest role assigned to my family in the national drama. On July 27, 1995, my sixteen-year-old nephew was shot and paralyzed.

Talking with friends in front of his house, Johnny saw a car he thought he recognized. He waved boisterously—his trademark—throwing both arms in the air in a full-bodied, hip-hop Y. When he got no response, he and his friends sauntered down the walk to join a group loitering in front of an apartment building. The car followed. The driver got out, brandished a revolver, and fired into the air. Everyone scattered. Then he took aim and shot my running nephew in the back.

Johnny never lost consciousness. He lay in the road, trying to understand what had happened to him, why he couldn't get up. Emotionlessly, he told the story again and again on demand, remaining apologetically firm against all demands to divulge the missing details that would make sense of the shooting but obviously cast him in a bad light. Being black, male, and shot, he must apparently be involved with gangs or drugs. Probably both. Witnesses corroborate his version of events.

Nearly six months have passed since that phone call in the night and my nightmarish headlong drive from Boston to Charlotte. After twenty hours behind the wheel, I arrived haggard enough to reduce my mother to fresh tears and to find my nephew reassuring well-wishers with an eerie sang-froid.

I take the day shift in his hospital room; his mother and grand-mother, a clerk and cafeteria worker, respectively, alternate nights there on a cot. They don their uniforms the next day, gaunt after hours spent listening to Johnny moan in his sleep. How often must his subconscious replay those events and curse its host for saying hello without permission, for being carefree and young while a would-be murderer hefted the weight of his uselessness and failure like Jacob Marley's chains? How often must he watch himself lying stubbornly immobile on the pavement of his nightmares while the sound of running feet syncopate his attacker's taunts?

I spend these days beating him at gin rummy and Scrabble, holding a basin while he coughs up phlegm and crying in the corridor while he catheterizes himself. There are children here much worse off than he. I should be grateful. The doctors can't, or won't, say whether he'll walk again.

I am at once repulsed and fascinated by the bullet, which remains lodged in his spine (having done all the damage it can do, the doctors say). The wound is undramatic—small, neat, and perfectly centered—an impossibly pink pit surrounded by an otherwise undisturbed expanse of mahogany. Johnny has asked me several times to describe it but politely declines to look in the mirror I hold for him.

Here on the pediatric rehab ward, Johnny speaks little, never cries, never complains, works diligently to become independent. He does whatever he is told; if two hours remain until the next pain pill, he waits quietly. Eyes bloodshot, hands gripping the bed rails. During the week of his intravenous feeding, when he was tormented by the primal need to masticate, he never asked for food. He just listened while we counted down the days for him and planned his favorite meals. Now required to dress himself unassisted, he does so without demur, rolling himself back and forth valiantly on the bed and shivering afterward, exhausted. He "ma'am"s and "sir"s everyone politely. Before his "accident," a simple request to take out the trash could provoke a firestorm of teenage attitude. We, the women who have raised him, have changed as well; we've finally come to

5

appreciate those boxer-baring, oversized pants we used to hate—it would be much more difficult to fit properly sized pants over his diaper.

He spends a lot of time tethered to rap music still loud enough to break my concentration as I read my many magazines. I hear him try to soundlessly mouth the obligatory "mothafuckers" overlaying the funereal dirge of the music tracks. I do not normally tolerate disrespectful music in my or my mother's presence, but if it distracts him now . . .

"Johnny," I ask later, "do you still like gangster rap?" During the long pause I hear him think loudly, I'm paralyzed, Auntie, not stupid. "I mostly just listen to hip-hop," he says evasively into his *Sports Illustrated*.

Miserable though it is, time passes quickly here. We always seem to be jerking awake in our chairs just in time for the next pill, his every-other-night bowel program, the doctor's rounds. Harvard feels a galaxy away—the world revolves around Family Members Living with Spinal Cord Injury class, Johnny's urine output, and strategizing with my sister to find affordable, accessible housing. There is always another long-distance uncle in need of an update, another church member wanting to pray with us, or Johnny's little brother in need of some attention.

We Dickerson women are so constant a presence the ward nurses and cleaning staff call us by name and join us for cafeteria meals and cigarette breaks. At Johnny's birthday pizza party, they crack jokes and make fun of each other's husbands (there are no men here). I pass slices around and try not to think, Seventeen with a bullet.

Oddly, we feel little curiosity or specific anger toward the man who shot him. We have to remind ourselves to check in with the police. Even so, it feels pro forma, like sending in those $2 rebate forms that come with new pantyhose: you know your request will fall into a deep, dark hole somewhere, but still, it's your duty to try. We push for an arrest because we owe it to Johnny and to ourselves as citizens. We don't think about it otherwise—our low expectations are too ingrained. A Harvard aunt notwithstanding, for people like Johnny, Marvin Gaye was right that only three things are sure: taxes, death, and trouble. At least it wasn't the second.

We rarely wonder about or discuss the brother who shot him because we already know everything about him. When the call came, my first thought was the same one I'd had when I'd heard about Rosa Parks's beating: a brother did it. A non-job-having, middle-of-the-day malt-liquor-drinking, crotch-clutching, loud-talking brother with many neglected children born of many forgotten women. He lives in his mother's basement with furniture rented at an astronomical interest rate, the exact amount of which he does not know. He has a car phone, an $80 monthly cable bill, and every possible phone feature but no savings. He steals Social Security numbers from unsuspecting relatives and assumes their identities to acquire large TV sets for which he will never pay. On the slim

10

chance that he is brought to justice, he will have a colorful criminal history and no coherent explanation to offer for his act. His family will raucously defend him and cry cover-up. Some liberal lawyer just like me will help him plea-bargain his way to yet another short stay in a prison pesthouse that will serve only to add another layer to the brother's sociopathology and formless, mindless nihilism. We know him. We've known and feared him all our lives.

As a teenager, he called, "Hey, baby, gimme somma that boodie!" at   15
us from car windows. Indignant at our lack of response, he followed up with, "Fuck you, then, 'ho!" He called me a "white-boy-lovin' nigger bitch oreo" for being in the gifted program and loving it. At twenty-seven, he got my seventeen-year-old sister pregnant with Johnny and lost interest without ever informing her that he was married. He snatched my widowed mother's purse as she waited in predawn darkness for the bus to work and then broke into our house while she soldered on an assembly line. He chased all the small entrepreneurs from our neighborhood with his violent thievery and put bars on our windows. He kept us from sitting on our own front porch after dark and laid the foundation for our periodic bouts of self-hating anger and racial embarrassment. He made our neighborhood a ghetto. He is a poster fool behind the maddening community knowledge that there are still some black mothers who raise their daughters but merely love their sons. He and his cancerous carbon copies eclipse the vast majority of us who are not sociopaths and render us invisible. He is the Siamese twin who has died but cannot be separated from his living, vibrant sibling; which of us must attract more notice? We despise and disown this anomalous loser, but for many he *is* black America. We know him, we know that he is outside the fold, and we know that he will only get worse. What we didn't know is that, because of him, my little sister would one day be the latest hysterical black mother wailing over a fallen child on TV.

Alone, lying in the road bleeding and paralyzed but hideously conscious, Johnny had lain helpless as he watched his would-be murderer come to stand over him and offer this prophecy: "Betch'ou won't be don' nomo' wavin', mothafucker."

Fuck you, asshole. He's fine from the waist up. You just can't do anything right, can you?

The Reader's Presence

1. Dickerson begins her essay with what rhetoricians call an "ethical" appeal: She tells the reader not about her subject but about herself, as a way of establishing her authority and good sense. What do you learn about Dickerson from the publications she

reads, the school she attends, and the attitude she has toward politics? Why do you think she wants her readers to know this information?

2. In paragraphs 14 and 15 Dickerson provides a long description of the man who shot her nephew. Is she saying that the same man did all those things? What does she mean when she compares the figure she describes to a "carbon copy" and a "Siamese twin"? Do Dickerson's generalizations about a whole group of young men strengthen or weaken her argument? Why? Could her argument be made if the focus were only on Johnny's attacker? Why or why not?

3. Some periodicals might have refused to print the obscenity with which Dickerson ends her piece. Could she have achieved the same effect without it? Try to come up with another ending that you feel is equally powerful. Does Dickerson's anger strengthen or weaken her authority to write on these events? Why, and in what ways?

93

Annie Dillard

Living Like Weasels

Annie Dillard (b. 1945) was awarded the Pulitzer Prize for general nonfiction in 1974 for Pilgrim at Tinker Creek, *which she describes (borrowing from Henry David Thoreau) as "a meteorological journal of the mind." She has also published poems in* Tickets for a Prayer Wheel *(1975) and* Mornings Like This: Found Poems *(1995), literary theory in* Living by Fiction *(1982), essays in* Teaching a Stone to Talk *(1982) and* For the Time Being *(1999), and autobiography in* An American Childhood *(1987). Dillard published her first novel,* The Living, *in 1992, and* The Annie Dillard Reader *appeared in 1994. From 1973 to 1982 she served as contributing editor to* Harper's *magazine, and since 1979 she has taught creative writing at Wesleyan University. "Living like Weasels" opens her book* Teaching a Stone to Talk.

In her book The Writing Life *(1989), Dillard writes, "One of the few things I know about writing is this: spend it all, shoot it, play it, lose it, all, right away, every time. . . . Something more will arise for later, something better. These things fill from behind, like well water. Similarly, the impulse to keep to yourself what you have learned is not only shameful, it is destructive. Anything you do not give freely and abundantly becomes lost to you."*

A weasel is wild. Who knows what he thinks? He sleeps in his underground den, his tail draped over his nose. Sometimes he lives in his den for two days without leaving. Outside, he stalks rabbits, mice, muskrats, and birds, killing more bodies than he can eat warm, and often dragging the carcasses home. Obedient to instinct, he bites his prey at the neck, either splitting the jugular vein at the throat or crunching the brain at the base of the skull, and he does not let go. One naturalist refused to kill a weasel who was socketed into his hand deeply as a rattlesnake. The man could in no way pry the tiny weasel off, and he had to walk half a mile to water, the weasel dangling from his palm, and soak him off like a stubborn label.

And once, says Ernest Thompson Seton[1] — once, a man shot an eagle out of the sky. He examined the eagle and found the dry skull of a weasel fixed by the jaws to his throat. The supposition is that the eagle had pounced on the weasel and the weasel swiveled and bit as instinct taught him, tooth to neck, and nearly won. I would like to have seen that eagle from the air a few weeks or months before he was shot: Was the whole weasel still attached to his feathered throat, a fur pendant? Or did the eagle eat what he could reach, gutting the living weasel with his talons before his breast, bending his beak, cleaning the beautiful airborne bones?

I have been reading about weasels because I saw one last week. I startled a weasel who startled me, and we exchanged a long glance.

Twenty minutes from my house, through the woods by the quarry and across the highway, is Hollins Pond, a remarkable piece of shallowness, where I like to go at sunset and sit on a tree trunk. Hollins Pond is also called Murray's Pond; it covers two acres of bottomland near Tinker Creek with six inches of water and six thousand lily pads. In winter, brown-and-white steers stand in the middle of it, merely dampening their hooves; from the distant shore they look like miracle itself, complete with miracle's nonchalance. Now, in summer, the steers are gone. The water lilies have blossomed and spread to a green horizontal plane that is terra firma to plodding blackbirds, and tremulous ceiling to black leeches, crayfish, and carp.

This is, mind you, suburbia. It is a five-minute walk in three direc-   5
tions to rows of houses, though none is visible here. There's a 55 mph highway at one end of the pond, and a nesting pair of wood ducks at the other. Under every bush is a muskrat hole or a beer can. The far end is an alternating series of fields and woods, fields and woods, threaded everywhere with motorcycle tracks — in whose bare clay wild turtles lay eggs.

So. I had crossed the highway, stepped over two low barbed-wire fences, and traced the motorcycle path in all gratitude through the wild rose and poison ivy of the pond's shoreline up into high grassy fields.

---

[1]*Ernest Thompson Seton* (1860–1946): American author and naturalist who founded the wildlife organization upon which the Boy Scout movement was later patterned.

Then I cut down through the woods to the mossy fallen tree where I sit. This tree is excellent. It makes a dry, upholstered bench at the upper, marshy end of the pond, a plush jetty raised from the thorny shore between a shallow blue body of water and a deep blue body of sky.

The sun had just set. I was relaxed on the tree trunk, ensconced in the lap of lichen, watching the lily pads at my feet tremble and part dreamily over the thrusting path of a carp. A yellow bird appeared to my right and flew behind me. It caught my eye; I swiveled around — and the next instant, inexplicably, I was looking down at a weasel, who was looking up at me.

Weasel! I'd never seen one wild before. He was ten inches long, thin as a curve, a muscled ribbon, brown as fruitwood, soft-furred, alert. His face was fierce, small and pointed as a lizard's; he would have made a good arrowhead. There was just a dot of chin, maybe two brown hairs' worth, and then the pure white fur began that spread down his underside. He had two black eyes I didn't see, any more than you see a window.

The weasel was stunned into stillness as he was emerging from beneath an enormous shaggy wild rose bush four feet away. I was stunned into stillness twisted backward on the tree trunk. Our eyes locked, and someone threw away the key.

Our look was as if two lovers, or deadly enemies, met unexpectedly   10
on an overgrown path when each had been thinking of something else: a clearing blow to the gut. It was also a bright blow to the brain, or a sudden beating of brains, with all the charge and intimate grate of rubbed balloons. It emptied our lungs. It felled the forest, moved the fields, and drained the pond; the world dismantled and tumbled into that black hole of eyes. If you and I looked at each other that way, our skulls would split and drop to our shoulders. But we don't. We keep our skulls. So.

He disappeared. This was only last week, and already I don't remember what shattered the enchantment. I think I blinked, I think I retrieved my brain from the weasel's brain, and tried to memorize what I was seeing, and the weasel felt the yank of separation, the careening splashdown into real life and the urgent current of instinct. He vanished under the wild rose. I waited motionless, my mind suddenly full of data and my spirit with pleadings, but he didn't return.

Please do not tell me about "approach-avoidance conflicts." I tell you I've been in that weasel's brain for sixty seconds, and he was in mine. Brains are private places, muttering through unique and secret tapes — but the weasel and I both plugged into another tape simultaneously, for a sweet and shocking time. Can I help it if it was a blank?

What goes on in his brain the rest of the time? What does a weasel think about? He won't say. His journal is tracks in clay, a spray of feathers, mouse blood and bone: uncollected, unconnected, loose-leaf, and blown.

I would like to learn, or remember, how to live. I come to Hollins Pond not so much to learn how to live as, frankly, to forget about it. That

is, I don't think I can learn from a wild animal how to live in particular—
shall I suck warm blood, hold my tail high, walk with my footprints precisely over the prints of my hands?—but I might learn something of
mindlessness, something of purity of living in the physical senses and the
dignity of living without bias or motive. The weasel lives in necessity and
we live in choice, hating necessity and dying at the last ignobly in its
talons. I would like to live as I should, as the weasel lives as he should.
And I suspect that for me the way is like the weasel's: open to time and
death painlessly, noticing everything, remembering nothing, choosing the
given with a fierce and pointed will.

I missed my chance. I should have gone for the throat. I should have   15
lunged for that streak of white under the weasel's chin and held on, held on
through mud and into the wild rose, held on for a dearer life. We could live
under the wild rose wild as weasels, mute and uncomprehending. I could
very calmly go wild. I could live two days in the den, curled, leaning on
mouse fur, sniffing bird bones, blinking, licking, breathing musk, my hair
tangled in the roots of grasses. Down is a good place to go, where the mind
is single. Down is out, out of your ever-loving mind and back to your careless senses. I remember muteness as a prolonged and giddy fast, where
every moment is a feast of utterance received. Time and events are merely
poured, unremarked, and ingested directly, like blood pulsed into my gut
through a jugular vein. Could two live that way? Could two live under the
wild rose, and explore by the pond, so that the smooth mind of each is as
everywhere present to the other, and as received and as unchallenged, as
falling snow?
    We could, you know. We can live any way we want. People take vows
of poverty, chastity, and obedience—even of silence—by choice. The
thing is to stalk your calling in a certain skilled and supple way, to locate
the most tender and live spot and plug into that pulse. This is yielding, not
fighting. A weasel doesn't "attack" anything; a weasel lives as he's meant
to, yielding at every moment to the perfect freedom of single necessity.

I think it would be well, and proper, and obedient, and pure, to grasp
your one necessity and not let it go, to dangle from it limp wherever it
takes you. Then even death, where you're going no matter how you live,
cannot you part. Seize it and let it seize you up aloft even, till your eyes
burn out and drop; let your musky flesh fall off in shreds, and let your
very bones unhinge and scatter, loosened over fields, over fields and
woods, lightly, thoughtless, from any height at all, from as high as eagles.

The Reader's Presence

1. Dillard begins her essay with two documented accounts of
   weasels, presumably drawn from her reading. What do these ac-

counts have in common? How do they establish the dominant characteristic of weasels and the theme of the essay?

2. "Our eyes locked," Dillard says in describing her encounter with the weasel. Why is this an appropriate image? How does the idea of "locking" run through the essay? She also uses the word *wild*. How does she characterize the wild? Could the wild be thought of differently, and in what ways?

3. Toward the end of her essay, Dillard contrasts the weasel's life of "necessity" to the human life of "choice." What does she mean by this contrast, and how does the essay illustrate it? Does Dillard give the impression that her wish to live like a weasel is sincere? If not, what is the significance of this hypothetical argument?

THE WRITER AT WORK

Annie Dillard's "Notes for Young Writers"

One of the nation's outstanding essayists, Annie Dillard is also a prominent creative writing teacher at Wesleyan University and the author of The Writing Life *(1989). After a series of lectures at the University of North Carolina at Chapel Hill, Annie Dillard sent the students the following afterthoughts about writing, which were subsequently published in* Image *magazine. The advice conveys her own tough-minded spirituality (see the preceding essay) and covers a great deal of valuable information in a compressed space. But suppose you have no interest in ever becoming a writer? Can you see how her advice might be applicable to whatever you decide to undertake?*

After I left Chapel Hill, I thought of many things I wish I'd said to you. Here are some of them.

Dedicate (donate, give all) your life to something larger than yourself and pleasure—to the largest thing you can: to God, to relieving suffering, to contributing to knowledge, to adding to literature, or something else. Happiness lies this way, and it beats pleasure hollow.

A great physicist taught at the Massachusetts Institute of Technology. He published many important books and papers. Often he had an idea in the middle of the night. He rose from his bed, took a shower, washed his hair, and shaved. He dressed completely, in a clean shirt, in polished shoes, a jacket and tie. Then he sat at his desk and wrote down his idea. A friend of mine asked him why he put himself through all that rigmarole. "Why," he said, surprised at the question, "in honor of physics!"

(Incidentally, he had been an illiterate little Arab boy without any schooling whatever, who had hitchhiked somewhere once when he was thirteen or fourteen. The driver who picked him up chatted with him for five hours, and recognized that the boy had a genius for mathematical thinking. Consequently the driver educated the boy, through his doctorate abroad, at his own expense. This sort of thing happens in Arabic countries, where the people actually practice their religion.)

If you have a choice, live at least a year in very different parts of the   5
country.

Never, ever, get yourself into a situation where you have nothing to do but write and read. You'll go into a depression. You have to be doing something good for the world, something undeniably useful; you need exercise, too, and people.

Read for pleasure. If you like Tolstoy, read Tolstoy; if you like Dostoevsky, read Dostoevsky. Push it a little, but don't read something totally alien to your nature and then say, "I'll never be able to write like that." Of course you won't. Read books you'd like to write. If you want to write literature, read literature. Write books you'd like to read. Follow your own weirdness.

You'll have time to read after college.

Don't worry about what you do the first year after college. It's not what you'll be doing for the rest of your life.

People in the arts, I read once, take about eight years just to figure   10
out which art they're in! Notify your parents.

MFA and MA writing programs are great fun, and many are cheap or free.

Learn grammar. Get a grammar book and read it two or three times a year (Strunk and White is classic.)

Learn punctuation; it is your little drum set, one of the few tools you have to signal the reader where the beats and emphases go. (If you get it wrong, any least thing, the editor will throw your manuscript out.) Punctuation is not like musical notation; it doesn't indicate the length of pauses, but instead signifies logical relations. There are all sorts of people out there who know these things very well. You have to be among them even to begin.

Check the spelling; proofread. Get someone else to proofread, too.

Don't use passive verb constructions. You can rewrite any sentence.   15

Don't misspell dialect. Let the syntax and words suggest the pronunciation.

Don't use any word for "walk" or "say" except "walk" or "say." I know your sixth-grade teacher told you otherwise. She told me otherwise, too, and is still telling her sixth graders otherwise.

Always locate the reader in time and space—again and again. Beginning writers rush in to feelings, to interior lives. Instead, stick to surface appearances; hit the five senses; give the history of the person and the place, and the look of the person and the place. Use first and last names. As you write, stick everything in a place and a time.

Don't describe feelings.

The way to a reader's emotions is, oddly enough, through the senses.   20

If something in your narrative or poem is important, give it proportional space. I mean, actual inches. The reader has to spend time with a subject to care about it. Don't shy away from your big scenes; stretch them out.

Writing in scenes doesn't mean in television scenes. No dull dialogue: "Honey, I'm home! Where's the beer?" "In the refrigerator!" (I think most fiction contains far too much dialogue.)

Capturing the typical isn't a virtue. Only making something new and interesting is. If you find life dull and people hateful, keep thinking until you can see it another way. Why would any reader pick up a book to read a detailed description of all that is most annoying in his daily life?

Don't use any extra words. A sentence is a machine; it has a job to do. An extra word in a sentence is like a sock in a machine.

Buy hardback fiction and poetry. Request hardback fiction and po- 25 etry as gifts from everyone you know. Give hardback fiction and poetry as gifts to everyone. No shirt or sweater ever changed a life. Never complain about publishing if you don't buy hardcover fiction and poetry regularly.

Buy books from independent booksellers, not chain stores. For complicated reasons, chain stores are helping stamp out literary publishing.

(Similarly, register and vote. If you don't vote, don't complain.)

Write for readers. Ask yourself how every sentence and every line will strike the reader. That way you can see if you're misleading, or boring, the reader. Of course it's hard to read your work when you've just written it; it all seems clear and powerful. Put it away and rewrite it later. Don't keep reading it over, or you'll have to wait longer to see it afresh.

Don't write about yourself. Think of books you like. Isn't it their subjects you like best? Boring people talk about themselves.

The work's unity is more important than anything else about it. 30 Those digressions that were so much fun to write must go.

Usually you will have to rewrite the beginning—the first quarter or third of whatever it is. Don't waste much time polishing this; you'll just have to take a deep breath and throw it away anyway, once you finish the work and have a clearer sense of what it is about. Tear up the runway; it helped you take off, and you don't need it now. This is why some writers say it takes "courage" to write. It does. Over and over you must choose the book over your own wishes and feelings.

Ignore your feelings about your work. These are an occupational hazard. If you are writing a book, keep working at it, deeper and deeper, when you feel it is awful; keep revising and improving it when you feel it is wonderful. When you are young and starting out, often it is better, however, to write something else than to labor over something that was a bad idea in the first place. Write something else; then write something else; then write something else. No matter how experienced you are, there is no correlation, either direct or inverse, between your immediate feelings about your work's quality and its actual quality. All you can do is ignore your feelings altogether. It's hard to do, but you can learn to do it.

When you are writing full-time (three to four hours a day), go in the room with the book every day, regardless of your feelings. If you skip a day it will take three painful days to get to believing in the work again. Have a place where you can leave the work out and open, so you don't have to get it all out and spread before you can start again.

The more you read, the more you will write. The better the stuff you read, the better the stuff you will write. You have many years. You can develop a taste for good literature gradually. Keep a list of books you want to read. You soon learn that "classics" are books that are endlessly interesting—almost all of them. You can keep rereading them all your life—about every ten years—and various ones light up for you at different stages of your life.

Don't find an interesting true story—a life, say, or a historical inci-   35 dent, and decide to turn it into a novel instead of a biography or a historical account. The novel based on fact is a muddy hybrid; readers can't tell what's true. Publishers won't touch these. Write it as nonfiction if you want to write it.

If you want to write novels (and if you buy hardcover novels regularly), go ahead and write novels. Publishing has changed, however, and novels are very difficult to publish. If you want to improve the odds that people will read what you write, write nonfiction narrative.

For fiction, poetry, or nonfiction, the more research you do, the more materials you will have to play with. You are writing for readers—a very educated bunch in this country. It's hard and interesting to tell them something they don't know. The more you read, the better you will know what they know.

No one can help you if you're stuck in a work. Only you can figure a way out, because only you see the work's possibilities. In every work, there's an inherent impossibility which you discover sooner or later— some intrinsic reason why this will never be able to proceed. You can figure out ways around it. Often the way around it is to throw out, painfully, the one idea you started with.

Publication is not a gauge of excellence. This is harder to learn than anything about publishing, and very important. Formerly, if a manuscript was "good," it "merited" publication. This has not been true for at least twenty years, but the news hasn't filtered out to change the belief. People say, "Why, Faulkner couldn't get published today!" as if exaggerating. In fact, Faulkner certainly couldn't, and publishers don't deny it. The market for hardback fiction is rich married or widowed women over fifty (until you all start buying hardback books). The junior editors who choose new work are New York women in their twenties, who are interested in what is chic in New York that week, and who have become experts in what the older women will buy in hardcover. Eight books of nonfiction appear for every book of fiction. The chance of any manuscript coming into a publishing house and getting published is 1 in 3,000. (Agents send in most of these manuscripts. Most agents won't touch fiction.)

When a magazine rejects your story or poem, it doesn't mean it   40
wasn't "good" enough. It means that magazine thought its particular
readers didn't need that exact story or poem. Editors think of readers:
what's in it for the reader? There is a cult of celebrity, too, in this country, and many magazines publish only famous people, and reject better
work by unknown people.

You need to know these things somewhere in the back of your mind,
and you need to forget them and write whatever you're going to write.

94

Gerald Early

Performance and Reality: Race, Sport, and the Modern World

Gerald Early (b. 1952) is Merle Kling Professor of Modern Letters and Di-
rector of African and Afro-American Studies at Washington University. An essay-
ist, poet, and editor, Early wrote his first book, Tuxedo Junction: Essays on
American Culture *(1990), while he was a postdoctoral fellow at the University of*
Kansas. Another collection of essays, The Culture of Bruising *(1994), won the*
National Book Critic's Circle Award. Most recently Early has edited Body Lan-
guage: Writers on Sports *(1998),* The Muhammad Ali Reader *(1998), and* Ain't
But a Place: An Anthology of African American Writings about St. Louis *(1998).*
He has contributed to a number of journals such as the Antioch Review, *the* New
York Review, Harper's, Callaloo, *and the* Nation, *in which "Performance and*
Reality" appeared in 1998.

Last year's celebration of the fiftieth anniversary of Jackie Robinson's
breaking the color line in major league baseball was one of the most pronounced and prolonged ever held in the history of our Republic in memory of a black man or of an athlete. It seems nearly obvious that, on one
level, our preoccupation was not so much with Robinson himself — previous milestone anniversaries of his starting at first base for the Brooklyn
Dodgers in April 1947 produced little fanfare — as it was with ourselves
and our own dilemma about race, a problem that strikes us simultaneously as being intractable and "progressing" toward resolution; as a
chronic, inevitably fatal disease and as a test of national character that we
will, finally, pass.

Robinson was the man white society could not defeat in the short
term, though his untimely death at age fifty-three convinced many that

the stress of the battle defeated him in the long run. In this respect, Robinson did become something of an uneasy elegiac symbol of race relations, satisfying everyone's psychic needs: blacks, with a redemptive black hero who did not sell out and in whose personal tragedy was a corporate triumph over racism; whites, with a black hero who showed assimilation to be a triumphant act. For each group, it was important that he was a hero for the other. All this was easier to accomplish because Robinson played baseball, a "pastoral" sport of innocence and triumphalism in the American mind, a sport of epic romanticism, a sport whose golden age is always associated with childhood. In the end, Robinson as tragic hero represented, paradoxically, depending on the faction, how far we have come and how much more needs to be done.

As a nation, I think we needed the evocation of Jackie Robinson to save us from the nihilistic fires of race: from the trials of O.J. Simpson (the failed black athletic hero who seems nothing more than a symbol of self-centered consumption), from the Rodney King trial and subsequent riot in Los Angeles and, most significant, from the turmoil over affirmative action, an issue not only about *how* blacks are to achieve a place in American society but about the perennial existential question: *Can* black people have a rightful place of dignity in our realm, or is the stigma of race to taint everything they do and desire? We know that some of the most admired celebrities in the United States today—in many instances, excessively so by some whites—are black athletes. Michael Jordan, the most admired athlete in modern history, is a $10 billion industry, we are told, beloved all over the world. But what does Michael Jordan want except what most insecure, upwardly bound Americans want? More of what he already has to assure himself that he does, indeed, have what he wants. Michael Jordan is not simply a brilliant athlete, the personification of an unstoppable will, but, like all figures in popular culture, a complex, charismatic representation of desire, his own and ours.

Perhaps we reached back for Jackie Robinson last year (just as we reached back for an ailing Muhammad Ali, the boastful athlete as expiatory dissident, the year before at the Olympics) because of our need for an athlete who transcends his self-absorbed prowess and quest for championships, or whose self-absorption and quest for titles meant something deeper politically and socially, told us something a bit more important about ourselves as a racially divided, racially stricken nation. A baseball strike in 1994–95 that canceled the World Series, gambling scandals in college basketball, ceaseless recruiting violations with student athletes, rape and drug cases involving athletes, the increasing commercialization of sports resulting in more tax concessions to team owners and ever-more-expensive stadiums, the wild inflation of salaries, prize money and endorsement fees for the most elite athletes—all this has led to a general dissatisfaction with sports or at least to some legitimate uneasiness about them, as many people see sports, amateur and professional, more and more as a depraved enterprise, as a Babylon of greed, dishonesty and hypocrisy, or as an industry out to rob the public blind. At what better moment to resurrect Jackie Robinson, a man who played for the competition and the glory, for the love of the game and the honor of his profession, and as a tribute to the dignity and pride of his race in what many of us perceive, wrongly, to have been a simpler, less commercial time?

What, indeed, is the place of black people in our realm? Perhaps, at   5
this point in history, we are all, black and white, as mystified by that question as we were at the end of the Civil War when faced with the prospect that slave and free must live together as equal citizens, or must try to. For the question has always signified that affirmative action—a public policy for the unconditional inclusion of the African-American that has existed, with all its good and failed intentions, in the air of American racial reform since black people were officially freed, even, indeed, in the age of abolition with voices such as Lydia Maria Child and Frederick Douglass—is about the making of an African into an American and the meaning of that act for our democracy's ability to absorb all. We were struck by Jackie Robinson's story last year because it was as profound, as mythic, as any European immigrant's story about how Americans are made. We Americans seem to have blundered about in our history with two clumsy contrivances strapped to our backs, unreconciled and weighty: our democratic traditions and race. What makes Robinson so significant is that he seemed to have found a way to balance this baggage in the place that is so much the stuff of our dreams: the level playing field of top-flight competitive athletics. "Athletics," stated Robinson in his first autobiography, *Jackie Robinson: My Own Story* (ghostwritten by black sportswriter Wendell Smith), "both school and professional, come nearer to offering an American Negro equality of opportunity than does any other field of social and economic activity." It is not so much that this is true as that Robinson believed it, and that most Americans today, black and white, still do or still want to. This is one of the important aspects of modern sports in a democratic society that saves us from being totally cynical about them. Sports are the ultimate meritocracy. Might it be said that sports are what all other professional activities and business endeavors, all leisure pursuits and hobbies in our society aspire to be?

If nothing else, Robinson, an unambiguous athletic hero for both races and symbol of sacrifice on the altar of racism, is our most magnificent case of affirmative action. He entered a lily-white industry amid cries that he was unqualified (not entirely unjustified, as Robinson had had only one year of professional experience in the Negro Leagues, although, on the other hand, he was one of the most gifted athletes of his generation), and he succeeded, *on merit,* beyond anyone's wildest hope. And here the sports metaphor is a perfectly literal expression of the traditional democratic belief of that day: If given the chance, anyone can make it on his ability, with no remedial aid or special compensation, on a level playing field. Here was the fulfillment of our American Creed, to use Gunnar

Myrdal's term (*An American Dilemma* had appeared only a year before Robinson was signed by the Dodgers), of fair play and equal opportunity. Here was our democratic orthodoxy of color-blind competition realized. Here was an instance where neither the principle nor its application could be impugned. Robinson was proof, just as heavyweight champion Joe Louis and Olympic track star Jesse Owens had been during the Depression, that sports helped vanquish the stigma of race.

In this instance, sports are extraordinarily useful because their values can endorse any political ideology. It must be remembered that the British had used sports—and modern sports are virtually their invention—as a colonial and missionary tool, not always with evil intentions but almost always with hegemonic ones. Sports had also been used by their subjects as a tool of liberation, as anti-hegemonic, as they learned to beat the British at their own games. "To win was to be human," said African scholar Manthia Diawara recently, and for the colonized and the oppressed, sports meant just that, in the same way as for the British, to win was to be British. Sports were meant to preserve and symbolize the hegemony of the colonizer even as they inspired the revolutionary spirit of the oppressed. Sports have been revered by fascists and communists, by free-marketers and filibusters. They have also been, paradoxically, reviled by all those political factions. Sports may be among the most powerful human expressions in all history. So why could sports not serve the United States ideologically in whatever way people decided to define democratic values during this, the American Century, when we became the most powerful purveyors of sports in all history?

Both the left and the right have used Jackie Robinson for their own ends. The left, suspicious of popular culture as a set of cheap commercial distractions constructed by the ruling class of postindustrial society to delude the masses, sees Robinson as a racial martyr, a working-class member of an oppressed minority who challenged the white hegemony as symbolized by sports as a political reification of superior, privileged expertise; the right, suspicious of popular culture as an expression of the rule of the infantile taste of the masses, sees him as a challenge to the idea of restricting talent pools and restricting markets to serve a dubious privilege. For the conservative today, Robinson is the *classic, fixed* example of affirmative action properly applied as the extension of opportunity to all, regardless of race, class, gender or outcome. For the liberal, Robinson is an example of the *process* of affirmative action as the erosion of white male hegemony, where outcome is the very point of the exercise. For the liberal, affirmative action is about the redistribution of power. For the conservative, it is about releasing deserving talent. This seems little more than the standard difference in views between the conservative and the liberal about the meaning of democratic values and social reform. For the conservative, the story of Robinson and affirmative action is about conformity: Robinson, as symbolic Negro, *joined* the mainstream. For the liberal, the story of Robinson and affirmative action is about resistance: Robinson, as symbolic Negro, *changed* the mainstream. The conservative does not want affirmative action to disturb what Lothrop Stoddard called "the iron law of inequality." The liberal wants affirmative action to create complete equality, as all inequality is structural and environmental. (Proof of how much Robinson figured in the affirmative action debate can be found in Steve Sailer's "How Jackie Robinson Desegregated America," a cover story in the April 8, 1996, *National Review,* and in Anthony Pratkanis and Marlene Turner's liberal article, "Nine Principles of Successful Affirmative Action: Mr. Branch Rickey, Mr. Jackie Robinson, and the Integration of Baseball," in the Fall 1994 issue of *Nine: A Journal of Baseball History and Social Policy Perspectives.*) Whoever may be right in this regard, it can be said that inasmuch as either side endorsed the idea, both were wrong about sports eliminating the stigma of race. Over the years since Robinson's arrival, sports have, in many respects, intensified race and racialist thinking or, more precisely, anxiety about race and racialist thinking.

Race is not merely a system of categorizations of privileged or discredited abilities but rather a system of conflicting abstractions about what it means to be human. Sports are not a material realization of the ideal that those who succeed deserve to succeed; they are a paradox of play as work, of highly competitive, highly pressurized work as a form of romanticized play, a system of rules and regulations that govern both a real and a symbolic activity that suggests, in the stunning complexity of its performance, both conformity and revolt. Our mistake about race is assuming that it is largely an expression of irrationality when it is, in fact, to borrow G. K. Chesterton's phrase, "nearly reasonable, but not quite." Our mistake about sports is assuming that they are largely minor consequences of our two great American gifts: marketing and technology. Their pervasiveness and their image, their evocation of desire and transcendence, are the result of marketing. Their elaborate modalities of engineering—from the conditioning of the athletes to the construction of the arenas to the fabrication of the tools and machines athletes use and the apparel they wear—are the result of our technology. But modern sports, although extraordinary expressions of marketing and technology, are far deeper, far more atavistic, than either. Perhaps sports, in some ways, are as atavistic as race.

THE WHITENESS OF THE WHITE ATHLETE

In a December 8, 1997, *Sports Illustrated* article, "Whatever Happened to the White Athlete?" S. L. Price writes about the dominant presence of black athletes in professional basketball (80 percent black), professional football (67 percent black) and track and field (93 percent of gold medalists are black). He also argues that while African-Americans make up only 17 percent of major league baseball players, "[during] the past twenty-five years, blacks have been a disproportionate offensive force, winning 41 percent of the Most Valuable Player awards." (And the number of blacks in baseball does not include the black Latinos, for whom baseball is more popular than it is with American blacks.) Blacks also dominate boxing, a sport not dealt with in the article. "Whites have in some respects become sports' second-class citizens," writes Price. "In a surreal inversion of Robinson's era, white athletes are frequently the ones now tagged by the stereotypes of skin color." He concludes by suggesting that white sprinter Kevin Little, in competition, can feel "the slightest hint—and it is not more than a hint—of what Jackie Robinson felt 50 years ago." It is more than a little ludicrous to suggest that white athletes today even remotely, even as a hint, are experiencing something like what Robinson experienced. White athletes, even when they play sports dominated by blacks, are still entering an industry not only controlled by whites in every phase of authority and operation but also largely sustained by white audiences. When Jackie Robinson departed the Negro Leagues at the end of 1945, he left a sports structure that was largely regulated, managed and patronized by blacks, inasmuch as blacks could ever, with the resources available to them in the 1920s, '30s, and '40s, profitably and proficiently run a sports league. Robinson's complaints about the Negro Leagues—the incessant barnstorming, the bad accommodations, the poor umpiring, the inadequate spring training—were not only similar to white criticism of the Negro Leagues but they mirrored the criticism that blacks tended to levy against their own organizations and organizational skills. As Sol White makes clear in his seminal 1907 *History of Colored Base Ball,* black people continued to play baseball after they were banned by white professional leagues to show to themselves and to the world that they were capable of *organizing* themselves into teams and leagues. When Robinson left the Kansas City Monarchs, he entered a completely white world, much akin to the world he operated in as a star athlete at UCLA. It was, in part, because Robinson was used to the white world of sports from his college days that Branch Rickey selected him to become the first black man to play major league baseball. Today, when white athletes enter sports dominated by blacks, they do not enter a black *organization* but something akin to a mink-lined black ghetto. (My use of the word "ghetto" here is not meant to suggest anything about oppression, political or otherwise.) Although blacks dominate the most popular team sports, they still make up only 9 percent of all people in the United States who make a living or try to make a living as athletes, less than their percentage in the general population.

What I find most curious about Price's article is that he gives no plausible reason for why blacks dominate these particular sports. He quotes various informants to the effect that blacks must work harder than whites at sports. "Inner-city kids," William Ellerbee, basketball coach at Simon

Gratz High in Philadelphia, says, "look at basketball as a matter of life or death." In a similar article on the black makeup of the NBA in the *Washington Post* last year, Jon Barry, a white player for the Atlanta Hawks, offers: "Maybe the suburban types or the white people have more things to do." Much of this is doubtless true. Traditionally, from the early days of professional baseball in the mid-nineteenth century and of professional boxing in Regency England, sports were seen by the men and boys of the poor and working classes as a way out of poverty or at least out of the normally backbreaking, low-paying work the poor male was offered. And certainly (though some black intellectuals may argue the point, feeling it suggests that black cultural life is impoverished) there probably is more to do or more available to amuse and enlighten in a middle-class suburb than in an inner-city neighborhood, even if it is also true that many whites who live in the suburbs are insufferably provincial and philistine.

Nonetheless, these explanations do not quite satisfy. Ultimately, the discussion in both articles comes down to genetics. There is nothing wrong with thinking about genetic variations. After all, what does the difference in human beings mean and what is its source? Still, if, for instance, Jews dominated football and basketball (as they once did boxing), would there be such a fixation to explain it genetically? The fact of the matter is that, historically, blacks have been a genetic wonder, monstrosity or aberration to whites, and they are still burdened by this implicit sense that they are not quite "normal." From the mid-nineteenth century—with its racist intellectuals like Samuel Cartwright (a Southern medical doctor whose use of minstrel-style jargon, "Dysesthaesia Ethiopica," to describe black people as having thick minds and insensitive bodies is similar to the talk of today's racist geneticists about "fast-twitch" muscles) and Samuel Morton (whose *Crania Americana* tried to classify races by skull size), Louis Agassiz, Arthur de Gobineau and Josiah Nott (who with George Gliddon produced the extremely popular *Types of Mankind* in 1854, which argued that races had been created as separate species)—to Charles Murray and Richard Herrnstein's most recent defense of intelligence quotients to explain economic and status differences among racial and ethnic groups in *The Bell Curve,* blacks have been subjected to a great deal of scientific or so-called scientific scrutiny, much of it misguided if not outright malicious, and all of it to justify the political and economic hegemony of whites. For instance, Lothrop Stoddard, in *The Revolt Against Civilization* (1922), a book nearly identical in some of its themes and polemics to *The Bell Curve,* creates a being called the Under-Man, a barbarian unfit for civilization. (Perhaps this is why some black intellectuals loathe the term "underclass.") "The rarity of mental as compared with physical superiority in the human species is seen on every hand," Stoddard writes. "Existing savage and barbaric races of a demonstrably low average level of intelligence, like the negroes [sic], are physically vigorous, in fact, possess an animal vitality apparently greater than that of the intellectually higher races." There is no escaping the doctrine that for blacks to be physically superior biologically, they must be inferior intellectually and, thus, inferior as a group, Under-People.

But even if it were true that blacks were athletically superior to whites, why then would they not dominate all sports instead of just a handful? There might be a more plainly structural explanation for black dominance in certain sports. This is not to say that genes may have nothing to do with it but only to say that, at this point, genetic arguments have been far from persuasive and, in their implications, more than a little pernicious.

It is easy enough to explain black dominance in boxing. It is the Western sport that has the longest history of black participation, so there is tradition. Moreover, it is a sport that has always attracted poor and marginalized men. Black men have persistently made up a disproportionate share of the poor and the marginalized. Finally, instruction is within easy reach; most boxing gyms are located in poor neighborhoods, where a premium is placed on being able to fight well. Male fighting is a useful skill in a cruel, frontierlike world that values physical toughness, where insult is not casually tolerated and honor is a highly sensitive point.

Black dominance in football and basketball is not simply related to 　15 getting out of the ghetto through hard work or to lack of other amusements but to the institution most readily available to blacks in the inner city that enables them to use athletics to get out. Ironically, that institution is the same one that fails more often than it should in fitting them for other professions: namely, school. As William Washington, the father of a black tennis family, perceptively pointed out in an article last year in the *New York Times* discussing the rise of tennis star Venus Williams: "Tennis, unlike baseball, basketball or football, is not a team sport. It is a family sport. Your immediate family is your primary supporting cast, not your teammates or the players in the locker room. . . . The experiences [of alienation and racism] start soon after you realize that if you play this game, you must leave your neighborhood and join the country club bunch. You don't belong to that group, and they let you know it in a variety of ways, so you go in, compete and leave." In short, because their families generally lack the resources and connections, indeed, because, as scholars such as V. P. Franklin have pointed out, black families cannot provide their members the cultural capital that white and Asian families can, blacks are at a disadvantage to compete in sports where school is not crucial in providing instruction and serving as an organizational setting for competition. When it comes to football and basketball, however, where school is essential to have a career, not only are these sports played at even the poorest black high schools, they are also the dominant college sports. If baseball were a more dominant college sport and if there were no minor leagues where a player had to toil for several years before, maybe, getting a crack at the major leagues, then I think baseball would attract more young black men. Because baseball, historically, was not a game that was invented by a school or became deeply associated with schools or education, blacks could learn it, during the days when they were banned from competition with white professionals, only by forming their own leagues. Sports, whatever one might think of their worth as activities, are extremely important in understanding black people's relationship to secular institutions and secular, non-protest organizing: the school, both black and white; the independent, nonprofessional or semi-professional league; and the barnstorming, independent team, set up by both whites and blacks.

Given that blacks are overrepresented in the most popular sports and that young black men are more likely than young white men to consider athletics as a career, there has been much commentary about whether sports are bad for blacks. The March 24, 1997, issue of *U.S. News & World Report* ran a cover story titled "Are Pro Sports Bad for Black Youth?" In February of that year Germanic languages scholar John Hoberman published *Darwin's Athletes: How Sport Has Damaged Black America and Preserved the Myth of Race*, to much bitter controversy. *The Journal of African American Men*, a new academic journal, not only published a special double issue on black men and sports (Fall 1996/ Winter 1997) but featured an article in its Winter 1995/96 number titled "The Black Student Athlete: The Colonized Black Body," by Billy Hawkins. While there are great distinctions to be made among these works, there is an argument about sports as damaging for blacks that can be abstracted that tends either toward a radical left position on sports or, in Hawkins's case, toward a militant cultural nationalism with Marxist implications.

First, Hoberman and Hawkins make the analogy that sports are a form of slavery or blatant political and economic oppression. Superficially, this argument is made by discussing the rhetoric of team sports (a player is the "property" of his team, or, in boxing, of his manager; he can be traded or "sold" to another team). Since most relationships in popular culture industries are described in this way—Hollywood studios have "properties," have sold and swapped actors, especially in the old days of studio ascendancy, and the like—usually what critics who make this point are aiming at is a thorough denunciation of popular culture as a form of "exploitation" and "degradation." The leftist critic condemns sports as a fraudulent expression of the heroic and the skilled in capitalist culture. The cultural nationalist critic condemns sports as an explicit expression of the grasping greed of white capitalist culture to subjugate people as raw resources.

On a more sophisticated level, the slavery analogy is used to describe sports structurally: the way audiences are lured to sports as a false spectacle, and the way players are controlled mentally and physically by white male authority, their lack of access to the free-market worth of their labor. (This latter point is made particularly about college players, since the breaking of the reserve clause in baseball, not by court decision but by union action, has so radically changed the status and so wildly inflated the salaries of many professional team players, regardless of sport.) Probably the most influential commentator to make this analogy of sport to slavery was Harry Edwards in his 1969 book, *The Revolt of the Black Athlete*. Richard Lapchick in his 1984 book, *Broken Promises: Racism in American Sports,* extends Edwards's premises. Edwards is the only black writer on sports that Hoberman admires. And Edwards is also cited by Hawkins. How convincing any of this is has much to do with how willing one is to be convinced, as is the case with many highly polemical arguments. For instance, to take up Hawkins's piece, are black athletes more colonized, more exploited as laborers at the university than, say, graduate students and adjunct faculty, who teach the bulk of the lower-level courses at a fraction of the pay and benefits of the full-time faculty? Are black athletes at white colleges more exploited than black students generally at white schools? If the major evidence that black athletes are exploited by white schools is the high number who fail to graduate, why, for those who adopt Hawkins's ideological position, are black students who generally suffer high attrition rates at such schools not considered equally as exploited?

What is striking is the one analogy between slavery and team sports that is consistently overlooked. Professional sports teams operate as a cartel—a group of independent entrepreneurs who come together to control an industry without giving up their independence as competitive entities. So does the NCAA, which controls college sports; and so did the Southern planters who ran the Confederacy. They controlled the agricultural industry of the South as well as both free and slave labor. The cartelization of American team sports, which so closely resembles the cartelization of the antebellum Southern planters (the behavior of both is remarkably similar), is the strongest argument to make about slavery and sports or about sports and colonization. This is what is most unnerving about American team sports as an industry, and how the power of that industry, combined with the media, threatens the very democratic values that sports supposedly endorse.

The other aspects of the sports-damage-black-America argument,   20
principally made by Hoberman, are that blacks are more likely to be seen as merely "physical," and thus inferior, beings; that society's promotion of black sports figures comes at the expense of promoting any other type of noteworthy black person; that black overinvestment in sports is both the cause and result of black anti-intellectualism, itself the result of virulent white racism, meant to confine blacks to certain occupations. Implicit in Hoberman's work is his hatred of the fetishization of athletic achievement, the rigid rationalization of sports as a theory and practice. He also hates the suppression of the political nature of the athlete, and hates, too,

both the apolitical nature of sports, mystified as transcendent legend and supported by the simplistic language of sportswriters and sports-apologist intellectuals, and the political exploitation of sports by ideologues and the powerful. As a critical theorist, Hoberman was never interested in proving this with thorough empiricism, and, as a result, was attacked in a devastatingly effective manner by black scholars, who blew away a good number of his assertions with an unrelenting empiricism. But he has got into deep trouble with black intellectuals, in the end, not for these assertions or for the mere lack of good empiricism. Hoberman, rather, has been passionately condemned for suggesting that blacks have a "sports fixation" that is tantamount to a pathology, a word that rightly distresses African-Americans, reminiscent as it is of the arrogance of white social scientists past and present who describe blacks as some misbegotten perversion of a white middle-class norm.

There is, however, one point to be made in Hoberman's defense. Since he clearly believes high-level sports to be a debased, largely unhealthy enterprise and believes that the white majority suffers a sports obsession, he would naturally think that blacks, as a relatively powerless minority and as the principal minority connected to sports, would be especially damaged by it. The black intellectual who most influenced Hoberman was Ralph Ellison,[1] and, as Darryl Scott pointed out in a brilliant analysis delivered at a sports conference at New York University this past April that dealt almost exclusively with Hoberman's book, Ellison might rightly be characterized as "a pathologist" and "an individualist." But he was, as Scott argued, "a pathologist who opposed pathology as part of the racial debate." Yet one of the most compelling scenes in *Invisible Man* is the Battle Royal, a surreal perversion of a sports competition in which blacks fight one another for the amusement of powerful whites. Although racism has compelled blacks to participate in this contest, the characters come willingly, the winner even taking an individualistic pride in it. Such participation in one's own degradation can be described as a pathology. How can an Ellison disciple avoid pathology as part of the debate when Ellison made it so intricately serve the artistic and political needs of his novel? Ellison may have loved jazz, and growing up black and poor in Oklahoma may have been as richly stimulating as any life, just as going to Tuskegee may have been the same as going to Harvard—at least according to Ellison's mythologizing of his own life— but he found black literature generally inadequate as art and thought that blacks used race as a cover to avoid engaging the issues of life fully. For Ellison, black people, like most oppressed minorities, intensely provincialized themselves.

This is not to say Hoberman is justified in adding his own patholo-

---

[1]See, for example, Ralph Ellison's "What America Would Be Like without Blacks" (page 367).—EDS.

gizing to the mix, but his reasoning seems to be something like this: If racism is a major pathology and if we live in a racist society, one might reasonably suspect the victims of racism to be at least as pathologized by it as the perpetrators. If the victims are not pathologized at all by it, why single out racism as a particularly heinous crime? It would, in that instance, be nothing more than another banal example of man's inhumanity to man.

In response to an article like *SI*'s "Whatever Happened to the White Athlete?" blacks are likely to ask, Why is it whenever we dominate by virtue of merit a legitimate field of endeavor, it's always seen as a problem? On the one hand, some blacks are probably willing to take the view expressed in Steve Sailer's August 12, 1996, essay in *National Review,* "Great Black Hopes," in which he argues that black achievement in sports serves very practical ends, giving African-Americans a cultural and market niche, and that far from indicating a lack of intelligence, blacks' dominance in some sports reveals a highly specialized intelligence: what he calls "creative improvisation and on-the-fly interpersonal decision-making," which also explains "black dominance in jazz, running with the football, rap, dance, trash talking, preaching, and oratory." I suppose it might be said from this that blacks have fast-twitch brain cells. In any case, blacks had already been conceded these gifts by whites in earlier displays of condescension. But black sports dominance is no small thing to blacks because, as they deeply know, to win is to be human.

On the other hand, what the *SI* article said most tellingly was that while young whites admire black athletic figures, they are afraid to play sports that blacks dominate, another example of whites leaving the neighborhood when blacks move in. This white "double-consciousness" — to admire blacks for their skills while fearing their presence in a situation where blacks might predominate — is a modern-day reflection of the contradiction, historically, that has produced our racially stratified society. To be white can be partly defined as not only the fear of not being white but the fear of being *at the mercy* of those who are not white. Whiteness and blackness in this respect cease to be identities and become the personifications not of stereotypes alone but of taboos, of prohibitions. Sports, like all of popular culture, become the theater where the taboos are simultaneously smashed and reinforced, where one is liberated from them while conforming to them. Sports are not an idealization of ourselves but a reflection.

THE PRINCE AND HIS KINGDOM

Arguably the most popular and, doubtless, one of the most skilled   25
boxers in the world today is the undefeated featherweight champion, Prince Naseem Hamed of England. (The "Prince" title is a bit of platonic self-romanticism; Naseem, of lower-middle-class origins — his father a corner-store grocer — has no blood tie to any aristocracy.) When he was a

boy, Hamed and his brothers fought all the time in the street, usually against white kids who called them "Paki." "I'd always turn around and say, 'Listen, I'm Arab me, not Pakistani,'" said Hamed in an interview some years later. "They'd turn around and say you're all the same." Indeed, Hamed was discovered by Brendan Ingle, his Irish manager, fighting three bigger white boys in a Sheffield schoolyard and holding his own very well. The fight was probably instigated by racial insult. Although his parents are from Yemen and Naseem is worshipped nearly as a god among the Yemeni these days, he was born in Sheffield, is a British citizen, never lived in Yemen and, despite his Islamic religious practices, seems thoroughly British in speech, taste and cultural inclination. Yet when Naseem was fighting as an amateur, he was sometimes taunted racially by the crowd: "Get the black bastard." Even as a professional he has sometimes been called "Paki bastard" and "nigger." He was once showered with spit by a hostile white audience. But Naseem was far more inspired than frightened by these eruptions, and was especially impressive in winning fights when he was held in racial contempt by the audience, as he would wickedly punish his opponents. For Hamed, these fights particularly became opportunities to rub white Anglo faces in the dirt, to beat them smugly while they hysterically asserted their own vanquished superiority. But his defiance, through his athleticism, becomes an ironic form of assimilation. He is probably the most loved Arab in England, and far and away the most popular boxer there. As he said, "When you're doing well, everyone wants to be your friend."

On the whole, these displays of racism at a sporting event need to be placed in perspective. For what seems a straightforward exhibition of racialist prejudice and Anglo arrogance is a bit more complex. And deeper understanding of the Naseem Hamed phenomenon might give us another way to approach the entangled subject of race and sports.

It must be remembered that professional boxing has been and remains a sport that blatantly, sometimes crudely, exploits racial and ethnic differences. Most people know the phrase "Great White Hope," created during the reign (1908–15) of the first black heavyweight boxing champion, Jack Johnson, when a white sporting public that had, at first, supported him turned against him in part because he flaunted his sexual affairs with white women; in part because he seemed to be so far superior to the white opponent, Tommy Burns, from whom he won the title. The advent of Johnson did not, by any means, invent the intersection of race and sports but surely heightened it as a form of national obsession, a dark convulsion in an incipient American popular culture. The expression "Great White Hope" is still used today, in boxing, track and field, and professional basketball, whenever a white emerges as a potential star.

But ethnicity and racialism in boxing has a more intricate history than white against black. Boxers have often come from racially and ethnically mixed working-class urban environments where they fought racial insults as street toughs. This was particularly true of white ethnic fighters—Jews, Italians and Irish—in the United States from the turn of the century to about the fifties, when public-policy changes widened economic and educational opportunities, and suburbanization altered white ethnic urban neighborhoods, changing the character of boxing and big-city life. John L. Sullivan, the last great bare-knuckle champion, may have been "white" when he drew the color line and refused to fight the great black heavyweight Peter Jackson (at nearly the same time that Cap Anson refused to play against blacks in baseball, precipitating a near-sixty-year ban on blacks in professional baseball), but to his audience he was not merely white but Irish. Benny Leonard was not just a white fighter but a Jewish fighter. Rocky Graziano was not merely a white fighter but an Italian fighter. Muhammad Ali, reinventing himself ethnically when the fight game became almost exclusively black and Latino, was not just a black fighter but a militant black Muslim fighter. Fighters, generally, as part of the show, tend to take on explicit ethnic and racial identities in the ring. One needn't be a deconstructionist to understand that race *aspires* to be a kind of performance, just as athletic performance aspires to be something racial. This is clear to anyone who has seriously watched more than, say a half-dozen boxing matches. Today, basketball is a "black" game not only because blacks dominate it but because they have developed a style of play that is very different from the style when whites dominated the pro game back in the fifties. It is said by scholars, writers and former players that Negro League baseball was different from white baseball and that when Jackie Robinson broke the color line, he introduced a different way of playing the game, with more emphasis on speed and aggressive base-running. In the realm of sports, this type of innovation becomes more than just performance. The political significance of race in a sporting performance is inextricably related to the fact that sports are also contests of domination and survival. It should come as no surprise that the intersection of race and sports reached its full expression at the turn of the century when social Darwinism was the rage (Charles Murray is our Herbert Spencer);[2] when sports, imitating the rampant industrialism of the day, became a highly, if arbitrarily, rationalized system; when business culture first began to assimilate the values of sports; when it was believed that blacks would die out in direct competition with whites because they were so inferior; when Euro-American imperialism—race as the dramaturgy of dominance—was in full sway.

In most respects, the racialism displayed at some of Naseem Hamed's fights is rather old-fashioned. This racialism has three sources. First, there

---

[2]**Charles Murray** is the coauthor of the controversial 1994 study of IQ, *The Bell Curve*, and **Herbert Spencer** (1820–1903) was the highly influential English philosopher who made Darwin's evolutionary theories part of social thought. It was Spencer, not Darwin, who coined the phrase "the survival of the fittest." Spencer believed in the superiority of the individual over society and thought that governments should play as little part as possible in social and economic affairs.—EDS.

is the old Anglo racism directed against anyone nonwhite but particularly against anyone from, or perceived to be from, the Indian subcontinent. (Hamed is insulted by being called a "Paki," not an Arab, a confusion that speaks to something specific in white British consciousness, as does the statement "they are all the same.") In short, in British boxing audiences, we see Anglo racism as a performance of competitive dominance as well as a belief in the superiority of "whiteness."

Second, there is the way that Hamed fights. "Dirty, flash, black bas-   30
tard," his audience shouts, meaning that Hamed has stylish moves, is very fast, but really lacks the heart and stamina to be a true boxer, does not have the bottom of a more "prosaic" white fighter. Hamed is derided, in part, because his showy, flamboyant style seems "black," although there have been several noted white fighters in boxing history who were crafty and quick, like Willie Pep. Hamed is immodest, something the white sporting crowd dislikes in any athlete but particularly in nonwhite athletes. He fights more in the style of Sugar Ray Leonard and Muhammad Ali than in the mode of the traditional stand-up British boxer. To further complicate the ethnicity issue, it must be remembered that famous black British boxers such as Randy Turpin, John Conteh and Frank Bruno have been very much accepted by the British sporting public because they fought in a more orthodox manner.

Third, traditional working-class ethnocentrism is part of most boxing matches, as it is a seamless part of working-class life. Hamed calls his manager "Old Irish," while Ingle calls him "the little Arab." A good deal of this ethnocentrism is expressed as a kind of complex regional chauvinism. Below the glamorous championship level, boxing matches are highly local affairs. Hamed has received his most racist receptions when fighting a local boy on that boy's turf. This almost always happens, regardless of ethnicity, to a "foreign" or "alien" boxer. In international amateur competitions, Hamed himself was constantly reminded that he was "fighting for England." It is all right if Hamed is a "Paki" as long as he is "our Paki."

What we learn from the example of Hamed is that race is a form of performance or exhibition in sports that is meant, in some way, for those at the bottom, to be an act of assertion, even revolt, against "how things are normally done." But also, in boxing, ethnic identities are performances of ethnic hatreds. As Jacques Barzun wrote, "In hatred there [is] the sensation of strength," and it is this sensation that spurs the fighter psychologically in the ring, gives him a reason to fight a man he otherwise has no reason to harm. So it is that within the working-class ethnic's revolt there is also his capitulation to playing out a role of pointless, apolitical resentment in the social order. This is why boxing is such an ugly sport: It was invented by men of the leisure class simply to bet, to make their own sort of sport of their privilege; and it reduces the poor man's rightful resentment, his anger and hatred, to a form of absurd, debased, dangerous entertainment. The Hameds of the boxing world make brutality a form of athletic beauty.

POSTSCRIPT: O DEFEAT, WHERE IS THY STING?

> She: Is there a way to win?
> He: Well, there is a way to lose more slowly.
>
> —Jane Greer and Robert Mitchum
> in *Out of the Past*

> I'm a loser
> And I'm not what I appear to be.
>
> —Lennon and McCartney

It is a certainty that sports teach us about defeat and losing, for it is a far more common experience than winning. It might be suggested that in any competition there must be a winner and a loser and so winning is just as common. But this is not true. When a baseball team wins the World Series or a college basketball team wins a national title or a tennis player wins the French Open, everyone else in the competition has lost: twenty-nine other baseball teams, sixty-three other basketball teams, dozens of other seeded and unseeded tennis players. Surely, all or nearly all have won at some point, but most sports are structured as elaborate eliminations. The aura of any sporting event or season is defeat. I am not sure sports teach either the participants or the audience how to lose well, but they certainly teach that losing is the major part of life. "A game tests, somehow, one's entire life," writes Michael Novak, and it is in this aspect that the ideological content of sports seems much like the message of the blues, and the athlete seems, despite his or her obsessive training and remarkable skill, a sort of Everyperson or Job at war, not with the gods but with the very idea of God. Sports do not mask the absurdity of life but rather ritualize it as a contest against the arbitrariness of adversity, where the pointless challenge of an equally pointless limitation, beautifully and thrillingly executed, sometimes so gorgeously as to seem a victory even in defeat, becomes the most transcendent point of all. Black people have taught all of us in the blues that to lose is to be human. Sports, on any given day, teaches the same.

My barber is a professional boxer. He fights usually as a light-heavyweight or as a cruiser-weight. He is thirty-four and would like to fight for a championship again one day, but time is working against him. He has fought for championships in the past, though never a world title. It is difficult to succeed as a boxer if you must work another job. A day of full-time work and training simply leaves a fighter exhausted and distracted. I have seen him fight on television several times, losing to such world-class fighters as Michael Nunn and James Toney. In fact, every time I have seen him fight he has lost. He is considered "an opponent," someone used by an up-and-coming fighter to fatten his record or by an established fighter who needs a tune-up. An opponent does not make much money; some are paid as little as a few hundred dollars a fight. My barber, I guess, is paid more than that. This is the world that most boxers occupy—this small-time world of dingy arenas and gambling boats, cramped dressing rooms and little notice. It is the world that most professional athletes occupy. He last fought on June 2 against Darryl Spinks for something called the MBA light-heavyweight title at the Ambassador Center in Jennings, Missouri. Darryl Spinks is the son of notorious St. Louis fighter and former heavyweight champion Leon Spinks. Spinks won a twelve-round decision, and my barber felt he was given "a hometown decision" in his own hometown, as he felt he decisively beat young Spinks. But Spinks is an up-and-coming fighter, and up-and-coming fighters win close fights. When I talked to my barber after the fight, he seemed to accept defeat with some equanimity. What upset him was that the local paper, or the local white paper, as it is seen by most blacks, the *St. Louis Post-Dispatch,* did not cover the fight. It was prominently covered by the *St. Louis American,* the city's black paper. I told him I would write a letter to the editor about that; he appreciated my concern. As things turned out, the fight was mentioned in the *Post-Dispatch* ten days later as part of a roundup of the local boxing scene. My barber's fight earned three paragraphs. It probably wasn't quite what he wanted, but I am sure it made him feel better. After all, a local fighter has only his reputation in his hometown to help him make a living. Nonetheless, I admired the fact that he took so well being unfairly denied something that was so important to him. Most people can't do that.

I might quarrel a little with my good friend Stanley Crouch,[3] who   35
once said that the most exquisite blues statement was Jesus, crucified, asking God why he had been forsaken. It's a good line Jesus said on the old rugged cross. But for us Americans, I rather think the most deeply affecting blues statement about losing as the way it is in this life is the last line of a song we learned as children and we sing every time we go to the park to see our favorite team: "'Cause it's one, two, three strikes you're out at the old ball game."

The Reader's Presence

1. What different meanings can you think of for the word *performance?* In what ways do sports figures—and sports audiences—"perform"? In what ways are famous minority figures forced to perform for a mainstream public? What "role" does Early assign Jackie Robinson in the drama of the struggles for equality and recognition? What "realities" does the piece contrast to performance? How does Early's view of performance differ from views

---

[3]*Crouch:* Stanley Crouch, the noted essayist and jazz critic, is the author of, among other books, *The All-American Skin Game, or, The Decoy of Race* (1995).—EDS.

you might see or hear in the sports pages or sports shows on radio and television?

2. What does Early find in common between sports and the concept of race in the beginning of the essay's fourth section? How does Robinson tie into both systems? How does this connection relate to Early's argument as a whole?

3. Early attaches a "postscript" to the main body of his piece. Why might this material be separate from the rest? What is the relation between Early's argument and the story about his barber? What is the relation of defeat to questions of sports and race?

95

Barbara Ehrenreich

Family Values

The writer, feminist, and Socialist Party leader Barbara Ehrenreich (b. 1941) wrote some of her first articles and books on the inefficiency and inhumanity of the American health care system. In Complaints and Disorders: The Sexual Politics of Sickness *(coauthored with Deirdre English, 1973) she critiques the unjust and unequal treatment women receive in the medical system. She has written over a dozen books, among them* The Hearts of Men: American Dreams and the Flight from Commitment *(1983),* The Worst Years of Our Lives: Irreverent Notes from a Decade of Greed *(1990), and* Kipper's Game *(1993). Ehrenreich is a contributing editor at* The Progressive *and* The Nation, *and her essays also appear regularly in magazines as varied as* Radical America, Time, Vogue, *and the* New York Times Magazine. *Her most recent books are* The Snarling Citizen: Essays *(1995) and* Blood Rites: Origins and History of the Passions of War *(1997).*

Asked whether she writes in a different voice for the alternative and the mainstream press, Ehrenreich replied, "I don't think it's really a different voice. . . . Obviously I assume more political sympathy for my views if I'm writing for Z or the Guardian *in England or the* Nation *than* Time, *but it might be the exact basic argument." She added, "An essay is like a little story, a short story, and I will obsess about what is the real point, what are the real connections, a long time before I ever put finger to keyboard."*

Sometimes in the eighties, Americans had a new set of "traditional values" installed. It was part of what may someday be known as the

"Reagan renovation," that finely balanced mix of cosmetic refinement and moral coarseness which brought $200,000 china to the White House dinner table and mayhem to the beleaguered peasantry of Central America. All of the new traditions had venerable sources. In economics, we borrowed from the Bourbons; in foreign policy, we drew on themes fashioned by the nomad warriors of the Eurasian steppes. In spiritual matters, we emulated the braying intolerance of our archenemies and esteemed customers, the Shi'ite fundamentalists.

A case could be made, of course, for the genuine American provenance of all these new "traditions." We've had our own robber barons, military adventures, and certainly more than our share of enterprising evangelists promoting ignorance and parochialism as a state of grace. From the vantage point of the continent's original residents, or, for example, the captive African laborers who made America a great agricultural power, our "traditional values" have always been bigotry, greed, and belligerence, buttressed by wanton appeals to a God of love.

The kindest — though from some angles most perverse — of the era's new values was "family." I could have lived with "flag" and "faith" as neotraditional values — not happily, but I could have managed — until "family" was press-ganged into joining them. Throughout the eighties, the winning political faction has been aggressively "profamily." They have invoked "the family" when they trample on the rights of those who hold actual families together, that is, women. They have used it to justify racial segregation and the formation of white-only, "Christian" schools. And they have brought it out, along with flag and faith, to silence any voices they found obscene, offensive, disturbing, or merely different.

Now, I come from a family — was raised in one, in fact — and one salubrious effect of right-wing righteousness has been to make me hew ever more firmly to the traditional values of my own progenitors. These were not people who could be accused of questionable politics or ethnicity. Nor were they members of the "liberal elite" so hated by our current conservative elite. They were blue-eyed, Scotch-Irish Democrats. They were small farmers, railroad workers, miners, shopkeepers, and migrant farm workers. In short, they fit the stereotype of "real" Americans; and their values, no matter how unpopular among today's opinion-shapers, are part of America's tradition, too. To my mind, of course, the finest part.

But let me introduce some of my family, beginning with my father, who 5 was, along with my mother, the ultimate source of much of my radicalism, feminism, and, by the standards of the eighties, all-around bad attitude.

One of the first questions in a test of mental competency is "Who is the president of the United States?" Even deep into the indignities of Alzheimer's disease, my father always did well on that one. His blue eyes would widen incredulously, surprised at the neurologist's ignorance, then he would snort in majestic indignation, "Reagan, that dumb son of a bitch." It seemed to me a good deal — two people tested for the price of one.

Like so many of the Alzheimer's patients he came to know, my father enjoyed watching the president on television. Most programming left him impassive, but when the old codger came on, his little eyes twinkling piggishly above the disciplined sincerity of his lower face, my father would lean forward and commence a wickedly delighted cackle. I think he was prepared, more than the rest of us, to get the joke.

But the funniest thing was Ollie North. For an ailing man, my father did a fine parody. He would slap his hand over his heart, stare rigidly at attention, and pronounce, in his deepest bass rumble, "God Bless Am-ar-ica!" I'm sure he couldn't follow North's testimony—who can honestly say that they did?—but the main themes were clear enough in pantomime: the watery-eyed patriotism, the extravagant self-pity, the touching servility toward higher-ranking males. When I told my father that many people considered North a hero, a representative of the finest American traditions, he scowled and swatted at the air. Ollie North was the kind of man my father had warned me about, many years ago, when my father was the smartest man on earth.

My father had started out as a copper miner in Butte, Montana, a tiny mountain city famed for its bars, its brawls, and its distinctly unservile work force. In his view, which remained eagle-sharp even after a stint of higher education, there were only a few major categories of human beings. There were "phonies" and "decent" people, the latter group having hardly any well-known representative outside of Franklin Delano Roosevelt and John L. Lewis, the militant and brilliantly eloquent leader of the miners' union. "Phonies," however, were rampant, and, for reasons I would not understand until later in life, could be found clustered especially thick in the vicinity of money or power.

Well before he taught me other useful things, like how to distinguish fool's gold, or iron pyrite, from the real thing, he gave me some tips on the detection of phonies. For one thing, they broadened the *e* in "America" to a reverent *ahh*. They were the first to leap from their seats at the playing of "The Star Spangled Banner," the most visibly moved participants in any prayer. They espoused clean living and admired war. They preached hard work and paid for it with nickels and dimes. They loved their country above all, but despised the low-paid and usually invisible men and women who built it, fed it, and kept it running.   10

Two other important categories figured in my father's scheme of things. There were dumb people and smart ones: a distinction which had nothing to do with class or formal education, the dumb being simply all those who were taken in by the phonies. In his view, dumbness was rampant, and seemed to increase in proportion to the distance from Butte, where at least a certain hard-bodied irreverence leavened the atmosphere. The best prophylactic was to study and learn all you could, however you could, and, as he adjured me over and over: always ask *why*.

Finally, there were the rich and the poor. While poverty was not seen as an automatic virtue—my parents struggled mightily to escape it—

wealth always carried a presumption of malfeasance. I was instructed that, in the presence of the rich, it was wise to keep one's hand on one's wallet. "Well," my father fairly growled, "how do you think they got their money in the first place?"

It was my mother who translated these lessons into practical politics. A miner's daughter herself, she offered two overarching rules for comportment: never vote Republican and never cross a union picket line. The pinnacle of her activist career came in 1964, when she attended the Democratic Convention as an alternate delegate and joined the sit-in staged by civil rights leaders and the Mississippi Freedom Democratic Party. This was not the action of a "guilt-ridden" white liberal. She classified racial prejudice along with superstition and other manifestations of backward thinking, like organized religion and overcooked vegetables. The worst thing she could find to say about a certain in-law was that he was a Republican and a churchgoer, though when I investigated these charges later in life, I was relieved to find them baseless.

My mother and father, it should be explained, were hardly rebels. The values they imparted to me had been "traditional" for at least a generation before my parents came along. According to my father, the first great steps out of mental passivity had been taken by his maternal grandparents, John Howes and Mamie O'Laughlin Howes, sometime late in the last century. You might think their rebellions small stuff, but they provided our family with its "myth of origins" and a certain standard to uphold.

I knew little about Mamie O'Laughlin except that she was raised as a   15
Catholic and ended up in western Montana sometime in the 1880s. Her father, very likely, was one of those itinerant breadwinners who went west to prospect and settled for mining. At any rate, the story begins when her father lay dying, and Mamie dutifully sent to the next town for a priest. The message came back that the priest would come only if twenty-five dollars was sent in advance. This being the West at its wildest, he may have been justified in avoiding house calls. But not in the price, which was probably more cash than my great-grandmother had ever had at one time. It was on account of its greed that the church lost the souls of Mamie O'Laughlin and all of her descendents, right down to the present time. Futhermore, whether out of filial deference or natural intelligence, most of us have continued to avoid organized religion, secret societies, astrology, and New Age adventures in spiritualism.

As the story continues, Mamie O'Laughlin herself lay dying a few years later. She was only thirty-one, the mother of three small children, one of them an infant whose birth, apparently, led to a mortal attack of pneumonia. This time, a priest appeared unsummoned. Because she was too weak to hold the crucifix, he placed it on her chest and proceeded to administer the last rites. But Mamie was not dead yet. She pulled herself together at the last moment, flung the crucifix across the room, fell back, and died.

This was my great-grandmother. Her husband, John Howes, is a figure of folkloric proportions in my memory, well known in Butte many decades ago as a powerful miner and a lethal fighter. There are many stories about John Howes, all of which point to a profound inability to accept authority in any of its manifestations, earthly or divine. As a young miner, for example, he caught the eye of the mine owner for his skill at handling horses. The boss promoted him to an aboveground driving job, which was a great career leap for the time. Then the boss committed a foolish and arrogant error. He asked John to break in a team of horses for his wife's carriage. Most people would probably be flattered by such a request, but not in Butte, and certainly not John Howes. He declared that he was no man's servant, and quit on the spot.

Like his own wife, John Howes was an atheist or, as they more likely put it at the time, a freethinker. He, too, had been raised as a Catholic — on a farm in Ontario — and he, too, had had a dramatic, though somehow less glorious, falling out with the local clergy. According to legend, he once abused his position as an altar boy by urinating, covertly of course, in the holy water. This so enhanced his enjoyment of the Easter communion service that he could not resist letting a few friends in on the secret. Soon the priest found out and young John was defrocked as an altar boy and condemned to eternal damnation.

The full weight of this transgression hit a few years later, when he became engaged to a local woman. The priest refused to marry them and forbade the young woman to marry John anywhere, on pain of excommunication. There was nothing to do but head west for the Rockies, but not before settling his score with the church. According to legend, John's last act in Ontario was to drag the priest down from his pulpit and slug him, with his brother, presumably, holding the scandalized congregation at bay.

I have often wondered whether my great-grandfather was caught up   20
in the radicalism of Butte in its heyday: whether he was an admirer of Joe Hill, Big Bill Haywood, or Mary "Mother" Jones, all of whom passed through Butte to agitate, and generally left with the Pinkertons on their tails. But the record is silent on this point. All I know is one last story about him, which was told often enough to have the ring of another "traditional value."

According to my father, John Howes worked on and off in the mines after his children were grown, eventually saving enough to buy a small plot of land and retire to farming. This was his dream, anyway, and a powerful one it must have been for a man who had spent so much of his life underground in the dark. So he loaded up a horse-drawn cart with all his money and belongings and headed downhill, toward Montana's eastern plains. But along the way he came to an Indian woman walking with a baby in her arms. He offered her a lift and ascertained, pretty easily, that she was destitute. So he gave her his money, all of it, turned the horse around, and went back to the mines.

Far be it from me to interpret this gesture for my great-grandfather, whom I knew only as a whiskery, sweat-smelling, but straight-backed old man in his eighties. Perhaps he was enacting his own uncompromising version of Christian virtue, even atoning a little for his youthful offenses to the faithful. But at another level I like to think that this was one more gesture of defiance of the mine owners who doled out their own dollars so grudgingly—a way of saying, perhaps, that whatever they had to offer, he didn't really need all that much.

So these were the values, sanctified by tradition and family loyalty, that I brought with me to adulthood. Through much of my growing-up, I thought of them as some mutant strain of Americanism, an idiosyncracy which seemed to grow rarer as we clambered into the middle class. Only in the sixties did I begin to learn that my family's militant skepticism and oddball rebelliousness were part of a much larger stream of American dissent. I discovered feminism, the antiwar movement, the civil rights movement. I learned that millions of Americans, before me and around me, were "smart" enough, in my father's terms, to have asked "Why?"— and, beyond that, the far more radical question, "Why not?"

These are also the values I brought into the Reagan-Bush era, when all the dangers I had been alerted to as a child were suddenly realized. The "phonies" came to power on the strength, aptly enough, of a professional actor's finest performance. The "dumb" were being led and abetted by low-life preachers and intellectuals with expensively squandered educations. And the rich, as my father predicted, used the occasion to dip deep into the wallets of the desperate and the distracted.

It's been hard times for a traditionalist of my persuasion. Long-   25
standing moral values—usually claimed as "Judeo-Christian" but actually of much broader lineage—were summarily tossed, along with most familiar forms of logic. We were told, at one time or another, by the president or his henchpersons, that trees cause pollution, that welfare causes poverty, and that a bomber designed for mass destruction may be aptly named the *Peacemaker*. "Terrorism" replaced missing children to become our national bugaboo and—simultaneously—one of our most potent instruments of foreign policy. At home, the poor and the middle class where shaken down, and their loose change funneled blithely upwards to the already overfed.

Greed, the ancient lubricant of commerce, was declared a wholesome stimulant. Nancy Reagan observed the deep recession of '82 and '83 by redecorating the White House, and continued with this Marie Antoinette theme while advising the underprivileged, the alienated, and the addicted to "say no." Young people, mindful of their elders' Wall Street capers, abandoned the study of useful things for finance banking and other occupations derived, ultimately, from three-card monte. While the poor donned plastic outerware and cardboard coverings, the affluent ran nearly naked through the streets, working off power meals of goat cheese, walnut oil, and crème fraîche.

Religion, which even I had hoped would provide a calming influence and reminder of mortal folly, decided to join the fun. In an upsurge of piety, millions of Americans threw their souls and their savings into evangelical empires designed on the principle of pyramid scams. Even the sleazy downfall of our telemessiahs—caught masturbating in the company of ten-dollar prostitutes or fornicating in their Christian theme parks—did not discourage the faithful. The unhappily pregnant were mobbed as "baby-killers"; sexual nonconformists—gay and lesbian— were denounced as "child molesters"; atheists found themselves lumped with "Satanists," Communists, and consumers of human flesh.

Yet somehow, despite it all, a trickle of dissent continued. There were homeless people who refused to be shelved in mental hospitals for the crime of poverty, strikers who refused to join the celebration of unions in faraway countries and scabs at home, women who insisted that their lives be valued above those of accidental embryos, parents who packed up their babies and marched for peace, students who protested the ongoing inversion of normal, nursery-school-level values in the name of a more habitable world.

I am proud to add my voice to all these. For dissent is also a "traditional value," and in a republic founded by revolution, a more deeply native one than smug-faced conservatism can ever be. Feminism was practically invented here, and ought to be regarded as one of our proudest exports to the world. Likewise, it tickles my sense of patriotism that Third World insurgents have often borrowed the ideas of our own African-American movement. And in what ought to be a source of shame to some and pride to others, our history of labor struggle is one of the hardest-fought and bloodiest in the world.

No matter that patriotism is too often the refuge of scoundrels. Dissent, rebellion, and all-around hell-raising remain the true duty of patriots.   30

The Reader's Presence

1. You may have been quite young in the 1980s. Do you believe, with Ehrenreich, that different periods in American history have carried different social values? Why or why not? What is your impression of the 1980s, and what sources have you derived it from? How does Ehrenreich characterize the 1980s? What elements of 1980s culture does she recall in supporting her claims?

2. One catch phrase frequently heard during Ehrenreich's radical college years was "the personal is political." In what ways were Ehrenreich's father's personal principles political, in her view? How does Ehrenreich's use of her father as a model make the personal political and the political personal? Does this intermingling

of the personal and the political undermine or enhance her larger argument? Why?

3. Ehrenreich uses her own impressions and experience as evidence in her argument. How might the essay read if it were argued in more objective terms (historical facts, statistics, etc.)? What sorts of examples does she use to make her point? Can you think of examples contrary to hers (counterexamples)?

96

Paul Fussell

A Well-Regulated Militia

A well-established English professor who taught at Rutgers before accepting a distinguished professorship at the University of Pennsylvania in 1983, Paul Fussell (b. 1924) did not successfully break with academic prose until he tired of writing what he was "supposed to write." After twenty years of writing critical works such as Poetic Meter and Poetic Form *(1965) and* The Rhetorical World of Augustan Humanism *(1965), Fussell published his first work of nonfiction for a general audience.* The Great War and Modern Memory *(1975) won the National Book Award and the National Book Critics Circle Award and received wide critical acclaim for its examination of how World War I changed what Frank Kermode called "the texture of our culture." Fussell continued to touch upon the subject of war in his subsequent books,* Abroad: British Literary Traveling between the Wars *(1980) and* The Boy Scout Handbook and Other Observations *(1982). Fussell then wrote* Class: A Guide through the American Status System *(1983) and edited* The Norton Book of Travel *(1987). Fussell returned to his favorite subject in his collection of essays* Thank God for the Atom Bomb and Other Essays *(1988), from which this selection is taken. Fussell's most recent publications are* Bad, or The Dumbing of America *(1991),* The Anti-Egoist, Kingsley Amis, Man of Letters *(1994), and* Doing Battle: The Making of a Skeptic (1996).

In the spring Washington swarms with high school graduating classes. They come to the great pulsating heart of the Republic—which no one has yet told them is Wall Street—to be impressed by the White House and the Capitol and the monuments and the Smithsonian and the space capsules. Given the state of public secondary education, I doubt if many of these young people are at all interested in language and rhetoric, and I imagine few are fascinated by such attendants of power and pressure as verbal misrepresentation and disingenuous quotation. But any who are can profit from a stroll past the headquarters of the National Rifle Association of America, its slick marble façade conspicuous at 1600 Rhode Island Avenue, NW.

There they would see an entrance flanked by two marble panels offering language, and language more dignified and traditional than that customarily associated with the Association's gun-freak constituency, with its T-shirts reading GUNS, GUTS, AND GLORY ARE WHAT MADE AMERICA GREAT and its belt buckles proclaiming I'LL GIVE UP MY GUN WHEN THEY PRY MY COLD DEAD FINGERS FROM AROUND IT. The marble panel on the right reads, "The right of the people to keep and bear arms shall not be infringed," which sounds familiar. So familiar that the student naturally expects the left-hand panel to honor the principle of symmetry by presenting the first half of the quotation, namely: "A well-regulated Militia, being necessary to the security of a free state, . . ." But looking to the left, the inquirer discovers not that clause at all but rather this lame list of NRA functions and specializations: "Firearms Safety Education. Marksmanship Training. Shooting for Recreation." It's as if in presenting its well-washed, shiny public face the NRA doesn't want to remind anyone of the crucial dependent clause of the Second Amendment, whose latter half alone it is so fond of invoking to urge its prerogatives. (Some legible belt buckles of members retreat further into a seductive vagueness, reading only, "Our American Heritage: the Second Amendment.") We infer that for the Association, the less emphasis on the clause about the militia, the better. Hence its pretence on the front of its premises that the quoted main clause is not crucially dependent on the now unadvertised subordinate clause — indeed, it's meaningless without it.

Because flying .38- and .45-caliber bullets rank close to cancer, heart disease, and AIDS as menaces to public health in this country, the firearm lobby, led by the NRA, comes under liberal attack regularly, and with special vigor immediately after an assault on some conspicuous person like Ronald Reagan or John Lennon. Thus *The New Republic,* in April 1981, deplored the state of things but offered as a solution only the suggestion that the whole Second Amendment be perceived as obsolete and amended out of the Constitution. This would leave the NRA with not a leg to stand on.

But here as elsewhere a better solution would be not to fiddle with the Constitution but to take it seriously, the way we've done with the First Amendment, say, or with the Thirteenth, the one forbidding open and avowed slavery. And by taking the Second Amendment seriously I mean taking it literally. We should "close read" it and thus focus lots of attention on the grammatical reasoning of its two clauses. This might shame the NRA into pulling the dependent clause out of the closet, displaying it on its façade, and accepting its not entirely pleasant implications. These could be particularized in an Act of Congress providing:

(1) that the Militia shall now, after these many years, be "well-regulated," as the Constitution requires.

(2) that any person who has chosen to possess at home a gun of any kind, and who is not a member of the police or the military or an appropriate government agency, shall be deemed to have enrolled automatically in the Militia of the United States. Members of the Militia, who will be issued identifying badges, will be organized in units of battalion, company, or platoon size representing counties, towns, or boroughs. If they bear arms while not proceeding to or from scheduled exercises of the Militia, they will be punished "as a court martial may direct."

(3) that any gun owner who declines to join the regulated Militia may opt out by selling his firearms to the federal government for $1,000 each. He will sign an undertaking that if he ever again owns firearms he will be considered to have enlisted in the Militia.

(4) that because the Constitution specifically requires that the Militia shall be "well regulated," a regular training program, of the sort familiar to all who have belonged to military units charged with the orderly management of small arms, shall be instituted. This will require at least eight hours of drill each Saturday at some convenient field or park, rain or shine or snow or ice. There will be weekly supervised target practice (separation from the service, publicly announced, for those who can't hit a barn door). And there will be ample practice in digging simple defense works, like foxholes and trenches, as well as necessary sanitary installations like field latrines and straddle trenches. Each summer there will be a six-week bivouac (without spouses), and this, like all the other exercises, will be under the close supervision of long-service noncommissioned officers of the United States Army and the Marine Corps. On bivouac, liquor will be forbidden under extreme penalty, but there will be an issue every Friday night of two cans of 3.2 beer, and feeding will follow traditional military lines, the cuisine consisting largely of shit-on-a-shingle, sandwiches made of bull dick (baloney) and choke-ass (cheese), beans, and fatty pork. On Sundays and holidays, powdered eggs for breakfast. Chlorinated water will often be available, in Lister Bags. Further obligatory exercises designed to toughen up the Militia will include twenty-five-mile hikes and the negotiation of obstacle courses. In addition, there will be instruction of the sort appropriate to other lightly armed, well-regulated military units: in map-reading, the erection of double-apron barbed-wire fences, and the rudiments of military courtesy and the traditions of the Militia, beginning with the Minute Men. Per diem payments will be made to those participating in these exercises.

(5) that since the purpose of the Militia is, as the Constitution says, to safeguard "the security of a free state," at times when invasion threatens (perhaps now the threat will come from Nicaragua, national security no longer being menaced by North Vietnam) all

units of the Militia will be trucked to the borders for the duration of the emergency, there to remain in field conditions (here's where the practice in latrine-digging pays off) until Congress declares that the emergency has passed. Congress may also order the Militia to perform other duties consistent with its constitutional identity as a regulated volunteer force: for example, flood and emergency and disaster service (digging, sandbag filling, rescuing old people); patrolling angry or incinerated cities; or controlling crowds at large public events like patriotic parades, motor races, and professional football games.

(6) that failure to appear for these scheduled drills, practices, bivouacs, and mobilizations shall result in the Militiaperson's dismissal from the service and forfeiture of badge, pay, and firearm.

Why did the Framers of the Constitution add the word *bear* to the phrase "keep and bear arms?" Because they conceived that keeping arms at home implied the public obligation to bear them in a regulated way for "the security of" not a private household but "a free state." If interstate bus fares can be regulated, it is hard to see why the Militia can't be, especially since the Constitution says it must be. *The New Republic* has recognized that "the Second Amendment to the Constitution clearly connects the right to bear arms to the eighteenth-century national need to raise a militia." But it goes on: "That need is now obsolete, and so is the amendment." And it concludes: "If the only way this country can get control of firearms is to amend the Constitution, then it's time for Congress to get the process under way."

I think not. Rather, it's time not to amend Article II of the Bill of Rights (and Obligations) but to read it, publicize it, embrace it, and enforce it. That the Second Amendment stems from concerns that can be stigmatized as "eighteenth-century" cuts little ice. The First Amendment stems precisely from such concerns, and no one but Yahoos wants to amend it. Also "eighteenth-century" is that lovely bit in Section 9 of Article I forbidding any "Title of Nobility" to be granted by the United States. That's why we've been spared Lord Annenberg and Sir Leonard Bernstein, Knight. Thank God for the eighteenth century, I say. It understood not just what a firearm is and what a Militia is. It also understood what "well regulated" means. It knew how to compose a constitutional article and it knew how to read it. And it assumed that everyone, gun lobbyists and touring students alike, would understand and correctly quote it. Both halves of it.

The Reader's Presence

1. Here is the Second Amendment of the Bill of Rights: "A well-regulated Militia being necessary to the security of a free state, the right of the people to keep and bear arms shall not be infringed."

Why does Fussell point out that the first part of the amendment does not appear on the marble facade of the National Rifle Association headquarters in Washington, D.C.? Why does he believe that the first half of the amendment is crucial to a correct understanding of the second half? Do you agree? Can you think of an alternative interpretation?

2. Though he is a proponent of gun control, why doesn't Fussell believe the Second Amendment should be repealed or revised? In what ways does his interpretation preserve the Second Amendment? Do you think the National Rifle Association would endorse Fussell's proposal? Do you think it would support any aspects of it? Explain.

3. Suppose Congress took Fussell's proposal seriously. Could it enact the kind of regulations Fussell recommends? What practical problems might arise? For example, how would the Militia be maintained? How expensive would it be? What parts of Fussell's plan do you think are meant to be taken seriously? What parts are intended as humorous? How can you tell the difference?

97

John Grisham

Unnatural Killers

Known for his best-selling suspense novels, John Grisham (b. 1955) received his law degree from the University of Mississippi in 1981 and practiced law for many years, specializing in criminal and civil law. While an elected member of the state house of representatives from 1983 to 1990, Grisham worked to improve the educational system in Mississippi. During the end of his tenure in the state legislature, Grisham, inspired by his legal experience, wrote his first novel, A Time to Kill (1989). His second novel, The Firm (1991), launched Grisham's successful writing career; it sold millions of copies and was on the New York Times bestseller list for forty-seven weeks. Grisham's other novels include The Pelican Brief (1992), The Rainmaker (1996), and The Testament (1999). "Unnatural Killers" appeared in the Oxford American in 1998.

The town of Hernando, Mississippi, has five thousand people, more or less, and is the seat of government for DeSoto County. It is peaceful and quiet, with an old courthouse in the center of the square. Memphis is only fifteen minutes away, to the north, straight up Interstate 55. To the west is Tunica County, now booming with casino fever and drawing thousands of tourists.

For ten years I was a lawyer in Southaven, a suburb to the north, and the Hernando courthouse was my hangout. I tried many cases in the main courtroom. I drank coffee with the courthouse regulars, ate in the small cafes around the square, visited my clients in the nearby jail.

It was in the courthouse that I first met Mr. Bill Savage. I didn't know much about him back then, just that he was soft-spoken, exceedingly polite, always ready with a smile and a warm greeting. In 1983, when I first announced my intentions to seek an office in the state legislature, Mr. Savage stopped me in the second-floor rotunda of the courthouse and offered me his encouragement and good wishes.

A few months later, on election night as the votes were tallied and the results announced to a rowdy throng camped on the courthouse lawn, it became apparent that I would win my race. Mr. Savage found me and expressed his congratulations. "The people have trusted you," he said. "Don't let them down."

He was active in local affairs, a devout Christian and solid citizen   5
who believed in public service and was always ready to volunteer. For thirty years, he worked as the manager of a cotton gin two miles outside Hernando on a highway that is heavily used by gamblers anxious to get to the casinos in Tunica.

Around five P.M., on March 7, 1995, someone entered Bill Savage's office next to the gin, shot him twice in the head at point-blank range, and took his wallet, which contained a few credit cards and two hundred dollars.

There were no witnesses. No one heard gunshots. His body was discovered later by an insurance salesman making a routine call.

The crime scene yielded few clues. There were no signs of a struggle. Other than the bullets found in the body, there was little physical evidence. And since Bill Savage was not the kind of person to create ill will or maintain enemies, investigators had nowhere to start. They formed the opinion that he was murdered by outsiders who'd stopped by for a fast score, then hit the road again, probably toward the casinos.

It had to be a simple robbery. Why else would anybody want to murder Bill Savage?

The townspeople of Hernando were stunned. Life in the shadows of   10
Memphis had numbed many of them to the idea of random violence, but here was one of their own, a man known to all, a man who, as he went about his daily affairs, minding his own business, was killed in his office just two miles from the courthouse.

The next day, in Ponchatoula, Louisiana, three hundred miles south, and again just off Interstate 55, Patsy Byers was working the late shift at a convenience store. She was thirty-five years old, a happily married mother of three, including an eighteen-year-old who was about to graduate from high school. Patsy had never worked outside the home, but had taken the job to earn a few extra dollars to help with the bills.

Around midnight, a young woman entered the convenience store and walked to a rack where she grabbed three chocolate bars. As she approached the checkout counter, Patsy Byers noticed the candy, but she didn't notice the .38. The young woman thrust it forward, pulled the trigger, and shot Patsy in the throat.

The bullet instantly severed Patsy's spinal cord, and she fell to the floor bleeding. The young woman screamed and fled the store, leaving Patsy paralyzed under the cash register.

The girl returned. She'd forgotten the part about the robbery. When she saw Patsy she said, "Oh, you're not dead yet."

Patsy began to plead. "Don't kill me," she kept saying to the girl who 15
stepped over her and tried in vain to open the cash register. She asked Patsy how to open it. Patsy explained it as best she could. The girl fled with $105 in cash, leaving Patsy, once again, to die.

But Patsy did not die, though she will be a quadriplegic for the rest of her life.

The shooting and robbery was captured on the store's surveillance camera, and the video was soon broadcast on the local news. Several full facial shots of the girl were shown.

The girl, however, vanished. Weeks, and then months, passed without the slightest hint to her identity making itself known.

Authorities in Louisiana had no knowledge of the murder of Bill Savage, and authorities in Mississippi had no knowledge of the shooting of Patsy Byers, and neither state had reason to suspect the two shootings were committed by the same people.

The crimes, it was clear, were not committed by sophisticated crimi- 20
nals. Soon two youths began bragging about their exploits. And then an anonymous informant whispered to officials in Louisiana that a certain young woman in Oklahoma was involved in the shooting of Patsy Byers.

The young woman was Sarah Edmondson, age nineteen, the daughter of a state court judge in Muskogee, Oklahoma. Her uncle is the Attorney General of Oklahoma. Her grandfather once served as Congressman, and her great uncle was Governor and then later a U.S. Senator. Sarah Edmondson was arrested on June 2, 1995, at her parents' home, and suddenly the pieces fell into place.

Sarah and her boyfriend, Benjamin Darras, age eighteen, had drifted south in early March. The reason for the journey has not been made clear. One version has them headed for Florida so that Ben could finally see the ocean. Another has them aiming at New Orleans and Mardi Gras. And a third is that they wanted to see the Grateful Dead concert in Memphis, but, not surprisingly, got the dates mixed-up.

At any rate, they stumbled through Hernando on March 7, and stayed just long enough, Sarah says, to kill and rob Bill Savage. Then they raced deeper south until they ran out of money. They decided to pull another heist. This is when Patsy Byers met them.

Though Sarah and Ben have different socioeconomic backgrounds, they made a suitable match. Sarah, a member of one of Oklahoma's most prominent political families, began using drugs and alcohol at the age of thirteen. At fourteen she was locked up for psychiatric treatment. She has admitted to a history of serious drug abuse. She managed to finish high school, with honors, but then dropped out of college.

Ben's family is far less prominent. His father was an alcoholic who   25
divorced Ben's mother twice, then later committed suicide. Ben too has a history of drug abuse and psychiatric treatment. He dropped out of high school. Somewhere along the way he met Sarah, and for awhile they lived the great American romance—the young, troubled, mindless drifters surviving on love.

Once they were arrested, lawyers got involved, and the love affair came to a rapid end. Sarah blames Ben for the killing of Bill Savage. Ben blames Sarah for the shooting of Patsy Byers. Sarah has better lawyers, and it appears she will also attempt to blame Ben for somehow controlling her in such a manner that she had no choice but to rob the store and shoot Patsy Byers. Ben, evidently, will have none of this. It looks as if he will claim his beloved Sarah went into the store only to rob it, that he had no idea whatsoever that she planned to shoot anyone, that, as he waited outside in the getaway car, he was horrified when he heard a gunshot. And so on.

It should be noted here that neither Ben nor Sarah have yet been tried for any of these crimes. They have not been found guilty of anything, yet. But as the judicial wheels begin to turn, deals are being negotiated and cut. Pacts are being made.

Sarah's lawyers managed to reach an immunity agreement with the State of Mississippi in the Savage case. Evidently, she will testify against Ben, and in return will not be prosecuted. Her troubles will be confined to Louisiana, and if convicted for the attempted murder of Patsy Byers and the robbing of the store, Sarah could face life in prison. If Ben is found guilty of murdering and robbing Bill Savage, he will most likely face death by lethal injection at the state penitentiary in Parchman, Mississippi. Juries in Hernando are notorious for quick death verdicts.[1]

On January 24, 1996, during a preliminary hearing in Louisiana, Sarah testified, under oath, about the events leading up to both crimes. It is from this reported testimony that the public first heard the appalling details of both crimes.

According to Sarah, she and Ben decided to travel to Memphis to see   30
the Grateful Dead. They packed canned food and blankets, and left the

---

[1]Darras received a sentence of life without parole, and Edmondson is currently doing thirty-five years in an Oklahoma prison. Her lighter sentence may not be due so much to her family connections as to the fact that her victim died of unrelated cancer in 1997.—EDS.

morning of March 6. Sarah also packed her father's .38, just in case Ben happened to attack her for some reason. Shortly before leaving Oklahoma, they watched the Oliver Stone movie *Natural Born Killers.*

For those fortunate enough to have missed *Natural Born Killers,* it is the repulsive story of two mindless young lovers, Mickey (Woody Harrelson) and Mallory (Juliette Lewis), who blaze their way across the Southwest, killing everything in their path while becoming famous. According to the script, they indiscriminately kill fifty-two people before they are caught. It seems like many more. Then they manage to kill at least fifty more as they escape from prison. They free themselves, have children, and are last seen happily rambling down the highway in a Winnebago.

Ben loved *Natural Born Killers,* and as they drove to Memphis he spoke openly of killing people, randomly, just like Mickey spoke to Mallory. He mentioned the idea of seizing upon a remote farmhouse, murdering all its occupants, then moving on to the next slaughter. Just like Mickey and Mallory.

We do not know, as of yet, what role Sarah played in these discussions. It is, of course, her testimony we're forced to rely upon, and she claims to have been opposed to Ben's hallucinations.

They left Memphis after learning the concert was still a few days away, and headed south. Between Memphis and Hernando, Ben again talked of finding an isolated farmhouse and killing a bunch of people. Sarah said it sounded like he was fantasizing from the movie. They left Interstate 55, drove through Hernando and onto the highway leading to the cotton gin where Bill Savage was working in his office.

Ben was quite anxious to kill someone, she says.   35

He professed a sudden hatred for farmers. This was the place where they would kill, he said, and told Sarah to stop the car a short distance away so he could test-fire the gun. It worked. They then drove to the gin, parked next to Bill Savage's small office. Ben told her to act "angelic," and then they went inside.

Ben asked Bill Savage for directions to Interstate 55. Sarah says that Mr. Savage knew they were up to something. As he gave directions, he walked around the desk toward Ben, at which point Ben removed the .38 and shot Mr. Savage in the head. "He threw up his hands and made a horrible sound," she testified. There was a brief struggle between the two men, a struggle that ended when Ben shot Mr. Savage for the second time.

Sarah claims to have been so shocked by Ben's actions that she started to run outside, then, after a quick second thought, decided to stand by her man. Together they rummaged through Mr. Savage's pockets and took his wallet.

Back in the car, Ben removed the credit cards from the wallet, threw the driver's license out the window, and found two one-hundred-dollar bills. According to Sarah, "Ben mocked the noise the man made when Ben shot him. Ben was laughing about what happened and said the feeling of killing was powerful."

You see, the Mickey character in *Natural Born Killers* felt much the   40
same way. He sneered and laughed a lot when he killed people, and then
he sneered and laughed some more after he killed them. He felt powerful.
Murder for Mickey was the ultimate thrill. It was glorious. Murder was a
mystical experience, nothing to be ashamed of and certainly nothing to be
remorseful about. In fact, remorse was a sign of weakness. Mickey was,
after all, a self-described "natural born killer." And Mickey encouraged
Mallory to kill.

Ben encouraged Sarah.

After the murder of Mr. Savage, he and Sarah drove to New Orleans,
where they roamed the streets of the French Quarter. Ben repeatedly assured Sarah that he felt no aftershocks from committing the murder. He
felt fine. Just like Mickey. He pressed her repeatedly to kill someone herself. "It's your turn," he kept saying. And, "We're partners."

Sarah, as might be expected, claims she was completely repulsed by
Ben's demands that she slay the next person. She claims that she considered killing herself as an alternative to surrendering to Ben's demands
that she shed blood.

But Sarah did not kill herself. Instead, she and Ben drove to Ponchatoula for their ill-fated meeting with Patsy Byers.

According to Sarah, she did not want to rob the store, and she cer-   45
tainly didn't wish to shoot anyone. But they were out of money, and, just
like Mickey and Mallory, robbery was the most convenient way to survive. Ben selected the store, and, through some yet-to-be-determined variety of coercion, forced her out of the car and into the store, with the gun.
It was, after all, her turn to kill.

In *Natural Born Killers,* we are expected to believe that Mickey and
Mallory are tormented by demons, and that they are forced to commit
many of their heinous murders, not because they are brainless young idiots, but because evil forces propel them. They both suffered through horrible, dysfunctional childhoods, their parents were abusive, etc. Demons
have them in their clutches, and haunt them, and stalk them, and make
them slaughter fifty-two people.

This demonic theme, so as not to be missed by even the simplest
viewer, recurs, it seems, every five minutes in the movie.

Guess what Sarah Edmondson saw when she approached the checkout stand and looked at Patsy Byers? She didn't see a thirty-five-year-old
woman next to the cash register. No.

She saw a "demon." And so she shot it.

Then she ran from the store. Ben, waiting in the car, asked where the   50
money was. Sarah said she forgot to take the money. Ben insisted she return to the store and rob the cash register.

We can trust the judicial systems of both Mississippi and Louisiana
to effectively deal with the aftermath of the Sarah and Ben romance. Ab-

sent a fluke, Sarah will spend the rest of her life behind bars in a miserable prison and Ben will be sent to death row at Parchman, where he'll endure an indescribable hell before facing execution. Their families will never be the same. And their families deserve compassion.

The wife and children and countless friends of Bill Savage have already begun the healing process, though the loss is beyond measure.

Patsy Byers is a quadriplegic for life, confined to a wheelchair, faced with enormous medical bills, unable to hug her children or do any one of a million things she did before she met Sarah Edmondson. She's already filed a civil suit against the Edmondson family, but her prospects of a meaningful physical recovery are dim.

A question remains: Are there other players in this tragic episode? Can fault be shared?

I think so.   55

Troubled as they were, Ben and Sarah had no history of violence. Their crime spree was totally out of character. They were confused, disturbed, shiftless, mindless—the adjectives can be heaped on with shovels—but they had never hurt anyone before.

Before, that is, they saw a movie. A horrific movie that glamorized casual mayhem and bloodlust. A movie made with the intent of glorifying random murder.

Oliver Stone has said that *Natural Born Killers* was meant to be a satire on our culture's appetite for violence and the media's craving for it. But Oliver Stone always takes the high ground in defending his dreadful movies. A satire is supposed to make fun of whatever it is attacking. But there is no humor in *Natural Born Killers*. It is a relentlessly bloody story designed to shock us and to further numb us to the senselessness of reckless murder. The film wasn't made with the intent of stimulating morally depraved young people to commit similar crimes, but such a result can hardly be a surprise.

Oliver Stone is saying that murder is cool and fun, murder is a high, a rush, murder is a drug to be used at will. The more you kill, the cooler you are. You can be famous and become a media darling with your face on magazine covers. You can get by with it. You will not be punished.

It is inconceivable to expect either Stone or the studio executives to   60
take responsibility for the aftereffects of their movie. Hollywood has never done so; instead, it hides behind its standard pious First Amendment arguments, and it pontificates about the necessities of artistic freedom of expression. Its apologists can go on, ad nauseam, about how meaningful even the most pathetic film is to social reform.

It's no surprise that *Natural Born Killers* has inspired several young people to commit murder. Sadly, Ben and Sarah aren't the only kids now locked away and charged with murder in copycat crimes. Since the release of the movie, at least several cases have been reported in which random killings were executed by troubled young people who claim they were all under the influence, to some degree, of Mickey and Mallory.

Any word from Oliver Stone?

Of course not.

I'm sure he would disclaim all responsibility. And he'd preach a bit about how important the film is as a commentary on the media's insatiable appetite for violence. If pressed, he'd probably say that there are a lot of crazies out there, and he can't be held responsible for what they might do. He's an *artist* and he can't be bothered with the effects of what he produces.

I can think of only two ways to curb the excessive violence of a film   65
like *Natural Born Killers*. Both involve large sums of money — the only medium understood by Hollywood.

The first way would be a general boycott of similar films. If people refused to purchase tickets to watch such an orgy of violence as *Natural Born Killers,* then similar movies wouldn't be made. Hollywood is pious, but only to a point. It will defend its crassest movies on the grounds that they are necessary for social introspection, or that they need to test the limits of artistic expression, or that they can ignore the bounds of decency as long as these movies label themselves as satire. This all works fine if the box office is busy. But let the red ink flow and Hollywood suddenly has a keen interest in rediscovering what's mainstream.

Unfortunately, boycotts don't seem to work. The viewing public is a large, eclectic body, and there are usually enough curious filmgoers to sustain a controversial work.

So, forget boycotts.

The second and last hope of imposing some sense of responsibility on Hollywood, will come through another great American tradition, the lawsuit. Think of a movie as a product, something created and brought to market, not too dissimilar from breast implants, Honda three-wheelers, and Ford Pintos. Though the law has yet to declare movies to be products, it is only one small step away. If something goes wrong with the product, whether by design or defect, and injury ensues, then its makers are held responsible.

A case can be made that there exists a direct causal link between the   70
movie *Natural Born Killers* and the death of Bill Savage. Viewed another way, the question should be: Would Ben have shot innocent people *but for* the movie? Nothing in his troubled past indicates violent propensities. But once he saw the movie, he fantasized about killing, and his fantasies finally drove them to their crimes.

The notion of holding filmmakers and studios legally responsible for their products has always been met with guffaws from the industry.

But the laughing will soon stop. It will take only one large verdict against the likes of Oliver Stone, and his production company, and perhaps the screenwriter, and the studio itself, and then the party will be over. The verdict will come from the heartland, far away from Southern California, in some small courtroom with no cameras. A jury will finally say enough is enough; that the demons placed in Sarah Edmondson's mind were not solely of her making.

Once a precedent is set, the litigation will become contagious, and the money will become enormous. Hollywood will suddenly discover a desire to rein itself in.

The landscape of American jurisprudence is littered with the remains of large, powerful corporations which once thought themselves bullet-proof and immune from responsibility for their actions. Sadly, Hollywood will have to be forced to shed some of its own blood before it learns to police itself.

Even sadder, the families of Bill Savage and Patsy Byers can only   75
mourn and try to pick up the pieces, and wonder why such a wretched film was allowed to be made.

The Reader's Presence

1. Grisham begins his argument with a story from his experience as a lawyer. Why does he choose Ben and Sarah to illustrate his point? Suppose he had not been personally acquainted with the case, but related it from a newspaper story, or instead listed statistics on "killers"? Would his argument be more, or less, effective? Why or why not?

2. Grisham proposes legal action to "curb the excessive violence" of such films like *Natural Born Killers*. Can you think of other possibilities, or counterproposals? Is Grisham's proposal convincing? Why or why not? Can Grisham's argument be applied to the 1999 high school murders in Columbine, Colorado? Why or why not?

3. The essay argues that life imitates popular culture. However, it might also be argued that Stone's film was based on the behavior of real-life killers—that is, that popular culture imitates life. Homicide had been a very common fact of American life long before movies, television, and electronic media were ever imagined. Why do we try to explain murder today by blaming the media?

98

Vicki Hearne

What's Wrong with Animal Rights

Vicki Hearne (b. 1946) has had a unique career as a poet, author, and animal trainer, and has taught creative writing at Yale University and at the University of California. She has written three volumes of poetry, Nervous Horses *(1980),* In the Absence of Horses *(1983), and* The Parts of Light *(1994). Hearne is known for her ability to train aggressive dogs (particularly pit bull terriers), and she wrote an account of her experiences in* Bandit: Dossier of a Dangerous Dog *(1991). Her other books include* Adam's Task: Calling Animals by Name *(1987),* The White German Shepherd *(1988), and* Animal Happiness *(1994). "What's Wrong with Animal Rights" was originally published in* Harper's *in 1991 and was selected for* The Best American Essays 1992.

Not all happy animals are alike. A Doberman going over a hurdle after a small wooden dumbbell is sleek, all arcs of harmonious power. A basset hound cheerfully performing the same exercise exhibits harmonies of a more lugubrious nature. There are chimpanzees who love precision the way musicians or fanatical housekeepers or accomplished hypochondriacs do; others for whom happiness is a matter of invention and variation—chimp vaudevillians. There is a rhinoceros whose happiness, as near as I can make out, is in needing to be trained every morning, all over again, or else he "forgets" his circus routine, and in this you find a clue to the slow, deep, quiet chuckle of his happiness and to the glory of the beast. Happiness for Secretariat is in his ebullient bound, that joyful length of stride. For the draft horse or the weight-pull dog, happiness is of a different shape, more awesome and less obviously intelligent. When the pulling horse is at its most intense, the animal goes into himself, allocating all of the educated power that organizes his desire to dwell in fierce and delicate intimacy with that power, leans into the harness, and MAKES THAT SUCKER MOVE.

If we are speaking of human beings and use the phrase "animal happiness," we tend to mean something like "creature comforts." The emblems of this are the golden retriever rolling in the grass, the horse with his nose deep in the oats, the kitty by the fire. Creature comforts are important to animals—"Grub first, then ethics" is a motto that would describe many a wise Labrador retriever, and I have a pit bull named Annie whose continual quest for the perfect pillow inspires her to awesome feats. But there is something more to animals, a capacity for satisfactions that come from work in the fullest sense—what is known in philosophy and in this country's Declaration of Independence as "happiness." This is a sense of personal achievement, like the satisfaction felt by a good woodcarver or a dancer or a poet or an accomplished dressage horse. It is a happiness that, like the artist's must come from something within the animal, something trainers call "talent." Hence, it cannot be imposed on the animal. But it is also something that does not come *ex nihilo*. If it had not been a fairly ordinary thing, in one part of the world, to teach young children to play the pianoforte, it is doubtful that Mozart's music would exist.

Happiness is often misunderstood as a synonym for pleasure or as an antonym for suffering. But Aristotle associated happiness with ethics—codes of behavior that urge us toward the sensation of getting it right, a kind of work that yields the "click" of satisfaction upon solving a problem or surmounting an obstacle. In his *Ethics,* Aristotle wrote, "If happiness is activity in accordance with excellence, it is reasonable that it should be in accordance with the highest excellence." Thomas Jefferson identified the capacity for happiness as one of the three fundamental rights on which all others are based: "life, liberty, and the pursuit of happiness."

I bring up this idea of happiness as a form of work because I am an animal trainer, and work is the foundation of the happiness a trainer and an animal discover together. I bring up these words also because they cannot be found in the lexicon of the animal-rights movement. This absence accounts for the uneasiness toward the movement of most people, who sense that rights advocates have a point but take it too far when they liberate snails or charge that goldfish at the county fair are suffering. But the problem with the animal-rights advocates is not that they take it too far; it's that they've got it all wrong.

Animal rights are built upon a misconceived premise that rights were created to prevent us from unnecessary suffering. You can't find an animal-rights book, video, pamphlet, or rock concert in which someone doesn't mention the Great Sentence, written by Jeremy Bentham in 1789. Arguing in favor of such rights, Bentham wrote: "The question is not, Can they *reason?* nor, can they *talk?* but, can they suffer?"

The logic of the animal-rights movement places suffering at the iconographic center of a skewed value system. The thinking of its proponents—given eerie expression in a virtually sado-pornographic sculpture of a tortured monkey that won a prize for its compassionate vision—has collapsed into a perverse conundrum. Today the loudest voices calling for—demanding—the destruction of animals are the humane

5

organizations. This is an inevitable consequence of the apotheosis of the drive to relieve suffering: death is the ultimate release. To compensate for their contradictions, the humane movement has demonized, in this century and the last, those who made animal happiness their business: veterinarians, trainers, and the like. We think of Louis Pasteur as the man whose work saved you and me and your dog and cat from rabies, but antivivisectionists of the time claimed that rabies increased in areas where there were Pasteur Institutes.

An anti-rabies public relations campaign mounted in England in the 1880s by the Royal Society for the Prevention of Cruelty to Animals and other organizations led to orders being issued to club any dog found not wearing a muzzle. England still has her cruel and unnecessary law that requires an animal to spend six months in quarantine before being allowed loose in the country. Most of the recent propaganda about pit bulls—the crazy claim that they "take hold with their front teeth while they chew away with their rear teeth" (which would imply, incorrectly, that they have double jaws)—can be traced to literature published by the Humane Society of the United States during the fall of 1987 and earlier. If your neighbors want your dog or horse impounded and destroyed because he is a nuisance—say the dog barks, or the horse attracts flies—it will be the local Humane Society to whom your neighbors turn for action.

In a way, everyone has the opportunity to know that the history of the humane movement is largely a history of miseries, arrests, prosecutions, and death. The Humane Society is the pound, the place with the decompression chamber or the lethal injections. You occasionally find worried letters about this in Ann Landers's column.

Animal-rights publications are illustrated largely with photographs of two kinds of animals—"Helpless Fluff" and "Agonized Fluff," the two conditions in which some people seem to prefer their animals, because any other version of an animal is too complicated for propaganda. In the introduction to his book *Animal Liberation,* Peter Singer says somewhat smugly that he and his wife have no animals and, in fact, don't much care for them. This is offered as evidence of his objectivity and ethical probity. But it strikes me as an odd, perhaps, obscene underpinning for an ethical project that encourages university and high school students to cherish their ignorance of, say, great bird dogs as proof of their devotion to animals.

I would like to leave these philosophers behind, for they are inept   10 connoisseurs of suffering who might revere my Airedale for his capacity to scream when subjected to a blowtorch but not for his wit and courage, not for his natural good manners that are a gentle rebuke to ours. I want to celebrate the moment not long ago when, at his first dog show, my Airedale, Drummer, learned that there can be a public place where his work is respected. I want to celebrate his meticulousness, his happiness upon realizing at the dog show that no one would swoop down upon him and swamp him with the goo-goo excesses known as the "teddy-bear complex" but that people actually got out of his way, gave him room to work. I want to say, "There can be a six-and-a-half-month-old puppy who can care about accuracy, who can be fastidious, and whose fastidiousness will be a foundation for courage later." I want to say, "Leave my puppy alone!"

I want to leave the philosophers behind, but I cannot, in part because the philosophical problems that plague academicians of the animal-rights movement are illuminating. They wonder, do animals have rights or do they have interests? Or, if these rightists lead particularly unexamined lives, they dismiss that question as obvious (yes, of course animals have rights, prima facie) and proceed to enumerate them, James Madison style. This leads to the issuance of bills of rights—the right to an environment, the right not to be used in medical experiments—and other forms of trivialization.

The calculus of suffering can be turned against the philosophers of festering flesh, even in the case of food animals, or exotic animals who perform in movies and circuses. It is true that it hurts to be slaughtered by man, but it doesn't hurt nearly as much as some of the cunningly cruel arrangements, meted out by "Mother Nature." In Africa, 75 percent of the lions cubbed do not survive to the age of two. For those who make it to two, the average age at death is ten years. Asali, the movie and TV lioness, was still working at age twenty-one. There are fates worse than death, but twenty-one years of a close working relationship with Hubert Wells, Asali's trainer, is not one of them. Dorset sheep and polled Herefords would not exist at all were they not in a symbiotic relationship with human beings.

A human being living in the "wild"—somewhere, say, without the benefits of medicine and advanced social organization—would probably have a life expectancy of from thirty to thirty-five years. A human being living in "captivity"—in, say, a middle-class neighborhood of what the Centers for Disease Control call a Metropolitan Statistical Area—has a life expectancy of seventy or more years. For orangutans in the wild in Borneo and Malaysia, the life expectancy is thirty-five years; in captivity, fifty years. The wild is not a suffering-free zone or all that frolicsome a location.

The questions asked by animal-rights activists are flawed, because they are built on the concept that the origin of rights is in the avoidance of suffering rather than in the pursuit of happiness. The question that needs to be asked—and that will put us in closer proximity to the truth—is not, do they have rights? or, what are those rights? but rather, what is a right?

Rights originate in committed relationships and can be found, both 15 intact and violated, wherever one finds such relationships—in social compacts, within families, between animals, and between people and nonhuman animals. This is as true when the nonhuman animals in question are lions or parakeets as when they are dogs. It is my Airedale whose excellencies have my attention at the moment, so it is with reference to him that I will consider the question, what is a right?

When I imagine situations in which it naturally arises that A defends or honors or respects B's rights, I imagine situations in which the relationship between A and B can be indicated with a possessive pronoun. I might say, "Leave her alone, she's my daughter" or "That's what she wants, and she is my daughter. I think I am bound to honor her wants." Similarly, "Leave her alone, she's my mother." I am more tender of the happiness of my mother, my father, my child, than I am of other people's family members; more tender of my friends' happinesses than your friends' happinesses, unless you and I have a mutual friend.

Possession of a being by another has come into more and more disrepute, so that the common understanding of one person possessing another is slavery. But the important detail about the kind of possessive pronoun that I have in mind is reciprocity: if I have a friend, she has a friend. If I have a daughter, she has a mother. The possessive does not bind one of us while freeing the other; it cannot do that. Moreover, should the mother reject the daughter, the word that applies is "disown." The form of disowning that most often appears in the news is domestic violence. Parents abuse children; husbands batter wives.

Some cases of reciprocal possessives have built-in limitations, such as "my patient / my doctor" or "my student / my teacher" or "my agent / my client." Other possessive relations are extremely limited but still remarkably binding: "my neighbor" and "my country" and "my president."

The responsibilities and the ties signaled by reciprocal possession typically are hard to dissolve. It can be as difficult to give up an enemy as to give up a friend, and often the one becomes the other, as though the logic of the possessive pronoun outlasts the forms it chanced to take at a given moment, as though we were stuck with one another. In these bindings, nearly inextricable, are found the origin of our rights. They imply a possessiveness but also recognize an acknowledgment by each side of the other's existence.

The idea of democracy is dependent on the citizens' having knowl-   20
edge of the government; that is, realizing that the government exists and knowing how to claim rights against it. I know this much because I get mail from the government and see its "representatives" running about in uniforms. Whether I actually have any rights in relationship to the government is less clear, but the idea that I do is symbolized by the right to vote. I obey the government, and, in theory, it obeys me, by counting my ballot, reading the *Miranda* warning to me, agreeing to be bound by the Constitution. My friend obeys me as I obey her; the government "obeys" me to some extent, and, to a different extent, I obey it.

What kind of thing can my Airedale, Drummer, have knowledge of? He can know that I exist and through that knowledge can claim his happinesses, with varying degrees of success, both with me and against me. Drummer can also know about larger human or dog communities than the one that consists only of him and me. There is my household—the other dogs, the cats, my husband. I have had enough dogs on campuses to know that he can learn that Yale exists as a neighborhood or village. My older dog, Annie, not only knows that Yale exists but can tell Yalies from townies, as I learned while teaching there during labor troubles.

Dogs can have elaborate conceptions of human social structures, and even of something like their rights and responsibilities within them, but these conceptions are never elaborate enough to construct a rights relationship between a dog and the state, or a dog and the Humane Society. Both of these are concepts that depend on writing and memoranda, officers in uniform, plaques and seals of authority. All of these are literary constructs, and all of them are beyond a dog's ken, which is why the mail carrier who doesn't also happen to be a dog's friend is forever an intruder—this is why dogs bark at mailmen.

It is clear enough that natural rights relations can arise between people and animals. Drummer, for example, can insist, "Hey, let's go outside and do something!" if I have been at my computer several days on end. He can both refuse to accept various of my suggestions and tell me when he fears for his life—such as the time when the huge, white flapping flag appeared out of nowhere, as it seemed to him, on the town green one evening when we were working. I can (and do) say to him either, "Oh, you don't have to worry about that" or, "Uh oh, you're right, Drum, that guy looks dangerous." Just as the government and I—two different species of organism—have developed improvised ways of communicating, such as the vote, so Drummer and I have worked out a number of ways to make our expressions known. Largely through obedience, I have taught him a fair amount about how to get responses from me. Obedience is reciprocal; you cannot get responses from a dog to whom you do not respond accurately. I have enfranchised him in a relationship to me by educating him, creating the conditions by which he can achieve a certain happiness specific to a dog, maybe even specific to an Airedale, inasmuch as this same relationship has allowed me to plumb the happiness of being a trainer and writing this article.

Instructions in this happiness are given terms that are alien to a culture in which liver treats, fluffy windup toys, and miniature sweaters are confused with respect and work. Jack Knox, a sheepdog trainer originally from Scotland, will shake his crook at a novice handler who makes a promiscuous move to praise a dog, and will call out in his Scottish accent, "Eh! Eh! Get back, get BACK! Ye'll no be abusin' the dogs like that in my clinic." America is a nation of abused animals. Knox says, because we are always swooping at them with praise, "no gi'ing them their freedom." I am reminded of Rainer Maria Rilke's account in which the Prodigal Son leaves—has to leave—because everyone loves him, even the dogs love him, and he has no path to the delicate and fierce truth of himself. Unconditional praise and love, in Rilke's story, disenfranchise us, distract us from what truly excites our interest.

In the minds of some trainers and handlers, praise is dishonesty.   25
Paradoxically, it is a kind of contempt for animals that masquerades as a
reverence for helplessness and suffering. The idea of freedom means that
you do not, at least not while Jack Knox is nearby, helpfully guide your
dog through the motions of, say, herding over and over—what one
trainer calls "explainy-wainy." This is rote learning. It works tolerably
well on some handlers, because people have vast unconscious minds and
can store complex preprogrammed behaviors. Dogs, on the other hand,
have almost no unconscious minds, so they can learn only by thinking.
Many children are like this until educated out of it.

If I tell my Airedale to sit and stay on the town green, and someone
comes up and burbles, "What a pretty thing you are," he may break his
stay to go for a caress. I pull him back and correct him for breaking. Now
he holds his stay because I have blocked his way to movement but not because I have punished him. (A correction blocks one path as it opens another for desire to work; punishment blocks desire and opens nothing.)
He holds his stay now, and—because the stay opens this possibility of
work, new to a heedless young dog—he watches. If the person goes on
talking, and isn't going to gush with praise, I may heel Drummer out of
his stay and give him an "Okay" to make friends. Sometimes something
about the person makes Drummer feel that reserve is in order. He responds to an insincere approach by sitting still, going down into himself,
and thinking. "This person has no business pawing me. I'll sit very still,
and he will go away." If the person doesn't take the hint from Drummer,
I'll give the pup a little backup by saying. "Please don't pet him, he's
working," even though he was not under any command.

The pup reads this, and there is a flicker of a working trust now stirring
in the dog. Is the pup grateful? When the stranger leaves, does he lick my
hand, full of submissive blandishments? This one doesn't. This one says
nothing at all, and I say nothing much to him. This is a working trust we are
developing, not a mutual congratulation society. My backup is praise
enough for him; the use he makes of my support is praise enough for me.

Listening to a dog is often praise enough. Suppose it is just after dark
and we are outside. Suddenly there is a shout from the house. The pup
and I both look toward the shout and then toward each other: "What do
you think?" I don't so much as cock my head, because Drummer is growing up, and I want to know what he thinks. He takes a few steps toward
the house, and I follow. He listens again and comprehends that it's just
Holly, who at fourteen is much given to alarming cries and shouts. He
shrugs at me and goes about his business. I say nothing. To praise him for
this performance would make about as much sense as praising a human
being for the same thing. Thus:

A. What's that?

B. I don't know. [Listens] Oh, it's just Holly.

A. What a goooooood human being!

B. Huh?

This is one small moment in a series of like moments that will culminate in an Airedale who on a Friday will have the discrimination and confidence required to take down a man who is attacking me with a knife and on Saturday clown and play with the children at the annual Orange Empire Dog Club Christmas party.

People who claim to speak for animal rights are increasingly devoted   30 to the idea that the very keeping of a dog or a horse or a gerbil or a lion is in and of itself an offense. The more loudly they speak, the less likely they are to be in a rights relation to any given animal, because they are spending so much time in airplanes or transmitting fax announcements of the latest Sylvester Stallone anti-fur rally. In a 1988 *Harper's* forum, for example, Ingrid Newkirk, the national director of People for the Ethical Treatment of Animals, urged that domestic pets be spayed and neutered and ultimately phased out. She prefers, it appears, wolves — and wolves someplace else — to Airedales and, by a logic whose interior structure is both emotionally and intellectually forever closed to Drummer, claims thereby to be speaking for "animal rights."

She is wrong. I am the only one who can own up to my Airedale's inalienable rights. Whether or not I do it perfectly at any given moment is no more refutation of this point than whether I am perfectly my husband's mate at any given moment refutes the fact of marriage. Only people who know Drummer, and whom he can know, are capable of this relationship. PETA and the Humane Society and the ASPCA and the Congress and NOW — as institutions — do have the power to affect my ability to grant rights to Drummer but are otherwise incapable of creating conditions or laws or rights that would increase his happiness. Only Drummer's owner has the power to obey him — to obey who he is and what he is capable of — deeply enough to grant him his rights and open up the possibility of happiness.

The Reader's Presence

1. Hearne writes from an "expert" perspective as an animal trainer. Suppose she were not an expert. How would that change your reading of her argument?

2. Hearne takes issue both with the common definition of "animal," protesting that not all animals are alike, and with the common notion of "happiness" as comfort (paragraphs 1 and 2). How do questions of these definitions form the basis of her argument? Is it

possible to disagree with Hearne's definitions and still support her overall argument, or vice-versa? Why or why not?

3. After discussing the notion of "slavery" (paragraph 17), Hearne lists other scenarios of ownership. How do these scenarios comment on the idea of slavery as it would apply to animals? In your opinion, are they legitimate comparisons? Why or why not?

99

Thomas Jefferson

The Declaration of Independence

Thomas Jefferson (1743–1826) was born and raised in Virginia and attended William and Mary College. After being admitted to the bar, he entered politics and served in the Virginia House of Burgesses and the Continental Congress of 1775. During the Revolutionary War he was elected governor of Virginia, and after independence was appointed special minister to France and later secretary of state. As the nation's third president he negotiated the Louisiana Purchase. Of all his accomplishments as an inventor, architect, diplomat, scientist, and politician, Jefferson counted his work in designing the University of Virginia among the most important, along with his efforts to establish separation of church and state and the composition of the Declaration of Independence.

In May and June 1776, the Continental Congress had been vigorously debating the dangerous idea of independence and felt the need to issue a document that clearly pointed out the colonial grievances against Great Britain. A committee was appointed to "prepare a declaration" that would summarize the specific reasons for colonial discontent. The committee of five included Thomas Jefferson, Benjamin Franklin, and John Adams. Jefferson, who was noted for his skills in composition and, as Adams put it, "peculiar felicity of expression," was chosen to write the first draft. The assignment took Jefferson about two weeks, and he submitted the draft first to the committee, which made a few verbal alterations, and then on June 28 to Congress, where, after further alterations mainly relating to slavery, it was finally approved on July 4, 1776.

Jefferson claims to have composed the document without research, working mainly from ideas he felt were commonly held at the time. As Jefferson recalled many years later, he drafted the document as "an appeal to the tribunal of the world" and hoped "to place before mankind the common sense of the subject, in terms so plain and firm as to command their assent." He claims that "neither aiming at originality of principle or sentiment . . . it was intended to be an expression of the American mind, and to give to that expression the proper tone and spirit called for by the occasion."

When in the Course of human events, it becomes necessary for one people to dissolve the political bands which have connected them with another, and to assume among the Powers of the earth, the separate and equal station to which the Laws of Nature and of Nature's God entitle them, a decent respect to the opinions of mankind requires that they should declare the causes which impel them to the separation.

We hold these truths to be self-evident, that all men are created equal, that they are endowed by their Creator with certain inalienable Rights, that among these are Life, Liberty and the pursuit of Happiness. That to secure these rights, Governments are instituted among Men, deriving their just powers from the consent of the governed. That whenever any Form of Government becomes destructive of these ends, it is the Right of the People to alter or to abolish it, and to institute new Government, laying its foundation on such principles and organizing its powers in such form, as to them shall seem most likely to effect their Safety and Happiness. Prudence, indeed, will dictate that Governments long established should not be changed for light and transient causes; and accordingly all experience hath shown, that mankind are more disposed to suffer, while evils are sufferable, than to right themselves by abolishing the forms to which they are accustomed. But when a long train of abuses and usurpations, pursuing invariably the same Object evinces a design to reduce them under absolute Despotism, it is their right, it is their duty, to throw off such Government, and to provide new Guards for their future security. — Such has been the patient sufferance of these Colonies; and such is now the necessity which constrains them to alter their former Systems of Government. The history of the present King of Great Britain is a history of repeated injuries and usurpations, all having in direct object the establishment of an absolute Tyranny over these States. To prove this, let Facts be submitted to a candid world.

He has refused his Assent to Laws, the most wholesome and necessary for the public good.

He has forbidden his Governors to pass Laws of immediate and pressing importance, unless suspended in their operation till his Assent should be obtained; and when so suspended, he has utterly neglected to attend to them.

He has refused to pass other laws for the accommodation of large 5 districts of people, unless those people would relinquish the right of Representation in the Legislature, a right inestimable to them and formidable to tyrants only.

He has called together legislative bodies at places unusual, uncomfortable, and distant from the depository of their Public Records, for the sole purpose of fatiguing them into compliance with his measures.

He has dissolved Representative Houses repeatedly, for opposing with manly firmness his invasions on the rights of the people.

He has refused for a long time, after such dissolutions, to cause others to be elected; whereby the Legislative Powers, incapable of Annihilation, have returned to the People at large for their exercise; the State remaining in the mean time exposed to all the dangers of invasion from without, and convulsions within.

He has endeavoured to prevent the population of these States;[1] for that purpose obstructing the Laws for Naturalization of Foreigners; refusing to pass others to encourage their migration hither, and raising the conditions of new Appropriations of Lands.

He has obstructed the Administration of Justice, by refusing his Assent to Laws for establishing Judiciary Powers.   10

He has made Judges dependent on his Will alone, for the tenure of their offices, and the amount and payment of their salaries.

He has erected a multitude of New Offices, and sent hither swarms of Officers to harass our People, and eat out their substance.

He has kept among us, in times of peace, Standing Armies without the Consent of our legislature.

He has affected to render the Military independent of and superior to the Civil Power.

He has combined with others to subject us to a jurisdiction foreign to   15 our constitution, and unacknowledged by our laws; giving his Assent to their acts of pretended Legislation:

For quartering large bodies of armed troops among us:

For protecting them, by a mock Trial, from Punishment for any Murders which they should commit on the Inhabitants of these States:

For cutting off our Trade with all parts of the world:

For imposing taxes on us without our Consent:

For depriving us in many cases, of the benefits of Trial by Jury: 20

For transporting us beyond Seas to be tried for pretended offenses:

For abolishing the free System of English Laws in a neighbouring Province, establishing therein an Arbitrary government, and enlarging its Boundaries so as to render it at once an example and fit instrument for introducing the same absolute rule into these Colonies:

For taking away our Charters, abolishing our most valuable Laws, and altering fundamentally the Forms of our Governments:

For suspending our own Legislatures, and declaring themselves invested with Power to legislate for us in all cases whatsoever.

He has abdicated Government here, by declaring us out of his Protec-   25 tion and waging War against us.

He was plundered our seas, ravaged our Coasts, burnt our towns, and destroyed the lives of our people.

He is at this time transporting large armies of foreign mercenaries to compleat the works of death, desolation and tyranny, already begun with circumstances of Cruelty & perfidy scarcely paralleled in the most barbarous ages, and totally unworthy the Head of a civilized nation.

---

[1]*prevent the population of these States:* This meant limiting emigration to the Colonies, thus controlling their growth. —EDS.

He has constrained our fellow Citizens taken Captive on the high Seas to bear Arms against their Country, to become the executioners of their friends and Brethren, or to fall themselves by their Hands.

He has excited domestic insurrections amongst us, and has endeavoured to bring on the inhabitants of our frontiers, the merciless Indian Savages, whose known rule of warfare, is an undistinguished destruction of all ages, sexes and conditions.

In every stage of these Oppressions We have Petitioned for Readdress 30 in the most humble terms: Our repeated Petitions have been answered only by repeated injury. A Prince, whose character is thus marked by every act which may define a Tyrant, is unfit to be the ruler of a free People.

Nor have We been wanting in attention to our British brethren. We have warned them from time to time of attempts by their legislature to extend an unwarrantable jurisdiction over us. We have reminded them of the circumstances of our emigration and settlement here. We have appealed to their native justice and magnanimity, and we have conjured them by the ties of our common kindred to disavow these usurpations, which, would inevitably interrupt our connections and correspondence. They too have been deaf to the voice of justice and of consanguinity. We must, therefore, acquiesce in the necessity, which denounces our Separation, and hold them, as we hold the rest of mankind, Enemies in War, in Peace Friends.

We, therefore, the Representatives of the United States of America, in General Congress, Assembled, appealing to the Supreme Judge of the world for the rectitude of our intentions, do in the Name, and by Authority of the good People of these Colonies, solemnly publish and declare, That these United Colonies are, and of Right ought to be Free and Independent States, that they are Absolved from all Allegiance to the British Crown, and that all political connection between them and the State of Great Britain, is and ought to be totally dissolved; and that as Free and Independent States, they have full Power to levy War, conclude Peace, contract Alliances, establish Commerce, and to do all other Acts and Things which Independent States may of right do. And for the support of this Declaration, with a firm reliance on the Protection of Divine Providence, we mutually pledge to each other our Lives, our Fortunes and our sacred Honor.

The Reader's Presence

1. How does Jefferson seem to define *independence?* Whom does the definition include? Whom does it exclude? How does Jefferson's definition of independence differ from your own? It has been

pointed out that Jefferson disregards "interdependence." Can you formulate an argument contrary to Jefferson's?

2. Examine the Declaration's first sentence. Who is the speaker here? What is the effect of the omniscient tone of the opening? Why does the first paragraph have no personal pronouns or references to specific events? What might Jefferson's argument stand to gain in generalizing the American situation?

3. As in classical epics and the Bible, Jefferson frequently relies on the rhetorical devices of repetition and lists. What is the effect of such devices? Would the piece be more, or less, effective written in "everyday" language? Why or why not? Try rewriting the long opening sentence in a more contemporary style.

100

June Jordan

Nobody Mean More to Me than You[1] *and the Future Life of Willie Jordan*

June Jordan (b. 1936) is professor of African American studies at the University of California, Berkeley. She is the author of novels, short stories, poetry, children's fiction, and biography. Her essays can be found in collections such as On Call *(1986),* Moving Toward Home: Political Essays *(1989),* Technical Difficulties: African American Notes on the State of the Union *(1992), and* Affirmative Acts: Political Essays *(1998). Jordan has also written a musical,* I Was Looking at the Ceiling and Then I Saw the Sky: Earthquake-Romance *(1995), for which John Adams wrote the music. The essay "Nobody Mean More to Me than You and the Future Life of Willie Jordan" is found in* On Call. *She has also published stories and poems in numerous national magazines; her latest collection of poems is* Kissing God Goodbye: Poems, 1991–97 *(1997).*

Jordan thinks of writing, and especially of poetry, as a way toward empowerment. "Why should power and language coalesce in poetry? Because poetry is the medium for telling the truth, and because a poem is antithetical to lies/evasions and superficiality, anyone who becomes a practicing poet has an excellent chance of becoming somebody real, somebody known, self-defined and attuned to and

---

[1]Black English aphorism crafted by Monica Morris, a junior at S.U.N.Y. at Stony Brook, October, 1984. — JORDAN'S NOTE.

listening and hungering for kindred real voices utterly/articulately different from his or her own voice."

Black English is not exactly a linguistic buffalo; as children, most of the thirty-five million Afro-Americans living here depend on this language for our discovery of the world. But then we approach our maturity inside a larger social body that will not support our efforts to become anything other than the clones of those who are neither our mothers nor our fathers. We begin to grow up in a house where every true mirror shows us the face of somebody who does not belong there, whose walk and whose talk will never look or sound "right," because that house was meant to shelter a family that is alien and hostile to us. As we learn our way around this environment, either we hide our original word habits, or we completely surrender our own voice, hoping to please those who will never respect anyone different from themselves: Black English is not exactly a linguistic buffalo, but we should understand its status as an endangered species, as a perishing, irreplaceable system of community intelligence, or we should expect its extinction, and, along with that, the extinguishing of much that constitutes our own proud, and singular identity.

What we casually call "English," less and less defers to England and its "gentlemen." "English" is no longer a specific matter of geography or an element of class privilege; more than thirty-three countries use this tool as a means of "international communication."[2] Countries as disparate as Zimbabwe and Malaysia, or Israel and Uganda, use it as their non-native currency of convenience. Obviously, this tool, this "English," cannot function inside thirty-three discrete societies on the basis of rules and values absolutely determined somewhere else, in a thirty-fourth other country, for example.

In addition to that staggering congeries of non-native users of English, there are five countries, or 333,746,000 people, for whom this thing called "English" serves as a native tongue.[3] Approximately ten percent of these native speakers of "English" are Afro-American citizens of the U.S.A. I cite these numbers and varieties of human beings dependent on "English" in order, quickly, to suggest how strange and how tenuous is any concept of "Standard English." Obviously, numerous forms of English now operate inside a natural, an uncontrollable, continuum of development. I would suppose "the standard" for English in Malaysia is not the same as "the standard" in Zimbabwe. I know that standard forms of English for Black people in this country do not copy that of whites. And, in fact, the structural differences between these two kinds of English

---

[2]*English Is Spreading, but What Is English?* A presentation by Professor S. N. Sridhar, Dept. of Linguistics, S.U.N.Y. at Stony Brook, April 9, 1985; Dean's Conversation among the Disciplines. — JORDAN'S NOTE.

[3]Ibid. — JORDAN'S NOTE.

have intensified, becoming more Black, or less white, despite the expected homogenizing effects of television[4] and other mass media.

Nonetheless, white standards of English persist, supreme and unquestioned, in these United States. Despite our multilingual population, and despite the deepening Black and white cleavage within that conglomerate, white standards control our official and popular judgments of verbal proficiency and correct, or incorrect, language skills, including speech. In contrast to India, where at least fourteen languages co-exist as legitimate Indian languages, in contrast to Nicaragua, where all citizens are legally entitled to formal school instruction in their regional or tribal languages, compulsory education in America compels accommodation to exclusively white forms of "English." White English, in America, is "Standard English."

This story begins two years ago, I was teaching a new course, "In   5
Search of the Invisible Black Woman," and my rather large class seemed evenly divided between young Black women and men. Five or six white students also sat in attendance. With unexpected speed and enthusiasm we had moved through historical narratives of the nineteenth century to literature by and about Black women, in the twentieth. I had assigned the first forty pages of Alice Walker's *The Color Purple,* and I came, eagerly, to class that morning:

"So!" I exclaimed, aloud. "What did you think? How did you like it?"

The students studied their hands, or the floor. There was no response. The tense, resistant feeling in the room fairly astounded me.

At last, one student, a young woman still not meeting my eyes, muttered something in my direction:

"What did you say?" I prompted her.

"Why she have them talk so funny. It don't sound right."   10

"You mean the language?"

Another student lifted his head: "It don't look right, neither. I couldn't hardly read it."

At this, several students dumped on the book. Just about unanimously, their criticisms targeted the language. I listened to what they wanted to say and silently marveled at the similarities between their casual speech patterns and Alice Walker's written version of Black English.

But I decided against pointing to these identical traits of syntax; I wanted not to make them self-conscious about their own spoken language—not while they clearly felt it was "wrong." Instead I decided to swallow my astonishment. Here was a negative Black reaction to a prize winning accomplishment of Black literature that white readers across the country had selected as a best seller. Black rejection was aimed at the one irreducibly Black element of Walker's work: the language—Celie's Black English. I wrote the opening lines of *The Color Purple* on the blackboard

---

[4]*New York Times,* March 15, 1985, Section One, p. 14: Report on study by Linguistics at the University of Pennsylvania.—JORDAN'S NOTE.

and asked the students to help me translate these sentences into Standard
English:

> *You better not never tell nobody but God. It'd kill your mammy.*
> Dear God,
>   I am fourteen years old. I have always been a good girl. Maybe you
> can give me a sign letting me know what is happening to me.
>   Last spring after Little Lucious come I heard them fussing. He was
> pulling on her arm. She say it too soon, Fonso. I aint well. Finally he
> leave her alone. A week go by, he pulling on her arm again. She say,
> Naw, I ain't gonna. Can't you see I'm already half dead, an all of the
> children.[5]

Our process of translation exploded with hilarity and even hysterical,
shocked laughter: The Black writer, Alice Walker, knew what she was
doing! If rudimentary criteria for good fiction includes the manipulation
of language so that the syntax and diction of sentences will tell you the
identity of speakers, the probable age and sex and class of speakers, and
even the locale—urban/rural/southern/western—then Walker had written, perfectly. This is the translation into Standard English that our class
produced:

> *Absolutely, one should never confide in anybody besides God. Your*
> *secrets could prove devastating to your mother.*
> Dear God,
>   I am fourteen years old, I have always been good. But now, could
> you help me to understand what is happening to me?
>   Last spring, after my little brother, Lucious, was born, I heard my
> parents fighting. My father kept pulling at my mother's arm. But she
> told him, "It's too soon for sex, Alfonso. I am still not feeling well." Fi-
> nally, my father left her alone. A week went by, and he began bothering
> my mother, again: Pulling her arm. She told him, "No, I won't! Can't
> you see I'm already exhausted from all of these children?"

(Our favorite line was "It's too soon for sex, Alfonso.")   15

Once we could stop laughing, once we could stop our exponentially
wild improvisations on the theme of Translated Black English, the students pushed me to explain their own negative first reactions to their spoken language on the printed page. I thought it was probably akin to the
shock of seeing yourself in a photograph for the first time. Most of the
students had never before seen a written facsimile of the way they talk.
None of the students had ever learned how to read and write their own
verbal system of communication: Black English. Alternatively, this fact
began to baffle or else bemuse and then infuriate my students. Why not?
Was it too late? Could they learn how to do it, now? And, ultimately, the
final test question, the one testing my sincerity: Could I teach them? Because I had never taught anyone Black English and, as far as I knew, no
one, anywhere in the United States, had ever offered such a course, the
best I could say was "I'll try."

[5]Alice Walker, *The Color Purple*, p. 11, Harcourt Brace, N.Y.—JORDAN'S NOTE.

He looked like a wrestler.

He sat dead center in the packed room and, every time our eyes met, he quickly nodded his head as though anxious to reassure, and encourage, me.

Short, with strikingly broad shoulders and long arms, he spoke with a surprisingly high, soft voice that matched the soft bright movement of his eyes. His name was Willie Jordan. He would have seemed even more unlikely in the context of Contemporary Women's Poetry, except that ten or twelve other Black men were taking the course, as well. Still, Willie was conspicuous. His extreme fitness, the muscular density of his presence underscored the riveted, gentle attention that he gave to anything anyone said. Generally, he did not join the loud and rowdy dialogue flying back and forth, but there could be no doubt about his interest in our discussions. And, when he stood to present an argument he'd prepared, overnight, that nervous smile of his vanished and an irregular stammering replaced it, as he spoke with visceral sincerity, word by word.

That was how I met Willie Jordan. It was in between "In Search of the Invisible Black Woman" and "The Art of Black English." I was waiting for Departmental approval and I supposed that Willie might be, so to speak, killing time until he, too, could study Black English. But Willie really did want to explore Contemporary Women's poetry and, to that end, volunteered for extra research and never missed a class.

Towards the end of that semester, Willie approached me for an independent study project on South Africa. It would commence the next semester. I thought Willie's writing needed the kind of improvement only intense practice will yield. I knew his intelligence was outstanding. But he'd wholeheartedly opted for "Standard English" at a rather late age, and the results were stilted and frequently polysyllabic, simply for the sake of having more syllables. Willie's unnatural formality of language seemed to me consistent with the formality of his research into South African apartheid. As he projected his studies, he would have little time, indeed, for newspapers. Instead, more than 90 percent of his research would mean saturation in strictly historical, if not archival, material. I was certainly interested. It would be tricky to guide him into a more confident and spontaneous relationship both with language and apartheid. It was going to be wonderful to see what happened when he could catch up with himself, entirely, and talk back to the world.

September, 1984: Breezy fall weather and much excitement! My class, "The Art of Black English," was full to the limit of the fire laws. And, in Independent Study, Willie Jordan showed up, weekly, fifteen minutes early for each of our sessions. I was pretty happy to be teaching, altogether!

I remember an early class when a young brother, replete with his ever present pork-pie hat, raised his hand and then told us that most of what he'd heard was "all right" except it was "too clean." "The brothers on the street," he continued, "they mix it up more. Like 'fuck' and 'motherfuck.' Or like 'shit.'" He waited, I waited. Then all of us laughed a good while, and we got into a brawl about "correct" and "realistic" Black English that led to Rule 1.

Rule 1: *Black English is about a whole lot more than mothafuckin.*

As a criterion, we decided, "realistic" could take you anywhere you   25
want to go. Artful places. Angry places. Eloquent and sweetalkin places. Polemical places. Church. And the local Bar & Grill. We were checking out a language, not a mood or a scene or one guy's forgettable mouthing off.

It was hard. For most of the students, learning Black English required a fallback to patterns and rhythms of speech that many of their parents had beaten out of them. I mean *beaten*. And, in a majority of cases, correct Black English could be achieved only by striving for *incorrect* Standard English, something they were still pushing at, quite uncertainly. This state of affairs led to Rule 2.

Rule 2: *If it's wrong in Standard English it's probably right in Black English, or, at least, you're hot.*

It was hard. Roommates and family members ridiculed their studies, or remained incredulous, "You *studying* that shit? At school?" But we were beginning to feel the companionship of pioneers. And we decided that we needed another rule that would establish each one of us as equally important to our success. This was Rule 3.

Rule 3: *If it don't sound like something that come out somebody mouth then it don't sound right. If it don't sound right then it ain't hardly right. Period.*

This rule produced two weeks of compositions in which the students   30
agonizingly tried to spell the sound of the Black English sentence they wanted to convey. But Black English is, preeminently, an oral/spoken means of communication. *And spelling don't talk.* So we needed Rule 4.

Rule 4: *Forget about the spelling. Let the syntax carry you.*

Once we arrived at Rule 4 we started to fly because syntax, the structure of an idea, leads you to the world view of the speaker and reveals her values. The syntax of a sentence equals the structure of your consciousness. If we insisted that the language of Black English adheres to a distinctive Black syntax, then we were postulating a profound difference between white and Black people, *per se*. Was it a difference to prize or to obliterate?

There are three qualities of Black English—the presence of life, voice, and clarity—that testify to a distinctive Black value system that we became excited about and self-consciously tried to maintain.

1. Black English has been produced by a pre-technocratic, if not anti-technological, culture. More, our culture has been constantly threatened by annihilation or, at least, the swallowed blurring of assimilation. Therefore, our language is a system constructed by people constantly needing to insist that we exist, that we are present. Our language devolves from a culture that abhors all abstraction, or anything tending to obscure or

delete the fact of the human being who is here and now/the truth of the person who is speaking or listening. Consequently, *there is no passive voice construction possible in Black English*. For example, you cannot say, "Black English is being eliminated." You must say, instead, "White people eliminating Black English." The assumption of the presence of life governs all of Black English. Therefore, overwhelmingly, *all action takes place in the language of the present indicative.* And every sentence assumes the living and active participation of at least two human beings, the speaker and the listener.

2. A primary consequence of the person-centered values of Black English is the delivery of voice. If you speak or write Black English, your ideas will necessarily possess that otherwise elusive attribute, *voice*.

3. One main benefit following from the person-centered values of Black English is that of *clarity*. If your idea, your sentence, assumes the presence of at least two living and active people, you will make it understandable because the motivation behind every sentence is the wish to say something real to somebody real.

As the weeks piled up, translation from Standard English into Black English or vice versa occupied a hefty part of our course work.

> Standard English (hereafter S.E.): "In considering the idea of studying Black English those questioned suggested—"
> (What's the subject? Where's the person? Is anybody alive in there, in that idea?)
> Black English (hereafter B.E.): "I been asking people what you think about somebody studying Black English and they answer me like this."

But there were interesting limits. You cannot "translate" instances of Standard English preoccupied with abstraction or with nothing/nobody evidently alive, into Black English. That would warp the language into uses antithetical to the guiding perspective of its community of users. Rather you must first change those Standard English sentences, themselves, into ideas consistent with the person-centered assumptions of Black English.

GUIDELINES FOR BLACK ENGLISH

1. Minimal number of words for every idea: This is the source for the aphoristic and/or poetic force of the language; eliminate every possible word.

2. Clarity: If the sentence is not clear it's not Black English.

3. Eliminate use of the verb *to be* whenever possible. This leads to the deployment of more descriptive and, therefore, more precise verbs.

4. Use *be* or *been* only when you want to describe a chronic, ongoing state of things.

He *be* at the office, by 9. (He is always at the office by 9.)
He *been* with her since forever.

5. Zero copula: Always eliminate the verb *to be* whenever it would combine with another verb in Standard English.

S.E.: She is going out with him.
B.E.: She going out with him.

6. Eliminate *do* as in:

S.E.: What do you think? What do you want?
B.E.: What you think? What you want?

Rules number 3, 4, 5, and 6 provide for the use of the minimal number of verbs per idea and, therefore, greater accuracy in the choice of verb.

7. In general, if you wish to say something really positive, try to formulate the idea using emphatic negative structure.   45

S.E.: He's fabulous.
B.E.: He bad.

8. Use double or triple negatives for dramatic emphasis.

S.E.: Tina Turner sings out of this world.
B.E.: Ain nobody sing like Tina.

9. Never use the *-ed* suffix to indicate the past tense of a verb.

S.E.: She closed the door.
B.E.: She close the door. Or, she have close the door.

10. Regardless of international verb time, only use the third person singular, present indicative, for use of the verb *to have,* as an auxiliary.

S.E.: He had his wallet then he lost it.
B.E.: He have him wallet then he lose it.
S.E.: He had seen that movie.
B.E.: We seen that movie. Or, we have see that movie.

11. Observe a minimal inflection of verbs. Particularly, never change from the first person singular forms to the third person singular.

S.E.: Present Tense Forms: He goes to the store.
B.E.: He go to the store.
S.E.: Past Tense Forms: He went to the store.
B.E.: He go to the store. Or, he gone to the store. Or, he been to the store.

12. The possessive case scarcely ever appears in Black English. Never   50
use an apostrophe ('s) construction. If you wander into a possessive case component of an idea, then keep logically consistent: *ours, his, theirs,*

mines. But, most likely, if you bump into such a component, you have wandered outside the underlying world-view of Black English.

S.E.: He will take their car tomorrow.
B.E.: He taking they car tomorrow.

13. Plurality: Logical consistency, continued: If the modifier indicates plurality then the noun remains in the singular case.

S.E.: He ate twelve doughnuts.
B.E.: He eat twelve doughnut.
S.E.: She has many books.
B.E.: She have many book.

14. Listen for, or invent, special Black English forms of the past tense, such as: "He losted it. That what she felted." If they are clear and readily understood, then use them.

15. Do not hesitate to play with words, sometimes inventing them: e.g. "astropotomous" means huge like a hippo plus astronomical and, therefore, signifies real big.

16. In Black English, unless you keenly want to underscore the past tense nature of an action, stay in the present tense and rely on the overall context of your ideas for the conveyance of time and sequence.

17. Never use the suffix *-ly* form of an adverb in Black English.   55

S.E.: The rain came down rather quickly.
B.E.: The rain come down pretty quick.

18. Never use the indefinite article *an* in Black English.

S.E.: He wanted to ride an elephant.
B.E.: He want to ride him a elephant.

19. Invariant syntax: in correct Black English it is possible to formulate an imperative, an interrogative, and a simple declarative idea with the same syntax:

B.E.: You going to the store?
      You going to the store.
      You going to the store!

Where was Willie Jordan? We'd reached the mid-term of the semester. Students had formulated Black English guidelines, by consensus, and they were now writing with remarkable beauty, purpose, and enjoyment:

I ain hardly speakin for everybody but myself so understan that. — Kim Parks

Samples from student writings:

Janie have a great big ole hole inside her. Tea Cake the only thing that fit that hole . . .
      That pear tree beautiful to Janie, especial when bees fiddlin with the

blossomin pear there growing large and lovely. But personal speakin, the love she get from staring at that tree ain the love what starin back at her in them relationship. (Monica Morris)

Love is a big theme in, *They Eye Was Watching God*. Love show people new corners inside theyself. It pull out good stuff and stuff back bad stuff . . . Joe worship the doing uh his own hand and need other people to worship him too. But he ain't think about Janie that she a person and ought to live like anybody common do. Queen life not for Janie. (Monica Morris)

In both life and writin, Black womens have varietous experience of love that be cold like a iceberg or fiery like a inferno. Passion got for the other partner involve, man or woman, seem as shallow, ankle-deep water or the most profoundest abyss. (Constance Evans)

Family love another bond that ain't never break under no pressure. (Constance Evans)

You know it really cold / When the friend you / Always get out the fire / Act like they don't know you / When you in the heat. (Constance Evans)

Big classroom discussion bout love at this time. I never take no class where us have any long arguin for and against for two or three day. New to me and great. I find the class time talkin a million time more interestin than detail bout the book. (Kathy Esseks)

As these examples suggest, Black English no longer limited the students, in any way. In fact, one of them, Philip Garfield, would shortly "translate" a pivotal scene from Ibsen's *Doll's House,* as his final term paper.

NORA: I didn't gived no shit. I thinked you a asshole back then, too, you make it so hard for me save mines husband life.
KROGSTAD: Girl, it clear you ain't any idea what you done. You done exact what I once done, and I losed my reputation over it.
NORA: You asks me believe you once act brave save you wife life?
KROGSTAD: Law care less why you done it.
NORA: Law must suck.
KROGSTAD: Suck or no, if I wants, judge screw you wid dis paper.
NORA: No way, man. (Philip Garfield)

But where was Willie? Compulsively punctual, and always thoroughly prepared with neatly typed compositions, he had disappeared. He failed to show up for our regularly scheduled conference, and I received neither a note nor a phone call of explanation. A whole week went by. I wondered if Willie had finally been captured by the extremely current happenings in South Africa: passage of a new constitution that did not enfranchise the Black majority, and militant Black South African reaction 60 to that affront. I wondered if he'd been hurt, somewhere. I wondered if the serious workload of weekly readings and writings had overwhelmed him and changed his mind about independent study. Where was Willie Jordan?

One week after the first conference that Willie missed, he called: "Hello, Professor Jordan? This is Willie. I'm sorry I wasn't there last week. But something has come up and I'm pretty upset. I'm sorry but I really can't deal right now."

I asked Willie to drop by my office and just let me see that he was okay. He agreed to do that. When I saw him I knew something hideous had happened. Something had hurt him and scared him to the marrow. He was all agitated and stammering and terse and incoherent. At last, his sadly jumbled account let me surmise, as follows: Brooklyn police had murdered his unarmed, twenty-five-year-old brother, Reggie Jordan. Neither Willie nor his elderly parents knew what to do about it. Nobody from the press was interested. His folks had no money. Police ran his family around and around, to no point. And Reggie was really dead. And Willie wanted to fight, but he felt helpless.

With Willie's permission I began to try to secure legal counsel for the Jordan family. Unfortunately Black victims of police violence are truly numerous while the resources available to prosecute their killers are truly scarce. A friend of mine at the Center for Constitutional Rights estimated that just the preparatory costs for bringing the cops into court normally approaches $180,000. Unless the execution of Reggie Jordan became a major community cause for organizing, and protest, his murder would simply become a statistical item.

Again, with Willie's permission, I contacted every newspaper and media person I could think of. But the William Bastone feature article in *The Village Voice* was the only result from that canvassing.

Again, with Willie's permission, I presented the case to my class in   65
Black English. We had talked about the politics of language. We had talked about love and sex and child abuse and men and women. But the murder of Reggie Jordan broke like a hurricane across the room.

There are few "issues" as endemic to Black life as police violence. Most of the students knew and respected and liked Jordan. Many of them came from the very neighborhood where the murder had occurred. All of the students had known somebody close to them who had been killed by police, or had known frightening moments of gratuitous confrontation with the cops. They wanted to do everything at once to avenge death. Number One: They decided to compose personal statements of condolence to Willie Jordan and his family written in Black English. Number Two: They decided to compose individual messages to the police, in Black English. These should be prefaced by an explanatory paragraph composed by the entire group. Number Three: These individual messages, with their lead paragraph, should be sent to *Newsday*.

The morning after we agreed on these objectives, one of the young women students appeared with an unidentified visitor, who sat through the class, smiling in a peculiar, comfortable way.

Now we had to make more tactical decisions. Because we wanted the messages published, and because we thought it imperative that our outrage be known by the police, the tactical question was this: Should the opening, group paragraph be written in Black English or Standard English?

I have seldom been privy to a discussion with so much heart at the dead heat of it. I will never forget the eloquence, the sudden haltings of speech, the fierce struggle against tears, the furious throwaway, and useless explosions that this question elicited.

That one question contained several others, each of them extraordinarily painful to even contemplate. How best to serve the memory of Reggie Jordan? Should we use the language of the killers — Standard English — in order to make our ideas acceptable to those controlling the killers? But wouldn't what we had to say be rejected, summarily, if we said it in our own language, the language of the victim, Reggie Jordan? But if we sought to express ourselves by abandoning our language wouldn't that mean our suicide on top of Reggie's murder? But if we expressed ourselves in our own language wouldn't that be suicidal to the wish to communicate with those who, evidently, did not give a damn about us/Reggie/police violence in the Black community? 70

At the end of one of the longest, most difficult hours of my own life, the students voted, unanimously, to preface their individual messages with a paragraph composed in the language of Reggie Jordan. *"At least we don't give up nothing else. At least we stick to the truth: Be who we been. And stay all the way with Reggie."*

It was heartbreaking to proceed, from that point. Everyone in the room realized that our decision in favor of Black English had doomed our writings, even as the distinctive reality of our Black lives always has doomed our efforts to "be who we been" in this country.

I went to the blackboard and took down this paragraph, dictated by the class:

... YOU COPS!
WE THE BROTHER AND SISTER OF WILLIE JORDAN, A FELLOW STONY BROOK STUDENT WHO THE BROTHER OF THE DEAD REGGIE JORDAN. REGGIE, LIKE MANY BROTHER AND SISTER, HE A VICTIM OF BRUTAL RACIST POLICE, OCTOBER 25, 1984. US APPALL, FED UP, BECAUSE THAT ANOTHER SENSELESS DEATH WHAT OCCUR IN OUR COMMUNITY. THIS WHAT WE FEEL, THIS, FROM OUR HEART, FOR WE AIN'T STAYIN' SILENT NO MORE.

With the completion of this introduction, nobody said anything. I asked for comments. At this invitation, the unidentified visitor, a young Black man, ceaselessly smiling, raised his hand. He was, it so happens, a rookie cop. He had just joined the force in September and, he said he thought he should clarify a few things. So he came forward and sprawled easily into a posture of barroom, or fireside, nostalgia:

"See," Officer Charles enlightened us, "most times when you out on   75 the street and something come down you do one of two things. Over-react or under-react. Now, if you under-react then you can get yourself kilt. And if you over-react then maybe you kill somebody. Fortunately it's about nine times out of ten and you will over-react. So the brother got kilt. And I'm sorry about that, believe me. But what you have to under-stand is what kilt him: Over-reaction. That's all. Now you talk about Black people and white police but see, now, I'm a cop myself. And (big smile) I'm Black. And just a couple months ago I was on the other side. But see it's the same for me. You a cop, you the ultimate authority: the Ultimate Authority. And you on the street, most of the time you can only do one of two things: over-react or under-react. That's all it is with the brother. Over-reaction. Didn't have nothing to do with race."

That morning Officer Charles had the good fortune to escape with-out being boiled alive. But barely. And I remember the pride of his smile when I read about the fate of Black policemen and other collaborators, in South Africa. I remember him, and I remember the shock and palpable feeling of shame that filled the room. It was as though that foolish, and deadly, young man had just relieved himself of his foolish, and deadly, explanation, face to face with the grief of Reggie Jordan's father and Reg-gie Jordan's mother. Class ended quietly. I copied the paragraph from the blackboard, collected the individual messages and left to type them up.

Newsday rejected the piece.

The Village Voice could not find room in their "Letters" section to print the individual messages from the students to the police.

None of the TV news reporters picked up the story.

Nobody raised $180,000 to prosecute the murder of Reggie Jordan.   80

Reggie Jordan is really dead.

I asked Willie Jordan to write an essay pulling together everything important to him from that semester. He was still deeply beside himself with frustration and amazement and loss. This is what he wrote, unedited, and in its entirety:

Throughout the course of this semester I have been researching the ef-fects of oppression and exploitation along racial lines in South Africa and its neighboring countries. I have become aware of South African po-lice brutalization of native Africans beyond the extent of the law, even though the laws themselves are catalyst affliction upon Black men, women, and children. Many Africans die each year as a result of the de-liberate use of police force to protect the white power structure.

Social control agents in South Africa, such as policemen, are also used to force compliance among citizens through both overt and covert tactics. It is not uncommon to find bold-faced coercion and cold-blooded killings of Blacks by South African police for undetermined and/or inadequate reasons. Perhaps the truth is that the only reasons for this heinous treatment of Blacks rests in racial differences. We should also understand that what is conveyed through the media is not always accurate and may sometimes be construed as the tip of the iceberg at best.

I recently received a painful reminder that racism, poverty, and the abuse of power are global problems which are by no means unique to South Africa. On October 25, 1984, at approximately 3:00 P.M. my brother, Mr. Reginald Jordan, was shot and killed by two New York City policemen from the 75th precinct in the East New York section of Brooklyn. His life ended at the age of twenty-five. Even up to this current point in time the Police Department has failed to provide my family, which consists of five brothers, eight sisters, and two parents, with a plausible reason for Reggie's death. Out of the many stories that were given to my family by the Police Department, not one of them seems to hold water. In fact, I honestly believe that the Police Department's assessment of my brother's murder is nothing short of ABSOLUTE BULLSHIT, and thus far no evidence had been produced to alter perception of the situation.

Furthermore, I believe that one of three cases may have occurred in this incident. First, Reggie's death may have been the desired outcome of the police officer's action, in which case the killing was premeditated. Or, it was a case of mistaken identity, which clarifies the fact that the two officers who killed my brother and their commanding parties are all grossly incompetent. Or, both of the above cases are correct, i.e., Reggie's murderers intended to kill him and the Police Department behaved insubordinately.

Part of the argument of the officers who shot Reggie was that he had attacked one of them and took his gun. This was their major claim. They also said that only one of them had actually shot Reggie. The facts, however, speak for themselves. According to the Death Certificate and autopsy report, Reggie was shot eight times from point-blank range. The Doctor who performed the autopsy told me himself that two bullets entered the side of my brother's head, four bullets were sprayed into his back, and two bullets struck him in the back of his legs. It is obvious that unnecessary force was used by the police and that it is extremely difficult to shoot someone in his back when he is attacking or approaching you.

After experiencing a situation like this and researching South Africa I believe that to a large degree, justice may only exist as rhetoric. I find it difficult to talk of true justice when the oppression of my people both at home and abroad attests to the fact that inequality and injustice are serious problems whereby Blacks and Third World people are perpetually short-changed by society. Something has to be done about the way in which this world is set up. Although it is a difficult task, we do have the power to make a change.

—Willie J. Jordan, Jr.
EGL 487, Section 58, November 14, 1984

It is my privilege to dedicate this book to the future life of Willie J. Jordan, Jr.

August 8, 1985

The Reader's Presence

1. How would you characterize Jordan's tone at the outset of this essay? When and how does her tone of voice change as the essay proceeds? How, for example, would you describe her voice when she takes up the subject of Black English, and more particularly its history and grammar? In what specific ways does her tone change when she discusses her class and her experiences with them? when she discusses Willie Jordan and her course in contemporary women's poetry? In what specific ways does her diction change in each of these parts of her essay? What, more specifically, do you make of the section where Jordan experiments with "translating" Alice Walker? What point does she make here about the adequacy of Standard English to represent the nuances of an important dimension of American culture?

2. Consider the "Rules and Guidelines" Jordan and her students formulate about Black English. Summarize the rationale for each, and comment on the extent to which you are convinced by the logic of each proposition. Assess the specific strengths and weaknesses of the examples Jordan presents from her students' own writing. Explain why the question of how the students should write their group preface to their message of protest is so sensitive. What sorts of issues are at stake in such a decision? What does Jordan mean when she says "our decision in favor of Black English had doomed our writings" (paragraph 72)? In what sense was the decision to write the protest in Black English courageous?

3. Reread the scene in which Officer Charles explains Reggie Jordan's death. What responses does this account elicit from the author? from her students? What diction and tone of voice does Jordan use to convey her attitude toward Officer Charles's apology for the system? What conclusions does Jordan draw from her experiences with this class? What connections does she make between the students' work with Black English and their response to Reggie Jordan's death?

Michiko Kakutani

The Word Police

Michiko Kakutani (b. 1955) was born in New Haven, Connecticut, and received a B.A. from Yale University in 1976. After graduation Kakutani worked as a reporter at the Washington Post *and later as a staff writer for* Time. *In 1979 she joined the cultural news department of the* New York Times *and has been the paper's senior book critic since 1983. She received the 1998 Pulitzer Prize for criticism for her "passionate, intelligent writing on books and contemporary literature." Kakutani has also published a collection of interviews,* The Poet at the Piano: Portraits of Writers, Filmmakers, Playrights, and Other Artists *(1988). "The Word Police" appeared in the* New York Times *in January 1993.*

This month's inaugural festivities, with their celebration, in Maya Angelou's words, of "humankind" — "the Asian, the Hispanic, the Jew/ The African, the Native American, the Sioux, / The Catholic, the Muslim, the French, the Greek / The Irish, the Rabbi, the Priest, the Sheik, / The Gay, the Straight, the Preacher, / The privileged, the homeless, the Teacher" — constituted a kind of official embrace of multiculturalism and a new politics of inclusion.

The mood of political correctness, however, has already made firm inroads into popular culture. Washington boasts a store called Politically Correct that sells pro-whale, anti-meat, ban-the-bomb T-shirts, bumper stickers and buttons, as well as a local cable television show called "Politically Correct Cooking" that features interviews in the kitchen with representatives from groups like People for the Ethical Treatment of Animals.

The Coppertone suntan lotion people are planning to give their long-time cover girl, Little Miss (Ms.?) Coppertone, a male equivalent, Little Mr. Coppertone. And even Superman (Superperson?) is rumored to be returning this spring, reincarnated as four ethnically diverse clones: an African-American, an Asian, a Caucasian and a Latino.

Nowhere is this P.C. mood more striking than in the increasingly noisy debate over language that has moved from university campuses to the country at large — a development that both underscores Americans' puritanical zeal for reform and their unwavering faith in the talismanic power of words.

Certainly no decent person can quarrel with the underlying impulse behind political correctness: a vision of a more just, inclusive society in which racism, sexism and prejudice of all sorts have been erased. But the methods and fervor of the self-appointed language police can lead to a rigid orthodoxy — and unintentional self-parody — opening the movement to the scorn of conservative opponents and the mockery of cartoonists and late-night television hosts.

It's hard to imagine women earning points for political correctness by saying "ovarimony" instead of "testimony" — as one participant at the recent Modern Language Association convention was overheard to suggest. It's equally hard to imagine people wanting to flaunt their lack of prejudice by giving up such words and phrases as "bull market," "kaiser roll," "Lazy Susan," and "charley horse."

Several books on bias-free language have already appeared, and the 1991 edition of the *Random House Webster's College Dictionary* boasts an appendix titled "Avoiding Sexist Language." The dictionary also includes such linguistic mutations as "womyn" (women, "used as an alternative spelling to avoid the suggestion of sexism perceived in the sequence m-e-n") and "waitron" (a gender-blind term for waiter or waitress).

Many of these dictionaries and guides not only warn the reader against offensive racial and sexual slurs, but also try to establish and enforce a whole new set of usage rules. Take, for instance, *The Bias-Free Word Finder, a Dictionary of Nondiscriminatory Language* by Rosalie Maggio (Beacon Press) — a volume often indistinguishable, in its meticulous solemnity, from the tongue-in-cheek *Official Politically Correct Dictionary and Handbook* put out last year by Henry Beard and Christopher Cerf (Villard Books). Ms. Maggio's book supplies the reader intent on using kinder, gentler language with writing guidelines as well as a detailed listing of more than 5,000 "biased words and phrases."

Whom are these guidelines for? Somehow one has a tough time picturing them replacing *Fowler's Modern English Usage* in the classroom, or being adopted by the average man (sorry, individual) in the street.

The "pseudogeneric 'he,'" we learn from Ms. Maggio, is to be avoided like the plague, as is the use of the word "man" to refer to humanity. "Fellow," "king," "lord" and "master" are bad because they're "male-oriented words," and "king," "lord" and "master" are especially bad because they're also "hierarchical, dominator society terms." The politically correct lion becomes the "monarch of the jungle," new-age children play "someone on the top of the heap," and the "Mona Lisa" goes down in history as Leonardo's "acme of perfection."

As for the word "black," Ms. Maggio says it should be excised from terms with a negative spin: she recommends substituting words like "mouse" for "black eye," "ostracize" for "blackball," "payola" for "blackmail" and "outcast" for "black sheep." Clearly, some of these substitutions work better than others: somehow the "sinister humor" of Kurt Vonnegut or *Saturday Night Live* doesn't quite make it; nor does the "denouncing" of the Hollywood 10.

For the dedicated user of politically correct language, all these rules can make for some messy moral dilemmas. Whereas "battered wife" is a gender-biased term, the gender-free term "battered spouse," Ms. Maggio notes, incorrectly implies "that men and women are equally battered."

On one hand, say Francine Wattman Frank and Paula A. Treichler in their book *Language, Gender, and Professional Writing* (Modern Language Association), "he or she" is an appropriate construction for talking about an individual (like a jockey, say) who belongs to a profession that's predominantly male—it's a way of emphasizing "that such occupations are not barred to women or that women's concerns need to be kept in mind." On the other hand, they add, using masculine pronouns rhetorically can underscore ongoing male dominance in those fields, implying the need for change.

And what about the speech codes adopted by some universities in recent years? Although they were designed to prohibit students from uttering sexist and racist slurs, they would extend, by logic, to blacks who want to use the word "nigger" to strip the term of its racist connotations, or homosexuals who want to use the word "queer" to reclaim it from bigots.

In her book, Ms. Maggio recommends applying bias-free usage   15
retroactively: she suggests paraphrasing politically incorrect quotations, or replacing "the sexist words or phrases with ellipsis dots and/or bracketed substitutes," or using "*sic*" "to show that the sexist words come from the original quotation and to call attention to the fact that they are incorrect."

Which leads the skeptical reader of *The Bias-Free Word Finder* to wonder whether "All the King's Men" should be retitled "All the Ruler's People"; "Pet Semetary," "Animal Companion Graves"; "Birdman of Alcatraz," "Birdperson of Alcatraz"; and "The Iceman Cometh," "The Ice Route Driver Cometh"?

Will making such changes remove the prejudice in people's minds? Should we really spend time trying to come up with non-male-based alternatives to "Midas touch," "Achilles' heel," and "Montezuma's revenge"? Will tossing out Santa Claus—whom Ms. Maggio accuses of reinforcing "the cultural male-as-norm system"—in favor of Belfana, his Italian female alter ego, truly help banish sexism? Can the avoidance of "violent expressions and metaphors" like "kill two birds with one stone," "sock it to 'em" or "kick an idea around" actually promote a more harmonious world?

The point isn't that the excesses of the word police are comical. The point is that their intolerance (in the name of tolerance) has disturbing implications. In the first place, getting upset by phrases like "bullish on America" or "the City of Brotherly Love" tends to distract attention from the real problems of prejudice and injustice that exist in society at large, turning them into mere questions of semantics. Indeed, the emphasis currently put on politically correct usage has uncanny parallels with the academic movement of deconstruction—a method of textual analysis that focuses on language and linguistic pyrotechnis—which has become firmly established on university campuses.

In both cases, attention is focused on surfaces, on words and metaphors; in both cases, signs and symbols are accorded more importance than content. Hence, the attempt by some radical advocates to remove *The Adventures of Huckleberry Finn* from curriculums on the grounds that Twain's use of the word "nigger" makes the book a racist text—never mind the fact that this American classic (written in 1884) depicts the spiritual kinship achieved between a white boy and a runaway slave, never mind the fact that the "nigger" Jim emerges as the novel's most honorable, decent character.

Ironically enough, the P.C. movement's obsession with language is   20
accompanied by a strange Orwellian willingness to warp the meaning of words by placing them under a high-powered ideological lens. For instance, the *Dictionary of Cautionary Words and Phrases*—a pamphlet issued by the University of Missouri's Multicultural Management Program to help turn "today's journalists into tomorrow's multicultural newsroom managers"—warns that using the word "articulate" to describe members of a minority group can suggest the opposite, "that 'those people' are not considered well educated, articulate and the like."

The pamphlet patronizes minority groups, by cautioning the reader against using the words "lazy" and "burly" to describe any member of such groups; and it issues a similar warning against using words like "gorgeous" and "petite" to describe women.

As euphemism proliferates with the rise of political correctness, there is a spread of the sort of sloppy, abstract language that Orwell said is "designed to make lies sound truthful and murder respectable, and to give an appearance of solidity to pure wind." "Fat" becomes "big boned" as "differently sized"; "stupid" becomes "exceptional"; "stoned" becomes "chemically inconvenienced."

Wait a minute here! Aren't such phrases eerily reminiscent of the euphemisms coined by the government during Vietnam and Watergate? Remember how the military used to speak of "pacification," or how President Richard M. Nixon's press secretary, Ronald L. Ziegler, tried to get away with calling a lie an "inoperative statement"?

Calling the homeless "the underhoused" doesn't give them a place to live; calling the poor "the economically marginalized" doesn't help them pay the bills. Rather, by playing down their plight, such language might even make it easier to shrug off the seriousness of their situation.

Instead of allowing free discussion and debate to occur, many gungho   25
advocates of politically correct language seem to think that simple sup-

pression of a word or concept will magically make the problem disappear. In the *Bias-Free Word Finder,* Ms. Maggio entreats the reader not to perpetuate the negative stereotype of Eve. "Be extremely cautious in referring to the biblical Eve," she writes; "this story has profoundly contributed to negative attitudes toward women throughout history, largely because of misogynistic and patriarchal interpretations that labeled her evil, inferior, and seductive."

The story of Bluebeard, the rake (whoops!—the libertine) who killed his seven wives, she says, is also to be avoided, as is the biblical story of Jezebel. Of Jesus Christ, Ms. Maggio writes: "There have been few individuals in history as completely androgynous as Christ, and it does his message a disservice to overinsist on his maleness." She doesn't give the reader any hints on how this might be accomplished; presumably, one is supposed to avoid describing him as the Son of God.

Of course the P.C. police aren't the only ones who want to proscribe what people should say or give them guidelines for how they may use an idea; Jesse Helms and his supporters are up to exactly the same thing when they propose to patrol the boundaries of the permissible in art. In each case, the would-be censor aspires to suppress what he or she finds distasteful—all, of course, in the name of the public good.

In the case of the politically correct, the prohibition of certain words, phrases and ideas is advanced in the cause of building a brave new world free of racism and hate, but this vision of harmony clashes with the very ideals of diversity and inclusion that the multicultural movement holds dear, and it's purchased at the cost of freedom of expression and freedom of speech.

In fact, the utopian world envisioned by the language police would be bought at the expense of the ideas of individualism and democracy articulated in the "The [*sic*] Gettysburg Address": "Fourscore and seven years ago our fathers brought forth on this continent a new nation, conceived in liberty and dedicated to the proposition that all men are created equal."

Of course, the P.C. police have already found Lincoln's words hope-   30
lessly "phallocentric." No doubt they would rewrite the passage: "Fourscore and seven years ago our foremothers and forefathers brought forth on this continent a new nation, formulated with liberty, and dedicated to the proposition that all humankind is created equal."

The Reader's Presence

1. Kakutani begins by dissecting what she sees as a current state of affairs. What kinds of words does she use to describe this state of affairs in paragraphs 1–3? Is she merely stating the facts or

beginning her argument? Why do you say so? Kakutani uses the word *police* (paragraph 5) to describe those who would alter the English language. What does this word imply? Is it justified?

2. The author humorously cites rather awkward word substitutions from *The Bias-Free Word Finder*. Is this example sufficient and fair as evidence? Why or why not? Does mockery strengthen or weaken Kakutani's case? Why? What response might a proponent of language change propose to counter her argument?

3. Kakutani agrees that old-fashioned language use can cause problems. What solution does she propose, if any? What solution might you propose that would avoid the excesses of either position? Kakutani wrote this essay in 1993. Have any of her examples changed since then?

102

Wendy Kaminer

A Civic Duty to Annoy

Wendy Kaminer (b. 1949), lawyer, author, and social critic, is the president of the National Coalition against Censorship, a public policy fellow at Radcliffe College, and a frequent commentator for National Public Radio's "Morning Edition." Kaminer's books include I'm Dysfunctional, You're Dysfunctional *(1992),* It's All the Rage: Crime and Culture *(1995), and* Sleeping with Extra-Terrestrials: The Rise of Irrationalism and Perils of Piety *(1999). She has written numerous essays and reviews for such publications as the* New York Times, *the* New Republic, *and the* Nation, *and is a contributing editor at the* Atlantic Monthly, *in which "A Civic Duty to Annoy" appeared in 1997.*

What is there about being in a room filled with people who agree with me that makes me want to change my mind? Maybe it's the self-congratulatory air of consensus among people who consider themselves and one another right-thinking. Maybe it's the consistency of belief that devolves into mere conformity. Maybe it's just that I can no longer bear to hear the word "empower."

At self-consciously feminist gatherings I feel at home in the worst way. I feel the way I do at family dinners, when I want to put my feet up on the table and say something to provoke old Uncle George. To get

George going, I defend affirmative action or the capital-gains tax.[1] To irritate my more orthodox feminist colleagues, I disavow any personal guilt about being born white and middle-class. I scoff every time I hear a Harvard student complain that she's oppressed.

I'm not alone in my irreverence, but feminist pieties combined with feminine courtesy keep most of us in line. Radcliffe College, where I am based, is devoted to nurturing female undergraduates. We're supposed to nod sympathetically, in solidarity, when a student speaks of feeling silenced or invisible because she is female, of color, or both. We're not supposed to point out that Harvard students are among the most privileged people in the universe, regardless of race or sex.

I don't mean to scoff at the discrimination that a young woman of any color may have experienced or is likely to experience someday. I do want to remind her that as a student at Harvard/Radcliffe or any other elite university she enjoys many more advantages than a working-class white male attending a community college. And the kind of discrimination that students are apt to encounter at Harvard — relatively subtle and occasional — is not "oppression." It does not systematically deprive people of basic civil rights and liberties and is not generally sanctioned by the administration.

Besides, everyone is bound to feel silenced, invisible, or unappreciated   5
at least once in a while. Imagine how a white male middle manager feels when he's about to be downsized. Like laments about dysfunctional families, complaints about oppression lose their power when proffered so promiscuously. Melodramatic complaints about oppression at Harvard are in part developmental: Students in their late teens and early twenties are apt to place themselves at the center of the universe. But their extreme sensitivity reflects frequently criticized cultural trends as well. An obsession with identity and self-esteem has encouraged students to assume that every insult or slight is motivated by racist, sexist, or heterosexist bias and gravely threatens their well-being. What's lost is a sense of perspective. If attending Harvard is oppression, what was slavery?

Sometimes nurturing students means challenging their complaints instead of satisfying their demands for sympathy. I've heard female students declare that any male classmate who makes derogatory remarks about women online or over the telephone is guilty of sexual harassment and should be punished. What are we teaching them if we agree? That they aren't strong enough to withstand a few puerile sexist jokes that may not even be directed at them? That their male classmates don't have the right to make statements that some women deem offensive? There would be no feminist movement if women never dared to give offense.

When nurturing devolves into pandering, feminism gives way to femininity. Recently a small group of female students called for disciplinary

---

[1]*capital gains tax:* Tax imposed on a profit from the sale of assets, such as bonds or real estate. — EDS.

proceedings against males wearing "pornographic" T-shirts in a dining hall. They found it difficult to eat lunch in the presence of such unwholesome, sexist images. Should we encourage these young women to believe that they're fragile creatures, with particularly delicate digestive systems? Should we offer them official protection from T-shirts? Or should we point out that a group of pro-choice students might someday wear shirts emblazoned with words or images that pro-life students find deeply disturbing? Should we teach them that the art of giving and taking offense is an art of citizenship in a free society?

That is not a feminine art. Radcliffe, for example, is an unfailingly polite institution. Criticism and dissatisfaction are apt to be expressed in a feminine mode, covertly or indirectly. It's particularly hard for many of us not to react with great solicitude to a student who declares herself marginalized, demeaned, or oppressed, even if we harbor doubts about her claim. If she seeks virtue in oppression, as so many do, we seek it in maternalism.

We tend to forget that criticism sometimes expresses greater respect than praise. It is surely more of an honor than flattery. You challenge a student because you consider her capable of learning. You question her premises because you think she's game enough to re-examine them. You do need to take the measure of her self-confidence, and your own. Teaching — or nurturing — requires that you gain students' trust and then risk having them not like you.

Sometimes withholding sympathy feels mean, insensitive, and uncaring; you acquire all the adjectives that aren't supposed to attach to women. You take on the stereotypically masculine vices at a time when the feminine virtue of niceness is being revived: Rosie O'Donnell is the model talk-show host, civility the reigning civic virtue, and communitarianism[2] the paradigmatic political theory. Communities are exalted, as if the typical community were composed solely of people who shared and cared about one another and never engaged in conflict.   10

In fact communities are built on compromise, and compromise presupposes disagreement. Tolerance presupposes the existence of people and ideas you don't like. It prevails upon you to forswear censoring others but not yourself. One test of tolerance is provocation. When you sit down to dinner with your disagreeable relations, or comrades who bask in their rectitude and compassion, you have a civic duty to annoy them.

The Reader's Presence

1. Kaminer writes that she refuses to accept "personal guilt about being born white and middle-class"; what sort of "guilt" is she referring to? How does she characterize this guilt? Who might make

---

[2]*communitarianism:* An influential contemporary political movement that, in general, emphasizes civic responsibility over individual rights. — EDS.

her feel guilty? Who does she feel is likely to claim similar guilt? Why does she resist it?

2. As a college professor, Kaminer writes from an "expert" perspective. How does the author's position of authority influence your reading of the piece? Suppose it were written from the perspective of a student or a custodian at the university. Would you read it differently? In what ways? Can you construct a similar argument about voicing disagreement from your own perspective, using examples from your own life?

3. The writer gives examples of specific cases of disadvantage and contrasts them with the seeming disadvantages of Harvard students. List these examples. Do they seem fair and sound? Can you think of other examples? Can you think of opposing examples?

103 ⸺⸺⸺⸺⸺⸺

Martin Luther King Jr.

Letter from Birmingham Jail

Martin Luther King Jr. (1929–1968) was born in Atlanta, Georgia, and after training for the ministry became pastor of the Dexler Avenue Baptist Church in Montgomery, Alabama. He became active in the civil rights movement in 1956 when he was elected president of the Montgomery Improvement Association, the group which organized a transportation boycott in response to the arrest of Rosa Parks. King later became president of the Southern Christian Leadership Conference, and under his philosophy of nonviolent direct action he led marches and protests throughout the South, to Chicago, and to Washington, D.C. In 1963 King delivered his most famous speech, "I Have a Dream," before 200,000 people in front of the Lincoln Memorial in Washington, D.C. and in 1964 he was awarded the Nobel Peace Prize, King was assassinated on April 3, 1968, in Memphis, Tennessee.

King was a masterful orator and a powerful writer. Along with his many speeches, King wrote several books, including Why We Can't Wait *(1963),* Where Do We Go from Here: Chaos or Community? *(1967),* The Measure of a Man *(1968), and* Trumpet of Conscience *(1968). "Letter from Birmingham Jail" appeared in* Why We Can't Wait.

King's best-known writings and speeches, including the letter reprinted here, are designed to educate his audiences and inspire them to act. "Through education we seek to break down the spiritual barriers to integration," he once said, and "through legislation and court orders we seek to break down the physical

*barriers to integration. One method is not a substitute for the other, but a mean-
ingful and necessary supplement."*

MARTIN LUTHER KING JR.
Birmingham City Jail
April 16, 1963

Bishop C. C. J. CARPENTER
Bishop JOSEPH A. DURICK
Rabbi MILTON L. GRAFMAN
Bishop PAUL HARDIN
Bishop NOLAN B. HARMON
The Rev. GEORGE M. MURRAY
The Rev. EDWARD V. RAMAGE
The Rev. EARL STALLINGS

My dear Fellow Clergyman,

While confined here in the Birmingham City Jail, I came across your recent statement calling our present activities "unwise and untimely." Seldom, if ever, do I pause to answer criticism of my work and ideas. If I
sought to answer all of the criticism that cross my desk, my secretaries
would be engaged in little else in the course of the day and I would have no
time for constructive work. But since I feel that you are men of genuine
good will and your criticisms are sincerely set forth, I would like to answer
your statement in what I hope will be patient and reasonable terms.

I think I should give the reason for my being in Birmingham, since
you have been influenced by the argument of "outsiders coming in." I
have the honor of serving as president of the Southern Christian Leadership Conference, an organization operating in every Southern state with
headquarters in Atlanta, Georgia. We have some eighty-five affiliate organizations all across the South—one being the Alabama Christian Movement for Human Rights. Whenever necessary and possible we share staff,
educational, and financial resources with our affiliates. Several months
ago our local affiliate here in Birmingham invited us to be on call to engage in a nonviolent direct action program if such were deemed necessary. We readily consented and when the hour came we lived up to our
promises. So I am here, along with several members of my staff, because
we were invited here. I am here because I have basic organizational ties
here. Beyond this, I am in Birmingham because injustice is here. Just as
the eighth century prophets left their little villages and carried their "thus
saith the Lord" far beyond the boundaries of their home town, and just
as the Apostle Paul left his little village of Tarsus and carried the gospel of
Jesus Christ to practically every hamlet and city of the Graeco-Roman
world, I too am compelled to carry the gospel of freedom beyond my particular home town. Like Paul, I must constantly respond to the Macedon-
ian call for aid.

Moreover, I am cognizant of the interrelatedness of all communities and states. I cannot sit idly by in Atlanta and not be concerned about what happens in Birmingham. Injustice anywhere is a threat to justice everywhere. We are caught in an inescapable network of mutuality tied in a single garment of destiny. Whatever affects one directly affects all indirectly. Never again can we afford to live with the narrow, provincial "outside agitator" idea. Anyone who lives inside the United States can never be considered an outsider anywhere in this country.

You deplore the demonstrations that are presently taking place in Birmingham. But I am sorry that your statement did not express a similar concern for the conditions that brought the demonstrations into being. I am sure that each of you would want to go beyond the superficial social analyst who looks merely at effects, and does not grapple with underlying causes. I would not hesitate to say that it is unfortunate that so-called demonstrations are taking place in Birmingham at this time, but I would say in more emphatic terms it is even more unfortunate that the white power structure of this city left the Negro community with no other alternative.

In any nonviolent campaign there are four basic steps: (1) collection   5
of the facts to determine whether injustices are alive; (2) negotiation; (3) self-purification; and (4) direct action. We have gone through all of these steps in Birmingham. There can be no gainsaying of the fact that racial injustice engulfs this community. Birmingham is probably the most thoroughly segregated city in the United States. Its ugly record of police brutality is known in every section of this country. Its unjust treatment of Negroes in the courts is a notorious reality. There have been more unsolved bombings of Negro homes and churches in Birmingham than any city in this nation. These are the hard, brutal, and unbelievable facts. On the basis of these conditions Negro leaders sought to negotiate with the city fathers. But the political leaders consistently refused to engage in good faith negotiation.

Then came the opportunity last September to talk with some of the leaders of the economic community. In these negotiating sessions certain promises were made by the merchants—such as the promise to remove the humiliating racial signs from the stores. On the basis of these promises Rev. Shuttlesworth and the leaders of the Alabama Christian Movement for Human Rights agreed to call a moratorium on any type of demonstrations. As the weeks and months unfolded we realized that we were the victims of a broken promise. The signs remained. As in so many experiences of the past we were confronted with blasted hopes, and the dark shadow of a deep disappointment settled upon us. So we had no alternative except that of preparing for direct action, whereby we would present our very bodies as a means of laying our case before the conscience of the local and national community. We were not unmindful of the difficulties involved. So we decided to go through a process of self-purification. We started having workshops on nonviolence and repeatedly asked ourselves the questions, "Are you able to accept blows without retaliating?" "Are you able to endure the ordeals of jail?"

We decided to set our direct action program around the Easter season, realizing that with the exception of Christmas, this was the largest shopping period of the year. Knowing that a strong economic withdrawal program would be the by-product of direct action, we felt that this was the best time to bring pressure on the merchants for the needed changes. Then it occurred to us that the March election was ahead, and so we speedily decided to postpone action until after election day. When we discovered that Mr. Connor[1] was in the run-off, we decided again to postpone so that the demonstrations could not be used to cloud the issues. At this time we agreed to begin our nonviolent witness the day after the run-off.

This reveals that we did not move irresponsibly into direct action. We too wanted to see Mr. Connor defeated; so we went through postponement after postponement to aid in this community need. After this we felt that direct action could be delayed no longer.

You may well ask, "Why direct action? Why sit-ins, marches, etc.? Isn't negotiation a better path?" You are exactly right in your call for negotiation. Indeed, this is the purpose of direct action. Nonviolent direct action seeks to create such a crisis and establish such creative tension that a community that has constantly refused to negotiate is forced to confront the issue. It seeks so to dramatize the issue that it can no longer be ignored. I just referred to the creation of tension as a part of the work of the nonviolent resister. This may sound rather shocking. But I must confess that I am not afraid of the word tension. I have earnestly worked and preached against violent tension, but there is a type of constructive nonviolent tension that is necessary for growth. Just as Socrates felt that it was necessary to create a tension in the mind so that individuals could rise from the bondage of myths and half-truths to the unfettered realm of creative analysis and objective appraisal, we must see the need of having nonviolent gadflies to create the kind of tension in society that will help men rise from the dark depths of prejudice and racism to the majestic heights of understanding and brotherhood. So the purpose of the direct action is to create a situation so crisis-packed that it will inevitably open the door to negotiation. We, therefore, concur with you in your call for negotiation. Too long has our beloved Southland been bogged down in the tragic attempt to live in monologue rather than dialogue.

One of the basic points in your statement is that our acts are untimely. Some have asked, "Why didn't you give the new administration   10

---

[1]*Mr. Connor:* Eugene "Bull" Connor and Albert Boutwell ran for mayor of Birmingham, Alabama, in 1963. Although Boutwell, the more moderate candidate, was declared the winner, Connor, the city commissioner of public safety, refused to leave office, claiming that he had been elected to serve until 1965. While the issue was debated in the courts, Connor was on the street ordering the police to use force to suppress demonstrations against segregation. — EDS.

time to act?" The only answer that I can give to this inquiry is that the new administration must be prodded about as much as the outgoing one before it acts. We will be sadly mistaken if we feel that the election of Mr. Boutwell will bring the millennium to Birmingham. While Mr. Boutwell is much more articulate and gentle than Mr. Connor, they are both segregationists dedicated to the task of maintaining the status quo. The hope I see in Mr. Boutwell is that he will be reasonable enough to see the futility of massive resistance to desegregation. But he will not see this without pressure from the devotees of civil rights. My friends, I must say to you that we have not made a single gain in civil rights without determined legal and nonviolent pressure. History is the long and tragic story of the fact that privileged groups seldom give up their privileges voluntarily. Individuals may see the moral light and voluntarily give up their unjust posture; but as Reinhold Niebuhr has reminded us, groups are more immoral than individuals.

We know through painful experience that freedom is never voluntarily given by the oppressor; it must be demanded by the oppressed. Frankly I have never yet engaged in a direct action movement that was "well timed," according to the timetable of those who have not suffered unduly from the disease of segregation. For years now I have heard the word "Wait!" It rings in the ear of every Negro with a piercing familiarity. This "wait" has almost always meant "never." It has been a tranquilizing thaliodomide, relieving the emotional stress for a moment, only to give birth to an ill-formed infant of frustration. We must come to see with the distinguished jurist of yesterday that "justice too long delayed is justice denied." We have waited for more than three hundred and forty years for our constitutional and God-given rights. The nations of Asia and Africa are moving with jet-like speed toward the goal of political independence, and we still creep at horse and buggy pace toward the gaining of a cup of coffee at a lunch counter.

I guess it is easy for those who have never felt the stinging darts of segregation to say wait. But when you have seen vicious mobs lynch your mothers and fathers at will and drown your sisters and brothers at whim; when you have seen hate-filled policemen curse, kick, brutalize, and even kill your black brothers and sisters with impunity; when you see the vast majority of your twenty million Negro brothers smothering in an air-tight cage of poverty in the midst of an affluent society; when you suddenly find your tongue twisted and your speech stammering as you seek to explain to your six-year-old daughter why she can't go to the public amusement park that has just been advertised on television, and see tears welling up in her little eyes when she is told that Funtown is closed to colored children, and see the depressing clouds of inferiority begin to form in her little mental sky, and see her begin to distort her little personality by unconsciously developing a bitterness toward white people; when you have to concoct an answer for a five-year-old son asking in agonizing pathos: "Daddy, why do white people treat colored people so mean?";

when you take a cross country drive and find it necessary to sleep night after night in the uncomfortable corners of your automobile because no motel will accept you; when you are humiliated day in and day out by nagging signs reading "white" men and "colored"; when your first name becomes "nigger" and your middle name becomes "boy" (however old you are) and your last name becomes "John," and when your wife and mother are never given the respected title "Mrs."; when you are harried by day and haunted by night by the fact that you are a Negro, living constantly at tip-toe stance never quite knowing what to expect next, and plagued with inner fears and outer resentments; when you are forever fighting a degenerating sense of "nobodiness";—then you will understand why we find it difficult to wait. There comes a time when the cup of endurance runs over, and men are no longer willing to be plunged into an abyss of injustice where they experience the bleakness of corroding despair. I hope, sirs, you can understand our legitimate and unavoidable impatience.

You express a great deal of anxiety over our willingness to break laws. This is certainly a legitimate concern. Since we so diligently urge people to obey the Supreme Court's decision of 1954 outlawing segregation in the public schools, it is rather strange and paradoxical to find us consciously breaking laws. One may well ask, "How can you advocate breaking some laws and obeying others?" The answer is found in the fact that there are two types of laws. There are *just* laws and there are *unjust* laws. I would be the first to advocate obeying just laws. One has not only a legal but moral responsibility to obey just laws. Conversely, one has a moral responsibility to disobey unjust laws. I would agree with Saint Augustine that "An unjust law is no law at all."

Now what is the difference between the two? How does one determine when a law is just or unjust? A just law is a man-made code that squares with the moral law or the law of God. An unjust law is a code that is out of harmony with the moral law. To put it in the terms of Saint Thomas Aquinas, an unjust law is a human law that is not rooted in eternal and natural law. Any law that uplifts human personality is just. Any law that degrades human personality is unjust. All segregation statutes are unjust because segregation distorts the soul and damages the personality. It gives the segregator a false sense of superiority and the segregated a false sense of inferiority. To use the words of Martin Buber, the great Jewish philosopher, segregation substitutes an "I-it" relationship for the "I-thou" relationship, and ends up relegating persons to the status of things. So segregation is not only politically, economically, and sociologically unsound, but it is morally wrong and sinful. Paul Tillich[2] has said that sin is separation. Isn't segregation an existential expression of man's tragic separation, an expression of his awful estrangement, his terrible

---

[2]*Paul Tillich* (1886–1965): Theologian and philosopher.—EDS.

sinfulness? So I can urge men to obey the 1954 decision of the Supreme Court[3] because it is morally right, and I can urge them to disobey segregation ordinances because they are morally wrong.

Let us turn to a more concrete example of just and unjust laws. An 15 unjust law is a code that a majority inflicts on a minority that is not binding on itself. This is *difference* made legal. On the other hand a just law is a code that a majority compels a minority to follow that it is willing to follow itself. This is *sameness* made legal.

Let me give another explanation. An unjust law is a code inflicted upon a minority which that minority had no part in enacting or creating because they did not have the unhampered right to vote. Who can say the legislature of Alabama which set up the segregation laws was democratically elected? Throughout the state of Alabama all types of conniving methods are used to prevent Negroes from becoming registered voters and there are some counties without a single Negro registered to vote despite the fact that the Negro constitutes a majority of the population. Can any law set up in such a state be considered democratically structured?

These are just a few examples of unjust and just laws. There are some instances when a law is just on its face but unjust in its application. For instance, I was arrested Friday on a charge of parading without a permit. Now there is nothing wrong with an ordinance which requires a permit for a parade, but when the ordinance is used to preserve segregation and to deny citizens the First Amendment privilege of peaceful assembly and peaceful protest, then it becomes unjust.

I hope you can see the distinction I am trying to point out. In no sense do I advocate evading or defying the law as the rabid segregationist would do. This would lead to anarchy. One who breaks an unjust law must do it *openly, lovingly* (not hatefully as the white mothers did in New Orleans when they were seen on television screaming "nigger, nigger, nigger") and with a willingness to accept the penalty. I submit that an individual who breaks a law that conscience tells him is unjust, and willingly accepts the penalty by staying in jail to arouse the conscience of the community over its injustice, is in reality expressing the very highest respect for law.

Of course there is nothing new about this kind of civil disobedience. It was seen sublimely in the refusal of Shadrach, Meshach, and Abednego to obey the laws of Nebuchadnezzar because a higher moral law was involved. It was practiced superbly by the early Christians who were willing to face hungry lions and the excruciating pain of chopping blocks, before submitting to certain unjust laws of the Roman Empire. To a degree academic freedom is a reality today because Socrates practiced civil disobedience.

---

[3]*1954 decision of the Supreme Court: Brown v. Board of Education,* the case in which the Supreme Court ruled racial segregation in the nation's public schools unconstitutional. —EDS.

We can never forget that everything Hitler did in Germany was   20
"legal" and everything the Hungarian freedom fighters[4] did in Hungary
was "illegal." It was "illegal" to aid and comfort a Jew in Hitler's Germany. But I am sure that, if I had lived in Germany during that time, I
would have aided and comforted my Jewish brothers even though it was
illegal. If I lived in a communist country today where certain principles
dear to the Christian faith are suppressed, I believe I would openly advocate disobeying those antireligious laws.

I must make two honest confessions to you, my Christian and Jewish
brothers. First I must confess that over the last few years I have been
gravely disappointed with the white moderate. I have almost reached the
regrettable conclusion that the Negroes' great stumbling block in the
stride toward freedom is not the White Citizens' "Counciler" or the Ku
Klux Klanner, but the white moderate who is more devoted to "order"
than to justice; who prefers a negative peace which is the absence of tension to a positive peace which is the presence of justice; who constantly
says "I agree with you in the goal you seek, but I can't agree with your
methods of direct action"; who paternalistically feels that he can set the
timetable for another man's freedom; who lives by the myth of time and
who constantly advises the Negro to wait until a "more convenient season." Shallow understanding from people of good will is more frustrating
than absolute misunderstanding from people of ill will. Lukewarm acceptance is much more bewildering than outright rejection.

I had hoped that the white moderate would understand that law and
order exist for the purpose of establishing justice, and that when they fail
to do this they become the dangerously structured dams that block the
flow of social progress. I had hoped that the white moderate would understand that the present tension in the South is merely a necessary phase
of the transition from an obnoxious negative peace, where the Negro passively accepted his unjust plight, to a substance-filled positive peace,
where all men will respect the dignity and worth of human personality.
Actually, we who engage in nonviolent direct action are not the creators
of tension. We merely bring to the surface the hidden tension that is already alive. We bring it out in the open where it can be seen and dealt
with. Like a boil that can never be cured as long as it is covered up but
must be opened with all its pus-flowing ugliness to the natural medicines
of air and light, injustice must likewise be exposed, with all of the tension
its exposing creates, to the light of human conscience and the air of national opinion before it can be cured.

In your statement you asserted that our actions, even though peaceful, must be condemned because they precipitate violence. But can this assertion be logically made? Isn't this like condemning the robbed man be-

---

[4]*Hungarian freedom fighters:* Those who fought in the unsuccessful 1956 revolt
against Soviet oppression. — EDS.

cause his possession of money precipitated the evil act of robbery? Isn't this like condemning Socrates because his unswerving commitment to truth and his philosophical delvings precipitated the misguided popular mind to make him drink the hemlock? Isn't this like condemning Jesus because His unique God consciousness and never-ceasing devotion to His will precipitated the evil act of crucifixion? We must come to see, as federal courts have consistently affirmed, that it is immoral to urge an individual to withdraw his efforts to gain his basic constitutional rights because the quest precipitates violence. Society must protect the robbed and punish the robber.

I had also hoped that the white moderate would reject the myth of time. I received a letter this morning from a white brother in Texas which said: "All Christians know that the colored people will receive equal rights eventually, but is it possible that you are in too great of a religious hurry? It has taken Christianity almost 2000 years to accomplish what it has. The teachings of Christ take time to come to earth." All that is said here grows out of a tragic misconception of time. It is the strangely irrational notion that there is something in the very flow of time that will inevitably cure all ills. Actually time is neutral. It can be used either destructively or constructively. I am coming to feel that the people of ill will have used time much more effectively than the people of good will. We will have to repent in this generation not merely for the vitriolic words and actions of the bad people, but for the appalling silence of the good people. We must come to see that human progress never rolls in on wheels of inevitability. It comes through the tireless efforts and persistent work of men willing to be co-workers with God, and without this hard work time itself becomes an ally of the forces of social stagnation.

We must use time creatively, and forever realize that the time is always ripe to do right. Now is the time to make real the promise of democracy, and transform our pending national elegy into a creative psalm of brotherhood. Now is the time to lift our national policy from the quicksand of racial injustice to the solid rock of human dignity.   25

You spoke of our activity in Birmingham as extreme. At first I was rather disappointed that fellow clergyman would see my nonviolent efforts as those of the extremist. I started thinking about the fact that I stand in the middle of two opposing forces in the Negro community. One is a force of complacency made up of Negroes who, as a result of long years of oppression, have been so completely drained of self-respect and a sense of "somebodiness" that they have adjusted to segregation, and of a few Negroes in the middle class who, because of a degree of academic and economic security, and because at points they profit by segregation, have unconsciously become insensitive to the problems of the masses. The other force is one of bitterness and hatred and comes perilously close to advocating violence. It is expressed in the various black nationalist groups that are springing up over the nation, the largest and best known being Elijah Muhammad's Muslim movement.[5] This movement is nourished by the contemporary frustration over the continued existence of racial discrimination. It is made up of people who have lost faith in America, who have absolutely repudiated Christianity, and who have concluded that the white man is an incurable "devil." I have tried to stand between these two forces saying that we need not follow the "do-nothing-ism" of the complacent or the hatred and despair of the black nationalist. There is the more excellent way of love and nonviolent protest. I'm grateful to God that, through the Negro church, the dimension of nonviolence entered our struggle. If this philosophy had not emerged I am convinced that by now many streets of the South would be flowing with floods of blood. And I am further convinced that if our white brothers dismiss us as "rabble rousers" and "outside agitators" — those of us who are working through the channels of nonviolent direct action — and refuse to support our nonviolent efforts, millions of Negroes, out of frustration and despair, will seek solace and security in black nationalist ideologies, a development that will lead inevitably to a frightening racial nightmare.

Oppressed people cannot remain oppressed forever. The urge for freedom will eventually come. This is what has happened to the American Negro. Something within has reminded him of his birthright of freedom; something without has reminded him that he can gain it. Consciously and unconsciously, he has been swept in by what the Germans call the *Zeitgeist*,[6] and his black brothers of Africa, and his brown and yellow brothers of Asia, South America, and the Caribbean, he is moving with a sense of cosmic urgency toward the promised land of racial justice. Recognizing this vital urge that has engulfed the Negro community, one should readily understand public demonstrations. The Negro has many pent-up resentments and latent frustrations. He has to get them out. So let him march sometime; let him have his prayer pilgrimages to the city hall; understand why he must have sit-ins and freedom rides. If his repressed emotions do not come out in these nonviolent ways, they will come out in ominous expressions of violence. This is not a threat; it is a fact of history. So I have not said to my people, "Get rid of your discontent." But I have tried to say that this normal and healthy discontent can be channeled through the creative outlet of nonviolent direct action. Now this approach is being dismissed as extremist. I must admit that I was initially disappointed in being so categorized.

But as I continued to think about the matter I gradually gained a bit of satisfaction from being considered an extremist. Was not Jesus an extremist in love? "Love your enemies, bless them that curse you, pray for them

---

[5]*Elijah Muhammad's Muslim Movement:* Led by Elijah Muhammad, the Black Muslims opposed integration and promoted the creation of a black nation within the United States. —EDS.

[6]*Zeitgeist:* A German word meaning "spirit of the time." —EDS.

that despitefully use you." Was not Amos an extremist for justice—"Let justice roll down like waters and righteousness like a mighty stream." Was not Paul an extremist for the gospel of Jesus Christ—"I bear in my body the marks of the Lord Jesus." Was not Martin Luther an extremist—"Here I stand; I can do none other so help me God." Was not John Bunyan an extremist—"I will stay in jail to the end of my days before I make a butchery of my conscience." Was not Abraham Lincoln an extremist—"This nation cannot survive half slave and half free." Was not Thomas Jefferson an extremist—"We hold these truths to be self evident that all men are created equal." So the question is not whether we will be extremist but what kind of extremist will we be. Will we be extremists for hate or will we be extremists for love? Will we be extremists for the preservation of injustice—or will we be extremists for the cause of justice? In that dramatic scene on Calvary's hill three men were crucified. We must never forget that all three were crucified for the same crime—the crime of extremism. Two were extremists for immorality, and thus fell below their environment. The other, Jesus Christ, was an extremist for love, truth, and goodness, and thereby rose above His environment. So, after all, maybe the South, the nation, and the world are in dire need of creative extremists.

I had hoped that the white moderate would see this. Maybe I was too optimistic. Maybe I expected too much. I guess I should have realized that few members of a race that has oppressed another race can understand or appreciate the deep groans and passionate yearnings of those that have been oppressed, and still fewer have the vision to see that injustice must be rooted out by strong, persistent, and determined action. I am thankful, however, that some of our white brothers have grasped the meaning of this social revolution and committed themselves to it. They are still all too small in quantity, but they are big in quality. Some like Ralph McGill, Lillian Smith, Harry Golden, and James Dabbs have written about our struggle in eloquent, prophetic, and understanding terms. Others have marched with us down nameless streets of the South. They have languished in filthy, roach-infested jails, suffering the abuse and brutality of angry policemen who see them as "dirty nigger lovers." They, unlike so many of their moderate brothers and sisters, have recognized the urgency of the moment and sensed the need for powerful "action" antidotes to combat the disease of segregation.

Let me rush on to mention my other disappointment. I have been so 30 greatly disappointed with the white Church and its leadership. Of course there are some notable exceptions. I am not unmindful of the fact that each of you has taken some significant stands on this issue. I commend you, Rev. Stallings, for your Christian stand on this past Sunday, in welcoming Negroes to your worship service on a nonsegregated basis. I commend the Catholic leaders of this state for integrating Springhill College several years ago.

But despite these notable exceptions I must honestly reiterate that I have been disappointed with the Church. I do not say that as one of those negative critics who can always find something wrong with the Church. I say it as a minister of the gospel, who loves the Church; who was nurtured in its bosom; who has been sustained by its spiritual blessings and who will remain true to it as long as the cord of life shall lengthen.

I had the strange feeling when I was suddenly catapulted into the leadership of the bus protest in Montgomery[7] several years ago that we would have the support of the white Church. I felt that the white ministers, priests, and rabbis of the South would be some of our strongest allies. Instead, some have been outright opponents, refusing to understand the freedom movement and misrepresenting its leaders; all too many others have been more cautious than courageous and have remained silent behind the anesthetizing security of stained glass windows.

In spite of my shattered dreams of the past, I came to Birmingham with the hope that the white religious leadership of the community would see the justice of our cause and, with deep moral concern, serve as the channel through which our just grievances could get to the power structure. I had hoped that each of you would understand. But again I have been disappointed.

I have heard numerous religious leaders of the South call upon their worshippers to comply with a desegregation decision because it is the law, but I have longed to hear white ministers say follow this decree because integration is morally right and the Negro is your brother. In the midst of blatant injustices inflicted upon the Negro, I have watched white churches stand on the sideline and merely mouth pious irrelevancies and sanctimonious trivialities. In the midst of a mighty struggle to rid our nation of racial and economic injustice, I have heard so many ministers say, "Those are social issues which the Gospel has no real concern," and I have watched so many churches commit themselves to a completely otherworldly religion which made a strange distinction between body and soul, the sacred and the secular.

So here we are moving toward the exit of the twentieth century with   35 a religious community largely adjusted to the status quo, standing as a tail-light behind other community agencies rather than a headlight leading men to higher levels of justice.

I have travelled the length and breadth of Alabama, Mississippi, and all the other Southern states. On sweltering summer days and crisp autumn mornings I have looked at her beautiful churches with their spires pointing heavenward. I have beheld the impressive outlay of her massive religious education buildings. Over and over again I have found myself asking: "Who worships here? Who is their God? Where were their voices

---

[7]***bus protest in Montgomery:*** After Rosa Parks was arrested on December 1, 1955, in Montgomery, Alabama, for refusing to give her seat on a bus to a white male passenger, a bus boycott began, which lasted nearly one year and was supported by nearly all of the city's black residents. — EDS.

when the lips of Governor Barnett[8] dripped with words of interposition and nullification? Where were they when Governor Wallace[9] gave the clarion call for defiance and hatred? Where were their voices of support when tired, bruised, and weary Negro men and women decided to rise from the dark dungeons of complacency to the bright hills of creative protest?"

Yes, these questions are still in my mind. In deep disappointment, I have wept over the laxity of the Church. But be assured that my tears have been tears of love. There can be no deep disappointment where there is not deep love. Yes, I love the Church; I love her sacred walls. How could I do otherwise? I am in the rather unique position of being the son, the grandson, and the great grandson of preachers. Yes, I see the Church as the body of Christ. But, oh! How we have blemished and scarred that body through social neglect and fear of being nonconformists.

There was a time when the Church was very powerful. It was during that period when the early Christians rejoiced when they were deemed worthy to suffer for what they believed. In those days the Church was not merely a thermometer that recorded the ideas and principles of popular opinion; it was a thermostat that transformed the mores of society. Wherever the early Christians entered a town the power structure got disturbed and immediately sought to convict them for being "disturbers of the peace" and "outside agitators." But they went on with the conviction that they were a "colony of heaven" and had to obey God rather than man. They were small in number but big in commitment. They were too God-intoxicated to be "astronomically intimidated." They brought an end to such ancient evils as infanticide and gladiatorial contest.

Things are different now. The contemporary Church is so often a weak, ineffectual voice with an uncertain sound. It is so often the arch-supporter of the status quo. Far from being disturbed by the presence of the Church, the power structure of the average community is consoled by the Church's silent and often vocal sanction of things as they are.

But the judgment of God is upon the Church as never before. If the Church of today does not recapture the sacrificial spirit of the early Church, it will lose its authentic ring, forfeit the loyalty of millions, and be dismissed as an irrelevant social club with no meaning for the twentieth century. I am meeting young people every day whose disappointment with the Church has risen to outright disgust.

Maybe again I have been too optimistic. Is organized religion too inextricably bound to the status quo to save our nation and the world? Maybe I must turn my faith to the inner spiritual Church, the church within the

40

---

[8]*Governor Barnett:* Ross R. Barnett, governor of Mississippi from 1960 to 1964. — EDS.

[9]*Governor Wallace:* George C. Wallace served as governor of Alabama from 1963 to 1966, 1971 to 1979, and 1983 to 1987. — EDS.

Church, as the true *ecclesia*[10] and the hope of the world. But again I am thankful to God that some noble souls from the ranks of organized religion have broken loose from the paralyzing chains of conformity and joined us as active partners in the struggle for freedom. They have left their secure congregations and walked the streets of Albany, Georgia, with us. They have gone through the highways of the South on torturous rides for freedom. Yes, they have gone to jail with us. Some have been kicked out of their churches and lost the support of their bishops and fellow ministers. But they have gone with the faith that right defeated is stronger than evil triumphant. These men have been the leaven in the lump of the race. Their witness has been the spiritual salt that has preserved the true meaning of the Gospel in these troubled times. They have carved a tunnel of hope through the dark mountain of disappointment.

I hope the Church as a whole will meet the challenge of this decisive hour. But even if the Church does not come to the aid of justice, I have no despair about the future. I have no fear about the outcome of our struggle in Birmingham, even if our motives are presently misunderstood. We will reach the goal of freedom in Birmingham and all over the nation, because the goal of America is freedom. Abused and scorned though we may be, our destiny is tied up with the destiny of America. Before the pilgrims landed at Plymouth, we were here. Before the pen of Jefferson etched across the pages of history the majestic words of the Declaration of Independence, we were here. For more than two centuries our foreparents labored in this country without wages; they made cotton "king"; and they built the homes of their masters in the midst of brutal injustice and shameful humiliation—and yet out of a bottomless vitality they continued to thrive and develop. If the inexpressible cruelties of slavery could not stop us, the opposition we now face will surely fail. We will win our freedom because the sacred heritage of our nation and the eternal will of God are embodied in our echoing demands.

I must close now. But before closing I am impelled to mention one other point in your statement that troubled me profoundly. You warmly commended the Birmingham police force for keeping "order" and "preventing violence." I don't believe you would have so warmly commended the police force if you had seen its angry violent dogs literally biting six unarmed, nonviolent Negroes. I don't believe you would so quickly commend the policemen if you would observe their ugly and inhuman treatment of Negroes here in the city jail; if you would watch them push and curse old Negro women and young Negro girls; if you would see them slap and kick old Negro men and young Negro boys; if you will observe them, as they did on two occasions, refuse to give us food because we wanted to sing our grace together. I'm sorry that I can't join you in your praise for the police department.

---

[10]*ecclesia:* The Latin word for church. — EDS.

It is true that they have been rather disciplined in their public handling of the demonstrators. In this sense they have been rather publicly "nonviolent." But for what purpose? To preserve the evil system of segregation. Over the last few years I have consistently preached that nonviolence demands that the means we use must be as pure as the ends we seek. So I have tried to make it clear that it is wrong to use immoral means to attain moral ends. But now I must affirm that it is just as wrong, or even more so, to use moral means to preserve immoral ends. Maybe Mr. Connor and his policemen have been rather publicly nonviolent, as Chief Pritchett[11] was in Albany, Georgia, but they have used the moral means of nonviolence to maintain the immoral end of flagrant racial injustice. T. S. Eliot has said that there is no greater treason than to do the right deed for the wrong reason.

I wish you had commended the Negro sit-inners and demonstrators   45
of Birmingham for their sublime courage, their willingness to suffer, and their amazing discipline in the midst of the most inhuman provocation. One day the South will recognize its real heroes. They will be the James Merediths,[12] courageously and with a majestic sense of purpose, facing jeering and hostile mobs and the agonizing loneliness that characterizes the life of the pioneer. They will be old, oppressed, battered Negro women, symbolized in a seventy-two year old woman of Montgomery, Alabama, who rose up with a sense of dignity and with her people decided not to ride the segregated buses, and responded to one who inquired about her tiredness with ungrammatical profundity: "My feets is tired, but my soul is rested." They will be young high school and college students, young ministers of the gospel and a host of the elders, courageously and nonviolently sitting in at lunch counters and willingly going to jail for conscience sake. One day the South will know that when these disinherited children of God sat down at lunch counters they were in reality standing up for the best in the American dream and the most sacred values in our Judeo-Christian heritage, and thus carrying our whole nation back to great wells of democracy which were dug deep by the founding fathers in the formulation of the Constitution and the Declaration of Independence.

Never before have I written a letter this long (or should I say a book?). I'm afraid that it is much too long to take your precious time. I can assure you that it would have been much shorter if I had been writing from a comfortable desk, but what else is there to do when you are alone

---

[11]*Chief Pritchett:* Pritchett served as police chief in Albany, Georgia, during nonviolent demonstrations in 1961 and 1962. Chief Pritchett responded to the nonviolent demonstrations with nonviolence, refusing to allow his officers to physically or verbally abuse the demonstrators. — EDS.

[12]*James Merediths:* Under the protection of federal marshals and the National Guard in 1962, James Meredith was the first black man to enroll at the University of Mississippi. — EDS.

for days in the dull monotony of a narrow jail cell other than write long letters, think strange thoughts, and pray long prayers?

If I have said anything in this letter that is an overstatement of the truth and is indicative of an unreasonable impatience, I beg you to forgive me. If I have said anything in this letter that is an understatement of the truth and is indicative of my having a patience that makes me patient with anything less than brotherhood, I beg God to forgive me.

I hope this letter finds you strong in the faith. I also hope that circumstances will soon make it possible for me to meet each of you, not as an integrationist or a civil rights leader, but as a fellow clergyman and a Christian brother. Let us all hope that the dark clouds of racial prejudice will soon pass away and the deep fog of misunderstanding will be lifted from our fear-drenched communities and in some not too distant tomorrow the radiant stars of love and brotherhood will shine over our great nation with all of their scintillating beauty.

> *Yours for the cause of*
> *Peace and Brotherhood*
> MARTIN LUTHER KING JR.

The Reader's Presence

1. King wrote this letter in response to the eight clergymen identified at the beginning of the letter, who had declared that the civil rights activities of King and his associates were "unwise and untimely." What does King gain by characterizing his "Fellow Clergymen" as "men of genuine good will," whose criticisms are "sincerely set forth"? What evidence can you point to in King's letter to verify the claim that his audience extends far beyond the eight clergymen he explicitly addresses? Comment on the overall structure of King's letter. What principle of composition underpins the structure of his response?

2. King establishes the tone of his response to the criticisms of the clergymen at the end of the opening paragraph: "I would like to answer your statement in what I hope will be patient and reasonable terms." As you reread his letter, identify specific words and phrases—as well as argumentative strategies—that satisfy these self-imposed criteria. In what specific sense does King use the word *hope* here? As you reread his letter, point to each subsequent reference to hope. How does King emphasize the different meanings and connotations of the word as he unfolds his argument? Do the same for his use of the word *disappointment.* What distinctions does he draw about the word *tension?* How are these distinctions related to his argument?

3. On what historical sources does King rely to create a precedent for his actions in Birmingham? With what religious figure does King most closely identify? With what effect? What more general analogy does he draw between the circumstances in Birmingham and elsewhere? What argument does he offer in support of this specific claim? Comment on the nature—and the extent—of his use of metaphors. Does he use metaphor primarily to clarify and reinforce a point? to introduce an element of emotion? some combination of these? something else? In what ways does King base his argument on an appeal to his readers' emotions? Point to particular examples to clarify and support your response. What purposes does he identify in his definition of—and justification of—"nonviolent direct action"?

104 _____

Barbara Kingsolver

Stone Soup

Barbara Kingsolver (b. 1955) writes about middle-American lives, and in both her fiction and her essays she searches for the common threads that bind people together. She has published stories in Homeland *(1989), poetry in* Another America *(1994), and four novels,* The Bean Trees *(1988),* Animal Dreams *(1990),* Pigs in Heaven *(1993), and* The Poisonwood Bible *(1998), which was nominated for the 1999 PEN/Faulkner Award for Fiction. She also contributes to numerous periodicals, including the* Progressive, Smithsonian, *the* New York Times Book Review, *and the* Los Angeles Times Book Review. *Her nonfiction works include* Holding the Line: Women in the Great Arizona Mine Strike of 1983 *(1989) and* High Tide in Tucson: Essays for Now or Never *(1995), in which "Stone Soup" appears.*

Regarding her work, Kingsolver remarks, "To me, writing is writing. . . . I believe there are some truths that are better told as fiction, and other truths that are most jarring and moving when you know they really did happen—like the Holding the Line *strike. There are moments of light that are best revealed in a poem, or a short story. . . . But the techniques, for me, remain the same."*

In the catalog of family values, where do we rank an occasion like this? A curly-haired boy who wanted to run before he walked, age seven now, a soccer player scoring a winning goal. He turns to the bleachers with his fists in the air and a smile wide as a gap-toothed galaxy. His own cheering section of grown-ups and kids all leap to their feet and hug each other, delirious with love for this boy. He's Andy, my best friend's son. The cheering section includes his mother and her friends, his brother, his father and stepmother, a stepbrother and stepsister, and a grandparent. Lucky is the child with this many relatives on hand to hail a proud accomplishment. I'm there too, witnessing a family fortune. But in spite of myself, defensive words take shape in my head. I am thinking: I dare *anybody* to call this a broken home.

Families change, and remain the same. Why are our names for home so slow to catch up to the truth of where we live?

When I was a child, I had two parents who loved me without cease. One of them attended every excuse for attention I ever contrived, and the other made it to the ones with higher production values, like piano recitals and appendicitis. So I was a lucky child too, I played with a set of paper dolls called "The Family of Dolls," four in number, who came with the factory-assigned names of Dad, Mom, Sis, and Junior. I think you know what they looked like, at least before I loved them to death and their heads fell off.

Now I've replaced the dolls with a life. I knit my days around my daughter's survival and happiness, and am proud to say her head is still on. But we aren't the Family of Dolls. Maybe you're not, either. And if not, even though you are statistically no oddity, it's probably been suggested to you in a hundred ways that yours isn't exactly a real family, but an impostor family, a harbinger of cultural ruin, a slapdash substitute — something like counterfeit money. Here at the tail end of our century, most of us are up to our ears in the noisy business of trying to support and love a thing called family. But there's a current in the air with ferocious moral force that finds its way even into political campaigns, claiming there is only one right way to do it, the Way It Has Always Been.

In the face of a thriving, particolored world, this narrow view is so   5
pickled and absurd I'm astonished that it gets airplay. And I'm astonished that it still stings.

Every parent has endured the arrogance of a child-unfriendly grump sitting in judgment, explaining what those kids of ours really need (for example, "a good licking"). If we're polite, we move our crew to another bench in the park. If we're forthright (as I am in my mind, only, for the rest of the day), we fix them with a sweet imperious stare and say, "Come back and let's talk about it after you've changed a thousand diapers."

But it's harder somehow to shrug off the Family-of-Dolls Family Values crew when they judge (from their safe distance) that divorced people, blended families, gay families, and single parents are failures. That our children are at risk, and the whole arrangement is messy and embarrassing. A marriage that ends is not called "finished," it's called *failed*. The children of this family may have been born to a happy union, but now they are called *the children of divorce*.

I had no idea how thoroughly these assumptions overlaid my culture until I went through divorce myself. I wrote to a friend: "This might be worse than being widowed. Overnight I've suffered the same losses — companionship, financial and practical support, my identity as a wife and partner, the future I'd taken for granted. I am lonely, grieving, and hard-pressed to take care of my household alone. But instead of bringing casseroles, people are acting like I had a fit and broke up the family china."

Once upon a time I held these beliefs about divorce: that everyone who does it could have chosen not to do it. That it's a lazy way out of marital problems. That it selfishly puts personal happiness ahead of family integrity. Now I tremble for my ignorance. It's easy, in fortunate times, to forget about the ambush that could leave your head reeling: serious mental or physical illness, death in the family, abandonment, financial calamity, humiliation, violence, despair.

I started out like any child, intent on being the Family of Dolls. I set   10
upon young womanhood believing in most of the doctrines of my generation: I wore my skirts four inches above the knee. I had that Barbie with her zebra-striped swimsuit and a figure unlike anything found in nature. And I understood the Prince Charming Theory of Marriage, a quest for Mr. Right that ends smack dab where you find him. I did not completely understand that another whole story *begins* there, and no fairy tale prepared me for the combination of bad luck and persistent hope that would interrupt my dream and lead me to other arrangements. Like a cancer diagnosis, a dying marriage is a thing to fight, to deny, and finally, when there's no choice left, to dig in and survive. Casseroles would help. Likewise, I imagine it must be a painful reckoning in adolescence (or later on) to realize one's own true love will never look like the soft-focus fragrance ads because Prince Charming (surprise!) is a princess. Or vice versa. Or has skin the color your parents didn't want you messing with, except in the Crayola box.

It's awfully easy to hold in contempt the straw broken home, and that mythical category of persons who toss away nuclear family for the sheer fun of it. Even the legal terms we use have a suggestion of caprice. I resent the phrase "irreconcilable differences," which suggest a stubborn refusal to accept a spouse's little quirks. This is specious. Every happily married couple I know has loads of irreconcilable differences. Negotiating where to set the thermostat is not the point. A nonfunctioning marriage is a slow asphyxiation. It is waking up despised each morning, listening to the pulse of your own loneliness before the radio begins to blare its raucous gospel that you're nothing if you aren't loved. It is sharing your airless house with the threat of suicide or other kinds of violence, while the ghost that whispers, "Leave here and destroy your children," has passed over every door and nailed it shut. Disassembling a marriage in these circumstances is as much *fun* as amputating your own gangrenous leg. You do it, if you can, to save a life — or two, or more.

I know of no one who really went looking to hoe the harder row, especially the daunting one of single parenthood. Yet it seems to be the most American of customs to blame the burdened for their destiny. We'd like so desperately to believe in freedom and justice for all, we can hardly name that rogue bad luck, even when he's a close enough snake to bite us. In the wake of my divorce, some friends (even a few close ones) chose to vanish, rather than linger within striking distance of misfortune.

But most stuck around, bless their hearts, and if I'm any the wiser for my trials, it's from having learned the worth of steadfast friendship. And also, what not to say. The least helpful question is: "Did you want the divorce, or didn't you?" Did I want to keep that gangrenous leg, or not? How to explain, in a culture that venerates choice: two terrifying options are much worse than none at all. Give me any day the quick hand of cruel fate that will leave me scarred but blameless. As it was, I kept thinking of that wicked third-grade joke in which some boy comes up behind you and grabs your ear, starts in with a prolonged tug, and asks, "Do you want this ear any longer?"

Still, the friend who holds your hand and says the wrong thing is made of dearer stuff than the one who stays away. And generally, through all of it, you live. My favorite fictional character, Kate Vaiden (in the novel by Reynolds Price), advises: "Strength just comes in one brand—you stand up at sunrise and meet what they send you and keep your hair combed."

Once you've weathered the straits, you get to cross the tricky juncture from casualty to survivor. If you're on your feet at the end of a year or two, and have begun putting together a happy new existence, those friends who were kind enough to feel sorry for you when you needed it must now accept you back to the ranks of the living. If you're truly blessed, they will dance at your second wedding. Everybody else, for heaven's sake, should stop throwing stones.

    15

Arguing about whether nontraditional families deserve pity or tolerance is a little like the medieval debate about left-handedness as a mark of the devil. Divorce, remarriage, single parenthood, gay parents, and blended families simply are. They're facts of our time. Some of the reasons listed by sociologists for these family reconstructions are: the idea of marriage as a romantic partnership rather than a pragmatic one; a shift in women's expectations, from servility to self-respect and independence; and longevity (prior to antibiotics no marriage was expected to last many decades—in Colonial days the average couple lived to be married less than twelve years). Add to all this, our growing sense of entitlement to happiness and safety from abuse. Most would agree these are all good things. Yet their result—a culture in which serial monogamy and the consequent reshaping of families are the norm—gets diagnosed as "failing."

For many of us, once we have put ourselves Humpty-Dumpty-wise back together again, the main problem with our reorganized family is that other people think we have a problem. My daughter tells me the only time she's uncomfortable about being the child of divorced parents is when her friends say they feel sorry for her. It's a bizarre sympathy, given that half the kids in her school and nation are in the same boat, pursuing childish happiness with the same energy as their married-parent peers. When anyone asks how *she* feels about it, she spontaneously lists the benefits: our house is in the country and we have a dog, but she can go to her dad's neighborhood for the urban thrills of a pool and sidewalks for roller-skating. What's more, she has three sets of grandparents!

Why is it surprising that a child would revel in a widened family and the right to feel at home in more than one house? Isn't it the opposite that should worry us—a child with no home at all, or too few resources to feel safe? The child at risk is the one whose parents are too immature themselves to guide wisely; too diminished by poverty to nurture; too far from opportunity to offer hope. The number of children in the U.S. living in poverty at this moment is almost unfathomably large: twenty percent. There are families among us that need help all right, and by no means are they new on the landscape. The rate at which teenage girls had babies in 1957 (ninety-six per thousand) was twice what it is now. That remarkable statistic is ignored by the religious right—probably because the teen birth rate was cut in half mainly by legalized abortion. In fact, the policy gatekeepers who coined the phrase "family values" have steadfastly ignored the desperation of too-small families, and since 1979 have steadily reduced the amount of financial support available to a single parent. But, this camp's most outspoken attacks seem aimed at the notion of families getting too complex, with add-ons and extras such as a gay parent's partner, or a remarried mother's new husband and his children.

To judge a family's value by its tidy symmetry is to purchase a book for its cover. There's no moral authority there. The famous family comprised of Dad, Mom, Sis, and Junior living as an isolated economic unit is not built on historical bedrock. In *The Way We Never Were*, Stephanie Coontz writes, "Whenever people propose that we go back to the traditional family, I always suggest that they pick a ballpark date for the family they have in mind." Colonial families were tidily disciplined, but their members (meaning everyone but infants) labored incessantly and died young. Then the Victorian family adopted a new division of labor, in which women's role was domestic and children were allowed time for study and play, but this was an upper-class construct supported by myriad slaves. Coontz writes, "For every nineteenth-century middle-class family that protected its wife and child within the family circle, there was an Irish or German girl scrubbing floors ... a Welsh boy mining coal to keep the home-baked goodies warm, a black girl doing the family laundry, a black mother and child picking cotton to be made into clothes for the family, and a Jewish or an Italian daughter in a sweatshop making 'ladies' dresses or artificial flowers for the family to purchase."

The abolition of slavery brought slightly more democratic arrange-   20
ments, in which extended families were harnessed together in cottage
industries; at the turn of the century came a steep rise in child labor in
mines and sweatshops. Twenty percent of American children lived in
orphanages at the time; their parents were not necessarily dead, but
couldn't afford to keep them.

During the Depression and up to the end of World War II, many millions of U.S. households were more multigenerational than nuclear.
Women my grandmother's age were likely to live with a fluid assortment of
elderly relatives, in-laws, siblings, and children. In many cases they spent
virtually every waking hour working in the company of other women — a
companionable scenario in which it would be easier, I imagine, to tolerate
an estranged or difficult spouse. I'm reluctant to idealize a life of so much
hard work and so little spousal intimacy, but its advantage may have been
resilience. A family so large and varied would not easily be brought down
by a single blow: it could absorb a death, long illness, an abandonment here
or there, and any number of irreconcilable differences.

The Family of Dolls came along midcentury as a great American experiment. A booming economy required a mobile labor force and demanded
that women surrender jobs to returning soldiers. Families came to be defined
by a single breadwinner. They struck out for single-family homes at an earlier age than ever before, and in unprecedented numbers they raised children
in suburban isolation. The nuclear family was launched to sink or swim.

More than a few sank. Social historians corroborate that the suburban
family of the postwar economic boom, which we have recently selected as
our definition of "traditional," was no panacea. Twenty-five percent of
Americans were poor in the mid-1950s, and as yet there were no food
stamps. Sixty percent of the elderly lived on less than $1,000 a year, and
most had no medical insurance. In the sequestered suburbs, alcoholism and
sexual abuse of children were far more widespread than anyone imagined.

Expectations soared, and the economy sagged. It's hard to depend on
one other adult for everything, come what may. In the last three decades,
that amorphous, adaptable structure we call "family" has been reshaped
once more by economic tides. Compared with fifties families, mothers are
far more likely now to be employed. We are statistically more likely to divorce, and to live in blended families or other extra-nuclear arrangements. We are also more likely to plan and space our children, and to rate
our marriages as "happy." We are less likely to suffer abuse without recourse, or to stare out at our lives through a glaze of prescription tran-
quilizers. Our aged parents are less likely to become destitute, and we're
half as likely to have a teenage daughter turn up a mother herself. All in
all, I would say that if "intact" in modern family-values jargon means living quietly desperate in the bell jar, then hip-hip-hooray for "broken." A
neat family model constructed to service the Baby Boom economy seems
to be returning gradually to a grand, lumpy shape that human families
apparently have tended toward since they first took root in the Olduvai

Gorge. We're social animals, deeply fond of companionship, and children love best to run in packs. If there is a *normal* for humans, at all, I expect it looks like two or three Families of Dolls, connected variously by kinship and passion, shuffled like cards and strewn over several shoeboxes.

The sooner we can let go the fairy tale of families functioning perfectly   25
in isolation, the better we might embrace the relief of community. Even the admirable parents who've stayed married through thick and thin are very likely, at present, to incorporate other adults into their families—household help and baby-sitters if they can afford them, or neighbors and grandparents if they can't. For single parents, this support is the rock-bottom definition of family. And most parents who have split apart, however painfully, still manage to maintain family continuity for their children, creating in many cases a boisterous phenomenon that Constance Ahrons in her book *The Good Divorce* calls the "binuclear family." Call it what you will—when ex-spouses beat swords into plowshares and jump up and down at a soccer game together, it makes for happy kids.

Cinderella, look, who needs her? All those evil stepsisters? That story always seemed like too much cotton-picking fuss over clothes. A childhood tale that fascinated me more was the one called "Stone Soup," and the gist of it is this: Once upon a time, a pair of beleagured soldiers straggled home to a village empty-handed, in a land ruined by war. They were famished, but the villagers had so little they shouted evil words and slammed their doors. So the soldiers dragged out a big kettle, filled it with water, and put it on a fire to boil. They rolled a clean round stone into the pot, while the villagers peered through their curtains in amazement.

"What kind of soup is that?" they hooted.

"Stone soup," the soldiers replied. "Everybody can have some when it's done."

"Well, thanks," one matron grumbled, coming out with a shriveled carrot. "But it'd be better if you threw this in."

And so on, of course, a vegetable at a time, until the whole suspicious   30
village managed to feed itself grandly.

Any family is a big empty pot, save for what gets thrown in. Each stew turns out different. Generosity, a resolve to turn bad luck into good, and respect for variety—these things will nourish a nation of children. Namecalling and suspicion will not. My soup contains a rock or two of hard times, and maybe yours does too. I expect it's a heck of a bouillabaisse.

The Reader's Presence

1. In paragraph 2, Kingsolver asks, "Why are our names for home so slow to catch up to the truth of where we live?" What are some of the old, outworn labels or buzzwords that Kingsolver identifies

directly or indirectly in this essay? What are some of the phrases she offers to replace them? What difference(s) might these new terms make?

2. Kingsolver draws on Stephanie Koontz's book *The Way We Never Were* to support her idea that the good old days for which many feel nostalgic were not really all that "good." What are some of the advantages, according to Kingsolver, of living in the contemporary world as opposed to in the past? In what particular ways have women's and children's lives changed for the better? What are some of the remaining social problems that Kingsolver believes the "policy gatekeepers" (paragraph 18) would do better to address?

3. Examine carefully the metaphors and analogies Kingsolver employs in this essay. Where, for instance, do comparisons with death and dismemberment arise, and to what effect(s)? What are some of the analogies she employs to describe the traditional and the modern family? Some of the analogies will require more interpretation than others. What, for example, does she mean when she writes that "arguing about whether nontraditional families deserve pity or tolerance is a little like the medieval debate about left-handedness as a mark of the devil" (paragraph 16)?

105

Paul Monette

Can Gays and Straights Be Friends?

A passionate advocate for a humane, swift, and urgent response to the AIDS crisis, Paul Monette (1945–1995) first became a national literary figure with his book Borrowed Time: An AIDS Memoir *(1988). In this book and in a collection of poems,* Love Alone: Eighteen Elegies for Rog *(1988), he mourned the loss of his partner Roger Horwitz and chronicled the early years of the epidemic. He continued to explore his rage against the AIDS crisis in two novels — Afterlife (1990) and* Halfway Home *(1991) — in which he also affirmed the experience of living with AIDS and fighting back against ignorance, prejudice, and fear. In 1992 Monette received a National Book Award for his autobiography,* Becoming a Man: Half a Life Story, *and shortly before his death from the disease he completed a collection of essays,* Last Watch of the Night: Essays Too Personal and Otherwise *(1994). "Can Gays and Straights Be Friends?" appeared in* Playboy *in 1993.*

Monette published a number of novels and volumes of poetry during the 1970s and 1980s, but endured many rejection notices in the process. In Last Watch of the Night *he wrote, "I spent twenty years being turned down because my work was considered 'too gay.' Which I came to regard as a compliment, and proof I was on the right track." Even after receiving his National Book Award, some of his essays were turned down by publishers because they were considered "too personal," which, Monette wrote, "I couldn't help but feel was even better than a compliment. For I grew up in a culture in which the personal was* verboten, *especially in polite company—a company I've long since sold my stock in."*

Radio call-ins are the worst, especially during drive time. Commuters sit gridlocked in traffic, their only way out by cellular phone to the local radio show. Some callers practically foam at the mouth, saying I deserve to die and my kind makes them want to puke. Usually, I've been talking about the skyrocketing rates of teen suicide, a third of which involves gays and lesbians. Or I'm describing the tyranny of the closet, the stunting of the heart by cruel stereotypes. "Excuse me," I said to the caller in Houston, "do I make you want to puke because I'm gay or because I have AIDS?"

It's not a meaningful distinction to your weed-variety homophobe. Over my desk hangs a picture of a young woman whose wet T-shirt reads: THANK GOD FOR AIDS. Such hatred pours across the airwaves daily from preachers wringing their hands over the sins of Sodom. Their diatribes rarely mention lesbians. To them it is a fight unto death between two breeds of men—the "real" ones and the "sick" ones.

Where do they come by this virulence? Is it an inherent code of pumped-up self-regard passed from dugout and locker room to cover a straight man's fear of being misperceived as queer? Is it a primal fear of being penetrated? A Seattle boy called in once, so cocksure at the age of 11, and asked with disdain, "Why would anyone want to be gay?" All he thought he needed was to score with a girl and his sexual issues would be eternally resolved. "In ten or fifteen years," I promised him, "you will grapple as hard as anyone, gay or straight, with problems of intimacy"—the lifelong struggle to somehow integrate *fuck* and *love.*

As for wanting to be gay, every young man who knows that he's "different" has already internalized society's ugly message. Gay kids become locked in a self-hatred that renders them meek, apologetic and invisible—their only safety the prison walls of their secret.

It's crucial to understand the difference between homophobia and   5
what I call homo-ignorance. There's much more of the latter, especially as gay and lesbian issues have surfaced more prominently in the news. Instinctively, people of goodwill rejected the paranoid philippic delivered in Houston by Pat Buchanan—a walking hate crime all by himself.

A straight friend of mine considers himself completely unhomophobic, he's that secure in his own manhood. Yet, when pinned down, he'll admit that the tactics of Queer Nation and Act Up make him, well, uncomfortable.

Uncomfortable is how the activists want him to feel. Even gays and lesbians juggle conflicting feelings about the guerrilla warriors in our midst. Sometimes I'm engulfed in the minutiae of political correctedness, labeled an enemy of my own people because I'm white, prosperous, and published. But I also feel juiced to have been part of the FDA takeover action in 1988 demanding the release of AIDS drugs. Our movement is only a generation old, and we've done it almost entirely without role models. Harvey Milk[1] was our Martin Luther King, but history texts have erased him. I studied Whitman at Yale for two years without hearing a mention of his homosexuality. Let alone Eleanor Roosevelt's. Or J. Edgar Hoover's.

It's easy to stay ignorant if gay never speaks its name. We need our straight allies to understand the nature of our struggle. It used to be said that a faggot was a homosexual gentleman who had just left the room. That can cease if enough heteros speak up and say "That's not funny" to fag jokes. Our families raise us the best they can, but it's a rare man who reaches adulthood without some legacy of racism, sexism and homophobia. We must confront these demons in ourselves, tolerance being the minimum goal of self-examination.

There's this thing that many straight men have about being on the team, one of the guys. This is the argument of the military brass who want to keep us out. What they really want is for us to continue hiding and lying. While the Joint Chiefs of Staff deliberate the earth-shattering problem of queers taking showers with straight men, the Armed Forces drown in sexual-harassment cover-ups. And the only thing they can offer by way of sensitivity training is "Don't bend over to pick up the soap."

I don't want to do it with a straight man any more that I want to "indoctrinate" his sons. I have no problem with straight men's sexuality, unless it harms or belittles women. I experience none of the homophobe's obsession with what others do in bed. That's sexual compulsion all its own, as if gay or lesbian had only carnal meaning. I think what disorients straight men today is how happy and fulfilled many gay lives are. We're supposed to be miserable, after all.

We all have closets to come out of. Gay isn't the enemy of straight. Heterosexual men have told me for years that, since college, they have no male friends to talk with. The emotional isolation caused by fear of intimacy is indifferent to sexual orientation. We're not boys anymore, trapped in the insecurities of the schoolyard. Our common enemy is ignorance, a sex-phobic bitterness and name-calling purveyed by those who are jealous of the joy of others because they have none of their own.

10

---

[1]*Harvey Milk* (1930–1978): An openly gay politician, Milk was elected to the San Francisco Board of Supervision in 1977. He and Mayor George Moscone were assassinated in 1978 by former city supervisor and police officer Don White. — EDS.

Nothing is more important to me than the freedom of being "out." I won't live to see 50, yet not even that can take away the happiness of having lived my life for real. Of course, you must realize you are in a closet before you can open the door. As gay and straight men, we can help one another over the great divide. We make terrific friends, we queers, perhaps because we have traveled so far to reach the free country of the heart. All men deserve to live there.

The Reader's Presence

1. The title of this essay poses a question: "Can Gays and Straights Be Friends?" How and where does Monette answer this question? What are some of the common grounds between gays and straights that Monette mentions or implies in his essay? What actions might heterosexual people take to ease gay-straight relations? What might homosexuals do? In what ways docs Monette's essay itself further the cause of gay-straight friendships?

2. What are the causes of homophobia? In developing your response, draw on both the essay and on your own personal experience. This essay was first published in *Playboy* magazine, which caters to heterosexual men. What signs do you find in the essay to suggest that Monette anticipates a measure of potential homophobia in his readers? Point to specific words and phrases to support your response. How effectively do you think he deals with the possible homophobia of his readers? Compare and contrast, for example, the discomfort felt by the radio call-ins in paragraph 1 and the discomfort intentionally caused by gay activists discussed in paragraph 7.

3. A popular gay slogan reads "Silence = Death." Comment on the kinds of silence that Monette refers or alludes to in this essay. When does silence very literally lead to death? What less literal consequences does it have?

106

Toni Morrison

Nobel Lecture, 7 December 1993

One of the most celebrated living American novelists, Toni Morrison (b. 1931) was awarded the Nobel Prize for literature in 1993 and the National Book Foundation Medal for Distinguished Contribution to American Letters in 1996. Her acceptance speech for the Nobel Prize is reprinted here as it appeared in the Georgia Review *in 1995. In extending this honor, the Nobel Committee applauded Morrison for eloquently and imaginatively exploring African American experience in her six novels, although Henry Louis Gates Jr. notes that the award would be deserved had she written only* Beloved *(1987). Morrison was born in Ohio, and the state figures prominently in her fiction, especially in* Beloved *and* Sula *(1973). Her novel,* Jazz *(1992), centers on characters from the rural South who settle in Harlem in the 1920s. Her most recent novel is* Paradise *(1998). In addition to writing novels, Morrison teaches at Princeton University, writes literary criticism and children's books, and lectures widely.*

She has written that fiction "should be beautiful, and powerful, but it should also work. It should have something in it that enlightens; something in it that opens the door and points the way. Something in it that suggests what the conflicts are, what the problems are. But it need not solve those problems because it is not a case study, it is not a recipe."

Members of the Swedish Academy, Ladies and Gentlemen:

Narrative has never been merely entertainment for me. It is, I believe, one of the principal ways in which we absorb knowledge. I hope you will understand, then, why I begin these remarks with the opening phrase of what must be the oldest sentence in the world, and the earliest one we remember from childhood: "Once upon a time . . ."

"Once upon a time there was an old woman. Blind but wise." Or was it an old man? A guru, perhaps. Or a *griot*[1] soothing restless children. I have heard this story, or one exactly like it, in the lore of several cultures.

"Once upon a time there was an old woman. Blind. Wise."

---

[1]*griot:* A storyteller in western Africa. — EDS.

In the version I know the woman is the daughter of slaves, black,   5
American, and lives alone in a small house outside of town. Her reputation for wisdom is without peer and without question. Among her people
she is both the law and its transgression. The honor she is paid and the
awe in which she is held reach beyond her neighborhood to places far
away; to the city where the intelligence of rural prophets is the source of
much amusement.

One day the woman is visited by some young people who seem to be
bent on disproving her clairvoyance and showing her up for the fraud
they believe she is. Their plan is simple: they enter her house and ask the
one question the answer to which rides solely on her difference from
them, a difference they regard as a profound disability: her blindness.
They stand before her, and one of them says,

"Old woman, I hold in my hand a bird. Tell me whether it is living or
dead."

She does not answer, and the question is repeated. "Is the bird I am
holding living or dead?"

Still she does not answer. She is blind and cannot see her visitors, let
alone what is in their hands. She does not know their color, gender, or
homeland. She knows only their motive.

The old woman's silence is so long, the young people have trouble   10
holding their laughter.

Finally she speaks, and her voice is soft but stern. "I don't know,"
she says. "I don't know whether the bird you are holding is dead or alive,
but what I do know is that it is in your hands. It is in your hands."

Her answer can be taken to mean: if it is dead, you have either found
it that way or you have killed it. If it is alive, you can still kill it. Whether
it is to stay alive is your decision. Whatever the case, it is your responsibility.

For parading their power and her helplessness, the young visitors are
reprimanded, told they are responsible not only for the act of mockery
but also for the small bundle of life sacrificed to achieve its aims. The
blind woman shifts attention away from assertions of power to the instrument through which that power is exercised.

Speculation on what (other than its own frail body) that bird in the
hand might signify has always been attractive to me, but especially so
now, thinking as I have been about the work I do that has brought me to
this company. So I choose to read the bird as language and the woman as
a practiced writer.

She is worried about how the language she dreams in, given to her at   15
birth, is handled, put into service, even withheld from her for certain ne-
farious purposes. Being a writer, she thinks of language partly as a system, partly as a living thing over which one has control, but mostly as
agency — as an act with consequences. So the question the children put to
her, "Is it living or dead?," is not unreal, because she thinks of language
as susceptible to death, erasure; certainly imperiled and salvageable only

by an effort of the will. She believes that if the bird in the hands of her visitors is dead, the custodians are responsible for the corpse. For her a dead language is not only one no longer spoken or written, it is unyielding language content to admire its own paralysis. Like statist language, censored and censoring. Ruthless in its policing duties, it has no desire or purpose other than to maintain the free range of its own narcotic narcissism, its own exclusivity and dominance. However, moribund, it is not without effect, for it actively thwarts the intellect, stalls conscience, suppresses human potential. Unreceptive to interrogation, it cannot form or tolerate new ideas, shape other thoughts, tell another story, fill baffling silences. Official language smitheried to sanction ignorance and preserve privilege is a suit of armor, polished to shocking glitter, a husk from which the knight departed long ago. Yet there it is; dumb, predatory, sentimental. Exciting reverence in schoolchildren, providing shelter for despots, summoning false memories of stability, harmony among the public.

She is convinced that when language dies, out of carelessness, disuse, indifference, and absence of esteem, or killed by fiat, not only she herself but all users and makers are accountable for its demise. In her country children have bitten their tongues off and use bullets instead to iterate the void of speechlessness, of disabled and disabling language, of language adults have abandoned altogether as a device for grappling with meaning, providing guidance, or expressing love. But she knows tongue-suicide is not only the choice of children. It is common among the infantile heads of state and power merchants whose evacuated language leaves them with no access to what is left of their human instincts, for they speak only to those who obey, or in order to force obedience.

The systematic looting of language can be recognized by the tendency of its users to forgo its nuanced, complex, midwifery properties, replacing them with menace and subjugation. Oppressive language does more than represent violence; it is violence; does more than represent the limits of knowledge; it limits knowledge. Whether it is obscuring state language or the faux language of mindless media; whether it is the proud but calcified language of the academy or the commodity-driven language of science; whether it is the malign language of law-without-ethics, or language designed for the estrangement of minorities, hiding its racist plunder in its literary cheek—it must be rejected, altered, and exposed. It is the language that drinks blood, laps vulnerabilities, tucks its fascist boots under crinolines of respectability and patriotism as it moves relentlessly toward the bottom line and the bottomed-out mind. Sexist language, racist language, theistic language—all are typical of the policing languages of mastery, and cannot, do not, permit new knowledge or encourage the mutual exchange of ideas.

The old woman is keenly aware that no intellectual mercenary or insatiable dictator, no paid-for politician or demagogue, no counterfeit journalist would be persuaded by her thoughts. There is and will be rousing language to keep citizens armed and arming; slaughtered and slaughtering in the malls, courthouses, post offices, playgrounds, bedrooms, and boulevards; stirring, memorializing language to mask the pity and waste of needless death. There will be more diplomatic language to countenance rape, torture, assassination. There is and will be more seductive, mutant language designed to throttle women, to pack their throats like pâté-producing geese with their own unsayable, transgressive words; there will be more of the language of surveillance disguised as research; of politics and history calculated to render the suffering of millions mute; language glamorized to thrill the dissatisfied and bereft into assaulting their neighbors; arrogant pseudo-empirical language crafted to lock creative people into cages of inferiority and hopelessness.

Underneath the eloquence, the glamour, the scholarly associations, however stirring or seductive, the heart of such language is languishing, or perhaps not beating at all—if the bird is already dead.

She had thought about what could have been the intellectual history 20 of any discipline if it had not insisted upon, or been forced into, the waste of time and life that rationalizations for and representations of dominance required—lethal discourses of exclusion blocking access to cognition for both the excluder and the excluded.

The conventional wisdom of the Tower of Babel story is that the collapse was a misfortune. That is was the distraction or the weight of many languages that precipitated the tower's failed architecture. That one monolithic language would have expedited the building, and heaven would have been reached. Whose heaven, she wonders? And what kind? Perhaps the achievement of Paradise was premature, a little hasty if no one could take the time to understand other languages, other views, other narratives. Had they, the heaven they imagined might have been found at their feet. Complicated, demanding, yes, but a view of heaven as life; not heaven as post-life.

She would not want to leave her young visitors with the impression that language should be forced to stay alive merely to be. The vitality of language lies in its ability to limn the actual, imagined, and possible lives of its speakers, readers, writers. Although its poise is sometimes in displacing experience, it is not a substitute for it. It arcs toward the place where meaning may lie. When a president of the United States thought about the graveyard his country had become, and said, "The world will little note nor long remember what we say here. But it will never forget what they did here," his simple words were exhilarating in their life-sustaining properties because they refused to encapsulate the reality of 600,000 dead men in a cataclysmic race war. Refusing to monumentalize, disdaining the "final word," the precise "summing up," acknowledging their "poor power to add or detract," his words signal deference to the uncapturability of the life it mourns. It is the deference that moves her, that recognition that language can never live up to life once and for all. Nor should it. Language can never "pin down" slavery, genocide, war.

Nor should it yearn for the arrogance to be able to do so. Its force, its felicity, is in its reach toward the ineffable.

Be it grand or slender, burrowing, blasting or refusing to sanctify; whether it laughs out loud or is a cry without an alphabet, the choice word or the chosen silence, unmolested language surges toward knowledge, not its destruction. But who does not know of literature banned because it is interrogative; discredited because it is critical; erased because alternate? And how many are outraged by the thought of a self-ravaged tongue?

Word-work is sublime, she thinks, because it is generative; it makes meaning that secures our difference, our human difference—the way in which we are like no other life.

We die. That may be the meaning of life. But we *do* language. That   25
may be the measure of our lives.

"Once upon a time . . ." Visitors ask an old woman a question. Who are they, these children? What did they make of that encounter? What did they hear in those final words: "The bird is in your hands"? A sentence that gestures toward possibility, or one that drops a latch? Perhaps what the children heard was, "It's not my problem. I am old, female, black, blind. What wisdom I have now is in knowing I cannot help you. The future of language is yours."

They stand there. Suppose nothing was in their hands. Suppose the visit was only a ruse, a trick to get to be spoken to, taken seriously as they have not been before. A chance to interrupt, to violate the adult world, its miasma of discourse about them. Urgent questions are at stake, including the one they have asked: "Is the bird we are holding living or dead?" Perhaps the question meant: "Could someone tells us what is life? What is death?" No trick at all; no silliness. A straightforward question worthy of the attention of a wise one. An old one. And if the old and wise who have lived life and faced death cannot describe either, who can?

But she does not; she keeps her secret, her good opinion of herself, her gnomic pronouncements, her art without commitment. She keeps her distance, enforces it and retreats into the singularity of isolation, in sophisticated, privileged space.

Nothing, no word follows her declaration of transfer. That silence is deep, deeper than the meaning available in the words she has spoken. It shivers, this silence, and the children, annoyed, fill it with language invented on the spot.

"Is there no speech," they ask her, "no words you can give us that   30
help us break through your dossier of failures? through the education you have just given us that is no education at all because we are paying close attention to what you have done as well as to what you have said? to the barrier you have erected between generosity and wisdom?

"We have no bird in our hands, living or dead. We have only you and our important question. Is the nothing in our hands something you could not bear to contemplate, to even guess? Don't you remember being young, when language was magic without meaning? When what you could say, could not mean? When the invisible was what imagination strove to see? When questions and demands for answers burned so brightly you trembled with fury at not knowing?

"Do we have to begin consciousness with a battle heroes and heroines like you have already fought and lost, leaving us with nothing in our hands except what you have imagined is there? Your answer is artful, but its artfulness embarrasses us and ought to embarrass you. Your answer is indecent in its self-congratulation. A made-for-television script that makes no sense if there is nothing in our hands.

"Why didn't you reach out, touch us with your soft fingers, delay the sound bite, the lesson, until you knew who we were? Did you so despise our trick, our modus operandi, that you could not see that we were baffled about how to get your attention? We are young. Unripe. We have heard all our short lives that we have to be responsible. What could that possibly mean in the catastrophe this world has become; where, as a poet said, 'nothing needs to be exposed since it is already barefaced'? Our inheritance is an affront. You want us to have your old, blank eyes and see only cruelty and mediocrity. Do you think we are stupid enough to perjure ourselves again and again with the fiction of nationhood? How dare you talk to us of duty when we stand waist deep in the toxin of your past?

"You trivialize us and trivialize the bird that is not in our hands. Is there no context for our lives? No song, no literature, no poem full of vitamins, no history connected to experience that you can pass along to help us start strong? You are an adult. The old one, the wise one. Stop thinking about saving your face. Think of our lives and tell us your particularized world. Make up a story. Narrative is radical, creating us at the very moment it is being created. We will not blame you if your reach exceeds your grasp; if love so ignites your words that they go down in flames and nothing is left but their scald. Or if, with the reticence of a surgeon's hands, your words suture only the places where blood might flow. We know you can never do it properly—once and for all. Passion is never enough; neither is skill. But try. For our sake and yours forget your name in the street; tell us what the world has been to you in the dark places and in the light. Don't tell us what to believe, what to fear. Show us belief's wide skirt and the stitch that unravels fear's caul. You, old woman, blessed with blindness, can speak the language that tells us what only language can: how to see without pictures. Language alone protects us from the scariness of things with no names. Language alone is meditation.

"Tell us what it is to be a woman so that we may know what it is to be a man. What moves at the margin. What it is to have no home in this place. To be set adrift from the one you knew. What it is to live at the edge of towns that cannot bear your company.

"Tell us about ships turned away from shorelines at Easter, placenta in a field. Tell us about a wagonload of slaves, how they sang so softly

35

their breath was indistinguishable from the falling snow. How they knew from the hunch of the nearest shoulder that the next stop would be their last. How, with hands prayered in their sex, they thought of heat, then sun. Lifting their faces as though it was there for the taking. Turning as though there for the taking. They stop at an inn. The driver and his mate go in with the lamp, leaving them humming in the dark. The horse's void steams into the snow beneath its hooves and the hiss and melt are the envy of the freezing slaves.

"The inn door opens: a girl and a boy step away from its light. They climb into the wagon bed. The boy will have a gun in three years, but now he carries a lamp and a jug of warm cider. They pass it from mouth to mouth. The girl offers bread, pieces of meat, and something more: a glance into the eyes of the one she serves. One helping for each man, two for each woman. And a look. They look back. The next stop will be their last. But not this one. This one is warmed."

It's quiet again when the children finish speaking, until the woman breaks into the silence.

"Finally," she says. "I trust you now. I trust you with the bird that is not in your hands because you have truly caught it. Look. How lovely it is, this thing we have done—together."

The Reader's Presence

1. Identify each of the narrative lines Morrison establishes in this essay. Consider carefully not only the first narrative Morrison tells, the one beginning "Once upon a time there was an old woman" (paragraph 4), but also the other narratives embedded in the essay. What knowledge might she hope her audience will absorb from each of the narratives (paragraph 2)? Discuss the overall function—and effects—of Morrison's use of narrative.

2. Although Morrsion is best known for her novels, she is also a respected literary and cultural critic. Discuss the function of interpretation in this essay. What are the possible interpretations of the bird in the young visitors' hands? In what specific ways are the different interpretations mutually exclusive, or do they work together to create a larger meaning? How do you interpret the significance of the final reference to the bird: "I trust you with the bird that is not in your hands because you have truly caught it" (paragraph 39)? What has led up to this riddle-like insight? Attentive readers interpret not only the words on the page but also the spaces. How do you read the space between paragraphs 25 and 26? Compare and contrast what comes before and after that space.

3. This is a difficult essay because not all the meaning lies readily accessible on the surface. Choose the paragraph that you found

most perplexing, and read it carefully, several times, making a comment or observation in the margins about every phrase. You might start by making sure you can identify the basics, such as the referents to each pronoun. Then move on to matters related to the writer's presence. What kinds of verbs does she use? What adjectives? What kinds of images? Are there patterns among the words and phrases you have marked, and do these patterns repeat in other parts of the essay? With what effect(s)?

107

Bertrand Russell

Why I Am Not a Christian

Mathematician, philosopher, logician, and social critic, Bertrand Russell (1872–1970) was born in England and is regarded as one of the greatest thinkers of modern times. Russell was an extremely prolific and influential writer, and his books, many of them highly readable, include Principia Mathematica, *a three-volume set published in 1910, 1912, and 1913;* Marriage and Morals *(1929); A* History of Western Philosophy *(1945);* Why I Am Not a Christian *(1957); and* The Autobiography of Bertrand Russell *(3 vols.: 1967–69). Russell is also known for his outspoken views on pacifism, advocacy of free love, and criticism of American foreign policy. "Why I Am Not a Christian," one of his most famous essays, was delivered as a lecture in 1927 to the National Secular Society.*

As your Chairman has told you, the subject about which I am going to speak to you tonight is "Why I Am Not a Christian." Perhaps it would be as well, first of all, to try to make out what one means by the word *Christian*. It is used these days in a very loose sense by a great many people. Some people mean no more by it than a person who attempts to live a good life. In that sense I suppose there would be Christians in all sects and creeds; but I do not think that that is the proper sense of the word, if only because it would imply that all the people who are not Christians — all the Buddhists, Confucians, Mohammedans, and so on — are not trying to live a good life. I do not mean by a Christian any person who tries to live decently according to his lights. I think that you must have a certain amount of definite belief before you have a right to call yourself a Christian. The word does not have quite such a full-blooded meaning now as it had in the times of St. Augustine and St. Thomas

Aquinas. In those days, if a man said that he was a Christian it was known what he meant. You accepted a whole collection of creeds which were set out with great precision, and every single syllable of those creeds you believed with the whole strength of your convictions.

WHAT IS A CHRISTIAN?

Nowadays it is not quite that. We have to be a little more vague in our meaning of Christianity. I think, however, that there are two different items which are quite essential to anybody calling himself a Christian. The first is one of a dogmatic nature—namely, that you must believe in God and immortality. If you do not believe in those two things, I do not think that you can properly call yourself a Christian. Then, further than that, as the name implies, you must have some kind of belief about Christ. The Mohammedans, for instance, also believe in God and in immortality, and yet they would not call themselves Christians. I think you must have at the very lowest the belief that Christ was, if not divine, at least the best and wisest of men. If you are not going to believe that much about Christ, I do not think you have any right to call yourself a Christian. Of course, there is another sense, which you find in *Whitaker's Almanack* and in geography books, where the population of the world is said to be divided into Christians, Mohammedans, Buddhists, fetish worshipers, and so on; and in that sense we are all Christians. The geography books count us all in, but that is a purely geographical sense, which I suppose we can ignore. Therefore I take it that when I tell you why I am not a Christian I have to tell you two different things: first, why I do not believe in God and in immortality; and, secondly, why I do not think that Christ was the best and wisest of men, although I grant him a very high degree of moral goodness.

But for the successful efforts of unbelievers in the past, I could not take so elastic a definition of Christianity as that. As I said before, in olden days it had a much more full-blooded sense. For instance, it included the belief in hell. Belief in eternal hell-fire was an essential item of Christian belief until pretty recent times. In this country, as you know, it ceased to be an essential item because of a decision of the Privy Council, and from that decision the Archbishop of Canterbury and the Archbishop of York dissented; but in this country our religion is settled by Act of Parliament, and therefore the Privy Council was able to override their Graces and hell was no longer necessary to a Christian. Consequently I shall not insist that a Christian must believe in hell.

THE EXISTENCE OF GOD

To come to this question of the existence of God: It is a large and serious question, and if I were to attempt to deal with it in any adequate manner I should have to keep you here until Kingdom Come, so that you will have to excuse me if I deal with it in a somewhat summary fashion. You know, of course, that the Catholic Church has laid it down as a dogma that the existence of God can be proved by the unaided reason. That is a somewhat curious dogma, but it is one of their dogmas. They had to introduce it because at one time the freethinkers adopted the habit of saying that there were such and such arguments which mere reason might urge against the existence of God, but of course they knew as a matter of faith that God did exist. The arguments and the reasons were set out at great length, and the Catholic Church felt that they must stop it. Therefore they laid it down that the existence of God can be proved by the unaided reason and they had to set up what they considered were arguments to prove it. There are, of course, a number of them, but I shall take only a few.

THE FIRST CAUSE ARGUMENT

Perhaps the simplest and easiest to understand is the argument of the   5
First Cause. (It is maintained that everything we see in this world has a cause, and as you go back in the chain of causes further and further you must come to a First Cause, and to that First Cause you give the name of God.) That argument, I suppose, does not carry very much weight nowadays, because, in the first place, cause is not quite what it used to be. The philosophers and the men of science have got going on cause, and it has not anything like the vitality it used to have; but, apart from that, you can see that the argument that there must be a First Cause is one that cannot have any validity. I may say that when I was a young man and was debating these questions very seriously in my mind, I for a long time accepted the argument of the First Cause, until one day, at the age of eighteen, I read John Stuart Mill's *Autobiography,* and I there found this sentence: "My father taught me that the question 'Who made me?' cannot be answered, since it immediately suggests the further question 'Who made God?'" That very simple sentence showed me, as I still think, the fallacy in the argument of the First Cause. If everything must have a cause, then God must have a cause. If there can be everything without a cause, it may just as well be the world as God, so that there cannot be any validity in that argument. It is exactly of the same nature as the Hindu's view that the world rested upon an elephant and the elephant rested upon a tortoise; and when they said, "How about the tortoise?" the Indian said, "Suppose we change the subject." The argument is really no better than that. There is no reason why the world could not have come into being without a cause; nor, on the other hand, is there any reason why it should not have always existed. There is no reason to suppose that the world had a beginning at all. The idea that things must have a beginning is really due to the poverty of our imagination. Therefore, perhaps, I need not waste any more time upon the argument about the First Cause.

THE NATURAL LAW ARGUMENT

Then there is a very common argument from natural law. That was a favorite argument all through the eighteenth century, especially under the influence of Sir Isaac Newton and his cosmogony. People observed the planets going around the sun according to the law of gravitation, and they thought that God had given a behest to these planets to move in that particular fashion, and that was why they did so. That was, of course, a convenient and simple explanation that saved them the trouble of looking any further for explanations of the law of gravitation. Nowadays we explain the law of gravitation in a somewhat complicated fashion that Einstein has introduced. I do not propose to give you a lecture on the law of gravitation, as interpreted by Einstein, because that again would take some time; at any rate, you no longer have the sort of natural law that you had in the Newtonian system, where, for some reason that nobody could understand, nature behaved in a uniform fashion. We now find that a great many things we thought were natural laws are really human conventions. You know that even in the remotest depths of stellar space there are still three feet to a yard. That is, no doubt, a very remarkable fact, but you would hardly call it a law of nature. And a great many things that have been regarded as laws of nature are of that kind. On the other hand, where you can get down to any knowledge of what atoms actually do, you will find they are much less subject to law than people thought, and that the laws at which you arrive are statistical averages of just the sort that would emerge from chance. There is, as we all know, a law that if you throw dice you will get double sixes only about once in thirty-six times, we do not regard that as evidence that the fall of the dice is regulated by design; on the contrary, if the double sixes came every time we should think that there was design. The laws of nature are of that sort as regards a great many of them. They are statistical averages such as would emerge from the laws of chance; and that makes this whole business of natural law much less impressive than it formerly was. Quite apart from that, which represents the momentary state of science that may change tomorrow, the whole idea that natural laws imply a lawgiver is due to a confusion between natural and human laws. Human laws are behests commanding you to behave a certain way, in which way you may choose to behave, or you may choose not to behave; but natural laws are a description of how things do in fact behave, and being a mere description of what they in fact do, you cannot argue that there must be somebody who told them to do that, because even supposing that there were, you are then faced with the question "Why did God issue just those natural laws and no others?" If you say that he did it simply from his own good pleasure, and without any reason, you then find that there is something which is not subject to law, and so your train of natural law is interrupted. If you say, as more orthodox theologians do, that in all the laws which God issues he had a reason for giving those laws rather than others — the reason, of course, being to create the best universe, although you would never think it to look at it—if there were a reason for the laws which God gave, then God himself was subject to law, and therefore you do not get any advantage by introducing God as an intermediary. You have really a law outside and anterior to the divine edicts, and God does not serve your purpose, because he is not the ultimate lawgiver. In short, this whole argument about natural law no longer has anything like the strength that it used to have. I am traveling on in time in my review of the arguments. The arguments that are used for the existence of God change their character as time goes on. They were at first hard intellectual arguments embodying certain quite definite fallacies. As we come to modern times they become less respectable intellectually and more and more affected by a kind of moralizing vagueness.

THE ARGUMENT FROM DESIGN

The next step in this process brings us to the argument from design. You all know the argument from design: Everything in the world is made just so that we can manage to live in the world, and if the world was ever so little different, we could not manage to live in it. That is the argument from design. It sometimes takes a rather curious form; for instance, it is argued that rabbits have white tails in order to be easy to shoot. I do not know how rabbits would view that application. It is an easy argument to parody. You all know Voltaire's remark, that obviously the nose was designed to be such as to fit spectacles. That sort of parody has turned out to be not nearly so wide of the mark as it might have seemed in the eighteenth century, because since the time of Darwin we understand much better why living creatures are adapted to their environment. It is not that their environment was made to be suitable to them but that they grew to be suitable to it, and that is the basis of adaptation. There is no evidence of design about it.

When you come to look into this argument from design, it is a most astonishing thing that people can believe that this world, with all the things that are in it, with all its defects, should be the best that omnipotence and omniscience have been able to produce in millions of years. I really cannot believe it. Do you think that, if you were granted omnipotence and omniscience and millions of years in which to perfect your world, you could produce nothing better than the Ku Klux Klan or the Fascists? Moreover, if you accept the ordinary laws of science, you have to suppose that human life and life in general on this planet will die out in due course: It is a stage in the decay of the solar system; at a certain stage of decay you get the sort of conditions of temperature and so forth which are suitable to protoplasm, and there is life for a short time in the life of the whole solar system. You see in the moon the sort of thing to which the earth is tending—something dead, cold, and lifeless.

I am told that that sort of view is depressing, and people will sometimes tell you that if they believed that, they would not be able to go on living. Do not believe it; it is all nonsense. Nobody really worries much about what is going to happen millions of years hence. Even if they think they are worrying much about that, they are really deceiving themselves. They are worried about something much more mundane, or it may merely be a bad digestion; but nobody is really seriously rendered unhappy by the thought of something that is going to happen to this world millions and millions of years hence. Therefore, although it is of course a gloomy view to suppose that life will die out — at least I suppose we may say so, although sometimes when I contemplate the things that people do with their lives I think it is almost a consolation — it is not such as to render life miserable. It merely makes you turn your attention to other things.

THE MORAL ARGUMENTS FOR DEITY

Now we reach one stage further in what I shall call the intellectual descent that the Theists have made in their argumentations, and we come to what are called the moral arguments for the existence of God. You all know, of course, that there used to be in the old days three intellectual arguments for the existence of God, all of which were disposed of by Immanuel Kant in the *Critique of Pure Reason;* but no sooner had he disposed of those arguments than he invented a new one, a moral argument, and that quite convinced him. He was like many people: In intellectual matters he was skeptical, but in moral matters he believed implicitly in the maxims that he had imbibed at his mother's knee. That illustrates what the psychoanalysts so much emphasize — the immensely stronger hold upon us that our very early associations have than those of later times.

Kant, as I say, invented a new moral argument for the existence of God, and that in varying forms was extremely popular during the nineteenth century. It has all sorts of forms. One form is to say that there would be no right or wrong unless God existed. I am not for the moment concerned with whether there is a difference between right and wrong, or whether there is not: That is another question. The point I am concerned with is that, if you are quite sure there is a difference between right and wrong, you are then in this situation: Is that difference due to God's fiat or is it not? If it is due to God's fiat, then for God himself there is no difference between right and wrong, and it is no longer a significant statement to say that God is good. If you are going to say, as theologians do, that God is good, you must then say that right and wrong have some meaning which is independent of God's fiat, because God's fiats are good and not bad independently of the mere fact that he made them. If you are going to say that, you will then have to say that it is not only through God that right and wrong came into being, but that they are in their essence logically anterior to God. You could, of course, if you liked, say

10

that there was a superior deity who gave orders to the God who made this world, or could take up the line that some of the gnostics took up—a line which I often thought was a very plausible one—that as a matter of fact this world that we know was made by the devil at a moment when God was not looking. There is a good deal to be said for that, and I am not concerned to refute it.

THE ARGUMENT FOR THE REMEDYING OF INJUSTICE

Then there is another very curious form of moral argument, which is this: They say that the existence of God is required in order to bring justice into the world. In the part of this universe that we know there is great injustice, and often the good suffer, and often the wicked prosper, and one hardly knows which of those is the more annoying; but if you are going to have justice in the universe as a whole you have to suppose a future life to redress the balance of life here on earth. So they say that there must be a God, and there must be heaven and hell in order that in the long run there may be justice. That is a very curious argument. If you looked at the matter from a scientific point of view, you would say, "After all, I know only this world. I do not know about the rest of the universe, but so far as one can argue at all on probabilities one would say that probably this world is a fair sample, and if there is injustice here the odds are that there is injustice elsewhere also." Supposing you got a crate of oranges that you opened, and you found all the top layer of oranges bad, you would not argue, "The underneath ones must be good, so as to redress the balance." You would say, "Probably the whole lot is a bad consignment"; and that is really what a scientific person would argue about the universe. He would say, "Here we find in this world a great deal of injustice, and so far as that goes that is a reason for supposing that justice does not rule in the world; and therefore so far as it goes it affords a moral argument against deity and not in favor of one." Of course I know that the sort of intellectual arguments that I have been talking to you about are not what really moves people. What really moves people to believe in God is not any intellectual argument at all. Most people believe in God because they have been taught from early infancy to do it, and that is the main reason.

Then I think that the next most powerful reason is the wish for safety, a sort of feeling that there is a big brother who will look after you. That plays a very profound part in influencing people's desire for a belief in God.

THE CHARACTER OF CHRIST

I now want to say a few words upon a topic which I often think is not quite sufficiently dealt with by Rationalists, and that is the question whether Christ was the best and the wisest of men. It is generally taken for granted that we should all agree that that was so. I do not myself. I think that there are a good many points upon which I agree with Christ a great deal more than the professing Christians do. I do not know that I could go with Him all the way, but I could go with Him much further than most professing Christians can. You will remember that He said, "Resist not evil: But whosoever shall smite thee on thy right cheek, turn to him the other also." That is not a new precept or a new principle. It was used by Lao-tse and Buddha some 500 or 600 years before Christ, but it is not a principle which as a matter of fact Christians accept. I have no doubt that the present Prime Minister,[1] for instance, is a most sincere Christian, but I should not advise any of you to go and smite him on one cheek. I think you might find that he thought this text was intended in a figurative sense.

Then there is another point which I consider excellent. You will re-   15
member that Christ said, "Judge not lest ye be judged." That principle I do not think you would find was popular in the law courts of Christian countries. I have known in my time quite a number of judges who were very earnest Christians, and none of them felt that they were acting contrary to Christian principles in what they did. Then Christ says, "Give to him that asketh of thee, and from him that would borrow of thee turn not thou away." That is a very good principle. Your Chairman has reminded you that we are not here to talk politics, but I cannot help observing that the last general election was fought on the question of how desirable it was to turn away from him that would borrow of thee, so that one must assume that the Liberals and Conservatives of this country are composed of people who do not agree with the teaching of Christ, because they certainly did very emphatically turn away on that occasion.

Then there is one other maxim of Christ which I think has a great deal in it, but I do not find that it is very popular among some of our Christian friends. He says, "If thou wilt be perfect, go and sell that which thou hast, and give to the poor." That is a very excellent maxim, but, as I say, it is not much practiced. All these, I think, are good maxims, although they are a little difficult to live up to. I do not profess to live up to them myself; but then, after all, it is not quite the same thing as for a Christian.

DEFECTS IN CHRIST'S TEACHING

Having granted the excellence of these maxims, I come to certain points in which I do not believe that one can grant either the superlative wisdom or the superlative goodness of Christ as depicted in the Gospels; and here I may say that one is not concerned with the historical question.

[1]Stanley Baldwin (1867–1947).—EDS.

Historically it is quite doubtful whether Christ ever existed at all, and if He did we do not know anything about Him, so that I am not concerned with the historical question, which is a very difficult one. I am concerned with Christ as He appears in the Gospels, taking the Gospel narrative as it stands, and there one does find some things that do not seem to be very wise. For one thing, He certainly thought that His second coming would occur in clouds of glory before the death of all the people who were living at that time. There are a great many texts that prove that. He says, for instance, "Ye shall not have gone over the cities of Israel till the Son of Man be come." Then He says, "There are some standing here which shall not taste death till the Son of Man comes into His kingdom"; and there are a lot of places where it is quite clear that He believed that His second coming would happen during the lifetime of many then living. That was the belief of His earlier followers, and it was the basis of a good deal of His moral teaching. When He said, "Take no thought for the morrow," and things of that sort, it was very largely because He thought that the second coming was going to be very soon, and that all ordinary mundane affairs did not count. I have, as a matter of fact, known some Christians who did believe that the second coming was imminent. I knew a parson who frightened his congregation terribly by telling them that the second coming was very imminent indeed, but they were much consoled when they found that he was planting trees in his garden. The early Christians did really believe it, and they did abstain from such things as planting trees in their gardens, because they did accept from Christ the belief that the second coming was imminent. In that respect, clearly He was not so wise as some other people have been, and He was certainly not superlatively wise.

THE MORAL PROBLEM

Then you come to moral questions. There is one very serious defect to my mind in Christ's moral character, and that is that He believed in hell. I do not myself feel that any person who is really profoundly human can believe in everlasting punishment. Christ certainly as depicted in the Gospels did believe in everlasting punishment, and one does find repeatedly a vindictive fury against those people who would not listen to His preaching—an attitude which is not uncommon with preachers, but which does somewhat detract from superlative excellence. You do not, for instance, find that attitude in Socrates. You find him quite bland and urbane toward the people who would not listen to him; and it is, to my mind, far more worthy of a sage to take that line than to take the line of indignation. You probably all remember the sort of things that Socrates was saying when he was dying, and the sort of things that he generally did say to people who did not agree with him.

You will find that in the Gospels Christ said, "Ye serpents, ye generation of vipers, how can ye escape the damnation of hell." That was said to people who did not like His preaching. It is not really to my mind quite the best tone, and there are a great many of these things about hell. There is, of course, the familiar text about the sin against the Holy Ghost: "Whosoever speaketh against the Holy Ghost it shall not be forgiven him neither in this World nor in the world to come." That text has caused an unspeakable amount of misery in the world, for all sorts of people have imagined that they have committed the sin against the Holy Ghost, and thought that it would not be forgiven them either in this world or in the world to come. I really do not think that a person with a proper degree of kindliness in his nature would have put fears and terrors of that sort into the world.

Then Christ says, "The Son of Man shall send forth His angels, and they shall gather out of His kingdom all things that offend, and them which do iniquity, and shall cast them into a furnace of fire; there shall be wailing and gnashing of teeth"; and He goes on about the wailing and gnashing of teeth. It comes in one verse after another, and it is quite manifest to the reader that there is a certain pleasure in contemplating wailing and gnashing of teeth, or else it would not occur so often. Then you all, of course, remember about the sheep and the goats; how at the second coming He is going to divide the sheep from the goats, and He is going to say to the goats, "Depart from me, ye cursed, into everlasting fire." He continues, "And these shall go away into everlasting fire." Then He says again, "If thy hand offend thee, cut it off; it is better for thee to enter into life maimed, than having two hands to go into hell, into the fire that never shall be quenched; where the worm dieth not and the fire is not quenched." He repeats that again and again also. I must say that I think all this doctrine, that hell-fire is a punishment for sin, is a doctrine of cruelty. It is a doctrine that put cruelty into the world and gave the world generations of cruel torture; and the Christ of the Gospels, if you could take Him as His chroniclers represent Him, would certainly have to be considered partly responsible for that.

There are other things of less importance. There is the instance of the Gadarene swine, where it certainly was not very kind to the pigs to put the devils into them and make them rush down the hill to the sea. You must remember that He was omnipotent, and He could have made the devils simply go away; but He chose to send them into the pigs. Then there is the curious story of the fig tree, which always rather puzzled me. You remember what happened about the fig tree. "He was hungry; and seeing a fig tree afar off having leaves, He came if haply He might find anything thereon; and when He came to it He found nothing but leaves, for the time of figs was not yet. And Jesus answered and said unto it: 'No man eat fruit of thee hereafter for ever' . . . and Peter . . . saith unto Him: 'Master, behold the fig tree which thou cursedst is withered away.'" This is a very curious story, because it was not the right time of year for figs, and you really could not blame the tree. I cannot myself feel that either in

20

the matter of wisdom or in the matter of virtue Christ stands quite as high as some other people known to history. I think I should put Buddha and Socrates above Him in those respects.

THE EMOTIONAL FACTOR

As I said before, I do not think that the real reason why people accept religion has anything to do with argumentation. They accept religion on emotional grounds. One is often told that it is a very wrong thing to attack religion, because religion makes men virtuous. So I am told; I have not noticed it. You know, of course, the parody of that argument in Samuel Butler's book, *Erewhon Revisited*. You will remember that in *Erewhon* there is a certain Higgs who arrives in a remote country, and after spending some time there he escapes from that country in a balloon. Twenty years later he comes back to that country and finds a new religion in which he is worshipped under the name of the "Sun Child," and it is said that he ascended into heaven. He finds that the Feast of the Ascension is about to be celebrated, and he hears Professors Hanky and Panky say to each other that they never set eyes on the man Higgs, and they hope they never will; but they are the high priests of the religion of the Sun Child. He is very indignant, and he comes up to them, and he says, "I am going to expose all this humbug and tell the people of Erewhon that it was only I, the man Higgs, and I went up in a balloon." He was told, "You must not do that, because all the morals of this country are bound round this myth, and if they once know that you did not ascend into heaven they will all become wicked"; and so he is persuaded of that and he goes quietly away.

That is the idea — that we should all be wicked if we did not hold to the Christian religion. It seems to me that the people who have held to it have been for the most part extremely wicked. You find this curious fact, that the more intense has been the religion of any period and the more profound has been the dogmatic belief, the greater has been the cruelty and the worse has been the state of affairs. In the so-called ages of faith, when men really did believe the Christian religion in all its completeness, there was the Inquisition, with its tortures; there were millions of unfortunate women burned as witches; and there was every kind of cruelty practiced upon all sorts of people in the name of religion.

You find as you look around the world that every single bit of progress in humane feeling, every improvement in the criminal law, every step toward the diminution of war, every step toward better treatment of the colored races, or every mitigation of slavery, every moral progress that there has been in the world, has been consistently opposed by the organized churches of the world. I say quite deliberately that the Christian religion, as organized in its churches, has been and still is the principal enemy of moral progress in the world.

HOW THE CHURCHES HAVE RETARDED PROGRESS

You may think that I am going too far when I say that that is still so.   25
I do not think that I am. Take one fact. You will bear with me if I mention it. It is not a pleasant fact, but the churches compel one to mention facts that are not pleasant. Supposing that in this world that we live in today an inexperienced girl is married to a syphilitic man; in that case the Catholic Church says, "This is an indissoluble sacrament. You must endure celibacy or stay together. And if you stay together, you must not use birth control to prevent the birth of syphilitic children." Nobody whose natural sympathies have not been warped by dogma, or whose moral nature was not absolutely dead to all sense of suffering, could maintain that it is right and proper that that state of things should continue.

That is only an example. There are a great many ways in which, at the present moment, the church, by its insistence upon what it chooses to call morality, inflicts upon all sorts of people undeserved and unnecessary suffering. And of course, as we know, it is in its major part an opponent still of progress and of improvement in all the ways that diminish suffering in the world, because it has chosen to label as morality a certain narrow set of rules of conduct which have nothing to do with human happiness; and when you say that this or that ought to be done because it would make for human happiness, they think that has nothing to do with the matter at all. "What has human happiness to do with morals? The object of morals is not to make people happy."

FEAR, THE FOUNDATION OF RELIGION

Religion is based, I think, primarily and mainly upon fear. It is partly the terror of the unknown and partly, as I have said, the wish to feel that you have a kind of elder brother who will stand by you in all your troubles and disputes. Fear is the basis of the whole thing—fear of the mysterious, fear of defeat, fear of death. Fear is the parent of cruelty, and therefore it is no wonder if cruelty and religion have gone hand in hand. It is because fear is at the basis of those two things. In this world we can now begin a little to understand things, and a little to master them by help of science, which has forced its way step by step against the Christian religion, against the churches, and against the opposition of all the old precepts. Science can help us to get over this craven fear in which mankind has lived for so many generations. Science can teach us, and I think our own hearts can teach us, no longer to look around for imaginary supports, no longer to invent allies in the sky, but rather to look to our own efforts here below to make this world a fit place to live in, instead of the sort of place that the churches in all these centuries have made it.

WHAT WE MUST DO

We want to stand upon our own feet and look fair and square at the world—its good facts, its bad facts, its beauties, and its ugliness; see the world as it is and be not afraid of it. Conquer the world by intelligence and not merely by being slavishly subdued by the terror that comes from it. The whole conception of God is a conception derived from the ancient Oriental despotisms. It is a conception quite unworthy of free men. When you hear people in church debasing themselves and saying that they are miserable sinners, and all the rest of it, it seems contemptible and not worthy of self-respecting human beings. We ought to stand up and look the world frankly in the face. We ought to make the best we can of the world, and if it is not so good as we wish, after all it will still be better than what these others have made of it in all these ages. A good world needs knowledge, kindliness, and courage; it does not need a regretful hankering after the past or a fettering of the free intelligence by the words uttered long ago by ignorant men. It needs a fearless outlook and a free intelligence. It needs hope for the future, not looking back all the time toward a past that is dead, which we trust will be far surpassed by the future that our intelligence can create.

The Reader's Presence

1. Summarize Russell's first and second paragraphs, each in a sentence. In a third sentence, describe and evaluate his strategy in opening with these paragraphs. What might be Russell's intention? What tone does Russell use in pursuing his points? Is this an expected tone for the subject matter? Does Russell's tone enhance or undermine the seriousness of his argument?

2. How does Russell characterize the "First Cause Argument"? Is this how its originators are likely to have characterized it? Can you understand the original argument from Russell's version of it? What sense of Russell's perspective do you gain from his "reading" of the original argument? What sort of audience do you think Russell was addressing? Why?

3. How does the beginning of the essay relate to the end? What themes do the paragraphs between them take up? Do you see a progression? Of what sort? Why might Russell have chosen this order for his arguments?

108

Scott Russell Sanders

The Men We Carry in Our Minds

Scott Russell Sanders (b. 1945) writes in a variety of genres: science fiction, realistic fiction, folktales, children's stories, essays, and historical novels. In all his work, however, he is concerned with the ways in which people live in communities. Some of his more recent books include The Paradise of Bombs *(1987), from which "The Men We Carry in Our Minds" is taken;* Staying Put: Making a Home in a Restless World *(1993);* Here Comes the Mystery Man *(1993);* Writing from the Center *(1995); and* Hunting for Hope: A Father's Journey *(1998). Sanders contributes to both literary and popular magazines. He is a professor of English at Indiana University.*

Sanders has said, "I believe that a writer should be a servant of language, community, and nature. Language is the creation and sustenance of community. . . . My writing is driven by a deep regard for particular places and voices, persons and tools, plants and animals, for human skills and stories. . . . If my writing does not help my neighbors to live more alertly, pleasurably, or wisely, then it is worth little."

"This must be a hard time for women," I say to my friend Anneke. "They have so many paths to choose from, and so many voices calling them."

"I think it's a lot harder for men," she replies.

"How do you figure that?"

"The women I know feel excited, innocent, like crusaders in a just cause. The men I know are eaten up with guilt."

We are sitting at the kitchen table drinking sassafras tea, our hands wrapped around the mugs because this April morning is cool and drizzly. "Like a Dutch morning," Anneke told me earlier. She is Dutch herself, a writer and midwife and peacemaker, with the round face and sad eyes of a woman in a Vermeer painting who might be waiting for the rain to stop, for a door to open. She leans over to sniff a sprig of lilac, pale lavender, that rises from a vase of cobalt blue.

5

"Women feel such pressure to be everything, do everything," I say. "Career, kids, art, politics. Have their babies and get back to the office a week later. It's as if they're trying to overcome a million years' worth of evolution in one lifetime."

"But we help one another. We don't try to lumber on alone, like so many wounded grizzly bears, the way men do." Anneke sips her tea. I gave her the mug with the owls on it, for wisdom. "And we have this deep-down sense that we're in the *right*—we've been held back, passed over, used—while men feel they're in the wrong. Men are the ones who've been discredited, who have to search their souls."

I search my soul. I discover guilty feelings aplenty—toward the poor, the Vietnamese, Native Americans, the whales, an endless list of debts—a guilt in each case that is as bright and unambiguous as a neon sign. But toward women I feel something more confused, a snarl of shame, envy, wary tenderness, and amazement. This muddle troubles me. To hide my unease I say, "You're right, it's tough being a man these days."

"Don't laugh." Anneke frowns at me, mournful-eyed, through the sassafras steam. "I wouldn't be a man for anything. It's much easier being the victim. All the victim has to do is break free. The persecutor has to live with his past."

How deep is that past? I find myself wondering after Anneke has left. 10 How much of an inheritance do I have to throw off? Is it just the beliefs I breathed in as a child? Do I have to scour memory back through father and grandfather? Through St. Paul? Beyond Stonehenge and into the twilit caves? I'm convinced the past we must contend with is deeper even than speech. When I think back on my childhood, on how I learned to see men and women, I have a sense of ancient, dizzying depths. The back roads of Tennessee and Ohio where I grew up were probably closer, in their sexual patterns, to the campsites of Stone Age hunters than to the genderless cities of the future into which we are rushing.

The first men, besides my father, I remember seeing were black convicts and white guards, in the cottonfield across the road from our farm on the outskirts of Memphis. I must have been three or four. The prisoners wore dingy gray-and-black zebra suits, heavy as canvas, sodden with sweat. Hatless, stooped, they chopped weeds in the fierce heat, row after row, breathing the acrid dust of boll-weevil poison. The overseers wore dazzling white shirts and broad shadowy hats. The oiled barrels of their shotguns flashed in the sunlight. Their faces in memory are utterly blank. Of course those men, white and black, have become for me an emblem of racial hatred. But they have also come to stand for the twin poles of my early vision of manhood—the brute toiling animal and the boss.

When I was a boy, the men I knew labored with their bodies. They were marginal farmers, just scraping by, or welders, steelworkers, carpenters; they swept floors, dug ditches, mined coal, or drove trucks, their forearms ropy with muscle; they trained horses, stoked furnaces, built tires, stood on assembly lines wrestling parts onto cars and refrigerators. They got up before light, worked all day long whatever the weather, and when they came home at night they looked as though somebody had been whipping them. In the evenings and on weekends they worked on their own places, tilling gardens that were lumpy with clay, fixing broken-down cars, hammering on houses that were always too drafty, too leaky, too small.

The bodies of the men I knew were twisted and maimed in ways visible and invisible. The nails of their hands were black and split, the hands tattooed with scars. Some had lost fingers. Heavy lifting had given many of them finicky backs and guts weak from hernias. Racing against conveyor belts had given them ulcers. Their ankles and knees ached from years of standing on concrete. Anyone who had worked for long around machines was hard of hearing. They squinted, and the skin of their faces was creased like the leather of old work gloves. There were times, study-ing them, when I dreaded growing up. Most of them coughed, from dust or cigarettes, and most of them drank cheap wine or whiskey, so their eyes looked bloodshot and bruised. The fathers of my friends always seemed older than the mothers. Men wore out sooner. Only women lived into old age.

As a boy I also knew another sort of men, who did not sweat and break down like mules. They were soldiers, and so far as I could tell they scarcely worked at all. During my early school years we lived on a mili-tary base, an arsenal in Ohio, and every day I saw GIs in the guardshacks, on the stoops of barracks, at the wheels of olive drab Chevrolets. The chief fact of their lives was boredom. Long after I left the Arsenal I came to recognize the sour smell the soldiers gave off as that of souls in limbo. They were all waiting—for wars, for transfers, for leaves, for promo-tions, for the end of their hitch—like so many braves waiting for the hunt to begin. Unlike the warriors of older tribes, however, they would have no say about when the battle would start or how it would be waged. Their waiting was broken only when they practiced for war. They fired guns at targets, drove tanks across the churned-up fields of the military reservation, set off bombs in the wrecks of old fighter planes. I knew this was all play. But I also felt certain that when the hour for killing arrived, they would kill. When the real shooting started, many of them would die. This was what soldiers were *for,* just as a hammer was for driving nails.

Warriors and toilers: those seemed, in my boyhood vision, to be the   15
chief destinies for men. They weren't the only destinies, as I learned from having a few male teachers, from reading books, and from watching tele-vision. But the men on television—the politicians, the astronauts, the generals, the savvy lawyers, the philosophical doctors, the bosses who gave orders to both soldiers and laborers—seemed as remote and unreal to me as the figures in tapestries. I could no more imagine growing up to become one of these cool, potent creatures than I could imagine becoming a prince.

A nearer and more hopeful example was that of my father, who had escaped from a red-dirt farm to a tire factory, and from the assembly line to the front office. Eventually he dressed in a white shirt and tie. He carried himself as if he had been born to work with his mind. But his body, remembering the earlier years of slogging work, began to give out on him in his fifties, and it quit on him entirely before he turned sixty-five. Even such a partial escape from man's fate as he had accomplished did not seem possible for most of the boys I knew. They joined the army, stood in line for jobs in the smoky plants, helped build highways. They were bound to work as their fathers had worked, killing themselves or preparing to kill others.

A scholarship enabled me not only to attend college, a rare enough feat in my circle, but even to study in a university meant for the children of the rich. Here I met for the first time young men who had assumed from birth that they would lead lives of comfort and power. And for the first time I met women who told me that men were guilty of having kept all the joys and privileges of the earth for themselves. I was baffled. What privileges? What joys? I thought about the maimed, dismal lives of most of the men back home. What had they stolen from their wives and daughters? The right to go five days a week, twelve months a year, for thirty or forty years to a steel mill or a coal mine? The right to drop bombs and die in war? The right to feel every leak in the roof, every gap in the fence, every cough in the engine, as a wound they must mend? The right to feel, when the lay-off comes or the plant shuts down, not only afraid but ashamed?

I was slow to understand the deep grievances of women. This was because, as a boy, I had envied them. Before college, the only people I had ever known who were interested in art or music or literature, the only ones who read books, the only ones who ever seemed to enjoy a sense of ease and grace were the mothers and daughters. Like the menfolk, they fretted about money, they scrimped and made-do. But, when the pay stopped coming in, they were not the ones who had failed. Nor did they have to go to war, and that seemed to me a blessed fact. By comparison with the narrow, ironclad days of fathers, there was an expansiveness, I thought, in the days of mothers. They went to see neighbors, to shop in town, to run errands at school, at the library, at church. No doubt, had I looked harder at their lives, I would have envied them less. It was not my fate to become a woman, so it was easier for me to see the graces. Few of them held jobs outside the home, and those who did filled thankless roles as clerks and waitresses. I didn't see, then, what a prison a house could be, since houses seemed to me brighter, handsomer places than any factory. I did not realize—because such things were never spoken of—how often women suffered from men's bullying. I did learn about the wretchedness of abandoned wives, single mothers, widows; but I also learned about the wretchedness of lone men. Even then I could see how exhausting it was for a mother to cater all day to the needs of young children. But if I had been asked, as a boy, to choose between tending a baby and tending a machine, I think I would have chosen the baby. (Having now tended both, I know I would choose the baby.)

So I was baffled when the women at college accused me and my sex of having cornered the world's pleasures. I think something like my bafflement has been felt by other boys (and by girls as well) who grew up in dirt-poor farm country, in mining country, in black ghettos, in Hispanic barrios, in the shadows of factories, in Third World nations — any place where the fate of men is as grim and bleak as the fate of women. Toilers and warriors. I realize now how ancient these identities are, how deep the tug they exert on men, the undertow of a thousand generations. The miseries I saw, as a boy, in the lives of nearly all men I continue to see in the lives of many — the body-breaking toil, the tedium, the call to be tough, the humiliating powerlessness, the battle for a living and for territory.

When the women I met at college thought about the joys and privi-   20
leges of men, they did not carry in their minds the sort of men I had known in my childhood. They thought of their fathers, who were bankers, physicians, architects, stockbrokers, the big wheels of the big cities. These fathers rode the train to work or drove cars that cost more than any of my childhood houses. They were attended from morning to night by female helpers, wives, and nurses and secretaries. They were never laid off, never short of cash at month's end, never lined up for welfare. These fathers made decisions that mattered. They ran the world.

The daughters of such men wanted to share in this power, this glory. So did I. They yearned for a say over their future, for jobs worthy of their abilities, for the right to live at peace, unmolested, whole. Yes, I thought, yes yes. The difference between me and these daughters was that they saw me, because of my sex, as destined from birth to become like their fathers, and therefore as an enemy to their desires. But I knew better. I wasn't an enemy, in fact or in feeling. I was an ally. If I had known, then, how to tell them so, would they have believed me? Would they now?

The Reader's Presence

1. Consider the title of the essay. Why does Sanders use the word *carry?* What image does the word convey? How is that image reinforced throughout the essay?

2. Sanders begins the essay by jumping directly into a conversation. What effect does this conversation have on the reader? What does Sanders want you to think of him during that conversation? (See paragraphs 1–9.) Do your first impressions of Sanders remain the same throughout your reading?

3. Why did Sanders once envy women? What did women possess that men didn't? Has his impression of women's lives changed or

does he still envy them? If not, why not? If so, have his reasons changed?

THE WRITER AT WORK

Scott Russell Sanders on Writing Essays

The well-known American essayist Scott Russell Sanders is also a professor of English at the University of Indiana and the author of several novels, short story collections, and books of criticism. In the following passage from "The Singular First Person," which was originally delivered as a keynote talk at an academic conference on the essay at Seton Hall University in 1988, Sanders argues for the relevance of essay writing in a society that increasingly relies on abstract and formulaic language. If you compare this passage with the style of argument Sanders makes in the preceding essay, you will see that he is a writer who practices what he preaches. He also raises an interesting question about the difference between essays and fiction that you might consider when reading the stories in the next chapter: Do essayists put more of themselves at risk than novelists and short story writers?

The essay is a haven for the private, idiosyncratic voice in an era of anonymous babble. Like the blandburgers served in their millions along our highways, most language served up in public these days is textureless, tasteless mush. On television, over the phone, in the newspaper, wherever humans bandy words about, we encounter more and more abstractions, more empty formulas. Think of the pablum ladled out by politicians. Think of the fluffy white bread of advertising. Think, Lord help us, of committee reports. In contrast, the essay remains stubbornly concrete and particular: it confronts you with an oil-smeared toilet at the Sunoco station, a red vinyl purse shaped like a valentine heart, a bow-legged dentist hunting deer with an elephant gun. As Orwell forcefully argued,[1] and as dictators seem to agree, such a bypassing of abstractions, such an insistence on the concrete, is a politically subversive act. Clinging to this door, that child, this grief, following the zigzag motions of an inquisitive mind, the essay renews language and clears trash from the springs of thought. A century and a half ago, Emerson called on a new generation of writers to cast off the hand-me-down rhetoric of the day, to "pierce this rotten diction and fasten words again to visible things." The essayist aspires to do just that.

As if all these virtues were not enough to account for a renaissance of this protean genre, the essay has also taken over some of the territory abdicated by contemporary fiction. Pared down to the brittle bones of plot, camouflaged with irony, muttering in brief sentences and grade-school

---

[1]See "Politics and the English Language," page 498. —EDS.

vocabulary, today's fashionable fiction avoids disclosing where the author stands on anything. Most of the trends in the novel and short story over the past twenty years have led away from candor—toward satire, artsy jokes, close-lipped coyness, metafictional hocus-pocus, anything but a direct statement of what the author thinks and feels. If you hide behind enough screens, no one will ever hold you to an opinion or demand from you a coherent vision or take you for a charlatan.

The essay is not fenced round by these literary inhibitions. You may speak without disguise of what moves and worries and excites you. In fact, you had better speak from a region pretty close to the heart, or the reader will detect the wind of phoniness whistling through your hollow phrases. In the essay you may be caught with your pants down, your ignorance and sentimentality showing, while you trot recklessly about on one of your hobbyhorses. You cannot stand back from the action, as Joyce instructed us to do, and pare your fingernails. You cannot palm off your cockamamie notions on some hapless character. If the words you put down are foolish, everyone knows precisely who the fool is.

To our list of the essay's contemporary attractions we should add the perennial ones of verbal play, mental adventure, and sheer anarchic high spirits. The writing of an essay is like finding one's way through a forest without being quite sure what game you are chasing, what landmark you are seeking. You sniff down one path until some heady smell tugs you in a new direction, and then off you go, dodging and circling, lured on by the songs of unfamiliar birds, puzzled by the tracks of strange beasts, leaping from stone to stone across rivers, barking up one tree after another. Much of the pleasure in writing an essay—and, when the writing is any good, the pleasure in reading it—comes from this dodging and leaping, this movement of the mind. It must not be idle movement, however, if the essay is to hold up; it must be driven by deep concerns. The surface of a river is alive with lights and reflections, the breaking of foam over rocks, but beneath that dazzle it is going somewhere. We should expect as much from an essay: the shimmer and play of mind on the surface and in the depths a strong current.

109

Arthur M. Schlesinger Jr.
The Cult of Ethnicity, Good and Bad

One of the most widely known historians, Arthur M. Schlesinger Jr. (b. 1917) has been a professor at Harvard University and at the Graduate Center of the City University of New York. Politically liberal, Schlesinger served as a special adviser to President Kennedy from 1961 to 1963. He has received numerous awards, including over two dozen honorary degrees, both a National Book Award and a Pulitzer Prize for A Thousand Days: John F. Kennedy in the White House *(1965), and a Pulitzer for* The Age of Jackson *(1945). His major historical work on the life of Franklin D. Roosevelt,* The Age of Roosevelt, *was published in three volumes:* The Crisis of the Old Order, 1919–1933 *(1957),* The Coming of the New Deal *(1958), and* The Politics of Upheaval *(1960). Most recently, Schlesinger has published* The Disuniting of America *(1991) and* Running for President: The Candidates and Their Images *(1994). "The Cult of Ethnicity, Good and Bad" appeared in* Time *in 1991.*

The history of the world has been in great part the history of the mixing of peoples. Modern communication and transport accelerate mass migrations from one continent to another. Ethnic and racial diversity is more than ever a salient fact of the age.

But what happens when people of different origins, speaking different languages and professing different religions, inhabit the same locality and live under the same political sovereignty? Ethnic and racial conflict—far more than ideological conflict—is the explosive problem of our times.

On every side today ethnicity is breaking up nations. The Soviet Union, India, Yugoslavia, Ethiopia, are all in crisis. Ethnic tensions disturb and divide Sri Lanka, Burma, Indonesia, Iraq, Cyprus, Nigeria, Angola, Lebanon, Guyana, Trinidad—you name it. Even nations as stable and civilized as Britain and France, Belgium and Spain, face growing ethnic troubles. Is there any large multiethnic state that can be made to work?

The answer to that question has been, until recently, the United States. "No other nation," Margaret Thatcher[1] has said, "has so successfully combined people of different races and nations within a single culture." How have Americans succeeded in pulling off this almost unprecedented trick?

We have always been a multiethnic country. Hector St. John de   5
Crèvecoeur, who came from France in the eighteenth century, marveled at the astonishing diversity of the settlers—"a mixture of English, Scotch, Irish, French, Dutch, Germans, and Swedes . . . this promiscuous breed." He propounded a famous question: "What then is the American, this new man?" And he gave a famous answer: "Here individuals of all nations are melted into a new race of men." *E pluribus unum.*[2]

The United States escaped the divisiveness of a multiethnic society by a brilliant solution: the creation of a brand-new national identity. The point of America was not to preserve old cultures but to forge a new *American* culture. "By an intermixture with our people," President George Washington told Vice President John Adams, immigrants will "get assimilated to our customs, measures and laws: in a word, soon become one people." This was the ideal that a century later Israel Zangwill crystallized in the title of his popular 1908 play *The Melting Pot.* And no institution was more potent in molding Crèvecoeur's "promiscuous breed" into Washington's "one people" than the American public school.

The new American nationality was inescapably English in language, ideas, and institutions. The pot did not melt everybody, not even all the white immigrants; deeply bred racism put black Americans, yellow Americans, red Americans, and brown Americans well outside the pale. Still, the infusion of other stocks, even of nonwhite stocks, and the experience of the New World reconfigured the British legacy and made the United States, as we all know, a very different country from Britain.

In the twentieth century, new immigration laws altered the composition of the American people, and a cult of ethnicity erupted both among non-Anglo whites and among nonwhite minorities. This had many healthy consequences. The American culture at last began to give shamefully overdue recognition to the achievements of groups subordinated and spurned during the high noon of Anglo dominance, and it began to acknowledge the great swirling world beyond Europe. Americans acquired a more complex and invigorating sense of their world—and of themselves.

But, pressed too far, the cult of ethnicity has unhealthy consequences. It gives rise, for example, to the conception of the United States as a nation composed not of individuals making their own choices but of inviolable ethnic and racial groups. It rejects the historic American goals of assimilation and integration. And, in an excess of zeal, well-intentioned people seek to transform our system of education from a means of

---

[1]*Margaret Thatcher:* Former prime minister of Great Britain.—EDS.
[2]*E pluribus unum:* Latin phrase and U.S. motto meaning "out of many, one."—EDS.

creating "one people" into a means of promoting, celebrating, and perpetuating separate ethnic origins and identities. The balance is shifting
from *unum* to *pluribus*.

That is the issue that lies behind the hullabaloo over "multicultural-   10
ism" and "political correctness," the attack on the "Eurocentric" curriculum and the rise of the notion that history and literature should be taught
not as disciplines but as therapies whose function is to raise minority self-
esteem. Group separatism crystallizes the differences, magnifies tensions,
intensifies hostilities. Europe—the unique source of the liberating ideas
of democracy, civil liberties, and human rights—is portrayed as the root
of all evil, and non-European cultures, their own many crimes deleted, are
presented as the means of redemption.

I don't want to sound apocalyptic about these developments. Education
is always in ferment, and a good thing, too. The situation in our universities,
I am confident, will soon right itself. But the impact of separatist pressures
on our public schools is more troubling. If a Kleagle[3] of the Ku Klux Klan
wanted to use the schools to disable and handicap black Americans, he
could hardly come up with anything more effective than the "Afrocentric"
curriculum. And if separatist tendencies go unchecked, the result can only
be the fragmentation, resegregation, and tribalization of American life.

I remain optimistic. My impression is that the historic forces driving
toward "one people" have not lost their power. The eruption of ethnicity
is, I believe, a rather superficial enthusiasm stirred by romantic ideologues
on the one hand and by unscrupulous con men on the other: self-
appointed spokesmen whose claim to represent their minority groups is
carelessly accepted by the media. Most American-born members of minority groups, white or nonwhite, see themselves primarily as Americans
rather than primarily as members of one or another ethnic group. A
notable indicator today is the rate of intermarriage across ethnic lines,
across religious lines, even (increasingly) across racial lines. "We Americans," said Theodore Roosevelt, "are children of the crucible."

The growing diversity of the American population makes the quest for
unifying ideals and a common culture all the more urgent. In a world savagely rent by ethnic and racial antagonisms, the United States must continue
as an example of how a highly differentiated society holds itself together.

The Reader's Presence

1. Why does the author use a Latin phrase in paragraph 5? Evaluate
   the use of this phrase. Is it a common phrase? Do you think most
   readers know what it means in English? Why does he use it twice
   in varying forms?

---

[3]*Kleagle:* An organizer or recruiter for the Ku Klux Klan.—EDS.

2. Schlesinger agrees that, historically, America has faced difficulties with ethnicity and assimilation, yet feels that in the current situation events have gone too far. Does he propose a different solution? Is this "commonsense" approach valid? Would a more fact-based approach be more, or less, convincing? Why? Can you think of an opposing argument? It might be counter argued that Schlesinger, hailing from a past generation of immigrants, is insensitive to the needs of current-day groups. How might Schlesinger answer that response? Can you think of an answer?

3. Why does Schlesinger discuss both the positive and negative aspects of what he calls "the cult of ethnicity"? Why does he present the positive points first? What does he conclude about this trend?

110

Elizabeth Cady Stanton

Declaration of Sentiments and Resolutions

Elizabeth Cady Stanton (1815–1902) was one of the leading figures in the women's suffrage movement. Along with Lucretia Mott, Stanton organized the first women's rights convention in 1848 at Seneca Falls, New York, where she read the "Declaration of Sentiments and Resolutions." Stanton did most of the writing for the movement, and she and Susan B. Anthony were editors for the group's newspaper, Revolution. *Stanton, Anthony, and Matilda Joslyn Gage edited the first three volumes of* The History of Woman Suffrage *(1881–1922). Shortly before her death, Stanton published her autobiography,* Eighty Years and More, 1815–1897 *(1898).*

When, in the course of human events, it becomes necessary for one portion of the family of man to assume among the people of the earth a position different from that which they have hitherto occupied, but one to which the laws of nature and of nature's God entitle them, a decent respect to the opinions of mankind requires that they should declare the causes that impel them to such a course.

We hold these truths to be self-evident: that all men and women are created equal; that they are endowed by their Creator with certain inalienable rights; that among these are life, liberty, and the pursuit of happiness; that to secure these rights governments are instituted, deriving their just powers from the consent of the governed. Whenever any form of government becomes destructive of these ends, it is the right of those who suffer from it to refuse allegiance to it, and to insist upon the institution of a new government, laying its foundation on such principles, and organizing its powers in such form, as to them shall seem most likely to effect their safety and happiness. Prudence, indeed, will dictate that governments long established should not be changed for light and transient causes; and accordingly all experience hath shown that mankind are more disposed to suffer, while evils are sufferable, than to right themselves by abolishing the forms to which they were accustomed. But when a long train of abuses and usurpations, pursuing invariable the same object, evinces a design to reduce them under absolute despotism, it is their duty to throw off such government, and to provide new guards for their future security. Such has been the patient sufferance of the women under this government, and such is now the necessity which constrains them to demand the equal station to which they are entitled.

The history of mankind is a history of repeated injuries and usurpations on the part of man toward woman, having in direct object the establishment of an absolute tyranny over her. To prove this, let facts be submitted to a candid world.

He has never permitted her to exercise her inalienable right to the elective franchise.

He has compelled her to submit to laws, in the formation of which   5
she had no voice.

He has withheld from her rights which are given to the most ignorant and degraded men—both natives and foreigners.

Having deprived her of this first right of a citizen, the elective franchise, thereby leaving her without representation in the halls of legislation, he has oppressed her on all sides.

He has made her, if married, in the eye of the law, civilly dead.

He has taken from her all right in property, even to the wages she earns.

He has made her, morally, an irresponsible being, as she can commit   10
many crimes with impunity, provided they be done in the presence of her husband. In the covenant of marriage, she is compelled to promise obedience to her husband, he becoming to all intents and purposes, her master—the law giving him power to deprive her of her liberty, and to administer chastisement.

He has so framed the laws of divorce, as to what shall be the proper causes, and in case of separation, to whom the guardianship of the children shall be given, as to be wholly regardless of the happiness of women—the law, in all cases, going upon a false supposition of the supremacy of man, and giving all power into his hands.

After depriving her of all rights as a married woman, if single, and the owner of property, he has taxed her to support a government which recognizes her only when her property can be made profitable to it.

He has monopolized nearly all the profitable employments, and from those she is permitted to follow, she receives but a scanty remuneration. He closes against her all the avenues to wealth and distinction which he considers most honorable to himself. As a teacher of theology, medicine, or law, she is not known.

He has denied her the facilities for obtaining a thorough education, all colleges being closed against her.

He allows her in Church, as well as State, but a subordinate position, claiming Apostolic authority for her exclusion from the ministry, and, with some exceptions, from any public participation in the affairs of the Church.

15

He has created a false public sentiment by giving to the world a different code of morals for men and women, by which moral delinquencies which exclude women from society, are not only tolerated, but deemed of little account in man.

He has usurped the prerogative of Jehovah himself, claiming it as his right to assign for her a sphere of action, when that belongs to her conscience and to her God.

He has endeavored, in every way that he could, to destroy her confidence in her own powers, to lessen her self-respect, and to make her willing to lead a dependent and abject life.

Now, in view of this entire disfranchisement of one-half the people of this country, their social and religious degradation—in view of the unjust laws above mentioned, and because women do feel themselves aggrieved, oppressed, and fraudulently deprived of their most sacred rights, we insist that they have immediate admission to all the rights and privileges which belong to them as citizens of the United States.

In entering upon the great work before us, we anticipate no small amount of misconception, misrepresentation, and ridicule; but we shall use every instrumentality within our power to effect our object. We shall employ agents, circulate tracts, petition the State and National legislatures, and endeavor to enlist the pulpit and the press in our behalf. We hope this Convention will be followed by a series of Conventions embracing every part of this country.

20

[The following resolutions were discussed by Lucretia Mott, Thomas and Mary Ann McClintock, Amy Post, Catharine A. F. Stebbins, and others, and were adopted:]

Whereas, The great precept of nature is conceded to be, that "man shall pursue his own true and substantial happiness." Blackstone in his Commentaries remarks, that this law of Nature being coeval with mankind, and dictated by God himself, is of course superior in obligation to any other. It is binding over all the globe, in all countries, and at all times; no human laws are of any validity if contrary to this, and such of them as are valid, derive all their force, and all their validity, and all their authority, mediately and immediately, from this original; therefore,

Resolved, That such laws as conflict, in any way, with the true and substantial happiness of woman, are contrary to the great precept of nature and of no validity, for this is "superior in obligation to any other."

Resolved, That all laws which prevent woman from occupying such a station in society as her conscience shall dictate, or which place her in a position inferior to that of man, are contrary to the great precept of nature, and therefore of no force or authority.

Resolved, That woman is man's equal—was intended to be so by the   25
Creator, and the highest good of the race demands that she should be recognized as such.

Resolved, That the women of this country ought to be enlightened in regard to the laws under which they live, that they may no longer publish their degradation by declaring themselves satisfied with their present position, nor their ignorance, by asserting that they have all the rights they want.

Resolved, That inasmuch as man, while claiming for himself intellectual superiority, does accord to woman moral superiority, it is preeminently his duty to encourage her to speak and teach, as she has an opportunity, in all religious assemblies.

Resolved, That the same amount of virtue, delicacy, and refinement of behavior that is required of woman in the social state, should also be required of man, and the same transgressions should be visited with equal severity on both man and woman.

Resolved, That the objection of indelicacy and impropriety, which is so often brought against woman when she addresses a public audience, comes with a very ill-grace from those who encourage, by their attendance, her appearance on the stage, in the concert, or in feats of the circus.

Resolved, That woman has too long rested satisfied in the circum-   30
scribed limits which corrupt customs and a perverted application of the Scriptures have marked out for her, and that it is time she should move in the enlarged sphere which her great Creator has assigned her.

Resolved, That it is the duty of the women of this country to secure to themselves their sacred right to the elective franchise.

Resolved, That the equality of human rights results necessarily from the fact of the identity of the race in capabilities and responsibilities.

Resolved, therefore, That, being invested by the Creator with the same capabilities, and the same consciousness of responsibility for their exercise, it is demonstrably the right and duty of woman, equally with man, to promote every righteous cause by every righteous means; and especially in regard to the great subjects of morals and religion, it is self-evidently her right to participate with her brother in teaching them, both in private and in public, by writing and by speaking, by any instrumentalities proper to be used, and in any assemblies proper to be held; and this being a self-evident truth growing out of the divinely implanted principles of human nature, any custom or authority adverse to it, whether modern or wearing the hoary sanction of antiquity, is to be regarded as a self-evident falsehood, and at war with mankind.

[At the last session Lucretia Mott offered and spoke to the following resolution:]

Resolved, That the speedy success of our cause depends upon the   35
zealous and untiring efforts of both men and women, for the overthrow of the monopoly of the pulpit, and for the securing to woman an equal participation with men in the various trades, professions, and commerce.

The Reader's Presence

1. Compare the first two paragraphs of this piece to Thomas Jefferson's Declaration of Independence. What has Stanton preserved from the original? What is different? Would you call her opening a "parody"? Is she imitating Jefferson to be funny? What benefit might Stanton gain by linking women's rights to human and national rights?

2. Beginning with paragraph 4, the indignities suffered by women appear in list form. What is the effect for the reader of the rhetorical devices of listing and repetition? Suppose the items on the list were presented in more conversational form. Would the piece be weakened or strengthened? Stanton refers to "man" in general as "he." What is the effect for the reader of this rhetorical choice?

3. This piece, like the Declaration of Independence, is a manifesto — a statement of a set of political views that will serve as the basis for action. The more conventional essay, by contrast, generally presents multiple sides of an issue; it may urge action, but primarily serves as a vehicle for contemplation. How might Stanton's manifesto read differently as a conventional essay? Which would be more effective? Why?

111

Shelby Steele

On Being Black and Middle Class

Shelby Steele (b. 1946) is a research fellow with the Hoover Institution at Stanford University. He has contributed articles and reviews to periodicals such as Confrontation, Black World, Harper's, *and the* Western Humanities Review. *Steele's writings on race relations in the United States have placed him in the center of the national debate on affirmative action and other issues. "On Being Black and Middle Class" appeared in* Commentary *in 1988. Steele published his first book,* The Content of Our Character: A New Vision of Race in America, *in 1990, and his most recent book is* A Dream Deferred: The Second Betrayal of Black Freedom in America *(1998).*

Steele told an interviewer, "Some people say I shine a harsh light on difficult problems. But I never shine a light on anything I haven't experienced or write about fears I don't see in myself first. I'm my own first target. I spill my own blood first."

Not long ago a friend of mine, black like myself, said to me that the term "black middle class" was actually a contradiction in terms. Race, he insisted, blurred class distinctions among blacks. If you were black, you were just black and that was that. When I argued, he let his eyes roll at my naiveté. Then he went on. For us, as black professionals, it was an exercise in self-flattery, a pathetic pretention, to give meaning to such a distinction. Worse, the very idea of class threatened the unity that was vital to the black community as a whole. After all, since when had white America taken note of anything but color when it came to blacks? He then reminded me of an old Malcolm X line that had been popular in the sixties. Question: What is a black man with a Ph.D.? Answer: A nigger.

For many years I had been on my friend's side of this argument. Much of my conscious thinking on the old conundrum of race and class was shaped during my high school and college years in the race-charged sixties, when the fact of my race took on an almost religious significance. Progressively, from the mid-sixties on, more and more aspects of my life found their explanation, their justification, and their motivation in race.

My youthful concerns about career, romance, money, values, and even styles of dress became subject to consultation with various oracular sources of racial wisdom. And these ranged from a figure as ennobling as Martin Luther King, Jr., to the underworld elegance of dress I found in jazz clubs on the South Side of Chicago. Everywhere there were signals, and in those days I considered myself so blessed with clarity and direction that I pitied my white classmates who found more embarrassment than guidance in the face of *their* race. In 1968, inflated by my new power, I took a mischievous delight in calling them culturally disadvantaged.

But now, hearing my friend's comment was like hearing a priest from a church I'd grown disenchanted with. I understood him, but my faith was weak. What had sustained me in the sixties sounded monotonous and off the mark in the eighties. For me, race had lost much of its juju, its singular capacity to conjure meaning. And today, when I honestly look at my life and the lives of many other middle-class blacks I know, I can see that race never fully explained our situation in America society. Black though I may be, it is impossible for me to sit in my single-family house with two cars in the driveway and a swing set in the back yard and *not* see the role class has played in my life. And how can my friend, similarly raised and similarly situated, not see it?

Yet despite my certainty I felt a sharp tug of guilt as I tried to explain myself over my friend's skepticism. He is a man of many comedic facial expressions and, as I spoke, his brow lifted in extreme moral alarm as if I were uttering the unspeakable. His clear implication was that I was being elitist and possibly (dare he suggest?) antiblack—crimes for which there might well be no redemption. He pretended to fear for me. I chuckled along with him, but inwardly I did wonder at myself. Though I never doubted the validity of what I was saying, I felt guilty saying it. Why?

After he left (to retrieve his daughter from a dance lesson) I realized   5 that the trap I felt myself in had a tiresome familiarity and, in a sort of slow-motion epiphany, I began to see its outline. It was like the suddenly sharp vision one has at the end of a burdensome marriage when all the long-repressed incompatibilities come undeniably to light.

What became clear to me is that people like myself, my friend, and middle-class blacks generally are caught in a very specific double bind that keeps two equally powerful elements of our identity at odds with each other. The middle-class values by which we were raised—the work ethic, the importance of education, the value of property ownership, of respectability, of "getting ahead," of stable family life, of initiative, of self-reliance, etc.—are, in themselves, raceless and even assimilationist. They urge us toward participation in the American mainstream, toward integration, toward a strong identification with the society—and toward the entire constellation of qualities that are implied in the word "individualism." These values are almost rules for how to prosper in a democratic, free-enterprise society that admires and rewards individual effort. They tell us to work hard for ourselves and our families and to seek our opportunities whenever they appear, inside or outside the confines of whatever ethnic group we may belong to.

But the particular pattern of racial identification that emerged in the sixties and that still prevails today urges middle-class blacks (and all blacks) in the opposite direction. This pattern asks us to see ourselves as an embattled minority, and it urges an adversarial stance toward the mainstream, an emphasis on ethnic consciousness over individualism. It is organized around an implied separatism.

The opposing thrust of these two parts of our identity results in the double bind of middle-class black. There is no forward movement on either plane that does not constitute backward movement on the other. This was the familiar trap I felt myself in while talking with my friend. As I spoke about class, his eyes reminded me that I was betraying race. Clearly, the two indispensable parts of my identity were a threat to each other.

Of course when you think about it, class and race are both similar in some ways and also naturally opposed. They are two forms of collective identity with boundaries that intersect. But whether they clash or peace-fully coexist has much to do with how they are defined. Being both black and middle class becomes a double bind when class and race are defined in sharply antagonistic terms, so that one must be repressed to appease the other.

But what is the "substance" of these two identities, and how does   10
each establish itself in an individual's overall identity? It seems to me that when we identify with any collective we are basically identifying with im-ages that tell us what it means to be a member of that collective. Identity is not the same thing as the fact of membership in a collective; it, rather, a form of self-definition, facilitated by images of what we wish our mem-bership in the collective to mean. In this sense, the images we identify with may reflect the aspirations of the collective more than they reflect re-ality, and their content can vary with shifts in those aspirations.

But the process of identification is usually dialectical. It is just as nec-essary to say what we are *not* as it is to say what we are—so that finally identification comes about by embracing a polarity of positive and nega-tive images. To identify as middle class, for example, I must have both positive and negative images of what being middle class entails; then I will know what I should and should not be doing in order to be middle class. The same goes for racial identity.

In the racially turbulent sixties the polarity of images that came to de-fine racial identification was very antagonistic to the polarity that defined middle-class identification. One might say that the positive images of one lined up with the negative images of the other, so that to identify with both required either a contortionist's flexibility or a dangerous splitting of the self. The double bind of the black middle class was in place.

The black middle class has always defined its class identity by means of positive images gleaned from middle- and upper-class white society, and by means of negative images of lower-class blacks. This habit goes back to the institution of slavery itself, when "house" slaves both mimicked the whites they served and held themselves above the "field" slaves. But in the sixties the old bourgeois impulse to dissociate from the lower classes (the "we-they" distinction) backfired when racial identity suddenly called for the celebration of this same black lower class. One of the qualities of a double bind is that one feels it more than sees it, and I distinctly remember the tension and strange sense of dishonesty I felt in those days as I moved back and forth like a bigamist between the demands of class and race.

Though my father was born poor, he achieved middle-class standing through much hard work and sacrifice (one of his favorite words) and by identifying fully with solid middle-class values—mainly hard work, family life, property ownership, and education for his children (all four of whom have advanced degrees). In his mind these were not so much values as laws of nature. People who embodied them made up the positive images in his class polarity. The negative images came largely from the blacks he had left behind because they were "going nowhere."

No one in my family remembers how it happened, but as time went   15
on, the negative images congealed into an imaginary character named Sam, who, from the extensive service we put him to, quickly grew to mythic proportions. In our family lore he was sometimes a trickster, sometimes a boob, but always possessed of a catalogue of sly faults that gave up graphic images of everything we should not be. On sacrifice: "Sam never thinks about tomorrow. He wants it now or he doesn't care about it." On work: "Sam doesn't favor it too much." On children: "Sam likes to have them but not to raise them." On money: "Sam drinks it up and pisses it out." On fidelity: "Sam has to have two or three women." On clothes: "Sam features loud clothes. He likes to see and be seen." And so on. Sam's persona amounted to a negative instruction manual in class identity.

I don't think that any of us believed Sam's faults were accurate representations of lower-class black life. He was an instrument of self-definition, not of sociological accuracy. It never occurred to us that he looked very much like the white racist stereotype of blacks, or that he might have been a manifestation of our own racial self-hatred. He simply gave us a counterpoint against which to express our aspirations. If self-hatred was a factor, it was not, for us, a matter of hating lower-class blacks but of hating what we did not want to be.

Still, hate or love aside, it is fundamentally true that my middle-class identity involved a dissociation from images of lower-class black life and a corresponding identification with values and patterns of responsibility that are common to the middle class everywhere. These values sent me a clear message: Be both an individual and a responsible citizen; understand that the quality of your life will approximately reflect the quality of effort you put into it; know that individual responsibility is the basis of freedom and that the limitations imposed by fate (whether fair or unfair) are no excuse for passivity.

Whether I live up to these values or not, I know that my acceptance of them is the result of lifelong conditioning. I know also that I share this conditioning with middle-class people of all races and that I can no more easily be free of it than I can be free of my race. Whether all this got started because the black middle class modeled itself on the white middle class is no longer relevant. For the middle-class black, conditioned by these values from birth, the sense of meaning they provide is as immutable as the color of his skin.

I started the sixties in high school feeling that my class-conditioning was the surest way to overcome racial barriers. My racial identity was pretty much taken for granted. After all, it was obvious to the world that I was black. Yet I ended the sixties in graduate school a little embarrassed by my class background and with an almost desperate need to be "black." The tables had turned. I knew very clearly (though I struggled to repress it) that my aspirations and my sense of how to operate in the world came from my class background, yet "being black" required certain attitudes and stances that made me feel secretly a little duplicitous. The inner compatibility of class and race I had known in 1960 was gone.

For blacks, the decade between 1960 and 1969 saw racial identification undergo the same sort of transformation that national identity undergoes in times of war. It became more self-conscious, more narrowly focused, more prescribed, less tolerant of opposition. It spawned an implicit party line, which tended to disallow competing forms of identity. Race-as-identity was lifted from the relative slumber it knew in the fifties and pressed into service in a social and political war against oppression. It was redefined along sharp adversarial lines and directed toward the goal of mobilizing the great mass of black Americans in this warlike effort. It was imbued with a strong moral authority, useful for denouncing those who opposed it and for celebrating those who honored it as a positive achievement rather than as a mere birthright.

The form of racial identification that quickly evolved to meet this challenge presented blacks as a racial monolith, a singular people with a common experience of oppression. Differences within the race, no matter how ineradicable, had to be minimized. Class distinctions were one of the first such differences to be sacrificed, since they not only threatened racial unity but also seemed to stand in contradiction to the principle of equality which was the announced goal of the movement for racial progress. The discomfort I felt in 1969, the vague but relentless sense of duplicity, was the result of a historical necessity that put my race and class at odds, that was asking me to cast aside the distinction of my class and identify with a monolithic view of my race.

If the form of this racial identity was the monolith, its substance was victimization. The civil rights movement and the more radical splinter groups of the late sixties were all dedicated to ending racial victimization,

20

and the form of black identity that emerged to facilitate this goal made blackness and victimization virtually synonymous. Since it was our victimization more than any other variable that identified and unified us, moreover, it followed logically that the purest black was the poor black. It was images of him that clustered around the positive pole of the race polarity; all other blacks were, in effect, required to identify with him in order to confirm their own blackness.

Certainly there were more dimensions to the black experience than victimization, but no other had the same capacity to fire the indignation needed for war. So, again out of historical necessity, victimization became the overriding focus of racial identity. But this only deepened the double bind for middle-class blacks like me. When it came to class we were accustomed to defining ourselves against lower-class blacks and identifying with at least the values of middle-class whites; when it came to race we were now being asked to identify with images of lower-class blacks and to see whites, middle class or otherwise, as victimizers. Negative lining up with positive, we were called upon to reject what we had previously embraced and to embrace what we had previously rejected. To put it still more personally, the Sam figure I had been raised to define myself against had now become the "real" black I was expected to identify with.

The fact that the poor black's new status was only passively earned by the condition of his victimization, not by assertive, positive action made little difference. Status was status apart from the means by which it was achieved, and along with it came a certain power — the power to define the terms of access to that status, to say who was black and who was not. If a lower-class black said you were not really "black" — a sellout, an Uncle Tom — the judgment was all the more devastating because it carried the authority of his status. And this judgment soon enough came to be accepted by many whites as well.

In graduate school I was once told by a white professor, "Well, 25 but . . . you're not really black. I mean, you're not disadvantaged." In his mind my lack of victim status disqualified me from the race itself. More recently I was complimented by a black student for speaking reasonably correct English, "proper" English as he put it. "But I don't know if I really want to talk like that," he went on. "Why not?" I asked. "Because then I wouldn't be black no more," he replied without a pause.

To overcome his marginal status, the middle-class black had to identify with a degree of victimization that was beyond his actual experience. In college (and well beyond) we used to play a game called "nap matching." It was a game of one-upmanship, in which we sat around outdoing each other with stories of racial victimization, symbolically measured by the naps of our hair. Most of us were middle class and so had few personal stories to relate, but if we could not match naps with our own biographies, we would move on to those legendary tales of victimization that came to us from the public domain.

The single story that sat atop the pinnacle of racial victimization for us was that of Emmett Till, the Northern black teenager who, on a visit to the South in 1955, was killed and grotesquely mutilated for supposedly looking at or whistling at (we were never sure which, though we argued the point endlessly) a white woman. Oh, how we probed his story, finding in his youth and Northern upbringing the quintessential embodiment of black innocence, brought down by a white evil so portentous and apocalyptic, so gnarled and hideous, that it left us with a feeling not far from awe. By telling his story and others like it, we came to *feel* the immutability of our victimization, its utter indegenousness, as a thing on this earth like dirt or sand or water.

Of course, these sessions were a ritual of group identification, a means by which we, as middle-class blacks, could be at one with our race. But why were we, who had only a moderate experience of victimization (and that offset by opportunities our parents never had), so intent on assimilating or appropriating an identity that in so many ways contradicted our own? Because, I think, the sense of innocence that is always entailed in feeling victimized filled us with a corresponding feeling of entitlement, or even license, that helped us endure our vulnerability on a largely white college campus.

In my junior year in college I rode to a debate tournament with three white students and our faculty coach, an elderly English professor. The experience of being the lone black in a group of whites was so familiar to me that I thought nothing of it as our trip began. But then halfway through the trip the professor casually turned to me and, in an isn't-the-world-funny sort of tone, said that he had just refused to rent an apartment in a house he owned to a "very nice" black couple because their color would "offend" the white couple who lived downstairs. His eyebrows lifted helplessly over his hawkish nose, suggesting that he too, like me, was a victim of America's racial farce. His look assumed a kind of comradeship: he and I were above this grimy business of race, though for expediency we had occasionally to concede the world it madness.

My vulnerability in this situation came not so much from the professor's blindness to his own racism as from his assumption that I would participate in it, that I would conspire with him against my own race so that he might remain comfortably blind. Why did he think I would be amenable to this? I can only guess that he assumed my middle-class identity was so complete and all-encompassing that I would see his action as nothing more than a trifling concession to the folkways of our land, that I would in fact applaud his decision not to disturb propriety. Blind to both his own racism and to me — one blindness serving the other — he could not recognize that he was asking me to betray my race in the name of my class. 30

His blindness made me feel vulnerable because it threatened to expose my own repressed ambivalence. His comment pressured me to choose between my class identification, which had contributed to my being a college student and a member of the debating team, and my desperate desire to be "black." I could have one but not both; I was double-bound.

Because double binds are repressed there is always an element of terror in them: the terror of bringing to the conscious mind the buried duplicity, self-deception, and pretense involved in serving two masters. This terror is the stuff of vulnerability, and since vulnerability is one of the least tolerable of all human feelings, we usually transform it into an emotion that seems to restore the control of which it has robbed us; most often, that emotion is anger. And so, before the professor had even finished his little story I had become a furnace of rage. The year was 1967, and I had been primed by endless hours of nap-matching to feel, at least consciously, completely at one with the victim-focused black identity. This identity gave me the license, and the impunity, to unleash upon this professor one of those volcanic eruptions of racial indignation familiar to us from the novels of Richard Wright. Like Cross Damon in *Outsider,* who kills in perfectly righteous anger, I tried to annihilate the man. I punished him not according to the measure of his crime but according to the measure of my vulnerability, a measure set by the cumulative tension of years of repressed terror. Soon I saw that terror in *his* face, as he stared hollow-eyed at the road ahead. My white friends in the back seat, knowing no conflict between their own class and race, were astonished that someone they had taken to be so much like themselves could harbor a rage that for all the world looked murderous.

Though my rage was triggered by the professor's comment, it was deepened and sustained by a complex of need, conflict, and repression in myself of which I had been wholly unaware. Out of my racial vulnerability I had developed the strong need of an identity with which to defend myself. The only such identity available was that of me as victim, him as victimizer. Once in the grip of this paradigm, I began to do far more damage to myself than he had done.

Seeing myself as a victim meant that I clung all the harder to my racial identity, which, in turn, meant that I suppressed my class identity. This cut me off from all the resources my class values might have offered me. In those values, for instance, I might have found the means to a more dispassionate response, the response less of a victim attacked by a victimizer than of an individual offended by a foolish old man. As an individual I might have reported this professor to the college dean. Or I might have calmly tried to reveal his blindness to him, and possibly won a convert. (The flagrancy of his remark suggested a hidden guilt and even self-recognition on which I might have capitalized. Doesn't confession usually signal a willingness to face oneself?) Or I might have simply chuckled and then let my silence serve as an answer to his provocation. Would not my composure, in any form it might take, deflect into his own heart the arrow he'd shot at me?

Instead, my anger, itself the hair-trigger expression of a long-repressed double bind, not only cut me off from the best of my own resources, it also distorted the nature of my true racial problem. The righteousness of this anger and the easy catharsis it brought buoyed the delusion of my victimization and left me as blind as the professor himself. 35

As a middle-class black I have often felt myself *contriving* to be "black." And I have noticed this same contrivance in others—a certain stretching away from the natural flow of one's life to align oneself with a victim-focused black identity. Our particular needs are out of sync with the form of identity available to meet those needs. Middle-class blacks need to identify racially; it is better to think of ourselves as black and victimized than not black at all; so we contrive (more unconsciously than consciously) to fit ourselves into an identity that denies our class and fails to address the true source of our vulnerability.

For me this once meant spending inordinate amounts of time at black faculty meetings, though these meetings had little to do with my real racial anxieties or my professional life. I was new to the university, one of two blacks in an English department of over seventy, and I felt a little isolated and vulnerable, though I did not admit it to myself. But at these meetings we discussed the problems of black faculty and students within a framework of victimization. The real vulnerability we felt was covered over by all the adversarial drama the victim/victimized polarity inspired, and hence went unseen and unassuaged. And this, I think, explains our rather chronic ineffectiveness as a group. Since victimization was not our primary problem—the university had long ago opened its doors to us—we had to contrive to make it so, and there is not much energy in contrivance. What I got at these meetings was ultimately an object lesson in how fruitless struggle can be when it is not grounded in actual need.

At our black faculty meetings, the old equation of blackness with victimization was ever present—to be black was to be a victim; therefore, not to be a victim was not to be black. As we contrived to meet the terms of this formula there was an inevitable distortion of both ourselves and the larger university. Through the prism of victimization the university seemed more impenetrable than it actually was, and we were more limited in our powers. We fell prey to the victim's myopia, making the university an institution from which we could seek redress but which we could never fully join. And this mind-set often led us to look more for compensations for our supposed victimization than for opportunities we could pursue as individuals.

The discomfort and vulnerability felt by middle-class blacks in the sixties, it could be argued, was a worthwhile price to pay considering the progress achieved during that time of racial confrontation. But what may have been tolerable then is intolerable now. Though changes in American society have made it an anachronism, the monolithic form of racial identification that came out of the sixties is still very much with us. It may be more loosely held, and its power to punish heretics has probably diminished, but it continues to catch middle-class blacks in a double bind, thus impeding not only their own advancement but even, I would contend, that of blacks as a group.

The victim-focused black identity encourages the individual to feel   40
that his advancement depends almost entirely on that of the group. Thus
he loses sight not only of his own possibilities but of the inextricable connection between individual effort and individual advancement. This is a
profound encumbrance today, when there is more opportunity for blacks
than ever before, for it reimposes limitations that can have the same oppressive effect as those the society has only recently begun to remove.

It was the emphasis on mass action in the sixties that made the
victim-focused black identity a necessity. But in the eighties and beyond,
when racial advancement will come only through a multitude of individual advancements, this form of identity inadvertently adds itself to the
forces that hold us back. Hard work, education, individual initiative,
stable family life, property ownership—these have always been the
means by which ethnic groups have moved ahead in America. Regardless
of past or present victimization, these "laws" of advancement apply absolutely to black Americans also. There is no getting around this. What
we need is a form of racial identity that energizes the individual by
putting him in touch with both his possibilities and his responsibilities.

It has always annoyed me to hear from the mouths of certain arbiters
of blackness that middle-class blacks should "reach back" and pull up
those blacks less fortunate than they—as though middle-class status were
an unearned and essentially passive condition in which one needed a large
measure of noblesse oblige to occupy one's time. My own image is of
reaching back from a moving train to lift on board those who have no
tickets. A noble enough sentiment—but might it not be wiser to show
them the entire structure of principles, efforts, and sacrifice that puts one
in a position to buy a ticket any time one likes? This, I think, is something
members of the black middle class can realistically offer to other blacks.
Their example is not only a testament to possibility but also a lesson in
method. But they cannot lead by example until they are released from a
black identity that regards that example as suspect, that sees them as
"marginally" black, indeed that holds *them* back by catching them in a
double bind.

To move beyond the victim-focused black identity we must learn to
make a difficult but crucial distinction: between actual victimization, which
we must resist with every resource, and identification with the victim's status. Until we do this we will continue to wrestle more with ourselves than
with the new opportunities which so many paid so dearly to win.

The Reader's Presence

1. Steele introduces his topic by means of a reported conversation he
   had with a friend. What effect does this have on the reader? If you
   rewrote his opening paragraph and eliminated the conversational

context, how would you then introduce the main topic? Try it and
see how it works.

2. Why does Steele's friend maintain that class and race are antagonistic terms? Do you agree? Would his argument apply to all races
and historical periods, or is it dependent only on present history?
What personal experiences would you offer either to confirm or
contradict Steele's friend's opening remark?

3. Steele's feeling of being in a "double bind" is seen exclusively in
the context of being middle class. How does Steele define *middle
class?* Would blacks from other economic groups feel differently?
For example, does Steele imply that blue-collar, working-class
black people feel greater racial solidarity? On the other hand,
would very wealthy blacks feel a greater conflict than Steele's?
Can you infer answers to these questions from Steele's essay?

112

Jonathan Swift

A Modest Proposal

*For Preventing the Children of Poor People in Ireland from
Being a Burden to Their Parents or Country, and for Making
Them Beneficial to the Public*

*Jonathan Swift (1667–1745) was born and raised in Ireland, son of English
parents. He was ordained an Anglican priest, and although as a young man he
lived a literary life in London, he was appointed against his wishes to be dean of
St. Patrick's Cathedral in Dublin. Swift wrote excellent poetry, but is remembered
principally for his essays and political pamphlets, most of which were published
under pseudonyms. Swift received payment for only one work in his entire life,*
Gulliver's Travels *(1726), for which he earned £200. Swift's political pamphlets
were very influential in his day; among other issues, he spoke out against English
exploitation of the Irish. Some of Swift's more important publications include* A
Tale of a Tub *(1704),* The Importance of the Guardian Considered *(1713),* The
Public Spirit of the Whigs *(1714), and* A Modest Proposal *(1729).*

*Writing to his friend Alexander Pope, Swift commented that "the chief end I
propose to my self in all my labors is to vex the world rather than divert it, and if
I could compass that designe without hurting my own person or Fortune I would
be the most Indefatigable writer you have ever seen."*

It is a melancholy object to those who walk through this great town[1] or travel in the country, when they see the streets, the roads, and cabin doors, crowded with beggars of the female sex, followed by three, four, or six children, all in rags and importuning every passenger for an alms. These mothers instead of being able to work for their honest livelihood, are forced to employ all their time in strolling to beg sustenance for their helpless infants: who as they grow up either turn thieves for want of work, or leave their dear native country to fight for the pretender in Spain,[2] or sell themselves to the Barbadoes.[3]

I think it is agreed by all parties that this prodigious number of children in the arms, or on the backs, or at the heels of their mothers, and frequently of their fathers, is in the present deplorable state of the kingdom a very great additional grievance; and, therefore, whoever could find out a fair, cheap, and easy method of making these children sound, useful members of the commonwealth, would deserve so well of the public as to have his statute set up for a preserver of the nation.

But my intention is very far from being confined to provide only for the children of professed beggars; it is of a much greater extent, and shall take in the whole number of infants at a certain age who are born of parents in effect as little able to support them as those who demand our charity in the streets.

As to my own part, having turned my thoughts for many years upon this important subject, and maturely weighed the several schemes of our projectors,[4] I have always found them grossly mistaken in their computation. It is true, a child just dropped from its dam may be supported by her milk for a solar year, with little other nourishment; at most not above the value of 2s.,[5] which the mother may certainly get, or the value in scraps, by her lawful occupation of begging; and it is exactly at one year old that I propose to provide for them in such a manner as instead of being a charge upon their parents or the parish, or wanting food and raiment for the rest of their lives, they shall on the contrary contribute to the feeding, and partly to the clothing, of many thousands.

There is likewise another great advantage in my scheme, that it will prevent those voluntary abortions, and that horrid practice of women murdering their bastard children, alas! too frequent among us! sacrificing the poor innocent babes I doubt more to avoid the expense than the   5

---

[1] *this great town:* Dublin. — EDS.

[2] *pretender in Spain:* James Stuart (1688–1766); exiled in Spain, he laid claim to the English crown and had the support of many Irishmen who had joined an army hoping to restore him to the throne. — EDS.

[3] *the Barbadoes:* Inhabitants of the British colony in the Caribbean where Irishmen emigrated to work as indentured servants in exchange for their passage — EDS.

[4] *projectors:* Planners. — EDS.

[5] *2s.:* Two shillings; in Swift's time one shilling was worth less than twenty-five cents. Other monetary references in the essay are to pounds sterling ("£"), pence ("d."), a crown, and a groat. A pound consisted of twenty shillings; a shilling of twelve pence; a crown was five shillings; a groat was worth a few cents. — EDS.

shame, which would move tears and pity in the most savage and inhuman breast.

The number of souls in this kingdom being usually reckoned one million and a half, of these I calculate there may be about 200,000 couple whose wives are breeders; from which number I subtract 30,000 couple who are able to maintain their own children (although I apprehend there cannot be so many, under the present distress of the kingdom); but this being granted, there will remain 170,000 breeders. I again subtract 50,000 for those women who miscarry, or whose children die by accident or disease within the year. There only remain 120,000 children of poor parents annually born. The question therefore is, how this number shall be reared and provided for? which, as I have already said, under the present situation of affairs, is utterly impossible by all the methods hitherto proposed. For we can neither employ them in handicraft of agriculture; we neither build houses (I mean in the country) nor cultivate land; they can very seldom pick up a livelihood by stealing, till they arrive at six years old, except where they are of towardly parts,[6] although I confess they learn the rudiments much earlier; during which time they can, however, be properly looked upon only as probationers; as I have been informed by a principal gentleman in the county of Cavan, who protested to me that he never knew above one or two instances under the age of six, even in a part of the kingdom so renowned for the quickest proficiency in that art.

I am assured by our merchants, that a boy or a girl before twelve years old is no salable commodity; and even when they come to this age they will not yield above 3£. or 3£. 2s. 6d. at most on the exchange; which cannot turn to account either to the parents or kingdom, the charge of nutriment and rags having been at least four times that value.

I shall now therefore humbly propose my own thoughts, which I hope will not be liable to the least objection.

I have been assured by a very knowing American of my acquaintance in London, that a young healthy child well nursed is at a year old a most delicious, nourishing, and wholesome food, whether stewed, roasted, baked, or broiled; and I make no doubt that it will equally serve in a fricassee or a ragout.[7]

I do therefore humbly offer it to public consideration that of the 120,000 children already computed, 20,000 may be reserved for breed, whereof only one-fourth part to be males; which is more than we allow to sheep, black cattle, or swine; and my reason is, that these children are seldom the fruits of marriage, a circumstance not much regarded by our savages; therefore one male will be sufficient to serve four females. That the remaining 100,000 may, at a year old, be offered in sale to the persons of quality and fortune through the kingdom; always advising the mother to

10

---

[6]*towardly parts:* Natural abilities. — EDS.
[7]*ragout:* A stew. — EDS.

let them suck plentifully in the last month, so as to render them plump and fat for a good table. A child will make two dishes at an entertainment for friends; and when the family dines alone, the fore and hind quarter will make a reasonable dish, and seasoned with a little pepper or salt will be very good boiled on the fourth day, especially in winter.

I have reckoned upon a medium that a child just born will weigh 12 pounds, and in a solar year, if tolerably nursed, will increase to 28 pounds.

I grant this food will be somewhat dear, and therefore very proper for landlords, who, as they have already devoured most of the parents, seem to have the best title to the children.

Infants' flesh will be in season throughout the year, but more plentiful in March, and a little before and after: for we are told by a grave author, an eminent French physician,[8] that fish being a prolific diet, there are more children born in Roman Catholic countries about nine months after Lent than at any other season; therefore, reckoning a year after Lent, the markets will be more glutted than usual, because the number of popish infants is at least three to one in this kingdom: and therefore it will have one other collateral advantage, by lessening the number of papists among us.

I have already computed the charge of nursing a beggar's child (in which list I reckon all cottagers, laborers, and four-fifths of the farmers) to be about 2s. per annum, rags included; and I believe no gentleman would repine to give 10s. for the carcass of a good fat child, which, as I have said, will make four dishes of excellent nutritive meat, when he has only some particular friend or his own family to dine with him. Thus the squire will learn to be a good landlord, and grow popular among the tenants; the mother will have 8s. net profit, and be fit for work till she produces another child.

Those who are more thrifty (as I must confess the times require) may   15 flay the carcass; the skin of which artificially[9] dressed will make admirable gloves for ladies, and summer boots for fine gentlemen.

As to our city of Dublin, shambles[10] may be appointed for this purpose in the most convenient parts of it, and butchers we may be assured will not be wanting: although I rather recommend buying the children alive, and dressing them hot from the knife as we do roasting pigs.

A very worthy person, a true lover of his country, and whose virtues I highly esteem, was lately pleased in discoursing on this matter to offer a refinement upon my scheme. He said that many gentlemen of this kingdom, having of late destroyed their deer, he conceived that the want of venison might be well supplied by the bodies of young lads and maidens,

---

[8]**French physician:** François Rabelais (c. 1494–1553), the great Renaissance humanist and author of the comic masterpiece *Gargantua and Pantagruel*. Swift is being ironic in calling Rabelais "grave." — EDS.

[9]**artificially:** Artfully. — EDS.

[10]**shambles:** Slaughterhouses. — EDS.

not exceeding fourteen years of age nor under twelve; so great a number of both sexes in every country being now ready to starve for want of work and service; and these to be disposed of by their parents, if alive, or otherwise by their nearest relations. But with due deference to so excellent a friend and so deserving a patriot, I cannot be altogether in his sentiments; for as to the males, my American acquaintance assured me from frequent experience that their flesh was generally tough and lean, like that of our schoolboys by continual exercise, and their taste disagreeable; and to fatten them would not answer the charge. Then as to the females, it would, I think, with humble submission be a loss to the public, because they soon would become breeders themselves: and besides, it is not improbable that some scrupulous people might be apt to censure such a practice (although indeed very unjustly), as a little bordering upon cruelty; which, I confess, has always been with me the strongest objection against any project, how well soever intended.

But in order to justify my friend, he confessed that this expedient was put into his head by the famous Psalmanazar[11] a native of the island Formosa, who came from thence to London about twenty years ago: and in conversation told my friend, that in his country when any young person happened to be put to death, the executioner sold the carcass to persons of quality as a prime dainty; and that in his time the body of a plump girl of fifteen, who was crucified for an attempt to poison the emperor, was sold to his imperial majesty's prime minister of state, and other great mandarins of the court, in joints from the gibbet, at 400 crowns. Neither indeed can I deny, that if the same use were made of several plump young girls in this town, who without one single groat to their fortunes cannot stir abroad without a chair,[12] and appear at the playhouse and assemblies in foreign fineries which they never will pay for, the kingdom would not be the worse.

Some persons of a desponding spirit are in great concern about the vast number of poor people, who are aged, diseased, or maimed, and I have been desired to employ my thoughts what course may be taken to ease the nation of so grievous an encumbrance. But I am not in the least pain upon that matter, because it is very well known that they are every day dying and rotting by cold and famine, and filth and vermin, as fast as can be reasonably expected. And as to the young laborers, they are now in as hopeful condition: They cannot get work, and consequently pine away for want of nourishment, to a degree that if at any time they are accidentally hired to common labor, they have not strength to perform it; and thus the country and themselves are happily delivered from the evils to come.

---

[11]*Psalmanazar:* George Psalmanazar (c. 1679–1763) was a Frenchman who tricked London society into believing he was a native of Formosa (now Taiwan). —EDS.
[12]*a chair:* A sedan chair in which one is carried about. —EDS.

I have too long digressed, and therefore shall return to my subject. I   20
think the advantages by the proposal which I have made are obvious and
many, as well as of the highest importance.

For first, as I have already observed, it would greatly lessen the
number of papists, with whom we are yearly overrun, being the principal
breeders of the nation as well as our most dangerous enemies; and who
stay at home on purpose to deliver the kingdom to the Pretender, hoping
to take their advantage by the absence of so many good Protestants, who
have chosen rather to leave their country than stay at home and pay tithes
against their conscience to an Episcopal curate.

Secondly, The poor tenants will have something valuable of their
own, which by law may be made liable to distress[13] and help to pay their
landlord's rent, their corn and cattle being already seized, and money a
thing unknown.

Thirdly, Whereas the maintenance of 100,000 children from two
years old and upward, cannot be computed at less that 10s. a-piece per
annum, the nation's stock will be thereby increased £50,000 per annum,
beside the profit of a new dish introduced to the tables of all gentlemen of
fortune in the kingdom who have any refinement in taste. And the money
will circulate among ourselves, the goods being entirely of our own
growth and manufacture.

Fourthly, The constant breeders beside the gain of 8s. sterling per
annum by the sale of their children, will be rid of the charge of maintaining them after the first year.

Fifthly, This food would likewise bring great custom to taverns,   25
where the vintners will certainly be so prudent as to procure the best receipts[14] for dressing it to perfection, and consequently have their houses
frequented by all the fine gentlemen, who justly value themselves upon
their knowledge in good eating; and a skilful cook who understands how
to oblige his guests, will contrive to make it as expensive as they please.

Sixthly, This would be a great inducement to marriage, which all
wise nations have either encouraged by rewards or enforced by laws and
penalties. It would increase the care and tenderness of mothers toward
their children, when they were sure of a settlement for life to the poor
babes, provided in some sort by the public, to their annual profit instead
of expense. We should see an honest emulation among the married
women, which of them would bring the fattest child to the market. Men
would become as fond of their wives during the time of their pregnancy
as they are now of their mares in foal, their cows in calf, their sows when
they are ready to farrow; nor offer to beat or kick them (as is too frequent
a practice) for fear of a miscarriage.

Many other advantages might be enumerated. For instance, the addition of some thousand carcasses in our exportation of barreled beef, the

13*distress* Seizure for payment of debt. — EDS.
14*receipts:* Recipes. — EDS.

propagation of swine's flesh, and improvement in the art of making good bacon, so much wanted among us by the great destruction of pigs, too frequent at our table; which are no way comparable in taste or magnificence to a well-grown, fat, yearling child, which roasted whole will make a considerable figure at a lord mayor's feast or any other public entertainment. But this and many others I omit, being studious of brevity.

Supposing that 1,000 families in this city would be constant customers for infants' flesh, besides others who might have it at merry-meetings, particularly at weddings and christenings, I compute that Dublin would take off annually about 20,000 carcasses; and the rest of the kingdom (where probably they will be sold somewhat cheaper) the remaining 80,000.

I can think of no one objection that will possibly be raised against this proposal unless it should be urged that the number of people will be thereby much lessened in the kingdom. This I freely own, and it was indeed one principal design in offering it to the world. I desire the reader will observe, that I calculate my remedy for this one individual kingdom of Ireland and for no other that ever was, is, or I think ever can be upon earth. Therefore let no man talk to me of other expedients: of taxing our absentees at 5s. a pound: of using neither clothes nor household furniture except what is of our own growth and manufacture: of utterly rejecting the materials and instruments that promote foreign luxury: of curing the expensiveness of pride, vanity, idleness, and gaming in our women: of introducing a vein of parsimony, prudence, and temperance: of learning to love our country, in the want of which we differ even from Laplanders and the inhabitants of Topinamboo:[15] of quitting our animosities and factions, nor acting any longer like the Jews, who were murdering one another at the very moment their city was taken:[16] of being a little cautious not to sell our country and conscience for nothing: of teaching landlords to have at least one degree of mercy toward their tenants: lastly, of putting a spirit of honesty, industry, and skill into our shopkeepers; who, if a resolution could now be taken to buy only our native goods, would immediately unite to cheat and exact upon us in the price the measure, and the goodness, nor could ever yet be brought to make one fair proposal of just dealing, though often and earnestly invited to it.

Therefore I repeat, let no man talk to me of these and the like expedi-   30
ents, till he has at least some glimpse of hope that there will be ever some hearty and sincere attempt to put them in practice.

But as to myself, having been wearied out for many years with offering vain, idle, visionary thoughts, and at length utterly despairing of success, I fortunately fell upon this proposal; which, as it is wholly new, so it has

---

[15]*Laplanders and the inhabitants of Topinamboo:* Lapland is the area of Scandinavia above the Arctic Circle; Topinamboo, in Brazil, was known in Swift's time for the savagery of its tribes. — EDS.
[16]*was taken:* A reference to the Roman seizure of Jerusalem (A.D. 70). — EDS.

something solid and real, of no expense and little trouble, full in our own power, and whereby we can incur no danger in disobliging England. For this kind of commodity will not bear exportation, the flesh being of too tender a consistence to admit a long continuance in salt, although perhaps I could name a country which would be glad to eat up our whole nation without it.

After all, I am not so violently bent upon my own opinion as to reject any offer proposed by wise men, which shall be found equally innocent, cheap, easy, and effectual. But before something of that kind shall be advanced in contradiction to my scheme, and offering a better, I desire the author or authors will be pleased maturely to consider two points. First, as things now stand, how they will be able to find food and raiment for 100,000 useless mouths and backs. And secondly, there being a round million of creatures in human figure throughout this kingdom, whose subsistence put into a common stock would leave them in debt 2,000,000£. sterling, adding those who are beggars by profession to the bulk of farmers, cottagers, and laborers, with the wives and children who are beggars in effect; I desire those politicians who dislike my overture, and may perhaps be so bold as to attempt an answer, that they will first ask the parents of these mortals, whether they would not at this day think it a great happiness to have been sold for food at a year old in the manner I prescribe, and thereby have avoided such a perpetual scene of misfortunes as they have since gone through by the oppression of landlords, the impossibility of paying rent without money or trade, the want of common sustenance, with neither house nor clothes to cover them from the inclemencies of the weather, and the most inevitable prospect of entailing the like or greater miseries upon their breed for ever.

I profess, in the sincerity of my heart, that I have not the least personal interest in endeavoring to promote this necessary work, having no other motive than the public good of my country, by advancing our trade, providing for infants, relieving the poor, and giving some pleasure to the rich. I have no children by which I can propose to get a single penny; the youngest being nine years old, and my wife past childbearing.

The Reader's Presence

1. Consider Swift's title. In what sense is the proposal "modest"? What is modest about it? What synonyms would you use for *modest* that appear in the essay? In what sense is the essay a "proposal"? Does it follow any format that resembles a proposal? What aspects of its language seem to resemble proposal writing?

2. For this essay Swift invents a speaker, an unnamed, fictional individual who "humbly" proposes a plan to relieve poverty in Ireland. What attitudes and beliefs in the essay do you attribute to the speaker? Which do you attribute to Swift, the author?

3. Having considered two authors (the speaker of the proposal and Swift), now consider two readers—the reader the speaker imagines and the reader Swift imagines. How do these two readers differ? Reread the final paragraph of the essay from the perspective of each of these readers. How do you think each reader is expected to respond?

113

Lewis Thomas

On Cloning a Human Being

Lewis Thomas (1913–1993) was trained as a physician and scientist, but his intellectual curiosity and his publications took him far beyond the practice of medicine. In 1971 he became a regular contributor to the New England Journal of Medicine, *writing a column called "Notes of a Biology Watcher." Several of these essays are collected in* The Lives of the Cell *(1974), which explores the many ways in which organisms relate to one another for their mutual benefit. Joyce Carol Oates praised this book, saying that it "anticipates the kind of writing that will appear more and more frequently, as scientists take on the language of poetry in order to communicate human truths too mysterious for old-fashioned common sense."*

Thomas also published The Medusa and the Snail: More Notes of a Biology Watcher *(1979), from which "On Cloning a Human Being" is taken. His later books expanded the range of his investigations into natural and social processes and include* Late Night Thoughts on Listening to Mahler's Ninth Symphony *(1984) and a collection of essays on language,* Et Cetera, Et Cetera: Notes of a Word Watcher *(1990).*

It is important to remember that Thomas wrote this essay in the late 1970s, long before cloning living creatures became a scientific actuality.

It is now theoretically possible to recreate an identical creature from any animal or plant, from the DNA contained in the nucleus of any somatic cell. A single plant root-tip cell can be teased and seduced into conceiving a perfect copy of the whole plant; a frog's intestinal epithelial cell possesses the complete instructions needed for a new, same frog. If the technology were further advanced, you could do this with a human being, and there are now startled predictions all over the place that this will in fact be done, someday, in order to provide a version of immortality for carefully selected, especially valuable people.

The cloning of humans is on most of the lists of things to worry about from Science, along with behavior control, genetic engineering, transplanted heads, computer poetry, and the unrestrained growth of plastic flowers.

Cloning is the most dismaying of prospects, mandating as it does the elimination of sex with only a metaphoric elimination of death as compensation. It is almost no comfort to know that one's cloned, identical surrogate lives on, especially when the living will very likely involve edging one's real, now aging self off to the side, sooner or later. It is hard to imagine anything like filial affection or respect for a single, unmated nucleus; harder still to think of one's new, self-generated self as anything but an absolute, desolate orphan. Not to mention the complex interpersonal relationship involved in raising one's self from infancy, teaching the language, enforcing discipline, instilling good manners and the like. How would you feel if you became an incorrigible juvenile delinquent by proxy, at the age of fifty-five?

The public questions are obvious. Who is to be selected, and on what qualifications? How to handle the risks of misused technology, such as self-determined cloning by the rich and powerful but socially objectionable, or the cloning by governments of dumb, docile masses for the world's work? What will be the effect on all the uncloned rest of us of human sameness? After all, we've accustomed ourselves through hundreds of millennia to the continual exhilaration of uniqueness; each of us is totally different, in a fundamental sense, from all the other four billion. Selfness is an essential fact of life. The thought of human nonselfness, precise sameness, is terrifying, when you think about it.

Well, don't think about it, because it isn't a probable possibility, not   5
even as a long shot for the distant future, in my opinion. I agree that you might clone some people who would look amazingly like their parental cell donors, but the odds are that they'd be almost as different as you or me, and certainly more different than any of today's identical twins.

The time required for the experiment is only one of the problems, but a formidable one. Suppose you wanted to clone a prominent, spectacularly successful diplomat, to look after the Middle East problems of the distant future. You'd have to catch him and persuade him, probably not very hard to do, and extirpate a cell. But then you'd have to wait for him to grow up through embryonic life and then for at least forty years more, and you'd have to be sure all observers remained patient and unmeddlesome through his unpromising, ambiguous childhood and adolescence.

Moreover, you'd have to be sure of recreating his environment, perhaps down to the last detail. "Environment" is a word which really means people, so you'd have to do a lot more cloning than just the diplomat himself.

This is a very important part of the cloning problem, largely overlooked in our excitement about the cloned individual himself. You don't have to agree all the way with B. F. Skinner to acknowledge that the environment does make a difference, and when you examine what we really mean by the word "environment" it comes down to other human beings. We use euphemisms and jargon for this, like "social forces," "cultural in-fluences," even Skinner's "verbal community," but what is meant is the dense crowd of nearby people who talk to, listen to, smile or frown at, give to, withhold from, nudge, push, caress, or flail out at the individual. No matter what the genome says, these people have a lot to do with shap-ing a character. Indeed, if all you had was the genome, and no people around, you'd grow a sort of vertebrate plant, nothing more.

So, to start with, you will undoubtedly need to clone the parents. No question about this. This means the diplomat is out, even in theory, since you couldn't have gotten cells from both his parents at the time when he was himself just recognizable as an early social treasure. You'd have to limit the list of clones to people already certified as sufficiently valuable for the effort, with both parents still alive. The parents would need cloning and, for consistency, their parents as well. I suppose you'd also need the usual informed-consent forms, filled out and signed, not easy to get if I know parents, even harder for grandparents.

But this is only the beginning. It is the whole family that really influ-   10
ences the way a person turns out, not just the parents, according to cur-rent psychiatric thinking. Clone the family.

Then what? The way each member of the family develops has already been determined by the environment set around him, and this environ-ment is more people, people outside the family, schoolmates, acquain-tances, lovers, enemies, car-pool partners, even, in special circumstances, peculiar strangers across the aisle on the subway. Find them, and clone them.

But there is no end to the protocol. Each of the outer contacts has his own surrounding family, and his and their outer contacts. Clone them all.

To do the thing properly, with any hope of ending up with a genuine duplicate of a single person, you really have no choice. You must clone the world, no less.

We are not ready for an experiment of this size, nor, I should think, are we willing. For one thing, it would mean replacing today's world by an entirely identical world to follow immediately, and this means no new, natural, spontaneous, random, chancy children. No children at all, except for the manufactured doubles of those now on the scene. Plus all those identical adults, including all of today's politicians, all seen double. It is too much to contemplate.

Moreover, when the whole experiment is finally finished, fifty years   15
or so from now, how could you get a responsible scientific reading on the outcome? Somewhere in there would be the original clonee, probably lost and overlooked, now well into middle age, but everyone around him would be precise duplicates of today's everyone. It would be today's same world, filled to overflowing with duplicates of today's people and their same, duplicated problems, probably all resentful at having had to go

through our whole thing all over, sore enough at the clonee to make end-less trouble for him, if they found him.

And obviously, if the whole thing were done precisely right, they would still be casting about for ways to solve the problem of universal dissatisfaction, and sooner or later they'd surely begin to look around at each other, wondering who should be cloned for his special value to soci-ety, to get us out of all this. And so it would go, in regular cycles, perhaps forever.

I once lived through a period when I wondered what Hell could be like, and I stretched my imagination to try to think of a perpetual sort of damnation. I have to confess, I never thought of anything like this.

I have an alternative suggestion, if you're looking for a way out. Set cloning aside, and don't try it. Instead, go in the other direction. Look for ways to get mutations more quickly, new variety, different songs. Fiddle around, if you must fiddle, but never with ways to keep things the same, no matter who, not even yourself. Heaven, somewhere ahead, has got to be a change.

The Reader's Presence

1. As a biologist, Thomas writes as an "expert." How would you read this essay differently if it were written by a nonscientist, rea-soning through common sense rather than inside knowledge of the subject? What sort of audience does Thomas appear to be writing for? What sorts of fears does he address? What is his general argu-ment?

2. In paragraphs 6–8, Thomas directs his writing toward the reader, creating hypothetical scenarios in which "you" participate. What is the effect of this technique? Why might Thomas have chosen it? Would the scenarios affect you differently if discussed in more general terms? Why?

3. Thomas concludes with advice pertinent both to genetic engineer-ing and life in general. How does Thomas link cellular and greater human concerns? Is this leap from biology to everyday life convincing? Why or why not? Does it undermine or enhance Thomas's authority?

114

Mark Twain

Corn-pone¹ Opinions

Mark Twain, the pseudonym of Samuel Clemens (1835–1910), was a master satirist, journalist, novelist, orator, and steamboat pilot. He grew up in Hannibal, Missouri, a frontier setting which appears in different forms in several of his novels, most notably in his masterpiece Adventures of Huckleberry Finn *(1869). His satirical eye spared very few American political or social institutions including slavery, and for this reason, as well as because it violated conventional standards of taste,* Huckleberry Finn *created a minor scandal when it was published. Nonetheless, with such books as* The Innocents Abroad *(1869),* Roughing It *(1872),* Old Times on the Mississippi *(1875),* The Adventures of Tom Sawyer *(1876), and* The Prince and the Pauper *(1882), Twain secured himself a position as one of the most popular authors in American history. Twain built his career upon his experiences in the western states and his travels in Europe and the Middle East, but he eventually settled in Hartford, Connecticut. His last years were spent as one of the most celebrated public speakers and social figures in the United States.*

Reflecting upon the experience of writing, Twain once wrote in his notebook, "The time to begin writing an article is when you have finished it to your satisfaction. By that time you begin to clearly and logically perceive what it is that you really want to say."

Fifty years ago, when I was a boy of fifteen and helping to inhabit a Missourian village on the banks of the Mississippi, I had a friend whose society was very dear to me because I was forbidden by my mother to partake of it. He was a gay and impudent and satirical and delightful young black man—a slave—who daily preached sermons from the top of his master's woodpile, with me for sole audience. He imitated the pulpit style of the several clergymen of the village, and did it well, and with fine passion and energy. To me he was a wonder. I believed he was the

---

¹*Corn pone:* Southern expression that dates from the mid-nineteenth century for a simple corn bread or muffin; *pone* comes from a Native American word for something baked. — EDS.

greatest orator in the United States and would some day be heard from. But it did not happen; in the distribution of rewards he was overlooked. It is the way, in this world.

He interrupted his preaching, now and then, to saw a stick of wood; but the sawing was a pretense — he did it with his mouth; exactly imitating the sound the bucksaw makes in shrieking its way through the wood. But it served its purpose; it kept his master from coming out to see how the work was getting along. I listened to the sermons from the open window of a lumber room at the back of the house. One of his texts was this:

"You tell me whar a man gits his corn pone, en I'll tell you what his 'pinions is."

I can never forget it. It was deeply impressed upon me. By my mother. Not upon my memory, but elsewhere. She had slipped in upon me while I was absorbed and not watching. The black philosopher's idea was that a man is not independent, and cannot afford views which might interfere with his bread and butter. If he would prosper, he must train with the majority; in matters of large moment, like politics and religion, he must think and feel with the bulk of his neighbors, or suffer damage in his social standing and in his business prosperities. He must restrict himself to corn-pone opinions — at least on the surface. He must get his opinions from other people; he must reason out none for himself; he must have no first-hand views.

I think Jerry was right, in the main, but I think he did not go far   5 enough.

1. It was his idea that a man conforms to the majority view of his locality by calculation and intention.

This happens, but I think it is not the rule.

2. It was his idea that there is such a thing as a first-hand opinion; an original opinion; an opinion which is coldly reasoned out in a man's head, by a searching analysis of the facts involved, with the heart unconsulted, and the jury room closed against outside influences. It may be that such an opinion has been born somewhere, at some time or other, but I suppose it got away before they could catch it and stuff it and put it in the museum.

I am persuaded that a coldly-thought-out and independent verdict upon a fashion in clothes, or manners, or literature, or politics, or religion, or any other matter that is projected into the field of our notice and interest, is a most rare thing — if it has indeed ever existed.

A new thing in costume appears — the flaring hoopskirt, for ex-   10 ample — and the passers-by are shocked, and the irreverent laugh. Six months later everybody is reconciled; the fashion has established itself; it is admired, now, and no one laughs. Public opinion resented it before, public opinion accepts it now, and is happy in it. Why? Was the resentment reasoned out? Was the acceptance reasoned out? No. The instinct that moves to conformity did the work. It is our nature to conform; it is a force which not many can successfully resist. What is its seat? The inborn requirement of self-approval. We all have to bow to that; there are no exceptions. Even the woman who refuses from first to last to wear the hoopskirt comes under that law and is its slave; she could not wear the skirt and have her own approval; and that she *must* have, she cannot help herself. But as a rule our self-approval has its source in but one place and not elsewhere—the approval of other people. A person of vast consequences can introduce any kind of novelty in dress and the general world will presently adopt it—moved to do it, in the first place, by the natural instinct to passively yield to that vague something recognized as authority, and in the second place by the human instinct to train with the multitude and have its approval. An empress introduced the hoopskirt, and we know the result. A nobody introduced the bloomer, and we know the result. If Eve should come again, in her ripe renown, and reintroduce her quaint styles—well, we know what would happen. And we should be cruelly embarrassed, along at first.

The hoopskirt runs its course and disappears. Nobody reasons about it. One woman abandons the fashion; her neighbor notices this and follows her lead; this influences the next woman; and so on and so on, and presently the skirt has vanished out of the world, no one knows how nor why, nor cares, for that matter. It will come again, by and by and in due course will go again.

Twenty-five years ago, in England, six or eight wine glasses stood grouped by each person's plate at a dinner party, and they were used, not left idle and empty; to-day there are but three or four in the group, and the average guest sparingly uses about two of them. We have not adopted this new fashion yet, but we shall do it presently. We shall not think it out; we shall merely conform, and let it go at that. We get our notions and habits and opinions from outside influences; we do not have to study them out.

Our table manners, and company manners, and street manners change from time to time, but the changes are not reasoned out; we merely notice and conform. We are creatures of outside influences; as a rule we do not think, we only imitate. We cannot invent standards that will stick; what we mistake for standards are only fashions, and perishable. We may continue to admire them, but we drop the use of them. We notice this in literature. Shakespeare is a standard, and fifty years ago we used to write tragedies which we couldn't tell from—from somebody else's; but we don't do it any more, now. Our prose standard, three quarters of a century ago, was ornate and diffuse; some authority or other changed it in the direction of compactness and simplicity, and conformity followed, without argument. The historical novel starts up suddenly, and sweeps the land. Everybody writes one, and the nation is glad. We had historical novels before; but nobody read them, and the rest of us conformed—without reasoning it out. We are conforming in the other way, now, because it is another case of everybody.

The outside influences are always pouring in upon us, and we are always obeying their orders and accepting their verdicts. The Smiths like the new play; the Joneses go to see it, and they copy the Smith verdict. Morals, religions, politics, get their following from surrounding influences and atmospheres, almost entirely; not from study, not from thinking. A man must and will have his own approval first of all, in each and every moment and circumstance of his life—even if he must repent of a self-approved act the moment after its commission, in order to get his self-approval *again:* but, speaking in general terms, a man's self-approval in the large concerns of life has its source in the approval of the peoples about him, and not in a searching personal examination of the matter. Mohammedans are Mohammedans because they are born and reared among that sect, not because they have thought it out and can furnish sound reasons for being Mohammedans; we know why Catholics are Catholics; why Presbyterians are Presbyterians; why Baptists are Baptists; why Mormons are Mormons; why thieves are thieves; why monarchists are monarchists; why Republicans are Republicans and Democrats, Democrats. We know it is a matter of association and sympathy, not reasoning and examination; that hardly a man in the world has an opinion upon morals, politics, or religion which he got otherwise than through his associations and sympathies. Broadly speaking, there are none but corn-pone opinions. And broadly speaking, corn-pone stands for self-approval. Self-approval is acquired mainly from the approval of other people. The result is conformity. Sometimes conformity has a sordid business interest—the bread-and-butter interest—but not in most cases, I think. I think that in the majority of cases it is unconscious and not calculated; that it is born of the human being's natural yearning to stand well with his fellows and have their inspiring approval and praise—a yearning which is commonly so strong and so insistent that it cannot be effectually resisted, and must have its way.

A political emergency brings out the corn-pone opinion in fine force   15
in its two chief varieties—the pocketbook variety, which has its origin in self-interest, and the bigger variety, the sentimental variety—the one which can't bear to be outside the pale; can't bear to be in disfavor; can't endure the averted face and the cold shoulder; wants to stand well with his friends, wants to be smiled upon, wants to be welcome, wants to hear the precious words, "*He's* on the right track!" Uttered, perhaps by an ass, but still an ass of high degree, an ass whose approval is gold and diamonds to a smaller ass, and confers glory and honor and happiness, and membership in the herd. For these gauds many a man will dump his lifelong principles into the street, and his conscience along with them. We have seen it happen. In some millions of instances.

Men think they think upon great political questions, and they do; but they think with their party, not independently; they read its literature, but not that of the other side; they arrive at convictions, but they are drawn from a partial view of the matter in hand and are of no particular value. They swarm with their party, they feel with their party, they are happy in their party's approval; and where the party leads they will follow, whether for right and honor, or through blood and dirt and a mush of mutilated morals.

In our late canvass half of the nation passionately believed that in silver lay salvation, the other half as passionately believed that that way lay destruction. Do you believe that a tenth part of the people, on either side, had any rational excuse for having an opinion about the matter at all? I studied that mighty question to the bottom—came out empty. Half of our people passionately believe in high tariff, the other half believe otherwise. Does this mean study and examination, or only feeling? The latter, I think. I have deeply studied that question, too—and didn't arrive. We all do no end of feeling, and we mistake it for thinking. And out of it we get an aggregation which we consider a boon. Its name is Public Opinion. It is held in reverence. It settles everything. Some think it the Voice of God.

The Reader's Presence

1. "Corn pone" was a dish eaten, in Twain's time, by poor Southerners. How might this image of a lowly, common foodstuff be tied to the opinions of Twain's commonsense slave "philosopher"? What is Twain's position on Jerry's everyday wisdom? What sort of audience does Twain appear to be writing for? How does Twain "translate" Jerry's statement?

2. Twain agrees with Jerry's statement, but feels he "did not go far enough." How do Twain's opinions differ from Jerry's? How does Twain use Jerry's opinions, starting in paragraph 9, to launch his own? Twain does not return to Jerry in the essay. How does the dramatic technique of ending the essay with topics far from those with which it was begun affect your reading of it?

3. Outline Twain's points in the final two paragraphs. Does he write from evidence or belief? Does Twain's reasoning in the body of his essay support his more general final conclusions? Are they convincing? Why or why not?

115

Gore Vidal

Drugs

Gore Vidal (b. 1925), author, playwright, screenwriter, essayist, and reviewer, is known for his satirical observations, acerbic wit, and eloquence. He is the author of twenty-four books, including The City and the Pillar *(1948),* Myra Breckinridge *(1968),* Myron *(1974), and* The Smithsonian Institution *(1998). Among Gore's irreverent historical novels are* Julian *(1964),* Burr *(1973),* 1876 *(1976), and* Lincoln *(1984). His best-known dramatic work is* Visit to a Small Planet *(1957), which was made into a movie. Most recently Vidal has published collections of his writings in* The Essential Gore Vidal *(1999) and* Gore Vidal, Sexually Speaking *(1999). The essay "Drugs" originally appeared in 1970 as an editorial in the* New York Times *and was later included in his book* Homage to Daniel Shays: Collected Essays 1952–1972 *(1972).*

It is possible to stop most drug addiction in the United States within a very short time. Simply make all drugs available and sell them at cost. Label each drug with a precise description of what effect—good and bad—the drug will have on the taker. This will require heroic honesty. Don't say that marijuana is addictive or dangerous when it is neither, as millions of people know—unlike "speed," which kills most unpleasantly, or heroin, which is addictive and difficult to kick.

For the record, I have tried—once—almost every drug and liked none, disproving the popular Fu Manchu theory that a single whiff of opium will enslave the mind. Nevertheless many drugs are bad for certain people to take and they should be told why in a sensible way.

Along with exhortation and warning, it might be good for our citizens to recall (or learn for the first time) that the United States was the creation of men who believed that each man has the right to do what he wants with own life as long as he does not interfere with his neighbor's pursuit of happiness. (That his neighbor's idea of happiness is persecuting others does confuse matters a bit.)

This is a startling notion to the current generation of Americans. They reflect a system of public education which has made the Bill of

Rights, literally, unacceptable to a majority of high school graduates (see the annual Purdue reports) who now form the "silent majority"—a phrase which that underestimated wit Richard Nixon took from Homer, who used it to describe the dead.

Now one can hear the warning rumble begin: If everyone is allowed to take drugs everyone will and the GNP will decrease, the Commies will stop us from making everyone free, and we shall end up a race of zombies, passively murmuring "groovy" to one another. Alarming thought. Yet it seems most unlikely that any reasonably sane person will become a drug addict if he knows in advance what addiction is going to be like.

Is everyone reasonably sane? No. Some people will always become drug addicts just as some people will always become alcoholics, and it is just too bad. Every man, however, has the power (and should have the legal right) to kill himself if he chooses. But since most men don't, they won't be mainliners either. Nevertheless, forbidding young people things they like or think they might enjoy only makes them want those things all the more. This psychological insight is, for some mysterious reason, perennially denied our governors.

It is a lucky thing for the American moralist that our country has always existed in a kind of time-vacuum: We have no public memory of anything that happened before last Tuesday. No one in Washington today recalls what happened during the years alcohol was forbidden to the people by a Congress that thought it had a divine mission to stamp out Demon Rum—launching, in the process, the greatest crime wave in the country's history, causing thousands of deaths from bad alcohol, and creating a general (and persisting) contempt among the citizenry for the laws of the United States.

The same thing is happening today. But the government has learned nothing from past attempts at prohibition, not to mention repression.

Last year when the supply of Mexican marijuana was slightly curtailed by the Feds, the pushers got the kids hooked on heroin and deaths increased dramatically, particularly in New York. Whose fault? Evil men like the Mafiosi? Permissive Dr. Spock? Wild-eyed Dr. Leary? No.

The government of the United States was responsible for those deaths. The bureaucratic machine has a vested interest in playing cops and robbers. Both the Bureau of Narcotics and the Mafia want strong laws against the sale and use of drugs because if drugs are sold at cost there would be no money in it for anyone.

If there was no money in it for the Mafia, there would be no friendly playground pushers, and addicts would not commit crimes to pay for the next fix. Finally, if there was no money in it, the Bureau of Narcotics would wither away, something they are not about to do without a struggle.

Will anything sensible be done? Of course not. The American people are as devoted to the idea of sin and its punishment as they are to making money—and fighting drugs is nearly as big a business as pushing them.

Since the combination of sin and money is irresistible (particularly to the professional politician), the situation will only grow worse.

The Reader's Presence

1. Writing in 1970, Vidal admits to having tried "almost every drug." What might the impact of such an admission by a public figure have been at that time? Would the impact be the same today? What sort of audience might Vidal's piece be directed to? Does his admission seem casual or calculated? Does it strengthen or weaken his argument? Why?

2. In paragraph 5, Vidal constructs a hypothetical scenario of what would happen if drugs were not illegal. Does he endorse or mock this scenario? Whose opinion does he seem to be representing? What sorts of words does he use to describe a drug-addicted world? Does his use of humor enhance or undermine his argument?

3. Vidal asserts that the U.S. government profits from drug sales and prosecution, and links the government to organized crime. Although these assertions have been made at times, the connection remains rather unexpected, or counterintuitive. How does Vidal present these counterintuitive statements? Are they backed up by evidence? Would a more fact-based approach strengthen or weaken Vidal's argument? Why?

116 _____

Cornel West

Race Matters

Philosopher, author, and social critic Cornel West (b. 1953) teaches in the Afro-American Studies Department at Harvard University and at Harvard Divinity School. Regarded as an inspiring and popular speaker, West has delivered speeches at churches, political rallies, and lecture halls, and has appeared on such television programs as The MacNeil/Lehrer Newshour *and William F. Buckley's* Firing Line. *As a scholar and author, he has fought persistently for the continuing relevance of Christianity and Marxism as means for battling white racism and oppression. He has also fought against what he calls "the closing of ranks" among African Americans who place racial allegiances before moral principles. He has published more than a dozen books, including* The Ethical Dimensions of Marxist Thought *(1991);* Race Matters *(1993), in which the following essay originally appeared;* Keeping Faith: Philosophy and Race in America *(1993); and* The Future of American Progressivism: An Initiative for Political and Economic Reform *(1998).*

Since the beginning of the nation, white Americans have suffered from a deep inner uncertainty as to who they really are. One of the ways that has been used to simplify the answer has been to seize upon the presence of black Americans and use them as a marker, a symbol of limits, a metaphor for the "outsider." Many whites could look at the social position of blacks and feel that color formed an easy and reliable gauge for determining to what extent one was or was not American.

Perhaps that is why one of the first epithets that many European immigrants learned when they got off the boat was the term "nigger"—it made them feel instantly American. But this is tricky magic. Despite his racial difference and social status, something indisputably American about Negroes not only raised doubts about the white man's value system but aroused the troubling suspicion that whatever else the true American is, he is also somehow black.

(Ralph Ellison,
"What America Would Be Like without Blacks" [1970])[1]

What happened in Los Angeles in April of 1992 was neither a race riot nor a class rebellion. Rather, this monumental upheaval was a multiracial, trans-class, and largely male display of justified social rage. For all its ugly, xenophobic resentment, its air of adolescent carnival, and its downright barbaric behavior, it signified the sense of powerlessness in American society. Glib attempts to reduce its meaning to the pathologies of the black underclass, the criminal actions of hoodlums, or the political revolt of the oppressed urban masses miss the mark. Of those arrested, only 36 percent were black, more than a third had full-time jobs, and most claimed to shun political affiliation. What we witnessed in Los Angeles was the consequence of a lethal linkage of economic decline, cultural decay, and political lethargy in American life. Race was the visible catalyst, not the underlying cause.

The meaning of the earthshaking events in Los Angeles is difficult to grasp because most of us remain trapped in the narrow framework of the dominant liberal and conservative views of race in America, which with its worn-out vocabulary leaves us intellectually debilitated, morally disempowered, and personally depressed. The astonishing disappearance of the event from public dialogue is testimony to just how painful and distressing a serious engagement with race is. Our truncated public discussions of race suppress the best of who and what we are as a people because they fail to confront the complexity of the issue in a candid and

[1]For the full essay, see page 367.—EDS.

critical manner. The predictable pitting of liberals against conservatives, Great Society Democrats against self-help Republicans, reinforces intellectual parochialism and political paralysis.

The liberal notion that more government programs can solve racial problems is simplistic—precisely because it focuses *soley* on the economic dimension. And the conservative idea that what is needed is a change in the moral behavior of poor black urban dwellers (especially poor black men, who, they say, should stay married, support their children, and stop committing so much crime) highlights immoral actions while ignoring public responsibility for the immoral circumstances that haunt our fellow citizens.

The common denominator of these views of race is that each still sees black people as a "problem people," in the words of Dorothy I. Height, president of the National Council of Negro Women, rather than as fellow American citizens with problems. Her words echo the poignant "unasked question" of W. E. B. Du Bois, who, in *The Souls of Black Folk* (1903), wrote:

> They approach me in a half-hesitant sort of way, eye me curiously or compassionately, and then instead of saying directly, How does it feel to be a problem? they say, I know an excellent colored man in my town. . . . Do not these Southern outrages make your blood boil? At these I smile, or am interested, or reduce the boiling to a simmer, as the occasion may require. To the real question, How does it feel to be a problem? I answer seldom a word.

Nearly a century later, we confine discussions about race in America to the "problems" black people pose for whites, rather than consider what this way of viewing black people reveals about us as a nation.

This paralyzing framework encourages liberals to relieve their guilty   5
consciences by supporting public funds directed at "the problems"; but at the same time, reluctant to exercise principled criticism of black people, liberals deny them the freedom to err. Similarly, conservatives blame the "problems" on black people themselves—and thereby render black social misery invisible or unworthy of public attention.

Hence, for liberals, black people are to be "included" and "integrated" into "our" society and culture, while for conservatives they are to be "well behaved" and "worthy of acceptance" by "our" way of life. Both fail to see that the presence and predicaments of black people are neither additions to nor defections from American life, but rather *constitutive elements of that life*.

To engage in a serious discussion of race in America, we must begin not with the problems of black people but with the flaws of American society—flaws rooted in historic inequalities and longstanding cultural stereotypes. How we set up the terms for discussing racial issues shapes our perception and response to these issues. As long as black people are viewed as a "them," the burden falls on blacks to do all the "cultural" and "moral" work necessary for healthy race relations. The implication is that only certain Americans can define what it means to be American — and the rest must simply "fit in."

The emergence of strong black-nationalist sentiments among blacks, especially among young people, is a revolt against this sense of having to "fit in." The variety of black-nationalist ideologies, from the moderate views of Supreme Court Justice Clarence Thomas in his youth to those of Louis Farrakhan today, rest upon a fundamental truth: white America has been historically weak-willed in ensuring racial justice and has continued to resist fully accepting the humanity of blacks. As long as double standards and differential treatment abound — as long as the rap performer Ice-T is harshly condemned while former Los Angeles Police Chief Daryl F. Gates's antiblack comments are received in polite silence, as long as Dr. Leonard Jeffries's anti-Semitic statements are met with vitriolic outrage while presidential candidate Patrick J. Buchanan's anti-Semitism receives a genteel response — black nationalisms will thrive.

Afrocentrism, a contemporary species of black nationalism, is a gallant yet misguided attempt to define an African identity in a white society perceived to be hostile. It is gallant because it puts black doings and sufferings, not white anxieties and fears, at the center of discussion. It is misguided because — out of fear of cultural hybridization and through silence on the issue of class, retrograde views on black women, gay men, and lesbians, and a reluctance to link race to the common good — it reinforces the narrow discussions about race.

To establish a new framework, we need to begin with a frank acknowledgment of the basic humanness and Americanness of each of us. And we must acknowledge that as a people — *E Pluribus Unum* — we are on a slippery slope toward economic strife, social turmoil, and cultural chaos. If we go down, we go down together. The Los Angeles upheaval forced us to see not only that we are not connected in ways we would like to be but also, in a more profound sense, that this failure to connect binds us even more tightly together. The paradox of race in America is that our common destiny is more pronounced and imperiled precisely when our divisions are deeper. The Civil War and its legacy speak loudly here. And our divisions are growing deeper. Today, 86 percent of white suburban Americans live in neighborhoods that are less than 1 percent black, meaning that the prospects for the country depend largely on how its cities fare in the hands of a suburban electorate. There is no escape from our interracial interdependence, yet enforced racial hierarchy dooms us as a nation to collective paranoia and hysteria — the unmaking of any democratic order.

The verdict in the Rodney King case, which sparked the incidents in Los Angeles, was perceived to be wrong by the vast majority of Americans. But whites have often failed to acknowledge the widespread mistreatment of black people, especially black men, by law enforcement agencies, which helped ignite the spark. The verdict was merely the occasion for deep-seated rage to come to the surface. This rage is fed by the "silent" depression ravaging the country—in which real weekly wages of all American workers since 1973 have declined nearly 20 percent, while at the same time wealth has been upwardly distributed.

The exodus of stable industrial jobs from urban centers to cheaper labor markets here and abroad, housing policies that have created "chocolate cities and vanilla suburbs" (to use the popular musical artist George Clinton's memorable phrase), white fear of black crime, and the urban influx of poor Spanish-speaking and Asian immigrants—all have helped erode the tax base of American cities just as the federal government has cut its support and programs. The result is unemployment, hunger, homelessness, and sickness for millions.

And a pervasive spiritual impoverishment grows. The collapse of meaning in life—the eclipse of hope and absence of love of self and others, the breakdown of family and neighborhood bonds—leads to the social deracination and cultural denudement of urban dwellers, especially children. We have created rootless, dangling people with little link to the supportive networks—family, friends, school—that sustain some sense of purpose in life. We have witnessed the collapse of the spiritual communities that in the past helped Americans face despair, disease, and death and that transmit through the generations dignity and decency, excellence and elegance.

The result is lives of what we might call "random nows," of fortuitous and fleeting moments preoccupied with "getting over"—with acquiring pleasure, property, and power by any means necessary. (This is not what Malcolm X meant by this famous phrase.) Post-modern culture is more and more a market culture dominated by gangster mentalities and self-destructive wantonness. This culture engulfs all of us—yet its impact on the disadvantaged is devastating, resulting in extreme violence in everyday life. Sexual violence against women and homicidal assaults by young black men on one another are only the most obvious signs of this empty quest for pleasure, property, and power.

Last, this rage is fueled by a political atmosphere in which images,   15
not ideas, dominate, where politicians spend more time raising money than debating issues. The functions of parties have been displaced by public polls, and politicians behave less as thermostats that determine the climate of opinion than as thermometers registering the public mood. American politics has been rocked by an unleashing of greed among opportunistic public officials—who have followed the lead of their counterparts in the private sphere, where, as of 1989, 1 percent of the population owned 37 percent of the wealth and 10 percent of the population owned 86 percent of the wealth—leading to a profound cynicism and pessimism among the citizenry.

And given the way in which the Republican Party since 1968 has appealed to popular xenophobic images—playing the black, female, and homophobic cards to realign the electorate along race, sex, and sexual-orientation lines—it is no surprise that the notion that we are all part of one garment of destiny is discredited. Appeals to special interests rather than to public interests reinforce this polarization. The Los Angeles upheaval was an expression of utter fragmentation by a powerless citizenry that includes not just the poor but all of us.

What is to be done? How do we capture a new spirit and vision to meet the challenges of the post-industrial city, post-modern culture, and post-party politics?

First, we must admit that the most valuable sources for help, hope, and power consist of ourselves and our common history. As in the ages of Lincoln, Roosevelt, and King, we must look to new frameworks and languages to understand our multilayered crisis and overcome our deep malaise.

Second, we must focus our attention on the public square—the common good that undergirds our national and global destinies. The vitality of any public square ultimately depends on how much we *care* about the quality of our lives together. The neglect of our public infrastructure, for example—our water and sewage systems, bridges, tunnels, highways, subways, and streets—reflects not only our myopic economic policies, which impede productivity, but also the low priority we place on our common life.

The tragic plight of our children clearly reveals our deep disregard for 20 public well-being. About one out of every five children in this country lives in poverty, including one out of every two black children and two out of every five Hispanic children. Most of our children—neglected by overburdened parents and bombarded by the market values of profit-hungry corporations—are ill-equipped to live lives of spiritual and cultural quality. Faced with these facts, how do we expect ever to constitute a vibrant society?

One essential step is some form of large-scale public intervention to ensure access to basic social goods—housing, food, health care, education, child care, and jobs. We must invigorate the common good with a mixture of government, business, and labor that does not follow any existing blueprint. After a period in which the private sphere has been sacrilized and the public square gutted, the temptation is to make a fetish of the public square. We need to resist such dogmatic swings.

Last, the major challenge is to meet the need to generate new leadership. The paucity of courageous leaders—so apparent in the response to the events in Los Angeles—requires that we look beyond the same elites and voices that recycle the older frameworks. We need leaders—neither saints nor sparkling television personalities—who can situate themselves within a larger historical narrative of this country and our world, who can grasp the complex dynamics of our peoplehood and imagine a future grounded in the best of our past, yet who are attuned to the frightening obstacles that now perplex us. Our ideals of freedom, democracy, and equality must be invoked to invigorate all of us, especially the landless, propertyless, and luckless. Only a visionary leadership that can motivate "the better angels of our nature," as Lincoln said, and activate possibilities for a freer, more efficient, and stable America — only that leadership deserves cultivation and support.

This new leadership must be grounded in grass-roots organizing that highlights democratic accountability. Whoever *our* leaders will be as we approach the twenty-first century, their challenge will be to help Americans determine whether a genuine multiracial democracy can be created and sustained in an era of global economy and a moment of xenophobic frenzy.

Let us hope and pray that the vast intelligence, imagination, humor, and courage of Americans will not fail us. Either we learn a new language of empathy and compassion, or the fire this time will consume us all.

The Reader's Presence

1. What is the relation of the beginning quotation from Ralph Ellison to the rest of West's piece? What is the effect of putting together, or juxtaposing, part of one piece with another? Compare West's piece with Ellison's "What America Would Be Like without Blacks" (see page 367). How might West's piece be seen to respond to Ellison's? Does West's piece stand on its own without the Ellison quote? How does the quote enhance it?

2. West is a Harvard professor and a well-respected figure in the African American religious community. Would you read the essay differently if it were written by an unknown author, or a white author? Why? Does West present evidence for his case? Does experience or expertise serve as a form of evidence in the piece? Is it convincing? Why or why not?

3. West's argument begins in a fairly accessible manner but subtly becomes complicated. Summarize each paragraph in a sentence, stopping at concepts you do not understand to note your questions. Through what steps does West's argument proceed? What is his final conclusion? Examine your first and last summary statements. How does tracing West's logical process enhance your understanding of his reasoning?

117

John Edgar Wideman
The Night I Was Nobody

John Edgar Wideman was born in 1941 in Washington, D.C., and grew up in Homewood, a Pittsburgh ghetto. Much of his fiction is set in Homewood or neighborhoods like it, and it explores issues facing the black urban poor in America. He has published over a dozen books, including Brothers and Keepers *(1984), a memoir that focuses on his brother Robby; the novel* Philadelphia Fire *(1990); and* The Stories of John Edgar Wideman *(1992). Other recent novels include* The Cattle Killing *(1996) and* Two Cities *(1998). Wideman was a Rhodes scholar at Oxford University (1963) and a Kent fellow at the University of Iowa Writing Workshop (1966). He is also an athlete and a member of the Philadelphia Big Five Basketball Hall of Fame. Recently he published* Fatheralong: A Meditation on Fathers and Sons, Race and Society *(1994). "The Night I Was Nobody" appeared in* Speak My Name: Black Men on Masculinity and the American Dream *(1995).*

When Wideman lived in Cheyenne and taught at the University of Wyoming (1975–1986), an interviewer inquired whether he felt a distance between his life and his fiction. "My particular imagination has always worked well in a kind of exile," he responded. "It fits the insider-outsider view I've always had. It helps to write away from the center of action." Currently he is affiliated with the University of Massachusetts at Amherst and lectures at colleges all over the United States.

On July 4th, the fireworks day, the day for picnics and patriotic speeches, I was in Clovis, New Mexico, to watch my daughter, Jamila, and her team, the Central Massachusetts Cougars, compete in the Junior Olympics Basketball national tourney. During our ten-day visit to Clovis the weather had been bizarre. Hailstones as large as golf balls. Torrents of rain flooding streets hubcap deep. Running through the pelting rain from their van to a gym, Jamila and several teammates cramming through a doorway had looked back just in time to see a funnel cloud touch down a few blocks away. Continuous sheet lightning had shattered the horizon, crackling for hours night and day. Spectacular, off-the-charts weather flexing its muscles, reminding people what little control they had over their lives.

Hail rat-tat-tatting against our windshield our first day in town wasn't exactly a warm welcome, but things got better fast. Clovis people were glad to see us and the mini-spike we triggered in the local economy. Hospitable, generous, our hosts lavished upon us the same hands-on affection and attention to detail that had transformed an unpromising place in the middle of nowhere into a very livable community.

On top of all that, the Cougars were kicking butt, so the night of July 3rd I wanted to celebrated with a frozen margarita. I couldn't pry anybody else away from "Bubba's," the movable feast of beer, chips, and chatter the adults traveling with the Cougars improvised nightly in the King's Inn Motel parking lot, so I drove off alone to find one perfect margarita.

Inside the door of Kelley's Bar and Lounge I was flagged by a guy collecting a cover charge and told I couldn't enter wearing my Malcolm X hat. I asked why; the guy hesitated, conferred for a moment with his partner, then declared that Malcolm X hats were against the dress code. For a split second I thought it might be that *no* caps were allowed in Kelley's. But the door crew and two or three others hanging around the entranceway all wore the billed caps ubiquitous in New Mexico, duplicates of mine, except theirs sported the logos of feed stores and truck stops instead of a silver X.

What careened through my mind in the next couple of minutes is essentially unsayable but included scenes from my own half-century of life as a black man, clips from five hundred years of black/white meetings on slave ships, auction blocks, plantations, basketball courts, in the Supreme Court's marble halls, in beds, back alleys and back rooms, kisses and lynch ropes and contracts for millions of dollars so a black face will grace a cereal box. To tease away my anger I tried joking with folks in other places. Hey, Spike Lee. That hat you gave me on the set of the Malcolm movie in Cairo ain't legal in Clovis.

But nothing about these white guys barring my way was really funny. Part of me wanted to get down and dirty. Curse the suckers. Were they prepared to do battle to keep me and my cap out? Another voice said, Be cool. Don't sully your hands. Walk away and call the cops or a lawyer. Forget these chumps. Sue the owner. Or should I win hearts and minds? Look, fellas, I understand why the X on my cap might offend or scare you. You probably don't know much about Malcolm. The incredible metamorphoses of his thinking, his soul. By the time he was assassinated he wasn't a racist, didn't advocate violence. He was trying to make sense of America's impossible history, free himself, free us from the crippling legacy of race hate and oppression.

While all the above occupied my mind, my body, on its own, had assumed a gunfighter's vigilance, hands ready at sides, head cocked, weight poised, eyes tight and hard on the doorkeeper yet alert to anything stirring on the periphery. Many other eyes, all in white faces, were checking out the entranceway, recognizing the ingredients of a racial incident. Hadn't they witnessed Los Angeles going berserk on their TV screens just a couple months ago? That truck driver beaten nearly to death in the street, those packs of black hoodlums burning and looting? Invisible lines were being drawn in the air, in the sand, invisible chips bristled on shoulders.

The weather again. Our American racial weather, turbulent, unchanging in its changeability, its power to rock us and stun us and smack us from our routines and tear us apart as if none of our cities, our pieties, our promises, our dreams, ever stood a chance of holding on. The racial weather. Outside us, then suddenly, unforgettably, unforgivingly inside, reminding us of what we've only pretended to have forgotten. Our limits, our flaws. The lies and compromises we practice to avoid dealing honestly with the contradictions of race. How dependent we are on luck to survive—*when* we survive—the racial weather.

One minute you're a person, the next moment somebody starts treating you as if you're not. Often it happens just that way, just that suddenly. Particularly if you are a black man in America. Race and racism are a force larger than individuals, more powerful than law or education or government or the church, a force able to wipe these institutions away in the charged moments, minuscule or mountainous, when black and white come face to face. In Watts in 1965, or a few less-than-glorious minutes in Clovis, New Mexico, on the eve of the day that commemorates our country's freedom, our inalienable right as a nation, as citizens, to life, liberty, equality, the pursuit of happiness, those precepts and principles that still look good on paper but are often as worthless as a sheet of newspaper to protect you in a storm if you're a black man at the wrong time in the wrong place.

None of this is news, is it? Not July 3rd in Clovis, when a tiny misfire 10 occurred, or yesterday in your town or tomorrow in mine? But haven't we made progress? Aren't things much better than they used to be? Hasn't enough been done?

We ask the wrong questions when we look around and see a handful of fabulously wealthy black people, a few others entering the middle classes. Far more striking than the positive changes are the abiding patterns and assumptions that have not changed. Not all black people are mired in social pathology, but the bottom rung of the ladder of opportunity (and the space *beneath* the bottom rung) is still defined by the color of the people trapped there—and many *are* still trapped there, no doubt about it, because their status was inherited, determined generation after generation by blood, by color. Once, all black people were legally excluded from full participation in the mainstream. Then fewer. Now only some. But the mechanisms of disenfranchisement that originally separated African Americans from other Americans persist, if not legally, then in the apartheid mind-set, convictions and practices of the majority. The seeds sleep but don't die. Ten who suffer from exclusion today can become ten thousand tomorrow. Racial weather can change that quickly.

How would the bouncer have responded if I'd calmly declared, "This is a free country, I can wear any hat I choose"? Would he thank me for standing up for our shared birthright? Or would he have to admit, if pushed, that American rights belong only to *some* Americans, white Americans?

We didn't get that far in our conversation. We usually don't. The girls' faces pulled me from the edge—girls of all colors, sizes, shapes, gritty kids bonding through hard clean competition. Weren't these guys who didn't like my X cap kids too? Who did they think I was? What did they think they were protecting? I backed out, backed down, climbed in my car and drove away from Kelley's. After all, I didn't want Kelley's. I wanted a frozen margarita and a mellow celebration. So I bought plenty of ice and the ingredients for a margarita and rejoined the festivities at Bubba's. Everybody volunteered to go back with me to Kelley's, but I didn't want to spoil the victory party, taint our daughters' accomplishments, erase the high marks Clovis had earned hosting us.

But I haven't forgotten what happened in Kelley's. I write about it now because this is my country, the country where my sons and daughter are growing up, and your daughters and sons, and the crisis, the affliction, the same ole, same ole waste of life continues across the land, the nightmarish weather of racism, starbursts of misery in the dark.

The statistics of inequality don't demonstrate a "black crisis"—that   15
perspective confuses cause and victim, solutions and responsibility. When the rain falls, it falls on us all. The bad news about black men—that they die sooner and more violently than white men, are more ravaged by unemployment and lack of opportunity, are more exposed to drugs, disease, broken families, and police brutality, more likely to go to jail than college, more cheated by the inertia and callousness of a government that represents and protects the most needy the least—this is not a "black problem," but a *national* shame affecting us all. Wrenching ourselves free from the long nightmare of racism will require collective determination, countless individual acts of will, gutsy, informed, unselfish. To imagine the terrible cost of not healing ourselves, we must first imagine how good it would feel to be healed.

The Reader's Presence

1. The incident Wideman recounts in this essay takes place on the eve of July Fourth, "the fireworks day, the day for picnics and patriotic speeches" (paragraph 1). Look closely at the modifiers he chooses to describe the Fourth of July. Given the events that took place in Clovis that night, comment on the significance of each phrase. How

else might he have described this holiday, and why might he have intentionally discarded those descriptions? Identify—and comment on the effectiveness of—other moments in the essay when Wideman refers to the Fourth of July in related themes.

2. An extended metaphor of weather runs through this essay. Trace the analogy through the comparisons and contrasts Wideman makes or implies. In what specific ways, for instance, are the townsfolk described in paragraph 2 like or unlike the weather? How does this change as the essay progresses? How does racism resemble and differ from the weather? Given this guiding metaphor, does Wideman leave his reader with much hope for an end to racism?

3. In paragraph 6, Wideman mentions several courses of action he might have taken in reaction to the bouncer at Kelley's bar. What would be the pros and cons of each possible reaction? How would each one measure up to the "individual acts of will, gutsy, informed, unselfish" that he mentions in the last paragraph? What other courses of action might he have considered? What factors made him choose the course he took? In paragraph 12 he recounts the beginning of a hypothetical dialogue with the bouncer, and in paragraph 13 he writes, "We didn't get that far in our conversation. We usually don't." In your judgment, would it be better or worse if we did engage in these dialogues? Might Wideman's essay itself be seen as an attempt to open such a dialogue? To what extent is the essay "as worthless as a sheet of newspaper to protect you in a storm" (paragraph 9)? If "law or education or government or the church" (paragraph 9) can't provide an end to racism, what can?

118

Patricia J. Williams

Hate Radio

Patricia J. Williams (b. 1951) is a law professor at Columbia University. She was an undergraduate at Wellesley College, received her J.D. from Harvard University, and was a fellow in the prestigious School of Criticism and Theory at Dartmouth College. She is a contributing editor to The Nation, *where she writes a column, "Diary of a Mad Law Professor." She has published* The Alchemy of

Race and Rights *(1990) and more recently,* The Rooster's Egg: On the Persistence
of Prejudice *(1995).*

Three years ago [1991] I stood at my sink, washing the dishes and listening to the radio. I was tuned to rock and roll so I could avoid thinking
about the big news from the day before—George Bush had just nominated Clarence Thomas to replace Thurgood Marshall on the Supreme
Court. I was squeezing a dot of lemon Joy into each of the wine glasses
when I realized that two smoothly radiocultured voices, a man's and a
woman's, had replaced the music.

"I think it's a stroke of genius on the president's part," said the female voice.

"Yeah," said the male voice. "Then those blacks, those African
Americans, those Negroes—hey 'Negro' is good enough for Thurgood
Marshall—whatever, they can't make up their minds [what] they want to
be called. I'm gonna call them Blafricans. Black Africans. Yeah, I like it.
Blafricans. Then they can get all upset because now the president ap-
pointed a Blafrican."

"Yeah, well, that's the way those liberals think. It's just crazy."

"And then after they turn down his nomination the president can say   5
he tried to please 'em, and then he can appoint someone with some intelligence."

Back then, this conversation seemed so horrendously unusual, so singularly hateful, that I picked up a pencil and wrote it down. I was certain
that a firestorm of protest was going to engulf the station and purge those
foul radio mouths with the good clean soap of social outrage.

I am so naive. When I finally turned on the radio and rolled my dial
to where everyone else had been tuned while I was busy watching Cosby
reruns, it took me a while to understand that there's a firestorm all right,
but not of protest. In the two, and a half years since Thomas has assumed
his post on the Supreme Court, the underlying assumptions of the conversation I heard as uniquely outrageous have become commonplace, popu-
larly expressed, and louder in volume. I hear the style of that snide
polemicism everywhere, among acquaintances, on the street, on television
in toned-down versions. It is a crude demagoguery that makes me heart-
sick. I feel more and more surrounded by that point of view, the assumptions of being without intelligence, the coded epithets, the "Blafrican"-
like stand-ins for "nigger," the mocking angry glee, the endless tirades
filled with nonspecific, nonempirically based slurs against "these people"
or "those minorities" or "feminazis" or "liberals" or "scumbags" or
"pansies" or "jerks" or "sleazeballs" or "loonies" or "animals" or "foreigners."

At the same time I am not so naive as to suppose that this is something new. In clearheaded moments I realize I am not listening to the
radio anymore, I am listening to a large segment of white America think
aloud in ever louder resurgent thoughts that have generations of histori-

cal precedent. It's as though the radio has split open like an egg, Morton Downey, Jr.'s[1] clones and Joe McCarthy's[2] ghost spilling out, broken yolks, a great collective of sometimes clever, sometimes small, but uniformly threatened brains—they have all come gushing out. Just as they were about to pass into oblivion, Jack Benny and his humble black sidekick Rochester get resurrected in the ungainly bodies of Howard Stern and his faithful black henchwoman, Robin Quivers. The culture of Amos and Andy has been revived and reassembled in Bob Grant's radio minstrelry and radio newcomer Darryl Gates's[3] sanctimonious imprecations on behalf of decent white people. And in striking imitation of Jesse Helm's nearly forgotten days as a radio host, the far Right has found its undisputed king in the personage of Rush Limbaugh—a polished demagogue with a weekly radio audience of at least twenty million, a television show that vies for ratings with the likes of Jay Leno, a newsletter with a circulation of 380,000, and two best-selling books whose combined sales are closing in on six million copies.

From Churchill to Hitler to the old Soviet Union, it's clear that radio and television have the power to change the course of history, to proselytize, and to coalesce not merely the good and the noble but the very worst in human nature as well. Likewise, when Orson Welles made his famous radio broadcast "witnessing" the landing of a spaceship full of hostile Martians, the United States ought to have learned a lesson about the power of radio to appeal to mass instincts and incite mass hysteria. Radio remains a peculiarly powerful medium even today, its visual emptiness in a world of six trillion flashing images allowing one of the few remaining playgrounds for the aural subconscious. Perhaps its power is attributable to our need for an oral tradition after all, some conveying of stories, feelings, myths of ancestors, epics of alienation, and the need to rejoin ancestral roots, even ignorant bigoted roots. Perhaps the visual quiescence of radio is related to the popularity of E-mail or electronic networking. Only the voice is made manifest, unmasking worlds that cannot—or dare not?—be seen. Just yet. Nostalgia crystallizing into a dangerous future. The preconscious voice erupting into the expressed, the prime time.

What comes out of the modern radio mouth could be the *Iliad,* the   10 *Rubaiyat,* the griot's song of our times. If indeed radio is a vessel for the American "Song of Songs," then what does it mean that a manic, adolescent Howard Stern is so popular among radio listeners, that Rush Limbaugh's wittily smooth sadism has gone the way of prime-time television, and that both vie for the number one slot on all the best-selling book

[1]*Morton Downey Jr.* was a talk-show host of the 1980s who often ridiculed his guests and took up controversial topics.

[2]*U.S. Senator Joseph R. McCarthy* (1909–1957), chair of the House Un-American Activities Committee, hunted and prosecuted suspected Communists and Communist sympathizers in the 1950s.

[3]*Darryl Gates* was Los Angeles police commissioner during the Rodney King beating affair of the early 1990s.

lists? What to make of the stories being told by our modern radio evangelists and their tragic unloved chorus of callers? Is it really just a collapsing
economy that spawns this drama of grown people sitting around scaring
themselves to death with fantasies of black feminist Mexican able-bodied
gay soldiers earning $100,000 a year on welfare who are so criminally de-
praved that Hillary Clinton or the Antichrist-of-the-moment had no
choice but to invite them onto the government payroll so they can run the
country? The panicky exaggeration reminds me of a child's fear. . . . *And
then, and then, a huge lion jumped out of the shadows and was about to
gobble me up, and I can't ever sleep again for a whole week.*

As I spin the dial on my radio, I can't help thinking that this stuff
must be related to that most poignant of fiber-optic phenomena, phone
sex. Aural Sex. Radio Racism with a touch of S & M. High-priest hosts
with the power and run-amok ego to discipline listeners, to smack with
the verbal back of the hand, to smash the button that shuts you up once
and for all. "Idiot!" shouts New York City radio demagogue Bob Grant
and then the sound of droning telephone emptiness, the voice of dissent
dumped out some trapdoor in aural space.

As I listened to a range of such programs what struck me as the most
unifying theme was not merely the specific intolerance on such hot topics
as race and gender but a much more general contempt for the world, a
verbal stoning of anything different. It is like some unusually violent
game of "Simon Says," this mockery and shouting down of callers, this
roar of incantations, the insistence on agreement.

But, ah, if you *will* but only agree, what sweet and safe reward, what
soft enfolding by a stern and angry radio god. And as an added bonus,
the invisible shield of an AM community of fans who are Exactly Like
You, to whom you can express, in anonymity, all the filthy stuff you
imagine "them" doing to you. The comfort and relief of being able to
ejaculate, to those who understand, about the dark imagined excess over-
taking, robbing, needing to be held down and taught a good lesson, needing to put it in its place before the ravenous demon enervates all that is
true and good and pure in this life.

The audience for this genre of radio flagellation is mostly young,
white, and male. Two thirds of Rush Limbaugh's audience is male. According to *Time* magazine, 75 percent of Howard Stern's listeners are
white men. Most of the callers have spent their lives walling themselves
off from any real experience with blacks, feminists, lesbians, or gays. In
this regard, it is probably true, as former Secretary of Education William
Bennett says, that Rush Limbaugh "tells his audience that what you believe inside, you can talk about in the marketplace." Unfortunately,
what's "inside" is then mistaken for what's outside, treated as empirical
and political reality. The *National Review* extols Limbaugh's conservative leadership as no less than that of Ronald Reagan, and the Republican
party provides Limbaugh with books to discuss, stories, angles, and public support. "People were afraid of censure by gay activists, feminists, en-

vironmentalists—now they are not because Rush takes them on," says Bennett.

U.S. history has been marked by cycles in which brands of this or that 15 hatred come into fashion and go out, are unleashed, and then restrained. If racism, homophobia, jingoism, and woman-hating have been features of national life in pretty much all of modern history, it rather begs the question to spend a lot of time wondering if right-wing radio is a symptom or a cause. For at least four-hundred years, prevailing attitudes in the West have considered African Americans less intelligent. Recent statistics show that 53 percent of people in the United States agree that blacks and Latinos are less intelligent than whites, and a majority believe that blacks are lazy, violent, welfare-dependent, and unpatriotic.

I think that what has made life more or less tolerable for "out" groups have been those moments in history when those "inside" feelings were relatively restrained. In fact, if I could believe that right-wing radio were only about idiosyncratic, singular, rough-hewn individuals thinking those inside thoughts, I'd be much more inclined to agree with Columbia University media expert Everette Dennis, who says that Stern's and Limbaugh's popularity represents the "triumph of the individual," or with *Time* magazine's bottom line that "the fact that either is seriously considered a threat . . . is more worrisome than Stern or Limbaugh will ever be." If what I was hearing had even a tad more to do with real oppressions, with real white *and* black levels of joblessness and homelessness, or with the real problems of real white men, then I wouldn't have bothered to slog my way through hours of Howard Stern's miserable obsessions.

Yet at the heart of my anxiety is the worry that Stern, Limbaugh, Grant, et al, represent the very antithesis of individualism's triumph. As the *National Review* said of Limbaugh's ascent, "It was a feat not only of the loudest voice but also of a keen political brain to round up, as Rush did, the media herd and drive them into the conservative corral." When asked about his political aspirations, Bob Grant gloated to the *Washington Post,* "I think I would make rather a good dictator."

The polemics of right-wing radio are putting nothing less than hate onto the airwaves, into the marketplace, electing it to office, teaching it in schools, and exalting it as freedom. What worries me is the increasing-to-constant commerce of retribution, control, and lashing out, fed not by fact but fantasy. What worries me is the re-emergence, more powerfully than at any time since the institution of Jim Crow, of a sociocentered self that excludes, "the likes of," well, me for example, from the civic circle and that would rob me of my worth and claim and identity as a citizen. As the *Economist* rightly observes, "Mr. Limbaugh takes a mass market—white, mainly male, middle-class, ordinary America—and talks to it as an endangered minority."

I worry about this identity whose external reference is a set of beliefs, ethics, and practices that excludes, restricts, and acts in the world on me, or mine, as the perceived if not real enemy. I am acutely aware of losing *my* mythic individualism to the surface shapes of my mythic group fear-someness as black, as female, as left wing. "I" merge not fluidly but irretrievably into a category of "them." I become a suspect self, a moving target of loathsome properties, not merely different but dangerous. And that worries me a lot.

What happens in my life with all this translated license, this permis-   20
sion to be uncivil? What happens to the social space that was supposed at the sweet mountaintop of the civil rights movement's trail? Can I get a seat on the bus without having to be reminded that I *should* be standing? Did the civil rights movement guarantee us nothing more than to use public accommodations while surrounded by raving lunatic bigots? "They didn't beat this idiot [Rodney King] enough," says Howard Stern.

Not long ago I had the misfortune to hail a taxicab in which the driver was listening to Howard Stern undress some woman. After some blocks, I had to get out. I was, frankly, afraid to ask the driver to turn it off—not because I was afraid of "censoring" him, which seems to be the only thing people will talk about anymore, but because the driver was stripping me too, as he leered through the rearview mirror. "Something the matter?" he demanded, as I asked him to pull over and let me out well short of my destination. (I'll spare you the full story of what happened from there—trying to get another cab, as the cabbies stopped for all the white businessmen who so much as scratched their heads near the curb; a nice young white man, seeing my plight, giving me his cab, having to thank him, he hero, me saved-but-humiliated, cabdriver pissed and surly. I fight my way to my destination, finally arriving in bad mood, militant black woman, cranky feminazi.)

When Yelstin blared rock music at his opponents holed up in the parliament building in Moscow, in imitation of the U.S. Marines trying to torture Manuel Noriega in Panama, all I could think of was that it must be like being trapped in a crowded subway car when all the portable stereos are tuned to Bob Grant or Howard Stern. With Howard Stern's voice a tinny, screeching backdrop, with all the faces growing dreamily mean as though some soporifically evil hallucinogen were gushing into their bloodstreams, I'd start begging to surrender.

Surrender to what? Surrender to the laissez-faire resegregation that is the metaphoric significance of the hundreds of "Rush rooms" that have cropped up in restaurants around the country; rooms broadcasting Limbaugh's words, rooms for your listening pleasure, rooms where bigots can capture the purity of a Rush-only lunch counter, rooms where all those unpleasant others just "choose" not to eat? Surrender to the naughty luxury of a room in which a Ku Klux Klan meeting could take place in orderly, First Amendment fashion? Everyone's "free" to come in (and a few of you outsiders do), but mostly the undesirable nonconformists are gently repulsed away. It's a high-tech world of enhanced choice. Whites choose mostly to sit in the Rush room. Feminists, blacks, lesbians, and gays "choose" to sit elsewhere. No need to buy black votes, you just pay them not to vote; no need to insist on white-only schools, you just sell the desirability of black-only schools. Just sit back and watch it work, like those invisible shock shields that keep dogs cowering in their own backyards.

How real is the driving perception behind all the Sturm und Drang of this genre of radio-harangue—the perception that white men are an oppressed minority, with no power and no opportunity in the land that they made great? While it is true that power and opportunity are shrinking for all but the very wealthy in this country (and would that Limbaugh would take that issue on), the fact remains that white men are still this country's most privileged citizens and market actors. To give just a small example, according to the *Wall Street Journal,* blacks were the only racial group to suffer a net job loss during the 1990–91 economic downturn at the companies reporting to the Equal Employment Opportunity Commission. Whites, Latinos, and Asians, meanwhile, gained thousands of jobs. While whites gained 71,144 jobs at these companies, Latinos gained 60,040, Asians gained 55,104, and blacks lost 59,479. If every black were hired in the United States tomorrow, the numbers would not be sufficient to account for white men's expanding balloon of fear that they have been specifically dispossessed by African Americans.

Given deep patterns of social segregation and general ignorance of   25
history, particularly racial history, media remain the principal source of most Americans' knowledge of each other. Media can provoke violence or induce passivity. In San Francisco, for example, a radio show on KMEL called *Street Soldiers* has taken this power as a responsibility with great consequence: "Unquestionably," writes Ken Auletta in *The New Yorker,* "the show has helped avert violence. When a Samoan teenager was slain, apparently by Filipino gang members, in a drive-by shooting, the phones lit up with calls from Samoans wanting to tell [the hosts] they would not rest until they had exacted revenge. Threats filled the air for a couple of weeks. Then the dead Samoan's father called in, and, in a poignant exchange, the father said he couldn't tolerate the thought of more young men senselessly slaughtered. There would be no retaliation, he vowed. And there was none." In contrast, we must wonder at the phenomenon of the very powerful leadership of the Republican party, from Ronald Reagan to Robert Dole to William Bennett, giving advice, counsel, and friendship to Rush Limbaugh's passionate divisiveness.

The outright denial of the material crisis at every level of U.S. society, most urgently in black inner-city neighborhoods but facing us all, is a kind of political circus, dissembling as it feeds the frustrations of the moment. We as a nation can no longer afford to deal with such crises by *imagining* an excess of bodies, of babies, of job-stealers, of welfare mothers, of overreaching immigrants, of too-powerful (Jewish, in whispers) liberal Hollywood, of lesbians and gays, of gang members ("gangsters" remain white, and no matter what the atrocity, less vilified than "gang members," who are black), of Arab terrorists, and uppity women. The reality of our social poverty far exceeds these scapegoats. This right-wing backlash resembles, in form if not substance, phenomena like anti-Semitism in Poland: There aren't but a handful of Jews left in that whole country, but the giant balloon of heated anti-Semitism flourishes apace, Jews blamed for the world's evils.

The overwhelming response to right-wing excesses in the United States has been to seek an odd sort of comfort in the fact that the First Amendment is working so well that you can't suppress this sort of thing. Look what's happened in Eastern Europe. Granted. So let's not talk about censorship or the First Amendment for the next ten minutes. But in Western Europe, where fascism is rising at an appalling rate, suppression is hardly the problem. In Eastern and Western Europe as well as the United States, we must begin to think just a little bit about the fiercely coalescing power of media to spark mistrust, to fan it into forest fires of fear, and revenge. We must begin to think about the levels of national and social complacence in the face of such resolute ignorance. We must ask ourselves what the expected result is, not of censorship or suppression but of so much encouragement, so much support, so much investment in the fashionability of hate. What future is it that we are designing with the devotion of such tremendous resources to the disgraceful propaganda of bigotry?

The Reader's Presence

1. Reread Williams's opening paragraph. Why do you think she begins her essay this way? What does the paragraph tell you about her? How does it prepare you for the rest of the essay? Suppose Williams began with an anecdote from her experience in law or teaching. Would the effect differ? How and why?

2. Williams writes: "It's clear that radio and television have the power to change the course of history, to proselytize, and to coalesce not merely the good and the noble, but the very worst in human nature as well" (paragraph 9). What is the significance of this statement relative to Williams's general argument? Williams cites the Orson Welles example. What correlation is implied between this and the "hate mongers" of radio?

3. What tone does the author take toward her subject in paragraph 10? What is its effect for the reader? Rewrite a few sentences in a more neutral tone. Does this change the general sense of the material? If so, in what way?

119

Terry Tempest Williams
The Clan of One-Breasted Women

The environmentalist and writer Terry Tempest Williams (b. 1953) lives in Utah, where she is active in the movement to expand federally protected wilderness areas. She was until recently a professor of English at the University of Utah and has also been naturalist-in-residence at the Utah Museum of Natural History. In Refuge: An Unnatural History of Family and Place *(1991), she documents the epidemic of cancer caused by nuclear weapons tested in Utah during the 1950s and meditates upon the meaning of this tragedy for her family. "The Clan of One-Breasted Women" appears in* Refuge. *Her first book,* Pieces of a White Shell: A Journey to Navajoland *(1984), received a Southwest Book Award. She is also the author of* Coyote's Canyon *(1989),* An Unspoken Hunger: Stories from the Field *(1994), and* Desert Quartet *(1995). More recently she has been coeditor of* Testimony: Writers of the West Speak on Behalf of Utah Wilderness *(1996) and* New Genesis: Mormons Writing on the Environment *(1999).*

Reflecting upon her motivation for writing about her personal experience with cancer, Williams notes, "Perhaps I am telling this story in an attempt to heal myself, to confront what I do not know, to create a path for myself with the idea that 'memory is the only way home.'"

I belong to a Clan of One-Breasted Women. My mother, my grandmothers, and six aunts have all had mastectomies. Seven are dead. The two who survive have just completed rounds of chemotherapy and radiation.

I've had my own problems: two biopsies for breast cancer and a small tumor between my ribs diagnosed as a "borderline malignancy."

This is my family history.

Most statistics tell us that breast cancer is genetic, hereditary, with rising percentages attached to fatty diets, childlessness, or becoming pregnant after thirty. What they don't say is that living in Utah may be the greatest hazard of all.

We are a Mormon family with roots in Utah since 1847. The "word of wisdom" in my family aligned us with good foods — no coffee, no tea, 5

845

tobacco, or alcohol. For the most part, our women were finished having their babies by the time they were thirty. And only one faced breast cancer prior to 1960. Traditionally, as a group of people, Mormons have a low rate of cancer.

Is our family a cultural anomaly? The truth is, we didn't think about it. Those who did, usually the men, simply said, "bad genes." The women's attitude was stoic. Cancer was part of life. On February 16, 1971, the eve of my mother's surgery, I accidentally picked up the telephone and overheard her ask my grandmother what she could expect.

"Diane, it is one of the most spiritual experiences you will ever encounter."

I quietly put down the receiver.

Two days later, my father took my brothers and me to the hospital to visit her. She met us in the lobby in a wheelchair. No bandages were visible. I'll never forget her radiance, the way she held herself in a purple velvet robe, and how she gathered us around her.

"Children, I am fine. I want you to know I felt the arms of God   10
around me."

We believed her. My father cried. Our mother, his wife, was thirty-eight years old.

A little over a year after Mother's death, Dad and I were having dinner together. He had just returned from St. George, where the Tempest Company was completing the gas lines that would service southern Utah. He spoke of his love for the country, the sandstoned landscape, bare-boned and beautiful. He had just finished hiking the Kolob trail in Zion National Park. We got caught up in reminiscing, recalling with fondness our walk up Angel's Landing on his fiftieth birthday and the years our family had vacationed there.

Over dessert, I shared a recurring dream of mine. I told my father that for years, as long as I could remember, I saw this flash of light in the night in the desert—that this image had so permeated my being that I could not venture south without seeing it again, on the horizon, illuminating buttes and mesas.

"You did see it," he said.

"Saw what?"   15

"The bomb. The cloud. We were driving home from Riverside, California. You were sitting on Diane's lap. She was pregnant. In fact, I remember the day, September 7, 1957. We had just gotten out of the Service. We were driving north, past Las Vegas. It was an hour or so before dawn, when this explosion went off. We not only heard it, but felt it. I thought the oil tanker in front of us had blown up. We pulled over and suddenly, rising from the desert floor, we saw it, clearly, this golden-stemmed cloud, the mushroom. The sky seemed to vibrate with an eerie pink glow. Within a few minutes, a light ash was raining on the car."

I stared at my father.

"I thought you knew that," he said. "It was a common occurrence in the fifties."

It was at this moment that I realized the deceit I had been living under. Children growing up in the American Southwest, drinking contaminated milk from contaminated cows, even from the contaminated breasts of their mothers, my mother — members, years later, of the Clan of One-Breasted Women.

It is a well-known story in the Desert West, "The Day We Bombed   20
Utah," or more accurately, the years we bombed Utah: above ground atomic testing in Nevada took place from January 27, 1951 through July 11, 1962. Not only were the winds blowing north covering "low-use segments of the population" with fallout and leaving sheep dead in their tracks but the climate was right. The United States of the 1950s was red, white, and blue. The Korean War was raging. McCarthyism[1] was rampant. Ike[2] was it, and the cold war was hot. If you were against nuclear testing, you were for a communist regime.

Much has been written about this "American nuclear tragedy." Public health was secondary to national security. The Atomic Energy Commissioner, Thomas Murray, said, "Gentlemen, we must not let anything interfere with this series of tests, nothing."

Again and again, the American public was told by its government, in spite of burns, blisters, and nausea, "It has been found that the tests may be conducted with adequate assurance of safety under conditions prevailing at the bombing reservations." Assuaging public fears was simply a matter of public relations. "Your best action," an Atomic Energy Commission booklet read, "is not to be worried about fallout." A news release typical of the times stated, "We find no basis for concluding that harm to any individual has resulted from radioactive fallout."

On August 30, 1979, during Jimmy Carter's presidency, a suit was filed, *Irene Allen v. The United States of America*. Mrs. Allen's case was the first on an alphabetical list of twenty-four test cases, representative of nearly twelve hundred plaintiffs seeking compensation from the United States government for cancers caused by nuclear testing in Nevada.

Irene Allen lived in Hurricane, Utah. She was the mother of five children and had been widowed twice. Her first husband, with their two oldest boys, had watched the tests from the roof of the local high school. He died of leukemia in 1956. Her second husband died of pancreatic cancer in 1978.

In a town meeting conducted by Utah Senator Orrin Hatch, shortly   25
before the suit was filed, Mrs. Allen said, "I am not blaming the

[1]*McCarthyism:* The practice of publicizing accusations of political disloyalty or subversion without sufficient regard to evidence. Associated with Senator Joseph McCarthy (1908–1957). — EDS.
[2]*Ike:* President Dwight D. Eisenhower (1890–1969) was known as "Ike." — EDS.

government, I want you to know that, Senator Hatch. But I thought if my testimony could help in any way so this wouldn't happen again to any of the generations coming up after us . . . I am happy to be here this day to bear testimony of this."

God-fearing people. This is just one story in an anthology of thousands.

On May 10, 1984, Judge Bruce S. Jenkins handed down his opinion. Ten of the plaintiffs were awarded damages. It was the first time a federal court had determined that nuclear tests had been the cause of cancers. For the remaining fourteen test cases, the proof of causation was not sufficient. In spite of the split decision, it was considered a landmark ruling. It was not to remain so for long.

In April 1987, the Tenth Circuit Court of Appeals overturned Judge Jenkins's ruling on the ground that the United States was protected from suit by the legal doctrine of sovereign immunity, a centuries-old idea from England in the days of absolute monarchs.

In January 1988, the Supreme Court refused to review the Appeals Court decision. To our court system it does not matter whether the United States government was irresponsible, whether it lied to its citizens, or even that citizens died from the fallout of nuclear testing. What matters is that our government is immune: "The King can do no wrong."

In Mormon culture, authority is respected, obedience is revered, and 30 independent thinking is not. I was taught as a young girl not to "make waves" or "rock the boat."

"Just let it go," Mother would say. "You know how you feel, that's what counts."

For many years, I have done just that—listened, observed, and quietly formed my own opinions, in a culture that rarely asks questions because it has all the answers. But one by one, I have watched the women in my family die common, heroic deaths. We sat in waiting rooms hoping for good news, but always receiving the bad. I cared for them, bathed their scarred bodies, and kept their secrets. I watched beautiful women become bald as Cytoxan, cisplatin, and Adriamycin were injected into their veins. I held their foreheads as they vomited green-black bile, and I shot them with morphine when the pain became inhuman. In the end, I witnessed their last peaceful breaths, becoming a midwife to the rebirth of their souls.

The price of obedience has become too high.

The fear and inability to question authority that ultimately killed rural communities in Utah during atmospheric testing of atomic weapons is the same fear I saw in my mother's body. Sheep. Dead sheep. The evidence is buried.

I cannot prove that my mother, Diane Dixon Tempest, or my grand- 35 mothers, Lettie Romney Dixon and Kathryn Blackett Tempest, along with my aunts developed cancer from nuclear fallout in Utah. But I can't prove they didn't.

My father's memory was correct. The September blast we drove through in 1957 was part of Operation Plumbbob, one of the most intensive series of bomb tests to be initiated. The flash of light in the night in the desert, which I had always thought was a dream, developed into a family nightmare. It took fourteen years, from 1957 to 1971, for cancer to manifest in my mother—the same time, Howard L. Andrews, an authority in radioactive fallout at the National Institutes of Health, says radiation cancer requires to become evident. The more I learn about what it means to be a "downwinder," the more questions I drown in.

What I do know, however, is that as a Mormon woman of the fifth generation of Latter-day Saints, I must question everything, even if it means losing my faith, even if it means becoming a member of a border tribe among my own people. Tolerating blind obedience in the name of patriotism or religion ultimately takes our lives.

When the Atomic Energy Commission described the country north of the Nevada Test Site as "virtually uninhabited desert terrain," my family and the birds at Great Salt Lake were some of the "virtual uninhabitants."

One night, I dreamed women from all over the world circled a blazing fire in the desert. They spoke of change, how they hold the moon in their bellies and wax and wane with its phrases. They mocked the presumption of even-tempered beings and made promises that they would never fear the witch inside themselves. The women danced wildly as sparks broke away from the flames and entered the night sky as stars.

And they sang a song given to them by Shoshone grandmothers: 40

Ah ne nah, nah	Consider the rabbits
nin nah nah	How gently they walk on the earth—
ah ne nah, nah	Consider the rabbits
nin nah nah	How gently they walk on the earth—
Nyaga mutzi	We remember them
oh ne nay	We can walk gently also—
Nyaga mutzi	We remember them
oh ne nay	We can walk gently also

The women danced and drummed and sang for weeks, preparing themselves for what was to come. They would reclaim the desert for the sake of their children, for the sake of the land.

A few miles downwind from the fire circle, bombs were being tested. Rabbits felt the tremors. Their soft leather pads on paws and feet recognized the shaking sands, while the roots of mesquite and sage were smoldering. Rocks were hot from the inside out and dust devils hummed unnaturally. And each time there was another nuclear test, ravens watched the desert heave. Stretch marks appeared. The land was losing its muscle.

The women couldn't bear it any longer. They were mothers. They had suffered labor pains but always under the promise of birth. The red hot pains beneath the desert promised death only, as each bomb became a stillborn. A contract had been made and broken between human beings and the land. A new contract was being drawn by the women, who understood the fate of the earth as their own.

Under the cover of darkness, ten women slipped under a barbed-wire fence and entered the contaminated country. They were trespassing. They walked toward the town of Mercury, in moonlight, taking their cues from coyote, kit fox, antelope squirrel, and quail. They moved quietly and deliberately through the maze of Joshua trees. When a hint of daylight appeared they rested, drinking tea and sharing their rations of food. The women closed their eyes. The time had come to protest with the heart, that to deny one's genealogy with the earth was to commit treason against one's soul.

At dawn, the women draped themselves in mylar, wrapping long streamers of silver plastic around their arms to blow in the breeze. They wore clear masks, that became the faces of humanity. And when they arrived at the edge of Mercury, they carried all the butterflies of a summer day in their wombs. They paused to allow their courage to settle.

The town that forbids pregnant women and children to enter because   45
of radiation risks was asleep. The women moved through the streets as winged messengers, twirling around each other in slow motion, peeking inside homes and watching the easy sleep of men and women. They were astonished by such stillness and periodically would utter a shrill note or low cry just to verify life.

The residents finally awoke to these strange apparitions. Some simply stared. Others called authorities, and in time, the women were apprehended by wary soldiers dressed in desert fatigues. They were taken to a white, square building on the edge of Mercury. When asked who they were and why they were there, the women replied, "We are mothers and we have come to reclaim the desert for our children."

The soldiers arrested them. As the ten women were blindfolded and handcuffed, they began singing:

> *You can't forbid us everything*
> *You can't forbid us to think —*
> *You can't forbid our tears to flow*
> *And you can't stop the songs that we sing.*

The women continued to sing louder and louder, until they heard the voices of their sisters moving across the mesa:

> *Ah ne nah, nah*
> *nin nah nah —*
> *Ah ne nah, nah*
> *nin nah nah —*
> *Nyaga mutzi*
> *oh ne nay —*

Nyaga mutzi
oh ne nay—

"Call for reinforcements," one soldier said.

"We have," interrupted one woman, "we have—and you have no idea of our numbers."

I crossed the line at the Nevada Test Site and was arrested with nine other Utahns for trespassing on military lands. They are still conducting nuclear tests in the desert. Ours was an act of civil disobedience. But as I walked toward the town of Mercury, it was more than a gesture of peace. It was a gesture on behalf of the Clan of One-Breasted Women.

As one officer cinched the handcuffs around my wrists, another   50
frisked my body. She found a pen and a pad of paper tucked inside my left boot.

"And these?" she asked sternly.

"Weapons," I replied.

Our eyes met. I smiled. She pulled the leg of my trousers back over my boot.

"Step forward, please," she said as she took my arm.

We were booked under an afternoon sun and bused to Tonopah,   55
Nevada. It was a two-hour ride. This was familiar country. The Joshua trees standing their ground had been named by my ancestors, who believed they looked like prophets pointing west to the Promised Land. These were the same trees that bloomed each spring, flowers appearing like white flames in the Mojave. And I recalled a full moon in May, when Mother and I had walked among them, flushing out mourning doves and owls.

The bus stopped short of town. We were released.

The officials thought it was a cruel joke to leave us stranded in the desert with no way to get home. What they didn't realize was that we were home, soul-centered and strong, women who recognized the sweet smell of sage as fuel for our spirits.

The Reader's Presence

1. Paragraph 3 reads, "This is my family history." Which parts of her essay are particular to her family, and what do they add to the larger social history of her time and place? How does her family's religion, Mormonism, play into the family history? What does she gain by drawing on the earlier spiritual tradition of the Shoshones, which is rooted in the same geographical area? What other "families," besides her nuclear and extended family, might Williams belong to?

2. Examine carefully—and discuss in detail—the role of dream and reality in this essay. Characterize the power of each. Consider also the relationship between dream and nightmare. How do you read the "dream" Williams recounts in paragraphs 39 and following? Characterize the relationship between that dream and the "civil disobedience" she recounts in the following section (paragraph 48 ff.).

3. Discuss the role of language in the essay. You might begin by examining instances of what might be termed Orwellian doublespeak. (In this context you might refer to Orwell's "Politics and the English Language" and/or Morrison's "Nobel Lecture, 7 December, 1993," both collected in this volume.) What are the dangers and ironies inherent in this euphemistic, obfuscating prose? Examine carefully Williams's own language and that of the Shoshones, as well as the written doctrines and documents to which Williams alludes or refers. Finally, reread paragraph 51, where she refers to her pen and paper as "weapons." How effective a weapon is this essay itself in the battle for social justice?

120

Howard Zinn

Growing Up Class-Conscious

Howard Zinn (b. 1922) is a historian, author, and a professor emeritus of political science at Boston University. As a political activist, Zinn was involved in both the civil rights movement and the Vietnam War protest, using these experiences in his books, SNCC: The New Abolitionists *(1964) and* Vietnam: The Logic of Withdrawal *(1967). He is perhaps best known for his revolutionary work,* A People's History of the United States *(1990), which provides alternative accounts of historical events as viewed from the perspectives of minorities and the working class. Other books of nonfiction include* The Politics of History *(1970),* Declarations of Independence *(1990), and* The Zinn Reader *(1997). He has also written three plays,* Emma *(1976),* Daughter of Venus *(1985), and* Marx in Soho *(1999). "Growing Up Class-Conscious" is from his autobiography,* You Can't Be Neutral on a Moving Train *(1994).*

I was in my teens when I wrote this poem:

Go see your Uncle Phil
And say hello.

Who would walk a mile today
To say hello,
The city freezing in the snow?

Phil had a news stand
Under the black El.
He sat on a wooden box
In the cold and in the heat.
And three small rooms across the street.

Today the wooden box was gone,
On top the stand Uncle Phil was curled,
A skeleton inside an Army coat.
He smiled and gave me a stick of gum
With stiffened fingers, red and numb.

Go see your Uncle Phil today
My mother said again in June
I walked the mile to say hello
With the city smelling almost sweet
Brand new sneakers on my feet.

The stand was nailed and boarded tight
And quiet in the sun,
Uncle Phil lay cold, sleep,
Under the black El, in a wooden box
In three small rooms across the street.

I recall these lines, certainly not as an example of "poetry," but because they evoke something about my growing up in the slums of Brooklyn in the thirties, when my father and mother in desperate moments
turned to saviors: the corner grocer, who gave credit by writing down the
day's purchases on a roll of paper; the kind doctor who treated my rickets
for years without charging; Uncle Phil, whose army service had earned
him a newsstand license and who loaned us money when we had trouble
paying the rent.

Phil and my father were two of four brothers, Jewish immigrants
from Austria, who came to this country before the First World War and
worked together in New York factories. Phil's fellow workers kept questioning him: "Zinn, Zinn—what kind of name is that? Did you change
it? It's not a Jewish name." Phil told them no, the name had not been
changed, it was Zinn and that's all there was to it. But he got tired of the
interrogations and one day had his name legally changed to Weintraub,
which from then on was the name of that branch of the family.

My father, looking to escape the factory, became a waiter, mostly at
weddings, sometimes in restaurants, and a member of Local 2 of the
Waiters Union. While the union tightly controlled its membership, on
New Year's Eve, when there was a need for extra waiters, the sons of the
members, called juniors, would work alongside their fathers, and I
did too.

I hated every moment of it: the ill-fitting waiter's tuxedo, borrowed   5
from my father, on my lanky body, the sleeves absurdly short (my father
was five-foot-five and at sixteen I was a six-footer); the way the bosses
treated the waiters, who were fed chicken wings just before they marched
out to serve roast beef and filet mignon to the guests; everybody in their
fancy dress, wearing silly hats, singing "Auld Lang Syne" as the New
Year began and me standing there in my waiter's costume, watching my
father, his face strained, clear his tables, feeling no joy at the coming of
the New Year.

When I first came across a certain e.e. cumming's poem, I didn't fully
understand why it touched me so deeply, but I knew it connected with
some hidden feeling.

> my father moved through dooms of love
> through sames of am through haves of give,
> singing each morning out of each night
> my father moved through depths of height. . . .

His name was Eddie. He was always physically affectionate to his
four boys, and loved to laugh. He had a strong face, a muscular body,
and flat feet (due, it was said, to long years as a waiter, but who could be
sure?), and his waiter friends called him "Charlie Chaplin" because he
walked with his feet splayed out—he claimed he could balance the trays
better that way.

In the Depression years the weddings fell off, there was little work,
and he got tired of hanging around the union hall, playing cards, waiting
for a job. So he became at different times a window cleaner, a pushcart
peddler, a street salesman of neckties, a W.P.A. worker in Central Park.
As a window cleaner, his supporting belt broke one day and he fell off the
ladder onto the concrete steps of a subway entrance. I was perhaps twelve
and I remember him being brought, bleeding, into our little flat. He had
hurt himself badly. My mother would not let him clean windows again.

All his life he worked hard for very little. I've always resented the smug
statements of politicians, media commentators, corporate executives who
talked of how, in America, if you worked hard you would become rich. The
meaning of that was if you were poor it was because you hadn't worked
hard enough. I knew this was a lie, about my father and millions of others,
men and women who worked harder than anyone, harder than financiers
and politicians, harder than *anybody* if you accept that when you work at
an unpleasant job that makes it very hard work indeed.

My mother worked and worked without getting paid at all. She was a   10
plump woman, with a sweet, oval Russian face—a beauty, in fact. She had
grown up in Irkutsk, in Siberia. While my father worked *his* hours on the
job, she worked all day and all night, managing the family, finding the food,
cooking and cleaning, taking the kids to the doctor or the hospital clinic for
measles and mumps and whooping cough and tonsillitis and whatever came
up. And taking care of family finances. My father had a fourth-grade edu-

cation and could not read much or do much arithmetic. My mother had gone as far as seventh grade, but her intelligence went far beyond that; she was the brains of the family. And the strength of the family.

Her name was Jenny. Roz [Zinn's wife] and I sat with her in our kitchen one day when she was in her seventies and had her talk about her life, with a tape recorder on the table. She told of her mother's arranged marriage in Irkutsk, of how "they brought a boy home, a Jewish soldier stationed in Irkutsk, and said, This is who you'll marry."

They emigrated to America. Jenny's mother died in her thirties, having given birth to three boys and three girls, and her father — against whom she boiled with indignation all her life — deserted the family. Jenny, the eldest but only a teenager, became the mother of the family, took care of the rest, working in factories, until they grew up and found jobs.

She met Eddie through his sister, who worked in her factory, and it was a passionate marriage all the way. Eddie died at sixty-seven. To the end he was carrying trays of food at weddings and in restaurants, never having made enough money to retire. It was a sudden heart attack, and I got the news in Atlanta, where Roz and I had just moved. I remembered our last meting, when my father was clearly upset about our little family moving south, so far away, but said nothing except "Good luck. Take care of yourself."

My mother outlived him by many years. She lived by herself, fiercely insisting on her independence, knitting sweaters for everybody, saving her shopping coupons, playing bingo with her friends. But toward the end she suffered a stroke and entered a nursing home.

As a child I was drawn to a framed photograph on the wall, of a   15
delicate-faced little boy with soft brown eyes and a shock of brown hair, and one day my mother told me it was her firstborn, my older brother, who died of spinal meningitis at the age of five. In our tape recording she tells how when he died they'd been in the country for a brief, cheap vacation, and how she and my father held the boy's body on the long train ride back to New York City.

We lived in a succession of tenements, sometimes four rooms, sometimes three. Some winters we lived in a building with central heating. Other times we lived in what was called a cold-water flat — no heat except from the coal cooking stove in the kitchen, no hot water except what we boiled on that same stove.

It was always a battle to pay the bills. I would come home from school in the winter, when the sun set at four, and find the house dark — the electric company had turned off the electricity, and my mother would be sitting there, knitting by candlelight.

There was no refrigerator, but an icebox, for which we would go to the "ice dock" and buy a five- or ten-cent chunk of ice. In the winter a wooden box rested on the sill just outside the window, using nature to keep things cold. There was no shower, but the washtub in the kitchen was our bathtub.

No radio for a long time, until one day my father took me on a long walk through the city to find a second-hand radio, and triumphantly brought it home on his shoulder, me trotting along by his side. No telephone. We could be called to the phone at the candy store down the block, and pay the kid who ran upstairs to get us two pennies or a nickel. Sometimes we hung out near the phone to take the call and race to collect the nickel.

And yes, the roaches. Never absent, wherever we lived. We'd come   20
home and they'd be all over the kitchen table and scatter when we turned on the light. I never got used to them.

I don't remember ever being hungry. The rent might not be paid (we moved often, a step ahead of eviction), no bills might be paid, the grocer might not be paid, but my mother was ingenious at making sure there was always food. Always hot cereal in the morning, always hot soup in the evening, always bread, butter, eggs, milk, noodles and cheese, sour cream, chicken fricassee.

My mother was not shy about using the English language, which she adapted to her purposes. We would hear her telling her friend about the problem she was having with "very close veins," or "a pain in my crutch." She would look in the dairy store for "monster cheese." She would say to my father if he forgot something, "Eddie, try to remember, wreck your brains."

My brothers—Bernie, Jerry, Shelly—and I had lots of fun over the years recalling her ways. She would sign her letters to us, "Your mother, Jenny Zinn." We laughed at those memories even while standing by in the hospital room where she lay in a coma, kept "alive" by a tangle of tubes, her brain already damaged beyond repair. We had signed that terrible order, "Do Not Resuscitate," shortly after which she coughed up her breathing tube and died. She was ninety.

We four boys grew up together—sleeping two or three to a bed, in rooms dark and uninviting. So I spent a lot of time in the street or the schoolyard, playing handball, football, softball, stickball, or taking boxing lessons from a guy in the neighborhood who had made the Golden Gloves and was our version of a celebrity.

In the time I did spend in the house I read. From the time I was eight I   25
was reading whatever books I could find. The very first was one I picked up on the street. The beginning pages were torn out, but that didn't matter. It was *Tarzan and the Jewels of Opar* and from then on I was a fan of Edgar Rice Burroughs, not only his Tarzan books but his other fantasies: *The Chessmen of Mars,* about the way wars were fought by Martians, with warriors, on foot or on horses, playing out the chess moves; *The Earth's Core,* about a strange civilization in the center of the earth.

There were no books in our house. My father had never read a book. My mother read romance magazines. They both read the newspaper. They knew little about politics, except that Franklin Roosevelt was a good man because he helped the poor.

As a boy I read no children's books. My parents did not know about such books, but when I was ten, the *New York Post* offered a set of the complete works of Charles Dickens (of whom they had never heard, of course). By using coupons cut out of the newspaper, they could get a volume every week for a few pennies. They signed up because they knew I loved to read. And so I read Dickens in the order in which we received the books, starting with *David Copperfield, Oliver Twist, Great Expectations, The Pickwick Papers, Hard Times, A Tale of Two Cities,* and all the rest, until the coupons were exhausted and so was I.

I did not know where Dickens fitted into the history of modern literature because he was all I knew of that literature. I did not know that he was probably the most popular novelist in the English-speaking world (perhaps in any world) in the mid-nineteenth century, or that he was a great actor whose readings of his own work drew mobs of people, or that when he visited the United States in 1842 (he was thirty), landing first in Boston, some of his readers traveled two thousand miles from the Far West to see him.

What I did know was that he aroused in me tumultuous emotions. First, an anger at arbitrary power puffed up with wealth and kept in place by law. But most of all a profound compassion for the poor. I did not see myself as poor in the way Oliver Twist was poor. I didn't recognize that I was so moved by his story because his life touched chords in mine.

How wise Dickens was to make readers feel poverty and cruelty 30 through the fate of children who had not reached the age where the righteous and comfortable classes could accuse them of being responsible for their own misery.

Today, reading pallid, cramped novels about "relationships," I recall Dickens' unashamed rousing of feeling, his uproariously funny characters, his epic settings — cities of hunger and degradation, countries in revolution, the stakes being life and death not just for one family but for thousands.

Dickens is sometimes criticized by literary snobs for sentimentality, melodrama, partisanship, exaggeration. But surely the state of the world makes fictional exaggeration unnecessary and partisanship vital. It was only many years after I read those Dickens novels that I understood his accomplishment.

For my thirteenth birthday, my parents, knowing that I was writing things in notebooks, bought me a rebuilt Underwood typewriter. It came with a practice book for learning the touch system, and soon I was typing book reviews for everything I read and keeping them in my drawer. I never showed them to anyone. It gave me joy and pride just to know that I had read these books and could write about them — on a typewriter.

From the age of fourteen I had after-school and summer jobs, delivering clothes for a dry cleaner, working as a caddy on a golf course in Queens. I also helped out in a succession of candy stores my parents bought in a desperate attempt to make enough money so my father could quit being a waiter. The stores all failed, but my three younger brothers and I had lots of milkshakes and ice cream and candy while they existed.

I remember the last of those candy store situations, and it was typical. 35 The six of us lived above the store in a four-room flat in a dirty old five-story tenement on Bushwick Avenue in Brooklyn. The streets were always full of life, especially in spring and summer, when everyone seemed to be outside — old folks sitting on chairs, mothers holding their babies, teenagers playing ball, the older guys "throwing the bull," fooling with girls.

I especially remember that time because I was seventeen and had begun to be interested in world politics.

I was reading books about fascism in Europe. George Seldes' *Sawdust Caesar,* about Mussolini's seizure of power in Italy, fascinated me. I could not get out of mind the courage of the Socialist deputy Matteotti, who defied Mussolini and was dragged from his home and killed by brown-shirted thugs.

I read something called *The Brown Book of the Nazi Terror,* which described what was happening in Germany under Hitler. It was a drama beyond anything a playwright or novelist could imagine. And now the Nazi war machine was beginning to move into the Rhineland, Austria, Czechoslovakia. The newspapers and radio were full of excitement: Chamberlain meeting Hitler at Munich, the sudden, astonishing nonaggression pact of the two archenemies, Soviet Russia and Nazi Germany. And finally, the invasion of Poland and the start of the Second World War.[1]

The Civil War in Spain, just ended with victory for the Fascist general Franco,[2] seemed the event closest to all of us because several thousand American radicals — Communists, socialists, anarchists — had crossed the Atlantic to fight with the democratic government of Spain. A young fellow who played street football with us — short and thin, the fastest runner in the neighborhood — disappeared. Months later the word came to us: Jerry has gone to Spain to fight against Franco.

There on Bushwick Avenue, among the basketball players and street 40 talkers, were some young Communists, a few years older than me. They had jobs, but after work and on weekends they distributed Marxist literature in the neighborhood and talked politics into the night with whoever was interested.

I was interested. I was reading about what was happening in the world. I argued with the Communist guys. Especially about the Russian

---

[1]*Chamberlain:* Neville Chamberlain (1869–1940) was the Conservative British prime minister (1937–1940) who pursued an appeasement policy with Nazi Germany. Hitler invaded Poland in 1939. — EDS.

[2]*Franco:* A conservative army officer, Francisco Franco Bahamonde (1892–1975), mutinied against the Spanish government in 1936 and thus launched a three-year civil war that took nearly one million lives. Franco received support from both Hitler and Mussolini. — EDS.

invasion of Finland. They insisted it was necessary for the Soviet Union to protect itself against future attack, but to me it was a brutal act of aggression against a tiny country, and none of their carefully worked out justifications persuaded me.

Still, I agreed with them on lots of things. They were ferociously antifascist, indignant as I was about the contrasts of wealth and poverty in America. I admired them—they seemed to know so much about politics, economics, what was happening everywhere in the world. And they were courageous—I had seen them defy the local policeman, who tried to stop them from distributing literature on the street and to break up their knots of discussion. And besides, they were regular guys, good athletes.

One summer day they asked me if I wanted to go with them to "a demonstration" in Times Square that evening. I had never been to such a thing. I made some excuse to my parents, and a little bunch of us took the subway to Times Square.

When we arrived it was just a typical evening in Times Square—the streets crowded, the lights glittering. "Where's the demonstration?" I asked my friend Leon. He was tall, blond, the ideal "Aryan" type, but the son of German Communists who were also nature worshippers and part of a little colony of health-conscious German socialists out in the New Jersey countryside.

"Wait," he said. "Ten o'clock." We continued to stroll.   45

As the clock on the Times tower struck ten, the scene changed. In the midst of the crowd, banners were unfurled, and people, perhaps a thousand or more, formed into lines carrying banners and signs and chanting slogans about peace and justice and a dozen other causes of the day. It was exciting. And nonthreatening. All these people were keeping to the sidewalks, not blocking traffic, walking in orderly, nonviolent lines through Times Square. My friend and I were walking behind two women carrying a banner, and he said, "Let's relieve them." So we each took an end of the banner. I felt a bit like Charlie Chaplin in *Modern Times,* when he casually picks up a red signal flag and suddenly finds a thousand people marching behind him with raised fists.

We heard the sound of sirens and I thought there must be a fire somewhere, an accident of some kind. But then I heard screams and saw hundreds of policemen, mounted on horses and on foot, charging into the lines of marchers, smashing people with their clubs.

I was astonished, bewildered. This was America, a country where, whatever its faults, people could speak, write, assemble, demonstrate without fear. It was in the Constitution, the Bill of Rights. We were a *democracy.*

As I absorbed this, as my thoughts raced, all in a few seconds, I was spun around by a very large man, who seized my shoulder and hit me very hard. I only saw him as a blur. I didn't know if it was a club or a fist or a blackjack, but I was knocked unconscious.

I awoke in a doorway perhaps a half-hour later. I had no sense of   50
how much time had elapsed, but it was an eerie scene I woke up to. There
was no demonstration going on, no policemen in sight. My friend Leon
was gone, and Times Square was filled with its usual Saturday night
crowd—all as if nothing had happened, as if it were all a dream. But I
knew it wasn't a dream; there was a painful lump on the side of my head.

More important, there was a very painful thought in my head: those
young Communists on the block were right! The state and its police were
not neutral referees in a society of contending interests. They were on the
side of the rich and powerful. Free speech? Try it and the police will be
there with their horses, their clubs, their guns, to stop you.

From that moment on, I was no longer a liberal, a believer in the self-
correcting character of American democracy. I was a radical, believing
that something fundamental was wrong in this country—not just the existence of poverty amidst great wealth, not just the horrible treatment of
black people, but something rotten at the root. The situation required not
just a new president or new laws, but an uprooting of the old order, the
introduction of a new kind of society—cooperative, peaceful, egalitarian.

Perhaps I am exaggerating the importance of that one experience. But
I think not. I have come to believe that our lives can be turned in a different direction, our minds adopt a different way of thinking, because of
some significant though small event. That belief can be frightening or exhilarating, depending on whether you just contemplate the event or *do*
something with it.

The years following that experience in Times Square might be called
"my Communist years," but that phrase would be easy to misunderstand
because the word "Communist" conjures up Joseph Stalin and the gulags
of death and torture, the disappearance of free expression, the atmosphere of fear and trembling created in the Soviet Union, the ugly bureaucracy that lasted seventy years, pretending to be socialism.

None of that was in the minds or intentions of the young working-   55
class people I knew who called themselves Communists. Certainly not in
my mind. Little was known about the Soviet Union, except the romantic
image, popularized by people like the English theologian Hewlitt Johnson, the Dean of Canterbury. In his book *The Soviet Power,* distributed
widely by the Communist movement, he gave idealists disillusioned with
capitalism the vision they longed for, of a place where the country belonged to "the people," where everyone had work and free health care,
and women had equal opportunities with men, and a hundred different
ethnic groups were treated with respect.

The Soviet Union was this romantic blur, far away. What was close
at hand, visible, was that Communists were the leaders in organizing
working people all over the country. They were the most daring, risking
arrest and beatings to organize auto workers in Detroit, steel workers in
Pittsburgh, textile workers in North Carolina, fur and leather workers in
New York, longshoremen on the West Coast. They were the first to speak

up, more than that, to demonstrate—to chain themselves to factory gates and White House fences—when blacks were lynched in the South, when the "Scottsboro Boys" were being railroaded to prison in Alabama.[3]

My image of "a Communist" was not a Soviet bureaucrat but my friend Leon's father, a cabdriver who came home from work bruised and bloody one day, beaten up by his employer's goons (yes, that word was soon part of my vocabulary) for trying to organize his fellow cabdrivers into a union.

Everyone knew that the Communists were the first antifascists, protesting against Mussolini's invasion of Ethiopia and Hitler's persecution of the Jews. And, most impressive of all, it was the Communists, thousands of them, who volunteered to fight in Spain in the Abraham Lincoln Brigade, to join volunteers from all over the world to defend Madrid and the Spanish people against the army of Francisco Franco, which was given arms and airplanes by Germany and Italy.

Furthermore, some of the best people in the country were connected with the Communist movement in some way, heroes and heroines one could admire. There was Paul Robeson, the fabulous singer-actor-athlete whose magnificent voice could fill Madison Square Garden, crying out against racial injustice, against fascism. And literary figures (weren't Theodore Dreiser and W. E. B. Du Bois Communists?),[4] and talented, socially conscious Hollywood actors and writers and directors (yes, the Hollywood Ten, hauled before a congressional committee, defended by Humphrey Bogart and so many others).

True, in that movement, as in any other, you could see the righteousness leading to dogmatism, the closed circle of ideas impermeable to doubt, an intolerance of dissent by people who were the most persecuted of dissenters. But however imperfect, even repugnant, were particular policies, particular actions, there remained the purity of the ideal, represented in the theories of Karl Marx and the noble visions of many lesser thinkers and writers.   60

I remember my first reading of *The Communist Manifesto,* which Marx and Engels wrote when they too were young radicals; Marx was thirty, Engels twenty-eight. "The history of all hitherto existing society is the history of class struggle." That was undeniably true, verifiable in any reading of history. Certainly true for the United States, despite all the promises of the Constitution ("We the people of the United States . . ." and "No state shall deny . . . the equal protection of the laws").

---

[3]*"Scottsboro Boys":* When nine black youths were tried for the alleged rapes of two white women in Scottsboro, Alabama, in 1931, it set into motion two landmark rulings of the Supreme Court. The case became a major cause for the American Communist party.—EDS.

[4]*Theodore Dreiser* (1871–1945) is the author of such American classics as *Sister Carrie* and *An American Tragedy; W. E. B. Du Bois* (1868–1963) is the author of numerous nonfiction books, including *The Souls of Black Folk.*—EDS.

The analysis of capitalism by Marx and Engels made sense: capitalism's history of exploitation, its creation of extremes of wealth and poverty, even in the liberal "democracy" of this country. And their socialist vision was not one of dictatorship or bureaucracy but of a free society. Their "dictatorship of the proletariat" was to be a transitional phrase, the goal a classless society of true democracy, true freedom. A rational, just economic system would allow a short work day and leave everyone freedom and time to do as they liked — to write poetry, to be in nature, to play sports, to be truly human. Nationalism would be a thing of the past. People all over the world, of whatever race, of whatever continent, would live in peace and cooperation.

In my teenage reading, those ideas were kept alive by some of the finest writers in America. I read Upton Sinclair's *The Jungle;* work in the Chicago stockyards was the epitome of capitalist exploitation, and the vision of a new society in the last pages of the book is thrilling. John Steinbeck's *The Grapes of Wrath* was an eloquent cry against the conditions of life wherein the poor were expendable and any attempt on their part to change their lives was met with police clubs.

When I was eighteen, unemployed and my family desperate for help, I took a much-publicized Civil Service examination for a job in the Brooklyn Navy Yard. Thirty thousand young men (women applicants were unthinkable) took the exam, competing for a few hundred jobs. It was 1940, and New Deal programs had relieved but not ended the Depression. When the results were announced, four hundred of the applicants had gotten a score of 100 percent on the exam and would get jobs. I was one of them.

For me and my family it was a triumph. My salary would be $14.40   65
for a forty-hour week. I could give the family $10 a week and have the rest for lunch and spending money.

It was also an introduction into the world of heavy industry. I was to be an apprentice shipfitter for the next three years. I would work out on "the ways," a vast inclined surface at the edge of the harbor on which a battleship, the USS *Iowa,* was to be built. (Many years later, in the 1980s, I was called to be a witness at the Staten Island trial of pacifists who had demonstrated against the placement of nuclear weapons on a battleship docked there — the USS *Iowa.*)

I had no idea of the dimensions of a battleship. Stood on end, it would have been almost as tall as the Empire State Building. The keel had just been laid, and our job — thousands of us — was to put together the steel body and inner framework of the ship. It was hard, dirty, malodorous work. The smell caused by cutting galvanized steel with an acetylene torch is indescribable — only years later did we learn that the zinc released in such burning also causes cancer.

In the winter, icy blasts blew from the sea, and we wore thick gloves and helmets, and got occasional relief around the little fires used by the riveters. They heated their rivets in these fires until the rivets were glow-ing globules which they then pulled from the fire and pounded into the steel plates of the hull with huge hammers driven by compressed air. The sound was deafening.

In the summer, we sweated under our overalls and in our steel-tipped boots, and swallowed salt pills to prevent heat exhaustion. We did a lot of crawling around inside the tiny steel compartments of the "inner bottom," where smells and sounds were magnified a hundred times. We measured and hammered, and cut and welded, using the service of "burners" and "chippers."

No women workers. The skilled jobs were held by white men, who   70
were organized in A. F. of L. craft unions known to be inhospitable to blacks. The few blacks in the shipyard had the toughest, most physically demanding jobs, like riveting.

What made the job bearable was the steady pay and the accompanying dignity of being a workingman, bringing home money like my father. There was also the pride that we were doing something for the war effort. But most important for me was that I found a small group of friends, fellow apprentices—some of them shipfitters like myself, others shipwrights, machinists, pipefitters, sheetmetal workers—who were young radicals, determined to do something to change the world. No less.

We were excluded from the craft unions of the skilled workers, so we decided to organize the apprentices into a union, an association. We would act together to improve our working conditions, raise our pay, and create a camaraderie during and after working hours to add some fun to our workaday lives.

This we did, successfully, with three hundred young workers, and for me it was an introduction to actual participation in a labor movement. We were organizing a union and doing what working people had done through the centuries, creating little spaces of culture and friendship to make up for the dreariness of the work itself.

Four of us who were elected as officers of the Apprentice Association became special friends. We met one evening a week to read books on politics and economics and socialism, and talk about world affairs. These were years when some fellows our age were in college, but we felt we were getting a good education.

Still, I was glad to leave the shipyard and join the Air Force. And it   75
was while flying combat missions in Europe that I began a sharp turn in my political thinking, away from the romanticization of the Soviet Union that enveloped many radicals (and others, too), especially in the atmosphere of World War II and the stunning successes of the Red Army against the Nazi invaders.

The reason for this turn was my encounter, which I described earlier, with an aerial gunner on another crew who questioned whether the aims of the Allies—England, France, the United States, the Soviet Union— were really antifascist and democratic.

One book he gave me shook forever ideas I had held for years. This was *The Yogi and the Commissar,* by Arthur Koestler.[5] Koestler had been a Communist, had fought in Spain, but he had become convinced—and his factual evidence was powerful, his logic unshakable—that the Soviet Union, with its claim to be a socialist state, was a fraud. (After the war I read *The God That Failed,* in which writers whose integrity and dedication to justice I could not question—Richard Wright, Andrew Gide, Ignazio Silone, and Koestler, too—describe their loss of faith in the Communist movement and the Soviet Union.)

But disillusionment with the Soviet Union did not diminish my belief in socialism, any more than disillusionment with the United States government lessened my belief in democracy. It certainly did not affect my consciousness of *class,* of the difference in the way rich and poor lived in the United States, of the failure of the society to provide the most basic biological necessities—food, housing, health care—to tens of millions of people.

Oddly enough, when I became a second lieutenant in the Army Air Corps I got a taste of what life was like for the privileged classes—for now I had better clothes, better food, more money, higher status than I had in civilian life.

After the war, with a few hundred dollars in mustering-out money, and my uniform and medals packed away, I rejoined Roz. We were a young, happy married couple. But we could find no other place to live but a rat-infested basement apartment in Bedford-Stuyvesant ("rat-infested" is not a figure of speech—there was that day I walked into the bathroom and saw a large rat scurry up the water pipe back into the ceiling).

80

I was back in the working class, but needing a job. I tried going back to the Brooklyn Navy Yard, but it was hateful work with none of the compensating features of that earlier time. I worked as a waiter, as a ditch-digger, as a brewery worker, and collected unemployment insurance in between jobs. (I can understand very well the feeling of veterans of the Vietnam War, who were *important* when soldiers, coming back home with no jobs, no prospects, and without the glow that surrounded the veterans of World War II—a diminishing of their selves.) In the meantime, our daughter, Myla, was born.

At the age of twenty-seven, with a second child on the way, I began college as a freshman at New York University, under the G.I. Bill of Rights. That gave me four years of free college education and $120 a month, so that with Roz working part-time, with Myla and Jeff in nursery, with me working a night shift after school, we could survive.

---

[5]***Arthur Koestler*** (1905–1983), the Hungarian-born British thinker and novelist, had at one time been a member of the Communist party and had been rescued by the British while condemned to death during the Spanish Civil War. His major books, besides those mentioned here by Zinn, are *Darkness at Noon* and *The Act of Creation.*—EDS.

Whenever I hear that the government *must not* get involved in helping people, that this must be left to "private enterprise," I think of the G.I. Bill and its marvelous nonbureaucratic efficiency. There are certain necessities—housing, medical care, education—about which private enterprise gives not a hoot (supplying these to the poor is not profitable, and private enterprise won't act without *profit*).

Starting college coincided with a change in our lives: moving out of our miserable basement rooms into a low-income housing project in downtown Manhattan, on the East River. Four rooms, utilities included in the rent, no rats, no cockroaches, a few trees and a playground downstairs, a park along the river. We were happy.

While going to N.Y.U. and Columbia I worked the four-to-twelve   85
shift in the basement of a Manhattan warehouse, loading heavy cartons of clothing onto trailer trucks which would carry them to cities all over the country.

We were an odd crew, we warehouse loaders—a black man, a Honduran immigrant, two men somewhat retarded mentally, another veteran of the war (married, with children, he sold his blood to supplement his small pay check). With us for a while was a young man named Jeff Lawson whose father was John Howard Lawson, a Hollywood writer, one of the Hollywood Ten. There was another young fellow, a Columbia College student who was named after his grandfather, the socialist labor leader Daniel DeLeon. (I encountered him many years later; he was in a bad way mentally, and then I got word that he had laid down under his car in the garage and breathed in enough carbon monoxide to kill himself.)

We were all members of the union (District 65), which had a reputation of being "left-wing." But we, the truck-loaders, were more left than the union, which seemed hesitant to interfere with the loading operation of this warehouse.

We were angry about our working conditions, having to load outside on the sidewalk in bad weather with no rain or snow gear available to us. We kept asking the company for gear, with no results. One night, late, the rain began pelting down. We stopped work, said we would not continue unless we had a binding promise of rain gear.

The supervisor was beside himself. That truck had to get out that night to meet the schedule, he told us. He had no authority to promise anything. We said, "Tough shit. We're not getting drenched for the damned schedule." He got on the phone, nervously called a company executive at his home, interrupting a dinner party. He came back from the phone. "Okay, you'll get your gear." The next workday we arrived at the warehouse and found a line of shiny new raincoats and rainhats.

That was my world for the first thirty-three years of my life—the   90
world of unemployment and bad employment, of me and my wife leaving our two- and three-year-olds in the care of others while we went to school or to work, living most of that time in cramped and unpleasant

places, hesitating to call the doctor when the children were sick because we couldn't afford to pay him, finally taking the children to hospital clinics where interns could take care of them. This is the way a large part of the population lives, even in this, the richest country in the world. And when, armed with the proper degrees, I began to move out of that world, becoming a college professor, I never forgot that. I never stopped being class-conscious.

I note how our political leaders step gingerly around such expressions, how it seems the worst accusation one politician can make about another is that "he appeals to class hostility . . . he is setting class against class." Well, class has been set against class in the realities of life for a very long time, and the words will disappear only when the realities of inequity disappear.

It would be foolish for me to claim that class consciousness was simply the result of growing up poor and living the life of a poor kid and then the life of a hard-pressed young husband and father. I've met many people with similar backgrounds who developed a very different set of ideas about society, and many others, whose early lives were much different from mine but whose world-view is similar.

When I was chair of the history department at Spelman and had the power (even a *little power* can make people heady!) to actually hire one or two people, I invited Staughton Lynd, a brilliant young historian, graduate of Harvard and Columbia, to join the Spelman faculty. (We were introduced at a historians' meeting in New York, where Staughton expressed a desire to teach at a black college.)

The summer before Staughton Lynd came south, we met in New England and decided to climb a New Hampshire mountain (Mt. Monadnock) together and get acquainted. My two children, Myla and Jeff, came with us. They were thirteen and eleven. When we reached the summit, tired and hungry, we found the remains of a pack of cigarettes, and the four of us — all nonsmokers, it is fair to say — sat down cross-legged and puffed silently, pretending we were characters in *Treasure of the Sierra Madre.*[6]

That mountain-climbing conversation was illuminating. Staughton came from a background completely different from mine. His parents were quite famous professors at Columbia and Sarah Lawrence, Robert and Helen Lynd, authors of the sociological classic *Middletown*. Staughton had been raised in comfortable circumstances, had gone to Harvard and Columbia. And yet, as we went back and forth on every political issue under the sun — race, class, war, violence, nationalism, justice, fascism, capitalism, socialism, and more — it was clear that our social philosophies, our values, were extraordinarily similar.

95

----

[6]*Treasure of the Sierra Madre* (1948) is a film classic staring Humphrey Bogart. It was based on B. Traven's novel and directed by John Huston, who won Oscars for best direction and best screenplay. — EDS.

In the light of such experiences, traditional dogmatic "class analysis" cannot remain intact. But as dogma disintegrates, hope appears. Because it seems that human beings, whatever their backgrounds, are more open than we think, that their behaviour cannot be confidently predicted from their past, that we are all creatures vulnerable to new thoughts, new attitudes.

And while such vulnerability creates all sorts of possibilities, both good and bad, its very existence is exciting. It means that no human being should be written off, no change in thinking deemed impossible.

The Reader's Presence

1. Zinn begins the piece with a poem he wrote in his youth. How does the poem relate to the rest of the piece? Does it express something the essay itself cannot? If so, how so? If not, what would Zinn need to add to the essay to incorporate the impressions and emotions conveyed by the poem?

2. "The personal is political" was a watchword of the radical era of the sixties. How does Zinn's essay link the personal to the political, and vice-versa? How does the highly descriptive story of Zinn's father's progression through working-class jobs (paragraphs 3–7) enrich the reader's understanding of his political commitment? How might the essay read if presented from a more objective or general viewpoint? What would be lost or gained?

3. In the last two paragraphs of the essay, Zinn concludes with statements concerning humanity in general. Do his statements seem justified? Why or why not? Can you construct an opposing argument about the possibility of social change based on your own experience?

Part V

The Voices of Fiction: Eight Modern Short Stories

121

Raymond Carver

Popular Mechanics

Raymond Carver (1938–1988) is best known for his tightly crafted, spare, and often grim short stories. In fact, his mastery of dialogue and his fine eye for detail have made his collections of short stories best-sellers in the United States and abroad. These collections include Will You Please Be Quiet, Please? *(1976);* What We Talk about When We Talk about Love *(1981), in which "Popular Mechanics" can be found;* Cathedral *(1984); and* Where I'm Calling From *(1988). In 1993 Robert Altman made the critically acclaimed film* Short Cuts *based on a number of Carver's short stories.*

Describing the process of writing fiction, Carver says, "I never start with an idea. I always see something. I start with an image, a cigarette being put out in a jar of mustard, for instance, or the remains, the wreckage, of a dinner left on the table. Pop cans in the fireplace, that sort of thing. And a feeling goes with that. And that feeling seems to transport me back to that particular time and place, and the ambience of time. But it is the image, and the emotion that goes with that image—that's what's important."

For more information on Raymond Carver, see page 69.

Early that day the weather turned and the snow was melting into dirty water. Streaks of it ran down from the little shoulder-high window that faced the backyard. Cars slushed by on the street outside, where it was getting dark. But it was getting dark on the inside too.

He was in the bedroom pushing clothes into a suitcase when she came to the door.

I'm glad you're leaving! I'm glad you're leaving! she said. Do you hear?

He kept on putting his things into the suitcase.

Son of a bitch! I'm so glad you're leaving! She began to cry. You   5
can't even look me in the face, can you?

Then she noticed the baby's picture on the bed and picked it up.

He looked at her and she wiped her eyes and stared at him before turning and going back to the living room.

Bring that back, he said.

Just get your things and get out, she said.

He did not answer. He fastened the suitcase, put on his coat, looked   10
around the bedroom before turning off the light. Then he went out to the
living room.

She stood in the doorway of the little kitchen, holding the baby.

I want the baby, he said.

Are you crazy?

No, but I want the baby. I'll get someone to come by for his things.

You're not touching this baby, she said.   15

The baby had begun to cry and she uncovered the blanket from
around his head.

Oh, oh, she said, looking at the baby.

He moved toward her.

For God's sake! she said. She took a step back into the kitchen.

I want the baby.   20

Get out of here!

She turned and tried to hold the baby over in a corner behind the stove.

But he came up. He reached across the stove and tightened his hands
on the baby.

Let go of him, he said.

Get away, get away! she cried.   25

The baby was red-faced and screaming. In the scuffle they knocked
down a flowerpot that hung behind the stove.

He crowded her into the wall then, trying to break her grip. He held
on to the baby and pushed with all his weight.

Let go of him, he said.

Don't, she said. You're hurting the baby, she said.

I'm not hurting the baby, he said.   30

The kitchen window gave no light. In the near-dark he worked on her
fisted fingers with one hand and with the other hand he gripped the
screaming baby up under an arm near the shoulder.

She felt her fingers being forced open. She felt the baby going from her.

No! she screamed just as her hands came loose.

She would have it, this baby. She grabbed for the baby's other arm.
She caught the baby around the wrist and leaned back.

But he would not let go. He felt the baby slipping out of his hands   35
and he pulled back very hard.

In this manner, the issue was decided.

The Reader's Presence

1. Carver begins his story in the middle of the action, without properly introducing his characters or the story's setting. What clues
   do you find within the opening ten paragraphs as to the charac-

ters' natures and relationship? What questions remain? How does this lack of detail affect your reading of the story? How might a more detailed opening description affect your reading? Why might Carver have chosen this narrative technique? The story also ends on a note of mystery. What do you think has happened at the end?

2. In the first paragraph, Carver writes: "Cars slushed by on the street outside, where it was getting dark. But it was getting dark on the inside too." In the thirty-first paragraph he writes: "The kitchen window gave no light." How does this description of the objective factor of light enhance the story's mood and influence your understanding of the characters' subjective experience?

3. Carver writes his dialogue without quotation marks. Does this make the dialogue seem different from that in the usual short story? If so, in what way? Would the dialogue read differently for you with quotation marks? If so, describe the difference. How does the author's "voice" influence the way you hear the characters' voices?

122

Jamaica Kincaid

Girl

Jamaica Kincaid became a professional writer almost by accident. Living in New York City in the 1970s, she befriended one of the staff writers at the New Yorker *and began to accompany him as he conducted research for the "Talk of the Town" section. Before long, she discovered that she could write and that her writing impressed the editors of the magazine. When her first piece of nonfiction was published, Kincaid remembers, "That is when I realized what my writing was. My writing was the thing that I thought. Not something else. Just what I thought." After working as a staff writer at the* New Yorker *for four years, she began to turn to fiction. "Girl" is the first piece of fiction she published; it appeared in the* New Yorker *in 1978.*

For more information on Jamaica Kincaid, see page 130.

Wash the white clothes on Monday and put them on the stone heap; wash the color clothes on Tuesday and put them on the clothesline to dry; don't walk barehead in the hot sun; cook pumpkin fritters in very hot sweet oil; soak your little clothes right after you take them off; when buying cotton to make yourself a nice blouse, be sure that it doesn't have gum on it, because that way it won't hold up well after a wash; soak salt fish overnight before you cook it; is it true that you sing benna[1] in Sunday School?; always eat your food in such a way that it won't turn someone else's stomach; on Sundays try to walk like a lady and not like the slut you are so bent on becoming; don't sing benna in Sunday School; you mustn't speak to wharf-rat boys, not even to give directions; don't eat fruits on the street — flies will follow you; *but I don't sing benna on Sundays at all and never in Sunday School;* this is how to sew on a button; this is how to make a buttonhole for the button you have just sewed on; this is how to hem a dress when you see the hem coming down and so to prevent yourself from looking like the slut I know you are so bent on becoming; this is how you iron your father's khaki shirt so that it doesn't have a crease; this is how you iron your father's khaki pants so that they don't have a crease; this is how you grow okra — far from the house, because okra tree harbors red ants; when you are growing dasheen,[2] make sure it gets plenty of water or else it makes your throat itch when you are eating it; this is how you sweep a corner; this is how you sweep a whole house; this is how you sweep a yard; this is how you smile to someone you don't like too much; this is how you smile to someone you don't like at all; this is how you smile to someone you like completely; this is how you set a table for tea; this is how you set a table for dinner; this is how you set a table for dinner with an important guest; this is how you set a table for lunch; this is how you set a table for breakfast; this is how to behave in the presence of men who don't know you very well, and this way they won't recognize immediately the slut I have warned you against becoming; be sure to wash every day, even if it is with your own spit; don't squat down to play marbles — you are not a boy, you know; don't pick people's flowers — you might catch something; don't throw stones at blackbirds, because it might not be a blackbird at all; this is how to make a bread pudding; this is how to make doukona;[3] this is how to make pepper pot; this is how to make a good medicine for a cold; this is how to make a good medicine to throw away a child before it even becomes a child; this is how to catch a fish; this is how to throw back a fish you don't like, and that way something bad won't fall on you; this is how to bully a man; this is how a man bullies you; this is how to love a man, and if this doesn't work there are other ways, and if they don't work don't feel too bad about giving up; this is how to spit up in the air if you feel like it, and this is how to move quick so that it doesn't fall on you; this is how to make ends meet; always squeeze bread to make sure it's fresh; *but what if the baker won't let me feel the bread?;* you mean to say that after all you are really going to be the kind of woman who the baker won't let near the bread?

[1] *benna:* Popular calypso-like music. — EDS.
[2] *dasheen:* A starchy vegetable. — EDS.
[3] *doukona:* Cornmeal. — EDS.

The Reader's Presence

1. Whose voice dominates this story? To whom is the monologue addressed? What effect(s) does the speaker seek to have on the listener? Where does the speaker appear to have acquired her values? Categorize the kinds of advice you find in the story. Identify sentences in which one category of advice merges into another. How are the different kinds of advice alike, and to what extent are they contradictory?

2. "Girl" speaks only two lines, both of which are italicized. In each case, what prompts her to speak? What is the result? Stories generally create the expectation that at least one main character will undergo a change. What differences, if any, do you notice between her first and second lines of dialogue (and the replies she elicits), differences that might suggest that such a change has taken place? If so, in whom? Analyze the girl's character based not only on what she says but on what she hears (if one can assume that this monologue was not delivered all in one sitting, but is rather the distillation of years' worth of advice, as heard by the girl).

3. Discuss the role of gender in this story. What gender stereotypes are accepted and perpetuated by the main speaker? Look not only at the stereotypes that affect women, but also those that define the roles of men. Find the references to men and boys in the story. What can you infer about the males, who remain behind the scenes? What can you infer about the balance of power between the genders in the community in which "girl" is being raised? What can you infer about the author's (as opposed to the narrator's) attitude toward these gender issues?

THE WRITER AT WORK

Jamaica Kincaid on "Girl"

To many readers, "Girl" appears to be an odd and confusing short story. It's far shorter than most published stories and consists almost entirely of a monologue spoken by a mother to her daughter. Readers may wonder: "What makes this a story?" In the following passage from an interview with Jamaica Kincaid, Allan Varda asks the author some questions about this intriguing little story and discovers behind its composition a larger agenda than we might perceive from a single reading. Do Kincaid's answers to Varda's questions help you better understand what's happening in the story? In what ways? After considering the story and interview, you also might want to turn (or return) to Kincaid's essay, "Biography of a Dress" (see page 130) and see how they enhance its autobiographical and social significance.

AV: There is a litany of items in "Girl" from a mother to her daughter about what to do and what *not* to do regarding the elements of being "a nice young lady." Is this the way it was for you and other girls in Antigua?

JK: In a word, yes.

AV: Was that good or bad?

JK: I don't think it's the way I would tell my daughter, but as a mother I would tell her what I think would be best for her to be like. This mother in "Girl" was really just giving the girl an idea about the things she would need to be a self-possessed woman in the world.

AV: But you didn't take your mother's advice?   5

JK: No, because I had other ideas on how to be a self-possessed woman in the world. I didn't know that at the time. I only remember these things. What the mother in the story sees as aids to living in the world, the girl might see as extraordinary oppression, which is one of the things I came to see.

AV: Almost like she's Mother England.

JK: I was just going to say that. I've come to see that I've worked through the relationship of the mother and the girl to a relationship between Europe and the place that I'm from, which is to say, a relationship between the powerful and the powerless. The girl is powerless and the mother is powerful. The mother shows her how to be in the world, but at the back of her mind she thinks she never will get it. She's deeply skeptical that this child could ever grow up to be a self-possessed woman and in the end she reveals her skepticism; yet even within the skepticism is, of course, dismissal and scorn. So it's not unlike the relationship between the conquered and the conqueror.

123 _____

Joyce Carol Oates

Shopping

The novelist, essayist, playwright, and poet Joyce Carol Oates (b. 1938) has published over two dozen novels and countless collections of poems, essays, short stories, and plays. Currently teaching at Princeton, she has received nominations for nearly every prestigious literary prize in the United States, and at age thirty-one was the youngest author ever to receive the National Book Award for fiction, awarded for her novel them *(1969). Oates writes comfortably in many different styles, voices, and moods, but she is especially celebrated for her talent to conjure suspense and terror in the gothic tradition. Several of her recent titles demonstrate this talent:* Haunted: Tales of the Grotesque *(1995),* American Gothic Tales *(1996),* Zombie *(1996), and* The Collector of Hearts: New Tales of the Grotesque *(1998). Oates has also recently published* My Heart Laid Bare *(1998),* Man Crazy: A Novel *(1997), and* Broke Heart Blues *(1999). Henry Louis Gates Jr., comments about Oates that "a future archeologist equipped with only her oeuvre could easily piece together the whole of postwar America." "Shopping" can be found in* Heat and Other Stories *(1991).*

When asked what advice she might give to young writers, Oates replied, "Just to write. The literal practice of writing, putting words down, getting a first draft. If you get a first draft, then you start feeling a little surge of power. You feel kind of happy about it, so you'll go on to the second draft. . . . Have an open and free attitude because writing should be playful and fun."

An old ritual, Saturday morning shopping. Mother and daughter. Mrs. Dietrich and Nola. Shops in the village, stores and boutiques at the splendid Livingstone Mall on Route 12: Bloomingdale's, Saks, Lord & Taylor, Bonwit's, Neiman-Marcus, and the rest. Mrs. Dietrich would know her way around the stores blindfolded but there is always the surprise of lavish seasonal displays, extraordinary holiday sales, the openings of new stores at the mall like Laura Ashley, Paraphernalia. On one of their mall days Mrs. Dietrich and Nola would try to get there at mid-morning, have lunch around 1 P.M. at one or another of their favorite restaurants, shop for perhaps an hour after lunch, then come home. Sometimes the shopping trips were more successful than at other times, but you have to have faith, Mrs. Dietrich tells herself. Her interior voice is calm, neutral, free of irony. Even since her divorce her interior voice has been free of irony. You have to have faith.

Tomorrow morning Nola returns to school in Maine; today will be spent at the mall. Mrs. Dietrich has planned it for days—there are numerous things Nola needs, mainly clothes, a pair of good shoes; Mrs. Dietrich must buy a birthday present for one of her aunts; mother and daughter need the time together. At the mall, in such crowds of shoppers, moments of intimacy are possible as they rarely are at home. (Seventeen-year-old Nola, home on spring break for a brief eight days, seems always to be *busy*, always out with her *friends*, the trip to the mall has been postponed twice.) But Saturday, 10:30 A.M., they are in the car at last headed south on Route 12, a bleak March morning following a night of freezing rain; there's a metallic cast to the air and no sun anywhere in the sky but the light hurts Mrs. Dietrich's eyes just the same. "Does it seem as if spring will ever come? It must be twenty degrees colder up in Maine," she says. Driving in heavy traffic always makes Mrs. Dietrich nervous and she is overly sensitive to her daughter's silence, which seems deliberate, perverse, when they have so little time remaining together—not even a full day.

Nola asks politely if Mrs. Dietrich would like her to drive and Mrs. Dietrich says no, of course not, she's fine, it's only a few more miles and maybe traffic will lighten. Nola seems about to say something more, then thinks better of it. So much between them is precarious, chancy—but they've been kind to each other these past seven days. Nola's secrets remain her own and Mrs. Dietrich isn't going to pry; she's beyond that. She loves Nola with a fierce unreasoned passion stronger than any she felt for the man who had been her husband for thirteen years, certainly far stronger than any she ever felt for her own mother. Sometimes in weak despondent moods, alone, lonely, self-pitying, when she has had too much to drink, Mrs. Dietrich thinks she is in love with her daughter, but this is a thought she can't contemplate for long. And how Nola would snort in amused contempt, incredulous, mocking—"Oh, *Mother!*"—if she were told.

("Why do you make so much of things? Of people who don't seem to care about you?" Mr. Dietrich once asked. He had been speaking of one or another of their Livingstone friends, a woman in Mrs. Dietrich's circle; he hadn't meant to be insulting but Mrs. Dietrich was stung as if he'd slapped her.)

Mrs. Dietrich tries to engage her daughter in conversation of a harmless sort but Nola answers in monosyllables; Nola is rather tired from so many nights of partying with her friends, some of whom attend the local high school, some of whom are home for spring break from prep schools— Exeter, Lawrenceville, Concord, Andover, Portland. Late nights, but Mrs. Dietrich doesn't consciously lie awake waiting for Nola to come home; they've been through all that before. Now Nola sits beside her mother looking wan, subdued, rather melancholy. Thinking her private thoughts. She is wearing a bulky quilted jacket Mrs. Dietrich has never liked, the usual blue jeans, black calfskin boots zippered tightly to mid-calf. Her delicate profile, thick-lashed eyes. Mrs. Dietrich must resist the temptation to ask, Why are you so quiet, Nola? What are you thinking? They've been through all that before.

Route 12 has become a jumble of small industrial parks, high-rise office and apartment buildings, torn-up landscapes: mountains of raw earth, uprooted trees, ruts and ditches filled with muddy water. Everywhere are yellow bulldozers, earthmovers, construction workers operating cranes, ACREAGE FOR SALE signs. When Mr. and Mrs. Dietrich first moved out to Livingstone from the city sixteen years ago this stretch along Route 12 was quite attractive, mainly farmland, woods, a scattering of small suburban houses; now it has nearly all been developed. There is no natural sequence to what you see—buildings, construction work, leveled woods, the lavish grounds owned by Squibb. Though she has driven this route countless times, Mrs. Dietrich is never quite certain where the mall is and must be prepared for a sudden exit. She remembers getting lost the first several times, remembers the excitement she and her friends felt about the grand opening of the mall, stores worthy of serious shopping at last. Today is much the same. No, today is worse. Like Christmas

5

when she was a small child, Mrs. Dietrich thinks. She'd hoped so badly to be happy she'd felt actual pain, a constriction in her throat like crying.

"*Are* you all right, Nola? You've been so quiet all morning," Mrs. Dietrich asks, half scolding. Nola stirs from her reverie, says she's fine, a just perceptible edge to her reply, and for the remainder of the drive there's some stiffness between them. Mrs. Dietrich chooses to ignore it. In any case she is fully absorbed in driving—negotiating a tricky exit across two lanes of traffic, then the hairpin curve of the ramp, the numerous looping drives of the mall. Then the enormous parking lot, daunting to the inexperienced, but Mrs. Dietrich always heads for the area behind Lord & Taylor on the far side of the mall, Lot D; her luck holds and she finds a space close in. "Well, we made it," she says, smiling happily at Nola. Nola laughs in reply—what does a seventeen year-old's laughter *mean?*—but she remembers, getting out, to lock both doors on her side of the car. Even here at the Livingstone Mall unattended cars are no longer safe. The smile Nola gives Mrs. Dietrich across the car's roof is careless and beautiful and takes Mrs. Dietrich's breath away.

The March morning tastes of grit with an undercurrent of something acrid, chemical; inside the mall, beneath the first of the elegant brass-buttressed glass domes, the air is fresh and tonic, circulating from invisible vents. The mall is crowded, rather noisy—it *is* Saturday morning— but a feast for the eyes after that long trip on Route 12. Tall slender trees grow out of the mosaic-tiled pavement; there are beds of Easter lilies, daffodils, jonquils, tulips of all colors. There are cobblestone walkways, fountains illuminated from within, wide promenades as in an Old World setting. Mrs. Dietrich smiles with relief. She senses that Nola too is relieved, cheered. It's like coming home.

The shopping excursions began when Nola was a small child but did not acquire their special significance until she was twelve or thirteen years old and capable of serious, sustained shopping with her mother. Sometimes Mrs. Dietrich and Nola would shop with friends, another mother and daughter perhaps, sometimes Mrs. Dietrich invited one or two of Nola's school friends to join them, but she preferred to be alone with Nola and she believed Nola preferred to be alone with her. This was about the time when Mr. Dietrich moved out of the house and back into their old apartment building in the city—a separation, he'd called it initially, to give them perspective, though Mrs. Dietrich had no illusions about what "perspective" would turn out to entail—so the shopping trips were all the more significant. Not that Mrs. Dietrich and Nola spent very much money; they really didn't, *really* they didn't, when compared to friends and neighbors. And Mr. Dietrich rarely objected: the financial arrangement he made with Mrs. Dietrich was surprisingly generous.

At seventeen Nola is shrewd and discerning as a shopper, not easy to please, knowledgeable as a mature woman about certain aspects of

10

fashion, quality merchandise, good stores. She studies advertisements, she shops for bargains. Her closets, like Mrs. Dietrich's, are crammed, but she rarely buys anything that Mrs. Dietrich thinks shoddy or merely faddish. Up in Portland, at the academy, she hasn't as much time to shop, but when she is home in Livingstone it isn't unusual for her and her girlfriends to shop nearly every day. Sometimes she shops at the mall with a boyfriend—but she prefers girls. Like all her friends she has charge accounts at the better stores, her own credit cards, a reasonable allowance. At the time of their settlement Mr. Dietrich said guiltily that it was the least he could do for them: if Mrs. Dietrich wanted to work part-time, she could (she was trained, more or less, in public relations of a small-scale sort); if not, not. Mrs. Dietrich thought, It's the most you can do for us too.

Near Baumgarten's entrance mother and daughter see a disheveled woman sitting by herself on one of the benches. Without seeming to look at her, shoppers are making a discreet berth around her, a stream following a natural course. Nola, taken by surprise, stares. Mrs. Dietrich has seen the woman from time to time at the mall, always alone, smirking and talking to herself, frizzed gray hair in a tangle, puckered mouth. Always wearing the same black wool coat, a garment of fairly good quality but shapeless, rumpled, stained, as if she sleeps in it. She might be anywhere from forty to sixty years of age. Once Mrs. Dietrich saw her make menacing gestures at children who were teasing her, another time she'd seen the woman staring belligerently at *her*. A white paste had gathered in the corners of her mouth.

"My God, that poor woman," Nola says. "I didn't think there were people like her here—I mean, I didn't think they would allow it."

"She doesn't seem to cause any disturbance," Mrs. Dietrich says. "She just sits. Don't stare, Nola, she'll see you."

"You've seen her here before? Here?"

"A few times this winter."   15

"Is she always like that?"

"I'm sure she's harmless, Nola. She just *sits*."

Nola is incensed, her pale blue eyes like washed glass. "I'm sure *she's* harmless, Mother. It's the harm the poor woman has to endure that is the tragedy."

Mrs. Dietrich is surprised and a little offended by her daughter's passionate tone but she knows enough not to argue. They enter Baumgarten's, taking their habitual route. So many shoppers! So much merchandise! Dazzling displays of tulips, chrome, neon, winking lights, enormous painted Easter eggs in wicker baskets. Nola speaks of the tragedy of women like that woman—the tragedy of the homeless, the mentally disturbed: bag ladies out on the street, outcasts of an affluent society—but she's soon distracted by the busyness on all sides, the attractive items for sale. They take the escalator up to the third floor, to the Clubhouse Juniors department, where Nola often buys things. From there

they will move on to Young Collector, then to Act IV, then to Petite Corner, then one or another boutique and designer — Liz Claiborne, Christian Dior, Calvin Klein, Carlos Falchi, and the rest. And after Baumgarten's the other stores await, to be visited each in turn. Mrs. Dietrich
checks her watch and sees with satisfaction that there's just enough time
before lunch but not *too* much time. She gets ravenously hungry, shopping at the mall.

    Nola is efficient and matter-of-fact about shopping, though she acts   20
solely upon instinct. Mrs. Dietrich likes to watch her at a short distance,
holding items of clothing up to herself in the three-way mirrors, modeling
things she thinks especially promising. A twill blazer, a dress with
rounded shoulders and blouson jacket, a funky zippered jumpsuit in
white sailcloth, a pair of straight-leg Evan Picone pants, a green leather
vest: Mrs. Dietrich watches her covertly. At such times Nola is perfectly
content, fully absorbed in the task at hand; Mrs. Dietrich knows she isn't
thinking about anything that would distress her. (Like Mr. Dietrich's betrayal. Like Nola's difficulties with her friends. Like her difficulties at
school — as much as Mrs. Dietrich knows of them.) When Nola glances
in her mother's direction Mrs. Dietrich pretends to be examining clothes
for her own purposes. As if she's hardly aware of Nola. Once, at the mall,
perhaps in this very store in this very department, Nola saw Mrs. Dietrich
watching her and walked away angrily, and when Mrs. Dietrich caught
up with her she said, "I can't stand it, Mother." Her voice was choked
and harsh, a vein prominent in her forehead. "Let me go. For Christ's
sake will you let me go." Mrs. Dietrich didn't dare touch her though she
could see Nola was trembling. For a long terrible moment mother and
daughter stood side by side near a display of bright brash Catalina beach-
wear while Nola whispered, "Let me go. *Let me go.*" How the scene
ended Mrs. Dietrich can't recall — it erupts in an explosion of light, like a
bad dream — but she knows better than to risk it again.

    Difficult to believe that girl standing so poised and self-assured in
front of the three-way mirror was once a plain, rather chunky, unhappy
child. She'd been unpopular at school. Overly serious. Anxious. Quick to
tears. Aged eleven she hid herself away in her room for hours at a time,
reading, drawing pictures, writing little stories she could sometimes be
prevailed upon to read aloud to her mother, sometimes even to her father,
though she dreaded his judgment. She went through a "scientific" phase a
little later; Mrs. Dietrich remembers an ambitious bas-relief map of North
America, meticulous illustrations for "photosynthesis," a pastel drawing
of an eerie ball of fire labeled RED GIANT (a dying star?), which won a
prize in a state competition for junior high students. Then for a season it
was stray facts Nola confronted them with, often at the dinner table. Interrupting her parents' conversation to say brightly, "Did you know that
Nero's favorite color was green? He carried a giant emerald and held it
up to his eye to watch Christians being devoured by lions." And, "Did

you ever hear of the raving ghosts of Siberia, with their mouths always open, starving for food, screaming?" And once at a large family gathering, "Did you all know that last week downtown a little baby's nose was chewed off by rats in his crib — a little *black* baby?" Nola meant only to call attention to herself, but you couldn't blame her listeners for being offended. They stared at her, not knowing what to say. What a strange child! What queer glassy-pale eyes! Mr. Dietrich told her curtly to leave the table; he'd had enough of the game she was playing and so had everyone else.

Nola stared at him, her eyes filling with tears. Game?

When they were alone Mr. Dietrich said angrily to Mrs. Dietrich, "Can't you control her in front of other people, at least?" Mrs. Dietrich was angry, too, and frightened. She said, "I *try*."

They sent her off aged fourteen to the Portland Academy up in Maine, and without their help she matured into a girl of considerable beauty. A heart-shaped face, delicate features, glossy red-brown hair scissor-cut to her shoulders. Five feet seven inches tall weighing less than one hundred pounds, the result of constant savage dieting. (Mrs. Dietrich, who has weight problems herself, doesn't dare inquire as to details. They've been through that already.) All the girls sport flat bellies, flat buttocks, jutting pelvic bones. Many, like Nola, are wound tight, high-strung as pedigreed dogs, whippets for instance, the breed that lives for running. Thirty days after they'd left her at the Portland Academy, Nola telephoned home at 11 P.M. one Sunday giggly and high, telling Mrs. Dietrich she adored the school she adored her suitemates she adored most of her teachers particularly her riding instructor Terri, Terri the Terrier they called the woman because she was so fierce, such a character, eyes that bore right through your skull, wore belts with the most amazing silver buckles! Nola loved Terri but she wasn't *in* love — there's a difference!

Mrs. Dietrich broke down weeping, *that* time.   25

Now of course Nola has boyfriends. Mrs. Dietrich has long since given up trying to keep track of their names. And, in any case, the Paul of this spring isn't necessarily the Paul of last November, nor are all the boys necessarily students at the academy. There is even one "boy" — or young man — who seems to be married: who seems to be, in fact, one of the junior instructors at the school. (Mrs. Dietrich does not eavesdrop on her daughter's telephone conversations but there are things she cannot help overhearing.) Is your daughter on the pill? the women in Mrs. Dietrich's circle asked one another for a while, guiltily, surreptitiously. Now they no longer ask.

But Nola has announced recently that she loathes boys — she's fed up.

She's never going to get married. She'll study languages in college, French, Italian, something exotic like Arabic, go to work for the American foreign service. Unless she drops out of school altogether to become a model.

"Do you think I'm too fat, Mother?" she asks frequently, worriedly, standing in front of the mirror, twisted at the waist to reveal her small round belly which, it seems, can't help being round: she bloats herself on diet Cokes all day long. "Do you think it *shows?*"

When Mrs. Dietrich was pregnant with Nola she'd been twenty-nine 30 years old and she and Mr. Dietrich had tried to have a baby for nearly five years. She'd lost hope, begun to despise herself; then suddenly it happened: like grace. Like happiness swelling so powerfully it can barely be contained. I can hear its heartbeat! her husband exclaimed. He'd been her lover then, young, vigorous, dreamy. Caressing the rock-hard belly, splendid white tight-stretched skin, that roundness like a warm pulsing melon. Never before so happy, and never since. Husband and wife. One flesh. Mr. Dietrich gave Mrs. Dietrich a reproduction on stiff glossy paper of Dante Gabriel Rossetti's *Beata Beatrix,* embarrassed, apologetic, knowing it was sentimental and perhaps a little silly but that was how he thought of her—so beautiful, rapturous, pregnant with their child. Her features were ordinarily pretty, her wavy brown hair cut short; Mrs. Dietrich looked nothing like the extraordinary woman in Rossetti's painting in her transport of ecstasy but she was immensely flattered and moved by her husband's gift, knowing herself adored, worthy of adoration. She told no one, but she knew the baby was to be a girl. It would be herself again, reborn and this time perfect.

Not until years later did she learn by chance that the woman in Rossetti's painting was in fact his dead wife Lizzy Siddal, who had killed herself with an overdose of laudanum after the stillbirth of their only child.

"Oh, Mother, isn't it *beautiful!*" Nola exclaims.

It is past noon. Past twelve-thirty. Mrs. Dietrich and Nola have made the rounds of a half dozen stores, traveled countless escalators, one clothing department has blended into the next and the chic smiling saleswomen have become indistinguishable, and Mrs. Dietrich is beginning to feel the urgent need for a glass of white wine. Just a glass. "Isn't it beautiful? It's *perfect,*" Nola says. Her eyes glow with pleasure, her smooth skin is radiant. Modeling in the three-way mirror a queer little yellow-and-black striped sweater with a ribbed waist, punk style, mock cheap (though the sweater by Sergio Valente, even "drastically reduced," is certainly not cheap), Mrs. Dietrich feels the motherly obligation to register a mild protest, knowing Nola will not hear. She must have it and will have it. She'll wear it a few times, then retire it to the bottom of a drawer with so many other novelty sweaters, accumulated since sixth grade. (She's like her mother in that regard—can't bear to throw anything away. Clothes, shoes, cosmetics, records; once bought by Nola Dietrich they are hers forever, crammed in drawers and closets.)

"*Isn't* it beautiful?" Nola demands, studying her reflection in the mirror.

Mrs. Dietrich pays for the sweater on her charge account. 35

Next they buy Nola a good pair of shoes. And a handbag to go with them. In Paraphernalia where rock music blasts overhead and Mrs. Dietrich stands to one side, rather miserable, Nola chats companionably with two girls—tall, pretty, cutely made up—she'd gone to public school in Livingstone with, says afterward with an upward rolling of her eyes, "God, I was afraid they'd latch onto us!" Mrs. Dietrich has seen women friends and acquaintances of her own in the mall this morning but has shrunk from being noticed, not wanting to share her daughter with anyone. She has a sense of time passing ever more swiftly, cruelly.

Nola wants to try on an outfit in Paraphernalia, just for fun, a boxy khaki-colored jacket with matching pants, fly front, zippers, oversized buttons, so aggressively ugly it must be chic, yes of course it *is* chic, "drastically reduced" from $245 to $219. An import by Julio Vicente and Mrs. Dietrich can't reasonably disapprove of Julio Vicente, can she. She watches Nola preening in the mirror, watches other shoppers watching her. My daughter. Mine. But of course there is no connection between them, they don't even resemble each other. A seventeen-year-old, a forty-seven-year old. When Nola is away she seems to forget her mother entirely—doesn't telephone, certainly doesn't write. It's the way all their daughters are, Mrs. Dietrich's friends tell her. It doesn't *mean* anything. Mrs. Dietrich thinks how when she was carrying Nola, those nine long months, they'd been completely happy—not an instant's doubt or hesitation. The singular weight of the body. A state like trance you are tempted to mistake for happiness because the body is incapable of thinking, therefore incapable of anticipating change. Hot rhythmic blood, organs packed tight and moist, the baby upside down in her sac in her mother's belly, always present tense, always *now*. It was a shock when the end came so abruptly, but everyone told Mrs. Dietrich she was a natural mother, praised and pampered her. For a while. Then of course she'd had her baby, her Nola. Even now Mrs. Dietrich can't really comprehend the experience. *Giving birth. Had a baby. Was born.* Mere words, absurdly inadequate. She knows no more of how love ends than she knew as a child, she knows only of how love begins—in the belly, in the womb, where it is always present tense.

The morning's shopping has been quite successful, but lunch at La Crêperie doesn't go well. For some reason—surely there can be no reason?—lunch doesn't go well at all.

La Crêperie is Nola's favorite mall restaurant, always amiably crowded, bustling, a simulated sidewalk café with red-striped umbrellas, wrought-iron tables and chairs, menus in French, music piped in overhead. Mrs. Dietrich's nerves are chafed by the pretense of gaiety, the noise, the openness onto one of the mall's busy promenades where at any minute a familiar face might emerge, but she is grateful for her glass of chilled white wine—isn't it red wine that gives you headaches, hangovers?—white wine is safe. She orders a small tossed salad and a creamed chicken crêpe and devours it hungrily—she *is* hungry—while Nola picks at her seafood crêpe with a disdainful look. A familiar scene: mother watching while daughter pushes food around on her plate. Suddenly Nola is tense, moody, corners of her mouth downturned. Mrs. Dietrich wants to ask, What's wrong? She wants to ask, Why are you unhappy? She wants to smooth Nola's hair back from her forehead, check to see if her forehead is overly warm, wants to hug her close, hard. Why, why? What did I do wrong? Why do you hate me?

Calling the Portland Academy a few weeks ago Mrs. Dietrich suddenly lost control, began crying. She hadn't been drinking and she hadn't known she was upset. A girl unknown to her, one of Nola's suitemates, was saying, "Please, Mrs. Dietrich, it's all right, I'm sure Nola will call you back later tonight—or tomorrow, Mrs. Dietrich? I'll tell her you called, all right, Mrs. Dietrich?" as embarrassed as if Mrs. Dietrich had been her own mother.   40

How love begins. How love ends.

Mrs. Dietrich orders a third glass of wine. This is a celebration of sorts, isn't it? Their last shopping trip for a long time. But Nola resists, Nola isn't sentimental. In casual defiance of Mrs. Dietrich she lights up a cigarette— yes, Mother, Nola has said ironically, since *you* stopped smoking *everybody* is supposed to stop—and sits with her arms crossed, watching streams of shoppers pass. Mrs. Dietrich speaks lightly of practical matters, tomorrow morning's drive to the airport and will Nola telephone when she gets to Portland to let Mrs. Dietrich know she has arrived safely? La Crêperie opens onto an atrium three stories high, vast, airy, lit with artificial sunlight, tastefully decorated with trees, potted spring flowers, a fountain, a gigantic white Easter bunny, cleverly mechanized, atop a nest of brightly painted wooden eggs. The bunny has an animated tail, an animated nose; paws, ears, eyes that move. Children stand watching it, screaming with excitement, delight. Mrs. Dietrich notes that Nola's expression is one of faint contempt and says, "It *is* noisy here, isn't it?"

"Little kids have all the fun," Nola says.

Then with no warning—though of course she'd been planning this all along—Nola brings up the subject of a semester in France, in Paris and Rouen, the fall semester of her senior year it would be; she has put in her application, she says, and is waiting to hear if she's been accepted. She smokes her cigarette calmly, expelling smoke from her nostrils in a way Mrs. Dietrich thinks particularly coarse. Mrs. Dietrich, who believed that particular topic was finished, takes care to speak without emotion. "I just don't think it's a very practical idea right now, Nola," she says. "We've been through it, haven't we? I—"

"I'm going," Nola says.   45

"The extra expense, for one thing. Your father—"

"If I get accepted, I'm going."

"Your father—"

"The hell with him too."

Mrs. Dietrich would like to slap her daughter's face. Bring tears to   50
those steely eyes. But she sits stiff, turning her wineglass between her
fingers, patient, calm; she's heard all this before; she says, "Surely this
isn't the best time to discuss it, Nola."

Mrs. Dietrich is afraid her daughter will leave the restaurant, simply
walk away; that has happened before and if it happens today she doesn't
know what she will do. But Nola sits unmoving, her face closed, impassive. Mrs. Dietrich feels her quickened heartbeat. It's like seeing your own
life whirling in a sink, in a drain, one of those terrible dreams in which
you're paralyzed—the terror of losing her daughter. Once after one of
their quarrels Mrs. Dietrich told a friend of hers, the mother too of a
teenaged daughter, "I just don't know her any longer; how can you keep
living with someone you don't know?" and the woman said, "Eventually
you can't."

Nola says, not looking at Mrs. Dietrich, "Why don't we talk about it,
Mother."

"Talk about what?" Mrs. Dietrich asks.

"You know."

"The semester in France? Again?"   55

"No."

"What, then?"

"You *know*."

"I don't know, really. Really!" Mrs. Dietrich smiles, baffled. She feels
the corners of her eyes pucker white with strain.

Nola says, sighing, "How exhausting it is."   60

"How *what?*"

"How exhausting it is."

"What is?"

"You and me."

"What?"   65

"Being together."

"Being together how?"

"The two of us, like this—"

"But we're hardly ever together, Nola," Mrs. Dietrich says.

Her expression is calm but her voice is shaking. Nola turns away,   70
covering her face with a hand; for a moment she looks years older than her
age—in fact exhausted. Mrs. Dietrich sees with pity that her daughter's
skin is fair and thin and dry—unlike her own, which tends to be oily—it
will wear out before she's forty. Mrs. Dietrich reaches over to squeeze her
hand. The fingers are limp, ungiving. "You're going back to school tomorrow, Nola," she says. "You won't come home again until June twelfth. And
you probably will go to France—if your father consents."

Nola gets to her feet, drops her cigarette to the flagstone terrace, and
grinds it out beneath her boot. A dirty thing to do, Mrs. Dietrich thinks,
considering there's an ashtray right on the table, but she says nothing. She
dislikes La Crêperie anyway.

Nola laughs, showing her lovely white teeth. "Oh, the hell with him," she says. "Fuck Daddy, right?"

They separate for an hour, Mrs. Dietrich to Neiman-Marcus to buy a birthday gift for her elderly aunt, Nola to the trendy new boutique Pour Vous. By the time Mrs. Dietrich rejoins her daughter she's quite angry, blood beating hot and hard and measured in resentment; she has had time to relive old quarrels between them, old exchanges, stray humiliating memories of her marriage as well; these last-hour disagreements are the cruelest and they are Nola's specialty. She locates Nola in the rear of the boutique amid blaring rock music, flashing neon lights, chrome-edged mirrors, her face still hard, closed, prim, pale. She stands beside another teenaged girl, looking in a desultory way through a rack of blouses, shoving the hangers roughly along, taking no care when a blouse falls to the floor. Mrs. Dietrich remembers seeing Nola slip a pair of panty hose into her purse in a village shop because, she said afterward, the saleswoman was so damned slow coming to wait on her; fortunately Mrs. Dietrich was there, took the panty hose right out, and replaced it on the counter. No big deal, Mother, Nola said, don't have a stroke or something. Seeing Nola now, Mrs. Dietrich is charged with hurt, rage; the injustice of it, she thinks, the cruelty of it, and why, and why? And as Nola glances up, startled, not prepared to see her mother in front of her, their eyes lock for an instant and Mrs. Dietrich stares at her with hatred. Cold calm clear unmistakable hatred. She is thinking, Who are *you?* What have I to do with *you?* I don't know *you,* I don't love *you,* why should I?

Has Nola seen, heard? She turns aside as if wincing, gives the blouses a final dismissive shove. Her eyes look tired, the corners of her mouth downturned. Anxious, immediately repentant, Mrs. Dietrich asks if she has found anything worth trying on. Nola says with a shrug, "Not a thing, Mother."

On their way out of the mall Mrs. Dietrich and Nola see the disheveled woman in the black coat again, this time sitting prominently on a concrete ledge in front of Lord & Taylor's busy main entrance, shopping bag at her feet, shabby purse on the ledge beside her. She is shaking her head in a series of annoyed twitches as if arguing with someone but her hands are loose, palms up, in her lap. Her posture is unfortunate— she sits with her knees parted, inner thighs revealed, fatty, dead white, the tops of cotton stockings rolled tight cutting into the flesh. Again, streams of shoppers are making a careful berth around her. Alone among them Nola hesitates, seems about to approach the woman—Please don't, Nola, please! Mrs. Dietrich thinks—then changes her mind and keeps on walking. Mrs. Dietrich murmurs, "Isn't it a pity, poor thing, don't you wonder where she lives, who her family is?" but Nola doesn't reply. Her pace through the first floor of Lord & Taylor is so rapid that Mrs. Dietrich can barely keep up.

But she's upset. Strangely upset. As soon as they are in the car, packages and bags in the back seat, she begins crying.

It's childish helpless crying, as though her heart is broken. But Mrs. Dietrich knows it isn't broken; she has heard these very sobs before. Many times before. Still she comforts her daughter, embraces her, hugs her hard, hard. A sudden fierce passion. Vehemence. "Nola honey, Nola dear, what's wrong, dear? everything will be all right, dear," she says, close to weeping herself. She would embrace Nola even more tightly except for the girl's quilted jacket, that bulky L. L. Bean thing she has never liked, and Nola's stubborn lowered head. Nola has always been ashamed, crying, frantic to hide her face. Strangers are passing close by the car, curious, staring. Mrs. Dietrich wishes she had a cloak to draw over her daughter and herself, so that no one would see.

The Reader's Presence

1. The story is related through the perspective of Mrs. Dietrich, yet we learn more about her and Nola than she herself knows. Reread the second paragraph. Where and how does Oates's "voice" seem to diverge from Mrs. Dietrich's? Where is the distinction unclear?

2. Rather than describing her characters, Oates reveals them through details of their daily lives. Reread paragraphs 6 and 7. What sort of person does Mrs. Dietrich seem to be? What sort of life does she seem to lead? What kinds of values does she seem to hold? Which small clues alert you to the "bigger picture"?

3. What might the painting *Beata Beatrix* (paragraphs 30 and 31) symbolize? What might the homeless woman (paragraphs 11–19 and 75) symbolize? What do these external figures reveal about the inner lives of the story's main characters?

124

Flannery O'Connor

A Good Man Is Hard to Find

Flannery O'Connor (1925–1964) was born in Savannah, Georgia, the only child of devout Catholic parents. At the age of thirteen, O'Connor moved with her parents to her mother's ancestral home in Milledgeville, Georgia, after her father became terminally ill with lupus. In 1945 she received an A.B. degree from

Georgia State College for Women, where she contributed regularly to the school's literary magazine. While earning an M.F.A. from the Writers' Workshop at the University of Iowa, O'Connor published her first short story. "The Geranium" in 1946. After graduation O'Connor was a resident at Yaddo, an artists' retreat in New York, and lived in New York City and in Connecticut until 1951, when she was diagnosed with lupus and returned to Georgia for treatment. She and her mother moved a short distance from Milledgeville to their family farm, Andalusia, where O'Connor lived until her death at the age of thirty-nine, raising peafowl, painting, and writing daily. During her short yet distinguished life, O'Connor published two novels, Wise Blood *(1952) and* The Violent Bear It Away *(1960), and a collection of short stories,* A Good Man Is Hard to Find *(1955). A book of essays,* Mystery and Manners *(1969); two other short story collections,* Everything That Rises Must Converge *(1965) and* The Complete Stories of Flannery O'Connor *(1971), winner of a National Book Award; and a collection of letters,* The Habit of Being *(1979), were published posthumously.*

The grandmother didn't want to go to Florida. She wanted to visit some of her connections in east Tennessee and she was seizing at every chance to change Bailey's mind. Bailey was the son she lived with, her only boy. He was sitting on the edge of his chair at the table, bent over the orange sports section of the *Journal*. "Now look here, Bailey," she said, "see here, read this," and she stood with one hand on her thin hip and the other rattling the newspaper at his bald head. "Here this fellow that calls himself The Misfit is aloose from the Federal Pen and headed toward Florida and you read here what it says he did to these people. Just you read it. I wouldn't take my children in any direction with a criminal like that aloose in it. I couldn't answer to my conscience if I did."

Bailey didn't look up from his reading so she wheeled around then and faced the children's mother, a young woman in slacks, whose face was as broad and innocent as a cabbage and was tied around with a green head-kerchief that had two points on the top like a rabbit's ears. She was sitting on the sofa, feeding the baby his apricots out of a jar. "The children have been to Florida before," the old lady said. "You all ought to take them somewhere else for a change so they would see different parts of the world and be broad. They never have been to east Tennessee."

The children's mother didn't seem to hear her but the eight-year-old boy, John Wesley, a stocky child with glasses, said, "If you don't want to go to Florida, why dontcha stay at home?" He and the little girl, June Star, were reading the funny papers on the floor.

"She wouldn't stay at home to be queen for a day," June Star said without raising her yellow head.

"Yes and what would you do if this fellow, The Misfit, caught you?" the grandmother asked.

"I'd smack his face," John Wesley said.

"She wouldn't stay at home for a million bucks," June Star said. "Afraid she'd miss something. She has to go everywhere we go."

5

"All right, Miss," the grandmother said. "Just remember that the next time you want me to curl your hair."

June Star said her hair was naturally curly.

The next morning the grandmother was the first one in the car, ready 10
to go. She had her big black valise that looked like the head of a hippopotamus in one corner, and underneath it she was hiding a basket with Pitty Sing, the cat, in it. She didn't intend for the cat to be left alone in the house for three days because he would miss her too much and she was afraid he might brush against one of the gas burners and accidentally asphyxiate himself. Her son, Bailey, didn't like to arrive at a motel with a cat.

She sat in the middle of the back seat with John Wesley and June Star on either side of her. Bailey and the children's mother and the baby sat in front and they left Atlanta at eight forty-five with the mileage on the car at 55890. The grandmother wrote this down because she thought it would be interesting to say how many miles they had been when they got back. It took them twenty minutes to reach the outskirts of the city.

The old lady settled herself comfortably, removing her white cotton gloves and putting them up with her purse on the shelf in front of the back window. The children's mother still had on slacks and still had her head tied up in a green kerchief, but the grandmother had on a navy blue straw sailor hat with a bunch of white violets on the brim and a navy blue dress with a small white dot in the print. Her collars and cuffs were white organdy trimmed with lace and at her neckline she had pinned a purple spray of cloth violets containing a sachet. In case of an accident, anyone seeing her dead on the highway would know at once that she was a lady.

She said she thought it was going to be a good day for driving, neither too hot nor too cold, and she cautioned Bailey that the speed limit was fifty-five miles an hour and that the patrolmen hid themselves behind billboards and small clumps of trees and sped out after you before you had a chance to slow down. She pointed out interesting details of the scenery: Stone Mountain; the blue granite that in some places came up to both sides of the highway; the brilliant red clay banks slightly streaked with purple; and the various crops that made rows of green lace-work on the ground. The trees were full of silver-white sunlight and the meanest of them sparkled. The children were reading comic magazines and their mother had gone back to sleep.

"Let's go through Georgia fast so we won't have to look at it much," John Wesley said.

"If I were a little boy," said the grandmother, "I wouldn't talk about 15
my native state that way. Tennessee has the mountains and Georgia has the hills."

"Tennessee is just a hillbilly dumping ground," John Wesley said, "and Georgia is a lousy state too."

"You said it," June Star said.

"In my time," said the grandmother, folding her thin veined fingers, "children were more respectful of their native states and their parents and everything else. People did right then. Oh look at the cute little pickaninny!" she said and pointed to a Negro child standing in the door of a shack. "Wouldn't that make a picture, now?" she asked and they all turned and looked at the little Negro out of the back window. He waved.

"He didn't have any britches on," June Star said.

"He probably didn't have any," the grandmother explained. "Little   20
niggers in the country don't have things like we do. If I could paint, I'd paint that picture," she said.

The children exchanged comic books.

The grandmother offered to hold the baby and the children's mother passed him over the front seat to her. She set him on her knee and bounced him and told him about the things they were passing. She rolled her eyes and screwed up her mouth and stuck her leathery thin face into his smooth bland one. Occasionally he gave her a faraway smile. They passed a large cotton field with five or six graves fenced in the middle of it, like a small island. "Look at the graveyard!" the grandmother said, pointing it out. "That was the old family burying ground. That belonged to the plantation."

"Where's the plantation?" John Wesley asked.

"Gone With the Wind," said the grandmother. "Ha. Ha."

When the children finished all the comic books they had brought, they   25
opened the lunch and ate it. The grandmother ate a peanut butter sandwich and an olive and would not let the children throw the box and the paper napkins out the window. When there was nothing else to do they played a game by choosing a cloud and making the other two guess what shape it suggested. John Wesley took one the shape of a cow and June Star guessed a cow and John Wesley said, no, an automobile, and June Star said he didn't play fair, and they began to slap each other over the grandmother.

The grandmother said she would tell them a story if they would keep quiet. When she told a story, she rolled her eyes and waved her head and was very dramatic. She said once when she was a maiden lady she had been courted by a Mr. Edgar Atkins Teagarden from Jasper, Georgia. She said he was a very good-looking man and a gentleman and that he brought her a watermelon every Saturday afternoon with his initials cut in it, E. A. T. Well, one Saturday, she said, Mr. Teagarden brought the watermelon and there was nobody at home and he left it on the front porch and returned in his buggy to Jasper, but she never got the watermelon, she said, because a nigger boy ate it when he saw the initials, E. A. T.! This story tickled John Wesley's funny bone and he giggled and giggled but June Star didn't think it was any good. She said she wouldn't marry a man that just brought her a watermelon on Saturday. The grandmother said she would have done well to marry Mr. Teagarden because he was a gentleman and had bought Coca-Cola stock when it first came out and that he had died only a few years ago, a very wealthy man.

They stopped at The Tower for barbecued sandwiches. The Tower was a part stucco and part wood filling station and dance hall set in a clearing outside of Timothy. A fat man named Red Sammy Butts ran it and there were signs stuck here and there on the building and for miles up and down the highway saying, TRY RED SAMMY'S FAMOUS BARBE-CUE. NONE LIKE FAMOUS RED SAMMY'S! RED SAM! THE FAT BOY WITH THE HAPPY LAUGH! A VETERAN! RED SAMMY'S YOUR MAN!

Red Sammy was lying on the bare ground outside The Tower with his head under a truck while a gray monkey about a foot high, chained to a small chinaberry tree, chattered nearby. The monkey sprang back into the tree and got on the highest limb as soon as he saw the children jump out of the car and run toward him.

Inside, The Tower was a long dark room with a counter at one end and tables at the other and dancing space in the middle. They all sat down at a board table next to the nickelodeon and Red Sam's wife, a tall burnt-brown woman with hair and eyes lighter than her skin, came and took their order. The children's mother put a dime in the machine and played "The Tennessee Waltz," and the grandmother said that tune always made her want to dance. She asked Bailey if he would like to dance but he only glared at her. He didn't have a naturally sunny disposition like she did and trips made him nervous. The grandmother's brown eyes were very bright. She swayed her head from side to side and pretended she was dancing in her chair. June Star said play something she could tap to so the children's mother put in another dime and played a fast number and June Star stepped out onto the dance floor and did her tap routine.

"Ain't she cute?" Red Sam's wife said, leaning over the counter.   30
"Would you like to come be my little girl?"

"No I certainly wouldn't," June Star said. "I wouldn't live in a broken-down place like this for a million bucks!" and she ran back to the table.

"Ain't she cute?" the woman repeated, stretching her mouth politely.

"Aren't you ashamed?" hissed the grandmother.

Red Sam came in and told his wife to quit lounging on the counter and hurry up with these people's order. His khaki trousers reached just to his hip bones and his stomach hung over them like a sack of meal swaying under his shirt. He came over and sat down at a table nearby and let out a combination sigh and yodel. "You can't win," he said. "You can't win," and he wiped his sweating red face off with a gray handkerchief. "These days you don't know who to trust," he said. "Ain't that the truth?"

"People are certainly not nice like they used to be," said the grand-   35
mother.

"Two fellers come in here last week," Red Sammy said, "driving a Chrysler. It was a old beat-up car, but it was a good one and these boys looked all right to me. Said they worked at the mill and you know I let them fellers charge the gas they bought? Now why did I do that?"

"Because you're a good man!" the grandmother said at once.

"Yes'm, I suppose so," Red Sam said as if he were struck with this answer.

His wife brought the orders, carrying the five plates all at once without a tray, two in each hand and one balanced on her arm. "It isn't a soul in this green world of God's that you can trust," she said. "And I don't count nobody out of that, not nobody," she repeated, looking at Red Sammy.

"Did you read about that criminal, The Misfit, that's escaped?" asked the grandmother. 40

"I wouldn't be a bit surprised if he didn't attact this place right here," said the woman. "If he hears about it being here, I wouldn't be none surprised to see him. If he hears it's two cent in the cash register, I wouldn't be a tall surprised if he . . ."

"That'll do," Red Sam said. "Go bring these people their Co'-Colas," and the woman went off to get the rest of the order.

"A good man is hard to find," Red Sammy said. "Everything is getting terrible. I remember the day you could go off and leave your screen door unlatched. Not no more."

He and the grandmother discussed better times. The old lady said that in her opinion Europe was entirely to blame for the way things were now. She said the way Europe acted you would think we were made of money and Red Sam said it was no use talking about it, she was exactly right. The children ran outside into the white sunlight and looked at the monkey in the lacy chinaberry tree. He was busy catching fleas on himself and biting each one carefully between his teeth as if it were a delicacy.

They drove off again into the hot afternoon. The grandmother took cat naps and woke up every few minutes with her own snoring. Outside of Toombsboro she woke up and recalled an old plantation that she had visited in this neighborhood once when she was a young lady. She said the house had six white columns across the front and that there was an avenue of oaks leading up to it and two little wooden trellis arbors on either side in front where you sat down with your suitor after a stroll in the garden. She recalled exactly which road to turn off to get to it. She knew that Bailey would not be willing to lose any time looking at an old house, but the more she talked about it, the more she wanted to see it once again and find out if the little twin arbors were still standing. "There was a secret panel in this house," she said craftily, not telling the truth but wishing that she were, "and the story went that all the family silver was hidden in it when Sherman came through but it was never found . . ." 45

"Hey!" John Wesley said. "Let's go see it! We'll find it! We'll poke all the woodwork and find it! Who lives there? Where do you turn off at? Hey Pop, can't we turn off there?"

"We never have seen a house with a secret panel!" June Star shrieked. "Let's go to the house with the secret panel! Hey Pop, can't we go see the house with the secret panel!"

"It's not far from here, I know," the grandmother said. "It wouldn't take over twenty minutes."

Bailey was looking straight ahead. His jaw was as rigid as a horse-shoe. "No," he said.

The children began to yell and scream that they wanted to see the   50
house with the secret panel. John Wesley kicked the back of the front seat and June Star hung over her mother's shoulder and whined desperately into her ear that they never had any fun even on their vacation, that they could never do what THEY wanted to do. The baby began to scream and John Wesley kicked the back of the seat so hard that his father could feel the blows in his kidney.

"All right!" he shouted and drew the car to a stop at the side of the road. "Will you all shut up? Will you all just shut up for one second? If you don't shut up, we won't go anywhere."

"It would be very educational for them," the grandmother murmured.

"All right," Bailey said, "but get this: this is the only time we're going to stop for anything like this. This is the one and only time."

"The dirt road that you have to turn down is about a mile back," the grandmother directed. "I marked it when we passed.

"A dirt road," Bailey groaned.   55

After they had turned around and were headed toward the dirt road, the grandmother recalled other points about the house, the beautiful glass over the front doorway and the candle-lamp in the hall. John Wesley said that the secret panel was probably in the fireplace.

"You can't go inside this house," Bailey said. "You don't know who lives there."

"While you all talk to the people in front, I'll run around behind and get in a window," John Wesley suggested.

"We'll all stay in the car," his mother said.

They turned onto the dirt road and the car raced roughly along in a   60
swirl of pink dust. The grandmother recalled the times when there were no paved roads and thirty miles was a day's journey. The dirt road was hilly and there were sudden washes in it and sharp curves on dangerous embankments. All at once they would be on a hill, looking down over the blue tops of trees for miles around, then the next minute, they would be in a red depression with the dust-coated trees looking down on them.

"This place had better turn up in a minute," Bailey said, "or I'm going to turn around."

The road looked as if no one had traveled on it in months.

"It's not much farther," the grandmother said and just as she said it, a horrible thought came to her. The thought was so embarrassing that she turned red in the face and her eyes dilated and her feet jumped up, upsetting her valise in the corner. The instant the valise moved, the newspaper top she had over the basket under it rose with a snarl and Pitty Sing, the cat, sprang onto Bailey's shoulder.

The children were thrown to the floor and their mother, clutching the baby, was thrown out the door onto the ground; the old lady was thrown into the front seat. The car turned over once and landed right-side-up in a gulch off the side of the road. Bailey remained in the driver's seat with the cat—gray-striped with a broad white face and an orange nose—clinging to his neck like a caterpillar.

As soon as the children saw they could move their arms and legs, they   65
scrambled out of the car, shouting, "We've had an ACCIDENT!" The grandmother was curled up under the dashboard, hoping she was injured so that Bailey's wrath would not come down on her all at once. The horrible thought she had had before the accident was that the house she had remembered so vividly was not in Georgia but in Tennessee.

Bailey removed the cat from his neck with both hands and flung it out the window against the side of a pine tree. Then he got out of the car and started looking for the children's mother. She was sitting against the side of the red gutted ditch, holding the screaming baby, but she only had a cut down her face and a broken shoulder. "We've had an ACCI-DENT!" the children screamed in a frenzy of delight.

"But nobody's killed," June Star said with disappointment as the grandmother limped out of the car, her hat still pinned to her head but the broken front brim standing up at a jaunty angle and the violet spray hanging off the side. They all sat down in the ditch, except the children, to recover from the shock. They were all shaking.

"Maybe a car will come along," said the children's mother hoarsely.

"I believe I have injured an organ," said the grandmother, pressing her side, but no one answered her. Bailey's teeth were clattering. He had on a yellow sport shirt with bright blue parrots designed in it and his face was as yellow as the shirt. The grandmother decided that she would not mention that the house was in Tennessee.

The road was about ten feet above and they could see only the tops   70
of the trees on the other side of it. Behind the ditch they were sitting in there were more woods, tall and dark and deep. In a few minutes they saw a car some distance away on top of a hill, coming slowly as if the occupants were watching them. The grandmother stood up and waved both arms dramatically to attract their attention. The car continued to come on slowly, disappeared around a bend and appeared again, moving even slower, on top of the hill they had gone over. It was a big black battered hearselike automobile. There were three men in it.

It came to a stop just over them and for some minutes, the driver looked down with a steady expressionless gaze to where they were sitting, and didn't speak. Then he turned his head and muttered something to the other two and they got out. One was a fat boy in black trousers and a red sweat shirt with a silver stallion embossed on the front of it. He moved around on the right side of them and stood staring, his mouth partly open in a kind of loose grin. The other had on khaki pants and a blue striped coat and a gray hat pulled down very low, hiding most of his face. He came around slowly on the left side. Neither spoke.

The driver got out of the car and stood by the side of it, looking down at them. He was an older man than the other two. His hair was just beginning to gray and he wore silver-rimmed spectacles that gave him a scholarly look. He had a long creased face and didn't have on any shirt or undershirt. He had on blue jeans that were too tight for him and was holding a black hat and a gun. The two boys also had guns.

"We've had an ACCIDENT!" the children screamed.

The grandmother had the peculiar feeling that the bespectacled man was someone she knew. His face was as familiar to her as if she had known him all her life but she could not recall who he was. He moved away from the car and began to come down the embankment, placing his feet carefully so that he wouldn't slip. He had on tan and white shoes and no socks, and his ankles were red and thin. "Good afternoon," he said. "I see you all had you a little spill."

"We turned over twice!" said the grandmother. 75

"Oncet," he corrected. "We seen it happen. Try their car and see will it run, Hiram," he said quietly to the boy with the gray hat.

"What you got that gun for?" John Wesley asked. "Whatcha gonna do with that gun?"

"Lady," the man said to the children's mother, "would you mind calling them children to sit down by you? Children make me nervous. I want all you all to sit down right together there where you're at."

"What are you telling US what to do for?" June Star asked.

Behind them the line of woods gaped like a dark open mouth. "Come 80 here," said their mother.

"Look here now," Bailey began suddenly, "we're in a predicament! We're in . . ."

The grandmother shrieked. She scrambled to her feet and stood staring. "You're The Misfit!" she said. "I recognized you at once!"

"Yes'm," the man said, smiling slightly as if he were pleased in spite of himself to be known, "but it would have been better for all of you, lady, if you hadn't of reckernized me."

Bailey turned his head sharply and said something to his mother that shocked even the children. The old lady began to cry and The Misfit reddened.

"Lady," he said, "don't you get upset. Sometimes a man says things 85 he don't mean. I don't reckon he meant to talk to you thataway."

"You wouldn't shoot a lady, would you?" the grandmother said and removed a clean handkerchief from her cuff and began to slap at her eyes with it.

The Misfit pointed the toe of his shoe into the ground and made a little hole and then covered it up again. "I would hate to have to," he said.

"Listen," the grandmother almost screamed, "I know you're a good man. You don't look a bit like you have common blood. I know you must come from nice people!"

"Yes mam," he said, "finest people in the world." When he smiled he showed a row of strong white teeth. "God never made a finer woman than my mother and my daddy's heart was pure gold," he said. The boy with the red sweat shirt had come around behind them and was standing with his gun at his hip. The Misfit squatted down on the ground. "Watch them children, Bobby Lee," he said. "You know they make me nervous." He looked at the six of them huddled together in front of him and he seemed to be embarrassed as if he couldn't think of anything to say. "Ain't a cloud in the sky," he remarked, looking up at it. "Don't see no sun but don't see no cloud neither."

"Yes, it's a beautiful day," said the grandmother. "Listen," she said, "you shouldn't call yourself The Misfit because I know you're a good man at heart. I can just look at you and tell." 90

"Hush!" Bailey yelled. "Hush! Everybody shut up and let me handle this!" He was squatting in the position of a runner about to sprint forward but he didn't move.

"I pre-chate that, lady," The Misfit said and drew a little circle in the ground with the butt of his gun.

"It'll take a half a hour to fix this here car," Hiram called, looking over the raised hood of it.

"Well, first you and Bobby Lee get him and that little boy to step over yonder with you," The Misfit said, pointing to Bailey and John Wesley. "The boys want to ast you something," he said to Bailey. "Would you mind stepping back in them woods there with them?"

"Listen," Bailey began, "we're in a terrible predicament! Nobody realizes what this is," and his voice cracked. His eyes were as blue and intense as the parrots in his shirt and he remained perfectly still. 95

The grandmother reached up to adjust her hat brim as if she were going to the woods with him but it came off in her hand. She stood staring at it and after a second she let it fall on the ground. Hiram pulled Bailey up by the arm as if he were assisting an old man. John Wesley caught hold of his father's hand and Bobby Lee followed. They went off toward the woods and just as they reached the dark edge, Bailey turned and supporting himself against a gray naked pine trunk, he shouted, "I'll be back in a minute, Mamma, wait on me!"

"Come back this instant!" his mother shrilled but they all disappeared into the woods.

"Bailey Boy!" the grandmother called in a tragic voice but she found she was looking at The Misfit squatting on the ground in front of her. "I just know you're a good man," she said desperately. "You're not a bit common!"

"Nome, I ain't a good man," The Misfit said after a second as if he had considered her statement carefully, "but I ain't the worst in the world neither. My daddy said I was a different breed of dog from my brothers and sisters. 'You know,' Daddy said, 'it's some that can live their whole life out without asking about it and it's others has to know why it is, and this boy is one of the latters. He's going to be into everything!'" He put on his black hat and looked up suddenly and then away deep into the woods as if he were embarrassed again. "I'm sorry I don't have on a shirt before you ladies," he said, hunching his shoulders slightly. "We buried our clothes that we had on when we escaped and we're just making do until we can get better. We borrowed these from some folks we met," he explained.

"That's perfectly all right," the grandmother said. "Maybe Bailey has   100 an extra shirt in his suitcase."

"I'll look and see terrectly," The Misfit said.

"Where are they taking him?" the children's mother screamed.

"Daddy was a card himself," The Misfit said. "You couldn't put anything over on him. He never got in trouble with the Authorities though. Just had the knack of handling them."

"You could be honest too if you'd only try," said the grandmother. "Think how wonderful it would be to settle down and live a comfortable life and not have to think about somebody chasing you all the time."

The Misfit kept scratching in the ground with the butt of his gun as if   105 he were thinking about it. "Yes'm, somebody is always after you," he murmured.

The grandmother noticed how thin his shoulder blades were just behind his hat because she was standing up looking down on him. "Do you ever pray?" she asked.

He shook his head. All she saw was the black hat wiggle between his shoulder blades. "Nome," he said.

There was a pistol shot from the woods, followed closely by another. Then silence. The old lady's head jerked around. She could hear the wind move through the tree tops like a long satisfied insuck of breath. "Bailey Boy!" she called.

"I was a gospel singer for a while," The Misfit said. "I been most everything. Been in the arm service, both land and sea, at home and abroad, been twict married, been an undertaker, been with the railroads, plowed Mother Earth, been in a tornado, seen a man burnt alive oncet," and looked up at the children's mother and the little girl who were sitting close together, their faces white and their eyes glassy; "I even seen a woman flogged," he said.

"Pray, pray," the grandmother began, "pray, pray . . ."   110

"I never was a bad boy that I remember of," The Misfit said in an almost dreamy voice, "but somewheres along the line I done something wrong and got sent to the penitentiary. I was buried alive," and he looked up and held her attention to him by a steady stare.

"That's when you should have started to pray," she said. "What did you do to get sent to the penitentiary that first time?"

"Turn to the right, it was a wall," The Misfit said, looking up again at the cloudless sky. "Turn to the left, it was a wall. Look up it was a ceiling, look down it was a floor. I forget what I done, lady. I set there and set there, trying to remember what it was I done and I ain't recalled it to this day. Oncet in a while, I would think it was coming to me, but it never come."

"Maybe they put you in by mistake," the old lady said vaguely.

"Nome," he said. "It wasn't no mistake. They had the papers on   115
me."

"You must have stolen something," she said.

The Misfit sneered slightly. "Nobody had nothing I wanted," he said. "It was a head-doctor at the penitentiary said what I had done was kill my daddy but I known that for a lie. My daddy died in nineteen ought nineteen of the epidemic flu and I never had a thing to do with it. He was buried in the Mount Hopewell Baptist churchyard and you can go there and see for yourself."

"If you would pray," the old lady said, "Jesus would help you."

"That's right," The Misfit said.

"Well then, why don't you pray?" she asked trembling with delight   120
suddenly.

"I don't want no hep," he said. "I'm doing all right by myself."

Bobby Lee and Hiram came ambling back from the woods. Bobby Lee was dragging a yellow shirt with bright blue parrots in it.

"Throw me that shirt, Bobby Lee," The Misfit said. The shirt came flying at him and landed on his shoulder and he put it on. The grandmother couldn't name what the shirt reminded her of. "No, lady," The Misfit said while he was buttoning it up, "I found out the crime don't matter. You can do one thing or you can do another, kill a man or take a tire off his car, because sooner or later you're going to forget what it was you done and just be punished for it."

The children's mother had begun to make heaving noises as if she couldn't get her breath. "Lady," he asked, "would you and that little girl like to step off yonder with Bobby Lee and Hiram and join your husband?"

"Yes, thank you," the mother said faintly. Her left arm dangled help-   125
lessly and she was holding the baby, who had gone to sleep, in the other. "Hep that lady up, Hiram," The Misfit said as she struggled to climb out of the ditch, "and Bobby Lee, you hold onto that little girl's hand."

"I don't want to hold hands with him," June Starr said. "He reminds me of a pig."

The fat boy blushed and laughed and caught her by the arm and pulled her off into the woods after Hiram and her mother.

Alone with The Misfit, the grandmother found that she had lost her voice. There was not a cloud in the sky nor any sun. There was nothing around her but woods. She wanted to tell him that he must pray. She opened and closed her mouth several times before anything came out. Finally she found herself saying, "Jesus, Jesus," meaning, Jesus will help you, but the way she was saying it, it sounded as if she might be cursing.

"Yes'm," the Misfit said as if he agreed. "Jesus thown everything off balance. It was the same case with Him as with me except He hadn't committed any crime and they could prove I had committed one because they had the papers on me. Of course," he said, "they never shown me my papers. That's why I sign myself now. I said long ago, you get you a signature and sign everything you do and keep a copy of it. Then you'll know what you done and you can hold up the crime to the punishment and see do they match and in the end you'll have something to prove you ain't been treated right. I call myself The Misfit," he said, "because I can't make what all I done wrong fit what all I gone through in punishment."

There was a piercing scream from the woods, followed closely by a   130
pistol report. "Does it seem right to you, lady, that one is punished a heap and another ain't punished at all?"

"Jesus!" the old lady cried. "You've got good blood! I know you wouldn't shoot a lady! I know you come from nice people! Pray! Jesus, you ought not to shoot a lady. I'll give you all the money I've got!"

"Lady," The Misfit said, looking beyond her far into the woods, "there never was a body that give the undertaker a tip."

There were two more pistol reports and the grandmother raised her head like a parched old turkey hen crying for water and called, "Bailey Boy, Bailey Boy!" as if her heart would break.

"Jesus was the only One that ever raised the dead." The Misfit continued, "and He shouldn't have done it. He thrown everything off balance. If He did what He said, then it's nothing for you to do but thow away everything and follow Him, and if He didn't, then it's nothing for you to do but enjoy the few minutes you got left the best way you can — by killing somebody or burning down his house or doing some other meanness to him. No pleasure but meanness," he said and his voice had become almost a snarl.

"Maybe He didn't raise the dead," the old lady mumbled, not know-   135
ing what she was saying and feeling so dizzy that she sank down in the ditch with her legs twisted under her.

"I wasn't there so I can't say He didn't," The Misfit said. "I wisht I had of been there," he said, hitting the ground with his fist. "It ain't right I wasn't there because if I had of been there I would of known. Listen lady," he said in a high voice, "if I had of been there I would of known and I wouldn't be like I am now." His voice seemed about to crack and the grandmother's head cleared for an instant. She saw the man's face twisted close to her own as if he was going to cry and she murmured, "Why you're one of my babies. You're one of my own children!" She reached out and touched him on the shoulder. The Misfit sprang back as if a snake had bitten him and shot her three times through the chest. Then he put his gun down on the ground and took off his glasses and began to clean them.

Hiram and Bobby Lee returned from the woods and stood over the ditch, looking down at the grandmother who half sat and half lay in a puddle of blood with her legs crossed under her like a child's and her face smiling up at the cloudless sky.

Without his glasses, The Misfit's eyes were red-rimmed and pale and defenseless-looking. "Take her off and thow her where you thown the others," he said, picking up the cat that was rubbing itself against his leg.

"She was a talker, wasn't she?" Bobby Lee said, sliding down the ditch with a yodel.

"She would of been a good woman," The Misfit said, "if it had been   140
somebody there to shoot her every minute of her life."

"Some fun!" Bobby Lee said.

"Shut up, Bobby Lee," The Misfit said. "It's no real pleasure in life."

The Reader's Presence

1. The grandmother is described only indirectly, through her words, actions, and interactions with others. Reread paragraphs 1–9. How does the grandmother appear to see herself? How do you see her? In what ways does the writer's "voice" influence your impression of the character?

2. What might the Misfit figure symbolize in relation to the grandmother and her family? Does his nickname have any significance? What sort of tone does O'Connor establish in the Misfit encounter? Is it eerie, comedic, or somewhere in between? Imagine the story as presented in a different tone; how would it differ? What does O'Connor's position on the characters and events appear to be? What clues in her approach lead you to your conclusion? (See also O'Connor's commentary on the story.)

3. In what sense is the grandmother responsible for the family's misfortunes? Consider the moment when she recognizes the Misfit. Why is this moment representative of the grandmother's behavior? Do you think the family would have been allowed to live if the grandmother had remained silent? Explain why or why not.

THE WRITER AT WORK

Flannery O'Connor on Her Own Work

Flannery O'Connor's "A Good Man Is Hard to Find" ranks as one of American fiction's most durable short stories. It has been reprinted and analyzed in critical periodicals hundreds of times since it first appeared in 1953. Ten years after its first publication and shortly before her untimely death, O'Connor was invited to read the story at Hollins College in Virginia, where she made the following remarks. Her comments on the story were then included in a collection of nonfiction published by her editor in 1969 under the very appropriate title "Mystery and Manners." As you consider the story, you may want to focus on these terms: mystery and manners. How does each word describe an important aspect of the story? How are they interrelated? You should also consider the story from the perspective O'Connor herself provides in the following selection. Do you think her comments on her own story are critically persuasive? Did you come

away from the story with a different sense of its significance? Do you think that
what an author says about his or her own work must always be the final word?

Last fall I received a letter from a student who said she would be
"graciously appreciative" if I would tell her "just what enlightenment" I
expected her to get from each of my stories. I suspect she had a paper to
write. I wrote her back to forget about the enlightenment and just try to
enjoy them. I knew that was the most unsatisfactory answer I could have
given because, of course, she didn't want to enjoy them, she just wanted
to figure them out.

In most English classes the short story has become a kind of literary
specimen to be dissected. Every time a story of mine appears in a Freshman anthology, I have a vision of it, with its little organs laid open, like a
frog in a bottle.

I realize that a certain amount of this what-is-the-significance has to
go on, but I think something has gone wrong in the process when, for so
many students, the story becomes simply a problem to be solved, something which you evaporate to get Instant Enlightenment.

A story really isn't any good unless it successfully resists paraphrase,
unless it hangs on and expands in the mind. Properly, you analyze to
enjoy, but it's equally true that to analyze with any discrimination, you
have to have enjoyed already, and I think that the best reason to hear a
story read is that it should stimulate that primary enjoyment.

I don't have any pretensions to being an Aeschylus or Sophocles and   5
providing you in this story with a cathartic experience out of your mythic
background, though this story I'm going to read certainly calls up a good
deal of the South's mythic background, and it should elicit from you a degree of pity and terror, even though its way of being serious is a comic
one. I do think, though, that like the Greeks you should know what is
going to happen in this story so that any element of suspense in it will be
transferred from its surface to its interior.

I would be most happy if you had already read it, happier still if you
knew it well, but since experience has taught me to keep my expectations
along these lines modest, I'll tell you that this is the story of a family of
six which, on its way driving to Florida, gets wiped out by an escaped
convict who calls himself the Misfit. The family is made up of the Grandmother and her son, Bailey, and his children, John Wesley and June Star
and the baby, and there is also the cat and the children's mother. The cat
is named Pitty Sing, and the Grandmother is taking him with them, hidden in a basket.

Now I think it behooves me to try to establish with you the basis on
which reason operates in this story. Much of my fiction takes its character from a reasonable use of the unreasonable, though the reasonableness
of my use of it may not always be apparent. The assumptions that underlie this use of it, however, are those of the central Christian mysteries.

These are assumptions to which a large part of the modern audience takes exception. About this I can only say that there are perhaps other ways than my own in which this story could be read, but none other by which it could have been written. Belief, in my own case anyway, is the engine that makes perception operate.

The heroine of this story, the Grandmother, is in the most significant position life offers the Christian. She is facing death. And to all appearances she, like the rest of us, is not too well prepared for it. She would like to see the event postponed. Indefinitely.

I've talked to a number of teachers who use this story in class and who tell their students that the Grandmother is evil, that in fact, she's a witch, even down to the cat. One of these teachers told me that his students, and particularly his Southern students, resisted this interpretation with a certain bemused vigor, and he didn't understand why. I had to tell him that they resisted it because they all had grandmothers or great-aunts just like her at home, and they knew, from personal experience, that the old lady lacked comprehension, but that she had a good heart. The Southerner is usually tolerant of those weaknesses that proceed from innocence, and he knows that a taste for self-preservation can be readily combined with the missionary spirit.

This same teacher was telling his students that morally the Misfit was 10 several cuts above the Grandmother. He had a really sentimental attachment to the Misfit. But then a prophet gone wrong is almost always more interesting than your grandmother, and you have to let people take their pleasures where they find them.

It is true that the old lady is a hypocritical old soul; her wits are no match for the Misfit's, nor is her capacity for grace equal to his; yet I think the unprejudiced reader will feel that the Grandmother has a special kind of triumph in this story which instinctively we do not allow to someone altogether bad.

I often ask myself what makes a story work, and what makes it hold up as a story, and I have decided that it is probably some action, some gesture of a character that is unlike any other in the story, one which indicates where the real heart of the story lies. This would have to be an action or a gesture which was both totally right and totally unexpected; it would have to be one that was both in character and beyond character; it would have to suggest both the world and eternity. The action or gesture I'm talking about would have to be on the anagogical level, that is, the level which has to do with the Divine life and our participation in it. It would be a gesture that transcended any neat allegory that might have been intended or any pat moral categories a reader could make. It would be a gesture which somehow made contact with mystery.

There is a point in this story where such a gesture occurs. The Grandmother is at last alone, facing the Misfit. Her head clears for an instant and she realizes, even in her limited way, that she is responsible for the man before her and joined to him by ties of kinship which have their roots deep in the mystery she has been merely prattling about so far. And at this point, she does the right thing, she makes the right gesture.

I find that students are often puzzled by what she says and does here, but I think myself that if I took out this gesture and what she says with it, I would have no story. What was left would not be worth your attention. Our age not only does not have a very sharp eye for the almost imperceptible intrusions of grace, it no longer has much feeling for the nature of the violences which precede and follow them. The devil's greatest wile, Baudelaire has said, is to convince us that he does not exist.

I suppose the reasons for the use of so much violence in modern fiction will differ with each writer who uses it, but in my own stories I have found that violence is strangely capable of returning my characters to reality and preparing them to accept their moment of grace. Their heads are so hard that almost nothing else will do the work. This idea, that reality is something to which we must be returned at considerable cost, is one which is seldom understood by the casual reader, but it is one which is implicit in the Christian view of the world. 15

I don't want to equate the Misfit with the devil. I prefer to think that, however unlikely this may seem, the old lady's gesture, like the mustard-seed, will grow to be a great crow-filled tree in the Misfit's heart, and will be enough of a pain to him there to turn him into the prophet he was meant to become. But that's another story.

This story has been called grotesque, but I prefer to call it literal. A good story is literal in the same sense that a child's drawing is literal. When a child draws, he doesn't intend to distort but to set down exactly what he sees, and as his gaze is direct, he sees the lines that create motion. Now the lines of motion that interest the writer are usually invisible. They are lines of spiritual motion. And in this story you should be on the lookout for such things as the action of grace in the Grandmother's soul, and not for the dead bodies.

We hear many complaints about the prevalence of violence in modern fiction, and it is always assumed that this violence is a bad thing and meant to be an end in itself. With the serious writer, violence is never an end in itself. It is the extreme situation that best reveals what we are essentially, and I believe these are times when writers are more interested in what we are essentially than in the tenor of our daily lives. Violence is a force which can be used for good or evil, and among other things taken by it is the kingdom of heaven. But regardless of what can be taken by it, the man in the violent situation reveals those qualities least dispensable in his personality, those qualities which are all he will have to take into eternity with him; and since the characters in this story are all on the verge of eternity, it is appropriate to think of what they take with them. In any case, I hope that if you consider these points in connection with the story, you will come to see it as something more than an account of a family murdered on the way to Florida.

125

Tillie Olsen

I Stand Here Ironing

Strongly influenced by her politically active Jewish parents and by her experiences as a union laborer, Tillie Olsen (b. 1913) writes about the struggles of the working class, the poor, and women. While raising four children and working a variety of jobs to support her family, Olsen was unable to devote herself to writing until 1956, when she received a Stanford University Creative Writing Fellowship after taking a writing course at San Francisco State University. Other recognition for her work includes an O. Henry Award for best short story, a Guggenheim Fellowship, a Rea Award for short fiction, and several honorary degrees. She has taught at various colleges, such as Amherst College, Massachusetts Institute of Technology, Kenyon College, and University of California at Los Angeles. "I Stand Here Ironing" is from Olsen's first book, a collection of four short stories entitled Tell Me a Riddle *(1961). Her only novel,* Yonnondio: From the Thirties *(1974), describes the plight of a poor family during the Depression. In her book of essays,* Silences *(1978), Olsen explores the difficulties writers encounter as a result of economic factors, racial prejudice, gender bias, or familial obligations. She is also editor of* Mother to Daughter, Daughter to Mother *(1984) and coeditor of* Mother and Daughter, That Special Quality *(1987).*

I stand here ironing, and what you asked me moves tormented back and forth with the iron.

"I wish you would manage the time to come in and talk with me about your daughter. I'm sure you can help me understand her. She's a youngster who needs help and whom I'm deeply interested in helping."

"Who needs help." . . . Even if I came, what good would it do? You think because I am her mother I have a key, or that in some way you could use me as a key? She has lived for nineteen years. There is all that life that has happened outside of me, beyond me.

And when is there time to remember, to sift, to weigh, to estimate, to total? I will start and there will be an interruption and I will have to gather it all together again. Or I will become engulfed with all I did or did not do, with what should have been and what cannot be helped.

She was a beautiful baby. The first and only one of our five that was beautiful at birth. You do not guess how new and uneasy her tenancy in her now-loveliness. You did not know her all those years she was thought homely, or see her poring over her baby pictures, making me tell her over and over how beautiful she had been—and would be, I would tell her— and was now, to the seeing eye. But the seeing eyes were few or nonexistent. Including mine.

I nursed her. They feel that's important nowadays, I nursed all the children, but with her, with all the fierce rigidity of first motherhood, I did like the books then said. Though her cries battered me to trembling and my breasts ached with swollenness, I waited till the clock decreed.

Why do I put that first? I do not even know if it matters, or if it explains anything.

She was a beautiful baby. She blew shining bubbles of sound. She loved motion, loved light, loved color and music and textures. She would lie on the floor in her blue overalls patting the surface so hard in ecstasy her hands and feet would blur. She was a miracle to me, but when she was eight months old I had to leave her daytimes with the woman downstairs to whom she was no miracle at all, for I worked or looked for work and for Emily's father, who "could no longer endure" (he wrote in his good-bye note) "sharing want with us."

I was nineteen. It was pre-relief, pre-WPA world of the depression. I would start running as soon as I got off the streetcar, running up the stairs, the place smelling sour, and awake or asleep to startle awake, when she saw me she would break into a clogged weeping that could not be comforted, a weeping I can hear yet.

After a while I found a job hashing at night so I could be with her days, and it was better. But it came to where I had to bring her to his family and leave her.   10

It took a long time to raise the money for her fare back. Then she got chicken pox and I had to wait longer. When she finally came, I hardly knew her, walking quick and nervous like her father, looking like her father, thin, and dressed in a shoddy red that yellowed her skin and glared at the pockmarks. All the baby loveliness gone.

She was two. Old enough for nursery school they said, and I did not know then what I know now—the fatigue of the long day, and the lacerations of group life in the kinds of nurseries that are only parking places for children.

Except that it would have made no difference if I had known. It was the only place there was. It was the only way we could be together, the only way I could hold a job.

And even without knowing, I knew. I knew the teacher that was evil because all these years it has curdled into my memory, the little boy hunched in the corner, her rasp, "why aren't you outside, because Alvin hits you? that's no reason, go out, scaredy." I knew Emily hated it even if she did not clutch and implore "don't go Mommy" like the other children, mornings.

She always had a reason why we should stay home. Momma, you look sick. Momma, I feel sick. Momma, the teachers aren't there today, they're sick. Momma, we can't go, there was a fire last night. Momma, it's a holiday today, no school, they told me.

But never a direct protest, never rebellion. I think of our others in their three-, four-year-oldness—the explosions, the tempers, the denunciations, the demands—and I feel suddenly ill. I put the iron down. What in me demanded that goodness in her? And what was the cost, the cost to her of such goodness?

The old man living in the back once said in his gentle way: "You should smile at Emily more when you look at her." What *was* in my face when I looked at her? I loved her. There were all the acts of love.

It was only with the others I remembered what he said, and it was the face of joy, and not of care or tightness or worry I turned to them—too late for Emily. She does not smile easily, let alone almost always as her brothers and sisters do. Her face is closed and sombre, but when she wants, how fluid. You must have seen it in her pantomimes, you spoke of her rare gift for comedy on the stage that rouses laughter out of the audience so dear they applaud and applaud and do not want to let her go.

Where does it come from, that comedy? There was none of it in her when she came back to me that second time, after I had to send her away again. She had a new daddy now to learn to love, and I think perhaps it was a better time.

Except when we left her alone nights, telling ourselves she was old enough.

"Can't you go some other time, Mommy, like tomorrow?" she would ask. "Will it be just a little while you'll be gone? Do you promise?"

The time we came back, the front door open, the clock on the floor in the hall. She rigid awake. "It wasn't just a little while. I didn't cry. Three times I called you, just three times, and then I ran downstairs to open the door so you could come faster. The clock talked loud. I threw it away, it scared me what it talked."

She said the clock talked loud again that night I went to the hospital to have Susan. She was delirious with the fever that comes before red measles, but she was fully conscious all the week I was gone and the week after we were home when she could not come near the new baby or me.

She did not get well. She stayed skeleton thin, not wanting to eat, and night after night she had nightmares. She would call for me, and I would rouse from exhaustion to sleepily call back: "You're all right, darling, go to sleep, it's just a dream," and if she still called, in a sterner voice, "now go to sleep, Emily, there's nothing to hurt you." Twice, only twice, when I had to get up for Susan anyhow, I went in to sit with her.

Now when it is too late (as if she would let me hold her and comfort her like I do the others) I get up and go to her at once at her moan or restless stirring. "Are you awake, Emily? Can I get you something?" And the answer is always the same: "No, I'm all right, go back to sleep, Mother."

They persuaded me at the clinic to send her away to a convalescent home in the country where "she can have the kind of food and care you can't manage for her, and you'll be free to concentrate on the new baby." They still send children to that place. I see pictures on the society page of sleek young women planning affairs to raise money for it, or dancing at the affairs, or decorating Easter eggs or filling Christmas stockings for the children.

They never have a picture of the children so I do not know if the girls still wear those gigantic red bows and the ravaged looks on the every other Sunday when parents can come to visit "unless otherwise notified"—as we were notified the first six weeks.

Oh it is a handsome place, green lawns and tall trees and fluted flower beds. High up on the balconies of each cottage the children stand, the girls in their red bows and white dresses, the boys in white suits and giant red ties. The parents stand below shrieking up to be heard and the children shriek down to be heard, and between them the invisible wall "Not To Be Contaminated by Parental Germs or Physical Affection."

There was a tiny girl who always stood hand in hand with Emily. Her parents never came. One visit she was gone. "They moved her to Rose Cottage," Emily shouted in explanation. "They don't like you to love anybody here."

She wrote once a week, the labored writing of a seven-year-old. "I am   30 fine. How is the baby. If I write my leter nicly I will have a star. Love." There never was a star. We wrote every other day, letters she could never hold or keep but only hear read—once. "We simply do not have room for children to keep any personal possessions," they patiently explained when we pieced one Sunday's shrieking together to plead how much it would mean to Emily, who loved so to keep things, to be allowed to keep her letters and cards.

Each visit she looked frailer. "She isn't eating," they told us.

(They had runny eggs for breakfast or mush with lumps, Emily said later, I'd hold it in my mouth and not swallow. Nothing ever tasted good, just when they had chicken.)

It took us eight months to get her released home, and only the fact that she gained back so little of her seven lost pounds convinced the social worker.

I used to try to hold and love her after she came back, but her body would stay stiff, and after a while she'd push away. She ate little. Food sickened her, and I think much of life too. Oh she had physical lightness and brightness, twinkling by on skates, bouncing like a ball up and down up and down over the jump rope, skimming over the hill; but these were momentary.

She fretted about her appearance, thin and dark and foreign-looking   35 at a time when every little girl was supposed to look or thought she should look a chubby blonde replica of Shirley Temple. The doorbell sometimes rang for her, but no one seemed to come and play in the house or to be a best friend. Maybe because we moved so much.

There was a boy she loved painfully through two school semesters. Months later she told me how she had taken pennies from my purse to buy him candy. "Licorice was his favorite and I brought him some every day, but he still liked Jennifer better'n me. Why, Mommy?" The kind of question for which there is no answer.

School was a worry for her. She was not glib or quick in a world where glibness and quickness were easily confused with ability to learn. To her overworked and exasperated teachers she was an overconscientious "slow learner" who kept trying to catch up and was absent entirely too often.

I let her be absent, though sometimes the illness was imaginary. How different from my now-strictness about attendance with the others. I wasn't working. We had a new baby. I was home anyhow. Sometimes, after Susan grew old enough, I would keep her home from school, too, to have them all together.

Mostly Emily had asthma, and her breathing, harsh and labored, would fill the house with a curiously tranquil sound. I would bring the two old dresser mirrors and her boxes of collections to her bed. She would select beads and single earrings, bottle tops and shells, dried flowers and pebbles, old postcards and scraps, all sorts of oddments; then she and Susan would play Kingdom, setting up landscapes and furniture, peopling them with action.

Those were the only times of peaceful companionship between her   40
and Susan. I have edged away from it, that poisonous feeling between them, that terrible balancing of hurts and needs I had to do between the two, and did so badly, those earlier years.

Oh there were conflicts between the others too, each one human, needing, demanding, hurting, taking—but only between Emily and Susan, no, Emily toward Susan that corroding resentment. It seems so obvious on the surface, yet it is not obvious; Susan, the second child, Susan, golden- and curly-haired and chubby, quick and articulate and assured, everything in appearance and manner Emily was not; Susan, not able to resist Emily's precious things, losing or sometimes clumsily breaking them; Susan telling jokes and riddles to company for applause while Emily sat silent (to say to me later: that was *my* riddle, Mother, I told it to Susan); Susan, who for all the five years' difference in age was just a year behind Emily in developing physically.

I am glad for that slow physical development that widened the difference between her and her contemporaries, though she suffered over it. She was too vulnerable for that terrible world of youthful competition, of preening and parading, of constant measuring of yourself against every other, of envy, "If I had that copper hair," "If I had that skin. . . ." She tormented herself enough about not looking like the others, there was enough of unsureness, the having to be conscious of words before you speak, the constant caring—what are they thinking of me? without having it all magnified by the merciless physical drives.

Ronnie is calling. He is wet and I change him. It is rare there is such a cry now. That time of motherhood is almost behind me when the ear is not one's own but must always be racked and listening for the child cry, the child call. We sit for a while and I hold him, looking out over the city spread in charcoal with its soft aisles of light. "*Shoogily,*" he breathes and curls closer. I carry him back to bed, asleep. *Shoogily.* A funny word, a family word, inherited from Emily, invented by her to say: *comfort.*

In this and other ways she leaves her seal, I say aloud. And startle at my saying it. What do I mean? What did I start to gather together, to try and make coherent? I was at the terrible, growing years. War years. I do not remember them well. I was working, there were four smaller ones now, there was not time for her. She had to help be a mother, and housekeeper, and shopper. She had to get her seal. Mornings of crisis and near hysteria trying to get lunches packed, hair combed, coats and shoes found, everyone to school or Child Care on time, the baby ready for transportation. And always the paper scribbled on by a smaller one, the book looked at by Susan then mislaid, the homework not done. Running out to that huge school where she was one, she was lost, she was a drop; suffering over the unpreparedness, stammering and unsure in her classes.

There was so little time left at night after the kids were bedded down. 45
She would struggle over books, always eating (it was in those years she developed her enormous appetite that is legendary in our family) and I would be ironing, or preparing food for the next day, or writing V-mail to Bill, or tending the baby. Sometimes, to make me laugh, or out of her despair, she would imitate happenings or types at school.

I think I said once: "Why don't you do something like this in the school amateur show?" One morning she phoned me at work, hardly understandable through the weeping: "Mother, I did it. I won, I won; they gave me first prize; they clapped and clapped and wouldn't let me go."

Now suddenly she was Somebody, and as imprisoned in her difference as she had been in anonymity.

She began to be asked to perform at other high schools, even in colleges, then at city and statewide affairs. The first one we went to, I only recognized her that first moment when thin, shy, she almost drowned herself into the curtains. Then: Was this Emily? The control, the command, the convulsing and deadly clowning, the spell, then the roaring, stamping audience, unwilling to let this rare and precious laughter out of their lives.

Afterwards: You ought to do something about her with a gift like that—but without money or knowing how, what does one do? We have left it all to her, and the gift has so often eddied inside, clogged and clotted, as been used and growing.

She is coming. She runs up the stairs two at a time with her light   50
graceful step, and I know she is happy tonight. Whatever it was that occasioned your call did not happen today.

"Aren't you ever going to finish the ironing, Mother? Whistler
painted his mother in a rocker. I'd have to paint mine standing over an
ironing board." This is one of her communicative nights and she tells me
everything and nothing as she fixes herself a plate of food out of the
icebox.

She is so lovely. Why did you want me to come in at all? Why were
you concerned? She will find her way.

She starts up the stairs to bed. "Don't get me up with the rest in the
morning." "But I thought you were having midterms." "Oh, those," she
comes back in, kisses me, and says quite lightly, "in a couple of years
when we'll all be atom-dead they won't matter a bit."

She has said it before. She *believes* it. But because I have been dredg-
ing the past, and all that compounds a human being is so heavy and
meaningful in me, I cannot endure it tonight.

I will never total it all. I will never come in to say: She was a child sel-   55
dom smiled at. Her father left me before she was a year old. I had to
work her first six years when there was work, or I sent her home and to
his relatives. There were years she had care she hated. She was dark and
thin and foreign-looking in a world where the prestige went to blondeness
and curly hair and dimples, she was slow where glibness was prized. She
was a child of anxious, not proud, love. We were poor and could not afford for her the soil of easy growth. I was a young mother, I was a distracted mother. There were other children pushing up, demanding. Her
younger sister seemed all that she was not. There were years she did not
want me to touch her. She kept too much in herself, her life was such she
had to keep too much in herself. My wisdom came too late. She has much
to her and probably little will come of it. She is a child of her age, of depression, of war, of fear.

Let her be. So all that is in her will not bloom but in how many does
it? There is still enough left to live by. Only help her to know—help
make it so there is cause for her to know—that she is more than this
dress on the ironing board, helpless before the iron.

The Reader's Presence

1. Olsen introduces the narrator solely through her own words.
   Reread paragraphs 1–7. What sort of person is she? To whom is she
   speaking? Can you understand more about her and her situation
   than she does? Through what means? What clues in the narrative
   lead you to distinguish the writer's "voice" from the narrator's?

2. The reader's view of the narrator's past is filtered both through her perspective and through time. In a few lines, recount Emily's growing-up as the narrator describes it. How might the narrator have viewed it at the time? What does hindsight seem to have added to or taken from it? Is the narrator a reliable source of information? Why or why not? Should the narrator's later version of the past be taken as more, or less, accurate? Does Olsen suggest a different interpretation than the one the narrator offers? If so, where do you see this division of "voice"?

3. The narrator compares her daughter to "this dress on the ironing board, helpless before the iron." What might the iron signify? Is the daughter the only helpless one? What might Olsen wish the reader to feel for the speaker? for her daughter? What does the writer refrain from saying? Do these omissions seem significant? If so, in what ways?

126

Amy Tan

Jing-Mei Woo: Two Kinds

"Two Kinds" is one of sixteen stories that compose Amy Tan's best-selling novel, The Joy Luck Club *(1989). Tan's success as a writer seemed to come about overnight, but she reminds us that writing is a process that can consume large amounts of time, energy, patience, and paper. When writing her second novel, Tan recalls, she started by writing—and throwing away—at least one thousand pages of manuscript that could have become several books. "But those books were not meant to become anything more than a lesson to me on what it takes to write fiction: persistence imposed by a limited focus. . . . The focus required of a priest, a nun, a convict serving a life's sentence."*

For more information on Amy Tan, see page 271.

My mother believed you could be anything you wanted to be in America. You could open a restaurant. You could work for the government and get good retirement. You could buy a house with almost no money down. You could become rich. You could become instantly famous.

"Of course you can be prodigy, too," my mother told me when I was nine. "You can be best anything. What does Auntie Lindo know? Her daughter, she is only best tricky."

America was where all my mother's hopes lay. She had come here in 1949 after losing everything in China: her mother and father, her family home, her first husband, and two daughters, twin baby girls. But she never looked back with regret. There were so many ways for things to get better.

We didn't immediately pick the right kind of prodigy. At first my mother thought I could be a Chinese Shirley Temple. We'd watch Shirley's old movies on TV as though they were training films. My mother would poke my arm and say, *"Ni kan"*—You watch. And I would see Shirley tapping her feet, or singing a sailor song, or pursing her lips in a very round O while saying, "Oh my goodness."

"Ni kan," said my mother as Shirley's eyes flooded with tears. "You already know how. Don't need talent for crying!"   5

Soon after my mother got this idea about Shirley Temple, she took me to a beauty training school in the Mission district and put me in the hands of a student who could barely hold the scissors without shaking. Instead of getting big fat curls, I emerged with an uneven mass of crinkly black fuzz. My mother dragged me off to the bathroom and tried to wet down my hair.

"You look like Negro Chinese," she lamented, as if I had done this on purpose.

The instructor of the beauty training school had to lop off these soggy clumps to make my hair even again. "Peter Pan is very popular these days," the instructor assured my mother. I now had hair the length of a boy's, with straight-across bangs that hung at a slant two inches above my eyebrows. I liked the haircut and it made me actually look forward to my future fame.

If fact, in the beginning, I was just as excited as my mother, maybe even more so. I pictured this prodigy part of me as many different images, trying each one on for size. I was a dainty ballerina girl standing by the curtains, waiting to hear the right music that would send me floating on my tiptoes. I was like the Christ child lifted out of the straw manger, crying with holy indignity. I was Cinderella stepping from her pumpkin carriage with sparkly cartoon music filling the air.

In all of my imaginings, I was filled with a sense that I would soon   10
become *perfect*. My mother and father would adore me. I would be beyond reproach. I would never feel the need to sulk for anything.

But sometimes the prodigy in me became impatient. "If you don't hurry up and get me out of here, I'm disappearing for good," it warned. "And then you'll always be nothing."

Every night after dinner, my mother and I would sit at the Formica kitchen table. She would present new tests, taking her examples from stories of amazing children she had read in *Ripley's Believe It or Not,* or *Good Housekeeping, Reader's Digest,* and a dozen other magazines she kept in a pile in our bathroom. My mother got these magazines from people whose houses she cleaned. And since she cleaned many houses each week, we had a great assortment. She would look through them all, searching for stories about remarkable children.

The first night she brought out a story about a three-year-old boy who knew the capitals of all the states and even most of the European countries. A teacher was quoted as saying the little boy could also pronounce the names of the foreign cities correctly.

"What's the capital of Finland?" my mother asked me, looking at the magazine story.

All I knew was the capital of California, because Sacramento was the   15
name of the street we lived on in Chinatown. "Nairobi!" I guessed, saying the most foreign word I could think of. She checked to see if that was possibly one way to pronounce "Helsinki" before showing me the answer.

The tests got harder—multiplying numbers in my head, finding the queen of hearts in a deck of cards, trying to stand on my head without using my hands, predicting the daily temperatures in Los Angeles, New York, and London.

One might I had to look at a page from the Bible for three minutes and then report everything I could remember. "Now Jehoshaphat had riches and honor in abundance and . . . that's all I remember, Ma," I said.

And after seeing my mother's disappointed face once again, something inside of me began to die. I hated the tests, the raised hopes and failed expectations. Before going to bed that night, I looked in the mirror above the bathroom sink and when I saw only my face staring back— and that it would always be this ordinary face—I began to cry. Such a sad, ugly girl! I made high-pitched noises like a crazed animal, trying to scratch out the face in the mirror.

And then I saw what seemed to be the prodigy side of me—because I had never seen that face before. I looked at my reflection, blinking so I could see more clearly. The girl staring back at me was angry, powerful. This girl and I were the same. I had new thoughts, willful thoughts, or rather thoughts filled with lots of won'ts. I won't let her change me, I promised myself. I won't be what I'm not.

So now on nights when my mother presented her tests, I performed   20
listlessly, my head propped on one arm. I pretended to be bored. And I was. I got so bored I started counting the bellows of the foghorns out on the bay while my mother drilled me in other areas. The sound was comforting and reminded me of the cow jumping over the moon. And the next day, I played a game with myself, seeing if my mother would give up on me before eight bellows. After a while I usually counted only one, maybe two bellows at most. At last she was beginning to give up hope.

Two or three months had gone by without any mention of my being a prodigy again. And then one day my mother was watching *The Ed Sullivan Show* on TV. The TV was old and the sound kept shorting out.

Every time my mother got halfway up from the sofa to adjust the set, the sound would go back on and Ed would be there talking. As soon as she sat down, Ed would go silent again. She got up, the TV broke into loud piano music. She sat down. Silence. Up and down, back and forth, quiet and loud. It was like a stiff embraceless dance between her and the TV set. Finally she stood by the set with her hand on the sound dial.

She seemed to be entranced by the music, a little frenzied piano piece with this mesmerizing quality, sort of quick passages and then teasing lilting ones before it returned to the quick playful parts.

"*Ni kan,*" my mother said, calling me over with hurried hand gestures, "Look here."

I could see why my mother was fascinated by the music. It was being pounded out by a little Chinese girl, about nine years old, with a Peter Pan haircut. The girl had the sauciness of a Shirley Temple. She was proudly modest like a proper Chinese child. And she also did this fancy sweep of a curtsy, so that the fluffy skirt of her white dress cascaded slowly to the floor like the petals of a large carnation.

In spite of these warning signs, I wasn't worried. Our family had no   25 piano and we couldn't afford to buy one, let alone reams of sheet music and piano lessons. So I could be generous in my comments when my mother bad-mouthed the little girl on TV.

"Play note right, but doesn't sound good! No singing sound," complained my mother.

"What are you picking on her for?" I said carelessly. "She's pretty good. Maybe she's not the best, but she's trying hard." I knew almost immediately I would be sorry I said that.

"Just like you," she said. "Not the best. Because you not trying." She gave a little huff as she let go of the sound dial and sat down on the sofa.

The little Chinese girl sat down also to play an encore of "Anitra's Dance" by Grieg. I remember the song, because later on I had to learn how to play it.

Three days after watching *The Ed Sullivan Show,* my mother told me   30 what my schedule would be for piano lessons and piano practice. She had talked to Mr. Chong, who lived on the first floor of our apartment building. Mr. Chong was a retired piano teacher and my mother traded house-cleaning services for weekly lessons and a piano for me to practice on every day, two hours a day, from four until six.

When my mother told me this, I felt as though I had been sent to hell. I whined and then kicked my foot a little when I couldn't stand it anymore.

"Why don't you like me the way I am? I'm *not* a genius! I can't play the piano. And even if I could, I wouldn't go on TV if you paid me a million dollars!" I cried.

My mother slapped me. "Who ask you to be genius?" she shouted. "Only ask you to be your best. For your sake. You think I want you to be genius? Hnnh! What for! Who ask you!"

"So ungrateful," I heard her mutter in Chinese. "If she had as much talent as she has temper, she would be famous now."

Mr. Chong, whom I secretly nicknamed Old Chong, was very   35 strange, always tapping his fingers to the silent music of an invisible orchestra. He looked ancient in my eyes. He had lost most of the hair on top of his head and he wore thick glasses and had eyes that always looked tired and sleepy. But he must have been younger than I thought, since he lived with his mother and was not yet married.

I met old lady Chong once and that was enough. She had this peculiar smell like a baby that had done something in its pants. And her fingers felt like a dead person's, like an old peach I once found in the back of the refrigerator, the skin just slid off the meat when I picked it up.

I soon found out why Old Chong had retired from teaching piano. He was deaf. "Like Beethoven!" he shouted to me. "We're both listening only in our head!" And he would start to conduct his frantic silent sonatas.

Our lessons went like this. He would open the book and point to different things, explaining their purpose: "Key! Treble! Bass! No sharps or flats! So this is C major! Listen now and play after me!"

And then he would play the C scale a few times, a simple chord, and then, as if inspired by an old, unreachable itch, he gradually added more notes and running trills and a pounding bass until the music was really something quite grand.

I would play after him, the simple scale, the simple chord, and then I   40 just played some nonsense that sounded like a cat running up and down on top of garbage cans. Old Chong smiled and applauded and then said, "Very good! But now you must learn to keep time!"

So that's how I discovered that Old Chong's eyes were too slow to keep up with the wrong notes I was playing. He went through the motions in half-time. To help me keep rhythm, he stood behind me, pushing down on my right shoulder for every beat. He balanced pennies on top of my wrists so I would keep them still as I slowly played scales and arpeggios. He had me curve my hand around an apple and keep that shape when playing chords. He marched stiffly to show me how to make each finger dance up and down, staccato like an obedient little soldier.

He taught me all these things, and that was how I also learned I could be lazy and get away with mistakes, lots of mistakes. If I hit the wrong notes because I hadn't practiced enough, I never corrected myself. I just kept playing in rhythm. And Old Chong kept conducting his own private reverie.

So maybe I never really gave myself a fair chance. I did pick up the basics pretty quickly, and I might have become a good pianist at that young age. But I was so determined not to try, not to be anybody different that I learned to play only the most ear-splitting preludes, the most discordant hymns.

Over the next year, I practiced like this, dutifully in my own way. And then one day I heard my mother and her friend Lindo Jong both talking in a loud bragging tone of voice so others could hear. It was after church, and I was leaning against the brick wall wearing a dress with stiff white petticoats. Auntie Lindo's daughter, Waverly, who was about my age, was standing farther down the wall about five feet away. We had grown up together and shared all the closeness of two sisters squabbling over crayons and dolls. In other words, for the most part, we hated each other. I thought she was snotty. Waverly Jong had gained a certain amount of fame as "Chinatown's Littlest Chinese Chess Champion."

"She bring home too many trophy," lamented Auntie Lindo that Sunday. "All day she play chess. All day I have no time do nothing but dust off her winnings." She threw a scolding look at Waverly, who pretended not to see her.   45

"You lucky you don't have this problem," said Auntie Lindo with a sigh to my mother.

And my mother squared her shoulders and bragged: "Our problem worser than yours. If we ask Jing-mei wash dish, she hear nothing but music. It's like you can't stop this natural talent."

And right then, I was determined to put a stop to her foolish pride.

A few weeks later, Old Chong and my mother conspired to have me play in a talent show which would be held in the church hall. By then, my parents had saved up enough to buy me a secondhand piano, a black Wurlitzer spinet with a scarred bench. It was the showpiece of our living room.

For the talent show, I was to play a piece called "Pleading Child"   50 from Schumann's *Scenes from Childhood*. It was a simple, moody piece that sounded more difficult than it was. I was supposed to memorize the whole thing, playing the repeat parts twice to make the piece sound longer. But I dawdled over it, playing a few bars and then cheating, looking up to see what notes followed. I never really listened to what I was playing. I daydreamed about being somewhere else, about being someone else.

The part I liked to practice best was the fancy curtsy: right foot out, touch the rose on the carpet with a pointed foot, sweep to the side, left leg bends, look up and smile.

My parents invited all the couples from the Joy Luck Club to witness my debut. Auntie Lindo and Uncle Tin were there. Waverly and her two older brothers had also come. The first two rows were filled with children both younger and older than I was. The littlest ones got to go first. They recited simple nursery rhymes, squawked out tunes on miniature violins, twirled Hula Hoops, pranced in pink ballet tutus, and when they bowed or curtsied, the audience would sigh in unison, "Awww," and then clap enthusiastically.

When my turn came, I was very confident. I remember my childish excitement. It was as if I knew, without a doubt, that the prodigy side of me really did exist. I had no fear whatsoever, no nervousness. I remember thinking to myself, This is it! This is it! I looked out over the audience, at my mother's blank face, my father's yawn, Auntie Lindo's stiff-lipped smile, Waverly's sulky expression. I had on a white dress layered with sheets of lace, and a pink bow in my Peter Pan haircut. As I sat down I envisioned people jumping to their feet and Ed Sullivan rushing up to introduce me to everyone on TV.

And I started to play. It was so beautiful. I was so caught up in how lovely I looked that at first I didn't worry how I would sound. So it was a surprise to me when I hit the first wrong note and I realized something didn't sound quite right. And then I hit another and another followed that. A chill started at the top of my head and began to trickle down. Yet I couldn't stop playing, as though my hands were bewitched. I kept thinking my fingers would adjust themselves back, like a train switching to the right track. I played this strange jumble through two repeats, the sour notes staying with me all the way to the end.

When I stood up, I discovered my legs were shaking. Maybe I had just been nervous and the audience, like Old Chong, had seen me go through the right motions and had not heard anything wrong at all. I swept my right foot out, went down on my knee, looked up and smiled. The room was quiet, except for Old Chong, who was beaming and shouting "Bravo! Bravo! Well done!" But then I saw my mother's face, her stricken face. The audience clapped weakly, and as I walked back to my chair, with my whole face quivering as I tried not to cry, I heard a little boy whisper loudly to his mother, "That was awful," and the mother whispered back, "Well, she certainly tried."   55

And now I realized how many people were in the audience, the whole world it seemed. I was aware of eyes burning into my back. I felt the shame of my mother and father as they sat stiffly throughout the rest of the show.

We could have escaped during the intermission. Pride and some strange sense of honor must have anchored my parents to their chairs. And so we watched it all: the eighteen-year-old boy with a fake mustache who did a magic show and juggled flaming hoops while riding a unicycle. The breasted girl with white makeup who sang from *Madama Butterfly* and got honorable mention. And the eleven-year-old boy who won first prize playing a tricky violin song that sounded like a busy bee.

After the show, the Hsus, the Jongs, and the St. Clairs from the Joy Luck Club came up to my mother and father.

"Lots of talented kids," Auntie Lindo said vaguely, smiling broadly.

"That was somethin' else," said my father, and I wondered if he was referring to me in a humorous way, or whether he even remembered what I had done.   60

Waverly looked at me and shrugged her shoulders. "You aren't a genius like me," she said matter-of-factly. And if I hadn't felt so bad, I would have pulled her braids and punched her stomach.

But my mother's expression was what devastated me: a quiet, blank look that said she had lost everything. I felt the same way, and it seemed as if everybody were now coming up, like gawkers at the scene of an accident, to see what parts were actually missing. When we got on the bus to go home, my father was humming the busy-bee tune and my mother was silent. I kept thinking she wanted to wait until we got home before shouting at me. But when my father unlocked the door to our apartment, my mother walked in and then went to the back, into the bedroom. No accusations. No blame. And in a way, I felt disappointed. I had been waiting for her to start shouting, so I could shout back and cry and blame her for all my misery.

I assumed my talent-show fiasco meant I never had to play the piano again. But two days later, after school, my mother came out of the kitchen and saw me watching TV.

"Four clock," she reminded me as if it were any other day. I was stunned, as though she were asking me to go through the talent-show torture again. I wedged myself more tightly in front of the TV.

"Turn off TV," she called from the kitchen five minutes later.   65

I didn't budge. And then I decided. I didn't have to do what my mother said anymore. I wasn't her slave. This wasn't China. I had listened to her before and look what happened. She was the stupid one.

She came out from the kitchen and stood in the arched entryway of the living room. "Four clock," she said once again, louder.

"I'm not going to play anymore," I said nonchalantly. "Why should I? I'm not a genious."

She walked over and stood in front of the TV. I saw her chest was heaving up and down in an angry way.

"No!" I said, and I now felt stronger, as if my true self had finally   70 emerged. So this was what had been inside me all along.

"No! I won't!" I screamed.

She yanked me by the arm, pulled me off the floor, snapped off the TV. She was frighteningly strong, half pulling, half carrying me toward the piano as I kicked the throw rugs under my feet. She lifted me up and onto the hard bench. I was sobbing by now, looking at her bitterly. Her chest was heaving even more and her mouth was open, smiling crazily as if she were pleased I was crying.

"You want me to be someone that I'm not!" I sobbed. "I'll never be the kind of daughter you want me to be!"

"Only two kinds of daughters," she shouted in Chinese. "Those who are obedient and those who follow their own mind! Only one kind of daughter can live in this house! Obedient daughter!"

"Then I wish I wasn't your daughter. I wish you weren't my mother,"   75
I shouted. As I said these things I got scared. It felt like worms and toads
and slimy things crawling out of my chest, but it also felt good, as if this
awful side of me had surfaced, at last.

"Too late change this," said my mother shrilly.

And I could sense her anger rising to its breaking point. I wanted to
see it spill over. And that's when I remembered the babies she had lost in
China, the ones we never talked about. "Then I wish I'd never been
born!" I shouted. "I wish I were dead! Like them."

It was as if I had said the magic words. Alakazam!—and her face
went blank, her mouth closed, her arms went slack, and she backed out
of the room, stunned, as if she were blowing away like a small brown
leaf, thin, brittle, lifeless.

It was not the only disappointment my mother felt in me. In the years
that followed, I failed her so many times, each time asserting my own
will, my right to fall short of expectations. I didn't get straight As. I didn't
become class president. I didn't get into Stanford. I dropped out of college.

For unlike my mother, I did not believe I could be anything I wanted   80
to be. I could only be me.

And for all those years, we never talked about the disaster at the
recital or my terrible accusations afterward at the piano bench. All that
remained unchecked, like a betrayal that was now unspeakable. So I
never found a way to ask her why she had hoped for something so large
that failure was inevitable.

And even worse, I never asked her what frightened me the most: Why
had she given up hope?

For after our struggle at the piano, she never mentioned my playing
again. The lessons stopped. The lid to the piano was closed, shutting out
the dust, my misery, and her dreams.

So she surprised me. A few years ago, she offered to give me the
piano, for my thirtieth birthday. I had not played in all those years. I saw
the offer as a sign of forgiveness, a tremendous burden removed.

"Are you sure?" I asked shyly. "I mean, won't you and Dad miss it?"   85

"No, this your piano," she said firmly. "Always your piano. You
only one can play."

"Well, I probably can't play anymore," I said. "It's been years."

"You pick up fast," said my mother, as if she knew this was certain.
"You have natural talent. You could been genius if you want to."

"No I couldn't."

"You just not trying," said my mother. And she was neither angry   90
nor sad. She said it as if to announce a fact that could never be disproved.
"Take it," she said.

But I didn't at first. It was enough that she had offered it to me. And
after that, every time I saw it in my parents' living room, standing in front

of the bay windows, it made me feel proud, as if it were a shiny trophy I had won back.

Last week I sent a tuner over to my parents' apartment and had the piano reconditioned, for purely sentimental reasons. My mother had died a few months before and I had been getting things in order for my father, a little bit at a time. I put the jewelry in special silk pouches. The sweaters she had knitted in yellow, pink, bright orange—all the colors I hated—I put those in moth-proof boxes. I found some old Chinese silk dresses, the kind with the little slits up the sides. I rubbed the old silk against my skin, then wrapped them in tissue and decided to take them home with me.

After I had the piano tuned, I opened the lid and touched the keys. It sounded even richer than I imagined. Really, it was a very good piano. Inside the bench were the same exercise notes with handwritten scales, the same secondhand books with their covers held together with yellow tape.

I opened up the Schumann book to the dark little piece I had played at the recital. It was on the left-hand side of the page, "Pleading Child." It looked more difficult than I remembered. I played a few bars, surprised at how easily the notes came back to me.

And for the first time, or so it seemed, I noticed the piece on the right-hand side. It was called "Perfectly Contented." I tried to play this one as well. It had a lighter melody but the same flowing rhythm and turned out to be quite easy. "Pleading Child" was shorter but slower; "Perfectly Contented" was longer, but faster. And after I played them both a few times, I realized they were two halves of the same song.

95

The Reader's Presence

1. The story opens with background information on the mother. What objective facts about her are conveyed in the opening section? What subjective impressions of her do you derive from this section? Whose "voice" is evident in this section—the writer's, the narrator's, or the mother's, or a mix? Reread the section sentence by sentence; which voices and perspectives do you hear in each? What is the effect of this writing technique for the reader?

2. Tan writes in the first person. Are the writer and narrator exactly the same? What leads you to your conclusion? Reread the second section, supposing that all the events recounted actually occurred to the young Tan. How are they edited and arranged to form a coherent, meaningful whole? What sorts of details are preserved? What sorts of details are left out?

3. Tan is able to control the reader's response by gradually shifting her point of view about the events as well as about what she calls the "raised hopes and failed expectations" at the dramatic center

of this story. Consider the scenes involving the piano lessons and the mother's relation to the television set. How are the shifts in point of view accomplished? What effect do they have on your reading of the story?

127

John Updike

A & P

Over the course of his career as a novelist, short story writer, poet, essayist, and dramatist, John Updike (b. 1932) has been awarded every major American literary award; in 1998 he was awarded the National Book Foundation Medal for Distinguished Contribution to American Letters. For one novel alone, Rabbit Is Rich *(1981), he won the Pulitzer Prize, the American Book Award, and the National Book Critics Circle Award. Among over a dozen published novels, his recurring themes include religion, sexuality, and middle-class experience. In his essays, Updike's concerns range widely over literary and cultural issues. One volume of his collected essays,* Hugging the Shore: Essays and Criticism *(1983), was awarded a National Book Critics Circle Award. His most recent publications include* Bech at Bay: A Quasi-Novel *(1998),* Toward the End of Time *(1997), and* More Matter: Essays and Criticism *(1999). "A & P" appears in* Pigeon Feathers and Other Stories *(1962).*

Updike has said, "I began my writing career with a fairly distinct set of principles which, one by one, have eroded into something approaching shapelessness." He does maintain one principle, however: "You should attempt to write things that you would like to read." Writing, he continues, is a process of rendering "your vision of reality into the written symbol. Out of this, living art will come."

In walks these three girls in nothing but bathing suits. I'm in the third checkout slot, with my back to the door, so I don't see them until they're over by the bread. The one that caught my eye first was the one in the plaid green two-piece. She was a chunky kid, with a good tan and a sweet broad soft-looking can with those two crescents of white just under it, where the sun never seems to hit, at the top of the backs of her legs. I stood there with my hand on a box of HiHo crackers trying to remember if I rang it up or not. I ring it up again and the customer starts giving me hell. She's one of these cash-register-watchers, a witch about fifty with rouge on her cheekbones and no eyebrows, and I know it made her day to trip me up. She'd been watching cash registers for fifty years and probably never seen a mistake before.

By the time I got her feathers smoothed and her goodies into a bag—she gives me a little snort in passing, if she'd been born at the right time they would have burned her over in Salem—by the time I get her on her way the girls had circled around the bread and were coming back, without a pushcart, back my way along the counters, in the aisle between the checkouts and the Special bins. They didn't even have shoes on. There was this chunky one, with the two-piece—it was bright green and the seams on the bra were still sharp and her belly was still pretty pale so I guessed she just got it (the suit)—there was this one, with one of those chubby berry-faces, the lips all bunched together under her nose, this one, and a tall one, with black hair that hadn't quite frizzed right, and one of these sunburns right across under the eyes, and a chin that was too long—you know, the kind of girl other girls think is very "striking" and "attractive" but never quite makes it, as they very well know, which is why they like her so much—and then the third one, that wasn't quite so tall. She was the queen. She kind of led them, the other two peeking around and making their shoulders round. She didn't look around, not this queen, she just walked straight on slowly, on these long white prima-donna legs. She came down a little hard on her heels, as if she didn't walk in her bare feet that much, putting down her heels and then letting the weight move along to her toes as if she was testing the floor with every step, putting a little deliberate extra action into it. You never know for sure how girls' minds work (do you really think it's a mind in there or just a little buzz like a bee in a glass jar?) but you got the idea she had talked the other two into coming in here with her, and now she was showing them how to do it, walk slow and hold yourself straight.

She had on a kind of dirty-pink—beige maybe, I don't know—bathing suit with a little nubble all over it and, what got me, the straps were down. They were off her shoulders looped loose around the cool tops of her arms, and I guess as a result the suit had slipped a little on her, so all around the top of the cloth there was this shining rim. If it hadn't been there you wouldn't have known there could have been anything whiter than those shoulders. With the straps pushed off, there was nothing between the top of the suit and the top of her head except just *her,* this clean bare plane of the top of her chest down from the shoulder bones like a dented sheet of metal tilted in the light. I mean, it was more than pretty.

She had sort of oaky hair that the sun and salt had bleached, done up in a bun that was unraveling, and a kind of prim face. Walking into the A & P with your straps down, I suppose it's the only kind of face you *can* have. She held her head so high her neck, coming up out of those white shoulders, looked kind of stretched, but I didn't mind. The longer her neck was, the more of her there was.

She must have felt in the corner of her eye me and over my shoulder   5
Stokesie in the second slot watching, but she didn't tip. Not this queen.
She kept her eyes moving across the racks, and stopped, and turned so
slow it made my stomach rub the inside of my apron, and buzzed to the
other two, who kind of huddled against her for relief, and then they all
three of them went up the cat-and-dog-food-breakfast-cereal-macaroni-
rice-raisins-seasonings-spreads-spaghetti-soft-drinks-crackers-and-cookies
aisle. From the third slot I look straight up this aisle to the meat counter,
and I watched them all the way. The fat one with the tan sort of fumbled
with the cookies, but on second thought she put the package back. The
sheep pushing their carts down the aisle — the girls were walking against
the usual traffic (not that we have one-way signs or anything) — were
pretty hilarious. You could see them, when Queenie's white shoulders
dawned on them, kind of jerk, or hop, or hiccup, but their eyes snapped
back to their own baskets and on they pushed. I bet you could set off dy-
namite in an A & P and the people would by and large keep reaching and
checking oatmeal off their lists and muttering "Let me see, there was a
third thing, began with A, asparagus, no, ah, yes, applesauce!" or whatever it is they do mutter. But there was no doubt, this jiggled them. A few
houseslaves in pin curlers even looked around after pushing their carts
past to make sure what they had seen was correct.

You know, it's one thing to have a girl in a bathing suit down on the
beach, where what with the glare nobody can look at each other much
anyway, and another thing in the cool of the A & P, under the fluorescent
lights, against all those stacked packages, with her feet paddling along
naked over our checkerboard green-and-cream rubber-tile floor.

"Oh Daddy," Stokesie said beside me. "I feel so faint."

"Darling," I said. "Hold me tight." Stokesie's married, with two babies chalked up on his fuselage already, but as far as I can tell that's the
only difference. He's twenty-two, and I was nineteen this April.

"Is it done?" he asks, the responsible married man finding his voice. I
forgot to say he thinks he's going to be manager some sunny day, maybe
in 1990 when it's called the Great Alexandrov and Petrooshki Tea Company or something.

What he meant was, our town is five miles from a beach, with a big   10
summer colony out on the Point, but we're right in the middle of town,
and the women generally put on a shirt or shorts or something before
they get out of the car into the street. And anyway these are usually
women with six children and varicose veins mapping their legs and nobody, including them, could care less. As I say, we're right in the middle
of town, and if you stand at our front doors you can see two banks and
the Congregational church and the newspaper store and three real-estate
offices and about twenty-seven old freeloaders tearing up Central Street
because the sewer broke again. It's not as if we're on the Cape, we're
north of Boston and there's people in this town haven't seen the ocean for
twenty years.

The girls had reached the meat counter and were asking McMahon something. He pointed, they pointed, and they shuffled out of sight behind a pyramid of Diet Delight peaches. All that was left for us to see was old McMahon patting his mouth and looking after them sizing up their joints. Poor kids, I began to feel sorry for them, they couldn't help it.

Now here comes the sad part of the story, at least my family says it's sad, but I don't think it's so sad myself. The store's pretty empty, it being Thursday afternoon, so there was nothing much to do except lean on the register and wait for the girls to show up again. The whole store was like a pinball machine and I didn't know which tunnel they'd come out of. After a while they come around out of the far aisle, around the light bulbs, records at discount of the Caribbean Six or Tony Martin Sings or some such gunk you wonder they waste the wax on, sixpacks of candy bars, and plastic toys done up in cellophane that fall apart when a kid looks at them anyway. Around they come, Queenie still leading the way, and holding a little gray jar in her hands. Slots Three through Seven are unmanned and I could see her wondering between Stokes and me, but Stokesie with his usual luck draws an old party in baggy gray pants who stumbles up with four giant cans of pineapple juice (what do these bums *do* with all that pineapple juice? I've often asked myself). So the girls come to me. Queenie puts down the jar and I take it into my fingers icy cold. Kingfish Fancy Herring Snacks in Pure Sour Cream: 49¢. Now her hands are empty, not a ring or a bracelet, bare as God made them, and I wonder where the money's coming from. Still with that prim look she lifts a folded dollar bill out of the hollow at the center of her nubbled pink top. The jar went heavy in my hand. Really, I thought that was so cute.

Then everybody's luck begins to run out. Lengel comes in from haggling with a truck full of cabbages on the lot and is about to scuttle into that door marked MANAGER behind which he hides all day when the girls touch his eye. Lengel's pretty dreary, teaches Sunday school and the rest, but he doesn't miss that much. He comes over and says, "Girls, this isn't the beach."

Queenie blushes, though maybe it's just a brush of sunburn I was noticing for the first time, now that she was so close. "My mother asked me to pick up a jar of herring snacks." Her voice kind of startled me, the way voices do when you see the people first, coming out so flat and dumb yet kind of tony, too, the way it ticked over "pick up" and "snacks." All of a sudden I slid right down her voice into the living room. Her father and the other men were standing around in ice-cream coats and bow ties and the women were in sandals picking up herring snacks on toothpicks off a big glass plate and they were all holding drinks the color of water with olives and sprigs of mint in them. When my parents have somebody over they get lemonade and if it's a real racy affair Schlitz in tall glasses with "They'll Do It Every Time" cartoons stenciled on.

"That's all right," Lengel said. "But this isn't the beach." His repeating this struck me as funny, as if it had just occurred to him, and he had 15 been thinking all these years the A & P was a great big dune and he was the head lifeguard. He didn't like my smiling—as I say he doesn't miss much—but he concentrates on giving the girls that sad Sunday-school-superintendent stare.

Queenie's blush is no sunburn now, and the pump one in plaid, that I liked better from the back—a really sweet can—pipes up, "We weren't doing any shopping. We just came in for the one thing."

"That makes no difference," Lengel tells her, and I could see from the way his eyes went that he hadn't noticed she was wearing a two-piece before. "We want you decently dressed when you come in here."

"We *are* decent," Queenie says suddenly, her lower lip pushing, getting sore now that she remembers her place, a place from which the crowd that runs the A & P must look pretty crummy. Fancy Herring Snacks flashed in her very blue eyes.

"Girls, I don't want to argue with you. After this come in here with your shoulders covered. It's our policy." He turns his back. That's policy for you. Policy is what the kingpins want. What the others want is juvenile delinquency.

All this while, the customers had been showing up with their carts   20 but, you know, sheep, seeing a scene, they had all bunched up on Stokesie, who shook open a paper bag as gently as peeling a peach, not wanting to miss a word. I could feel in the silence everybody getting nervous, most of all Lengel, who asks me, "Sammy, have you rung up their purchase?"

I thought and said "No" but it wasn't about that I was thinking. I go through the punches, 4, 9, GROC. TOT—it's more complicated than you think, and after you do it often enough, it begins to make a little song, that you hear words to, in my case "Hello (*bing*) there, you (*gung*) hap-py pee-pul (*splat*)!"—the *splat* being the drawer flying out. I uncrease the bill, tenderly as you may imagine, it just having come from between the two smoothest scoops of vanilla I had ever known were there, and pass a half and a penny into her narrow pink palm, and nestle the herrings in a bag and twist its neck and hand it over, all the time thinking.

The girls, and who'd blame them, are in a hurry to get out, so I say "I quit" to Lengel quick enough for them to hear, hoping they'll stop and watch me, their unsuspected hero. They keep right on going, into the electric eye; the door flies open and they flicker across the lot to their car, Queenie and Plaid and Big Tall Goony-Goony (not that as raw material she was so bad), leaving me with Lengel and a kink in his eyebrow.

"Did you say something, Sammy?"

"I said I quit."

"I thought you did."   25

"You didn't have to embarrass them."

"It was they who were embarrassing us."

I started to say something that came out "Fiddle-de-doo." It's a saying of my grandmother's, and I know she would have been pleased.

"I don't think you know what you're saying," Lengel said.

"I know you don't," I said. "But I do." I pull the bow at the back of   30
my apron and start shrugging it off my shoulders. A couple customers
that had been heading for my slot begin to knock against each other, like
scared pigs in a chute.

Lengel sighs and begins to look very patient and old and gray. He's
been a friend of my parents for years. "Sammy, you don't want to do this
to your Mom and Dad," he tells me. It's true, I don't. But it seems to me
that once you begin a gesture it's fatal not to go through with it. I fold the
apron, "Sammy" stitched in red on the pocket, and put it on the counter,
and drop the bow tie on top of it. The bow tie is theirs, if you've ever
wondered. "You'll feel this for the rest of your life," Lengel says, and I
know that's true, too, but remembering how he made the pretty girl blush
makes me so scrunchy inside I punch the No Sale tab and the machine
whirs "pee-pul" and the drawer splats out. One advantage to this scene
taking place in summer, I can follow this up with a clean exit, there's no
fumbling around getting your coat and galoshes, I just saunter into the
electric eye in my white shirt that my mother ironed the night before, and
the door heaves itself open, and outside the sunshine is skating around on
the asphalt.

I look around for my girls, but they're gone, of course. There wasn't
anybody but some young married screaming with her children about
some candy they didn't get by the door of a powder-blue Falcon station
wagon. Looking back in the big windows, over the bags of peat moss and
aluminum lawn furniture stacked on he pavement, I could see Lengel in
my place in the slot, checking the sheep through. His face was dark gray
and his back stiff, as if he'd just had an injection of iron, and my stomach
kind of fell as I felt how hard the world was going to be to me hereafter.

The Reader's Presence

1. The story is written in very colloquial or everyday language.
   Reread the first two paragraphs. What does the narrator's style of
   expression convey about him? What effect does the narrator's
   style of expression have upon your reading of the story? Are you
   more, or less, inclined to believe his words? Suppose the same
   story were recounted in a more conventional English. Would its
   meaning differ? If so, in what ways? How do you think Updike
   wishes the reader to view the narrator? Does Updike seem to
   agree, partially agree, or disagree with the narrator's point of
   view? What clues in the narrative lead you to your conclusion?

2. A great deal of the story hinges upon what the narrator doesn't
   know or say. Is the girls' attire the only issue in the confrontation?
   What other tensions are evident in the store and in the town?

What impression of the situation do you glean "between the lines"? How does the writer convey information beyond the scope of what the narrator is able to articulate?

3. Reread the final paragraph, beginning in the present tense and ending with the narrator's retrospective estimation of "how hard the world was going to be to me hereafter." How do the present and past tenses mingle in the paragraph? How do present and past perceptions intersect in the story?

128

Alice Walker

Everyday Use

Alice Walker is well known for both her essays and her fiction. Her novel The Color Purple *(1982) received many prestigious awards, including the Pulitzer Prize and the American Book Award, and was made into a successful film. Two of her most famous essays, "Beauty: When the Other Dancer Is the Self" and "In Search of Our Mothers' Gardens," are collected in previous chapters of this book and offer interesting comparisons with the following short story. "Everyday Use" is from Walker's 1973 short story collection* In Love and Trouble: Stories of Black Women.

For additional information on Alice Walker, see pages 285 and 588.

For Your Grandmama

I will wait for her in the yard that Maggie and I made so clean and wavy yesterday afternoon. A yard like this is more comfortable than most people know. It is not just a yard. It is like an extended living room. When the hard clay is swept clean as a floor and the fine sand around the edges lined with tiny, irregular grooves, anyone can come and sit and look up into the elm tree and wait for the breezes that never come inside the house.

Maggie will be nervous until after her sister goes: She will stand hopelessly in corners, homely and ashamed of the burn scars down her arms and legs, eying her sister with a mixture of envy and awe. She thinks her sister has held life always in the palm of one hand, that "no" is a word the world never learned to say to her.

You've no doubt seen those TV shows where the child who has "made it" is confronted, as a surprise, by her own mother and father, tottering in weakly from backstage. (A pleasant surprise, of course: What would they do if parent and child came on the show only to curse out and insult each other?) On TV mother and child embrace and smile into each other's faces. Sometimes the mother and father weep, the child wraps them in her arms and leans across the table to tell how she would not have made it without their help. I have seen these programs.

Sometimes I dream a dream in which Dee and I are suddenly brought together on a TV program of this sort. Out of a dark and soft-seated limousine I am ushered into a bright room filled with many people. There I meet a smiling, gray, sporty man like Johnny Carson who shakes my hand and tells me what a fine girl I have. Then we are on the stage and Dee is embracing me with tears in her eyes. She pins on my dress a large orchid, even though she has told me once that she thinks orchids are tacky flowers.

In real life I am a large, big-boned woman with rough, man-working   5 hands. In the winter I wear flannel nightgowns to bed and overalls during the day. I can kill and clean a hog as mercilessly as a man. My fat keeps me hot in zero weather. I can work outside all day, breaking ice to get water for washing; I can eat pork liver cooked over the open fire minutes after it comes steaming from the hog. One winter I knocked a bull calf straight in the brain between the eyes with a sledge hammer and had the meat hung up to chill before nightfall. But of course all this does not show on television. I am the way my daughter would want me to be: a hundred pounds lighter, my skin like an uncooked barley pancake. My hair glistens in the hot bright lights. Johnny Carson has much to do to keep up with my quick and witty tongue.

But that is a mistake. I know even before I wake up. Who ever knew a Johnson with a quick tongue? Who can even imagine me looking a strange white man in the eye? It seems to me I have talked to them always with one foot raised in flight, with my head turned in whichever way is farthest from them. Dee, though. She would always look anyone in the eye. Hesitation was no part of her nature.

"How do I look, Mama?" Maggie says, showing just enough of her thin body enveloped in pink skirt and red blouse for me to know she's there, almost hidden by the door.

"Come out into the yard," I say.

Have you ever seen a lame animal, perhaps a dog run over by some careless person rich enough to own a car, sidle up to someone who is ignorant enough to be kind to him? That is the way my Maggie walks. She has been like this, chin on chest, eyes on ground, feet in shuffle, ever since the fire that burned the other house to the ground.

Dee is lighter than Maggie, with nicer hair and a fuller figure. She's a   10 woman now, though sometimes I forget. How long ago was it that the other house burned? Ten, twelve years? Sometimes I can still hear the flames and feel Maggie's arms sticking to me, her hair smoking and her dress falling off her in little black papery flakes. Her eyes seemed stretched open, blazed open by the flames reflected in them. And Dee. I see her standing off under the sweet gum tree she used to dig gum out of; a look of concentration on her face as she watched the last dingy gray board of the house fall in toward the red-hot brick chimney. Why don't you do a dance around the ashes? I'd wanted to ask her. She had hated the house that much.

I used to think she hated Maggie, too. But that was before we raised the money, the church and me, to send her to Augusta to school. She used to read to us without pity; forcing words, lies, other folks' habits, whole lives upon us two, sitting trapped and ignorant underneath her voice. She washed us in a river of make-believe, burned us with a lot of knowledge we didn't necessarily need to know. Pressed us to her with the serious way she read, to shove us away at just the moment, like dimwits, we seemed about to understand.

Dee wanted nice things. A yellow organdy dress to wear to her graduation from high school; black pumps to match a green suit she'd made from an old suit somebody gave me. She was determined to stare down any disaster in her efforts. Her eyelids would not flicker for minutes at a time. Often I fought off the temptation to shake her. At sixteen she had a style of her own: and knew what style was.

I never had an education myself. After second grade the school was closed down. Don't ask me why: In 1927 colored asked fewer questions than they do now. Sometimes Maggie reads to me. She stumbles along good-naturedly but can't see well. She knows she is not bright. Like good looks and money, quickness passed her by. She will marry John Thomas (who has mossy teeth in an earnest face) and then I'll be free to sit here and I guess just sing church songs to myself. Although I never was a good singer. Never could carry a tune. I was always better at a man's job. I used to love to milk till I was hooked in the side in '49. Cows are soothing and slow and don't bother you, unless you try to milk them the wrong way.

I have deliberately turned my back on the house. It is three rooms, just like the one that burned, except the roof is tin; they don't make shingle roofs any more. There are no real windows, just some holes cut in the sides, like the portholes in a ship, but not round and not square, with rawhide holding the shutters up on the outside. This house is in a pasture, too, like the other one. No doubt when Dee sees it she will want to tear it down. She wrote me once that no matter where we "choose" to live, she

will manage to come see us. But she will never bring her friends. Maggie
and I thought about this and Maggie asked me, "Mama, when did Dee
ever *have* any friends?"

She had a few. Furtive boys in pink shirts hanging about on washday   15
after school. Nervous girls who never laughed. Impressed with her they
worshiped the well-turned phrase, the cute shape, the scalding humor
that erupted like bubbles in lye. She read to them.

When she was courting Jimmy T she didn't have much time to pay to
us, but turned all her faultfinding power on him. He *flew* to marry a
cheap city girl from a family of ignorant flashy people. She hardly had
time to recompose herself.

When she comes I will meet—but there they are!

Maggie attempts to make a dash for the house, in her shuffling way,
but I stay her with my hand. "Come back here," I say. And she stops and
tries to dig a well in the sand with her toe.

It is hard to see them clearly through the strong sun. But even the first
glimpse of leg out of the car tells me it is Dee. Her feet were always neat-
looking, as if God himself had shaped them with a certain style. From the
other side of the car comes a short, stocky man. Hair is all over his head a
foot long and hanging from his chin like a kinky mule tail. I hear Maggie
suck in her breath. "Uhnnnh," is what it sounds like. Like when you see
the wriggling end of a snake just in front of your foot on the road.
"Uhnnnh."

Dee next. A dress down to the ground, in this hot weather. A dress so   20
loud it hurts my eyes. There are yellows and oranges enough to throw
back the light of the sun. I feel my whole face warming from the heat
waves it throws out. Earrings gold, too, and hanging down to her shoulders. Bracelets dangling and making noises when she moves her arm up to
shake the folds of the dress out of her armpits. The dress is loose and
flows, and as she walks closer, I like it. I hear Maggie go "Uhnnnh"
again. It is her sister's hair. It stands straight up like the wool on a sheep.
It is black as night and around the edges are two long pigtails that rope
about like small lizards disappearing behind her ears.

"Wa-su-zo-Tean-o!" she says, coming on in that gliding way the
dress makes her move. The short stocky fellow with the hair to his navel
is all grinning and he follows up with "Asalamalakim, my mother and
sister!" He moves to hug Maggie but she falls back, right up against the
back of my chair. I feel her trembling there and when I look up I see the
perspiration falling off her chin.

"Don't get up," says Dee. Since I am stout it takes something of a
push. You can see me trying to move a second or two before I make it.
She turns, showing white heels through her sandals, and goes back to the
car. Out she peeks next with a Polaroid. She stoops down quickly and
lines up picture after picture of me sitting there in front of the house with
Maggie cowering behind me. She never takes a shot without making sure

the house is included. When a cow comes nibbling around the edge of the yard she snaps it and me and Maggie *and* the house. Then she puts the Polaroid in the back seat of the car, and comes up and kisses me on the forehead.

Meanwhile Asalamalakim is going through motions with Maggie's hand. Maggie's hand is as limp as a fish, and probably as cold, despite the sweat, and she keeps trying to pull it back. It looks like Asalamalakim wants to shake hands but wants to do it fancy. Or maybe he don't know how people shake hands. Anyhow, he soon gives up on Maggie.

"Well," I say. "Dee."

"No, Mama," she says. "Not 'Dee,' Wangero Leewanika Kemanjo!"   25

"What happened to 'Dee'?" I wanted to know.

"She's dead," Wangero said. "I couldn't bear it any longer, being named after the people who oppress me."

"You know as well as me you was named after your aunt Dicie," I said. Dicie is my sister. She named Dee. We called her "Big Dee" after Dee was born.

"But who was *she* named after?" asked Wangero.

"I guess after Grandma Dee," I said.   30

"And who was she named after?" asked Wangero.

"Her mother," I said, and saw Wangero was getting tired. "That's about as far back as I can trace it," I said. Though, in fact, I probably could have carried it back beyond the Civil War through the branches.

"Well," said Asalamalakim, "there you are."

"Uhnnnh," I heard Maggie say.

"There I was not," I said, "before 'Dicie' cropped up in our family,   35 so why should I try to trace it that far back?"

He just stood there grinning, looking down on me like somebody inspecting a Model A car. Every once in a while he and Wangero sent eye signals over my head.

"How do you pronounce this name?" I asked.

"You don't have to call me by it if you don't want to," said Wangero.

"Why shouldn't I?" I asked. "If that's what you want us to call you, we'll call you."

"I know it might sound awkward at first," said Wangero.   40

"I'll get used to it," I said. "Ream it out again."

Well, soon we got the name out of the way. Asalamalakim had a name twice as long and three times as hard. After I tripped over it two or three times he told me to just call him Hakim-a-barber. I wanted to ask him was he a barber, but I didn't really think he was, so I didn't ask.

"You must belong to those beef-cattle peoples down the road," I said. They said "Asalamalakim" when they met you, too, but they didn't shake hands. Always too busy: feeding the cattle, fixing the fences, putting up salt-lick shelters, throwing down hay. When the white folks poisoned some of the herd the men stayed up all night with rifles in their hands. I walked a mile and a half just to see the sight.

Hakim-a-barber said, "I accept some of their doctrines, but farming and raising cattle is not my style." (They didn't tell me, and I didn't ask, whether Wangero (Dee) had really gone and married him.)

We sat down to eat and right away he said he didn't eat collards and   45
pork was unclean. Wangero, though, went on through the chitlins and corn bread, the greens and everything else. She talked a blue streak over the sweet potatoes. Everything delighted her. Even the fact that we still used the benches her daddy made for the table when we couldn't afford to buy chairs.

"Oh, Mama!" she cried. Then turned to Hakim-a-barber. "I never knew how lovely these benches are. You can feel the rump prints," she said, running her hands underneath her and along the bench. Then she gave a sigh and her hand closed over Grandma Dee's butter dish. "That's it!" she said. "I knew there was something I wanted to ask you if I could have." She jumped up from the table and went over in the corner where the churn stood, the milk in it clabber by now. She looked at the churn and looked at it.

"This churn top is what I need," she said. "Didn't Uncle Buddy whittle it out of a tree you all used to have?"

"Yes," I said.

"Uh huh," she said happily. "And I want the dasher, too."

"Uncle Buddy whittle that, too?" asked the barber.   50

Dee (Wangero) looked up at me.

"Aunt Dee's first husband whittled the dash," said Maggie so low you almost couldn't hear her. "His name was Henry, but they called him Stash."

"Maggie's brain is like an elephant's," Wangero said, laughing. "I can use the churn top as a centerpiece for the alcove table," she said, sliding a plate over the churn, "and I'll think of something artistic to do with the dasher."

When she finished wrapping the dasher the handle stuck out. I took it for a moment in my hands. You didn't even have to look close to see where hands pushing the dasher up and down to make butter had left a kind of sink in the wood. In fact, there were a lot of small sinks; you could see where thumbs and fingers had sunk into the wood. It was beautiful light yellow wood, from a tree that grew in the yard where Big Dee and Stash had lived.

After dinner Dee (Wangero) went to the trunk at the foot of my bed   55
and started rifling through it. Maggie hung back in the kitchen over the dishpan. Out came Wangero with two quilts. They had been pieced by Grandma Dee and then Big Dee and me had hung them on the quilt frames on the front porch and quilted them. One was in the Lone Star pattern. The other was Walk Around the Mountain. In both of them were scraps of dresses Grandma Dee had worn fifty and more years ago. Bits and pieces of Grandpa Jarrell's Paisley shirts. And one teeny faded blue piece, about the size of a penny matchbox, that was from Great Grandpa Ezra's uniform that he wore in the Civil War.

"Mama," Wangero said sweet as a bird. "Can I have these old quilts?"

I heard something fall in the kitchen, and a minute later the kitchen door slammed.

"Why don't you take one or two of the others?" I asked. "These old things was just done by me and Big Dee from some tops your grandma pieced before she died."

"No," said Wangero. "I don't want those. They are stitched around the borders by machine."

"That'll make them last better," I said.   60

"That's not the point," said Wangero. "These are all pieces of dresses Grandma used to wear. She did all this stitching by hand. Imagine!" She held the quilts securely in her arms, stroking them.

"Some of the pieces, like those lavender ones, come from old clothes her mother handed down to her," I said, moving up to touch the quilts. Dee (Wangero) moved back just enough so that I couldn't reach the quilts. They already belonged to her.

"Imagine!" she breathed again, clutching them closely to her bosom.

"The truth is," I said, "I promised to give them quilts to Maggie, for when she marries John Thomas."

She gasped like a bee had stung her.   65

"Maggie can't appreciate these quilts!" she said. "She'd probably be backward enough to put them to everyday use."

"I reckon she would," I said. "God knows I been saving 'em for long enough with nobody using 'em. I hope she will!" I didn't want to bring up how I had offered Dee (Wangero) a quilt when she went away to college. Then she had told me they were old-fashioned, out of style.

"But they're *priceless!*" she was saying now, furiously; for she has a temper. "Maggie would put them on the bed and in five years they'd be in rags. Less than that!"

"She can always make some more," I said. "Maggie knows how to quilt."

Dee (Wangero) looked at me with hatred. "You just will not under-   70
stand. The point is these quilts, *these* quilts!"

"Well," I said, stumped. "What would *you* do with them?"

"Hang them," she said. As if that was the only thing you *could* do with quilts.

Maggie by now was standing in the door. I could almost hear the sound her feet made as they scraped over each other.

"She can have them, Mama," she said, like somebody used to never winning anything, or having anything reserved for her. "I can 'member Grandma Dee without the quilts."

I looked at her hard. She had filled her bottom lip with checkerberry   75
snuff and it gave her face a kind of dopey, hangdog look. It was Grandma Dee and Big Dee who taught her how to quilt herself. She stood there with her scarred hands hidden in the folds of her skirt. She looked at her sister with something like fear but she wasn't mad at her. This was Maggie's portion. This was the way she knew God to work.

When I looked at her like that something hit me in the top of my head and ran down to the soles of my feet. Just like when I'm in church and the spirit of God touches me and I get happy and shout. I did something I never had done before: hugged Maggie to me, then dragged her on into the room, snatched the quilts out of Miss Wangero's hands and dumped them into Maggie's lap. Maggie just sat there on my bed with her mouth open.

"Take one or two of the others," I said to Dee.

But she turned without a word and went out to Hakim-a-barber.

"You just don't understand," she said, as Maggie and I came out to the car.

"What don't I understand?" I wanted to know.   80

"Your heritage," she said. And then she turned to Maggie, kissed her, and said, "You ought to try to make something of yourself, too, Maggie. It's really a new day for us. But from the way you and Mama still live you'd never know it."

She put on some sunglasses that hid everything above the tip of her nose and her chin.

Maggie smiled; maybe at the sunglasses. But a real smile, not scared. After we watched the car dust settle I asked Maggie to bring me a dip of snuff. And then the two of us sat there just enjoying, until it was time to go in the house and go to bed.

The Reader's Presence

1. The story is told in the first person. Are the writer and narrator the same person? What sort of person is the narrator? Which clues lead you to your conclusions? Reread the first and second sections. Whose "voice" do you hear — the writer's, the narrator's, or a mix? How do you think Walker wishes the reader to view the narrator?

2. How might the fire and its aftermath (section 3) symbolize other elements of the story? How is this external event used to mirror the internal states of the characters? Reread the last section. What might the quilt symbolize? How might the fire and the quilt be related to the theme of "tradition" and "heritage"? Do these elements seem coincidental to the events in the story, or carefully chosen? Where can you see the writer's "craft" at work in this seemingly straightforward narrative?

3. Reread the final paragraph. Is there more to the events — Maggie's smile, Maggie and her mother's settling back into the yard — than meets the eye? What has transpired, emotionally, between Dee, Maggie, and their mother? How are those emotional events concluded? Through what means does Walker convey a sense of meaning in the paragraph beyond the simple facts related?

Alternate Tables of Contents_____

Selections Arranged by Common Rhetorical Modes and Patterns of Development

CONSTRUCTING NARRATIVES

937

WRITING DESCRIPTION: PERSONS, PLACES, THINGS

SUPPLYING INSTANCES AND EXAMPLES

CLASSIFYING IDEAS

ANALYZING AND DESCRIBING PROCESSES

ESTABLISHING CAUSES AND EFFECTS

FORMING ANALOGIES

FASHIONING ARGUMENTS: EIGHT METHODS

Selections Arranged by Contemporary Issues

IMMIGRATION

THE CHANGING AMERICAN FAMILY

THE POWER OF THE MEDIA

GUNS AND VIOLENCE

REGULATING SPEECH

LIVING WITH OTHER CREATURES

THE BODY

Selections Arranged by Research Techniques and Use of Information

SUPPLYING STATISTICAL AND QUANTITATIVE INFORMATION

EMPLOYING SUMMARY AND PARAPHRASE

OBTAINING INFORMATION THROUGH INTERVIEWS AND ORAL HISTORY

Acknowledgments (continued from page iv)

Russell Baker. "Gumption" from *Growing Up* by Russell Baker. Copyright © 1985 by Russell Baker. Used with permission of NTC/Contemporary Publishing Group Inc.

James Baldwin. "Stranger in the Village" from *Notes of a Native Son* by James Baldwin. Copyright © 1955, renewed 1983, by James Baldwin. Reprinted by permission of Beacon Press, Boston.

Robert Bly. "Men's Initiation Rites," *Utne Reader,* April–May 1986. Copyright © 1986 by Robert Bly. Reprinted with the permission of Robert Bly.

Rachel Carson. "Saturday" and "Dunes" from *Lost Woods: The Discovered Writing of Rachel Carson* edited by Linda Lear. Copyright © 1998 by Roger Allen Christie. Reprinted by permission of Beacon Press, Boston.

Stephen L. Carter. "The Insufficiency of Honesty" from *Integrity*. Copyright © 1996 by Stephen L. Carter. Reprinted by permission of Basic Books, a member of Perseus Books, L.L.C.

Raymond Carver. "My Father's Life," reprinted by permission of International Creative Management, Inc. Copyright © 1984 by Tess Gallagher. First published in *Esquire*. "Popular Mechanics" from *What We Talk about When We Talk about Love* by Raymond Carver. Copyright © 1981 by Raymond Carver. Reprinted by permission of Alfred A. Knopf, a Division of Random House, Inc.

Judith Ortiz Cofer. "Silent Dancing" by Judith Ortiz Cofer is reprinted with permission from the publisher of *Silent Dancing: A Partial Remembrance of a Puerto Rican Childhood* (Houston: Arte Público Press–University of Houston, © 1991).

K. C. Cole. "Calculated Risks" from *The Universe and the Teacup: The Mathematics of Truth and Beauty* by K. C. Cole. Copyright © 1998 by K. C. Cole. Reprinted by permission of Harcourt, Inc.

Bernard Cooper. "A Clack of Tiny Sparks: Remembrances of a Gay Boyhood." Copyright © 1990 by *Harper's Magazine*. All rights reserved. Reproduced from the January 1991 issue by special permission.

William Cronon. "The Trouble with Wilderness; or, Getting Back to the Wrong Nature" from *Uncommon Ground: Toward Reinventing Nature* by William Cronon, editor. Copyright © 1955 by William Cronon. Reprinted by permission of W. W. Norton & Company, Inc.

Amy Cunningham. "Why Women Smile," copyright © 1993 by Amy Cunningham. Reprinted by permission of the author. First appeared in *Lear's*.

Edwidge Danticat. "We Are Ugly, But We Are Here," *Barnard Magazine,* Summer 1994. Copyright © 1994. Reprinted by permission of the author.

Toi Derricotte. "October" and "July" from *The Black Notebooks: An Interior Journey* by Toi Derricotte. Copyright © 1997 by Toi Derricotte. Reprinted by permission of W. W. Norton & Company, Inc.

Alan Dershowitz. "Shouting 'Fire!'" Copyright © 1989 by Alan Dershowitz. First published in *The Atlantic Monthly*. Reprinted by permission of the author.

Debra Dickerson. "Who Shot Johnny?" from *Best American Essays* 1997. Copyright © 1996 by Debra Dickerson. First published in *The New Republic*. Reprinted by permission of the author.

Joan Didion. "On Keeping a Notebook" from *Slouching Towards Bethlehem* by Joan Didion. Copyright © 1966, 1968 and copyright renewed © 1996 by Joan Didion. Reprinted by permission of Farrar, Straus & Giroux, LLC.

Annie Dillard. "Living like Weasels" from *Teaching a Stone to Talk* by Annie Dillard. Copyright © 1982 by Annie Dillard. Reprinted by permission of HarperCollins Publishers, Inc. "Notes for Young Writers," *Image* 16 (Summer 1997). Copyright © 1997. Reprinted by permission of the author.

Gerald Early. "Performance and Reality." Reprinted with permission from the August 10, 1998, issue of *The Nation*.

Barbara Ehrenreich. "Family Values" excerpted from *The Worst Years of Our Lives* by Barbara Ehrenreich. Copyright © 1990 by Barbara Ehrenreich. Reprinted by permission of Pantheon Books, a division of Random House, Inc.

Lars Eighner. "On Dumpster Diving," copyright © 1993 by Lars Eighner. From *Travels with Lizbeth* by Lars Eighner. Reprinted by permission of St. Martin's Press, LLC.

Loren Eiseley. "How Flowers Changed the World" from *The Immense Journey* by Loren Eiseley. Copyright © 1957 by Loren Eiseley. Reprinted by permission of Random House, Inc.

Ralph Ellison. "What America Would Be Like without Blacks" from *Going to the Territory* by Ralph Ellison. Copyright © 1986 by Ralph Ellison. Reprinted by permission of Random House, Inc.

Nora Ephron. "A Few Words about Breasts," reprinted by permission of International Creative Management, Inc. Copyright © 1972 by Nora Ephron.

Louise Erdrich. "Skunk Dreams" from *The Blue Jay's Dance* by Louise Erdrich. Copyright © 1995 by Louise Erdrich. Reprinted by permission of HarperCollins Publishers, Inc.

Kai Erikson. "The Witches of Salem Village" from *Wayward Puritans: A Study in Social Deviance* by Kai Erikson. Copyright © 1966 by Allyn & Bacon. Reprinted by permission.

James Fallows. "Throwing Like a Girl," *The Atlantic Monthly,* August 1996. Reprinted by permission of the author.

Anne Frank. "Things That Lie Buried Deep in My Heart," "Back to My Diary," and "A Sweet Secret," from *Anne Frank: The Diary of a Young Girl* by Anne Frank. Copyright © 1952 by Otto H. Frank. Used by permission of Doubleday, a division of Random House, Inc.

Ian Frazier. "Pride," *Outside Magazine,* June 1997. Copyright © 1997 by Ian Frazier. Reprinted by permission of the author.

Paul Fussell. "A Well-Regulated Militia" from *Thank God for the Atom Bomb* by Paul Fussell. Copyright © 1988 by Paul Fussell. Reprinted by permission of the author.

Henry Louis Gates Jr. "In the Kitchen" from *Colored People* by Henry Louis Gates Jr. Copyright © 1994 by Henry Louis Gates Jr. Reprinted by permission of Alfred A. Knopf, a Division of Random House, Inc. "On the Writer's Voice" from the Introduction to *Colored People* by Henry Louis Gates Jr. Copyright © 1994 by Henry Louis Gates Jr. Reprinted with permission of the author.

Mary Gordon. "The Ghosts of Ellis Island" [originally published as "More than Just a Shrine: Paying Homage to the Ghosts of Ellis Island"], *New York Times Magazine* Part 2, November 3, 1985. Copyright © 1985 by the New York Times Co. Reprinted by permission.

Stephen Jay Gould. "Sex, Drugs, Disasters, and the Extinction of Dinosaurs," copyright © 1984 by Stephen Jay Gould, from *The Flamingo's Smile: Reflections in Natural History* by Stephen Jay Gould. Reprinted by permission of W. W. Norton & Company, Inc.

John Grisham. "Unnatural Killers," from *The Oxford American,* Spring 1996. Copyright © 1996. Reprinted by permission.

Michihiko Hachiya, M.D. "What had happened?" and "Pikadon" from *Hiroshima Diary: The Journal of a Japanese Physician, August 6–September 30, 1945* by Michihiko Hachiya, translated by Warner Wells, M.D. Copyright © 1955 by The University of North Carolina Press. Used by permission of the publisher.

Kathryn Harrison. "What Remains," *Harper's Magazine,* December 1995. Copyright © 1995 by Kathryn Harrison. Reprinted by permission of International Creative Management, Inc.

Linda M. Hasselstrom. "Why One Peaceful Woman Carries a Pistol" from *Land Circle: Writings Collected from the Land* by Linda Hasselstrom. Copyright © 1991. Reprinted by permission of Fulcrum Publishing, Inc.

Vicki Hearne. "What's Wrong with Animal Rights." Copyright © 1991 by *Harper's Magazine.* All rights reserved. Reproduced from the September issue by special permission.

Edward Hoagland. "The Courage of Turtles" from *The Courage of Turtles* by Edward Hoagland. Published by Lyons & Burford. Copyright © 1968, 1993 by Edward Hoagland. This usage granted by permission of Lescher & Lescher, Ltd.

Linda Hogan. "Dwellings" from *Dwellings: A Spiritual History of the Living World* by Linda Hogan. Copyright © 1995 by Linda Hogan. Reprinted by permission of W. W. Norton & Company, Inc.

John Hollander. "Mess" from *The Yale Review* 83:2, April 1995. Copyright © 1995. Reprinted by permission of Blackwell Publishers.

Langston Hughes. "Salvation" from *The Big Sea* by Langston Hughes. Copyright renewed © 1968 by Arna Bontemps and George Huston Bass. Reprinted by permission of Hill and Wang, a division of Farrar, Straus & Giroux, LLC. "How to Be a Bad Writer (in Ten Easy Lessons)" from *The Langston Hughes Reader.* Copyright © 1950 by Langston Hughes. Reprinted by permission of Harold Ober Associates Incorporated.

Zora Neale Hurston. "How It Feels to Be Colored Me" from *World Tomorrow* II (May 1928). Used with the permission of the Estate of Zora Neale Hurston.

June Jordan. "Nobody Mean More to Me than You and the Future Life of Willie Jordan" from *On Call: Political Essays* by June Jordan. Copyright © 1985 by June Jordan. Reprinted with the permission of the author.

Michiko Kakutani. "The Word Police," *New York Times,* February 1, 1993. Copyright © 1993 by the New York Times Co. Reprinted by permission.

Wendy Kaminer. "A Civic Duty to Annoy" from *True Love Waits: Essays and Criticisms* by Wendy Kaminer. Copyright © 1996 by Wendy Kaminer. Reprinted by permission of the author and Perseus Books Publishers, a member of Perseus Books, L.L.C.

Jamaica Kincaid. "Biography of a Dress" from *Grand Street* 43, vol. 11, #3 (1992). Copyright © 1992 by Jamaica Kincaid. Reprinted by permission of The Wylie Agency, Inc. Photograph of Jamaica Kincaid, c. 1951. Reprinted by permission of The Wylie Agency, Inc. "Girl" from *At the Bottom of the River* by Jamaica Kincaid. Copyright © 1983 by Jamaica Kincaid. Reprinted by permission of Farrar, Straus & Giroux, LLC. "An Interview with Jamaica Kincaid" from *Face to Face: Interviews with Contemporary Novelists,* edited by Allan Vorda (Houston: Rice University Press, 1993). Reprinted by permission.

Martin Luther King Jr. "Letter from Birmingham Jail." Reprinted by arrangement with The Heirs to the Estate of Martin Luther King Jr., c/o Writers House, Inc., as agent for the proprietor. Copyright © 1963 by Martin Luther King Jr., copyright renewed 1991 by Coretta Scott King.

Barbara Kingsolver. "Stone Soup" from *High Tide in Tucson* by Barbara Kingsolver. Copyright © 1995 by Barbara Kingsolver. Reprinted by permission of HarperCollins Publishers, Inc.

Maxine Hong Kingston. "Maxine Hong Kingston and Writing for Oneself" excerpted from "'Pig in a Poke': An Interview with Maxine Hong Kingston" by Diane Simmons, *Crab Orchard Review* 3:2 (Spring/Summer 1998), 96–116. Copyright © by Diane Simmons. Used by permission of Diane Simmons. "No Name Woman" from *The Woman Warrior* by Maxine Hong Kingston. Copyright © 1975, 1976 by Maxine Hong Kingston. Reprinted by permission of Alfred A. Knopf, a Division of Random House, Inc.

Chang-rae Lee. "The Faintest Echo of Our Language" from *New England Review,* Summer 1993. Copyright © 1993 by Chang-rae Lee. Reprinted by permission of the author.

Barry Lopez. "A Passage of the Hands" from *About This Life: Journeys on the Threshold of Memory* by Barry Lopez. Copyright © 1998 by Barry Holstun Lopez. Reprinted by permission of Alfred A. Knopf, a Division of Random House, Inc.

Nancy Mairs. "On Being a Cripple" from *Plain Text* by Nancy Mairs. Copyright © 1986 The Arizona Board of Regents. Reprinted by permission of the University of Arizona Press. "On Finding a Voice" from *Voice Lessons* by Nancy Mairs. Copyright © 1994 by Nancy Mairs. Reprinted by permission of Beacon Press, Boston.

Malcolm X. "Homeboy" from *The Autobiography of Malcolm X* by Malcolm X, with the assistance of Alex Haley. Copyright © 1964 by Malcolm X and Alex Haley. Copyright © 1965 by Alex Haley and Betty Shabazz. Reprinted by permission of Random House, Inc.

David Mamet. "The Rake: A Few Scenes from My Childhood" from *The Cabin* by David Mamet. Copyright © 1992 by David Mamet. Reprinted by permission of Random House, Inc.

Frank McCourt. "First Communion Day," Chapter IV of *Angela's Ashes: A Memoir* by Frank McCourt. Copyright © 1996 by Frank McCourt. Reprinted with the permission of Scribner, a Division of Simon & Schuster, Inc.

Marvin Minsky. "Will Robots Inherit the Earth?" from *Scientific American,* October 1994. Copyright © 1994 by Scientific American, Inc. Reprinted by permission of the author. All rights reserved.

N. Scott Momaday. "The Way to Rainy Mountain," first published in *The Reporter,* January 26, 1967. © 1969, 1997. Reprinted by permission of the University of New Mexico Press.

Paul Monette. "Can Gays and Straights Be Friends?" Originally appeared in *Playboy* Magazine, May 1993. Reprinted by permission of Wendy Weil Literary Agency on behalf of the author's literary estate.

Toni Morrison. "Nobel Lecture, 7 December 1993." © The Nobel Foundation, 1993. Reprinted by permission.

Bharati Mukherjee. "Two Ways to Belong in America," *New York Times,* September 2, 1996. Copyright © 1996 by the New York Times Co. Reprinted by permission.

Scott Russell Sanders. "The Men We Carry in Our Minds" from *The Paradise of Bombs* by Scott Russell Sanders, copyright © 1984 by Scott Russell Sanders. First appeared in *Milkweed Chronicle*. Reprinted by permission of the author and the Virginia Kidd Agency, Inc.

Luc Sante. "Résumé" from *The Factory of Facts* by Luc Sante. Copyright © 1998 by Luc Sante. Reprinted by permission of Pantheon Books, a division of Random House, Inc.

Arthur Schlesinger Jr. "The Cult of Ethnicity, Good and Bad," *Time*, July 8, 1991. Copyright © 1991 Time Inc. Reprinted by permission.

Richard Selzer. "Room without Windows" from *Confessions of a Knife* by Richard Selzer. Copyright © 1974 by Richard Selzer. Reprinted by permission of John Hawkins & Associates, Inc.

Jane Smiley. "Reflections on a Lettuce Wedge," *Hungry Mind Review*, Fall 1993. Copyright © 1993 by Jane Smiley. Reprinted by permission of the author.

Gary Soto. "The Childhood Worries, or Why I Became a Writer," copyright © 1995 by Gary Soto. First appeared in *The Iowa Review*, Spring/Summer 1995. Reprinted by permission of the author.

Benjamin Spock. "Should Children Play with Guns?" from *Baby and Child Care* by Benjamin Spock. Copyright © 1945, 1946, 1957, 1968, 1976, 1985, 1992 by Benjamin Spock, M.D.; copyright renewed © 1973, 1974, 1985, 1996 by Benjamin Spock, M.D. Reprinted with the permission of Pocket Books, a Division of Simon & Schuster, Inc.

Brent Staples. "From *Parallel Time*" excerpted from *Parallel Time* by Brent Staples. Copyright © 1994 by Brent Staples. Reprinted by permission of Pantheon Books, a division of Random House, Inc. "Just Walk on By: A Black Man Ponders His Power to Alter Public Space," copyright © 1986 by Brent Staples. Reprinted by permission of the author.

Shelby Steele. "On Being Black and Middle Class," *Commentary*, January 1998. Reprinted by permission of the author; all rights reserved.

Brad Stroup. "The Koans of Yogi Berra," *Tricycle: The Buddhist Review* 8.1 (Fall 1998). Reprinted by permission of the author.

Amy Tan. "Jing-Mei Woo: Two Kinds" from *The Joy Luck Club* by Amy Tan. Copyright © 1989 by Amy Tan. Used by permission of Putnam Berkley, a division of Penguin Putnam Inc. "Mother Tongue," copyright © 1990 by Amy Tan. First appeared in *The Threepenny Review*. Reprinted by permission of the author and the Sandra Dijkstra Literary Agency.

Deborah Tannen. "Listening to Men, Then and Now," by Deborah Tannen, *The New York Times Magazine*, May 16, 1999. Copyright © 1999 Deborah Tannen. Reprinted by permission.

Lewis Thomas. "On Cloning a Human Being" from *The Medusa and the Snail* by Lewis Thomas. Copyright © 1974, 1975, 1976, 1977, 1978, 1979 by Lewis Thomas. Used by permission of Viking Penguin, a division of Penguin Putnam Inc.

James Thurber. "University Days" from *The Thurber Carnival* by James Thurber. Copyright © 1945 by James Thurber. Copyright renewed 1973 by Helen Thurber and Rosemary A. Thurber. Reprinted by arrangement with Rosemary Thurber and The Barbara Hogenson Agency.

Sallie Tisdale. "A Weight That Women Carry." Copyright © 1993 by *Harper's Magazine*. All rights reserved. Reproduced from the March issue by special permission.

Calvin Trillin. "A Traditional Family" from *Too Soon to Tell* published by Farrar, Straus & Giroux. Copyright © 1991, 1995 by Calvin Trillin. This usage granted by permission of Lescher & Lescher, Ltd.

Garry Trudeau. "My Inner Shrimp," *New York Times Magazine*, March 31, 1996. Copyright © 1996 by the New York Times Co. Reprinted by permission.

Barbara W. Tuchman. "'This Is the End of the World': The Black Death" from *A Distant Mirror* by Barbara W. Tuchman. Copyright © 1978 by Barbara W. Tuchman. Reprinted by permission of Alfred A. Knopf, a Division of Random House, Inc.

John Updike, "A & P" from *Pigeon Feathers and Other Stories* by John Updike. Copyright © 1962 by John Updike. Reprinted by permission of Alfred A. Knopf, a Division of Random House, Inc. Originally appeared in *The New Yorker*.

Gore Vidal. "Drugs" from *Homage to Daniel Shays* by Gore Vidal. Copyright © 1970 by Gore Vidal. Reprinted by permission of Random House, Inc.

Alice Walker. "Beauty: When the Other Dancer Is the Self" from *In Search of Our Mothers' Gardens: Womanist Prose*, copyright © 1983 by Alice Walker. "In Search of Our Mothers' Gardens" from *In Search of Our Mothers' Gardens: Womanist Prose*, copy-

Index of Authors and Titles ─────────